# The
# Great
# Game

# THE GREAT GAME

*Past Imperative*
*Present Tense*
*Future Indefinite*

DAVE DUNCAN

PAST IMPERATIVE Copyright © 1995 by Dave Duncan
        Printing History: Morrow/AvoNova Hardcover October 1995

PRESENT TENSE Copyright © 1996 by Dave Duncan
        Printing History: Avon Books Hardcover November 1996

FUTURE INDEFINITE Copyright © 1997 by Dave Duncan
        Printing History: Avon Books Hardcover August 1997

Excerpt from *Mahatma Gandhi: Essays on His Life and Works* edited by S. Radhakrishan used by permission of HarperCollins Publishers Ltd.

Excerpt from "Reflections on Gandhi" in *Shooting an Elephant and Other Essays* by George Orwell, copyright 1950 by Sonia Brownell Orwell and renewed 1978 by Sonia Pitt-Rivers, reprinted by permission of Harcourt Brace & Company; copyright the estate of Sonia Brownell Orwell and Martin Secker and Warburg Ltd., reprinted by permission of A.M. Heath & Company Limited.

Published by arrangement with:
William Morrow/AvoNova and
Avon Books
Divisions of
The Hearst Corporation
1350 Avenue of the Americas
New York, New York 10019

ISBN: 1-56865-462-6

Visit our website at **http://www.sfbc.com**
Visit Avon Book's website at **http://AvonBooks.com**
Visit Dave Duncan's website at **http://www.cadvision.com/daveduncan**

Printed in the United States of America.

# Contents

# PAST
# IMPERATIVE

I see you stand like greyhounds in the slips,
Straining upon the start. The game's afoot.

SHAKESPEARE
*Henry V*, III, i

"Come, Watson, come!" he cried. "The game is afoot."

SIR ARTHUR CONAN DOYLE
*The Return of Sherlock Holmes:*
"Adventure of the Abbey Grange"

Hear all peoples, and rejoice all lands, for the slayer of Death comes, the Liberator, the son of Kameron Kisster. In the seven hundredth Festival, he shall come forth in the land of Suss. Naked and crying he shall come into the world and Eleal shall wash him. She shall clothe him and nurse him and comfort him. Be merry and give thanks; welcome this mercy and proclaim thine deliverance, for he will bring death to Death.

FILOBY TESTAMENT, 368

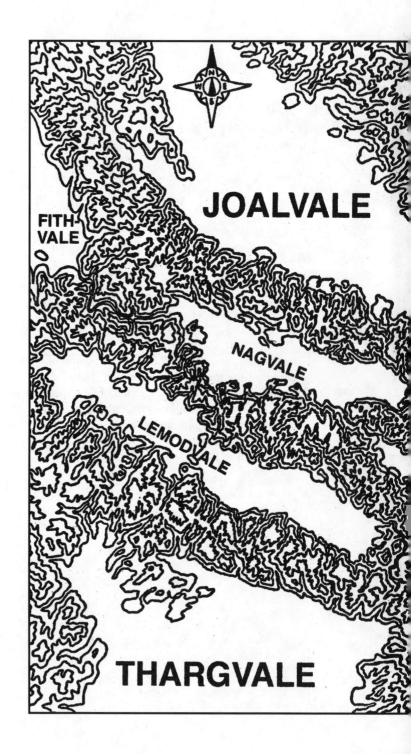

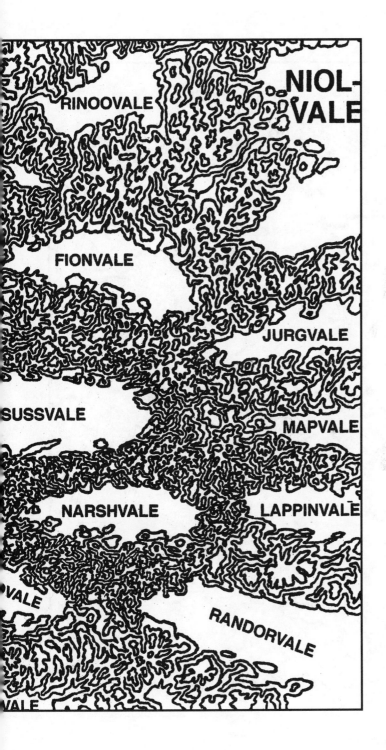

NIOL-
VALE

RINOOVALE

FIONVALE

JURGVALE

SUSSVALE

MAPVALE

NARSHVALE

LAPPINVALE

VALE

RANDORVALE

VALE

# Contents

# *Translator's Note*

In Joalian and related dialects, a geographic name usually consists of a root modified by a prefix. English equivalents (for example Narshland, Narshvale, Narshia, etc.) fail to convey all the subtleties of the original. Joalian alone has twelve words to describe a mountain pass, depending on its difficulty, but no word for a mountain range.

The flora and fauna of the Vales are quite unrelated to terrestrial types, but convergent evolution has tended to fill similar ecological niches with species of similar appearance. Form follows function—a beetle is more or less a beetle anywhere, airborne species lay eggs so that they need not be burdened with immature young, and so on. To avoid overloading the reader's memory with names and the page with italics, I have either coined descriptive terms ("bellfruit") or assigned names on the basis of appearance. A rose is a rose is, sort of, a rose. The correspondence may be superficial; a "moa" is a bipedal mammal.

Time and distance have been converted to familiar units.

Spelling has been made as phonetic as possible, based on common English pronunciation. *G* is hard; *c* is used only in *ch*, *x* and *q* not at all.

Masculine gender words begin with hard consonants (b,d,g,k,p,t), feminine with vowels or aspirates (a,e,i,o,u,y,h), and neuter with soft consonants (f,j,l,m,n,r,s,th). Abstract concepts have their own declensions and begin with v,ch,w, or z.

Dissimilar vowels are pronounced separately, as if marked with a dieresis: *Eleal* is pronounced *El-eh-al*, not *Eleel*. Double vowels indicate a long sound: *aa* as in *late*, *ee* as in *feet*, *ii* as in *fight*, *oo* as in *goat*, *uu* as in *boot*.

The English word *candle* is pronounced *cand'l*. Joalian contains many such unvoiced vowels, which are indicated with an apostrophe. The initial consonant in *D'ward* would be stressed more than in English *dwarf*.

# The Gods

The five great gods of the Pentatheon are—

**Visek**  The Supreme Parent is often regarded as male, but also as a triad: Father, Mother, and First Source. Visek may be spoken of in the singular or plural, as masculine, feminine, or abstract in ways that will not readily translate into English. The Light, the All-Knowing, the Father of Gods, etc., may take on attributes of other deities, such as wisdom, creation, justice. There are hints of monotheism in Visek worship. Except in Niol, where his main temple stands, Visek seems too remote and abstract a god to be truly popular with the masses. He is associated with the sun, fire, silver, and the color white.

His many avatars include **Chiol** (destiny) and **Wyseth** (the sun).

**Eltiana**  The Lady is goddess of love, motherhood, passion, childbirth, crops, agriculture, transition. Her clergy wear red; her symbol is ⌀ and her main temple is at Randor. She is the only major deity to be directly identified with one of the four moons.

Her avatars include **Ois**, goddess of mountain passes.

**Karzon**  The Man is the god of creation and destruction, and thus of war, strength, courage, virility, vengeance, pestilence, nature, and animal husbandry. His clergy wear green, his symbol is a hammer. His main temple is at Tharg and he is associated with the moon Trumb.

As **Zath** he is god of death, and hence the most feared of the gods. Then his color is black and his symbol a skull. Other avatars include **Garward** (strength), **Ken'th** (virility), and **Krak'th** (earthquakes).

**Astina**  The Maiden is goddess of purity, duty, justice, patron of warriors and athletes. Her clergy wear blue and her symbol is a five-pointed star. Her main sanctuary is at Joal. She is associated with Ysh, the blue moon.

Her avatars include **Iilah** (athletes), **Irepit** (repentance), **Ysh** (constancy and duty), and **Ursula** (justice).

**Tion**  The Youth is god of art, beauty, science, knowledge, healing. His clergy wear yellow. His main temple is at Suss. The unpredictable yellow moon Kirb'l is identified with his avatar the god of humor.

His avatars include **Ember'l** (drama), **Kirb'l** (the Joker), **Gunuu** (courage), **Yaela** (singing), and **Paa** (healing).

# The Trong Troupe

Trong Impresario

Ambria Impresario, Trong's second wife

K'linpor Actor, Trong's son

Halma Actor, K'linpor's wife

Uthiam Piper, Ambria's daughter

Golfren Piper, Uthiam's husband

Yama Actor, Ambria's cousin

Dolm Actor, Yama's husband

Piol Poet, brother of Ambria's first husband

Gartol Costumer, Trong's cousin

Olimmiar Dancer, Halma's sister

Klip Trumpeter, Gartol's stepbrother

Eleal Singer, an orphan

# Overture

# 1

The summer of 1914 was the finest in living memory. All over Europe the sun shone, day after day, from a sky without a cloud. Holidaymakers traveled as they wished across a continent at peace, reveling in green woods and clean, warm seas. They crossed national borders unimpeded. Almost no one noticed the storm building on the political horizon; even newspapers mostly ignored it. The war struck with the suddenness of an avalanche and carried everything away.

There was never to be another summer like it.

Toward the end of June in that year the Greek steamship *Hermes,* preparing to depart from Port Said and having a vacant stateroom, embarked at short notice a gentleman whose name was entered in the log as Colonel Julius Creighton. He was polite and aloof and inscrutable. During the crossing of the Mediterranean, he remained extremely reticent about both himself and his business. He was without question an English *milord,* but beyond that obvious deduction, neither the officers nor the other passengers were able to progress. Everyone was intrigued when he chose to disembark at Cattaro, in Montenegro, which was not on the road to anywhere. The English, they agreed, were crazy. They would all have been considerably more surprised had they been able to follow his subsequent travels.

He set foot on European soil on the twenty-eighth of June, which by coincidence was the day Archduke Francis Ferdinand's death in Sarajevo opened the first crack of the collapse that was to bring down the whole world. The Montenegro border was less than fifty miles from Sarajevo. The reader is therefore cautioned that Colonel Creighton had absolutely nothing to do with the assassination.

He progressed rapidly north and east, traveling mainly on horseback through wild country, until he reached the vicinity of Belgrade. In a wagon in a wood, he was granted audience by a gypsy *voivode,* whose authority transcended national borders.

Creighton continued eastward and spent a night as guest of a certain count of ancient lineage, lord of a picturesque castle in Transylvania. In Vienna he met with several people, including a woman reputed to be the most skilled courtesan in Austria, with the fairest body in Europe, but the substance of their meeting was unrelated to such matters.

By the fifteenth of July he had reached St. Petersburg. Although the Russian capital was racked by workers' strikes, he succeeded in spending several hours talking with a monk celebrated for both his holiness and his political connections.

On the twenty-third, when Austria issued its ultimatum to Serbia, Colonel Creighton arrived in Paris, having wasted a couple of days in a cave in the Black Forest. Paris was in the throes of the Caillaux scandal, but he ignored that, conferring with two artists and a newspaper editor. He also took an overnight train south to Marseilles to visit Fort St. Jean, European Headquarters of the Foreign Legion. He spent most of his time there in the chapel, then returned to the capital.

On July 28, when Austria declared war on Serbia, he obtained a berth on the next boat train to London—a surprising feat, considering the near-panic in the Gare du Nord.

On reaching England, he completely disappeared.

# 2

Edward arrived in Greyfriars on the 4.15 from London. It was the Saturday of August Bank Holiday weekend, and the little station was almost deserted. Paris had been in panic. London was a riot of trippers fighting their way out of town, heading for the seaside. Greyfriars was its usual sleepy country self.

He emerged from the station, bag in hand, to find the Bodgley Rolls at the curb, with Bagpipe himself at the wheel.

Edward said, "Damned good of you to put me up, Bodgley," and climbed in.

Bagpipe said, "Good to see you, old man. Care to go for a spin?" He was trying not to swallow his ears at being allowed to drive the Rolls.

So Timothy Bodgley drove Edward Exeter home to Greyfriars Grange by a somewhat roundabout route, but took care that they arrived in decent time to get ready for dinner. Edward thanked Mrs. Bodgley for taking him in at such short notice—and at his own request, of course, but that part of it was too painful to mention. She insisted he was always welcome.

Then there was a gap. This is a common result of head injuries.

He retained no record at all of the next hour. After that came a few scattered images of dinner itself, random pages saved from a lost book. His most vivid recollection was to be of his own intense embarrassment at being in blazer and flannels, like a stray dog that had wandered into the thoroughbred kennel. One of his cases had been stolen in Paris, and he had had no time to hire evening clothes on his dash through London. He had had no English money, either, and the banks were closed on Saturdays.

The nine or ten faces around the table remained only a blur. The Bodgleys themselves, of course, he knew well: Bagpipe and his parents—the large and booming Mrs. Bodgley, and the peppery general with his very red face and white mustache. There was a Major Someone, an ex-India type. There was a Dowager Lady Somebody and the vicar. And others. The scraps of conversation he did remember were all about the imminence of war. The major explained at length how easily the French and the Russians between them would roll up the Boche. Everyone agreed it would all be over by Christmas.

Later, when the ladies had withdrawn and left the men to the port and cigars, the talk was of the need to teach the Germans a damned good lesson, and which regiment Edward Exeter and Timothy Bodgley should join, and how lucky they were to be young enough to serve.

The evening concluded with patriotic songs around the piano, and everyone turned in early because the general was scheduled to read the lesson in church the next morning.

Later still, Edward sprawled on the window seat in his room while Bagpipe in pajamas and dressing gown sat on the chair, and the two of them nattered away like old times in the junior dorm. Bagpipe raved about the book he was reading, *The Lost World,* and promised to lend it to Edward as soon as he had finished. They reminisced about their schooldays, amused to discover that a mere week away had already wreathed Fallow in a haze of nostalgia. They returned to the subject of the war, and Bagpipe waxed bitter.

"Me enlist? It's not meant, old man. Won't pass the medical. Not Pygmalion likely!" Even as he said it, his lungs sounded like a dying cat. He had asthma; he had never been able to run even the length of cricket pitch without turning blue, but he was a straight enough chap in spite of it. He would miss the war, and Edward was at a loss to know how to comfort him, although he babbled nonsense about valuable alternatives, like intelligence work.

Then Bagpipe shrugged it off and tried to hide his chagrin. "What say we go down and raid the larder, like old times?"

Edward must have agreed, although he retained no recollection of doing so. A trivial boyish prank like that should have been beneath their dignity, but perhaps it suited the mood of unreality that had so suddenly descended upon their lives. They had emerged from the ordered, cloistered discipline of school into a world poised on the brink of madness.

The kitchen was in the oldest part of the Grange, a vast stone barn of echoes and monumental furniture and unsettling, unexplained shadows. There, for Edward Exeter, reality ended altogether.

After that there were just a few confused frozen images, like blurred photographs in newspapers, or line drawings in the *Illustrated London News.* There was a girl screaming, her screams reverberating in that cavernous stone scullery. She had wild eyes and hair that hung down in long ringlets. There was a knife. There was blood—a porcelain sink with blood pouring into it. He retained a very foggy memory of people beating on the door, trying to get in, and of himself fending off the knife-wielding maniac with the aid of a wooden chair. There was a terrible pain in his leg.

Then darkness and nightmare.

# 3

It was the hour before dawn. A gale left over from winter rolled clouds through the sky, continually veiling or unveiling the moons, so that sometimes the narrow streets were inky as coal cellars, and at others a man could read the storekeepers' signs creaking to and fro in the wind. Over the slate rooftops, far behind the chimneys, the ice-capped peaks of Narshwall glimmered like teeth with black tongues of cloud-shadow lolling over them.

Dragon claws scratching on cobblestones betrayed the progress of a watchman, riding slowly along Straight Way, making his rounds. It was a living, if not a very lucrative one, nor especially prestigious. It was a cursed cold living on a night like this, and his thoughts were mainly of the snug, wife-warmed bed awaiting him at sunrise. He wore a metal-and-leather helmet and a steel breastplate over a layer of fur and two of wool. He switched his lantern from one hand to the other, feeling its warmth even through his gloves. He was in more danger of freezing his fingers than of meeting with trouble at night in Narsh.

Narsh was a peaceable place, but long ago the city fathers had decreed a curfew, so someone must uphold it. Illicit love affairs were the main cause of curfew-breaking, but most nights the watchman met not a single soul. Any evildoers that might be skulking around heard his dragon approach or saw his light and took cover until he had gone. The ban applied only to persons on foot, of course. It excluded dragon riders and coaches, and thus it did not restrict the city fathers or their friends.

*Scritch, Scritch,* went the dragon's claws. The wind rattled shutters and moaned in high eaves. Total blackness enveloped Straight Way, except where the watchman's lantern cast an uncertain beam on doors and the gaping mouths of alleys. Through a momentary gap in the clouds he caught a glimpse of the fourth moon, Eltiana, a gory red star in the east. He thought a silent prayer—his usual prayer to the Lady, emphasizing the undesirability of her sending further progeny to swell the household he must feed on his meager pay.

Then great green Trumb soared into view, as if springing out from ambush, his mighty half disk illuminating the town, highlighting the spires of the Lady's temple . . . and revealing a double line of people shuffling along the street just ahead of the watchman. For a moment he was struck speechless. Then he barked a command to speed his mount: *"Varch!"*

The dragon was perhaps also surprised, for it was accustomed to amble the night streets at a comfortable *Zaib* and had probably not been required to go faster in many years. After a brief pause, as if it were trying to recall the training of its youth, it increased its pace obediently, and the night watch of Narsh bore down upon the lawbreakers.

There were about a dozen of them, arranged roughly by height, from a tall couple up front to a child trailing at the rear. They all bore bulky packs. The watchman rode past them, shining his lantern on them, heading for the leaders. They were not residents, he concluded, for few of them were clad in the all-enveloping Narshian furs. Most of them were hunched and shivering. Strangers! Curfew breakers!

He drew ahead, spoke orders to his dragon, and came to a halt, barring their way. They stopped. Many of them lowered their burdens to the ground with evident relief. They peered up at him. He peered back down at them with all the majesty of the law.

The law's majesty was not as awe-inspiring as he would have liked. The dragon was not much of a dragon. Its scales were so worn and scuffed where the stirrups had rubbed at them over the years that it had been double-docked—the pommel plate removed so that the saddle could be placed farther forward than was normal, or truly comfortable. Its rider was thus seated on a slight slope and could not lean back in comfort against the baggage plate.

The dragon studied the malefactors with as much interest as the watchman, while puffing pearly clouds for the wind to disperse. Its eyes glowed pale green. Ferocious as dragons seemed, they were the gentlest of beasts, and most people knew that. The watchman was not quite certain what he was supposed to do when faced with a dozen lawbreakers at once, and half of them women.

He said, "Ho!" Then he added, "Identify yourselves!"

The leader was a tall man in a flowing robe that swirled continuously in the wind. So did his white patriarchal beard. When he doffed his hat and bowed, he revealed a bald pate surrounded by a mane of long white locks, and the wind began playing with them also. Nonetheless, he was a striking figure under the green moonlight, and his voice rang out with the sonority of a peal of bells.

"I am Trong Impresario and these are my associates in the troupe that bears my name—singers, musicians, actors, wandering players, seeking only to serve the Lord of Art."

Wandering beggars, more like, but the watchman recalled that he had seen a playbill outside the Shearing Shed a couple of days ago.

"You are abroad before first light, and such is forbidden!"

The Trong man swung around to regard the east. With dramatic suddenness, he threw out a long arm. "Behold, sir! Already the dewy dawn blushes to look upon the deeds of night!" He spoke with a Joalian accent, but that did not mean he could see the horizon through a two-story building.

"Forgive us if we have offended!" proclaimed his companion. She was almost as tall as he, and her voice seemed even more resonant, carrying a hint of clashing steel. It was not as readily identifiable, but certainly not homely Narshian. " 'First light' is not a precise term. We are strangers and may have misconstrued your local usage."

The watchman could not imagine why anyone would waste good money going to hear this rabble of outlanders recite poetry or even sing, if that was what they did. It seemed very un-Narshian behavior, but if anyone attended those performances, they would be the wealthier citizens—and their wives, of course. To make trouble for this band of tattered beggars might possibly land him in disfavor with important persons.

"State your business!" he demanded, to give himself time to think.

"We proceed," Trong declaimed, "to the temple to make sacrifice. Our wandering feet lead us onward to the Festival of Holy Tion in Suss, and we would seek the favor of Ois before hazarding fearsome Rilepass."

Ah! In his youth, the watchman had attended the Festival of Tion a few times. He had competed in the boxing contests until his face became so battered that he had been refused admittance. Of course a troupe of actors would be heading that way at this time of year, and no one in his right mind would venture a mammoth ride over Rilepass without making an offering at the temple. As goddess of passes, Ois was liable to drop avalanches on travelers who displeased her.

He cast another quick look at the sky and again saw the red moon peering through a narrow gap in the clouds. Ois was an avatar of the Lady, Eltiana, who was not only one of the Five, but also specifically identified with the red moon. She was watching him to see what he was going to do. She might disapprove of him harassing pilgrims on their way to worship one of her manifestations. He had best let these vagabonds proceed about their business.

"You should have waited until daybreak!"

The woman spoke up quickly. "But our need to reach Suss is urgent. You must know that this is the seven hundredth festival, and very special. There are many like us, seeking passage, and the lines are long this year. Our impatience was inspired by our piety, Watchman."

It was true that Narsh had seen an unusual number of festival-goers passing through in the last fortnight, although the watchman's wife had told him that the normal contingent of artists, athletes, and cripples was much the same. Surplus priests and priestesses were to blame.

"Go in peace," he proclaimed, moving his dragon out of the way. "But next time observe the law more strictly."

They heaved their packs higher on their shoulders and tramped off in unhappy silence.

Trumb dipped into cloud again and the street darkened. The last the watchman saw of the actors as they faded out was the child at the rear. Stooped under her bulky pack, she walked with a marked limp. He could guess why that one was going to the Tion Festival.

# ACT I

## *Tragedy*

# 4

*M*urder! It never bleeding rained but it bloody poured.

Carruthers had taken his family to Harrogate, Robinson was hiking in Scotland, Hardy had broken his pelvis, and Newlands was in bed with acute appendicitis. Meaning Mister Muggins Leatherdale was left running the whole shop. Meaning simple Inspector Leatherdale, just six months short of retirement, poor sod, was now expected to do the work of a superintendent, a deputy superintendent, a squad of detective inspectors, and earn not a ha'penny more for it.

On top of all that there had been threats of civil war in Ireland last week and real war breaking out all over Europe now—the Boche and the Russkis at each other's throats already and the Frogs mobilizing—with resultant official warnings to look out for all sorts of un-English activities, like riots and marches. Half the force was away on holiday.

And now a murder, the first in the county in twenty years. Not just your drunken brawl in a pub, charge reduced to manslaughter. Not just some sordid backstreet quarrel over a woman, oh no! Nothing so simple for poor Muggins Leatherdale. No, the chief constable's own son murdered in the chief constable's own house and the Old Man himself two-thirds off his rocker with grief and shock.

Howzat for pouring?

*Bloody Noah's Flood*!

The bells of St. George's were pealing as the big car purred through Bishops Wallop. Leaning back on the leather cushions with his bowler on his lap, Leatherdale heard them with a strange sense of unreality. He'd been routed out of bed at midnight and his eyelids felt thick as muffins. Shameful. He was getting too old to be a real copper.

The sun was baking hot already, a perfect Bank Holiday weekend in a perfect summer. War and murder and insanity, and yet the bells of Bishops Wallop pealed as they always had. They had rung like that when Leatherdale was a boy, spending holidays with his grandparents in a cottage whose thatched roof and ceilings had seemed uncomfortably low even then. The tenor bell had sounded a tiny fraction flat in those days, and it did now. It had probably seemed that way to Richard the Lionheart.

Church bells were still ringing as he was whisked through Sternbridge, and he wondered what his grandfather would have said to that miracle. Or his father, for that matter. Toffed out in their Sunday best, the worthy folk ambled along the street to worship, very much as their forebears had done for centuries. Dogs barked to repel the intruder and probably thought their efforts successful, for the motor accelerated as it left the village and raced up the hill beyond. It must have been doing forty when it reached the long avenue of beeches and chestnuts.

He watched the great canopy of summer foliage rushing overhead as the vehicle traversed the green tunnel. All his life he had gone to work on his bike, in uniform. On his bike he would be able to hear the thrushes and the woodpeckers and see butterflies working the hedgerows, but he had asked the chauffeur to lower the black leather hood so he could enjoy the breeze, scented with thyme and clover. England in August! The hayfields were deserted today, their crop half cut. Down in the bottoms horses swished their tails at flies. Everywhere he looked, the hazy skyline was ornamented with church spires and towers rising over the trees. Once he could have named them all and probably still could if he had a moment to think—St. Peter's in Button Bent, St. Alban's in Cranley . . . Norman, High Gothic, Perpendicular. For a thousand years, every Englishman had dwelt within walking distance of a church.

He had pulled out his watch before he realized that the bells had just told him the time. Elsie would be pulling out the stops in St. Wilfred's about now. He was going to be early for his appointment.

This jaunt was all a waste of time anyway. Leatherdale had a corpse and a killer and an open-and-shut case. The motive might not be obvious to nice-thinking folks, but a copper knew about the seamy side of life. Such things could happen even in drowsy little Greyfriars, where a runaway horse was a month's excitement. They happened; they just weren't talked about. This jaunt to Fallow had been Mrs. Bodgley's idea and the Old Man had been ready to agree to anything. So Leatherdale got a ride in a Rolls Royce. He yawned.

Fallow? He had passed the gates a few times, never been inside. It was outside his manor. Outside his ken, too—educational establishment for young gentlemen. Snob factory. Fallow boys would show up around Greyfriars sometimes, on day outings with their parents, like tailors' dummies in their school uniform, top hat and tails, each one like every other one. All speaking alike with the *proper* accent and polite as Chinese mandarins, all of 'em.

He'd thought to quiz the police doctor about Fallow, but the answer had been very much what he'd expected. A highly respected public school, Watkins had said. Not Eton or Harrow, of course. Second eleven, but probably about the best in the second eleven. Has a very solid relationship with the Colonial Office. Turns out the men who run the Empire—something of a specialty of the house, you might say. A chap'll bump into Old Fallovians all over the globe, in just about every Crown Colony everywhere. Running them, of course. White Man's Burden, palm and pine, and all that.

Dear Mrs. Bodgley could not imagine anything on God's green earth that would turn a tailor's dummy, right-spoken, frightfully polite Fallow boy into a savage killer. Or her equally well-mannered son into a victim.

But Leatherdale could. Not nice. Not nice at all!

# 5

The sky was growing lighter as the Trong Troupe approached the temple. They were still arrayed in approximate order of size, although that was not a conscious arrangement. Trong Impresario led the way, like some peripatetic monument, with the statuesque Ambria at his side. Last of all came little Eleal Singer. The wind was still just as bitter and boisterous, whirling scattered snowflakes along the canyon of the street.

Hobbling under the weight of her pack, Eleal was immediately behind Klip and Olimmiar. She hated Narshvale. It was her least favorite of all the lands the troupe visited each year. Narshvale was cold, with leaden skies always seeming just about to spill snow. In Narsh itself the streets stank, because of the coal the Narshians burned to warm their ugly stone houses—grimy stone with roofs of black slate. The people stank, too, probably because they didn't wash their clothes. You couldn't wash llama fleece, it wouldn't dry before next winter.

She especially disliked the temple and Ois, its goddess, although of course no one would ever say such a thing out loud. Ambria probably felt the same way, because she always told Eleal to wait outside. If the old hussy thought Eleal did not know what went on in there, then she was sorely misinformed. In some of the villages the troupe played, they all had to share the same sleeping room. Eleal knew perfectly well what happened in the dark, under the covers. Uthiam and Golfren did it a lot, because they'd been married less than a year. K'linpor Actor and Halma did it too, and Dolm Actor and Yama, but not as often. Even Trong and Ambria did it sometimes. Everyone had to pretend not to hear, and nobody ever mentioned it, although when one couple started it, they often set off others.

They were married and did it because they wanted to and must like it. What happened in the temple of Ois was different. It involved money, and was supposed to be a sacrifice to the goddess, but no other god or goddess that Eleal knew of demanded that. She often wondered how the priestesses felt about it. She'd even asked Uthiam once if that was what the men did on their annual visit. Uthiam had become indignant and said of course not, Trong Impresario would never allow them to, not even the bachelors.

"You mean it's wrong?" Eleal had asked, very sweetly.

"Certainly not!" Uthiam had declared, one must not presume to judge what the gods decree. She had turned very pink and changed the subject.

Up front, Trong and Ambria had rounded the corner. They would stop at the temple door for everyone else to catch up, and then Ambria would order Eleal to wait outside.

Well, Eleal saw no reason why she should walk all that way and then back again with this heavy pack. She was not going to wait outside and freeze to death—she had other plans!

Checking that Uthiam and Dolm were still talking and paying no attention to her, she ducked into a doorway and made herself as flat as paint.

She felt breathless and her heart was thumping faster than usual. She had eaten no breakfast, yet there was a tight feeling in her insides. The annual mammoth ride over Rilepass always affected her like this. The summit was very scary, with huge masses of ice and snow liable to break off and crash down. Sometimes even a surefooted mammoth could slip and fall miles down, into a gorge. It was very exciting.

Everyone sacrificed to Ois before crossing Rilepass. On the other hand, the goddess was not likely to worry very much about one twelve-year-old girl, and even the goddess couldn't drop an avalanche on her without also dropping it on all the other people riding in the same howdah. Eleal was going to go and pray to Tion instead. She had some very special prayers to make.

She risked a glance around the corner, but Dolm and Uthiam were still in sight, and a few of the others also. She pulled back into her hiding place, grateful to be out of the wind, puffing on the tip of her nose to warm it.

Some big cities boasted several temples, but even towns like Narsh that had only one temple would also have at least one shrine to each member of the Pentatheon, either in person or to an aspect. Ois was an aspect of Eltiana, the Lady in her role as custodian of passes. Narsh also had a shrine to Kirb'l, the Joker, and the Joker was an aspect of Tion, the Youth.

It was very curious that the dour Narshians should have chosen that particular Tion persona to be his local representative. Narshians had less humor than any people she knew. Whereas most people never left the land they were born in, Eleal was very well traveled. The troupe visited seven of the Vales on their annual circuit. This year they had spent half a fortnight in Narsh. They had staged the comedy three times and the tragedy four times, without taking in enough to pay for the groceries, so Ambria said. Mill owners and ranchers, she grumbled—the meanest people in the world. They certainly had no sense of humor, so why should they honor the Joker so?

Piol Poet said that humor was the highest form of art, because it made people rejoice. He was joking when he said so.

Another glance showed Eleal that the coast was now clear. She left the alcove and hurried back the way she had come, her mismatched boots going *clip, clop, clip, clop.* Some of the locals were emerging now, as dawn approached, all bundled up in their smelly fleeces and furs. Miserable troglodytes! Trong Impresario had been stupendous as Trastos, especially when he was dying, but Narsh had just sat on its hands.

Piol had written speaking parts for Eleal into both plays this year, small ones. She played a gods' messenger in the tragedy—she sang offstage, of course—and a young herald in the comedy, where she could use the staff to hide her limp. So she had played Narsh for the first time in her life, being received with wild indifference. Her curtain calls and standing ovations had totaled zero, exactly. In Lappin her acting had won applause one night; her singing in the masque always did. Tonight she would play in Sussland. Sussvale was a warmer, nicer place and did not stink of coal smoke. The Sussians would clap for her.

She turned a corner. Fortunately, there seemed to be a law everywhere that holy places must bunch together. The shrines in Narsh all adjoined the back wall of the Lady's temple, like chicks huddled under a hen's wing. There was one for Visek the Parent, one for Karzon the Man, one for Astina the Maiden, and the Youth's was at the far end of the street. What all the other buildings were, she did not know. Priests' houses, perhaps.

*Clip, clop, clip, clop . . .*

She would not have much time. She had her prayers all planned. First she would ask the god to see her safely to his Festival, of course—just in case Ois took offense. Then she would pray for her friends, that the troupe might win the drama contest, Piol Poet for the play itself, and others for their individual performances. It was a bad year when the Trong Troupe did not collect at least three roses. Especially she must pray for Uthiam, who had been practicing *Ironfaib's Polemic* for months and could still bring tears to Eleal's eyes with it. Uthiam was married now. Next year she would either be the wrong shape or have a baby to look after.

Not far to go. *Clip, clop . . .* She was panting, sweating in her llama fleece coat, despite the icy wind. She slowed down a little. If she were too much out of breath, she would not be able to sing for the god.

And the last prayer . . . It was not so very much to ask. The Youth was god of art, and therefore the god most favored by actors. He was also god of beauty, which was why ugly or deformed people could not enter his Festival. And he was god of healing. Every year, at the closing ceremonies, he would grant at least one miracle cure to some fortunate pilgrim. Was it so much to ask that Eleal Singer's leg be made whole, so that in future years she, too, could enter his festival and sing for his glory?

The shrine was marked by an archway, painted yellow. Heaving her pack higher on her aching shoulders, Eleal limped inside.

She had never considered that there might be someone else there.

The shrine was a smallish, squarish room, lit by the doorway and some high windows. It contained only a low altar for offerings, with two tall candlesticks—which she strongly suspected were not real gold—and a large frog, carved out of yellow stone. She had come here many times. She thought that the god of beauty ought to have arranged for a more esthetic shrine, but she supposed its simplicity was sort of artistic . . . if you liked sheds. The frog was one of the Youth's symbols, associated especially with Kirb'l, who was not only the Joker but also the golden moon, the one that did not behave like the other moons. So the frog itself was all right. It was the leer on its face and its skewed eyes that secretly annoyed her.

The man annoyed her much more. He was tiny and bent, and without his voluminous fur robe he would be tinier still. He was busily sweeping the floor with a scrawny broom, raising clouds of dust for the wind to stir.

Seeing her shadow, perhaps, he stopped his sweeping and turned around to peer at her. Inside his hood, all that showed was a face with a million wrinkles and eyes that did not look in the same direction. He must be even older than Piol Poet.

"Blessings upon you, missy!" he slobbered, leering at her cheerfully with toothless gums.

All she could think of to say was, "I came to pray to the god!" Which was obvious, of course.

"And make an offering, I hope? My breakfast, I hope?" He rolled one eye in the direction of her pack.

To her disgust, she saw a hem of dirty yellow protruding from under his furs. This rag doll must be the resident priest. She had never seen him here before, or even wondered who tended the shrine and removed each day's offerings. So she could not just ask him to leave. She did not want a nosy old priest eavesdropping on her prayers. And the only real offering she might give was a single copper coin, which she had not intended to give.

Still, she had come and had best get on with her business so she could run back to the temple door and wait for the others. Or perhaps she could just meet them out at the mammoth pens.

"I was planning to sing for the god."

The old man sighed, although his toothless grin did not fade. "Then I must enjoy your song. It will be a lighter breakfast than yesterday's, although probably more memorable. That's the best you can do?" he added wistfully.

She was nettled, as any true artist would be by such an attitude. He was making fun of her. "Music is my profession!"

He pursed his lips in wonder and turned to lean the broom in a corner. "May your offering be worthy of the god. What is your name, child?"

"Eleal Singer."

"*Who?*" The old man spun around with surprising agility. Both his eyes had opened very wide, although only one was looking at her. "You are *Eleal?* But where is the Daughter?"

She had been just about to wriggle out of her pack straps. This inexplicable reaction made her pause. "What daughter?"

The priest took a step toward her, anxiously rubbing his hands. His fingers were twisted, white with cold. "The Daughter of Irepit, of course! Don't you know about the prophecy? Don't you realize that you are in terrible danger? There is a reaper in town! You are so much younger than I expected!" Still babbling, he followed Eleal as she backed away. His wrinkles writhed in anguish. "Surely death will seek you out to break the chain! Who is looking after you, child? Your father? Parents?"

She had no parents, but she was not about to explain that to this crazy old man with his ravings of reapers and danger and chains and daughters of Irepit, whoever she might be. He was more than a few seats short of a full house. Someone had shuffled his script.

"Thank you for the warning," she said. Her retreat had brought her to the door. "I'll go and look after that right away!"

She turned and ran, pack and all. *Clipclopclipclopclip* . . .

# 6

The big car purred in through the gates of Fallow. Leatherdale peered out sourly at the ivy-shrouded Gothic buildings, the shady elms, the central lawn basking in the sunshine. He'd played billiards on worse. The Gothic was of the Railway Nabob variety, but pleasantly aged now—best part of a century, at a guess. Pretty soon it would class as old, even by English standards. He wondered what it cost a man to send his son to a place like this, even as a day boy. If you had to ask, you couldn't afford it.

Had Elsie given him a son, the boy would have followed his father's footsteps through Parish Boys' School in Greyfriars. He'd have learned the Three R's and been gone at fourteen, most likely. Not for him the inside track of a public school—classical education, university entrance, front of the queue when the posh jobs were handed out. This was where the bosses came from, the officers, the cabinet ministers, the men who ran the Empire. The Old Boys' Network began here, at the snob factory.

The car glided to a stop in front of an imposing doorway, flanked by steps. There was no drawbridge or portcullis, but the architecture implied that there should be. The morning was magically peaceful, with doves cooing somewhere and a few faint clicks and puffings from the engine.

"Tudor House, sir," said the chauffeur, opening the door. He must know, having driven the Young Master here often enough.

Leatherdale stepped down. "Shan't be more than twenty minutes, I expect, but you've got time to go find a cuppa round the back if you want."

A respectful smile thawed the man's professional inscrutability. "Why, I'd trust 'em with my life, sir! But I'll stay here."

Eight boys had condensed out of the summer morning to examine the car. They ranged in height from not much over four feet to not much less than six. They wore toppers and tails and not one hand was in a pocket. They were standing back, carefully not crowding close enough to the machine to provoke its guardian, murmuring technical details without raising their voices: "Guff! She'll do more'n that . . ." "Bags more'n thirty horsepower!"

These unfortunates must be boarders with no homes to go to, residing at Fallow over the summer holidays. Lordie, what would it cost even to clothe a boy here? On a Sunday morning, Leatherdale would have expected them to be marched off to church parade. Then he realized that the tallest boy was Oriental and three of the others various shades of brown. Perhaps none of them were Christians. Rather startled by that possibility, he set off up the steps.

"Inspector Leatherdale?" The speaker was standing in the doorway, a bearded, paunchy man with a marked resemblance to the late King Edward.

Who else would it be, coming to ruin a perfect summer Sunday?

"Mr. Jones?"

Jones was staring past his visitor at the thousand-guinea motor. Perhaps his query had not been totally inane. Policemen did not normally travel in quite such style.

The hallway was dim and baronial, so full of silence that it seemed to echo with it, smelling of polish and chalk, exercise books and blotting paper. Marble stairs flanked by iron railings led up to mysterious heights. The room to which the visitor was led was equally institutional, furnished with aging armchairs and an ingrained reek of pipe smoke. Despite the windows open at the top, the air was stuffy and dead. Stern portraits of elderly gentlemen peered down disapprovingly between bookshelves, and the linoleum by the door was dangerously worn.

"Masters' common room," Jones explained quite needlessly. "May I offer you some tea, Inspector?"

Leatherdale declined the tea and accepted a chair with his back to the windows. It was more comfortable than it looked, and much too comfortable for a man who had been granted only two hours' sleep.

Jones took a chair opposite, first removing a copy of the *Times,* which he brandished to demonstrate indignation. "Seen this morning's news? The Prussian rogues have invaded Luxembourg! And declared war on Russia. Belgium, Holland, Sweden—all mobilizing. Bounders!"

"Bad business," Leatherdale agreed.

"The Kaiser's a maniac! Doesn't he realize that we mean what we say? England's made it perfectly plain, hasn't it, for years, that if Luxembourg or Belgium is invaded, then we'll have to fight? Don't the blighters understand that our word is our bond? That they're going to bring the British Empire in against them?" He slapped the paper down angrily. "May as well get it over with, I suppose. The Hun has made it pretty clear that he plans to smash France and Russia first and then deal with us later."

Leatherdale made sounds of assent. Jones's resemblance to the late king was astonishing, except that he wore pince-nez, which flashed in the light from the window. From lifetime habit Leatherdale quantified his estimates—middle fifties, five-foot-eight or -nine, weight close to fourteen stone, well dressed, hair brown turning gray at the temples, full beard likewise.

"I mean we have no choice, have we?" Jones persisted. "When a chap already has the world's biggest army and keeps adding to it, and then his neighbors justifiably start to get alarmed and add a few guns of their own and the Germans scream that they're being encircled . . ." Having apparently lost the thread of his sentence, he scowled into silence and leaned back to regard his visitor. "Madmen!" he added. "Huns!"

His accent was pure Oxbridge, a long way from the mining valleys of his ancestors, the sort of drawl that always carried hints of arrogance, whether intentional or not. He wore a brown suit of good Harris tweed and a pair of stout brogues—and also an entirely inappropriate old boy tie. Leatherdale decided he resented that tie. Whatever school or university or regiment it represented, it was around that shiny white collar at the moment only to impress him.

"I shan't keep you from your ramble any longer than I have to, Mr. Jones." He pulled out his notebook. "I need some background information. To be specific, I need to see the personal files on two of your boys. Technically old boys, now, I believe."

"I'm frightfully sorry, Inspector, but that will not be possible." Jones blinked solemnly. Was he enjoying himself baiting the rustic policeman? Or was he merely the chicken left in charge of the farm, scared to do anything at all while the watchdogs took their holidays at the seaside?

"This is not a matter of cribbing apples, Mr. Jones." Did he think Leatherdale had nothing better to do on summer Sundays?

The master tapped his beard with the tips of his steepled fingers. "I do not doubt that the matter is important. I should be happy to assist you in any way I can, but the filing cabinets are locked and I have no keys."

Without question, his first priority would be to protect the school's reputation. He could have been picked out as a schoolmaster a furlong off. He had the diffident, mannered speech, the air of tight control, and even the curious blunting of masculinity that sometimes showed in men who must constantly guard their tongues. Clergymen had it also. He was a book whose pages were becoming yellow and dog-eared, the binding threadbare and gilt lettering worn. It would open to predictable pages.

Now he reached for the arms of his chair, as if to pull himself out of it and end the interview. "I do wish you had mentioned documents when you telephoned, Inspector. I could have saved you the journey. You only said you wanted information, and you will recall that I did explain that the Head will not be back until Thursday at the earliest, and any statements really ought to come from him. I am just *in loco magistri,* you might say, not authorized to comment at all." The pince-nez glinted.

He was not a material witness, who must be played like a ten-pound salmon on a five-pound line. Far from it—he was just a watchdog that could be brought to heel. Yet the man could help, if he would. Juries hated to convict without being shown a motive. Jones could clarify the motive in this case. Which one was the pouncer—the killer or the victim? Or both?

Leatherdale decided to try a couple more drops of honey before applying vinegar. "Now, if I may have your full name, sir?"

"David Jones. French master."

How many hundreds of boys had been processed into speaking French with that accent? "You have been here how long?"

"Ten—no, eleven years now. Before that—"

"Not necessary, sir. I just wanted to know how well you are acquainted with the boys in question."

The fancy spectacles shone white and inscrutable. "I am not sure that I might not be in breach of confidence were I to discuss any of our pupils without the Head's authorization or perhaps the advice of a solicitor, Inspector."

Yes, he was enjoying himself.

"The keys to the filing cabinets? Who has them?"

"The Head, of course. Dr. Gibbs."

"And the duplicate set? There must be a duplicate set?"

"I don't know. I certainly don't know where they are, if they exist."

"Mr. Jones, the matter cannot wait until Thursday. How may I get in touch with the Headmaster?"

A gold tooth flashed as Jones smiled. "I don't think you can, Inspector. He was on his way to Crete to visit Evans's dig. He has four senior boys with him, and two more are on their way to join him—or they were. Dr. Gibbs and his companions got as far as Greece. With the present turmoil, I suspect their journey home may take longer than expected."

Leatherdale favored him for a moment with a blandly thoughtful expression. Then he said, "Technically the board of governors would have overall authority over the premises?"

Jones flinched. "I suppose they must, but the board have always—"

"In a sense, sir, you and I work for the same man. General Bodgley is not only chairman of your board, but also my chief constable. I should perhaps have brought a note from him, but I assumed you would cooperate without it."

"Cooperate? I assure you—"

"Actually that is his car and chauffeur outside. Perhaps if we can reach him by telephone . . ."

The watchdog was in full retreat already. "Inspector, er, Leatherdale, I assure you that I am trying my best! I do not know where the keys to the cabinets are kept. I do not know exactly where the Head is. I can show you his telegram, but it was dispatched from some railway station in Austria and will not help you. The bursar is touring in Switzerland. If General Bodgley does not have a duplicate set of keys, and I would not expect him to, then I cannot imagine who else does." Jones clawed at his beard with his left hand.

"Dr. Gibbs does not employ a secretary?"

"Paddling at Blackpool, I believe. This is August Bank Holiday weekend, Inspector! England is closed. However, if any Fallow boy is in trouble, then of course I am more than ready to assist your inquiries in any way I can."

Better. Leatherdale nodded. "I just need information about a couple of them, that's all."

"Their names?"

"Edward George Exeter?"

Jones stiffened. "Exeter? Oh, Lord! You don't mean they got caught up in the Balkan imbroglio, too?"

"Nothing to do with the Balkans that I know of, sir."

"But Exeter and Smedley were on their way to join Dr. Gibbs. The two I mentioned."

"They were forced to cancel. They returned home from Paris."

"Well that's a relief! A great relief! I was quite concerned about them and I—" Jones's smile vanished as fast as it had come. "You mean there's been an accident?"

"No, sir."

This time the shock was obvious. "Exeter is in *trouble?*"

"What can you tell me about him, sir?"

The teacher drew a deep breath. "Exeter was house prefect in his final year! An excellent boy in every way. He was here in Tudor! I was his housemaster, Inspector, so I know him well. Exeter would be almost the last boy I would expect to fall afoul of the law! That is the case, isn't it? You're telling me that he is being investigated by the British police?"

"I am afraid that is the case."

Looking stunned, Jones pulled a linen handkerchief from his pocket and dabbed his forehead. His distress and astonishment seemed quite genuine. "I mean, he has definitely not just met with an accident or something?"

"Too early to say, sir. No charges have been laid as yet, but at the moment the situation does look grave."

"God bless my soul!" Jones sprawled back in his chair. "Exeter? I nominated him for my house prefect, Inspector, and he performed every bit as well as I expected. I cannot give you a higher character reference than that—cannot give any boy a higher recommendation. You did not say that . . . I mean, I have notes of my own on boys in Tudor. I shall gladly make them available." Again he moved as if to rise, although now it was an obvious effort.

"Later, sir, I shall appreciate seeing them. Meanwhile, tell me what you know of him. His character, his background. His family, particularly."

Jones sank back again, fumbling with his handkerchief. He paused for a moment to gather thoughts, then spoke without looking up. "Leadership, Inspector. Leadership is our product. They come here as children. They leave as young men. Rather innocent young men by the world's standards, I suppose, but well molded to take their place in the service of the Empire. Many a lad has walked out of here and in three or four years been running a chunk of country somewhere half the size of England—dictator, judge, soldier, engineer, tax collector, policeman, all rolled into one. Not for power, not for money, but purely out of a sense of duty!"

Leatherdale waited.

Jones's glasses glittered. "Latin and Greek and all that—none of it really matters. It isn't what you know that matters in this world, it's what you are! *Esse non sapere*— school motto. We teach them honor, honesty, and fair play. They take it from there. Not all of them, of course, not by a long shot. But the best ones are as good as you'll find anywhere. I'd have classed Exeter with the best." He looked across defiantly at the policeman.

Mrs. Bodgley had said very much the same.

"Some specifics, if you please."

Jones stuffed the handkerchief back in his trouser pocket. "Edward Exeter? Born in British East Africa—in '96, I suppose. Came here when he was about twelve. Left officially a week ago. Good pupil, credit to the school. Turned down a chance to play for the county this summer."

He paused then. Still Leatherdale waited, sensing better game on its way.

"Exeter's had more than his share of tragedy already. I'm sure you recall the Nyagatha affair?"

"Vaguely."

"Exeter's father was the district officer. He and his wife were among the dead. They were due to go on leave within days."

"The general mentioned something about it. He was, er, rather vague." That was an understatement of elephantine proportions.

Jones pulled a face. "You'd best look up the official report if you're interested. The whole thing was just one of those senseless episodes of bloodshed that seem to be the inevitable price of progress. Less than ten years ago that whole area was just uncharted bush, you know. Barbarism is still very close below the surface. The trouble did not even originate in Exeter's district. Some disaffected warriors of a neighboring tribe—Meru, or some name like that—outlaws, hungry, raiding for food . . . massacre, atrocities, followed by retribution. So history rolls along, leaving a few more gravestones by the roadway to be mourned for a generation." Mr. Jones sighed at the folly of mankind.

"How old would Exeter have been, then, sir?"

"Sixteen."

"He was here, in Fallow? How did he take it?"

"Oh, really! How do you think? He was shattered, of course. The news came in on a weekend and no one in Whitehall bothered to notify him. The first he knew was when the newspapers arrived on Monday morning. He hadn't seen his parents in four years, and was looking forward to a reunion that summer."

"No brothers or sisters?"

Jones sighed again. "None. He made a wonderful recovery. Tremendous pluck. His marks hardly dipped. And then, just as he seemed to be over the worst of it, the board of inquiry report came out and opened all the wounds again."

"Spell the name of that place, sir, if you please. And the exact date, or as close as you can recall?" Leatherdale knew he was getting full cooperation now. He felt no satisfaction from so easy a victory. "How did it open the wounds, sir?"

"Well, it opened wounds for Exeter." Jones removed his pince-nez and wiped them on his tie. He dabbed one eye surreptitiously with a knuckle. "His father was cleared of any blame in the atrocity itself. As I said, the perpetrators were just a band of malcontents wandering off the reserve. But Exeter was severely criticized for not maintaining a garrison of trained native troops handy to defend the post. Young Exeter will tell you—and I can almost sympathize with his views—that his father was being condemned for being too good at his job. If he'd been a worse governor and ruled by terror as some of them do, then he would have had protection to hand! Another of the ironies of history, mm? But Exeter has already passed through the Valley of Shadows, young as he is."

"And his legal guardian?"

Jones replaced his glasses and peered incredulously. "Why do you need to ask? Can't he speak for himself? Is he missing?"

"No, sir." Leatherdale flipped back a couple of pages. " 'Concussion, compound fracture of the right leg, extensive minor contusions.' He was just starting to come around when I left."

"Good God!" Jones paused, as if shocked by his own profanity, then added, "His guardian is his uncle, the Reverend Roland Exeter, director of the Lighthouse Missionary Society."

He spoke as if everyone knew the Reverend Dr. Exeter, and admittedly Leatherdale had heard of him. He did not reveal that he had already spoken with the holy gentleman on the telephone early that morning, nor that it had taken the Reverend Exeter's house-keeper considerable time to persuade him even to come to the phone. When he had come, he had explained at length that his religious beliefs forbade him to travel on Sundays—no, not even to visit an injured nephew involved in a murder case.

"Exeter also corresponded with a chap in the Colonial Office," Jones said, frowning. "I have his name and address somewhere, I'm sure. A Mr. Oldcastle, as I recall. In such cases, His Majesty's Government takes an interest, of course, and quite rightly so."

"No other relatives?"

"Only a cousin, so far as I know."

Leatherdale's antennae quivered, but he said, "Family friends?"

"None I have ever heard mentioned."

"Does the name 'Jumbo' mean anything to you, Mr. Jones?"

"Common nickname, that's all. We have a Jumbo Little in Fourth Form."

"No. Tell me about the cousin."

"Miss Alice Prescott. I have her address also, I believe."

"They are close?"

Jones forced a thin smile of acknowledgment. "Exeter went to her twenty-first a couple of months ago. Until she reached her majority, they were both wards of their reverend uncle. I have not met the lady for several years, but I believe the young man is seriously smitten. I do not know how she feels about him. He is three years her junior and they are first cousins."

"I shall see she is informed, sir."

"Thank you. I'm sure Exeter will be grateful, and if she is anything like he thinks she is, she will respond."

A good housemaster was much more than a jailer. Leatherdale raised his estimation of David Jones. In the case of at least one of his charges, he had obviously won trust and friendship.

"Tell me of the boy himself, sir."

"Solid!" Jones thought for a moment. "Fair athlete, but not exceptional, except at cricket. There he was one of the best fast bowlers we've had for some time. A bit of a loner, especially since the tragedy, but popular despite that. He made an excellent prefect. Born leader—kept the youngsters in line and never raised his voice. They worshiped him. Damnably weak in maths—can't seem to see the point of 'em. A real flair for languages. Walked off with the medals in Greek and German and came close in Latin, too. More competition in French," he added vaguely.

This sort of stuff would be deadly in court.

"So he has left school. What are his ambitions, can you say?"

Jones hesitated. "If I know Exeter, then he's panting to get into uniform like all the others. Teach the Hun a lesson, by Jingo!"

"And if there's no mobilization?"

"He was going up to Cambridge. Looks like he has his choice of two or three colleges—there is money in the family for that sort of thing."

"To follow in his father's footsteps? Colonial Office?"

Pause. "Oh, no. Modern languages."

Leatherdale made a note. The witness was holding something back. Probably young Exeter resented the organization that had condemned his father for being too good at his job. His ambitions could hardly be relevant to the murder, though.

*Motive?* Leatherdale wanted the motive. What turned a model public schoolboy into a savage killer?

"No family on his mother's side?"

"Exeter himself knows of none. She was a New Zealander."

"Of European stock?"

Jones laughed contemptuously. "You're looking for a touch of the tar brush, Inspector? I admit he has black hair, and he takes a good tan, but those eyes! Blue as they come. Looks Cornish, I'd say."

Nettled in spite of himself, Leatherdale said, "I didn't see his eyes, sir. They were closed." He shrugged and took up his quest again. "What of his private life? Any wild oats in his background?"

The French master had aged several years since he sat down. The condescension had long since faded from his manner, but that remark brought an angry flush to his cheek. "I have already given you my appraisal of Exeter. He is a young English gentleman."

"A direct answer, if you please, Mr. Jones."

Jones snorted. "Boys in public school have no private life. What happens in the holidays is beyond my ken, but I should doubt it very much, in his case. Schools such as Fallow are a great deal more celibate than any monastery the church ever knew. I told you—I think Master Exeter has his heart set on his cousin. I simply cannot imagine his being promiscuous."

Reluctantly, Leatherdale noted the reply. "Forgive this next question, but it must be asked. How about, 'The love that dares not breathe its name'?"

"No! Any hint of that in Fallow is cause for immediate sacking—boys or masters!" Jones glared for a moment, then sighed. "Of course it is always a potential problem in any all-male community. Some otherwise exemplary schools . . . you know, I'm sure. We are not naive. We watch for it. We haven't had a case in several years. Cold baths and constant vigilance, Inspector!"

"Not Exeter?"

"Absolutely not."

He seemed to be sincere. He might not be quite as shrewd a judge of his charges as he believed. A storm of passion of one sort or another was the only credible motive in the case. Leatherdale toyed with his pen for a moment, wondering if there was anything more he need ask about Exeter. The housemaster's enthusiasm for the boy was worrisome. However misplaced, it would go down well with a jury.

When he looked up, Jones seemed to brace himself in his chair. "And the other boy you are interested in, Inspector? Smedley, I suppose?"

"Timothy Fitzjohn Bodgley."

*"What?"* Jones could not have displayed greater shock had he been informed that he had been chosen to tutor the Prince of Wales in Hebrew. "Explain!"

"At the moment the details are confidential, Mr. Jones. It missed the Sunday papers, but some of it will most certainly be in tomorrow's."

The master moaned. "For God's sake tell me! This is awful!"

"First your comments on young Bodgley, if you please. Was he also in your house?"

"Yes he was. He and Exeter were close chums as juniors and the friendship lasted—they don't always, of course. It's less on Exeter's side than Bodgley's, I'd say. Exeter is more, er, self-sufficient." Jones began polishing his glasses again, gazing blankly meanwhile, as if he could not see without them. "Bodgley's a delicate boy. He is frequently troubled by asthma. This has kept him back in games . . . He was known as Bagpipe."

"His father is an Old Etonian." Leatherdale did not mention that he had researched his chief constable in that worthy gentleman's own copy of *Who's Who*.

Jones smiled faintly at nothing. Then he replaced his spectacles and seemed to come back to life. "You are wondering why he did not send his own son there? Because of the asthma. Fallow is closer to home than Eton. Or are you wondering why our chairman is not an Old Fallovian? That's a matter of politics—money and influence, Inspector. And if you are wondering whether young Bodgley was of better family than most of our boys, the answer to that is yes. The blood runs blue in the Bodgley veins. His future in the Empire, if any, will be at the level of British resident, far above the district officerships to which Exeter might aspire. Foreign Office and *corps diplomatique* would be more his field. He's a bit spoiled, pampered and oversheltered, and inclined to feel sorry for himself. I might just be persuaded that he had been led into wrongdoing by an older, stronger character—which I would not believe of Exeter—but basically he's a fine young man, and I am convinced that whatever you suspect these two of, your information is incorrect."

He tried to smile, but the result was grotesque. "There! I have been completely frank, have I not? Now will you inform me of the trouble they appear to be in? Less than a week ago I saw my young friends walk out into a world that looked ready to throw itself at their feet. I asked Exeter to sacrifice a glass of retsina to Poseidon in my name. Now you tell me he is back in this country and under suspicion of wrongdoing."

"I can tell you a little." Leatherdale did not close his notebook. "The preliminaries you already know. When Smedley's parents called him back from Paris, Exeter returned also. He apparently found himself with nowhere to go, but he had a standing invitation to visit Greyfriars Grange. . . . Where did he normally spend his holidays, when his parents were alive?"

"Here," Jones said quietly. "He has lived at Fallow since he was twelve, except for a few odd breaks, such as OTC camp or school outings or visiting his friends. Many of our boys are children of parents living overseas. Other parents will often take pity on their sons' chums in such case—invite them to stay over Christmas, for example."

"Never with his uncle?"

"Rarely. I gathered that the experience was always mutually unpleasant."

Leatherdale made a note. "And as an old boy, he could not just return to Fallow?"

Jones shook his head sadly. "Inspector! He had just *left school!* Don't you remember how huge that milestone loomed in your own life? Even if the alternative was his friend's charity . . . The raven had been released from the ark!"

Interesting point, Leatherdale thought. The youth must have been in an agitated state of mind. His uncle had been surprised to learn he was back in England.

"Exeter telegraphed to the Bodgleys from Paris and was accepted. He arrived yesterday." Watching carefully, he continued. "I can outline the statement released to the newspapers. General Bodgley's household at Greyfriars Grange was awakened shortly after midnight this morning by the sound of an altercation in the kitchen quarters. Investigation revealed Mr. Edward George Exeter injured and unconscious, and the mortal remains of Mr. Timothy Fitzjohn Bodgley. Foul play is suspected."

"Good God!" All the color drained from Jones's face, leaving a parchment marred by brown age spots. He licked his lips and even his tongue seemed pale. "Dead! How?"

"The nature of his injuries is not being released, sir."

"Inspector! I have known these boys for years. They are my friends and my life's work and until last week they were my wards!"

Leatherdale decided to trust him. It might prove to be an indiscretion, but he was in charge of the investigation. He had the right to make his own mistakes. "In strict confidence, then, sir? I do not wish the press to get its hands on this."

Jones licked his lips. "I may tell Dr. Gibbs when he returns?"

"That would be in order. Exeter fell or was thrown down the cellar steps. He sustained the injuries I mentioned. Bodgley had been stabbed to death with a carving knife."

Jones's mouth moved for a while before he croaked, "Just the two of them there?"

"That is implied in the official statement. I cannot say any more, sir."

"But why in Heaven? . . ."

"Motive? A good question. Why should two young men raid a kitchen at that time of night? Since the cellar is used to store the general's wine, we might speculate that they were after more than a cup of tea."

"I suppose some such prank is not impossible," Jones admitted hoarsely.

"If it was a prank, it rapidly became something else." Leatherdale waited hopefully, but if Jones guessed what he wanted to hear, he did not oblige. Pity. Leatherdale was curious to know which one of the two had started the hanky-panky and which had resisted. In spite of his considerable advantage in height and weight, Exeter's only possible defense was self-defense. It would not get him off or even reduce the charge to manslaughter, but it might wring a recommendation of mercy out of a sympathetic jury.

He closed his notebook. He had an open-and-shut case. He had failed to uncover a motive, but the Crown was not obliged to establish motive. At the next assizes, learned counsel would explain to the jury how Exeter had stabbed his friend and then, in a panicky attempt to flee from the scene of the crime, had fallen down the cellar steps.

The defense would drag in the vague reports of a woman screaming—they would not be able to explain her disappearance through doors bolted on the inside. They were welcome to propose that Bodgley had thrown his guest into the cellar and subsequently thrust a steel carving knife in his own back so hard that he had nailed himself to a teak draining board.

The jury would deliberate and then the judge would don the black cap to order Edward George Exeter hanged by the neck.

Suddenly Leatherdale was seized by a frightful desire to yawn. It was time to go. He could do no more good at Fallow, if indeed he had done any good at all. He should be grateful for a rare opportunity—the thrill of a murder investigation without the tedious follow-up, for it would all be taken out of his hands by tomorrow at the latest. He had everything he needed to brief Scotland Yard when the Old Man came to his senses. Even if the Old Man didn't, Robinson should be back by then, if he could find his way through Bank Holiday traffic.

A telephone rang somewhere in the distance.

"That is probably the press already," he said wearily. "I advise you not to say anything at all." He levered himself out of the chair. "If you will look out for those notes you mentioned, sir?"

Jones stayed where he was, staring up at his visitor as if felled by shock. When he spoke, though, it was obvious that he had been thinking hard. "The general's son was murdered in his own house and yet he, as chief constable, is titular head of the investigation? Is he not placed in an impossible situation, Inspector?"

"Awkward, sir. I expect he will call in Scotland Yard in due course."

When he came to his senses, he would—or when he was allowed to, for Leatherdale had a strong suspicion that the formidable Mrs. Bodgley was meddling in police business.

"The Home Secretary may have something to say when he hears of it, I shouldn't wonder," Jones said drily. His eyes were invisible behind white reflections again. The instant Leatherdale left the building, David Jones would be on the phone to some senior members of the board of governors.

"Not up to me to question orders, sir."

The two men stared at each other.

"I don't envy you, Inspector," the schoolmaster said softly.

Leatherdale sensed the offer of the Old Boys' Network. "We all do our duty as best we can, sir."

Jones scratched his beard. "Normally, of course, the Home Secretary's sacred weekend would never be disturbed by anything as petty as willful homicide. But I'm afraid times are not normal. The Cabinet is in almost continuous session because of the crisis. On a weekend? Incredible! On August Bank Holiday weekend in particular? Epochal! It may take a little time for Whitehall to catch up on routine matters, you realize?"

Leatherdale had not even thought of that. What the damned Frogs and Huns and Wops got up to on the Continent was their business, and he hoped His Majesty's Government would keep the country out of it. Let them all kill one another off, as far as he was concerned. But he realized that this snotty French master had made a good point. If Bodgley continued to behave like an idiot, then London might not crack the whip over him as fast as it normally would.

"I expect you're right, sir. Now—"

"If you had evidence of an intruder, you would not have come here today!"

"I really am not at liberty to comment further, sir."

Why was the schoolmaster smirking?

"Are you familiar with our burglary, Inspector?"

"*Your* burglary, Mr. Jones?"

"At Whitsun there was a burglary—here, in Tudor House. Any criminal who attempts a break-in where there are a hundred sets of young lungs available to sound the alarm is excessively rash, wouldn't you say, Inspector? Besides, what could there be worth stealing beyond the odd illicit packet of Gold Flake?"

Behind the spectacles, Jones's eyes were gleaming bright.

Leatherdale felt a hint of uneasiness. "I fail to see how this is relevant, sir." A break-in at Fallow would not have been reported to Greyfriars—wrong county.

Jones showed his teeth in a snarl of frustration. "Perhaps not. Yet the coincidence . . . I believe—" His smile vanished as if a new idea had struck him. He sprang to his feet with surprising agility. "Inspector, where is Exeter now?" he demanded shrilly.

"Albert Memorial Hospital in Greyfriars."

"Under guard, Inspector? You said no charges had been laid, but you do have someone there to guard him, don't you?"

# 7

Still thinking *crazy old man!* Eleal Singer limped out through the city gate. How could she possibly be in danger? Why should death seek her out?

Here in the open, the wind blew like an avalanche. She pulled her hat down firmly and wished she did not keep thinking about avalanches. The low sun shone on a scene of hubbub and bustle. Traders were erecting stalls; ranchers were arriving with herds of llamas, brought down from Narshslope for sale. In the distance stood the ominous, ice-cloaked peaks of Narshwall. From them the land descended in bare hills and grassy ridges to the plain of Narshflat. Narshwater was the color of dirty milk, its banks still bearing grubby remnants of winter ice floes among the reeds.

A wide space of muddy grass separated the river from the city. Here the mammoths were kept during the summer and fall, when the pass was open. Here the farmers and herders came to trade. Most cities would hold festivals and games on a common like this, although Eleal doubted that the dour folk of Narsh were capable of appreciating either, any more than they appreciated theater.

Soon she was clear of the market and could see the mammoths, a dozen great gray-brown mountains with tusks. They would step over the puny rail fence around them with no trouble, so it must be intended more to keep people out than mammoths in. Mammoths were bigger and stronger than anything, and their little eyes gleamed with intelligence. As she hurried through slower-moving knots of people, one of the bulls curled up his trunk and trumpeted. She decided to take that as a welcome.

But the crowds! She had never seen so many people here before, milling around the rickety flight of steps where the travelers paid their fares and mounted. She scanned the group urgently. If everyone she could see was hoping to leave today, then there would simply not be room! A dozen mammoths and ten or twelve passengers per howdah meant . . . meant . . . well, not enough seats to empty the meadow, certainly. Where was the troupe? Loading had not yet begun, so they could not have left yet, but where were they?

Not everyone was there because of the mammoths, though. A troop of men drilled with pikes, another squad practiced archery. She also noticed a camp of three or four tents and a small herd of dragons. They were too far off for her to be sure, but that was probably T'lin Dragontrader's outfit. T'lin was her special friend. He trekked around the Vales with his herd, so she often ran into him, but this year she had not seen him since winter, in Jurgland. It was a pity she would not have time to speak with him before the mammoths left, because she had information for him.

The first mammoth was plodding over to the steps to load. The old mahout astride its neck looked like a doll, he was so high. There was still no sign of the rest of the troupe. Eleal began to feel seriously worried. Had they waited for her at the temple? Had they sent someone back to the hostel to look for her?

The seven hundredth Festival of Tion was attracting a far larger attendance than usual. All about her, people were making weepy farewells, issuing instructions and warnings. A surprising number were priests and monks, their colored gowns peeking out from under drab llama fleece robes added for warmth. Some were merchants, accompanied by bearers to carry their wares and even by armed guards. Others were athletes, large young men heading for the festival, receiving last-minute instructions from the fathers or uncles or friends who had trained them. She noted the usual cripples and invalids and blind people, going to seek a miracle. The remainder, men and women, could be assumed to be just pilgrims.

She squirmed through the crowd, hampered by her pack and her limp.

"Eleal!"

She spun around with a gasp of relief. It was Uthiam Piper—all alone, and without her pack. Uthiam was Ambria's daughter. She was eighteen, and the most *beautiful* actor: her looks, her voice, her grace. At the moment she looked cold as ice in her woolen robe, but she was still beautiful—and so welcome!

"You little chump! Where did you get to?"

"Oh . . ." Eleal said airily. "I went to pray to Kirb'l." Then she realized that she hadn't. "Where is everyone? What's keeping them? So many people—"

"And more to come! The temple is packed."

"But the festival starts on Thighday!" And this was Ankleday! "If we don't—"

"The portents were bad!"

"Huh?"

Uthiam's face was grave. She bent to whisper, for the crowd had closed in around them. "Trong Impresario offered a white cockerel as usual. When the priests went to read its entrails, they discovered that it had no liver."

That was ridiculous! How could a cockerel not have a liver? What a terrible omen! Eleal's vision of a journey over Rilepass today suddenly dimmed. The goddess must be very displeased about something.

"So what is happening?"

"We have to wait until the priests have dealt with all the others. We shall have to offer a greater sacrifice."

The look on Uthiam's face gave Eleal cold shivers. "You don't mean . . ."

"Oh, no! At least, I don't think so." She obviously wasn't sure, though. "The priests suggested a dragon foal."

Eleal gasped. "Ambria will have a foaming fit!" A dragon foal would cost more money than the troupe would take in in weeks. This was going to be a very expensive day. Hard times for the troupe meant thin eating.

Uthiam smiled. "But they'll probably settle for an alpaca."

Old Ambria was still going to have a fit. Even an alpaca would cost several nights' take, especially the take in tightfisted Narsh, but the big woman would bridle her tongue for fear of upsetting the goddess further.

"We may not get away today," Uthiam said, straightening. "I'd better go back to the temple." Obviously the prospect did not please her.

"Me too?"

"No need for you to come. Wait here, just in case. I think I saw T'lin Dragontrader, didn't I?"

"Who?" Eleal demanded. Her friendship with T'lin was supposed to be a secret. Uthiam's amused expression indicated that she knew that and it wasn't. But Eleal would have time to visit with T'lin. She could wander around . . . Then she recalled the crazy priest's warning that she was in danger.

"Uthiam, isn't Irepit goddess of something? What's a Daughter of Irepit?"

Uthiam looked understandably surprised. "They're a sect of nuns—down in Nosok-vale, I think. They—"

"Rinoovale," said a croaky voice, "not Nosokvale."

Eleal spun around angrily. "Eavesdropping is a sin!"

Uthiam's hand thumped the side of her head so hard she staggered. That was unfair—she had only been repeating what Ambria had told her lots of times.

The woman who had spoken was a nun, her flowing woolen garb conspicuous amid the leather-draped multitude. Whatever height she might once have had was now lost in a stoop and a hump, so she stood barely taller than Eleal. Her face was dominated by a long thin nose that seemed to be the only part of it not crumpled in wrinkles—it was red, with a shiny drop at the end of it, while her cheeks were an antique yellow, although the cold had added a purplish tint to them. Her hair and neck were hidden by a wimple, which, like her habit, had once been blue, although now both were threadbare and almost colorless. She was blinking at Eleal with eyes that likewise seemed faded to a colorless, blurry gray; they were watering copiously in the icy wind.

"Forgive her, holy lady," Uthiam said. "She is a wayward brat." She shook Eleal's shoulder. "Apologize!"

"The follies of youth are easily forgiven!" the woman muttered. Her pale moist eyes were still fixed intently on Eleal, whose ears were ringing. "In the Blue Scriptures, the *Book of Alyath*, it is written, 'Time is the gods' wages.' Is that why the young, whose life is most enjoyable, should be so eager to see it pass, while the old, who have lost most of their capacity for joy, savor every moment?" She blinked more, apparently waiting for an answer.

A naked sword hung at her side, its point almost touching the ground.

"M-mother?" Eleal said, staring at that incongruous weapon.

"Sister," said the nun. "Sister Ahn." Her lips were almost as blue as her eyes, yet she seemed unaware of the cold. She turned her watery gaze on Uthiam. "Is it not wonderful how many are heeding the prophecies?"

"Prophecies, Sister?" Uthiam spoke loudly also.

The sword was a real weapon, a really-truly shiny blade, and it bore no speck of rust. Yet now Eleal noticed the woman's right hand resting on a staff. It also was blue, and the fingers were so twisted that they probably could not grasp a hilt firmly enough to draw. Just looking at this shivering crone made her feel cold.

Blue was the color of Astina, the Maiden, who was goddess of lots of things: justice and soldiers and athletes, among others. That might explain the sword, but why should Astina be goddess of soldiers, when the Man was god of war? And why athletes? They should be the concern of the Youth—who ever heard of a female athlete? The universe ought to be more logical, and an armed geriatric nun was carrying things altogether too far.

"The seven hundredth festival!" Sister Ahn suddenly smiled, revealing a few yellow pegs of teeth. "Great wonders are foretold. Praise to the god. But should we not approach the young man selling tickets?"

However well-intentioned, the old woman's smile was quite the most gruesome Eleal could ever recall seeing. Her accent was unfamiliar, but perhaps that was because her speech was smeared by lack of teeth.

Uthiam was studying the nun with an oddly wary expression. "We are waiting on friends to join us, Sister. May the Lady bless your journey."

"Ah." The old woman sighed. "Ask rather that the Maiden grant you safe return. Many who see the wonders will not carry word of them home." Muttering to herself, she tottered away, leaning on her staff, the point of her sword almost trailing on the grass. Understandably, the crowd eased open to let her through.

"Don't wander too far," Uthiam said. "And stay out of trouble for once." She turned and pushed off through the mob.

Eleal decided she might as well go and see T'lin Dragontrader.

# 8

A dozen or so city children lurked around the dragons, being ordered away by two men shouting in clipped Fionian accents. T'lin himself stood by the tents, talking with two more of his assistants.

Dragontrader was a big man with a monstrous copper beard. His face was roughened and scarred by weather and he usually sported a showy sword and outrageously bright clothes. In Narshvale, he bundled up in llama hide like everyone else, but his boots were dyed blue, his leggings yellow, and a green scabbard hung out from under his red coat. Above all that he wore a black turban. Undoubtedly he would have a white shirt or something on underneath—no god in the Pentatheon would ever be able to complain of being neglected by T'lin. He seemed almost as large as one of his dragons.

As Eleal approached, his eyes flickered over her with no sign of recognition, but almost at once he clapped one of his companions on the shoulder, ending the discussion. He stalked away in amongst the dragons, pulling a rag from his pocket. Eleal doubled around the herd to approach from the other side, glad that he had not been trading with a customer.

A few of the great shiny beasts were standing, munching at bales of hay, flapping their frills up and down softly in pleasure. Most had lain down to chew their cud, but the fences of horny plates along their backs rose higher than her head and concealed her admirably. The long scaly necks stood up like palm trees. She caught glimpses of Dragontrader's turban and worked her way in his direction.

She loved dragons. That was how she had met T'lin—hanging around his herd. Sometimes he had only five or six, sometimes forty or more. Today she thought about fifteen or twenty, so he might be either buying or selling. When she was young she had toyed with dreams of marrying T'lin and being with the dragons all the time. They looked so ferocious and they were so gentle. They smelled good, and they spoke in funny belching noises. As she went by them, she trailed fingers over the shiny scales, admiring the play of light on them. Bright green eyes watched her under heavy brow-ridges, jewels in caves. In darkness, dragon eyes actually glowed.

She made out Starlight and detoured to greet him, T'lin's own mount. No dragon was ever a real black, but Starlight was what was called deep twilight, and the twinkle of light on his scales had given him his name. He truly resembled a starry night. The two long frills that extended back from his neck were magnificent, longer than any others she had ever seen, like small wings. He lowered his head to snuffle and belch hay scent quietly at her. She liked to think he remembered her, but that was probably just wishful thinking.

T'lin was standing beside one of the cud-chewers, a five- or six-year male of the color called Osby slate, a sort of blue-gray. It was not yet docked, the long crest of plates standing unbroken along its back. The big beast purred softly as T'lin busily polished its flank with his rag. He bent over as if to examine its claws. Then he squatted down on his heels and grinned at Eleal through his bush of beard. His face was still not very much lower than hers. They were quite private here, between the Osby slate and a glacier blue female. They were also sheltered from the wind.

"And how is the Beloved of Tion, the Friend of the Gods, the great singer?"

"She is very well, thank you," Eleal said politely.

He looked oddly weary for so early in the day. Perhaps he had been traveling all night. She noticed a small gold ring in his left ear and wondered if that was new, for she could not recall seeing it before. How odd! And why only one ear?

"How is the goddess-impersonating business?" he asked.

"Slow, in Narsh at least. Tonight we shall meet with more fitting recognition. The citizens of Sussia appreciate art. If the gods will," she added.

T'lin snorted loudly. That was a habit of his. She suspected he had picked it up from listening to his dragons' belchings.

"You do not care for the worthy burghers of Narsh? You prefer that maniac rabble in Sussland?" He shook his big head in disbelief. "They are born mad and then go crazy."

Eleal racked her brains. "Narshians are so mean they won't even give you a cold." She had been practicing repartee recently, and thought that remark showed it.

T'lin's green eyes twinkled. "Sussians don't know an assembly from a riot!"

She went on the attack. "How is the dragon-rustling business?"

T'lin covered his face with his big rough hands and wailed. "As the gods are my witness, the child wrongs me! No more honest trader ever crossed a pass."

That remark reminded her of the troupe's problem and stopped her from indulging in more banter.

"I have some information for you," she said.

T'lin's shaggy red eyebrows shot up. "I await it eagerly. You are an invaluable source of information to aid a poor honest man in wresting a living."

He was joking of course, but his quick green eyes had noted her worry. Probably very little Eleal told him was ever news to him. Sometimes the troupe played in rich people's houses, and even in rulers' houses, and then she might hear or see things he could not learn elsewhere. Everything else was mere gossip or obvious to any sharp eye, although he never said so. He was curious about all sorts of things: the chatter in the forum or bazaar, the price of foodstuffs, the lives of the rich, the grumbles of the poor, the edicts of the gods, the crops, the roads.

"When I buy a dragon," T'lin had told her once, "I do not just look at its claws. I look at every scale, every tooth. I look in its eyes and its ears. Sometimes very small things can tell me very important things, especially if they can be added together, yes? Now, a young dragon with his saddle plate already docked but no wear on his claws and no girth marks on his scales—do you know what those mean, Avatar of Astina? Why, it means that he has never done much work, does it not? So he has been a lucky young dragon, yes? Or he has a problem, maybe. A bad temper, maybe. Now when I come to a land to trade, I do not just ask the going price of dragons, because no one would tell me. Well, they would tell me, but I would not believe them. No, I look at everything in that land—in the whole vale, everything! Finally I decide what the price of dragons should be, and whether I want to buy or sell there."

Then he would smile triumphantly and stroke his copper beard, and she could never tell if he spoke seriously or in jest.

When Eleal Singer reported to T'lin Dragontrader, therefore, she reported everything she could think of. He never said he already knew something, he never said that anything did not interest him. When she had finished, he would pick out an item or two from her list and ask for details, but she never knew which topics he would choose, or whether he was really any more interested in those than the others or was just being a good trader. His face never changed expression by as much as one red beard hair.

At the end, he would reward her. When she had been little, the reward had been a ride on a dragon, but now he gave her money—sometimes only a few coppers, once a whole Joalian silver star, but he would rarely tell her what she had said to earn it. Sometimes he would comment that she had reported well, or that she should have observed this or that, things she had missed.

She had learned how to note Things That May Interest T'lin as she went about her life. She had learned how to remember them and keep them organized in her head. Actors were good at memorizing, of course.

She took a deep breath and began with the floods in Mapland. Then she described the riot in Lappin with six people killed and two houses burned, and the unusual number of monks and priests on Fandorpass—all colors, white, red, blues, yellows, greens— and how there were as many waiting to get on the mammoths, although he would have noticed that for himself. She mentioned the magistrate who had died here in Narsh and the assembly to be held next Headday to elect his replacement. That reminded her . . . "I am told there is a reaper in town!"

The glacier blue female belched thunderously and turned its long neck to stare at her reprovingly, as if she had made that disgraceful noise.

"There's a lot of Thargians in the city," she finished proudly. "I've heard them talking. They were trying to disguise their voices, but we theater people are very attuned to accents. There were two blue monks at the show two nights ago, and three well-dressed women last night, although I only heard one of those speak. I heard two young men in the baker's. There was a fat man with a local merchant and his wife I've seen before. And I overheard a white priest in the street. They were all trying to speak Joalian-style, and the men had beards, but I'm sure they were all from Thargia. Well, from somewhere in Thargdom, anyway." She thought quickly for a minute, and said, "That's all."

During her whole recital T'lin had just stared at her, motionless as a statue, balanced on his toes. She would not be his only informant in Narsh. Often she had seen him talking with people who could not be customers—children, beggars, priests. Most of them must be locals; she was probably the only one who traveled as he did. Once or twice he had remarked on that. Residents knew a lot, he had said, but travelers who came rarely saw changes better and noticed differences between places.

Now he took his rag and began to polish the Osby slate dragon thoughtfully. The monster purred. A dragon purr was an awesome sepulchral sound, like a hollow metal shell full of bluebottles.

"Men die all the time," T'lin murmured. "Not every unexpected death is caused by a reaper."

"But some are!"

"And not all Thargians are spies."

"Then why do they try to disguise their voices?"

He shrugged. "What set off the riot in Lappinvale?"

"Followers of D'mit'ri Karzon attacked a house they said was being used by worshipers of the Prime. The house was burned and six people killed. The governor did not punish anyone," she added. That should intrigue him. The Thargians usually kept very strict order in lands they ruled, although Thargland itself was said to be a rowdy place.

After a moment T'lin said, "In Lappin there is a temple to Zoan, the god of truth, who is an aspect of Visek, the Prime. Why should the whites need to worship him in a house instead of the temple? And why should Karzon followers care anyway?"

"That was what I heard."

He scratched his beard thoughtfully. "Are you sure it was the Parent they were supposed to be worshiping? Tell me the exact words you heard."

T'lin Dragontrader had never admitted before, as far as she could remember, that anything she had told him was news to him. She felt rather excited, wondering how much he would pay her this time. She closed her eyes and thought very hard. Then she looked at him again.

"The One?"

"Are you sure or are you guessing?"

"Mostly guessing," she admitted.

His eyes were like hard green stones. "What do you know of the One?"

"Well . . . Usually it means Visek, the Parent, the Source. Or one of his aspects, like Zoan."

"Blessed are the avatars of Visek, father and mother of gods, blessed be his name. You said 'usually'? Who else is the One?"

"Dunno." Theology was confusing, and not something she had ever known T'lin to show an interest in before.

Now he polished the dragon in silence until Eleal began to fidget.

"There is a god whose real name is never mentioned," he said solemnly. "He is called the One True God, or the Undivided."

"Visek."

The dragon trader shook his head. "The Parent was not called the One like that until this other came. Other gods do not approve of the Undivided. He has few followers in Lappin, I expect. Fewer now, you tell me. He has no shrine or temple there."

Eleal nodded, perplexed by his sudden interest in gods. Probably it was a blind anyway, for he suddenly changed the subject.

"These Thargian visitors? Can you describe any of them so I would know them? Any squints or cauliflower ears?"

"Of course not! What sort of a spy would he be? But the fat one I saw with the locals . . . the local was Gaspak Ironmonger. He's thought to have a slight chance of being the new magistrate and if he supports the Joalians instead of the Thargians—"

T'lin chuckled and rose to his feet. "Did you ever hear of the chicken farmer who bought a leopard to rid his land of foxes?"

"No," she said, bewildered.

"Joalians are the foxes."

"Oh! And the Thargians are leopards?"

Dragontrader laughed. He fumbled in a pocket. "Indeed, you are a mountain of useful knowledge, Beloved of Tion. Here!"

She held out her hands and he sprinkled silver into them without bothering to count it. She gasped in delight at this shower of riches.

"Well done, Leading Lady of the World," T'lin said. "Give my love to Suss."

"If we can get there . . . T'lin! Dragons can go over mountains!"

"Yes," he said warily.

"Then, since the mammoths are so busy this year, and we *need* to get there more than, oh, a merchant say, or a priest—I mean, our art is important! I was just wondering . . ." She saw a glint in his eyes.

"Yes, I could put you and your friends on my dragons and be a ferryman, but I wouldn't get away with it twice. Do you know who owns those mammoths, Aspect of Astina?" He bared his teeth. "The temple of Ois! And the priests would not appreciate competition. They would have my trading license canceled."

"Oh."

"Yes. So you stick to acting! Good fortune at the festival."

How could he be so tactless? Did he not know the rules? "I have decided my art is not yet mature enough for me to enter."

T'lin shrugged. "Well, good luck in Sussland, anyway."

# 9

The straps of her pack were cutting through even her heavy fleece clothes as she trudged back to the mammoths across the muddy meadow. *Squish, squash, squish, squash* . . . Her hip hurt, and she could feel a stitch starting in her side.

As she neared the loading point, the line of mammoths was already moving out, the leaders wading across the river. One last shaggy bull stood by the stair, and he raised his trunk to trumpet, perhaps calling on the others to wait for him. The loading had gone quickly. There had not been time for the others to complete another sacrifice in the temple; Uthiam Piper had known where Eleal was; they would not have left without her. Another night in miserable cold Narsh!

When she reached the crowd squashed in around the steps, she could see no sign of the troupe. She began squeezing her way through, ignoring angry protests about what the world was coming to and the usual mutters that children had no respect for their elders these days.

She could not see the huckster, but she heard voices raised in frantic competition as the customers bid for seats in the last howdah. Even if T'lin had given her enough money for a ticket—and it sounded as if the offers were being made in gold—she could not just go on by herself. Not without telling the others. It would have been a good idea to send her on ahead, though, because Gartol Costumer had left two days ago to make arrangements for a performance in Filoby tonight. He would wonder what had happened. A missed show meant patrons disappointed and more money lost. What a disastrous day!

The festival started in three more days! To miss the festival would be a tragedy.

Then she thought of even worse disaster. Ois was goddess of all passes. Suppose she would not turn aside her anger, and the troupe was stuck in horrible Narshvale forever? Even Fandorpass could be dangerous.

Something poked hard in her back. "Child!" said a sharp voice.

She wriggled around in the crush, and discovered the ancient blue nun peering at her accusingly. It was her staff that had done the poking.

"Is your name Eleal?"

"Yes! Do you have a message for me?"

"Oh, no!" Sister Ahn's long nose seemed redder than ever, her faded eyes even moister. "But that explains why we keep meeting."

"Do you know if my friends have left?"

"Friends?" She shook her head sadly. "Oh, your friends are irrelevant, child. You are the only one mentioned."

Suddenly the crowd moved like leaves in the wind. The two men in front of Eleal backed up so fast she was almost knocked over. She staggered, recovered, and found that she and the blue nun were alone in an empty space, looking across at the huckster. He was a beefy, red-faced young man, and there was an expression of comical astonishment on his pudgy features.

"Well, that helps," Sister Ahn murmured, almost inaudibly. "Come, child." She leaned a twisted hand on Eleal's shoulder and pushed with surprising firmness.

Eleal resisted. "I can't go without my friends!"

"You are the one who matters!" the nun snapped. "Is it not written, *Eleal shall be the first temptation?*"

"Written?" The crazy old priest had mumbled something about a prophecy. "Written where? Written what?"

"If you do not know, then it is probably destined that you shall not know. Come!"

She pushed harder. Peering down nervously to make sure the unsheathed sword was not about to cut her off at the ankles, Eleal found herself being propelled toward the huckster. She looked up suddenly as he uttered a wail of horror.

A man had come forward to the base of the steps—probably a man, possibly a tall woman. He was swathed in a heavy robe, like a monk's, keeping his head bent so the hood would hide his face. He was black, all black. Even the cord around his waist was black. The hand that reached out to offer a coin to the huckster wore a black glove.

The huckster dropped his satchel with a loud jangle and leaped back, colliding with the mammoth's leg. He tried to speak and made no sound at all. His eyes bulged; his face had gone comically pale. Trong Impresario himself could not have depicted terror more convincingly.

Again the black-robed stranger tried to offer payment. Again the huckster refused it, sidling away farther, clearly determined not to let that fateful hand come close to him. With a shrug the dark monk turned to the steps and proceeded to climb slowly up to the howdah. The mahout stared down in horror as this sinister passenger made his approach.

The crowd was scattering in sullen silence, many of them running.

"Truly the gods reward those who have faith," proclaimed the blue nun. "Come, my dear, let us see what the price of a seat is now." She hobbled forward on her staff, urging Eleal along also, but she had taken only a couple of steps before the huckster grabbed up the satchel he had dropped, dived through under the mammoth, and took to his heels as if Zath himself were after him.

"Wait!" cried the nun, but the wind swept the word away. The black monk had taken his seat. Nine seats around him remained empty. The stairs were empty.

"You can go now if you want," Eleal said. Her mouth was dry, but surely the man in black could not be what she suspected he was.

"We must both go, for so it is written, but we cannot go until we have *paid,*" Sister Ahn wailed. "And now that young man who sells the tickets has departed."

She sounded confused. She was probably crazy. On the other hand, the rest of the world did not seem to be much saner. One man had been given a seat at no charge and no one else except Sister Ahn seemed willing to share the howdah with him, although the seats were now available for free. How to explain that miracle? In tightfisted Narsh, too! The mahout had eased himself up the mammoth's neck until he was almost sitting on its head, as far from the solitary passenger as he could get.

"Perhaps that driver up there will negotiate a price," Sister Ahn muttered, but at that moment he spoke to the mammoth, and the big beast rolled forward.

Eleal looked around despairingly, but the onlookers were leaving. She was alone with the old woman. No one else had been willing to ride with the man in black. What else could he be? "Was that a reaper?"

Sister Ahn was still staring after the departing mammoth, apparently at a loss. She glanced at Eleal in bleary surprise. "He is a holy one, a servant of Zath. Yes, what they call a reaper."

Eleal's heart turned a cartwheel, her knees wobbled violently, and something seemed to squeeze her throat shut. "I've never seen a reaper before," she croaked. "In daylight?" Reapers were never discussed, or at least only in whispers—or croaks. But the mad old priest had mentioned him.

The nun chuckled. "You certainly wouldn't be able to see him in the dark, my dear!" she said, her good humor apparently restored. "And why not in daylight? He's only human. He must do something between sunrise and sunset."

That was even worse! "You mean he goes around in *disguise?*"

"He doesn't normally wear his habit, no. You can see the effect it has." The old woman shook her head disapprovingly. "No one would sit beside him."

"You would have?"

All the innumerable wrinkles around Sister Ahn's mouth puckered up in one of her gruesome smiles, although her watery eyes gave it an incongruous sadness. She raised her long nose so she could look down it. "Why not? If he wanted to gather my soul for Zath now, he could have done so. I am sure he can run much faster than I. In the Green Scriptures, Canto 2578, it is written, *"All gods play dice, but Zath's never lose."*

The worst part of this insanity was that she had expected Eleal to accompany her. "Then why did you not go?"

"Because I had not paid, of course. We children of Irepit are not permitted to accept charity. Everything must be paid for somehow—a story, or a lesson, usually. I had offered to give lessons on the journey, but the young man refused my bid." Her eyes were wandering even more than before, and she seemed puzzled that her companion did not understand. "When the other offers were withdrawn, I hoped he would reconsider."

The reaper must have been present in the crowd earlier. When the ticket price became unreasonable, he had donned his robe and revealed his avocation. Eleal shivered.

"What is a reaper doing here?"

"Earning his living by day, I expect," Sister Ahn said off-handedly, uninterested in reapers. "Gathering souls by night."

Eleal looked up at the sky apprehensively. The big moon would be setting about

now, but the sky was cloudy. Trumb had not eclipsed for at least a fortnight; he must
be about due.

> *When the green man turns to black,*
> *Then the reaper fills his sack.*

Which did not mean he didn't fill it other nights also.

In the distance the mammoth plodded into Narshwater, and across, and out the far
side, gradually catching up with the others and dwindling into the distance. The tiny
black figure sat alone with nine empty seats around him. Soon he became hard to see
... Why was the reaper traveling to Sussland? Who had earned the enmity of Zath?
Trumb must start eclipsing again soon. Where was the troupe? Should she go to the
temple?

Worried, shivering in the icy wind, she glanced around the meadow. It seemed almost
deserted without the mammoths, although there were llamas and dragons in the distance, and market stalls set up near the city gate. The other team would arrive tonight
from Sussvale. The pen stood deserted, a flimsy rail fence around a patch of mud and
mammoth dung. Klip Trumpeter was sitting on his pack with his head in his hands
and his back to her. Apparently he had missed the reaper drama altogether!

Eleal hurried over to him at her fastest skip: *clop!clip! . . . clop!clip! . . .*

Apart from her, Klip was the youngest member of the troupe. He had played women's
parts last year. Now he couldn't and he wasn't ready for men's, so he worked mostly
as a roustabout. His pimples were as many as the stars and his opinion of himself as
both man and musician was as high. Olimmiar, who was a couple of months older,
considered him still only a boy. Golfren Piper would not perform with him. Why had
he come? And why alone?

"Did you see who—"

He looked up. She recoiled at the pallor of his face. "What's wrong?"

"The alpaca," he said hoarsely.

"What about it?" She saw that Klip had lost three years somewhere since dawn. The
arrogant self-styled musician was just a frightened boy now, and the change scared her.

"It was beautiful, Eleal, beautiful! All white and silky! Not a dark hair on it. Not a
scratch on its hooves. Ambria paid five Joalian stars for it!"

*Five!* "And?"

Trumpeter's face crumpled as if he wanted to weep. "And its insides were all rotten.
Black, and foul. Horrible. The stench filled the whole temple."

Eleal was already trembling with cold. Fear was no help. First a crazy priest, then an
even crazier nun, then a reaper, and now this! She dropped her pack beside Klip and
sat down, tucking her hands into her sleeves. At least the reaper had left town.

"What have we done to anger the Lady so?"

Klip's tongue moved over his lips. His acne showed as ugly purple blemishes on his
ashen cheeks. "The Lady herself, or just Ois? We don't know. The priests say . . . Have
you ever been to her temple?"

"No."

"That may be it. None of us worship at the temple here, except when we are about to leave. It may not have been enough."

Eleal felt sick. "And?"

Klip swallowed hard. "Now we have to make amends."

*"All of us?"*

"The women. Ambria tried to get Olimmiar excused, saying she was only fifteen and a maiden. The priests just said that made her service specially potent." Trumpeter groaned and buried his face in his hands. He mumbled something that might have been, "Meaning they can charge more."

Eleal waited . . . and waited. She could count the thumps of her heart. Finally she had to ask.

"Me too?"

He looked around sharply; she saw that the wind had filled his eyes with tears also. "No, no! Oh, I'm sorry, Eleal! I should have said! No, not you! Ambria asked, but the priests said no, not if the Lady has not blessed you yet and made you a woman."

She felt a rush of relief and despised herself for it. The others' sacrifice would lift the Lady's anger and she would not have contributed. She did not want to, but neither did they.

"Maybe next year?" Klip smiled sourly.

"Maybe," she said uneasily. It was certainly possible. Many girls received the Lady's blessing at thirteen or even earlier. She was oh-so-glad it was not this year, though! "So what do we do now?"

"Go back to the hostel and wait until their service is complete."

"You mean it may take a long time?"

"That's up to the priests, to decide when the goddess is appeased. Days, maybe."

Tion's Festival began in three days!

Klip rose suddenly and lifted the two packs. Eleal reached for hers and he moved it out of her reach.

"I can manage!" she shouted.

"I want the exercise," he said gruffly. "I'm trying to make my shoulders stronger."

She detested people taking pity on her because of her leg, but she decided to believe him and let him take both packs. As they began to walk, she concluded Klip Trumpeter was not so bad after all.

"I'll let you into a secret," she said. "If you promise not to repeat it. A couple of days ago Olimmiar remarked how big and muscular you were getting. You mustn't tell her I said so!"

He glanced down at her with a wan smile. "I won't tell her because I don't believe a word of it."

"Well it's true!"

"No it isn't."

Eleal sniffed and tossed her head. She had only been trying to cheer him up. The least he could have done was pretend to believe her. Just for that, she wouldn't tell him that she had overheard Trong say he would make a good actor one day.

They trudged in silence toward the gate. Then Trumpeter said miserably, "I think it was Uthiam all the time!"

"What was?"

"The priests asked for her specially."

"By name? They knew her name?"

"The one who played Herinia two nights ago, they said—was she there? It was all a plot, Eleal! Don't you see? Some rich man saw her as Herinia and coveted her. He prayed to the Lady, and offered gold, and she granted his prayer! The priests had been instructed."

"Klip!" She put a hand on his sleeve. "You mustn't say such things about the Lady!"

He glowered at her. "I'll say them about Ois, then, even if she is a goddess! They took Uthiam away from the others—so they could send word to the man that she was available now, see? And he could be first. Uthiam's the sweetest, most beautiful—"

"Yes, she is. But—"

"Golfren was going crazy! He offered ninety-four stars if he could be the man to lie with her, the only man. Ninety-four!"

Ninety-four stars? That was a fortune! Eleal had long wondered why Golfren wore a money belt, which he probably thought no one except Uthiam knew about. "How could a wandering troubadour like Golfren Piper ever have collected so much money?"

"Dunno. I think he was planning to offer it to Tion in Suss to grant victory to Uthiam in the festival!"

"The priests refused?"

"They said husbands didn't count. I thought he was going to *hit* them!"

"Oh, Klip! Poor Golfren!"

Poor Uthiam!

Suddenly Trumpeter stopped and threw down one of the packs, so he could wipe his nose on his sleeve. He glared at Eleal with red-rimmed eyes. "I'll see you back at the hostel!"

She nodded sadly and limped away among the market stalls and the people.

•

# 10

Aₛ she reached the cluster of traders' stalls by the gate, Eleal realized that she was very hungry. She felt she should not be thinking of personal comfort when her friends were making so terrible a penance, but she had not eaten since the previous evening—and she no longer had Rilepass to look forward to. She wandered in among the fleece-wrapped servants and housewives, inspecting the wares. Mostly the offerings were of vegetables, for these were farmers' stalls. Eventually a savory scent drew her and she discovered a booth dispensing meat pies.

T'lin had given her money, of course, but she wanted to keep that. Many women were crowding around that table, competing for the trader's attention. Eleal moved in close at one end, and knelt as if to tie a lace. A moment later, as a customer clinked coins in payment, a small hand made a deft grab between two bulky customers. A pie vanished from the display.

Gleefully clutching her prize close to her, Eleal rose and walked away. When she reached a safe distance, she produced her loot and simultaneously bumped into a tiny woman in blue.

"This is kind of you, my child," Sister Ahn said, taking the pie in her twisted fingers. "It is long since I last ate. My, this smells delicious!" Her eyes were faded, watery, and filmed by age. They were also quite free of guile.

After a brief pang of annoyance, Eleal decided to be magnanimous. To feed this batty old crone would be meritorious. The Maiden would notice and might intercede with the Lady to turn aside her anger. And there were lots more pies where that one had come from.

"Oh, you are welcome, Sister! You really ought to be taking better care of yourself. A good llama fleece coat is what you need. Do you have somewhere warm to sleep?"

"I cannot accept charity," the nun mumbled, gazing longingly at the pie she held. "It is written, *Everything has its price.*"

"Payment is not necessary. One of my business ventures proved unexpectedly profitable this morning, so I can easily afford it."

The old woman still appeared frozen in her skimpy wool habit, and still unaware of the fact. The tip of her nose was turning white. "Here is what we shall do," she said, looking around vaguely, as if in search of a table and chairs. "We shall share this and I shall explain to you about the reaper. Take care of it for a moment." She returned the booty while she settled herself on the grass—an awkward procedure for which she leaned on her staff with one hand and adjusted the sword with the other, so as not to cut herself. Eleal wondered why the wind did not blow her over.

"Well, I do have pressing business engagements," she said, dropping to the ground. "But I admit I should like to know about the reaper and why you journey to Suss and why you carry a sword and several other things."

Sister Ahn took the pie in her grotesquely warped fingers, broke it in half, murmuring a grace, and then offered Eleal the larger piece. It was rich and juicy and delicious, still faintly warm from the oven.

"So you are Eleal!" she said, chewing vigorously. "Younger than I expected. What trade do you follow?"

"Eleal Singer. Actually I am more of an actor now, but we have so many Actors in the troupe that it seemed wise—"

The nun frowned. "What do you act?"

"Both tragedy and comedy. And I sing in—"

"What," Sister Ahn demanded, removing a piece of gristle from the mouth, "is the difference?"

Carefully not showing how shocked she was by the old woman's ignorance, Eleal explained. "Comedies are just about people. Tragedies have gods in them. People too, of—"

"Mmph! You portray goddesses?"

"Sometimes. I mean, I shall when I am tall enough."

"Then you must learn how goddesses think. You will travel to the festival tomorrow?"

Eleal told of the cockerel and the alpaca. When she started to explain what the other women in the troupe were doing, she felt nauseated and stopped eating.

Sister Ahn continued to work on the pie with her few teeth. The skin of her cheeks was like crepe, with all the underlying flesh underneath wasted away. A wisp of pure white hair had escaped from under her headcloth.

"Their penance may last a long time," she mumbled with her mouth full, "and the festival is soon. You will have to go without them."

"I can't! I mustn't!"

The nun waved a hand dismissively. "It has been foreseen that you will. You can't fight destiny. History awaits you."

"I am *not* going to leave Narsh without my friends! I must stand by them in their hour of distress."

The nun pursed her already shriveled lips. "Your religious education has been woefully neglected. Why 'distress'?"

"It seems so horrible!"

"Oh it is. That is why it is valuable. Have you not been taught that everything has a purpose? The purpose of life is to learn obedience to the gods."

"Of course." Eleal forced herself to take another bite of pie. She did not want to think about what was happening in the Lady's temple. Before she could ask about the sword and the reaper instead, the lecture resumed.

"The gods made us to serve them." Sister Ahn wiped gravy from her chin with a gnarled hand. "In this world we learn to do their will. When we have completed our apprenticeship, Zath gathers us to their judgment, to serve in whatever manner we have shown ourselves best fit for. In the Red Scriptures, the *Book of Eemeth*, it is written, *Among the heavens and the constellations thereof shall they be set, lighting the world as the lesser gods.*"

Eleal had never understood the attraction of being hung in the sky like laundry for all eternity.

"To do what we want is easy," the nun said, still chewing. "To do what the gods want may not be. The reaper upset you, and a deal of other people also, but he worships Zath as Zath commands him. To take life is a sin for most of us. To obey the dictate of a god is never sin. A reaper can slay with a touch of his hand, but only because Zath has given him that power. Likely the god gave him other powers also, to help him in his unhappy task. He must put the god's gifts to their intended use. What for you or me would be murder is for him both a sacrament and a duty."

Eleal shivered. "And the Lady?"

"Likewise. To offer your body to a man for money would be a crime most foul. To do so as a sacrifice to the Lady when she commands it is a holy, precious thing. Obedience is all."

The faded gray eyes turned from Eleal to stare blankly across the windy meadow. "I have never lain with a man. I have never killed anyone. That does not make me better than those who do such things in holy service. I am sworn to obey another goddess in other ways, that is all."

A troop of armed citizens went striding past, returning from their drill. They all seemed to glance sideways at Eleal's odd companion, and she realized that no other passersby had come as close. Apparently a Daughter of Irepit was to be avoided—not given as wide a berth as a reaper would merit, but wide enough to remind Eleal of Uthiam's wary expression when she faced this cryptic crone.

"What goddess? Irepit? Is she an avatar of the Maiden?"

"Of course—Astina in her aspect as goddess of repentance. A stern goddess! Not as stern as Ursula, her aspect of justice, but—"

"Why drag that sword around if you don't use it?"

The old woman smiled her gruesome smile happily. "Because the Holy Irepit has so commanded, of course. It is a reminder and a burden, a burden I bear gladly."

"A reminder of what?"

"A reminder of mortality and obedience." She pointed a bony finger at Eleal's right boot, with its two-inch sole. "You also bear a burden, child."

"Not willingly!" Eleal was annoyed to feel her face flushing.

"But perhaps the gods had their reasons for laying it upon you."

It was very impolite to discuss people's infirmities. The sword was not the same thing at all.

"Swords are valuable! Suppose some man covets it and threatens to kill you for it?"

The nun shrugged her narrow shoulders. "Then I refuse and he kills me. If he takes it without killing me, then I must kill myself in penance for whatever evil he may someday do with it. I said it was a burden."

"You may never use it?"

"Only in ritual. Some of my sisters have frozen to death rather than profane their swords by chopping wood with them."

"Well!" Eleal said crossly. "You tell me that everything has a purpose. Obviously the purpose of a sword is to kill people, er, men, I mean."

"Oh, I never said it had not killed people!" The nun patted the hilt of the weapon lovingly. "It has belonged to my order for a long time, so I expect it has been the death of many."

That made no sense at all. The woman was as crazy as the equally ancient priest who had first mentioned her. The two of them must be in cahoots somehow. Feeling very uneasy, Eleal scrambled to her feet.

"To endure without complaint, to obey without question," Sister Ahn said, as if unaware of the movement, "this is what life is for. It is written in the *Book of Shajug* how holy P'ter, having ruled over the Thargians for tenscore years and seven—"

"Why are you traveling to Suss?"

The nun sighed. "The play was written long ago. By your definition it is a tragedy, for the gods are involved. There is a part in this play for one of my order. I deemed . . . I was deemed the most expendable."

"And me? You knew my name!"

"Your part is written also."

"Namely?"

Sister Ahn peered up awkwardly at this impertinent young questioner. Tears were trickling down her cheeks. "So many questions! In the Blue Scriptures, the *Book of Alyath,* we read, *Ask not lest the answer displease you; seek not lest you become lost; knock and you may open a dangerous door.*"

Crazy as a drunken bat!

"I really must be off!" Eleal said royally. "Business, you know. I do wish you would find yourself some warmer garments. Now, pray excuse me."

She stalked away. She half expected to hear an order that she stay and listen to more, but it did not come.

# *11*

Sunday never really existed for Edward Exeter. From time to time the pain in his leg would solidify out of the fog and he would open his eyes and see the mess of bandages and ropes and discover that he could not move. His head throbbed. He faded in and faded out. Often he would try to turn over and again be balked by those ropes and that leg stuck up in the air. He was vaguely aware of nurses coming around at intervals and talking to him. As soon as he grunted a few words, they would go away satisfied. Sometimes they tucked thermometers under his tongue and scolded when he went to sleep and dropped them. There was a nasty business with a bottle, too.

Often the world was filled with silent music, sometimes music soaring like a Puccini aria, sometimes funny music, like a Gilbert and Sullivan patter song, although he heard no words.

Once or twice he noted the drab brown walls and the stink of carbolic and ether. Then he would deduce yet again that he must be in a hospital and therefore was being cared for and could safely drift off again. At other times he thought he was back in Paris and reflected that Smedley's uncle kept jolly hard beds. Once he had a memory of pain and streaming blood; he started to cry out then. Someone came and jabbed a needle in him and the music returned.

A voice he knew spoke his name, very far away. His eyelids were heavy as coffin lids, but he forced them open and saw Alice.

"I'm dead, aren't I?" His tongue was too thick, his lips too stiff.

"Not very."

"Then why am I seeing angels?"

She squeezed his hand. "How do you feel?"

"Not quite as good as usual."

"You'll be better tomorrow, they say."

He blinked to try and make his eyes work correctly. There was an electric light up there. "What time is it?"

"Evening. Sunday evening. You had a bang on the head. I told them there wasn't much brain there to start with."

He tried to say, "Tell me you love me and I'll die happy." He wasn't sure if he managed to. They woke him later to give him a back rub, but Alice had gone.

# 12

Eleal had been wandering aimlessly around the city's dreary gray streets until eventually her feet brought her into the temple quarter. The house of Ois was easily the tallest building in town, but no less ugly than any of the others. She did not want to visit that! Old Sister Ahn might describe what was happening there as a great and holy sacrifice, but Eleal still felt that it was degradation, and she would not witness her friends' shame.

Then she recalled the silver in her pocket. She was the only member of the troupe who had not made an offering that day, unless half a pie to a nun counted. She decided she would go to Tion's shrine and sacrifice some money there. If the crazy old priest was still there, she could reassure him that she was obviously in no danger and the reaper had left town anyway.

But why just the Youth? Why not visit all the shrines? She could pray to the Parent for comfort and the Maiden for justice and even to the Man for courage. She could ask them all to intercede with the Lady. She headed for the street behind the temple. The area was busy now, full of hurrying Narshian troglodytes.

She had often come along this street, so she knew the first shrine was Visek's, although she had never entered it before. Its imposing archway, which must once have been white, was now a grubby drab color and the faded sun symbol of the mother and father of gods was barely visible. She walked in boldly, to the small and shadowy courtyard, overgrown with somber trees and roofed by black branches and gray sky. The walls were smeared with lichen. Faint scents of stale incense cloyed the air. There was no one else present.

The statue of the Father opposite the entrance was crude, spattered with bird droppings and shedding flakes of white paint like dandruff. It depicted a stern, bearded man wearing a crown and long robes. The contorted Narshian script on the plinth was obscured by moss, but the god had only one eye and one ear, in his aspect as Chiol, god of destiny. She hoped he had his one ear turned her way now, to hear her prayer. Chiol had a very splendid temple in Joal, which she had seen but never visited—she never had problems with destiny.

She knelt before the figure. To pray to the All-Knowing, one should wear something white. Well, the inside of her fleece coat was *sort-of* white, so that was all right. She pulled out two of the silver coins Dragontrader had given her, unable to see what they were in the gloom.

There were other offerings lying on the plinth: a few coppers, two jars and a bottle, a cold leg of goose with flies crawling on it, a hank of wool, and a string of beads, which was probably somebody's most precious thing. She resisted a temptation to open the jars and sniff at the contents. She laid the silver beside them.

She bowed her head and repeated a prayer from the White Scriptures: "Father of Gods, Mother of Mortals, Giver of Truth, grant us comfort in our sorrows and forgive us our sins."

That was very appropriate, she thought, and in a moment she did feel better. Surprisingly better—but then she had never offered silver to a god before. She murmured the first thanksgiving she thought of; it was from the Blue Scriptures, but that would not matter.

Eleal limped out cheerfully, into a swirl of snow.

White flakes danced around in the streets, sticking only to people, it seemed, and not settling on the ground. They made it hard to see where she was going. Tugging her collar tighter, she set off between the hurrying pedestrians, the carts, and wagons. The high wall continued, marked by unwelcoming doors. Trees poked over the top in places, suggesting private gardens. The next shrine was Karzon's, in his aspect of Krak'th, god of earthquakes. She had rarely prayed to the Man before, and certainly never to Krak'th. She had no more problems with earthquakes than she did with destiny.

The afternoon was drawing to a close already; she was cold and weary. Her hip hurt. Blinking into the snowflakes, she saw a familiar figure stalking toward her. Anyone could recognize Dolm Actor at a distance by his height and rolling gait. Normally, of course, she would run to him. Dolm was a gangly, cheerful man, almost as tall as Trong Impresario, but much younger. He had a wonderful voice, although he moved poorly and his gestures were graceless. She could just remember when Dolm had been young enough to play the Youth. Now he usually portrayed the Man when the troupe performed tragedies, lovers or warriors in the comedies.

But Dolm would not be cheerful today, with Yama sacrificing in the temple. Dolm was very probably doing what she was doing—making a pilgrimage to all the shrines of Narsh—and in that case he was heading for Karzon's, as she was. She did not want Dolm to listen to her prayers.

She did not think she was wicked enough to listen to his. It wouldn't be easy to arrange, anyway. She stepped behind a parked wagon to let him go in unmolested. As he came closer, she decided that there was something strange about the way he was behaving. He passed by without seeing her, and without entering the shrine.

Curiosity is a sin, Ambria Impresario scolded.

Curiosity is a great talent, T'lin Dragontrader said.

So Eleal watched, and in a few minutes she decided that her hunch was correct, and Dolm Actor was being furtive. She stepped out from behind the cart and followed, keeping close to a rumbling wagon of bales. He walked faster than the yaks plodded, but every few minutes he would pause and look behind him.

He was tall and she was small. She could be a lot more inconspicuous than he could, and on a gloomy afternoon in a riot of snowflakes, she could be downright invisible.

Perhaps he was going to Chiol's shrine, to begin there, as she had. Why should he make such a mystery of it, though?

Without warning, Dolm vanished. Eleal caught a brief glimpse of a closing door. She stamped her heavy boot with annoyance.

Curiosity howled in frustration. Like her, Dolm visited Narsh only once a year, and briefly, yet he had obviously known exactly which door he wanted. As it was just a spread of timber in a featureless stone wall, with no name or marker on it, he must have been here before. The wall was too high to climb, even had she dared try such a thing in a busy street. Shrubbery protruded over the top, so there was a garden beyond. It might be a back gate to the temple, or else another courtyard, like Chiol's shrine.

Another courtyard, *next* to Chiol's shrine!

Without pausing to think, Eleal sprinted back to the archway and through, into the gloomy shrine. There was still nobody there. Without a word of apology to the god, she hurried to the sidewall. Cursing her cumbersome boot and her heavy Narshian fleece, she scrambled up a tree until she could peek over.

Below her lay a larger courtyard, enclosed by high mossy walls, overgrown with old trees and gangly shrubs. It had an air of neglect and decay about it, as if no one ever came. It was another shrine, although never in her life had she heard of a sacred place being kept secret. Despite the snow swirling in the air, she had a clear view across the wet cobbles to the god.

The figure was so lifelike that it stopped her breath. She had never seen finer, even in the grandest temples. It was larger than mortal, wrought in bronze, a male in a loincloth. The Youth was usually shown nude and Karzon fully clad, but this must be the Man, for he was a heavyset mature adult, not a slim-waisted adolescent. Besides, he bore a skull in one hand and a hammer in the other. He was also weathered to a muddy green, and green was the color of Karzon, the Man. He stood in a sort of thicket of implements that stuck up around his feet: a spade, a sword, a scythe, a shepherd's crook, and other attributes of his many aspects. All of those were also of green bronze, except the sword, which was red with rust—she hoped it was rust.

That was no minor local god. That must be Karzon himself, god of creation and destruction. She had never been to his temple because it was in Tharg. So the Man had two shrines in Narsh—a public one to Krak'th and a private one of his own. Curious!

Then she saw Dolm, sitting on the ground below her, bare to the waist. While she watched, he hauled off his leggings and stood up, wearing nothing except a black cloth tied around his loins. He was visibly shivering as the snow settled on his shoulders and the prominent bald spot on top of his head, but the fact that he had stripped off everything except that one monocolored garment meant that he was about to perform some special ritual sacred to one god. Black meant *Zath* Karzon, the Man's avatar as god of death.

She wanted to vanish, but mad curiosity froze her to her perch on the branch. Even if Dolm looked up, he would not notice her face peering at him through the foliage. Yet outsiders prying into secret rites were asking for very serious trouble. Trouble from *Zath?*

And *Dolm?*

Dolm Actor, her friend?

Piol Poet would never eat fish. Ambria belonged to a women's cult that she would never discuss, and recently had begun taking Uthiam along to meetings, whenever they could get away. Eleal had overheard them talking about it when they did not know she was listening, but she had not learned much more than that it had something to do with Ember'l, who was goddess of drama, avatar of Tion in Jurg. Probably many people had sworn special allegiance to some particular god or goddess. A twelve-year-old was not likely to be told about such private matters.

Oh, Dolm!

Soldiers always wore something black. Many other men did—but an actor? An actor worshiping *Zath?*

She stared in disbelief as that lanky, bony man strode forward to stand before the god and raise his lean arms in supplication. He was almost as tall as the idol. She did not recognize the words he began to chant—they sounded Thargian, but not a dialect she recognized.

It was a complex ritual. Dolm turned around several times—he had an extremely hairy chest, Dolm. He dropped to his knees and touched his face to the ground. He sprang up, legs astride, and recited something else. He touched his toes, crouched, rose, bowed, in careful sequence, chanting softly all the time in his sonorous actor's voice. He dropped on hands and knees and barked three times like a dog. And finally he wriggled forward on his belly to the base of the plinth. Eleal shivered at the thought of all that cold, wet stone, and snow.

Dolm Actor rose to his knees, and grasped the sword with his left hand. It came free of the plinth easily. He recited another formula and kissed the rusty blade. He stretched out his right arm, laying his hand at the god's feet, palm upward. For the first time his voice faltered and he seemed to hesitate. Then he slashed down at his wrist as if trying to sever it completely.

He cried out, dropping the sword. A torrent of blood spilled from the cut arteries.

Eleal's hair rose straight up, or at least felt as if it did.

Steadying the wounded arm with his left hand, Dolm lifted it so the red fountain of his own life's blood gushed down upon his own balding head. The injured hand hung limp and useless.

That last obscenity snapped the spell that had rooted Eleal. This was no normal worship! This was no little clique of gossipy women muttering secret prayers. This was some arcane invocation. Hiding from Dolm Actor was child's play, but she could not hide from the god of death if he came in person.

Teeth chattering, she slithered wildly downward through the branches until she collapsed on the leaf-strewn ground. Then she sprang to her feet and fled.

# ACT II

*Mystery*

# 13

The New Hotel in Greyfriars was a gloomy Victorian structure of red brick, a short walk from the High Street, flanked by *Robinson & Son Drapers* on one side and *Wimpole Bros. Chemists* on the other. Its prices were reasonable—four shillings and sixpence for bed and breakfast. It was convenient to the station and much favored by commercial travelers. On Bank Holiday weekend, it was as vivacious as the inside of a sealed tomb. No games of auction bridge would liven its Residents' Lounge this evening. Very few pairs of shoes would be set outside its bedroom doors tonight for Boots to polish before morning.

The entrance hall was dark, but still stuffy from the day's heat. Permanent odors of yeast and stale cigar smoke lingered amid the aspidistras drooping in the windows and the horsehair sofas flanking the dead hearth. Walls and woodwork were a uniform, sad brown; the elaborate plaster ceiling was stained to the color of old tea. As the revolving door hissed to a stop behind her, Alice Prescott mentally prepared for a few hours of dread boredom before she could sleep. Her room would still be hot, and it overlooked the shunting yard. The bed was surely the lumpiest south of the Humber.

The West Country could never be as unbearable as London, but she longed to reach her room and shed a few clothes. Africa had been hotter, but in the Colonies a woman was not required to wrap herself in *quite* such absurd creations of Oriental silk under-skirts and ankle-length cotton voile gowns and broad silk sashes. Or, if she were, then she would not be expected to spend an afternoon trudging around a county town.

Her plumed hat was going to come off before anything else did.

Most Sunday evenings in Greyfriars would offer nothing whatsoever in the way of entertainment except Divine Service at St. Michael and All Angels'. Today, however, there had been an impromptu meeting in the park, which had provided some unexpected excitement. Mr. Asquith, God Bless Him, had been three-cheered several times, the Kaiser had been loudly booed. The mayor had spoken a few words about the Empire on Which the Sun Never Sets and England Expecting Every Man to Do His Duty. A hastily gathered band from the Boys' Brigade had played some martial music, and everyone had sung "Land of Hope and Glory" and "God Save the King." Then the crowd had quietly dissolved, slinking away as if ashamed of having displayed emotion in public.

Alice headed for the desk to collect her room key. She could see it dangling on the board with the others, well out of reach. There was no message in her pigeonhole, and no news was good news because the only people who knew where she was staying were the hospital and the police.

She hoped D'Arcy had found the note she had left for him in the sitting room—at times he could be quite astonishingly unperceptive, blind as a mole. She teased him about that. She had left another note on the pillow: "See note on mantelpiece." She wondered what he had done this morning without her. Perhaps this Sunday he had actually gone to church! She would send a telegram to his chambers in the morning. Unless Edward took a grave turn for the worse, she absolutely must get back to town tomorrow.

The clerk was not in evidence. Before she could lift the little brass bell thoughtfully placed on the desk for just such an emergency, a man spoke from the far end of the hall.

"Miss Prescott?"

She jumped and turned.

He must have been sitting in the corner armchair. Now he had risen. He was large, portly, dressed like a banker in his Sunday best, waistcoat and gold watch chain.

"I am she."

He nodded and walked over to her, taking his time, carrying his bowler. She closed her fingers on the bell. His hair was thinning, his graying mustache turned up in points like the Kaiser's.

"Inspector Leatherdale of the County Constabulary, Miss Prescott. Wonder if I might have a word with you?"

Alice released the bell. Her heart was behaving disgracefully. "Of course, Inspector. I hope you can inform me what has transpired. I did inquire at the station, but the officer there was most uncommunicative."

The policeman nodded, as if that was to be expected. He gestured to the heavy sofas by the fireplace. "There are some gentlemen in the Residents' Lounge, ma'am. This should be private enough."

She led the way over there and perched carefully on an edge, keeping her back straight as a musket. The cushion sagged so low that her knees tilted uncomfortably to the side. She stood her parasol upright against the arm and removed her gloves. Leatherdale pulled up the creases of his trouser legs at the knees in thrifty middle-class fashion, then settled deeply into the sofa beside hers. He produced a notebook and fountain pen.

He looked annoyingly comfortable. She hoped she appeared more composed than she felt, because she felt like a felon caught red-handed, which was ridiculous. Dear Uncle Roland would consider her sense of guilt very fitting if he knew of it and knew what caused it. He could not know, of course, but absence of evidence would never lead him to doubt. He had been convinced of her depravity as soon as she moved out on her own, and that had been long before she met D'Arcy. Immorality was not a criminal offense. It just felt like it at the moment.

"Now, Inspector! I understand that—"

"Your full name, please, ma'am. For the record."

He took charge of the conversation so effectively that she found herself waiting in obsequious silence while he wrote down every answer. What did her age have to do with Edward's accident? Or her address? Or that she had been born in India, raised in British East Africa, was self-supporting, taught piano?

"Edward George Exeter is your first cousin?"

"He is. He is also seriously injured, Inspector. I was told he fell down some stairs, but I have yet to learn—"

The inspector looked up with eyes as cold and penetrating as the iceberg that sank the *Titanic.* "We do not know how he came to fall down those stairs, Miss Prescott. That is something we hope to establish when he is well enough to answer questions."

"You mean it was not an accident?"

"What happened to Exeter may or may not have been an accident. The other young man involved was stabbed to death. I can tell you, though, that there seems to have been no one else present at the time. As of this date your cousin has not been charged, but he is an obvious suspect in a clear case of murder."

The ensuing silence had the impact of bells. Stabbed to death? Murder?

*Edward?* She felt herself opening and closing her mouth like a fish.

The questions began to roll again. She did not hear them, and yet she could hear her voice answering them.

"Anything I can do to help . . . caught the first train . . . uncle's housekeeper sent me a telegram . . . very fond, extremely fond of Edward . . . more like brother and sister . . ."

It was unbelievable. Edward would never murder anyone! Murder was something that happened in the slums of Limehouse. Murder was Jack the Ripper or Dr. Crippen, not Edward! There had been some horrible mistake.

She must have said so, because the inspector was nodding understandably. "I know how you must feel," he said, and suddenly he seemed avuncular and less intimidating. "Between ourselves, I am much inclined to agree with you, Miss Prescott. Your cousin seems like a very promising young man, well thought of, of good family . . ."

He must have asked, or she had volunteered, because she discovered that she was telling him all about their family, and about herself.

". . . other sahibs fled town when the cholera arrived. My parents were both doctors, though . . . sent me away and they stayed . . . I don't remember them at all . . . mother had two brothers. I was sent off to Kenya on the mail boat, like a parcel. Uncle Cameron, Aunt Rona . . . like parents to me . . ."

She was telling of Africa, the only childhood she could recall . . . Why should the policeman care about that? Yet he was still making notes, apparently managing to keep up with the story pouring out of her.

"And you came Home when exactly?"

"In 1906. Edward followed in '08, when he was twelve."

"You do not live with your uncle now, though?"

"I am of age, Inspector."

"But you have lived on your own for some time?" he asked, watching her shrewdly under bushy gray brows.

She took a deep breath. She knew the conclusions men drew when a woman lived on her own. That those conclusions were now true in her case made them no less unfair.

They would have been there had she never met D'Arcy. There had been no one before D'Arcy.

"Uncle Roland is not an easy man to live with."

"Your cousin shares that opinion?"

To describe Edward's opinions of Holy Roly could not help, although they were starting to look appallingly accurate. "The relationship is cool on both sides. It was all right at first, but since Aunt Griselda died, my uncle has become . . . well, difficult."

The inspector nodded thoughtfully and studied his notebook for a moment. Hooves and wheels clattered past the windows.

"Exeter rarely stayed with his uncle, even in holiday time?"

"My uncle goes out of town a lot. He . . . He tends to distrust young people. He preferred not to leave us in the care of the servants. I was more fortunate. My father was survived by two elderly maiden aunts. I mostly spent my summers with them in Bournemouth." The Misses Prescott had been reluctant to put up with their great-niece. They had had no use for an adolescent boy about the house, a boy unrelated to them.

"So he lived year-round at Fallow?"

"Not completely. Friends would often invite him to visit during the holidays. He has been to the Continent several times, France and Germany, staying with families to learn the language. The school arranges such things."

The more she could tell about Edward the better, surely? Then the police would see how absurd it was to suspect him of anything.

"You know, I don't believe Edward has ever told a lie in his life, Inspector? He—"

The policeman donned his fatherly smile. "Your family seems to have been very dedicated to the Empire, Miss Prescott. Let me see if I have them pegged correctly. Mr. Cameron Exeter, Edward's father, was a district officer in British East Africa. Dr. Roland Exeter was a missionary in the South Pacific for the Lighthouse Missionary Society, of which he is now director. Your mother, Mrs. Mildred Prescott, was a doctor in India?"

Alice laughed for the first time. "I think we all have guilty consciences. My great-grandfather was a nabob. He made a fortune in India. Loot, Edward calls it."

Leatherdale made another note. "Your family has money still, then?"

"Some, Inspector. We are by no means wealthy, though."

That might be more true than she meant it to be. More and more it looked as if Edward was right and Holy Roly had poured the whole lot into his blessed Missionary Society. She had not seen a penny of her inheritance yet. But surely that scrap of dirty family laundry was irrelevant? Surely this whole family history was irrelevant?

The policeman did not seem to think so. Was he truly on Edward's side as he had claimed, or was he somehow trying to trap her into saying something she should not? But what on earth could she reveal that would be damaging? Nothing!

"Your uncle, the Reverend Roland Exeter, is an elderly man?"

"In his seventies, yes."

"Seventy-two, actually," Leatherdale said offhandedly. "Born in 1842. And your mother?"

Puzzled and oddly uneasy now, Alice said, "I'd have to work it out. She was thirty-eight when I was born. I can't recall why I know even that much."

Leatherdale scribbled. "So 1855 or '56. And Roland in '42. How about Cameron?"

"I don't know. I never saw them after I left Africa, remember. But he must have been much younger."

The bushy brows flickered upward. "According to *Who's Who,* your uncle Roland was the second son—meaning Cameron was the oldest child."

She smiled and shook her head. "I'm quite sure he wasn't! I remember how shocked I was at how old Uncle Roland was when I met him. Perhaps it's a misprint?"

"Possibly." The inspector seemed to change the subject. "It seems odd that your adoptive parents never came Home on leave. District officers are usually granted leave every two years or so, aren't they?"

"I don't know. Yes, I suppose so. Nyagatha is very remote. It was even more remote in those days." That seemed irrelevant, somehow. All the Empire was remote.

"Your cousin Edward. Last week he was on his way to Crete. When he had to cancel his plans—when he came back to England—why did he come to Greyfriars?"

"I'm not sure."

"Did he get in touch with you?"

Alice shook her head. "He dropped me a postcard on his way through London. I am not on the telephone, you know. He just said the trip was off and he was coming here, to stay with General and Mrs. Bodgley."

"He did not wish to stay with his uncle," Leatherdale said. "Why not with you?"

She felt herself blushing, but it would not matter. "I could not put him up!"

"Why not?"

Her cheeks felt warmer yet. "Really, Inspector! If the highly respectable ladies who employ me were to hear that a *young man* had been seen entering and leaving my flat, then they would never allow me across their doorsteps again! They would not let me near their pianos, let alone their children!"

Which was true, but not the real reason. What if Edward had stumbled on something of D'Arcy's lying around? His dressing gown, for example? Edward was a romantic. It would kill him.

"You are on good terms, though?"

"Oh, yes! I told you, I regard him as a brother."

"And what are his feelings toward you?"

She turned and stared at the empty fireplace. "You had best direct that question to him, Inspector."

"Murder is no respecter of privacy, Miss Prescott!"

She turned to him in horror. "Heavens! You don't mean I am going to find myself pilloried in the gutter press? *The News of the World?*" If the reporters ever scented a scandal as well as a murder and dragged D'Arcy in, his career would be completely ruined. His wife was a vindictive bitch.

The big man shrugged. "In normal times I expect you would. I believe the Kaiser will save you in this instance."

"Well, that is certainly a relief!"

"So will you answer my question, ma'am?"

"My cousin believes he is in love with me."

"Believes?"

She turned again to the fireplace. "Edward has led a very sheltered life, and in many ways an extremely lonely one. He last saw his parents when he was twelve. They died in very horrible circumstances four years later. I was the only person he could turn to. I am three years older, which is a lot at that age. Some of his letters were heartbreaking!"

And just when the pain was easing, Cameron's reputation had been stamped into the mud by the board of inquiry. For Edward, that had been a toboggan trip through Hell.

She forced herself to meet the policeman's steady stare. "I am literally the only girl he knows! Can't you see? Edward has a romantic Celtic streak to him. He believes he is in love with me. Now he has left school . . . in a few months . . . when he has had a chance to meet other girls . . ."

Edward would not meet many girls if he had to spend those next few months in jail.

# 14

About the only good thing Ambria Impresario ever found to say about Narsh—and Eleal agreed with her on this—was that it had a very good hostel. True, it was shabby and none too clean, like the rest of the city, but it was located conveniently close to the shearing barn where the plays were performed. It provided innumerable poky rooms, and it was never busy so early in the spring, when the troupe needed it. There was no embarrassing pretending to be asleep when the troupe played Narsh.

Snow was starting to pile up in alleys and the light was failing when Eleal at last found her way back there—thinking gloomily that they should all be down in warm Filoby by now, getting ready for the evening's performance.

She was still very shaky from her narrow escape, but no terrible gods had come after her. Dolm Actor himself might have bled to death, if his rites had failed. He would have been in too much pain to notice any noise she had made in leaving, and the snow had not been lying then, so she should have left no tracks.

Now that she had recovered from her fright, she felt angry, which was strange. Perhaps she should feel sorry for Dolm, who served so terrible a god, but she couldn't feel sorry. Murdering people was wrong, no matter what old Sister Ahn might say. Dolm had deceived her all her life, and she just felt angry.

She wondered what T'lin Dragontrader would say when she told him about that bizarre performance. He would believe her. To mention it to anyone else was unthinkable—even if Dolm Actor never returned, the troupe would not credit her story. She would be the only one who would ever know what had happened to him.

The hostel was a welcome sight in the dusk. There was no smoke rising from the chimney, though, as she had hoped there would be by now. She found the key in its usual cranny under the step. The door opened into the big communal kitchen that took up most of the ground floor, big enough and high enough to house a family of mammoths. Another door led out to toilets and washrooms; a wooden stair against one wall led up to sleeping rooms above.

She stood for a while, sniffing the familiar smells of ancient cooking and old tallow, listening to wind rattling the casements and whining in the eaves. There seemed to be no one else in the familiar old warren. She decided she would take off her coat first, comb her hair, and then kindle a fire to heat up wash water. She felt limp and sore from a long day. Only a llama should be expected to spend so long inside a heavy fleece.

She set off up the staircase that clung to the high, raw-stone wall. From long habit, she stepped on the ends of the treads. Ambria was always accusing her of sneaking, but she hated the sound of her uneven gait and had learned to move quietly in consequence. *Our Lady Mouse,* Golfren called her sometimes.

In some cities the troupe slept in one big room, while in Jurg they stayed in the king's house. The Narsh hostel lay somewhere between those two extremes. It was so large and so empty at this time of year that Eleal had a room all to herself, not having to share with Olimmiar. She walked down the long corridor, turned the corner, and saw her pack lying abandoned by Klip Trumpeter's door. Muscle building only went so far, obviously.

As she stooped to lift it, she detected a faint rasping coming from the room itself. The door was ajar, but whatever was making that odd noise was not visible through the crack.

One of the really nice things about the Narsh hostel was the size of its keyholes. Trumpeter was standing with his back to her, stripped to his breechclout as Dolm Actor had been. But Klip was not engaged in any arcane holy ritual. The cloth was white, anyway, although not as white as it should have been. He had a brick in each hand, and he was swinging them up and down, up and down. His bony back and shoulders gleamed with sweat, and the noise was his panting. He sounded almost ready to collapse.

He was really serious about those muscles! Perhaps he had believed her little lie after all? She sensed interesting opportunities for teasing—she might mention bricks at supper and smile at him innocently. That would make Trumpeter's face glow like one big all-over pimple.

Amused, Eleal took up her pack and tiptoed off along the corridor. Then she came to another open door, and her heart jumped into her mouth and stayed there.

This was Yama and Dolm's room. Like the others, it contained no furniture except a straw pallet, but their packs were lying there. Someone must have brought all the baggage back. Shivering with a sort of sick excitement, Eleal stared at this deadly opportunity.

When she had been little, she had found people's packs absolutely irresistible. There was always something interesting in them! Once she had found a hand-tinted print of a naked woman in K'linpor Actor's, and had produced it at lunch for everyone to admire. That had been a painful experience all round.

She had grown more discreet after that, but about two years ago Ambria had caught her going through Trong's pack and had taken a belt to her. That had really hurt. And then Ambria had said that Eleal Singer was nothing but a stray fledgling and the troupe had no duty to care for her and feed her and if she was ever caught prying like that again, she would be thrown out on the street where she belonged. That had hurt even more.

Since then, she had mostly managed to resist personal packs. They were a bad habit.

This, however, was different! This was important.

This was crazy—the man served Zath.

He was almost certainly dead, victim of his own clumsiness in botching a ritual. If he wasn't, there might be evidence in that baggage that would convince the others.

There was no one else in the building except muscle-man Klip, and he was busy.

All packs looked much alike. Whoever had brought the baggage back could easily have made a mistake. About three heartbeats after that last thought, Eleal Singer was limping along the corridor carrying Dolm Actor's pack instead of her own. It was very little heavier.

Panting like a cat, she laid it on her pallet, then spared a moment to lock and bolt her door.

Her hands trembled so much that she could hardly manage the buckles. Gasping for breath, she began hauling out clothes, spare boots, a printed book containing extracts from the Green and the Blue Scriptures, a couple of manuscript copies of plays—this year's repertoire. A makeup kit. A wig that ought to be in the prop box and had probably been left over after last night's performance. And a little bag of dream pods—well! Ambria Impresario would be very interested to know about them.

When Eleal had taken out everything, she looked for secret pockets like those in Golfren and Klip's packs. This one was a little trickier to figure out, but she managed it. It contained exactly what she had feared, a black garment. She did not even dare pull it out to inspect it. She had no need to. It was bulky enough.

A door banged, and voices came drifting up from downstairs. Almost retching with terror, Eleal began stuffing everything back in what she hoped was the right order, making a frantic muddle.

*Curiosity is a sin!*

Curiosity is a great talent, but this time that talent had worked too well.

Only a reaper would ever dress all in black. Sister Ahn had said, murder was both a sacrament and a duty for reapers. She had not mentioned whether their powers included the ability to know when someone had been ransacking their packs.

With her hair combed, wearing her shawl over her warmer dress, Eleal approached the stairs. She was an actor, wasn't she, sort of? Very well, she must act as if she still believed that Dolm was just an innocent, none too talented, actor. Holding her head high, she began to pick her way carefully down the stairs, holding the banister.

Then she saw that she had no need to act. Only Piol Poet and Golfren Piper had returned, and they were in no state to be an audience. Dull evening light struggled through high barred windows to show plank tables and the black iron range. The big kitchen was as bleak and cold as the streets outside. If there was no snow on the flagstone floor, Eleal could imagine it just by looking at Golfren Piper's face.

Wizened little Piol Poet knelt at the grate, trying to start a fire and producing nothing but smoke. He was the oldest of them all, but practical and helpful, a quiet soul who never said an unkind word. His wife had died years ago, so he was less intensely involved than the others in today's disaster.

Golfren Piper had perched on a stool and was gazing sickly at some empty, cobwebby shelves as if the end of the world had come and gone and left him behind. His pale blue eyes flicked round to look at Eleal, though. He raised eyebrows inquiringly. She nodded reassuringly. He forced a faint smile of approval and looked away again. She liked Golfren. He was slim and fair and would have been well suited to playing gods had he not been so wooden on stage that he resembled a tree with rheumatism. Piol wrote walk-on parts for him, but his main value to the troupe was as a musician and as Uthiam's husband.

Klip Trumpeter was probably still upstairs, giving himself a rubdown. Gartol Costumer had gone on ahead to Suss and would soon be wondering what had happened to everyone. That left three men unaccounted for, including Dolm Actor.

Eleal tried to muffle an immense sigh of relief. She dallied for a moment with the idea of racing back upstairs to rearrange Dolm's pack better. Then she decided someone might come to investigate, and Dolm himself might still return any minute anyway—she could not be certain he had died.

She sat down on a chair and looked around, being calm as the Mother on the Rainbow Throne in *The Judgment of Apharos*.

"You feeling all right?" Golfren asked, frowning.

"Yes. Yes, quite all right. Er, where's everybody?"

He shrugged. "Don't know. Trong and K'linpor went to consult their brothers. Dolm and Trumpeter—"

"I'm here," Klip said, clattering down the stairs, rubbing his hair with a grubby towel. "What brothers?"

Golfren pulled a face. "Local lodge of the Tion Fellowship. Forget I mentioned it."

Klip glanced thoughtfully at Eleal and then asked, "Any news from the temple?"

Golfren shook his head mournfully.

Piol rose stiffly from the range, where faint flickers of light showed success. He scowled at his hands and took the towel from Klip to wipe them. The murderous silence was broken by thumping of boots on the stoop. The door creaked open, swirling snowflakes, sucking smoke from the range. Trong Impresario slunk in. His son followed, closing the door with an angry bang.

As always, Trong bore the haggard, tragic expression to be expected of a man who died two hundred times a year. Usually he walked tall, a rawboned giant with a mane of long silver locks and beard, striding through the world without deigning to notice it, his mind far away among divine wonders of poetry and fate. Tonight he shuffled across the room in silence and crumpled onto a chair like a wrecked wagon, gangling limbs awry. That was not the way he depicted sorrow on stage, but it was more evocative.

K'linpor Actor looked nothing like his father. He was round-faced and pudgy—a fair actor, except that his voice lacked power. K'linpor was also a surprisingly agile acrobat in the masques. He sat down by the table and laid his head on his arms in utter dejection. He would be thinking of Halma, of course. Their marriage was even more recent than Golfren and Uthiam's.

"What news, sir?" Golfren inquired.

Trong shook his head without looking up. "None." His voice had lost its usual resonance. "It's just us, apparently. They have heard no word of the Lady banning others."

"Nothing they can do?"

"Pray. They will sacrifice a yak this evening on our behalf."

Silence fell. Eleal wondered who "they" were. Important, rich citizens, apparently, if they could afford to donate a yak. And was it to be sacrificed to the Lady, or to Tion?

Dolm Actor had offered a lot more than that to his chosen deity.

Trong roused himself with a sudden surge. The big man straightened and glared around in his god aspect.

"We have a free night before us. It is a fortuitous opportunity to rehearse the *Varilian*. The child can stand in for Uthiam—"

K'linpor raised his face slightly. "Father, you are talking *dung.*" He laid his head back on his arms.

Trong looked shocked, then slowly melted back to his former desolated posture and stared at the floor.

Men without women . . . The range was crackling cheerfully, gushing smoke. Eleal pulled herself away from awful thoughts of reapers. She stood up, marched across, and flicked a lever.

"It helps to open the flue first!"

Old Piol scratched at the silver stubble on his jowl. He smiled and started to say something; it became an attack of coughing.

Eyes stinging, Eleal moved away from the range. "We must eat," she said in her best goddess voice, because that was what Ambria would say. "I don't feel like it either," she told the disgusted expression all around, "but we should. The markets will close soon."

"She's right," Golfren said, rising. "You will be our keeper tonight, Eleal. I'll come with you."

"I'll get my coat . . ."

Boots thumped on the step outside. Heads turned.

The door flew open, swirling snow and smoke and cold air. Dolm Actor swept in with a basket on his arm. He slammed the door and glanced around with an inquiring grin.

Eleal looked down quickly at the greasy flagstones, unable to meet his eyes. Invoking Zath! Self-mutilation! Black gown in pack! *Reaper!* She scurried back to her seat by the table and hunched herself very small, trying to hide her shaking.

Dolm's resonant voice rang out, reverberating in the big room. "Well, you're a glum lot! Nobody thought about food, I suppose?"

K'linpor straightened up, soft face flushing. "Where have you been?"

There was a momentary silence. Eleal did not glance up, frightened that Dolm might be watching her.

"Me? I went back to the temple."

Golfren roared, *"What?"* and stepped backward, knocking over his stool with a crash.

"I didn't see any of our ladies there, if that's what's worrying you," Dolm said soothingly. He stepped to the table beside Eleal and laid his basket on it. He was so close that she could smell the wet leather of his coat.

"I did what we should have all done . . . except Klip Trumpeter maybe. Yet, why not him, too? He's a staunch young man now. I dropped some of my own hard-earned silver in the bowl, and I made sacrifice to the Lady."

*Liar!* Eleal thought. *Liar! Liar!*

Trong bellowed, *"No!"* in a voice that seemed to shake the house. His craggy features flamed red.

"Yes," Dolm said calmly. "I saw it as my duty. I chose the oldest, ugliest woman I could find. She was immensely grateful."

"That is utterly foul!" Golfren Piper yelled.

"It was a holy ritual! Do you criticize the goddess?"

Silence. Eleal stole a glance at Golfren. He was as red as Trong—redder even, because his face was fair-skinned and clean-shaven. His knuckles were white. She wondered if there was about to be a fight.

Yes, she thought, it was foul. She thought of Dolm's long, hairy limbs and body, and she shivered. Goddess or not, it was foul to make a woman submit to that against her will.

"Well?" Dolm Actor inquired.

Piper growled, "No."

"Wise! The woman in question had been assigned a penance. I did not ask for what, naturally." Dolm was always a cheerful, almost boisterous person, but now he sounded exuberant, excited. Eleal wondered if he had been drinking, but she could not smell wine on him, only the wet leather.

Dolm laughed. "She had been waiting there every day for two fortnights, she told me. Of course she was grateful! I trust the Lady approved. It wasn't my most enjoyable experience, I admit, but I did my duty in a spirit of proper humility, with prayer."

Golfren muttered an obscenity and turned his back.

"I find I cannot disapprove under the circumstances," Trong Impresario declaimed with obvious reluctance.

"Good!"

Eleal was still shaking, hoping no one would notice, too terrified to move, still staring at the disgustingly dirty floor. Dolm was lying! No matter how brief the remainder of his horrible ritual had been, there had not been time for him to recover and go to the temple and then visit the markets and come back here. He had not been running, or he would be puffing. Running? Lying with a woman? After losing so much blood? He had been soaked in blood while she watched, and more blood still pumping out of him.

"Furthermore," Dolm said, "we all . . ."

Alerted by the silence, Eleal glanced up.

He had sensed something wrong. He raised his head as if sniffing. He looked slowly around the big room, studying each face in turn. Finally he dropped his eyes to hers.

Then he smiled, and the recognition in his dark eyes was obvious—fond reproof. *He knew!* He knew she knew. She was the one.

Slowly, agonizingly slowly, Dolm reached down with his left hand to scratch his right, which rested on the handle of the basket beside her. His sleeve slid back. She could see his bony, hairy wrist. There was no mark on it, no scar, no bandage . . . No bloodstains, even!

She looked up again at his face.

No blood on it, no blood in his hair—and the hair combed over his bald pate was lank, showing no sign that it had been recently washed.

He was still smiling, like a snow cat.

"This must have been a difficult day for you, child!" he said softly. "Are you feeling all right?"

She started to turn her head away and his hand shot out to grasp her chin. The touch of a reaper!

Eleal screamed and leaped away from him. She hurtled across the room and threw herself against Golfren Piper, hugging him fiercely. She needed Ambria, but he would have to do. Everyone seemed to shout, "What?" at the same moment.

Golfren put his arms around her and lifted her bodily, as if she were a child. He muttered soothing noises. "Yes, she's had a very hard day!" he said.

The door flew open with a crash and Ambria Impresario made an Entrance.

# 15

Ambria was an imposing woman on the most trivial occasion. She could peel a tuber dramatically or ladle gruel with majesty. These days the heavy breasts sagged and the hair was dyed, but no more convincing goddess had ever trod the boards, and she blazed with authority in that kitchen doorway. Taller than most men, deep-voiced, big-boned, she had been known to silence a hall of drunken miners with a single gesture. Now one arm was extended shoulder high from hurling open the door; her hood was back, letting her dark hair flow to her waist, framing aquiline features normally pale, ashen in her present distress. The snow-mottled cloak hung to her boots, making her seem taller than ever.

"We are all here." Her voice rang through the vast room. "We are all unharmed, save a few bruises." She swung aside in a swirl of leather to let the others enter.

The men cried out in joy. Uthiam Piper ran in, heading for Golfren, who dropped Eleal instantly. She caught a brief glimpse of a livid welt on Uthiam's cheek before it was hidden in an embrace.

Yama Actor ran to Dolm; Halma to K'linpor. Olimmiar stepped inside last, holding a rag over one eye. She stopped beside Ambria and stood with face lowered. Trong rose, moved one foot forward a pace, and spread his arms in welcome.

Ambria swung the door halfway closed and halted it there. "Hold!" Her deep voice boomed like a thunderclap, silencing everyone. "There is no need for us all to repeat the sordid details. I shall tell the tale." Her compelling eyes raked the room in challenge. Everyone watched; no one spoke. The door remained half closed.

"We did as we were bidden." The spectacular voice dropped to a lower register. "We offered ourselves in the service of the Lady. A man came to each of us—"

"Three," Olimmiar said with a sob.

Ambria enveloped her in a powerful arm and pulled her close without looking down. "Each of us was accepted, then. Not one of the men was able to . . ." She drew a deep breath. ". . . complete the holy ritual. The goddess refused our sacrifice."

"You mean they were all *impotent?*" Dolm Actor barked.

Ambria slammed the door so the building shook. Everyone jumped. "Yes," she admitted. "The priests are deeply concerned, naturally. But none of you husbands need worry about, er, consequences."

"That's insane!" Dolm said, and suddenly laughed shrilly. Everyone glared at him, even Eleal. "And three tried with Olimmiar, one after the other?" His eyes flicked inquiringly to Uthiam.

"Two."

"So a total of eight—"

"We need not discuss sordid trivia," Ambria Impresario proclaimed. She strode majestically across the big chamber toward Trong, one hand extended, the other sweeping Olimmiar Dancer along beside her. "Some of the men became violent in their distress, but the priests stopped them before there was any serious damage. Now you know. The matter is closed." She stepped into her husband's embrace.

"No it's not!" Dolm was grinning and quite unabashed by her anger. Eleal had never seen any member of the troupe defy Ambria openly like that, but then Dolm had been bubbling like a kettle since he came in, and a reaper certainly need not fear an aging female actor.

Ambria whirled around in wrath. Olimmiar looked up in astonishment, revealing a puffy swelling around her eye. K'linpor's mouth was hanging open.

"It's a miracle!" Dolm jeered. "A holy miracle! Of course we must discuss it. Were they all old, fat factory owners?"

Ambria's ivory cheeks flamed scarlet in a way Eleal would never have believed possible. "No they were not!" Echoes rang. "In my case, as I remained unchosen, the priests went out and found a twenty-year-old quarry worker who has already fathered two children. Does that satisfy your prurient curiosity, Dolm Actor?"

He sniggered. "Did it yours? Well, now what happens? Are we free to depart from Narsh, as Ois has apparently no use for us?"

The big woman seemed to shrink slightly. "No. We are summoned to the temple at dawn. The priests will seek an oracle to discover the Lady's will."

Even Dolm Actor flinched.

There was a moment's silence, and then he said softly, "All of us?"

"All of us."

Everyone turned to look at Eleal Singer.

When times were good, the troupe was one big happy family. When times were otherwise, which was more frequent, it was still one big family, and rarely too unhappy. Everyone was related to everyone else in some contorted fashion. Old Piol Poet was the brother of Ambria's first husband and thus Uthiam's uncle. Even Klip Trumpeter was a stepbrother of Gartol Costumer, who was Trong Impresario's cousin. Everyone was family except Eleal Singer. Although she could recall no trace of her life before the troupe took her in, she was the outsider, the waif, the stray.

Normally she never thought about that distinction. Certainly nobody ever mentioned it, not even Olimmiar at her most catty. That evening Eleal could smell it. She was the only one who had not been to the temple of the Lady. She was the last hope. All other efforts had failed, so in the morning they would take her there and she would be unmasked as the cause of the trouble. It was obvious.

Perhaps Sister Ahn's lunatic babbling had been true, and the gods were staging some great cosmic tragedy that involved little Eleal Singer.

Wives clung to husbands. Olimmiar Dancer had attached herself to Halma, her sister. Old Piol fussed around, preparing a meal in tactful silence. Trumpeter soon went up to his room and came down muffled in llama fleece. He announced briefly that he was going out for a walk, and vanished rapidly through the door into a near-blizzard, followed by a puzzled frown from Ambria, a glare of outrage from Trong, and a sardonic smile from Dolm. Young Klip knew an opportunity when he was handed one.

He might be heading for a disappointment, though—he did not know that Dolm had been lying about going back to the temple.

Every time Eleal risked a glance in Dolm's direction, he was directing his sardonic smile at her. She wondered about her chances of living through the night. No one ever spoke of reapers; to denounce one was probably suicide. To denounce Dolm Actor would be an act of rank madness. The others would just assume that the stressful day had unhinged her mind—he was Ambria's cousin's husband, one of the family! The only evidence Eleal could hope to produce was that black garment hidden in his pack and she was certain that it would have gone elsewhere by now. Even if it could be produced, he could always claim that it was an old stage costume and then accuse her of having stolen something.

Maybe it *was* only an old costume, although she could not imagine any audience tolerating a play with a reaper in it. Maybe she had imagined the loathsome ritual. Maybe she had gone crazy.

As the evening dragged on in quiet confidential whispers, she realized that everyone was planning to head off to be alone very early. Actors were night birds by profession, but tonight wives wanted to be alone with husbands and husbands wanted to be alone with wives.

Larger and larger in her mind grew an image of her cubicle door, with its heavy lock and its thick iron bolt. Not even a reaper was going to break through those without waking everybody!

Then Dolm himself stretched his long arms overhead and yawned.

Eleal realized that she must leave before he did, or she might find him waiting for her in her room.

"G'night!" she snapped, jumping to her feet.

She scampered across the room to the stairs—*Clip, clop.*

"I'm very sleepy," she explained, racing up them two at a time.

*Clip, clop* . . . "See you in the morning," she shouted back as she tore along the corridor.

She dashed into her room—took a hurried glance around to make sure it was un-occupied—closed the door. It creaked loudly, but at the last minute she slowed it so it would not slam. She turned the key gently, wrestled the bolt over, and flopped down on the floor, panting as if she had run over Rilepass carrying a mammoth.

The window was barred. The walls were solid stone, the floor and ceiling thick planks. If anywhere was safe from a reaper, this was it. As an afterthought, she took the big key out and tucked it in her pack. She stuffed a sock into the keyhole.

Preparing for bed was never a lengthy process in chilly Narsh. She donned her woolly nightgown, rolled up her second-best dress to be a pillow, and laid her llama fleece coat on the pallet as a cover. Then she knelt and took hold of her amulet to say her prayers.

The amulet was a little golden frog that Ambria had given her a long time ago, as soon as she could be trusted not to swallow it. It looked like gold, but it left green stains on her chest. It seemed a very frail defense against the god of death, whom she had probably offended mightily by spying on his sacred ritual.

The wind rattled the casement hungrily. Her usual prayers seemed grievously inadequate this night. She extemporized a long addition, addressed to Kirb'l Tion, asking for his aid in letting the troupe travel to the Tion Festival in safety. Shivering with cold, then, she whispered an apology to the Man for spying on holy ceremony in his shrine. After all, the shrine itself had not been specifically dedicated to *Zath* . . . she could not speak that name.

At last she snuggled in under the heavy fleece. Cockerel with no liver, alpaca white outside and black inside, a reaper on a mammoth and another in the troupe, men stricken impotent by the Lady . . . She would not be able to sleep a wink!

But she did.

# *16*

Nights in hospitals are much longer than days. Edward Exeter had discovered this truth during his first term at Fallow, when the unfamiliar diseases of England had made him a frequent patient in the san. He rediscovered it in Albert Memorial.

A nurse came around with a light, checking on people.

"Where am I?" he asked.

She told him.

"What happened?"

"You had an accident. Do you want another needle?"

"No. I'm all right." He did not like the silent music the drugs brought.

"Try to sleep," she said, and went away.

Trouble was, he seemed to have been sleeping for weeks. The shock was wearing off, he decided. His leg lashed him with a sickening beat of pain, he was stiff with staying in the same position so long. He kept trying to remember, and when he did remember, he didn't want to. His recollections were very patchy and most of them must be nightmares.

When he did sleep, he was tormented by those same nightmares. He would wake up in a state of shivering funk, soaked with sweat and remember nothing of what had so frightened him. For the first time he began to wonder what on earth he had done to himself. Not playing rugby at this time of year. Train accident? There was a bandage around his head and his leg was in splints.

Yet the strangest dream that came in that endless night was amazingly sharp and memorable, so that in the morning he was to wonder whether it had really been a dream at all.

Light was shining in the door, and the room was a mass of confusing shadows. This time he seemed to have just wakened naturally, not frightened. His leg throbbed with a regular pulse that seemed to go all the way through him. He studied the ropes holding it up and then turned his head on the pillow. There was a window there with no curtains, and the sky outside was black. He rolled his head over to the other side to look up at the man standing there.

"Behold the limpid orbs," the man said, "reflecting the sense within, the very turning of the soul. Prithee, then, this maiming of thy shin, it does not pain thee o'ermuch?"

Edward said, "It's not too bad, sir." It wasn't, really.

"To dissemble thus becomes thee more than honesty."

The visitor was an odd little man—quite old, with a fuzz of silver curls and a wrinkled, puckish face, clean-shaven. He was stooped, so his face stuck out in front of him. His overcoat had a very old-fashioned Astrakhan collar and seemed slightly too large for him. He was holding an equally antique beaver hat in one hand and a walking stick with a silver handle in the other.

"We have not come into acquaintance beforetimes although ink in veritable tides has flowed between us. I am your worship's servant, Jonathan Oldcastle." He bowed, clutching the topper to his heart.

"Mr. Oldcastle!" Edward said. "You're . . . You're not what I expected, sir." In the way of dreams, Mr. Oldcastle's appearance seemed perfectly acceptable for an officer in His Majesty's Colonial Office. Yet none of the letters he had written to Edward in the past two years had read like Mosley Minor's atrocious efforts to extemporize Shakespeare.

The little man chuckled, beaming. "I fain perfect attainments beyond expectation. This council needs be consummated with dispatch. Pray you, Master Exeter, being curt and speedy in response, advise me what befell, what savage circumstance contrived this havoc upon thy person and thy fortunes. Discover to me the monument of thy memory that we may invent what absences the dickens may have wiped thereof."

He had a broad accent, which Edward could not place, and his speech would certainly have been unintelligible had this not all been a dream.

"I don't remember much, sir. I went . . . I went to the Grange, sir, didn't I? To stay with Bagpipe."

Mr. Oldcastle nodded. "I so surmise."

"Just for a few days. They said they didn't mind, and I was welcome. I'm planning to enlist as soon as mobilization starts of course, but until then . . ."

There hadn't been anywhere else to go. Words caught in his throat and he was afraid he was going to start piping his eye.

"Comfort thyself!" Oldcastle said soothingly. "I think someone approaches. Tarry a moment."

Edward must have drifted off to sleep again, because he jumped when Oldcastle said, "Now, my stalwart? What else lurks in thy recollection?"

"Dinner? I didn't have any proper togs. It's all very vague, sir."

Mr. Oldcastle breathed on the silver head of his cane and wiped it on his sleeve. "And after that?"

"We turned in. The general was going to be reading the lesson in church next morning."

"Yes?"

A curious smell of mothballs was overpowering even the ever-present stink of carbolic.

"Then Bagpipe came and said did I feel like some tuck, and why didn't we raid the larder."

"And you did. And what then befell?"

Screaming? Long curly hair? Porcelain sink. . . .

*"Nothing!"* Edward said quickly. "Nothing! I can't remember."

"Be not vexed," Mr. Oldcastle said, matter-of-factly. "Oftentimes a wounding of the head will ruptures cause upon the spirit withall. Thou cannot fare hence upon the morrow, good young coz. Dost peradventure know by rote the speech of bold King Harry before Harfleur?"

" 'Once more into the breach,' you mean, sir?"

"The same."

"I should. I played the king when Sixth Form did *Henry V* last Christmas."

"Be it that, then. No bardic fancy ever better nailed the spirit of a man. Now mark me well. Here are you well cosseted and I shall set a palliation about thee, but if thy foes evade my artifice and so distrain thee, do thou declaim that particular poesy. Wilt keep this admonition in thy heart?"

"Yes, sir, I'll remember," Edward said solemnly. In the way of dreams, the instructions seemed very important and logical.

"I wish thee good fortune, Master Exeter."

"Goodnight, Mr. Oldcastle. I'm very pleased to have met you at last, sir."

He slept better after that.

# 17

A click from the bolt wakened Eleal. The lock turned, making much less noise than it had for her. In utter darkness, all she could see was the window, a lopsided patch of not-quite light, distorted by clinging snow. Yet somehow there was enough light for her to know how the door swung open, with not a hint of its usual squeak.

He glided in, blacker than black, making no sound. The door closed, equally silent. Moving like smoke, he approached. He stopped at her feet and she supposed he was looking down at her, but she could see no face, no eyes, only a pillar of darker dark.

All she could hear was her heart.

"You saw." It was a whisper, but even a whisper had resonance when it came from Dolm Actor.

The words were not a question and she was incapable of answering anyway.

"Normally that would seal your fate in itself," said the whisper.

*Normally?* Was there a shimmer of hope there? Would she die of terror before she found out?

Obviously he knew she was awake. "You are an incredible little snoop. I always wondered if you would ransack my pack one day. I would have known, of course. It is given to us to know when we are detected. Then I should have had to send your soul to my master. I hoped it would not be like that, Eleal Singer. We do have feelings, you know. We are not monsters. We mourn the necessity."

Pause.

Not quite a chuckle . . . yet when the deadly soft voice spoke again, it held a hint of amusement. "I thought I was the problem, you see. I thought it was my master's print on my heart that had displeased the Lady. Yes, my master is he whom you call Zath—the Unconquerable, the Last Victor. I reported to my master, as you saw, seeking guidance. I was told that it is you who are the problem, not me."

She wanted to scream, *Why me?* and her mouth was as dry as ashes. Her nails were digging into her palms and her insides were melting to jelly. Her teeth continued to chatter.

"The *Filoby Testament* . . . but you will not have heard of that. Never mind. The gods have decreed, Eleal Singer, that you shall not journey to Sussland. That is all. Your presence there might change the world. I was instructed to ensure it does not happen."

She thought of the priest and Sister Ahn. She could not even scream.

The reaper sighed. "Please believe, the necessity distressed me. I am not evil. I am not vindictive. I honor my master with the gift of souls—that is all. True, he grants me great rapture when I perform this service, but I would rather offer strangers, really I would."

Dolm, who was always so jovial . . .

The reaper moved. Without exactly seeing, she knew that he had knelt down at her side—within reach.

She could not hear him breathing. Did he breathe when he was being a reaper?

"But here tonight I learned that it will not be necessary. Holy Ois knows who you are and how to stop you. She has the matter in hand. I was told I need not meddle within her domain. In the morning she will do what she wills, whatever that may be. You will not be journeying to Sussland."

That did sound like Eleal Singer was not going to die now.

The morning could look after itself.

"Is there anyone you wish to die?" the reaper inquired softly.

Eleal's teeth chattered.

"Well?" he asked. "Answer!"

She stuttered, "N-n-no!"

"Pity. Because if you wish to see someone die, Eleal Singer, then you need only tell that person that I am a reaper. I shall know, and they will die. Is that clear?"

She nodded in the dark, and knew he knew that.

"If by any chance Holy Ois does allow you to go to Suss, then of course I shall have to act." Dolm sighed, and floated erect again. "And I must go and act now. Act? Actor?"

He chuckled drily, as Dolm did when he was about to make a joke. "Ironic, is it not? That rare performance you saw had but one spectator, yet she does not have to pay. Others must pay, strangers must pay. An expensive performance! He will want two at least, perhaps three if they are not young. Sleep well, little spy."

The blackness drifted toward the door. Then it stopped.

"I only came," said a whisper more definitely in Dolm's usual offhand tone, "because I thought your remarkable curiosity had earned an explanation."

The door opened, closed. The bolt slid. The lock shut.

Eleal drew great sobbing breaths of icy air. She was going to live through the night. Compared to that, nothing else mattered, not even her wet bed.

# *18*

Patients were wakened at six o'clock so they could be washed and fed and have their beds made before the doctors' rounds. Shaving in bed was bad enough, but other things were worse. Bedpans were the utter end.

The nurse wanted to give Edward another needle, but he refused it, preferring to put up with the pain, rather than have porridge for brains.

She was quite pretty, in a chubby sort of way, with a Home Counties accent and a brusque manner. She would tell him nothing except he'd had an accident and Doctor Stanford would explain. His dream kept coming back to him and the memories he'd had in his dream—he could remember remembering them, sort of. Bagpipe was in there somewhere.

He was in hospital, in Greyfriars. He still could remember almost nothing after those awful images of dinner and him with no evening dress. After dinner . . . nothing, just fog. And nightmares.

He was worried about Bagpipe. He asked about him, Timothy Bodgley.

"No one by that name in the hospital," the nurse said, and then just kept repeating that Doctor Stanford would explain. She wouldn't even say how she was so certain that there was no one by that name in the hospital when she had not even gone to check. She did admit that this was Monday, and visiting hours were from two till four. "You've got a fine collection of stitches under that bandage," she added, changing the subject clumsily, "but your hair should hide most of the scar."

"You mean it won't spoil my striking good looks?" he asked facetiously, and was shaken when she blushed.

He surprised himself by eating the greasy ham and eggs he was given for breakfast. The tea was cold, but he drank it. He had a private room, and that worried him. He had a broken leg—a badly broken leg—and that worried him even more. He could not enlist with a broken leg, so he might be going to miss the war. Everyone agreed it would be over by Christmas.

He asked for a newspaper to find out what was happening in the crisis, and the nurse said that was up to the doctor.

He was left alone for a long time, then. Eventually a desiccated, graying man in a white coat marched in holding a clipboard. He had a stethoscope protruding from one pocket. Right behind him came Matron, armored in starch, statuesque as Michelangelo's *Moses*.

"Doctor Stanford, Mr. Exeter," she said.

"How are we this morning?" The doctor looked up from the clipboard with an appraising glance.

"Not bad, sir. Worried."

The doctor frowned. "What's this about you refusing a needle?"

"It doesn't hurt too much, sir," Edward lied.

"Oh, doesn't it? You can overdo the stiff-upper-lip business, young fellah. Still, I'll leave it up to you."

A few questions established that the only real problem was the leg. The many-colored patches Edward had discovered on his hips and arms were dismissed brusquely. Eyes and ears, fingertips on his wrist and a beastly cold stethoscope on his chest . . .

The doctor changed the bandage on Edward's head. "Eighteen stitches," he said admiringly. "Most of the scar won't show unless you want to try a Prussian haircut." He scribbled on the clipboard and handed it to Matron. "Get the blanks filled in now he's conscious, will you?"

He stuffed his hands in the pocket of his white coat. "You have a badly broken leg, Exeter, as I'm sure you know by now. In a day or two we'll take off the splints and see if we can put it in a cast. Depends on the swelling, and so on. We may have to load you in an ambulance and take you to have it x-rayed, but we hope that won't be necessary. You're a healthy young chap; it should heal with no permanent damage. In a year you'll have forgotten all about it. For the time being, though, you have to endure the traction."

"How soon can I enlist?"

Stanford shrugged. "Three months."

"May I see a paper?"

"If you take it in small doses. Don't persist if you get a headache. Anything else you need?"

"I'd like to know how I got here."

"Ah! How much can you remember?"

"Very little, sir. Greyfriars Grange? Bagp . . . Timothy?"

The look in the doctor's eye told him before the man said it. "He wasn't as lucky as you."

The ham and eggs rose and then subsided. Edward swallowed hard a few times and then said, "How?"

"He was murdered."

"*Murdered?* Who by?"

"Don't know yet. Do you feel up to answering some questions for the police?"

"I'll try. I don't remember very—"

In strode a large, heavyset man. He must have been waiting by the door. He was dressed like a banker, but he had *Roberto* written all over him, and the look of a man who might have been a first-rate rugby fullback. Getting a ball past him would be like swimming up Victoria Falls, even now, with a staunch bow window stretching the links of his watch chain. His mustache spread out like the horns on a Cape buffalo, turning up in points at the end.

"Five minutes, no more," the doctor said.

The policeman nodded without a glance at him. The doctor departed. Matron followed him to the door, but in a way that suggested she was not going far.

"Inspector Leatherdale, Mr. Exeter." He pulled up the chair. "I am not asking for a formal statement. You do not need to tell me anything, but I would appreciate hearing what you can recall of the events which led to your injuries."

Edward told what he could, mostly while studying the way the inspector's hair was combed over his bald spot. His memories were so patchy that he thought he must sound like an absolute ass.

"That's the lot, sir. Er . . ."

"Take your time. Even vague impressions may be helpful to us."

"Crumpets? Crumpets and strawberry jam on a deal table."

"Why crumpets at your age? Why not raid the sherry?"

Edward started to smile and then remembered Bagpipe. "We tried that three years ago and were sick as dogs. It was a tradition, that's all." Never again, Bagpipe!

"Anything else you recall?"

"A woman with long curly hair?"

The rozzer's face was as unmoving as a gargoyle's. "What color hair?"

"Dark brown, I think. It hung in ringlets, sort of a Gypsy look. Very pale face."

"Where did you see her? What was she doing?"

Edward shook his head on the pillow. "Screaming, I think. Or shouting."

"What was she wearing?"

"Don't remember, sir."

"But this might have been hours earlier, and you don't know where?"

"Yes. No. Yes it might have been and no I don't know why I remember her."

"What more?"

"A . . . A porcelain sink turning red, scarlet. Blood running into a sink. A *stream* of blood." He felt a rush of nausea and bit his lip. He was shaking—lying flat on his back and shaking like a stupid kid!

Leatherdale studied him for a minute, and then rose. "Thank you. We shall require a formal statement as soon as you are up to it."

"Bodgley's dead?"

The massive head nodded. "You fell down some steps. He was stabbed."

"And you think I did it?"

Inspector Leatherdale went very still, and yet seemed to fill the room with menace. "Why should I think that, Mr. Exeter?" he asked softly.

"Private room, sir. You said I didn't need to tell you anything. Nobody would answer my questions."

The man smiled with his mouth but not with his eyes. "No other reason?"

"I didn't!" Edward yelled.

"Five minutes are up, sir," Matron said, sailing in like a dreadnought, clipboard ready and fountain pen poised. "Your full name and date of birth, Mr. Exeter?"

"Edward George Exeter . . ."

The inspector moved the chair back to where it had been without taking his eyes off Edward.

"C. of E.?" Matron said, writing busily.

"Agnostic."

She looked up with a Medusa stare of disapproval. "Shall I just put, 'Protestant'?"

Edward was certainly not going to support any organization that tolerated Holy Roly as one of its advocates. The Nyagatha horrors had been provoked by meddling, addle-headed missionaries, and that was another reason.

"No, ma'am. Agnostic."

She wrote unwillingly. "Diseases?"

He listed what he could recall—malaria and dysentery in Africa, and all the usual English ones he'd caught when he came Home: mumps, measles, whooping cough, chicken pox.

Then he saw that the policeman was still standing in the doorway, watching him.

"You want to ask me some more questions, Inspector?"

"No. Not now. We'll take a statement later, sir." His mouth smiled again. "Normally I would ask you to keep yourself available, but I don't expect you'll be going anywhere for a day or two."

# 19

A bleak dawn was breaking, but even the beggars were still asleep, huddled in doorways and corners under their dusting of snow. Somewhere back in the temple precincts doomed cockerels screamed defiance at the coming day. The troupe had assembled as instructed, and they were the day's first business for the temple.

Inside the long hall, night had not yet ended. Even the many candles glittering upon the altar before Ois could not brighten that big, cold place. Off to the sides, in the shadows, a few fainter glows showed where lamps burned under some of the innumerable arches. Those few bright alcoves amid so much dark somehow reminded Eleal of Sister Ahn's scattered teeth.

Shivering with cold and apprehension, she knelt between Trong and Ambria, seeking comfort from their huge solidity—although even Ambria seemed cowed today. The floor was cold and hard on the knees. They knelt in a circle, all of them except the missing Gartol Costumer; twelve counting Eleal. She had been placed with her back to the door, facing almost straight at the goddess. She clutched a gold coin, the first real gold she had ever held. The cold of the floor was seeping into her bones.

In the center of the circle stood a silver bowl, containing a feather, two eggs, and a white pebble. The priests had placed them there with great ceremony to begin the ritual.

The image of the Lady was the largest Eleal had ever seen, but it was a picture, not a statue. It filled the end wall, the full height of the temple, crafted from shiny white tiles, but her nipples gleamed scarlet, like rubies. Darker tones shadowed her belly and the undersides of her great breasts; her face was barely visible in the high darkness. At her feet an old man warbled holy writ in continuous monotone. In time he would be relieved by another, and another, until the entire Red Scripture had been pronounced. Then they would begin at the beginning again. So it had always been. He was not always audible, but he never stopped.

A half dozen or so priests had chanted a service to the Lady. Now a drummer began a low, menacing rhythm while a new group executed a strange, posturing dance. They were all young, obviously, and their shaven heads showed that they were priests, despite their curious close-fitting garments, which left arms and shins bare. In the candlelight the cloth seemed almost black, but it was red, in honor of the Lady. Eleal was fascinated by their ritual, very measured and deliberate, more like stylized gymnastics than any dance she had ever seen.

One of the illuminated alcoves blinked in the corner of her eye. Then a second. She leaned back slightly to see. A man was walking along the wall, followed by a priestess. He obscured another lamp, and stopped. A woman rose beyond him, apparently from a seat inside the alcove. She opened her robe. He walked on and she sat down again—unwanted, rejected. Eleal shuddered, tasting a sourness rising in her throat. Ambria hissed angrily and she turned her face back to the ceremony.

In a moment, though, the man progressed to where she could see him without moving her head. Her eyes insisted on straying in his direction. She watched how he found a woman he fancied and paid the priestess. The priestess walked away, he entered the alcove and began to undress.

The acrobatics ended in a flurry of drum strokes. Again Eleal returned her attention to where it belonged. A priest approached and gestured; the actors scrambled to their feet. There was a pause. She felt even smaller now, standing between tall Ambria and taller Trong. She studied the goddess to keep her mind off what was happening in that alcove. The Lady was emerging from darkness as daylight began to seep in through the high windows. The stone face bore a curious expression, eyes almost closed, scarlet lips parted, a hint of tongue showing. It was not a merciful face. It gave no clue why a mighty goddess should be so wroth at little Eleal Singer.

Drums thundered, making her jump. They sank into an irregular, disturbing beat.

"State your age first. . . ."

A priest and a priestess had entered the circle and placed themselves in front of Golfren. The voice, however, came from outside, from an older man standing behind him, muttering instructions. Then Golfren spoke, his voice higher-pitched than usual:

"I am twenty-six years old, my name is Golfren Piper. I am married and childless. I revere the Lady and beseech her to have mercy upon me." A coin clinked.

The priest behind the little priestess put a hand on her shoulder and guided her along to stand before the next supplicant.

"I am twenty years old, my name is K'linpor Actor. I am married and childless. I revere the Lady and beseech her to have mercy upon me." Another clink.

Eleal caught a glimpse of the older priest, the one on the outside. His red robe was sumptuously embroidered and begemmed, it bulged over his belly. He carried a lit taper in a soft, plump hand, light gleaming like wax on his shaven head and doughy jowls, sparkling on his jeweled fingers.

The priestess was very young, little more than a child, yet her head, too, was shaven. A cord around her neck supported a golden vase, dangling between her small breasts. She was barefoot, seemingly wearing only her robe—and that was so thin that the bumps of her nipples showed through it. She must be frozen.

The priest behind her was a large youth, one of the gymnasts, still breathing hard from his exertions. His hairy shins and forearms contrasted oddly with the shiny smoothness of his head and face.

"I am forty-five years old, my name is Ambria Impresario." Ambria's splendid voice was hoarse and uncertain this grim morning. "I am . . . I have been married twice, Father . . ."

The outside priest muttered questions, directions. The little priestess turned and began to walk away. The young priest grabbed her arm and pulled her back. When he released her, she stayed where she had been put, like a chair, but her hands and head twitched oddly.

Eleal clenched her fists against her thighs to stop them shaking. She was next after Ambria. She felt the gold coin sticky on her palm.

"I am forty-five years old, my name is Ambria Impresario. I am widowed and re-married and have borne one child. I revere the Lady and beseech her to have mercy upon me."

Suddenly the priestess started to laugh. The young priest behind her grabbed her shoulders and shook her until she stopped. Then he pulled her along to stand in front of Eleal. Her eyes were vacant, her jaw slack. Drool shone on her chin and darkened the bodice of her robe.

The priest outside the circle had arrived also. Eleal sensed him at her back and caught a whiff of a scent like lilac.

An actor must not falter over such simple lines: "I am twelve years old," she said clearly, "my name is Eleal Singer. I am unmar—"

"If you are a virgin, then you must specify."

Her teeth chattered briefly. She swallowed. "I am twelve years old, my name—"

A thunderstorm rumble from Trong drowned her out. "Her true name is not Singer but Impresario. She is my granddaughter."

Eleal cried, *"What?"* very shrilly. The sound seemed to soar like a bat up into the dark recesses of the roof. The drums rumbled.

The priest made an irritated sound. "Explain. Quickly!"

"I had a daughter," Trong growled, staring fixedly up at the goddess. "She shamed herself, and then died. I have reared the bastard in obedience to holy scripture. Her name is Eleal Impresario."

His face was hidden from Eleal's vantage by his silver mane. She looked up at Ambria in disbelief. Ambria nodded, smiling sadly.

Again the idiot priestess started to laugh. Her husky keeper shook her, but she continued. He shook her harder—viciously, like a floor mat, her head lolling back and forth, the gold vase thumping to and fro on its cord. He finally managed to stop the fit, but he retained a hold on her after that.

The older priest was sounding annoyed at the interruptions to his ritual, but was obviously determined to proceed in proper form. "Name her by the father's trade."

"I don't know it!" Trong growled, sounding as if this disclosure was hurting him badly. He was so upright himself, it was hard to imagine him having raised a wanton child.

"Your daughter would not name the man?"

"She could not! She disappeared for a fortnight. When we found her, her wits had gone and the damage was done. She never spoke a rational word after."

The priest grunted. "Use the Impresario name."

Eleal was one of the family! But joy was debased by a surge of anger. Why had they never told her so? Why had Ambria once threatened to throw her out as a stray?

"Make your appeal!" the priest snapped.

Eleal pulled her wits together and spoke the words rapidly. "I am twelve years old, my name is Eleal Impresario. I am a virgin. I revere the Lady and beseech her to have mercy upon me." She dropped her coin in the vase and was surprised to hear it plop into liquid.

The moronic priestess sniggered, her eyes moving vaguely and somehow wrongly. Her muscular attendant looked seriously worried now. She hung limp as a towel in his grip. He moved to dangle her in front of Trong. The drumbeat was growing faster, urgent.

Eleal Impresario? That did not sound right! She would continue to call herself Eleal Singer. After all, her singing brought her wages—token wages, perhaps, but real copper money. Trong Impresario's granddaughter! Why had he never told her? It wasn't her fault her mother had been wicked! What of her mother? What had she been called? Had she been an actor? Beautiful? Ugly? How old when she died? How had she died?

Eleal glanced around at the others, wondering if any of them had known this secret. Surely K'linpor must have! He was avoiding her eye, watching the priest and priestess working their way around the circle. *Uncle* K'linpor!

"I am sixty-five years old, my name is Piol Poet . . ."

The whole temple was emerging from night now as the high windows began to shine. Luridly tinted carvings covered every surface. Walls and pillars were mantled in gods and flowers of painted stone, the floor was bright mosaic, dominated by the Ø symbol of the Lady. Reds and greens, ivory and gold leaf . . . Eleal had never guessed there could be so much riotous color in drab Narsh. Perhaps all the color in Narshvale had flowed into this holy place.

A flicker of movement caught her eye. The solitary male worshiper had emerged from the alcove and was heading for the door, his sacrifice completed. The woman appeared also, fastening her robe, hurrying after him. Was she heading home to husband and family, and had she been performing a penance or merely offering sacrifice to win the Lady's favor?

"I am thirty-three years old, my name is Dolm Actor . . ." The reaper contributed his coin, then flashed a triumphant smile across at Eleal. How many souls had he gathered to Zath since leaving her room?

Eleal looked away quickly, and watched a line of red-robed priestesses filing in from some unknown doorway. Each took up station in an alcove. Early-rising worshipers were appearing also, peering curiously at the ceremony in progress.

The drums thundered and stopped. At the Lady's feet, the hoarse recitation became audible again. Supporting the priestess's deadweight, the young priest lowered her until she was sitting on the floor. He knelt at her side. Steadying her with one brawny arm, he lifted the vase to her lips.

"Join hands!" commanded the fat man. Eleal's hands were grabbed by Ambria and Trong. The drums started again. The young priest forced the girl's head back and tilted the vase—enough for her to drink, not enough to spill the coins. Scarlet fluid dribbled over both of them, but she coughed and choked, apparently taking some of it in her mouth. Satisfied, he lifted the loop over her head and passed the vessel out to a waiting hand. Then he dragged her to the center of the circle and left her there, lying like a corpse alongside the silver bowl. He stood back and watched intently.

Many more priests and priestesses had surrounded the troupe. They began to chant—softly at first, rapidly growing louder. Blurred by their own echoes, the words were an archaic form of classic Joalian. Eleal gathered only that they praised the Lady and beseeched her to vouchsafe guidance. The beat was capricious, unsettling. Her heart thumped painfully.

The little priestess had begun to twitch. The singing surged higher. She screamed. She beat her fists on the floor. Louder and faster went the drums. She thrashed as if in pain, yet her face was flushed. The silver bowl went clattering across the floor, splashing eggs. She paused, lifted her head, and looked around the circle that confined her, madness in every move, every twist of her face. Her hands clawed at her robe and ripped it off, revealing a willowy, wasted body, flushed and sweating.

Without warning she was on her feet, lurching at Eleal, hands clawing for her, eyes burning with hatred. Eleal tried to leap back; Trong and Ambria staggered but did not release her. The priest caught the maniac just in time and tried to haul her back to the center, but she fought him in frenzy, screaming and frothing. Amazingly, it became a real fight. The priest was as tall as Trong, young and husky; she was a scrawny stripling half his size with limbs like spade handles, but in moments she had bitten and mauled him, shredded his robe and opened bloody tracks on his face with her nails. Twice she almost broke free altogether, heading for Eleal, twice he caught her in time. He was trying to restrain her without doing hurt; she had no such scruples. They fell to the floor and struggled more there. The drums and singing echoed deafeningly.

In another bewildering change, she cried out and went rigid, head back, limbs spread, sprawling over her opponent. The man threw her off and backed away on hands and knees, bleeding and gasping as if he had been wrestling bear cats.

Her eyes flicked open. *"Athu!"* she roared, in a voice as deep and resonant as Trong's—an impossible voice for that child-sized body. The drumming and singing stopped instantly. *"Athu impo'el ignif!"*

It was the voice of the oracle. Outside the circle, priests began scribbling on parchment as the words of the goddess reverberated through the temple. Again the dialect was too archaic for Eleal to follow. She thought she heard her name a few times, but then she thought she heard several names she knew, and probably none of them was intended. The priests seemed to make sense of the torrent, though, for their pens moved rapidly.

It died away into animal gurgles and stopped. A drum tapped. The singing resumed, a triumphant paean of thanks and praise.

Red-robed priestesses pushed in to attend the unconscious oracle. The circle fell apart. Wives and husbands embraced in relief at the end of the ordeal. Trong released Eleal's hand. Ambria hauled her close and hugged her fiercely. In a moment she felt wetness. Bewildered, she looked up and realized that the big woman was weeping.

# 20

It was obvious why the temple rarely asked the Lady for an oracle. The little priestess had been carried off, wrapped in a blanket. Her burly guardian had limped out, clutching a rag to his bleeding face and leaning on a friend. A young boy had brought a bucket and knelt to wash stains from the floor.

The richly adorned priest with the big belly was chuckling as he pawed over a group of parchments, discussing them with other elderly priests and priestesses. They all seemed pleased.

The troupe stood apart, huddled together, waiting to hear what the goddess had decreed. Eleal clung tight to Ambria's big hand and tried not to see Dolm Actor's patronizing sneer.

Then the fat priest waddled over to them, still clutching the records. "The Lady has been most generous!" he boomed. "I have never seen clearer, more explicit directions."

There was a worried pause. "Tell us!" Ambria said.

"Just the two of them, I think." He checked one page against another. "Yes, just two. The one named Uthiam Piper?"

Uthiam whimpered. Golfren's arm tightened around her.

"Three fortnights' service, it would seem," said the fat man. He shrugged his pillowed shoulders. "Not as severe a penance as I would have expected, really."

Uthiam's cheeks were ashen. She raised her chin defiantly. "I have to whore here for forty-two days?"

Shocked, the priest raised his shaven brows. "Sacrifice!"

"For what?"

"For your sins and your friends' sins, naturally. They are free to go—except one, of course. One remains. I am sure you made out that much. It is a small price to win so much favor and forgiveness, for yourself and your loved ones. Many women learn to enjoy it." He leered slyly.

He had eyes like a pig's.

Little Piol Piper cleared his throat. "I thought—" He stopped. He was the scholar. If any of the laity had understood those ancient words, it would be Piol.

"You thought what?"

The old man clawed at his silvery, stubbly beard. "I thought an alternative was offered?"

The priest nodded, his dewlaps flapping. "But not a reasonable alternative for a band of wandering players, I am sure."

"How much?" Golfren yelped. His fair-skinned face was paler than any.

The fat man sighed. "One hundred Joalian stars."

"Ninety-four, you mean! You know we have that much!"

The priest pursed his thick lips sadly. "You cannot bargain with a goddess, actor."

"But I was to give that money to Tion that he might favor my wife in the festival."

"Your wife will not be attending the festival this year. She will be serving the goddess, here in the temple. The mammoth herders who risk their lives daily in the pass will certainly not be rash enough to offend Holy Ois." His fat smirk left no doubt that the men would be advised of the danger.

Golfren looked close to tears. "That gold was my father's farm and his father's before him! And we only have ninety-four."

Everyone looked at Ambria, Uthiam's mother.

Her hand in Eleal's was sweating. Her voice was hoarse: "If we make up the differ-ence, Holy One, it will leave us penniless. The fare to Suss is reputedly higher this year than it has ever been. We are poor artists, Father! Our expenses are heavy. The festival is our only hope of recouping our fortunes so that we may eat next winter. Will the Lady ruin us?"

The priest's eyes narrowed inside their bulwarks of lard, appraising her. "If you travel with the Lady's blessing," he said reluctantly, "I believe the temple could arrange passage for you." It was indeed possible to bargain.

"Today! The festival begins tomorrow. We must travel today!" Hints of the old Ambria were emerging.

"One hundred stars and you go today," the priest agreed.

Ambria sighed her relief. "And the other one?"

"Mm?" He chuckled and consulted the parchments again, comparing them. "Oh, yes. Eleal Singer . . . or Eleal Impresario . . . the goddess called her something else . . . No matter. She must remain. Must enter the service of Great Ois."

Somehow Eleal had expected this. She shivered. She felt Ambria's hand tighten on hers.

"There is no ransom for her?" Piol demanded.

The fat man scowled. "Ransom? Watch your tongue, actor!" He looked around suspiciously. "Are you offering one?"

"You have taken every copper mite we possess!" Ambria shouted.

"Ah!" He shook his head sadly and consulted the scripts again. "In any case, we are given no choice in her case." He glanced at Trong, who was projecting utter despair. "The, er, misadventure occurred in Jurg?"

"Yes," the big man muttered, showing no surprise.

"Of course!" The priest chuckled, shaking his head in mock disapproval. "Mighty Ken'th again! But the Lady is a jealous goddess! She demands the child." He glanced around the group. "Come, you are being let off lightly! A hundred stars and the girl."

Eleal also looked around. No one would meet her eye except Dolm Actor, who wore a distinctly I-told-you-so sneer.

"She will be well cared for," the priest said. "Trained in the Lady's service. It will be an easier, more rewarding life than you can offer her." He waited, and no one replied. "In a couple of years . . . But you know that."

Getting no response, he beckoned with his fat soft fingers, summoning a woman almost as large as himself. "Take this one and guard her closely. Farewells would be inappropriate," he added.

Ambria released Eleal's hand.

# 21

Inspector Leatherdale had left a man outside the door, as Edward soon realized. Conversations came along the hallway, stopped while they should have been going by, and then resumed again in the distance. Beds and carts slowed and squeaked as they were navigated around the obstacle. Perhaps the jailer had been there all the time, but he was one more indication that Edward was a murder suspect. As the guard could hardly be intended to prevent the criminal escaping, he must be hoping to eavesdrop on conversations. There was no other conceivable reason to waste a policeman's day, was there?

The room was depressingly square. The walls were brown up to about shoulder height, where there was a frieze of brown tiles; above that the plaster was beige. Having nothing better to do, Edward catalogued his assets. Item, one brass bed with bedclothes, pillow, and overhead frame. Item, one chair, wicker-backed, hard. Item, one bedside cupboard in red mahogany. Item, one small chest of drawers to match . . . one bellpull just barely within reach . . . one iron bed table on wheels, with a flip-up mirror . . . one wicker wastepaper basket. . . . He had a jug of tepid water, a tumbler, an ashtray, and a kidney-shaped metal dish suitable for planting crocus bulbs. The cupboard contained a bedpan and a heavy glass bottle with a towel around it. Robinson Crusoe would have been ecstatic.

A distant church tower was the only thing visible outside. The window was open as wide as it would go, but no air seemed to be coming in—it couldn't be this hot outdoors, surely? What a summer this had been!

So he had left school at last and in little over a week become prime suspect in a friend's murder. He thought of Tiger, the school cat, and how he had liked to sit under the tree where the robins nested, waiting for the fledglings—two fledglings.

Poor old Bagpipe! He'd never had a fair shake with his wheezing. And now this. There'd have to be an inquest, of course. How would their classmates take the news? How many would believe Edward Exeter capable of such a crime? He decided they would judge by the evidence, just as he would. At least this was England and he would be tried by British Justice. It wasn't as if he must deal with Frenchies, who made you prove yourself innocent. British Justice was the best in the world, and it did not make mistakes.

At least, he did not think it did. Trouble was, he had no idea what the case against him might be. Could he possibly have gone insane, a sort of Doctor Exeter and Mr. Hyde? Was that why he couldn't remember? Lunatics were not hanged, they were shut up in Broadmoor and quite right, too! If he had a Hyde half who went around stabbing people, then his Exeter half would have to be locked up also.

The bobby had treated him with kid gloves, and that was a rum go. A mere witness would be quizzed much harder than that—especially a witness who couldn't remember anything. He was a minor and an invalid, and the policeman had been very careful and respectful so that he could not be accused of bullying. Edward could recall much worse wiggings from Flora-Dora Ferguson, the maths master. Leatherdale must be absolutely sure his case was watertight, so he was in no special hurry to hear what the suspect might testify.

At that point in his brooding, Edward heard a familiar voice raised in the corridor and thought, *No! Please no!* Visiting hours began at two o'clock and it couldn't possibly be even nine in the morning, and yet he knew that voice. He also knew its owner would not be blocked by any hospital rule in Greyfriars, nor by any matron, no matter how intimidating. Nor even by a uniformed constable from the sound of it.

"Gabriel Heyhoe, don't be absurd. You've known me all your life. I dried your eyes when you wet your pants at King Edward's coronation parade. If you want to prowl through this bouquet in search of hacksaws, then go ahead, but meanwhile stand aside."

Mrs. Bodgley swept into the room like Boadicea sacking Londinium. She was large and loud. She overawed, and yet normally she somehow combined a booming jollity with as much majesty as Queen Mary herself. She had been the star attraction at Speech Day for as long as Edward could remember and the boys of Fallow worshiped her.

Today she swung a familiar battered suitcase effortlessly in one hand, and she was dressed all in black from her shoes to her hat. A black glove threw back her veil.

"Edward, poor chap! How are you feeling?"

"Fine. Oh, Mrs. Bodgley, I am so sorry!"

Warning beacons flamed in her eyes, as a policeman loomed in the doorway behind her, his helmet almost touching the lintel. "What exactly do you mean by that statement, Edward?"

"I mean I'm sorry to hear the tragic news about Timothy, of course."

"That's what I thought you meant, but you must learn to guard your speech more carefully at present!" She towered above him, peering over her ample black bosom as Big Ben looks down on the Houses of Parliament. "The remark might have been construed as an apology. I brought your things. Your money I extracted and gave to Matron. I put the receipt for it in your wallet. And I brought this book for you. Here."

He stuttered thanks as she thrust the book at him. "But—"

"Timothy was enj . . . said it was the best book he had ever read, and I thought you would need something to pass the time. No, don't bother thanking me. I'm sure he would have wanted you to have it. And apart from that I had better not stay and chatter or Constable Heyhoe here will suspect me of perverting the course of justice. I want you to know that we—I mean I—do not for one moment believe that you had anything whatsoever to do with what happened and nothing will ever convince me otherwise. I for one know that there was a woman's voice in that cacophony, even if the general . . . but we must *not* discuss details of the case, Edward. Furthermore, I intend to see that you have the best legal advice available and if there is any need for money for your defense, should things come to that unhappy pass, then it will be forthcoming. I have already so instructed my solicitor, Mr. Babcock of Nutall, Nutall, & Shoe. So you are not to worry, and Doctor Stanford assures me that your leg can be expected to mend with no lasting ill effects."

He opened his mouth and she plunged ahead before he could say a word.

"Timothy always spoke very well of you, and the few times we have met I have been greatly impressed with you, Edward. I know that your housemaster and Dr. Gibbs rated you highly and I trust their judgment—most of the time and certainly in this. So do not fret. The whole terrible affair will be solved, I am quite sure. Now we must not say another word on the matter!"

With a grim smile, she swirled around and flowed out of the room, the policeman backing ahead of her. Edward looked down at the book he was holding, and it was a blur.

A nurse entered, bearing a vase of dahlias that had probably been growing in the grounds of Greyfriars Grange less than an hour ago. She lifted the suitcase from the floor onto the bed.

"If you want to go through this and take out whatever you need, sir, then I'll take it away. Matron does not approve of luggage lying around in rooms."

He muttered a response without looking. The book was *The Lost World,* by Sir Arthur Conan Doyle.

He opened it at random and a bookmark fell out.

# 22

Two flights up, the priestess was puffing and leaning a sweaty hand on Eleal's shoulder. They turned along another corridor smelling of incense and soap and stale cooking. Eleal was too numb for fear or sorrow. Mostly she felt a sense of loss: loss of her friends, her newfound family, loss of liberty, loss of career, loss even of her pack, which had been refused her. The distant chanting had died away into silence as if she were sinking into the ground, away from the living world. She reached an open door and was pushed inside.

The room was poky and plain, seemingly clean enough despite its musty smell. Bare stone formed the walls, bare boards the floor and ceiling. It contained a fresh-looking pallet, a chair, a little table, a copy of the Red Scriptures, nothing more. A beam of sunlight angled in through a small window, seeming only to emphasize the shadows. No lamp, no fireplace.

The priestess released her captive then and sank down gladly on the chair, which creaked—the bulges of her sweat-patched robe suggested a large body. She wiped a sleeve across her forehead. Her hair was hidden under her scarlet headcloth; her face was saggy, padded with chins and rolls of fat, and yet Eleal thought it was the hardest face she had ever seen.

"My name is Ylla. You address me as 'Mother.' "

Eleal said nothing.

Ylla's smile would have curdled milk. "Kneel down and kiss my shoe."

Eleal backed away. "No!"

"Good!" The smile broadened. "We shall make that the test, then, shall we? When you are ready to obey—when you cannot take any more—tell me you are ready to kiss my shoe. Then we shall know that we have broken your spirit. We shall both know. You are entering upon a life of unquestioning obedience."

She waited for a reply. Not getting one, she narrowed her eyes. "We can try a whipping now if you want."

"What about Ken'th?"

Ylla laughed loudly, as if she had been waiting for the question. "Boys and old men pray to Ken'th. Men perform his sacrament willingly enough, but few would be seen dead near his temple!"

Few women went near his temple either, for Ken'th was god of virility. "Is he my father?"

"Perhaps. The goddess hinted at it. And it would fit with what your grandfather said. Women taken by a god aren't much use afterward."

That much Eleal knew from the old tales—Ken'th and Ismathon, Karzon and Harrjora. When the god withdrew his interest, the woman died of unrequited love. How strange that Piol Poet had never used either of those two great romances as the basis of a play! (She would never see a Piol play again.)

How strange to hear Trong described as her grandfather!

There was no hint of sympathy in the priestess's stony face. "But don't think that makes you special. A mortal's child is a mortal, nothing more."

Usually less, according to common belief. To call a man *godspawn* was about the worst insult possible. It implied he was a liar, a wastrel, and a bastard, and his mother had been as bad.

Eleal thought of Karzon's shrine and that powerful, potent bronze figure. Ken'th also was the Man. What if she prayed to Karzon? She did not even know her mother's name.

"If you are thinking of appealing to him," Ylla said contemptuously, "then save your breath. Gods sire bantlings like mortal men spit. I suggest you don't mention it. You are an acolyte in the service of Holy Ois, and older than most, so I must explain a few things."

She folded her plump hands in her lap. "We get many unwanted girls, usually much younger than you, but most of us are temple bred. My mother was a priestess here, and her mother before her. For eight generations we have served the Lady."

"And your father?"

"A worshiper." Ylla showed her teeth. "A hundred worshipers. Don't try to lord it over me for that, godspawn. In a year or two the Lady will bless you. You will be consecrated by priests, then, and thereafter you will serve her that same way. You will regard it as a great honor."

"No I won't!"

The fat priestess laughed, flesh rippling under her robe. "Oh, but you will! When properly instructed, you will be eager to begin. I am forty-five years old. I have borne eight children to her honor and I think I am about to bear another. You also, in your time."

They would have to chain her to the bed, Eleal thought. She would rather starve in a gutter. She said nothing, just stared at the floor.

"Why do you limp?"

"My right leg is shorter than the other."

"I can see that. Why? Were you born like that?"

"I fell out a window when I was a baby."

"Stupid of you. But it won't matter. It won't show when you're on your back, will it?"

Eleal gritted her teeth.

"I asked you a question, slut!"

"No it won't."

"Mother."

"Mother."

Ylla sighed. "You will begin your service by plucking chickens. By this time next year, you will be able to pluck chickens in your sleep. Scrubbing floors, washing clothes . . . good, honest labor to purify the soul. Normally we should start with your oath of obedience. However—"

She frowned. "However, in your case the Lady gave explicit instructions."

"What sort of instructions?"

"Mother."

"What sort of instructions, Mother?"

"That for the next fortnight you are to be kept under the strictest confinement. I don't know if we can even take you to the altar for the oath—I'll ask. And guards on the door!" The old hag looked both annoyed and puzzled by that.

"The *Filoby Testament!*"

Ylla stared. "What of it?"

Eleal had blurted out the name without thinking and wished she hadn't. "It mentions me."

The woman snorted disbelievingly. "And who told you that?"

"A reaper."

Ylla surged to her feet, astonishingly fast for her size. Her thick hand took Eleal in the face so hard she stumbled and fell prostrate on the pallet, her head ringing from the blow and a taste of blood in her mouth.

"For that you can fast a day," Ylla said, stamping out, slamming the door. Bolts clicked.

\*    \*    \*

The room faced east, offering a fine view of the slate roofs of Narsh. The wall beneath it was sheer, and although the stonework was rough and crumbly, Eleal had no hope of being able to climb down it. It was quite high enough to break her legs. Upward offered no hope either, for her cell was a full story below the cornice—they had thought of that.

Below her lay a paved courtyard, part of the temple complex, enclosed by a row of large houses in high-walled grounds. She could see through the gaps to the street beyond, where people went about their business, enjoying freedom. She could even see parts of the city wall, Narshwater, farms, grasslands. If she leaned out as far as she dared, she could just see the meadow with the mammoth pen.

To north and south Narshflat became Narshslope, rising to join the mountains of Narshwall. She had a fine view down the length of Narshvale. Indeed she thought she could see to the end of it, where sky and plain and mountains all converged. It was a small land and a barren one. She wondered why Joalia and Thargia would bother to quarrel over it.

Later she saw the mammoth train leave and even thought she heard faint trumpeting. She was too far away to make out the people. The mammoths themselves were small as ants, but she hung over the sill for a long time, watching them go.

*Farewell Ambria! Farewell Grandfather Trong, you cold, proud man! Farewell Uthiam and Golfren—and good luck in the festival! May Tion keep you.*

*Remember me.*

If she listened at the door, she could hear her guards muttering outside, but she could not make out the words. A choir of students practiced for a while in the courtyard below.

Not long after noon, Ylla returned, bringing some burly assistance in case it might be needed. She made Eleal strip, and gave her a red robe too large for her, a skimpy blanket, a jug of warm water, and a pungent bucket. She even confiscated Eleal's boots, leaving her a pair of sandals instead. Eleal stooped to pleading over that—walking was much harder for her without her special boots. The priestess seemed pleased by the pleading, but refused to change her mind.

Then she departed, taking everything Eleal had been wearing when she entered the temple, even her Tion locket, and leaving her a sack of chickens to pluck—eviscerated sacrifices, caked with blood and already stiff.

The rest of the day went by in boredom, fear, anger, and despair in various mixtures. The prisoner raged at her split lip, the goddess, the priestess, the fat priest, the chickens and all their feathers, Dolm the reaper, the *Filoby Testament*—whatever that was—her unknown father, her unknown mother, Trong and Ambria for deserting her and betraying her and lying to her. She refused to open the book of scripture. She seriously considered throwing it out the window, then decided that such an act of open defiance would merely provide an excuse to whip her. By late afternoon she knew that whippings would not be necessary. A few days of this confinement and she would be willing to kiss every shoe in the temple.

A year of it and she would be ready for the naked men in the alcoves.

# 23

The dahlias were merely the leaders of a parade of flowers that staggered Edward. They came from his old housemaster Ginger Jones on his own behalf, with another on behalf of all the masters, from the president of the Old Boys' Club, from Alice, and from a dozen separate friends. The word must have spread across all England, and he could not imagine how much money had been spent on trunk calls. The nurses teased him about all the sweethearts he must have. They set vases on the dresser and then ranked them along the wall he could see best, turning the drab brown room into a greenhouse. He could hardly bear to look at them. It was Bagpipe who needed the flowers, wasn't it?

Somewhere in that floral parade, someone smuggled in a copy of the *Times*. He suspected the plump nurse with the London accent, but he wasn't sure. It was just lying there on his bed when he looked.

Mr. Winston Churchill had ordered the fleet mobilized. Some holiday excursion trains had been canceled. France and Russia were preparing for war with Germany, and there had been shooting at border points. He found his own name, but there was nothing there that he did not already know. In normal times the yellow press would make a sensation out of such a story, a general's son murdered under his own roof by a house-guest, complete with nudge-nudge hints about public school pals. Just now the war news was sensation enough, but the press might be one more reason why there was a policeman outside his door.

The *Times* made his eyes swim, so he stopped reading for a while. He had just picked up *The Lost World* when he heard another voice he recognized, and all his muscles tensed. Had he not been tethered he might have rolled under the bed or jumped out the window. As it was, he tucked his book under the covers in case it might be snatched away from him, then waited for a second visitor who would not be restrained until formal visiting hours.

The Reverend Roland Exeter was a cadaverous man, invariably dressed in black ecclesiastical robes. His elongated form was reminiscent of something painted by El Greco in one of his darkest moods, or a tortured saint in some Medieval church carv-ing—a resemblance aided by his natural tonsure of silver hair, a homegrown halo. His face was the face of a melancholy, self-righteous horse, with a raucous, braying voice to match. Celebrated preacher and lecturer, Holy Roly was probably better known than the Archbishop of Canterbury. Alice called him the Black Death.

He strode into the room clutching a Bible to his chest with both arms. He came to a halt and regarded his nephew dolefully.

"Good morning, sir," Edward said. "Kind of you to come."

"I see it as my Christian duty to call sinners to repentance, however heinous their transgressions."

"Caught the early train from Paddington, did you?"

"Edward, Edward! Even now the Lord will not turn his face from you if you sincerely repent."

"Repent of what, sir, exactly?"

Holy Roly's eyes glittered. He was probably convinced of his ward's guilt, but he was not fool enough to prejudge the criminal matter with a policeman listening outside the door. "Of folly and pride and willful disbelief, of course."

There had been no need for him to come all the way to Greyfriars to deliver the sermon again. He could have written another of his interminable ranting letters.

"I don't feel up to discussing such solemn matters at the moment, sir." Edward's fists were clenched so hard they hurt, but he had tucked them under the sheet. This was not going to work. The two Exeters had exchanged barely a dozen friendly words in the two years since his parents died. Fortunately, the guv'nor's will had stipulated that Edward be allowed to complete his education at Fallow, or Roly might well have pulled him out. Roly had had no choice there, but his idea of pocket money for a public school senior had been five shillings per term, probably less than any junior in the place received.

Also fortunately, Mr. Oldcastle had provided generously and regularly. Edward was resolved to have his affairs audited as soon as he reached his majority, for he strongly suspected that his parents' money had long ago vanished into the bottomless pit of the Lighthouse Missionary Society. Meanwhile he must endure his minority for almost another three years.

Holy Roly's wrinkles had twisted into an expression of mawkish pity. "You see that you have thrown it all away, don't you?"

"Thrown all what away, sir?"

"All the advantages you were given. You don't imagine Cambridge will accept you now, do you?"

"I understood that every Englishman was innocent until proven guilty."

"Then you are a fool. Even if you do not get your neck snapped on the scaffold, all doors are closed to you now."

There might be a hint of truth in what the old bigot was saying, but he was obviously enjoying himself, preparing to heap hellfire on an immobilized sinner. His voice descended to an even more melancholy range. "Edward, will you pray with me?"

"No, sir. I have told you before that I will not add hypocrisy to my shortcomings."

His uncle came closer, opening the Bible. "Will you at least hear the Word of God?"

"I should prefer not, sir, if you don't mind." Edward began to sweat. Normally at this point he excused himself as politely as possible and left the room, but now he was trapped and the bounder knew it. That might be the main reason he had come.

"Consider your sins, Edward! Consider the sad fate of the young friend you led into evil—"

*"Sir?"* That was too much!

"The First Epistle of Paul to the Corinthians," Roly announced, opening the Bible, "beginning at the thirteenth chapter." His voice began to drone like an organ.

*Blackened sepulchre!* He had not come to ask after his nephew's health, or to ask what really happened, or what he could do to help, or to display faith in his innocence. He had come to gloat. He had been predicting Edward's perdition since the day they met and now believed it had happened even sooner than expected. He had to come and drool over it.

How could two brothers have been so unalike?

Edward closed his eyes and thought about Africa.

He thought of Nyagatha, high in the foothills of Mount Kenya, amid forest and gorges, glowing with eternal sunshine, as if in retrospect the rainy seasons had been suspended for the duration of his childhood. He savored again the huge dry vistas of Africa under the empty sky, the velvet tropical nights when the stars roamed just above the treetops like clouds of diamond dust. He saw the dusty compound with the Union Jack hanging limp in the baking heat, scavenging chickens, listless dogs, laughing native children in the village. He recalled the guv'nor handing out medicines in the sanitarium; the mater teaching school in the shade of the veranda to a score of wriggling black youngsters and three or four whites; tribal elders arriving after treks of days or weeks to conclave in the black shadow of the euphorbia trees and listen solemnly to Bwana's advice or judgment; visiting Englishmen passing through the district, drinking gin and tonic at sundown and amusing themselves by talking to the boy, the future builder of Empire. It had all seemed quite natural—was not this how all white people grew up?

Above all he remembered the leggy, bony girl in pigtails, who bossed him and all the other children of every color—who chose the games they would play and the places they would visit and the things they must do and the things they must not do, and with whom he never argued. He remembered again his horror when she had to go Home, to England, to the mystical ancestral homeland her parents had left before her birth.

"Edward?"

Hospital and pain returned. "I beg your pardon, sir. What did you say?"

Holy Roly closed his eyes in sorrow. "Why can you not see that prayer and repentance are your only hope of salvation, Edward? He will make allowance for your doubts. *Lord I believe; help thou mine unbelief!*"

His sepulchral, ivy-coated bleating was probably comforting the ward next door. It was giving his nephew prickly heat.

"I appreciate your kindness in coming all this way to see me, sir."

Hints were wasted on Uncle Roland.

"Edward, Edward! Your father was a misguided apostate and look where it got him!"

Edward tried to sit up and his leg exploded in flame. He sank back on the pillow, streaming sweat.

"Good-*bye,* sir!" he said through clenched teeth. The pain was making him nauseated. "Thank you for coming."

A flush of anger showed in the sallow cheeks. Roly slammed the bible shut. "Do you still not see? *Exodus,* chapter twenty-one, the fifth verse: *Thou shalt not bow down thyself to them, nor serve them: for I the Lord thy God am a jealous God, visiting the iniquity of the fathers upon the children unto the third and fourth generation of them that hate me.*"

"I never quite saw that as fair play, somehow," Edward said, wondering what insanity was boiling inside the old maniac now. "Bowing down to what?"

"Idols! False gods! The Father of Evil! Your father was a disgrace to his country and his calling and his race! Read what the board of inquiry wrote about him, how he betrayed the innocent savages placed in his care—"

"Innocent savages? They were innocent until you Bible-bangers got to work on them! My parents would be alive today if a bunch of meddling missionaries—"

"Your father turned away the Word of God and frustrated the laws of his own people and sold his soul to the Devil!"

That did it. *"Out!"* Edward screamed, hauling on the bellpull. "Go away or I shall throw things at you."

"I warned him that the Lord would not be mocked!"

"Nurse! Constable! Matron!"

*"Wherefore, seeing we are encompassed about . . ."* declaimed his uncle, rolling his eyes up to inspect the electric lighting.

The lanky policeman appeared in the doorway. Footsteps were hurrying along the corridor.

"Get this maniac out of here!" Edward yelled.

*". . . sin which does so easily beset . . ."*

"Nurse! Matron! He's driving me as mad as he is. He's insulting my parents."

*"And it is also written—"*

"He's preaching sedition. Remove him!" To emphasize the point, Edward grabbed up the kidney-shaped dish and hurled it, aimed to bounce off the book his uncle was again clutching to his breast. It was unfortunate that at that moment the old man started to turn. The dish, in cricket parlance, broke to leg. As Matron steamed into the room, a loud shattering announced that Edward had bowled a vase.

She impaled him with a glance of steel. "What is the meaning of this?"

"He insulted my father. . . ."

Too late the expression on Holy Roly's cadaverous face registered. Edward could not call back the words, nor the act itself.

He had resorted to violence!

Matron spoke again and he did not hear her; he did not see an ample, whaleboned lady in a stiff white cap and starched uniform. He saw instead the crown prosecutor in black silk and wig. He heard himself being forced to admit to the jury the damning answer he had just given, and he heard the question that would follow as surely as night must follow day:

"Do you remember discussing your father with Timothy Bodgley?"

# 24

The Suspect had traveled to Paris and back with Julian Smedley, who was therefore an obvious witness. The Smedleys resided at "Nanjipor," Raglan Crescent, Chichester, and Leatherdale could justify another drive in that spiffy motorcar General Bodgley had placed at his disposal.

"Nanjipor" was a terrace house. It had an imposing facade fronted by a garden of roses, begonias, and boxwood topiary hedges. From the outside, therefore, it was identical to all the other houses in its row. The interior was suffocatingly hot and resembled a museum of Oriental art—wicker chairs, gaudy rugs, brass tables, lacquer screens in front of the fireplaces, idols with innumerable arms, hideously garish china vases, ebony elephants. The English had always been great collectors.

A chambermaid ushered Leatherdale into a parlor whose heavy curtains had been drawn, leaving the room so dark that the furnishings were barely visible. There he met Julian Smedley.

For Bank Holiday, young Smedley wore flannel trousers with a knife-edge crease, a brass-buttoned blazer, and what must obviously be an Old Fallovian tie—he was too young to lay claim to be an Old-Anything-Else. His shoes shone like black mirrors. He sat very stiffly on the edge of a hard chair, his hands folded in his lap, staring owlishly at his visitor. He added, "sir," to every statement he uttered. He gave his age as seventeen; he did not look it.

A certain amount of reticence could be expected in anyone who found himself involved in a very nasty murder case and Smedley was probably shy at the best of times. He might have been more forthcoming had Leatherdale been able to speak with him alone.

His father was present and had a right to be, as the boy was a minor. Sir Thomas Smedley was ex-India, a large, loud, and domineering man. He apologized for not being at his best: "Just recovering from a touch of the old malaria, you know." He certainly did not look well—he was sweating profusely and his hands trembled. Tropical diseases were something else the English collected while bringing enlightenment to the backward races of the world.

Sir Thomas had offered sherry and biscuits, which were declined. He had thereupon opened the interview with a ten-minute diatribe against the Germans: "Blustering bullies, you know. Always have been. Stand up to them and they crawl, try to be reasonable and they brag and threaten. Absolutely no idea how to handle natives, none at all. Made a botch of their colonies, all of them. Thoroughly hated, everywhere. Southwest Africa, Cameroons, East Africa—it's always the same with the Boche. The Hottentots taught them a thing or two, back in '06, you know. Never did get the whole story there. Now they think they can make a botch of Europe. Might is Right, they say. Well, they've got a surprise coming. Russians'll be in Berlin by Christmas, if the French don't beat them to it."

And so on.

When Leatherdale forced the conversation around to his case, Sir Thomas glowered and shivered, listening as his son confirmed the story. Then the father came in again, explaining why he had sent the telegram to Paris ordering Julian home, stressing his vision and common sense in doing so.

With his companion recalled and the Continent bursting into flames, with the strong possibility that he might be unable to join up with the rest of the party, young Exeter had chosen to return to England also. Any other decision would have demonstrated very bad judgment. Sir Thomas gave no hint, however, that he had offered hospitality to his son's friend, suddenly at a loose end. Had young Julian thought to do so? If not, why not? If he had, why had Exeter chosen the embarrassing alternative of an appeal to the Bodgleys' charity? While Leatherdale was considering how to ask those questions, he put another:

"What was Exeter's state of mind?"

"State of mind, sir?" The boy blinked like an idiot.

"Was he disappointed?"

"At first, sir. But eager to get his own back, of course—sir."

Leatherdale felt the thrill of a hound scenting its prey. "His own back on *who?*"

"On the Germans, sir. We're going to enlist together, sir."

Red herring.

Sir Thomas uttered a snort of potent scorn.

"Exeter has broken his leg," Leatherdale said. "It will be some time . . ."

The scorn registered. The lack of invitation clicked into place also. He confirmed some times and dates while he shaped his questions, then turned to the father. "You know Exeter, Sir Thomas?"

"Believe Julian introduced him last Speech Day."

There was strong disapproval there. That was the first indication Leatherdale had found that the entire world did not approve wholeheartedly of Edward Exeter. Another quarry had broken cover.

"How would you judge him, sir?"

Smedley Senior drummed his fingers on the arm of his chair. Suddenly he was being cautious. "Can't say I know the boy well enough to pass an opinion, Inspector."

That might well be true, but it did not mean that Sir Thomas did not have an opinion, and it would be based on something, however inadmissible it might be as evidence.

"His housemaster speaks very highly of him," Leatherdale said.

Sir Thomas made a *Hrumph!* noise.

"You thought enough of him to approve him as your son's companion on a trip across Europe."

*Hrumph!* again. "Well, they were chums." Father eyed son with a See-How-Wrong-You-Were? expression. "It was only for a few days, till they joined Dr. Gibbs and the others . . ."

Leatherdale waited.

Again Sir Thomas cleared his throat. "Must admit I have nothing against the boy himself. Deucedly good bowler. He may be straight enough. Guilty until proved innocent, what? I've seen Fallow work wonders. There was a young Jew boy there in my time . . . Well, that's another story."

Another silence. Leatherdale knew the road now.

"Do you know his *family* at all, Sir Thomas?"

"Only by reputation."

"And that is?"

"Well the Nyagatha affair, of course."

"Tragic?"

"Damned scandal! Read the board of inquiry report, Inspector!"

"I intend to. Can you give me the main points, though?"

That was all the encouragement Sir Thomas required. "Shocking! If Exeter had survived, he'd have been drummed out of the Service. Lucky not to be thrown in the clink. A band of malcontents wanders out of the jungle and burns a Government Station? White women raped and murdered! Children! Not a single survivor. Shameful! If Exeter had maintained a proper force of guards as he should, damned business would never have happened. Disgraceful! And there was all sorts of other dirt came out, too."

"Such as?"

"His overall performance. Aims and motivations. The man had absolutely *gone native,* Inspector! Tribal barbarities that had been stamped out in other districts had been allowed to persist. Witch doctors and such abominations. Roads that should have been built had not been. Missionaries and developers had been discouraged—virtually thrown out, in some cases. The commissioners were extremely critical. Gave his superiors a very stiff wigging for not having kept a better eye on him."

In the shadowed room, Sir Thomas's glare was as ferocious as any of the sinister idols'. His son was staring at the floor, fists clenched, saying nothing. His back was still ramrod-stiff.

So young Exeter had perhaps spent his childhood in unusually primitive surroundings, even by Colonial standards. That was not evidence. But it did help explain a certain curious document that Leatherdale had found in the suspect's luggage.

"Mr. Smedley?" Leatherdale said gently.

Julian looked up nervously. "Sir?"

"Did Edward Exeter ever express any ambition to follow in his father's footsteps? In the Colonial Office, I mean?"

Sir Thomas snorted. "They wouldn't touch another Exeter with a forty-foot pole."

"Hardly fair to the boy, sir?"

The invalid shivered and produced a linen handkerchief to dab his beaded forehead. "There are some names you don't want around on files to remind people, Inspector! Have you any further questions to put to my son?"

"Just one, I think. What do you think of Edward Exeter, Mr. Smedley?"

Julian glanced briefly at his father and seemed to make an effort to sit up even straighter, which was not physically possible.

"He's white!" he said defiantly. "A regular brick!"

# 25

Slower than a plague of snails crawled the hospital minutes. Lunch lay in Edward's stomach like a battleship's anchor: pea soup, mutton stew, suet pudding, lumpy custard. He was trying, with very little success, to write a sympathy letter to the Bodgleys.

Amid his foggy memories of his visit to the Grange, he had a clear vision of old Bagpipe cursing the asthma that would keep him out of the war—and now here he was himself, flat on his back with his bloody leg in pieces. Three months! It would be all over by then, and even if it wasn't, then all his chums would be three months ahead of him. What bloody awful luck!

Not quite as bloody as Bagpipe's of course. . . . His birthday present from Alice had been a handsome leather writing case, which fortunately had not been pilfered in Paris. It bore his initials in gold and had pockets for envelopes and stamps and unanswered correspondence. Abandoning the Bodgley letter, he pulled out two well-thumbed sheets that he had stored away in one of those pockets. He knew the text by heart now, but he read it all over again. Then he set to work copying it out, word for word.

It was dated the day of the Nyagatha massacre, and the writing was his father's.

*My dear Jumbo,*

*It was with both surprise and of course delight that Mrs. Exeter and I welcomed Maclean to our abode last night. Although conditions have improved vastly over the last few years, his journey from the Valley of the Kings was as arduous as might be expected. Had he been delayed only another three days at Mombasa, I fear he would have missed us here altogether. Indeed, delivery of this letter cannot precede by more than a week our personal arrival Home. Needless to say, the tidings he brought concerning your own crossing were equally agreeable to us. Without implying that any incentive beyond that of being reunited with our son and adopted daughter is necessary to motivate us to visit the Old Country, your presence there and the resulting prospects of riotous revelry in your company are a joyous prospect!*

Who was Jumbo? Who was Maclean? The casualties of the massacre had included a "Soames Maclean, Esq., of Surrey," but the board of inquiry report had given no explanation of who he was, or what he had been doing at Nyagatha, except to describe him as a visitor. Just an old friend? Nothing odd about that. But then the letter turned strange.

> *Your new interpretation, of which Maclean has advised me, I find very convincing and in no small measure disturbing! You are to be congratulated on perceiving something that should have been perfectly obvious to all of us and me in particular, but of course was not. (He was named after Mrs. Exeter's father!) Unfortunately, in this case insight, which should promote increase in understanding and alleviation of apprehension, has tended rather to promote proliferation of enigmas!*

The only person Edward knew who had been named after his grandfather was himself, but why should that matter to Jumbo, whoever Jumbo was? The letter then mentioned him directly.

> *While friendship, gratitude, and personal respect all incline me to acquiesce, dear Jumbo, the awesome responsibilities of fatherhood dissuade me from permitting a personal interview. The boy is not yet old enough to understand the implications. Rest assured that he will be fully informed before the critical date, and while he will still be very young even then, the decision will be his alone. We have given the Kent group strict instructions not to reveal his whereabouts to anyone at all. You will understand that no personal slight is intended.*
>
> *His mother agrees with me wholeheartedly in this. Perhaps we are being over-cautious, but we both feel "better safe than sorry"!*
>
> *You will be relieved to hear that I am still strongly in favor of breaking the chain. Soapy has been trying to convert me with all his customary eloquence, but so far without success.*

Five days ago, in the middle of the Champs Élysées, Edward had realized that a man named Soames Maclean might very likely be known as "Soapy" behind his back, especially if he were noted for his eloquence.

> *I still disapprove of turning a world upside down. The effects of good intentions are well-known and my work here has merely hardened my conviction that paving with better intentions only makes the road descend more slowly. One cannot take away half of a culture and expect the remainder to thrive. I have at least kept out the worst of the busybodies and preserved as many of the indigenous customs as I dare.*
>
> *For example, I have not prohibited warfare among the young men of Nyagatha, although all the other districts banned it at once. It is not war as the Europeans understand war, nor is it done for slavery or conquest. It is a ritual combat with shields and clubs that rarely results in serious injury to the men themselves and never harms*

*women and children. It is very little rougher than a county rugby match, and it is the basis of their whole concept of manhood. In neighboring districts, the culture has virtually collapsed without it.*

*I doubt that information concerning my irregular activities can much longer be kept from the local powers in London. I shall be severely criticized, but that is of no consequence. I hope and believe that we have softened the inevitable blow.*

*As for religion, I need not tell you of the dangers of tampering there! Even a bad faith, if it provides stability, may be better than the turmoil . . .*

There it stopped, in mid-sentence. His last words.

*Criticized? Oh, guv'nor, how they criticized you! They tore your corpse to shreds in their elegant Whitehall meeting rooms. They hung your parts on bridges for the world to mock.*

Three days after those words had been written, a white-faced boy had been hastily summoned to the Head's study at Fallow, but not before he had seen the morning papers. The telegram from London had arrived a couple of hours later. That had been bad enough. Much worse had been the letters from the dead that had trickled in over the next two months, full of cheerful plans for the journey Home and the family reunion. Every week another ship would dock and the wound would be reopened before it had even had a chance to scab. A year later, when a thin crust had begun to form so that his heart was not always a stone and he could even smile again without feeling guilty— then that awful board of inquiry report had started him bleeding all over again.

And a couple of months after that, even, some idiot, well-meaning, thoughtless lawyer had forwarded a box of his parents' possessions that had somehow survived the fire. Fortunately, Holy Roly had forgotten to mention them. They had lain in his attic until a week ago. Edward had stopped a night in Kensington on his way to Paris, dropping off all the gear he had accumulated at Fallow. Only then had he discovered that box, and in it that extraordinary letter.

What did it all mean? Who was Jumbo? What was the Valley of the Kings? Mr. Oldcastle of the Colonial Office lived in Kent—was he somehow related to the Kent group mentioned? The only person who might be able to answer any of those questions was Mr. Oldcastle himself. Now he had time on his hands, Edward was going to send him a copy of the letter. The original he would keep forever, his father's last words.

A patter of feet and rush of voices in the corridor announced the start of visiting hours. Alice would be prompt, she always was. Edward put away his writing and crossed his fingers. How exactly did one bait breath? . . .

Alice had been the first good thing he had seen in England, come to Southampton to meet him, a poised young lady of fifteen standing on the docks with her aunt Griselda—Roland had been too busy to leave town. Edward had met him that evening and they had disliked each other on sight. Dislike had flowered rapidly to mutual contempt. Alice and Griselda had probably kept the frightened twelve-year-old from madness or suicide in his first few weeks of that strangely green, soggy, solid England, full of mists and pale faces.

He had gone up to Fallow in the autumn, and what had been a nightmare of alienation and homesickness for all the other new boys had been a blessed release for him. That winter Griselda had faded away altogether, a mousy, kindly woman unable to withstand her famous, fanatical, power-crazy husband. Roland had grown steadily worse ever since, shriller, more eccentric, more bigoted.

Alice had been an absent relation, rarely seen, but her letters and Edward's had flashed across England in a single day, not to be compared to the twelve-week round trip to Kenya, and he had been grateful for her and to her. Whenever the loneliness had overflowed, he had written to Alice, and two days later her replies had arrived, full of stern comfort and practical advice.

The years had crept by. In retrospect, he should have informed his parents how things stood between him and the Reverend Roland, but it would have seemed like tattling, so he never had. He had given no thought to words like *tragedy, probate, executor.* . . . Plans for the family reunion had been seeded, nourished, cultivated—and ultimately blasted by that inexplicable massacre just days before the Exeters were due to leave Nyagatha. The ship that should have brought them Home had brought details of their deaths.

Even before the disaster, Roland Exeter had displayed a driving ambition to convert his niece and nephew to his own brand of religious fervor. His brother's will had named him guardian of the orphaned boy and the twice-orphaned girl, and he had reacted like a missionary given a personal gift of two cannibals to win from the darkness.

Alice had left school by then. Her uncle had expected her to remain and keep house in the dread Kensington mausoleum which was home to both him and his Lighthouse Missionary Society. When she had moved out and set up her own establishment, he had denounced her as a scarlet woman, damned to hellfire for eternity. That was Roly's standard way of expressing disapproval.

Edward had remained at Fallow, but there he had raised the banner of liberty and manned the barricades, a staunch upholder of his father's skepticism, fighting his guerrilla war at long distance. He had not set foot in a church since the Nyagatha memorial service.

The corridors had gone quiet again. Was she not coming? Had she been forced to return to London, or had he merely dreamed her presence yesterday?

*Were I a praying man, I should pray now.*

Most girls made him squirm and shuffle and stutter. With Alice he could just stand and smile for hours. His face ached after being with her, just from smiling.

He had not seen her since her birthday. He had obtained a somewhat irregular exeat to attend the celebration—irregular in that his guardian had neither requested it nor known of it. Ginger Jones had stuck his neck out there, but the shrewd old housemaster had known for years how the wind blew.

The three years' age difference had dwindled now. In Africa it had represented the gulf between big child and small child. In England between boy and young woman. Now she was twenty-one, but he was a man in all but legal status. He was five feet, eleven and three-quarters inches tall.

In the spring he had even grown a mustache. It had not been wholly satisfactory, and Alice had obviously not thought much of it, so he had shaved it off when he got back to Fallow. The principle was what mattered.

Feminine heels clicked in the now-silent corridor. He held his breath.

Alice walked in. The sun came out and birds sang. She could always do that to rooms now, even drab brown hospital rooms.

She walked straight to the bed and for an intoxicating moment he wondered if she would kiss him, but she raised her eyebrows archly and handed him a string shopping bag full of books. He laid them on the bed.

She dressed very well, considering her limited means. She was wearing dove gray, to match her eyes—masses of striped cotton, from wrists to ankles, with a broad sash around her waist. Heaven knew what else ladies wore underneath. She must be cooked on a day like this, and yet she did not seem so. She removed her rose-bedecked hat, laying it and her parasol on the foot of the bed. Then she pulled up the chair. Her eyes were assessing him.

He realized that he had been staring at her like a stuffed stag. "Thank you for coming."

"I had to promise we will not discuss the case." She flicked a thumb at the open door and mimed someone writing. "You are much better!" She smiled. "I'm glad."

"Actually the treatment of choice in such cases is a kiss."

"No, that's a discredited superstition. Kisses overexcite the patient."

"They are good for the heart and stimulate the circulation."

"I'm sure they do. Seriously, how are you feeling?"

"Bored."

"Doesn't your leg hurt?"

"Throbs a bit once in a while. No, I'm in tip-top shape."

"You shaved off your mustache!"

"Actually that gale in early June did for it."

Alice glanced over the floral display with appreciation. "Impressive! Are all of them from barristers and solicitors or are some of them personal?"

She was not conventionally beautiful. Her hair was a nondescript brown, although bright and shiny. Her teeth were possibly on the large side, her nose might have been better had it been a thirty-second of an inch shorter. Overall, her face could almost be described as horsey—although not safely in Edward's hearing—but she had poise and humor and he would rather gaze at her than any woman in the world.

"Has Uncle been to see you?"

"He has. Have you got your money out of him yet?"

"These things take time," she said confidently.

"Till the Nile freezes? He's spent it all on his lousy cannibals! He's brought light to the heathen by burning your five-pound notes!"

"I think it's just his very muddled accounting."

She shrugged and glanced at the watch on her slim wrist—his present for her twenty-first, bought with money saved out of Mr. Oldcastle's regular donations. "We'll see.

Let's not waste time talking about the Black Death. Mrs. Peters has been a love, but I absolutely must catch the 3.40. Tell me what happened the weekend before Whitsun."

"Before Whitsun? By Jove, that was when I took the most gorgeous girl in the world out to the park and explained—"

"Not in London. At Fallow." Again she glanced warningly at the door, where the copper must be writing all this down. "I was tracked down at the hotel by your Ginger Jones. He gave me those books for you. He wants them back. I gather they're all racy French novels he didn't dare let you read when you were a pupil."

"They don't sound like my cup of tea."

She grinned momentarily—that intimate, secretive grin that had meant mischief in their childhood and now hinted at vastly more magnificent possibilities. Or at least he hoped it would, one day soon.

"You're a big boy now. You're going to be even taller if that leg stretches much, you know. Do you suppose the other one will reach the ground? The weekend before Whitsun you got an exeat and while you were gone there was a burglary at Tudor."

Why was this important, when they had only an hour to be together and the entire future threatened to crumble in ruins?—his personal future, the Empire, Europe. . . . Why talk about a nonsensical schoolboy prank? But her expression said it was important, and he would not argue with her.

"Ginger knows more about it than I do. He never really convinced anyone else that it was a burglary. The bobbies listened politely and yawned. The front door was still bolted on the inside. Some chaps in Big School were in on the wheeze, whatever it was, but their door was bolted, too. A couple of juniors claimed they saw a woman wandering through the dorms, but they couldn't have been very convinced at the time, because they just went back to sleep. It was dodgy, all right, but no one ever did work it out." He stared at her doubt and then said, "We are discussing a community of three hundred juvenile males. Do you expect sanity?"

Alice reached for the *Times* on the bed and began using it as a fan. "He said something about a spear."

"Oh?" Ginger had mentioned that, had he? "A Zulu assegai from the Matabele display in Big School was left in my room in Tudor. That seems to have been the whole point, if you'll pardon an obscure pun. Possibly there had been scandalous rumors about what I was doing in town that night. Prefects sometimes make enemies, if they wallop a little too hard or too often, although I had been remarkably self-controlled for weeks before that, in anticipation of seeing you. Apart from that, nothing was missing or . . . What's wrong?"

"Where exactly was this spear when you found it?"

"Ginger found it. He made a complete search. He has keys to all the rooms, of course."

"Thrust right through your mattress?"

"So he said. Why is he riding this hobbyhorse again?"

Alice glanced at the door, giving him a view of her profile. She looked best in profile, rather like Good Queen Bess in her prime.

"Mr. Jones is wondering now if you were supposed to be present when the spear was rammed through your bed. Your name was on your door, right? Whoever it was broke into Big School and located your house in the files—someone had been rummaging there, too, he said. Then the intruder pulled two steel brackets off the wall to get the assegai, went across to Tudor and found your room. You were missing, and in a fit of frust—"

Edward started to laugh and jarred his leg. "Bolting and unbolting doors from the wrong side? A lock is one thing, but a bolt is another! The old coot's off his rocker!"

Alice did not seem to have noticed his wince. She smiled. "He did admit he reads the penny dreadfuls he confiscates." Then she sobered. "He now assumes that there has been a second attempt, and this time the wrong man . . ." She raised an eyebrow archly, waiting for Edward to complete the thought.

"Strewth! I always thought the old leek was one of the sanest men there. Why should anyone try to kill me, of all people? I have no money. Even if Holy Roly's left anything of the family fortune for me to inherit, it will be only a few hundred quid. I have no enemies that I can think of."

*Once more into the breach, dear friends, once more; Or close the wall up with our English dead.* . . . Why had he thought of those lines? Oh yes, that weird dream of a Dickensian apparition claiming to be Mr. Oldcastle. Two nights ago, and yet it still stuck in his memory. Dear friends?

"Anyone can have enemies," Alice said emphatically.

He thought of the letter, but he would not worry her with that until Mr. Oldcastle had commented on it.

"You refer to my brains, good looks, and personal magnetism, of course. Admittedly they arouse enormous envy wherever I go, but that's only to be expected. Rival suitors are the real threat. Seeing the burning love you bear me in every bashful glance, consumed with jealousy, some dastard seeks to clear me from the field. Who can it be, this wielder of spears who opens bolts from the wrong side of . . ."

Alice raised both eyebrows and he stopped, feeling stupid. She did not speak, but her eyes said a lot. Ginger must have his reasons. Explain one impossible intruder and you might be able to claim another? Did a bolted door in the Grange case make Edward Exeter the only possible suspect in the killing of Timothy Bodgley?

"It's an interesting problem," she said, toying with her gloves. "What about the woman the boys thought they'd seen? Did they mention her before or after the unbolted door was found?"

"I have no idea! I can't believe you'd swallow any of this. You are usually so level-headed!"

"Reliable boys?"

"Good kids," he admitted.

"Mr. Jones said that perhaps you, as prefect, uncovered some hints that the masters didn't. Often happens, he said."

"Not in this case. Most of the chaps tried to blame the suffragettes. The Head was pretty steamed. He canceled a half holiday because no one would own up."

"Is that usual?"

"Communal punishment, or no one having the spunk to own up?"

"Both."

"Neither," he admitted. And even rarer was the absence of any retaliation on the culprits by those who had suffered unjustly, but there had been none of that at all, or he'd have heard of it.

Into his mind popped a sudden image of solemn little Codger Carlisle, nervousness making all his freckles show like sand, babbling of a woman with long dangling curls and a very white face. *He could have been describing that half memory from the Grange that still haunted Edward!* Codger would never be capable of telling a convincing lie if he lived to be a hundred. It must be coincidence! Or else in his drugged stupor in the hospital Edward had remembered that testimony and converted one fiction into another.

He returned Alice's stare for a moment before he realized that she was genuinely worried. "Forget the silly prank, darling! It was months ago. It has nothing whatsoever to do with what happened at the Grange, the thing we mustn't talk about. Let's talk about us!"

"What about us?"

"I love you."

She shook her head. "I love you dearly, but not that way. There is nothing to discuss, Edward. Please don't let's go through all that again! We're first cousins and I'm three years older—"

"That matters less and less as time goes by."

"Nonsense! In 1993 I shall be a hundred years old and you will only be ninety-seven and still pursuing wenches when I need you to wheel me around in my Bath chair. I hope we shall always remain the best of friends, Eddie, but never more than that."

He heaved himself into a more comfortable position, although he had tried them all and none of them was really comfortable now.

"My darling Alice! I am not asking you for a commitment—"

"But you are, Edward."

"Nothing final!" he said desperately. "We're both too young to go that far. All I'm asking is that you consider me as an eligible suitor like any other young man. I just want you to think of me as—"

"That was your final offer. You asked a lot more than that when you started!"

Her fanning had grown more vigorous. He ran a hand through his sweaty hair. Ladies' garments were even less suitable than gentlemen's for this unusually hot summer. In a way he was fortunate to be wearing only a cotton nightgown, but how could man woo maid when he was flat on his back with one leg in the air? "Then I'm sorry I was so precipitate. Put it down to transitory youthful impatience. You said you had no intention of making any final—"

"Edward, stop!" Alice slapped the newspaper noisily on her knee. "Listen carefully. Our ages don't matter very much, I'll agree with you on that. That is not the problem. First, I will never marry a cousin! Our family is odd enough already without starting to inbreed. Secondly, I do not think of you as a cousin."

"That's promising!"

"I think of you as a brother. We grew up together. I love you very much, but not in the way you want. Girls do not marry their brothers! They do not *want* to marry their brothers. And thirdly, you are not the sort of man I should ever want to marry."

He winced. "What's wrong with me?"

She smiled sadly. "I'm looking for an elderly rich industrialist with no children and a very dickey heart. You're a starry-eyed romantic idealist student and strong as a horse."

Edward sighed. "Then may I be your second husband and help you spend the loot?"

Eventually they found their way to happier ground, talking about their childhood in Africa. The whites they had known had all died in the massacre, of course, but their native friends had survived. They speculated on who would now be married to whom. They talked of all sorts of other things, but not what he wanted to talk about, which was their future together. He discovered several times that he was lying there like a dead sheep, smiling witlessly at her, just happy to be in her presence. And at last Alice glanced at her watch and gave a little shriek and jumped to her feet.

She clutched his hand. "I must run! Take care of yourself! Look out for Zulu spears."

He felt a heavenly touch of lips on his cheek and smelled roses. Then she was gone.

Later he looked through the books Ginger had sent and decided that they were definitely not the sort of thing he wanted to read in a hospital bed, and probably not ever. That came of being a romantic, starry-eyed idealist, he supposed. Most of them were suspiciously tatty, as if the old chap had read them many times, or they been passed around a lot. Then he chanced upon a flyleaf bearing an inscription in green ink:

*Noël, 1897*

*Vous Inculper,*
  *Avant de savoir ce lui qui est arrivée,*

*Gardez-vous Bien.*

Every book contained a similar inscription, each in a different ink and handwriting. It was a reasonable assumption that Constable Heyhoe knew no French. Arranging the volumes in alphabetical order by title and reading the fragments as a single message, Edward translated:

"The back door was bolted on the inside; the door from the kitchen premises to the house was locked, but the key is missing. They cannot charge you until they discover where it has gone. Beware of admitting anything that may be used against you."

Two men in a locked room, one dead, one injured—from which side had the door been locked? Yes, that was just mildly critical, wasn't it?

*Three cheers for the devious Welsh!*

# 26

Eleal awoke shivering, lying on her pallet in darkness. She could not remember going to sleep. Cold and hunger had wakened her—distant sounds of evensong from the temple told her that the hour was not late. The troupe would be in Sussvale now, very likely still performing *The Fall of Trastos* for the kindly folk of Filoby. Curse Filoby and its cryptic testament!

Her fingers were sore from plucking chickens. She had left the casement open—never a wise move in Narshland. She scrambled up stiffly and limped across to close it.

Below her, lights showed in windows, here and there. In the crystal mountain air the skies were bright with a myriad of sparkling diamond stars, and two moons. Narshians bragged about their stars. Eltiana was a baleful red spot, high in the east, gloating over her prisoner, perhaps. Below her, just rising at the far end of the valley, Ysh's tiny half disk cast an eerie blue glow on the peaks of Narshwall. Of green Trumb there was no sign at all. Eleal leaned out and scanned the sky to make sure—*and Kirb'l appeared right before her eyes!*

She had never actually seen him do that before. Always she had just realized that the night had become brighter or darker, that she had just gained or lost a shadow, and looked up to see that Kirb'l had come or gone, as the case might be. This time she had been watching! One minute there had been only stars at the crest of the sky, and the next moment there was Kirb'l's brilliant golden point, putting them to shame. She even thought she could make out a disk. Usually Kirb'l, like Eltiana, was merely a starlike point, although no star was ever so bright, or such a clear gold.

All the moons went in and out of eclipse, but none so abruptly as he. Sometimes Kirb'l even went the wrong way, and a few minutes' watching were enough to show her now that his light was indeed moving against the stars, sinking in the east. He was also heading southward, to avoid Eltiana and Ysh. Kirb'l, the moon that did not behave like the others—wandering north and south, moving the wrong way, sometimes bright, sometimes faint—Kirb'l was also the Joker, Kirb'l the god, avatar of Tion in Narsh. Was that a sign to her that she must not give up hope? Or was the Joker laughing at her plight? Kirb'l the frog had given her a sign! Good sign or bad?

She decided to treat it as a good sign. She closed the casement, wrapped herself in her blanket, and knelt down to say some prayers. She prayed, of course, to Tion. She would not pray to the goddess of lust, nor to the god of death, not to the Maiden who withheld her justice. Chiol the Father had taken her coins and thrown a very cruel destiny upon her. But Tion was god of art and beauty and in Narsh he was Kirb'l and he had given her a sign.

# 27

"Your full name, if you please."

Edward supplied his name and date of birth. He felt as he did when he faced an unfamiliar bowler. The opening balls would be simple and straightforward while the opponents summed each other up. Then the googlies would start.

It was Tuesday afternoon, a full day since Alice had departed. The most exciting thing that had happened in those twenty-four hours was the bandage around his head being replaced with a sticking plaster, half of which was on scalp and sure to hurt like Billy-o when it came off.

He was half-insane from boredom, and a battle of wits with the law was a most welcome prospect. Being not guilty, he had nothing to fear if the game was played fair; if the deck was stacked, then devil take him if he could not outwit this country bumpkin copper. Anything he said might be used in evidence. He had never expected to hear the dread words of the official caution directed at himself.

"You feel well enough to answer questions now, Mr. Exeter?"

"Yes, sir. I'll do anything I can to help you catch the killer."

"What do you recall of the events of Sunday last, August first? . . ."

Leatherdale looked weary. The man was suffering from his weight and the heat. His face was more florid than ever, gleaming with perspiration, his neck bulged over his collar, and the points of his waxed mustache were drooping instead of standing up proudly. Edward had considered inviting him to remove his jacket and even his waistcoat and had then decided that fair play could be carried too far. Leatherdale for his part was not being at all sporting—he had set chair back almost against the wall, so Edward must keep his head turned hard over on the pillow to see him. The uniformed sergeant was on the other side of the bed, evidenced only by an occasional scratch from his pen.

However absurd his apparel, Edward was much more comfortable than either of his visitors, except for the strain on his neck. His leg had stopped hurting much except when he moved it. Let the game begin!

Next question: "You are familiar with the kitchen premises at Greyfriars Grange?"

"Yes. I've stayed there before. Timothy and I always raided the larder after everyone else went to bed. It was a tradition we started when we were kids. We used to feel frightfully depraved, but I expect Mrs. Bodgley knew what we were up to and didn't care."

"Would she have cared on Sunday?"

"What?" Edward almost laughed. "Timothy could have treated me to the best Napoleon brandy and his parents wouldn't have minded. I expect we'd have felt a pair of real mugs if anyone had walked in on us sitting there by candlelight . . ."

"You would have been embarrassed if anyone had found the two of you in the kitchen at that hour of the night?"

"Mildly embarrassed," Edward conceded, realizing that the conversation was coming around to—

"Was that why you locked the door?"

"We didn't." He must not reveal what Ginger Jones had told him about missing keys. He must not show any interest in keys.

"You say your memories of the night's events are foggy, and yet you recall a detail like that? You would testify under oath that neither you nor your companion locked the kitchen door?"

"I would testify that I do not recall locking it or seeing Bagpipe lock it—neither that night nor any of the half dozen or so times we had been there under similar circumstances before. I do remember people beating on the door later, trying to get in, so somebody must have locked it." It was hard not to smile at that point.

"Or bolted it."

"There's no bolt on that door . . . is there?"

Leatherdale smiled placidly. "I'll ask the questions, if you don't mind."

He continued to send down simple balls and Edward continued to stonewall them. He had recalled quite a lot in the past two days, but it was patchy—Bagpipe showing him to his room, the talk of war over the port, Bagpipe coming to chat, Bagpipe raving about *The Lost World*.

The inspector reached out and took the book off the bed table and eyed the title. "Sir Arthur Conan Doyle? Good man. Liked what he wrote about the war and those Boers. Well, it would be his Mr. Sherlock Holmes we would be needing now, wouldn't you say, sir?" With his homely, West Country voice he might have been discussing the prospects for the harvest, but he was not fooling Edward.

"Run through the clues for me, Inspector, and I shall solve the case lying here in my bed."

"I hope you do." Leatherdale twirled his mustache and somehow made that commonplace gesture seem sinister.

Edward resolved to make no more jokes.

If what Ginger Jones had reported was correct, then there was no chance of Edward Exeter being kept under unofficial arrest much longer. At the end of this interview he would ask to be moved out of solitary. A ward full of other men would be infinitely preferable, even if they were all farmers and tradesmen. At least there would be the crisis to talk about. The order mobilizing the army was going to be signed today. Belgium had rejected the German ultimatum. If the Prussian jackboot came across that border, then Britain would be in the war. Meanwhile he must be nice to the rozzer. . . .

"Had the rest of the household retired to bed?"

"I don't remember, sir."

"What exactly did you do in the kitchen?"

"All I recall of the kitchen is what I already . . ."

The sensation was oddly like being called to walk the carpet, but he had not been in serious trouble at Fallow since his wild youth in the Upper Fourth, and he knew the stakes now were considerably higher than a breeching or a few hours' detention. His neck was growing devilish stiff. He addressed his next few answers to the ceiling, aware that the foe was still watching him and he could not see the foe.

Of course the most likely explanation of the tragedy was that the two of them had blundered into a gang of burglars and tried to be heroes. In the resulting fracas the intruders had stabbed Bagpipe, thrown Edward down the stairs, and departed. But if Ginger's information was correct, they had not escaped out the back door, which had been bolted, but had gone through into the main house, locking the door and taking the key. Although Ginger had not mentioned the front door and other means of escape, there must be a possibility that the killer or killers had not been intruders at all, but someone in General Bodgley's household. As Bodgley was practically lord of the manor around Greyfriars, this investigation must be much more than a routine for Inspector Leatherdale. He would be under terrific pressure; he would play every trick he knew. Even a romantic, starry-eyed idealist knew the googlies must start soon.

The voices droned, the constable's pen squeaked, and faint sounds of carts and motors drifted in through the open window. Visitors' voices wandered up and down the corridor, and Leatherdale continued to use up Edward's visiting hours. Quite possibly Ginger Jones or others might be cooling their heels outside there somewhere, waiting to be admitted.

"But you had never seen this woman before?"

"I'm not sure I even saw her then, Inspector. I have only a few very vague images. She may have been a delusion." Should he have admitted that?

"You threw something at your uncle yesterday?"

*Googly!*

Edward turned to look at Leatherdale quizzically, and then reached up to the bedside table.

"No. I did heave this dish, or one just like it."

"Why?"

He resisted the temptation to say, "I didn't know what else it was for." Instead he explained calmly, "I threw it at the book he was holding. Had I wanted to hit him instead, I would have hit him. I can hit a sixpence at the far end of a cricket pitch." He raised the dish. "Choose any flower in the room and I'll hit it for you, even lying flat like this."

"That won't be necessary. Why did you throw the dish at Dr. Exeter?"

"I didn't."

"Why did you throw the dish at the Bible, then?"

"Because my uncle is a religious fanatic. I'd say a religious maniac, but I'm not qualified to judge that. For years he has been trying to convert me to his beliefs, and he is absolutely unstoppable when he gets going. I could not leave, and the only way I could think of to get rid of his ranting was to make a scene. So I made a scene."

"You did not just ask him to leave?"

"I did try, sir."

"You could have rung for a nurse and asked her to show him out."

"He is my legal guardian and a well-known divine. He would have resisted and probably won."

"Trying to convert you from what?" Leatherdale changed topics like a juggler moved balls.

"From believing what my parents believed."

"And what is that?"

"My father told me, 'Don't talk about your faith, show it.' "

"You refuse to answer the question?"

"I did answer the question." What on earth did this have to do with Bagpipe's death? "I was taught that deeds count and words don't. The guv'nor was convinced that rabid, bigoted missionaries like my uncle Roland did incalculable harm to innumerable people by thrusting an alien set of beliefs and values on them. They finish up confused and adrift, with their tribal ways in a shambles and no real understanding of what they are expected to put in their place. He used to quote . . ."

*May be used as evidence* . . . Even if Leatherdale himself was broad-minded and tolerant—and there was no evidence of that—the average English jury would certainly contain some dogmatic, literal-minded Christians. Edward took a long breath, cursing his folly at letting his tongue run away with him. "He believed a man should advertise his beliefs by making his life an example to others and to himself and to whatever god or gods he believed in. You don't really want a sermon, do you, Inspector?"

"And this provoked you to throw the dish?"

Another curved one! "He insulted my father." As Leatherdale was about to speak, Edward decided to get the words on the record. "He accused him of worshiping Satan." Try putting that before twelve honest men and true!

"Those exact words, 'worshiping Satan'?"

"Close enough. How would you react if someone—"

"It is your reactions we are investigating, sir. Do you normally become violent when someone makes an insulting remark about your father?"

"I don't recall anyone else ever being such a boor."

As the interrogation continued, Leatherdale's West Country growl seemed to be growing broader and broader. Edward wondered if his own public school drawl was also becoming more marked. He ought to try and curb it, but he had no spare brain cells to put in charge of the attempt. He had also realized that the policeman disliked him for some reason, and was enjoying this.

"Why would your uncle have made such an accusation?"

Edward rubbed his stiffening neck. "Ask him. I do not understand my uncle's thinking."

"In his youth he was a missionary himself."

"I know that much."

"Where were you born, Mr. Exeter?"

What did this have to do with Bagpipe's murder? "In British East Africa. Kenya."

The questions jumped like frogs—Kenya, Fallow, the Grange. Any time Edward questioned a question for relevancy, Leatherdale would change the subject and then work his way back again. The ceiling could do with a coat of paint.

"And how did your father treat missionaries in Nyagatha?"

"I have no idea. I was only twelve when I left there. I was only twelve when I last spoke to my father. Boys of that age barely regard their parents as mortals, let alone question them on such topics."

"That was not what you said earlier."

"That's true," Edward admitted, angry with himself. "I know what he said to me about missionaries, but I don't know what he did about them in practice. I remember missionaries visiting the station and being made welcome."

"Can you name any of them?"

"No. It was a long time—"

"And the Reverend Dr. Exeter is your father's brother?"

"Was my father's brother. My father died when I was sixteen."

Leatherdale twirled his mustache. "Your father's younger brother?"

"Hardly! Much older."

"Have you any evidence of that, Mr. Exeter?"

"I knew them both very well."

"Any documentary evidence?"

Edward stared. "Sir, what does this have to do with what happened at Greyfriars Grange?"

"Answer the question, please."

"I expect the guv'nor's age is recorded on my birth certificate. I don't remember. I don't read my birth certificate very often."

Manners! He was growing snippy. Was that a glint in Leatherdale's eye? He was against the light, so it was hard to tell.

"When a British subject is born in the colonies, who issues the birth certificate?"

"The nearest district officer, I expect."

"So your father made out your birth certificate?"

"Perhaps he did. I'll look and see when I get out of hospital."

"I was asking about your father's age. Have you any evidence handy at the moment—a photograph, for instance?"

Impudence! Unmitigated gall! The bounder had gone through Edward's wallet when he was unconscious! The urge to try and take him down was becoming dangerously close to irresistible.

"I have a photograph."

"Will you show me that photograph, please?"

Glowering, Edward opened the drawer and took out his wallet. "Be careful of it, please. It is fragile and it is the only picture of my parents I have."

Leatherdale hardly glanced at it.

"This shows you and your parents in Africa?"

"Yes. It was taken by a visitor who had a portable camera. He sent it to us just before I left."

"So it was taken around when?"

What the devil was all this leading to?

"In 1908. I would be eleven, almost twelve."

"And how old would you say the man in this picture is, sir?"

Without releasing it, Leatherdale held the photograph out for Edward to see.

"Around forty, I suppose. Not fifty. More than thirty." It was hard to tell. The image had always been blurred, and six years in his wallet had worn it almost blank, as if a heavy fog had settled on that little group on the veranda. His mother's face was in shadow. He was standing in front of his parents, his father's hand on his shoulder, and he was grinning shyly.

"Your father was Cameron Exeter, son of Horace Exeter and the former Marian Cameron, of Wold Hall, Wearthing, Surrey?"

Edward was completely at sea now. He had a strange sensation that the bed was rocking. This was worse than a geometry exam. *Prove that angle ADC equals angle DCK. . . .*

"I think so. I don't know where they lived, except it was somewhere in Surrey. I'm not even certain of their names."

Leatherdale nodded as if a trap had just clicked. "Their eldest child, Cameron, was born in 1841, Mr. Exeter. That would make him sixty-seven in 1908. How old did you say this man seems to you?"

Edward desperately wanted a drink of water, but he dared not reach for one in case his hands shook. "Forty?"

"His mother, your grandmother, died in 1855, almost sixty years ago."

"You've made a mistake somewhere. Tricky stuff, maths."

"Has your uncle seen this picture?"

"I have no idea. I may have shown it to him when I first came Home. I don't recall."

"Try."

"It was a long time ago. I really don't remember, sir. What are you suggesting?"

"I am suggesting that the man in the picture is either not your father or else your father was not who he said he was."

This conversation made no sense at all! It must be a ruse to rattle him. Bemused, Edward ran a hand through his hair and realized that it was soaked—he was soaked. He turned his head to ease his neck, and watched the sergeant finish writing a sentence, then look up, waiting for more.

He turned back to Leatherdale, who was impassively twirling his mustache again. That, apparently, was a bad sign. But the man could not possibly be as confident as he was pretending.

"You've been busy, Inspector!" He was ashamed to hear a quaver in his voice. "Unfortunately, you've been misinformed. Yesterday was Bank Holiday. I suppose you telegraphed to Somerset House first thing this morning, or the Colonial Office, perhaps?

Whitehall must be in turmoil just now with war about to break out. Someone has blundered."

"I obtained the information from your uncle."

Oh, Lord! Edward reined in his tongue before it ran away with him. "I suggest you obtain confirmation of anything he says. Check with the Colonial Office."

"Ah, yes. Can you give me the name of someone to get in touch with there, sir?"

With a rush of relief, Edward said, "Yes! Mr. Oldcastle. I'm sorry I don't know his title. I always wrote to him at his home."

"His full name?"

"Jonathan Oldcastle, Esquire."

"And do you remember his address?"

"I should do! I've written to him every week or two for the last couple of years. The Oaks, Druids Close, Kent."

Leatherdale nodded and eased himself on the chair. "That was the address in the school records, Sergeant?"

Pages rustled. "Yes, sir," said the sergeant.

"And this Mr. Oldcastle replied to your letters, sir?"

"Religiously. He was very kind—and generous."

Again the thick fingers caressed that gray mustache. "Exeter, there is nowhere in Kent called Druids Close. There is nowhere in Great Britain by that name."

"That's impossible!"

"Sergeant, will you confirm what I just told the witness?"

"Yes, sir."

After a moment Edward said, "I think I need a glass of water."

From then on it got worse, much worse. Having succeeded in rattling him, Leatherdale gave him no chance to recover. Suddenly they were back in Greyfriars Grange—

"Did you stab Timothy Bodgley?"

"No!"

"You're sure of that? You remember?"

"No, sir, I don't remember, but—"

And back in Africa—

"Who is 'Jumbo'?"

"Who?" Edward said furiously. Bounder! The letter!

"Is there anyone in England now who knew your father?"

"I don't know."

And back in the Grange—

"Had you ever been down in the cellar before?"

"No, sir. Not that I remember."

"Would a schoolboy forget visiting a fourteenth century crypt?"

"Probably not. So I suppose I never—"

"You heard people banging on the door while the woman was still screaming? How long did she scream at you? How long did you hold her off with the chair? . . ."

Eventually, inevitably, Edward blundered.

"Do you recognize this, Mr. Exeter?"

"Oh, you found it!" *Oh, you muggins!*

Leatherdale pounced like a cat. "You knew it was lost?"

"That's a key. I don't know what it's the key to, though . . . No, I don't recognize it. . . . Lots of keys look like that, big and rusty . . ." Avoid, evade, distract . . . "I assumed that since you asked earlier about the door . . ." It was hopeless. In ignominious defeat, the suspect told of the message Ginger had sent him. *Traitor! Snitch! Nark!*

Leatherdale followed up his victory, slashing questions like saber blows.

"Why did you kill him?" "Why did you argue with him?" "Why were you shouting?" "What were you shouting?" "What secret had he discovered about you?" "Describe the kitchen."

"Big. High. Very old. Why?"

"How high? How high is the ceiling?"

Edward wiped his wet forehead. "How should I know? Fifteen feet?"

"Twenty-one. Do you remember the shelves on the wall under the bells?"

"I remember shelves, and dressers, I think bells . . ." A long row of bells, one for every room in the house.

Leatherdale smiled grimly. "Yes, this is the key to the kitchen quarters at Greyfriars Grange. We found it, Mr. Exeter, in a pot on the topmost shelf."

"Oh."

"Twenty feet up in a poor light. There were no marks in the dust on the lower shelves, Mr. Exeter. What do you say about that?"

"What do you say about it, sir?"

"I say that the only way it could have been put in that pot was to throw it up there and bounce it off the wall just under the ceiling. Whoever managed to do that first try in a poor light must be a very expert thrower indeed. A bowler, perhaps?"

When at last the ordeal ended, Edward watched in misery as Ginger's books were impounded as evidence, along with his cherished photograph, the most precious thing he possessed in the world. The policemen departed.

He had not confessed. He had not been charged, either, but obviously that was only a matter of time now.

# 28

Eleal had endured a second day in her lonely prison, plucking chickens. Her fingers were worn raw. She had done the work conscientiously because anything else would have just brought her more hunger and perhaps a beating. She had been given boiled chicken and chicken soup to eat. She never wanted to see another chicken ever again.

Tomorrow the festival began and she would not be there. She would never see another festival, never sing for a real audience again, never be an actor. Worst of all was the certainty that she could not stand many more days of this torment without breaking. Soon she would kneel and kiss Ylla's shoe, just to beg for some company, someone to talk to.

She hadn't done so yet, though.

She had cried herself to sleep.

She awoke in darkness. It was not like the time the reaper had wakened her. She swam up from sleep slowly, reluctantly, annoyed by an exasperating noise. She tried to pull the skimpy blanket up over her ear and succeeded only in exposing her toes to the cold.

There it came again! Something tapping.

Angrily she lifted her head.

Tapping at the window! . . .

She scrambled to her knees. She could barely make out the squares of the casement. There was *something* out there, though! Tap, tap! Not just wind in a tree.

A momentary fear was followed by a rush of excitement. Still clutching her blanket around her, she stumbled to her feet and stepped over. The end of a rope was swinging against the glass: *tap! tap!*

She struggled with the hasp in frantic impatience and hauled the little casement open. She leaned over the sill and peered up, but she could see nothing. Clouds scudded over the sky, their edges tinted with blood by Eltiana's ominous red. No other moons were in sight, and that was ominous—only the Lady!

A wicked breeze blew through Eleal's hair and chilled her skin. The rope slithered up a few feet and then dropped down in her face. She grabbed it and pulled it inside the room with her. Fumbling in the dark, she established that there was a loop tied in the end of it. It was not a noose, but the association of ideas made her uneasy. She pulled in the slack while she tried to work out what she was supposed to do with it. Light faded as Eltiana vanished behind a cloud. Was that an omen?

Then the rope reversed direction as the unknown prankster on the roof hauled it in.

She hung on, thinking, *Wait! Wait! I need some time!* She was dragged to the window. She hung tight, refusing to let this opportunity escape her. The rope slackened.

Obviously someone was signaling intentions. She pulled the noose over her shoulders and scrambled up on the sill. The gap was small, even for her, but she was agile. She twisted around and wriggled, until she was sitting on the hard ledge, with most of her outside and only her legs inside. She clung very tightly to the sides of the opening. The wind tugged at her robe, which was no warmer than a nightgown would have been and definitely not a garment she would have chosen for midnight acrobatics two stories above a very hard-looking courtyard. Better not to think about that! Her face was against the stone above the lintel. She waited for the pull, feeling all knotted up inside as she did on a mammoth, crossing Rilepass.

The noose tightened on her, and then stopped before it had taken her weight. Teeth chattering, she peered anxiously up at the dark clouds. The cornice was barely visible, but then a faint glimmer showed over it—a face? Checking that she was doing what he wanted? She dared not shout, and neither did he. She hoped he had big, strong hands and arms. She thought he waved. She assumed it was a man. No woman would be mad enough to try this. She waved back. He disappeared.

She was going to freeze to death if he didn't do something soon. The cold and the discomfort of her perch were making her eyes water. The rope tightened under her arms, cutting into her back. She pulled herself up on the line and pushed herself out with one foot, prepared to walk up to the roof. She did not look down. For a moment a pinkish glow heralded Eltiana's reappearance, but then it faded behind the clouds again. *Hurry!* she thought. *Before the goddess sees!*

The rope slackened. Taken by surprise, she tipped backward with a squeal of alarm. She swung free and banged her knees into the wall below the window. Now she realized she was expected to walk *down* the wall, not up. It was cold and rough against her bare toes. She tried to forget that awful drop below her.

Her rescuer must be immensely powerful, for he was letting the rope out very evenly and smoothly. She saw the next window coming and avoided it—lucky the openings were so small. Then there would be another window on the ground floor. There was, and it was larger, but at last she felt cold, cold cobbles under her feet. With a gasp of relief, she leaned against the wall and muttered a prayer of thanks to every deity she could think of. Except the Lady Eltiana in all her aspects, of course.

Several rooms away to the right, a single window at ground level showed light. The rest of the temple slept. If the goddess knew of this violation of her sacred precincts, she had not yet roused her guardians.

Eleal slipped free of the rope, which continued to descend and collect at her feet. Shivering violently, she began to gather it up in coils. Good rope was expensive. She should have thought to bring her sandals. A scratching noise made her look up—and jump back in disbelief as small fragments of stone rattled down on her. A huge shape showed against the sky, dark against dark, and two eyes glowed faintly. The dragon began to descend the sheer face of the wall. The noises became dangerously loud as its claws struggled for purchase. She moved farther out of the way, having no desire to be struck by a falling dragon and no chance of being able to catch one effectively. She had always known that dragons were skilled climbers, but she had not known they could scale a sheer masonry wall.

A dark forked tail came into view, swinging vigorously from side to side. It felt the ground and then swung up out of harm's way as the hindquarters followed. A *very* dark tail! Of course this could only be Starlight, and her rescuer must be T'lin himself— what other dragon owners did she know? She resisted a desire to call out to him. Clawed feet reached the cobbles. Starlight balanced on them for a moment, his frills extended and flapping for balance like small wings. He tipped around and down and settled on all fours, puffing. His eyes glowed faintly green, and blinked.

Eleal ran to him and looked up. "T'lin Dragontrader!"

"No," said a whisper. "But his dragon. It won't hurt you." The rider had twisted around to untie the rope attached to the baggage plate at his back. It had been Starlight who had lowered her down the wall.

"Of course he won't. He's Starlight."

"Oh. Well, up with you!" He reached down.

She hesitated only a fraction of a second. Whoever he was, she had already trusted her life to him. She accepted the hand and waited for the heave. It came in the form of an ineffective tug. She realized that the hand she was holding was far too small and smooth to be T'lin's.

"Mmph!" said the whisperer angrily. "You're too heavy. *Choopoo!*" The dragon twisted its neck around and blinked at him. "*Choopoo!*" he repeated. "Oh, *Wosok!* I mean."

Starlight sighed and obediently folded his legs, sinking into a crouch.

"Now!" said the rider. "Step on my foot. Squeeze in here, in front."

He was hardly more than a boy, not nearly large enough to be T'lin Dragontrader, but Eleal was not about to look gift dragons in the mouth now. She scrambled into the saddle in front of him. It was a very uncomfortable position, for her robe pulled up to expose her legs and she was squeezed between the rider and the bony pommel plate. Two leather-clothed arms closed around her.

A light came on in the nearest window.

"Oops!" said that young voice in her ear. "Hang on for all you're worth! *Wondo! Zomph!*"

Telling Starlight to *zomph* turned out to be a miscalculation. *Varch* would have been more prudent. He was up and off across the courtyard like an arrow in flight. He sprang to the top of the wall and over, and an instant later was racing through shrubbery and trees. Branches cracked and whipped. Eleal choked down a scream and doubled over, clinging for her life to the pommel plate. Fortunately Starlight had folded his frills back tightly out of harm's way, and she managed to tuck her head underneath one. Leaning on her back, her companion cursed shrilly.

A tooth-jarring leap almost unseated her as the dragon bounded to the top of another wall. Coping stones fell loose and they all descended into the road beyond with a crash in the night. Having been given no further instructions, the dragon might well have crossed the road and proceeded to scramble up the house opposite, but fortunately he wheeled to the right and began to gather speed.

"Five gods!" yelled the youth. "What's the word for *slow down?*"

"*Varch!*" Eleal shouted, straightening up.

Starlight reluctantly slowed to a breathtaking run. The night streamed past in a rush of cold air and a clattering of claws. Luckily the street was deserted.

"Phew! Thanks. I'm Gim Sculptor."

"Eleal Singer."

"Glad to hear it. Would be bad manners to rescue the wrong damsel. Which is left and which is right? I've forgotten already."

"*Whilth* and *chaiz.* You mean you don't know how to do this?"

"*Chaiz!*" Gim ordered. "No. I've never been on a dragon in my life before. The god will preserve us! He sent me."

# 29

Edward spent the hours after Inspector Leatherdale's departure stewing in misery, going over and over the ghastly interrogation and wishing he could call back a lot of his answers. His bragging about the accuracy of his bowling had been the worst sort of side—it might not justify a hanging, but it seemed likely to provoke one now. From what he recalled of the Grange kitchen, the feat the bobbies were suggesting was absolutely impossible. Far more likely, that key was an unneeded duplicate that had been lying in the pot for years, but if there was no other explanation for the locked room, then a jury would accept the police version. The only alternative was magic, and English juries were notoriously disinclined to believe in magic.

So was he.

The mystery of his father's age was maddening, although it seemed completely irrelevant to the murder. His knowledge of his family was the knowledge of a twelve-year-old, for he had never discussed such things with Holy Roly. He knew that the brothers had not met since Cameron had emigrated to New Zealand; he thought he could recall the guv'nor saying once that Roland had been in divinity college then. The old bigot had probably been ordained sometime in the late sixties, judging by his present age. Edward's parents had been married in New Zealand and had then returned to England, briefly, before going out to Africa. There had been no family reunion, because by then the Prescotts had been in India and Roland still in Fiji or Tonga or somewhere. That was as much as Edward knew.

On the face of it, though, Leatherdale had a case. If Cameron Exeter had been a clerk in government service in New Zealand in the sixties, how could he have been forty years old in Kenya, forty years later?

But if District Officer Exeter had been an impostor, then why had that fact not emerged at the board of inquiry? Edward had read the hateful report a hundred times and there was no hint of any such mystery in it. It did not mention his father's background at all. In his present state of dejection that curious omission suddenly seemed ominous, like a potential embarrassment swept under a rug.

Obviously Holy Roly must know more than he had ever revealed, and Edward might yet have to grovel to him for enlightenment. Had he shown his uncle that photograph when he arrived in England? He could not remember, but it would have been odd if he had not. Assume he had. The old bigot must have seen right away that the fortyish man in it could not be his brother. So why had he not said so at once? Why had he not said so four years later, after the massacre, when he was landed with custody of the impostor's son?

In order to lay his hands on the rest of the family money?

*The Crown proposes* that when Grandfather Exeter died and left the remains of the ill-gotten family fortune to his three children, the genuine Cameron Exeter was already dead and buried at the far side of the world. Somehow a much younger man assumed his identity, was accepted in his stead, pocketed the loot, and promptly left New Zealand, where he was known by his real name. Thereafter he could never be unmasked as long as he stayed away from the dead man's brother and sister. My Lud, the prosecution rests its case.

*Learned counsel for the defense* expresses disbelief. Why would such a rogue then go and bury himself in the African bush?

Because, counters the prosecution, the Reverend Roland Exeter had retired from active missionary service and was on his way Home. The impostor would be exposed.

But why Africa? Why not Paris, or Vienna, or even America?

Edward tried to consider the question as judge and ended as a hung jury. He could not deny the evidence of the photograph; he could not believe that the father whose memory he cherished had been such a villain. When Mildred Prescott died, the guv'nor had become Alice's guardian and therefore custodian of her share of the dwindling family fortune. He had taken the child in and treated her as his own daughter; he had not rushed off to Europe to spend her money. He had remained to serve the people of Nyagatha until his death.

What if, four years before that death, Roland Exeter had seen the photograph? That made nonsense of the hypothesis! Holy Roly would have blown the gaff, denounced the impostor, reclaimed the money, and thrown Edward out in the gutter. Wouldn't he?

So Edward could not have shown the guv'nor's picture to Roland. He would certainly give odds that it was presently on its way to London so the reverend gentleman might view it now. The mystery could have nothing to do with the murder at Greyfriars Grange, but surely no copper would resist a chance to solve a twenty-year-old fraud case so easily.

Edward barely touched the leathery slab of haddock that came at teatime.

*     *     *

By nine o'clock the nurses were making their rounds—giving the patients back rubs, bedding them down for the night, removing the flowers because it was not healthy to sleep with flowers in the room. Germany had invaded Belgium, Britain had declared war. Men were enlisting by the thousands. Even that stirring news failed to penetrate Edward's black mood. He was out of it for at least three months, until his leg mended, and death on the gallows now seemed much more likely than glory in battle.

He noticed a change in the nurses' attitude. They passed on the latest news, but they did not seem to want to talk with him. Even when he roused himself to be cheerful and chatty, they failed to respond. Now they knew he was a murderer.

He tried to read the last chapter of *The Lost World,* and the words were a blur. All he could take in was the awful relevance of the title.

The lights were turned off. The hospital fell quiet and gradually the clamor of hooves and engines outside faded into night. Greyfriars would never be a riotous place in the evening, and tonight most men would be at home with family and friends, coming to grips with the catastrophe that had so suddenly befallen the world. If there was a patriotic rally in progress somewhere, it was being held out of earshot of Albert Memorial.

Completely unable to sleep, he squirmed and fretted in his sweat-soaked bed. To-morrow he must ask to see the solicitor Mrs. Bodgley had mentioned. Or would that be an admission of guilt? Should he wait until Leatherdale arrived with the warrant? Who could possibly have killed old Bagpipe, and how, and why? Nothing made any sense anymore.

The only certainty was that he had no choice but to stay and face the music. Even if he were able to run, he had no one to run to—except Alice, and he would never impose on her like that. He could never impose on anyone like that. As it was, he could not walk, he had no money or clothes; he would not even be able to pull his trousers on over his splints. If he even had a proper cast on his leg . . .

Suppose he *had* shown the photograph to Holy Roly? Suppose Roly had recognized his brother, but his brother thirty years younger than he should be? That would explain his references to devil worship. He had been implying that Cameron, like Dr. Faustus, had sold his soul to the devil in return for eternal youth.

Oh, Lord! That was even madder than keys jumping into pots or murderers going out through locked doors.

He might have been asleep, he was not sure. Sudden light startled him as the door swung wider and a nurse entered, making her rounds. He saw her only as a dark shape. He raised a hand in greeting.

"Not sleeping?" she asked. "Pain?"

"No. Bad news."

"Oh, they'll hold the Germans off until you get there." She laid an appraising hand on his forehead.

"Not that. Personal bad news."

"I'm sorry. Anything I can do to help?"

"Find me a good solicitor."

She said, *"Oh!"* as if she had just remembered who he was. "Want me to ask the doctor for a sleeping draft for you?"

He thought about it.

He very nearly said yes.

"No. I'll manage."

"I'll look back later." She floated away and the room filled again with darkness, except for one thin strip of light along the doorjamb.

He went back to his worries. Eventually a new thought penetrated—the nurse's belated reaction suggested that Leatherdale had removed his watchdog. Perhaps he had been needed for more urgent duties tonight. Marvelous! Now the suspect could tiptoe out of the hospital and run off to Brazil or somewhere. When the nurse came back he'd ask her for a set of crutches.

Again a sudden flowering of light startled him out of semiconsciousness. He blinked at the same dark shape against the brightness. He wondered why she'd removed her cap at the same moment as he registered her long braids and realized that this was no nurse.

"Dvard Kisster?" The voice was husky and heavily accented. It jarred loose an avalanche of memory.

He flailed like a landed fish, half-trying to sit up, half-trying to reach for the bell rope, and the result was that he jolted his leg. It hurled a thunderbolt of pain at him. He yelled.

Then he saw a glint of metal in her hand and screamed at the top of his lungs.

She left the door, coming around on his right. *Danger!*

He began to yell for help, using the first words that came into his head. *"Once more into the breach, dear friends!"* Grabbing the nearest weapon, which happened to be the kidney-shaped dish, he continued to shout. *". . . once more; or close the wall up with our English dead. In peace . . ."*

He hurled the dish with all his strength. *". . . so becomes a man as modest stillness and humility . . ."* She had not expected his attack and the missile took her full in the face. She stumbled back with a cry; the dish clanged and clattered on the linoleum. *". . . imitate the action of the tiger; stiffen the sinews . . ."*

He started to reach for the bell again, but it meant extending himself and would leave him open. He needed that hand for throwing. *". . . hard-favored rage . . ."* She flashed toward him, cursing in some foreign tongue and raising her blade. *". . . then lend the eye a terrible aspect . . ."* He hurled the water carafe, she flailed it aside; glass crashed. Where was everybody? *". . . like the brass cannon; let the brow . . ."* He followed with the tumbler and scored a hit. *". . . galléd rock o'erhang . . ."* He was o'erhanging the side of the bed now, earthquakes of agony running through his leg.

She was holding back, watching him, a sinister dark shape. He continued to scream out his speech as loudly as he could: *"Now set the teeth and stretch the nostril wide . . ."* He had Bagpipe's book ready. Why, why, was no one coming? *". . . on, you noble English, whose blood...*" She lunged forward and he hurled Conan Doyle. He thought it hit her, but she laughed, and spoke again in her guttural accent. "What next, Dvard?"

She was right; he was running out of missiles. Why could no one hear him? He had never been louder in his life. *"Be copy now to men of grosser blood, And teach them how to war."* She came, fast as an adder. He swung farther to the right as she slashed down at him, flailing his pillow around with his left hand, parrying the blow. But he had almost fallen off the bed, and the jolt on his leg brought a howl to his throat. That was the worst ever—he thought he would faint, and thrust the possibility away. Feathers swirled like smoke. He scrabbled with his right hand and found the empty urinal bottle. "*... none of you so mean and base...*" He swung it as a club against her arm as she struck again, wishing it had been weighted with contents. She cried out and dropped the knife on the floor. He tried to grab her dress with his left hand, thinking he might be able to strangle her if he could pull her close, but she slipped away. Oh—his leg again!

His throat was sore with shouting, *"I see you stand like greyhounds in the slips..."* She made a dive to snatch up the knife. He swung the bottle at her head and missed. She came at him again and this time he thought it was all over "*... straining upon the start. THE GAME'S AFOOT!*"

"Desist!" said a new voice in the corner.

The woman spun around with a shriek.

Edward had not seen him come in, but without question this was the same Mr. Oldcastle he had imagined before. Even in his fur-collared overcoat, with his ancient beaver hat set square on his head, he was a small and unimpressive ally. Yet, with one hand pointing his cane at the armed madwoman and the other tucked in his pocket, he was certainly the calmest person present.

"Begone, strumpet! Go lick thy scurvy masters' boots in penance lest they feed thy carrion carcass to the hounds."

The woman hesitated, then fled out the door without a word. Her footsteps seemed to fade away almost instantly.

The crisis was over.

"Hey!" Edward gasped. "Stop her!"

"Nay, nay, bully lad, it were no profit to deed her to the watch." Mr. Oldcastle removed his hat and brushed it absently with his sleeve. "That wight has been accorded arts to rook their locks and manacles. Wouldst sooner close a cockatrice in a cock-boat than jail yon jade."

"You mean," Edward said, easing himself back onto the bed, "she can get out through a bolted door?" He was soaked and shaking, his heart seemed to be running the Grand National, jumps and all, but he was alive. He was almost sobbing with the pain, but he was alive.

"Aye, or in withal. Had they who seek thy soon demise invested her with deeper skills, thou hadst not fared so well." The little man chuckled. "The recitation was most gamely done! It wanted something in smoothness of phrasing, methinks, but 'twas furnished well in vehemence. Hal himself could not have seasoned the lines with greater spice."

He stepped over to the bed and peered down at Edward with an intent expression on his puckish, wrinkled face. He brought a strange odor of mothballs with him. "The pain in thy leg is not beyond thy strength to bear."

"Er. No, it's not too bad." Edward panted a few times. "Amazingly good, considering." It was not what he would describe as comfortable. He did not need a bullet to bite on, but he was making his teeth work hard.

"It needs suffice for the nonce. Compose thyself a moment. I shall return betimes."

With that Mr. Oldcastle laid his hat and cane carefully on the bed and bustled over to the door. Edward caught a brief glimpse of his tiny, stooped shape against the light, and he had gone.

"Angels and ministers of grace defend me!" he muttered, as this seemed to be Shakespeare night. "What in the name of glory is going on here?" His heartbeat was gradually returning to normal. He was definitely awake and not dreaming. Feathers and water and sparkles of glass on the lino—and splatters of blood also, so he must have scored a hit, perhaps with the tumbler.

And certainly an antique hat and stick lay on the bed, so Mr. Jonathan Oldcastle had really been present and did intend to return. Perhaps he had popped over to Druids Close, the town that received mail and did not exist? *Steady, old chap! We'll have no hysterics here.*

Strangest of all—why was the hospital not in chaotic uproar? The racket should have wakened every patient on the floor and brought every nurse for miles. Edward thought about trying the bell and then decided to wait for his mysterious guardian to come back.

That did not take long. The little man minced in with a pale garment over his shoulder, carrying a pair of crutches almost as long as himself. His stoop and the forward thrust of his head made him seem to be hurrying even when he was not.

"Thy baggage waits without, Master Exeter." He uttered the little cackling chuckle that was now starting to sound very familiar. "And thy breakage must wait within! Do don this Oxford." He handed Edward a recognizable left shoe and threw down a dressing gown across his chest.

"Hold a minute, sir! I can't walk on this leg!"

"Indeed you will have to make like the wounded plover, dangling a limb to lure the plunderer from the nest. Be speedy, my brave, for worse monsters than the harlot may soon snuff thy scent, such as may overtop my wilted powers." Mr. Oldcastle proceeded to fumble with the tackle that held Edward's leg in traction.

"But running away is an admission of guilt!"

"Staying will be a demonstration of mortality."

Edward's response was stifled by a searing jolt of pain as the leg settled on the bed. He glared up at the old man until he had caught his breath and wiped the sweat out of his eyes.

The puckish face frowned. "Ah, my young butty, dost not know that dragons of war are now full awakened? Beacon fires shall become funeral pyres and flames will consume a generation. Horror soon bestrides the world."

"Yes, but what has that to do—"

"Master Edward, those same elements that spawned this evil dissonance can now turn satisfied from that labor and address their intent to destroying *thee*. Until now they minded more those weightier matters particular to their desires. Thee they gave but little thought, for you are a mere favor they perform for other parties—who shall shortly be discovered to you. Thus thy foes dispatched to your dispatch only that demented trollop who has thrice ineptly sought to undo thee. Now at greater leisure they will loose such grievous raptors to contrive thy demise that thou surely will not see another dawn unless you now take urgent flight."

In other words: *Beat it!*

Absurd as it sounded, his convoluted speech carried conviction. There was no arguing with his obvious sincerity—after all, he had undoubtedly saved Edward's life a few moments ago. Edward pulled up his left leg and struggled into the shoe.

The next few minutes were a stroll on the cobbles of Hell. He made the distance, but only because he chose to regard it as a test of manhood. He sat up and donned the dressing gown. His right foot was lowered to the floor with much help from Mr. Oldcastle, and he pushed himself up to stand on the left. Then he was on his crutches, heading across the litter of feathers to the door. To hold his right leg up was agony; to let it touch the ground was infinitely worse.

It wasn't going to work, of course. The nurses would see him and take him back. They would telephone the police. But he had no breath to argue, and he sweated every step in silence along the wide, dim corridor, wobbling on his crutches with Mr. Oldcastle at his side. The little man had recovered his hat and silver-topped walking stick, and seemed to be fighting back a case of fidgets at the cripple's tortoise pace.

The duty desk was deserted. His old battered suitcase stood beside it, his boater resting on top. Mr. Oldcastle placed this on his head for him at a jaunty angle and took charge of the case. Then he went ahead and opened the door to the stairs.

Edward tried to say, "There's a lift," but he had his teeth so tightly clenched that the words would not come out. Mr. Oldcastle might think that the rackety old cage would bring nurses and orderlies running, or perhaps he did not understand modern machinery. Edward went down three flights of stairs on one foot, one crutch, and a white hand gripping the rail. Mr. Oldcastle carried the other crutch. From the way he managed the suitcase, he must be much stronger than he looked.

There was no one about, no one even tending the admittance desk by the front door. Edward reeled out of the hospital into the cool night air, wondering if he had left a trail of sweat all the way from his bed.

# 30

"*Wosok!*" Gim commanded firmly, but nothing happened. Starlight had his head down, buried in T'lin Dragontrader's loving embrace, and was purring so hard he could not hear the order.

"*Wosok!*" T'lin murmured. The dragon sank down on his belly, still nuzzling his owner and purring loud enough to waken the neighborhood.

There could be few places in cramped Narsh where a dragon might be hidden, but a sculptor's yard was one of them. Even so, Starlight was squeezed in between blocks of stone and half-completed monuments, and the space was hardly enough. A man with a lantern had just closed the gates.

Eleal swung a leg hastily over the pommel plate and slid to the ground in an undignified rush, wincing as her bare feet struck gravel. She had barely rearranged her robe when Gim landed beside her, stumbled, and pitched over with a shrill oath. That was not a very dignified descent for a noble hero on what must surely be his first chivalrous exploit. He scrambled up, muttering and sucking an injured palm.

Eleal had taken two unsteady steps toward T'lin when a portly woman came rushing out of the house with another lantern.

"My dear! You must be frozen! Come inside quickly." She propelled Eleal bodily over the sharp gravel and into a cozy, fragrant kitchen, brightened by no less than four candles. Swathed in llama wool blankets, Eleal was tucked into a chair close to the big iron range. The woman swung the door open and clattered a poker in among the glowing coals. Then she began stoking it with big lumps of coal from a shiny brass scuttle, using brass tongs. Shiny copper pans hung on one wall. There was a tasseled rug on the floor; painted china plates stood along a shelf so the pictures on them were visible. Gim's family might not live in a palace like the king of Jurg, but they were wealthy compared with a troupe of actors.

Eleal began to shiver uncontrollably. She could not tell whether that was from the change of temperature or from nervous reaction, but she felt in danger of falling apart.

"Hot soup!" the woman proclaimed as if invoking a major god. Granting the range fire a few moments' mercy, she knelt to bundle her visitor's feet in her own still-warm fleece coat.

Eleal forced her reply through chattering teeth. "That would be wonderful, thank you."

"Vegetable or chicken broth?"

"No chicken please!"

"I'm Gim's mother, Embiliina Sculptor, and you must be Eleal Singer."

"Yes, but how—"

"Explanations later!" Embiliina insisted. She was much less bulky without her coat and hood. In fact, she was slim and surprisingly youthful to be mother of a boy as old as Gim. Her features were fine-drawn, her complexion pale and speckled with millions of tiny fair freckles. Her hair was a spun red-gold, hanging in big loose curls to her shoulders. She wore a quality dress of the same blue shade as her eyes. She wore a smile.

T'lin Dragontrader strode in, filling the room, black turban almost touching the ceiling. His weather-beaten face and coppery beard seemed vulgar and barbaric alongside Embiliina's more delicate red-gold coloring. He began to peel off outer garments, scowling at nothing with a taut, grim expression. When he stepped closer to warm his fingers at the range, he was still avoiding Eleal's eye.

And the door closed behind the man who must be Gim's father. He was of middle height and husky, although he looked small alongside the dragon trader. He clasped Eleal's icy hand in one twice as large and rough as a rasp, studying her with solemn coal black eyes. He was as swarthy as his wife was fair.

"I am Kollwin Sculptor."

"Eleal Singer."

He nodded. "You are younger than I imagined. If you did what I think you did, then you're a brave lass." He spoke with great deliberation, as if reading his words.

"I d-d-didn't have time to think! The honor is G-g-gim's."

The dark man shook his head. "The honor is the god's. Gim has gone to thank him for a safe return. When you are ready, you will wish to visit him also?"

"Of course! At once." Eleal stood up shakily.

"Later!" Embiliina said, clattering pots. "The child's half-froze to death and the soup—"

Eleal had almost resumed her seat when the sculptor said, "First things first." His voice was slow, but not to be argued with. "You will promise not to discuss or reveal the place I am about to take you?"

That settled Eleal's indecision—her curiosity reared like a startled dragon. "Of course! I swear I never shall," she said eagerly.

The sculptor nodded and turned to T'lin. "Dragontrader?"

But T'lin had found himself a chair and spread out his long legs. He was a startling, many-colored sight in variegated leggings and a doublet of embroidered quilting. He was also a figure of menace. His long sword in its green scabbard lay by his feet, he still wore his black turban. He shook his head. "Secrets make me nervous. They are more often evil than good."

Kollwin's ruddy face seemed to bunch up with shock at the refusal. "It is no great secret, a shrine to Tion. Just . . . private."

T'lin's green eyes stared back coldly. "Then why require oaths of secrecy?"

"Because there are valuables there and I do not want them talked around. Not everyone is above stealing from a god."

"Gods can afford the loss better than us poor workers. No, I shall give thanks in my own fashion later."

Kollwin scratched a dark-stubbled cheek in contemplation. "Has that ring in your ear some special significance, Dragontrader?"

T'lin drooped his red eyebrows menacingly. "If it has, then it did not deter your god when he needed my assistance."

The sculptor thought for a moment and seemed to accept the reasoning, although he was not pleased. "Come then, Eleal Singer."

"Just a moment!" Embiliina barred the way like an enraged deity. "You are not to drag that poor child outside again on a night like this in her bare feet."

There was a minor delay while Eleal donned her hostess's boots and fleece coat, all much too large for her. There was another minor delay when Kollwin tried to go out and came face-to-face with a dragon. Starlight, being as nosy as any of his kind, had wriggled forward to see what was going on and his head filled the doorway.

"Try opening the drape," T'lin said drily from his chair. "And close the door before he tries to come in."

That worked. The great head swung over to peer in the window, and then the sculptor was able to squeeze out past the scaly shoulder, followed by Eleal, stepping over claws like sickles.

Ysh's tiny disk shed her cold blue light through a gap in the clouds, sparkling like frost on the dragon's scales. Carrying a lantern, Kollwin Sculptor led Eleal all around the dragon to reach a small shed against the wall of the yard. The door was open, but she noticed that the timber was thick and it bore at least three locks. If that was merely "private," then what was "secret" like? The inside was cluttered with all the litter she might have expected: tools and balks of wood and oddly shaped scraps of stone or metal. More interesting than those was the trapdoor in the floor, and a staircase descending.

The sculptor went first, lighting the way. "This is very old." His voice echoed up eerily. "There was probably a temple here, once upon a time."

And now there was a shrine. The room was small and low, more like an oddly shaped volume of shadow than a chamber, a bricked-off portion of an ancient cellar. Where the walls were visible, some parts were of very rough, crude masonry, others had been cut out of living rock. The only light came from a pair of braziers standing on a rug, thick and richly colored and oddly out of place. Those were the only furniture. The air was chill and yet headily scented with incense.

Beyond the rug was an alcove, and in the alcove stood the god.

Gim knelt on stone in the center of the chamber, but he must have concluded his devotions, because he scrambled to his feet and turned to smile a welcome as the newcomers approached. It was the first time Eleal had really seen him. He was still bulky as a bear in his coat, but he had removed his hat, revealing a floppy tangle of gold curls, and his eyes were as blue as his mother's. His lip bore a faint pink fuzz, which he probably thought of as a mustache. Politely disregarding that, she concluded that her rescuer could be considered a very handsome young man—how appropriate! She returned his smile. Only then did she look at the god.

The image had not been set in the alcove. Rather, the mottled yellow stone of the cave had been dug out to leave Tion in high relief, exquisitely carved. He was life-size, identifiable by a beardless face and by the pipes he held. The Youth was most often depicted nude, but here he wore a narrow scarf around his loins—an impractical garment that would rapidly fall off any mortal. He was striding forward out of the rock, one foot on the floor and the other still buried in the wall. He held his head slightly bent and turned, as if he were about to put the pipes to his lips or had just finished playing, while his eyes looked out at the visitors with a curiously enigmatic smile. As the creeping flames of the braziers danced, reflections moved on his limbs, his shadow fidgeted on the back of the hollow. He almost seemed to breathe.

"He's gorgeous!" Eleal whispered. "You made him yourself, Sculptor? Oh, he is beautiful!" Then she took a longer look at that perfect face and swung around to stare down at Gim, who bent his head quickly.

"I'm sorry," she muttered. "I didn't mean . . . Well, I did, but—"

"I did not bring you here to admire art, Singer," Kollwin growled, but he was fighting back a smile.

"Oh, but . . . Gim? Look at me."

Gim looked up, redder than a bloodfruit in the dim light. He smiled a little . . .

The likeness was exact! Or would be. He was not quite old enough, but the faces were already the same. Gim seemed taller only because he was wearing boots; otherwise he would be the same height as the god stepping out of the wall.

"An older brother, Kollwin Sculptor? Or did you imagine him as he will be in another couple of years?"

"My son was not the model. I never use models."

She could only stare from the god's inscrutable smile to Gim's scarlet embarrassment and back again.

"Tell her, Father. Please?"

"I carved the blessed likeness long ago," Kollwin said in his ponderous way. "The night I completed it I thanked the god and went up to the house and was told my wife was in labor."

She dared another glance at Gim, and he was redder yet, but wearing an idiotic grin now.

"Then the god? . . ." The god had fashioned the boy to the statue!

"The carving is the older," the sculptor said. "Gim takes after his mother and I was very much in love with her—and still am, of course. That may explain any resemblance you see, but we came here to give thanks, not to discuss art."

Eleal was about to kneel, then saw that Kollwin had more dissertations to intone.

"I think you are old enough to keep a secret, Eleal Singer. I will risk a word of explanation, if you will swear never to carry it outside this holy place."

She swore, anxious to learn the purpose of a covert shrine. This was almost as exciting as escaping down a wall in the middle of the night and much less nightmarish.

He rubbed his chin with a raspy noise. "I am not sure how much I may say, though."

Gim was staying very quiet.

"The Tion Fellowship?" she prompted.

Kollwin's eyes glinted; his swarthy face seemed to darken.

Error? "All I know," she said hastily, "is that Trong Impresario and his son came, er, *went* to a meeting two nights ago. A mutual friend said they belonged to some club he called the Tion Fellowship. They did not mention it themselves." But now she knew where they had come.

The sculptor sniffed grudgingly. "The Tion Mystery is not a club! But, yes, they asked their brethren of the Narsh Lodge for aid. Of course we offered prayer and sacrifice on their behalf, both here and in the Lady's temple. Our pleas seemed to be heard." He cleared his throat awkwardly, looking up at the god. "We know what happened, because we had one of our local brothers in the temple anyway."

Doing what, she wondered? But of course special dedication to one god would not reduce anyone's obligations to worship all the others also. The ceremony had been public.

Kollwin smiled—a slow process like sunshine moving on mountains. "We sent along someone who would understand the ancient speech, just to be on the safe side. The priests did not reveal everything the oracle had said, but they did not distort the holy words unduly. The goddess specifically directed that you were to be taken into her clergy. She insisted you be kept locked up and guarded for a fortnight. She said the rest of the troupe must contribute a hundred stars to her temple treasury, either by donation or service, and then should be run out of town as soon as possible.

"So it seemed that the Lady had turned aside her anger and all but one of the troupe was free to leave." The sculptor cleared his throat harshly. "Frankly, that one seemed of very little importance to us. The youngest, dispensable. . . . One cracked egg in a dozen is not a disaster. We thought the problem had been solved.

"But Holy Tion did not think so! He looks after those who serve him, as we should have remembered. It so happened—and this is what I ask you not to repeat—that my son had begun his initiation into the Tion Mystery." He hesitated, then shrugged. "The ceremony includes a period of prayer and fasting, which concludes when Kirb'l next appears. That night the skies were clear and Kirb'l appeared."

"I saw him." Eleal stole a glance at Gim. He smiled down at her shyly.

"At the conclusion of the ceremony," his father continued, "the initiate sleeps before the figure of the god. Here, on the floor, Gim was vouchsafed a remarkable dream, indeed a vision. Tell her, lad."

Gim rubbed his upper lip with a knuckle. His blue eyes sparkled in the candlelight. "I saw myself on a black dragon, riding to the temple." His voice rose in excitement. "Just as it happened! I knew which window, and exactly what to do with the rope. It all came true! And I knew it wasn't just an ordinary dream! I mean, I've never even touched a dragon before! So I told Father and—"

The older Sculptor chuckled. "He hauled my bedcovers off at dawn! Understand: Gim was not present when the actors came! He had not been told of the oracle, or of Eleal Singer. Yet here he was babbling about rescuing a girl held against her will in the Lady's temple! I knew then that the god had heard our prayers and issued instructions.

We inquired and learned that there was a dragon trader in town, so we went to talk with him. And he did have a black dragon in his herd. And he knew you personally."

This was something out of one of Piol Poet's dramas! "And?" Eleal demanded.

Kollwin Sculptor chuckled. "And I think he should be in on the rest of the telling. Your soup must be ready. My wife will skin me. You know enough now to know who to thank."

"It was the god who rescued you, Eleal," Gim said modestly.

Yes. But why why why?

And which aspect of Tion had answered the prayers? Dropping to her knees, Eleal took a harder look at the image that so much resembled the young man now kneeling beside her. The enigma in the smile, she decided, came from the turn of the head and eyes—lips smiling in one direction, eyes in another. He held Tion's pipes, but a god who would steal a girl away from a goddess's temple by sending a dragon and a boy who had never ridden one before might well be the same god who was causing that boy to grow up as an exact replica of his father's masterpiece—Kirb'l, the Joker.

Kollwin had somehow contrived to put her in the center. It was his shrine, so she waited for him to begin. One of the nice things about the Youth was that he spurned written texts. There were red, green, white, and blue scriptures, but no yellow.

While she was preparing words in her head, Kollwin addressed the god. Even in conversation with mortals he sounded as if he were reading a text; his prayer was a monumental inscription. "Lord of art and youth and beauty, I thank you for the safe return of my son this night, for the trust you have shown in us, and for the chance to be of service. As always, I am grateful for the blessings of the day passed and the opportunities of the day ahead. Amen."

Gim said, "Amen," so Eleal did also. This intimate sharing of religion was unfamiliar to her, but obviously it was her turn now. She looked up at the god; his eyes smiled back with infinite patience and the same mysterious amusement as before.

"Thank you, Holy Tion, for rescuing me from the most disgusting, degr—"

The sculptor barked, *"Careful!* You must not blaspheme against the Lady!"

Eleal took a deep breath and began again. "Then I'll just say that I am very grateful for being rescued. . . . Thank you, Lord." She paused, the others waited. "And I promise to serve, er, the lord of art and beauty as well as I can." She thought of the festival, and tried to imagine Uthiam mounting the steps in the great temple to receive a scarlet rose from the hand of the god. "And I ask you to look after my friends, because they have suffered because of me, and, well, I'd like them to do well in your festival. To your honor, of course. Amen."

Gim said, "Amen."

His father coughed. "I am no priest, Eleal Singer—but may I make a suggestion?"

"Please do."

"If your trouble was caused by some offense you committed against Holy Ois, or against Holy Eltiana herself, then you might perhaps ask Lord Tion to intercede for you."

"I didn't do anything. . . . I don't think it was anything I did," Eleal said. "But yes.

Please, Holy One, keep me safe from the other gods' anger and whatever is prophesied. Amen."

That had not come out quite as she had intended. Again Gim echoed her amen, but there was a distinct pause before his father did—Kollwin had noted the cryptic reference in her prayer. Gim was still too stirred up by his adventure to be concerned with anything else.

"I already spoke my thanks to Holy Tion, Father, but I will do so again if you want to hear."

The sculptor chuckled. "You are not a child that I need supervise your prayers, but I can understand if your heart is still full, and anything I can understand must be very obvious to a god."

Gim needed no more encouragement than that. He raised his hands in supplication to the image. "Lord of art, I thank you again for the opportunity to serve you and for giving me such an adventure and bringing me back safely. All I ever want is to serve you, Lord, and I especially hope to serve you by bringing more beauty into the world in art or music, but I dedicate my whole life to pleasing you in any way I can. Amen."

"Amen," Eleal said.

The sculptor bowed his head to the floor and said, "Amen" loudly as he straightened again. Then he clambered to his feet to indicate that the ceremony was over.

Ambria Impresario had been known to complain more than once that the gods had given Eleal Singer exceptionally sharp ears. She knew that Kollwin Sculptor had whispered a few other words—quickly, softly—in that sudden genuflection. *"Lord, remember he is very young!"* She had heard. Gim almost certainly had not. Had the god?

# ACT III

## *Road Show*

# *31*

"So I had visitors," T'lin Dragontrader said. "A very lovely lady named Uthiam Piper came to see me, with a distraught young man named Something Trumpeter. They both seemed to know my business better than I did. How was I ever going to get any work done in Narsh if people kept cornering me to pour out tragic sagas of young women adopted by a goddess?"

His tone was amused. His expression was not. There was tension in that cozy kitchen. Dragontrader had refused to visit the family shrine. That was a very unusual act, which might be taken as a serious insult. The fact that the sanctuary was more than that—was the center of a mystery—might help a little, or perhaps it made things even worse, for he had probably declined a very rare honor.

Eleal was no stranger to late hours and odd sleep patterns, but this was the middle of the night. The soup had been hot and delicious. Embiliina had insisted on tucking her into her chair with loads of blankets. She was feeling woozy.

"What did they think I could do against a goddess?" T'lin said, rolling his green eyes. "Did they think I was crazy?" He was very large. Although he sprawled at ease, legs and arms spread, his size and beard and black turban were daunting in that kitchen. His sword lay within reach. "They did not even know where missy was. I threw them out, and they went away on the mammoths."

Kollwin Sculptor had stripped down to a threadbare, well-washed yellow cotton smock and battered old leather leggings. He sat hunched forward on his chair, leaning meaty forearms on his knees, mostly scowling at the range but sometimes at the dragon trader. His arms and his feet were bare. Such informality was surprising and perhaps deliberate. Although he could not match T'lin for sheer bulk, he was a broad, thick man, and he was showing he was not intimidated by his visitor.

Two enormous green eyes kept watch through the window. Dragons looked ferocious, but they were pretty harmless usually.

Gim was still so jittery with excitement that he could barely sit still. His mother kept telling him to stop fidgeting. He, too, had stripped off his fleeces, losing half of himself in the process. In cotton smock and woolen leggings, he was all long limbs and grin. His resemblance to the god in the crypt was astonishing, but his bare arms showed that he needed to fill out yet; the divine artist needed a few more years to produce a perfect replica of the model.

Eleal wondered sleepily what his trade was. His hand had been smooth and he lacked his father's brawn, so he was probably not a sculptor, and yet he retained the family name. He was certainly old enough to be apprenticed to something, though.

"The next morning I had two more visitors," T'lin said, "and those two they told me a god wanted me to get involved! How, I asked them, is a man ever going to earn a living in this city?"

Gim grinned and ran a hand through his golden curls. Yes, he was even more handsome than Golfren Piper and he would make Klip Trumpeter look like a gargoyle. Eleal wondered sleepily if he had any talent for acting. Even now he would be a natural as the Youth in the tragedies! She must offer to give him lessons. That idea was amusing, except he seemed to have forgotten her altogether. He would be regarding her as a mere child, of course. She would have to demonstrate her maturity.

What more could she do to impress him than climb down a wall in the dark on a rope?

"Madness!" T'lin grumbled. "They wanted to borrow my favorite dragon for a kid who didn't know *Whilth* from *Chaiz!*"

"What persuaded you?" Embiliina Sculptor asked quietly. She was the only one of the group who seemed at ease, playing the role of hostess beautifully, passing around homemade biscuits. There was no hint of worry in her eyes.

Had Eleal's mother been as pretty as she? She had never had a chance to be motherly.

T'lin grunted. "I needed peace and quiet to earn a living. Besides, I was sure the brat would break his neck and I could trust Starlight to come home to me."

Gim grinned again.

"Why didn't you ride him yourself?" Eleal asked.

T'lin's green eyes registered horror. "Me? I'm much too heavy for escapades like that. Obviously Holy Tion had chosen a racing jockey for the task. To be honest," he admitted ruefully, "and you know I am always honest, Jewel of the Arts, I did not expect such success. I thought it was suicide."

Gim chuckled with delight.

"What if the temple guards had caught him, though?"

T'lin stroked his copper beard complacently. "Then I would have denounced him as a thief to get my dragon back."

Gim's jaw dropped.

A sour smile crossed his father's face. "You hadn't thought of that? You'd have been hanged!"

"But it worked," T'lin said in disgust. He fixed his cold green gaze on Eleal, and she started at his frown. "I came here to trade dragons and I have earned the enmity of the senior divinity of the city! I must leave quickly and never return." He gripped the arms of his chair with his big hands. "The priests and guards will be scouring the streets already. Well, you have her, Sculptor. I have done my part. I must go!"

For a moment Eleal toyed with the idea of staying in this cozy family kitchen forever—forsaking drama and travel . . . becoming one of this kindly family. . . . It did have a certain appeal in her present condition, but she knew that it was not going to happen.

"Not so fast," Kollwin growled, eyeing her. "Now we need to know why! Why did

Eltiana want this girl so badly? Why has Kirb'l Tion snatched her away? And what on earth are we supposed to do with her now she is here? Explain, Singer!"

"My part is done," T'lin repeated, but he settled back in his chair to listen.

Four sets of eyes were waiting, five counting the dragon's, although he was having trouble because he kept steaming up the window. Two sets of blue, two green, one black . . .

Eleal swallowed a yawn. She decided she must tell the tale with the majesty it deserved, although it needed Piol Poet to do it justice. She would have to stick to prose. She threw off the blankets and sat up like the Mother on the Rainbow Throne in *The Judgment of Apharos*.

"Are you feeling all right, dear?" Embiliina asked anxiously.

"Quite all right, thank you. Dost any of you mort . . . do any of you know what the *Filoby Testament* is?"

T'lin and Kollwin said, "Yes," as Gim shook his head.

"Book of prophecies," his father explained. "About eighty years ago some priestess over in Suss went out of her mind and began spouting prophecies. The others wrote them down. Her family had it printed up as memorial. What about it?"

T'lin uttered his dragon snort. Eleal knew she could never guess what he was thinking, and yet somehow she felt sure that he was surprised by this mention of the *Testament*. He seemed displeased, and certainly wary.

"Most prophecy is so thin you could drink it," he growled. "Quite a lot of the Filoby stuff turned out to be hard fact—so I've heard. What about it?"

"It is prophesied therein," Eleal declared mysteriously, "that should I happenstance attend the festival of Tion in Suss this year, then the world may be changed."

There was a thoughtful silence. The range crackled. Starlight's green eyes blinked at the window.

"Does she often behave like this?" Gim asked.

"No," T'lin said, staring hard. "She's putting on airs, but she's telling the truth as she knows it. Carry on, Avatar of Astina."

"The oracle proclaimed me a child of Ken'th."

"Yecch!" T'lin's red beard twisted in an expression of disgust.

"It's not my fault!" Eleal protested,

"No. Nor your mother's either. Can you confirm that, Kollwin Sculptor?"

"I was told that the oracle implied it. The Lady is always enraged when her lord philanders with mortals."

Embiliina said, "Oh dear!" and patted Eleal's hand. "It doesn't matter, dear."

Eleal recalled Ambria in *The Judgment of Apharos* again. "Peradventure, it may. Both the Lady and the Man decreed that I must not be allowed to fulfill the prophecy."

"Eltiana yes," T'lin said. "How do you know about Karzon?"

Eleal drew a deep breath.

"A reaper told me."

Gim sniggered. He looked at his father . . . at the dragon trader . . . at his mother. His eyes widened.

"Go on," T'lin said, his eyes cold marble.

Eleal told the story carefully, leaving out Dolm's name. She described him only as "a man I know."

It was a very satisfying performance. When she had finished, Embiliina seemed ready to weep, Gim's eyes were as big as Starlight's, and the two men were staring hard at each other. Dragontrader chewed at his copper mustache. Sculptor had clasped his great hands and was cracking knuckles.

"By the four moons!" T'lin growled. "Your god is the Joker!"

"He is," Kollwin said stubbornly, "but he is my god. We are supposed to get her to the festival, I think."

"That would be my interpretation."

Eleal protested. "I'm not sure I want—"

"You have no choice, girl!"

"Apparently not," the dragon trader agreed.

"Is it possible?"

T'lin did not answer that. He clawed at his beard with one hand, staring morosely at the range. "We seem to have been sucked into a serious squabble in the Pentatheon! I did not tell you of my first visitor—a doddering old crone trailing an unsheathed sword."

The others waited in silence. Embiliina moved her lips in prayer.

"A blue nun, of course," T'lin continued. "Of all the lunatic regiments of fanatics that harass honest workingmen . . . It was barely dawn and I had a hangover. I listened with a patience and politeness that will assuredly let my soul twinkle in the heavens for all Eternity. Then I sent her away!" He clenched a red-hairy fist. "I thought she was senile. I should have known better, I suppose."

Kollwin raised heavy black brows, pondering in his deliberate fashion. "She came *before* the oracle spoke?"

"Before the holy hag could have scampered down there from the temple, at any rate. She babbled about Eleal Singer being in trouble. I pretended I did not know who she was talking about. She smiled as if I was an idiot child, then tottered away, saying she would return. I told my men I would flatten every one of them if she ever got near me again."

"Who are these blue nuns?" Gim asked, worried.

"Followers of the goddess of repentance," said his father. "A strange order, rarely seen in these parts. Harmless pests."

T'lin shook his head. "But the stories . . . When Padsdon Dictator ruled in Lappin—him they called the Cruel—one day he was haranguing the citizens from a balcony and a sister in the crowd pointed her sword up at him and began calling on him to repent. Padsdon's guards could not reach her, and he either could not or would not depart. Before she had finished, he leaped from the balcony and died!"

Kollwin shrugged dismissively. "You believe that?"

"I do," T'lin said with a scowl. "My father was there."

In the ensuing silence, the range uttered a few thoughtful clicking sounds.

"So the Maiden is on Eleal's side—the Youth's side," Embiliina Sculptor said softly, blue eyes filled with concern now. "What of the Source? Have we any word of the All-Knowing?"

Her husband shook his head. "If the Light has judged, the others would not be still at odds."

"That is obvious!" Eleal declared. "Tragedies always end with the Parent deciding the issue. It's not time for Visek yet."

Gim grinned, but no one argued.

"You must take the girl to Sussland, T'lin Dragontrader," the sculptor said heavily.

The big man groaned. "Why me?"

"Who else? The priests will be scouring the city already. The Lady . . ." Kollwin shrugged, looking thoughtfully at his son. "It is possible?"

"Normally I would say it was," T'lin growled. "Normally I would say I could run over to Filoby and be back before dark. But Susswall is treacherous at the best of times. How will it be now, with the Lady of Snows enraged and bent to stop us? May colic rot my guts! And when I arrive I may find armies of reapers waiting for me!"

Eleal had already thought of that complication—how could she return to the troupe when Dolm was there?

Gim was wilting under his father's stare.

The sculptor cracked his knuckles again. "I shouldn't ask this. Don't answer if you don't want—"

Gim relaxed and smirked. "No I didn't."

"Didn't do what?" his mother demanded.

Kollwin laughed and clapped his son's knee. "When he took his vows last night . . . the night before last I suppose it is now . . . When he prayed to Tion, he was going to ask to go to the festival. Right, lad?"

Gim nodded wistfully, looking much more like a child than a romantic hero of damsel-rescuing prowess. "I thought about it, but you asked me not to. So I didn't."

Now approval shone in his father's smile. "I noticed you didn't actually promise! I was sure you wouldn't be able to resist the opportunity. I'm proud that you did. But the holy one knew how much you want to go. He has overruled us."

Gim's grin returned instantly. "You mean I get to go?"

"You have to go, son! You were the one who profaned the Lady's temple. Her priests will blunt their knives on your hide if they catch you. It is your reward, I suppose. You will do this for us, Dragontrader?"

"It won't take much more avalanche to bury three of us than two," T'lin agreed morosely.

Kollwin uttered a snort that would not have shamed the dragon trader. "Four! You think the blue sister has gone back to her nunnery?"

T'lin threw back his head and howled, but whether from rage or merriment Eleal could not tell. Starlight's answering belch rattled the casement.

"Oh that does it!" the big man said, heaving to his feet. "That'll waken half the city. That'll fetch every priest in the Lady's temple!"

Eleal stood up, but he frowned at her.

"I can't take you! Every lizard in the streets is going to be stopped and questioned. Can you dress this troublesome wench to look like a boy, Embiliina Sculptor?"

Gim's mother looked Eleal over and pursed her lips. "I think we have some old castoffs that will fit."

"Excellent!" T'lin turned a thoughtful gaze on Gim. "Never knew a city without a lovers' gate."

"I know a way over the wall, sir," the boy said.

T'lin nodded. "Have you a trade yet, stripling?"

Gim smiled nervously. "I am apprenticed to my uncle, Golthog Painter. I play the lyre, but . . ."

"As of now you're Gim Wrangler!" Dragontrader pulled a face. "Remember I hired you in Lappin last Neckday and I pay you one crescent a fortnight." He grinned. "But I may make it two. I don't usually pay that for greenies, understand, but you made a good start on impressing me tonight. Bring the girl down to my outfit as soon as she's ready. You'll impress me a lot more if you make it."

"Very generous of you, sir!" Gim straightened his shoulders. "The god will guard us."

"He'll have to." T'lin on his feet could not have dominated the kitchen more effectively had he been one of his dragons. He swung around to the sculptor. "What of you and your lovely wife? The priests will be after you also."

Husband and wife exchanged glances. "Us and our other fledglings?" Kollwin said. "What sort of a family picnic are you planning to conduct over Narshwall, T'lin Dragontrader?" He shook his head. "We have friends who will help us offer penance to assuage the Lady's wrath."

T'lin did not argue—he had scowled at the mention of children. "Probably cost you a whole new temple." He stooped to cup Eleal's chin in his raspy hand. He tilted her face up and frowned at her menacingly. "Most women wait until they have tits. You have set the world on its ears already, minx!"

Eleal had been thinking the same, but she knew Ambria would not tolerate such vulgarity. She assumed her most disapproving expression. "Wait 'till you see what I'm going to do in Suss, Dragontrader," she said.

# 32

A dogcart stood under the gaslights. The driver jumped down and came trotting up the steps. He wore a sporty suit and a bowler hat, but no overcoat. He was scowling under a bristly hedge of eyebrows. He had a clipped, military-style mustache, and a clipped, military-style bark: "You brought him!"

"Aye!" Mr. Oldcastle chortled. All Edward could see of him was the crown of his hat and his Astrakhan collar. "I bring thee a doughty cockerel for thy flock—truly a recruit of sinew."

"The devil you do! But I'm not at all sure I want him, don't you know?"

"Well, thou hast him now. Present thyself by whatever name thou deemest most fitting."

The man eyed Edward disapprovingly. "Name's Creighton. I knew your father." He began to offer a hand, then realized that both of Edward's were engaged. He was obviously an army man, very likely Army of India, for there was a faint lilt to his speech that such men sometimes picked up after years of commanding native troops.

"Pleased to meet you, sir," Edward said. Balanced precariously on one foot and his crutches, he was shaking so violently that he was frightened he might fall, and the thought was terrifying.

"By Jove!" Creighton said. "The man looks all in. Couldn't you have made things easier for him, sir?"

Mr. Oldcastle thumped the ferrule of his walking stick on the granite step with a sharp crack. "I have already expended resources I would fain husband!"

Creighton's reaction was surprising. As a class, Anglo-Indian officers were self-assured in the extreme, yet he recoiled from the little old civilian's testiness. "Of course, sir! I meant no criticism. You know we are extremely grateful for your assistance."

"I know it not, sirrah, when you presume so." Then came the familiar dry chuckle. "Besides, I let him demonstrate his mettle. He tests an admirable temper in the forge."

"I expect he does," Creighton said offhandedly. "But he cannot cross over with that leg."

"It shall be attended to, Colonel."

"Ah!" Creighton brightened. "Very generous of you, sir. Well, lean on me, lad. We'd best get you out of here, since you obviously can't go back."

Edward could tell he was not welcome, but that was hardly surprising. War or not, there was going to be a hue and cry after him very shortly. "I have no desire to cause trouble, sir."

"You already have. Not your fault. And my esteemed friend here has made a good point. I know spunk when I see it. Just what I would expect of your father's son. Come."

After that remark, Edward had no choice but to descend the steps and install himself in the dogcart without screaming even once.

Creighton took the reins, with Mr. Oldcastle sitting beside him. Edward sprawled along the backward-facing bench behind them. The pony's hooves clattered along the deserted road. Soon the gaslights of Greyfriars were left behind, and they were clopping along a country lane under a bright moon. He had been rescued from both the law and the knife-wielding woman, but he was now a fugitive from justice, utterly dependent on Mr. Oldcastle and this Colonel Creighton. He did not know who they were or what their interest in him was.

He was wearing a shift and a dressing gown, one shoe and a straw hat—hardly the sort of inconspicuous garb he would have chosen for a jailbreak, and certainly not enough for small hours travel in England, even in August. He shivered as the cool air dried his sweat. His leg throbbed maliciously with every bounce and lurch. He suspected it was swelling inside the bandages; he wondered what more damage he had done to the shattered bones. He felt utterly beat.

"Gentlemen?" he said after a while. "Can you tell me what's going on?"

Creighton snorted. "Not easily. Ask."

"I didn't kill Timothy Bodgley—did I?"

"No. The objective was to kill you. He got in the way, I presume. Damned shame, but lucky for you."

"Why, sir? Why should anyone want to kill me?"

"That I am not prepared to reveal at this time," Creighton said brusquely. "But the culprits are the same people who killed your parents."

After a moment, Edward said, "With all due respect, sir, that is not possible. The Nyagatha killers were all caught and hanged."

Creighton did not turn his head, concentrating on the dark road ahead. His rapid-fire speech was quite loud enough to be heard, though.

"I don't mean that bunch of blood-crazed nigs. They were dupes. I mean the ones who incited them to go berserk."

"The missionaries who threw down their idols? But they were the first—"

"The Chamber was behind that Nyagatha incident, and even then the purpose was to kill you."

"Me?" Edward said incredulously. "What chamber?"

"You. Or prevent you from being born, actually. There was a misunderstanding. It's a very long story and you couldn't possibly believe it if I told you now. Wait a while."

That ended the conversation. He was right—Edward could not even believe what he had already seen and heard. To be suspected of killing Bagpipe was bad enough. To be held responsible for his parents' death and the whole Nyagatha bloodbath would be infinitely worse.

And yet that cryptic Jumbo letter had hinted at unknown dangers and secrets his parents had not lived to tell him. Whoever Jumbo was, he had never received that letter.

Damnation! He had forgotten to bring the Jumbo letter! It was back at the hospital.

Obviously there was not going to be any logical, mundane explanation. Mr. Oldcastle had said that those behind this whole horrible mystery were involved in the outbreak of a worldwide war, and he had claimed that the ringlets woman had occult abilities to bypass locks—implying that she had both entered Fallow and exited Greyfriars Abbey through bolted doors. The little man himself had sent her away without any visible use or threat of force. One or the other of them had most certainly arranged for the patients and staff of the hospital to be smitten with inexplicable deafness, at the very least. Where had all the nurses gone? Had they met the same fate as Bagpipe? How had Mr. Oldcastle himself arrived in answer to Edward's Shakespearean summons?

None of it made real-world sense, nor ever would. You could not expect Sherlock Holmes if you already had Merlin.

The only brightness in the murky affair was the thought of Inspector Leatherdale's face when he learned of his suspect's disappearance.

A halt and sudden stillness jerked Edward out of a shivery daze. Creighton jumped down at the same moment. He went to open a gate and lead the pony through it. After it was shut again, he scrambled back to the bench and the dogcart went lurching slowly across a meadow, climbing gently. The sky was starting to brighten in the east, and the moon was just setting.

Edward was not sure how long they had been traveling—an hour, perhaps—and he had no idea where he was, but then his familiarity with the country around Fallow did not extend as far as Greyfriars. Lately Mr. Oldcastle had been giving directions, so Colonel Creighton did not know either.

He was stiff and cold. His leg throbbed abominably. But he was alive, and at the moment he was free. Both conditions might be transitory.

Beyond another gate the track was thickly overgrown, winding into the patch of woodland that crowned the little hill. The pony picked its way cautiously, brush crackled under the wheels, and overhead the sky was almost hidden by foliage. The air smelled heavily of wet leaves. After about ten minutes of that, the trail ended completely, ferns and high grass giving way to bracken and broom. No farmer's cattle grazed here. A faint predawn light was evident, but not enough to show colors, only shades of gray.

Creighton reined in. "We get out here, Exeter. I'll give you a hand down."

Getting out of the dogcart was even worse than getting in. The accursed leg felt ready to burst the bandages and the splints as well. The grass was cold and wet.

"Leave one crutch and lean on me," Creighton said. "Just a few steps. And leave your hat, too."

In that undergrowth, a few steps were plenty. Eventually Edward reeled and almost fell.

"Two more yards'll do it," Creighton said. "Other side of this stone. Good man. Now, you'd best sit down. No—on the grass. I expect it'll be chilly on your you-know-what, but this shouldn't take long."

Edward was already aware that the long grass was soaked with dew, and he did not see why he should not try to make himself comfortable on the wall instead, but he was hugely relieved just to sit, leaning back with his hands in the dewy leaves, his legs stretched out before him. He took a moment to catch his breath and then looked around. Creighton was kneeling at his side, bareheaded. It was highly unusual to see an Englishman out of doors without a hat.

"Where's Mr. Oldcastle?"

"He's around somewhere," Creighton said softly. "He can undoubtedly hear what you say. Any guesses as to what this place is?"

Puzzled, Edward took another look. The trees were mostly oaks, but very thickly grown together, mixed with a few high beeches. The stillness was absolute—not a bird, nothing. Eerie! He was tempted to start cracking jokes, and knew that was merely a sign of funk. Funk would also explain his teeth's strong desire to chatter, however much he might prefer to blame the cold.

The low wall at his side was not a wall at all, but a long boulder, mossy and buried in the undergrowth. Eventually he made out a tall shape within the bracken at the far side of the glade. Then another, and he realized that he was within a circle of standing stones. Scores of them dotted the countryside of southwestern England, relics of a long-forgotten past. Sometimes the stones were still upright, sometimes they had fallen or been pushed down by followers of newer gods. The great boulder beside him had been part of the circle.

Feeling very uneasy, he said, "It makes me think of The Oaks, Druids Close, Kent."

"You're on the right track. It's very old. And what we are about to do is very old, also—there's a price to pay. You're going to have to trust me in this."

Creighton had produced a large clasp knife. He unfastened his right cuff and pulled back his sleeve to uncover his wrist. He drew the blade across the back of it, holding it to the side, well clear of his pants. He stretched out his arm and let the blood dribble on the mossy boulder. In the gloom it seemed black.

He passed the knife to Edward.

It was exam time.

Edward wondered what Uncle Roland would say if he were present, and thought he could guess the exact words.

The cutting hurt more than he expected, like cold fire, and his first attempt was a craven scratch that hardly bled at all. He gritted his teeth and slashed harder. Blood poured out, and he adorned the stone with it—like a dog peeing on a post, he thought.

"Good man," Creighton muttered. He accepted the knife back, closed it one-handed, and dropped it in his pocket.

"Now what, sir?"

The reply was a whisper. "Wait until it stops dripping. Don't speak—and it may be best if you keep your eyes down and don't look too directly at, er, anything you may notice."

Edward himself could refrain from speech, but his teeth were going to chatter. His fingers and toes were icy. Even his leg seemed to have gone numb; it hardly throbbed at all now.

Something moved at the far side of the circle, a shadow in the undergrowth. He tried not to stare, but that was not easy. Whatever or whoever was moving might have been very hard to see clearly in any case.

The shape flitted from stone to stone, peering around this one, over that one, darting to and fro, pausing to study the visitors like a squirrel or a bird inspecting a tempting crust. A man? A boy, perhaps? He made no sound. He was a darkness in the shrubbery, as if shadow went with him, or was deeper where he was. He would grow brave and approach with a mincing, dancing step, then suddenly scamper back as if he had taken fright or had decided that the other way around the circle would be a safer approach.

Gradually Edward built a picture in his mind: no clothes, thin, terribly thin, and no larger than a child. His head seemed clouded with silver hair, but without taking a direct look, Edward could not decide if it was a juvenile ash-blond or white with age. He was too small and much too young to be Mr. Oldcastle, and yet there was something familiar about him—the way he held his head forward, perhaps? Or perhaps he was much too *old* to be Mr. Oldcastle. He was not an illusion.

He was not human, either, and the grove was silent as a grave.

Advance, retreat, advance . . . At last the numen was only ten or twelve feet away, behind the closest of the standing pillars. He peeked round one side, then the other. There was a pause. Then he repeated the process. Suddenly the decision was made. With a silent rush, he scampered through the undergrowth and took refuge on the far side of the fallen boulder, out of sight but more or less within reach.

Edward discovered that he was growing faint from holding his breath too long. *What* was now on the other side of this rock? Out of the corner of his eye he watched the streaks of blood, half-expecting them to disappear, but they didn't.

The voice when it came was very soft, like a single stirring of wind in the grass. "Take off the splints, Edward."

There was no doubt about the words, though, nor the meaning, and no Shakespearean mumbo jumbo either. Exam time. Finals.

Edward looked down at the white cocoon of bandage that extended from his toes to the top of his thigh. Then he looked at Creighton, who was staring back at him expectantly.

A cripple on the run could hardly be any worse off. Edward began to fumble with pins and bandages. In a moment, Creighton handed him the knife again. Then it went faster. No use wondering how he was going to wrap the whole thing up again.

He wasn't. He knew that. He ripped and tugged until his leg was uncovered—damned good leg, not a thing wrong with it.

Creighton doubled forward until his face was on his knees, and stayed there, arms outstretched.

*Oh, Uncle Roland, what do you say now?*

Edward pulled his legs in under him—no trace of stiffness, even—and adopted the same position, kneeling with head down and arms extended.

God or devil, it was only right to thank the numen for mercy received, wasn't it?

A few moments later, the pony jingled harness and began to munch grass. A bird chirruped, then others joined in, and soon the glade exploded into song. The sky was light, leaves rustled in a breeze that had not been there a minute before. The world had awakened from an ancient dream.

Creighton straightened up. Edward copied him. Then they scrambled to their feet, not looking at each other. There was no one else present, of course.

Edward closed the knife and offered it.

"Leave it," Creighton said gruffly. "And the bandages also." He strode over to turn the pony.

Feeling very thoughtful, Edward gathered up the bandages, the splints, the crutch. He laid them tidily alongside the bloodstains. He limped after Creighton in one shoe and one bare foot, but when he reached the dogcart, Creighton silently handed him the second crutch.

He hobbled all the way back to the circle again. The grass was trampled where he and Creighton had knelt. On the other side of the stone, where the numen had been, there was no sign that it had ever been disturbed. What else would you expect?

He stooped to lay his burden with the other offerings. Then he changed his mind and deliberately knelt down first. He bowed his head again and softly said, "Thank you, sir!"

He thought he heard a faint chuckle and an even softer voice saying, "Give my love to Ruat."

It was only the wind, of course.

# 33

When playing chilly Narsh, the troupe was forced to compromise on classical costuming. In her herald role, Eleal had worn long Joalian stockings under her tunic and still shivered; she had never experimented with real Narshian menswear. It was even more fiendishly uncomfortable than she had suspected—and difficult! In warmer lands the deception would not have been possible at all, for although she had not matured in the way T'lin had so crudely mentioned, she had progressed to the point where she would not be mistaken for a boy if she paraded around in just a loincloth. So there were advantages to the Narshland climate after all, but she would never have managed to dress without Embiliina's motherly assistance.

The breechclout was a band with a tuck-over flap. Then came well-darned wool socks and the diabolical fleece leggings, cross-gartered all the way up, the tops held by a web strap that looped around the back of her neck. How fortunate that she had little bosom yet to worry about! On top went a wool shirt for the mountains, so often washed that it was thick as felt, and a smock that reached halfway down her thighs; then boots. She pinned up her hair under a pointed hat that tickled her ears. She eyed herself disapprovingly in the looking glass. As she had been warned, the garments were all shabby castoffs. One of her leggings had a hole in the knee and the other was patched.

"How does it feel?" Embiliina Sculptor said, smiling.

"Drafty!"

"Mmm." Gim's mother chuckled mischievously. "Men seem to like the freedom. If you need to, er . . . well, pick a good thick bush to go behind, won't you, dear?"

Her smile was so inviting that for a moment Eleal wanted to throw herself into this so-kindly lady's arms. Her eyes prickled and she turned away quickly. She was no longer a mere waif supported by a troupe of actors and given odd jobs to make her feel useful. In some way she did not understand in the slightest she was important—a Personage of Historic Significance! She must behave appropriately. Perhaps in a hundred years poets like Piol would be writing great plays about her.

She headed for the bedroom door. Without her specially made boot, her walk was very awkward. Not just *Clip, clop,* but rather *Step, lurch* . . . "Fortunately," she said brightly, "my dramatic training has taught me how to portray boys."

"Er . . . yes. This way, dear."

Gim was waiting in the kitchen, bareheaded, but otherwise already wrapped in out-door wear. He had a lyre case slung on his shoulder. He smirked bravely when he saw Eleal, but the smirk faded quickly. His eyelids were pink, as if he was fighting back tears. It was all very well to trust a god, but she wished Tion had provided a more convincing, experienced champion to escort her.

His father looked even more worried, trying to act proud.

"Oh, dear!" Embiliina said. "Have you said good-bye to your sisters?"

"They're asleep, Mother!"

"Yes, but did you go in and see them so I can tell them you did?"

"Yes, Mother," Gim said with exaggerated patience. He turned to his father. "I don't suppose I can go and say good-bye to Inka, can I?"

Kollwin shook his head. "I don't think Dilthin Builder would be very happy to have you hammering on his door at this hour. Your mother will tell Inka in the morning and give her your love."

"And tell her I'll write?"

"And tell her that you'll write. Now you must hurry. The entire watch must be searching for Eleal Singer by now. The priests will have half the city roused. Keep your eyes open. Hurry, but don't be rash. And especially look out for pickets around the trader's camp—they must know she escaped on a dragon."

Gim's fair face seemed to turn even paler. "What'll I do then?"

"You're the hero, son. I think you leave the girl by the wall and go on alone to investigate—but you'll have to make your own judgment."

Gim nodded unhappily. "The guards may just arrest Dragontrader and seize his stock!"

"No. That'd need a hearing before the magistrates—but I suppose they may even drag them out of bed for something this big. Off with you, my boy, and trust in the god."

The ensuing farewells became openly tearful. Eleal turned her back and tried not to listen. She could not help but think that no one had ever said good-bye to her like that.

She had no baggage except a few odd clothes Embiliina had insisted on giving her, and they were easily tucked into the top of Gim's pack. He was already burdened with the lyre, but he made indignant noises when Eleal offered to carry either. He strode off along the dark, windy street, long legs going like swallows' wings. Suddenly he slowed down and peered at her.

"Why're you limping?"

"I'm not. It's just your imagination."

"Good!" Gim said, and speeded up again. He seemed to have forgotten that she was the heroine and he only her guardian, but she would never ask him to go more slowly, not ever! Soon she was panting in the heavy fleece coat that had been added to all her other ridiculous garments. She grew hot, except where the night wind reached. Perhaps men would be better behaved if they dressed more comfortably.

At the first corner Gim stopped and peered around cautiously. Then he strode off again into the wind.

"Who's Inka?" she asked.

"My girlfriend, of course."

"Pretty?"

"Gorgeous!"

"You love her?"

"Course!"

"Does she love you?"

"Very much! You scared?"

"Yes. You?"

"Horribly."

He was supposed to be a strong, comforting supporter! He had not studied his role very well. "You weren't scared on the dragon, were you?"

Gim turned into a narrow alley. "Yes I was—and Holy Tion had shown me that bit! He didn't show me this at all. Along here. Besides, all I had to do was shout *Choopoo!* and close my eyes and hang on. I'm a painter, not a hero!"

Of course he was brave! Of course he must be a hero if the god had chosen him. She decided Gim Sculptor's modesty was more admirable than Klip Trumpeter's pretenses.

"And I'm an actor, not a Historic Personage."

He chuckled. "I wouldn't believe you were either if the gods didn't keep saying so. What you need instead of me, Eleal Singer, is someone like Darthon Warrior."

"You came?" she exclaimed.

"Dad took me. Just the *Varilian*. Couldn't follow half of it. Wish you'd done a masque."

"So do I. I get to sing three songs in the masque."

He did not ask for details, so she prompted, "Was I a convincing herald?"

"You were all right," Gim conceded, "if heralds were ever girls."

Eleal did not say another word to him for quite some time.

He led her along narrow lanes, down smelly alleys, across cramped, sinister courtyards. Soon she was hopelessly lost, but he insisted this was a shortcut. She kept thinking of Kollwin Sculptor's warnings about the guard, but the streets seemed to hold no people, only windy darkness. Bats flittered overhead, and a couple of times she noted small eyes glinting in garbage-strewn corners.

Ysh shone bright blue in the east and that should be a good omen if the Maiden was supporting Tion's rescue efforts. But Eltiana dominated the sky, glaring red, and that was bad. There was no sign of Trumb, who must be due to eclipse one night soon. That was always a bad omen, and it would be especially scary now.

*When the green moon turns to black,*
*Then the reaper fills his sack.*

"What's a lovers' gate?" Eleal asked.

"A way over a city wall. You'll understand when you're older." Gim stopped at a dark archway.

"I understand now."

He hissed. "Sh! Watch your step in here."

"Here" was a black tunnel. He felt his way, leading her by the hand.

They emerged into a well enclosed by sheer walls stretching up to a tiny patch of sky where two bright stars were visible. There was no visible exit except the tunnel arch and one stout wooden door that looked very determinedly shut. The smell was nauseating.

"Made a mistake?" Eleal inquired in a whisper.

"Not if you can climb like my sisters. Hold this a moment. And be careful with it." He handed her his lyre case while he removed his pack. Then he showed her the handholds and footholds in the walls, leading up to a patch of not-quite-so-dark darkness. She had missed it because it was higher than even his head and a long way above hers.

"I'll pass the pack up," he said, taking his lyre back for safer keeping.

"What's on the other side?"

"Kitchen yard. Private house. Don't expect they're hanging out washing at this time of night."

"Can you fit through there?"

"Could last fortnight. Up with you."

Leggings did have some advantages over long skirts when it came to climbing. Eleal scrambled up, feeling the stones icy cold in her hands, but it was an easy climb, as he had said. The opening had once been a barred window, although which side had been "inside" and which "outside" she could not tell. Now it was a gap between two yards, only one bar remained, and there was room for a child or a slim adult to squeeze through—the sort of illegal shortcut every child in the city would know about and love to use. She wriggled her head and shoulders through and then stopped.

The yard was small, not large enough to hang very much washing, just house on one side and sheds on the other. No lights showed, but moonlight revealed that the way was definitely not clear. She looked back down at Gim, his face a barely visible blur.

"There's a small problem," she whispered.

Gim said, "What?" impatiently.

"A dragon."

"*What?*" He sounded as if he did not trust her to know a dragon from a woodpile. She was blocking the preferred route, but he stepped on his pack, leaped up with long arms and legs and a scrabbling of boots on stone, catching a grip on the bar and hauling himself up beside her, dangling by one hand and one elbow.

"I'm so sorry," Eleal said in his ear. "I see it's only a watchcat after all."

It was Starlight. He was crouched directly below her, and he knew she was there, for he was snuffling inquiringly. With his neck almost straight up, the soft glow of his eyes seemed close enough to touch. Any minute now he might decide to recognize her and issue an earsplitting belch of welcome. He would probably dislike having people drop packs and lyres and themselves on him.

Gim grunted. "Better take the long way round." He let go and dropped. He had forgotten his pack. The sounds of body parts thumping stone seemed to go on rather a long time.

Eleal clambered down cautiously. By then he had stopped using bad words and was sitting up, trying to rub his head and an elbow at the same time.

"You didn't dirty your coat, I hope?" she inquired solicitously.

"Shuddup!"

"Whose house is that?"

Gim clambered painfully to his feet, rubbing his hip. "Gaspak Ironmonger's."

"Do you suppose he has a private shrine, too? Do you think T'lin Dragontrader belongs to another mystery?"

"Probably. Most men do."

Interesting! She'd suspected that. "Not Tion's, though? Then whose?"

"Why do girls talk so much? Keep quiet." Gim hoisted his pack again, but he made no objection when Eleal slung the lyre strap over her shoulder.

They crept back to the tunnel. This time the way was easier, for Ysh's eerie beams shone in from the street entrance.

Now Eleal had a whole new problem to consider. T'lin had said he would give thanks to the gods in his own way. That suggested that he had gone to seek out the Narshian lodge of whatever god bore his particular allegiance.

Would he be giving thanks or seeking instructions? And what god would he favor? Obviously not Tion, or he would have prayed at Sculptor's shrine, nor Eltiana, or he would not have aided in Eleal's rescue. She could not imagine T'lin dedicating himself to the Maiden. Astina was the patron goddess of warriors, true, and athletes, oddly enough, but her attributes included justice and duty and purity. None of those sounded like T'lin Dragontrader's preference. Visek was the All-knowing, of course, but he was rather an aloof god, and not easily swayed, god of destiny and the eternal sun. T'lin ought to be more concerned with commerce and domesticated animals, and the gods for those were avatars of Karzon, the Man.

Who was also Zath, who had told his reaper not to let her reach Sussland alive.

Who was also Ken'th.

Daddy.

Gim grabbed Eleal's arm and pulled her back into a doorway.

She waited, but he did not explain what he had seen, or thought he had seen. Of course the guard would not necessarily parade around on dragonback with bands playing. It might be skulking in alleyways just as she and Gim were.

Gim did not move for some time. Shivering at his side, Eleal realized that T'lin might have more mundane concerns than gods. She had told him about the Thargians, and she had specifically mentioned the Narshian she had recognized in their company—Gaspak Ironmonger. The dragon trader had laughed then, and made a joke about farmers buying leopards to guard chickens.

Perhaps T'lin Dragontrader was a Thargian spy himself.

The lyre was becoming unpleasantly heavy on her shoulders when Gim reached his objective.

"We scramble up this trunk," he said, "along that branch, and across the roof to the wall. Think you can manage that?"

"No. You'll have to carry me."

"Stay here then." He reached for the first branch. "There's quite a drop on the other side, so don't break any ankles."

A couple of minutes later, they were outside the city. Neither of them had broken an ankle, although Eleal's hip was hurting now, missing her special boot. Gim yanked her back into shadow while he scanned the moonlit meadow. Light shone on a bend of Narshwater in the distance, and the mammoth steps stood like a monument to a forgotten battle. The pen was invisible. Although this was spring, the grass seemed covered with a shimmer of silver frost. Perhaps it was only dew. T'lin's camp was an isolated patch of darkness, from which the wind brought faint belching noises.

"See anyone?" Gim asked nervously.

"No."

"This is ridiculous! There's *gotta* be soldiers out there waiting for us! Dad said so. T'lin did too, more or less."

Eleal yawned. She knew she ought to be excited and keyed-up, and she very definitely did not want to be captured and dragged back to Mother Ylla, but . . . she yawned again. The night had gone on too long.

She understood what was worrying Gim, though. There were few dragons in Narsh and those mostly belonging to the watch. Ranchers owned dragons, but the guard would very soon have accounted for all the dragons in the city itself and learned that none of them had been involved in her escape. The next move would have been to investigate the trader's camp outside the wall. It was absolutely certain that there would be soldiers there still.

Furthermore, the camp was visible from the city gate, which was closed and guarded until dawn. Two people walking away from the wall would be as visible as a bear in a bed.

"Why're they making all that noise?" Gim muttered.

"Dragons always make that noise. If there were strangers around, they'd be making a lot more."

"Really?"

"Really," Eleal said with a confidence she did not feel at all. She yawned again.

"Come on, then!" Gim said. "It's trust the god or freeze to death!" He marched off across the meadow, leaning into the wind. Eleal followed by the light of the moons.

As they reached the huddle of sleeping dragons, a tall shape stepped forward to meet them.

"Name?" The voice was low, and not T'lin's.

"Gim, er, Wrangler and, ah—my cousin, Kollburt Painter."

"Goober Dragonherder. Follow me, Wrangler." He led them to a tent, dark and heavily scented by the leather it was made of. It thumped rhythmically in the wind, but the inside seemed almost warm after the meadow. "Sit," said the man.

There was a pause while he laced up the flap, and another while he flashed sparks from a flint. Eventually a very small lantern glowed dimly, showing a few packs and a rumpled bedroll, no furniture, three people kneeling on the blankets, and beyond them the dark walls and roof swallowed the light, so that there was nothing more in the world.

Goober was a thin-faced man with a dark beard, solemn as if he never smiled. Gold glinted faintly in the lobe of his left ear. He was garbed in the inevitable llama skin garments, plus a black turban. He pointed to it. "Can you tie one of these?"

"No," said the fugitives together.

He produced two strips of black cloth and wrapped their heads up. Then he made them practice. To Eleal's fury, Gim caught the knack much faster than she did. She was too sleepy.

"You'll do, Wrangler," Dragonherder said. "You keep trying, Small'un. You look like a boiled pudding. Don't uncover the lantern until you've laced up the door again. Wrangler, you come with me."

"To do what?"

"To learn how to saddle a dragon and stop asking questions. I'm told you know the commands."

By the look on Gim's face, he had already forgotten them, but he did not say so. The two departed. Left on her own, Eleal struggled with the infernal turban until it felt as if she had it right. Then she had nothing else left to do except wait.

She inspected the mysterious packs—not opening them, in case she was interrupted, but feeling them carefully. She decided they contained little else but spare clothes.

Sudden weariness fell on her like . . . like an avalanche. Why did she keep thinking about avalanches? She leaned back against a pack. There had been no guards around the dragons, so the god was still helping her, right? Right.

Goober Dragonherder had known she was coming, so T'lin had returned here from Kollwin Sculptor's and then gone back into the city again to visit Gaspak Ironmonger. Right?

That must be right, too, but it seemed very odd. What had that meeting been about, and what had T'lin learned that evening that had made it necessary?

# 34

Edward jumped down to open the first gate. He deliberately closed it from the wrong side so he could vault over it, dressing gown and all. He felt a whirling sense of wonder as he swung back up to the bench, agile as a child. Being a cripple had been a pretty stinky experience. The dogcart set off across the meadow.

"Is his name really Oldcastle, sir?"

Creighton shot him a frown, as if warning that they were not out of earshot yet.

"No it isn't. There is no Mr. Oldcastle. Oldcastle is a sort of committee, or a nom de plume. Our friend back there is . . . He's just that, a friend. He's been there a long, long time. I don't know his name. Probably nobody does anymore."

The dogcart rattled down the slope toward the next gate. In daylight the land was bright with goldenrod and purple thistles.

"Robin Goodfellow?"

"That was the name of the firm. He would have been the local representative."

No wonder his face had seemed *Puckish*. "Why blood? I thought a bowl of milk and a cake was his offering?"

Creighton's tone had not encouraged further questions, but he must appreciate a chap's normal curiosity when he had just received a miracle.

He cleared his throat with a *Hrrmph!* noise. "Depends what you're asking him to do, of course—or not to do, in his case. The value of a sacrifice is in what it costs. Blood's pretty high on the list." He stared ahead in silence for a while, then said, "He would have lost on the exchange, though. You heard him say he husbands his resources. The *mana* he used to cure your leg he has probably been hoarding for centuries, and he can't replace it now—I don't suppose he gets any worshipers at all these days. We wouldn't have given him much, even with the blood. He's one of the Old Ones, but he does not belong to any of the parties involved in this. My associates here were desperately shorthanded and asked him to help, as he lives in the neighborhood. He agreed, much to everyone's surprise. For that you should be very, very grateful."

Edward licked the cut on the back of his wrist. "I am, of course. Anything else I can do, sir?"

"Yes. As soon as you've opened this gate, you go behind the hedge and get dressed. You look like a bloody whirling dervish in that rig-out."

As he stripped, Edward discovered that his assorted scrapes and bruises had not been cured, only his leg. The flannel bags and blazer he wanted were badly crumpled, but he found a presentable shirt. His cuff links seemed to have disappeared altogether, his collars were all limp. He detested tying a tie without a looking glass, so he left that to be attended to on the road. In record time, he tossed his case into the dogcart and scrambled up beside Colonel Creighton, once more a presentable young gentleman.

Except that he had only one shoe.

As the pony ambled forward, he adjusted his boater at a debonair angle to cover the sticking plaster, and began fighting with his tie. Beautiful morning. Health and freedom! Breakfast now?

In the light of day, Creighton was revealed as a man of middle years, spare and trim and indelibly tanned by a tropic sun. His close-cropped mustache was ginger, his eyebrows were red-brown and thick as hedges. His nose was an arrogant ax blade. He was staring straight ahead as he drove the pony, with his face shadowed by the brim of his bowler. As he seemed in no hurry to make conversation, Edward remained silent also, content to wait and see what the day would offer to top the night's marvels.

Pony and cart clattered along the hedge-walled lanes, already growing warm. As they passed a farm gate, a dog barked. The damp patches on Creighton's trouser legs were drying. Somewhere a lie-abed cock was still crowing.

Suddenly the colonel cleared his throat and then spoke, addressing his remarks to the pony's back.

"You have seen a wonder, you have been granted a miracle cure. I trust that you will now be receptive to explanations that you might have rejected earlier?"

"I think I can believe anything after that, sir."

"*Hrrmph!*" Creighton shot him a glance, hazel eyes glinting under the hedge of red-brown eyebrow. "Did you *feel* anything unusual up there, by the way, even before our friend appeared?"

Edward hesitated, reluctant to admit to romantic fancies. "It did seem a 'spooky' sort of place."

Creighton did not scoff as a hard-bitten army man might be expected to. "Ever felt that sort of 'spookiness' before?"

"Yes, sir."

"For example?"

"Well, Tinkers' Wood, near the school. Or Winchester Cathedral on a school outing. I didn't tell anyone, though!"

"Wise of you, I'm sure. Probably several of your classmates would have felt the same and kept equally quiet about it, but there's really nothing to be ashamed of. Sensitivity's usually a sign of artistic talent of one sort or another. Celtic blood helps, for some reason. It doesn't matter either way. When you get to . . . Well, never mind that yet. There are certain places that are peculiarly suited to supernatural activities. We call them 'nodes.' They have what we call 'virtuality.' Some people can sense it, others can't. They seem to be distributed at random, some more marked than others, but here in England you'll almost always find evidence that they've been used, or are still being used, for worship of one kind or another—standing stones, old ruins, churches, graveyards."

"That was why Mr. Old . . . er, Mr. Goodfellow . . . why he didn't cure my leg in the hospital?" Edward had wondered why he had been made to endure that journey.

"Of course. It would have been much harder for him to do it there than at home in his grove, on his node. Perhaps even impossible for him nowadays."

Creighton turned out of one lane into another, apparently confident that he knew where he was heading. For a while he said no more. Edward began to consider his options. To go to any local enlistment center might be dangerous. Of course the police would be much more inclined to look for him in a nursing home than at a recruiting office, but near Greyfriars he might be recognized by someone. His best plan was probably to head up to town and join all the thousands enlisting at Great Scotland Yard.

Then the colonel began addressing the pony's arse again. "Officially I am Home on leave. Unofficially, I intended to observe the developments in Europe, do a bit of recruiting, and keep an eye on you."

Edward said, "Yes, sir," respectfully.

"Things went—*Hrrnph!*—a little askew. The European thing sort of ran away with us. You see, the nature of prophecy is that it usually comes in a frightful muddle, with most incidents undated. Nevertheless, it describes a single future, so it must relate to a unitary stream of events, right?"

"Er. I suppose so." What had prophecy to do with anything?

"Some foretellings you'd think you can do nothing about—storms or earthquakes. Others you obviously can. If a man is prophesied to die in battle and you poison him first at his dinner table, then you have invalidated the entire prophecy, you see? Prophecy is by nature a chain, so that breaking one link breaks the whole thing. If any one statement is clearly discredited, then the future described is no longer valid and none of the rest of the prophecy applies anymore. If the prophecy foretelling a man dying in battle also foretells a city being wrecked by an earthquake, then by poisoning the man, you can prevent the earthquake."

Edward muttered, "Good Lord!" and nothing more. He seemed to have stumbled into a mystical world that was definitely going to take some getting used to.

"It's all or nothing," Creighton said. "Like a balloon. Poke one hole in it and the entire thing fails. And you were mentioned in a prophecy."

"I see." The Jumbo letter had mentioned a chain! Why had Edward been such a fool as to leave it behind?

"About twenty years ago," Creighton continued, "someone tried to kill your father, Cameron Exeter. The attempt did not succeed, but an investigation revealed that he was mentioned in a certain well-substantiated prophecy, the *Vurogty Migafilo*. *Vurogty* is a formal, legal statement. *Miga* means a village, like the English *ham* or *by*, in the genitive case. So in English *Vurogty Migafilo* would be something like *Filoby Testament*. It has been around for many years, and many events foretold in it have already come to pass. Many more remain. You see that to be mentioned in such a document is virtually a death sentence?"

He paused, as if to let Edward make an intelligent comment, which seemed an unlikely possibility.

"Because anyone who does not like anything else in the prophecy will try to block its fulfillment?" That felt reasonably intelligent, considering the hour.

"Right on! Good man! In this case, the specific prophecy about your father was particularly unwelcome to the Chamber, and of course that increased his danger considerably."

The trap jingled and joggled along the lane. A thrush sang in the hedgerow. The dawn clouds glowed in decorous pinks. It was all very normal—no genies going by on magic carpets, no knights in armor tilting at dragons.

"What was that specific prophecy, sir?"

"It was foretold that he would sire a son."

"*Sir!*" This was starting to sound suspiciously like a leg-pull in very poor taste.

"Furthermore, the date was specified very clearly."

"June first, 1896, I presume?"

"No. Sometime in the next two weeks."

Edward said, "Oh." He studied the thick hedges passing by. Life had been much simpler a few days ago. "Well, that's impossible, so this *Testament* has now failed?"

*Hrrnph!* "No again. The date was a misinterpretation. The seeress may not have understood correctly herself, and she expressed herself poorly—the ordeal drove her insane and she died soon after. Prophecy requires an enormous amount of mana, which is why it's so rare. The person who had given her the talent miscalculated. He was utterly drained by her outburst. Almost died himself, or so it's said. That's beside the point. Anyway, the Service decided that your father had better go into hiding until the danger was past. And so he did."

"He left New Zealand?"

"He went back to New Zealand! Ultimately he went on to Africa. A year or so later he was blessed with a son, namely you." Creighton spoke in sharp, authoritative phrases, as if he were instructing recruits in the mysteries of the Gatling gun. If he had been, then at least one recruit would have been totally at sea.

Edward was tempted to ask if the prophecy had saved him from being a girl, but that would sound lippy.

Creighton was still talking. "The Service has rather mixed feelings about the *Filoby Testament,* but all in all we tend to favor the future it describes. So he fulfilled that element of the prophecy and stayed where he was, at Nyagatha, killing time until the—"

"*Killing time?* Sir, he was—"

"I know what he was!" Creighton barked. "I dropped in there in '02 and met you. Cute little fellow you were, lugging a leopard cub around under your arm everywhere. Nevertheless, take my word for it, as far as your father was concerned, Africa was merely an extended working holiday."

"A twenty-year holiday, sir?"

"Why not? Exeter, when I say that your father belonged to the Service, I am not referring to His Majesty's Colonial Office. The Service to which I belong and your father belonged is something else entirely, and probably a great deal more important."

Edward muttered "Yes, sir," wondering how to bring up the question of his father's true age.

Creighton did not give him the opportunity. "Now you understand why I waited until you saw your leg healed before I tried to tell you any of this."

"It will take a little time to adjust, sir."

Creighton might be crazy, but he seemed to know exactly where he was heading. The dogcart was entering a fair-sized village. A baker's wagon was making its rounds, but otherwise the streets were still deserted.

"Time is something we don't have," he said testily. "The opposition have tried three times to nobble you, Exeter. Five times, if you count the first attempt on your father and the Nyagatha massacre. They probably assumed they'd got you that time, by the way. That would explain why they left you alone for so long afterward. But this spring a certain building was buried by a landslide, and then everybody knew that the *Filoby Testament* was still operative. Your parents were definitely dead, so you must be alive. They set the hounds on you again. You can't expect your luck to hold indefinitely."

"How can they find me now, sir? If I can hide from the law, then I can hide from . . . Who exactly are the opposition? I mean, if someone's out to kill me, I'd like to know who."

Creighton directed the pony down a side road. He made his *Hrrnph!* noise. "Ultimately the people who are so eager to put your head over their fireplace are the group we refer to as the Chamber. It has no official name and its membership varies from time to time. This is a little hard to . . . Look at it this way. You know that His Majesty's Colonial Office doesn't operate in England. The Home Office doesn't operate overseas. But the two would cooperate if—oh, say a dangerous criminal wanted by one of them escaped into the other's territory. They'd pass the word. With me so far?"

"Yes, sir."

"Well the Chamber doesn't operate here—its members have no power at all in this, er, environment. The Service that I belong to doesn't operate here either, but we're allied with a sort of local branch that we usually refer to as Head Office, although the relationship is informal. We help each other out from time to time—in matters like this, in recruiting, and so on. They were the ones who got your father appointed D.O. at Nyagatha, of course, as a favor to us. He, in turn, did certain favors for them while he was there. The two organizations have similar aims and goals, so we cooperate with them and they with us, but you understand that here I am only a private citizen, with no authority."

*Hrrnph!* "Now, the opposition here is as variable and poorly defined as the Chamber—knock one down and two more spring up—but at the moment Head Office is tangled with a really hard bunch they're calling 'the Blighters.' It's a very apt description! Blighters here and Chamber there both oppose the aims that the Service and Head Office aspire to, so they're natural allies. It's the Blighters who killed your father and who are after your hide, as a favor to the Chamber."

Which was all very clear, Edward thought, but it had told him nothing except mean-ingless names. "Would you mind defining a couple of terms, sir? Where exactly do you mean by 'here'? If the Service you refer to is not the Colonial Office, then what is it? What sort of people make up the Chamber, and the Blighters?"

"That's a deuce of a lot of defining. As for what sort of people, well Mr. Goodfellow is one example, although he has always remained neutral until now."

This was definitely too much to swallow on an empty stomach. "Sir, are you telling me these groups are made up of *gods?*"

Creighton sighed. "No, they're not gods, not in the sense you mean. They may act like gods, and they do have supernatural powers. The one you met is a faint shadow of what he would have been in Saxon or Celtic times, and he cured your leg out of kindness, because he'd taken a fancy to you. Snap of the fingers, you might say."

"If he's not a god, then he's some sort of numen, or woodland spirit, or a demon, or—"

"He's a man, like us. Born of woman. He's a *stranger,* that's all."

"Well certainly! But—"

"And I won't define 'stranger' either. Not yet. He has a store of mana and I'm sure that a long time ago he was much more powerful than he is now. Yet he was probably always a pygmy in his class, whereas some of the Blighters are giants—look what they've achieved in the last month. This bloody war in Europe was provoked by them. Head Office have been struggling to prevent it for years. The Blighters outmaneuvered them. Now it's happened, utter disaster. But on that level the battle is over, and the big bad wallahs can sit back and savor their rewards. They can also turn their attention to other things. Like you."

Mr. Goodfellow had said very much the same thing about the war, Edward recalled, and whoever or whatever Mr. Goodfellow was, he was no ordinary mortal.

The dogcart had left the village and was bumping across a common on the far side, heading for some trees by the river.

"You see," Creighton added in a terse tone, as if he was tired of explaining things to a very thick child, "part of the trouble has been that both Head Office and the Blighters have been so occupied with political conniving these last few months, that they had no real assets to spare for peripheral matters such as doing favors for friends. That's why they just sent a crazy woman against you. They say she truly is crazy, by the way. She's a Balkan anarchist with a bad case of bloodlust. In other circumstances, they could have disposed of you without any trouble. On the other hand, had things been normal, Head Office could have defended you better."

"So it canceled out?"

"Perhaps it did. But now Head Office are in disarray. They have lost badly and will need time to lick their wounds. The Blighters are about to reap an enormous harvest of mana. This is definitely a good time to do a bunk!"

"But I don't have any choice—" Edward said, and then stopped in astonishment. The dogcart had rounded the trees and was almost into an encampment of Gypsies— half a dozen wagons and a couple of tents. Smoke trickled up from a central fire. Small children were running for cover and several dark-garbed men had turned to inspect the visitors. *Gypsies?*

"Any choice of what?" Creighton demanded, reining in the pony.

"I mean I'm going to enlist, of course. There's a war on!"

Creighton turned to him with an air of exasperation. "Yes," he said. "So there is. I've been trying to tell you."

# 35

"You should have turned out the lamp before you went to sleep," T'lin grumbled. "Waste of oil. Come on."

Rubbing her eyes, Eleal stumbled out of the tent behind the big man and hobbled after him as he strode in among the sleeping dragons. There was no sign of Gim or Goober. She was stiff and cold. She must have slept a couple of hours, because the sky was bright, and she could see the mountains. The stars had almost gone, but Ysh's tiny blue half disk and Eltiana's fiery point still shone. It was going to be a fine day.

"This is Lightning," T'lin said, stopping so suddenly Eleal almost bumped into him. The dragon twisted his long neck around to inspect her. She rubbed the big browridges automatically, and he snorted warm hay scent at her, perhaps approving of her size.

T'lin inspected the girths. "He's not as young as he used to be, but he's wise, and he won't even notice your weight." He lifted Eleal effortlessly to the saddle and began adjusting the stirrup leathers.

"Hill straps?" she said apprehensively. Lightning was large, making her feel very far from the ground already. She had never ridden except on the flat. Truth be told, her riding experience could be described as *extremely limited.*

"Just buckle them loose for now, so they don't flap. I'll tell you when to tighten them. There. Now let's see how far you can make him go. That way." He pointed west, upstream.

"That's not the way to Rilepass."

T'lin's big hand closed fiercely on her knee. His face in the twilight was hard as rock. "I know that, Little Missy. And understand one thing: You don't argue or talk back on this journey, all right? This isn't a joyride to amuse a usefully nosy little child anymore. This is serious, and I didn't ask for the job of rescuing you."

"I'm sorry."

"Good." He snorted. "Your business is costing me a lot of money. It may cost me my life, or even my soul. And when I say 'Do this!' you do it. Don't waste a moment. Clear?"

If he was trying to frighten her, he was succeeding. She had never heard him speak so sternly. "Yes, Dragontrader." She gripped the pommel plate with chilled fingers. "Lightning, *Wondo!*"

Lightning turned his head around again and stared at her with big eyes, their glow still just visible in the fast-brightening dawn.

"*Wondo!*" Eleal shouted.

Lightning lifted his head high and looked over the rest of the herd. Then he faced Eleal and yawned insolently, showing teeth as big as her hand.

"Shouting doesn't help," T'lin sighed. "Kick him."

Eleal kicked in her heels. "*Wondo! Zaib!*"

Uttering a muffled belch of disgust, Lightning lurched to his feet and Eleal found herself staring down at the top of T'lin Dragontrader's turban. The dragon strolled insolently forward, picking his way between his sleeping mates, but in a moment he began to curve around. He did not want to leave the herd.

With much kicking and directions of *Whilth!* and *Chaiz!* she directed him to the open meadow and tried *Varch!* He eased into a feeble pretence at a run, but in a moment he looked behind him and slowed down again. Then he began to curve to the left. Eleal drummed her heels on his scales and scolded. He straightened momentarily but soon started edging around to the right. In a few minutes she admitted defeat, afraid she was about to be taken ignominiously all the way back. "*Wosok!*" she said, and was relieved when her stubborn mount accepted the compromise. He lay down, still disgustingly close to the herd and facing toward it.

Another dragon had risen from the mass and was approaching at a slow run. It came willingly as far as Lightning, and then balked. Gim shouted angrily; Eleal was secretly pleased that he did no better than she had done. His mount settled on the grass, nose-to-nose with Lightning as if to compare notes on this disgraceful waste of valuable sleeping time.

"Stupid lizards!" Gim muttered. His pack and lyre were strapped alongside the baggage plate at his back. His face was pale and unweathered under the black turban, unconvincing as the face of a wrangler. "Why all this *wosok* and *varch* stuff anyway? Why not teach them to understand good, honest Joalian?"

Eleal restrained a snigger—what Gim Wrangler spoke was a long way from true Joalian. "Because common words like 'run' may differ between the dialects. The dragon commands are the same all over the Vales, and they're very old. So T'lin says," she added to forestall argument.

Gim grunted.

"You'll like Sussland," she said cheerfully. "It's much warmer and more fertile than Narshland."

"And the people riot all the time."

"Sussia's a democracy." She hoped that was the right word. "They meet every year to elect the magistrates."

"So do we. The adult men, anyway."

"But in Narsh the elections are a foregone conclusion. In Suss it's always a free-for-all. So T'lin says."

Gim mumbled something sadistic about the dragon trader, ending the conversation. The two of them sat in shivering silence, not even looking at each other.

The east was growing brilliant and color had returned to the world. Lightning was revealed as a nondescript dun, Gim's mount was a glacier white. Eleal realized that the city gate was clearly visible now, so she must be visible to the guards on the parapet. Eventually she could stand the quiet no longer. "He's not bringing the whole herd?"

"Evidently not." Gim twisted around in his saddle to see what was happening. Nothing was. "Maybe they're going to head off in the opposite direction after we leave," he added, sounding as if he'd just thought of that. "Lay a false trail."

Then a third dragon emerged from the herd and came racing toward them. It was dark-colored and soon recognizable as Starlight, but he seemed to have no rider. He slowed as he reached the watchers. Someone cried, *"Zomph!"* shrilly, and he continued on at a smooth run.

"Gods preserve me!" Gim said, kicking angrily. *"Wondo,* Beauty, you scaly horror! *Zomph!"*

Beauty and Lightning rose as one, taking off after the newcomer. The meadow rushed past so fast that the wind seemed to fade away. Dragons were a smooth ride.

*"Zomph!"* Gim yelled again, but Beauty and Lightning were already going flat out. Gradually Beauty fell behind, despite Gim's curses. Starlight was still pulling ahead, making a race of it.

Then he veered to avoid a clump of bushes and Eleal caught sight of a small figure cowering over in the saddle, almost hidden by a bulky pack strapped to the baggage plate. Garments streamed in the wind, stirrup leathers and hill straps were flapping free. The light flashed on a strip of steel, but she had already guessed that the rider must be Sister Ahn.

Apparently Gim had not realized that T'lin was missing. He could do nothing about it even if he did. Eleal twisted around and stared back at the dawn. Already the camp was invisible and the city was receding into the distance, with the spires of the temple dominating its skyline. Another dragon was coming in pursuit.

The old woman must certainly be crazy. She would be killed if she fell off. *"Zomph!"* Eleal yelled, kicking madly. Lightning could go no faster, though. He was breathing hard, while white steam poured from his nostrils. Starlight was younger.

The river had disappeared. The bizarre little caravan was racing along an obvious track now, with scattered cottages and dry stone walls. The hills of Narshslope marched alongside to the north, drawing no closer. The sun rose suddenly and in minutes the dragons were chasing their own long shadows over dry wheel ruts and scraggly grass.

So Eleal Singer had escaped from Narsh, if not yet from Narshvale. As far as she could remember, the western end was closed. Rilepass led north to Sussland and Fandorpass east to Lappinland. There were other passes to the south that she did not know, leading to Tholand and Randorland, but she recalled none to the west. Soon she thought she could see brightness in the distance, probably morning sun sparkling on the dew-wet thatch roofs of a village. That must be where this road went, and probably where it ended.

Then a largish stream blocked the way. The trail dipped to a ford and Starlight balked, because dragons disliked water. He wheeled around, apparently with no objection from his rider. Lightning made gasping sounds of approval, and slowed. The three dragons came together, uttering joyous roars, nuzzling each other in greeting.

Gim's jaw dropped when he saw the old woman crumpled in the saddle. He leaped down, shouting *"Wosok,* Starlight! *Wosok!"*

Eleal made Lightning crouch before she dared dismount, and then she went to help Gim. The old woman seemed unconscious, but her twisted hands still held a fierce grip on her staff and the pommel plate. Carefully avoiding the sharp-looking sword, the youngsters dragged her from the saddle and lowered her to the grass like a heap of washing.

She blinked up at them, her eyes watering. When she spoke, though, her creaky voice sounded amazingly calm. "The Maiden be with you, child. Introduce your friend."

"Gim Wrangler, Sister."

"He is not mentioned," Sister Ahn proclaimed, as if dismissing Gim from consideration. She struggled up to a sitting position and began tucking white strands of hair back under her wimple.

"He rescued me from the temple."

"The god rescued her!" Gim said.

Sister Ahn nodded. "Praise to the Youth. But the Maiden is worthy of thanks also. I did not injure the dragon with my sword, did I?"

Gim bent and inspected Starlight's flank. Starlight turned round and puffed grass-scented steam at him.

"A couple of faint scratches on his scales. Nothing serious."

"How did you make him leave the herd?" Eleal demanded.

"I gave him some nice hay and told him how beautiful he was. It is always best to pay in advance, whenever possible."

"The dragon trader didn't know, did he?" Eleal said.

Sister Ahn frowned at her, and then suddenly smiled. Probably her smile was well intentioned, but it seemed just as gruesome as it had two days ago, involving much crunching of wrinkles and a display of lonely yellow teeth. "Sometimes action must come before explanation," she explained wryly. "I always wanted to try a ride on a dragon!"

She took a firm grip on her staff and held out an arm. Gim helped her rise, studying her with rank disbelief.

"You've never done it before?"

"I implied that, did I not? Had I not overheard you, young man, I would not have known the correct command. Now, what place is that?" Apparently her watery eyes were not as useless as they seemed.

"Morby, sister. Just a little place."

"Never heard of it." Her tone implied that it was therefore of no consequence.

"It has a wonderful bakery," Gim said wistfully.

The fourth dragon arrived in a scramble of claws, being greeted by belches from the others. T'lin Dragontrader seemed to hit the ground running before it had even stopped. His face was flushed with fury and he towered over the nun.

Sister Ahn attempted to straighten, but the move merely emphasized her hump. Her long nose was about level with the middle of his chest.

"You *stole* my dragon!" His fists were clenched.

"Borrowed it, merely. Time was short and you would have argued."

"By the moons, I would have argued! And now I suppose you expect to accompany us to Sussland?"

He was speaking much louder than usual. The dragons were all watching curiously. Eleal caught Gim's eye. He did not seem to know whether to be amused or concerned. Neither did she.

"Accompany you? I don't know anything about you," the old woman proclaimed. "You are not mentioned. It is written, *Before the festival, Eleal will come into Sussvale with the Daughter of Irepit.* This is Thighday. The festival begins tonight, does it not? You don't expect to negate holy prophecy when the goddess Ois failed, do you?"

T'lin shook his fists futilely and then grabbed his beard with both hands as if to keep them from doing violence to the maddening old woman. Starlight was Dragontrader's personal mount. They had been together as long as Eleal could remember. She had never seen rage portrayed so clearly, not even when Trong Impresario played Kaputeez in *The Vengeance of Hiloma.*

"Is that so? Really so? As I understand your discipline, sisters of the sword always offer value in return for service."

Sister Ahn nodded complacently. "Always."

"Today the price for passage to Sussland is one million stars, payable in advance!" T'lin pushed his bristling red beard almost into her face. "Well?"

She raised hairless brows. "Or something greater?"

"Greater? Name it!"

"Your life, my son. Without me you would presently be chained in the city cells."

T'lin made a choking noise.

"Why do you think the guard did not come after you?" she asked pityingly. "Do you believe they are all so stupid, or that the priests of Our Lady are?"

T'lin wavered. "What did you do?"

"I told them I had seen a black dragon with two people aboard climbing over the wall and heading in the direction of Nimpass. A mounted patrol left immediately and all the rest went back to—"

"You *lied?*"

"Certainly *not!*" Again Sister Ahn tried to look down her long nose at him, but he was still much too tall. "I was vouchsafed a vision of this, in a dream. It was very clear."

T'lin Dragontrader moaned and covered his face with his hands. Eleal bit her lip to restrain a snigger. There was silence, until Gim said hesitantly, "It was odd that the guard did not come after us, sir."

"Not odd at all!" the nun sniffed. "I gave them my oath that I had seen what I said. Sisters of my order are impeccable witnesses. Courts have accepted the sworn word of a Daughter over the testimony of phalanxes of magistrates. You owe me your life, Dragontrader. Or if not, at the very least they would have impounded all your worldly goods. I have paid fairly."

# 36

Creighton seemed to have an infinite capacity to astonish. First he had produced ancient woodland gods out of pagan legend, and now Gypsies. Gypsies were thieves, poachers, charlatan fortune-tellers, and altogether not the sort of people whose company any self-respecting gentleman would cultivate. Nor was this encounter a sudden impulse, for he had obviously been recognized. A man was approaching. There was no smile of welcome on his face, but he was not scowling either.

"Get your bag," Creighton said, "and then wait here." He jumped down.

Edward followed and retrieved his suitcase. Without a word, the Gypsy took charge of the dogcart and pony. He was nattily dressed, although his clothes had more elaborate pleats and stitching than those of any ordinary Englishman. His waistcoat was too fancy, his hat brim too wide, and he had a colorful kerchief around his neck. He returned Edward's smile with a sullen glance and led the pony away. Only now did Edward register that the dogcart was an outlandishly gaudy affair of shiny brass fittings and bright-hued paints. So were three or four of the wagons, in varying degrees. Others were plainer, scruffy by comparison.

Creighton was already in conversation with an elderly woman sitting by the fire. She was so muffled up in bright-colored clothes that she resembled nothing more than a heap of rainbows. She said something, nodding, then looked up to stare across at Edward. Even at that distance he sensed the piercing dark eyes of the true Gypsy. He tried not to squirm.

Waving to him to follow, Creighton headed for one of the gaudiest of the wagons. When Edward arrived, he was regarding it with distaste.

"I don't suppose the police can put the bite on you in here, old man," he said, "but I can't answer for fleas." With that, he trotted up the ladder. Edward followed. By the time he was inside, Creighton had stripped off his hat and jacket.

There was barely room for the two of them to stand between the chairs and table and stove and shelves and various bundles and boxes. The air was heavy with an unfamiliar scent, and everywhere there was color—reds and greens and blues rioting on walls, furniture, garments, and bedding. The ceiling had not been designed for a six-footer. At the far end were two bunks, one above the other. From the assortment of clothes littered everywhere, this was home to a large family, and the lower bunk had pillows at both ends. In the middle of it lay a notably new and clean pigskin suitcase. Edward assumed it had been stolen, but when Creighton had stripped to his undervest, he began stowing his shirt and waistcoat in it.

"Close the door, man! They said we could help ourselves to anything we find. I don't suppose there's much here that will fit you. Have to do the best you can."

Edward began to undress. "Sir, you said the guv'nor was killing time in Africa. My uncle Roland accused him of engaging in devil worship because—"

"Terminology depends on whose side you're on. One man's god is another man's devil. I'll explain about your father later." Creighton was rummaging through heaps of garments.

"And where does Christianity fit into this?"

"Anywhere you want. Good King George and his cousin the Kaiser worship the same god, don't they?" Creighton held up a pair of pleated black trousers and frowned at them. "Britain and Germany pray to the same god. So do the French and the Russians and the Austrians. They all trust him to grant victory to the righteous, meaning them-selves. Here—these look like the longest." He handed them over. Then he selected a pink- and-blue shirt and wrinkled his nose.

"Something wrong, sir?" Edward inquired, discovering that the pants did not reach his ankles.

*Hrrmph!* "Just wondering about, you know, cleanliness."

"I don't think you need worry. They will. You must be paying them handsomely? Or Head Office must be?"

Creighton shot him a glare that would have softened horseshoes. "Just what're you implying?"

"Well, anything that's been worn by a *gorgio* will be *mokadi,* and will be burned as soon as we leave."

"What?"

*"Mokadi*—ritually unclean. In fact I suspect they'll burn the whole wagon."

"Burn the? . . ." The hazel eyes scowled out from under hedges of eyebrow in the sort of glare Edward had not faced since he was one of the crazy imps of the Fourth Form. "What the devil do you know about Gypsies?"

"They quite often camp at Tinkers' Wood, sir, near the school," Edward said blandly. "A family named Fletcher." He reached for a rainbow-embroidered shirt.

"Out of bounds, I hope?"

"Er, yes, sir."

"They're swindlers and horse thieves!"

"Oh, of course!" Fascinating people—even as a prefect, Edward had sneaked out at night to visit them. "They'll steal and lie and cheat any *gorgio* who comes within miles.

That's just their way. But isn't it also true, sir, that they've been known for centuries as the finest spies in Europe?"

A reluctant smile twitched the corner of Creighton's mouth. "I daresay."

"The true Rom are about the most fastidious people in the world." Edward was enjoying this. "They make high-caste Brahmins look like slobs."

*Hrrnph!* "I suppose their fleas are frightfully *pukka,* too?"

"I doubt if they're as fussy, sir."

Creighton laughed approvingly, and proceeded to dress. Edward wondered if he'd just been tested in some way. . . .

"You feel spooky at all?"

"No, sir. Should I?"

"This is a node, I think."

"It is?"

"Well, of course here I'm no more certain than you are. I can always detect virtuality on Nextdoor, but here's trickier. The Rom prefer nodes for campsites, for obvious reasons. The headman's name is Boswell, by the way, but the real power is his mother. You look awfully sweet in that shirt. Old Mrs. Boswell's a *chovihani*—a witch, and a good one. Be respectful."

"Oh gosh, sir! I grant you I saw a miracle this morning. I met Puck himself, an Old One. I know I would not have believed this yesterday and it was the experience of a lifetime—but please! Do I have to believe in Gypsy witches now?"

Creighton flashed him another menacing, hazel glance. "Caesar, Alexander, Napoleon, Bismarck, Jenghis Khan. . . . You ever study any of those men in your fancy school, Exeter?"

"Some of them."

"They all had a lot of what's called *charisma.* Know what I mean by that?"

"Er, leadership?"

"More than that, much more. It's a faculty to absorb their followers' admiration and focus it. A charismatic leader can persuade men to believe what he tells them to believe, to die for his smile, to follow him anywhere he goes; the more he demands of them, the more they are willing to give. He grows by their loyalty and induces more loyalty because of it. Generals, politicians, prophets—sometimes actors have charisma."

Creighton paused in his dressing, and sighed. "I once saw Irving play Hamlet! Incredible! Half the audience was weeping, and I don't just mean the ladies. You must believe in faith healing? Well, in extreme cases, a charismatic leader can literally inspire miracles. And a *chovihani* has charisma. You'll see."

Hunger and lack of sleep had made Edward short-tempered. Argument burst out of him before he could stop it. "Come, sir! Charisma is one thing. Magic's something else!"

"Is it? Sometimes it's hard to tell where one ends and the other begins. So you plan to enlist, do you?"

Thrown off-balance, Edward said, "Of course!" His country was at war—what else could he do? Let the beastly Prussians take over Europe? If they won, they'd attack the British Empire right afterwards anyway. They had to be stopped now.

Creighton sighed, and bent to scrabble through a pile of socks. "Well, I suppose I might have felt the same at your age. Do you know Germany has invaded Belgium? The British and French are going to try and stop them, and sheer hell is going to stalk the plains of Flanders. The oracular reports are terrifying. The last few days have darkened the entire century. But I suppose at your age you feel immortal."

"It is my duty!"

The colonel straightened up and scowled. "I think you have a greater duty, although you don't know it yet. I think I have a duty to your father to save his only son from being hanged for a crime he did not commit. But I'll make a bargain with you. My friends and I saved you from an assassin. We've rescued you from a murder charge that would undoubtedly have sent you to the gallows. We've cured your leg. I think you owe us a little something, don't you?"

Put like that, the question had only one answer.

"I owe you a lot, sir, a devil of a lot."

"Too bloody Irish you do! I'm calling in my debt, Exeter. Pay now."

"Pay what?" Edward asked grumpily.

"Parole. I want you to—I demand that you—put yourself under my orders. You will obey without question!"

"For how long?"

"One day. Until dawn tomorrow."

"That's all? Then we're quits?"

"That's all."

"You're asking for a blank check!"

"How much did you have in your account last night?"

Creighton was not without charisma himself. Edward could not meet those eyes glittering under the hedgerow brows.

"Thruppence! Very well, sir, I agree."

"Right. Word of honor, of course?"

*Strewth!* What did the cocky little bastard expect? Edward stared cold fury at him and said, "I beg your pardon?"

Creighton nodded placidly. "Good. Then make yourself respectable and come on out. Rabbit stew for breakfast, I expect. Or pheasant, if we're lucky." He pushed rudely past Edward and headed for the door.

"Sir? What did you mean—"

"Without question!" Creighton snapped, and disappeared down the steps.

There was indeed stew for breakfast, and it might have contained rabbit. It certainly contained many other things, and it tasted delicious to a hungry man. Edward tried not to think about hedgehogs and succeeded so well that he emptied his tin plate in record time.

He sat on the ground in an irregular circle of Gypsies, mostly men. Women flitted around in attendance, never walking in front of a man. The women's garb was brighter, but even the men seemed dressed more for a barn dance than for country labor. There were about a score of adults in the band, and at least as many children, most of whom were hiding behind their elders and peering out warily at the strangers. The campsite was an untidy clutter of wagons and tents and basket chairs in various stages of assembly. Heaps of pots and clothespins indicated other trades. A dozen or so horses grazed nearby, and the skulking dogs seemed to belong.

Creighton sat at the far side, deep in conversation with the ancient *chovihani*. Edward could hear nothing of what was being said, although there seemed to be some hard bargaining in progress. The few words he overheard near him were in Romany. He could not but wonder what the masters at Fallow would say if they could see him now in his grotesque garb. His wrists and ankles stuck out six inches in all directions. He was barefoot because he had been unable to find any shoes to fit him. The only part of his apparel not too small for him was his hat, and that kept falling over his eyes.

A slender hand reached down to his plate. "More?" asked a soft voice.

"Yes, please! It's very good."

He watched as she carried the plate over to the communal pot and heaped it again with a ladle. Her dress made him think of Spanish dancers, and she was very pretty, with her head bound in a bright-colored scarf and her dangling earrings flashing in the sun. Her ankles . . . Some ancient instinct caused him to glance around then. He saw that he was the object of suspicious glowers from at least half a dozen of the younger men. Good Lord! Did they think? . . . Well, maybe they were right. Not that he had been considering anything dishonorable, but he had certainly been admiring, and that was forbidden to a *gorgio*. Nevertheless, he smiled at her when she gave him back the plate. She smiled back shyly.

Eating at a nomad's campfire, he could not help feeling he was slumming, yet he knew that these were a proud people, and to them he was probably as out of place as a naked Hottentot at a dons' high table in Oxford. There was a lesson there and he ought to be learning from it. The guv'nor would have been able to put it into words.

The second helping he ate more slowly, feeling sleepiness creeping over him—he hadn't really slept at all in the night. There were so many things to think about! Could he trust Creighton, in spite of what the man had done for him? He was certainly being evasive. He claimed to have visited the guv'nor at Nyagatha, and he had known about Spots. He had pointedly avoided saying where he had come from, except for cryptic references to somewhere called "Nextdoor." He had contrasted it with "Here," without stipulating whether "Here" meant England or all Europe. The Service he talked about— what government did it serve? Some semiautonomous Indian potentate? The Ottoman Empire? China? China was in disarray, wasn't it?

Everywhere was in disarray now, and yet Creighton had never once hinted at the possibility of the war interfering with whatever his precious Service served. And what could the Chamber be? He had certainly implied that it was in some sense supernatural; if it was, then the Service must be also.

So what on Earth did that make *Nextdoor?*

Replete, Edward returned his plate to the owner of the ankles and wiped his mouth on the back of his hand. He wanted a wash and a shave, but sleep would do for starters.

Creighton called his name and beckoned.

He walked around the fire, being careful not to step on anything sharp. Creighton was paying court to the old woman. Perhaps she really was a *phuri dai,* a wisewoman, but Edward knew enough about Gypsies to know that their leaders were invariably male. Furthermore, the man beside her was sitting on a wooden chair, while everyone else was on the ground. That made him unusually important. Edward went to the man.

Boswell was probably in his sixties, thick and prosperous looking, with a patriarchal silver mustache. His face was the face of a successful horse trader, unreadable.

Edward doffed his hat respectfully and said, *"Latcho dives."*

The man's mustache twitched in a smile. *"Latcho dives!* You speak *romani?"*

"Not much more than that, sir."

Still, Edward had scored a point. Boswell said something very fast in Romany—probably addressed to his mother, although he was watching Edward to see if he understood, which he did not.

Edward bowed and squatted down before her, alongside Creighton. She looked him over with the most extraordinary eyes he had ever seen. Her gaze seemed to go right through him and out the other side and back again. He barely noticed anything else about her, except that she was obviously very old. Only her lustrous Gypsy eyes.

"Give me your hand," she said. "No, the left one."

He held out his hand. She clutched it in gnarled fingers and pulled it close to her face to study. He was able to glance away, then. He raised a quizzical eyebrow at Creighton, who frowned. Then the old woman sighed and closed his fingers into a fist. Here it came, he thought—you will go on a long journey, you will lose a close friend, your dearest love will be true to you although you may be troubled by doubts, *et* blooming *cetera.* She was going to be disappointed when she told him to cross her palm with silver.

She was looking at him again, darn it!

"You 'ave been unjustly blamed for a terrible crime." Her voice amused him. It was straight off the back streets of London, almost Cockney.

"That is true!" He tore his eyes away and reproachfully glanced at Creighton.

"I told Mrs. Boswell nothing about you, Exeter."

Oh, really? Edward would have bet a five-bob note—if he had one—that Creighton had told the old crone a lot more than he thought he had.

"You will go on a long journey," she said.

Well, Belgium was a good guess, and quite a long journey.

"You will have to make a very hard choice."

That could mean anything—pie or sausage for supper, for instance. "Can you be more specific, ma'am?"

Creighton and Boswell were listening and watching intently. So was everyone else within earshot.

Mrs. Boswell twisted her incredibly wrinkled face angrily, as if recognizing Edward's disbelief. Or perhaps she was in pain. "You must choose between honor and friendship," she said hoarsely. "You must desert a friend to whom you owe your life, or betray everything you hold sacred."

Edward winced. That sounded *too* specific!

"If you make the right choice, you will live, but then you will have to choose between honor and duty."

"I beg your pardon, ma'am. How can honor and duty ever come in conflict?"

She turned her head away suddenly in dismissal, and he thought she would not answer, but then she added: "Only by dishonor will you find honor."

*Bunk!* Edward thought, more nettled than he wanted to admit, even to himself. "Honor or friendship, then honor or duty . . . Do I get a third wish?"

She did not reply for a long moment. Just when he had concluded that she would not, she whispered, "Yes. Honor or your life." Then she waved him away without looking around.

Soon the Gypsy caravan was ambling along the lanes of summer England, heading Edward knew not where. Creighton, having snared his victim with an oath of obedience, now refused to answer questions, or even hear them. Time for forty winks, he said.

"How are you at dancing?" he inquired brusquely while they were undressing.

Edward admitted he could probably manage a slow waltz.

"And how are your teeth? Any fillings?"

"Two."

"Pity." Creighton stretched out on the lower bunk in his underwear.

"Are those necessary qualifications in recruits to the Service?" Edward clambered into the upper berth, banging his head in the process. Even with the windows open, the wagon was stuffily hot.

"Very much so," said a smug voice from below him. "A knack for languages helps. How many can you speak?"

"Usual school set: French, Latin, Greek. A bit of German."

"You took the medal in German. How about African?"

"Bantu."

"Which Bantu?"

"Embu, of course, and Kikuyu. A smattering of Meru and Swahili." That sounded like bragging, so he added, "Once you've got a couple of them, the others come easily. Anyone can read Italian or Spanish if he knows French and Latin."

Creighton chuckled at something. "A faculty for language helps, but you're far too young. If it wasn't for the *Filoby Testament,* I'd throw you back. I was looking for men in their fifties or sixties. Women even better. Didn't find any."

In five minutes the man was snoring.

# 37

Dragons had a notorious dislike of water, but when Dragontrader had coaxed Starlight to cross Narshwater, the others had followed. He had relegated Sister Ahn to the fourth mount, named Blaze, and insisted that her sword be bound to its pack. There had been another fight over that, but she had yielded when he pointed out that the hilt would still be within her reach.

"What pass is this?" Eleal asked wonderingly as the procession raced northward over the grassy hills of Narshslope.

"No pass," he growled. He was still mad. "Dragons don't need passes. Your hill straps all right?"

She nodded. In fact the belt was uncomfortably tight, but having seen Starlight scramble down a temple wall, she had a strong suspicion she was going to need it.

The sun was climbing higher, shedding real heat. Soon a valley enclosed them, providing shelter from the wind, and she began to feel warm—a rare sensation in Narshvale. A few hours' sleep would be nice, and she remembered Gim's remark about the bread shop in Morby with regret, but obviously the fugitives must hurry on their way. The Narsh guard would discover Sister Ahn's deception soon enough.

Dragons in motion spread out and she had no one to talk with. The saddle had begun to chafe already. Yesterday at this time she had just begun plucking chickens— she cocked a mental snoot at the temple. *Pluck your own fowls, Mother Ylla!* The day before, the oracle had spoken, and the day before that she had unmasked Dolm. On Ankleday she had been an aspiring actor looking forward to a ride on a mammoth. Life had been very simple back then.

For half an hour or so the fugitives raced up a brush-filled valley, climbing steeply alongside rapids and waterfalls. Trees were rare in Narshvale, and no other obstacle was a hindrance to dragons. Eventually the valley curved off T'lin Dragontrader's preferred path; he put Starlight at the slope. At the top, he called a halt to let the mounts catch their breath, and they automatically closed up near one another.

Eleal was astonished how high they were already—perched on a windy, grassy ridge with all of Narshland spread out before them, cupped within the icy peaks of Narshwall and dappled by shadows of clouds. Even in summer it was more tawny than green; hard country good only for grazing. Here and there she saw the scars of mines. Gim was staring at it all openmouthed.

"Never seen it like this before?" she asked.

He shook his turbaned head. "I'm not like you. I've never been anywhere! Well, I've been everywhere down there." He waved at the valley. "We go on picnics sometimes, Mom and Dad and the girls and me. Thunder Falls, up there. Daisy Meadow over there. You know, you can walk across the whole land and back in a day, if you own some good boots. You can walk from one end to the other in two days—Dad did, once."

Eleal would not want to try that, but a strong man probably could. "There are smaller vales," she said helpfully. "And some larger. In Joalvale there are places there where you can hardly see mountains at all!"

Gim looked suitably impressed. "Sussland is much bigger, isn't it?"

"It's broader," she said. "Not much longer, maybe. Lower, hotter."

"Tell me about the festival," Gim said, but mention of their destination had reminded Eleal that she had prophecies to fulfill.

Sister Ahn was sitting as erect as she could on Blaze, one gnarled hand behind her, clutching her precious sword. Her haggard face seemed relatively content and unthreatening. Before Eleal could question her, though, T'lin Dragontrader intervened.

"Sister, I don't suppose your prophecies tell you which is the best way through this?" He waved irritably at the jagged rock and ice filling the northward sky—gray and white, with hardly a speck of green in view anywhere.

"No."

"Or whether Ois will contest our passage?"

"She may." The nun sniffed. "She wishes to stop Eleal and myself, but you and the boy may die also. I cannot say."

T'lin uttered his inevitable snort. "Religion is such a comfort in times of need!"

"Holy Tion will shield us," Gim said devoutly. "We are pilgrims to his festival."

"Indeed?" For the first time, Ahn showed some interest in him. "You plan to play your lyre for the god?"

"I'll enter if Dragontrader will permit me to."

T'lin snorted again. "Think you can win a rose, do you?"

"Oh, no!" Gim looked down at his boots and mumbled, "I'd be honored just to try."

The red beard parted in a toothy smile. "You might win the gold one."

The idea had occurred to Eleal a moment before T'lin spoke. Gim turned his face away quickly and said nothing.

The dragon trader shrugged, apparently regretting his ridicule. "Oh, never mind. I think we'll try for that gap there. Looks like a good place to be eaten by snow tigers."

Eleal saw her chance. "Sister, will you tell me now what is going to happen in Sussland?"

The old woman frowned, and then nodded. "Certainly! In fact I should probably give you some instructions as soon as possible, because the holy testament does not specify exactly which day the wonderful event will occur."

"Instructions?"

"Yes. There may not be time after we arrive, you see? Unless you are already experienced, of course."

"Experienced in what?"

At that moment T'lin shouted, *"Zomph!"* and Eleal was thrown back against the baggage plate as the dragons flashed into high speed. Whatever Sister Ahn said was lost in the wind.

The ridge curved as the valley had done; T'lin led his troupe down a steep slope and straight up the other side. Dragons were in their element in mountain terrain. Roaring with excitement, they raced one another up hills and slid down long scree slopes in showers of gravel. Eleal understood then why they stayed so far apart, and she also realized this crossing might take much less time than the plodding mammoths needed for their long trek over Rilepass. Soon the air grew cold, although the wind was not as fierce as she would have expected. Even grass became rare and gray stone stretched out everywhere.

Starlight was chief dragon, but he labored under T'lin's substantial weight. With his much lighter burden, Lightning took to challenging him for the lead position, and then the pace became fierce indeed. As T'lin had said, the old dun was wily, with a good eye for the easiest routes. The two females, Blaze and Beauty, scorned to play such foolish games and were soon left far behind.

Eventually they vanished altogether, and T'lin called a halt. Eleal rode up beside him. Starlight and Lightning belched weakly at each other, puffing clouds of steam into the wind. The dragon trader himself was flushed and grinning.

"You know what that is, Jewel of the Mountains?" He gestured at a wall of dirty white blocking the valley ahead from side to side. It was bleeding a torrent of frothy green water.

"It remarkably resembles snow, but I am sure you would not have asked if the answer was so obvious."

He nodded, uncorking his canteen. "It's an old avalanche."

Eleal looked around uneasily. On either side the valley walls rose in cliffs and scarps and impossible slopes, mostly still mantled with winter snow. At the top sunlight glinted on parapets of ice, a white frame around deep blue sky.

"Meaning this place is dangerous?"

He took a long drink. He nodded as he wiped his mouth. "If Ois wants it to be. Listen!"

She listened. There was only the dragons' puffing and the chatter of the stream and . . . a distant rumble of thunder?

"There goes another!" T'lin said with an unconvincing smirk.

They peered around, but the wall of snow prevented a proper view of the valley ahead.

"We should ride along the top," she said. "Then nothing can fall on us."

"It might fall on us as we went up. It might fall when we were on top of it. Praise the goddess." T'lin sighed, staring back the way they had come. "What does holy scripture tell us about squabbles between the gods?"

"Scripture I leave to the priests. I can tell you what happens in drama, though."

"So what happens in drama, Embodiment of Ember'l?"

"They usually appeal to the Parent."

"And what happens then, Wisdom?" His green eyes fixed on her with a quizzical expression she could not read.

"He sends them away. That's in Act One. In Act Three he renders judgment. Then we all come out and bow and pass the plate again."

Dragontrader busied himself replacing his canteen in his pack.

"You think that's what's happening?" she asked. "You think the Lady has gone to appeal to Visek?"

He shrugged and smiled. "I am only a humble dragon trader. You are the fountain of the arts, the Avatar of Astina. If you don't know, then what mortal can understand the gods?"

She thought over all the tragedies she could remember. "Prophecy's one of Visek's attributes. Being god of destiny, he will not allow the others to block the fulfillment!"

"Truly your insight is comforting. Have you discovered yet what the prophecy prophesies for you?"

"No. Sister Ahn was about to tell me at the last stop, and you interrupted." And he had done so deliberately.

"It says that during the seven hundredth Festival of Tion—that's now, starting tonight—that the Liberator will be born." T'lin raised a coppery eyebrow to ask what Eleal thought about that.

"Who's the Liberator?"

"His name is not given. He is the son of Kameron Kisster."

"Who's he, and what's a Kisster?"

The dragon trader shrugged his bulky shoulders. "I do not know these things! Perhaps it is all his given name—Kameronkisster?"

Eleal searched his face for signs that he was making all this up, in some stupid, stupid game. T'lin might, but Sister Ahn had displayed no signs of a sense of humor, and reapers had to be taken seriously.

"Who or what does the Liberator liberate?"

"And from whom? Or from what? That is not so clear at all. The *Testament* implies he will be very, very important, but it sort of takes that for granted and does not say how, except for one sort of hint."

"What sort of hint?" she snapped.

"It implies he will kill Death."

"I think I would class that as an important act."

"It probably doesn't mean what it seems to mean, though. What it does say is that he will be born sometime in the next few days, in Sussvale."

T'lin had not known this in Embiliina Sculptor's kitchen, or at least had not admitted knowing it. His obvious amusement was very irritating.

"And what does it say about me?" she demanded crossly.

"Ah. Here come the others now."

"You are being deliberately aggravating!" Eleal said in Ambria's most disapproving tone.

He stroked his red beard. "I think I would wager that you do not have the right sort of experience. You had best take those lessons from the old hag at the earliest possible opportunity."

"Lesson in what?" Eleal demanded through clenched teeth.

"Delivering babies."

"*What!?*"

"That is correct, Beloved of the Gods. *Naked and crying he shall come into the world and Eleal shall wash him. She shall clothe him and nurse him and comfort him.* That's what it says about you." T'lin shook with silent mirth, so that Starlight turned his head around and peered at him curiously. "I don't suppose 'nursing' means 'suckling,' unless there are some miracles mentioned I missed."

Personage of Historic Importance?

"That's all? There isn't any more? I don't believe you! Why would I be threatened by a reaper and imprisoned for life by a goddess if all I'm going to do is help some woman have a baby?" Let Kameronkisster go hire a midwife!

"But a very important baby! Even I was small and helpless when I was born. Beautiful, of course, because of my beard. All the witnesses agreed that they had never seen so—"

"So that's where you went last night? That's why you weren't at the camp when Gim and I arrived. You went to visit someone who has a copy of the *Testament?*"

Seeing a glint of suspicion in Dragontrader's eye, Eleal hastily added, "Some rancher friend, I suppose—outside the city?"

"A very shrewd guess, Goddess of Curiosity."

"There isn't any more about me, or you didn't have time to read any more?"

The other two dragons were closing in, puffing.

T'lin chuckled. "All right! No, I didn't have time to read the whole thing, or anything like the whole thing. It's a terrible jumble. There may be more about you in there—I don't know." He turned Starlight to face the newcomers.

That, she decided, was better.

Delivering babies? Yuu-uck!


A little later, walking their heated mounts up the valley, they saw an avalanche descend in white smoke and, later, thunder. It did not come close. Just a warning, Eleal thought, a sign that the Lady was still angry. She made the sign of Tion, and probably Gim did also. Sister Ahn clasped her hands in a prayer to Astina. T'lin made a gesture Eleal did not quite see.

The ascent out of the gorge was almost vertical, it ended in a scramble up a face of sheer ice. Nothing but a dragon could have gone that way, except birds. The surface of the glacier was a jagged nightmare, blindingly bright and swept by a cruel wind. It formed a saddle between two jagged peaks, and the mountains ahead were lower.

Soon it dipped. It dipped more steeply. Then Lightning launched himself like a toboggan and went sweeping off with Eleal screaming, *"Zappan!"* on his back and T'lin shouts of warning fading in the distance. She was too scared even to close her eyes. Cold wind rushed past, peppering her face with gritty snowflakes. Faster and faster, and she had heart-stopping visions of hurtling out over a precipice.

She did not. The crafty old dragon seemed to know what he was doing. He came to rest in a flat snowfield far below, belching contentedly to himself and twisting his long neck to watch the others follow the trail he had laid out.

"When we get to Sussland, lizard," Eleal said grimly, "I shall take off these accursed leggings and strangle you with them."

Going down was usually faster than going up, but Eleal—as an *experienced* traveler— knew that this descent would take longer than the climb, because Sussland lay so much lower than Narshland. Yet soon the snow had been left behind and what had seemed to be more snow ahead turned out to be the tops of clouds. Mist crept in on every hand, transforming the sun to a glowing silver disk and the world itself to a circle of rock no larger than the amphitheater at Suss. Always the dragons headed downward; the air grew steadily warmer and damper. The dragons had a discerning eye for the easiest path, although several times Eleal found herself leaning on the pommel plate and staring straight down while Lightning negotiated a near-vertical face. Once he turned around and descended backward, as Starlight had at the temple.

Grass appeared and eventually straggly shrubs, silvery with dew. It was still not yet noon when the first blighted trees emerged from the fog and T'lin called Starlight to a halt. The other dragons closed in, scales shining wetly, breath cloudy.

"Looks like a good spot for lunch," he said. "Strip off the tack and let them graze, Wrangler. Food's in that pack. *Wosok!*"

T'lin was in a good mood. He helped Sister Ahn dismount. She was probably too stiff to have managed by herself, although she did not utter as much as a wince. He retrieved her sword and attached it to her belt; then he escorted her over to the little stream where Eleal was already gulping ice-cold water.

With both men thus occupied, Eleal slipped off into the rocks to make some necessary adjustments. Already she was far too hot, and in Sussland itself the heat would be stifling. She removed her wool sweater, replaced the smock and coat, and headed back to see what Gim was unpacking.

With the suddenness of a cock crow, the sun's disk brightened. The sky turned from white to blue as if the gods had drawn back curtains. The mist dispersed and Sussland was laid out far below like a painting, framed between two massive cliffs. Gim was kneeling with a loaf of bread forgotten in his hands, staring openmouthed.

"There it is," Eleal said cheerfully. "Green, isn't it? Suss itself is over there. I don't suppose you can make out the city, but that bright spot is sunlight on the roof of the temple. It's gold, you know. The gap in the mountains beyond is Monpass, to Joalvale. I've been over that one lots of times. The place in the middle with all the trees is Ruatvil, but that's mostly ruins. I know—I've been there. The Thargians still call this Ruatland, did you know that? The gorge is Susswater. It's a *much* bigger river than Narshwater, and it flows west, not east. There's only two places you can cross it. Filoby is over there." She pointed to the right, although she suspected that Filoby itself might be behind the mountain.

Gim nodded, then sprang back into motion as T'lin came striding over. Eleal turned to him.

"We're coming down right on top of Thogwalby, Dragontrader."

"Or will do, if we can find a way through the forest." He flopped down on the grass and produced his knife. As he reached for the bread, Eleal sat down also.

"Aren't you going to say grace?"

T'lin shot a penetrating green glare at her. "No. I earned this. You can thank the gods or thank me, as you prefer."

Even Eleal was surprised by that, and Gim looked truly shocked, but he said nothing. Sister Ahn was hobbling over to them, leaning on her staff and weighted down with her ridiculous sword.

"What's at Thogwalby?" Gim asked. He was apparently waiting for the nun to arrive before starting to eat.

Eleal bit into a peach. "A monastery."

"Not much else," T'lin said with his mouth full. "Green brothers. Don't allow women near the place."

"Not even these two?" Gim grinned shyly.

Dragontrader shook his head.

"Garward Karzon, god of strength," Eleal explained. "Men go there to train for the festival." She had never been to Thogwalby and was annoyed to hear that she might miss it this time. "Some of them stay there year after year!"

"And never see a woman," T'lin agreed. "Lot of sacrifice for a miserable flower in their hair, if you ask me."

Gim bristled. "The principle is that all mortal achievement is transitory, sir, and the roses fade after—"

"I know the principle, lad. It's the practice that would bother me."

Gim clenched his lips and did not reply.

Sister Ahn settled awkwardly to the ground, clasped her hands in prayer, then helped herself to a slice of bread and a piece of cheese. Apparently she considered the cost of food to be included in the fare, because she did not offer additional payment. Her face was gray with fatigue.

T'lin chewed for a while, studying her. Finally he said, "Sister? We're going to come down somewhere near Thogwalby. Where do we deliver our Maiden of Destiny?"

The nun blinked her faded, filmy eyes at him. "I am not familiar with the geography, T'lin Dragontrader. The prophecies do not specify a location. I am sure the gods will provide."

"One way or the other? According to our little Toast of the World, there are at least two reapers skulking around Sussia now, and at least one of them knows her and will kill her on sight."

*"Two* reapers?" Sister Ahn turned her head stiffly to look at Eleal. "Tell me, child."

All the taste had gone out of the food. Eleal recounted the tale of Dolm Actor again.

The nun frowned as if worried, but did not comment. There was a long silence while everyone waited for her to finish chewing, but she just kept on and on. Dragons crunched grass in the background.

"Why don't you mention his name?" Gim asked. "You didn't last night, either."

"Because if you know a reaper, he will know you know him! I am trying to spare your life, that's all."

Gim gulped, and looked at the other two for confirmation. The nun was still chewing, staring at the ground. T'lin was frowning. After a while he said, "The convent at Filoby will take you in, Sister."

The old woman nodded, not looking up.

"And the girl also."

"*Zappan* to that!" Eleal said. "I did not escape from the red just to be trapped by the blue. To be a priestess is not my ambition, T'lin Dragontrader!"

"No self-respecting goddess would have you anyway, minx. You want to go to Suss and join your friends?"

"Er, no." One of those "friends" was a reaper, and from the glint in T'lin's eye he had guessed as much.

"The sisters will grant you shelter while the festival is on, I'm sure." T'lin popped a last fragment of cheese in his mouth. "What happens after depends on what happens during. Maybe nothing."

Life, Eleal decided, had become very much like that journey in the mist—straight down with no clear future in sight. What happened after she had delivered that unthinkable baby? Would Tion reward her when she had fulfilled the prophecy? Would the Lady bear a grudge, so she would have to wander the world forever like Hoinyok in *The Monk's Curse?*

"Eleal?" Gim said, "tell me about the festival." He was smiling wistfully. Sister Ahn had drifted off to sleep where she sat, head down, a small huddle of threadbare blue cloth. T'lin had stretched out on the grass, soaking up sunshine.

"Well!" Eleal pondered. "It would take me all day to tell you everything. It always begins on Thighday evening, with a service in the temple. That's not in the city, it's outside. The next day there's the dedication. Then all the athletes go off on the circuit and the artistic events begin."

"Circuit of what?"

"Sussvale. It takes four days. They stay at Thogwalby, and Filoby, and Jogby. Every day the last few are disqualified and lots just drop out."

Gim's blue eyes widened. "Why?"

"Exhaustion, of course! Sussland's always hot as an oven. At Thogwalby they honor Garward. At Filoby they have another dedication, to Iilah. She's goddess of athletes. They spend the night in the sacred grove there." She sniggered. "One year there was a thunderstorm and they all caught colds! Next day they march to Jogby."

"What do they do there?"

"Lick their blisters."

"I mean what god do they worship?" Gim said crossly.

Eleal could not recall ever hearing of a temple at Jogby. "None! You don't *have* to go round by Jogby to get to Suss, so I've never been there. I suspect it's just a ploy to keep them out of the way. By the time the brawn gets back to Suss, we artists've usually got most of the individual performances out of the way, and a lot of the plays, too. The end is on Headday, of course. The roses are awarded and the winners parade into the temple to thank Tion, and all the cripples and invalids are brought in and the god performs a miracle . . . What are you grinning about?"

Gim scrambled to his feet and went sauntering off as if to admire the view. Eleal went after him.

"What's the matter?"

He grinned sheepishly. "Nothing."

"Tell me! I told you about the festival!"

He was turning pink. "Oh, I was just wondering if Holy Tion looks anything like . . . like Dad's statue of Kirb'l."

"He doesn't look at all! Don't you even know that? There's no image of Tion in the temple. No mortal artist could do justice to the lord of beauty."

"Oh. Dad's carving . . ." Gim squirmed.

"I'm sure it comes very close!"

His milky complexion reddened perceptibly. "Little monster!"

"That's what T'lin meant by the gold rose. There's one yellow rose given out, and the winner of that stands before the altar and represents Tion. He hands out the red roses."

Gim glowered. "I know that!"

"I am sure you will win the gold rose!"

She had thought that his face was red, but it had been barely pink compared with what it now turned. Scarlet spread from the roots of his hair to the collar of his smock. His misty mustache became fairer in contrast. She was fascinated. She couldn't recall ever managing to provoke such an all-encompassing blush, like a stormy sunset all over the sky.

"Go jump off a mountain!" Gim spun on his heel.

She hobbled after him. "But it's a very great honor to portray a god, and in your case you would be entering as a likeness of your father's carving. Perhaps the god is telling us that he wants your father brought here to make—"

Gim spun around furiously. "Go away and stop pestering me, little girl!"

*Oo!* "But I am drawn to your beauty as stenchbugs to honey—"

"Stenchbugs get stamped on!"

"But beauty should be recognized and all women—"

"What's the argument?" asked T'lin Dragontrader, strolling over to them. He had stripped down to a smock and baggy Joalian breeches, both colored like a flock of rainbow birds. His sword dangled at his belt. The little gold ring glinted in his earlobe.

"Nothing!" Gim barked.

"I was just explaining about the gold rose."

"Ah." T'lin shrugged. "Myself, I don't think good looks are anything to brag about. But they're nothing to be ashamed of, either, and you'll grow out of them soon enough. Don't let this little queen bee get under your skin, lad. How well can you play that lyre of yours?"

"I'll show you!" Gim said, eager for a distraction.

"I'm no judge."

"I am," Eleal said.

T'lin folded red-hairy arms. "You keep out of this, pest. Can you twang a note or two well enough to enter? Not win, necessarily, just reasonably enter?"

"Think so."

"Good. Then you'll do that. You can be our scout at the festival."

Gim frowned. "The festival is to honor the—"

"Then why are there reapers there? Your god told you to rescue this half-size belly-ache, didn't he?"

Both men looked down at Eleal while she tried to think of a witty alternative to kicking Dragontrader's shins.

"I'm suggesting your responsibilities aren't over yet," T'lin said. "We've got her here, you and me, and we've got to try to keep her alive. Or do you put your trust in Sister Ahn's swordsmanship?"

Gim smiled. "No, sir."

"Ah, the old bag's awake, we can be on our way. Let's see you saddle up, Wrangler. Come, Jewel of the. . . ."

Eleal spun around to see why T'lin was staring. She saw smoke. Something big was burning in Sussland.

# *38*

"Piol Poet was planning to write a drama called the *Zoruatiad,* about the siege of Ruat," Eleal explained, "so of course that year we went there to let him look over the place. He never did write it, though. Once this was all Ruatland, and Ruat was a fair and mighty city. There was a bridge there in those days. Then came the Lemodland War. Ruatia fought for the Thargians, but the Joalians won, at least hereabouts, and Trathor Battlemaster razed the city and threw down the bridge. They made Sussby into the new capital, on their side of the river, but there's still only the two bridges, at Rotby and Lameby. So Sussby grew up to became Suss, Ruatwater became Susswat—"

"Do you *ever* stop talking?" Gim asked.

"Not when faced with such an abundance of ignorance in need of instruction." That was a quote from last year's comedy, and quite witty under the circumstance, Eleal decided. She would forgive him, then. Besides, he had smiled enough to take the sting out of his words and Gim Wrangler's smile would melt a statue of the Maiden. His face was scorched by the sun already and so coated with road dust that his eyebrows and mustache had vanished altogether. The latter looked much better when it wasn't visible.

T'lin was in the lead. Behind him Sister Ahn lolled in Blaze's saddle like a bag of cordroot. Even if she was as unconscious as she looked, she was well strapped on. The youngsters were bringing up the rear. They had gained enough control over their mounts now that they could ride side by side and converse.

The descent of Susslope had been easier than Eleal had expected, following the steepest route to avoid trees and then down avalanche cuts. Those in turn had led to a sizable river, which had soon entered a cultivated valley, and since then it had been all dirt road and dust and sweat. She had forgotten just how hot Sussvale was, or else the quick descent had given her no time to adjust. She had stripped down to breechclout and smock. Her legs were getting burned. So were Gim's, because he was wearing no more than she was.

Dragons did poorly in heat, and T'lin was holding them to a gentle *zaib*. On either hand sun blazed on lurid green paddy fields, where brown-chested men in wide straw hats would straighten from their work to inspect the travelers, and sometimes return their waves. Eleal suspected the water round their legs would be as warm as a hot bath. Some crop she should recognize and didn't was flowering in acres of pale pink, scenting the air like custard. Once in a while the road passed through orchards of the great dark bellfruit trees, and the black shade was a blessing. Sometimes, too, watchcats would yowl from the little farms as the four dragons ran by.

In Suss itself, and in the villages, men and women dressed in smocks that were no more than tubes of cotton with shoulder straps. Here the field hands wore only loin-cloths. For everyone, though, the brutal sun of Sussvale made the wheel-sized straw hats essential wear. Turbans were just not adequate. T'lin outfitted himself and his companions by buying hats right off the heads of children who ran out to see the dragons. Four copper mites bought four serviceable hats, which the original owners could replace with a few minutes' work. Even Sister Ahn made no complaint when T'lin leaned over and placed one on her head.

"We're still heading northeast," Eleal said. "So we're not going to come out near Thogwalby at all. Probably nearer Filoby. And I wish I knew what that smoke was!"

The black pillar had not dispersed; indeed it still seemed to be thickening. It stood almost dead ahead, towering over the hills like a menacing giant. The top spread out in a sooty layer, drifting gently westward, but for most of its height it was a vertical scar upon the hot, still afternoon.

"I expect we'll find out soon enough," she added. The side valley was about to enter Sussvale proper.

"How big is Filoby?"

To avoid saying she had no idea, Eleal risked a guess. "About a hundred homes, more or less."

Gim nodded. "Built of what?"

"Er. White stuff. Like those." She pointed to a cluster of farm buildings.

"Adobe. That doesn't burn very well. What else is there at Filoby?"

"A waterfall."

Gim rolled his eyes and joined in her laugh.

"The Convent of Iilah," she said.

"Describe it."

"I'm not sure," she admitted. "I've only passed by. The buildings are mostly hidden in the trees. There's this sacred grove, you see. It's a little round hill covered with mighty oaks. The temple is quite small. All you can see is the dome and some red tile roofs."

"Tiles need beams. Anything else?"

"No," she admitted, worried.

"Then there's your answer," Gim said with a frown. He nodded at the smoke. "The late sacred grove."

Almost imperceptibly, the valley widened into Sussflat. The peaks of Susswall came into sight to the north, shimmering behind veils of heat haze. The rich plain was familiar to Eleal—a mosaic of orchards, bright green crops, tiny white hamlets—but she knew it must seem strange to Gim, native of a bleaker land. At times a star flashed in the distance; she pointed it out to him, explaining that it was sunlight reflecting from the temple roof in Suss itself. To the east, the ominous smoke still crawled into the sky.

Red dirt tracks between the fields led eventually to the main Filoby–Thogwalby highway, which was no more than a wider version of the same rutted trail. In this hottest part of the day traffic was light: scrawny herds being driven to fresh pasture, a few ox wagons. Once Gim cried out in astonishment and pointed to a party of men riding long-legged moas in the distance. Eleal suspected they were soldiers and was relieved to have missed them.

Eventually T'lin halted Starlight and waited for the others to gather around. "We must take a break," he said, scowling at the mounts. "They can't take this heat." He nodded at a hillock ahead, capped by tall trees. "Head over there; I'll catch up with you." He rode off toward a cluster of farmhands, who were gaping at the dragons.

Normally the others would have tried to follow Starlight, but now they were too dispirited to argue. Gim persuaded Beauty to move. Lightning and Blaze followed. The trees were smooth pillars, erupting into green canopies very high from the ground. Their shade seemed dark as a cave, and nothing else grew in it.

Gim said, *"Wosok!"* and beamed when all three dragons obeyed him. He looked around approvingly at the grove. "Cool!"

Eleal slithered down from Lightning's saddle, feeling as old and stiff as Sister Ahn. "It isn't really. It just seems cool after the heat outside."

"You have to argue, don't you? What are these trees called?"

"Parasol trees."

"Do you know that, or are you guessing?"

"I know that, of course." After all, she had just called them parasol trees, so they were called parasol trees by her, even if other people had other names for them. She sat down on the sand and leaned back against one of the great leathery trunks. The air did feel sort of cool. Filoby could not be much more than five or six miles away; even the flames were visible now.

Gim had helped the nun dismount. The old woman seemed barely conscious. She did not ask for her sword, which was a bad sign.

Ahn had never said that she was Eleal Singer's protector. Although the sword seemed to imply that, the nun had firmly denied that it was a weapon. Nor had she ever claimed that the Maiden had sent her, only that she was fulfilling the prophecy. The Youth had designated Gim to rescue Eleal from the temple, but had sent him no further orders, no vision of later events. T'lin Dragontrader was Eleal's guardian and keeper now. Her secret friend had turned out to be the most important person in her life. He was big and gruff, and she knew he had secrets she did not share, but she had no one else to trust. She wished she knew which god had sent him.

T'lin joined them in a few minutes. He sat down, wiping his forehead with a brawny arm. His face was as red as his beard, and he was glaring. "Well, that's the sacred grove, as we thought. Last night a large group of men went by here, heading for Filoby. Fifty or sixty of them. They joked that they were going to call on the goddess."

"What?" Eleal shouted. "You mean it was deliberate?"

"Typical Sussian atrocity."

Defile the abode of a goddess? "Who were these savages?"

Gim was frowning. Sister Ahn was slumped over, apparently barely conscious.

T'lin's green eyes were cold as ice. "The trainees from Garward's monastery, led by some of the monks. At dawn they roused the people of Filoby to join them, and they sacked the convent. Anyone who refused to help was beaten and his house destroyed."

"Why would they do such a thing, sir?" Gim asked softly.

"What happened to the nuns?" Eleal demanded.

T'lin shrugged, apparently in answer to both queries.

Despite the heat, Eleal now felt thoroughly chilled. "Last night you said there was a serious squabble in the Pentatheon, didn't you?"

"Seems I was right, then."

She was a token in a game being played by the gods. Garward was another avatar of Karzon and apparently just as much involved in this affair as Zath. The Man and the Lady were against her in all their aspects. The Youth was helping her, and now it seemed that the Maiden was on her side also—or at least on the opposite side from the Man, which must mean the same thing . . . mustn't it? And the stake in this whole evil game was the Liberator, a baby.

Sister Ahn stirred and tried to sit up straight. She still wore her woolen habit, which must now be intolerably hot. Somehow her face was both flushed and haggard. After a moment she spoke in a surprisingly firm voice: *Woe to the Maiden, for the Man shall ply his strength against her. Woe to her holy place. Virgins are profaned. See blood and ashes paint the face of sanctity. The sacred place yields to the strength of the Man and only lamentation remains.*"

"I suppose that's part of your precious prophecy?" T'lin sneered.

She nodded, blinking tears. "It is so written in the *Testament,* but there is no date given. I weep to see it."

"Me too. Doesn't make any sense until it's too late, does it?" He scowled contemptuously. "We need a change of plan. The thugs are probably on their way to Suss and the festival now, but there's no point in us going to Filoby. We certainly can't risk Thogwalby after this." He eyed Eleal shrewdly. "And we can't take you to Suss, either, can we?" He had guessed about Dolm Actor.

"Wouldn't I be safe if I took refuge in Tion's temple?"

"Would you? Would the priests let you? Besides, we must stop soon—the dragons can't take this heat." He was looking at Sister Ahn, though, who had slumped over again in abject exhaustion.

"That only leaves one choice, sir, doesn't it?" Gim said calmly. "We go to Ruatvil."

"There's nothing there!" Eleal protested, and then realized that *no*-thing might be a very *good* thing under the circumstances.

T'lin cocked a coppery eyebrow. "Know it, do you?"

"Oh, yes!"

"Nowhere to stay?"

"Well, yes. There's a hostelry."

"And do you know the Sacrarium?"

"Of course," she said, relieved that he had asked something easy.

"Good. Then let's *zaib!*"

The big man rose to his feet and headed for the dragons before Eleal had a chance to find out why T'lin Dragontrader should want to go sightseeing. It seemed out of character.

It was not true that there was nothing at Ruatvil. There were ruins, and trees, and hummocky pasture. As Eleal explained to Gim while they were riding in—repeating what Piol Poet had told her two years before—much of mighty Ruat had been built of clay bricks, and those parts had collapsed to mud once their roofs had gone. The stone buildings stood as isolated walls, broken towers, and stark, useless arches. Some families dwelt in shanties within these relics, in constant risk of death from storm or earth tremor. Other cottages had been constructed from fallen masonry and then roofed with turf, so that goats grazed on them. The result was a strangely widespread settlement, a village scattered like seed corn over the grave of a metropolis.

"I think I could have worked all that out for myself," Gim said, looking around disparagingly.

"If you win the gold rose, the priests will make you shave off your mustache."

"What has that to do with anything?"

"I've been meaning to ask you the same question."

They were all weary. None of them had slept much in the previous night, and the journey had been hard.

Ruatvil was not completely abandoned. The main street was still wide, although its paving lay buried in grass and heaved by tree roots. A few inhabitants were going about their business—herding goats, bearing loads of food and charcoal. They all paused to stare at the dragons.

Eleal directed T'lin to the hostelry, which he would doubtless have found quite easily by himself. It brought back memories for her, yet it was smaller than she remembered. Once the building must have been some rich man's mansion or a public edifice, and the walls still stood three stories high. Now only the ground floor was in use, and sky showed through the empty arches of the windows, for the roof had long since vanished. The entrance was an imposing portico, but the doors themselves had cooked meals for persons long dead, and only their rusty hinges remained.

Piit'dor Hosteler was a large, ruddy-faced man with a gray-streaked beard and a prominent wart on his nose. Playing his role in traditional fashion, he rubbed his hands gleefully when T'lin flashed gold, gabbling at length how he anticipated an invasion of refugees from Filoby, and how the civic authorities of Ruatvil would require him to provide them with shelter, but if the noble guests were already in residence, of course, then they would not be disturbed, and fortunately his very best accommodation was still available . . . and so on.

Gim was already unbuckling the straps that held Sister Ahn in her saddle. T'lin eased him out of the way. "Civic authorities!" he muttered under his breath. "Ten to one they're his brother."

He lifted the old woman bodily in his arms, her sword dangling. Piit'dor Hosteler flinched with astonishment. His joviality vanished, and he backed away until he stood squarely before the steps to his front door, all the while staring hard at that sword.

"Something wrong?" T'lin demanded.

The hosteler began to mutter about evil omens.

"All of us or none! Which is it?" T'lin was still holding the old woman as if she weighed nothing. He rolled forward menacingly.

"She is ill?"

"Merely fatigued."

Obviously unhappy, Piit'dor faltered. Daughters of Irepit must be rare in Ruatvil, but visitors with real money would not be common either. He forced an ingratiating simper. "Oh, my lord is most welcome, and all his companions. The reverend lady shall be fittingly attended." He scurried up the steps muttering, "My wife . . ."

"I'll bet the ceilings leak," Gim said.

"Yes, they do." Suddenly Eleal began to yawn. She was too weary to relate how much it had rained on her previous visit. It had not seemed funny at the time. She thought that even a cloudburst as bad as that one would not waken her tonight, once she found somewhere to lie down.

\*　　　\*　　　\*

Hayana Hosteler was even larger than her husband, boisterous and motherly, with a matching mole on her nose. She knew all the traditional business of her role—the smear of flour on the forehead, the fast shuffle on flat feet, the wiping of hands on apron— and she arrived with an entourage of several adolescent assistants. Displaying no super- stitious dread of a Daughter of Irepit, she bemoaned the poor sister's distress, saw her laid on a mattress, and then chased the men away.

Furnished with a bucket of water of her own in a corner of the big room, Eleal set to work to remove the sediment of her journey. Although her inclination was just to fall over and sleep, she could not do so until Hayana and her brood stopped fussing around Sister Ahn. They were to share the same bedchamber. That mattered little; there would have been ample room for a couple of the dragons as well.

Sunlight poured in two huge empty window arches, so there was no privacy—and no security either, for anyone could approach through the woodland outside. The roof was partly composed of the original beams and upstairs flooring, now sagging badly. Where it had collapsed, the holes had been patched with tree trunks. The beds were oddly placed, obviously in the driest locations, for much of the mosaic floor was grimed by dry watercourses, relics of rain.

She had no garment other than the smock Embiliina Sculptor had given her, and it was red with dust. With her hair still damp and her feet still bare, she found herself hustled off to eat. Gim was already doing so, sitting in lordly solitude in a vast room furnished with rough-hewn tables and benches. Faded fragments of frescoes clung to the walls. His hair was as damp as hers, but he did have a clean smock. There was no sign of T'lin, who was probably fussing over his precious dragons.

Lunch—or perhaps dinner, or maybe supper—comprised heaps of fruit and hot bread and goats' milk cheese. Gim, his new cleanliness emphasizing his sunburn, tried each sort of fruit in turn, demanding to know its name. Eleal told him, making up suitable noises when she wasn't sure. Apart from that, neither spoke much.

Eventually she could keep her eyes open no longer, although she knew the sun would not set for a couple of hours yet. "I am going to bed!" she announced firmly.

Gim donned a superior, tough-male expression. "I am going to practice my lyre, unless Dragontrader needs me."

"You can practice drums and you won't keep me awake," Eleal said, and headed off to her room.

A mattress in one corner was invitingly empty. Another near the center bore a snoring Sister Ahn. No matter! Eleal would sleep if—*Eek!*

A man was peering in the window. It took her a moment to realize that it was T'lin Dragontrader in a straw hat and a drab-colored local smock. She had never seen him without his turban, and there was something odd about his beard.

"Only me!" He dropped a bundle over the sill. "Brought you something to wear. Up all night—expect you want to sleep now?"

"Oh, yes!"

"Just tell me how to find the Sacrarium."

Fogged by fatigue, Eleal regarded him blankly for a moment. He had apparently smeared his beard with charcoal, dulling its normal copper red. Why did Dragontrader want to be inconspicuous?

And why did he not just ask one of the locals to give him directions?

"You can't miss it," she said. "Follow the main road north to the old bridge. It's east of the road, 'bout half a mile. There's a sign, and a path."

"Oh. Good. Er . . . anything you need before you kip?"

Eleal yawned and stretched divinely. "Can't keep my eyes open."

"Right." T'lin eyed her with bright green suspicion. "If you do wake up when I'm not around . . . Well, this isn't Narsh or Suss, remember. You stay here!"

Eleal walked over to her mattress and sat down, promising faithfully that she would go no farther from the hostelry than the dragons, which she could hear belching faintly.

"Just remember what happened at Filoby this morning," T'lin said thoughtfully. "They catch bigfangs hereabouts sometimes, too."

She went on the offensive. "Are you trying to keep me away from something, T'lin Dragontrader?"

"No, no! You sleep well." He disappeared.

Perhaps food had revived her. Perhaps it was only curiosity. Either way, she knew she could not sleep now. She rushed over to the bundle he had tossed in, discovering a smock and a pair of sandals. He would almost certainly hang around for a while and watch the window in case she tried to follow him. She changed quickly into the clean smock, grabbed up the sandals, and ran out the door. *Slop slap slop slap . . .*

# 39

Edward had not expected to sleep, but he did. The wagon was hot and noisy. From time to time he would become aware of snores, wheels rumbling, axles squeaking, and the clopping of hooves. Very rarely a lorry would go by or children would shout abuse at the hated Gypsies. Dogs barked hysterically. At such times his worries would surge in on him again and for a while he would stare at the painted slats above his nose while plot and counterplot raced around in his mind. What proof of age or identity would he need to enlist? He would not dare use his own name. His OTC Certificate would be useless and was unobtainable now anyway, back in Kensington, so he could not hope for early routing into officer training. Well, he would not mind the ranks. But how long could he conceal his identity? How long until word filtered back to Fallow and Greyfriars?

Sometime during the morning the caravan halted for a while. He did not bother to investigate the reason for the stoppage. He did not think it would be a police roadblock looking for him, but if it were, the Gypsies could handle it. They had centuries of practice at dealing with rozzers. Creighton continued to snore.

By now Alice must have heard of his disappearance. She would be worried crazy. On the other hand, he thought with much satisfaction of his uncle's reaction, wishing he could somehow take him to that hilltop grove and introduce him to Puck. He wondered how Head Office had contrived the Oldcastle sham for the last two years. A committee, Creighton had said, and yet all his letters had been answered in the same handwriting.

The wagon rolled again. He slept again.

He dreamed of his parents and awoke shaking.

In the dream they had been sitting on the veranda at Nyagatha, writing a letter together like a committee of two, and in the way of dreams he had known they were writing to him.

That Jumbo letter was what was bothering him. It tied in so well with what Creighton had told him! Without it, he probably would dismiss all of the colonel's story as rubbish—mended leg or no mended leg.

"I see you're awake at last." Creighton was stripped to his undervest, shaving with a straight razor. "Was that the sleep of the just, or just sleep?"

"Yes, sir," Edward said, with what he thought was admirable self-control. He felt limp and sweaty in the noon heat. There was no room for him to climb down. The wagon was still moving and he might jostle Creighton and make him cut his throat. The man was infuriatingly tight-lipped, but that would be going a bit far.

The wagon lurched as Creighton stooped to see in the looking glass, preparing a stroke. He cursed under his breath.

"Will you tell me where we are, sir?"

"Halfway to where we're going. We'll be there tonight."

"And where is that?"

"Stonehenge."

Edward sensed a leg-pull and then realized. "A node, of course?"

"The most powerful in Britain, so I'm told."

"And who do we meet there? Druids?"

"Druids? I suppose they would have used it, but I suspect it was ancient even in their time." Creighton aimed another stroke at his neck. Apparently he was in a more informative mood now, for he carried on talking as he wiped the razor. "It has no resident genius now, so far as I know—so far as my friends in Head Office know. Nodes have another purpose, many of them. They can be used as portals."

He had just confirmed something Edward had been afraid of.

"Portals to where?"

"Various places. Most of the European ones connect with a territory known as the Vales, but that may just be a peculiarity of the keys we know—something to do with the languages or the cultural trends in rhythm. Try this." He laid down his razor and beat a rapid tattoo on the table. "Can you do that?"

Edward reached up to the roof in front of his nose and repeated the beat.

Creighton whistled. "First time? That was perfect, I think. Do it again."

Edward did it again, wondering what the catch was.

"Let's see if you can do the whole thing then!" This time Creighton repeated the refrain and continued drumming. The whole thing was long and extremely complex, but obviously just a series of variations and syncopation. Edward played it back to him exactly.

"Exeter, you're a wonder! How the deuce did you manage that? I thought it would take you all afternoon to get it."

"I was raised in Africa. The natives have far more complicated beats than that. Try this one." His fingers were rusty, and it really needed two drummers, but he managed a fair imitation of one of the simpler Embu rhythms.

Creighton listened in silence, and then suddenly laughed. It was the first real laugh Edward had heard him utter, a raucous bray. "I could never come close! Well, that takes care of one problem. How are you at learning stuff off by heart?"

"Average, I suppose."

"Modesty? You played the king in *Henry V.* That's a tough part."

"How did . . . You read my letters to Mr. Oldcastle?"

"A summary of what you've been up to." Creighton seemed to have forgotten that half his face was coated with soap. "Repeat this:

*"Affalino kaspik, fialybo tharpio,*
*Noga nogi theyo fan*
*Affaliki suspino."*

"What's it mean?"

"Lord knows. It's in no known language. Probably older than the pyramids. Try it."

That was tougher. It took him several tries and repeats.

"They go together, don't they?" he said. "What's the melody?" He began to sing the words to the beat.

"Stop!" Creighton barked. "Do not mix the ingredients until I say so!"

"Sir?" Edward wondered yet again if the man was crazy.

"Beat, words, melody, and dance. You must learn them separately. Together they're a key."

"A key to what?"

"A key to a portal, of course. I hope it's one of the keys to Stonehenge. Let's try the next verse."

"A key to a portal to where?" Edward said angrily.

"Obedience without question! Second verse—"

"Sir!

They glared at each other, but Edward was so riled now that it was Creighton who looked away. He smirked into the looking glass and picked up his razor again.

"The keys are all very ancient," he remarked cheerfully. "Shamanistic, most of 'em. Been used for thousands of years. We've got a chappie at Olympus who's made quite a study of them, trying to figure out how they work. Not all keys work at all nodes. In fact we know how to work very few of them as portals, and not all of those lead to Nextdoor, although most of them do—that's why it's called Nextdoor, I suppose. The European ones are definitely biased in favor of the Vales and *vice versa,* he says, but there are exceptions. There's one in Joalland itself that connects to one in New Zealand. Does that surprise you?"

"No," Edward admitted. "And another in the Valley of the Kings?"

Creighton cut his cheek and barked out an oath that would have had any boy at Fallow sacked on the spot.

"What do you know about *that?*"

Apparently Edward had poked a very sensitive tooth, which he found highly satisfying. "It's sometimes called the Valley of the Tombs of Kings. Near Luxor. A bunch of pharaohs were buried there."

Creighton glared, blood streaming down his neck. "Answer my question, boy!"

"Will you first answer some of mine?"

"No, I will not! I am not playing games!" He was, though. "This is a matter of life and death, Exeter—your death, certainly. Possibly mine too. Now tell me how you learned of the Valley!"

Reluctantly, Edward conceded. "A letter my father wrote just before his death, sir."

"Where did you see this letter? Where is it now?"

"Back at the hospital."

With another oath, the colonel took up a perfectly good shirt and dabbed at his cut. "Who was he writing to? Not you."

"No, sir. A chappie called Jumbo. The letter was never sent, obviously. I found it in his papers last week."

Creighton grunted. "Well, you're right. Jumbo is one of us. There is a portal in Egypt. Now the opposition may learn of it! Damn it to hell! I wonder if I can send a telegram from one of these villages?" He glared wordlessly at the shirt.

"I expect the police will impound my belongings, sir."

"You think that will stop the Blighters? Well, you didn't know; it's not your fault. The Luxor portal is handy because it leads directly to Olympus. Some others do, but they're better known. This key I'm teaching you usually leads to somewhere in the Vales. What else was in that letter?"

"I think," Edward said icily, "that you cheated."

"Absolutely unthinkable," Creighton told his reflection blandly.

"I think that when my parole ends, you will have made it impossible for me to enlist!"

"Did I ever say I wouldn't?"

"That," Edward snarled, "is hairsplitting! Bloody lawyer talk!"

Creighton made his *Hrrmph!* noise and glared again. "And that is insubordination!"

"You extracted my word of honor. Where's your honor?"

"Insolence! Impudent puppy!"

They were both shouting now.

Edward swung his legs around, dropped to the floor, and straightened up to confront the colonel. He cracked his head resoundingly against the roof, seeing blue flames.

Creighton snorted mockingly. "See? You can't even stand on your own two feet. You're a dead man without me around to save you, Exeter. You'd never get into uniform. The Blighters will track you down, and this time they won't beat around the bush. They'll snuff you like a candle."

Edward sank down on a suitcase to massage his scalp. Trouble was, he had every reason to believe the maniac. "One of the first things I heard you say, at the hospital, was, 'He cannot cross over with that leg.' Cross over to where?"

Not getting an answer, he looked up. Creighton was regarding him sourly. Then he shrugged. "Nextdoor, I hope. Nobody's ever tried Stonehenge before, that I know of, but we'll have to risk it. If it doesn't work, we'll head over to the big circles at Avebury and try there. All our usual portals in England will be under surveillance. According to the *Filoby Testament*, my lad, you arrive at one of the nodes in Sussland, which is in the Vales, on Nextdoor. We must trust the prophecy."

"*On* Nextdoor? Not *in* Nextdoor? Nextdoor's an island?"

Creighton turned back to the looking glass. "No," he said. "Not an island. Nextdoor is a lot more than an island."

"And that's where the guv'nor was living before he *came back* to New Zealand? The missing thirty years when he did not grow old?"

"You're a sharp little nipper, you are!" Creighton said. "Give me that first verse again."

# *40*

Susswater was said to be the least navigable river in the Vales. Muddy yellow, it roared along the bottom of a canyon whose sides were hundreds of feet high and usually sheer. In only three places was it narrow enough to bridge, and the bridge at Ruat had been the first and most splendid. When Trathor Battlemaster had laid siege to the city he had begun by throwing down the stone arch on the north bank. The south arch still stood, a notable landmark dangling vestiges of its ancient chains and straddling a paved road now trod by none. From its base the towers of Suss were clearly visible to the north, the sun glinting on the roof of Tion's temple. They seemed but an hour's stroll away, yet it would take a strong walker all day to reach them. The citizens of Suss had blocked any effort to rebuild the bridge, lest Ruatvil rise again as a rival.

So Piol Poet had said.

The Sacrarium must once have been a noble and imposing monument, standing by itself near the edge of the cliffs. It was revered as the oldest holy building in the Vales, its builders long forgotten. Even Trathor had not dared violate a temple so sacred, but time, storm, and earthquake had done it for him. All that could now be seen was a pentagonal platform of giant blocks bearing remains of a circle of pillars. Many were represented only by their bases, less than a dozen still retained their full height. What sort of roof or lintels they might once have supported was unknown, and theologians could not explain why they had originally numbered thirty-one. Pilgrims still came, although rarely, and devout persons had kept the inside of the circle clear of rubble. The surrounding land had been too holy to plow; it had grown a forest instead, and now the lonely ruin was buried in jungle.

Eleal was confident she could find a shortcut. Rather than follow the old highway and the pilgrim path, she would head directly northeast until she reached the edge of the gorge and then approach the Sacrarium from the other side. Holding her hat on with one hand and her sandals in the other, she ran barefoot through the grassy woodland of Ruatvil, skirting its stony ruins. A few young goatherds watched her, but no one challenged her or jeered at her awkward lope. Puffing and sweating in the heat, she came to the woods and realized her error. She had forgotten how dense the jungle was.

Thorns and brambles became so thick that she was slowed to a stumbling walk. Masses of stone lay hidden everywhere. She found the way hard going in sandals, but she forced her way through, being as quiet as she could. Her hat kept catching in branches; she took it off and carried it in front of her to shield her face from twigs. The grove was utterly silent in the heat of the afternoon. Not a bird sang. Even insects seemed to be sleeping.

Then she discovered a stream by almost falling into it. Where had that come from? It crossed her path in a deep gully, whose sides were muddy and crumbly. She slid and floundered down to the water, and was infuriated to discover that it was flowing from right to left. As far as she could remember, the pilgrim path never crossed a creek, so she must be on the correct side already. She struggled back up again, and set off to follow the gully—it could only flow to the river, and the cliff.

It certainly did not flow *directly* to the river. It wound and twisted until she lost all sense of direction and began to think that the sun was setting in the east. Her legs shook with weariness; her hip ached fiercely. Soon she was tempted to turn back and forget stupid T'lin Dragontrader and his idiotic interest in ruins. Trouble was, she would have to follow the stream all the way.

In the distance, someone began whistling a solemn refrain. She halted and listened. It was not a tune she knew. It stopped suddenly. She started to move again, heading in that direction. Soon she saw steps rising out of the undergrowth, the edge of the plinth. Directly above her stood a stub of stone pillar as thick as a man's outstretched arms and furred with dense ivy.

She heard a murmur of someone speaking.

Step by step she approached. When she reached the base of the mossy, crumbling stair, the voice was clearer, and apparently coming from just behind that same pillar.

Barefoot again, she tiptoed up until she stood beside its ivy-coated bulk, and then she could make out the words.

"... the boy to bring her to my camp. I went and told my men to expect them. Then I went back into town and reported to Narsh Prime."

T'lin himself!

That was better. Eleal eased around the curve of the stone like growing moss.

A man chuckled. "And what did he make of all that?"

A Thargian! He was speaking Joalian, but the guttural accent was unmistakable.

T'lin again: "He thought the Service would be interested."

"He was right, of course."

T'lin sighed. "Glad to hear that! Well, we thumbed through the *Testament*—as much as we had time for—and found her name, as she had said. Funny, that! I've known the brat for years and never guessed she was anyone of consequence. She's an incredible little busybody. I always thought she might make a good recruit when she's older."

"Sounds like she might."

"Well, Prime agreed I ought to bring her if I could. When I got back to my camp, I found the kids had arrived safely—much to my surprise. So I loaded them up on mounts. What I hadn't realized was that the old nun was skulking in the herd. I geared up my own dragon and turned my back for a moment. Before I knew it, she'd scrambled into the saddle and taken off." He paused, then added diffidently, "In the end I had to bring her also."

The other man chuckled. He sounded quite young. Peering with one eye around the pillar, Eleal made him out. He was seated on a fallen block of stone, his back to her. T'lin must be at his side. They were facing into the empty paved space within the Sacrarium.

"I'm not surprised! The *Filoby Testament* has turned out to be astonishingly accurate. It said the girl would come with a blue nun, so she came with a blue nun. Only a miracle could have prevented it."

"It's a miracle I didn't strangle the old witch!"

The Thargian chortled loudly, as if that were a good joke. "Violence is not advisable with her kind!"

Eleal eased herself a few more inches around the ivy so she could watch with both eyes. The two men were sitting in shade, and had removed their hats. The Thargian was as tall as T'lin, but he was leaning back on his arms, and they were sinewy, youthful arms, well burned by the sun. He was a much younger man. His hair was black and when he turned his head she saw that he was clean-shaven.

He wore a small gold circle in his left ear!

"She's back at the hostelry now, sir," T'lin said. "So what do I do with her?"

*Sir?* T'lin Dragontrader addressed this stripling as *Sir?*

"Good question!" The Thargian straightened up and ran his fingers through his hair. "What do you get when you cross a wallaby and a jaguar?"

T'lin said, "Huh? Oh! 'Fraid I don't know, sir."

"That's all right. Just means there are some things I'm not supposed to tell you.

Don't feel slighted, now! I'm sure you have secrets in the political branch that I don't know. This is a religious matter, that's all."

T'lin uttered his familiar snort. "I had gathered that! Subversion and infiltration I can understand. I'm totally out of my depth with something like this."

"You're not the only one, believe me! How much have you put together?"

"Very little. There's supposed to be some child born in Sussland during the festival. The girl delivers it. The Karzon and Eltiana faction is trying to prevent this. Tion and Astina seem to be in favor. I gather the Service is in favor also?"

The younger man grunted. "We are. Zath and Ois are opposed, certainly. Karzon and Eltiana, probably. But don't ever trust Tion! He plays his own dirty games."

Eleal gasped. *Blasphemy!*

"Tion sent the boy to rescue the girl," T'lin demurred.

"Kirb'l did, you mean! I shudder to think what his reasons may be. Kirb'l is an outright maniac. Astina herself is staying out of things at the moment."

"That was her grove got burned this morning."

The Thargian sighed. "No! That was Iilah's grove. Iilah is more or less on our side—or she was. She may be dead now. Listen, I'll tell you some things I'm not supposed to, so be discreet, all right? The priests' theology is totally muddled, understandably. Their idea of five great gods, the Pentatheon, is a useful simplification, but it has definite limits. Yes, the five are all very powerful—Visek, Karzon, Eltiana, Astina, Tion. But some of the others carry a lot more weight than you'd expect, and their loyalties are not always what you'd expect either. All the aspect-avatar business is stable washings. Iilah is not Astina; Kirb'l is not Tion; Garward is not Karzon! Ois is not Eltiana, either. She's an utter bitch, that one, with her ritual prostitution—and immensely powerful because of it, of course. She probably can cause avalanches as she claims. For all his patronage of art and sport, Tion is just about as depraved as she is."

This was foul, foul heresy! Why was T'lin Dragontrader listening to such blasphemy?

"Fortunately," the stranger added, "they don't all support the Chamber. There's some decent types, and a lot of fence-sitters."

After a moment, T'lin laughed ruefully. "And I thought politics was complicated! Thargdom's going to annex Narshia, you know. Any day now."

"Doesn't surprise me," the Thargian said. "And the Joalians won't stand for it. Idiots! But that doesn't matter much compared to this. Wars come and wars go. The Liberator may turn out to be far more important than any war. You arrived in Sussland after dawn?"

"Well after. After noon."

"Ah! Garward's mob sacked the Filoby grove before that. So he didn't succeed."

Silence followed. Eleal resisted a temptation to scream. She was relieved when T'lin said, "Succeed in what?"

There was another pause then. The Thargian bent over and produced a bottle from near his feet. He drank and passed it to T'lin. "I'll have to explain a few things. First of all, the birth thing is a misinterpretation. We're not expecting a baby. This Liberator the *Testament* mentions will be a grown man."

T'lin chuckled. "My young friend will be relieved. She did not enjoy hearing she was going to be a midwife."

"Don't tell her any of this!" the Thargian said sharply.

"Of course not, sir. I won't tell anyone."

"Right. She has to act on her own volition. If she knows what's expected of her, she may do the wrong thing altogether. Not that I know what is expected of her either, so it probably doesn't matter, but we mustn't risk upsetting the prophecies now. The Chamber's been trying to do that for years, and whatever they want we don't want, if you follow me." He paused again. "That's why Garward sacked Iilah's grove this morning—he wanted to break the chain of prophecy. I think he just strengthened it. He's a headstrong bully and none too bright."

*This was a god he was insulting!*

"Nevertheless," the blasphemer continued, "the Chamber has much greater resources in this than the Service does, Seventy-seven. Zath is deeply involved, for one."

"Death!"

"The person who claims to be Death. The Liberator sounds like a personal threat to him."

"He's got a couple of his reapers here, apparently."

"More than just a couple. We're pretty sure he's done a foreseeing of his own—he's plenty strong enough to risk it. He probably knows exactly where the Liberator is going to arrive, and we don't." The young man laughed ruefully. "At least we didn't until you came. I thought I had an easy watch here, and now you've thrown me right in the thick of things."

"Bringing the girl, you mean?"

The Thargian made an affirmative sound as he tipped the bottle again.

"I should have left her at some handy farmhouse and come on alone!" T'lin said, sounding annoyed.

The other passed him the bottle. "Maybe. Maybe that would have fouled up everything—who knows? Why did Narsh Prime send you here, to Ruatvil?"

T'lin wiped his lips. "Didn't. He suggested I go to Filoby and report to Thirty-nine. He mentioned this place as a backup. Said there was sure to be someone from religious branch here."

He tried to pass back the bottle and the Thargian said, "Finish it. See, as far as we know, there's only six places in Sussland where the Liberator can realistically be expected to appear. Tion's temple is one, the Thogwalby monastery's another. If he picks either of those, the Chamber's got him and he's dead meat. We were banking on Iilah's grove at Filoby, because she'd have sheltered him. Probably she would. Garward's taken care of that possibility! You can bet your favorite organ that he's left some henchmen there to look after matters if the Liberator does arrive. There's a roadside campground just outside Filoby that has loads of virtuality . . ."

"Loads of what?"

"Forget that. I just mean it's another possible choice. That leaves this place, the

Sacrarium, and another node . . . place, I mean . . . up in the hills near Jogby. That was our second choice, after Filoby, because it's unoccupied."

"You've lost me, sir."

"Nothing there, I mean. No temple or shrine. Too obvious, perhaps? Well, never mind. Question is what to do now. The festival starts tonight."

He thought for a moment. "First, you've got to dump the boy. If he really is a Tion Cultist, then Kirb'l may have marked him in some way. So give him some money and send him off to the festival. That's easiest. After that, he can fend for himself. He'll never be any good to us. There's still a couple of hours of light. Take your dragons over to Filoby and see if you can help ferry survivors to Rotby. Go back and forth several times. You've drawn attention to this place with the dragons, so you'll have to try and muddy the waters."

T'lin seemed to swell. "They're tired, sir!"

"Kill 'em if you have to and put it on your expense account!"

The dragon trader subsided again. "Yes, sir."

"Sorry, but the stakes in this are higher than you can imagine. Leave the girl at the hostelry."

"I'd best keep her away from this place, you think, sir?"

The young man laughed. "You can try, but I'll put my bets on the prophecy."

Eleal liked him a little better for that remark. She was fighting an urge to walk out and ask T'lin if he'd had any trouble finding the Sacrarium, just so she could see his face.

The Thargian stretched his ropy arms and yawned. "We've got a courier coming round tomorrow on a fast moa, so I'll pass word to the others and hope they can spare me some reinforcements. It's not likely. Got all that?"

And again the strangely humble T'lin said, "Yes, sir."

"It's a pity the Chamber identified the mysterious Eleal before we did, but perhaps our turn is coming. I suppose there couldn't be *two* Eleals, could there? She sounds too young."

"She's twelve, I'm sure."

"Mmph! Mostly she just appears in the bit that sounds like delivering a baby, but another passage says she will be the first temptation. Little hard to relate temptation to a twelve-year-old, isn't it?"

T'lin uttered a dragon snort. "There's many a time I've been tempted to thump her ear, sir!"

*I will get even with you for that remark, Dragontrader!*

The Thargian chuckled. "How about cavemen, then? You haven't run into any cavemen in your adventures, have you?"

"Cavemen, sir?"

"One of my favorite verses: *Many mighty shall go humbly, even as Eleal took him to the caveman for succor, then they are going mightily again.* That's about average for clarity."

"It doesn't mention the Liberator."

"No, it may have nothing to do with him at all. Or it may refer to events years from now, because there's lots of unrelated stuff about him: The-Liberator-comes-into-Joal-crying-Repent! sort of thing. But Eleal is only mentioned four times and that sounds like she is still helping the Liberator, so it may be relevant to what's about to happen this fortnight. Just wondered."

"No cavemen," T'lin growled. "I wouldn't like anything to happen to the kid, sir."

"Nor I," the Thargian said, rising. He was very tall and skinny. "But you could put the whole Joalian army around her and it couldn't protect her from the Chamber. Until the Liberator himself arrives, she's the obvious weak link in the chain. If Zath's reapers find her, she's dead. Nobody in the world could do anything for her then."

T'lin rose also. "The saints, sir?"

The younger man cleared his throat harshly. "Ah, yes. Well, of course we must pray to the saints to intercede with the Undivided. Come over to the tent and . . ."

The two men strolled away across the bare stone floor of the ruined temple. Eleal heard no more.

# 41

Eleal stumbled down the steps and pushed off into the bush.

The enormity of what she had overheard stunned her. She had trusted T'lin Dragon-trader! Gim was only a boy, Sister Ahn a senile maniac, but she had thought that T'lin was a strong man and reliable and a friend. Now she knew that he bore no loyalty to her at all, except some vague idea of one day enlisting her to work for his diabolical "Service," whatever that was. Her last protector had failed her.

T'lin had taken orders from the Thargian. He had not spoken out against the blasphemy. He was probably a Thargian spy himself! Eleal had never pondered her own political convictions very deeply. Had she been forced to declare her loyalties, she would probably have claimed to be a Jurgian, because she spent more time in Jurg than any-where else and she liked the king, who clapped when she sang for him. She approved of the Joalians' artistic principles and the concept of Joaldom, which gave peace to the lands she knew, and she had always heard bad things about the Thargians and their harsh military ways. Spying for them seemed like betrayal.

Her religious loyalties were in no doubt at all. Tion was lord of art and beauty. Ember'l, the goddess of drama, was an avatar of Tion. So was Yaela, the goddess of singing.

The Thargian had done one good thing, though—he had unwittingly told Eleal a lot about the *Filoby Testament.* She would not be required to deliver any messy baby. A grown man was going to arrive—young and handsome, undoubtedly—either here or somewhere . . . how? Nobody had said *how* he would arrive, she decided. And when the Liberator arrived, Eleal Singer was going to help him. Wash him and clothe him, T'lin had said that morning. She could do with a good wash again herself, to get rid of all the mud and perspiration. The flies had reappeared. Her smock was ripped and filthy. Her legs were so weary they would hardly hold her up.

She staggered and lurched through the thickets, stumbling over hidden blocks of stone. If she kept the sun on her right, she would come to the city.

What she would do when she arrived was another problem altogether. To return to the hostelry would be to put herself back in the hands of the despicable dragon trader and his Thargian overlord, but she had no money and no other friends. Gim would jump at the chance of going to the festival and would probably be gone before she returned anyway.

She must seek out some sympathetic peasant family to take her in and let her stay a while. She could wash dishes or something for them in return for her keep. Sew, maybe—she was handy with a needle. She would pretend to be a refugee from Filoby! *My name is Antheala Battlemaster. My father is chief of the Jurgian army and loves me dearly. He plans to betroth me to one of the king's sons when I am a little older. Fearing that his enemies would strike at him by kidnapping me, he sent me to Iilah's convent for safekeeping.* That had been two fortnights ago, she decided, so she had not had time to learn very much about the convent, in case she was asked. The green monks had arrived at dawn and there had been terrible shouting and raping and she had fled out into the dark and had walked all day until . . .

She stepped where there was no ground. Her short leg betrayed her, and she pitched forward through the shrubbery—smashed her shoulder into something—twisted her ankle—screamed—landed hard on her side—rolled—fell again—banged her head—slithered down a steep hill—pitched into a torrent of icy-cold water—was twirled around, thumped against a rock or two, and then wrapped around a submerged tree trunk. She flailed wildly, struggled against the deadly press of the current, and finally managed to get her head up. Spluttering and gasping, she could breathe again. She would freeze to death. How could water be so cold in this hot land? She shook her ears dry and was horrified by the roar of the stream. She must be very close to the edge of the canyon, and might even have been swept into a waterfall had she not caught on the tree.

Struggling back to the bank was fairly easy. Clambering up the long, steep slope was not. Near the precipice, the little brook had dug a canyon of its own, narrow and dark. Eventually she hauled herself up into the bushes and just lay there, sore and cold and shaking.

*Tion!* she thought, *Tion, lord of art and youth, hear my prayer. I do not believe what those men said about you. I do not believe in that heretical Undivided god of T'lin's. Tion, save me!*

\*          \*          \*

After a while she concluded that her sufferings were not going to elicit a miracle. Perhaps Tion could not hear her prayer over the racket of the stream. Bigfangs had sharp hearing. The sun was close to setting. She tried to imagine climbing a tree to sleep in. She would surely fall out, and a tree would be a very uncomfortable bed anyway. Scrambling wearily to her feet, she set off along the edge of the little gorge again, limping through the prickles. The stream had stolen her sandals, but it would guide her back to Ruatvil. Thorns tugged at her smock and scraped her limbs.

In just a few moments there were no more trees ahead, only shrubs, with the sky above them. She had reached the town already! She could see the peaks of Susswall glowing pink, and off to the right, just rising clear of them, the green disk of Trumb. When Trumb rose shortly before sunset, he was due to eclipse. Reapers . . .

As she pushed her way out of the last of the bushes, her foot came down on nothing. Everything happened in a flash and yet seemed to take hours. She yelled in terror; she grabbed at a shrub; the ground crumbled away beneath her heel. She realized where she was—gazing at the sky, she had not been watching where she was going. She had climbed out of the stream on the far side, and followed it the wrong way. Her seat hit the ground and seemed to bounce her out into space. Her right hand had hold of something. The left joined it.

Her shoulders struck rock, skidded, and stopped. The one green cane she clutched so tight had bent double, like a rope, but not broken—yet. She dangled from it, a sharp edge digging into her back, her arms above her head, and her legs flailing in empty air. Hundreds of feet below her, muddy Susswater roiled in its canyon.

"Help!" she screamed. Then she just screamed. Off to her left, the stream emerged from its narrow gorge and sprayed out in a shiny cataract that faded away to the river below. It was much louder than she was.

There was no one around to hear her, anyway.

Her feet could find no purchase; nothing at all. The cane was liable to come out by the roots any minute, and her hands were crushed between it and the rock, so she could not even free them to try and pull herself back up.

Her hands were slipping on the sappy twig.

She tried to swing a leg up to the rock, but it wouldn't reach, and the bush made ominous cracking noises. She tried to turn over, and couldn't.

"Help! Oh, help! Tion!" Her cries were a croak: she could not breathe against the pressure on her back and her arms were about to pull out of their sockets.

*I don't want to die! I don't want to fulfill any stupid prophecies! I am only twelve years old! I don't want to deliver babies or wash grown men or do any of those things! I don't want to be a holy whore for Ois. I don't want to be a Historic Personage. I don't want to be killed by a reaper! I just want to be Eleal Singer and a great actor and faithful to Tion and beautiful! I didn't ask for all this and I don't want it and it isn't fair! And I don't want to die!*

Then strong fingers gripped her wrist and hauled her upward.

# 42

The Thargian had mentioned a caveman.

Eleal had found him.

Where the stream neared the great canyon of Susswater, it had undercut its bank on one side, to make a hollow roofed with rock and paved with sand and fine gravel. Ferns masked the entrance, so no one would ever find it. Someone had planted those ferns. Someone had made the shelter deeper and fitted it out with a little hearth, a bed of boughs covered with a fur robe, a store of firewood, a few misshapen jars and baskets. Someone was living there.

He was sitting there now with his skinny legs crossed and a crazy leer on his face. His hair and beard were white, flowing out in all directions. He wore only a loincloth of dirty fur. His skin was dried leather. In the flickering light of the tiny fire, he looked more like a bird's nest than a man.

Eleal sat on the bed, bundled inside another robe, and gradually managing to stop shaking. She was even nibbling some of the roots and berries the hermit had brought her, just to please him. She just couldn't stop talking, though. She was telling him the whole story for at least the third time.

He was not speaking. He couldn't speak.

He did not look as scary now as he had when she first saw him, but perhaps she had just grown used to him. He had explained with signs, and by writing on sand, that his name was Porith Molecatcher. He had lived here for many years—he did not seem to know how many. She was the first visitor who had ever come to his cave. He was originally from Niolland, which was many vales away. He had been a priest of Visek until he had been convicted of blasphemy and his tongue had been cut out. At that point Eleal concluded he was fantasizing. Visek's temple at Niol was supposed to be the greatest in all the Vales and hence the greatest in the world. On the other hand, she could not recall any other crime for which tongues were punished.

He was not totally without human contact. He traded skins with someone in Ruatvil for the few essentials he needed—salt and needles and perhaps others. A comb would be an excellent innovation, Eleal thought, regarding the undergrowth in his beard.

He listened to her story with mad grimaces. He frowned when she mentioned reapers, leered when she talked about crazy old Sister Ahn, and pulled faces of fierce disapproval when she described the harlots in the temple, but he might be just reacting to her tone or facial expressions.

She wondered what T'lin and Sister Ahn had made of her disappearance. They would expect her to come staggering out of the forest all repentant. Well, she wasn't going to! She could stay here, with Porith. Tion had sent the caveman to help her.

Night had fallen. The festival would be starting about now, with the service in the temple. Funny—the temple was only a few miles from Ruatvil. She might even be able to see the lights of the procession if she went out to the cliff edge. She wasn't going to, though. Of course it was on the other side of the river and to reach it on foot would be a very long day's walk.

*To break the chain of prophecy*—that was how the Thargian had described Garward Karzon's attack on Iilah's sacred grove. *The world may be changed,* Dolm Actor had said. Dolm must still believe she was safely locked up in Ois's temple in Narsh, plucking chickens—unless Zath had informed him otherwise. Who could hide from the god of death?

Well, another god could, because gods were immortal. She must not forget that Tion had rescued her from prison and sent Porith to pull her up the cliff. Tion was on her side! He would protect her still.

"Trumb will eclipse tonight, won't he?" she said, and Porith nodded, pulling faces.

Why was she so apprehensive about an eclipse of the big moon? It happened just about every fortnight, if the weather was good. Sometimes Trumb eclipsed twice in a fortnight, and then the temples were filled as the priests sought to avert misfortune. There were even stories of *three* eclipses in one fortnight, which meant someone very important was about to die.

She was worried over that silly rhyme about reapers filling sacks, that was all. In a couple of days, very likely, Wyseth would eclipse too, and day turn to night. That ought to be a lot more hair-raising, but somehow it never was.

She chewed another root. She must not expect first-class fare while she stayed with a caveman. Seven days would do it. If her host would let her stay with him until the end of the festival, then she would feel safe to return to civilization, because the prophecy would no longer apply.

Tion had provided the aid she had prayed for. He had brought her to this sanctuary.

What did the god want in return, though? The prophecy fulfilled? If she had been saved by a miracle, then surely it must have been so that she could fulfill her destiny. She was a Historic Personage. She was to help the Liberator—*Eleal shall wash him* and so on. The Liberator would bring death to Death.

Death was Zath, Dolm's god, the god who had sent the reapers after her. If Eleal Singer wanted anything, surely she ought to want to get her own back on Zath?

Trumb would eclipse tonight. The festival had begun. The Liberator might come tonight. Maybe tomorrow or any other time in the next half fortnight—by night, she thought, not by day. And Trumb would eclipse tonight.

She looked across the glowing embers and their tiny flickering flames to mad old

Porith, who was hugging his knees with arms like brown ropes, and watching her through the crazy glitter of his eyes.

"I have to go to the Sacrarium, don't I?" she whispered.

He nodded.

"Holy Tion brought me here to Sussland so that the prophecy can be fulfilled," she said, working it out. *Nod.* "If I am ever to succeed in my chosen career as an actor, I must do as my god commands." *Nod.* "He guided my steps today so I could overhear those two blasphemers, because I learned a lot from them."

For some reason Eleal Singer had to wash and clothe a grown man and then the world would be changed.

The Liberator was coming. If she did not go and watch, she would never forgive herself. Just watch—she need not *do* anything.

"That horrible Ois wants me kept away, so that means I should go!" *Nod.* "And afterward I'll be safe, too, because I'll have played my part in the prophecy!" *Nod.* "The Thargian said something about, 'until the Liberator arrives!' He meant that as soon as that happens, then the reapers will go for him and not me!" *Nod, leer.* "Then I won't matter to anyone anymore. So I'd better do what I have to do and get it over!"

*Nod.*

"Will you come with me?"

Porith shook his head violently.

She felt disappointed by that, but of course he was not protected by any god specially and not mentioned . . . yes he was! "But I'll bring the Liberator back here?"

Another violent shake—so violent that the old man's white hair and beard seemed to lash to and fro.

"It is prophesied! I told you!"

Porith cringed down as if he were sinking into the ground. He made little whimpering noises. Probably he hid in his burrow if anyone came near—it was only her youth and distress that had persuaded him to reveal his existence to her. He was a crazy old recluse.

"The *Testament* doesn't say I bring the Liberator to the *cave!*" Eleal said sharply. "It says I bring him to the *caveman!* That's you! For succor. So you stay here and be prepared to give succor!"

The sky was darkening, Trumb glowing brighter. She felt sick with fear, but she had known that feeling before. It was only stage fright. That thought cheered her up. This was her greatest role! Tonight she played for history and the gods themselves were in the audience! All the same, she had better get on with it or she might lose her resolve. She might even faint.

"Now, what's the quickest way to the Sacrarium? Can I walk around the cliff edge?"

*Nod.*

She frowned at her bare feet, already sore and blistered. She eyed the pile of furs—

moleskins, she assumed. "Could you make a pair of slippers? Just furs with sort of laces, maybe, to keep them on?"

Porith leered and nodded again, but made no move.

"Well, get started, then!" she said.

# ACT IV

## *Duet*

# 43

The cliff edge was easier walking than the jungle, because there was a lot of bare rock there. At times she had to choose between undergrowth and hair-raising acrobatics, but she made good progress. Soon she saw a distant twinkle of lights and guessed they were the bonfires at the temple.

*I do your bidding, Holy Tion. Watch over me!*

She began to worry that she might go right past the Sacrarium without seeing it. She should have asked the mad old hermit to give her directions. Well, if she arrived at the ruined bridge, she would know she had gone too far. And in the end there was no doubt. The forest thinned and she saw bare pillars standing over the trees, palely shining in Trumb's uncanny light.

Then she became very cautious. The distance was not great, but she moved one step at a time, feeling for her footing so she would not crack twigs or stumble on rocks. Her fur slippers were very good for that. She lifted branches out of the way; she stooped and at times even crawled on hands and knees. She clambered carefully over the fragments of masonry strewn around. There was no hurry—she had all night. She assumed that the forest was full of reapers, and that helped her to concentrate.

When she came to the steps, she sat down and took a breather. Then she wriggled up on her tummy through the litter of leaves and twigs until she could see into the court, staying close to a pillar. The ruin was empty and apparently deserted, haunted in the bright moonlight.

Well, if anyone else was around, he would be keeping quiet as she was. He would be flat on his belly as she was. He would be breathing very quietly as she was.

The mossy stone was cold. She should have brought one of Porith Molecatcher's fur blankets. But then she might have gone to sleep. She might have snored!

The Sacrarium seemed completely deserted. Not even the owls were making noises tonight. From the looks of the place, no one had come here in a hundred years. She had a deep conviction, though, that she was not the only one watching that circle of paving. The Thargian would be around somewhere, and perhaps the reinforcements he hoped for. Zath would have a reaper or two. T'lin Dragontrader? Sister Ahn?

Tion? Garward? Eltiana?

Even the gods would be watching.

But no one coughed. No one cracked a twig.

Why was the jungle so quiet?

Trumb climbed slowly up the sky.

The shadows played strange tricks. Eventually Eleal became convinced that there was a reaper standing on the far side of the Sacrarium, alongside one of the unbroken pillars. She told herself firmly that she was imagining things. No man would stand when he might have to wait for hours—he would sprawl on the ground as she did. Nevertheless, her eyes insisted on telling her that there was a dark figure standing beside that pillar, a man in a black gown with a hood. She thought she could even make out the paler glimmer of his face. Of course it had to be a delusion, a trick of the light.

She was too cold and uncomfortable to sleep, too frightened now to go away. No reaper would find her unless he stepped on her. Aware that she might have to wait until dawn, she stayed where she was, and the forest made no sounds at all.

# 44

An hour or so after midnight, the dogcart clattered through Amesbury and began the gentle climb westward to Stonehenge. The moon was barely past the full, playing hide-and-seek in the clouds. A chill wind was blowing—the weather had turned nasty.

Creighton was on the rear-facing seat, idly tapping on one of the little drums the Gypsies had made for him. Edward was talking with the driver, Billy Boswell. Billy was about Edward's age, short and swarthy and naturally reticent. Under the *gorgio*'s blandishments he had gradually been persuaded to talk about his life and himself. Now he was telling his worries that he might have to go and fight a war. That was exactly what Edward did want, but he was having trouble transferring his viewpoint to the Gypsy. He did not know how the Rom fared in Germany, and the greater benefits of English civilization were somewhat irrelevant to a man who spent most of his year on the road selling clothespins.

"Now, I was born in Africa—"

"Never 'eard of it."

*Mm!* Edward tapped his feet in counterpoint to the drum.

"By the way," Creighton said suddenly at their backs, "where did you get the fancy shoes, Exeter?"

"Billy gave them to me after we passed through Andover this afternoon. Very kind of him, I thought." They were a size too small, but a man must not look a gift shoe in the tongue. . . .

"Didn't cost nuffin'," Billy said in his Cheapside accent.

*Mm!* again.

Creighton stiffened, and pointed. "See lights over there?"

"Yes," said the front bench unanimously.

"Where's that?" Edward added.

"It must be the Royal Artillery Barracks at Larkhill. Means we're getting close."

Salisbury Plain, apparently, was not a plain. The road dipped into another hollow.

Edward felt scruples. This sneaking around in the small hours of the morning with a Gypsy and a highly suspect character like Creighton was probably going to involve him in trespassing at the very least, and Lord knew what else. "Does anyone live at Stonehenge, sir? Who owns it?"

"It's owned by Sir Edmund Antrobus. There's a policeman lives in a cottage about quarter of a mile to the west. Let us trust that the worthy constable does not suffer from insomnia." After a moment Creighton added, "The aerodrome's even closer, but I don't suppose there will be anyone there in the middle of the night."

Edward looked up as a patch of cloud began to glow fiercely silver. He shivered.

"Ah!" Creighton said. "You feel it too? How about you, Boswell?"

The Gypsy muttered something in Romany.

"Incredibly strong, if we can feel it here. There it is!"

The moon sailed out from behind its veils. Glimmering on the skyline a short way ahead stood the ghostly circle of trilithons—ruined, sinister, inexplicable. At first it seemed very small, surrounded by so much emptiness. As the cart grew closer, the height of the stones began to register. Who would have erected such a thing in so desolate a spot, and above all *why?* It was archaic insanity in stone, alone in the wind and time. The pony continued to trot along the dusty track, unaffected by such morbid wonderings.

Edward's scalp prickled. "Are you sure we couldn't try somewhere a little less spooky first, sir? Not so much 'virtuality'?"

"We could, but I have my reasons for wanting to start here. The Chamber knows the prophecy too, remember. There are only five or six nodes in Sussland, so it would not be an impossible task to interdict them against you."

"I don't think I quite follow that. In fact I'm sure I don't."

"Think of a magic spell: 'No one named Edward Exeter may come this way.'"

"Magic is that specific?"

"Call it mana, not magic. If it's strong enough, it can be. I'm hoping that a portal this powerful will overcome that sort of blockage, if it's been tried." *Hrrmph!* "It's a great mistake to assume that your enemy is infallible, you know. They may have forgotten that you have a middle name."

Edward wished Creighton's words would justify the confidence in his tone. "What about guards at the other end? I mean, if the Blighters are hunting me here, why won't the Chamber be waiting for me there?"

"I'm sure they will be," Creighton said breezily. "I hope some of our chaps will be on hand to make a fight of it. I'll be on my own turf, too, in a manner of speaking."

*Affalino kaspik* . . . The nonsense words were going around and around in Edward's head. He could feel the complex stirrings of the rhythm, too. Was that some sort of response to the occult power of the node? Sheer funk, more like.

"There's a fence!" He hoped that the fence would be the end of the matter and they could go home now, but he didn't really expect that. It was a confident-looking barbed wire fence strung on steel posts.

"Yes, and the attendant is not on hand to accept our sixpences or whatever they charge."

"We can climb that."

"We could, but Mr. Boswell can deal with the fence for us, can't you, Mr. Boswell?"

Billy said nothing while the cart dipped where the track crossed a wide hollow and a bank. Then he reined in the dogcart alongside the fence. "Didn't tell me t'bring me tools. Can just 'eave it dahn fo' ya."

"Why not?" Creighton said, jumping out of the gig. "Devil take it! Beastly bad form to disfigure a national treasure that way." His obnoxious heartiness was probably concealing the same sort of eerie nervousness as Edward was feeling. "Now, Exeter, I have bad news."

Edward sighed. "Yes, sir."

"You can take nothing with you when you cross over. Nothing can translate except a human being, not even the fillings in his teeth. You needn't worry about those, but clothes are an impediment."

"We have to go through with this rigmarole in the nude?"

"Starkers." Creighton tossed his hat into the dogcart and began unbuttoning. "Quick, while there's moonlight."

Groaning, Edward began to strip also. He removed his shoes with relief. Dawn would appear in about two hours, he thought. The moment the sun's edge showed above the horizon he would be free of his oath, and then he was going to shed his lunatic companion, even if the only way to do it was to walk into a police station and give himself up.

Billy led the pony forward a few feet. A section of fence tried to follow with a long squeal of agony, the posts pulling free from the chalk. "'At aw'a do ya," the Gypsy remarked, and backed up the cart so he could recover his rope.

Edward looked nervously at the lights of Larkhill to the north; he stared across the dark plain to the vague shapes that might be the aerodrome buildings, but no lights had come on in their windows. He tossed his socks into the wagon.

"Splendid fellow!" Creighton said patronizingly. "Now, Boswell, you'll wait here for twenty minutes or so, won't you? Just in case. Hate to have to walk to Salisbury in my birthday suit."

He reached into the dogcart for the drums. He hung one around his own neck and looped the other over Edward's.

"Come, Exeter!" he barked cheerfully, stepping carefully over the fallen wire. He set off across the turf, a ghostly white shape in the moonlight.

Still fumbling with the buttons of his fly, Edward suddenly said, "No!"

Creighton stopped and wheeled around. "Word of honor!" he barked.

"Sir, you extracted that by unfair means. I have a duty to King and Country."

"You have a duty to your father's memory and his life's work, also."

"Sir, I have only your word for that. You have not been fair with me."

Creighton growled. "You have no concept of what is going to happen in this war. Millions of men are going to die! The mud of Europe will be soaked with blood!"

"I have a duty!"

"Idiot! Even if you managed to get to the front—which I doubt very much—you would be nothing there but more cannon fodder. Your destiny lies on Nextdoor. Shut up and listen to me! You don't know what the prophecy calls you—the Liberator!"

"Me?"

"You! Why do you think the Chamber fears you? These are the people who killed your parents, Exeter! If you refuse to come with me now, then your mother and father died in vain!"

Edward shivered in silence for a moment, the night air icy cold on his bare chest. "I have your word on that, sir?"

"I swear it as your father's friend."

With a sigh, Edward unfastened his trousers.

Naked, he followed Creighton through the gap in the fence, shivering with both cold and a bitter apprehension. Nudity seemed only fitting, somehow. The last few days had progressively stripped him of everything—his good name, his prospects for a career, his chance to fight in a war, his future inheritance, his most precious possessions, like his parents' picture and that last letter to Jumbo, even Fallow, which had been in fact his home. Alice. He might never even know how *The Lost World* turned out at the end, he thought bitterly. All gone.

"Might as well go right to the center," Creighton remarked. "We'll be less conspicuous there if anyone should happen to come along the road."

What would Billy Boswell do in that case? Better not to think about it. Better not to think about anything. Edward followed his leader between the towering stones, into moonlit mystery. At close range, Stonehenge was not just a clutter of standing stones, it was a building—a ruined building, but an awe-inspiring one.

Creighton's teeth gleamed at him in a smile. "One last warning!"

"Tell me."

"Passing over is quite a shock to the system, especially the first time. You'll be badly disoriented. I should react better, although it's a bit like seasickness—you can never predict. It may last some time. I hope we'll have some friends there to help. They won't speak any English, of course."

"How can I tell if they're friends or enemies?"

"Well, look out for johnnies in black gowns like monks. They're called 'reapers' and they're deadly. They can slay a chap with a touch. Otherwise—friends will help you. If they try to kill you, assume they're enemies."

"Why didn't I think of that?" Edward muttered under his breath. "Lay on, Macduff!"

Creighton turned his back, and began to pat out the rhythm on the drum with his hands. In a moment he said, "One—two—three!" and began the chant.

Jumping, jiggling, gesturing, singing, they pranced around, following each other in a small circle. *Inso athir ielee ... paral inal fon. ...* The moonlight faded, then brightened.

There were a lot of beastly sharp stones in the grass.

Edward decided he was not cut out to be a witch doctor. This was the most ridiculous thing he had ever done in his life. He would freeze to death. And it was wrong! Those great pillars looming over him in the darkness were an ancient mystery, sanctified in ways he could not imagine. He was profaning something mighty, consecrated by the hands of time itself. . . .

He cried out and stumbled to a halt, shivering and sweating simultaneously, shaken to the core by a sense of revulsion and awe. "No, no!"

Silence returned to the night.

"Aha!" Creighton said triumphantly. "You felt that?"

"No. Nothing. I felt nothing!"

*"Hrrmph!* Well I did! It was starting. So it works. It's going to take us somewhere, even if not where we want to go. Sure you felt nothing?"

"Quite sure," Edward said, jaw chattering. "Quite certain."

"Mm? Clench your teeth." Creighton reached out and prized up a corner of the sticking plaster on Edward's forehead. "Now!"

Yank!

"Ouch! You scalped me!"

"Let's see if that helps. All right, we'll start from the beginning again. Now, concentrate! Be sure and get the movements right. Ready? . . ."

"No!" Edward shouted, backing away. "Oh, no!" He was naked and cold and he had been duped into behaving like a lunatic. "You're just trying to fulfill the prophecy, aren't you? That's what all this is about!"

"I'm trying to save your life! If what we do fulfills the prophecy, then so be it. You'd prefer to die? Take it from the beginning—"

"I won't! I'm not coming."

"Boy!" the colonel thundered. "You gave me your word!"

Edward backed away farther. "You cheated. You lied to me!"

"I did not!"

"You said the Service supports the prophecy! You said my father was one of them— you said he did, too! But the guv'nor didn't, did he? He wanted to break the chain! He said so in that letter!"

After a long moment, Creighton sighed. "All right, old man. You're right. I never lied to you, but you're absolutely right. Cameron Exeter did not approve of all the things prophesied about the Liberator. Some, yes, certainly, but not all. He split with the majority on this. He did not want any son of his to be the Liberator."

Edward backed up another step and cannoned into a monolith. It was hard and cold and jagged. He recoiled. "The guv'nor did not approve of turning worlds upside down! That's what he said."

"That was partly it—what you will do to the world. But it was more what the world will do to you."

"What do you mean: 'What the world will do to me'?"

"He didn't think you could possibly be man enough to . . ." Creighton shivered.

"Look, you haven't any alternative now, have you? Trust me! When you get to Olympus we'll give you the whole story from beginning to—"

The silence of the night exploded in noise. Something enormous roared nearby, the sound merging into the pony's scream of terror. Billy howled curses as the dogcart rattled and jangled away into the distance, taking him with it and leaving the two men stranded, naked, on Salisbury Plain.

"What in the name of Jehoshaphat was *that?*" Creighton demanded, staring into the darkness.

The hair on Edward's neck was rising. "That was a lion!"

"No!"

"Oh yes it was! That's the grunt they use to scare their prey when they're hunting. How do lions get to Stonehenge, Colonel?"

"Ask rather what they eat at Stonehenge. Let's try the key again, shall we? And this time it had better work."

Edward thought he agreed with that. He had heard lions often enough, but never so horribly close. That fence would never stop a hungry lion, and there was a gap in it now anyway.

"Ready?" said Creighton. "One—Two—Three . . ."

*Affalino kaspik* . . . The drumbeats throbbed. Arms and legs waved—even head movements were supposedly important, and he kept wanting to watch the wall of trilithons, to see what might be coming through. To look for green eyes in the night.

The moon sailed into a cloud and died.

Half the beat stopped as if cut off by a guillotine, and so did Creighton's voice. His drum bounced and rolled away on the grass. Edward stumbled to a halt. He was alone.

# 45

It began as a faint sigh in the distance. It came closer. It was a rushing of wind through the trees and soon seemed all around, everywhere but where Eleal lay in the darkness. At last it arrived and the leaves stirred. Boughs creaked, thrashed. Gradually it faded, traveling on, and the night stilled. Trumb shone unchallenged in a cloudless sky, drowning out the stars with his baleful splendor.

She shivered, wondering what god had sent that wind sign. She was cramped and cold. She flexed herself, one limb at a time, frightened of making any noise among the trash of leaves and branches that covered the steps. She had no idea how long she had been lying there, too tense even to doze. Her neck was appallingly stiff.

Her eyes were still insisting that there was a reaper on the far side of the court. It could not be just a trick of the light, for the big moon had moved a long way since she arrived, and was very bright. It must be a tree stump, perhaps a dead sapling coated in ivy. No man could stand for so many hours like that.

Trumb *must* eclipse soon! There had been a hint of shadow on one side of his disk when he rose, but now it was a perfect circle and that meant . . .

A scream rent the silence of the night and a man rolled to the paving only a few yards from her. His limbs flailed and he cried out again. Her hair rose. *Where had he come from?*

Naked, a grown man—this must be the Liberator! He sounded as he was in terrible pain. She started to rise and then stopped, hearing feet slap on stone. Another man came running out of the darkness on her right, and then a second from the left.

The first was T'lin—big, and heavily bearded, and wearing a black turban that barely showed in the moonlight, so that the top half of his head seemed to be missing. He carried a bundle. And the other was the lanky Thargian, drawing a sword and looking around as he ran.

Huh! Well if those two were here, they could attend to all the washing and nursing required. Eleal's services were not needed, not wanted. She could have enjoyed a good night's rest instead.

The Liberator's cries of pain had faded to grunts and moans. He retched and vomited, then groaned again.

"*You,* sir!" the Thargian exclaimed. "We expected someone else." He knelt, and helped the man sit up.

T'lin stayed standing, peering around warily at the darkness with his hand on the hilt of his sword.

"Gover?" The Liberator retched again, and doubled up as if cramped—except that the Thargian had implied that this was not the Liberator. "Good to see you."

"We should leave!" T'lin growled.

"Calm down, Seventy-seven!" the Thargian snapped. "If there was anyone out there, they'd be all over us by now."

"Yes, but—"

"Just wait a minute! Can't you see the man's in pain? Bad crossing, sir?"

The reply was a suppressed bubbling shriek from the newcomer, as another spasm took him. The Thargian put an arm around his shoulders and cradled his head like a child's.

"All right, Kriiton," he muttered. "You're among friends. It'll pass."

The comforting seemed to help. In a moment Kriiton muttered, "Thanks!" and pushed himself free. "Where's Kisster?" He looked around. "God Almighty! He . . . He didn't make it?"

"No sign of anyone else, sir."

The reply was lost in another groan, another spasm of cramps. Again the Thargian cuddled the sufferer, and again the physical comforting seemed to ease the pain.

The men were fading! Eleal tore her eyes away and looked up in sudden terror. Trumb was well into eclipse already. Darkness raced over the great disk.

"Gotta go back 'n get'm!" Kriiton mumbled.

"You're in no state for another crossing, sir! It would kill you! We've got no key for it anyway, not that I know of."

"Where is this?"

"The Sacrarium at Ruatvil."

Kriiton sighed. The others were almost invisible now; his bare skin showed up better. "In Sussland! So it should have worked! Let's hope he keeps trying!"

"First time is hardest sometimes, isn't it?" the Thargian said.

The Kriiton man suppressed a groan, as if he was being racked by more cramps. "Can be. Maiden voyage. Trouble is, the opposition was moving in on us."

Trumb had dwindled to a thin line, a sword cut in the sky. The darkened disk was faintly visible, black against the reborn stars.

"Opposition may move in here, too, sir," the Thargian said. "Seventy-seven's right. We ought to go, soon as you're ready. Damned moon'll be back in a minute. We've brought some clothes so let's get you up now and—"

T'lin uttered a yell of warning. Another figure had entered the darkened courtyard, gliding swiftly over the ancient stones, black and infinitely menacing. Eleal thought of flight, her limbs twitched uncertainly, and then she just froze, like a small animal facing a large predator. Dolm had been able to see in the dark!

"Up!" Kriiton yelled. "Get me up!"

The other two grabbed his arms and hauled him to his feet. Trumb's final crescent had gone. Starlight flashed as the Thargian brandished his sword in the reaper's face.

The reaper stopped just out of reach and chuckled. "You expect to block me with that, Gover Envoy?" That was not Dolm Actor's voice! Eleal was too terrified to move an eyelid, barely even to think, but she knew that was not Dolm's voice she was hearing.

The Thargian cried out and his sword clanged to the ground.

"Don't fandangle with me, Reaper!" Kriiton croaked. He was leaning hard on T'lin's shoulder, as if unable to straighten properly. "Go now and I'll spare you."

"But I will not spare you! Prepare to meet the Last Victor."

The men were half-seen shapes in the faint gleam of stars. Trumb's disk was a round black hole in the stars, the moon of Zath. The reaper stretched forth his hand and took a step forward.

*Flash!* Thunder!

Ruins and jungle jumped out of the night and then vanished again.

Eleal cried aloud and jerked back, her ears ringing from the crash. Her eyes burned with a dazzling afterimage, as if she had been blinded. *Lightning out of a clear sky?* She wiped away tears with shaking hands.

"By the moons, sir!" Gover Envoy was shouting, but his voice sounded muffled through the hum in her ears. "You answered his arguments!" He laughed shrilly.

T'lin was muttering. Forcing her eyes to work, Eleal saw that he had fallen on his knees in prayer. The reaper was stretched out flat on his back, motionless. Envoy was supporting Kriiton. There was a strange, tingling scent in the air.

"Crude!" Kriiton muttered. "Lost control."

"It worked!" said the Thargian. "That one filled no sacks."

"Worked too well. Drained me. Far too much!" He made an effort to stand by himself. "I wanted to stun him, not fry him. All right, where are those clothes?"

Eleal's eyes were recovering. Her ears still buzzed. In the heavy darkness, tiny red fireflies shone on the body of the reaper, and she did not understand those. She heard, more than saw, that T'lin had scrambled to his feet and unrolled his bundle.

So where was the Liberator? And what was this Kriiton, who appeared out of empty air and called down thunderbolts? Was he man or god? His paleness faded away as he hauled a smock over his head, and then he was just a dark shape like the others. He staggered, and Envoy reached out an arm to steady him, but obviously he was recovering.

"Right," he grunted. "Shoes? Fornication! I had D'ward right with me. Damned good kid, too, from what I saw."

A razor cut of light in the sky in the background heralded the return of Trumb. The pillars glimmered back into view and the stars faded. Puzzled, Eleal strained to make out what the men were doing. There seemed to be four of them. There *were* four of them! She opened her mouth to yell a warning, but her dry throat made no sound. Another reaper had joined the group.

Two men went down in fast succession, without a sound. They thrashed on the ground and then she heard some muffled choking, but that was all.

The third one yelled, and leaped back. Then he turned and fled. His feet slapped noisily over the stones.

The reaper laughed, a deep and horribly familiar sound. "Come back! I want you!" It was Dolm Actor! He also ran, but in total silence, a black cloud flowing swiftly across the court. His quarry vanished between the pillars, and shrubbery crashed as he plowed into it. The reaper followed him out without a rustle. The two dying men lay still.

Gone!

The sounds of the fugitive's flight had stopped, but that might be either because he had reached the path or because the reaper had caught him—and would then return, perhaps.

Eleal felt sick. Her heart was hammering its way out of her chest and there was a bitter swirling sensation in her head. Swift, unwelcome brightness was flooding the Sacrarium as if a door was opening, revealing the carnage. She wanted to cry *Stop!* She preferred the dark. Three bodies, three men dead, and probably one more corpse out in the woods now. Dolm Reaper might come back at any moment, to gather more souls for Zath. Hers.

She couldn't leave dying men, however little she expected to be able to help.

And she had to know which ones they were.

Quick, then! She staggered to her feet and tried to run forward. It was only a few yards, but she was so stiff and unsteady from lying still that she nearly fell. She stumbled to her knees beside the Thargian, almost on top of his fallen sword. Gover Envoy lay on his side because his back was bent like a bow, his limbs twisted behind him. His mouth was still dribbling blood, black in the green light, and his dead eyes bulged as if he had perished in terrible agony. He had not made a sound, but obviously a reaper death was not an easy one.

The first reaper lay on his back, spread-eagled. He had a gaping black hole in his chest, and there was a nasty scent of scorched cloth and charred meat around him, but at least his ending had been quick. His cowl had fallen back to expose his face. She had never seen him before, a bearded man of middle years. His eyes were rolled up, the whites shining green in the light of his god.

The third corpse lay in the same contorted arch as Envoy, but he was on his belly, head and limbs bent up grotesquely. His face was distorted by the same rictus of agony—teeth exposed, dead eyes bulging, and a puddle of blood congealing under his mouth. He was not T'lin, and therefore had to be the strange Kriiton, whose powers had been able to slay one reaper but not defend against another. His nose was prominent, his eyebrows heavy, and he had a stubbly mustache. Man or demon, he was very obviously as dead as the other two.

So T'lin Dragontrader had escaped, if he had managed to run fast enough. *Run, T'lin, run!* Very faintly, she heard a dragon burp in the distance.

Nothing Eleal could do here.

She scrambled to her feet and glanced around to make sure no reapers were approaching. Right before her eyes, a man rolled to the paving out of empty air. He thrashed a whirl of bare limbs, and screamed.

# 46

When Edward saw Creighton's drum rolling on the grass, he felt as if time itself had stopped. He knew his heart had. He was conscious of the darkness, the wind on his heated skin, and utter disaster. Billy and the dogcart had gone and would not return.

To be arrested stark naked on Salisbury Plain would certainly reinforce a plea of insanity, but he did not want to spend the rest of his life locked up in Broadmoor. That might be the better choice, though, if his only alternative was to be eaten by lions. He did not for one moment believe that some escaped circus animal had chanced to wander past Stonehenge. There might or might not be a flesh-and-blood carnivore out there, but without doubt there was an enemy.

Time had not stopped, and he had none of it to waste. For a brief moment he considered trying some of the African chants and dances he knew, but he saw at once that those might take him to the wrong place. He must believe what Creighton had told him. He must follow Creighton; without Creighton he would be hopelessly lost. As he was about to start tapping, he heard laughter in the darkness, human laughter.

He did not look. He began the ritual again, concentrating on the beat, trying not to think about the interdiction Creighton had mentioned.

Laugh away, friends! We'll try this again.

He let the rhythm grow in his mind, shutting out everything else. *De-de-de-DAH-de, DAH-de*... He began the beat. Creighton had been taking it too slowly. He began the dance. *Affalino kaspik*... He ignored the laughter. *DAH de-de-DAH Affaliki suspino ayakairo*...

Faster, faster! He let the rhythm flower, seeking its subtleties, its complex cross-beats, three against four, left against right, four against five, tasting it in his mind, living it. The words rolled and jigged. The movements flowed. He absorbed the ritual soaking through him, bearing him back to childhood and farther yet, to atavistic tribal memories. My fathers danced here in the Dreamtime! He felt the response, the surge of power, the thrill, rising like a life force, a thrill permeating his whole body.

Now the aura of awe and sanctity swelled in wonder.

*Here it comes! DAH-de, DAH-de-de*... The power grew up around him. Waves of excitement surging—he could feel them in his blood and along his bones. His heart moved in time. He felt awe, sanctity, power. The laughter had stopped. Legs, head, elbows—hands beating the intricate rhythm, primitive, primal. *Kalafano Nokte! Finothoanam*... Stronger, harder. He was one with the world and the pulse of worlds. The power roared. Something tried to block it and he overrode it, wielding strength and will. A voice howled in sudden fury. The cosmos opened for him and he plunged through.

He had a momentary sensation of flying. He felt himself as infinitely tiny, swept past shapes infinitely large. Dark and cold. Speed.

*Impact!*

Were it possible to be smashed flat and live, then that was the sensation. Not physical pain—emotional. He had never guessed at anything approaching such shame, such sorrow and despair. All his muscles knotted up in horror, and then it was physical also. He heard himself screaming and he wanted to die.

Someone was hugging him, soothing him. In his wrenching abyss of misery, he sensed a spark of human compassion. He clung, clung desperately. Agonies of cramps, waves of nausea—but someone cared, and that was salvation. The spark was there, life amid the measureless void of death.

There was a hand over his mouth, but he could not stop screaming. Every muscle strained, every tendon was pulling free of his bones. His gut was a fire pit and his heart was tearing itself to ribbons. *Die, die, oh please die!*

A voice shouted his name, over and over.

He opened his eyes and saw the moon. *Godfathers!* What had happened to the moon? The screaming had started again. Was that him?

Who was this he was crushing to him?

He was rolling around on cold stone, hugging someone. In the dark. The air was hot and scented. Moonlight, *green* moonlight.

Nextdoor was much more than just an island.

# 47

The man fell still, his muscles too exhausted to do more than quiver like leaves in a wind. His arms had been holding Eleal in iron bands, and now they dropped away limply. His eyes were open, staring, but they did not seem to be looking at anything. His breath came in frightening, irregular gasps.

She backed off a few feet on hands and knees. "Liberator?"

"Yes," said Dolm's resonant voice. "I fancy that is the Liberator this time."

Eleal opened her mouth to scream and nothing happened. She stared up in paralyzed silence at the reaper looming over her, immensely tall and dark against the sky. He shook his cowled head sadly. His face was in shadow, but she could not mistake the voice.

"I have no option, Eleal. You do understand that?"

She wriggled farther away.

"Running will not save you," Dolm said. "You belong to my master now. First the Liberator, then you."

"No!" she whimpered.

"You are young and your soul is worth much."

"All souls are worth much," said another voice.

The reaper turned in a swirl of black cloth to regard the newcomer as she hobbled across the courtyard, pounding her staff with one hand, trailing her sword in the other. Its point scraped across the stone with a bloodcurdling scratching.

Dolm laughed. "Yours is not, old woman. Depart and cherish the days that are left to you. If you are gone when I have taken these two, then I shall not pursue you."

Eleal leaped to her feet and raced around the litter of corpses to Sister Ahn's side. The bent old crone dropped her stick and rested her gnarled hand on Eleal's shoulder instead. She kept her eyes on the reaper, though. "Repent, Minion of Zath!"

He paced toward them. "I have nothing to repent, hag."

"Not the deeds you commit in his name, no." Her harsh, corroded voice was surprisingly powerful. "But there is another, or he would not have enlisted you to his dread band. Repent, I say, and be free!"

"Never!"

"Here, my dear," Sister Ahn said. "Lift this sword with me. Both hands. We must fulfill a prophecy."

It did not occur to Eleal to refuse. Trembling, she took hold of the hilt around the nun's frail grasp, and between them they raised the long blade until it pointed unsteadily at the man in black.

Dolm laughed again, a grotesque parody of that jovial laugh Eleal knew so well. "You know that weapons are useless against a reaper! Come then, to my master!"

He strode forward. In a creaky chant, Sister Ahn gabbled something so fast that Eleal made out few words. "Holy-Irepithear . . . transferthesin . . . thathemaysee . . . pay here not elsewhere . . ." The sword seemed to swing of its own accord. The reaper screamed and fell. Sister Ahn crumpled. The sword dropped clanging to the stone.

Eleal staggered away with a shriek of fright. For a moment the temple swayed about her and she stuffed knuckles in her mouth. Her knees wobbled. Then she saw that the danger was gone. Dolm Actor was a shapeless, motionless heap of black. The old woman was sitting on the ground, doubled over, her head between her knees.

Eleal knelt down to hug Sister Ahn's thin shoulders.

"Sister! Sister!"

The nun fell sideways and rolled on her back. Dark blood was already soaking through the front of her habit.

Eleal uttered a shrill sob that was almost a scream. "What happened?" The blade had never touched the nun, she was certain.

Eyes flickered open. The emaciated face twisted into a smile. The pallid lips moved, but Eleal heard nothing.

"What?" she leaned closer on hands and knees, frightened now even to touch the old woman's garments. So much blood!

"My part is over, child," Sister Ahn said, soft but clear. "Yours begins. Eleal has the stage now—for a little while."

A moment later, her eyes rolled up, lifeless. As Eleal watched in horror, death and moonlight smoothed out the wrinkles like melting wax, leaving only a hint of a smile. The sword had never touched her, but it had obviously slain her. One dead woman and four dead men and . . .

The Liberator was trying to sit up.

Eleal ran across to him. He would explain what was happening. He could defend her against whatever other horrors the night might bring. He was a much younger man than she had expected, only a very tall boy—unless he shaved off his whiskers, of course, in which case she supposed he might count as a grown man. His hair was dark, yet his wide-stretched eyes were light. Blood from a gash on his head had painted one side of his face and dribbled down his neck and chest, black in the greenish moonlight.

"Liberator?"

He stared blankly at her for a moment, then seemed to realize that he had no clothes on. He moved his hands to cover himself. The movement brought on a spasm of cramp; he gurgled and doubled over.

Eleal found a garment, one that T'lin had dropped. She took it to the Liberator; he tried to take it from her and again went into convulsions. Eleal put it over his hands, one at a time, and then lifted his arms to let it drop around his neck. With difficulty, frequently twisting and writhing with cramps, he managed to pull it down and tuck the hem over his thighs. Then he looked up and again tried to speak, but what he said was still gibberish. It ended in a sob of pain and despair.

*Naked and crying he shall come into the world and Eleal shall wash him. She shall clothe him and nurse him and comfort him.*

She would have to do something about that blood.

"Are you the Liberator?" she shouted.

More gibberish. Partly he had trouble even speaking, for the least movement seemed to start all his muscles into cramps. Partly he was using some language she had never heard. It was not Thargian, or even Niolian.

"Eleal," she said, tapping her chest. "Liberator?" She pointed at him.

He said something that sounded like, "*Ed*ward."

She sniggered at that. "D'ward?"

He nodded faintly.

"Good! Come, we must go! There must be some sandals you can have."

More gibberish—"Kriiton?" He had his back to the corpses.

She pointed. The youth turned carefully to see and gave a cry. He tried to rise, only to collapse in a whimpering tangle. Then he began dragging himself over the ground, moving one limb at a time. Obviously the effort was agony for him, but he persevered. Her efforts to help merely hindered him, so she stood aside and let him crawl. She tried to warn him about more reapers coming, but he paid no heed. He hauled himself all the way to Kriiton's body and peered at the face.

He shuddered, then gently reached out and closed the eyes, muttering something Eleal could not understand. She brought him sandals and Sister Ahn's staff and pointed urgently to the north. He nodded, and began the ordeal of rising to his feet.

Leaning heavily on the walking stick and the child's shoulder, Edward moved his feet one at a time in the direction she had suggested.

The night was a blur of nightmare for him. He knew he was in deep shock and should not try to make sense of anything until he had recovered. Creighton had warned him, but he had not expected so much pain, so much confusion and weakness. Half his muscles were useless and he did not know how much he could trust his senses. Was that really Creighton lying there? Who were the others? Reapers, Creighton had said, but all the clothes had seemed black. The moon was pure hallucination—three or four times the size a moon ought to be and a lurid green. The markings on it looked like a hammer. Its light drowned out the stars.

The building was a vague echo of some ruined Greek temple, with remains of a circle of pillars on a paved plinth. Beyond that lay jungle. It had a humid, tropical smell. There were mosquitoes, although any attempt to swat them—any sudden movement at all—brought on the terrible muscle cramps. Even resting, his whole body ached from them.

His tongue had found two gaping holes in his teeth. They felt enormously larger than they would look, of course, but again Creighton's prediction had been correct. The fillings were back on Earth, in the grass of Wiltshire. So were his stitches and sticking plaster; his face was caked with blood from the reopened wound on his temple. It drew insects.

Bodies all over the place, five of them. Expect friends or enemies, Creighton had said, but obviously both had been waiting. There had been an ambush and a battle. Had Edward crossed over at the same time as Creighton, would he also now be stiffening in that charnel house? He might as well be—for what did a man do in a strange world when he could not speak the language, had no friends, no money, nor even any concept of who his friends and enemies were? Why had Bloody Idiot Creighton been so secretive about what Edward was to expect?

And the girl—who had brought her here and why? Was one of these dead men her father, perhaps? She was understandably terrified, of course, shaking almost as much as he was. Every few minutes she would jump at some shadow, but for her age she was doing amazingly well. She had a pronounced limp, which made her an unsteady support. Every lurch, every effort to lift the staff, threatened to make his muscles cramp up in knots.

She seemed pathetically eager to help and please. And since she showed no signs of wanting to add Edward's corpse to the collection, he must assume that she was a friend. Her impatience suggested that she had some associates waiting, or a safe refuge. Transportation, perhaps. At the very least she would know how to get word to the Service that Cameron Exeter's son had arrived on Nextdoor.

# 48

Thinking *money*, Eleal awoke at first light, having slept very little, and poorly. The bed she had chosen was gravelly, but the only reasonably flat area near the shelter. D'ward had suffered even in his sleep. His moans and cries had disturbed her often and she had gone to inspect him several times.

She threw off her rug and went to take another look. He was sleeping peacefully. She had washed the blood from his face, but the pad of moss she had bound to his head was caked. She had also bathed as many of his scrapes as she could without being indecent, although by the time she and Porith had brought him in, he had been more or less unconscious.

She glanced around the shadowy gully. Where was the mad old hermit? Very likely he was curled up under a bush somewhere nearby, but she did not know where. With any luck he was already out hunting breakfast, three breakfasts. Well, she would enlist his aid later. Right now she had some pillage to attend to.

She clambered up the bank and set off back to the Sacrarium. The bodies would have to be buried, or disposed of in some other way if Porith had no spade, and she had seen no signs of one. T'lin's friends or more of Zath's reapers might investigate the ruin soon, and there was always the chance of a stray pilgrim. Whoever found those five corpses would surely raise a hue and cry. She did not want that, so she would have Porith remove them. First they should be looted. Almost certainly there would be money on some of those dead men and she did not see why she should share it with Porith Molecatcher. He had no use for silver and she did.

She would also collect Sister Ahn's magic sword and present it to the Liberator. Anyone with so many enemies should be armed, and tall, lean men like D'ward always looked good with swords dangling at their belts. It would certainly look better on him than it had on Sister Ahn.

The walk seemed much shorter than it had the night before, especially when she had been half-carrying D'ward. Grown men were heavy, even young, skinny ones. From that point of view, a baby would have been much easier to manage.

The sun rose while she was working her way along the cliff top. It warmed her and revived her. Birds sang cheerfully. She saw the pillars and turned away from the cliff, moving with more care amid the trees. Soon she passed the spot where D'ward had collapsed. She had left him there while she went and fetched Porith. He had been very unwilling—she had almost had to punch him to make him come back and help her. Stupid, crazy old man!

She reached the Sacrarium steps . . .

The bodies had gone.

She stood like a tree, staring in disbelief. Nothing stirred. Eventually she crept forward and took a closer look. There were dried bloodstains on the stone, nothing more.

She soon discovered a trampled trail through the woods, leading to the cliff. Someone had dragged the corpses along there—probably just one man, she thought, or the weeds would not be so crushed. She found a fragment of black cloth snagged on a thorn.

At the edge she lay on her tummy and peered over. Far below her, Susswater was a slowly roiling yellow snake. She could guess that it would be a deafening torrent if she were down there, but from up here its motion was barely detectable, just a hint of life, like muscle moving below skin. Specks of birds were circling about halfway up the cliff, so some of the bodies might have caught on rocks.

Who could have done this? Certainly no stray pilgrim would have chanced by in the middle of the night. Old Porith Molecatcher was too frightened of the reapers. There might be more reapers about, and she reminded herself that she could not recognize a reaper unless he was wearing his work clothes. T'lin Dragontrader might have escaped and returned. Or the Service he had mentioned might have sent more agents. The reapers she did not want. The Service blasphemed, so she thought she probably did not want that either. In any case, she had no idea who the Service was, or where it could be found. D'ward must know, and he could decide.

She found Porith drinking at a pool some distance upstream from his shelter. She knelt down on the edge of the gully and remarked cheerfully, "Good morning!"

He jumped like a frog and then scowled up at her.

"Did you move the dead bodies from the Sacrarium?" she demanded.

He shook his head, mad eyes wide.

"What's for breakfast?"

He scowled even more at that, and shook his head. Then he pointed in the general direction of the cave and made a "Git!" motion.

"You wish my friend and myself to depart?"

*Emphatic nod.*

"I'm sure we will withdraw as soon as he is rested. But right now he's still very weak and must be fattened up and strengthened for the journey. Red meat and lots of it!"

She tried a winning smile and it was poorly received.

"Don't you make obscene gestures at me, Porith Molecatcher! You're a priest, you said. Well, this is gods' work. You're mentioned in the prophecy, the *Filoby Testament,* and Holy Visek is god of prophecy. So the gods know you and what you're doing, and they expect you to give succor to the Liberator. The seeress said so!"

*Glare.*

"Breakfast, if you please?"

Eleal rose and walked away with as much dignity as her limp allowed. Ambria Impresario would have been proud of her.

She found D'ward sitting outside the cave. He smiled weakly at her and said, "Eleal!"

"Godsbless, D'ward! Have you remembered how to speak yet?"

He looked at her blankly. His eyes were intensely blue, although his hair was as black as any she had ever seen. She would not call him handsome, she decided. He was plain. He was bony. On the other hand he was certainly not ugly.

It was hardly fair to judge him now. His features were pale and drawn, his arms and legs a mess of scrapes and bruises. Caked blood disfigured his bandage and his mouth was swollen where he had bitten his lips. All in all, though, he was alert and probably on the mend. He seemed older than he had in the night. Lots of men shaved their faces, especially Thargians. Golfren and K'linpor did because they played juvenile roles sometimes and could add a false beard when they needed one. Boys like Klip Trumpeter did, because their whiskers were still patchy.

"Drink?" she said. She mimed drinking and pointed to the stream. "Water?"

He nodded. "Drink."

She took a gourd down and brought it back full. She taught him *I drink* and *you drink.*

"I drink," he said, and drank. His hands trembled. Smile, gibberish.

"Thank you."

"Thank you?"

She nodded.

He tapped his bandage and said, "Thank you," again. He had a very winning smile.

Eleal made herself comfortable and began lessons: man, woman, boy, girl, tree, sky, fingers, happy, sad, angry . . .

\*     \*     \*

Edward was one big ache. Every muscle was bruised from the cramps, and he had battered all his bones repeatedly against stone paving. The spasms had stopped, though, and his head was clearing. He felt giddy if he tried to stand, but he would be all right in a day or so.

Nextdoor was surprisingly Earthlike—gravity and temperature, sky and clouds and sun all much the same. The plants looked like vegetation he had seen in the south of France, and the day was going to be hot accordingly. Nevertheless, this was not Earth. The moon had been very wrong. The beetles had eight legs.

Ridiculous! His mind rejected the evidence. He would wake up soon and find himself back in Albert Memorial. And when he did, he would refuse any more drugs!

He could recall seeing metal swords in the night, but not firearms. That put the culture somewhere between the Stone Age and the Renaissance, quite a gap. Both Eleal and he were dressed in very simple garments like overgrown undervests, leaving arms and shoulders and lower legs exposed. Natives in Kenya could get by in such costumes, or even less, but he would be arrested if he tried to walk along an English beach like this. The homespun material had never seen the looms of Manchester. That did not mean that there was no advanced civilization around somewhere. Earth had its Nyaga-thas as well as its Londons. A world was a big place and he must not judge this one by a hole in the woods.

The accommodation left a lot to be desired. He did not remember arriving at the cave. The girl could not have carried him by herself, so she had friends around some-where. And probably enemies also, else why was she hiding him here? Her obvious intent to teach him the language suggested that she was not expecting any English-speaking collaborators to arrive in the near future. He'd learned German by spending a summer in Heidelberg with the Schweitzes, but Frau Schweitz had been proficient in English. It would be tougher without an interpreter to clear up misunderstandings, even if he did have a knack for languages.

Eleal was a pretty thing, with curly hair and a snub nose. He guessed she was eleven or twelve, no more. She had a deformed leg. She was certainly Caucasian, and could even have been English as far as looks went. And she was a sharp little dolly. Once they had gone through everything she could point to, she fetched a fur rug and spread it out on a flat rock. It was full of fine brown sand and she used this as a drawing board. Then the conversation began to grow interesting.

*Four* moons? Trumb, Ysh, Eltiana, Kirb'l. Two men, two women—meaning gods and goddesses, of course. The sun was Wyseth and both, which seemed odd. Well, now he was starting to get a feel for the genders. All languages except English had gender problems, and even in English ships and whales were feminine.

Eleal, Ysh, Eltiana. That was why the girl laughed when he tried to correct her pronunciation of his name—it must sound feminine to her. She was as fussy as a Frenchman about pronunciation. He tried his surname, Exeter, and she grinned again. "Kisster?"

He decided he would rather be D'ward than Kisster.

He sketched the ruined temple, and learned its name, or the word for temple. Or the word for ruin? She began to tell him the story with gestures and illustrations. She had gone there by herself, apparently—he wondered why. Creighton had appeared and her word, "Foop!" sounded much like the "Plop!" he might have used. She knew Creighton's name! Then two men had run in, separately, T'lin and Gover. She looked inquiringly; he shook his head to show that the names meant nothing to him.

He tried "Service" and "Chamber," but those meant as little to her. Nor did "Olympus," which Creighton had mentioned as if it were the Service's headquarters. But all those words were obviously codes, club talk that members of the Service used among themselves. The inhabitants of this world would not call it Nextdoor, nor yet the equivalent of that expression. They would just call it the World. Olympus might be a private house in some city as far from here as London was from Stonehenge.

A whole world to explore? Even Columbus had not blundered into anything quite so unthinkable.

Columbus had not wanted to rush home and enlist in the army, either, but Edward did. The only way he could do that was to locate the Service, and that meant he must learn to talk. He hauled his mind back to work.

Then he recalled two words he already knew in this unnamed language.

"Vurogty Migafilo?"

The girl started and clapped her hands in delight. She pointed southeast. "Magafilo!"

*Migo,* Creighton had said, meant a village in the genitive case, so *maga* must be nominative or dative. The language was inflected, like Latin.

At that moment a third person joined the group. Edward had not heard the apparition approach and his start of surprise gave him a shocking spasm of cramp in his back.

Robinson Crusoe, or the Wild Man of the Woods? No it was Ben Gunn, straight out of *Treasure Island.* Emaciated and weather-beaten, with untamed white hair and beard, this near-naked scarecrow could pass as an Indian fakir. Obviously he was the owner of the cave and Edward had slept in his bed. The glint in his crazy eyes was distinctly unfriendly, implying that hermits did not appreciate uninvited guests. He had brought a bag of berries and some dirty tubers. He dropped them and spun on his leathery heel to leave.

Edward said the words that seemed to mean, "Thank you."

The girl spouted a long, angry speech. The hermit turned back and fixed his glittery, Ancient Mariner gaze on Edward. He could not possibly be as deranged as he looked, could he?

Edward pointed to the cave and said, "Thank you," again.

The hermit showed his teeth in a sneer and stalked away without a word. Unfriendly chappie!

"Porith," Eleal said, pointing at the scrawny back vanishing upstream. She stuck her tongue out and cut it off with a finger.

Edward thought *Good God!* and confirmed his understanding with more gestures. Why would anyone cut out a man's tongue? Perjury? Sedition? Blasphemy, perhaps?

He tried to convey the question but either did not succeed or did not understand the answer.

One look at Porith's offering made him nauseous. He explained that with more gestures and pushed it all to the girl. She ate while continuing her story of the night's events. Eleal was quite a storyteller. Even understanding less than a tenth of her words, Edward could appreciate her dramatic performance. She rolled her eyes and waved her hands until he was hard put to keep a straight face.

She began using berries and roots to denote the characters on stage. The roots were the baddies. She explained them by cutting imaginary corn with a sickle. He nodded, recalling Creighton's warning of *reapers*. Soon, though, his head ached with the effort of trying to memorize so many words at one sitting. He would forget most of them. It was like playing charades with no one to tell you if you had guessed right. What did she mean by reapers, the sun, a crescent, and kneeling?

The reapers sounded very much like the dreaded thugs of India, the murderous worshipers of Kali. The British had struggled for years to wipe out thuggee.

They went back to the temple story and Eleal dropped a hint of advanced technology. Possibly she was fantasizing or had made a mistake, but it sounded as if Creighton had killed one of the reapers with a loud noise—a gun, obviously!

The picture was becoming clearer. Eleal had gone to spy, by herself. Creighton had crossed over, arriving dazed and shocked. The next two arrivals, T'lin and Gover . . . how did Eleal know their names? Those words might not be names at all but visible categories like "policeman" or "Chinaman." Whoever or whatever they were, the "t'lin" and the "gover" had welcomed Creighton, so they were almost certainly Service. They must have brought a gun for him, because then the first reaper had attacked and Creighton had shot him dead.

The girl's observations might be more reliable than her beliefs. She thought the reapers came from the god of death. Of course! Earthquakes came from Poseidon and thunder from Thor, yes? The reapers belonged to, or were agents of, the Chamber. But who were the Chamber? Who were the Service?

The T'lin man had escaped. He was Edward's road to sanity and assistance. He was the lead to the Service and Home and duty.

"T'lin! Er, *want?* T'lin!" he said.

Eleal scowled and said something about T'lin and gods and bad.

Nextdoor certainly seemed to have gods in both abundance and variety.

"No religion is wholly bad," the guv'nor had told him often enough. "Without gods of some sort, life seems to have no meaning, so mortals need gods. But no religion is wholly good, either. Every religion at some time or another has persecuted strangers, stoned prophets, burned heretics, or extorted wealth from the poor."

Edward did not believe in gods. He believed in progress and love and tolerance and ethics. He did not think Nextdoor was going to change his mind.

Eleal tired of the word game. Teaching D'ward to speak good Joalian was going to take much longer than she had expected. His accent was worse than a Niolian's and he kept forgetting things she had told him. Just when she thought she was making progress, he would come out with absolute nonsense like, "Onions sings bluer gentle?"

The day was hot and still. All her nights seemed to be full of wild adventures now, and her days needed for sleep. He was yawning too. She sent him off to the cave to rest, and he went without argument, moving as stiffly as a very old man. It would be cooler in there for him. She climbed up the bank and stretched out on a mattress of ferns under a tree.

For a while her mind kept racing. Obviously Porith Molecatcher wanted her to leave and take her Liberator with her, and he could probably starve her into obedience. Somewhere farther from the Sacrarium would be much safer. Perhaps tomorrow D'ward would be strong enough to go.

Go where?

Go to Tion, of course! Her god was a just and benevolent god. He had saved her from Eltiana's jail and Zath's reapers. The Maiden had helped by sending Sister Ahn to kill Dolm Actor, but Irepit's convent was many vales away, in Nosokland, wherever that was. Here in Sussland the Maiden's grove had been destroyed. So that left Tion, and now it was safe for Eleal to rejoin the troupe, because Dolm was dead. So she would deliver the Liberator safely to Tion's temple in Suss, and Tion would reward her.

Reward her how?

Paa, the god of healing, was another avatar of Tion. Tion, therefore, was god of healing as well as god of art and beauty. Tion could cure sicknesses—and deformities! Eleal drifted off to sleep, thinking about the reward she would like best of all.

Porith shook her awake. The crazy old man was so excited he was hooting like a goose and drooling all over his beard. He made beckoning gestures, he tugged her hand. Grumpily she rubbed her eyes and stood up.

*Come!* he said in sign language. *Come quickly!*

She followed on dragging feet. The afternoon was half-gone, the air as hot as fresh milk. Porith kept running ahead and having to wait for her.

Soon she realized that he was following a faint trail. Many branches hung across it, so it was never visible for more than a few feet, but it was an easier way through the forest than any she had found. It must be a path of his own making, for no one else would come here. It led past the Sacrarium on the side away from the cliff. Just beyond there, Molecatcher plunged through some bushes and made more wild whooping sounds.

She followed, and found him capering alongside a tent. It was a small tent, of good linen, colored a very inconspicuous green, and well concealed in the undergrowth.

"Oh, wonderful!" she cried, suddenly as excited as he. "I heard Gover Envoy invite T'lin to his tent! So whoever stole the bodies didn't know about this! And the man who owned it is dead, so we can have it!"

Apparently that was all the reassurance the old man needed. He knelt to fumble with the ties. Then he plunged inside on hands and knees with Eleal at his heels. The interior was a cavern of riches, straight out of *The Fall of Tarkor*. There were six or seven bales and packs there, leaving barely room for a man to lie down. Some spare clothes and a couple of straw hats lay on top of them, and a pair of good-looking boots, also. Eleal's fingers itched to start exploring this wealth, but she knew she must wait until it had been transported back to Molecatcher's cave. Gover Envoy just might have friends who knew where his camp was. He had mentioned a courier on a fast moa.

They needed two trips to transfer all their treasure, and by the time they brought in the last of it, D'ward was awake and sitting beside the first load. Eleal was relieved to see he had not opened anything, because she thought she deserved that pleasure. It would be like a birthday feast, with presents. He seemed strangely interested in the packs themselves, studying the fastenings and the stitching. In some ways D'ward Liberator was very odd!

She began with the lumpiest pack, because that seemed likely to be the most interesting. Most of the others smelled like food—bacon and onions and dried fish. Right at the top she found a bronze mirror and a razor. The Thargian had been clean-shaven, so these confirmed that the tent had belonged to him and not a reaper who might come in search of it. D'ward's blue eyes had lit up at the sight of them, so she gave them to him as a gift. The soap she kept, but she would let him share.

Next came two iron cooking pots. She gave those to Porith, because she would not be able to carry them away and he was host, and cook. He gibbered over them. And then—wonder of wonders! A leather-bound book—the *Filoby Testament* itself!

She beamed in joy and held it up for the others to see.

D'ward snatched it out of her hand.

A printed book, by George! A hide-bound, gold-embossed beautiful book! Nightmares of the Stone Age vanished, the Renaissance dawned in certainty, and even the Industrial Revolution began to seem possible.

Then the title jumped off the cover at him:

βυρογε μιγαφιλο

*Vurogty Migafilo!* He flicked the pages. The language was jabber, but the letters were unmistakable. There were a few unfamiliar accent marks and obviously some of the pronunciations had changed—β was V, as in modern Greek—but overall the alphabet used was too close to classical Greek to be coincidence.

He barely noticed as Eleal grabbed the book back from him. Creighton had said that the keys to the portals were very ancient. Edward had not understood the significance of that at the time. While the Earth had been inventing steam engines and hot air balloons and now aeroplanes, it had been forgetting the antique wisdom of the shamans and witch doctors. People must have been crossing between worlds for thousands of years. Not many of them, but enough to found races and influence culture. They could have brought nothing with them, no tools or domestic animals, nor even fillings in their teeth, but their memories had come.

Someone had brought the art of writing from Earth to Nextdoor, or someone had taken the art of writing from Nextdoor to Earth. The Greeks were supposed to have copied the alphabet from the Phoenicians and improved it, but perhaps both had come from outside. The Greek alphabet had spawned the Latin and the Cyrillic and many others. This language of Eleal's was written in yet another variant of the Greek alphabet.

What else, who else, had crossed between worlds? For example, Edward thought—wishing he had someone to argue this with—Prometheus, who had stolen fire from the gods, might be an ancient memory of some interworld traveler. Perhaps many myths would make sense as muddled records of people vanishing mysteriously or appearing even more mysteriously. Suppose a man, or woman, popped out of nowhere into the middle of a druid ceremony at Stonehenge—would not the newcomer be hailed as a god?

With a squeal of delight, Eleal found her name where someone had marked a passage. She showed it to Edward. He nodded and smiled, but his mind was busily chipping out a whole new view of human history.

# 49

By evening, he was feeling much stronger. With Porith's fumbling help, Eleal had pitched the tent in thick shrubbery on the east side of the stream. She probably hoped that any reapers who came snooping around would not venture to cross the gully. The old hermit was so delighted to have his own house back that he had become almost jovial; at sundown the three of them ate a celebratory feast outside his cave.

Edward's appetite had come back with a rush. He suffered a stabbing toothache in consequence, but did not inquire about local dentists. His muscles and joints were recovering from their bruising, so he no longer moved like a centenarian. Later he managed to scramble up the bank for the first time, and then Eleal led him to the edge of the cliff.

The sun had just set. The view was superb—not merely the breathtaking canyon and the waterfall plunging into it, but also the many little white farmhouses standing out clearly on the far bank as if arranged there by an artist. Each had its own cluster of heavy shade trees and lighter, feathery things like palms or frozen green fountains. A background of fertile countryside faded off into distant foothills and a jagged frame of mountains. The land was prosperous, and obviously either tropical or subtropical, because the sun had been overhead at noon. It was better watered than his Kenya birth-place, he decided, and probably at a lower elevation—judging by terrestrial standards, which might not fit the case at all. Westward the ranges were a dark saw-edge against the last glow of evening. To the east the icy summits burned in gold and pink, and some of those peaks could match anything the Alps had to offer. Another range loomed over the forest behind him. The basin itself was about the width of the Mittelland at Lausanne, but closed off to east and west. The river was much bigger than the Rhine, the largest he had ever seen.

Waving an all-encompassing arm, Eleal explained that this was *Something*-Suss, which he assumed was what Creighton had translated as Sussland. When Edward asked the names of the ranges to north and south, they were both *Something-else*-Suss. The river was *Yet-Another*-Suss, and so was the little town he could see in the distance. He had a lot to learn.

Still, the town was promising. A gleam of reflected light there was somehow related to another god, Tion—a good god, apparently. Nice to hear that some of them were not horrors! Having discovered that Eleal had strong religious convictions, Edward had resolved to be very cautious on the subject of gods.

She indicated that tomorrow she was going to take him to that Town-Suss. He could manage that, he thought, five miles or so. Then he asked with gestures about crossing the canyon and learned that there would have to be a detour to the east, to Maganot. Still thinking in English, he translated that to Village-Not . . . Notham? Notting? Notby?

"Magathogwal," she explained, pointing the other way, and then, "Magalame, Magajot."

He pointed straight down. "Query name."

"Ratharuat."

*Ratha* must be yet another geographical prefix, perhaps meaning "forest" or "place smaller than a village" or "old ruins, nobody lives there now." *Ruat?* That name sounded familiar, but his memory was reeling from overwork and he could not place it.

The two of them sat in contented silence as the stars came out. Birds or something were making a strange racket in the trees and once in a while his stomach would rumble loudly, provoking Eleal to giggles. Then she began to sing. He could not follow the words, but the melody was pleasant. She was a competent little songstress.

She was a pretty girl, too, although she would never be a classical beauty; her nose tipped up and her hair was more frizzy than curled. She had a quick smile and a remarkable self-confidence. He suspected she was short for her age, but of course he was only guessing, for the local population might be stunted by twentieth century European standards. He wondered what had happened to her leg. It could not be rickets in this climate.

The song ended. The singer glanced up to see what her audience thought of it. Edward clapped, not sure if that was the local sign of applause. Apparently it was, because she beamed. On impulse he smiled, took her hand, and squeezed it. She blushed. He released it quickly, recalling Miss Eleal's dramatic tendencies. She was probably old enough to start having romantic notions also. He had no wish to provoke an embarrassing juvenile crush. Call me in five or six years, perhaps.

Five or six *years?* Five or six *days* ago, he had been on the boat train from Paris. Now he seemed to be stranded for the rest of his life on a world unknown, more exotic than anywhere Haggard ever Rode or Rudyard ever Kipled.

The giant green moon, Trumb, seemed to have disappeared. A small blue light just above the sunset was Ysh, Eleal said, and then she became excited and pointed to a brighter, yellow star. That was Kirb'l, and apparently seeing Kirb'l was an honor, or a good omen, or something. Kirb'l Tion, she said, and gestured toward Suss town.

Gods again! To change the subject Edward asked about her home and parents. She evaded the question and asked about his. They still conversed in baby talk and gestures, and that could become a bad habit. He decided to give himself one more day of that and then insist on using proper grammar.

The stars were lighting up with tropical swiftness. He could see the Great Bear low over the mountains to the northeast and Arcturus above that. He asked Eleal about their names, and again she became evasive. She would never admit ignorance. He wondered what other planets might circle this sun, but did not embarrass her by asking, and he probably could not have made himself understood anyway. He located Vega and the Summer Triangle. Then he turned around and peered up the stream gorge, which gave him a south view through the trees. There was the Centaur, which the guv'nor had pointed out to him when he was only—

He uttered a grunt of astonishment that made Eleal jump. Impossible! These were the stars of Earth.

Even before he went to sleep, he knew he was in for trouble. In the middle of the night it arrived. He crawled out of the tent without waking the girl.

Don't drink the water—but if he was going to be stranded on Nextdoor for the rest of his life, he must drink the water, and his insides would just have to learn to deal with the local germs. He'd suffered from the traveler's curse in France and in Germany and lived through it, but he was not familiar with the interplanetary variety. What he needed now was a good dose of codeine, Dover Pills. Without that he might be in for a severe case of Delhi Belly.

By morning he had a corker.

There was no question of leaving that day. He could barely crawl in and out of the tent, and eventually he stayed outside. He tried to reassure Eleal, but lacked the strength to explain the cause of the problem. She fussed and worried and prayed. She brought him water to drink, and made some thin soup, which he sometimes managed to keep down. Her concern was very touching, and she demonstrated remarkable patience at just fanning flies off him, although she was annoyed that he would not continue the language lessons. Another day ought to do it, he thought.

The next day he was running a high fever and things were looking dicey. His first term at Fallow he had caught every disease known to childhood, although he must have had as much inbred immunity as any native-born English boy. Those mumps and measles and whooping cough would have killed his Embu friends at Nyagatha. He had inherited some resistance to English diseases, and he was better fitted to survive as an adult in Africa than any homebred white man, but he was not equipped for Nextdoor.

He began to wander in and out of delirium, never recognizing it until it was past.

He did not want to die here, so far from home and everyone he knew. Where was *home?* Not Fallow. Nor Nyagatha. Certainly not Uncle Roly's house in Kensington. How ironic to escape the hangman's noose only to succumb to fever on another world! Oh, Alice, Alice! Perhaps he would have fallen to a German bullet had things turned out otherwise, but that would at least have had a certain dignity. Interplanetary disease had killed H. G. Wells's Martians.

Little Eleal was distraught, not knowing what to do. He tried to tell her that she was doing everything possible, but he could remember nothing of the language except her name. Alexander the Great had sighed for new worlds to conquer. They would have killed you, Alec.

O, brave new world! Lost world.

He did not want to die.

The next day he was weakening fast. The girl brought him drinks and washed away his sweat and held his hand. He was immeasurably grateful and could not tell her so. She was a gritty little thing. He heard her berating the old hermit. He tried to say that she should leave and go home to her parents. She didn't understand the King's English, poor child.

A whole new world and he was going to die without ever seeing more than a few square feet of it. He had so much wanted to find Olympus and talk to people who had known his father.

Creighton came to see him, fading in and out of illusion, talking of strangers.

Mr. Goodfellow came, sorrowfully. "I can do nothing, Edward," he said, clutching his beaver hat. "I have no authority here."

Why was the girl still hanging around? What was her interest in Edward? The way she bullied old Ben Gunn was really very funny. What day was this?

That night—whatever night it was—a monstrous thunderstorm lashed the jungle, while Edward raved in delirious arguments with Inspector Leatherdale, trying to convince him that miracles still happened and could open bolted doors. Poor Bagpipe Bodgley came by and talked of the *Lost World,* asking how the story had ended.

Then he found himself in jail, explaining to the doctor that his broken leg had been cured by a minor god left over from Saxon prehistory.

Eleal was praying again.

"That won't do any good!" he said crossly, aware that she could not understand.

"Well, you never know, old man," Creighton said. "Let's just hope nobody hears, that's all. I told you that they're not gods, but may behave like gods. But even if somebody does hear, well they're not all horrors."

"Did you give my love to Ruat?" Mr. Goodfellow asked.

His fever broke that night, and he lived. By morning he was lucid, but as weak as a newborn babe. He watched the dawn steal in through the leaves and smelled the new, wet scent of a cleansed world; he was infinitely grateful just to be alive.

He hoped he could stay that way, but obviously it would not be easy. Daylight had brought enlightenment. Sometime in his madness he had worked out who the opposition was, and why the Service referred to it as the Chamber.

The Chamber of Horrors, of course.

He was young and superbly fit, and he recovered quickly. One day he was a raving maniac and the next he was sitting up and very shakily trying to shave himself. The looking glass showed him the narrowness of his escape. That afternoon he began the language lessons again. The next day he was managing small walks.

Porith had hidden most of the food. Eleal screamed and threatened until he produced it. She wanted it for D'ward, to build up his strength.

With much glee she showed him the passages in the *Filoby Testament* that mentioned her, and the others that mentioned him—Δωαρδ. He was also sometimes identified by a title that Eleal did not even try to translate but which must be the "Liberator" Creighton had mentioned, and once he was called the son of Καμερον Κιστρ. That was a fair attempt to transliterate a name that must surely have been unique on Nextdoor. The reference had worked well enough to bring death to his parents and might yet do the same to him.

Edward knew that Eleal was keeping secrets from him. She could follow his pidgin and gestures perfectly well when she wanted to. When he asked some question she preferred not to answer, he became completely incomprehensible and remained so until she could change the subject.

She was very impatient to leave. He suggested that she go on ahead and he would follow or wait for her to return, but she refused, and for that he felt very grateful. He owed her his life, but to embark on a walk of perhaps several days' duration before he recovered his strength would be real folly, risking a complete relapse. He tried to explain that.

She managed to explain the need for haste—she had friends who would be leaving soon. He made her a promise: He must stay one more day, and he would do some walking to build up his strength, but they would leave the day after.

# 50

The next morning Eleal took D'ward eastward along the cliff edge. He leaned heavily on Sister Ahn's staff and persevered until they reached cultivated fields. He needed a rest before he could walk back. In all they had covered no more than a couple of miles, yet he was exhausted and slept through the whole afternoon.

In the heat of the day she lay on the grass and swatted flies and wondered how

Uthiam had made out with *Ironfaib's Polemic*, and the others in their individual pieces. She even wondered if young Gim had done well with his harp or won the gold rose for his beauty. How that would embarrass him!

She also thumbed through the *Filoby Testament*. It was a terrible muddle. She had found the four references to her that Gover Envoy had mentioned. That had not been difficult, as he had marked them all in the book. The order did not seem to matter.

Verse 386 was the important one, about clothing and washing. In Verse 401, she brought "him" to the caveman for succor, and "him" had been D'ward of course.

Verse 475: *Before the festival, Eleal will come into Sussvale with the Daughter of Irepit. The minion of Zath seeketh out the Liberator, but he will be called to repentance.* Well, they had done all that! What use was a prophecy after you'd done it?

The only Eleal prophecy she had not yet fulfilled came right at the end of the book. Out of 1102 verses altogether, there she was again in number 1098: *Terrible is the justice of the Liberator; his might lays low the unworthy. He is gentle and hard to anger. Gifts he sets aside and honor he spurns. Eleal shall be the first temptation and the prince shall be the second, but the dead shall rouse him.*

What prince? Tempting to do what? A lot of the prophecies were like that—they almost meant something but not quite. Like Verse 114: *Men plot evil upon the holy mountain. The servants of the one do the work of the many. They send unto D'ward, mouthing oaths like nectar. Their voices are sweet as roses, yea sweeter than the syrup that snares the diamond-fly. He is lured to destruction by the word of a friend, by the song of a friend he is hurled down among the legions of death.*

The book spoke of D'ward and the Liberator separately and never said they were the same man—perhaps she was in there under other names too. Nor did it ever say who or what he was supposed to liberate.

Sussians were very fond of liberators. This year's tragedy was called *The Tragedy of Trastos,* and it was about Daltos Liberator, one of their ancient heroes, who had slain Trastos Tyrant, his own father, and brought democracy to Sussland. It was a very good tragedy, with lots of gods and goddesses. Suss would love it. At the festival it would have won the rose for the best play easily . . . maybe! Dolm Actor had played major roles in both the tragedy and the comedy. Dolm had been slain by Sister Ahn's sword. K'linpor was his understudy, but Golfren was K'linpor's, and Golfren acted like a rock.

This was Neckday and the festival would end tomorrow. Eleal did not want to think about that. Usually the troupe stayed on in Suss, because the winning group was allowed free use of the temple amphitheater and many citizens would come to see the winning play. Those performances often brought them more money than any others in their year. But without Dolm they could not stage either the *Varilian* or *Trastos,* only the masque, and unless they had won the rose, they would not have a free theater available.

In other words, there was a very good chance that the Trong Troupe would leave the following day, Toeday, and there was no hope of D'ward reaching Suss before then. Once the troupe had crossed Monpass, it might wander almost anywhere in Joalland.

Eleal might never manage to get him to Suss at all, because she had no money to pay the toll over the bridge at Notby.

There! She backed up a page in the *Testament* and yes, there was D'ward's name again.

*D'ward shall become Tion. He shall give heart to the king and win the hearts of the people. D'ward shall become Courage.*

What in the world did that mean? There was nothing to say that it referred to the Liberator. What a terrible muddle! Well, at the least it proved that she would be right to take D'ward to Tion's temple.

# *51*

They planned to leave at dawn the next morning, to make progress before the day grew hot. Edward had no idea what dangers lurked out there in the world: slavers, press-gangs, or knights in armor challenging passersby to joustings? He would have to rely on Eleal to lead him safely to wherever she thought he ought to be—for his benefit or hers. Clearly, she had plans, and they had involved careful preparation and much discussion with old Porith.

Whatever those plans were, he would have to go along with them. He could not spend the rest of his life in a jungle tent, certainly not while there was a war on that he must fight in.

Judging by garments looted from the dead Gover's baggage, standard dress in Sussland was a smock of drab gray material with a touch of bright-colored embroidery on hem or shoulder strap. Eleal had been improving on one of these costumes. Below the neckband she had stitched a jagged sunburst of white cloth, cut from a flour bag. Below that again, out to either side, she had attached a green hammer and a red Ø, and underneath them, but closer together, a yellow triangle and a blue star. The colors were vital—having nothing else green to hand, she had cut a piece out of the tent to use for the hammer. This armorial creation was to be Edward's wear. He concluded that anything so lacking in sense must obviously be very holy.

○

⊤            Ø

△   ★

That evening she repeated her instructions solemnly and emphatically, a ragged urchin sitting cross-legged in the dirt, literally wagging a finger at him. He was to be a *gods' man,* walking to gods' houses—a pilgrim, in other words—and he was not to speak to anyone. She would do the talking. He was not sure if she was to be his guide, pupil, or assistant, but the role seemed to be formal and well-defined. He would play the lama, she the chela. His only communication was to be a gesture of blessing, and she made him practice that.

The idea was ingenious and might save him considerable trouble if he attracted the attention of the authorities. Nextdoor had no British consuls to stand bail or threaten to send gunboats. On the other hand, all cultures he knew of imposed certain obligations on their able-bodied young men—honest labor and military service being two that came to mind at once. This handy cop-out as a pilgrim might work for the elderly, but he worried that his ingenious young accomplice was overlooking some snag. He certainly put no faith in the addled wits of old Porith, the ex-priest. Nevertheless, having no better plan of his own to propose, Edward agreed that he would be a holy man. He just hoped he would not be called upon to perform some sacred ritual. Public flagellation, for example.

Before the sun rose, the travelers left their tent for the last time and ate a hurried breakfast. They scrambled down the bank and called at Porith's cave to say farewell. Eleal gave him a kiss, which flustered him. The crazy old man was much richer than he had been before she arrived, because he had inherited all the valuables from the tent. He had resented Edward when they first met. The last couple of days he had become quite friendly.

Edward was not sure of the proprieties of handshaking and was certainly not inclined to kiss the shaggy old gargoyle, so he used his pilgrim-blessing gesture instead, a raised palm with fingers spread. The hermit stared at him for a moment, and then sank to his knees and bowed his head.

Eleal and Edward exchanged startled glances and took to their heels before they began to laugh. They looked back from the top of the bank, and the old man was still on his knees, as if in prayer.

Edward trudged along the jungle path with Eleal hobbling eagerly ahead. Besides his pilgrim's smock, he wore sandals and an absurd Chinese coolie straw hat like a wheel, all looted from the dead Gover. He leaned on his walking stick, which had belonged to some woman called Ahn, who had slain the second reaper. He was still not sure who she had been or how she had died.

He thought he might manage five miles if he were lucky. If he were unlucky, then he would discover that beggars were set to work picking oakum or mending roads. He had already identified the first snag in Eleal's pilgrim deception—by the rules of the game, neither of them could carry any baggage, not even a packed lunch, although he had slipped the razor and a lump of soap into his pocket when she wasn't looking.

When he neared the ruined temple, his skin rose in gooseflesh. The eerie sensation he had known in Winchester Cathedral and at Stonehenge was enormously magnified, into a dread sense of cold and dark and sanctity. He remembered Creighton saying he could always recognize virtuality on Nextdoor. Apparently the talent was amplified in strangers and Edward was a stranger here.

Did portals work in both directions? He still knew the key; he could easily make himself a primitive drum. But would that key take him back to Stonehenge, or on to some other world? Even if he dared take the risk and did reach Stonehenge, he would arrive there penniless and stark naked. By now Inspector Leatherdale would have a warrant out for his arrest. There was no easy way out of this mess.

He was glad to leave the temple behind. Beyond it the path was much clearer and in half a mile or so it emerged from the forest close to another ruin, a monumental arch. Despite Eleal's protests, Edward went to inspect it. Once it had anchored the end of a suspension bridge. Corroded remains of chains still hung from it, and the base of a matching arch was discernible on the far side of the gorge. Had he seen its like on Earth, he would have guessed that it dated from Roman times. Here it might be more recent, but no traveler had crossed Susswater at this point for several centuries.

The ancient road it had served was still evident, leading southward through a curiously diffuse settlement, a hodgepodge of farmland, trees, ruins, and cottages. No one else was about yet, so he was free to chat with Eleal. He soon established that this was Ruatvil. He learned how the language distinguished between small, medium, and large places—villages like Notby, towns like Ruatvil, cities like Suss. He suspected that even a city would seem very small by his standards. London or Paris would fill the whole valley.

"Hello, Ruat!" he said in English. "Mr. Goodfellow sends his love."

Eleal looked up quickly to frown at him. Her hat fell off and they laughed.

He felt very strange, walking under a tropic sun again, disguised as a peasant, but he had been seven days in this new world now and was eager to see more of it.

Beyond the remains of Ruatvil, he noticed real peasants toiling in the fields under coolie hats like his. People could pass through the portals, animals could not. The concept of agriculture could; the domesticated species would have to be local. He saw beasts of burden and herds of others that might be edible. They had a rough similarity to oxen and goats, and he thought he recognized geese until he observed that they had fur instead of feathers. The vegetation was unfamiliar, but none of it would have seemed out of place in a terrestrial land he had not visited before.

The biggest surprise of the morning was a man racing past on the back of something shaped like an ostrich. It was gone before Edward had time to see it properly. Soon two more riders approached from the south, and then he had time to observe that their mounts had hair and hooves. They moved very fast. Eleal told him they were *mothaa,* so he classified them in his mind as moas, although they must be more mammal than bird. He was trying hard to think in the local language, but he had not succeeded yet.

The road now was merely a red dirt trail, rutted and pocked with weeds. Hedges defined the fields and he saw no barbed wire, no eyeglasses or steam engines. He no longer believed in Creighton's gun—he had another theory now to explain the reaper's death—but he still hoped that the culture of Ruatvil did not represent the limits of Nextdoor's technology. An interplanetary traveler arriving at some isolated Chinese or African village would not find motorcars or telegraph wires.

No policeman asked to see the travelers' papers, no highwayman demanded their money or their lives. By and large the population just ignored them—field workers, herders, men driving oxcarts. The only exceptions were a few pedestrians coming along the trail in the opposite direction. They mostly regarded the holy man with surprise or disapproval, and in some cases with open amusement. Edward tried giving his sign of blessing, but that met with outright laughter and ribald comments. Thereafter he maintained a dignified impassivity, but obviously an eighteen-year-old prophet was no more convincing on Nextdoor than he would have been on Earth. He needed old Porith's white beard.

To his shame, he soon found himself hard put to keep up with the crippled child at his side. Eleal might have less than two complete legs, but she made good use of what she had. He wondered why she did not wear a built-up shoe to make her stride more even.

The road continued to wander south. As their destination lay to the north, he concluded that the detour was going to be sizable, probably dictated by the availability of bridges. After five or six miles he had reached his limit. Happily, just there the road crossed a small knoll, capped by a grove of tall trees like gigantic umbrellas, casting black velvet shadow. Eleal pulled faces, but agreed to let him rest.

An hour or so later, they set off again and soon came to a junction. Eleal turned to the east. A short distance on this new road brought them to a fast-flowing river, whose milky water told of its glacial origin, like streams Edward had seen in the Alps. He was staggering now, his legs trembling. He had a nagging toothache and blisters from the unfamiliar footwear.

"Rest!" he said as he staggered down the incline to the ford. Such weakness was humiliating, but his illness had drained him of strength.

Clutching her hat, Eleal looked up at him with a worried frown. "Not speak!"

"Not speak," he agreed. The last thing he needed now was the strain of trying to make conversation.

She led the way over a long line of stepping stones, into a small grove on the far bank. Several groups of travelers were taking a noontime break in a wayside campground. Two oxcarts stood by the road; a few of the strange moa bipeds grazed on tethers under trees resembling beeches. Watchdogs that looked more like oversized shaggy cats guarded a herd of goatlike creatures. Flower-bedecked shrubs brightened the grove. Almost all the blossoms were some shade of red, and he had noted the same thing at Ruatvil. It reminded him of Kenya, where blue and yellow flowers were similarly rare. Delicious odors of cooking came wafting from the fires.

Eleal pointed to a log near an unoccupied hearth, seeming to imply that Edward should sit on it, so he did. He thought he heard his knees utter sighs of relief. He felt like one big ache. He had a sunburn, and he was trembling with fatigue.

Was it *all* fatigue? He looked around uneasily at the pillared tree trunks. Something creepy . . . Then he realized that it was virtuality again. This campground was a node—not on the scale of the Ruat temple or Stonehenge, but awesome enough to make his skin prickle. He could see no shrine or ruins; he could only hope that it had no resident numen.

Eleal had gone hobbling over to the largest group of wayfarers, eight or nine men busily eating and arguing. They broke off their conversation to inspect her. Then they scowled across at her pilgrim companion.

Undeterred, she began to make a speech. Edward could not understand any of it. One of the men shouted angrily, waving her away. They were a nondescript gang, rough and weather-beaten. A couple of the youngest wore only loincloths, the rest were clad in the customary drab smocks, their straw hats lying on the grass beside them. Every man had a knife at his belt and they all sported beards. Most were stocky and dark-complexioned. Apart from their clothes, they could have been rural Italians.

Eleal was never easily discouraged. She continued her harangue, gesturing dramatically in Edward's direction—no doubt explaining how holy and worthy he was. He did not feel holy and worthy, but he did feel hungry, and unbearably weary. The throb in his tooth hurt almost as much as his feet.

One of the younger men said something witty and all the others laughed. The oldest, a graybeard, shouted at her again. They were not speaking the language Eleal had been teaching Edward, and neither was she. It had a more guttural sound to it, but he caught a word or two and decided it might be only a dialect variation. She grew shriller and more insistent. Graybeard stood up and advanced on her menacingly. Evidently her plan to elicit charity for her pilgrim was not going to work. Nice try.

Abandoning hopes of lunch, Edward rose also. He limped forward and laid a hand on Eleal's shoulder. She jumped, and fell silent. He had intended to draw her away, but she did not move and that turned his gesture into one of protection and support. Suddenly there was confrontation. Graybeard was no longer threatening a child, but a man both younger and taller than himself. He could not possibly back down now.

From the looks of him, Graybeard was a seasoned old rover. His face was burned by the sun, with lines of red road dust marking its wrinkles. His shoulders were impressively hairy and beefy, his dark eyes bloodshot and menacing. He said something contemptuous; the words could have been Chinese for all Edward knew, but the tone was an unmistakable warning that certain young scroungers should go and find themselves honest work before they had the living daylights knocked out of them. His companions jeered their agreement.

*Oh, is that so?* Before he realized it, Edward had raised his eyebrows in challenge. He was not going to take that remark, whatever it meant, from a gang of vagrant peddlers. *Never let them see you're afraid of them. . . .*

Too late he registered that his Fallow training might have betrayed him. He was not dressed to play the role of the young gentleman; these were not insubordinate English navvies. He was not His Majesty's District Officer, backed by the invincible might of the British Empire. He was not even Bwana's son at Nyagatha. He was exactly what these men thought he was, a beggar. Public school airs were inappropriate under the circumstances.

Too bad! To back down now would only make things worse.

He returned the man's stare with contempt, holding the eye contact: *Do your worst!* Graybeard shouted again.

*Really? You don't say?*

Doubt flickered over the other man's craggy features. Had he never seen blue eyes before? He asked a question.

Still Edward said nothing. Eleal said nothing. The doubt curdled into worry. The old man turned away; he strode quickly back to the fire and returned bearing a stick with a sizzling lump of charred meat on it. Eleal snatched it from him and peremptorily demanded another, holding out her hand. Another man hurried over with a second.

Edward nodded in acceptance, and offered his spread-hand blessing. Both men laid palms on their hearts and bowed low, apparently relieved.

The holy man returned to his log, trying not to limp on his blisters. He did not sit immediately, but took a careful look around to make sure the trouble was over. He had won the attention of the whole campground. Eleal came to stand beside him. Her face was paler than usual, but she flicked him a wink. He kept his features impassive, deciding it would be safe to eat.

But then one of the younger men followed and knelt to offer Eleal a bowl of cereal mush. Edward gravely blessed him as she accepted it. Another came with a gourd of water. One by one, men hurried over to kneel and buy the holy man's blessing. Other men from other groups joined in, bringing food from their own meals. Soon there was a feast spread out around the venerable pilgrim's feet.

Eleal's eyes grew wider and wider every time she looked up at him. Edward remained inscrutable, as if this sort of tribute was no more than his due. Eventually he realized what was expected of him—he sat down to show that he was satisfied. Then the offerings stopped coming. He hoped the two of them could do justice to such a banquet. He had collected half the food in the campground, enough to feed a monasteryful of starving monks.

His mouth was watering. He bit into the meat, feeling delicious hot fat run down his chin. His tooth had stopped aching.

Graybeard's oxcart was piled high with what seemed to be small blue carrots. They did not make a very comfortable throne, but Edward sat cross-legged on the top under the shade of his hat and made the best of the ride into Filoby. He clutched his staff, trying to look holy and ineffable, dribbling unholy sweat in the heat of the afternoon. Eleal sat beside the old man and chattered imperiously. God knew what sort of tale she was spinning, although Edward heard his name being mentioned. Her religious scruples were starting to seem surprisingly flexible. Every now and again she would twist around and address some remark to him, but he rarely caught more than a couple of words. *Migafilo* was one.

Eventually they came to another river. A ford and a steep hill out of the valley brought them into a village of whitewashed cottages with roofs of red tiles. This must be Filoby, the Magafilo of the prophecy. It was an unimpressive clutter of narrow clay lanes and perhaps fifty homes, but a rank odor of charred wood hung in the air. Several cottages had been burned—recently, for repairs were under way. There were more people around than might have been expected at that time of day. They looked up with interest at the pilgrim on his chariot.

Then worse destruction came in sight. Beyond the village rose a small conical hill, spiky with black tree trunks. As the oxcart approached, Edward began to feel the now-familiar sense of virtuality. He shivered despite the heat. That hill was a node and a sacred place. It must be the birthplace of the *Filoby Testament,* and it had been ravaged by fire. Gutted ruins of many buildings stood stark amid the ashes of the grove. From what Creighton had told him about prophecy, he could only assume that this destruction was more work of the Chamber, striving to block fulfillment of the *Testament.* The people who had devastated Nyagatha had struck here also, the killers of his parents, the enemies who would still be seeking his death.

Here Graybeard's road parted from his. The holy pilgrim descended from the carrots with as much dignity as he could contrive in his skimpy frock.

Mumbling apologetically, the old man knelt in the dirt and removed his hat to receive the pilgrim's final blessing. Feeling mischievous, Edward went so far as to lay his out-spread hand on the man's head. That must be a signal honor, for when the old rascal rose to his feet, tears were cleaning small tram lines down the dust on his weather-beaten cheeks. He gabbled thanks, fumbling with his hat.

Edward turned and walked briskly in the direction his small disciple indicated. He could not see her face under her hat and he wondered what she was thinking. It was not like Eleal to remain silent.

The street was narrow. He was constantly passing close to people. Almost without exception, they bowed to him. One or two women knelt as he went by. He responded with his sign of blessing and saw faces light up.

This was all very creepy! Not everyone was dark-eyed and swarthy—he saw auburn hair, some mousy brown. He saw hazel eyes and gray eyes. His own blue eyes might be rare, but they could not be unique in the world, so they were not what was provoking superstitious respect. He was tall by local standards, but again not uniquely so. His was not the single white face among a thousand black. Above all, he was only a youth. Why should his pilgrim garb merit this sudden veneration? Were the inhabitants of Filoby so much more devout than those of Ruatvil, who had laughed at him that morning?

No, something had changed when he faced down Graybeard in the campground. That confrontation had given him confidence, of course, which might be part of it, but his wildest theories were starting to seem believable.

He could not ask Eleal to comment, for now the road was busy and a pilgrim must not speak. Even when he had left the village behind, there was no lack of travelers. As soon as one party had passed, another was in sight. They all seemed to be heading south, and he did not understand that. He was going the wrong way.

Nor were they all peasants. Well-dressed folk rode past on swift moas or in gigs drawn by animals resembling pony-sized greyhounds. Many of the pedestrians wore colored robes, and he guessed that those were priests and priestesses. Even they greeted him with respectful gestures—clasped hands, touches to breast or forehead. He responded with his five-finger blessing, and no one accused him of irreverence.

The travelers were more varied than the locals. He saw fairer skins, even some blond hair and eyes as blue as his own. One or two could have been Saxons or Scandinavians. Others might have been Indians or Arabs. Clothes showed more diversity, also—tunics and baggy pants like Turkish pajamas, gowns, simple loincloths. Men were bearded or clean-shaven or mustachioed, their limbs smooth or hairy. Noses were hooked or straight, broad or narrow. The population of Nextdoor was a cross section of European types, but of course that was to be expected. Creighton had said that most of the European portals connected with a territory he had called the Vales. Of course the racial types would be similar if people had been crossing to and fro for thousands of years, keeping the bloodlines mingled.

Fascinated, Edward strode along the dusty track. Heat and sweat and insects were minor inconveniences. He eyed the sprouting crops in the fields, the hedges, the livestock, the farmhouses. Many trees stood on carpets of fallen blossom—in England it was August, but in the Vales it was spring.

A troop of six armed men approached, streaking along on moas. As they came near, their leader drew his sword. For a moment Edward's muscles all tightened up in alarm, but the man merely raised the blade in salute and kept on going.

Suddenly Eleal took a grip on her hat and tilted her head to look up at him. Her face was flushed and worried. "Rest?" she pleaded. She was panting, her smock soaked with sweat.

He was so surprised and ashamed that he almost broke his presumed vow of silence. Nodding, he slowed down—blessing a passing pair of monks at the same time. Eleal limped to the shade of a hedge and flopped down on the grass. Edward joined her, lowering himself with more dignity. He had forgotten that his legs were so much longer than hers. He had run the poor cripple off her feet. How could he have been so thoughtless! And why had she not said something sooner? Obviously it was not only his teeth that were feeling better—he had recovered his physical strength, too.

Two well-dressed men stopped and offered canteens of water, inquiring solicitously after the holy man's health. Eleal replied in the same clipped dialect, obviously explaining that it was she who was weary. They nodded understandingly. Grateful for the drink, Edward sent them on their way with a blessing.

Whatever his magic was, it worked on Eleal also. She was regarding him with awe and delight and adoration.

He waited for a gap in the stream of passersby and risked a question. "Query many men going."

She replied with a long dissertation about the god Tion and the city of Suss, but he did not understand and had no chance to question her further. She seemed to know the reason for this migration and she was obviously not worried by it, so he could forget theories of plague or marauding Goths coming out of the hills. He would just have to wait and see. He hoped she would revive soon, so they might continue on their way.

Another half hour or so brought them to Rotby, which was much like Filoby, or slightly larger. The natives were just as respectful to the young pilgrim, just as pleased to receive his blessing, so the effect was showing no signs of wearing off. If anything, it seemed to be growing stronger.

The bridge beyond Rotby was marked by a great megalithic arch, a twin of the relic at Ruatvil. Another stood on the far bank of the gorge, several hundred feet away. The green-bronze chains looped between them supported a wooden roadbed barely wide enough for a single oxcart. Despite the steady flow of travelers approaching, few were heading north—Edward still wished he understood that imbalance—so there was no great press of people ahead of him at the massive timber gates. There were enough for him to work out the procedure, though, and to see that the men in metal helmets and leather armor were collecting a toll.

Eleal took his hand and squeezed it warningly.

He thought *Phooey!* Obviously a holy pilgrim who had taken an oath of silence and a vow of poverty could not be expected to have money.

He might be required to find some rich layman to pay his way for him, of course.

He laid a comforting hand on Eleal's shoulder as they approached the gate. Two guards were taking the cash, checking it carefully, and then dropping it in a bag—one doing the actual work, the other mostly keeping a careful eye on him, although sometimes they would both have to bite a coin before reaching a decision. Three other guards lounged on a bench in the shade behind, chatting in bored fashion. All five wore swords.

A peasant and his wife passed through. Edward and Eleal were next. The guard held out a horny hand.

Edward gave him his respect-compelling stare.

The soldier demanded money in unmistakable, no-nonsense terms.

Edward said nothing.

The soldier scowled, hesitated, and glanced at his companion. He, in turn, swung around and said something to the three on the bench. The man on the left and the one in the middle both looked to the one on the right. Obviously military procedures did not vary much from one world to another.

The one on the right was a grizzled bull of a man, and his expression as he sized up the juvenile prophet suggested that he would like nothing better in the whole world than a chance to have that stripling under his command for a few hours. Edward waited. For a long, unhappy moment there was challenge and confrontation, as there had been in the campground.

Then the leader rose to his feet, his two companions an instant behind him. He marched forward four steps as if to take a closer look at Edward's blue eyes. He stamped his feet, barked an order, and the whole squad came to attention. He saluted. Edward gave him a blessing and led Eleal through the gate, onto the bridge.

*When I grow up,* he thought, *I am going to be Pope.*

The gorge was especially narrow there. The walls fell sheer to the spray—in fact the north side looked undercut, which suggested that one day soon the Rotby bridge might be taken out of service by the river itself. Even upstream and downstream from this notch the canyon was much deeper than it was wide, the river barely visible in the shadowy depths. Its voice was a constant, threatening mumble, sensed more through the soles of the feet than the ears. The chains creaked softly. Many roadbed timbers were in need of repairs and the road itself had a worrying dip to the center. Edward decided he would be evermore content to remain on the far side when he reached it.

Other travelers stepped aside for him and bowed. The driver of an oxcart brought it to a halt—no easy task, for the roadbed sloped steeply at that point. The guard at the north gateway saluted as the pilgrim passed through.

A few cottages stood to the right; a grove of trees to the left was clearly another of the wayfarers' campsites. Several early bird groups were setting up tents and at least one hearth trickled smoke already. After the banquet he had eaten at noon, Edward did not expect to be hungry for several days, and his legs had found some sort of second wind—he could cheerfully have carried on walking—but the girl was flagging again and would appreciate a break. She must have come to that conclusion herself, because she turned off into the campground without hesitation.

He sensed no virtuality this time. This was not a node, but it was an attractive enough spot, well shaded and cool. Between the trees, massive flowering bushes shaped like giant puffballs displayed innumerable shades of red, from orange through almost to violet. Some of them were bigger than armchairs. Taking a second look, he wondered if each bush might be a single enormous blossom. Half a dozen moas were grazing off to the side, and he decided to go and take a look at those interesting . . .

A man shouted, "Eleal!" and came running forward.

Eleal screamed. She grabbed Edward's hand and hauled at him.

*"Reaper!"* she shrieked. *"Reaper!"*

Edward stayed where he was, ignoring her frantic tugging while he summed up the man who had provoked her terror. Seeing the effect he had produced, the stranger had halted, so he was no immediate danger. He was standing about twenty feet away, staring. There was nothing threatening about his appearance—he was taller than most and in his late twenties or early thirties, but he bore no visible weapon. There was a rawboned awkwardness even to the way he was standing. He wore a yellow tunic and loose pants down to his knees.

Eleal was babbling, *"Reaper!"* and trying to pull Edward away.

He could see no danger in the man. His expression was one of extreme distress—pain, perhaps, or fear, or any one of several things, but more suffering than any desire to cause suffering. Both ignorance of the language and the role he was playing prevented Edward from arguing with the girl, but he was much stronger than she was. Effortlessly towing her along beside him, he strode forward to take a closer look.

# ACT V

*Ensemble*

# 52

"It is the way of the Daughters," Dolm Actor said sadly. "Irepit is goddess of repentance."

The three of them were sitting on the ground around an empty hearth of blackened pebbles. It was a private corner of the campground, almost surrounded by cloud blossoms. Eleal was cuddling very close to D'ward, for she did not trust the former reaper.

Yet Dolm had obviously changed. His face was haggard, and he seemed much thinner than she remembered. There were gray streaks in his hair she did not recall either. His eyes were bloodshot and underlined with darkness.

"I thought you had died," she muttered. "The sword moved by itself. I had both hands on it and Sister Ahn had one and yet it felt as if it moved by itself."

Dolm groaned and covered his face. "It did not touch me."

"I did not feel it touch you," she admitted.

D'ward was listening intently, but she could not tell how much he understood. They were speaking Joalian, which was what she had been teaching him, and his bright blue eyes flickered back and forth as she and Dolm spoke, but he could not be catching very much of this, surely. He was still playing his pilgrim role, being very relaxed and confident. Whenever she looked at him he smiled at her reassuringly.

"Did you not hear what she said?" Dolm asked. "She took my sin upon herself and then I saw what . . ."

"Saw what?"

"Saw what I had become, what I had been doing."

"You really aren't a reaper anymore?"

He shook his head, not looking at her.

She glanced at D'ward. He nodded to show he understood.

"What happened at the festival?" she asked.

Dolm straightened, wiping his eyes with the back of his hand.

"Disaster! Well, Uthiam won a rose for her solo."

"Praise to Tion!" Eleal clapped her hands.

"But she was the only one. I didn't get there in time, you see." Dolm shook his head sorrowfully. "I had orders to go to Ruatvil."

"Orders?"

"Orders from Zath. When we arrived at Filoby, I left the group without telling anyone. Zath's orders override anything. I had been instructed to meet up with another . . . with a colleague."

"That was the one the Kriiton man killed?"

He nodded, staring at the stones of the hearth. "I don't know his name. The next night I was at the Sacrarium. You know."

"But if you weren't killed," she said, working it out, "then it must have been you who removed the bodies!"

Again he nodded. "I buried the nun—dug her grave with her sword and my bare hands. That seemed the least I could do. The others I dropped over the cliff. I looked for you, couldn't find you, and decided you had gone off somewhere with the Liberator." He looked across at D'ward, who was frowning in exasperation.

"So then what happened?" Eleal demanded impatiently.

"I went to Suss," Dolm said reluctantly. "I was too late. They presented the *Varilian*, because it's easier. K'linpor took my part and Golfren took his."

"Oh no!"

"Oh yes."

How awful! A yak could act better than Golfren, fine musician though he was. "So what are they doing now?"

Dolm picked up a thin twig and poked idly at the cold ashes. "Starving."

*"Starving?"*

"Almost. The priests in Narsh took all their money. They don't even have enough to get out of Sussvale, Eleal. And it's all my fault!"

This did not make any sense! "But you were back. Even if they didn't compete, or win, they can stage performances, surely? They're well-known in Suss! Surely people would—"

"I can't act anymore!" Dolm shouted. He put his face down on his knees, huddled in misery. "Trong fired me yesterday."

"Can't act?"

"No. I'm terrible! I forget my lines, I fall over my feet. It's all gone."

Again Eleal glanced at D'ward. He shrugged, obviously at a loss.

"So what are they doing?"

"Trying to hire a replacement for me," Dolm said, speaking to the ground. "As soon as he's learned his lines, they'll stage the *Varilian*."

Eleal sighed. This was awful! "What does Yama—"

The immediate expression of agony on Dolm's face told her she was an unkind, blundering idiot.

"Do you really think I would tell her?" he said bitterly. "Or any of them?"

How strange!—she felt sorry for him now. This was a very different Dolm.

"What *did* you tell them?"

"That I went on a binge, drinking." He laughed, a very hollow sound. "It's better to be thought a lush than a mass murderer."

"Oh. I won't tell them, Dolm. I know I'm nosy, but I can keep secrets if I want to."

"I know you can, Eleal. Thank you. Thank you very much. It doesn't really matter, because they won't see me again, but I'd feel happier . . . Somehow."

The evening must be cooling, for she felt little goose bumps on her skin.

"Who won the gold rose?"

He shrugged. "Some pretty boy, of course."

"You didn't hear his name?"

"No. A musician, I think . . . There was some story that the judges told him to throw his lyre in the river and report to the chief priest. No one else had a look-in, they said. Why?"

"I met a boy named Gim."

"Yes, maybe that was his name, now you mention it."

"And how many miracles?"

Dolm's eyes flickered to her leg and then away again quickly. He smiled his stage smile. "One or two—the priests couldn't decide which. When the time came for the boy to call out a name, he called two names. They were sisters, identical twins, and all their lives they'd had a terrible skin disease. Even from where I was standing, they looked just horrible."

"And Tion healed them!"

"Oh yes! He laid his hands—laid your friend's hands—on their heads and they were cured."

That was beautiful! "Were they pretty? How old are they? What are their names?"

Dolm had lost interest in telling her about the festival. He was studying D'ward with a puzzled expression. "Why is the Liberator still here, in Sussland? Doesn't he know that Zath has reapers out looking for him? Doesn't he know he's in terrible danger?"

She sniggered. "He doesn't seem to know anything. He doesn't know the language, or the gods, or anything!"

Dolm's cavernous eyes widened. "The seeress described him as a baby! Why on earth is he going around dressed as a pilgrim?"

"I decided he would be safest that way, since he can't talk. And, Dolm, he's a wonderful actor! He's being making everyone think he really is a holy man!"

A pained smile twisted the actor's gaunt face. "Oh, Eleal, little idiot! Of course he can act a holy man! Don't you see what you've done?"

She bristled. "I've been ingenious and, er, resourceful under trying conditions! He's been terribly sick!" She looked to D'ward for support and he smiled encouragingly. How odd! Except for the red wound on his forehead, he looked as if he'd never been sick in his life. "And he doesn't know anything about the world at all, but I thought he ought to get to Suss and appeal to Tion, and this seemed—"

"You are a small chump!" Dolm said. "Zath has I-don't-know-how-many reapers out looking for him, and you dress him like a pilgrim? Don't you understand? He's the Liberator! Of course he could make people think he was a holy man! He *is* a holy man! You disguised him as what he really is, you frog-brain!"

Eleal said, "Oh! . . . Oh?" Well, that might help explain a few of the surprising things that had been happening today.

"And I'm not at all sure about taking him to Tion," Dolm said uncertainly. "Some of the passages in the *Testament* suggest that the Liberator . . . All of Sussia's been talking about the birth of the Liberator. Well, never mind. I wish I'd thought of the pilgrim idea for myself, though. That's what I need to do! I shall don the holy pentacle and see if I can cleanse my soul." Another painful smile flickered over his haggard features. "I wonder if he'd—"

He turned to his pack and began unlacing it. Eleal recalled how she'd rummaged through that pack less than a fortnight ago and found a reaper's gown.

Dolm pulled out a tunic and pants. He held them out to D'ward. D'ward's blue eyes lit up and he looked to Eleal for her approval.

"Just what are you suggesting, Dolm Actor?" she demanded.

"I'll trade with him. I'll have to come back with you to Suss and start at Tion's temple, of course."

Eleal shivered. The Holy Circuit of the five great temples took at least a year—a year of begging and poverty, of penance and complete silence.

"But he really can't talk! What if someone asks him questions?"

Dolm shrugged. "You're planning to rejoin the troupe and take him with you, aren't you? It's only a few hours' walk. I'll come with you to the city. He can have my pack, too."

Eleal nodded uncertainly—she had nowhere to go except back to the troupe. D'ward grabbed the garments and jumped up. He strode off into the cloud blossoms. A moment later he came marching out again in his new clothes, grinning shyly. He and Dolm were about the same height and the garments were intended to be loose—but not so loose. If he let go of the pants, they would fall down. Chuckling, Dolm dug in his pack again and produced a length of cord.

"Better!" D'ward said, laughing. "Not women frighten. Talk now?"

"Talk now," Eleal agreed.

He sat down and smiled at Dolm. "D'ward!" He held out a hand.

"Dolm Actor." They shook hands. Dolm stuffed the pilgrim smock in his pack. "I tried to kill you!"

D'ward nodded. "Remember. Saw your voice under the night."

"He doesn't speak very well, does he?" Dolm said wonderingly.

"He's learning very fast!"

"Was reaper?" D'ward asked.

Dolm nodded solemnly.

"Better now?"

"Better."

"Good!" Again D'ward offered a hand to shake.

Dolm looked startled, and then accepted. He stared at D'ward afterward as if hunting something he could not identify.

"We can stay here tonight, can't we?" Eleal said. The sun must have slipped behind Susswall, for the grove was growing dark.

"I have a little food," Dolm said. "But only one blanket."

"We should have left D'ward a holy man. He just has to look at people and they throw charity at him."

Dolm scratched his scanty hair. "Where do you want to go, sir?"

Eleal turned away to hide a smile. She did not think Dolm had even realized that he had called a boy, "sir."

D'ward took a moment to work out the question. "Olympus."

"Who's she?"

"I don't know," Eleal sighed. "He raved about her when he was delirious."

D'ward said, "Query town. Query village."

"That's a woman's name!" she protested. "He must mean *Limpus.*"

Edward shrugged.

"Limpusvil?" Dolm said thoughtfully. "Limpusby? I never heard of either. Your first problem will be to escape from Sussvale. Zath set watches on the nodes and you slipped by us. Now he has all the passes guarded. Only four passes." At Edward's frown he explained more slowly, with gestures, scratching a map in the dirt.

"We need T'lin Dragontrader again!" Eleal said. Then she remembered and said, "Oh!"

Dolm's clouded face brightened momentarily. "He escaped me, if that's what you're wondering. The way he took off on that dragon, I don't suppose he stopped this side of Nosokland." He turned again to study D'ward. "Taking him to Tion is probably the best idea, I suppose, since none of us has any money."

"Tion god?" D'ward said, frowning. "No gods!"

Dolm raised his eyebrows. "Like that, is it? *The gods shall flee before him; they shall bow . . .*" He pondered. "Perhaps you weren't so foolish after all, Eleal Singer—disguising him as a holy man, I mean. The reapers wouldn't be looking for him in that role. And taking him to Suss but not going to the temple may be the same sort of thing. The best place to hide a man is in a crowd of men. Unless they're keeping an eye out for you also, of course."

"What do you mean?" Eleal demanded, feeling a cold shiver.

"They know you're involved, so they may be watching the troupe, in case you try to return. They're probably hunting me, too," he said sadly. "I don't think ex-reapers live very long."

She switched into Sussian, which D'ward would not understand. "Tion!" she said firmly. "We must go and seek the aid of our god!"

"I suppose you're right," Dolm agreed, shooting a worried glance at the Liberator.

# 53

At Suss the canyon was much wider than at Ruatvil. The land descended in steps and cliffs, a red and green landscape fretted by intricate wadis. Tion's temple stood on an isolated mesa, a sprawling palace on a giant plinth, its gilded dome blazing under the tropic sun. It was a giant's cake of white marble, decorated and ornamented in pillars and cornices of bright color, in form like nothing Edward had ever seen, although unquestionably fair. If it resembled anything on Earth, perhaps "out of the Taj Mahal by the Kremlin," would sum it up best. Innumerable lesser buildings spread out over the steps of the valley wall, all set in gardens and park, lush vegetation contrasting with the ruddy soil. The whole complex was larger than the little walled town beyond it. Yes, it was beautiful. And so it should be, for Tion was god of art and beauty. It was vastly impressive—and so it should be, for Tion was one of the five paramount deities of the Vales.

It would be a node, of course, but it stood too far from the road for Edward to sense virtuality. Unlike Stonehenge and the Sacrarium, this node was *occupied*. He did not know whether the numen who dwelt there belonged to the Chamber or the Service. Eleal insisted that Tion was a benevolent god, but the teams in this game did not wear colored jerseys. Edward was not about to walk into any den until he had learned more about the lion. So far his only instructors had been a child and a confessed mass murderer.

Dolm Actor was the first adult he had been able to talk with since he arrived on Nextdoor. However willing and precocious, Eleal had a child's limitations. Dolm spoke clearly and slowly, repeating himself in ingenious variations to convey his meaning. He had a quick wit for untangling Edward's efforts to reply, the patience to correct his grammar, plus an actor's ear for pronunciation. He was a very good coach, but he explained that any wandering entertainer in the Vales must soon become a language expert. Every valley had its own dialect. The farther from home, the greater the difference.

How many valleys? How many peoples?

Dolm could not give an answer, barely even a guess. There were three main languages, Joalian, Thargian, and Niolian, and at least half a dozen variants of each. A score was the absolute minimum.

How many gods? That question produced a lecture on theology, the five great gods—Parent, Lady, Man, Maiden, Youth—and the many minor gods who were the five also. Edward recalled his father saying that people could believe anything they wanted to believe.

By the time noon rolled around and the weary travelers were approaching the turnoff to Tion's spectacular temple, he was often able to understand what was said at the first attempt. Speaking was harder, of course. Nevertheless, he had never picked up a language so quickly. There were uncanny things going on, and he was becoming more and more uneasy about them. He was a stranger here. Mr. Goodfellow . . . Oh, stuff it! That way led madness. *Here be dragons.*

The roads were almost deserted. Yesterday's traffic had been heavy because people had been heading home from Tion's Festival, which sounded like a sort of annual Olympic Games. That train of thought shunted Edward off onto a siding. He spent several minutes asking if there was any great home for all the gods—a sacred mountain, perhaps. Neither Dolm nor Eleal could recall hearing of such a place. Every god and goddess had a temple and important deities might have outlying shrines and chapels as well, but there was no central clubhouse where they were known to assemble. If they threw parties for one another, they did so at home. Scratch that thought. "Olympus" was only a nickname.

Eleal had been feeling ignored all morning and was being obnoxious in consequence. Dolm started asking her about her arrival in Sussland and her replies confirmed Edward's suspicions that she was keeping secrets from him. Having learned of her theatrical background, he could understand her affected airs and dramatics. She claimed that she had been kidnapped by a goddess and rescued by a god. Doubting most of this, Edward still moved Eleal to the head of his list of things to investigate as soon as he had mastered the language. He would like to hear much more about the T'lin man who had brought her to Sussland and had been Creighton's friend also—and especially so when Dolm confirmed that the man had managed to escape. He was an itinerant horse trader, although Edward had seen no horses so far.

But why was the Service so much less conspicuous than the Chamber? Why were enemies so much easier to find than friends? The goddess who had imprisoned Eleal in Narsh was an obvious Horror. Her ritual prostitution sounded exactly like Herodotus's tales of the temple of Aphrodite in Babylon that always so intrigued the Greek scholars of Fifth Form. Zath was another, with his reapers. Was Tion with them or against them? Was he with the Service or against it?

Tion was too much of a risk. The T'lin man had been a friend of Creighton's and was a much safer bet. He must find T'lin. Only if that proved impossible would he risk Tion.

The entrance to the temple precincts was a resplendent arch, ornamented with much gold and many symbols of the god: roses and triangles and animals that looked like frogs. A few worshipers were coming and going, ignored by half a dozen pike-bearing guards, who caught Edward's attention more than anything else did. A squad of fifty or so was being drilled in the distance. Their armor looked like solid gold but obviously couldn't be, or the poor beggars would collapse in heaps. Why should a god need such a force? To stop tourists writing on the pillars? Or just because they looked good standing there? As far as he could judge without going close, they were all at least as tall as he was and very well turned out—the Coldstream Guards of Nextdoor. Were they only for show, or were they an elite force? Smart troops were effective troops. None showed that better than the British Army.

Dolm hesitated, but it was not the guards that deterred him. This was where his pilgrimage must begin. "I'll walk a little farther with you," he muttered. "I think I can find the troupe for you." It was a reasonable excuse to put off the awful moment. The three of them carried on toward the city.

Suss occupied a salient of high ground protected on three sides by cliffs. It was no more than a small town by Edward's standards, and the sight of its walls was a shock, a reminder that he was living in a primitive world. He might have to acquire a sword! He had fenced during his stay in Heidelberg, but not enough to qualify as a swordsman.

As it neared the city gates, the road crossed a series of arched bridges spanning small tributary canyons. On one of these Dolm stopped and peered over the rail. He unslung his pack.

"Yes," he said. "Right first time. Down there. Rehearsing."

The valley below was wooded, but there was a clearing below the bridge; there two men and a woman were apparently having an argument. Other people lounged around in the shade, watching. Voices drifted up unintelligibly. The grouping was staged and unnatural.

Dolm groaned. "By the moons! They've taken on that idiot Tothroom Player!" He mumbled something about women and fighting.

Eleal was jumping up and down and clapping her hands. "Come on!" she said urgently.

"You go," Dolm said. "I will go back now."

"Come, D'ward!" she commanded.

"You'd better not tell them who he is," Dolm said.

That was hardly fair play! "Tell!" Edward said. He tapped his chest. "Danger to them? Tell them."

Eleal hesitated, looking from one to the other.

"Yes, perhaps you had better warn them," Dolm said, giving Edward an odd look.

Then he sighed and went down on his knees to her. "Eleal Singer, I want you to know that I am deeply sorry for what happened. I frightened you terribly and I intended to kill you. I do not ask you to forgive me, because I can never forgive myself, but if you could give me your blessing for the future, it would make me very happy, and very grateful."

Eleal was momentarily at a loss. Then she raised her chin. "Of course I forgive you, Dolm Actor!" she proclaimed magnanimously. "I pray that Holy Tion will protect you and that you will find peace." She hugged Dolm and kissed his cheek. Then she glanced sidelong at Edward to see if he had appreciated her performance.

"Thank you!" Dolm said, and his gratitude seemed genuine.

"Come, D'ward!" she repeated.

"You go," Edward said. "Warn them. I am following."

She pouted at him suspiciously.

"I must change into that pilgrim robe you made, which will always remind me of you," Dolm said. "Then I will give D'ward my pack. He will come."

Edward nodded his agreement. Reassured, Eleal went skipping off to the end of the bridge, and disappeared down a steep path.

The two men looked at each other.

"Tell me," Edward said.

Dolm shuddered and shook his head. "Never!" He unfastened his pack and pulled out the smock with the pentacle on it. Then he stood up and looked apprehensively at Edward.

"Tell me!" Edward repeated. "Tell of Zath. I need to know."

"Need?"

"Need! Am the Liberator."

Frowning, the actor leaned his lanky frame on the rail and stared down at his former friends far below.

"I did a terrible thing," he said quietly. "I hurt a woman, hurt her badly. I was an animal. I was drunk." He mimed drinking and touched his groin. "Understand? Next day I learned that she was likely to die. I went to the temple of Zath and prayed that he would take my life and spare the woman—that I would die, she would not die." He acted it out, pausing frequently to be sure that the stranger understood. "A priest said I must go to her and touch her, lay my hand on her, like this. It was dark, nighttime. Doors opened for me. Bolts slid. No one saw me. She was asleep, or unconscious. I touched her."

He shivered, staring out over the rail.

"She died at once. I felt great pleasure, a rush of joy. Perhaps you don't know yet what it is like to lie with a woman, or perhaps you do, but it was like that, only much more. Much more! I went back to the temple and was initiated. I became a reaper. At night the lust would come upon me. Not every night, but often. I would go out and walk the streets or enter into houses, and I would gather souls for Zath. They died in silence, but in fearful agony. They knew. They died terribly and I felt rapture."

He was weeping, his gaunt cheeks shining wet.

"Always I would feel that joy," he said, his voice breaking. "Especially if they were young and strong. Many, many of them."

Blood was pretty high on the list, Creighton had said. What could be higher than human sacrifice?

"Not you doing this," Edward said awkwardly. How could anyone console a man who bore such a burden? "The god was doing it, not you."

"But it was my crime that led me to him."

"Sister Ahn kill your, er . . ."

"Guilt? Sister Ahn took away my guilt?"

"Thank you. Sister Ahn took away your guilt."

"Yes. And gave me repentance instead. I was happy in my evil. Now I can never be happy again. I think I will kill myself."

"No. Sister Ahn died. You die also, her dying is no thing."

Dolm turned his head to stare at Edward with red-rimmed eyes. "She died for me!"

"You die also, then Zath wins!" How, Edward wondered, had he ever gotten himself into this? He was not qualified to be a spiritual advisor. He was a sanctimonious school prefect lecturing a mass murderer. Holy Roly would be proud of him. He barely knew enough of the language to ask for a drink of water, let alone argue ethics. But he could not stop now.

"Sister Ahn gave you back your life. You must take it. You must use it. Do good!"

"Maybe when I have been a pilgrim and made the Holy Circuit."

Edward thought about that. "No. Pilgrim is running away."

"What else can I do?" Dolm said angrily. "I can't act anymore!"

Their eyes locked.

This was Graybeard again, and the soldier at the bridge. This was Dusty Miller of the Lower Fourth, who'd broken an ankle playing rugby and been terrified to put on his studs after that. This was the First Eleven after they'd lost three in a row and were going up against the top of the league. But Edward did not have the words he had used on those occasions. All he had was baby talk. "Yes you *can*, Dolm. You *can* act. You *can* remember lines. You *can* move without tripping. Acting not changed. Nothing has changed."

He saw the resistance. He felt himself failing. He reached out and gripped Dolm's shoulders with both hands.

"You *can!*" he said. "I say you can!"

Dolm's eyes widened. Edward saw doubt rooting and pressed harder, using every scrap of conviction he could muster. "You can! *I* say you can. Trust me. I am D'ward Liberator! *Trust me!*"

Without warning, the actor screamed. He pushed Edward away and turned, doubling over the rail, racked by sobs. Edward staggered back, appalled at what he had done. The bridge seemed to sway under his feet. A terrible weariness came crashing down on him.

Dolm was weeping helplessly, hysterically, like a child, pounding his fists on the balustrade. He sounded as if he were choking to death.

Edward could find no more words. *I had no right to torture the poor man, so! I should have left him to do what he wanted to do and suffer as he wanted to suffer.*

Angrily he limped away. He did not try to take the pack, because he did not think he could lift it. He was only two days off his sickbed and he must have walked fifty miles. He was crushed by exhaustion. He had blisters all over his feet and his teeth hurt.

There were too many people. He reeled down the path on jellied legs, stumbling with weakness and hanging on to trees, and when at last he had descended to the valley floor and found the clearing, there were just too many people. A dozen or more of them were clustered around Eleal's tiny form. They were enjoying collective hysterics.

They had not known. Dolm had not been able to tell them that Eleal had escaped from Narsh, because he dared not reveal how he knew. Now, suddenly, she had come skipping out of the bushes to join them. She was the center of attention and loving it—hugging and kissing and telling her adventures all at the same time. They must know of the *Testament* with its mention of Eleal and the Liberator, because all Suss had been talking of it. Their god had worked a miracle for them. Their baby was back. Everyone was talking at once, men swearing oaths, women weeping. High drama!

Were actors as superstitious on Nextdoor as they were reputed to be on Earth? She was their mascot, Edward thought, watching the reunion. They must see that! Their little crippled mascot had returned to them and now their luck would change. Or would it? The Tion presence in the temple must know of him, or would surely learn shortly. Zath's reapers might be watching the troupe. The Liberator could bring only trouble to these humble players. He must leave now, at once, before they saw him. Too many people!

Perhaps Dolm would have left the backpack on the bridge. With that, and the smattering of language he had attained, Edward could survive on his own somehow—couldn't he? It was the thought of trying to climb that hill again so soon that delayed him. Then someone saw him.

Screaming with excitement, Eleal came skipping choppily over the grass to him, the whole troupe running in pursuit. Too many people. He staggered back a few paces and leaned against a tree for support.

He soon identified the leaders. The figurehead was the middle-aged giant with the silvery mane, Trong Impresario. He declaimed in a voice like distant gunfire. He rumbled platitudes and struck dramatic poses. The real power was his wife, Ambria, a woman taller than Edward, with steel in her eyes and a tongue like a lash. She was all bone and angles, and yet strangely reminiscent of the irrepressible Mrs. Bodgley of Greyfriars Abbey. The brains of the group might well be that little man with the stubbly white beard. Names, names, and more names . . . Good-looking men, handsome women, all putting on airs. Handshakes and thumps on the back and effusive gratitude for restoring their darling . . .

And then came reaction and withdrawal as they realized that this youth meant more trouble in their lives, not less. He was involved with the gods in ways they did not understand and were not likely to approve if they did. He could not give a straight answer or frame a grammatical sentence. He would be one more mouth to feed and could give nothing in return.

Excitement faded into a murk of uneasiness. The group began to break up and drift away in twos and threes to whisper.

The big Ambria woman said something to her husband. At once he began shouting orders for the rehearsal to continue. Edward sank down on a tussock and put his head in his hands. He should curl up and have a sleep—perhaps they would just take the chance to creep away and leave him.

"Hungry? Thirsty?" asked a voice. A woman was kneeling at his side. She was offering a clay flask and a slab of bread and cheese.

She was the sort of girl that turned a boy's thoughts to desert islands built for two, and her smock would have barely made one good dish towel. Edward was not accustomed to seeing so much beautiful skin—he felt daring when he caught a glimpse of Alice's calves. He knew his face was turning redder than that wilted blossom in her hair. He nodded dumbly several times before he found his voice.

"Thank you. Yes. Um, query name."

She smiled in vision of pearls. "Uthiam. Thanks to you for bringing Eleal back to us."

"Er, Eleal me brought! I fear I bring trouble."

She laughed joyfully. "Eleal is always trouble!"

And he laughed also, and thought that maybe things might be going to turn out not quite so bad as he had feared.

Possibly the food revived him. He sat by himself, staying out of sight and mind, and he watched the troupe's activities with growing interest. Some of the younger folk were engaged in juggling and acrobatics, but they seemed more interested in exercise and enjoyment than in polishing their skills. The main event was a rehearsal of a drama, and everyone was intent on that.

Trong portrayed Grastag King, a tragic, aging figure facing a young challenger. The gallant hero, Darthon Warrior, was being played by Tothroom, replacement for the failed Dolm. The newcomer clutched a script, to which he had to make frequent reference. This might be his first attempt at the role. Even allowing for such handicaps, his performance was insipid. Grastag had stolen his wife, but Tothroom was playing the role as though he had lost a hairbrush.

At first the ornate, high-flown poetry was quite beyond Edward's comprehension. By the fifth or sixth repetition it began to fit together. Like Shakespeare's, the words had a music that soared beyond literary sense, so that meanings missed here and there were of no importance. At times Trong's delivery soared close to opera, where meaning did not matter at all, only emotion. Tothroom mumbled and stuttered and barely seemed to understand his lines himself. Over and over the two men performed the same scene until Trong would roar, "Cut!" and begin bawling instructions. Then he would take it all from the beginning again.

The problem was mostly Tothroom. He was a sallow, pinch-faced man, sadly lacking in stage presence. The plot required him to accost Grastag at his prayers. At first Grastag would respond with contempt and indignation, but then Darthon was supposed to take over the scene, to overwhelm the older man with vituperation and a catalogue of his crimes, to achieve dominance, to grind him into repentance and despair. It was not happening that way, because Tothroom was simply no match for Trong. He was a sheep trying to cow a lion. Trong was at fault also, for he did not seem able to bridle his own flamboyance. He would not lie down unless he was bludgeoned into submission.

And whenever the action was broken off, he would scream more insults than instructions. Instead of encouraging his new recruit, he was browbeating him and threatening. Some team captain he was!

Thinking of the Sixth Form's *Henry V,* Edward began to reflect that even he might have more dramatic talent than this inept Tothroom—and at least he would understand that Trong's ranting should be ignored. He glanced around the clearing. The melancholy expressions on all the other faces suggested that Tothroom was not going to survive the day as a member of the troupe. It was quite clear why Dolm Actor, in his guilt and anguish, had been unable to portray the arrogant swashbuckling Darthon Warrior. Given Hamlet to play in his present mood, he would have dampened every eye in Sussland.

"You foulness clad in kingly," Darthon said mildly. "Raiment. Earth's bowels have never issued forth," he remarked, "more loathsome leech to suck"—he fumbled with the script and then found the place—"to suck the merit. From the people and," he continued apologetically, "warp their aspirations like, er, your own, too. Baseness?"

Trong bellowed, "Cut!" and loosed another torrent of abuse that Edward was glad not to understand.

Eleal bounced down to sit beside him. She was still flushed with excitement at being reunited with her family.

Trong, she said proudly, was her something.

"Query," Edward sighed.

"Father of mother."

"Ah. I see the likeness."

She giggled with delight, then frowned severely. "Darthon Warrior is not good!"

"No."

"Sh! They're starting again!"

"Insolent spawn of lowborn vermin!" Trong declaimed, giving the cue.

*"You foulness clad in kingly raiment!"* roared a new voice from the trees. Tothroom jumped and dropped his script. *"Earth's bowels,"* Dolm bellowed, striding out, brandishing a stick with such menace that it seemed to reflect the sun, *"have never issued forth more loathsome leech to suck the merit from the people and warp their aspirations, like your own, to baseness."*

The troupe was on its feet. Tothroom's jaw hung slackly.

"Say you so?" Trong fell back a pace, hands raised to ward off this attack. "Easier 'tis for whippersnapper to crack the air with words and slight his betters than man to balance judgment and uphold the laws with deeds."

*"Uphold the laws?"* Dolm stormed, advancing on him and leaving his unfortunate replacement completely out of the scene. A barrage of words exploded from the newcomer, an avalanche of scorn fell on Trong. Carillons of poetry soared far beyond Edward's comprehension, but the sense was obvious. Grastag King defied, argued, pleaded, and finally cringed, while Darthon Warrior thundered over him like a volcano.

The scene ended when Trong fled howling into the bushes. For a moment the grove was silent.

"Oh, that was much better!" Eleal remarked judiciously as the riot of welcome converged on Dolm. She turned to Edward with a puzzled frown. "He was never that good before. What did you do to him?"

"I just—"

*No! No! No!* Everything clicked into place and Edward could only stare at Eleal in horror.

# 54

Now there was no question of the troupe rejecting Edward, for Dolm was restored to form and favor, and he was a strong Edward supporter. In fact no one gave a thought to the newcomer for the rest of the day except Eleal, who kept him advised of what was happening.

The incompetent Tothroom having been sent packing, performances could begin as soon as arrangements were made. The big amphitheater at the temple was still being used by the Golden Book Players, who had won that year's rose—a very inferior troupe, Eleal insisted—but the town had a smaller one just outside the walls. By nightfall, she was coaching Edward in the art of coloring placards, lettered in the strange Greek-style script. He shared his new friends' meager meal; he slept in a borrowed blanket in the shed they had rented. It was normally used to store some sort of root crop and had a strong smell of ginger. As a dorm for fourteen people it was embarrassingly intimate, but he had been accepted as one of the band, at least for the time being.

The next day he walked the streets of Suss carrying sandwich boards. He was still shaky and footsore, but the job was within his capabilities; Dr. Gibbs had stoutly maintained that the chief benefits of a classical education were versatility and adaptability. Edward found himself in trouble only once, when a visiting merchant asked him for directions to Boogiil Wheelwright's.

Suss was tightly cramped within its walls, yet prosperous. The walls themselves suggested that artillery was still unknown in the Vales, but he noted promising signs of technology. A few people wore spectacles. Stores sold printed books and musical instruments and tailored clothes, while food stalls offered a wide variety of crops. He saw very few beggars. The sewer system was underground and drinking water was piped to communal outlets. He had seen many towns on Earth less favored. He could still hold out hopes that Nextdoor had a London or a Paris somewhere.

That evening he peeled yamlike tubers for the cooks, fetched firewood, washed clothes, and helped to lay out the evening meal. The fare was sparse, but tomorrow should bring better fortune. The day's rehearsals had gone well. Old friends in Suss had promised to attend the opening night.

That evening, sprawled on the grass outside their hut, the players for the first time had leisure to discuss their new recruit. Understandably, they wanted to know just who he was and where he had come from and what he was planning to do. He explained as well as he could that he was a visitor from a very far country and did not know why the gods had brought him to Sussland. He would eagerly help in any way he could in return for his daily bread and a roof over his head. Eleal's tale was being regarded with justifiable incredulity, but Dolm vouched for him. The discussion went on a long time as those voluble, arty people passed a rare free evening doing what they enjoyed doing most—talking.

In the end the decision was made by the formidable Ambria. Edward would not be discussed outside the group, she decreed. The name "Liberator" would not be mentioned. He would be a traveling scholar from Nosokland, which was sufficiently distant that no one would question his mangled grammar and peculiar accent. "Choose a name!" she commanded.

Edward shrugged.

"D'ward's a *nice* name!" Eleal said. Everyone laughed.

It was certainly not uncommon, Piol remarked, being the name of a minor Tion avatar, god of heralds and envoys.

"Then D'ward Scholar he shall be!" Ambria decreed. Talk turned to other topics.

Probably only Edward knew how she came by her infallibility, for he had been trained in leadership. He had watched her read the group's wishes and put them into words, sensing where her followers wished to go before they themselves knew. Then she had led them there. She displayed no doubts. A man could learn from her.

Thus D'ward Scholar became one of the Trong Troupe.

He, in turn, accepted them. They were a strange group, but they had many admirable qualities. They were devoted to their art, cheerfully enduring poverty and hardship for its sake. They had a strong mutual affection and they rarely bickered. They knew one another's strengths and weaknesses, and worked within them. Politics and commerce they ignored, their religion was simple, their god benevolent. A world of such people would not be a bad place.

The following morning he again walked the streets with his placards, and he chose some odd parts of the city in which to advertise drama. He had observed waterwheels outside the walls, but the factories were not mechanized. Nevertheless they were true factories, employing dozens of people, with clear divisions of labor. He discovered something that he thought was a small blast furnace, although it was not in use. He saw both coal and coke. This was a culture waiting for an industrial revolution.

In the afternoon he went with Dolm Actor to purchase firewood, which was apparently an artistic necessity. Suss was one of the better towns of the Vales, Dolm said— proud to be the home of a major god and anxious to live up to his standards. Its citizens were devoted to freedom and democracy, which often meant social chaos. New laws must be approved by an assembly of all the citizens, leading to riot, destruction of property, and even deaths, but such mishaps were regarded as the price of liberty. In their own eyes Sussians were a sturdy, self-reliant people; their neighbors thought they were crazy anarchists. Of course, Dolm explained with a chuckle, Joalvale lay over the next pass and in reality Sussia was part of Joaldom. Edward decided that further understanding must await mastery of the language.

That afternoon he joined the whole troupe in a late lunch, another skimpy repast of fruit and vegetables. The first performance of the *Varilian* in Suss would begin just before sundown, and everyone was in a state of nerves. Again they had gathered on the grass outside the shed. The shade was welcome, the sun ferocious. Insects buzzed around the sweaty people, biting painfully whenever they had the chance. Tempers were touchy. It was no secret that the finances were exhausted. Only a favorable reception of the play lay between the band and disaster.

Edward was just as edgy as they were. His feet and legs ached and his sore tooth was hammering a red-hot chisel into his jaw. He feared he had another attack of diarrhea pending, when he had not properly recovered from the last one. An able-bodied scrounger might be acceptable if he were willing to help, but he could not expect the troupe to care for a useless invalid. He knew that the unfamiliar diseases of this world might kill him sooner rather than later.

Conversation turned to the evening's proceedings, with Ambria distributing responsibilities.

"And what will D'ward do?" asked Klip Trumpeter, a pimply adolescent. More than anyone else, he seemed to resent the freeloader—possibly because his own value to the troupe was questionable at best.

"D'ward will help pass the hat," Dolm said, dark eyes gleaming with amusement. "I think he will do very well at that."

"He will collect gold!" Eleal proclaimed. Everyone ignored that absurdity and went on with their various discussions.

Edward was sitting across from the charming Uthiam, not entirely by accident. She was married, but he enjoyed looking at her. "Tell me, please," he said. "Query . . . T'lin?"

She looked surprised, doing lovely things with her eyebrows. "T'lin Dragontrader? Eleal's friend?"

He had learned now that names were trades. What exactly this T'lin traded in, he was uncertain, except that it was something to ride on. He nodded.

She shrugged. "He comes and goes. A bit of a rascal, I think, but he seems fond of Eleal. If you believe her story, he helped rescue her from the temple in Suss. We run into him two or three times a year."

He got all that on the first try, except for the last bit, which he asked her to repeat. Two or three times a year? How long was a year? Could he bear to wait that long, or must he risk appealing to Tion?

Uthiam said, "Why do you want T'lin Dragontrader, or is that a rude question?"

"I think he may be able to help me."

She gave him a thousand-ship smile. "He must know the Vales as well as anyone. Stay with us and you'll meet him sooner or later."

"You're all very kind. I wish I could be more useful."

"You are useful! Have you ever done any acting?

*One schoolboy production?* "A little."

Heads turned.

"Would you care to say a few words?" asked Piol Poet. The little man was genuinely interested, his eyes bright. He wrote the plays; he was the scholar, a likable old gentleman.

"You would not understand them, sir."

"But we may see if you have talent!"

Only if they had very sharp eyes, Edward thought. But a good laugh would help cheer them up and could not hurt him. He finished chewing a mouthful of the carroty root with the ginger flavor. "All right." He rose to his feet. If he were being honest with himself, he would admit that what he really had in mind was a test of some of his wild-eyed theories.

Other quiet conversations ceased. More heads turned to watch him. Reviewing his very limited repertoire, he chose the Agincourt speech.

"I'll give you a speech by a warrior named . . ." *Henry* would sound female to them.

"Kingharry. His men must fight many more men." He struggled to put his thoughts into words. "He begins with scorn for those who want to leave. He says that they can go if they want to. He has too many . . . no . . . he has *enough* men that their deaths will hurt their land if they lose, understand? And then he tells of the glory that will be theirs if they win against such great odds."

"Sounds like Kaputeez Battlemaster's speech in the *Hiloma*," Trong pontificated.

Edward left the shade, out into the scorching sunlight. He detoured by a stack of properties to arm himself with a wooden sword, then took up his stance before a group of shrubs, his knees starting to quiver with stage fright. He must just hope that Shakespeare would sound as impressive to them as Piol's poetry did to him. He was going to perform in a foreign language before an audience of professionals? He was crazy! He reviewed the opening lines, wiped sweat from his forehead. *Idiot show-off!* Then he turned to face the watchers under the trees, the eyes, the expectant silence. He noticed the secret smiles. He took a deep breath. Mr. Butterfield, the English master, had always told him to speak to a deaf old lady in the back row. He spoke to Piol Poet, who was slightly deaf and well to the rear.

*"What's he that wishes so?"* he said sharply. *"My cousin Westmoreland? No, my fair cousin: If we are marked to die, we are enow to do our country loss."*

He saw the frowns, the shock as they realized that this was a language like none they had ever heard before.

*"I am not covetous for gold . . ."*

He began to raise his voice. He had caught the poet's interest already—Piol's eyes were wide.

*"We would not die in that man's company that fears his fellowship to die with us! This day is called the feast of Crispin . . ."*

Dolm was smiling. Eleal was agog. Trong, old ham, was frowning. But he had them! It was working! Creighton had known.

*"Then shall our names, familiar in his mouth as household words, Harry the King, Bedford and Exeter, Warwick and Talbot . . ."*

The excitement was rising. He could feel their empathy, their professional response. Not his minuscule talent, not the roll of the bard's poetry, not challenge and bluster— no, there was other magic at work here. Fallow would have laughed him to shreds had he blustered like this, but ham was what the troupe enjoyed, so he gave them ham. He postured and flailed and roared the deathless words.

*"And Crispin Crispian shall ne'er go by,*
*From this day to the ending of the world,*
*But we in it shall be rememberéd:*
*We few, we happy few, we band of brothers—"*

The troupe was totally caught up in the bravado, and so was he. He stalked the field of Agincourt before them, a juvenile warlord reviling the potent French multitude, defying death in the name of fame. He was one with his audience. The troupe's joy flowed out to him, he ate it up and sent it back to them in glory.

*"And gentlemen in England now abed*

*Shall think themselves accursed they were not here,*
*And hold their manhood cheap while any speaks*
*That fought with us upon Saint Crispin's Day!"*

He waited, puzzled that no one had picked up the cue. The greatest inspirational English ever penned faded away into the alien trees. Suddenly he was back in the dusty orchard before the ramshackle hut, and the troupe was on its feet, cheering and applauding and screaming for more.

Laughing with relief, he bowed in acknowledgment.

His gut had stopped hurting and so had his tooth. He felt tremendous.

Creighton had called it *charisma.*

Generals, politicians, prophets, and sometimes actors.

# 55

Eleal had known all along that D'ward would be a wonderful actor, and she was delighted by the family's reaction to his performance. As soon as she saw Trong going off by himself, she ran over to him and said, "Grandfather?"

The big man jumped and looked at her as if he had never seen her before. Then he went down on one knee and—much to her astonishment—hugged her tightly. His beard tickled. She noticed how rough and coarse his face was, scarred by years of makeup.

"Darling Granddaughter! I missed you! It is wonderful to have you safely restored to us."

Well! He might have said so two days ago!

"I missed you, too. And one day you must tell me all about my mother."

He turned his face away, registering extreme pain. "It is a tragic tale, child."

"I expect it is, but we don't have time for it now. I have a suggestion."

"Indeed?" His astonishment seemed somewhat excessive.

"Indeed!" Eleal said. "I think D'ward would be much better as Tion in the *Trastos* than Golfren Piper is."

She had feared he would dismiss the idea out of hand, but the old man considered it seriously. "He has a very strange accent, Eleal."

"But Tion has very few lines to say, and I know D'ward could learn to say those clearly. Besides, would it even matter? Do you think the audience would notice? He would be so convincing!"

Trong smiled, which he rarely did. In fact she could not recall him ever actually smiling at her before. "Perhaps he would! But it would hardly be fair to Golfren."

"If he didn't mind, would you?"

"Well, I don't know. Tion is usually shown with fair hair, and D'ward is dark. And the Youth never wears more than a loincloth. D'ward may have a very hairy chest, and that would not look right."

"He can use a wig and he doesn't have any hairs on his chest." He did have marvelous eyelashes, though.

Trong flinched. "Oh. Well, I will think about it."

"Thank you, Grandfather!" Eleal said, and kissed him. He was still kneeling, staring after her, as she skipped away.

She had thought that the priests of Ois had stolen her pack, but apparently Ambria had saved it. So she had its familiar weight on her shoulders as the troupe set out for the amphitheater. She had a proper built-up boot again, too, which made walking much easier. She sidled next to Golfren, and waited until she had him to herself.

"Golfren?"

"Eleal? Up to your tricks again?"

"Certainly not. I mean, what tricks? I just wanted to ask your opinion of something."

He smiled down at her, eyes twinkling. Golfren had nice eyes, but they were not nearly as bright a blue as D'ward's. D'ward was altogether more handsome.

"I smell trouble. Ask away."

"Don't you think it would be nice," Eleal said carefully, "if we could give D'ward a small part in one of the plays? So as he could feel like one of the group?"

Golfren cleared his throat. "Well, that depends. What part did you have in mind?"

"Oh, I was thinking he would make a very good Tion, in the right sort of play."

"You were, were you? Well I think he might—in the right sort of play."

"I knew you would agree with me," Eleal said.

Piol was talking with D'ward all the way, and Eleal did not get a chance to talk with him until after they had arrived at the amphitheater. She changed quickly into her herald costume. As this was not Narsh, she did not need extra clothes to keep warm. She went in search of Piol, and found him in the middle of a circle of props, spread out on the grass.

"Piol Poet?"

"Yes?" he muttered abstractly. The trouble with Piol was that he so often had his mind on other things.

"Don't you think D'ward is a wonderful actor?"

Scratching his stubbly beard, the little man said, "Mm?" and then, "Hmm? Yes, I do." He glanced at his list and then peered all around.

"Good! Don't you think it would be advisable to give him a small part in one of the plays?"

"Mmm? But which part?"

"I think he would make a great Tion in the *Trastos!* Golfren thinks so too, and Trong agrees."

"Can you see Karzon's sword anywhere?"

Eleal sighed and picked up the sword, which was lying right by her feet. She poked at Piol's tummy with it. "Why not let D'ward play Tion when we do the *Trastos?*"

Piol spoke to his list. "What? Who? But Tion has to play his pipes!"

Sussians preferred plays that made Tion seem like the most important god in the Pentatheon, of course, but this year Piol had ignored tradition, as he so often did. He had written Tion's part for Golfren. Golfren looked splendid in a skimpy loincloth, but he couldn't act. So Tion mostly just stood by while the other gods argued. D'ward could do that just as well as Golfren, even if he didn't have golden curls!

At the end, when the doomed Trastos Tyrant fell into despair and called on Tion to help him—when the audience would be expecting Tion to make a big speech—Golfren came in and played his pipes instead. It was a big surprise. It had gone over well in Mapvale, fairly well in Lappinvale. What Narshians thought didn't matter.

"No he doesn't!" Eleal said crossly. "You just wrote it that way because you don't trust Golfren not to butcher his lines!"

"We can talk about it some other time. Take this flask over to the spring and fill it, will you? And stop threatening me with that sword!"

"No, listen!" Eleal poked him again. "Tion inspires Trastos with courage to go and fight even though he knows he's doomed. Of *course* you could give Tion more lines to speak instead of the silly piping, so the audience would know what it meant. A rousing speech like the one D'ward did tonight, but in Joalian, of course, and why are you laughing?"

"Me, laughing? I wasn't laughing! I was thinking about the soldier in the *Varilian.*"

That was Golfren Piper's other role, and he was just terrible in it.

"What of it?" she demanded warily.

"We could turn him into a general."

"D'ward could do that very well, too," she said. "But we can't change the *Varilian* now, in the middle of a run. And it really wouldn't be fair to steal all Golfren's parts. No, I think D'ward should play Tion in the *Trastos.*"

"I'll think about it." Piol knelt down to look in the makeup box. "Golfren might not mind losing his lines, but he loves to play his pipes. Fetch that water."

Fortunately Eleal had a spare string for her lute. "This is a tragedy we're talking about, not a masque! Now admit it—the only reason you have Tion play his pipes to encourage the tyrant is that Golfren can't act. Well, why not have Tion play his pipes to summon Gunuu?"

Piol finished counting greasepaint and closed the box. He reached for a pile of . . . He looked up. "Who?"

"Gunuu, god of courage," Eleal said airily. "An avatar of the Youth, of course. He's not very well known hereabouts, I admit, because his temple's down in Rinooland or somewhere, and there are some arguments about where he fits in the Pentatheon." She had accosted a pair of priestesses in the street that morning and asked them all about courage and who was god of courage, and she must know a lot more about Gunuu at the moment than Piol Poet did.

"What sort of arguments?" Piol was interested now.

"Oh, one school of thought considers him an aspect of Astina, as she is goddess of warriors. But no one will argue that in Suss. So Tion pipes and Gunuu comes on stage and speaks! A god can summon one of his own avatars, can't he?"

Piol stared at her as if she was crazy. "I never heard . . . Visek preserve me! Side by side?"

"Why not?" Eleal laid down the sword. "I think D'ward would make an ideal god of courage, don't you? He's a born actor!"

"And you're a born playwright!" The old man was staring blankly into space already. Recognizing the signs of genius at work, she crept quietly away to let him concentrate. She was glad to have that settled! Not that she'd been in any doubt how the conversation would turn out. It was written in the prophecy: *D'ward shall become Tion, D'ward shall become Courage.*

The amphitheater was a natural hollow on the cliff edge outside the walls. It was not as large as the one at the temple, but Eleal thought it had better acoustics, and there were two shacks in the bushes for the cast dressing rooms. The arena at the temple had only one dressing room.

Members of the troupe moved around with the money bowls as the audience trickled down the path. Later she overheard Gartol Costumer wondering how D'ward had managed to collect twice as much as he had. The play began at sunset, with Klip blowing a fanfare on his trumpet. The first act was played in twilight. The bonfires were lit during the intermission and again players went around with the bowls. This time everyone was interested to know how the play was being received, and again D'ward had collected the most.

In the second act Eleal made her entrance as the herald and said her line. She had played in Suss for the first time in her life! As she walked off into the shadows, wielding her staff so her limp would not show, someone began to clap, and then the whole audience followed, and that really did sound like the biggest applause of the evening. She had a strong suspicion that it had been D'ward who had begun that clapping, but she couldn't be sure, and of course she was too proud to ask.

At the end, as the audience trooped out under the moons, the actors offered the bowls again, and then some people did put real gold in D'ward's, exactly as Eleal Singer had predicted. He had not even had a part in the play, but he had such a nice smile!

# 56

The next day the troupe moved to more respectable quarters and the meals improved considerably.

Before that, though, Ambria announced that she was going to the temple. Her expression suggested that everyone ought to go to the temple. There were a few grumbles, but most people nodded to show they thought this was a good idea. Eleal knew that she should go, to thank Tion for returning her safely to her family, certainly D'ward should. Obviously he did not want to.

"I shall not," he said firmly. "And I should be very grateful if you would not mention the Liberator in your prayers. Do you need someone to stay behind and look after your baggage?"

Ambria disapproved, but she could hardly force him to go to the temple against his will, and even she was not proof against his smile. Piol announced that he had some work to do, so he would stay behind also. Everyone else went.

Nothing special happened. Eleal thanked the god for rescuing her from Narsh, and from the reapers, and restoring her to her family. She did not mention D'ward, although it was very hard not to think about him while she was praying. And nothing special happened! She limped when she departed just as much as she had limped when she arrived. Perhaps she was being presumptuous in hoping that her efforts would be rewarded with a miracle—or had she not finished her task? She had not actually brought D'ward to Tion's temple.

Later the troupe moved into the Suss hostelry, which was a very good one. Piol Poet disappeared. Eleal found him in the attic, writing busily. She was confident then that he was working on a new speech for the *Tragedy of Trastos*. She left him alone and later, when Halma was looking for him, she said he had gone to the market.

It was wonderful to be back with her family again. They all told her how much they had missed her; she thought they appreciated her more now. Perhaps she even appreciated them more. That very afternoon, to her complete astonishment, Trong took her aside and sat her down and told her all about her mother, Itheria Impresario. It was a very sad story, and they were both weeping before it was finished.

An hour later, when Eleal was helping Ambria hang out washing, the big woman said, "Did Trong speak to you?"

Eleal nodded. She should have guessed whose idea that had been.

"Don't be too hard on him," the big woman said gruffly, standing on tiptoe to peg things on the highest rope. "He has never forgiven himself for letting you fall out the window when he was supposed to be looking after you."

"What has that to do with my mother?"

"Well, nothing, I suppose. He shouldn't have made us keep that a secret from you. It is still very difficult for him to talk about."

"But," Eleal said loyally, feeling her eyelids start to prickle all over again, "if it was a god who, er, I mean . . . Well, if she fell in love with a god, then that really wasn't her fault, was it?"

"You mean it was the god's fault?"

*Um!* "Well, yes. It must have been."

"That's what Trong finds so hard to talk about. Be careful with that blouse, now!"

D'ward was becoming quite fluent in Joalian and everyone was very careful to speak clearly and correctly around him, so he would not pick up the terrible local growl. He asked Eleal to give him reading lessons, too, and of course she graciously consented to set aside some time for this. He wanted to find a copy of the *Filoby Testament* and practice on that, but she explained that it was written in Sussian, and would be bad for him.

"How about some of Piol's plays, then?" he asked.

"No!" she said firmly. "They're in *classical* Joalian. If you try speaking that in the streets people will think you are very odd."

He smiled. "That speech I recited from *Kingharry* was like that."

So they went with Uthiam to a secondhand bookstore. Eleal picked out a famous romance, but D'ward refused it and instead chose an *exceedingly* dull book about the moons and stars. Teaching him to read with that awful thing was not nearly as much fun as she had expected. He seemed amazed to learn that Trumb went through his phases in only four and a half days, making solemn-faced jokes that Trumb wasn't really a big moon, therefore, only close to the Earth. He was even surprised to learn that the fortnight came from Ysh, who took exactly fourteen days to go from eclipse to eclipse. He spent *hours* studying Kirb'l and became almost surly in consequence. He claimed he had not known that there were three hundred sixty-four days in a year! At times, the Liberator was definitely *strange.*

She was not the only one to have noted his smile. Olimmiar Dancer was making a perfect fool of herself, following him around like a lapcat and blushing every time he looked at her, until Eleal wanted to scream. The married women were almost as bad. If their husbands noticed, they did not comment. Everybody knew that D'ward was an honorable man.

Piol produced his ode to courage and Trong started rehearsing the *Trastos,* although the *Varilian* was still drawing full houses every night.

Eleal sat down with D'ward to help him learn his speech. He had trouble working out exactly what it said, of course, and then he seemed very unhappy with it.

"It's all, er—what do you call a thing that says something everybody knows already?"

Eleal wasn't sure, so they called over Golfren, who said the word was "platitude."

"This is all platitudes!" D'ward announced.

Golfren read over the speech. "Yes, it is. But isn't most poetry like that? It isn't what it says that matters, it's the way it says it."

D'ward pondered, then laughed and agreed.

He was absolutely horrified when Gartol Costumer produced his costume.

"You mean I have to go out in front of hundreds of people wearing only *that*? But there will be ladies present!"

"It's traditional," the old man said, "and the ladies will love it."

D'ward looked very shocked and turned red.

He was interested in all sorts of things—politics and customs and geography and business. Especially, though, he was interested in the gods. One day Eleal actually overheard him ask Trong which were the good gods and which were the bad gods.

Trong, of course, was horrified. "The gods are good and know not evil, my son!" he said, which was a line from *The Judgment of Apharos,* although D'ward would not know that.

"So where does evil come from?"

"Evil comes from mortals, when they do not obey the gods."

"Then you approve of what women must do in the temple in Narsh?" D'ward sounded more puzzled than impertinent.

Trong growled, "Certainly!" and stalked away.

The very next day, D'ward took Piol Poet off to a corner of the dining area and started writing something. It so happened that Eleal was helping Uthiam hunt for an earring she had lost, and while she was looking under a nearby table she chanced to hear some of what was being said. Piol seemed to be listing all the gods and goddesses he could think of, and D'ward was writing them down. Actually, he only wrote down some of them, and later he left the list lying around where anyone could pick it up and read it. There was no pattern to the ones he'd chosen: *P'ter, D'mit'ri, Ken'th, D'ward, Alis.*

He'd spelled most of them wrong anyway. And his handwriting was terrible.

Another day, when they were rehearsing in the park under the bridge and D'ward was sitting with Dolm in front of some bushes, Eleal just happened to pass by on the other side of the bushes.

"I know T'lin Dragontrader," Dolm was saying, "but only by sight. He's probably spying for someone, maybe both sides, maybe four or five sides. Most traveling merchants do. The Vales are always conspiring—Joalia, Thargia, Niolia, and all their vassal states."

"How about traveling actors?"

"Of course. When we return to Jurg in the fall, Ambria files reports with the Niolian ambassador."

Eleal had not known that! She moved to a more comfortable position, a little closer.

"Political spying?" D'ward said. "Do the gods play the same sort of game among themselves?"

"Likely they do, some of them."

"I suppose one tries everything in a few thousand years?"

Dolm chuckled. "I expect so. I was required to report to Zath if I ever learned anything that might interest him—a war brewing, or a plague, for example. I only had reason to do it once, and that was in Narsh last fortnight."

"How did you? Do you write reports to gods?"

"I had a ritual, of course."

"Explain that, please."

How typical of D'ward, not to know what a ritual was!

But Dolm did not laugh. "A ritual is a procedure decreed by a god. A priest will sacrifice a chicken in a particular way for a foretelling, another way for a blessing or a healing, right? It works because the god has arranged it so."

"So it's sort of like writing a name and address on a message? When you do certain things in a certain order, the god knows he's being called and what's expected of him?"

"I never thought of it that way, but yes, it must be."

How like D'ward to see things in a way nobody else did!

Dolm continued. "I had been given a ritual to summon the god in person. Obviously that is not something one undertakes lightly, especially when one's personal god is Zath. Parts of the ceremony had been made deliberately unpleasant, but of course that is to be expected." He laughed nervously. "Fortunately he approved of my presumption, and I must admit that he rewarded me well."

"May I ask how?"

Dolm sighed. "With rapture, mostly. But he also cured the wound I had inflicted on myself as part of the ritual. Otherwise I would have bled to death."

D'ward asked the question that was making Eleal want to burst: "What does Zath look like?"

There was a long pause before Dolm answered. "Hard to say. He wears a reaper gown with a hood. I never saw him properly, not really."

"This was what Eleal saw?"

"She saw the ritual, at least. I'm sure she'd run away before Zath arrived, or she would not be around now. I never met anyone one quarter as snoopy as that child!"

How *dare* he call her a child!

D'ward had not finished with his questions. "Why did you call Zath that time?"

"Because of what happened in the temple. Trong sacrificed to Ois. The priest was extremely surprised by the portents. Minor rituals like that are normally routine, so I knew the goddess was taking a personal interest. Thinking she objected to my evening activities, I reported to my master. Zath knew what was happening, though. He said Eleal was the problem, and I could leave her to the goddess."

There was a silence, then, broken only by Trong's rantings in the distance.

Dolm chuckled. "You look worried. What else do you want to know?"

"This story about Eleal's mother."

Eleal bristled. It was not polite of them to discuss her when she wasn't there! Or not supposed to be there, at least.

"Is it a common event—a god raping a mortal?"

"Not *raping!*" Dolm protested. "She would have submitted very willingly. It's not exactly common. But I don't think it's truly rare, either. You know the athletes from the festival here always spent a night at Iilah's grove? There's a common belief that at least one husky young man will always have an interesting experience that night."

"It sounds like rape to me, if the victims can't resist. And when it's a god and a woman—do the women always kill themselves?"

"No. But men or women, they're never much good for anything else. They never speak of it, but how could they ever be happy again, after having known the love of a god? Excuse me. I've got to go. My cue's coming up."

D'ward just sat there then, by himself, thinking. Eleal crept away.

He was accepted as one of the troupe. Even Klip could not dislike him. If he had a fault, it was that he would persist in regarding Eleal as a mere child. For example, one afternoon when he was in the kitchen, helping Uthiam Piper make supper—he was peeling blueroots, Uthiam baking bread . . .

"I am worried about Eleal," he said, and again that was very rude of him to discuss someone who was not there.

Uthiam laughed. "Why on earth are you worried about her?"

"Well, I'm grateful to her for what she did for me, of course. I should certainly have died without her help. I am very grateful to all of you, also, but I was brought here against my will. Somehow I must find a way to go home again and . . . attend to certain important duties."

"We shall miss you. We enjoy your company. You more than pay your way with the collections—I wish I knew how you did that! But what has this to do with Eleal?"

"She seems to think she owns me! I can't stay with you forever, and I don't want to hurt the child's feelings."

*Child?* Eleal fumed.

"I am sorry for her," D'ward continued. "She is so convinced that she will be a great actor when she grows up! Can she? With that game leg? She won't be able to compete in the Tion Festival or—"

"You needn't worry about that small hussy," Uthiam said. "I would back her against the entire Sussian militia any day. In fact, if you were to peek around that door, there, right now, I suspect you would find a pair of very sharp ears, attached to the sides of Eleal Singer's head."

Eleal took off along the corridor as if Zath himself were after her.

Following six well-received performances of the *Varilian,* the Trong Troupe announced *The Tragedy of Trastos.* In the smallest print on the playbills, D'ward Scholar was mentioned in the role of Gunuu, god of courage. Rehearsals had not gone well. D'ward seemed very wooden and not at all the fiery young man who had played Kingharry for the troupe.

"Bigger, bigger!" Trong told him, over and over. "It's almost dark, remember! You're standing in firelight, not sunlight. Exuberate! Wave your arms! *Declaim!*"

But D'ward continued to play the part in the same dull way, almost as if he hoped they would cancel his appearance.

Even on the morning of the first performance, Trong was doubtful. Piol insisted it would be all right on the night, and even if it wasn't it would not spoil the show.

Eleal was sure it would be all right.

It was more than all right. It was spectacular.

Eleal had no costume to worry about in the *Trastos* because she sang her gods' messenger part offstage. She did it very well, but she won no applause. Nobody was being applauded. The collection at intermission had been pitiful. In backstage whispers, the actors agreed they had never met a harder audience. The trouble might be that Trastos was a historical villain in Suss, so Sussians did not enjoy seeing him portrayed as a tragic hero. Piol had bent tradition too far.

D'ward's scene came near the end. Eleal slipped out through the bushes to sit on the edge of the crowd and watch. The doomed Trastos, having defied the gods' command to abdicate in favor of a democracy and then challenged the rebels to send forth a champion to meet him in single combat, had now learned that this champion would be his own son, Daltos Liberator. Trong proclaimed his despair in a long soliloquy, crumbling by stages to the grass. He ended lying prone, howling out the cue: "Gods, send me courage!"

Golfren entered, wearing the golden loincloth that identified him as Tion. Even in Narsh, the audience had reacted a little to this dramatic confrontation. The Sussians sat in stony silence to hear what the god might say to rescue the evening from disaster.

"I will send you courage!" Golfren announced, and began to play. Eleal heard a few angry whispers near her. Golfren, too, sensed the crowd's displeasure, for he shortened his solo, raising the music swiftly to the rallying call that was D'ward's cue.

"I am Courage!" D'ward Scholar strode into the light of the fires, tall and lean, wearing an identical costume and holding a symbolic lantern high. How handsome he was! Surely every woman in the amphitheater must have felt her heart quicken at the sight of him! Surely every man would identify with his youthful bravado? The spectators gasped to see a god and one of his own aspects on stage together.

Piol had written better poetry, Eleal thought, but she had never heard any of it better spoken, and in a fine Joalian accent, too:

> *Courage alone is bone to shape our flesh.*
> *Without such spine of mettle, man remains*
> *Earthbound, a carrion worm perceiving death*
> *In every shiver of a grassy blade.*
> *Look up, look up! Behold the beck'ning stars!*
> *Spurn not the gods who loaned you life to be*
> *The wherewithal of deeds, not end itself.*

*Affection, reputation, pride and joy*
*Are but frail branches sprung from sturdy stem*
*Of valor, which defies the storms of fate,*
*Onslaught of age, the petty and the base,*
*To raise a crown above the common line*
*And stand one sunlit hour as mark and gauge*
*Of what may sometimes be . . .*

And so on, in forty or fifty lines of rousing verse. It built to a satisfying climax with a local Sussian reference or two. All the time old Trong was recovering, rising with the poetry—to his knees, to one knee, until at the end he was erect and defiant, brandishing his sword at the stars and roaring out an echo of the final line, inspired to die bravely.

The audience was on its feet also. The hollow rang with cheers. D'ward had to come out again and repeat the entire thing twice. Then he and Trong had to take a special bow, while the audience screamed hysterically and threw gold coins.

Never had Eleal seen such a triumph! Later she limped around through the crowd with a bowl. Money clinked into it like rain until it became unpleasantly heavy. The others' bowls were filling up as well. She saw smiling faces everywhere. There was a huge throng around D'ward—mostly women, she was annoyed to notice—and she hoped he was managing the conversation successfully. Probably none of it was very subtle. She could not even get close to him.

Eventually she sidled up to Trong, to hear what was being said by all the admiring citizens clustered around him. Many of them were old friends she recognized from past years, who might have a kind word to say about her own debut. One of the others was an ancient priest from the temple, conspicuous in his splendid yellow robe. He seemed to be somebody special, for everyone was deferring to him.

Then Klip came lounging by, empty-handed.

"Here!" she said, thrusting the weighty bowl at him. "Some more loot!"

Klip whistled as he took it. "You've done well, Eleal!"

The old priest turned around. "Eleal? Is your name Eleal, my daughter?"

She curtsied. "I am Eleal Singer, Your Holiness. You heard me earlier, in my role as the gods' messenger. I have an onstage part in our other play where I—"

He must have sharp ears to have overheard Klip. He had very sharp eyes, too. His hair was silver, his shaven, wizened face had a snowy texture. "And this remarkable young actor we witnessed this evening . . . D'ward?"

"D'ward . . . Scholar, Your Holiness." Staring into that needling gaze, she felt a sudden uneasiness. "He's from Rinoovale."

"Is he, indeed?" The old man glanced around at his companions. "Excuse us a moment." He laid a spidery hand on Eleal's shoulder and urged her back a few paces, away from onlookers. He bent over, putting his face very close to hers, and he smiled in a grandfatherly sort of way. "There is an Eleal mentioned in the *Filoby Testament*. There is a D'ward mentioned there, too. What can you tell us about this strange coincidence, child?"

*Curtain*

# 57

Edward was screwed—scammered, corned, fried, paralyzed, and plastered. Intoxicated, in other words. He had not been drinking. First there had been that explosion of adulation from the audience. Now he had been backed against a bush with worse thorns than a wait-a-bit by a gaggle of gabbling, animated women. Some of them were old enough to be his mother; some of them weren't. Some of them couldn't keep their hands off him; some of them weren't. He wasn't wearing much more than a lace doily and terrible things were starting to happen. "Thank you, thank you, that's very kind of you, well, I'd love to, but . . ." They kept peppering him with invitations to parties, dinners, dances until his head spun—he thought he'd already accepted at least three for Thighday. And somewhere deep down inside, under all the fizz, if he could only have an instant to think about it, lurked the certainty that he'd made an epochal blunder.

Rescue arrived in the shape of old Trong, who came barging into the melee, thundering apologies while parting the crowd like a charging bull. Assisting him was Ambria. Behind them came a bent, elderly man in sumptuous gold vestments. The admirers fell back.

"Here he is, Your Holiness!" Ambria declaimed. "D'ward Scholar. D'ward, we are greatly honored by the presence here tonight of the Holy Kirthien Archpriest." Ambria was never serene, but she seemed more genuinely agitated now than he had ever seen her—why?

Having no idea how to greet a senior clergyman in Sussland, Edward merely bowed low. When he straightened up and saw the razor glint of mind in the age-ravaged face, his head cleared with a rush. Epochal blunder! And there was Eleal, at the old man's side. She was so flushed that her face looked fevered in the firelight; she was hopping up and down on the grass, up and down, up and down . . . Worse than epochal?

A word from the Archpriest worked wonders. Trong and Ambria shepherded the spectators back, aided by a couple of younger, lesser clerics. Edward was left alone with Kirthien Archpriest and Eleal. Sweat dried cold all over him.

"D'ward Scholar?" the old man murmured. "That is, of course, merely your stage name?" His withered lips wore a smile, but his eyes were as deadly as snakes'.

"It is, er, Your Holiness. I have reasons for not divulging my identity." He took another glance at the effervescing Eleal and knew that she had blown the gaff. She was precocious, but she would be no match for that sly Kirthien.

The priest chuckled softly. "Your performance tonight was a revelation to us, my son."

"Er, thank you, Your Holiness." Oh, damn! damn! damn! Why had he ever been such an idiot?

"Such virtuosity can only be a blessing from the Lord of Art." Kirthien was playing with his prey. "It behooves you to give thanks to him in person, my son. You have visited his temple recently?"

Edward stammered. "I do intend to go there . . . come . . . very shortly. Tomorrow, or . . . Soon . . . Thighday?"

"You will be welcome to ride back with us in our carriage—now."

That was an order.

"Er . . ."

"Oh, yes, D'ward!" Eleal cried, clutching at his hand. "You must come and give thanks to Tion and he will cure my leg!"

"What?"

"His Holiness says so!" She was beside herself with excitement and hope, terrified that he would not cooperate.

Kirthien tut-tutted. "Now, child! I made no promises! I merely said that I thought there was an excellent chance that the noble god would look with favor upon you for your assistance to the Liberator."

"Please, D'ward! Please? Oh, please!"

"I must change just a minute excuse me I will be back directly . . ." Edward ran.

He dodged past more of his starry-eyed admirers and hurried along the path to the shack that served as the men's dressing room, as fast as he dared go in bare feet.

Why had he been such a muggins? He should never have taken part in the play. It had felt like a way of repaying the troupe's kindness to him, even good camouflage, making him seem like one of them. He had not intended to create a sensation. The audience's enthusiasm had struck him in a tidal wave and swept him away. A rank novice had upstaged Trong Impresario, an old trouper with considerable talent and more than thirty years' experience—but only because that novice had the charisma of a stranger. Did the old priest know of that vital distinction, or had he merely made a shrewd guess? It didn't matter now, because he had obviously extracted the truth from Eleal.

Was Tion Robin or the Sheriff of Nottingham? Did he play for the Service or the Chamber? Edward was about to find out. If he did not submit to the archpriest's orders, then the old man could summon all those efficient-looking gold-plated guardsmen. Suss was too small a town to hide in. There were only four passes out of the vale. The population was fiercely loyal to its patron god and would not harbor a fugitive. All in all, the chances of escaping from Tion now were nonexistent, even without allowing for the workings of magic. The astonishing thing, really, was that Edward had evaded detection for so long.

He reached the shack. He should have brought a lantern. A three-quarter Trumb lit the sky, but the trees were casting heavy shadows.

As he threw open the door to the black interior, someone spoke behind him: "By George, you really let the bally cat out of the bag, didn't you?"

The voice was unfamiliar, but the words were in English.

\*    \*    \*

He spun around, stubbed his toe on a rock, and almost fell into a bush.

"Who? . . ."

There were two of them. One was a youth of his own age, or perhaps slightly younger. He was slim, golden-haired, and wearing even less than he was—wearing, in fact, nothing but an inexplicably self-assured smile.

It was the woman who had spoken, though. She was tall by Sussian standards, and her smock revealed thin arms and bony shoulders. He could make out almost nothing of her face.

"Monica Mason," she said. "Delighted to make your acquaintance, Mr. Scholar. May I have your autograph? I suspect it will shortly acquire rarity value."

He resisted a mad impulse to fall on his knees and kiss her feet. He found his voice somewhere. "Delighted to meet you, also, ma'am. You are with the Service, I presume?"

"Of course. I am usually known as Onica, by the way. What the hell were you doing, making an exhibition of yourself like that?"

"It was indiscreet."

"Indiscreet? Indiscreet, the man says!" She moved closer, and the moonlight gleamed on a hard, mannish face, framed by longish dark hair, hanging loose. She was wearing the standard local smock as if it were a coronation gown. "There are reapers in town, you dunderhead! Even if there weren't any in the audience, they're going to hear about you soon enough. And if they don't, then Tion will!"

"Tion already has! I mean his high priest or someone did. He knows who I am. He wants me to go back to the temple with him."

She snorted. "I came here to rescue you, not bury you. That is, if you want rescuing?"

"Want? Of course I do! Creighton was killed by—"

"I heard! The dragon trader told us. Well, if you want to come with me, then you'd better get some clothes on. Running around in that getup isn't going to help. You look like a bloody cherub sprouted in a dark cupboard."

Clothes . . . He pulled his wits together, stifling a swarm of questions buzzing around in his head. He turned to the blackness of the shed. "I need a lantern."

"Never mind! Even a pinafore would be better than that. Grab whatever you can. Move!"

She shoved him. He stepped into the dark and promptly stubbed his toe on a stool. The youth came in after him and raised a hand. Instantly a faint glow illuminated the plank walls, the rough benches strewn with clothes, the footwear lying around the floor.

He dived for his smock and sandals. "Gosh! Is this mana?"

The boy just smiled.

Edward repeated the question in Joalian, but still received no answer. Pulling his smock over his head, he went out. "Where are we going?" Home, Home!

Mason was a rangy black shape against the moonlight. "Anywhere we can, I suppose. Zath has his dogs loose, and as soon as that priest gets word back to the temple . . . He can probably notify Tion directly from here, actually. He's not on a node, but it's not far. He's bound to have some ritual or other."

Edward fumbled into his sandals. There was nothing else he needed. Naked he had come into this world; he had acquired no possessions yet. The woman turned and he began to follow . . . Then he remembered Eleal. His mouth went dry and his heart froze in his chest.

"Wait! What happens if I go to the temple?"

She stopped and looked around. "Can't say. Tion may turn you over to Zath. You're not serious?"

"The girl, Eleal. She saved my life! She stayed and nursed me when I was ill, although she knew the reapers were hunting me."

"You don't . . . What of it?"

"She's a cripple. The priest says that Tion will cure her limp."

Mason snorted again, a very unladylike noise. "And you have a huge honorable schoolboy lump of guilt, I suppose? Well, it's your neck. I'm leaving, and leaving pronto, because I value my skin. One reaper I might just be able to handle, if I saw him in time. Several reapers I can't, and God knows I wouldn't have a hope against Tion." She did not move, though.

Oh, hell! He clenched his fists in agony. "Would Tion cure her? I know he can. Would he?"

"Impossible to say. He's mad as a hatter. They all are. A few hundred years of omnipotence boils up their brains."

"He's one of the Chamber?"

She shrugged. "Probably not, and he can't be very happy having Zath's killers all over his manor." She frowned. "Tion fancies himself as a collector of beauty—pretty girls, pretty boys. He has unorthodox tastes in what he does with them. You would most likely find yourself in the temple guard, I'd think. He favors that role for tall young men."

"My preferences wouldn't matter, of course?"

"Not in the slightest. He's quite capable of turning you into a woman, if that takes his fancy, but he can do whatever he likes with you. You'll probably enjoy it, although I can't guarantee that, even. He's better than some, but I shouldn't want him as a friend."

Judging by her companion, who wandered around so shamefully in the altogether, she had liberal tastes in friendship.

"But Eleal saved my life!"

Mason tapped her foot on the path. "Make up your mind. Tion may very well appoint you a god, you know. That's what's prophesied. Whether that comes after the hanky-panky or instead of, I don't know."

"Make me a *god?*"

"There is no god of courage—hasn't been for a couple of hundred years. Gunuu was one of Tion's but he switched allegiance. You must know about the *Testament* by now, surely?"

"I haven't read it. What does it say?"

He could hear voices. Someone was coming, probably looking for him. The woman had heard them also. She glanced around as she spoke. *"D'ward shall become Tion. He shall give heart to the king and win the hearts of the people. D'ward shall become Courage.* That's it. Come on, laddie! Time to go."

Eleal! Blasted, meddling Eleal! Giving him the part of Gunuu had been all her idea. She had arranged the whole debacle. She must have found that passage in the copy of the *Testament* they had left back in Ruatvil. That was how the old priest had guessed. But . . .

"I fulfilled that prophecy tonight, in the play!" Bless you, Eleal!

Mason uttered a harsh bark of laughter. "Damn my eyes! I suppose you did. Actually, that's quite a relief, old man. We were worried about that one. Good show." She took a couple of steps and then looked back. "Are you coming or not?"

Time! He needed time to think. He turned to the youth, who merely shrugged, seeming amused but not about to offer any helpful suggestions. He had not spoken a word so far.

"Good luck in your new career, whatever it is," Monica Mason said. "Give my love to Zath, or Tion, whichever gets you first." She disappeared into the shrubbery. The youth went with her.

"Eleal saved my life!" Edward wiped his forehead. With a crippled leg, she could never have the stage career she craved, could never enter Tion's Festival. She had braved the deadly reapers to stay and nurse him through his fever. He had always thought that honor enabled a man to choose between good and evil. He had never seriously considered that a decision might lie between two evils. Be a god? Be plaything to an omnipotent pervert?

That damnable Gypsy witch, Mrs. Boswell, had defined the conflict exactly: *You must choose between honor and friendship. You must desert a friend to whom you owe your life, or betray everything you hold sacred.*

Fallow had not prepared him for this.

The approaching voices were louder, just around the last bend.

"Wait!" Edward said. "Where are you going to take me? What does the Service want of me?"

There was no answer. He could hear Mason and her young friend moving through the bushes, the sound growing fainter as they retreated. He shouted, "Wait!" and ran after them.

All that nattering about courage and then he ran away.

# 58

They slipped out of the theater area, apparently unseen. Trumb's green brilliance suffused the landscape, but red Eltiana and blue Ysh added a strange mix of tints to the shadows. There could be reapers . . . Over the last week, Edward had almost forgotten the reapers, and now he was too tormented by thoughts of Eleal to worry about them. Mrs.—or Miss—Mason seemed to know exactly where she was going. She did not head for the city gate, but struck off down an unused, overgrown track, heading roughly in the direction of the river. He stumbled blindly along between her and the youth. Half a mile or so away, the temple dome shone points of colored light back at the moons.

Eleal was a likable kid. Her extreme nosiness was more funny than annoying. She was brave, amusing, dedicated. He owed his life to her, and now he was walking out on her. She could have what she wanted most in the world, and he was denying it to her. His betrayal might ruin her entire life.

Mr. Goodfellow had healed broken bones, which would have healed anyway. Eleal's trouble was more than that. *"Could* Tion cure a deformed leg, ma'am?"

"Call me Onica. Of course he could, easily. Didn't Creighton explain? Tion's a stranger, and strangers have charisma. We absorb mana. It makes us immortal, or almost so, and in large quantities gives us supernatural powers." She fell silent to work her way through a tangle of thorny shrubs.

Edward followed carefully. The boy just pushed through as if they were long grass.

Yes, Edward had worked it out—and even seen glimmers of it in himself after he had played holy man in the campground. Obviously the effect disappeared if the stranger returned to his home world. Creighton had possessed no "authority" back on Earth, but as soon as he had returned to Nextdoor, he had been able to smite a reaper with a thunderbolt. Mr. Goodfellow had been a stranger on Earth, an immigrant from Ruatvil.

"I think I picked up some tonight—a sort of tingle? Can I work miracles?"

She shook her head. "Unless you're on a node, it's pretty much impossible to collect enough to produce physical effects."

The campground where he had faced down old Graybeard had been a node, and he'd acquired real mana there. He had used that power to learn the language so swiftly and to cure Dolm's guilt. All the same, his tongue could find no cavities in his teeth now. What should be surprising about minor repairs? The guv'nor had lived somewhere in this world for thirty years without aging a day.

Even the charisma itself was dangerous. Edward Exeter could be the greatest actor in the world if he wanted. He could pluck women like daisies. He could enter politics and be a dictator in no time. He could raise an army and conquer the world. Now he knew why Creighton had wanted older recruits—they might be able to handle this sort of power without being corrupted by it. How long would Edward be able to resist adulation on that scale? How long before his moral standards collapsed like a wet soufflé? At last he understood why the guv'nor had wanted to break the chain and prevent him from becoming the Liberator.

But Eleal! . . . What sort of rotter was he to walk out on her like this?

They were past the bushes. He fell into step with Onica.

"What constitutes worship? Blood? Degradation? Public prostitution?"

She stalked on without looking at him. "Sometimes. They don't all go that far. The general principle is that sacrifice must hurt. The believer must voluntarily do something he doesn't want to do—give money or perform unpleasant acts. The greater the pain, the greater the crop of mana. Adoration works too. Tion's better than most in that regard. He bribes his worshipers with roses. He probably gains more mana from one hard-fought singing contest on his node than Zath does from any of his distant murders."

"Human sacrifice is the most powerful source?"

"With one exception. Look out for the burrower holes here."

They were closer to the temple now, and well below the city. Its roofs were a jagged blackness against the sky. Good-bye, Suss! Oh, Eleal!

"What does a god of courage do?" he asked miserably.

"He gives supplicants courage, of course. It isn't difficult to make young men behave like suicidal maniacs." Onica's voice held traces of the adenoidal accent of Lancashire. "The fact that they're still worshiping there on a node that's been unoccupied for two hundred years shows that most of the effect is wishful thinking. As I recall Gunuu's rituals, they're quite honest. The worshiper offers blood and is granted courage, but it's conditional on abstinence. As soon as he takes a woman, the deal is off. That must bring in lots of return business in the course of a long campaign."

He remembered what Piol had told him about the monastery at Thogwalby. "The god of strength works the same sort of swizz, doesn't he?"

"Garward?" The woman chuckled. "Yes, that's a potent sacrifice! All those young men in training, right on his node, forbidden even to think about their groins. Every night the mana must just pour in. Insomnia to the glory of god! They've been at this for centuries, remember. They've worked out all sorts of twists. Why? Are you seriously—"

She stopped and listened. "Blast! We're being followed!"

"How can you tell?" He could hear nothing.

"Come on!" She began to run down the slope. He loped along beside her, stumbling more often than she did. Either of them might break an ankle any minute. The youth went out in front, jogging steadily. His lack of shoes seemed to make him more sure-footed, although he must have feet like hooves to run on this terrain.

"Who's after us?" Edward panted. "Tion? Or Zath?"

"Zath. Reapers. I can smell them. Look, make up your mind, Exeter! Do you want to come with me to Olympus, or don't you? Go to the bloody temple if you want to bare your neck for Tion. Or bare anything else, for that matter."

"Would he really make me god of courage?"

"He might. It's prophesied. Strangers are in short supply, and he needs to reclaim that attribute."

Eleal! Eleal was the problem. Tion might cure her leg out of gratitude, or Edward himself would be able to as soon as he had collected enough mana. A god did not have to be evil, surely? He could do good. A few years on Nextdoor, like the guv'nor . . .

But the guv'nor's case was different. There was a war on now. Edward had a duty to King and Country. Even his debt to Eleal must take second place to that call. He certainly couldn't trust Tion.

Could he even trust the Service? He stumbled wildly, caught his balance. "Never mind what I want. What does the Service want with me?"

"Save you from Zath. Cameron's son."

Mana or not, she was panting harder than he was. How much farther?

"Suppose you do. Then what? Creighton told me you were divided over the *Filoby Testament.*"

"Obviously. Oh darn it!"

A peculiar, rumbling explosion rent the night. Edward shied to a halt as he registered two huge green eyes glowing at him from the darkness.

"What in Hades is *that?*"

Onica had gone on to the monster and was embracing its huge head, provoking more belching rumbles. "This is Cuddles. She's a dragon. Quick! They're closing on us."

She scrambled up into the saddle. "Up here, behind me. Hang on. Cuddles, *Zomph!*" She held out a hand for him.

As she hauled him aboard, the saddle simultaneously shot skyward. He grabbed at the woman's arm and a pannier, was almost thrown as the huge brute launched itself forward. He caught a glimpse of two black shapes and cried out at a sudden pain in his leg like a jolt of electricity. He started to overbalance, then the spasm passed and he could grip again. A nasty pins and needles remained, but was already fading. The rush of wind in his face told him they were racing over the ground, although the ride was as smooth as the Bodgleys' Rolls.

"All right?" the woman yelled.

"Fine. Reapers?"

"Not quite within lethal range, fortunately." The wind caught her words and flung them past him. "They can't catch us now. You can relax."

He had been that close to death and he was expected to relax?

He shouted, "Righto!" and passed the word to his insides: relax! That was not so easy when he was perched on the rim of the saddle with a bony plate digging into his back.

Dragon? He had thought the word referred to something like a horse—T'lin Horsetrader. This thing was more like the stegosaurus in *The Lost World,* bigger than a full-grown rhino. She had a ridge of high plates along her back, one of which had been cut out to make room for the rider. A couple of wicker panniers were strapped to the one behind the gap. Dragon was a fitting name for the beast, though—she even had long winglike frills stretching back from her shoulders.

The monster raced along a flat, treeless terrace. Rugged hillocks and cliffs flowed by, pale in the moonlight, casting multitoned shadows. There was a gully ahead. Onica's hair kept flying in his face, and conversation was impossible. Cuddles hurtled down into the gully and up the other side with a stomach-churning lurch. They were heading east, passing the temple at a lower level.

Three or four gullies later, Onica yelled, "Hang on now. *Whilth!*"

The dragon swung to the left and headed straight up a fifty-degree slope. Edward toppled back, steadying himself against the panniers. He was deucedly uncomfortable. Onica had the advantage of a flat seat and stirrups.

When they reached the level again, she said, *"Varch!"* Cuddles dropped to a slower pace. No reins or handlebars—she was entirely controlled by voice commands and must be at least as smart as a dog.

In a few minutes Onica told her, *"Zappan! Wosok!"* Cuddles stopped and crouched down. "Off!"

Edward assumed that meant him, and gratefully scrambled to the ground. She slid down beside him. They were in another gully, a smaller one. It was dry and shadowed.

"Come on!" She hurried up the slope.

He strode beside her, his longer legs giving him an advantage.

The boy strolled along at his side. Edward turned to him and met the same inscrutable smile as before. He forgot what he had been about to ask.

"Well?" the woman said. "Which is to be, Exeter? The temple, or Olympus? If you want the temple, you can walk from here."

He could see it, not half a mile away, and the city beyond. "I want to go Home. To England. We're at war with Germany."

"I heard about that. We'll see you get Home, then, if that's what you want. Yes, we're of two minds about the Liberator, but if that's your decision, then I'm certain the committee will consent."

They crested the rise, coming to flat farmland. Onica headed for a clump of palmlike trees.

"Do you mind explaining what we're doing?" he asked politely.

"Wondered when you'd start wondering. I want to go west, to Lameby. I'm hoping the opposition will be deceived and give chase. We can watch the road from here."

A low stone wall ran through the grove. She sat down on it and wiped her face, puffing. "May be a long wait. They'll have to run back up to the town and find mounts."

"What sort of mounts?" Setting himself beside her, he tried to visualize a midnight chase of dragons.

"Moas."

"I thought moas were one-rider animals?"

"They are, but I suspect reapers can get around that. They probably have moas of their own, anyway."

They were in shadow, and now he could see the dirt track that was the main highway across Suss, a couple of hundred yards away. It was deserted at this time of night. The countryside slept peacefully under the light of three moons, which was much brighter than the moonlight he knew. Only a week or so ago, he had come along there with Dolm and Eleal.

Again he turned to say something to the youth sitting beside him, and again that cryptic smile distracted him.

Onica said, "Tell me what happened after T'lin escaped from the reapers."

"I arrived . . ." Edward told what he knew from his own blurred memories and what Eleal had recounted.

When he had done, she said, "*Hrrnph!* We thought you'd been knocked off, of course. I came to investigate. Arrived last night, detected reapers still around. That made me wonder if you might be alive after all, keeping under wraps somewhere."

"How did you find me?"

"Sheer chance. I saw the playbill, saw a D'ward listed. Good job I made the connection before Zath's thugs did, you bloody idiot."

A change of subject was called for. "Tell me about Olympus."

"It's in a little side canyon. There's hundreds of those, of course, but that one's a beautiful spot. We try to keep it an outpost of real civilization—it's not unlike Nyagatha, actually."

"You know Nyagatha?"

"Dropped in there with Julian in '02. Met you—solemn, stringy kid, brown as walnut. Could have been a native, except for those blue eyes. You'll feel right at home in Olympus. We don't fly a Union Jack, but we do dress for dinner."

Mm! It sounded as if the Service was not unlike Holy Roly's Lighthouse Missionary Society, bringing enlightenment to the heathen. The guv'nor had supported it, so it must do some good.

He asked about dragons and received a long lecture on their habits and strengths. Mason was obviously an enthusiastic dragon-lover and made them sound like the finest riding beast in the Universe. Eleal had raved about them, although without thinking to describe what they looked like. When he had learned much more about the lizards than he wanted to, he managed to ask something more relevant.

"What about Gunuu? Why is there no god of courage?"

"How much do you know about the Great Game?"

He could say, "It means the struggle between England and Russia to control Afghanistan and the Northwest Frontier, which has been going on for more than a hundred years," and he would sound like a complete muffin. In the Vales there was a similar political rivalry between Joalia and Thargia, the major powers of the Vales, which he had privately classed as equivalents of Athens and Sparta, with Niolland, off to the north, roughly corresponding to Corinth. Obviously that was not what was meant either.

He said, "Nothing."

Onica grunted. "Immortality gets boring. The strangers compete among themselves. Earth has five great powers, right?—England, France, Russia, Germany, and Austria. So have the Vales, except here they're called Visek, Karzon, Eltiana, Astina, and Tion."

So the teams did wear colored jerseys! "Yes?"

"The priests' doctrine of the Pentatheon is a rough approximation—the Parent, the Man, the Lady, the Maiden, and the Youth. Those are the parts, but the actors change from time to time. Each one has a supporting cast of avatars. They're all strangers, like us—from Home or other worlds. There's plenty backstabbing goes on within the teams, but mostly the Game is played between the five. They change alliances all the time."

"Sounds like a feudal system."

"Very much so," Onica said approvingly. "Especially since it all rests on the backs of the peasants, whose worship provides the mana. A couple of hundred years ago, Gunuu got subverted. He announced that he was an avatar of the Maiden, not the Youth—Gunuu Astina, not Gunuu Tion. He ordered his priests into blue instead of yellow, and so on. Tion wasn't willing to lose a profitable source of mana, so he retaliated. Normally the Game's played by Queensberry rules: Natives are fair game for anything, but stranger doesn't usually make a direct attack on stranger. That's a waste of mana and can be dangerous if your opponent turns out to have more power than you expected. In this case, Tion got nasty, very nasty."

Edward glanced at the youth, who shrugged sadly. He still had not spoken one word, and yet his reactions suggested he understood English.

"Pour encourager les autres?"

Onica chuckled. "Exactly! Since then Gunuu's node has been unoccupied. To recruit a substitute stranger, Tion would have to visit another world, and he's not likely to take that risk."

Creighton had commented on the problems of recruitment.

"He could send a helper, an avatar?"

"It's done, but then the new boys may have loyalty problems, what?"

"So, now, when people pray to Gunuu, where does the mana go?"

"Most of it's wasted. If they pray to Gunuu Tion, then Tion will get some of it. If they pray to Gunuu Astina, then the Maiden will."

"They play rough, don't they? Just before I arrived, Garward's monks sacked Iilah's grove at Filoby."

"Sounds fairly typical—the rough work would be done by locals. Iilah herself would not be hurt. If a lot of nuns were raped or killed . . . well, they're only natives, you see. Garward's a fool. He'll pay for that, I'm sure."

"Pay to whom?"

"To his master Karzon, of course. Let's see . . . The Thargians are brewing a war. The warriors will seek portents from their patron goddess, Astina. The omens will be bad. Karzon will complain to Astina; she will demand justice for Filoby, because Iilah's one of hers. Karzon will pull strips off Garward's hide until she is satisfied. There may even be a change of resident at Thogwalby. Quite typical."

Quite disgusting! The guv'nor's support for the Service was starting to seem more understandable.

Edward squirmed. The wall was only slightly less uncomfortable than his perch on the dragon had been. How could the bare-arsed boy sit there without even fidgeting? He seemed quite content, listening to what was being said with calm amusement.

Something that sounded like a miniature pipe organ began singing in the branches overhead.

"What the dickens? . . ."

"We call them nightingales. They look more like squirrels, though."

Damn! Why did this world have to be so interesting? "It was Iilah who created the *Filoby Testament,* I suppose?"

Onica covered a yawn. "Apparently not. Even the big players rarely meddle with foretelling. Prediction involves holding a mirror up to memory, to recall the future. That can be dangerous! One can forget who one is and how to let go. The situation may become permanent. It also costs an incredible amount of mana. None of them likes to squander mana. I told you Garward's an idiot. The story is that he'd seduced Sister Ashylin—he's always in among the nuns there—and for some reason he gave her the gift of prophecy in return. He botched the ritual. The first time she invoked it, it drove her out of her mind with prophecy. It completely drained Garward himself, serves him right. She went mad and died. He almost died."

After a moment she added, "The future doesn't interest them. Most of them are centuries old. Nothing can harm them. The only thing they fear is boredom. Boredom kills them all in the end. That's why they play the Great Game. . . . *Look!*"

Two dark figures were racing along the road, coming from the town, going far faster than a man could run, or even a horse. The moas' long legs were a blur of ten-foot strides. The hooded riders crouched on their backs were barely distinguishable at that distance, and yet infinitely sinister in the green moonlight. Like silent motorcyclists, they disappeared along the Rotby road.

Edward suppressed a shiver. He glanced at his other, silent companion, who was frowning angrily. Then he met Edward's eye and smiled again. . . .

"Looks like they took the bait," Onica said. "We'll give them a few minutes, just to be sure they keep going. Then we head west."

"There's a bridge at Lameby? Then where?"

"The road goes on over Rothpass, to Nagvale." She hesitated. "You definitely want to go Home? You don't want to stay on Nextdoor and try to fulfill the prophecy?"

"No, ma'am. I definitely want to go Home."

She eyed him curiously. "You're an odd fish! A boy of your age, offered a whole new world to explore, a chance at fame and power . . . yet you refuse?"

He resented being called a boy, but Onica Mason must be a great deal older than she seemed.

"I'd love to stay," he admitted. "I'd love to see more of the Vales, and meet the people who knew my father. At any other time, I'd jump at it. Now—there's a war on. I must go Home and do my bit."

"Does you credit, I suppose," she muttered. "You'll have time to change your mind if you want to, because I can't take you straight to Olympus. Cuddles can go across country, but not with two riders. I did not expect to find you living, Mr. Exeter. I didn't bring a spare mount. I didn't bring warm clothes for two. You'd freeze your arse up there." She gestured at the towering peaks of Susswall.

The conversation was not heading in favorable directions.

"You can go over *that?*"

"Dragons can. They don't like the heat down here, and Nagland's even hotter. Furthermore," she added, "to take a dragon into Nagland would be like riding one down Whitehall."

"Conspicuous?"

"Quite. Rothpass is ranked as easy. By Valian standards, that means you can walk over it if you have the legs of a goat. I'll take you to the summit, though, and set you adrift there. I'll go over the hills to Olympus and report. You go down into Nagvale. The first village you come to is Sonalby. Ask for Kalmak Carpenter. He's one of ours, in the religious branch. The code question is, 'What do you get when you cross a wallaby and a jaguar?' "

"And what's the answer?"

"The kids' answer is, 'A fur coat with pockets.' If you get that, then you've found the wrong man. If he says, 'Sunrise over five peaks,' then he's sound."

Straight out of *Kim!* "And what do I do with Kalmak Carpenter when I've got him?"

"Mostly keep your mouth shut. He's a local, so he doesn't know what you know, but he's trustworthy, a good man. Stay with him until we send someone for you."

"How long?" he asked, trying not to show his doubts.

"Couple of weeks. Travel's slow here. I'll have you Home inside two fortnights, Exeter, promise." She twisted her awkward mouth in a smile. "A month, that means."

What could he say? "Fair enough."

She glanced at him quizzically.

He shrugged. "They all say the war'll be over by Christmas."

"So keen to kill? How long till Christmas?"

That she had to ask was a shock, a reminder of how very far away England was.

# 59

"Well, they obviously didn't sense us," Mason said. "Let's go."

Edward rose from the wall with relief. "What happens if they turn back and follow us?"

"Down here, they'd catch us easily. This is moa country. They can't handle heights, though. We'd have to try to get to the hills." She walked on for a few minutes, then added, "But we wouldn't make it."

"You know, you're full of cheerful information."

She chuckled. "If there's only two, I may manage to handle them."

He wondered how the members of the Service came by their mana. It might be an impertinent question.

The three of them walked in silence back down to the dragon, and again Edward had to squeeze himself into the gap between Mason and the bony plate. It was about as comfortable as riding on handlebars.

Once on the road, though, Cuddles ran smoothly. They sped by the temple, detoured around the town, and rushed on through the night, heading west.

He tried to keep watch behind. He felt worn-out by this interminable day. A few hours' sleep and he would be ready for anything. Talk was too difficult, so he just sat without speaking, wishing he could dismount from his uncomfortable perch—wishing, too, that he had not been such an unmitigated bounder as to walk out on Eleal when she needed his help.

After half an hour or so, Onica pulled the dragon in behind a copse of trees and made her lie down so the riders could dismount. There they were hidden from view but could look back along the dirt track crossing wide meadows of moonlit grass. They would see the reapers if they came.

"Just a short break," she said, stretching. "Hungry?"

"If you are going to eat, I could nibble something."

"Like a roast ox?"

"With potatoes and gravy, please."

She rummaged in one of the panniers and produced a small bundle wrapped in a cloth. She sat down and opened it, revealing some lumps of a hard bread. Edward was more than happy to sink to the grass and stretch out, finding new joints to put his weight on. He bit into one of the crusts. It was nutty and fresher than it looked, with a pleasant spicy flavor.

The golden-haired youth squatted down and took one also.

Edward said, "How the devil? . . ."

The boy smiled at him, chewing.

"What?" Onica asked.

"Nothing. Forgot what I was going to say. Tell me about Zath."

She grimaced. "What do you want to know?"

"Well, I don't like having an enemy who tries to kill me for something I haven't done and don't intend to do. Suppose I wrote him a note—"

"He'd never believe you! Zath's the worst of them all. I told you the native theology is only an approximation. The Man has always been god of both creation and destruction, symbolized by his hammer. Zath was his persona as god of death, but no one ever assumed the role—who would want to? About . . . oh, about a hundred years ago or so, someone did. Whether he asked Karzon for the post or it was all Karzon's idea, I haven't the foggiest. Doesn't matter. Zath invented the reapers. He may have stolen the idea from Indian thuggee."

"Their murders give him mana?"

"In spades. Human sacrifice died out a long time ago on Nextdoor, just as it did at Home, but it generates huge amounts of mana. He's enormously powerful because of it, although his technique's very wasteful—the deaths don't happen on a node, and they're mostly a long way away from Zath himself. It's just that there are so many of them. In doctrine he's only an aspect of Karzon, but in fact he's by far the stronger now. The Five are worried about him, worried he may decide to promote himself to full Pentatheon membership."

"Can't they gang up on him?"

She laughed grimly. "Honor among thieves? Who bells the cat? Mana is power and power always has friends."

He looked at the youth, who grinned, shrugged, and went on eating.

Mason fell silent too. She seemed to be thinking hard, so Edward respected her silence. He had decided that Onica Mason knew what she was doing. She was a very competent . . . whatever she was.

Cuddles was grazing without standing up. She could probably do so for quite a long time before eating everything within the reach of that serpentine neck. Trumb was setting behind the peaks. Yellow Kirb'l had appeared, low in the south. He considered asking for an explanation of that rogue moon's motion but decided he was too fagged out at the moment to take in a lecture on astronomy.

Onica reached for the cloth. "Finished? Time to be on our way."

"Yes, thank you, ma'am." He stood up and peered back along the road. He could see no sign of the reapers. As they walked back to the dragon, he blurted: "Did you know my father?"

"Yes."

"I'd like to hear about him some time. I feel I hardly knew him."

She clambered into the saddle, keeping her back to him as she answered. "I knew him intimately. Does that shock you?"

"Of course not!" It did, though. He had never imagined the guv'nor having a lover. The information saddened him, emphasizing that his knowledge of his parents was that of a twelve-year-old. He had never really known them, and never would. They had died because of Zath and the *Filoby Testament.*

Onica held down a hand and helped him up with a surprisingly powerful heave. He wondered how old she was.

"He was a fine man, widely respected. I was very much in love with him. We drifted apart later. It was long before he met your mother, of course. All right, Cuddles, old girl. I know you're tired. *Wondo!*"

Did that long-ago affair explain why Monica Mason had come to aid Cameron's son? But why had she gone visiting her former lover at Nyagatha? That sounded like bad form, or was he just naive? There were too many questions to ask, too many pitfalls and unforeseeable hurts lurking in the possible answers.

\*     \*     \*

He lost track of time. Uncomfortable as he was, he began to find the motion of the dragon soporific. He tried to keep watch behind them, but in the moonlight he probably would not have been able to see the reapers approaching until it was too late to do anything about them. Trumb and Ysh had set; now golden Kirb'l ruled the sky. The night was taking on a sense of nightmare, one of those awful dreams that never end.

Then Onica shouted something and pointed.

Houses. Lameby.

She skirted the hamlet, cutting across fields. Cuddles turned out to be as skilled as a horse at jumping fences, although Edward found the landings exceedingly unpleasant. Then they were on the road again, and it angled down into a narrow ravine, a dry streambed. A steady, low-pitched roar must be the voice of Susswater.

"Damn!" Onica said. *"Zappan!"*

The dragon stopped, claws scrabbling in gravel.

Silence, except for the bone-jarring rumble of the river, not even a whisper of wind, here in this little gorge . . . Walled on either side by steep cliffs, the track disappeared around a sharp bend about fifty yards ahead. The gap showed a glimpse of mightier, moonlit cliffs in the distance, and the far end of a bridge. Like the one he had seen at Rotby, it was suspended from heavy chains, but here there were no towers. The anchors must be set in the rock of the canyon itself. The near side was hidden around the corner.

"Trouble?" he whispered.

"At least two of them," Onica said. She sighed. "It's a logical place for an ambush. I should have thought of it."

"We can go back?"

"And then where? Cuddles needs rest, even if you don't. I think we'll try the direct method. Saint George and the dragon will now perform! Get down."

"Ma'am, I—"

*"Get down!"*

The command was spoken quietly, but it must have been backed with mana, because his feet hit the dirt an instant later. He staggered.

"Here goes the charge of the Light Brigade," Onica said.

"No, wait!"

"You can't help. Keep your fingers crossed, Exeter. Remember Kalmak Carpenter. *Zomph!"*

Cuddles shot forward, claws spraying stones. She hurtled like an arrow along the road, leaned into the curve, and disappeared.

He choked back a shout of anger. He stood there on the gravel, feeling like a pampered brat. The smirk on the youth's face did nothing to help his feelings. Bloody young exhibitionist, parading around in the nude!

"Well, come on!" he snapped. "Let's try to help!" He began to run, and the youth loped along at his side without a word.

The worst part was that he heard nothing at all—no screams, nothing. Cuddles came into view again, streaking across the bridge like a runaway lorry. Her claws must have made a considerable racket on the timbers, but the roar of the river below muffled it completely. At the far end, the dragon did not turn to follow the road, but went straight up the cliff face like a gigantic fly. She had no rider. In moments she vanished over a ledge. He caught one more glimpse of her, higher up, and then she had gone.

He stopped in dismay. The river rumbled, his heart thumped madly.

He wondered if he was the victim of some horrible hoax and rejected the notion as madness. *Something* had spooked that dragon!

If Onica were alive, she would come back. If she had died, she would not have accounted for all the reapers.

Now what? Eleal had explained that ordinary weapons were useless against reapers. Onica might be lying on the road, hurt and in need of help. If any of the enemy had survived, then they might well be able to sense him as Mason had sensed them—he did not know the extent of their powers. He bent and fumbled in the gravel until he had found a couple of rounded rocks that would fit his grip. He put one in his pocket and stood up. He would not likely have time for more than two shots.

What was the reapers' range? He racked his brain to recall that brief glimpse he had caught earlier. Fifteen yards? Hard to say in the dark, just two black shapes in the night. He had better allow twenty, at least. A cricket pitch was twenty-two yards long.

He turned to his cryptic companion, who was watching him with amused contempt.

"Are you going to help or just stand there displaying yourself?"

This time he got an answer. He had spoken in English, but the reply came in Joalian:

"You go ahead, D'ward dear. I'll be very interested to see what happens."

With a snort of disgust, Edward started forward. He walked as quietly as he could, although he knew the river would mask any sounds he made. The youth sauntered along beside him.

Edward ignored him, keeping his eyes on the corner ahead, rolling the stone in his hand, forced his breathing to stay slow. The corner was not a knife-edge, just a very sharp bend. He moved close to the wall, crept forward more slowly. One step at a time now . . .

He saw a body. And a dark-robed form bending over it. *Now! Quickly!*

He sprinted forward. The reaper looked up, surprised, then rose, brightly lit by moonlight. He raised an arm. . . .

Edward pivoted and bowled his best fast ball. For a moment he thought he had left it too late—a spasm of pain shot through his arm.

He hadn't, though. The reaper had no chance to dodge a missile moving at that speed. The rock took him between the eyes with an audible crunch. He went down, as if he had been hit by a sledgehammer.

Edward stumbled to a halt, rubbing his tingling hand and fighting waves of nausea. He did not want to think what that rock would have done to a human face. He had probably killed a man, or at least maimed him horribly. Worse, if the reaper was not dead, then he could still be dangerous. Dare Edward go closer to finish him off? Could he kill an injured man in cold blood? There were other bodies, but no one standing or moving.

He hurried forward. The first two were both reapers, and the one he had struck down was still twitching. The next was another reaper, sprawled in a contorted way that suggested he was very dead indeed.

Onica lay at the beginning of the bridge. She was dead, too. Her face was a lurid color in the green light, and twisted as if she had died in agony. A black trickle of blood had flowed from her mouth. He closed her eyes as he had closed Creighton's.

First Bagpipe, then Creighton and the Gover man—now Mason, too! How many deaths must he trail behind him?

Sudden realization made him leap to his feet. He turned to face his companion, the youth with the golden curls, the one who wore nothing but the light of the joker moon, the one who had not ridden on the dragon but had turned up at every stop. He had appeared at the theater with Mason, but she had not brought him. Mason had not even known he was there.

The two stood and looked at each other, the youth smiling, Edward fighting against tides of fury and despair, racking his brains. Out of the frying pan! *I demand to see the British Consul! Bring in the gunboats!*

What was the proper form for greeting a god? A local chieftain could be accorded respect, within limits, but Tion was not a secular authority, nor even a high priest or witch doctor. He was a brigand, a parasite, a first-class fraud. A native would undoubtedly throw himself in the dirt at this point, but no Englishman should grovel like that to anyone, and this young bugger ranked lower than a Sarawak pirate. *Grovel?* Edward wanted to smash that pretty face to pulp.

"I suppose you're Tion?"

The boy uttered a high-pitched laugh. "And you are the Liberator! Do you like this body? It was a present from Kirb'l." He turned around to display it. "He's a maniac, but he does appreciate my tastes."

"A present?"

"Or you could say I won it in the festival. I win one every year—my prize! Do you like it?"

Was there any good answer to that?

"It's a fine representation of the young Apollo."

Apparently Tion understood the reference, for he flashed white teeth in a smile of pleasure. "Thank you! You're quite nice-looking yourself, you know. I say so, and I am the ultimate authority on such matters."

Fury! He must be mad as a March hare and dangerous as a hungry shark. With his superhuman power, he had turned up like a *deus ex machina* and then done nothing at all! "Why didn't you save her?"

The god pouted. "Why should I? She was only one of those meddling, idealistic nobodies from the Service! They won't last. It's been tried before. I've been around a lot longer than the Service, and I shall be around when they're all dead and forgotten."

"I'm sorry she's dead!"

"Well, you shouldn't be!" The Youth sounded peeved. Then he smiled. "We mustn't leave the evidence lying around, though. It's unsightly, having bodies all over the place. Drop them in the river."

"I won't take orders—"

"Yes you will," Tion said quietly.

Before he knew it, Edward had bent to take hold of Onica's feet. He tried to let go, but his hands refused to open. His feet started to move, and he began dragging her out onto the bridge. There the roar of the river was deafening. A cold, misty wind blew along the canyon. The planks were slippery.

"Damn you!" he shouted. "She deserves a decent burial at least!"

"No she doesn't. This should be far enough."

Sick at heart, Edward pushed the body out through the chains and watched it dwindle away to a speck before it vanished in the surging foam of Susswater, far below.

He found himself hurrying back to the corpses, and then he stopped resisting the compulsion. He did not care about the reapers, but he felt shamed at having treated the woman so, even if he had had no choice. Tion strolled beside him, making no effort to assist. Manual labor must be beneath a god's dignity.

"This one she ran down with the dragon," he remarked. "But too late to avoid his power, of course. And you got the last of them, dear boy! Nasty vermin. You are a very good thrower, aren't you?"

Edward almost choked on his anger. "Why didn't you save the woman?"

"Because I chose not to, of course. She was trespassing. So were the others. I warned Zath to keep his trash off my lawn. Giving powers like that to natives is quite disgusting."

When Edward came to the man he had felled, though—trying not to look at the bloody wreckage inside the hood—he discovered that the victim was still moaning.

"This one's not dead!"

"A purely temporary state of affairs, dear boy. Go on."

Unable to refuse, Edward dragged the man to the bridge and disposed of him as he had disposed of the bodies. He felt more nauseated by that than by anything else that had happened. He was really a murderer now. The Vales' equivalent of Inspector Leatherdale would be justified in swearing out a warrant for the arrest of D'ward Liberator.

The last reaper followed the others. When morning came, travelers crossing Lameby Bridge would see no evidence of the massacre.

"There, that's better!" Tion sighed. "And I suppose I must let you be on your way, tempting though you are. Mustn't upset any of the prophecies! The pass is clear, you'll have no trouble. You did frightfully well to dispose of that reaper without mana—but you are altogether the most *interesting* thing to come along in centuries, dear boy! I can't imagine how you're going to settle that horrible Zath, but I do so hope you succeed! I can't wait to see how you do it."

"You heard what I told Mrs. Mason—I'm not fulfilling any prophecies! I am going Home."

The Youth shrugged disbelievingly. "Beware the Service, D'ward Liberator. Remember Verse 114!"

Edward Exeter must be the only man on Nextdoor who had not read the *Filoby Testament.* "Which one's that?"

"Oh, let me think. . . . How does it go now? *Men plot evil upon the holy mountain. The servants of the one do the work of the many. They send unto D'ward, mouthing oaths like nectar. Their voices are sweet as roses, yea sweeter than the syrup that snares the diamond-fly. He is lured to destruction by the word of a friend, by the song of a friend he is hurled down among the legions of death.* Horrible prose, but you see what I mean, darling?"

If he was telling the truth, that did sound ominous. *Holy mountain* must refer to Olympus, because there was no other holy mountain. It was odd that Tion had made the connection, but he had known of Apollo, too.

"Well, that completes the night's business," Tion said. "It's been a most entertaining evening. Bye-bye!"

"Wait!"

The Youth cocked an eyebrow, almost as if he had been waiting for the word. "Yes?"

Edward braced himself to plead with this monster. "If you enjoyed the show, let's pass the hat. The girl who's mentioned in the *Testament,* Eleal—she deserves the credit for staging it. She's only a child. She has a crippled leg."

Tion switched on a smile that was too sudden to be genuine. "You want me to heal her for you?"

"Would you, sir?" It was hard to be respectful to this seeming-boy who had so callously let four people die, but Mason had said he was not as bad as some of the other strangers. "She'll go mad with joy."

"That's trivial, D'ward! Nothing to it. Delighted to do you a favor."

There was bound to be a catch, though. Cautiously, Edward said, "Thank you, sir! I'd be very grateful—and she'll be ecstatic!"

"You can't have omelette and roast goose, of course."

Trapped!

Tion's smile grew broader.

Edward wiped his forehead. He owed his life to Eleal, but to repay that debt would force him to stay here on Nextdoor, and inevitably he would find himself fighting in the wrong war. His war lay on another world.

What would his father have done?

Zath and the Chamber had killed his parents . . . but he had only Creighton's word for that.

Zath had killed Creighton. What sort of chap did not try to avenge his friends? But he had only Eleal's word for that.

He could cause Eleal's limp to be cured and thus repay her for saving his life . . . but he had only Tion's word for that.

Tion was smiling gleefully. "You understand what I mean?"

"You mean I can't have my cake and eat it, too."

The boy smiled sweetly. "I mean, if we're into doing favors . . . You have an Eleal problem, I have a Gunuu problem, that unmanned aspect. You'd make an excellent god of courage, D'ward, you really would." The childish face glowed with innocent appeal. "Even a beginner ought to be able to raise that much mana in a fortnight or so. To pay me back. I mean, that would only be fair, wouldn't it?"

"A fortnight? Just a fortnight?"

Tion pursed his cherub lips. "Perhaps a little longer. It's hard to say. . . . I'd have to see how you perform." His pale eyes shone very bright.

*Speak ye one word in elfin land* . . . If Edward bit, he would be hooked, somehow. Perhaps forever.

Where did honor lie in this morass? Where were courage and duty?

King and Country! There were no doubts about those. They took precedence over anything else.

"I cannot accept a favor from you on those terms, sir. I withdraw my request."

Tion sighed, but he did not seem surprised. "Good-bye, then, D'ward Liberator! I wish you luck—god knows you'll need it, and I speak with authority." He shrieked with childish glee and faded away.

Edward was alone.

He didn't even have Eleal to look after him now. *Oh, Eleal!*

Would the dragon find her way home to Olympus? Would she return in search of her mistress? He could not control her if she did. The only course of action open to him was to head on over the pass and find Kalmak Carpenter.

Having nothing else to do, he walked over the bridge and began climbing the trail on the other side.

He was going Home! That was what mattered, he told himself. Duty called. Onica's death gnawed at his conscience. So did his despicable betrayal of the child who had saved his life, but there he had made his own choice and it was too late to back out now.

Nextdoor was a snare and a temptation. He must answer his country's call. Zath was not his proper foe. He would go Home and enlist to fight in the war he was meant to fight in.

There a man at least could know who was right and who was wrong. There a man fought with bullet and bayonet, not hideous sorcery. There a man could hope for honor, trust in courage, believe in a cause.

# *Acknowledgements*

I have been granted willing assistance by many people. Some merely confirmed a single fact, others slaved over the manuscript for me word by word. To list them in anything but alphabetical order would be invidious, but to all of them I extend my sincere thanks:

J. Brian Clarke, Janet Duncan, Michael Duncan, Jean Greig, Betty Hutton, the Public Library of Wiltshire County Council, Jean-Louis Trudel, and John Welch. All responsibility for the text, however, is mine.

The Embu and Meru are authentic tribes of Kenya, although I have taken some liberties with their history.

I have no desire to offend anyone's religious sensibilities. To the best of my knowledge, there never was a Lighthouse Missionary Society. This is a work of make-believe. Even on its own terms, the "gods" it depicts are divine only in the eyes of those foolish enough to worship them.

# PRESENT
# TENSE

For
Jacinta, Richard & Michael

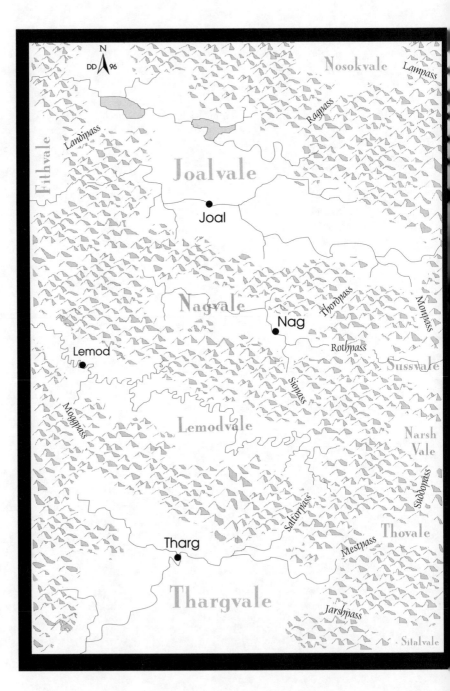

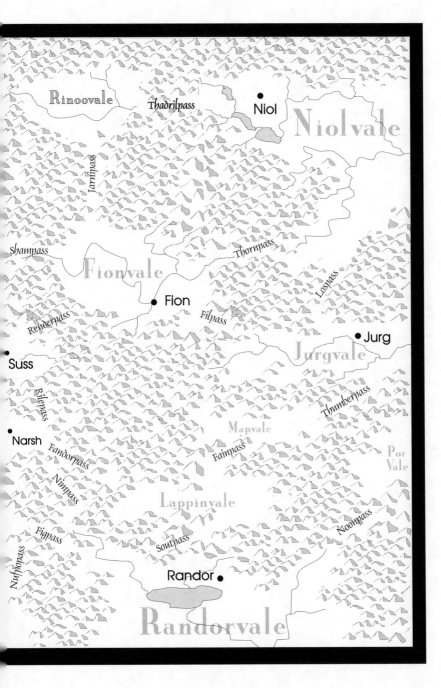

Rinoovale

Thadrilpass

Niol

Niolvale

Jarnipass

Shampass

Fionvale

Thornpass

Renderpass

Fion

Filpass

Lospass

Suss

Jurg

Jurgvale

Rilepass

Thumberpass

Narsh

Fandorpass

Mapvale

Fainpass

Por
Vale

Nimpass

Lappinvale

Fignass

Noorpass

Nuthopass

Soutpass

Randor

Randorvale

But war's a game, which, were their subjects wise, Kings would not play at.

COWPER, The Task

Men plot evil upon the holy mountain. The servants of the one do the work of the many. They send unto D'ward, mouthing oaths like nectar. Their voices are sweet as roses, yea sweeter than the syrup that snares the diamond-Øy. He is lured to destruction by the word of a friend, by the song of a friend he is hurled down among the legions of death.

FILOBY TESTAMENT, 114

# Contents

# I

# *Pawn en Passant*

*1*

The incident occurred on August 16, 1917, during the battle of Third Ypres. The following day, Brig.-Gen. Stringer instituted an informal board of inquiry, consisting of Capt. K. J. Purvis, the medical officer of 26th (Midland Scottish) Battalion, and Capt. J. J. O'Brien, the brigade padre. This procedure was highly improper. The choice of Father O'Brien implies that rumors of a miracle were circulating already.

Apprehension of a suspected spy should certainly have been reported at once to division headquarters, and from there it should have been relayed to Corps and Army, and eventually GHQ. In this case there is considerable doubt that the news ever reached higher than brigade level. Published dispatches and official histories contain no mention of the bizarre affair. Apart from a few cryptic comments in some of the diaries and letters of the period, the only documentary evidence resides in the Stringer family archives.

The four witnesses were examined separately. All four were privates in C Company of the Royal Birmingham Fusiliers, which officially had been held out of the battle on the sixteenth. All four were either eighteen or nineteen years old, and all from the Midlands. Stretcher-bearing duty, to which the four had been assigned, was little less hazardous than combat. They had been on their fourth mission of the day and had been under fire almost continuously. Without question, they were all physically exhausted. Their mental and emotional condition should be borne in mind when evaluating their evidence.

Of the four accounts, that of Chisholm is the most detailed and seems the most convincing. He was the eldest by a few months; he had been a printer's apprentice and had benefitted from two more years' education than the others, Pvts. W. J. Clark, P. T. White, and J. Goss, who had all left school at fourteen.

Considering the danger, the inhuman conditions, and the extreme fatigue under which they had been laboring, the witnesses' evidence is remarkably uniform. They disagree on a few minor details, but—as the board observed in its report—completely identical accounts would be cause for suspicion.

They had paused for a rest in the lee of a fragment of masonry wall, probably the remains of a church which the maps showed in approximately that location. Over the roar of the heavy guns they could hear the repeated *ping* of bullets and shrapnel striking the stones; from time to time a shell would come close enough to spray mud at them. They lay in pairs, two men on either side of a flooded shell hole.

Chisholm later claimed that he had risen to his knees and called on the party to start moving again. None of the other three mentioned this, but in the racket and their own fatigue, they might not have heard or noticed. The important point is that Chisholm was apparently looking toward the rear at the crucial moment, and he insisted that the newcomer did not come from that direction.

The men were unanimous in stating that the fifth man fell into the shell hole between them with considerable force, as if he had dropped "out of the sky." No amount of questioning could shake their testimony on this point. They all claimed to have been splashed by the water thrown up. Three of them insisted that he could not have jumped or fallen down from the top of the wall. The fourth, Pvt. Clark, considered that he might have done, but did not think it likely.

The newcomer floundered and struggled, apparently unable to stand. Clark and Goss waded into the water and hauled him out, choking and still struggling, and completely coated in mud. It was only then that they realized just how remarkable the mysterious newcomer was.

"I saw the man had no tin hat," Pvt. Clark related in the sort of bloodless prose that has obviously been clerically improved. "But the rest of him was just mud. I reached for his arm and at first it slipped through my fingers. I realized he had no coat on. When we got him out, we saw that he had no clothes on at all."

The witnesses agreed that the stranger was having some sort of fit. His limbs thrashed and he seemed to be in considerable pain. He was incapable of answering questions, and they were unable to make sense cf what he was saying.

Each of them was asked to report whatever he could remember of the man's words. There the testimonies diverge. Chisholm thought he heard mention of July, railways, and bed socks. White opted for cabbage and ladders and Armentières. The other two had similar unlikely lists, and we can only assume that they were equally mistaken. They all agreed that some of the talk was in English, some of it was not.

They did all agree on a few words: *spy, traitor, betrayed, treason.*

They had come to rescue wounded soldiers. This man had no visible wounds except some minor bleeding scratches caused by his convulsions. He was apparently incapable of standing, let alone walking, even had he been suitably clothed.

That he was a British soldier must have seemed extremely improbable to them, even then. That he was a German soldier was even less likely. Under questioning, they admitted discussing the possibility that he was a spy. Any man apprehending a spy automatically received leave in England, and they did not deny that they were aware of that regulation, although they all claimed that it had not influenced their decision.

Whatever their motives, they loaded the stranger on their stretcher, tying him down securely. They covered him with muddy greatcoats taken from corpses, and waded off through the bog to deliver him to the regimental aid post. It is difficult to see what else they could have done.

The report wastes little time discussing the conditions on the battlefield, which were only too familiar to the examining officers.

Those conditions can be reconstructed from other sources, although at this distance in time the reader's reaction is mostly incredulity. Superlatives pile up in a mental logjam, and the reader is left wondering if any words could ever be adequate. Even the photographs fail to convince. The mind recoils, refusing to believe that men actually fought over such terrain or that any of them could have come out alive to tell of it.

By the summer of 1917, the Belgian plain had been contested for almost three years, and yet the front line had scarcely changed position. The trenches, like insatiable bloody mouths, had subducted the youth of Europe. For three years men had marched in from east and west with intent to kill each other. On both sides they had succeeded. On both sides they had died in hundreds of thousands, yet still they came. Since 1914 the introduction of aircraft and poison gas had improved the technology of death tremendously, but repeated campaigns had barely changed the maps. At the opening of the battle of the Somme, in the previous year, the British Army alone lost over 57,000 men—killed, wounded, or missing—*in one day.* (This is numerically equal to the death toll suffered by the United States in the whole of the Vietnam War, half a century later.)

The battle of Third Ypres lasted for months and much of it was fought in torrential rain. The monotonously flat ground was completely waterlogged, repeatedly churned up by shells. Nothing of the original countryside remained. Nothing at all remained except mud, often thigh deep and in some places capable of sucking men and mules down to their death. It was laced throughout with broken timbers and old barbed wire, with rotting bodies of men, mules, and horses. There was no cover, for every hollow was filled with slime and water, commonly scummed with blood and fragments of flesh. Old corpses thrown up by the explosions lay amid the dying.

Over all this watery desolation hung the reek of death and decay, the garlic odor of mustard gas, the stench of the mud itself. Even a minor wound could cause a man to drown, and in those days there were no antibiotics to combat the frightful infections. The soil was poisoned by gas and virulent microbes. The roar of artillery never ceased. The ground shook as if Earth itself were suffering. Mule trains struggled forward with ammunition; the walking wounded staggered toward the rear. The British Army was attempting to advance across the desolation, while the Germans tried to mow it down with howitzers, machine guns, shrapnel, and poison gas. The field was swept by unrelenting fire and unrelenting rain.

Through this maelstrom of death went stretcher parties looking for wounded. Four men to a stretcher was a bare minimum. Often eight or ten were required, and even then it was not uncommon for the whole party to stumble and tip the wounded man to the ground. After a journey back to the field dressing station—which might take hours—the stretcher-bearers would go back for another. The work had to be done in daylight, for at night there were no landmarks.

Peculiar as the incident itself was, the subsequent behavior of the Army command structure was even stranger.

Suspicion must be directed at the brigade commander, Brig.-Gen. J. G. Stringer, although in all other respects his reputation is unclouded. The son of an Army of India officer, Brig.-Gen. (later Major-Gen.) Stringer had a distinguished career as a professional soldier. Born in India in 1882, he was educated in England at Fallow and Sandhurst. He was a noted athlete, playing cricket for Hampshire and serving as master of the Dilby Hunt. When war broke out in August 1914, he held the rank of major in the Royal Fusiliers, which formed part of the British Expeditionary Force dispatched to France. His subsequent rise was dramatic. He was well-thought-of by both his superiors and his subordinates. He was to die tragically in a motor accident in 1918, shortly before the end of the war.

One man did not testify at the inquiry—the mysterious stranger himself.

Even when the stretcher party had set off with their mysterious patient, their troubles were not over. The British began bringing up reinforcements. The Germans laid down a barrage to stop them. The stretcher-bearers had to run the gauntlet of high-explosives, shrapnel and, at one point, poison gas shells. They took a gas helmet from a corpse for their patient, but some of his exposed skin was blistered.

Their estimates of the time this journey took varied from two and a half to three and a half hours. By the time they arrived at the dressing station, the unknown man was unconscious and incapable of explaining anything.

# 2

Two men sat in a garden and talked about hell. One of them had been there.

The time was a Saturday afternoon in early September 1917. The site was a sunny corner in the grounds of Staffles, which had been an English country house since the seventeenth century and was now a hospital for wounded returning from the Great War.

The two sat side by side at the top of a short flight of steps leading up to a set of glass doors. Inside those doors, a row of beds prevented anyone from coming out or going in, so the speakers would not be disturbed. It was a sheltered spot. The younger man had found it, and it was probably the best place in the entire hospital for a private chat. He had always had a knack for coming out on top like that. He was not greedy or selfish, yet even as a child he had always been the one to land the best bed in the dorm. Draw a name from a hat, and it would almost always be his.

The steps led down to crazy paving and a lichen-stained stone balustrade. Beyond that, a park sloped to a copse of beeches. The grass badly needed cutting, the rosebushes were straggly, and the flower beds nurtured more weeds than blossoms. Hills in the distance were upholstered with hop fields, their regular texture like the weave of a giant green carpet. Autumn lurked in the air, although the leaves had not yet begun to turn.

Once in a while a train would rush along behind the wood, puffing trails of smoke. When it had gone, the silence that returned was marred by a persistent faint rumbling, the sound of the guns across the Channel. There was another big push on in Flanders. Every man in Staffles knew it. Everyone in southern England knew it.

Men in hospital blues crowded the grounds, sitting on benches or strolling aimlessly. Some were in wheelchairs, some on crutches. Many had weekend visitors to entertain them. Somewhere someone was playing croquet.

In front of the two men stood a small mahogany parlor table, bearing a tea tray. One plate still bore a few crumbs of the scones which had come with the tea. The sparrows hopping hopefully on the flagstones were well aware of those crumbs.

The younger man was doing most of the talking. He spoke of mud and cold, of shrapnel and gas attacks, of days without rest or relief from terror, of weeks in the same clothing, of lice and rheumatism, of trench foot and gas gangrene. He told of young subalterns like himself marching at the head of their men across the wastes of no-man's-land until they reached Fritz's barbed wire and machine guns scythed them down in their ranks. He told of mutilation and death in numbers never imagined possible in the golden days before the war.

Several times during the tea drinking and scone eating, he had reached out absent-mindedly with his right sleeve, which was pinned shut just where his wrist should have been. He had muttered curses and tucked that arm out of sight again. He chain-smoked, frequently reaching to his mouth with his empty cuff. At times he would try to stop talking, but his left eye would immediately start to twitch. When that happened, the spasms would quickly spread to involve his entire face, until it grimaced and writhed as if it had taken on an idiot life of its own. And then he would weep.

At such times the older man would tactfully pretend to be engrossed in watching other men in the distance or studying the swallows gathering on the telephone wires. He would speak of the old days—of the cricket and rugby, and of boys his companion had known who were now men. He did not mention the awful shadow that lay on them as they waited for the call that would take them away and run them through the mincer as it ran their older brethren. A war that had seemed glorious in 1914 was a monster now. He did not mention the ever-growing list of the dead.

He was middle-aged, approaching elderly. His portly frame and full beard gave him a marked resemblance to the late King Edward VII, but he wore a pair of pince-nez. His beard was heavily streaked with gray, and his hat concealed a spreading baldness. His name was David Jones and he was a schoolmaster. For more than thirty years he had been known behind his back as Ginger, not for his temperament or his coloring, but because in his youth Ginger had gone with Jones as Dusty went with Miller.

The gasping, breathless sobs beside him had quietened again.

"The swallows will be heading south soon now," he remarked.

"Lucky buggers!" said the young man. His name was Julian Smedley. He was a captain in the Royal Artillery. He was twenty years old. After a moment he added, "You know that was my first thought? There was no pain at all. I looked down and saw nothing where my hand should be and that was my first thought: *Thank God! I am going Home!*"

"And you're not going back!"

"No. Even better." There was another gasp. "Oh, God! I wish I could stop piping my eye like this." He fumbled awkwardly for a cigarette.

The older man turned his head. "You're not the worst, you know. Not by a long shot. I've seen many much worse."

Smedley pulled a face. "Wish you'd tell the guv'nor that."

"It's the truth," Jones said softly. "Much worse. And I will tell your father if you want me to."

"Hell, no! Let him brood about his yellow-livered, sniveling son. It was damned white of you to come, Ginger. Do you spend all your weekends trailing around England, combing the wreckage like this?"

"Paying my respects. And, no, not every weekend."

"Lots, I'll bet." Smedley blew out a long cloud of smoke, then dabbed at his cheeks with his empty sleeve. He seemed to be talked out on the war, which was a good sign.

"Ginger . . . ?"

"Mm?"

"Er, nothing."

It wasn't nothing. They'd had that same futile exchange several times in the last two hours. Smedley had something to say, some subject he couldn't broach.

Jones glanced at his watch. He must not miss his bus. He was running out of things to talk about. One topic he had learned never to mention was patriotism. Another was Field-Marshal Sir Douglas Haig.

"Apart from school, how are things?" Smedley muttered.

"Not so bad. Price of food's frightful. Can't find a workman or a servant anywhere."

"What about the air raids?"

"People grumble, but they'll pull through."

Smedley eyed the older man with the ferocity of a hawk. "How do you think the war's going?"

"Hard to say. The papers are censored, of course. They tell us that Jerry's done for. Morale's all gone."

"Balls."

"Oh. Well, we don't hear rumors at Fallow. The Americans are in, thank God."

"They're in America!" Smedley snapped. "How long until they can build an army and move it to France—if the U-boats don't sink it on the way? And the Russians are out! Good as. Did you know that?"

Jones made noncommittal noises. If the Hun could finish the Russians before the Yanks arrived, then the war was lost. Everyone knew it. No one said it.

"Do you recall a boy called Stringer? Before my time."

The schoolmaster chuckled. "Long Stringer or Short Stringer?"

"Don't know. A doctor."

"That's Short Stringer. His brother's a brigadier or something."

"He drops in here once in a while. I recognized the school tie."

"A surgeon, actually. Yes, I know him. He's on the board of governors. Comes to Speech Days."

Smedley nodded, staring out over the lengthening shadows in the garden. He sucked hard on his cigarette. Jones wondered if the unspeakable, whatever it was, was about to be spoken at last. It came in a rush.

"Tell me something, Ginger. When war broke out I was in Paris, remember? Edward Exeter and I were on our way to Crete. Came home from Paris just before the dam broke."

"I remember," Jones said, suddenly wary. "Dr. Gibbs and the others never made it back, if that's what you're wondering. Never did hear what happened to them."

"Interned?"

"Hope so, but there's never been word."

Smedley dismissed the topic with a quick shake of his head, still staring straight ahead. "Tough egg! No, I was wondering about Exeter. We parted at Victoria. I was heading home to Chichester. He was going on to Greyfriars, to stay with the Bodgleys, but he wanted to send a telegram or something. I had to run for my train. Next thing I knew, there was a copper at the house asking questions."

He turned to look at Jones with the same owlish stare he had had as a boy. He'd always been a shy, quiet one, Smedley, not the sort you'd have ever expected to be a hero and sport those ribbons. But the war had turned thousands of them into heroes. Millions of them.

"Young Bodgley was murdered," Jones said.

"I know. And they seemed to think Exeter had done it."

"I didn't believe that then and I don't now!"

"What innocents we were . . . fresh out of school, thinking we were debonair young men of the world . . ." The voice wavered, then recovered. "Wasn't old Bagpipe stabbed in the back?"

Jones nodded.

Smedley actually smiled, for the second time that afternoon. "Well, then! That answers the question, doesn't it? Whatever Exeter may have done, he would never stab anyone in the back. He *couldn't* stab anyone in the back! Not capable of it." He lit a new cigarette from the previous butt.

"I agree," Jones said. "He wasn't capable of any of it—a stabbing or killing a friend or any of that. A quick uppercut to the jaw, yes. Sudden insanity even. Can happen to . . . But I agree that the back part is conclusive proof of his innocence."

"Bloody nonsense," the young man muttered.

"Even Mrs. Bodgley refused to believe he killed her son."

The owlish stare hardened into a threatening frown. "Then what? He escaped?"

"He totally vanished. Hasn't been seen since."

"Go on, man!" Suddenly the pitiful neurotic invalid was a young officer blazing with authority.

Jones flinched like some lowly recruit, even while feeling a surge of joy at the transformation. "It's a total mystery. He just disappeared. There was a warrant issued, but no one ever heard from him again. Of course things were in a pretty mess, with war breaking out and all that."

Apparently none of this was news to Smedley. He scowled with impatience, as if the recruit were being more than usually stupid. "The copper told us he had a broken leg."

"His right leg was smashed."

"So someone helped him? Must have."

Jones shrugged. "An archangel from the sound of it. Or the Invisible Man. The full story never came out."

"And you genuinely believe it was a put-up job? Still? You still think that, Ginger?"

Jones nodded, wondering what lay behind the sudden vehemence. After being through what this boy had been through, why should he brood over the guilt or innocence of a schoolboy chum? After seeing so much death, why become so agitated over one long-ago death? It had been three years. It had happened in another world, a world that was gone forever, butchered in the mud of Flanders.

The mood passed like a lightning flash. Smedley slumped loosely. He leaned his arms on his knees and reached for his cigarette with the wrong arm. He cursed under his breath.

Jones waited, but he would have to run for the bus soon or he would not see his bed tonight. Nor any bed, if he got trapped in the city. Not the way London was these days.

"Why?"

"I don't know," Smedley muttered. He seemed to be counting the litter of butts around his feet.

Nonsense! The man needed to get something off his chest. Well, that was why Jones had come. He crossed his legs and leaned back to wait. He'd slept on station waiting room benches before now. He could again.

"Shell shock, they call it," his companion told the dishes on the table—slowly, as if dragging the words out of himself. "Battle fatigue. Tricks of the mind. Weeping, you know? Facial tics, you know? Imagining things?"

"Maybe. Maybe not. Man has to trust something."

"There's lots here worse off than me, you know?" Smedley jerked his thumb over his left shoulder. "They call it the morgue. West wing. Don't know who they are, some of them. Or think they're the bleeding Duke of Wellington. All lead-swingers and scrimshankers, I expect."

"I doubt that very much."

Smedley looked up with a tortured, frightened grimace.

Jones's heart began to thunder like all the guns on the Western Front. "So?"

"There's one they call John Three. They have a John Two, and there was a John One once, I expect. No name or rank. Doesn't speak. Can't or won't say who he is or what unit he was in."

Jones sucked in a long breath of the chilling air.

"I'd forgotten how blue his eyes are," Smedley whispered.

"Oh, my God!"

"Bluest eyes I ever did see."

"Is he . . . Is he injured? Physically, I mean?"

"Nothing major. Touch of gas burn or something." Smedley shook his head. With another of his abrupt mood changes he sat up and laughed. "I expect I was imagining it."

"Let's just pretend you weren't, shall we? Did you speak to him?"

"No. He was with his keeper. Being exercised. Walked around the lawn like a dog. I wandered over. He looked right through me. I asked his keeper for a light. Said thanks. Trotted off."

Of course Exeter would have enlisted as soon as his leg had mended. It was impossible to imagine him not doing so. False name . . . Tricky, not impossible . . .

"One thing you should know," Smedley said shrilly. "He doesn't look a day older than he did in Victoria Station, three years ago. So a chap really has to assume that he's just a little bit more shell-shocked than he hoped he was, wouldn't you say? Imagining things like that?"

"You're all right, man!" Jones said sharply. "But Exeter? Amnesia? He's lost his memory?"

Smedley's eye had begun to twitch again. He threw down his cigarette and stamped on it. "Oh, no! No, no, old man, that's not the problem at all. He knew me right away. Turned white as a sheet, then just stared at the horizon. That's why I didn't speak to him. Chatted up the keeper to keep him busy till Exeter got his color back, then left without a glance at him."

"He's faking it?"

"No question. Unless I imagined it."

"You didn't imagine this!"

"Oh, I wouldn't say that!"

"Don't be a fool, man!" Jones snapped. "Have you had other delusions? Seen any other ghosts?"

"No."

"Then you didn't this time. He can't reveal his name without going on trial for a murder he didn't commit!"

The eye twitched faster. "He'd better find himself a name pretty soon, Mr. Jones! Very soon! I've been asking a few discreet questions." The twitch had spread to his cheek. "He turned up at the front line under very mysterious circumstances. No uniform, no papers, nothing. They think he's a German sp-p-py!"

"What!"

"That's one th-th-theory." Smedley was having trouble controlling his mouth now. "So he's got the choice of being hanged or sh-sh-shot, do you see?"

"My god!"

"What'n hell're we going to do, Ginger? How can we help him?" Smedley buried his face in one hand and a sleeve. He began to weep again.

# II

# *White Knight*

# 3

As soon as the nurse turned her back, Smedley spat out the sleeping pill. When the light was turned off, he placed it carefully under his pillow. He would need it later. He rolled onto his back and prepared to wait.

His right hand throbbed. The fingers were tightly clenched, the nails digging into his palm. They were all somewhere back in Belgium, but he could feel exactly what they were doing . . . hurt like hell sometimes. Just part of the trouble of going bonkers.

Staffles had not been designed as a hospital. He shared a room with two other men, and there was barely room to walk between the beds. Rattray tossed and scuffled on the right; Wilkinson wheezed and bubbled on the left, his lungs ruined by gas. Very shortly both men were snoring—those pills packed a punch like twelve-inch howitzers.

Light filtered in from the corridor. The sounds of the hospital dwindled into silence. Once in a while it trembled as a train clattered by, London to Dover or Dover to London . . . no question which was the better way to be heading these days. The guns were still throbbing.

He needed a fag, but the nurses gathered up every cigarette in the building at lights-out. Staffles was one giant firetrap.

He lay and brooded, trying to fit what he had learned about the anonymous John Three in the west wing to the Exeter story he had heard from Jones—how that man had aged! An impossible disappearance and an impossible reappearance? Somehow that was appropriate. At least it made sense to a loony with a bad case of shell shock who couldn't sit still for ten minutes without having an attack of the willies.

*I would kill for a cigarette.*

He should have done something about Exeter days ago, but he hadn't really been able to believe himself. It had taken Ginger's reassurance to convince him of his own story, to persuade him he wasn't that far gone in the head. Not quite. Close, but not on target.

Exeter had vanished from Albert Memorial Hospital in Greyfriars. Somehow he had passed by the nurses on duty and the doorman, all of whom had sworn he had not. The night nurse had discovered his room wrecked, blood on the floor, and yet no one had heard a thing. Impossible, but Ginger believed, although he admitted it was hearsay. Hearsay from Mrs. Bodgley was good as Holy Writ.

John Three had been brought in from the battlefield with no uniform on. With *nothing* on, so the rumors said—shows how far gone the poor sod must be. No sane skulker would go so far as to strip to the buff in that rain-swept, bullet-swept, shell-swept hell. Mad as a March hare.

There were only two ways into no-man's-land. Either he had come from the British lines or the German lines. Or perhaps he'd cracked up an aeroplane. But why bare arsed? The mud had been known to suck off a man's boots and trousers but not his tunic. Shell blast could collapse his lungs or his brain and kill him without leaving a visible mark on him, but stripping him naked without otherwise harming him seemed rather too freakish even for shell blast.

*I would give my right arm for a fag. It's no damn use anyway.*

Why John Three? Could he speak at all? Why not invent a name?

Name, rank, and serial number.

The alternative was a bullet.

Why had Exeter not been shot out of hand? Why was he not in a provost cell, at least, instead of a low-security mental ward? There were weird rumors. Or at least there were rumors of rumors, tales of people who knew more than they were able to tell but rolled their eyes expressively.

He might not have been faking when he was brought in. Men picked up in battlefields were usually in bloody rotten shape. The journey back on a stretcher would be enough of an ordeal to drive a chap bonkers all by itself. So perhaps Exeter had genuinely been unable to talk when he was brought in, although Smedley himself had walked on his own feet into the casualty clearing station and tried to shake hands with—never mind.

Exeter had been putting up a stall on Wednesday. He had known Smedley. And if there was one thing Smedley had learned to recognize in Belgium, it was terror.

Exeter hadn't even given him a don't-give-me-away look. It had been an attempt at an I-don't-know-you look. That rankled a little, but if he couldn't trust an old pal not to give him away, then he was in something very deep and ever so smelly.

How long could he swing it? The medicals weren't dumb; they knew a skulker when they saw one. They'd use all kinds of tricks—sneak up behind him and bark orders, ask unexpected questions, leave newspapers lying around. . . .

Thinking about that, Smedley began to sweat. How long could a man go without speaking? It would be like solitary, but solitary in the middle of a crowd. Voluntary Coventry? Never speaking, never admitting that you could understand? Hour after hour. Day after day. It would crack a man. If Exeter wasn't already off his rocker, the strain of pretending to be would make it so. Playing crazy, he'd go crazy!

Smedley realized with a shock that he hadn't been weeping or even twitching. Just lying there, thinking and wishing for a Player's. The Exeter puzzle had given his mind something to chew on.

He had a strange jumpy feeling, not altogether unpleasant. He wasn't going to be in any personal danger. Hell, he could paint his face green or dance hornpipes on the piano and no one would do anything more than sigh and write a note on his file.

The danger would be to Exeter. If Smedley got caught showing interest in the mystery man, then someone might put two and two together. If anyone ever made the Fallow connection, then the jig would be up. Which might be why Exeter was keeping his mouth shut instead of spinning a yarn. An Englishman's voice would place him within a county. Or his school. Put Professor Higgins on the case and he'd say, "Fallow!" in two shakes.

Smedley awoke with a blast of terror, sweating torrents and choking back a scream. He had been asleep! Without a pill! Jolly good! First time since . . . since never mind. Snores to the right of him, snores to the left of him, volleyed and thundered. So he hadn't actually shrieked aloud. He had slept! Perhaps he was getting a little better, just a little? Please, Lord?

He tried to see his watch and couldn't. Still, it felt like time to go. He swallowed the ashtray taste in his mouth and eased back the blankets.

Dressing one-handed was bad enough in daylight. From now on he'd have his suits made with flies that buttoned on the left. He had thought to pull his shoes off without untying them, but getting them on again was harder. Neckties were an invention of the devil. . . . Hairbrush . . .

One wan bulb lit the corridor, invoking vast shadows. He set off on tiptoe, thinking of the poor sods in the trenches in Belgium, going over the top. At least in the artillery he'd never had to do that. Primary target: the linen closet down the hall. Pray it wasn't locked.

It was. Hellfire!

In two weeks he had snooped everywhere in Staffles—upstairs, downstairs, in any chamber he was allowed into—hoping he was doing it from boredom and because it was better than sitting still, frightened he was doing it because his loose brains were looking for bogeys.

Secondary target: one of the doctors' rooms.

He found a doctors' cubbyhole that was not locked, that did have a white coat hanging behind the door. Some kind saint had even left a stethoscope in the pocket. Now that was really shockingly careless! Take that man's name, Sergeant.

His fingers were shaking so much he could barely fasten the buttons. Nelly! He hung the stethoscope around his neck like a gas mask. He tucked a pencil behind his ear and his stump in his pocket and a clipboard under his arm. Then he stiffened his upper lip and marched off boldly in the direction of the west wing.

The house was dim and silent. It stank of disinfectant and the eternal stench of stale cigarette smoke.

A real doctor was the worst danger, and there would be one on duty somewhere. A nurse might be overawed by the stethoscope. Guards . . .

One guard, reading a newspaper.

"Don't get up!" the doctor said, and walked right by him.

It would not have worked in a proper hospital, but Staffles was not a proper hospital. The night nurses were not sitting out at a duty desk where they could view the corridor. Light pouring from an open door was the best they could manage, and apparently no one noticed the white shape flit past. The west wing had been servants' quarters—low ceilings, painted plaster walls. Feeling the guard's eyes boring into his backbone, Smedley chose a room at random.

There were two beds crammed in there. One was empty. The man in the other was bandaged beyond recognition, but he sounded asleep.

Would the guard register that the doctor had not turned on the light?

Smedley waited a couple of minutes, about two thousand heartbeats.

Then he peeked cautiously. The guard was back in his newspaper. The light from the duty room shone unobstructed.

The next room was not the right one either.

Nor the next.

The next was.

A fair-haired head. Asleep. Just a kid, but lying on his back and breathing noisily. Exeter's black hair on the other pillow.

Suddenly Smedley was back in Paris, three years ago, staying at Uncle Frank's on his way to Crete, sharing a room with Exeter. His heart twisted in his chest. Ye gods and little fishes, man! How can you still look so *young?*

He left the door open. To close it would attract attention if a nurse had to pass by. He squeezed in between the bed and the wall, on the right side. He knelt down, dropping the clipboard. He laid his hand over Exeter's mouth.

A wild reaction almost blew the gaff. Bedsprings creaked. Arms and legs flailed; a hand grabbed his wrist so hard he thought it would crack.

"Shush, you idiot! It's me. Smedley. Julian!"

A grunt. A groan. Exeter subsided. The kid in the other bed paused in his breathing—and then resumed. Smedley's heart crawled back where it belonged.

He leaned close. "I know who you are," he whispered. "This is on the level. No one put me up to this. I swear that! I want to help."

The blue eyes were silver gray in the dark, even with his, staring at him from the pillow.

"Ginger Jones came calling today."

Exeter sucked in a long breath and sighed it out again. He was drugged and still mostly asleep. Dopey, trying not to show any reaction.

"I don't believe you killed—I don't think Bagpipe's death was your doing. Ginger doesn't, either. I know you disappeared mysteriously from a hospital. Can you disappear from this one?"

Pause. Very slightly, Exeter shook his head.

That was a very deniable shake. Why wouldn't he trust an old friend?

"Can you talk?"

An almost imperceptible nod.

"You won't fool them for long, Edward! Do you want help getting out of here?"

A stronger nod. More blinks, as if Julian Smedley might not be the only man in the world with eye troubles.

"Can you tell me what's going on?" Smedley begged.

Another faint shake.

"For God's sake, man! Trust me!" He felt his cheek beginning to twitch. Any minute now the tears would start. Then where would trust go?

He waited stubbornly, sweating, gritting his teeth, fighting against twitching and weeping. He thought he wasn't going to get an answer. Then it came, a tenuous sound, like a whisper from beyond the grave and yet so close that he could smell the breath that brought it.

"You couldn't believe me."

"From the rumors I've heard, I can believe anything."

A shake: no.

"Look, I'm not going to be here much longer. I don't know how to get you out of here, and I don't know where I could take you that would be safe. Have you any ideas? Any suggestions? Anyone who needs to be told?"

Exeter's fingers reached out and took the pencil from behind Smedley's ear.

Smedley fumbled awkwardly to retrieve the clipboard. It had slipped under the bed. He passed it up. Exeter turned over the top sheet and wrote on the back of it. He handed them both back.

Smedley took the pencil in his left hand and tried to take the clipboard with his stump.

"Oh, my *god!*"

Exeter had spoken aloud, almost shouted. The kid on the next bed fell silent. Smedley crouched down low, out of sight. He was shaking. He must get out of here before he had an attack of the willies! In a moment the slow breathing resumed.

When he straightened up again, Exeter's hand gripped his shoulder and squeezed like a vise. They stared at each other.

Well! So there were other men who had trouble with watery eyes these days? Lot of it going around.

"Edward—"

Somebody screamed farther along the hall. Then screamed again.

Smedley wanted to dive under the bed. He forced himself to stand up and go to the door. Confused voices rising in protest, more screams . . . Some poor bugger having nightmares. A nurse hurried by. Then another.

Then the heavy tread of the guard. They all went by. Splendid!

He glanced around. Exeter was sitting up straight, face pale, eyes wide.

"Enfilading fire, old man!" Smedley said cheerily. He waved his stump and departed.

If one of the nurses came out to fetch something and saw a doctor in the corridor— but that didn't happen.

Smedley went back to bed and wept until his sleeping pill took effect.

On Sunday it rained most of the day. He practiced left-handed writing all morning. In the evening he walked down to the village and posted two letters, to the addresses Exeter had given him.

# 4

Fallow in holiday time was a morgue these days. In another week the inmates would start to trickle back, and the school year would start up again. Meanwhile, only a half dozen or so masters and three or four wives remained on the premises. Before the war there had always been a few boys in permanent residence, sons of parents abroad. The problems of finding staff, both academic and domestic, had forced the board of governors to abandon the practice of providing year-round board *in the meantime*. A revolution was sweeping England "in the meantime," and only the far future would show how many of those expedients were temporary.

Early on Tuesday, David Jones cycled into Wassal and caught the local train to Greyfriars. The service was extremely poor on that line now, but rural buses were worse, almost as rare as dodoes in the England of 1917. After a twenty-minute wait, he entrusted his mortal coil to the Great Western Railway Company once more and was borne eastward toward London. The express was packed with people, many of them servicemen. At first he thought he would have to stand in the corridor the whole way, but a young gunner rose and donated his seat to the elderly gent, for which the same was suitably grateful. Considering that Jones was bound on paying his respects to the military, the tribute was ironic.

A couple of hours brought him to Paddington. From there he took the tube to Cannon Street and emerged into a dreary, drizzly gray morning, rank with the stench of coal and petrol. Letting the scurrying crowds rush by him, he strolled across London Bridge at a leisurely pace to his destination, Guy's Hospital.

He spent the remainder of the morning in conversation with William Derby, another Fallow old boy—not so old, really. He could not be more than twenty-five. He had been broken and blinded on the Somme, but his morale was heartrending. The ones that needed cheering up were almost easier. Like Julian Smedley, most of them were so happy to be out of the fighting that they regarded their disabilities as blessings. In time the reality would sink in.

By lunchtime, Jones's task was done. He did not like London. Before the war he had rarely come up to town except to pass through on his way to somewhere else. It was too big, too busy, too grimy. The war had brought to it a frantic, hothouse exuberance that did nothing to change his feelings. His new, self-imposed assignment of visiting the wounded had taken him there a dozen times in the last two months. One precaution he had learned from bitter experience was to bring his lunch with him, so today he sat on a damp bench on the Victoria Embankment and ate his sandwiches. Ten years ago all the taxicabs in London had been pulled by horses. Now there was hardly a horse to be seen anywhere. The smell of the city had changed, but petrol fumes were hardly an improvement.

He had the rest of the day before him. There were many other maimed young men he could call on, although none he knew of whom he had not visited at least once. He was haunted by the problem of one he could not visit, Edward Exeter.

In more than thirty years of teaching, he could recall no boy so cursed. His parents had been foully slaughtered in a native uprising in Kenya. He himself had been implicated in another murder, and seriously injured. Now he was in danger of being shot as a spy. It was madness! What had he ever done to provoke the Furies so? Out of all the hundreds of boys Jones had taught in his career, he would have ranked none ahead of Edward Exeter.

The only help he could think to provide was to track down Alice Prescott. He had last met her in 1914, when she had rushed down to Greyfriars to visit her young cousin in hospital. She had been a very self-possessed miss even then. Exeter had been suffering from a severe case of puppy love, but her heart—so Jones had suspected—had been mortgaged elsewhere. She had been fond of Edward, without question, because they had grown up together in Africa, but she had not spoken of him as a prospective lover.

Jones had written to her a couple of times afterward, relaying what skimpy information he had been able to gather about Exeter's disappearance. The correspondence had withered for lack of purpose. When her famous uncle, the Reverend Roland Exeter, died a couple of years later, Jones had sent a sympathy card to her last known address. It had been returned, recipient unknown. The war had raged ever more wildly since then. She might well be married or driving an ambulance in Palestine by now.

But he had promised Julian Smedley that he would try to devise some way of assisting Exeter, assuming that the mysterious John Three confined in Staffles was truly the missing man. In the days since, Jones had experienced no brain waves, had achieved nothing practical. He had written a careful note to the widowed Mrs. Bodgley, but she could hardly be expected to assist a boy she had barely known, one suspected of murdering her only son. The only possible helper in this affair was Alice Prescott. To the best of his knowledge, she was the only family Exeter possessed.

He fed his crusts to the restless pigeons and headed for the underground again. Miss Prescott's last known address had been in Chelsea, a modest location that would have been handy for her clients. She had been a teacher of piano, and the nearby area of South Kensington would have provided many wealthy families with children in need of such social improvement.

He found the flat. There was nobody home, which was hardly surprising in the middle of the afternoon. He rang a few doorbells in the vicinity, spoke with a few harried, suspicious women, and eventually found one who remembered Miss Prescott. It had only been three years, after all. He spun a yarn about news of a long-lost relative; either that or his accent convinced the lady that he was not a bill collector. After a long wait in a dim corridor, he was rewarded with an address in Hackney. Doffing his hat in salute, David Jones departed in search of the nearest tube station.

Hackney, of course, lay on the other side of the City. He could not afford taxis, so he had a choice of bus, tram, or tube. The advantage of the tube was that it displayed maps in all the stations. Even a country yokel could not get lost on the underground.

How often could a young lady change her address in three years?

Twice.

Three times, and apparently never for the better. There had been money in the family once.

The rain had started again. By the time darkness fell, he was in Lambeth, south of the river, and not very far from his starting point at Guy's Hospital. Whatever Miss Prescott was doing in that grim, working-class area, she was not likely to be teaching piano to the pampered offspring of rich matrons.

It had been an exhausting day, and his feet throbbed. Darkness was true darkness, too, for the threat of German air raids had imposed blackout. He knew in a purely cerebral way that the bombs did very little damage and caused few casualties—relative to the millions of people exposed, that is—but emotionally he had no desire to become a statistic.

He found the entrance beside a tobacconist's shop and was happily surprised to see that Miss Prescott did not inhabit one of the horrible egg-crate tenements of the back streets. This was a three-story corner building, proudly bearing the date, 1896. Its yellow brick was stained by the ever-present soot of London, but it was a reasonably appealing edifice. He plodded wearily up two flights of hard, steep stairs, inhaling aromas of boiled cabbage and cooking fat. At the top he was faced with a door, four bell pushes, and four labels he could not read in the gloom. He flipped a mental coin in the dark and pressed.

With surprisingly good reflexes, the door cracked open almost at once. Light knifed out at him. He blinked.

He raised his hat. "I am looking for a Miss Alice Prescott."

"I am she," said an educated, non-Lambeth voice.

Praise the Lord! "David Jones, Miss Prescott."

The cultured voice said, "Christ!" and the door shut.

Jones could not recall ever having heard a woman use that particular blasphemy, and few men either. Before he could catch his breath, the chain rattled and the door swung open.

"Come in, Mr. Jones! This is a welcome, if rather alarming surprise. Let me take your coat. I have just brewed a pot of tea. . . ."

She was a very practical young lady, and self-possessed to boot. He was ushered out of the cramped entrance hall into a small sitting room and urged to take a chair. He glanced around, at first with surprise and then with something closer to astonishment.

The address might be questionable and the wallpaper regrettable, but the furnishings were not. The tiny space was almost filled by an upright rosewood piano, two armchairs, and a sofa; they were old, yet neither worn nor faded. The rug underfoot was thick and bright. The curtains were velvet, the little tables oak. The mantel above the gas fire bore several Royal Doulton figurines and a silver-framed photograph of a man in uniform.

A marble-topped cupboard with a two-ring gas cooker and a gently steaming kettle served as kitchen. The cup and saucer were Spode.

The crusts of the family fortune had taken refuge in Lambeth.

His wondering gaze turned to the walls and the watercolors.

"Yes, they are genuine Constables," Miss Prescott said drily. "You will have a cup of tea with me since you are here?"

One of the more embarrassing problems of advancing years . . . "If I may just freshen up first?"

"Of course! First door on the right. Let me find you a towel."

The WC was the size of a chicken coop. The bathroom opposite was little larger, but any indoor plumbing at all ranked the flat well above average for the neighborhood. She would share the facilities with the other tenants on the floor, of course. Considering the housing situation in London at the moment, she was doing very well. Her plain, serviceable suit had suggested that she was in some sort of clerical work, certainly not munitions, like so many thousands of British women now. Idiot!—there were no munitions factories in the heart of London. As he dried his hands, Jones decided that Alice Prescott was almost certainly a secretary of some sort, and she could walk to Whitehall from here.

He returned to the sitting room. She smiled up at him and said, "One lump or two?" Thus might a Roman matron have invoked the household gods.

She was not classically beautiful—her nose and teeth were too prominent. Had she possessed her cousin's jet-black hair and startlingly blue eyes, she might have been striking. Even with nondescript coloring, she was a handsome young woman.

Jones accepted the tea with gratitude, took a sip, and found himself impaled by a very direct gaze.

She wasted no words. "Where is he, Mr. Jones?"

"I am not certain of this, I have not seen him, but . . . Do you remember Julian Smedley?"

"Yes."

"He says Exeter is in Staffles, a temporary hospital in Kent."

"Under what name?"

"A pseudonym, of course. 'John Three.' He is pretending to be suffering from amnesia, but Smedley is certain it's your cousin."

Alice bit her lip. All she said was, "Go on."

With tea soaking through his fibers like ambrosia, Jones recounted the tale. His feet were throbbing and burning inside his shoes; his knees ached. He did not want to think of the journey home that awaited him, but hotel rooms in London were an impossibility now.

She murmured an apology and held out a plate of biscuits. They had not been in evidence when he came in. He limited himself to one. As he talked, he became vaguely aware of other changes in the room. The fire had been lit . . . a table moved . . . Ah! The photograph had disappeared from the mantel. Interesting!

When his tale was done, she did not at first comment, which was a surprise. Instead she said, "And how are things at Fallow?"

"Much the same. We feel the pinch less than most, I expect."

She raised her eyebrows in frank disbelief. "Then how does it feel to be raising the next crop of cannon fodder?"

"Not good."

She smiled bitterly. "How bright and glorious it seemed at the beginning! When I last saw Edward, he was far more upset at his broken leg keeping him out of the war than he was about being a suspected murderer. Another cup? And now we all know better, don't we?"

Uneasy at hearing such defeatist sentiment, Jones accepted another cup.

As she poured, she said, "Edward turning up in Flanders I can understand. He would have enlisted as soon as his leg healed. No question. But to enlist he would have needed an identity. Turning up without any clothes on sounds . . ."

Again she turned her intimidating stare on her visitor. It would not have disgraced Queen Mary. "I do not attend séances, Mr. Jones. I do not read fortunes in tea leaves, nor consult Gypsy witches at fairgrounds. And yet I am convinced that whatever my cousin was mixed up in three years ago was more than natural."

Jones sighed. "I have been trying to avoid that conclusion ever since it all happened, but I think I agree with you. There were too many locked doors, too much of the inexplicable. A rational explanation . . . There wasn't one!"

"Edward thought he was in love with me."

What was the difference between thinking one was in love and actually being in love? "He made no secret of it."

"I mention that only because I really believed he had died. He would never have departed voluntarily without at the very least dropping me a note. Now you say he has returned under equally mysterious circumstances. . . . May I suppose that he was taken against his will and has now escaped?"

"Out of the frying pan?"

She smiled and turned to study the hissing gas.

"I must see him."

"I told Smedley I would visit him again on Friday."

"No, we have departmental minutes on Fridays." A wicked gleam shone in her eyes. "One advantage of being female, Mr. Jones, is that a male employer is always too embarrassed to ask for details if you request a day off."

Shocked again, he coughed awkwardly. "Yes."

"So will you stay over tonight?"

*Oh, yes please!* "Oh, I couldn't possibly—"

"The settee is quite comfortable, my friends tell me. I doubt if the neighbors will notice, and we must hope the zeppelins don't. Not many zeppelins now, anyway—they have these big bombers instead. I have a largish haddock we can share, and potatoes are back in the shops, thank goodness. If you can manage on half a haddock, two potatoes, and a sofa, then you are more than welcome."

"That is exceedingly generous of you!"

"I am most grateful to you for coming here, Mr. Jones," Alice said somberly. "You must tell me how you tracked me down. What is your normal procedure for organizing jailbreaks?"

# 5

Wednesday brought Smedley disaster. Three disasters.

Whatever the war had done, it had not seriously damaged the Royal Mail, which delivered the first two disasters by the morning post. Miss Alice Prescott was "not known" at the Chelsea address. Whether or not Jonathan Oldcastle, Esq. still resided at The Oaks, Druids Close, Kent, the Post Office was not about to admit being aware of the address.

With one hand and a foot, Smedley tore both letters into fragments. Then he had a quiet weep.

The third disaster was even worse. He was told to pack his bags.

He begged. He pleaded. He groveled. Damned tears wouldn't come when they might be useful. The thought of being buried alive in Chichester was the living end. Since his mother had died the house was a tomb. With no servants available now, he would be completely alone with his father. Worse, next Sunday was his twenty-first birthday, so every aunt and cousin and uncle from Land's End to John o' Groats would descend on the returning hero. He would gibber and weep buckets and shock the whole brood of them out of their wits.

"Those are orders, Captain," the medic said coldly. "Besides, we need the beds, old man."

His discharge would take effect as soon as he had been up to the palace to get his medal. Meanwhile he was on sick leave. There was a bus at 12:10. Ta-ta!

Then he remembered Exeter, who would wait and wait and never know why his savior did not return. Ginger Jones was coming back on Friday with whatever plans he had been able to concoct, but Smedley could do nothing by himself. The willies came then. His face did its octopus dance. Tears streamed in torrents. He shook so hard he expected the dressing to fall off his wrist. He gabbled.

"Well . . ." the doctor said unwillingly. "We've got a new lot coming in on Friday. Can put you up till then, I suppose."

Smedley could not even get his thanks out. Two more days! He wanted to kiss the man's hand like a dago.

\*     \*     \*

It felt like midnight, and it was still not lunchtime. He wandered out into the entrance hall, which was almost the only public space in the building. On a rainy day, like this one, it was crammed with uniformed men, those mobile enough to leave their beds. Amid all the bandages and crutches and wheelchairs there were dominoes and draughts, bridge and newspapers, and much desultory, bored conversation.

Dr. Stringer came marching in the main door.

Smedley made an about-turn. He headed back to his room and changed into civvies. He would get away with that for about twenty minutes, if he was lucky. He asked a red-haired nurse to tie his Old Fallovian tie for him, so it would look nice.

"Mr. Stringer is extremely busy!" the secretary snapped.

Surgeons were never called "doctor," but fortunately Smedley had remembered that. He should have guessed that surgeons, like golden fleeces, would be guarded by monsters. This particular monster had fortified a stronghold of her own; her rolltop desk was probably armor plated, the wall of filing cabinets behind her cut off half the hallway. Her outer defenses of chairs and tables could not have been bettered by the German high command. It would need at least a full division to advance to that decidedly closed door.

If she could not actually breathe fire, she could certainly look it. "You are not one of his patients, Captain—er . . ."

"Oh, I shan't keep him more than a jiffy! It's a family matter."

The old hussy pouted disbelievingly. "Family?" A surgeon as eminent as Mr. Stringer could not possibly be related to anything lower than a colonel.

"Sort of." Wilting under the glare, Smedley fingered his tie. "Just wanted to pay my respects, don't you know."

Perhaps she had been a schoolmistress in her youth. She wore her hair in a bun and must be at least thirty. Her features had been chipped from granite, but the basilisk eyes narrowed as she appraised the tie. "I'll see if he can spare you a moment, Captain Smedley. Pray take a seat."

He sat on a hard wooden chair and sweated it out. Stringer was another Old Fallovian, but he could not have known Exeter, who had been long after his time. Even by talking to the man, Smedley was breaking trust. But what choice did he have? In less than two days he would be evicted from Staffles and lose all hope of helping Exeter. This was the only lead he had. He need not give John Three's real name. Just make a few inquiries. Find out what the score was. Face seems familiar, maybe? Dare he go that far?

And if the surgeon called his bluff, the provost sergeant would break Smedley into pieces in seconds.

He studied the *Illustrated London News* and saw not a line of it. Oddly enough, though, his hand was so steady that the paper wasn't even shaking. Funny, that. No accounting for the willies.

"Mr. Stringer will see you now, Captain."

*     *     *

The office was a cramped oblong with a small, high window and green-painted walls. It had probably been a butler's pantry originally, because scars on the wall showed where built-in cupboards had been ripped out when the Army took over. There was barely room for a desk, two filing cabinets, and a couple of chairs. The chair behind the desk looked comfortable. The one in front was not.

Stringer rose and extended his left hand. Smedley had not yet decided whether he appreciated that courtesy or regarded it as patronizing. In this case it had been offered to show that the surgeon had fast reactions.

He was short, fortyish, starting to grow plump, and his fair hair was parted in the middle. His suit had cost fifty guineas on Savile Row. His manner was brusque and arrogant, which was to be expected of surgeons. He had an unhealthy hospital pallor, as if he rarely went outdoors. His eyes were fishily prominent, and they had registered the tie.

"Do take a seat, Captain. Smoke?" He offered a carved mahogany box, English and Egyptian.

Smedley accepted a chair and a Dunhill. Stringer took the same and lit both fags with a vesta. He leaned back to put his visitor at ease. He smiled politely.

"I was not aware that we were related."

"Adopted family, sir."

*"Esse non sapere?"*

"That certainly applied in Flanders!" *To be, not to know.*

Stringer nodded approvingly. "Fallow has more than done its share in this war, Captain. Forty-four old boys have made the Supreme Sacrifice, last I heard. I feel sorry for the youngsters there now. Grim lookout, what?"

"Bloody awful."

The lookout for a sixth former now was a great deal worse than the lookout for a successful surgeon with a prosperous Harley Street practice, who probably regarded his weekly consultation at Staffles as all the Empire could legitimately expect from him in the way of war effort. Field hospitals would be beneath a man of his eminence.

He was smiling the sort of smile that medical professors taught their best students. "You are assured of an honored place in the school annals yourself, Captain. Sorry I hadn't registered you were here. Jolly good show. We can all be proud of you."

Willies gibbered in the rafters. Smedley shuddered and fought them back.

Stringer's eyebrows rose fractionally. "And what can I do for you today?"

What Smedley wanted to say was, *Don't let them send me away from here!*

What he did say was, "Er . . ."

"Yes?"

"Er . . ." He was choking, he could not breathe. "Er . . . er . . ."

Stringer patiently trimmed the ash on his cigarette in the ashtray, looking at that and nothing else.

"Er . . ."

Still the doctor kept his eyes down. "Take your time, old man. It just takes a little while to get it out of your system. You're still fresh out of Hades."

"Er . . ."

"We've got lots worse than you. Not my specialty, of course. Not my patients, most of them. Can't amputate memories, unfortunately."

They all *said* this sort of guff at Staffles, but it wasn't what they *thought*. What they thought was *coward* and *weakling,* just like the guv'nor did. When Smedley was thrown out of here, he was going to have to face a world that thought like that.

Still Stringer studied his cigarette, while Smedley's face burned like a sunset and twitched and twitched. His lips and tongue would do nothing but slaver. Why had he come here? Any minute he would blurt out something about Exeter. . . .

"Some poor devils can't even remember their own names," Stringer said offhandedly, putting his cigarette back in his mouth. He took a letter from a wire basket and scanned it. "Got one chappie upstairs hasn't spoken a word since the day he was brought in. Understands English, though. He reacts—tries not to, but he does. Understands German, too."

*Good God! He knew!*

"But I don't really think the German's too significant," Stringer remarked, frowning at the page.

"Probably not," Smedley agreed. Exeter had always been a sponge for languages. Stringer knew who he was!

"Interesting chappie. Picked up in the middle of a battle without a stitch on him, just outside Ypres. No account of how he got there. And he can't tell us. Or won't, perhaps. There was some talk of just standing him up against a wall and shooting him."

"Why didn't they?" said a voice astonishingly like Smedley's own.

Stringer looked up cautiously and seemed to approve of what he saw. He dropped the letter back in the tray. "Well, it's a rum do. His hair, for one thing."

"Hair, sir?"

"He had a full beard and his hair was down over his ears, like a woman's. I needn't quote King's Regulations to you, Captain, and I dare say the Kaiser feels the same way about lice." Stringer drew on his cigarette, eyebrows cocked quirkily to indicate that this was all frightfully jolly and nobody need get overwrought. The fishy eyes gleamed. He spun his chair around and opened a drawer in one of the filing cabinets. "At any rate," he said over his shoulder, "our mystery man was no soldier. That's certain. And then there was his tan. I suppose the south of France is a possibility."

"Tan, sir?" Hospital pallor?

"He had a tan. A corker of a tan." Stringer spun around to face his visitor again, thumbing through a file. "Yes, here it is. 'When stripped, the patient appeared to be wearing white shorts. This pigmentation is only compatible with recent, extended exposure to a tropical climate.' Then he turns up outside Ypres in the wettest summer in fifty years. Odd, isn't it?"

Now the surgeon put his arrogant stare to work, but Smedley was past noticing. Now he knew why Exeter had not been shot as a spy. But he wasn't much further forward. There was still a murder in the background, and now there was also the problem of how Stringer had known. . . .

The surgeon was smiling.

"How?" Smedley asked weakly.

Smirking. "Best fast bowler the school's had this century. Saw him get that hat trick against Eton."

Lord, who would ever forget that day! The willies grabbed Smedley's eyeballs and squeezed.

"Astonishing thing is that no one else's recognized him yet!" Stringer sighed. "What the hell are we going to do?"

"You? You, sir? You'll help, sir?"

"Don't you want me to?"

"Yes, oh, yes! Would you? I mean he was just about my best friend and I'll do anything I can to get him out and clear his—"

"Ah, yes. There is that, isn't there?"

Smedley considered the awful prospect that he had walked into a trap. He had never spoken to this man before, and now he had betrayed his pal. The chance that Stringer would jeopardize a notable career and even risk a prison sentence for abetting the escape of a suspected spy was not the sort of hypothesis even a shell-shocked . . .

But the doctor had already known.

"Nothing too serious physically," Stringer muttered, perusing the file. "He picked up some scratches in the mud, of course, and that stuff swarms with microbes. Gas gangrene, tetanus—we have antitoxins now, thank the Lord. Not like 1915. And he got some mustard gas blisters." He looked up warily. "But he's basically sound, physically that is. You said you were chums? I'd have thought he was a year or two behind you."

"He seems to have worn well." Smedley had not. "Sir, I will never believe Exeter stabbed a man in the back!"

Stringer pulled a face. "Not what they taught at Fallow in my day! The investigation was thoroughly botched, you know. Some country bobby who'd never dealt with anything worse than poaching. The Home Office sacked the general over it. That wasn't the story, but it's true. He should have called in Scotland Yard or shouted for aid from the next county."

But what did they do now?

"Just as well," Stringer said, glancing at his watch. "No fingerprints on file. So Mrs. Bodgley tells me. I have to make my rounds right away. We'll have the man in here after and talk it over. You can manage for a half hour or so?"

He smiled quietly and eased the file across to the other side of his desk. Then he stubbed out his cigarette, rose to his feet, and pranced out the door in his fifty-guinea suit. Smedley's mouth was still hanging open.

# 6

Had Smedley really thought about it, he would have said that he could no more sit still for half an hour in that cramped little office than his battery could have shelled Berlin from Flanders. Yet he did not go off his rocker. The walls did not fall on him. The willies stayed away, although it was probably nearly a whole hour before he was interrupted.

He had serious planning to do. He must devise a way to smuggle Exeter out of Staffles. After a while he decided that could be arranged. But where could the fugitive run to once he was outside the walls?

He considered Chichester and his gorge rose. In theory an empty house with no tattling servants around would be an ideal hideout, but there would be recurring plagues of aunts. Worse, the guv'nor had no use for Exeter. He blamed Exeter's father for the Nyagatha massacre, claiming the man had gone native. He'd accepted the son's guilt in the Bodgley case right away. Scratch Chichester!

There was Fallow. Term did not start for another ten days. Ginger could arrange something.

So that was settled. Now he had to think of a way to pass the information to Exeter when he was brought in, and right under Stringer's nose, too—another midnight expedition to the west wing would be tempting the gods. He found paper in the desk drawer. Writing left-handed was a bugger. Do *not* begin, "Dear Exeter!"

*Tomorrow night will set off fire alarm. Try to slip away in the confusion. Left at bottom of stair. The yard wall is climbable. Go right. Look for Boadicea's chariot at crossroads, half a mile. Good luck.*

He added: *God bless!* and felt a little shamefaced about that.

Even folding a paper one-handed was tricky, but he wadded the note small and slipped it in his trouser pocket. Then he sat back to examine the file Stringer had so generously left for him.

Boadicea's chariot was Ginger's Austin roadster. Smedley could write a quick letter and catch the evening post with it. It would reach Fallow in the morning—perhaps. If it did not arrive until the afternoon, that would cut things very fine. He had better walk down to the village after dinner and telephone.

He realized that he was staring blankly at some appalling handwriting and medical jargon. He pulled his wits together—what was left of them—and began to read. He was not much wiser when he got to the end than he had been at the beginning, except on one point. The doctors knew that John Three was a shirker. He would certainly be thrown in the clink very shortly.

Two points. The stretcher-bearers who had witnessed his arrival all swore he had dropped out of the sky.

Smedley jumped as the door swung open. It swung a long way, hiding him from whoever was outside.

"Hand me that chair, would you, Miss Pimm?" Stringer's voice said with breezy authority. In a hospital, a surgeon ranked just above God. "I am not to be disturbed. You needn't wait, Sergeant. We'll send word when we need to ship him back. Come in here, Three."

There was barely room for another chair and two more men and a closing door. Exeter had not expected Smedley. His blue eyes flickered anger for a moment and then went stony blank. He was wearing flannels, a tweed jacket, and a shirt with no tie. He stood like a tailor's dummy as the surgeon squeezed past him to reach his desk.

Stringer sat down and gazed up fishily at the patient.

Smedley shrank back on his seat.

Exeter just stood and looked at the wall. He was tall and lean, as he'd always been. In daylight his cheekbones still bore the inexplicable tan. But his chin and ears . . . long hair like a woman's? *Exeter?*

"Sit down, Exeter," the surgeon said. Nothing happened, and he sighed. "I know you, man! I shook your hand in June 1914. I have discussed your strange disappearance extensively with Mrs. Bodgley. I have read the reports on your equally mysterious reappearance. I know more about your odd goings-on than anyone in the world, I expect."

Still no reaction. How could the man *stand* it? According to the file, he had not spoken a word in three weeks.

"You'll be more comfortable sitting down, Exeter," Stringer said sharply. He would not meet defiance very often. "Cigarette?"

Nothing. Smedley's skin crawled. As the box came his way he shook his head. He needed another Dunhill, but he also needed his hand free.

"Captain?" said the surgeon. "You try."

"I didn't tell him, Edward. He already knew."

No reaction at all.

Smedley felt the willies brush over his skin. Exeter thought he was a traitor. Stringer was scowling at him, as if this were all his fault. Didn't they realize he was just a broken coward, a shell-shocked wreck of a man? Didn't they know he was liable to crack up and start weeping at the first sign of trouble? Please, lord, don't let me get the jitters now!

"I'm leaving here the day after tomorrow, Edward. Dr.—Mr. Stringer showed me your file. They're on to you! I wrote to those two people you named and both letters came back this morning, addressees unknown." He stared up at that unchanging witless expression and suddenly exploded. *"For god's sake, old man! We're trying to help you!"*

He might as well have spoken to the desk. Exeter did not move a muscle.

Stringer chuckled drily. "The most remarkable case of *esse non sapere* I ever saw."

Smedley discovered he was on his feet, eye to eye with Exeter, which must mean he was on tiptoe, because he was three inches shorter. He grabbed at lapels with one hand and a stump, and Exeter staggered back under the assault.

"You bastard!" Smedley shrilled. "We're trying to help! You don't trust me! Well, screw you, you bastard!" Shriller yet. He had not planned this, but he might as well use it. He had his back to Stringer. He stuffed the note down inside Exeter's shirt collar. "I didn't go through all that the other night to help an ungrateful *bastard* who—who—" He was weeping, damn it! His face was going again. Full-fledged willies!

"Sorry, old man," Exeter said quietly, easing him aside. "Mr. Stringer?"

The surgeon rose and reached across the desk. "I'm honored once again to shake the hand that humbled the fearsome ranks of Eton."

"Those were the days," Edward said in a sad voice. He sat down. "You have a good memory for faces, sir."

"Good memory for cricket. Did you kill Timothy Bodgley?"

"No, sir."

"Are you a traitor to your King?"

"No, sir."

Happy to be ignored, Smedley sat down also, and shook like a jelly. He had done it! He had passed the note. "Perhaps I do need that fag, sir," he muttered. He helped himself and leaned forward to the march, sucking a blessed lungful of smoke.

Stringer, too, drew on his cigarette, eying his prisoner.

Exeter gazed back with an unnerving steely calm.

The surgeon blew a smoke ring. "You say you're not a traitor, and I accept your word on it. But when you made your dramatic appearance amidst the battle's thunder, you were talking."

"Just shock, sir. It hits those who—Just shock."

"Daresay. But you were babbling about treason and spies. If you have any important information, I want it. It's your duty to—"

Exeter was shaking his head. "Nothing to do with the war, sir."

"Tell me anyway."

"Friends of mine in another war altogether. I was not expecting to arrive where I arrived. I was tricked, betrayed."

"You'll have to do better than that."

"I can't, sir. You would dismiss it as lunatic babbling. It has nothing to do with the Germans, the Empire, the French . . . no concern of yours at all, sir. You have my oath on it."

The two stared bleakly across the desk at each other.

"You're saying that someone wants you dead, is that it?"

"That is very much it, sir. But I can't even try to explain."

Exeter's foot pressed down on Smedley's instep.

He choked on a mouthful of smoke, remembering Ginger Jones sitting on that bench on Saturday.

"Someone tried to kill him at Fallow," the schoolmaster had said. "They ran that spear right through his mattress. Someone tried to kill him at the Grange and got young Bodgley instead. When he disappeared from Albert Memorial I was afraid that they had scuppered him at last. Now you say he's turned up in the middle of a battlefield? It sounds as if he's a hard man to kill."

*Stringer?*

Exeter was trying to say that the surgeon wanted to kill him?

Perhaps Captain Smedley was not the worst case of shell shock in Staffles after all.

Suddenly Stringer defused the confrontation with a patronizing chuckle. "Not just the public hangman?"

"Him too, sir. But private enemies also."

"All right! I shall accept your word on this also." He beamed and sat back in his comfortable chair. "All the more reason why we've got to get you out of here, what?"

Smedley gulped.

Exeter showed no change of expression at all. "Why? Why risk your career to help a fugitive escape from justice?"

The surgeon smiled with smug, professional calm. "Not justice, just the law. We can't have the school name dragged in the mud, what? And if some private thugs are after you as well, then that's even more reason. If we can get you out, is there anyone who would take you in?"

Exeter turned a sad look on Smedley. "I thought there might be. Apparently not."

"I think I can arrange a place for him," Smedley said.

"Ah! Somewhere secure?" the surgeon inquired blandly.

Why ask? And Exeter's foot was warning him again.

"No names, no pack drill, sir."

Stringer's chuckle did not quite reach his eyes—or was that just another illusion? "If he is apprehended, Captain, then my part in the affair may become known. I must be sure you have a safe haven ready for him."

*Shot while trying to escape?*

This was totally crazy! A distinguished surgeon was offering to let a suspected murderer and spy escape from his care, and the aforesaid spy was hinting that the aforesaid surgeon was actually trying to kill him, and Julian Smedley was believing both of them. He had definitely cracked.

"A school friend, sir, Allan Gentile. He and I were in the Somme cock-up together. He got a Blighty."

"A what?" Exeter said.

Smedley and the surgeon exchanged shocked glances.

"A wound. Brought him Home to Blighty—England."

"Ah."

Where had the man been for the last three years not to have heard that expression? Still, Allan Gentile had died of scarlet fever in 1913, and Exeter must remember that, so he would know this was all drip.

Stringer seemed satisfied. "Good. Now, how do you propose to get him off the premises?"

"He can go as me, sir." Smedley fished out his pay book and flourished it. "I've got a chit for the bus to Canterbury, a chit for a railway ticket to Chichester." He turned to Exeter and leaned a foot on his instep. "The window in your WC is directly above the washing shed roof. Sneak out just before dawn on Friday."

Exeter waited inscrutably. He still looked like the peach-faced boy of 1914, but something inside him must be a hundred years old.

Smedley ad-libbed some more. "There's a derelict summer house about halfway down the drive, on the left. Meet me there. My pay book will get you through the gate."

"It will be a very close run thing," Exeter said impassively. "They'll miss me when they do the morning rounds."

"They'll search the house first," Smedley snapped. It was a wet rag of a plan. It would not convince the present audience if Exeter himself started picking holes in it.

Stringer frowned, tapping ash from his cigarette with a surgeon's thick finger. "I'll try and get down here again tomorrow evening and stay over. If I'm around in the morning I may be able to muddy the waters a little."

Now that was definitely going too far! The surgeon had just strayed right out of bounds. Smedley felt a shiver of joy as if the spotters had reported he had found the range. He nudged Exeter's foot.

"I'll look like a scarecrow in your togs," Exeter complained.

"You look like a scarecrow already. I'll try and filch something better from the laundry. If you've got a better idea, spit it out."

"I haven't. But what happens to you?"

"I shall be discovered eventually, bound and gagged in my underwear. How could you do such a thing to a cripple, you rotter?"

"You'll freeze!" Stringer protested. He eyed Smedley suspiciously. "You may be there for hours. Can you really take that in your condition, Captain?"

It would drive him utterly gaga in ten minutes. But it wasn't going to happen. "I'll manage."

"Good show!" Stringer said approvingly. "Now we know how you collected all those medals. It's audacious! And ingenious! You agree, Exeter?"

"I'm very grateful to both of you."

"Just a small recompense for some of the finest cricket I ever saw. Now, where does he find Gentile?"

Smedley almost said, "Who?"

Again the man was showing too much curiosity. Chichester itself would sound a little too convenient. Somewhere handy? "Bognor Regis. Seventeen Kitchener Street, behind the station."

Stringer glanced at his watch and reached for the cigarette box. "Excellent! Now, Exeter, I have a small favor to ask."

"Sir?"

"I want to hear where you've been these last three years—how you escaped from Greyfriars, how you turned up in Flanders. Just to satisfy my own curiosity."

For the first time, Exeter's stony calm seemed to crack a little. "Sir, if I even hint at my story, you will lock me up in a straitjacket and a padded cell!"

"No. I accept that there are things going on around you that have no obvious rational explanation. You can't spout any tale taller than the things I have already tried to imagine to account for your appearances and disappearances." The surgeon was brandishing his full authority now. "I don't expect I shall ever see you again after you walk out of this room. So I want the story. The truth, however mad it may be." The smile did not hide the threat: no story, no escape.

Exeter bit his lip and glanced at Smedley.

"Don't mind me, old chap!" Smedley said. "I'm already round the bend, as the sailors say."

Exeter sighed. "There are other worlds."

Stringer nodded. "Sort of astral planes, you mean?"

"Sort of, but not this world at all. Another planet. Sir, won't you let me leave it at that?"

"No. I can see that there must be some paranormal explanation for the way you come and go, and I won't go to my grave wondering. Talk on."

Exeter sighed again and crossed his legs. "I was on another world, which we call *Nextdoor*. It's a sort of reflection of Earth—very like in some ways, very different in others. The animal life's different, the geography's different, but the sun's the same, the stars are the same. The people are indistinguishable from Europeans, everything from Italians to Swedes."

He paused to study Stringer's reaction. "See? You can't possibly believe I'm not raving or spinning a cuffer."

"It sounds like Jules Verne," the surgeon admitted. "How did you get to Elfinland?"

"I went to Stonehenge, took all my clothes off, and performed a sacred dance." Exeter pulled a shamefaced smile. "You sure you want to hear any more?"

"Oh, absolutely! Why Stonehenge?"

"It's what we—what they call a node. They're sort of naturally holy places. There are lots of them, and they often have churches or old ruins on them or standing stones. You know that creepy feeling you get in old buildings? That's what they call *virtuality*, and it means you're sensing a node. If you know a suitable key—that's the dance and chant—then a node can act as a portal. Somehow the nodes on this world connect with nodes on Nextdoor or one of the other worlds. People have been going and coming for hundreds . . . probably thousands, of years. You have to know the ritual, though."

Smedley wondered how Exeter had managed to dance with a broken leg, but Stringer did not seem to have thought of that. He was nodding as if he could almost believe—or was he just humoring the maniac?

"How do they work, though?"

"I don't know, sir, I really haven't the foggiest. The best explanation I ever got was from a man named Rawlinson, but it was mostly just wordplay. Let's see if I can remember how he put it. It was about a year ago. . . . I'd been on Nextdoor for two years by then, and I'd finally met up with . . . call them *strangers*—other visitors, like me—people who understand all this. Some of them have been back and forth lots of times. They call themselves the Service.

"The Service have a station—much like a Government station in the colonies somewhere. In fact, it's not unlike Nyagatha, where I was born, in Kenya. Prof Rawlinson's made a study of the crossing-over business and come up with some theories. . . ."

Exeter had always carried conviction. As he continued to talk, Smedley found himself caught up in what had to be the strangest story he had ever heard, and somehow he found himself slipping into unwilling belief.

# 7

"What Rawlinson said was, 'It's a matter of dimensions. We live in a three-dimensional world. Can you imagine a two-dimensional world?'

"Of course I had to tell him that maths had never been my long suit. Then he produced a pack of cards. . . ."

That wasn't quite true, Edward recalled. The cards had been lying on the other table at the far end of the veranda, at least twenty feet away, so Rawlinson had not fetched them himself. He had shouted for a Carrot, and the Carrot had come and brought over the cards to him. That was how the *tyikank* did things in Olympus. But how could anyone ever explain Olympus to these two—the surgeon, as smug in his chair as a Persian cat, almost purring with self-satisfaction . . . or Smedley, poor sod, with the skin of his face stretched so tight over the bone that it looked ready to split open, with glimmers of hellfire inside his eyeballs and little nervous ticks of smiles jerking the corner of his mouth every few seconds as he listened to poor crazy old Exeter talking himself into a lifetime padded cell.

"He pulled out a king and a jack. Two two-dimensional people, he called them—length and width, but no thickness. He put them face-to-face and then asked me, could they see each other? I said I supposed not.

"He said, 'Right. They can't, because they're not in quite the same plane. They're separated by a very small thickness, and their world contains no thickness.' "

Edward remembered how triumphantly Rawlinson had beamed, then. Prof was a spare, sandy-haired man with the fussy, pedantic manner of an Oxford don, but he looked no more than twenty, most of the time. His English had an odd burr, which might be more historical than geographical. He knew a lot and his mind was quick, but there was something essentially impractical about Prof, a hint of that most damning of all indictments: *not quite sound.* If you needed a detailed report with graphs and illustrations and references, fine—very good chap. Else put him in charge of the sports program.

Materially, he was doing very well. His bungalow was large, one of the inner circle of residences surrounding the node, and he must own one of the finest collections of books in the Vales, where printing was a very recent innovation. He had at least a dozen servants, all rigged out in snowy white livery.

But Stringer and Smedley would not be interested in all that.

"I said, 'You're telling me that Nextdoor and Earth are separated in some other dimension?' and he said, 'It's more complicated. If it were only one dimension, then Home would have only two neighbors, but there are at least six worlds that can be reached directly from Home. We know of only two others from Nextdoor, but then we don't know very much about this world outside the Vales. So we must be dealing with more than one extra dimension. I know it's hard enough to think in four dimensions without throwing five or six at you.'"

Edward was alarmed to hear himself chuckle. "I remember taking a long drink at that point. I couldn't cope with this while sober."

All the time he'd been on Nextdoor, he'd been homesick for Earth. And now he was Home, he felt his heart twisting as he talked of Olympus. He recalled the dry fragrance of the air, tantalizing scents of spice or dried flowers; hot by day, cooling off rapidly in the evening when the *tyikank* gathered on their verandas to drink gin and blue . . .

He looked again at his audience—Stringer's eyes half closed as he dribbled smoke, Julian's wide, too wide.

"I warned you this was going to take a lot of swallowing! It even stuck in my throat, and I'd *done* it—I mean, I'd actually crossed over to another world. No offense, Mr. Stringer, but this is a too practical, down-to-earth setting for fairy tales. I told you you wouldn't be able to believe me. I had trouble believing Prof, although I knew I wasn't on Earth, and hadn't been for two years. Look here: desk, papers, telephone, filing cabinet! Whereas I was sitting in a wicker chair drinking what they call gin, but isn't, on a veranda with screens around it. The trees had an African look to them, you know?— airy traceries with foliage hovering around the branches more like clouds of smoke or insects than leaves. There were mountains like white teeth behind them, going straight up into a pale, bloodless blue sky. My drink had been brought by a liveried servant who addressed me as *Tyika* Kisster. Prof and I were dolled up in white tie and tails—he'd asked me to come a little early so we could have a private chat, but a dozen or more other guests would be arriving shortly and his wife was indoors overseeing the final touches."

Chattering like this was madness! The sparkle in Smedley's eyes was welcome. The poor devil seemed to be enjoying the guff, and anything that took his mind off his own personal internal hell for even a few minutes was worth doing. But Stringer wasn't going to believe a word of it. Edward Exeter, alias John Three, was cutting his own throat with all this babbling. Trouble was, he'd been silent for so long that now he'd started to speak, he couldn't stop himself. . . .

\*       \*       \*

The veranda fronted on a garden of flowering shrubs and carefully scythed lawn, a surprise of green fertility in the khaki dryness of Olympus. Teams of servants must water it frequently to keep it so lush.

Scattered amid the woods were more of the *tyikank*'s sprawling bungalows, clustered around the node. An irregular line of denser, dark-foliaged trees marked the course of the Cam. The natives' village lay a mile or so downstream.

To the west, the jagged sword of the Matterhorn towered over everything, a stark silhouette. Opposite stood Mount Cook and Nanga Parbat and Kilimanjaro's perfect cone, a poem in itself. All three were flushing pink and salmon and peach in the sunset. The valley lay like a palm between them, the Matterhorn being the thumb and the other three raised fingers. Several minor summits might qualify as the pinkie. He had not learned all their names yet.

"They're two slightly different aspects of the same world," Prof said, "two cards in the same pack, no two identical. Make two slices through, oh, say a Stilton cheese, and you won't get exactly the same pattern of maggot holes each time, what?"

Edward thought longingly of Stilton cheese. "The stars are the same."

"Ah! You noticed that? Small things are different, big things are the same. The beetles have eight legs. The sun looks exactly the same. The planets are very much the same, so far's I've been able to find out. The year's a little shorter, this world's axial tilt's a little less, days are about three minutes longer."

"How can you know that? You can't bring a watch over with you."

Rawlinson smiled knowingly. "But you can go back and forth. Sometimes you arrive at the same time of day, sometimes later or earlier. It works out to about three minutes' lag per day."

Edward had walked into that one. Even so . . . "Nextdoor has four moons. Moons are not exactly small."

"You're wrong!" Prof beamed excitedly. "Oh, they're big, but they may be caused by very small effects. A trumpet can't knock down a forest, can it?"

"No." Edward could not see what a trumpet had to do with moons, but he knew he was about to find out.

"But suppose there's an avalanche poised to fall? Then the trumpet call might set off the avalanche! There goes your forest. Now, it's generally agreed that the Moon was knocked off the Earth by a giant meteor, you know. The Pacific Ocean is the scar remaining. A meteor hit is a very chancy business. If the meteor comes by even a second or two earlier or later, it will miss the Earth altogether. Both bodies are moving at tremendous speed, remember! So it struck Nextdoor slightly differently. The debris coalesced into four small moons instead of one large one. Even Trumb is quite small. It just looks big because it's very close." Prof reached for his glass triumphantly. "Or perhaps there were several hits."

"How about the other worlds?"

"Other slices, remember? More variations. Gehenna has two moons, or so I've been told. Never been there." Rawlinson took a long drink. He was just hitting his stride, glad of an audience. "Back to our flat friends. We agree that they can't see each other, because they're not in the same plane. These cards can't be perfect planes, can they? No such thing as a perfectly flat surface. But if they're face-to-face, then they must touch here and there, what?"

"The nodes!"

"Right you are! The flat cards touch at a few points. And where worlds touch, you have a node—a portal, a hole in reality."

"And the keys pull you through that hole!"

"Across. Or through, I suppose. Apparently."

"But how do they work?"

The enthusiasm faded slightly. "Good question. It's all mental, of course."

"It is?"

"Absolutely. Only people can cross over. You can't bring anything with you—no clothes, no money, nothing."

"Not even the fillings in my teeth."

Rawlinson raised his sandy eyebrows. "Do the cavities bother you?" He grinned, seemingly suddenly very juvenile.

"I picked up some mana, and they healed themselves." Edward could also recall a scar on his forehead that had vanished and certain other scars on his chest that had persisted in trying to disappear when he had wanted them not to.

"That's what usually happens," Prof said smugly. "But whatever makes crossing over possible is something only the human brain can achieve. The keys themselves don't do it, I'm sure. They're not magical incantations; they only work internally. You could teach a parrot the song, but it wouldn't work. Rhythm, words, dance—somehow they induce a particular vibration or something in the mind, a resonance. The music of the spheres, what? The mind soars in splendor, it roams, it drifts across the gap. Then it hauls the rest of you after it. I think that's why we feel so bloody awful afterward. The brain's in shock."

Edward squirmed. "Does it always work? I mean, from what you say, then sometimes the mind might go and the body not follow? Can that happen?"

"Yes, it can. Sometimes. You ready for a refill?"

"Not yet, thank you. Now explain mana to me."

"Wish I could. How much have you learned already?"

How much should he admit to knowing? His report was going to be completely truthful, of course, but there were certain episodes in his recent past that he . . . did not intend to stress.

"I know that Colonel Creighton talked about charisma. I know it's something that only happens to strangers. He had no occult power on Earth, but as soon as he arrived back on Nextdoor he could throw thunderbolts."

"Because he hadn't been born here," Rawlinson agreed. "Where you're born is what matters. If you ever father a son here, my lad, then he'll be a native. Take him back to Earth and he'd be a stranger there. I can't give you an explanation, but I'll give you another picture. Suppose we're all born with a sort of shield, a kind of mental armor.

Suppose that it doesn't cross over with us—that fits the case, doesn't it? Without the shield, you can absorb mana. With a shield there, very little can get through."

"And what is mana?"

Rawlinson sighed like an old, old man. "I wish I knew!" he said wearily. "It comes from admiration. It comes from obedience. It comes from just plain old faith. We breathe it in and blow it out again as power. It works most easily on the mind, of course. You must have discovered the authority you have here! Give orders and the natives will jump to obey 'em.

"At higher levels, mana can work on the body, as in faith healing or those yogi chappies who can sit around on an ice field in the altogether. In really high concentrations, it can influence the physical world. Then you're into miracles, Indian rope trick, teleportation, and all that." He discovered his glass was empty. "Carrot!"

A servant hurried out from the house door. He was probably sixty or older, although still trim and alert. His close-cropped hair had once been a fiery red; now the embers were streaked with ash. He wore white trousers with knife-edge creases down the front, a white tunic buttoned to a high collar. Very smart. His shoes were a shiny black.

"Ah, there you are," Prof said. "Sure you're not ready for another, old man?"

"Not just yet, thank you, sir."

The servant bowed slightly and withdrew.

The natives were always referred to as Carrots. Edward wondered if they had any idea what the word implied. He rather hoped they did not. They must have a name for themselves in their own language. Nextdoor's vegetation was completely unlike Earth's; it included some carrotlike vegetables, but they were not carrot colored.

Prof was off on his hobbyhorse again. "Strangers have the ability to absorb mana and redirect it as magic, but even natives can have it in some measure. 'Charisma' is as good a term as you'll find. Napoleon obviously had it. His soldiers worshiped him. He led them into the jaws of hell—they followed him and loved him for it. Caesar the same. Mohammed." He eyed Edward with wry amusement. "You can think of others, I'm sure."

"But Napoleon could not work miracles!"

"Couldn't he? Some of his opponents thought he did. And he was only a native, not even a stranger. Where do you draw the line? If a general or a statesman inspires his followers with a rousing speech, is that magic?"

Edward conceded the point. "No."

"Even if they are moved to superhuman efforts?"

"Probably not."

"Then how about faith healing? Mental telepathy? Foretelling the future? Where do you draw the line? When does the uncanny become the impossible?"

"When scientists can't measure it?"

"They can't measure love either. Don't you believe in love?"

Edward chuckled. Obviously this speech had been made many times before.

"You came through an untried portal, I hear." Rawlinson rubbed his chin. "That's very interesting! Creighton took a hell of a risk there. Could have landed you anywhere on Nextdoor or on some other world altogether."

"He was relying on the prophecy. It said I would appear in Sussvale."

"I wouldn't have risked it. Still, all's well that ends well. And you arrived in the Sacrarium? That's useful to know. What key did you use?"

Edward tapped out a beat on the table with his fingers. *"Affalino kaspik . . ."*

"Oh, yes, that one," Prof said, watching the Carrot replace his empty glass with a full one. "Don't try that rascal here at Olympus, my boy! It'll flip you to Gehenna. Nasty spot! *Affalino* was a sound choice, though. It does seem to connect Europe to the Vales pretty often. It works the other way sometimes. There's a portal in Mapvale it opens to somewhere in the Balkans. Near Trieste, I think. And others."

The servant stepped backward a couple of paces and bowed before turning away.

Almost like being back in Africa . . . not quite. The natives of the Vales were whites, and in this valley they were all redheads. It happened that way quite often. Blue eyes here, brown eyes there. In one valley the women would all be flat-chested, in the next breasts would be heavy as melons and lush as ripe peaches. The larger vales had varied populations of several "European" types; the little side glens, when they were habitable at all, each cut their sons and daughters from a single cloth. Olympians had hair as red as any Gael. They also had green eyes and skin like sand beaches, freckles on freckles on freckles.

Edward had a houseboy of his own now. Dommi was about the same age as he, but shorter and wider. And freckles! Every time he blinked, Edward expected to see freckles flake off his eyelids. He was a tough little mule. He wore nothing but a loincloth, even first thing in the morning when the valley was decidedly nippy. The soles of his feet were as thick as steaks and hard as iron; he could run along a gravel path like a gazelle. He was as much a white man as Edward—even whiter, really—but he was a native and Edward was a stranger. So he was the servant and Edward the *tyika.*

After roughing it for so long, formal evening wear felt very odd. Three days had not begun to blunt the strangeness of Olympus. Nor had they taught the newcomer all the intricacies of accepted social behavior. Even speaking English again was alien to him now.

The natives spoke a version of Randorian, which was pretty much a dialect of Thargian. They would have their own names for the Cam River and Kilimanjaro and the Matterhorn. They probably did not call the *tyika* settlement Olympus. Edward wondered what they did call it.

The strangers spoke English among themselves. They sprinkled it with Thargian words—or even Joalian—but by and large their English would have been understood on Regent Street. Yet they always referred to themselves as *tyikank.* Odd, that. Why not use the English equivalent, "masters"?

They had a childish fondness for nicknames. Rawlinson was known as Prof, and he seemed to cultivate a dry, academic style. Edward was still "Exeter" to the men, "Mr. Exeter" to the women. Once his status and duties became established, he would probably pick up some informal title of his own. He already suspected it would be "Tinker." His

identity as the Liberator was officially a secret, for if the Chamber ever learned where
he was, then even Olympus itself might not be safe for him.

"You know mana exists, Exeter!" Prof lowered his voice and leaned closer. "They
say you've actually met two of the Pentatheon?"

Edward nodded and emptied his glass. He had not yet learned the levers and switches
in Olympus; he did not know who was supposed to know what. The *Filoby Testament*
strongly hinted that there were traitors here, in the very heart of the Service. For all he
knew, Rawlinson could be one of them.

"Well, you must know that they can work miracles! They draw their power from
their worshippers' adoration and sacrifices."

Edward had been expecting questions about his own experience with mana, so Rawlinson evidently knew less than he thought he did. As for his "explanations," they were
slick enough, but they left an aftertaste of bamboozlement. The words did not really
mean anything.

"Mostly on nodes? How does that fit your picture, Prof? I can see the nodes being
portals, but why do they increase the flow of mana?"

"Temperature."

"Temperature?"

"Not real temperature, but something like temperature. After all, if another world is
especially close just there, then there could be a leakage of something across the gap.
You must have sensed that feeling of awe we call 'virtuality'? Imagine the nodes as being
in some way hot and the rest of the world as cooler. Now suppose the shield effect is
dependent on this 'temperature.' Sensitive to heat, or whatever the force is. That would
explain why the stranger absorbs the mana best on a node and why his worshippers'
sacrifices are more potent there."

More mumbo jumbo, and yet it did have a sort of logic to it.

"What's the limit?" Edward asked. "Telepathy and prophecy—how far does it go?"
He knew it could kill.

"A long way. Healing, certainly. And prophecy, as you well know. Legends tell of
earthquakes and thunderbolts. Earthly myths do the same. It goes all the way to magic.
Miracle, if you prefer." Rawlinson flashed his boyish smile and laughed. He was starting
to display the results of the gin. "I have no science to give you, old chap! All I can do
is draw pictures."

"They fit the facts," Edward agreed politely. He was becoming a little fizzy, too, and
a long evening loomed ahead. He did believe in miracles. He had worked one himself.

Rawlinson peered around angrily at the door. "Where in the world has my wife got
to, do you suppose? *Carrot!*"

Edward had a few more questions about keys—who had invented them and who
ever dared test a new one—but his host suddenly changed the subject.

"Oh, by the way?"

"Yes?"

"The others'll be here shortly. . . . You hired a houseboy, I understand."

"Jumbo's cook recommended him. A grandson or nephew or something, I expect."

Rawlinson coughed. "Yes. Well, my wife was going by your place this afternoon and saw him. She suggested I drop you a quiet hint."

"I'd appreciate any help you can give me," Edward said, having trouble not adding, "sir," to every sentence. He felt as if he were back at Fallow and had been called into the Head's office. Consciously or unconsciously, Rawlinson was radiating mana at him now.

The manservant glided in, to wait expectantly near the *tyika*'s chair.

Rawlinson did not seem to notice him. "Well, it's just this, old man. We don't encourage the Carrots to run around like savages, you know. That's all very well down in their own wallow, but up here we try to teach them more civilized ways."

Back in the baking heat of the afternoon, young Dommi had scrubbed every floor in the bungalow and most of the walls as well. He'd been working like a horse and sweating like a pig. Shiny shoes and white uniform?

"I'll have a word with him."

"And do see he cuts his hair, old man. Shipshape and Bristol fashion, what?"

Dommi's hair hung down his back like a flag of burnished copper. He was very proud of it.

"It seems clean enough," Edward protested.

Rawlinson pulled a disapproving face. "They look much better with it short. More civilized. You mustn't let them get away with a thing, or you'll never get any work out of them at all. Bone lazy, the lot of them."

Edward had suggested Dommi take the evening off and go courting his beloved Ayetha. The youngster had been shocked. The *tyika*'s house was not yet completely cleaned up. There were still many dishes to unpack and wash. There were the *tyika*'s clothes to iron, and food to be fetched and prepared, and the garden must be dug over. His father would be horrified if he took time off while there was work waiting to be done.

Dommi was pathetically anxious to please.

"So far he had shown no signs of laziness at all! He works like a . . . He works very hard."

"Just you wait!" Rawlinson said. "As soon as he's saved up a few shillings he'll buy himself a wife and that'll be the last you'll see of any work out of him." He frowned up at the waiting Carrot. "What's the *Entyika* doing, d'you know?"

"She is supervising the cooks, *Tyika*."

Rawlinson grunted angrily. "Remind her we have a guest here, will you?" He waved the man away. "Bone lazy," he repeated, "the whole lot of 'em."

# 8

"Incredible!" Stringer muttered. He coughed, stubbing out a cigarette. His bulging eyes were red from the bite of the smoke that filled the little office.

Smedley's mind was spinning. *Incredible* did not do justice! And yet no one who knew Exeter would ever doubt his word. He spoke always with a quiet deliberation that compelled belief. Lying would be beneath him, even if his life depended on it. He had always been like that.

"These magical places?" the surgeon demanded. "There was one in Flanders?"

"Must have been," Exeter agreed hoarsely. "There may have been a church there before the war or a cemetery."

"And another in the hospital in Greyfriars?"

"Er, no, sir."

"So someone rescued you and took you elsewhere?"

Exeter set his jaw. After a moment he said, "No names, no pack drill, sir."

Stringer let his annoyance show. Then he glanced at his watch. "By Jove! I must be gone. Dining with some bigwigs tonight! Well, it's a fascinating tale! Wish I had time to hear more of it." His arrogant gaze settled a frown on Smedley, as if he did not belong there. "This meeting has gone on too long anyway. I think you should wriggle out unobtrusively now, Captain. Don't want anyone prefiguring your association with the escaped prisoner, do we?"

He was making sure the two of them had no chance for a private word. But that did not matter. The plan he had been told was not the one Exeter would learn from the note inside his shirt. And already Smedley was drawing up Plan Three in his mind. Other worlds!

He mumbled something and rose, holding out his hand. Exeter stood up also, to clasp it in an awkward grip.

"See you on Friday, old man!" Smedley said, nudging foot on foot.

"Good of you. Damned grateful."

By good luck, the formidable Miss Pimm was absent from her desk, probably having lunch, and Smedley walked away along the hall. He would have to change back into uniform if he expected to eat at the King's expense.

The big hall was almost deserted. Everyone must be in the mess.

Yes, the plan would have to be changed. Stringer was a nark, no question about it. Even if he was not quite low enough for the shot-while-trying-to-escape villainy, he was at least a nark. Exeter caught walking out the gate in a stolen uniform would be exposed as a scrimshanker and the jig would be up. Stringer thought the escape was going to happen on Friday morning, so it must happen sooner. Tonight!

Which was cutting things very fine indeed. Smedley must hare down to the village and phone Ginger to get the chariot fired up right away. How many hours would it take to drive from the West Country to Kent, even supposing the car did not break down completely or have too many bursts?

"Ah, there you are, sir! Been looking for you."

Smedley's eyes came back into focus, seeing the wan face of his roommate Rattray. "Lieutenant?"

"Couple of visitors for you, sir."

Smedley turned to look, and caught a wave.

Alice Prescott! And Ginger Jones!

Oh, hell! *That's torn it!*

He put his good arm around Alice and kissed her cheek. Despite her astonishment she did not bite him. He could tell she was tempted, though. Quite a gal, Miss Prescott. He laid his stump across Ginger's shoulders and propelled both visitors toward the door.

"I say, darned good of you to come! You haven't eaten yet, have you? Let's trot down to the Black Dragon and grab a bite." Then he had them outside.

It was raining and his greatcoat was upstairs. Oh, well.

"What was all that about, Captain Smedley?" Miss Prescott demanded as they walked down the driveway, footsteps crunching on the gravel.

"All what?"

"I have never been thrown out of a pub, but I imagine the sensation would be somewhat similar."

"Edward. He'll be brought through there in a couple of shakes, and seeing you two might rattle him."

"You've talked to him?" Ginger demanded.

"Yes. He's well."

"No amnesia?"

"No, he's in tip-top shape, actually."

What else could Smedley say? *He's been to visit another world, where he has magical powers. The magic took him there because it was prophesied it would, and he was tricked into coming back by people who want to kill him, who happen to include the doctors here.* And after that, of course, Smedley could explain that he was inclined to believe most of this. *You'd look neat upon the seat of a straitjacket built for two. . . .*

"He's slinging it, then?" Ginger demanded.

"Ah, yes. Odd thing, though. Stringer, the surgeon, knew who he was! Met him at the Eton match, apparently. He's been covering for him. Old School Tie and all that."

The rain was merely a drizzle. The fresh air smelled wonderful, all leafy and earthy. They walked hurriedly, and Smedley told the Fallow part of the story. He left out the Olympus bit altogether. He was asked, of course. He hedged: "He just dropped a few hints."

By the time he had finished, they had reached the Black Dragon. It was a favorite outing for the walking wounded from Staffles, serving good English ale and quite respectable lunches. The lounge was packed with patients and visitors, of course, with more men waiting hopefully on the sidelines, but luckily a group vacated a small table right under Smedley's nose and he grabbed it. Before his claim could be disputed, Miss Prescott sat down and the challengers angrily withdrew.

"My favorite table!" Smedley said with satisfaction.

"I wish I knew how you do that," Ginger muttered.

"Do what?"

"Never mind. A drink, Miss Prescott?"

She requested a sherry. Smedley ordered mild and bitter. Ginger went to fetch them.

Alice had changed very little. Her face had always been a little on the horsey side and still was, but not hard to smile at. Edward had been head over heels back in '14. She was not wearing a ring. How did she feel about Edward? How had she ever felt about him, for that matter? She was two or three years older. She was even older now, and Edward . . .

Recalling how oddly youthful Exeter still looked, Smedley suddenly recalled the remark about curing cavities in teeth. Was that why he still seemed young? He *was* still young? He had not aged at all on his other world. Hell's bells!

"Something wrong, Captain?" Miss Prescott inquired coldly.

He had been staring right through her. "No, nothing . . ."

Ginger laid a foaming tankard on the table; Smedley grabbed for it, cursed, switched arms, and drank. Son of a bachelor!

The fact was, he *believed* in Nextdoor and Olympus! That a man of twenty-one still had rosy cheeks was a very flimsy piece of evidence. Lots did, although lately they had been aging much faster than usual. But it was another piece in the puzzle. There had to be some explanation for that tropical tan turning up in Flanders.

"All they have left is the Melton Mowbray pie." Ginger had brought a beer for himself, but was still standing.

"It's usually pretty fair," Smedley said.

Alice nodded acceptance. Ginger went off to order lunches. Service was something else that had gone to hell since the war started. Now Smedley had his chance to hobnob with a girl and see how often he could make her smile.

"Having a good war, Miss Prescott?"

"You used to call me Alice."

"Horrid little bounder, wasn't I? You called me Spots, as I recall."

"And now I ought to call you Gongs! Well done! I hear you're going up to the palace for . . ."

Oh, God! His eye had begun to twitch. He leaned his face on his hand to hide it. No good—he was starting a full-fledged attack of the willies. He wanted a drink, but he couldn't lift the beer with his stump, and . . . *Hell and damnation!* He scrambled to his feet and blundered toward the door.

\*    \*    \*

The cool rain helped. When the tears stopped and he could breathe again, he went back inside. The other two were quietly eating pork pie, discussing the terrible price of food in the shops. They did not say a word as he sat down again, ignoring him as if all grown men had hysterical fits all the time, perfectly normal. He did not try to apologize, for that would just set him off again.

What was the use, now? How could they trust anything he said after that performance? He struggled to cut the hard crust with a fork, keeping quiet in his misery. His companions made small talk across him. As they finished eating, the adjoining tables suddenly emptied and stayed that way. So it was time to talk about the business of the meeting, and he wondered if he could do even that much without foaming at the mouth.

"First," Alice said, as matter-of-factly as if jailbreaks were all in her day's work, "we must get him out of Staffles. Second, we must get him up to London before they bring out the bloodhounds." She had finished her food, but she was still nursing her drink. "And third we must find him a safe refuge so he can stay at liberty. Have I omitted anything?"

She glanced at Smedley. He nodded, not trusting himself to speak.

"I think that's enough to be going on with." Ginger was scratching at his beard. His expression suggested that he was wondering how he had ever managed to get himself involved in such lunacy.

"Good!" she said. "Item one: Can we get him out of the building?"

Smedley nodded again.

"That's your part, Julian," she said. "But how?"

"Two plans," he said hoarsely, clenching his fist under the table, struggling not to let his voice quaver.

"Why two?"

"Because we can't trust Stringer! He was altogether too inquisitive. I think he wants Edward to give himself away by trying to escape."

"I see."

He knew what she was thinking.

"I know it sounds crazy. . . ." Oh, what was the use? He *was* crazy! They both knew that as well as he did.

Ginger grunted. "You say Stringer said he knew Exeter?"

"Shook his hand the day he got the hat trick."

"No, he didn't."

"What?"

Ginger removed his pince-nez and wiped it on his sleeve. It was a trick of his when he was upset. "Short Stringer never had any use for games. It was his brother who was the cricketer. Long Stringer was the one who was there that day at Eton. I know. I was there too. I sat right behind him. I remember Exeter being mobbed. I know there were dozens of admirers around him, but I'd swear Short Stringer wasn't there."

An unfamiliar sensation around his mouth told Smedley that he must be smiling. Another piece of evidence sliding into place! If distrusting doctors was proof of insanity, then Ginger Jones belonged to the club too.

"Long Stringer's the soldier?" Alice said. "Could he be involved in this? Could he have recognized Edward in Belgium and tipped off his brother?"

"I don't think we can trust anyone," Smedley said. "Just the three of us." That was funny, asking them to trust a babbling lunatic.

"I agree! Tell us your two plans."

Keeping Plan Three to himself for the time being, Smedley outlined Plan One, the blind for Stringer's benefit, and then Plan Two, the fire alarm.

His audience did not leap to its feet and applaud.

"Hardly cricket," Ginger said dourly, "to shout 'fire!' in a hospital full of disabled men."

"It's damned near a public service! They haven't had a fire drill since I got there, and the place is a death trap. I just hope the alarm works, that's all." Truth to tell, Smedley was uneasy about the ethics of Plan Two, perhaps trying to convince himself as much as his listeners.

"You're sure it will work?" Alice demanded.

"Certain. There will be chaos unlimited! The yard wall's only head high. Exeter could vault it one-han—easily."

She shrugged and did not argue. "Good. You've taken care of the first problem. How about the second, the manhunt? Spiriting him up to London?"

"That's Ginger's part. He'll have to be waiting with the getaway car. There's a concealed gateway . . ."

He was facing two stares of dismay.

"What car?" Ginger growled.

"Boadicea's chariot."

"The Chariot's out of commission. Up on blocks. There's no private motoring now."

"I—I didn't know!" Smedley felt a surge of panic and struggled against it.

"It's not quite illegal," Alice said quickly. "Not yet. I'm sure it soon will be. There's all kinds of restrictions."

"And the price of petrol!" Ginger added. "It just went up to four and sixpence a gallon! Nobody can afford that!"

Smedley cursed under his breath. He should have thought of this. Bicycles? Horses? No, Plan Two had just sunk with all hands. Oh, God, did that mean he would have to go through with Plan One?

"How much time will he have?" Alice asked.

"He'll be missed pretty soon. I can't cut the telephone wires, or I would. If he can just get up to London, he'll be in great shape, but he's got to go through Canterbury or Maidstone." The coppers could set up roadblocks and picket the railway stations. Kent was a dead end in wartime, with the ports closed. Stringer must have seen that.

"An hour?"

"At the most."

"The same problem would arise with Plan One, wouldn't it?"

Smedley shivered. Cold torrents ran over his skin as he thought of himself lying bound and gagged in the little summerhouse—that tiny, walls-falling-in, *trench*-sort-of suffocating summerhouse. "If Stringer snitches, Plan Two's a dead duck. If not, then my paybook and chits will get Exeter clean away. Just depends how long until they find me." Find a screaming, eye-rolling, mouth-foaming lunatic . . .

Alice eyed him thoughtfully for a moment. She laid down her glass. "I think Plan Two is better. You'll do it tomorrow?"

"Tonight would be even better, but—"

"I know a car I can borrow."

"You do?" Smedley wanted to hug and kiss her. The expression on her face sobered him.

"But I can't drive."

He opened his mouth and then closed it. He felt a twinge of the willies and suppressed them. He would never drive a car again.

"Edward can't," Alice said, "unless he's learned how in the last three years."

"I don't think that's too likely. And it doesn't get the car here, anyway."

"I've only ever driven a little bit," she said, "and I'm certainly not up to driving in London."

They looked at Ginger.

He pawed at his beard, alarmed. "Neither am I! Strictly a back roads driver, I am! And I've never driven anything except the chariot. My license is back at Fallow anyway."

"Come on, old man!" Smedley said. "It's only fifty miles to London from here, and the A2's the straightest damned highway in the country, Watling Street. The bloody Romans built it."

Ginger glowered at Alice. "Where is this vehicle?"

"Notting Hill."

"Don't know London. That's north?"

"West."

"So it's on the wrong side!" The old chap was scowling ferociously, but he had not quite said no—not quite.

Alice drummed fingers on the table. An old, familiar glint shone in her eyes. "Captain Smedley, can you suggest anyone else who might be qualified and willing to assist us in rescuing my cousin?"

"Dozens of chaps, Miss Prescott. All the fellows in his class at school would jump at the chance."

"And where can I find them?"

"Ask around in Flanders. Most of them are there, still fighting the lousy Boche or filling up the cemeteries. The ones back here in Blighty have all had their legs blown off. So they can't help you. Frightfully sorry."

Ginger snarled. "Damn you both! What sort of car?"

"A Vauxhall, I think," Alice said. "Bloody great big black box on four wheels. You won't get wet."

"Does it have electric lights?"

Alice pursed her lips, a gesture which definitely did not improve her appearance. It suggested hay. "I'm not sure. I've never been out in it in the dark."

"Time, gentlemen!" called the landlord.

"We must go," Smedley said.

Jones did not budge. "You're sure the owner will be willing to lend us this vehicle?"

"He would not mind!" she said firmly. "I have the key to the lockup."

"And what will he say if I ram a taxi in the Strand?"

"I am sure it is insured." Her face was bleak. Best to ask no more, obviously.

Ginger polished his glasses vigorously. "Tomorrow night?"

The old chap was not short of courage and definitely long on loyalty. How would Fallow react if one of its senior masters was caught driving the getaway car in a jailbreak?

"Good man!" Smedley said. "But not tomorrow. Tonight! We must get the jump on Stringer and his gang."

Ginger flinched. "Tonight?"

"This is Plan Three! I tried to hint to Exeter that it would not wait until Friday. Even if he didn't understand my hint, though, he'll know as soon as the alarm goes off. I'll bring some spare togs along, in case he has to run in his pajamas." Smedley sighed happily. "I'm coming too, you see."

Other worlds!

# 9

Suddenly there was urgency. Smedley recalled that the next bus was almost due, so the three of them ran. Jumpy and chattery, he waited at the bus stop with them until the bus arrived, a creaky old double-decker. Alice and Jones both found seats, but not together, so they had no chance to talk.

Alice was beside a verbose middle-aged lady with pronounced—loudly pronounced—opinions on the Germans, the war, prices, food shortages, the need for rationing, and many, many other topics. Letting this blizzard of complaint drift around her, Alice sat back and marveled at the sudden emergency that had disrupted her life.

She had met Julian Smedley four times previously, with a lapse of years between each encounter. He had always been one of Edward's closest friends at Fallow, and always more of a follower than a friend. It might be more accurate to say that Edward had always been Smedley's friend, for Edward was one of those people who had friendships thrust upon them. Her memories of Smedley were like photographs in an album. Weedy little boy on page one, then pimply adolescent, and now wounded hero on page five. Each memory was strangely different. He had been shy and owlish, yet mischievous and quietly witty. Moreover, as Ginger had pointed out on the train down, Julian Smedley had always possessed a gift for falling on his feet. When the cake was passed out, the largest piece would usually land on his plate, yet nobody ever disliked him.

Perhaps even a missing hand counted as a largish piece of cake in 1917. He had been buried alive by a shell burst and dug out in time. Now he was out of the war, which was what mattered. Ginger said he had medals galore, although she would never have marked Julian as a potential hero. Why had she made that *stupid, stupid* remark about them? Buried alive!

Shell-shocked or not, Julian Smedley had talked Jones and herself into this madness very slickly. She might lose her job over it, although jobs were no problem now. She might even go to jail, although that prospect was sufficiently improbable not to trouble her unduly. She was not the one in danger. If things went wrong, the police would want to know by what right she had taken a motorcar belonging to Sir D'Arcy Devers. The danger was scandal.

The bus groaned into Canterbury at five minutes to three, and there was a branch of the Midland Bank directly across the street. With a wave to Jones, she ran over to it and managed to cash a check just before it closed. Ready money might be useful.

After that she had a chance to talk with her fellow conspirator. They walked side by side to the station. He looked haggard and worried. Jones she had met only once before, and now suddenly they were plotting an illegal undertaking together. He seemed so much a typical, dull schoolmaster, a stolid rock, pitted and barnacled by wave after wave of untiring youth. He was obviously close to retirement, possibly due to having been put out to pasture before now had the war not intervened, a tweedy badger of a man. By no means cuddly, but unthinkable as a criminal.

"Have we both gone insane," she asked him, "or are we merely bewitched?"

"You've been wondering that too, have you? I decided that it's something to do with the war. It's stripping away all our pretenses, layer after layer."

"Pretenses?"

"Our veneer of culture. Illusions. Everything we hid behind for so long. We see those young men who have gone out into hell to fight for a cause, and we realize that they now know something we don't. Life and youth seem infinitely more precious than they did three years ago. Many other things have become trivial and meaningless."

She considered that thought and decided it was more profound than it had sounded at first. He had an aching conscience, this Mr. Jones.

"I am extremely grateful to you, and—I confess—more than a little surprised that you would let yourself become involved in this for the sake of my cousin."

The schoolmaster cleared his throat. "Ahem! Your cousin is an admirable young man. I feel very sorry for his many misfortunes. But I should be less than honest were I not to admit that my primary interest is Julian Smedley."

"He has severe emotional problems," she said warily.

"He has been horribly damaged, both physically and mentally. We old men who have stayed home and sent the young to fight for us—we do have certain obligations. At least I feel that way. And you cannot conceive the difference between the Smedley you met today and the one I saw last Sunday."

She remembered the tears. "Better?"

"Infinitely better. His efforts to aid his old friend are working a miracle cure on our young hero."

So that was why he had let Smedley talk him into this! What would Smedley think if he knew that? That reasoning would not sound convincing in the witness box at the Old Bailey. How would Smedley react if they failed?

"I wish he were not coming!" she said. "If he would just set off the alarm and then stay with the other inmates, then no harm could come to him." But they had both argued that case, and Smedley had insisted.

"I am sure he has his reasons. We must show him that we trust him. It is the best treatment he could get."

"Your sentiments do you honor," she murmured. "Have you ever had children of your own, Mr. Jones?"

He laughed feebly. "A highly improper question to put to a lifelong bachelor! I suppose I could be platitudinous and say I have had hundreds of sons, but that would not be true. Perhaps twenty-five, a little less than one a year. I always hoped that a year would bring forth at least one. Sometimes it did, sometimes it didn't. Rarely two. Two of them are involved in this."

She squeezed his arm. "I hope they appreciate you."

"Perhaps they will one day. Not now."

They turned into the station. It was ominously crowded.

"They are sending all the engines to France, you know," Jones complained. "And some of the rails, too! Let us go look at the board."

According to the board, there was a train in fifteen minutes. The waiting room was packed to the doors. By mutual consent, they wandered along the platform together, taking the chance to talk.

"May I inquire about this automobile, Miss Prescott?"

It was a very fair question.

"I told you I have the key. Its owner would certainly not object to my using it. He has let me drive it before."

"And why do you think it has petrol available? Why do you believe it to be in operating condition?"

Alice sighed and decided that there had better be honor among thieves. "His wife is a woman with a great deal of influence."

She glanced sideways at her companion, expecting to see a bristling of shock. But Jones had a trick of using his pince-nez to mask his eyes, and his face gave away nothing.

"Does she know you have the key?"

"She does not know I exist. I am certain of that. You know it's illegal now to employ men between the ages of eighteen and sixty-one in nonessential industries, and yet she still has a chauffeur. What strings she pulls I cannot imagine, but she does. Admittedly she is not in good health, but I feel that morally Captain Smedley has a greater claim on the vehicle tonight than she does."

Jones uttered his quiet chuckle again. "Learned counsel would hesitate to present such an argument in court. And what happens if we are caught and the lady finds out?"

Alice winced. "She will not lay charges, I am sure. It would cause tongues to wag."

That was not true at all. Lady Devers would trumpet it to the four corners of the earth. She was a vindictive, malicious *bitch*. Alice would not tell Mr. Jones that. He was more shocked by bad language than he was by confessions of adultery.

A porter began shouting, "London train!" and they had no further chance for private conversation.

They reached London. They struggled through the traffic, which was already mounting toward the evening rush. They stopped to do some shopping for supper and came at last to her flat.

As always, her hand was trembling when she unlocked the door. The day's post lay on the mat, where it had fallen through the slot. She snatched it up and peered at the envelopes. What she dreaded was not there, and she was another day closer to the end of the war.

The official notice would not come to her, of course—it would go to the bitch in Notting Hill—but D'Arcy had taken his sister into his confidence before he was posted overseas, and Anabel had promised faithfully that she would notify Alice if the dread announcement ever came. Alice could not bring herself to trust that arrangement. Every day she read the obituaries and casualty lists in the *Times,* although no one knew how out-of-date those might be. On Sundays she would sometimes go up to Notting Hill and walk past the house, looking for the drawn blinds that would be evidence of mourning. That was how she knew about the chauffeur.

She made tea and prepared a drab meal. She suggested that Jones take a nap, in preparation for a sleepless night, but he was too anxious about the coming ordeal to relax. They must be out of town before dark, he insisted. He dare not try to drive in traffic in the dark.

Alice prepared some sandwiches from the ugly wartime bread. She dressed in the warmest tweeds she possessed. She took the precious key from her bottom drawer, and pressed a kiss on D'Arcy's photograph. Then she went back into the sitting room and found Jones nodding before the gas fire. He looked up with a guilty start.

"Come, my lord!" she said. "We must embark upon our pilgrimage to Canterbury, as in days of yore. You shall be my verray, parfit gentil knyght!"

He hauled himself out of the chair, blinking behind his pince-nez. "And you, my lady? The prioresse?"

"The wif of Bathe, I think, is more my role. Shall I tell you a tale upon the way to lighten the journey?"

Mr. Jones looked deeply shocked that she should even know that story.

They sallied out into the streets again. They took the tube, and then a bus, and so they came to Notting Hill. It seemed a very mundane way to embark on a mission of romance and high adventure. And all those long miles must be retraced.

The lockup was one of six, in what had been a stable until five or six years ago. There was no one else about in the gloomy little yard. The rain had ended, but the skies remained gray and gravid.

The key still worked. Jones groaned loudly when he saw the size of the motorcar. The great black dragon almost filled its kennel, so that there was hardly room to move around it. Alice had only been here two or three times, and she could not recall why D'Arcy had ever given her the key. She could remember every drive she had ever had in the car, though—wonderful, intoxicating journeys out of town with her lover, stolen hours of happiness together.

Jones inspected every inch of the monster. Alice fidgeted, fearing that some neighbor would come driving in and think to investigate the strangers, although it was more than probable that the cars in the other lockups had been abandoned for the duration of the war. Adjacent houses overlooked the yard. Would some kind friend think to telephone Lady Devers and inform her that her car was being stolen?

Jones checked the fuel tank with the dipstick and examined the jerry can chained on the running board. Both seemed to be full, he said glumly. He had been hoping for a last-minute stay of execution, perhaps. The oil in the lamps was low, he said, and he could find no spare oil. They must stop somewhere and buy some before the garages closed.

That was not enough excuse to give up the expedition. Alice found a motoring rug in the back. She adjusted it over her knees as she settled herself in the seat next the driver's. Jones turned the crank. The motor caught at once. He backed the car out of the lockup and went to shut the doors. The adventure had begun.

Sometime in the small hours, Julian Smedley would set off the fire alarm in Staffles. Edward, who would not be expecting the signal this night, would be jerked out of his sleep by bells ringing to signal his escape. . . .

# III

## *Illegal Move*

# 10

Escape! Escape!

Edward Exeter had escaped from Sussvale.

He stalked along happily, encrusted in red dust. His boots were rubbing his toes, but the ache in his legs was almost pleasurable. Rothpass was one of the easier passes in the Vales, and now the road led downward. He matched strides with Goathoth Peddler, who was also on his way to Nagvale and enjoyed company on the road. Ahead of them trudged the peddler's packbeast, to whom Edward had not been introduced, but which generally resembled a jackass designed by a committee of iguana. Goathoth was expounding on his daughter-in-law's childbearing problems in a Sussian accent like a knife on a tin plate, quite unaware how little his young friend understood. Neither of them was particularly worried by trivia on such a fine morning.

"——," said the peddler, "another miscarriage. That made three. A few fortnights later they went to —— and sacrificed a —— to ——"

"A very wise decision," Edward remarked.

Jagged peaks towered on either hand. Once in a while the trail would emerge from forest and offer a glimpse of scenery ahead. From that height the world stretched out forever. Nagvale was another intermontane basin, of course. It seemed narrower than Sussvale, but he could not discern the end of it; the bordering ranges trailed away into hazy distance.

He was enjoying himself, although his conscience said he should not be. He had betrayed little Eleal, who had befriended him and saved his life. He had left a trail of dead friends and would-be helpers—Bagpipe, Creighton, Gover, Onica—not to mention an unknown number of slain foes, one of whom he had dispatched personally.

By all rights, he should have died in Sussland. Zath had been waiting for him to arrive there, as the *Filoby Testament* prophesied he would. The god of death had set his deadly reapers to trap the expected Liberator. Julius Creighton and Gover Envoy had died, but Edward had escaped. Zath's killers had set another ambush for him, and Onica Mason had died; but again Edward had beaten the odds and escaped. Tion, Suss's patron god, had let him go, which he had never expected either.

He could claim very little credit for himself, but he had escaped from Sussvale. He was going Home. In a few more weeks, he would be back in England, ready to fight for King and Country—under an assumed name, of course, but in time to help humble the Prussian Bully. Nextdoor would be nothing but an incredible memory, a month missing from his life.

A party of pilgrims came riding up the western slope, taking it easy to spare their moas. They waved cheerily at the two men heading down but did not break off their conversation. Clearly they had seen nothing odd in either of the two. They had probably not noticed the younger one taking an unusually hard look at their mounts.

Edward, for his part, was amused at how easily he now accepted the idea of creatures that had hooves and fur and yet looked like birds. In less than two weeks, he had already adjusted to the lesser oddities of Nextdoor. It was a fascinating place. Perhaps one day, after the war was over, he might try to come back, to explore it in detail—or even fulfill a prophecy or two.

"———" Goathoth announced triumphantly, "bouncing baby boy! Named him —— after his ———!"

"May the gods be praised!"

Tangles of purple and bronze creepers in the woods sent out waves of pungent scents, while shrieking birds fluttered and stalked around—feathery birds and furry birds also, for Nextdoor had a wide variety of bipeds.

Just once, near the summit, Edward had sensed the eeriness of virtuality, but very weak and localized. An ancient mossy shrine stood there, a curved wall around a weathered statue of a woman, which would be some aspect of Eltiana, the Lady. His companion had lingered to say a prayer; Edward stayed well back from it, although he doubted that there would be any resident numen at such a minor node. They had continued on their way unmolested.

The previous day he had stopped at a lonely farmhouse in the mountains and offered to work a few hours in return for a meal and a place to sleep. He had chopped wood and milked goats. He had raised some blisters and been butted a couple of times and enjoyed himself thoroughly. The food had been tasty and filling, the soft hay fragrant. The farmer's eldest daughter had offered more than customary hospitality and been mildly peeved when her advances were declined, but apart from that all parties had been satisfied by the arrangement. A stranger's charisma would take care of most problems; youth and honest labor guaranteed untroubled rest.

He had certainly had an interesting couple of weeks since leaving Paris.

"——— Thargians," the peddler grumbled. "All over Narshland like ——— around a mating ———!"

"Murderous scum," Edward agreed.

Joalia versus Thargia was another war, but one he must stay clear of. He was just the right age to be handed a spear and told to form up. He wondered which side Goathoth spied for. It soon became evident that Goathoth was wondering the same about him, for he began spinning a string of leading questions.

Oh, the temptation to tell the truth!—*I'm D'ward, the Liberator whom the* Filoby Testament *predicts will kill death. I'm a stranger in this world. When I get down to Sonalby, I'm going to seek out an agent of the Service, which is another group of strangers. They will send me Home. In another couple of fortnights, I'll be in England. That's on Earth. Yes, Earth. Well, I'd never heard of Nextdoor until a couple of weeks ago. Any other questions?*

It was not on. Instead, Edward explained that he was a wandering scholar from

Rinooland, a vale far enough away to explain his accent and his ignorance of the geography.

Joal versus Tharg was one war. There was another, older war that he must also stay out of. Odious as Tion had turned out to be, the Youth was not as despicable as some of the others, the ones known as the Chamber—Zath and his allies. Obviously Tion conspired against other members of the Pentatheon—the Parent, the Man, the Lady, the Maiden. That was the Great Game, which the strangers played to relieve the tedium of immortality. His personal recreations might be vicious, but the Lord of Art did not use murder to earn his mana. He seemed to keep his subordinates under reasonable control. He was certainly not a member of the Chamber, or he would never have released the Liberator to find his foretold destiny. Did he disapprove of Zath on ethical grounds, or was he merely resentful of his ill-gotten influence in the Great Game?

The struggle between the Service and the Chamber was yet a third war. Somewhere in a place nicknamed Olympus, the organization Edward sought was trying to do something about the appalling injustice of a deceitful religion, to bring enlightenment to an oppressed and benighted population. It was a new version of the White Man's Burden. His father had favored the cause, and anything the guv'nor had supported would be worthy of Edward's loyalty also.

But that was not his war either, no matter what the *Testament* predicted. He had duties elsewhere, a fourth war.

He must not—could not—stay and play missionary in this alien world while his friends were dying for England. He heard Alice's voice whispering *starry-eyed romantic idealist!* in his mind's ear, and he chuckled. Long might he remain one!

A bend brought another breathtaking glimpse of the great valley ahead, framed between rocky spurs. Sunlight gleamed on a winding river.

"Susswater again?" he asked.

The peddler frowned. "Nagwater."

Well, that was absurd! Susswater flowed west. The road had followed it for a while, detouring into the hills when the gorge became too narrow. Now both trail and river had emerged from the mountains. Obviously that was the same river!

But apparently it was not the same river to Goathoth Peddler, so each vale must have its own river. That was a strange concept of geography, another stumbling block to understanding the language—the many languages.

"Those mountains? What are they named?"

This time the peddler's sun-reddened eyes were frankly incredulous. "Nagwall, of course!"

Edward thought about that for a few paces. He used gestures to aid his next question. "Nagwall this side. What name on the other side?"

"Joalwall there." The peddler waved his stick northward. Then southward. "Lemodwall there."

"And in the middle what are they called?"

The old man seemed completely at a loss. "What pass are you looking from?"

What a range was called depended on where it was seen from? If mountains were all about you, always, then perhaps you had no concept of classifying mountains, like fish in an ever-present sea?

Why did Nextdoor have to be confoundingly interesting?

It was late afternoon when he limped into Sonalby. His feet hurt and his legs ached, and Nextdoor no longer seemed quite so fascinating as it had done in the morning. The peddler had stopped off to trade at an isolated ranch house, leaving him to walk alone for the last couple of hours.

Nagvale was different. Where Sussvale had been lushly tropical, with farms and orchards packed in from wall to mountain wall, here the flat land was semidesert. The grass was scrubby and well grazed; trees were rare and spiny. There were no hedges or fences; houses were grouped into small, widely scattered settlements, which he assumed were ranches. The only industry he had detected so far was herding. The livestock were gangling, hairless beasts as angular as camels would be without humps. The males sported elaborate branched antlers and looked potentially dangerous. He was relieved that none came near the road.

The herders were grown men, and they carried spears and big circular shields. Many of them were astride moas or had moas tethered nearby. He wondered if the weapons were for defense against the male cattle or against predators, and if those predators had four legs or two.

Sonalby was a larger village than any he had seen in Sussvale, although smaller than Suss itself. It had no wall or palisade around it, which meant either that Nagland was peaceful or that the inhabitants relied on their weapons for defense. It sprawled for more than a mile along the bank of a wide, reedy river, which clearly provided building material as well as drinking water. The houses were wicker walled and thatched, none higher than one story. There seemed to be no pattern to them, no streets.

He was parched, footsore, hungry. His first need was to locate Kalmak Carpenter and enlist the aid of the Service. Onica had not lived to carry word to Olympus, so he would have to improvise. Kalmak himself was only a native, not a stranger, but he would recognize the password and put Edward on the road Home.

Nagvale looked more like Kenya than England. From the road he had seen Nagians only at a distance, but he began to catch closer glimpses of them as he approached the town. They were about the color of well-tanned Spaniards or Italians. Most were lanky and leathery, their dark hair and beards long and untrimmed. Seeing both sexes dressed in leather kilts or loincloths, he found himself thinking of them as savages and that discovery annoyed him. Their way of life was well adapted to the climate. They might have a sophisticated literature and culture for all he knew to the contrary, although Eleal had never mentioned the troupe performing in Nagland.

Women going around bare-breasted had seemed quite unremarkable during his childhood in Africa. He found them more interesting now.

The village had no wall or stockade, or even any well-defined borders. He passed the first houses without being challenged. To his left a group of women pounded meal, to his right young men were practicing spear-throwing. Neither group seemed especially promising—or especially interested—although he was an obvious outsider in his Sussian smock. His hair was as black as theirs, but he doubted that anyone else had blue eyes. He had decided to go on a little farther when faint sounds of shouting came drifting out from the town.

The warriors stopped their spear-throwing. The women looked up.

Then the men took up their spears and began to run. The women rose to their feet, hastily gathered small children, and set off to follow.

So did Edward. Pushing his blistered feet faster, he hurried after them. Soon the shouting grew louder; he saw more people running. Something of importance was happening. It could have nothing to do with him, but if everyone was there, then he had better attend also. A stranger caught skulking around deserted houses would be suspected of ill intentions.

He saw smoke. One of the houses was burning, which could hardly be a rare event in a village built like this one. The houses were spaced well apart, undoubtedly for just that reason. With no set street pattern, the people were heading more or less straight to the emergency. He followed until he reached the assembled crowd. He peered over heads. Half the building had gone already, red flames shooting skyward. Through a window he could see the interior glowing like a furnace and could feel the heat on his face, even at that distance.

He sensed something amiss. However strange the language, he could read the tone of the shouting. There ought to be wailing and lamentation. There wasn't. He heard jeering and anger. This was a mob. Someone was in trouble, and ten to one that house had been deliberately torched.

He located the center of the agitation, the men in charge of this riot. Their green robes, their shaven heads and faces, all confirmed that they were priests. They were haranguing the crowd, rousing it to ever-greater fury.

His skin prickled. An outsider had no place in a nasty business like this. Mobs were fickle. Furthermore, green was the color of Karzon, the Man, one of the Five. In the popular mind, Zath was an avatar of the Man, but in Zath's case the vassal was the stronger of the two. Zath was certainly one of the Chamber, and Karzon must be assumed to be so also. This affair might very well concern Edward, therefore, and the sooner he made himself scarce the better.

He stepped back one pace, then stopped as the crowd howled, a hungry, bestial sound. Four men came forward, carrying another prone between them. The priests yelled something. The crowd howled again.

Then the lynch party ran forward to the flaming house, two holding their victim's ankles, two his wrists. They swung in unison, and hurled him bodily through the doorway. They beat a hasty retreat from the heat. The man screamed from inside the furnace. Edward watched, appalled and helpless. He thought he saw the wretch rise to his feet, already wreathed in flame, only to stumble and collapse. There was one more scream and then nothing but the roar of the fire and the wild hollering of the mob.

"Karzon!" they screamed. "Krobidirkin Karzon! Karzon Krobidirkin!"

The priests waved a signal, and the execution squad came forward again. This time they were carrying a woman.

Edward began to push his way through the crowd. He was a stranger; he had charisma; he might be able to do something. He was too late. Sickened, he turned away, hearing the lustful howl of the mob and the woman's horribly prolonged dying shriek.

An elderly man stood beside him. His graying beard hung to his waist, but it did not hide old ritual scars on his scraggly chest. The wrinkled face above the beard was painted with a complex design, mostly in white, but with minor elements in the other sacred colors. He was grinning and rubbing his hands on his leather skirt.

"What have they done?" Edward demanded in Joalian. "What is their crime?"

Filmy eyes inspected the stranger suspiciously. Then the old man bared his teeth and barked out a string of words.

Edward caught very little of the explanation, except for one name: Kalmak. Another howl from the crowd made him look around. He caught a glimpse of an adolescent boy cartwheeling through the air, following his parents into the pyre.

So the priests of Karzon had just taken care of Kalmak. They had also destroyed Edward's only lead to the Service. Without the help of the Service, he could not return to Earth.

No escape! No escape!

He was trapped on Nextdoor, with no way to escape.

He watched in dismay as all his hopes went up in flames.

*What was that confounded noise? He was in a bed. A bell ringing? A fire alarm. Not on Nextdoor any longer. Eyes gritty with sleep, head like a swamp. Back on Earth, in England. Dreaming of three years ago. Smedley had set off the alarm to help him escape from Staffles. . . .*

# *11*

Again Julian Smedley had disposed of his sleeping tablet. Again he struggled to push his feet into laced shoes. This time he had pulled his greatcoat on over his civvies—no old campaigner ever forgot his greatcoat. He had noted where Rattray had put his blues. Rattray was roughly Exeter's height, although much broader. With a stolen bundle under his maimed arm, Smedley stole out into the dim, hushed corridor.

The fire alarm was right beside the bathroom door—a real spot of luck, because he was going to provoke a very fast reaction, and he did not want to be caught in the act. He paused for a moment, heart pounding, wondering for the thousandth time if there was any horrible miscalculation in his plan. Suppose nothing at all happened?

*Over the top!* he thought, and pulled the lever. Noise roared through the silent mansion, louder than the guns opening up at the start of a major battle. He turned the door handle the wrong way and began to panic; he almost fell into the bathroom—should have opened the door first, of course—he counted to ten and then emerged again. Other men were coming out of other doors, nurses flitting like moths already, lights dazzling bright.

He had expected to be first down the stairs, but several men were ahead of him, staggering in the way of the newly awakened. They might be cursing, but the clamor of the bells drowned out all sound. More were already streaming out into the chilly night, some on crutches, some helping the disabled. Like him, many had thought to pull on their greatcoats. Then he was outside on the lawn.

His first error! He had expected darkness, but light was streaming from every window—so much for regulations! The sky was almost cloudless and a gibbous moon had etched the grounds into a silver lithograph. His companions had stopped to take stock, muttering angrily. He pushed past and kept on going, around the west wing and the big greenhouse, past the sheds, across the rose garden, and through a narrow arch into the yard.

Second error! The yard was already full of men, and more were pouring out the kitchen door. He should have foreseen that! And the light would make it impossible to climb the wall unobserved. Oh . . . heck. Keep calm! It could be done yet. All it needed was a cool head.

Some meddling officer began shouting, ordering everyone out to the garden. The yard was too close to the house.

Splendid! Smedley backed away and then stood against the wall near the arch, watching the faces coming by him—pale blurs, but he could imagine the angry, unshaven faces, the tousled hair. Cold, shivering men in pajamas. If they knew who had ruined their sleep, they would lynch him. And indoors, the bedridden, the crippled, the crazy . . .

Where was Exeter? Could he have vaulted that wall and gone on ahead? Not without raising a hue and cry, surely? Had he been rounded up by a guard? If Stringer had reported that the malingerer was preparing to break out, then anything was possible.

Then one of the taller ones . . .

"Exe—er, *Edward!*"

Exeter parted from the mob and grabbed Smedley's shoulder.

"Where to?"

"This way."

They moved along the side of the wall, and Smedley plunged into bushes. He heard crackling behind him. A voice shouted, "I say!" in the background. He kept on going. Twigs scratched and clawed at his face, tugged his clothing. There were no more shouts.

The shrubbery offered no foothold, only obstruction. Then it ended. Ahead was a lawn, and there were men on it, although none near the wall. They would all be looking toward the house, wouldn't they? Not staring out into the night?

"This'll have to do!" He panted. "There's glass on top here. Can you manage?" He thrust Rattray's uniform at his companion.

Exeter eyed the height. "I think so. Thanks, old son! You've been a real brick. Never forget this." He chose a spot clear of branches and swung the garments up to cover the glass.

"Wait! I'm coming too."

Exeter turned to stare at him. "Why?"

"I just am. Don't waste time arguing. I'll need a hand."

Funny ha-ha.

"Don't be an idiot! There's nothing to connect you with this. Don't stuff your neck in a noose!"

"I want to come!"

Exeter put his fists on his hips. "What are you planning?"

"Nextdoor. You're going back, aren't you? Take me!"

"No, I'm not going back! I don't know that I could, even if I wanted to. I don't know how to get in touch with Head Office. I'm not sure that you can cross over with only one hand. No. You stay here."

They were wasting precious seconds! This was madness.

"Exeter!" Smedley heard his voice crack. He felt his face starting to twitch. "Please!"

"Look here, there's no need to implicate yourself! I'll get in touch with you later. Your people still in Chichester? That's where you're going?"

"The coppers!" Smedley said, choking. "They'll watch me!" He was sobbing already. Must he beg, too? Must he explain that if they locked him up he would go out of his mind? "Please, Exeter! They'll question me. I'll give the others away! Ginger Jones! For God's sake—"

"Oh, right-oh!" Exeter stooped and cupped his hands.

Smedley placed a foot and jumped. He got his arms over the wall and heard glass crack, felt pain. He swung a leg up, banged his stump, scrabbled, and tipped over. Fire tore at his leg as it dragged over the coping. He fell bodily onto the grass verge. Impact knocked all the breath out of him. God almighty!

He hurt. He felt sick.

Exeter came down with a curse and hauled Smedley to his feet. Then he tried to pull the uniform loose from the wall. There was a loud ripping noise.

"That's torn it! Leave it. Come on!"

They began to run along the lane, through blackness under tree branches. Smedley could feel hot blood on his ankle. He lurched and stumbled; Exeter steadied him as they ran. The road was muddy and uneven.

"We're going to look like a pair of real ninnies if the car isn't there," Exeter said.

Smedley tried to explain about the concealed driveway, but he lacked breath. He should have remembered the glass on the wall sooner and brought his own blues as well as Rattray's. Or another greatcoat. Exeter in pajamas would have a deuce of a lot of explaining to do if they ran into anyone.

Twin orange moons dawned ahead of them, reflecting on puddles, shedding uncertain light on the hedges.

"Someone's coming!" Exeter said. "Into the ditch!"

"No! Be . . . Ginger . . ." He'd have seen the lights going on in Staffles.

"Too big for the chariot!"

Smedley made a gasping sound of disagreement. The car went spraying by them and stopped. A door flew open, and Alice's voice yelled, "Edward!"

He should have had the wit to go in the front, beside Ginger. The back was roomy enough, but the other two fell into the car and each other's arms and on top of him, all at the same time. Even before the door slammed, he was in a scrum.

By the time he had escaped to the fringes, the big car had swept past Staffles and was hurtling recklessly along the dark lane. He sank back with a shivery feeling of release. Done it! They had done it! Exeter was bubbling his thanks to Alice and Ginger. The old man was managing the driving very well. All they needed now was a burst tire.

Miss Prescott took Smedley's face in both hands and kissed him as if she really meant it.

"Well done!" she said, sounding quite emotional.

"My pleasure, ma'am. I should warn you . . ."

"What?"

"Nothing."

He was bleeding like a pig all over her fancy automobile. But there was no light, so it would have to wait. It would stop soon.

"Yes, well done," Exeter said from the far side. "Anyone mind if I wrap up in this rug?" His teeth rattled.

Alice squeaked in a motherly fashion and helped him. Smedley thought about offering his greatcoat, but that seemed like a lot of effort.

Ginger roared, "Crossroads! Which way?"

"Left," Smedley said, and they rushed through the village.

"Lights?" Exeter asked, peering back. "What's wrong with the streetlights?"

"Blackout," Alice said. "The lamps're painted so they just throw light downward . . . German planes."

There was a moment's silence, then he said incredulously, "They drop bombs?"

"On London, yes. They used to use zepps—zeppelins. *Airships.* We started shooting those down, so now they use aeroplanes. Big jobbies, with four or five engines."

"But bombs? On *civilians?* Women and children?"

"Indeed they do. Now you tell me exactly where you've been these last three years, baby Cousin, because I'm—"

"No! First you tell me all about this war!"

"You don't—You really have been away? You don't know?"

"I don't know a thing except what I've overheard when I wasn't supposed to be listening. I saw a bit of a battlefield. I thought I'd died and gone to hell. It's still going on, after three years? I'd never imagined it would be like that!"

"Nobody did! It turned out much worse than anyone ever thought it would be."

Smedley was trying to remember the way in case Ginger needed guidance. He stopped listening as Alice talked about the war—planes and U-boats and trenches, the Tsar deposed and the Yanks coming someday. He fingered his leg and discovered his pants leg and sock were soaked. He had gashed his calf in two places. It was sticky, but he thought the bleeding had more or less stopped. It throbbed nastily. It was his right one, unfortunately, hard for him to reach.

A lorry rumbled by in the opposite direction, and he realized that they were on a main road now. If it didn't go to Canterbury, it would go somewhere. Every mile made their escape more likely, as long as they didn't end up at Dover. He was shivering with reaction.

"Speak up!" Ginger shouted over his shoulder.

"Sorry," Exeter said. He had started to tell his story. "I've been in another world. Can you believe that?"

"We'll try," Alice said. "How did you get out of the hospital in Greyfriars?"

"I had supernatural aid. Call him Mr. Goodfellow. I don't know his real name. Perhaps he doesn't, any more."

"He made you invisible? No one saw you."

"I didn't see them. I just walked out, on crutches. Then we were met by a man named Creighton. Colonel Julius Creighton. Said he dropped in at Nyagatha once. Remember him?"

"Can't say I do."

"Average height . . . Doesn't matter. He was Service. And so was the guv'nor."

It was strange to hear that old familiar voice, would know it anywhere. Those dry, quiet tones in the dark, bringing back memories, bushels of memories.

"No, not the Colonial Office. This is another Service altogether. There's two Services, really. The one on this world we call Head Office, but it's not really in charge of the Service on Nextdoor. They're more just allies, sort of in cahoots. Service and Head Office are the goodies. There are also baddies, which on Nextdoor are the Chamber and here are the Blighters. I don't know very much about them here, except that they had a lot to do with starting this awful war. Mr. Goodfellow took us to his, er, residence, and he cured my broken leg."

"Snap of the fingers cured?"

"Pretty much. Yes. Then Creighton and I traveled down to Wiltshire. I didn't want to, of course, but he insisted I owed him that much. There's a portal there, a magic door. It let us cross over to Nextdoor. Trouble was, there were baddies waiting on the other side, and Creighton got killed. So there I was—stranded. Stuck. All washed up. Robinson Crusoe."

Ginger was following a lorry. Its stronger headlights were lighting the road for him, and they were doing a steady thirty at least.

"I really wanted to come back and do my bit in the war," Exeter said. "But the only way I could come back here was to find the Service, and I didn't know how to do that. I had what I thought was a lead, but it didn't pan out. When I did get in touch, they were pretty reluctant to help me. Three years, it's taken. You see, there's a prophecy about me."

Houses now. Perhaps this was Canterbury already. Smedley was feeling dizzy. Perhaps he had banged his head falling off the wall. Perhaps he was suffering from lack of sleep. He wouldn't have nurses popping pills at him every night now, so he might not sleep much in future. But he did have a strange tingling in his head.

The car jerked, coughed, and then purred again.

Alice: "What was that?"

Jones: "Dunno."

Dirt in the petrol, likely. That would put the hen among the foxes, wouldn't it? If the car broke down with Exeter in nightclothes and him with blood all over his bags . . . Even a modestly intelligent bus conductor might be suspicious enough to blow the whistle.

"You cross over," Exeter was explaining, "by doing a dance, a particular mixture of chanting and rhythm and words, done at a particular place. It used to be quite a common accident, I think, because the nodes are very often holy places. You know that sort of *awe* you feel in old churches? You're sensing what the Service calls 'virtuality,' although no one knows what it really is. So in primitive times, when the shaman called the tribe together to do their sacred leap-about, they would do it at a node. And if the routine was good, they'd feel that virtuality more strongly. Why do you think people sing in church? The shamans would experiment with the ritual, I expect. Try different words, different movements, to increase that sense of the holy presence or whatever they thought it was. And one day—one night, more likely—someone would hit the right mixture and *pouf!* Clarence and Euphemia had disappeared. Big feather in shaman's cap! Do it again next Thursday."

The car coughed again, twice, and then resumed its low rumble. Everyone was silent, but nothing more happened.

Smedley jerked his head up. He seemed to be drifting off to sleep. His leg had stopped throbbing. Come to think of it, his leg was numb. Were legs usually numb?

". . . set themselves up as gods," Exeter said from a long way away. "I expect many of the old myths relate to strangers from Nextdoor or one of the others: Hercules, Apollo, Prometheus. And on Nextdoor, they may be from either this world or one of the others. The more worship they get, the stronger they become. The stronger they become, the more worship they can demand."

"Absolute power corrupts absolutely," Alice muttered.

"It certainly does. On Nextdoor . . . Well, actually, the area I know is called the Vales. It's not much bigger than England and I haven't seen all of the Vales even. So there's an awful lot of the world I know nothing at all about. But in the Vales, there are five or six dominant gods. Well, they call themselves gods, but they're really just magicians."

Oh, that made things a lot more believable, Smedley thought drowsily.

"Each one has a retinue of lesser gods. Some of them are jolly nasty types. The Service refers to those as the Chamber of Horrors, and they're the ones trying to kill me, because of the prophecy. The worst is Zath, who calls himself god of death." Exeter paused for a moment. "I know this must sound dodgy, but they caused the Nyagatha business."

"That sounds dodgy," Alice agreed, "but keep talking."

"You know when the guv'nor was born?"

"Yes. Roly told me. He certainly didn't look his age."

"Because he'd spent thirty years or so on Nextdoor. You pick up mana even without trying. . . . He helped found the Service there. Then Zath tried to kill him, and failed. That brought the prophecy to light. The prophecy foretold that Cameron Exeter would father a son who would be a sort of messiah, who would kill death. It's very muddled, most of it, but that bit was clear enough."

The car coughed again.

When nothing more happened, Exeter continued. "So Zath was gunning for the guv'nor. He went to earth. That's a joke, actually."

"I expect you're out of practice. Carry on."

"Well, it was very ironic. Zath tried to stop me being born, but the attempt drove the guv'nor into coming Home—meaning home to Earth—and about the first thing he did was meet the mater and fall in love and, whoops, there was me. These things happen.

"If Zath had only known it, the guv'nor wasn't in favor of the prophecy either. It leads to all sorts of evil complications. So both sides in this business wanted to break the chain! The guv'nor thought that all he had to do was stay out of the Chamber's reach until after the prophesied date, which would have been August 1914 by our reckoning, and then keep Baby Exeter, that's me, from crossing over. Then the chain would be broken and nothing else would apply. Head Office wangled him into the Colonial Office and got him posted to Nyagatha . . ."

His voice kept fading away and coming back. Smedley was having a deuce of a job keeping his eyes open. Funny, that. Heavenly choirs.

". . . like everyone to take Home leave every few years. A little refresher course as a mortal is very humbling, and it keeps people in touch with the language and customs, and so on . . . Jumbo Watson and Soapy Maclean dropped in on Head Office in 1912. Jumbo inquired about the guv'nor . . . when he heard about me the penny dropped. Edward is a common enough name in England, but it begins with a vowel, which would make it feminine in the Vales; the masculine would be D'ward.

"There's actually more about D'ward in the *Filoby Testament* than there is about the Liberator, but nowhere did the seeress say that they were one and the same chappie. Soapy headed for Nyagatha to explain this and find out if the guv'nor was still opposed to the prophecy. Somebody tipped off the Chamber's agents—or perhaps they followed him. Anyway, Soapy arrived the day before the massacre. . . ."

Bad business, that massacre, but perhaps Exeter Senior had not been as much as fault as everyone had thought. . . . Smedley started awake. He had dozed off but not for very long. Exeter seemed to be talking about the gods again.

"Some of them aren't so bad. I've met a couple of the Pentatheon, the five Great Ones. When I first crossed over, Zath's assassins were waiting for me and almost nobbled me. They're rather like Kali's thugs, in India . . . wander around killing people at random. Fortunately that was in Sussland. That's Tion's manor, and he was miffed. . . . Tion's one of the five, the Youth. He's a sort of Apollo figure, if you believe his advertisements, god of art, and beauty, and sport. He holds a big festival every year, like a miniature Olympic Games."

"Sounds all right," Alice said.

"Well, he's not very *likable*, but he let me go so I could settle Zath's hash. He did warn me about the prophecy that said the Liberator would be betrayed by his friends and thrown among the legions of death. That's exactly what happened. There's a traitor in the Service, and I know who it is, and I absolutely must get the word back to Olympus."

Alice spoke from a long way away. "But you did find the Service in the end?"

"I found the Service right away, the next day. But I was too late. Zath got to their agent before I did. I saw him being burned alive by—"

"Excuse me," Smedley said. "Frightfully sorry and all that, but I think I'm going to faint."

# *12*

The priests were still haranguing the crowd.

As subtly as drifting snow, the young men of Sonalby closed in around the stranger in their midst. Just as unobtrusively, women, children, and older men left his vicinity, leaving Edward surrounded by youths. They all seemed intent on the funeral pyre, but he knew better than to try to escape.

Most of them leaned on spears, and some had shields also. Every one had a wooden club dangling at his side; none wore more than a leather loincloth. Their hair and beards were trimmed short, so they could not be caught hold of in battle, and they all had painted faces. They all had scars on their ribs, too regular to be accidental—some old and healed, others still raw and oozing.

The Carpenter house collapsed into ashes, and there were no more heretics to burn. The priests departed, and the mob began to disperse.

The young men turned to the next item of business, the stranger in town. They opened up into a circle around him and proceeded to discuss him as if he were a piece of furniture. He was footsore and thirsty and melting in the heat. The debate seemed likely to go on for the rest of the day. It might eventually conclude with a decision to put him to death or perform something less fatal but more unpleasant.

There were two factions involved, one slightly younger than the other. The younger group were clean shaven or just beardless, and their faces were painted in a complex design, mainly yellow, with very minor amounts of blue, white, red, and green. The older group had beards and another pattern, in which blue predominated, with lesser amounts of the other colors and an ominous addition of black.

Had Edward been a native-born Englishman, he would probably have demanded at that point to be taken before the village headman, and that would have been a very serious error. Fortunately, he had been raised among the Embu of Kenya, so he had some idea of what he was dealing with, although he could not make out a word of the jabbering talk.

Finally heads began to nod; some sort of agreement had been reached. One of the blue-painted older ones said in heavily accented Joalian, "Do you wear merit marks?" He tapped the scars on his ribs.

Sussian smocks left arms bare, but concealed chests. "It is not the custom of my people."

The debate resumed, as incomprehensibly as before.

Then the same man asked a second question. "How old are you?"

"Eighteen."

"How long since you shaved your face?"

Edward rubbed his stubble. "Two days ago."

There were grunts, then. And more jabber. At last the younger, yellow-faced youths just melted away. They had conceded that the beardless stranger belonged to the other group.

He belonged to them outright. He was fairly certain that he was theirs to do with as they pleased. There would be no headman, no council of elders to whom he could appeal. A young male stranger in town was a matter for the young warriors.

There must have been fifty of them around him now. By and large they were too swarthy to be a typical crowd in England, but they would not have been out of place in Southern Europe. They varied from lithe to beefy, from short to tall, although few were six-footers like himself. They were all about his own age. Now they were debating who should interrogate the prisoner, with much pointing. Eventually one of the tall ones was selected; he stepped forward and the rest fell silent.

"Foreigner, what is your name?"

Edward had already given that matter considerable thought. He had decided to stick with D'ward, having learned that it was not uncommon, the name of some minor god or other—who might be an interesting stranger to meet sometime, possibly a fellow countryman. To use an alias would be to concede to himself that he was frightened of the Chamber. D'ward he would remain, but in the Vales a man's name included his trade. He could think of only one skill he possessed that might be of any value at all in Sonalby.

"I am D'ward Spearthrower," he said.

It was an insane gamble. He would have to prove himself in the eyes of men who had been practicing all their lives, and he had no idea of the technique required for their weapons. But he had always had a knack for throwing things. He had set a school record with the javelin.

Now he had won the interest of his age group. They marched him back out of town in very short order, to the practice field he had seen on the way in. An audience of women and the younger youths watched curiously from the sidelines.

He would need to work a miracle. He had done so once, after picking up mana by playing holy man on a node. Later he had absorbed some from the audience in the theater, but that had been trivial and he must have used it up in the exertions of the last two days. Now he was so tired he doubted he could summon up any charisma at all.

A couple of warriors offered him a choice of spears. They were heavier than he had expected, with leaf-shaped metal blades. He selected one of medium length and weight and hefted it a few times. At that point someone thrust one of the round shields at him, a massively heavy circle of wood and thick leather. He was supposed to hold *that* while throwing *this!* His confidence plummeted.

"This weight is not familiar to me," he announced brashly. "I shall try for distance first." After that he might attempt to hit a moderate size barn at close quarters. He nudged the tall man with the edge of his shield. "Give me a mark." He could watch how it was done.

He expected the tall man to run, but he barely moved. He just leaned back, took one long pace with his left foot, and hurled. The spear flashed in the sky and dropped into the scrubby grass about a hundred miles down range.

Merciful *heavens!* Wasn't that out of bounds?

"Good throw!" Edward said. He could sense that it was a good throw from the reactions around them. He steadied himself for the roll of the dice, braced his left arm to support that pestilential shield. . . . He threw.

His spear fell well short of the other, but he heard no sniggers. He thought he sensed some grudging approval. He snarled angrily.

"Let me try again, with a longer pole!"

He was given a longer spear. This time he did better, and the audience was moderately pleased.

"Good throw!" said the tall man. "I am Prat'han Potter." He gripped Edward's left shoulder and squeezed. Edward did the same for him.

Then the fifty or so others went through the same procedure, each announcing his name in perfectly understandable Joalian, although the accent was harsh. Their trades were not what he had expected—tanner, shoemaker, tentmaker, yes, but also wheelwright, silversmith, printer, musician, and many others.

Now Edward must show that he could hit a target, and he discovered just how seriously young Nagians took their spear-throwing. One of them stalked forward about thirty paces, then turned and waited. His shield covered him from his shoulders to halfway down his thighs, but that still left far too much of him exposed. The blades were not honed to battle sharpness, but they could still maim.

"I will not throw against that target!"

Suddenly the blue-painted faces were dangerous again. The circle seemed to close in with menace.

"Your spears are not what I am accustomed to!" he protested.

"You are so good that Gopaenum cannot block your cast?"

"I don't mean that. It is unfair to the man to throw against him until I have practiced more."

"It is perfectly fair," Prat'han said. "That is a very easy shot. You throw to Gopaenum Butcher's shield. Then he throws to yours. Throw, D'ward!"

Hmm! Like that, was it?

"It is still not fair. He is at much greater risk than I shall be."

He provoked another debate. Did they *never* sit down in Nagvale? The human target was called back for the discussion, but in the end nothing was changed. Edward asked that Gopaenum stand closer, which was folly because now he had complicated the matter with questions of courage. Of course Gopaenum went out even farther than before, making the range greater. They really did seem to think the shot was an easy one.

Fortunately there was no wind. Wiping a sweaty palm on his smock, Edward summed up the problem. His bluff had been called. Only the most incredible luck would let him hit that shield, and even then he might be expected to repeat the throw. Gopaenum probably could block a single spear, and obviously this exercise was shield practice as well as spear practice, but Edward would not risk wounding a man just to carry off a fraud. It is better to have leaped and lost than never to have stuck your neck out. . . .

He missed the shield. His spear passed three feet over Gopaenum's head, and that was still a yard closer than he had planned. The audience burst into howls of ironic laughter. Their accent suddenly became incomprehensible again.

Out in the field, Gopaenum Butcher retrieved the spear and turned to throw.

The spectators moved back a pace or two, but probably only so the marksman could see his target more easily. None of them expected Gopaenum to miss.

Edward looked around for a safe place to hide, and of course there was none. The sprawling village was the only settlement in sight. Beyond the river, bare plain stretched out to the misty peaks, shimmering in the awful heat, and behind him the rocky face of Nagwall. At best he would be driven out to die of thirst and hunger. At worst the warriors would all use him for spear practice.

He should have claimed to be a traveling scholar. Then they would have assumed he was a spy, but they might have allowed him a night's sleep before they ran him out of town. He had gambled and lost.

He put down the shield, lower edge resting on the ground just in front of his toes, upper edge leaning against his thighs, leaving valuable parts unprotected. He straightened and folded his arms.

"What are you doing, foreigner?" Prat'han demanded.

"Waiting for Gopaenum."

The target was the same, but now the human part of it could not dodge or move to block the throw. Edward felt a strange tingle as his words registered; he knew it for the touch of mana. In the end these warriors would be more impressed by courage than by anything else. He had never thought of himself as being particularly brave—in fact, he was sure he was not—but he was not going to have them laughing at him, even if this mess he was in was all his own fault. Now he had captured their imagination.

Someone shouted an explanation to the waiting Gopaenum Butcher.

Gopaenum hesitated, then raised his spear. He hefted it a few times, judging the throw. Edward wished he would get on with it.

He felt a spasm of terror as the pole arced through the air. It struck the shield on the extreme end, jerking it away from him. Even so, he felt as if someone had kicked his knee. He almost fell over. He winced, staggering to regain his balance and wondering if a direct hit would have broken his legs. Gopaenum had either almost missed altogether or had deliberately aimed off to the side. The blade had gone right through the wood and leather—a possibility that Edward had not even considered.

The audience broke into cheers and rushed forward to thump him on the back. Their admiration sent intoxicating waves of mana surging through him. Willing hands thrust a spear at him and retrieved his shield. Gopaenum was waiting for the next throw. Again?

Oh, hell! How could he fail now? Too elated to stop and consider the risk, Edward drew back his arm, stepped forward, and hurled with all his strength. He could not tell how much he used mana on his arm and how much on the missile. Probably most of it went on himself, because to influence material objects must require far more power. He felt the sudden loss, the drain of mana, exactly like the time he cured Dolm Actor's despair. Again the results surprised him. The spear flashed over the field in an arrow's flat trajectory. Gopaenum did not have to move his shield an inch and perhaps did not even have time to react. The spear struck it dead center. The impact threw him flat on his back, the pole quivering upright. The spectators yelled out an incredulous whoop, and Edward felt his confidence return with a rush, greater than ever. Bizarre!

Honor was satisfied. Gopaenum came running up to give D'ward a hug of congratulation. There was much laughter and shoulder squeezing. Then the entire age group trotted off to their barracks to discuss the situation over warm beer. At last their visitor had a chance to sit down.

The barracks was a long building of wicker and thatch, as barren inside as an empty bottle. What need for closets when you owned only one garment? Where else would warriors sleep but on the bare ground with their shields as pillows?

The culture was not organized in quite the same way as the Kenyans', but there were strong similarities. These were the young men of the village. They had no designated leaders, for everything was resolved by consensus, but some were more respected and listened to than others. They had been together since they were children. Forty years from now the survivors would still be together, but by then they would be elders, with other responsibilities. There was a class of senior warriors three or four years ahead of them, and another of adolescents close behind, the yellow-faced Boy Scouts who had contested jurisdiction over the visitor.

The newcomer was questioned closely, because any traveler in the Vales was automatically assumed to be spying for someone, probably several someones. He did not mention the Service, which was obviously out of favor just then. Again he said he hailed from Rinoovale, because that was a long way away. Ah, they said—Rinoo was a vassal state of Nioldom, so he was a Niolian spy, was he? No, he was traveling because he was curious to see the world. They all thought that a very weak excuse. How would he ever earn enough money to buy a wife?

After more beer and prolonged debate, though, the junior warriors of Sonalby decided that D'ward Spearthrower was acceptable. Niol was too far away to worry about. He was given a leather loincloth, which was manly wear; his boots were removed, probably going in trade for it. Two of his new brethren brought paints and proceeded to decorate his face, instructing him carefully in the meaning of each of the symbols they had chosen for their mark. Blue spears and shields were for Olfaan Astina—blue was sacred to the Maiden. The black skulls showed that they served Zath and did not fear him. Two yellow triangles and a frog because they still owed allegiance to the Youth. Blue crescent, hand, and scroll for other aspects of Astina. A small white sunburst as a token to Visek. No red yet, because they were virgins. The green hammer of the Man for strength, and so on and so on.

There was a brief debate about whether he had earned one merit mark or two, and they agreed on two—one for being accepted and another for his dare with the shield. Raucous, tipsy, but probably not very dangerous, the age group set out to escort D'ward Spearthrower to the shrine of Olfaan Astina. In this aspect the Maiden was goddess of warriors and also patron deity of all Nagland, her main temple being located in Nag itself.

When they reached their destination, Edward could feel virtuality from the node, but the shrine seemed to be on the edges of it. He was now fairly confident that a shrine, unlike a temple, would contain no resident numen. This one was only a shabby— and smelly—leather tent enclosing an altar and a carved image of a young woman in armor. The figure was about half life size and surprisingly well made; he wondered if it had been looted from somewhere, sometime. If there was no numen present he was probably in no danger from Astina or any of her vassals.

But directly adjacent stood the temple of Krobidirkin the Herder, an aspect of Karzon. He was a definite threat. Kalmak Carpenter's auto-da-fé had been organized by priests of the Man, and the timing was too slick to be a coincidence. Either Karzon or Zath had guessed that the Liberator would seek out the Service, and might suspect he was in Nagvale. Edward had a strong hunch that a stranger would be able to detect the presence of another on his own node.

Yet he could think of no way to avoid the ordeal his classmates had planned for him. Merit marks were awards, a source of pride, recognition from his peers. His newfound brethren cheerfully inked lines on his ribs for him to cut along. They provided the stone knife; they offered the salt he had to rub in to stop the bleeding and create a lasting scar. Then they watched critically to see how he would perform. It was a sacrifice to the goddess, of course. It was a demonstration of his manhood. It was a damnable risk, because he was a stranger. The mana that should flow to Olfaan might stick to him and be detected by Krobidirkin Karzon, or he might be drained of the little he had collected that afternoon, or . . . or all sorts of things.

But he had no choice, so he cut and rubbed and shook away the tears before they could smudge the paint on his face. He felt nothing except anger and extreme pain. The first touch of the salt was the worst shock he could remember. The second time his hand shook so much that he cut too deep and the salt hurt even more. But nothing miraculous occurred. He was probably too exhausted and too intoxicated by the rotten beer to notice mana now.

His brothers carried him back shoulder-high to the barracks and cheerfully informed him that it was his turn to be cook.

Still, he had found a home and without it he might well have been facing starvation or execution. A few weeks to polish his skill with the language and he could hope to set off in search of the Service somewhere else.

If the Service was still worth finding, that was.

The only Service personnel he ever met always died very quickly.

# 13

"There's a horse trough!" Ginger was braking. "He can get a drink there."

Smedley had admitted to feeling thirsty. Mostly he was feeling very foolish, and everyone kept pestering him, asking if he was all right. The gash on his calf was not serious. He did not think he had lost very much blood, he had just lost it rather quickly. They had bandaged his leg with strips of blanket, but he was respectable again, keeping it stretched out along the seat. He was all right now, just thirsty.

The car came to a halt alongside the trough. Where else could one find anything to drink at two o'clock in the morning? Windows overlooked it; Jones turned off the engine, which shuddered into silence broken by irritated tickings.

"Damn!" Alice said. "We don't have anything to drink out of."

"I can walk!" Smedley protested. "Really, you're all making a frightful fuss about nothing."

Exeter opened the door and climbed out. Smedley moved to follow.

*Humiliation!* "Where did my shoes go?"

Alice tied the laces for him.

He shook off Exeter's helping hand and limped over to the water pipe, feeling nothing worse than a little shakiness. He bent his head to the stream, he drank and drank. That definitely helped. The sky was streaked with silvery clouds, the moon playing peekaboo. Moonlight showed the black blood all over his clothes. Exeter joined him, bundled up in the greatcoat. Even the greatcoat had blood on it. By the time they returned to the car, Jones had brought one of the oil lamps and was inspecting the interior.

It looked like a slaughterhouse.

"I hate to ask this," Exeter said, "but whose car is it?"

"It's stolen!" Alice said quickly.

He yowled like a hyena.

"Quiet, ninny!" she snapped, looking at the cottages flanking the road.

"Seriously, whose is it?"

"Don't worry about it. How much farther, Mr. Jones?"

"Oh, we're about halfway, almost at Chatham. Once we cross the Medway, we could get off the A2."

"What do you think, General Smedley?" Alice asked.

"Backroads'll be slower. I'd say keep on making a run for it."

"I won't argue," Jones said. He sounded very weary. "On irregular French verbs, yes. On strategy, no. Where do we go in London? Your flat, Miss Prescott, I assume?"

"Why don't we drop our jailbirds off there, then you and I go and return the car?"

He grunted agreement and took the lamp away. In a few moments he turned the crank and the engine caught at once. It had not done its worrisome coughing for some time. The car pulled smoothly away from the curb and resumed its journey.

Smedley had arranged himself along the back seat again, with the other two fitted in around him. He was starting to feel quite hopeful. True, they might yet blunder into a police blockade at any minute. The coppers could react very quickly at times, but would they in this case? Officially Exeter was just a shell-shocked soldier with amnesia. To reclassify him as an escaped German spy would require some explanations. The news of his disappearance must be in Whitehall by now, but at this time of night who was going to waken whom to do what or find which file where?

Whose car was it anyway? Alice had been reticent yesterday. Today she seemed even more determined that they not know.

"So I needn't have worried at all!" she said brightly. "Here I thought the Devil himself had carried you off bodily to hell, and all the time you were running around with a spear, stealing cattle?"

"It wasn't hell," Edward admitted, sounding as if he was smothering a yawn. "Actually it was almost fun. They were a likable bunch in their way. A different sort of college."

"But what did you do all day? Throw spears and rustle cattle?"

"No rustling at all. As for what we did . . . Well we all began by jumping in the river, except the day's cook, who made breakfast. Then we divided up in pairs and painted each other's faces. After that we went to work, usually."

Incredible! Smedley shuddered to think what his father would say about the Exeter family if he ever heard this confession. The fellow had gone completely native, it seemed—scars and war paint and all. This Nagland story was quite unlike the hints he'd dropped earlier about Olympus, where people had houseboys and dressed for dinner.

"What sort of work?" Alice asked. "Silversmithing, you said?"

"All sorts of work." Exeter chuckled, not sounding at all ashamed of himself. "Nobody worked very hard or very long, but we all had some sort of morning job. In the afternoon, we usually knocked off to go fishing or spear-throwing. Sports, exercise. We taught the juniors, the seniors taught us. In the evening we sat around and made weapons, gambled, or just talked about girls. None of us knew anything about them, of course."

"How long did you stay there?" Smedley asked, trying not to sound disapproving.

"Much longer than I intended. I soon learned that Kalmak Carpenter had been martyred because he was involved with a new sect, the Church of the Undivided. I could guess that the Service was behind it—the only way to break the tyranny of the Pentatheon would be to start a completely new religion, so that made sense. But the persecution had not been restricted to Sonalby; it had happened all over Nagland. The order had come from Karzon, but no doubt Zath was behind it, so I was probably the immediate cause. I was not very happy when I thought of all the innocent people who had died because of me.

"The new church might put me in touch with the Service, but it had been wiped out in Nagvale and nobody seemed to know anything about it—or even want to discuss it. If my interest in it got back to the wrong ears, then I might wake up dead one morning. I had no other leads, so I just stayed where I was and waited to be rescued. That wasn't very likely, of course. I knew the Service believed the reapers had killed me in the Sacrarium, the night I crossed over. It had sent Onica Mason to confirm this, and she had disappeared also. So the chances that it was still searching for me were about two thirds of zero.

"All I could do, I concluded, was try to find out as much as I could about the Vales. And learn the local jabber, of course. Perhaps one day I might pick up some mention of the Church of the Undivided that would tell me where to look for it. My group brethren were as informative as anyone, which wasn't informative at all. At least I could trust whatever they told me, which was more than you could say for anyone else. Most of them had never been outside Nagvale in their lives, and never expected to be, but there were a dozen or so who had jobs that required them to travel—peddlers and drovers, mostly. A couple had gone off to work in the capital, Nag. As they drifted back home, to stay a while before their next excursion, I got to know them and questioned them. I didn't learn much. I was lazy, I suppose, or just windy. Having nowhere to go, I kept putting off my departure.

"Obviously I needed a job. The group talked it over and decided I was tall and would be good on roofs, so about a dozen of them took me along to see Gopaenum's uncle's brother, Pondarz Thatcher. They suggested he hire me. He didn't argue, because a village has to support its militia. Also, he had a daughter."

"Aha!" Alice said. "Describe this daughter."

"Absolutely gorgeous. About ten, I think . . . I don't know, I never set eyes on her. I never saw much of my supposed wages, either. They went toward her bride price. It didn't matter to me, as long as I ate twice a day. All I had to do was toss bundles of reeds up to the workmen on the roof. The job was well within my capabilities.

"But I agree that the original purpose must have been cattle stealing, just as in Africa. In the olden days—whenever those may have been—a young man's occupation in that herding society would be stealing the neighbors' livestock. He would give his loot to some older man of the village as payment on a wife. When he had paid enough cows and proved his mettle in more or less serious battles, he would marry the girl he had bought and retire. Thereafter he would just watch his own herds grow and his wife do all the work. War he would then leave to the young men, because that was their business."

"If that were true here," Ginger Jones said, "then we might not be in the mess we're in."

Nobody commented for a while. The car roared on through the night. Smedley decided that the remark had been very close to defeatist. The war existed, so it must be won. He had done his bit.

When Exeter spoke again, his tone was more somber than before.

"You can't imagine how strange it feels to be back in England, spinning through the night in a motorcar like this! It feels odder than all these things I've been telling you. I'm sorry to chatter so much. It's such a relief to be able to talk again."

"We're all enjoying it," Alice said. "It is better than having Baron Munchausen along. You're leading up to something. You're going into all this sociology for some reason?"

"Absolutely! You remember Nyagatha and the Embu. A lot of Bantu peoples had that sort of age-group arrangement, or something similar. When the English arrived they usually said, 'Take me to your headman,' and the natives would look blank, not knowing what they meant. Who you talked to depended on what your business was! So the English would appoint a headman and tell him to stop the cattle raiding. Then they wondered why the whole culture collapsed. What astonished me about the Nagians was that they had managed to make a transformation to a money economy without losing their social structure. A lot of the Vales are very close to an industrial revolution, you see, although they don't have guns yet, thank goodness. The Joalians play the part of the English, but without firearms Joalia can't ever make a real colony out of Nagia. They had imported a mercantile culture, though, and yet the traditional ways had very largely persisted. The Nagians had managed to blend the old and the new. I was very intrigued to know how they'd done it. The answer was obvious, but I didn't think of it."

"But who do the warriors fight?" Smedley asked.

Exeter chuckled. "Nobody. Oh, they have periodic brawls with neighboring villages, but they're prearranged, show affairs. A few bones get broken and teeth knocked out and a deuce of a lot of betting goes on, and that's about it. I never saw one.

"The most exciting thing that happened in my first few fortnights there was that Toggan Silversmith got married. His father had money, of course. He was the first of our age group to tie the knot, and it was a big milestone for all of us. I swear it took half a fortnight to decide how our face design should be changed. We could add some more green emblems, you see, because that is the color of manhood. We could introduce some red, which represents the Lady, Eltiana, who's goddess of motherhood and, um, related matters. But if we overdid it, the senior warriors would get in a snit and the juniors might start crowding us on the blue. So we had to appoint delegates to negotiate with other age groups. Everyone found it fascinating.

"As soon as Toggan got married, he wasn't a warrior anymore, but he was still one of the group. He slept with his wife and came around in the morning to get his makeup on. After the first fortnight, we saw a lot more of him than she ever did. Being a warrior just seemed like being in a boarding school. So I assumed. Until the war came."

"Followed you, did it?" Alice said. "Oh, sorry! I didn't mean—"

"No, this was a different war. The first I knew of it was when a priest turned up one evening, an elderly chap in a green robe. I smelled trouble right away. He sat down and negotiated with us. I suppose there were about sixty of us there, sitting around sharpening spears. We didn't stop because of him, either! He said that the temple had learned that the junior warrior age group had adopted a foreigner. Well, the whole village had known that for fortnights. He said that Krobidirkin was Sonalby's patron god, and the foreigner really ought to make a sacrifice to the god and ask for sanctuary—matter of protocol, you see.

That debate lasted all night. A lot of the fellows said the priests just wanted a free meal, but eventually the group decided that it was a good idea. I considered making a break for it, but Krobidirkin must have known about me all along anyway. Moreover, I could see that if I did a bunk, I would get my pals in trouble with the numen and probably with the elder groups. And I was curious.

I couldn't be expected to take part in an important ceremony without the backing of my peers, so the next afternoon the whole age group assembled. We bought a bullock from Gopaenum's uncle and drove it along to the temple.

There we were right on the node. The virtuality made my scalp prickle, as usual. There were shrines to Olfaan, and Wyseth—he's the sun god, and in that climate you don't ever forget the sun. And there was one to Paa Tion, the god of healing, and one to Emthaz, goddess of childbirth. The usual Pentatheon representation. But the temple was the center of the village, and it was Krobidirkin the Herder's.

It was one story high, made of leather and poles. If you can imagine a leather labyrinth, that's what it was. Smelly and hot. The others knew what to expect because they'd been there before, but all the way in I was shivering from the sanctity and thinking I would never find my way out again. The middle was open, a big courtyard: sand underfoot and the sky overhead. There was a paved place for making sacrifices. The priests were waiting eagerly, because they would have red meat for supper afterward. And there was a small, round tent in one corner. A yurt, I think they're called. That was the house of the god. If there was an image of him, it was in there. All we could see was the tent.

I was introduced as D'ward Roofer and put in the front. We all knelt down on the sand and bowed our heads and the ceremony began, chanting and praying and so on.

In a few minutes I looked up. The flap of the tent had been pulled aside, and there was a little man standing there, holding it. He smiled at me and beckoned, and I knew that he was the numen himself, Krobidirkin. I could see no alternative, so I just stood up and walked over, and the priests did not notice. I was surprised they couldn't hear my knees knocking.

He took me inside, and the inside was much larger than the outside. There were several rooms to it, and flaps of the roof had been opened to let in the air and light. There were rugs and cushions. It smelled of spices. Someone was playing a zither or something softly in another room, and I could not hear the temple priests doing their awful wailing. It was exotic, but quite pleasant.

"Do sit down, Liberator," he said. "I regret that I cannot offer you tea, but I have a reasonable substitute."

We settled on the cushions, and he poured from a silver pot that stood on a brazier. The cups were beautiful porcelain.

You can't tell how old a stranger is from his appearance. They have a sort of age-lessness. Krobidirkin was small, as I said, but tough and wiry looking. He had the serenity of a landscape and could have been eighty, but he had the skin of a youth. He wore only the local leather loincloth, and his face was quite the ugliest I had ever seen, all slanty eyes and squashed nose. His ears stuck out, and his mustache turned down at the ends. He had a whimsical grin that I found reassuring.

It took me a minute or two to find my voice. This numen was a vassal of Karzon's, remember, and therefore an ally of Zath, the god of death, whom I was prophesied to kill and who had been doing his level best to kill me. I had met Tion and escaped unharmed, but he was not allied with the Chamber. This Krobidirkin must be. He had immolated Kalmak Carpenter and his family, and here he was offering me tea!

"I am honored to meet you, sir," I said, or some such nonsense.

He chuckled. "No, the honor is mine. May I say that your father would be proud of you?"

I spilled half a cup of scalding tea down my chest.

"You knew my father, sir?"

The little man was much amused by my reaction. "Yes, indeed. I met him several times. A good man. He made a special journey all the way from his home world to consult with me. He even gave me a picture of you."

I think that was probably the biggest surprise I have ever had in my life. There I was, an infinite distance from home, a stranger in a very strange land indeed, and this all-powerful local god handed me a photograph of the station at Nyagatha! It showed the mater, and you, Alice, and me. We were sitting on the veranda. The gramophone was there, and the parrot's cage, and all sorts of details I had forgotten. I was about three, I suppose. I had never seen that picture before. I made rather an ass of myself over it.

Of course Krobidirkin was pleased, because that was the effect he had wanted to produce. He refilled my cup.

And then I said, "But surely this is impossible! I thought nothing could cross over except people?"

He chuckled, as if he had been waiting for me to work that out in my dim-witted way. "Memories can cross over," he said. "And there is mana." He took the photograph from me—it did seem to be a real, honest-to-god photograph, black-and-white, not colored—and he turned it over. I expected to see the photographer's name there, but it was blank. Then he waved his hand and the back showed another picture. It was the guv'nor, sitting in that very tent, where I was sitting, wearing a Nagian loincloth and smiling.

Well, that floored me.

"May I guess?" I said when I recovered. "He had been put in charge of some people who had once had a society very similar to the Nagians', and he knew that you had managed to preserve their institutions in the face of progress, so he came to ask your advice?"

Krobidirkin's ugly face split in a wide grin. "Of course! Unfortunately, it takes mana to guide such a development, and in the post he then held, Kameron was only another native. A culturally advanced native, and a well-intentioned one, but not a stranger in his own world."

"You have been a good father to your people, sir," I said. "You also are from our world?"

He smiled and nodded. "A very long time ago, yes. I can recall very little of my youth, I am afraid. One forgets. A new world brings a new life, and the old days become unimportant when one decides one will never return. I do remember that my people were very warlike. We had a notable leader, named . . . I forget. He led us against a civilization of great cities, and we were badly defeated. The next year he tried again, and this time he was turned aside by an army led by a priest. The mana was very strong, and he retreated before it, knowing that he could not win against the god power. He died not long after."

That may have been the second worst shock, I suppose. It is one thing to know intellectually that strangers live a long time. To run into a man who remembers battles fought fifteen hundred years ago—that brings it home with a vengeance. "Was his name Attila?" I asked.

The little Hun clapped his hands and said, "That's it! A wonderful leader of men! Great native charisma."

So we sat and talked about the battle of Châlons—which was fought sometime in the middle of the fifth century, in case you forget—and Pope Leo, who somehow persuaded the Huns to withdraw from Italy the following year. How he did it has always been a great historical mystery. My host was delighted to learn that his comrades in arms were still remembered after so long, but I was careful not to go into details about their reputation. He probably wouldn't have minded. Krobidirkin had been a sort of medicine man with the horde, and in his old age he had accidentally crossed over to Nextdoor and become a god.

He soon eased the conversation around to the *Filoby Testament* and the Liberator.

"I greatly regret what happened to the carpenter and his family," he said. "I had direct orders, and I dared not disobey them. One hates to treat one's people so, however misguided their heresies."

"And what of me?" I asked. "Have you direct orders about me?"

"Oh, yes. But you are the son of my old friend Kameron! Zath does not know where you are. He does not know that I know, and he is furious that you have escaped him. He is a very frightened god!"

"He need not be," I said. "I have no plans to kill him."

The little man chortled. "The prophecy says you will! Zath has tried everything he can think of to break the chain of events and failed every time. So he fears you, and rightly so."

"What of Karzon?"

He screwed up his ugly little face, making it even uglier. "He fears Zath! And that brings me to the reason I invited you here, D'ward. Zath has decreed that there must be war, and more war. War brings him mana, and he is hungry for all the mana he can get, because the Liberator is a threat to him. Now it has begun—in Narshia, which was part of Joaldom, but lies between Thargvale and Lappinvale. Lappinvale has been a Thargian colony for half a century, you know? But recently the Randorians have been stirring up trouble there, urging rebellion and independence."

He looked expectantly at me and I nodded as if it all made sense. I was actually thinking that it didn't, but it still sounded less insane than all Europe exploding over the death of one Austrian nobleman.

Krobidirkin chuckled. "Thargians dislike being inconvenienced or worried by uncertainty. They had been trying to subvert the Narshian government for years, and this summer they ran out of patience. They invaded Narshland. The Joalians plot reprisal." He sighed. "It will be bloody, I fear, and Zath will benefit greatly."

As you may guess, I was not very happy to hear this. "What has it got to do with me?"

He smiled cryptically. "The Joalians plan a lightning raid on Tharg itself, while the Thargian army is absent—that is exceedingly brave of them! To reach Thargvale, they must cross both Nagvale and Lemodvale. Lemodia is part of Thargdom, but we belong to Joal. Our queen is a Joalian puppet. Their vanguard is already here, in Nag, demanding her help. She will muster her warriors as they demand."

I felt ill, and the more I thought about it, the more ill I got.

"I must give myself up!" I said. I probably didn't mean that, of course. It was just the first thing that came into my head.

Krobidirkin looked shocked. "Oh, no! That will not help at all! The war is inevitable now. No, I wish to ask a favor."

"Sir . . . ask!" I owed him my life, remember. He had given me sanctuary, even if I had not realized it until then.

He nodded, well pleased. Numens usually get their own way.

"The summons will arrive soon. I knew you would be tempted to leave. This is not your cause, after all—or at least, you would not have thought it so, had I not invited you here and told you. The Joalians will require each village contingent to have a leader.

Nagians prefer to debate and argue, but they do appoint leaders in time of war. In this case they will have to. There is no question whom the Sonalby contingent will choose."

I could not argue with that, because I knew they reacted to my stranger's charisma no matter how much I tried to hide it. "I know little of war, especially this sort of war."

"It is not necessary that you do. The Joalian generals will provide all the skill needed to spill all the blood possible. And I think you would have been my boys' choice even had you not been a stranger." That was just flattery, of course.

"What do you want of me?" I asked gloomily.

"Stay and lead them, D'ward! With you at their head, they will not suffer quite so much. More of them will return to their homeland. Believe me, this is so. You will ease the suffering and reduce the deaths. I fear for my people if their young men are dragged into this without your guidance."

What could I say to that?

I hedged at first. "I was hoping to find the Service and enlist their help in going Home."

He scowled and tugged at his droopy mustache. "Beware the Service, D'ward! They will betray you—it is foretold."

Everyone seemed to have read that damnable *Filoby Testament* but me! In the end I agreed to accept the leadership of the warriors. One cannot easily refuse a numen, and he had obviously kept my presence in Nagland a secret from Zath. He had probably taken quite a risk doing that. Although he did not labor the point, I knew I was in his debt.

"Your presence honors my humble tent," he said then. "I would be happy to keep you here and talk. I should have invited you before, but it is not safe for either of us. Zath suspects me, and he is far stronger than any of us."

It was dismissal. We rose. He offered to give me the picture. I was sorely tempted, but I had no pockets. Reluctantly I declined it, and promised that one day I would come back, after the war. He showed me to the door. The priests were still at their work, and they did not see me return to my place.

That was the third time I had met a god. He was a true father to his people, the most impressive of the three by far. And he had been one of Attila's Huns! In my innocence, I thought that very wonderful.

Much of what he had told me was true, actually. I later confirmed that the guv'nor did make a flying visit to Nextdoor in August of ninety-nine, and he did go to Nagland. The picture may well have been what Krobidirkin said it was, although he could just have pulled all the images out of my memories as easily as out of the guv'nor's. What the Herder was really doing was playing the Great Game. By enlisting the Liberator in the war, he had made a very cunning move—from his point of view, at least.

# 14

Smedley awoke with a start. That time he had really been asleep. The car was doing its coughing and stuttering again. He peered out the window and saw buildings, darkened shops. The blackened streetlights threw tiny puddles of brightness; here and there another vehicle showed or a chink of window high up.

"Where are we?"

"Greenwich," Alice said.

London! They must be safe now!

The car choked, slowed, and then picked up again.

"Does anyone know anything about the workings of these infernal contraptions?" Ginger demanded.

Alice and Exeter said, "No," simultaneously.

"A little," Smedley said. "Have we any tools on board?"

"No," said Ginger.

"Is it short of petrol?"

"No."

That settled that, then. Nothing to be done.

London never slept, but it was pretty drowsy out in the suburbs at this time in the morning. There were no traffic policemen at the intersections, but usually Ginger had the right-of-way. He was driving quite slowly. The old boy must be completely exhausted.

Smedley's leg throbbed. So did his missing hand. Perhaps in time he would discover that this was a sign of rain or thunder or something.

Exeter had refused to talk any more, claiming he was hoarse. He had demanded to know more about the war, about what this Lawrence character was up to in Palestine, about zeppelins and poison gas, and what sort of allies the Italians and Japanese were. Alice had talked for a while. Smedley had stayed out of it, and started nodding off.

"Somebody talk!" Ginger said. "I'm getting sleepy."

Smedley roused himself. "So that's what you've been doing these last three years? Fighting with spears?"

Exeter sighed. "Not all of it, no. But some. I knew there had been an out-of-valley campaign about twenty years ago. As soon as we left Krobidirkin's temple, I went off to talk to the fathers at their clubhouse. The whites, we called them, because Visek's— doesn't matter. That evening I brought a couple of them to the barracks and got them to tell us about it. I said I'd had an inspiration in the temple. Everyone assumed it was a message from the god, which was perfectly true.

"They told us how the Joalians had made them march in rows, and I suggested we practice that. There was a lot of grumbling, but I could always get my way when I wanted, being a stranger. A couple of days later the queen's envoy arrived in Sonalby. He went to the senior warriors and eventually they summoned us. We marched up in a phalanx and their eyes just about popped out of their heads."

Alice chuckled, although it sounded forced. "So you were elected general?"

"Of course. My group all voted for me, and we outnumbered the seniors. Half of them were married and didn't count—married men stay home as defensive reserves. We roped in a few of the big ones from the cadet class. In a day or two we set off for Nag, about a hundred of us."

The car coughed, coughed, coughed. It faded to a stop, then suddenly lurched forward. Everyone breathed again.

"Keep talking!" Alice said.

"Lordie! I'm sure you don't want to hear all that. Nag is a fair-sized city by Vales standards. Not like Joal or Tharg, of course, about the size of Suss. We'd call it a modest market town. That was where I met the heir apparent, Prince Goldfish."

"You are making that up!"

"No. Cross my heart! Well, it was pronounced more like 'Golbfish,' but I always thought of him as Goldfish. He was the queen's oldest son and his name was Golbfish Hordeleader. He was in his late twenties, I suppose, and one of the tallest, biggest men in Nagland. He was rich, had three gorgeous concubines, and he was heir to the throne. What more can a man want?"

"To play the mouth organ?" Smedley said grumpily.

"I told you you wouldn't want to hear all this."

"Yes, we do!" Alice said. "What about Goldfish?"

"And he was absolutely miserable! To start with, he was big, but he was shaped like a pear. Also—"

The car coughed and slowed, the motor silent.

Ginger guided it into the curb, and it came to a halt right by a streetlight. It hissed and clinked.

Alice said, "Hell's bells!"

Ginger had slumped over the wheel. After a moment he turned around. "Anyone got any ideas?"

"It may just have overheated," Smedley said. "Let's give it a few minutes and then try cranking it." If he had some tools he might be able to do something, or at least show Exeter how to do something . . . but he hadn't.

A lorry went rumbling by.

"We're not supposed to park here," Alice said, her voice brittle. "And I don't imagine the buses are running yet. Care to explain all that blood on your coat, Edward? Or your trousers, Julian?"

"Or why I am wearing pajamas," Edward said. "The old crate's done very well."

"But not well enough!" Now there was no hiding the overtones of panic in her voice.

"How about a taxicab?"

"At this time of night? Away out here? Explain the bloodstains?"

"Just a thought."

"Telephone the Royal Automobile Club," Smedley suggested.

"Don't be stupid! We have no papers!"

They sat in brooding silence for a while.

Failure was a bitter taste in Smedley's throat. So near and yet so far! The sun would be up soon, and they must look a hopeless bunch of guys. You could get away with a lot in London, but marching around covered in blood was not one. Without his folly, the others would have had a good chance, even yet. All his fault.

Lorries rumbled by in both directions. There were no pedestrians in sight, but the capital awoke early. Covent Garden would be stirring by now, and Billingsgate.

Smedley stiffened. He must be imagining things. That wasn't just traffic he was hearing. It must be! Or was he starting to have delusions in addition to all his other madness?

"What's that noise?" Exeter said.

"Oh no!" Alice said. "Look!"

A policeman had just passed under the next streetlight. He was heading their way with the solid, unhurried tread of the bobby on his beat.

"I don't have my license!" Ginger wailed.

"I don't have anything at all," Exeter growled. "Will he take me for a deserter?"

"Julian," Alice said wildly, "you're on convalescent leave, and we're taking you to my home in—"

"I don't have my hospital discharge yet and why at four in the morning and Exeter has no papers at all and the blood—"

There was no innocent explanation! No one answered. They all just stared helplessly as their nemesis approached relentlessly along the pavement. With his helmet on, he looked about eight feet tall. He would have to stoop to see in the window.

He did.

"Morning, Officer!" Ginger said in his best Cambridge drawl.

Pause. "Good morning, sir."

"The jolly old engine's overheated, you see. Just giving it a moment to calm down, and then we'll be on our way."

Pause. "Will you tell me the purpose of your journey this morning, sir?" The copper glanced at the three passengers in the back. He did not shine his light on them, not yet.

Ginger said, "Er . . ."

# 15

Ginger said, "Er . . ." again.

Smedley could feel Alice shaking. Or maybe it was him.

*Somebody think of something!*

"Yes, sir?" said the voice of the law. A regulation notebook appeared in the bobby's hand.

"Well, it's like this," Ginger said and fell silent.

"Convalescent leave!" Smedley said loudly, and leaned forward to wave his paybook at the policeman.

The law was becoming suspicious. "In a moment, sir. First may I see your driving license, sir?"

Ginger drawled, "Well, actually, officer—"

Behind the car, the night exploded in fire. Not a furlong away, a building sank to its knees and toppled forward into the street. The car jumped bodily. Gravel rattled on roof and windows. The policeman vanished. Before the roar had died away, another . . . and another . . . and another . . . all around. Glass tinkled in deadly rain.

"Out!" Exeter shouted, struggling with the door.

"Get down!" Smedley barked. The others jumped at his tone of authority. "This is as safe as anywhere. It's raining glass out there."

He pushed Alice down on the floor. Exeter went on top of her. As Smedley followed, he caught a glimpse of the policeman, on his feet again, staggering toward the nearest burning ruin. *Boom! Boom!* The car rocked. *Boomboom!* Hail spattered on the roof. Guns crumped regularly in the background between the bomb blasts. *Boom!* The car leaped, windows shattering. People were screaming right outside, they must be pouring out of the houses, idiots.

From underneath, Alice said, "My God!"

"This is nothing!" Smedley said scornfully. "Throwing darts. It'll take a direct hit to hurt us." Or the adjacent building falling on them, of course. He felt quite unworried. Odd, that. After the creeping barrages of the Western Front, this was a very pathetic fireworks display. The last few bombs had been farther away. The noise was mostly people yelling and the roar of fires.

*Boomboomboom!* Closer again.

"Nothing, you say?" Exeter's voice sounded strained. This was not spear-throwing and shield banging.

"Kids' stuff. You all right, Ginger?"

A distant voice said, "I just died of fright, that's all."

"Good show."

Heartbeat—beat—beat—beat—beat—

"Is it over?" Alice said. "Someone is kneeling on my kidneys."

"Wait and see. Later planes aim for the fires."

*BOOM!* The car rose a foot and fell back with protesting squeaks. Something sizable struck the roof, but now the clamor of hail was briefer.

"No, it's not over."

Minutes crawled by. Distant clanging of a fire engine bell. A lot of shouting and cursing now, some very close. More explosions very far away. The futile hammering of guns.

"I think we can risk it," Smedley said. "Watch out for glass in here." He sat up. The car had lost all its windows. A fiery dawn lit the street and the frightened crowds, many people still in their night attire. "Exeter, old man, I do believe you're wearing the proper kibosh now."

They emerged cautiously from the battered vehicle. Ginger had lost his hat and his pince-nez, he was blinking and mumbling. Apparently all four of them had escaped uninjured. The same could not be said for the inhabitants of Greenwich, or possibly this was Deptford. There were bodies on the road, wailing children, and hundreds of people in night attire. Policemen were trying to move the crowds back and let the ambulances and fire engines through. No one was interested in the fugitives now.

"That was very tricky timing," Smedley said. "How far is it from here?" He looked at the other three, who were staring aghast at the burning buildings. *"Alice!* How far is it from here?"

"What? Oh, miles!"

"Let's get started, then! Don't wait to say good-bye to everybody."

Alice stared at him. "How can you make jokes?" she shouted. "There are people dying, bodies—"

"If you don't laugh you cry. Come on!"

"But you can't walk in your condition!"

"Then you can carry me. Come on! No one's going to question how we're dressed! Or where the blood came from." Smedley took Ginger's arm and urged him into motion. He assumed Exeter and Alice were following, but he did not look back. He felt the same wild exuberance he had known when he lost his hand—saved! No matter the cost, deliverance was what mattered. They could explain their bizarre appearance now, if they were asked. It could not be more than five miles or so to Lambeth, and he was sure he could manage that. He had walked almost that far with a tourniquet on his bleeding stump. Alice would find it harder in her fashionable shoes.

That was a very strange journey along the winding darkened streets of the great city. Half the population had emerged to look at the fires and the searchlight beams playing on the clouds. They cursed the Hun and called out condolences in incomprehensible accents.

About half an hour later, as the fugitives emerged from the affected area, they began to attract more attention. People started asking questions. It could not be long before another policeman appeared. Then a lorry pulled up and asked in very thick Cockney if they needed help. Alice rode in the cab with the driver, denouncing the bombs and explaining about going to stay with a mythical aunt. The men rode in the back, and a few minutes later they all arrived safely at her flat.

# 16

Alice had never had four people in her sitting room before. She had far too much furniture, and it was all designed for greater, grander rooms. The three men standing there, blinking in the harsh light, seemed to fill every inch. This was the first time she had been able to see Edward properly. He had not changed in the slightest from the gangling, fresh-faced boy he had been three years ago. Except that now his expression was murderous.

"Do sit down, please!" she said. "And I'll make some tea."

They were all beat, as if they had mud smeared under their eyes. The two youngsters were blue chinned, old Mr. Jones's beard was frazzled. His thin hair lay all awry over his bald crown, while his fingers kept touching the bridge of his nose, feeling for lost specs. She probably looked a hag herself. She ought to be exhausted, yet she seemed to be floating in unreality, a bubble on a sea of illusion.

"So the old bastard did steal it all?" Edward said.

"Don't speak ill . . . You do know he died?"

"Glad to hear it. And for all eternity, he will wonder why he's in hell!"

*"Edward!* Go and wash out your mouth."

Still glowering, he removed the greatcoat and spread it on the sofa, bloodstains out. He gestured for Julian to sit there, while he flopped into a chair, apparently unaware that his pajamas were blood spattered also. Mr. Jones sank into the other with a long sigh, like a collapsing balloon. Alice took the kettle from the counter and headed for the bathroom to fill it, stepping over feet.

She heard Julian say, "Your late lamented uncle Roland, I presume?"

Edward growled something she did not catch; probably just as well. She returned to put the kettle on the gas ring, then stepped over all the feet again and went into the bedroom. D'Arcy's photograph was safely hidden in the drawer. She had only one other thing to remember him by, the bottle-green velvet dressing gown he had kept at her flat in Chelsea. Many of her favorite memories of him involved that gown—sitting on his lap, watching him take it off, or taking it off for him, or stepping inside it with him and feeling its soft touch on her back as he closed it around them both, body against body. . . . *Every day I do not hear is one day closer to the end of the war.*

D'Arcy would not mind her lending his dressing gown to Cousin Edward. Young Cousin Edward had been a little too friendly in the car. He should have grown out of his romantic illusions by now.

She went back into the sitting room and dropped the gown on him. "Here. You can make yourself a little more respectable."

Then she went to the cupboard and began taking out cups and saucers, not watching what was happening behind her back. Edward must have risen and donned the gown and sat down again, because she heard the chair squeak. Presumably three grown men knew a man's garment when they saw one. The silence was pregnant. *Extremely* pregnant.

She turned enough to see Julian. If that was an owlish look in his eye, then it was an owl trying very hard not to hoot.

"We must take a gander at your leg," she said. "It may need a doctor."

He blinked solemnly. "Then it won't get one. It's only a gash. A scar there won't ruin my looks."

Scar! She spun around to look at Edward. His eyes had never been bluer, but she did not read in them what she had expected—reproach, self-reproach, humiliation, anger, all of them? No, Edward was amused, and suddenly it was her face that was burning. He had seen through her little ploy. However he looked on the outside, there was an older, more experienced Edward inside there.

Ignoring the embarrassment she had brought on herself, she touched his forehead. He jerked his head away.

"You had stitches!" she said.

He smiled sardonically. "Now you believe me?"

"I believed you before." But that physical evidence made her feel creepy. He had no scar at all, which was impossible.

"The sawbones have some new techniques," Julian said. "They're using them on the—" He yawned. " 'Scuse me! On the wounded. They say they can put a chap back together so the scars don't show."

"They couldn't three years ago. Get those bags off, old man," Edward said without taking his mocking gaze away from Alice. *We're all men of the world here.* "Want to take a look at your leg."

Julian yawned again. "In a minute. Alice, how safe are we here? How about the neighbors?"

She turned back to the kettle, feeling it. "The old lady across the hall is as nosey as they come but deaf as a pole. The two couples at the end are away all day. You may be noticed when you go to the loo, though."

"Do it in squads and march in step?" He grinned wanly. "Or do you have a bucket we can use?"

"Good idea," she said. Julian had a foxy streak, an echo of his boyhood mischief.

She sat down on the end of the sofa, and all her bones seemed to creak. The bubble had burst. She felt old. She wished the watched pot would boil. She did not want tea, she wanted a mattress. "Two of you can share the bed. If we—"

"Tommyrot!" Julian said. "I can sleep in two feet of mud with shells falling all around. Nagian warriors lie on the ground, so I'm told."

" 'Sright." Edward yawned also. "That's why they sleepwalk so much."

Well, well! Big boy now.

"I'll remember to lock my door."

Jones, too, was having trouble keeping his eyes open. "And I made out very well on the settee last night, or whenever it was. Feels like a week ago."

"We'd better draw up some plans, though," Edward said sadly. "A couple of hours' shut-eye until the shops open won't hurt, but we can't stay here longer."

"Why not?" Alice had been wondering about that, and had decided that they had left no trail. "There's nothing to connect the car to us." She had dropped the lockup key down a drain in Bermondsey.

"No. It's Stringer. If he was telling the truth, we're all right, of course. If he was just protecting the Old School Tie, you see. But if he was trying to trap me and calls in the law . . . He knows who I am."

Now it was Jones who hid a yawn. "I tracked you down in one afternoon, Miss Prescott. The police should be faster."

Edward nodded and rubbed his eyes. "And if Stringer is on the side of the Blighters, then I've put you all in mortal danger."

The kettle began singing a warning.

"The who?" Alice said.

"The Blighters." He glanced around bleakly, as if expecting to see doubt in the weary faces. "They're the Chamber's allies in this world. They contrived the massacre at Nyagatha. They're a damned sight more dangerous than the law, although they can warp the law to their own ends if they want to. They have powers you can't imagine. They killed Bagpipe."

Alice caught Ginger's eye, and his expression frightened her. He believed. Timothy Blodgley, she recalled, had been nailed to a draining board with a butcher knife. In a locked room.

"How could they know you were in Staffles in the first place?" she demanded. "And if they're so clever, why not kill you on the spot? Why ever let you reach England alive?"

He shrugged.

"Well?" she demanded. "You can't just issue cataclysmic warnings and then not explain them!"

"The man who tricked me into landing in Flanders expected me to die," Edward said. "But he knows I'm extremely hard to kill, because of the prophecy. So it would make sense for him to have put a mark on me, like a ring on a pigeon. Then the Chamber passes word:

*"Dear Messrs. Blighters,*

*"The indicated subject has just returned to your manor. If he is alive, would you please stop him breathing at your earliest convenience. If you will do same, you will oblige,*

*"Your humble servants, etc.*

"The car broke down exactly where the bombs were going to fall! Or vice versa. I really oughtn't involve you lot anymore, but I'm frightened that the Blighters may decide to take you off as witnesses or even just for spite. In that case, my luck may help shield you also."

Ginger said, "Good Lord!"

"They're not infallible," Julian said sleepily. "The bombs missed. You are heading back to Nextdoor, aren't you? To pass a message, you said."

"No."

Alice rose and stepped over Edward's feet to reach the kettle. She poured some water into the pot to warm it. She wondered why Smedley was so eager to cross over to this other world of Edward's. Running around with spears did not sound like his cup of tea, especially since he would have to throw with his left hand and carry the shield on his stump. Did he seriously believe that magic could give him back his hand?

After a moment, Julian said, "Why not? Why aren't you going back?"

"Lordie!" Edward said. "You should know! Because I came back here to fight in the war I'm supposed to fight in, that's why! How much identification will I need to enlist?"

"If you can breathe you're in," Jones growled.

It would not be that easy, Alice thought. And how long could he stay in? Her indestructible cousin was trailing a remarkable history behind him now. Too many people knew of him and knew him by sight. The thought of another loved one at the Front was a horror, and yet that confession made her feel guilty and unpatriotic. He would have to enlist under a false name, so she could no more be listed as his next of kin than she could be D'Arcy's. She would have two names to look for in the casualty lists.

"What about this prophecy?" she asked. "Did you kill the Zath character?"

"No. And I never will."

She made the tea and covered the pot with the cozy. "So that's all? You walk out of here at daylight and enlist?" The night's efforts seemed strangely futile if all they had achieved was to deliver another living body to the abattoir.

"There's one thing I must do first," Edward said through a yawn. "And that's get word to Head Office about the traitor back in Olympus. I hope they can tell me if the Blighters are still after me."

"I thought only people could cross over?" Julian said. "Letters won't? So how do you get word back to the Service?"

"I've got three leads. Yes, one of them might require a trip back, but if I do have to go, it won't be for long. They all require heading down to the West Country. You going back to Fallow, Ginger?"

"I must. First thing."

"Then I'll come with you. Soon as I have something to wear. Can you think of anywhere I can lay low for a couple of days?"

Jones fingered the bridge of his nose and jerked his hand away angrily. "I do have one idea. If we can't trust Stringer, then the school itself's too obvious."

Edward nodded, yawning again. "Smedley?"

They all looked at Julian.

"I'll tag along," he said quietly.

"Tea, anyone?" Alice said, but it turned out nobody wanted tea. Probably, like her, they wanted only to close their eyes and disappear. "Well, if you men are sure you'll be all right in here . . ."

Today was Thursday. She would likely be sacked if she missed a second day's work, but she knew she could not just walk out of this affair now.

# IV

# Queen's Gambit

# 17

Daylight around the curtains wakened her. She fumbled for her watch. *Ten o'clock!* Now she could hear the rumble of traffic to tell her that business swirled as usual through the city. She reeled out of bed, buttoned up her housecoat, disciplined her hair viciously, and then hurried through to the sitting room.

A man in a bottle-green dressing gown was reading yesterday's *Times.* The sight was a stake through her heart, but of course it was only Edward. He lurched to his feet as she entered. He smiled, all blue eyes and white teeth.

No one else around—damn! She was not awake enough yet for the bleeding-hearts scene. "They can't both be in the bathroom. Is there a cup left in that pot?"

"Yes. It's fresh. Ginger went out shopping."

She moved to the counter, turning her back on him. She laid out cup and saucer, bracing for the inevitable questions. She heard a floorboard squeak as he moved to the fireplace, a rustle of paper.

"Tell me about him," Edward said.

"No." Perhaps when she was properly awake.

Or perhaps not.

She poured the tea. It looked well stewed.

Edward said, "He's rich, but his wife controls the money. He smokes cigars. He's a barrister and probably in the army."

The teapot clattered on the counter. She spun around, heart pounding madly.

Edward's smirk changed to alarm. "I say! Didn't mean to startle you!"

"Is this some of your witchcraft?"

He blushed like a child caught in wickedness. "Of course not! Not in this world!"

"Then how do you know all that?"

He shrugged, smiling thinly. "The cigars I can smell on this dressing gown. You don't wear a ring, so he's probably married. He buys his clothes at Harrods and drives a cathedral-size car, so he's rich. But you live in a slum, so he can't afford to give you money. Reasonable guess that he's in the Army, living on the King's shilling."

"And a barrister?"

Edward hesitated. Looking thoroughly ashamed now, he pulled a paper from his pocket. "Envelope addressed to Sir D'Arcy Devers, QC, at Gray's Inn."

She took up her tea with shaking hands and went to the sofa. "Elementary, my dear Watson!"

"Bloody cheap trick," he muttered. "I'm sorry. Soldier by choice or conscription?"

"By choice."

Edward said, "Oh!" and there was silence.

She finished the tea and laid down the cup and saucer.

"And you used to call me a starry-eyed romantic idealist!" he said.

She did not look at him. "They're all over the place. He was in line for a judgeship. A messy divorce would have finished that. His wife is vindictive and well-connected."

" 'I could not love thee, dear, so much, Loved I not honor more'?"

"You could say that."

"Herrick said that, actually."

"It was Lovelace. And, no, it doesn't feel good to come second to a war."

"Oh, Alice!" he said sadly. "Oh, my poor Alice!"

"Save your pity. I was a kept woman and happy in the work, until the Kaiser spoiled the show." She forced herself to meet his stare. "I should have told you. I nearly did, but you had so many other troubles. I'm sorry."

"That long?"

"Since October 1913."

"Oh." He winced and turned to face the mantelpiece. "I must have seemed a bloody fool!"

"No. Not a fool. Young men in love are foolish, but not fools. I told you, I love you as a brother."

"A kid brother!" he said angrily. "I was eighteen and you were twenty-one. I'm still eighteen!"

"And I'm an old crone of twenty-four!" He looked more like sixteen standing on a box, but she could hardly tell him so. "I still love you as a brother."

He turned back to her and smiled. It was a brave effort, but his eyes were glistening.

"And you're not eighteen on the inside, Edward. In some ways you seem older than Julian, who's been tempered in the flames of hell. What have you been through, to do that?"

"Nothing like what he's seen. Just experience."

Grim, grim experience, she thought.

"You didn't grow out of it?" she asked sadly. "Did you really carry a torch for me all those years on your magic world?"

He bit his lip. "I still had hopes, I suppose. You were another reason for wanting to come Home."

"Oh, come on!" she persisted teasingly. "You have all my secrets. In the car you displayed a certain assertiveness I do not recall noticing before. You've had practice in clinches."

He squirmed. "No love affairs! But—but there could have been." When she let the silence age, he said, "She indicated that she was inclined in that direction."

He sounded so incredibly Victorian she almost laughed aloud. He was still the paradigm of the romantic.

"Go back to her and try a few more of those clinches," she said.

He stared down at the cold gas fire. "I am never going back, so it isn't possible. It wasn't possible then. I had given my word to you."

She rose to go and dress. "But I had refused. You were under no obligation to me." She turned her back on him and suddenly his arms were tight around her.

"I expect I was using you as my excuse," he said in her ear. "How could I let myself fall in love on a world I was trying to leave? Yes, I was tempted, very tempted. It was my memory of you that sustained me."

Her baby foster brother was a man now, and this was the first time she had really appreciated the difference. Not being able to see his face helped. A man was embracing her, a determined, strong-willed man. No boy.

"Let me go, please."

"I'm not going to rape you. I just want to know if you're happy."

"If the war would end and D'Arcy come back safe, then I would be very happy. His wife's an invalid; she won't live much longer."

"You trust him?"

She would not take this inquisition from anyone else, but he was not anyone else. "Absolutely."

"Because if you have doubts . . . If you want to change your mind, Alice darling, then you still can. You can go to Nextdoor."

"What?"

"I'll go fight the Kaiser. You go to Nextdoor. In six years we'll be the same age."

"Edward! That is not the problem! Now let me go and stop talking nonsense!"

He released her. When she turned, she saw that he was furious. His voice had given no hint of that.

"You'd rather stay and fester in this slum? Uncle Roland blew it all on his precious Bibles, didn't he?"

She sighed. She was not at her best first thing in the morning. "Not really. Some man he had trusted embezzled it."

"Someone in his precious Missionary Society, of course?"

She nodded. "He had no idea. He wept when he told me, Edward. I think it killed him."

"So it should have!" He scowled at her frown. "Oh, I don't care about the money. It was his damned sanctimonious holier-than-thou-ness! I hate people who think they know what's best for the whole world."

There were probably many good responses to that, but she could not think of one. "There's a little left, your share. Just a few hundred quid, and it's all tied up in chancery or something."

"Garn! Cheese in a mousetrap?"

"Not worth your neck to claim, no."

With relief she heard the door open. Julian came limping into the room. His hair was wet, but he was unshaven and his clothes were still caked with dried blood. His eyes flickered appraisingly from one to the other.

"Good morning," he said.

"Good morning. How's the leg?"

"Stiff, that's all. I made a mess of your clean towels, I'm afraid. Have you found any breakfast? We cleaned out the larder like a herd of locusts."

"Horde," Edward said. "Horde of locusts."

"Plague," said Alice. They were playing silly games to cover the tension, and it annoyed her. "I'll go and get dressed before Ginger comes back."

The bell rang then. Julian went. Ginger entered with bulky brown-paper parcels under each arm. He blinked short-sightedly in her direction.

"Morning, Miss Prescott."

"Morning, Mr. Jones. My, you have been busy! I apologize for being such a terrible hostess."

"Nonsense. The old need very little sleep." He dropped the parcels. "This one's five-nine, eleven stone. This is five-foot eleven and three-quarters, ten stone seven pounds." He reached in pockets. "Razor, shaving soap, brushes of diverse types, all as per your favor of today's date."

"Savile Row?"

"Off a barrow." He sat down heavily. His hard night still showed. "I made a phone call and I have a refuge for you."

Edward sighed. "Ginger Jones, you are a prince among men! I am so grateful I could weep."

"So could we all," Julian agreed.

Jones coughed disapprovingly. "Steady, there!" He was genuinely embarrassed.

"Where is this haven, then?" Edward asked.

"The Dower House at Greyfriars."

Edward's eyes widened in shock, making his bony face seem skull-like. "The *Grange?*"

"Mrs. Bodgley lives in the Dower House now. The general died, you know."

"No, I didn't. I'm truly sorry to hear that. The lady hasn't had much luck, has she!"

"But she knows you were not the cause, and she is anxious to meet you. And a friend. I didn't give your name, Smedley, in case of accidents. There's a train in a little over an hour. Think we could make that?"

Julian and Edward dived for their respective parcels.

"Wait!" Alice said. "I hate to be rushed. Why don't we travel separately? Wouldn't that be safer?"

"All four of us?" Jones asked, frowning, touching his nose.

"Two and two. You and Julian. Me and Edward on the next train."

Everyone looked to Edward.

He nodded. "It can't be any riskier, can it? If I write a letter, Ginger, would you post it in the Fallow box for me?"

The schoolmaster raised his eyebrows and again reached to adjust his absent pince-nez. "Why should it matter what box I put it in?"

"I think it does," Edward said. "And the handwriting will. It may even matter whether you pop it in the box or I do, but we can try this first."

Julian made a snorting noise of disbelief. "May I borrow your bedroom, Alice? I'm slow, I'm afraid."

"Go ahead." Alice wondered how she could ever dispose of such horribly blood-stained clothes.

He limped out, carrying his parcel. When the bedroom door clicked shut, Ginger turned to her and smiled triumphantly—the invalid was shedding no tears today.

"What's so funny?" Edward demanded, seeing her answering smile.

"Nothing," she said.

"Next train's not till four-something," Ginger said.

Alice relaxed. "Then you and Julian go first. Edward and I can follow."

They would have time to hammer out his emotional problems, and she could hear more of his adventures in that magical world of his. She had a suspicion that he had been harping on the Nagian savages to discourage Smedley's interest. There must be a brighter side to Nextdoor—perhaps that mysterious Prince Goldfish he had mentioned.

# *18*

Golbfish slammed the bedroom door on Ymma's mocking laughter and stamped off to face his ordeal. He stopped stamping quite soon, because he was barefoot.

His honor guards were waiting in the antechamber. He had expected them to be dressed much as he was, but they all wore Joalian-style armor of shiny bronze. The colored symbols of their devotion to Olfaan and the other gods were marked on the armor, not slobbered in paint all over their faces. The leader saluted. Puish Lordservant bowed and waved forward two flunkies. One presented Golbfish with a spear, and the other a circular shield. It was so massively ornamented with gold that he almost dropped it. Anything less useful for battle had never been invented.

He glowered around the guards, searching for any hint of a smirk hiding inside a helmet, but their expressions were all studiously noncommittal. Growling angrily, he strode off without a word, leaving them to follow in any order they liked.

For the first—and, he fervently hoped, the last—time in his life, he was clad in the traditional garb of a Nagian warrior. Not that there was much garb to it—a skimpy leather loincloth. He felt naked. His face was ludicrously painted up with colored hi-eroglyphics. His hair and beard had been trimmed short, because that was warrior style, but he knew how it emphasized the smallness of his head. He felt a freak. He knew he looked a freak, too. Perhaps there was a funny side to it, and someday, at some elegant dinner party, he would laugh with his friends, relating how he had been forced to dress

up as a barbarian. Perhaps. But if his friends back in Joal could see him now they would
. . . they would laugh just as hard as that slut on the bed was laughing.

He was not the right shape. His torso tapered upward instead of downward, although
that did not stop him worrying that his absurd garment might slide right off him in
the sweltering heat. With both hands occupied, he would be able to do little to stop it
if it tried. He had no hair on his chest—and no ritual scars, either. If Mother thought
he would rouse the warrior caste of her primitive kingdom to blood lust and patriotic
fervor, then she was going to be sadly disappointed.

Even stupid Ymma knew that. Her mocking words still rang in his ears: "What will
they think of you? What will your precious friends think of you when they see you like
that? What verses will your poets compose, what songs will your singers sing? And that
sculptor man—will he carve your likeness?" She had started to laugh again—hard, cruel
laughter like the strokes of a lash.

Golbfish shuddered. Fortunately his best friends were all far away in Joal, and the
few he had in Nag would not be close enough to see any of the details. They were
civilians all, talented artists whom he had brought back from Joal to aid him in his
efforts at improving the cultural life of the kingdom. Civilians would be kept to the
back of the temple.

*The Joalians will understand!* he told himself. *They know I must conform to local custom
in raising the horde. They trust me, as they will never trust Tarion. It was the Joalians who
insisted Mother appoint me hordeleader.*

But Tarion had been made cavalryleader, and Golbfish did not understand why the
Joalians had agreed to that. They were relying on the Nagian cavalry far more than on
the Nagian infantry, which would be of little help to them. Nagland had plenty of moas,
but no tradition of using them in warfare. Joalian lancers were as good as any in the
Vales—except the Thargians, of course—but they had not been able to bring their
mounts over Thordpass. A moa was a one-man steed that needed many fortnights to
be imprinted by a new rider. Little brother Tarion would be technically under the
hordeleader's command, but he was far more likely to win glory in the coming war than
Golbfish himself was.

He was not looking forward to the war at all. He was a patron of the arts, not a
fighter. He was looking forward to this afternoon's mustering ceremony least of all. He
would rather face a horde of armed Thargians than go before his own people dressed
like this, but there was no way he could escape the ordeal. Joalia had demanded the
support of its ally, and the horde must be mustered in the ancient ways.

What Joal wanted, Joal got. That was the law in Nagia.

The palace was a dingy affair of endless stone corridors, badly designed and poorly
built, an insipid imitation of Joalian architecture. There was no decent building stone
near Nag, not like the lustrous variegated marbles of Joal. Everything was made of the
same drab, purplish sandstone. It was so soft it crumbled, and the floors were permanently gritty. Nagland had no tradition of building in stone.

Nagia had no tradition of hereditary monarchs, either. The Joalians had imposed the
monarchy by force of arms when they put his grandfather on the throne. His mother,

it must be admitted, had astonished everyone by managing to hang on to it, crushing the predictable revolts with Joalian help and ruthless cruelty. It was true she favored Tarion as her successor, for she made no secret of the fact. She maintained that Golbfish was not sufficiently ruthless. She was right about that, but was ruthlessness necessary anymore? After three generations, he thought, the Nagians had adjusted to the situation. They would tolerate a king to keep the Joalians quiet, just as long as he was benevolent and well intentioned.

Mother did not agree.

Golbfish's left foot was already sore by the time he reached the Garden of Blessings, which was a feeble copy of the Garden of Blessings in Joal. Anyone who had seen the original found this one pitiful. Imported Joalian seeds never thrived, and Nagian vegetation just did not have the same luster. The wickertrees gave a feeble shade, the sunblooms and starflowers were almost invisible amid their rioting leathery leaves. Now, in late summer, the fountains had run dry and the ornamental pools looked scummy and dead, as if they should have fish floating belly-up in them. The statuary had been carved from the inevitable purplish sandstone, so that most of the figures were weathered to faceless mummies already.

The honor guard had halted somewhere. Golbfish advanced alone, following the winding path through the shrubbery. He heard voices ahead, many voices, and felt a twinge of uneasiness. He had expected only Mother and Kammaeman, the Joalian commander. Possibly Tarion. He could hear a large party in progress.

Rounding a tangle of bamboo, ruby bushes, and salmon vines, he came in sight of the throne. The queen was holding court, elevated above the crowd. She seemed to be the only woman present. As he approached, he searched in vain for signs of anyone at all gaudied up as he was. Some were clad in bronze, gleaming and warlike, the rest were dressed in the loose breeches and tunics of Joalian civilians. He recognized the usual ministers, envoys, and secretaries. He could understand their being here, but there were others he would never have expected. Mother seemed to have invited every officer in the visiting Joalian army, plus all the court officials and most of the important local notables—and all Golbfish's personal friends, too! There were dozens of faces he had never seen within the palace before: Toalmin Sculptor, Gramwil Poet, Gilbothin Historian, and innumerable others. These were the people he had happily assumed would be relegated to the back of the temple. Why had they been invited to this reception?

And why was the reception being held at all? He had not been told of it. He wondered if Ymma had known about this.

He reached the back of the crowd and said, "Excuse me." The closer men looked around and gaped in astonishment. Then they backed out of his path, but their eyebrows soared high as flags.

*I shall run my spear into any man who smiles!* he thought, and then realized he would have to commit a massacre. Faces were averted, but he dared not look behind him to see what effect he was leaving in his wake. He could hear much coughing.

"Excuse me, please!" he said again. And again . . .

The one advantage of his grotesque war paint was that his blushes would not show. He could feel his ears glowing hot, though.

He was tall enough that he made out Kammaeman Battlemaster even before he reached the throne. The Joalian leader was standing at the foot of the steps, joking with the queen. Despite the gray in his beard, he was still one of the best warriors Joalia had produced in a generation. Kammaeman could be relied on to lead the combined armies with imagination and the necessary ruthlessness. The Thargians would not find him an easy opponent. He was also a shrewd politician, shrewdness in politics being an important survival trait in Joal. Golbfish had met him there often enough, but their friendship had been purely ceremonial.

Needless to say, Golbfish intended to leave all the military decisions to Kammaeman. He also intended to stay very close to him during the battles. An heir to a throne could not take risks like other men.

There was Tarion Cavalryleader, also close to the queen, smirking ominously.

Admittedly Tarion was only his half brother, but the two of them could not have been less alike. He was a pure Nagian type—lean as a whip, tireless, brown skinned, and dark haired—and touchy and dangerous. No one ever outrode Tarion; he seemed to merge with his moa and make it part of himself. If anyone else in this assembly ought to be exhibited in a loincloth and emblazoned with war paint like Golbfish, it should be Tarion, leader of the cavalry. But no. There he was, undeniably handsome in a shiny bronze helmet and Joalian riding wear of blue cotton, bearing himself with all the menace of a naked sword. He was good, and he knew it.

At last Golbfish came to the steps of the throne, stopped, and nodded his head in an excuse for a bow. He dare not ask why his mother was not also wearing national dress for the solemn occasion. If her subjects expected to see the scrawny royal bosom bared, they were going to be disappointed. Her blue gown was as Joalian as could be. She was tiny and frail, her thin white hair hidden by a jeweled tiara. Her face was painted even more heavily than his, but in her case the covering was wax and rouge, to hide the lines of pain and the yellowing skin.

Emchainne was dying. Everyone knew it, even she, and nobody dared say so. A few months at best were all she had left, but the illness that racked her had not yet blunted her will. She was still queen; she ruled Nagia yet, as implacably as she had ruled it for thirty years.

How had anyone so puny ever produced him? He was half again as tall as she was. At the moment, though, her eyes were higher than his, and they glared.

"You're late!" she snapped. "Have you already forgotten the correct form of military salute?" Her voice was croaky.

Grumpily, Golbfish slammed his shield with his spear and almost let it slip from his sweaty fingers. A couple of the onlookers leaped back out of harm's way.

The queen of Nagia looked over her older son with undisguised contempt. "And do you not also salute your commander in chief?"

Now there Golbfish felt he was on firmer ground, if there could be any firm ground in this quagmire of intrigue. He favored Kammaeman with a nod. "Battlemaster?" Then he turned back to the queen. "You are our commander in chief, Mother. I am your appointed deputy. The battlemaster is merely commander of our allies. Of course, I defer to his overall leadership, but by treaty we are equals. We march together against the common foe."

The older man raised a grizzled eyebrow.

With sudden apprehension, Golbfish glanced around the onlookers. Most of them were making an effort to conceal amusement. Not Tarion, though. His helmet did not disguise his sneer. He must know something Golbfish did not. Had Ymma also known it? Did everyone know but him?

"Ah, yes!" The queen glanced over the nearer courtiers. "Who has a copy of my son's speech?"

Golbfish could feel himself starting to grow angry, which was an unfamiliar feeling and an unwelcome one. When he lost his temper he usually became very shrill; he tended to stamp his feet. "I know my part, Mother!"

"We have decided to make a small addition to the ceremony."

"The form is traditional!"

Emchainne sighed, but the glint in her eyes showed that she was enjoying herself. "Monarchy is not. Historically, hordeleaders were elected, not appointed. You are our heir apparent. We have concluded that you are too precious, Golbfish, dear. We have decided we cannot allow you to risk yourself in battle. Nobody doubts your courage, of course. We know how you must regret this, but our Joalian allies agree—do they not, Battlemaster? So you will have to remain here in Nag, with us, my son."

His first reaction was a surge of relief. Tents and coarse food and sleeping on hard ground held very little appeal. Feather beds and silver spoons were more to his taste. Then he remembered Tarion's cryptic joy and knew that there were snakes here somewhere.

"But—" he said.

"No argument! Where is that speech? Ah, yes. Give it to him."

Gragind Chancellor thrust a paper at Golbfish. Having a shield on one arm and a spear in his other hand, he ignored it.

"Tell me!"

Faint cracks showed in the wax coating on his mother's face, as if a smile were struggling to break out. "At the conclusion of the oath-taking, when all the warriors have sworn allegiance to you, Hordeleader, you will announce that you are unable to lead them in person and therefore you transfer their loyalty to Kammaeman Battlemaster."

"What?" Golbfish screamed. "They swear to die for me and then I tell them I am staying home?"

"It is a regrettable necessity, son."

"I cannot do that! No man could!"

Satisfaction glowed in his mother's eyes. "You refuse a direct order from your sovereign, Hordeleader?"

That was a capital offense.

"No," Golbfish moaned. "Of course not! But—"

"No buts!" Emchainne said firmly, glancing askance at Kammaeman to see his re-action.

The barbarians would never stand for it!

Tarion was smirking from one ear guard to the other.


# *19*


Two terrible hours later, Golbfish stood beside the altar, a few steps up from the temple floor, his head almost level with the goddess's toes. The heat beating down off the rock behind him was a torment.

Astina, the Maiden, was one of the Five, the Pentatheon. Her temple in Joal was one of the wonders of the Vales.

In her aspect as Olfaan, goddess of warriors and presiding deity of Nagvale, she had to make do with very much less. The Joalian influence that had transformed the secular capital had been balked when it tried to replace the ancient sanctuary with something more dignified and artistic. Golbfish's grandfather had laid out foundations for a great religious complex on the far side of the city. The priestesses had refused to sanctify it, whereupon the people had downed tools and offered to die before they would offend Holy Olfaan. So the old temple had remained much as it had always been. Queen Emchainne had added a grandiose pillared entrance, but that was the only change.

Visitors, especially the all-important Joalian visitors, were always astonished by it. They complained that a hole in the ground was not truly a temple, and of course they were right. Not that it was strictly a hole—only half a hole, a semicircular embayment in a cliff. Its floor was a plain of shingle that often flooded in the rainy season. The image of the goddess had been carved into the vertical stone many eons ago. On dull days it was hard to make out, but when the sun shone, as it usually did, her outline was clearly visible. Nagians could boast that their goddess was the largest in the world and the acoustics were splendid. But it was still only a hole in the ground, and on a day like this it was a god-sized pit oven.

Before Golbfish, in massed array, stood the young warriors of Nagland, summoned from all over the vale to pledge their loyalty in the ancient ritual. Interspersed among them was a very large contingent from the Joalian army, presently encamped just north of the capital. Officially they had assembled to honor the goddess and their allies. Unofficially they were there to see that nothing went wrong, and the way they had segregated the Nagians into small groups proved that.

At the back of all this blade and muscle stood the queen's civilian subjects, come to watch their sons and brothers be inducted to fight a war that no Nagian truly cared a spit for. They had cheered Her Majesty when she was borne in. They had sung the praises of Holy Olfaan with a genuine verve that had probably been audible halfway up Nagwall, thanks to those superb acoustics. All in all, they were putting a brave face on this latest evidence of Nagvale's lowly status as a colony of Joalia.

After the initial invocation, the priestesses had slunk back to their caves. This was strictly a military ritual.

It had been going on for hours, and had a long way to go yet. The queen's litter had been located well off to one side, its draperies closed against the raging sun. Her attendants kept peering in at her. Golbfish assumed that she must be having one of her bad turns. There was nothing he could do about it, and he could not help thinking that it served her right. Admittedly she could not have refused the Joalian demands, but she had certainly used the situation to dispose of her elder son. He was doomed to die here today. Tarion had won.

The brawny young warrior on the other side of the altar took up the arms he had dropped earlier. He saluted Golbfish and the goddess overhead, then stalked away down the steps, following the last of his contingent. The steps were spotted with blood.

In the center of the altar a stone knife lay on a drying red stain. Beside it were half a dozen gold dishes. Three were empty now. The others were heaped with sparkling white salt, too brilliant to look upon.

Golbfish sighed and glanced down at the handwritten list that had been placed on the stone table to prompt him, weighted with gold coins in case a wind developed later. No such luck! The air was still, the temple an oven.

"I call on Her Majesty's loyal warriors from Rareby!" His throat was parched as the Western Desert. He seemed to have stopped sweating. Probably he had just run dry, like the palace fountains. Earlier, he had worried that he might have washed all the paint off his face.

A massive young man came striding up the steps, bearing his shield and spear. Now that was how a warrior should look! His shoulders were as broad as a wagon, his hips slender. The muscles of his calves bunched as he walked. Golbfish squirmed with shame to look at him.

The giant laid his shield and spear on the altar and spoke the words of the dedication. "Her Majesty's warriors of Rareby swear obedience to Holy Olfaan and to all your commands, Hordeleader." He had a strong voice, in keeping with his appearance, and the cliff threw it back over the weary multitude who had heard all this so often before. "They offer their blood and their lives and their absolute allegiance. They pray to Olfaan to guide them, protect them, and make them worthy of her service."

"Amen," Golbfish said for the eighth or ninth time that afternoon.

The man was sweating like a burrowpig, of course, but that could charitably be attributed to the heat. The way he set his teeth as he lifted the knife could not. He was dreading his ordeal. He already bore four merit marks on his ribs, but that knife must be thoroughly blunted by now.

He surreptitiously scraped it on the edge of the altar. That was not part of the service, but he was not the first to do so, and the marks there showed that these warriors' forefathers had done the same thing many times in past centuries. One scrape would not add much sharpness.

Then he slashed at his ribs.

Golbfish never watched this part. The sight of blood made him nauseous. He heard a faint gasp as the warrior rubbed the salt on his cut. Gods, how that must hurt! Two youngsters had fainted earlier and been dragged away by their friends. Officially they had to be put to death for that display of frailty, but more likely they would be allowed to escape and flee the country.

The troopleader sighed with relief as the pain eased. Then he stepped to the far side of the altar. The first of his men came hurrying up, eager to undergo his ordeal and get it over with. He had hardly stopped moving before he hurled down his shield and spear and grabbed for the knife. He made his cut so fast that Golbfish barely had time to avert his eyes.

"Not enough!" snapped the troopleader.

The warrior scowled at him and cut again. He let the blood run for a moment, as if waiting to be told it would suffice. Then he reached for the salt.

Barbaric! Unspeakably barbaric! The Joalians present would be appalled. When they sacrificed to Olfaan, or even to Astina herself, they offered a chicken, or a calf at most. They would think this deliberate self-mutilation utterly depraved, as did Golbfish himself. It was a primitive, savage custom.

He bore no merit marks. Because of that alone, he must have seemed a very spurious war leader to the real Nagians when he paraded through the town on his way here. He had been secretly ashamed, but he had certainly never considered mutilating himself just to please the rabble.

The warrior retrieved his weapons and departed. Another Rarebian followed, and another. At least they were moving quickly. Some villages tried to drag it out.

Golbfish ought to want it to last. Almost certainly he would die at the end of it. When the last warrior had sworn, he would have to make that dread speech that had been laid out for him. If he didn't, then the Joalians would know that he had disobeyed a direct command from his queen, and they would not tolerate an untrustworthy officer. So they would not help him.

The Nagians would not, either. They had laughed aloud as he marched through the city. Everyone else had been in armor, or mounted on moas like handsome brother Tarion. Only the hordeleader had been stripped down to a loincloth, to show his flabby hips, his narrow shoulders, and his hairless, unscarred chest. The queen had very cruelly demonstrated to her Joalian visitors that her elder son had no following among the people.

Tarion and his cavalry had been cheered! That rankled worse than anything. Tarion cared nothing for the people. Tarion did not know a sonnet from a drinking song. He had no interest in advancing Nagian culture and raising the people from barbarism, as Golbfish had. The Joalians did not trust Tarion, which was wise of them, but now they would have to. Tarion would go off and earn military glory in the war. Golbfish, even if he managed to escape assassination this afternoon, must needs skulk at home in the palace, and everyone would assume he was a coward. He wasn't a very brave man, but he would have gone to the war if he'd been given the chance. It was not fair!

His final act of the ceremony, rejecting all these oaths, was very likely going to be his last. The bloodied warriors would not stand for such an insult. A hundred spears would flash in the sunlight, and Golbfish's blood would mingle with theirs on the steps. A hundred? There were close to a thousand of them out there, and it would only take one.

The heat might kill him first. He lacked the lifelong tan of the peasant. His skin was being fried by the sun. What penalty did the ancient rituals prescribe if the hordeleader himself were to faint during the ceremony?

Oh, goddess! The troopleader was scooping up his shield. Next village, then. Had that one been Rareby or Thoid'lby? For a moment Golbfish almost panicked. Then he decided it had been Rareby, and called for Thoid'lby. No one corrected him.

The Thoid'lby leader was older than most, an ugly, weathered man. A widower, likely. His look at Golbfish was openly contemptuous as he spat out the oath.

The bloodshed continued.

The temple shimmered in the hellish glare.

Only one more village to go! Death was moving in very close to Golbfish Hordeleader now. He could think of no way out. If he did not resign his command as ordered, he would be arrested and executed for mutiny. If he did, the warriors would riot and use him for target practice. And even if by some miracle they didn't, then Tarion would see that he did not remain around long as a rival claimant to the throne. Not one Nagian or Joalian would lift a finger to save him.

He was doomed.

Warrior followed warrior. Cut followed cut.

He wanted to shout out that they were going too fast. Life had become a blur.

Thoid'lby completed its ordeal, and its surly troopleader departed.

The last village! He worked his mouth until he could find enough spit to speak.

"I call on Her Majesty's loyal warriors from Sonalby!"

A murmur of surprise rustled through the temple. Golbfish's eyes snapped back into focus. The Sonalby contingent was not milling forward in a mob, as all the others had done. It was marching four abreast, with its spears on its shoulders in parallel rows like the teeth of combs. Every foot moved in perfect unison as if an invisible band were playing somewhere. The Joalian infantry drilled no better.

"Troop—halt!"

A hundred feet came down together. Their hundred partners joined them, and the warriors stood motionless at the base of the steps. Not a spear wavered. Another bark, the poles sprang to the vertical, then the butts struck the ground. Somebody cheered at the back of the temple and was hushed.

Kammaeman Battlemaster had laughed out loud at the idea of teaching proper drill to Nagians. Past experience showed that it would be a waste of time, he insisted. But Sonalby must have found a veteran leader, one who had at some time served in the

Joalian army and learned the advantages of discipline. Somehow he had trained this band.

Who had worked that miracle?

This man?

The troopleader alone had continued. He came marching up the steps toward Golbfish.

Yet he was only a boy, although a very tall one. He bore only three merit marks. One was very recent, probably acquired when he was elected troopleader, but even the others were still red and therefore not more than a dozen or so fortnights old. As he came to a halt, Golbfish saw with astonishment that the youngster's eyes were brilliant blue, bluer than the blue of his face paint, a shade Golbfish could not recall ever seeing combined with hair so black.

For a moment the two stared at each other, and there was a significance in that steady gaze that startled Golbfish utterly. He could not place it. It was something he had never met before. He thought it mattered greatly.

Then, very slightly, the boy smiled.

Bewildered, Golbfish smiled back, and felt an inexplicable sense of relief.

With a couple of smart military movements, the young troopleader discarded his shield and spear. He spoke the words of the oath loudly and clearly, and if as he meant them. He had a faint, unfamiliar accent.

Never taking his eyes off Golbfish, he took up the knife and cut his chest. He salted the wound without a flinch, as if he were barely aware of what he was doing, and all the time that steady blue gaze was asking some impossible question.

He marched to his place at the far end of the altar, and swung around. Again he looked meaningfully at Golbfish. Who was this cryptic youngster? What message was he trying to pass? He seemed almost to be offering sympathy, as if he were aware of the terrible problem. That was impossible!

Then the first of his followers arrived to perform the ritual, and the young leader turned his attention on him.

One by one, a hundred men and boys came to shed their own blood before the goddess and their so-temporary hordeleader. But this time there was a curious difference. They did not look up at the goddess. They did not even seem to notice Golbfish. They watched their leader, and he watched them, and each time Golbfish detected a curious little smile of encouragement pass. The youngster's lips did not move, but his eyes brightened, and every man of the hundred seemed to appreciate that tiny signal, as if they drew inspiration from this juvenile soldier. *I did it. It's not so terrible.*

Then it was done. The last man marched smartly away.

The leader came over, picked up his arms, shouldered his spear. For a moment his eyes wandered past Golbfish and he frowned slightly, then smiled.

Golbfish looked around uneasily. There was no one there, only the bare rock of the cliff, radiating heat like a forge. He turned back to confront that same blue, quizzical stare. The barbaric face paint made the expression difficult to read. Now the boy would go and leave Golbfish alone, to meet his fate.

But he didn't. Instead he raised his eyebrows in a question. What? A suggestion? An invitation? He almost seemed to be offering to stay and help as if . . .

Merciful Goddess! Perhaps there *was* a way out!

Golbfish's knees began to tremble. Mindful of the phenomenal acoustics, he spoke in a tiny whisper. "Could you make me a warrior too?"

The boy smiled, pleased. He spoke as softly. "Only you can do that, sir. But I can show you how."

Golbfish nodded in bewilderment.

The boy marched back to the far end of the table, grounded his spear, and stood at attention—watching Golbfish! Again a mutter of surprise rustled through the crowd.

The prince glanced over to the queen's litter. A curtain had been raised so she could witness his coming resignation—and death. The monarchy had always mattered more to her than her disappointing son did. Golbfish was the product of a loveless, dynastic marriage. Tarion had been born of passion.

Tarion was a bastard in every sense of the word.

The shadows made Mother invisible. Kammaeman Battlemaster stood alongside her litter, tense and expectant. A glance to the cavalry at the other side of the temple showed Tarion—too far off for his gleeful smirk to be seen, although it could be imagined.

*I shall cheat you all yet!*

Golbfish took one last look at the boy from Sonalby, and received that same little smile of reassurance and encouragement that the others had.

At least one man was on his side!

He ignored the written speech. His voice burst out clear and strong, so suddenly that he hardly knew it was himself speaking. "Warriors of Nagland! I have accepted your oaths in the ways of our ancestors!" That was how the prepared text began, and it was a lie because he had not one drop of Nagian blood in his veins. Tarion did. Tarion was the son of a palace guard.

Golbfish sucked in another deep breath. "I shall be honored to fight at your side—but I am not a general. I am not worthy of your allegiance! I now command you all, in the first and last order I shall give you, to obey the noble Joalian battlemaster, who can lead us to victory in our righteous struggle against Thargian aggression."

He paused, sweating and shaking. Could he really go through with this? Rip his own flesh? He glanced again at the Sonalby troopleader, and again the boy smiled approvingly, urging him to continue. A low but rising growl from the audience warned him he must decide quickly.

"As for me, warriors, I shall fight as one of you, in the ranks."

He turned and took up that odious knife with a shaking hand. He poked the edge with his thumb and knew he would have to strike very hard to make a visible cut—it must be visible. To his horror, he felt a stirring in his groin, a rising thrill of sexual excitement. What foul perversion was that?

In a quick gesture of revulsion, he cut. It felt like molten iron poured on his skin. He had never known real pain before. It was frightful, worse than he had ever imagined.

But at least it had banished the deviant surge of lust. He felt panic in its place. Hot blood trickled down his ribs. He was bleeding!

He stared doubtfully at the salt. That would be a hundred times worse. Could he bear even that? Supposing he screamed? Frozen in terror between fear of pain and fear of bleeding, he looked again to his inspiration.

Again that nod, that smile. *I know how you feel,* the steady blue eyes said. *A thousand men and boys have done it already.*

Golbfish grabbed a handful of the gritty stuff and did it. Gods, gods, gods! Agony coursed through every nerve, every vein. He bit hard on his lip. He would faint! He must faint! Then the torment slowly faded to a fiery burn. He was still bleeding. Not so much, but still bleeding. Unable to suppress a moan, he took another handful and the torture came again. He blinked at the tears.

"Come," said the boy softly.

Golbfish staggered back to his own spear and shield. His head swam when he stooped, but he managed to lift them. He tottered down the steps behind his new leader. A hundred astonished Sonalby faces stared up in amazement at the unexpected recruit. The whole, vast congregation had frozen into statues.

The boy barked an order. The warriors snapped their spears to their shoulders. Another word and they spun around to face the other way. One error and those poles would have tangled in chaos, but there was no error. A third order, and they began to march. Their commander followed, and Golbfish tottered along at his side, struggling to keep in step.

He might die in battle, the rigors of training might kill him, but he had survived the ceremony! He stole a glance sideways at the lanky youth who had inspired his dramatic gesture. He felt a strange conviction that his newfound leader would look after him. He had found a friend. He had found someone he could trust.

# *20*

"So what did she look like, this goddess?" Alice demanded.

"Didn't get much of an eyeful," Edward said. "She was there and then she was gone. You've seen one goddess, you've seem them all."

The two of them were strolling through St. James's Park, Edward casually swinging her overnight bag. It was a beautiful autumn afternoon. They had lots of time, and a straight line from Lambeth to Paddington would take them through the fairest parts of London—over Westminster Bridge, past the Houses of Parliament, across St. James's Park, Green Park, and Hyde Park. Then they would be almost there.

It was wonderful to have Edward back, after three years of wondering and worrying and almost but not quite giving up hope. He was more than just a cousin. He was her foster brother, her only living relative. She had not yet plumbed all the changes in him—strength and firmness of purpose. The schoolboy honor would be more deliberate and perhaps more practical, but no less firm.

This should be a marvelous day, a day to savor and remember, yet she could not shake off a creepy sensation that she was being followed. She glanced behind her once in a while, although reason told her that any follower could hide amid the milling crowds.

Edward noticed, of course. "What's the matter? You're jumpy as a grasshopper."

"Guilty conscience. I ought to be at work."

"They'll hold the war for you. What sort of work do you do, anyway?"

"Can't talk about it. Official Secrets Act." If he were to guess that pianists made good typists and very few secretaries in London could type Kikuyu, he would not be far off.

Policemen bothered her. She kept thinking they were staring at her.

Half a dozen young men walked past talking loudly. Edward glanced back in surprise. "Americans?"

"Canadians, I expect. On leave."

He shook his head disbelievingly. "The whole world at war! It's mind-boggling."

"They all seem to come to London," she said. "I don't know how they stand it—a few days in civilization, knowing they have to go back to the trenches, to be scarred and tortured—or killed."

Edward said nothing.

"That wasn't exactly tactful of me, was it? Edward, are you sure your duty is here?"

He looked down at her quickly, then away. He pointed. "Never thought I'd see guns in London. Antiaircraft, I suppose?"

"Answer me!"

He frowned. "Of *course* my duty is here! You know! We weren't born in England, you and I, but this is our native land. Nextdoor isn't."

"But you know you can achieve something worthwhile there, in your storybook world, because of that prophecy! Here you may just become another number, one of millions."

"I will not be less than those millions!"

"But you could be one *in* millions."

He scowled. "Alice, can't you understand? You might have talked me out of it before, but now I've seen what it's like! Those men carried me for hours across that hell, and I saw. I had never imagined war could be so horrible. I had never imagined *anything* could be so horrible. But now I've seen it. Now I know. I have to go back there! I can't run away now."

That seemed a very stupid, masculine way to think. "We have to win the war," she said. "It's cost so much that we can't stop now. But I don't know that you belong in it." Or D'Arcy, either. "We aren't all called to serve in the same way. You don't pull carts with racehorses."

"You don't make pets of them, either."

They paced on. The park was surprisingly crowded. She took his hand, though she had promised herself she wouldn't. He squeezed her fingers without looking down at her.

"What amazes me," he said after a while, "is how you all seem to accept my story. I'd have expected you to have me locked up in Colney Hatch as a babbling loony."

"You carry conviction. You always did. Have you ever told a lie in your life?"

"Course I have! Don't be ridiculous! Everyone has."

"About anything important?"

He took some time to answer, staring woodenly at nothing. "Lying isn't important. Betraying friends, now . . . that's worse."

"I won't believe you ever have."

"Well, that's where you're wrong!" he snapped. "Twice! That damned prophecy keeps trying to make me a god. . . . And I keep thinking of Holy Roly. . . . Telling people what they must do—what's right and what's wrong!" He looked down, and she was astonished to see that his eyes were shiny with tears.

She reminded herself that something had changed him and to pry might be needless cruelty. This day was much too precious to spend quarreling. "Tell me what magic feels like?"

He smiled. "That's impossible! Like describing color to a blind man. When you have mana you know it, but I can't say how. It's a little like having a bag of money, so you can feel the weight of the coins. You're a great pianist—"

"I had some talent."

"How did you *know* your talent? Mana's like that. How does an athlete know his strength? It's a fizz in the head. It's an excitement. I thought I knew what it was like, but I didn't really. Not until that day in Olfaan's temple. Oh, I'd picked up scraps now and then, but nothing like that. Having a troop of warriors to lead had been giving me some, but we hadn't been on a node. Nodes make all the difference. That's why strangers find themselves nodes and become numens—gods, if you want to call them that. As soon as we marched in, my chaps realized that my drill had made them superior to all the other contingents. They were thinking, *Good old D'ward!* and I could feel that pride and admiration like a shot of hot brandy."

"You weren't frightened of the numen, Olfaan?"

He laughed. "I was a complete innocent! I still trusted Krobidirkin, you see. I thought he would have foreseen that ceremony and warned Olfaan I was coming and won her approval. Astina's lot were not part of the Chamber—so I thought, and in a very rough sense I was right about that. I was wrong about Krobidirkin. The Herder was just using me. There's the palace!"

"It's usually around here somewhere."

They stopped at the curb, looking across at Buckingham Palace, waiting for the policemen controlling the traffic.

"Ugly heap, isn't it?" Edward said. "You'd think that the King-Emperor of a quarter of the world would have a more impressive residence. Pity he isn't home, or we could drop in for tea." The royal standard was not flying.

"He's doing his bit. He does a lot for the troops."

"So he damned well should! They're certainly doing enough for him."

Alice glanced up, surprised. "What's wrong?"

"Oh . . . nothing."

"Come on! Out with it."

He shrugged, frowning. "I wish I understood how it works here. That was something we didn't talk about much in Olympus. A couple of thousand years ago, yes. Then it worked on Earth very much as it still does on Nextdoor. I think there really was a god at Delphi, then. When the Greeks went to consult the oracle, there was a numen present and the prophecies were genuine. Or some of them at least. When the Romans prayed in the Capitol to Jupiter Optimus Maximus, someone was listening. But things changed a few centuries back."

Alice had been wondering about that. "Nietzsche? 'God is dead'?"

"No. The gods are not dead. They're still here, or else there are new gods. People stopped taking them literally when the Enlightenment came, but they didn't die. They've taken some other form."

"You're not saying King George is a stranger?"

He laughed. "Hardly!" His mood darkened. "No. Creighton said the Blighters started this war, but there's no nominal god of death receiving the sacrifices. That doesn't mean the sacrifices aren't being made. Who is lapping up the mana?"

"Edward! Are you saying that all gods—*all* gods—throughout history . . . that *all* gods and *all* religions have been fakes, frauds?"

He hesitated. "No. No, I'm not saying that. You see, what the Service is trying to introduce in the Vales is a system of ethics that you would recognize. You would approve. I do. It has a lot of Christianity in it, and a lot of Buddhism. . . . The Golden Rule, mostly—the sort of thing that has cropped up in our world and in that world many times. It has to come from somewhere and—Come on!"

The policeman was waving. They crossed the road. She kept trying to release his hand, but he was holding her fingers tightly. Passersby shot them disapproving looks.

"It's incredible to be back here," he said. "To see all the old familiar sights again."

"And yet the differences? What do you notice?"

"Crowds. The whole population of the Vales would not fill London. People over-dressed, because of the climate. Walking their dogs! How absurdly, typically English! Mothers pushing babies in prams. Tourists and late holidaymakers, soldiers on leave. Policemen. Do those barrage balloons really do any good?"

They talked of the war for a while. They crossed Piccadilly and entered Hyde Park. His sinister talk of sacrifice bothered her, though, and eventually she asked him how it worked.

He sighed. "Know that, and you would understand all mysteries! The essence of sacrifice is that you do something you don't want to do because you think it will please your god. If you're lucky, you get a pat on the head and feel good. If I hadn't known that before, then I'd have learned it that day in Nag. All those warriors from Sonalby sacrificed to *me!* They didn't mean to. They didn't even know they were doing it, but each of them had to perform a very unpleasant ritual with a blunt knife and a handful of salt. They thought they were doing it for their own manhood, their goddess, and poor old Golbfish, but I was their leader and their friend, and there I was, right on the node. I had charisma! So they did it for me, and pretty soon I was gibbering drunk with mana."

"That was what you used on Golbfish?"

"Not really. I didn't use anything on him except charisma, and I couldn't help that. Oh, I suppose I was being a little more than naïve. Right at the beginning, as soon as he went up to the altar, I knew he was a very worried man. Probably no one else knew. I had no idea what the matter was, but I felt sorry for him. When I finally got my chance to march up the steps, I tried to give him a bit of cheering up. I gave him one of those looks you do when you want to tell someone something without actually speaking, you know? He sort of grabbed at it, and I realized that he was in mortal terror."

"Then the goddess came?"

"At the end she did. If I was tipsy, she must have been completely bung-eyed by that time. She'd all those thousands of people singing hymns to her and then hundreds of men offering blood and pain, all right on her node—mana in torrents! I don't suppose she'd had a feast like that in a generation. And suddenly it was cut off. It was all coming to me, see? So she came to find out what was going on. I'm sure nobody else saw her. I caught a glimpse and thought, *Whoops!* and she saw me and I'm sure she guessed right away who I was. I was very bad news, because I might queer her with Zath or Karzon or with major intriguing in the Pentatheon. The lady did not want to be involved! So she scarpered."

"But what did she look like?"

"Nothing special, as I recall," he said vaguely. "Big woman. Hardly saw her. It was like two friends passing in a busy street. They tip their hats to each other and are gone. I was more worried about Golbfish."

"Why? Why did you decide to help him?"

Edward shrugged, almost shyly. "I didn't do anything, really. He needed a friend and my charisma made him trust me. He thought up his own way out. I was amused to discover I now had a prince under my command. I wasn't thinking too clearly, as I said. I felt invincible! Good day for sailing boats!"

Alice looked to where the children were playing by the Serpentine.

"Is that what you want to do? Stop and play with toy boats on a lake, just let the world go by? Two worlds?"

"I want to enlist."

"Edward, what exactly is prophesied about you in the other world? What does the Liberator actually *do?*"

He turned on her in sudden anger. "I told you: He kills Death. Not real death, just

Zath, of course. And that's disaster! It leads to disaster! There's only one way it could be done, and that's for me to set myself up as a god and collect more mana than Zath—and he's been at it for a hundred years. I can't imagine what horrors I'd have to invent to squeeze worship on that scale out of the masses, and what happens after? What happens to me? What happens to them? All that just to kill one stranger, who'll probably be replaced by another in two shakes? Zath's the first one nasty enough to claim to be god of death, but it's such a great swindle he invented that he certainly won't be the last. The guv'nor saw all that, and when I finally got to read the bloody Filoby thing, I saw too, and I won't have anything to do with it! I came Home to enlist, but I also came Home to break the chain, and I'm never going back! Never! I won't! I mean it! That's final!" He spun on his heel and stalked away, walking faster than before.

She ran after him. "No, I don't see. Are you sure you can't kill Zath without using mana?"

"Absolutely certain."

"Then you could take the god of death office yourself, to make sure it isn't abused."

"Faugh! No. Don't worry about it. It won't happen. I'd rather stop a German bullet any day. What else do you want to know, apart from that?"

"What happened to Golbfish?"

Edward sighed. "Ah, that's quite a story. If it wasn't for Golbfish I wouldn't be here. First thing, of course, when we'd barely left the temple, was that a couple of heralds appeared, demanding that he return to the palace."

"And?"

Edward grinned, looking suddenly very juvenile. "I told them that Golbfish Warrior was now under my command and I refused to release him. I had a hundred spearsmen with me, so the argument was brief."

Alice glanced at her watch. They still had an hour before train time.

"Of course," he said, "I realized that I had blundered into a major political crisis. We'd hardly got back to camp before I was summoned to appear before Kammaeman Battlemaster, the Joalian general. I was told to bring my new recruit with me, but I didn't. I went alone and explained that the prince couldn't come—he was too busy digging latrine ditches. After that, they sort of lost interest in us."

"Never mind your confounded modesty! What did you really do?"

"Nothing much," Edward said blandly.

# 21

"Two friends are better than one," said Dosh Houseboy, kneading Tarion's calf, "especially if they are enemies."

"Sounds like one of my dear brother's aphorisms. It's enough to send a whole dining room of sycophants into hysterics."

"It's from the Green Scriptures, Canto 1576." Dosh turned his attention to the other leg.

Tarion was stretched out naked on an auroch hide. The tent was dim and hot. It smelled of leather, his own sweat, and the fragrant oil Dosh was using. After hours of standing in the temple, a massage felt very good. Massages from Dosh always did—he had skill and his hands were much more powerful than they looked. All the thousands of other people who had endured that ceremony would perhaps appreciate similar treatment, but none of them would be getting it.

"What two friends do you have in mind?" he asked sleepily.

Dosh chuckled throatily. "You and Golbfish."

"The Joalians can still play us off against each other, of course."

"Of course. And the fat man did not die . . . which may have been the plan, possibly?"

Tarion chuckled. "Do my thighs now." He sighed sensuously as those powerful fingers began to work on the muscle.

"So you will have to behave yourself, or they can bring him back," Dosh said, phrasing the words in time with his thrusts. "They do not trust my beloved master." He was as nosy as an old woman.

After a while Tarion roused himself to answer. "Mother cannot last much longer. Then the Joalians will have to decide which of us to put on the throne. I think we shall have just time to slaughter a few Lemodians before then. Before the terrible news arrives."

It would be better for Tarion himself if the time was insufficient for the Lemodian's Thargian allies to arrive on the scene—Thargians were dangerous—but that was in the lap of the gods. "It seems most unlikely that my dear brother will survive more than an hour or two of infantry training. He has the muscle tone of a milk pudding. His comrades will laugh him to death. There must be a limit to the amount of humiliation even that man can absorb. Besides . . . Do you want to hear a little secret, dear boy?"

"You know I love secrets."

"Then work harder. Harder! I won't break. Ah! Lovely! My whimsical brother took refuge in the Nagian infantry. You know what the Joalians think of the Nagian infantry?"

"They think it a useless rabble," Dosh said, panting with effort as he pummeled.

"Exactly! Our cavalry—*my* cavalry I mean . . . They will allow us to play some minor part. Nothing too critical, I am sure. I hope showy. But the infantry is a mob. A peasant's idea of fighting is to throw his spear at his opponent's shield and then charge him with a club. Even Lemodians can massacre Nagians. They always have in the past. Start on my back now. Kammaeman will hurl the Nagians in first to use up the Lemodians' arrows. That's what they're for. Dear Golbfish's chances of surviving his first battle may charitably be defined as, 'remote.' "

He grunted as Dosh's strong hands pressed down on his torso. He had allowed none of his subordinates to bring personal body servants along to the war, and only the very senior Joalians had them. As leader of the cavalry, though, he needed someone to attend to his mount, his weapons, and equipment. And his more personal needs. Dosh was a real joy, in every way.

"The Joalians do not trust you, master," Dosh repeated.

"I am heartbroken," Tarion said drowsily. "I wonder why not?"

"Because two friends are better than one, especially when they are enemies."

Tarion spun over on his back, grabbed a handful of Dosh's hair, and hauled him down. Dosh squealed in surprise and ended leaning on one elbow, nose to nose with his prince and frantically trying not to spill the oil bottle in his other hand.

"What are you implying?" Tarion said menacingly.

He saw none of the fear he had hoped to provoke, only amusement.

"Oh, beloved!" Dosh said in a fake whine of humility. "Who am I to lecture my master on political affairs?"

"Did I ever tell you you had beautiful eyes?"

"I don't think so. You've praised just about every other part of me excessively, but I don't recall you mentioning eyes."

"I do so now only to stress that I should hate to have them put out with red-hot irons. That would spoil your perfection. What were you saying?"

Dosh still showed no alarm. He smiled, as if this bullying were a form of foreplay—which it probably was, Tarion realized.

The beautiful eyes twinkled. "I mean that Thargia would be very happy to see Nagland recover its independence. Thargia is not close enough to be a threat to you in itself. I think you are a man of Nagvale, beloved master."

"My father was a peasant," Tarion agreed. "And then a palace guard, and then royal gigolo." He twisted the boy's hair. "Is this what is said about me—that I would sell out to Thargia?"

"It is what is thought. Nobody says it. Ouch! That hurts!"

"It is meant to. Do you spy on me for the Thargians or the Joalians?"

With his head bent over at a critical angle, Dosh regarded the prince sideways and then said, "Both. Whoever pays me."

"Good. I appreciate honesty and a proper respect for money. Spy all you want, but remember this—while you are mine, you let no other man touch you! Unless I say so, of course."

"Of course not. I have my standards."

Tarion chuckled and released him. Then he put an arm around Dosh's neck and hauled him closer. "I love you, you little monster! When we have overrun a village or two in Themodvale, we shall enjoy the spoils of war. What would you like me to bring you? Girls or boys?"

Dosh's white teeth shone. "Either, as long as they are young and pretty. Like you, I am not fussy."

"I am extremely fussy."

"I am flattered."

From outside the tent flap came the unmistakable sound of a spear being thumped against a shield.

"Curses!" Tarion said, pushing his body servant off his body. "Just when things were starting to become interesting! See what he wants."

Dosh rose, straightened his hair, adjusted his loincloth, and took the oil bottle with him.

Tarion sat up, hearing the Joalian voice outside summoning him to the battlemaster's tent. He had half expected this, and of course he must go. He would be very surprised if his beloved half brother Golbfish was not the first item on the agenda.

The camp was not large enough to justify riding; the two men walked. With the sun now dipping toward Nagwall, the temperature was becoming bearable, but Kolgan Coadjutant set a very leisurely pace. When the second-in-command of the Joalian army came in person to conduct a mere Nagian to a meeting, one could reasonably assume that he had an ulterior motive. Tarion was now Nagian heir designate and Kolgan was an important Joalian politician. They had never spoken in private before.

The camp bustled all around them. Troopleaders were drilling long-shadowed squads on the dusty plain; moas were mewing for their evening meal. Smoke trickled up reluctantly from cooking fires.

"How soon do you expect the final contingents from Joalvale, sir?" Tarion inquired politely.

"In a few days." Kolgan was very tall, and even his armor failed to make him look broad. He had a hatchet face and a reddish beard.

"I hope we shall move out at once. The enemy must know about us by now."

The tall man chuckled. "And the army is eating the heart out of your capital?" Tents ran off in rows for miles, enough to hold five thousand hungry men.

"Certainly. Mother will have to raise taxes to pay for it." On the other hand, the crown's levy on brothels must be paying royally just now.

"Ah. But the queen's health distresses us all. That unpopular task may fall to her successor."

"Or, if Karzon favors our cause," Tarion prompted, "loot from Lemodvale may solve the problem?" But would the Joalians let the Nagians have a significant share?

"Possibly," Kolgan said vaguely. "Do you know how I got to be where I am, Tarion Cavalryleader?" He glanced down with a meaningful glint in his eye.

"Not in detail," Tarion said diplomatically, "but I have heard how the people's assembly in Joal rejected the Clique's nominee for the position of coadjutant and demanded you instead. Riot was threatened. A great tribute to your reputation, of course."

"A great tribute to graft. I have no military experience to speak of. I had been sponsoring public games on a scale not seen for many years."

The People's Assembly was the ultimate authority in Joal, but it was very expensive to buy. Tarion distrusted candor. Candor was dangerous to both candorer and candoree. "How wonderfully public-spirited of you!"

"I staked everything I possessed and everything I could borrow. Unless I return gloriously victorious and loaded with loot, then I am a ruined man."

"We must trust in the gods and the justice of our cause," Tarion said, wondering what this frankness could possibly be leading up to.

Kolgan's angular face twisted in a grin—or possibly a sneer. It was hard to tell under his helmet. "And you, Prince? How did you come to be where you are?"

Candor was for others. "Mother has long believed that I would make a better king than my poor brother."

"Quite!" Kolgan Coadjutant snapped. "But her Joalian allies have never agreed with that viewpoint. Our distinguished ambassador recently switched his support to you— in direct breach of the Clique's instructions."

"He did," Tarion agreed blandly. The Joalian ambassador was effectively the resident Joalian governor of Nagland, although one did not say so openly. Bondvaan was another devious politician, a human snake.

The commander's tent was in sight now. Kammaeman had appropriated the best campsite, under the only decent shade trees. He was sitting on a stool, still wearing armor and watching his subordinates approach. Beside him sat that very same Bondvaan.

"Three years ago," Kolgan said, "the old man spent five million stars, bribing the Clique to appoint him. I am sure he has made it all back by now."

"In his first ten fortnights here, or so he boasts."

"Well, then!" Kolgan said triumphantly. "Bribery on his scale would be well beyond your means. How did you work it?"

"Mother persuaded him."

This time the sneer was unmistakable. "That is not what I heard. I had hoped we might exchange confidences, Tarion Cavalryleader."

Tarion sighed. "What did you hear?"

"He is a notorious lecher. He hosts orgies of the foulest perversions. What his age makes impossible for him personally now, he stages to watch. I heard you participated in certain memorable performances at his residence."

Tarion had never found a smile harder. "I am no prude, but I prefer not to be reminded of those nights." Candor!

"Understandably!" The tall man chuckled coarsely. "Great causes require great sacrifices?"

"Yes."

"Do we appreciate each other now? Do you know why I dismissed the messenger and came for you myself?"

Tarion gritted his teeth. "Of course. Kammaeman Battlemaster must be aware of your need for personal glory. A wise Joalian commander never turns his back on his deputy. By arriving with me, you are undermining my reliability in his eyes, and thus hope to enlist me to your side."

Kolgan laughed. "We do understand each other! Let us make an agreement, then. Help me come out on top in this and I shall give you Bondvaan Ambassador's privates on a plate. Interested?"

"Fervently," Tarion said. "Fried."

The guards let the visitors pass. They came to a halt and saluted the man who was at the moment autocrat of Nagland. Kammaeman's word could stop any heart in the vale.

He was close to sixty, a seasoned warrior. He must also be one of the most successful and ruthless politicians in Joal, as he had hung on to his membership in the Clique for more than ten years. The fact that he had dared take command of the army in person and thus absent himself from the city showed how firm his grip must be. He was physically powerful, too. His armor covered his torso and shins, but his bearlike, matted arms and thighs were exposed. Dust and sweat had muddied in the wrinkles in his weathered face and in his beard. His eyes were inflamed by the sun. He nodded at the newcomers without rising or even offering them a seat, although there were stools standing unused at his back.

Beside him—silver-haired, short, and blubbery—Bondvaan Ambassador favored Tarion with a buttery smile that awakened memories to make his skin crawl.

Kammaeman was peering up at him from under grizzled brows thicker than many men's mustaches. Black hairs sprouted from his ears and nostrils.

"Did you enjoy the ceremony today, Cavalryleader?"

Kolgan alone had been bad enough. Tarion braced himself to deal with three of them. "I hope someday to wean my people from ritual scarring, sir. It is a holdover from our barbaric past and contrary to the enlightened civilization that Joal has brought us, for which we are all so grateful. However, the sight of blood excites me, and you certainly cannot doubt the young men's courage."

"I can doubt their sanity. Did you find the conclusion at all surprising?"

"Astonishing!" It would be more truthful to call the conclusion deeply disappointing. Some blood would be more exciting than others. "I never suspected my brother of such patriotism."

Without even looking, Tarion could sense the smirk on Bondvaan's suety face. Oh, he must be pleased! The Joalians still had a second string to their bow in Nag.

"That was not quite what I . . . Ah!" Kammaeman gestured for Tarion and Kolgan to step aside. "Here comes the man I want to see."

Tarion watched with interest as the guards confiscated the new arrival's spear. He was a fairly typical Nagian—black haired, slender, and tall; taller than most. Still bearing his shield, he marched up to the commander and slapped a palm on it in salute. Then he stood stiffly at attention, staring over the commander's helmet. His grotesque face paint made his expression almost unreadable.

Having seen him earlier only at a distance, Tarion had not realized how young he was. He felt a stir of interest. A straight diet of Dosh Houseboy would soon pall. If rank did not suffice, a few coppers would seem like a fortune to such a peasant.

"Your name?" Kammaeman demanded, looking the youth up and down, mostly up.

"D'ward Troopleader, sir."

"And before that?"

"D'ward Roofer."

"From Sonalby?"

"Yes, sir." He had a faint accent that Tarion could not place. He was showing no signs of nervousness, which was exceedingly curious.

"I ordered you to bring your new recruit with you."

The young man did not look down. "With respect, sir, my oath was made to another, who then transferred it to you. I take orders only from you directly."

Kammaeman's face reddened under the dust. His hairy fists clenched.

"If you order me to go and fetch him now, sir," the youth told the tent in the background, "then of course I shall obey."

"That is exceedingly kind of you!"

Tarion detected a suitable moment to win the boy's gratitude. "If I may speak, Battlemaster? Technically he is correct. That is the way things stand at the moment. He cannot be expected to understand proper military procedures."

The youth glanced briefly at the speaker and Tarion saw with astonishment that he had brilliantly blue eyes. How bizarre! How very intriguing!

And why was he not quaking in his shoes—apart from the fact that he was barefoot, of course? This lad must definitely be investigated more closely. Nasty, fat old Bondvaan had obviously had the same idea. He was almost slobbering on his stool.

"I see!" Kammaeman growled, mollified. "Well, I can't have a dozen troopleaders pestering me all day. I have to appoint an overall commander for the Nagian infantry, do I? Someone responsible to me?"

Tarion opened his mouth and then hastily closed it. The question had been directed to the peasant.

"As I understand, sir, there are no precedents. No hordeleader has ever resigned before."

He was not speaking like an ignorant rustic. He was quite right, though, and Kammaeman's proposal was the only possible solution. Tarion had carefully not mentioned the problem earlier, but he was prepared to undertake the additional responsibilities if they were offered. Then he would command the entire Nagian army. He did not say so yet, for Kammaeman was still intent on the youngster.

"What military experience do you have?"

"None, sir."

"Who taught your squad to drill?"

"I did, sir. I asked some of the elders in the village how Joalians made war." He was showing no pride or satisfaction or . . . or anything! He was as impassive as a veteran of innumerable campaigns. His confidence was positively eerie. Tarion wondered if Kammaeman might order him flogged, just on principle. But there was nothing in the boy's manner to indicate insubordination or hidden mockery. He was being completely factual, and his manner carried conviction.

"How long did it take you?"

"Two days, sir, was all I had—I do have a request, sir."

"Yes?"

"I have nothing more to teach them. If you could send us a Joalian instructor, he could further their training."

Kammaeman snorted disbelievingly. "It has been tried before! Nagian warriors insist on fighting in their traditional fashion. They will not listen to a Joalian."

"They will listen if I tell them to, sir."

At Tarion's side, Kolgan Coadjutant chuckled. Kammaeman shot him a glance that silenced him, and then looked back to D'ward. Up to D'ward.

"Give me your oath on that, subject to a flogging if you are wrong."

"I so swear," the boy said at once, still staring over his head.

Tarion felt a stab of alarm. What was going on here? Was the old rogue going to take the word of a raw laborer? He glanced at Kolgan and saw a scowl that mirrored his own feelings exactly.

Kammaeman said, "Kneel."

The boy knelt. That put their eyes on the same level.

"So you can make them march in step," the commander said. "I admit that. I admit that I am surprised by that. But how do you make them remember that spears are for thrusting? In the heat of battle, they will throw their spears away! They always have in the past."

"I was planning to tie the poles to their wrists with leather thongs," D'ward said simply, "to remind them."

"Indeed?" Kammaeman raised those jungly eyebrows. He was obviously impressed. "How long would it take you to train the rest of the Nagian contingents to the same standard you have brought Sonalby's?"

Even the youth looked startled, but he barely hesitated. "I can talk to them this evening, sir. If you will assign a Joalian instructor to each troop in the morning, I will guarantee that they will obey him and do their best."

The battlemaster scratched his beard. "On the same penalty? No, I'll raise the stakes. Make that two floggings."

The boy grinned. "Done!"

"By the five gods, lad, you're either crazy or just insane! Your new recruit? What is he doing now?"

"Digging a latrine ditch, sir."

Tarion exploded. Oh, *joy!* Oh, perfection!

Kammaeman shot him a disapproving glare, but he was having trouble hiding his own amusement. "Why that?"

The boy seemed surprised, as if the answer were obvious. "I told him that was the worst job I could give him. Once he has done that, then he has nothing more to fear."

The Joalians exchanged glances. Old Bondvaan ran soft fingers through his skimpy silver hair. Kolgan was chewing his lip thoughtfully. Kammaeman seemed to be at a loss. "Did your group accept him?"

"Yes, sir."

"Oh? What did you tell them?"

"I said we were very honored to have the prince enlist with us. That they need not show him any special favor, but they should try to be patient with him, because he has had a deprived upbringing and has everything to learn about true manhood."

This time even the commander grinned. He turned to Kolgan.

"Well, Coadjutant? Do we have a native military genius here?"

"He appears to have flair, sir."

"Stand up!" Kammaeman said, heaving himself to his feet. Even in his boots and helmet, he was shorter than the boy, but twice as wide. "Take good care of him!"

"Yes, sir."

"We don't want him to have any accidents—do we, Cavalryleader?" He favored Tarion with a threatening glare.

"I hope my brother survives to dig many, many latrine ditches, sir," Tarion said crossly. If the Nagian rabble was to be turned into an effective fighting force, he could no longer count on Golbfish dying in the customary massacre. How annoying!

Kammaeman thrust out a hairy arm and grasped the youth's brown shoulder.

"I shall make you a wager! D'ward Troopleader, I appoint you acting commander of the Nagian infantry. Any instructors you need, just ask this man. His name is Kolgan Coadjutant. Three days from now, you will parade your horde for me. I shall then either confirm your appointment or have you beaten to jelly. Do you accept those terms?"

"Yes, sir," the youth said calmly. "Thank you, sir."

"My pleasure! Dismissed."

With a smart salute, the new troopleader spun around and marched away. The guards gave him back his spear.

Kammaeman watched him go and then turned to his deputy with the sleepy content of a bearcat that has just eaten a band of hunters. "You are dismissed also. Give him the best men you can, all the help you can. You two gentlemen wait a moment."

Kolgan flickered anger, but he saluted and marched away.

Tarion moved forward. Bondvaan rose, looking completely perplexed. Tarion hoped his own face did not show his fury. That young upstart was doomed!

"You two gentlemen," Kammaeman repeated as soon as Kolgan was out of earshot, "were both making slobbering spectacles of yourself. Keep your filthy habits to yourselves, do you understand? Leave D'ward alone!"

"Sir!" Tarion protested. "I don't underst—"

"You understand perfectly! He is not to be molested in any way. *Any* way! I think I may have found a secret weapon in this war."

Tarion decided he had better make some new plans.

# 22

His first few days in the infantry were continuous torment for Golbfish. Going without shoes, he shredded the soles of his feet; his skin blistered in the sun; his ritual cut suppurated. The sheer physical exertion was worse than all of those. He dug ditches, he marched, he ran. Every muscle in his carcass throbbed and ached. He fainted and was kicked awake and told to stop slacking. Time and again he came to the breaking point, when even death seemed preferable to this unending torture.

But whenever that happened, by some curious coincidence, he would look up to see a pair of steady blue eyes watching him. He would hear a few words of encouragement and recall that this youth had saved him in the temple at no small risk to himself. Somehow, then, Golbfish would find the strength to struggle on a little longer. He owed it to D'ward, who had trusted him.

He fully expected one of Tarion's assassins to come calling on him with a thin dagger, but that never happened. He awoke every morning, never quite sure whether to be surprised or disappointed. And by the fifth or sixth day, he realized that he was going to live through this and be a warrior. Even more astonishing, he came to understand that his rough companions were sympathetic to his sufferings and approved of his efforts. Then a thin sliver of pride began to glow in the darkness.

Just when he had begun to cope with life in camp, the army moved out, almost seven thousand strong. About a quarter were Nagians, a thousand on foot and eight hundred riding moas. Their road took them east, past Sonalby, and then south into the wilds of Siopass. For three days they made a cautious ascent of the winding valley, through dripping forest and along stony watercourses. The march brought Golbfish new impossibilities of fatigue and hardship.

It also brought danger, for every military campaign in the Vales inevitably began with a contested pass. The Lemodians could not but know that the combined might of Joalland and Nagland was coming against them. Already they must have reinforced their defenses and called for help from their fearsome Thargian masters. There were very few places where an army could cross the ranges.

Fortunately, there had not been time for Tharg's assistance to arrive. The battle was fought long before the Nagian contingent reached the summit. Word was sent back down the line that the pass was cleared and Lemodvale lay open before the invaders. Then the warriors cheered and sang songs as they marched. Golbfish saw the bodies as he stumbled past, but he was not involved in the fighting. He had no breath for singing, and he did not know the words of those songs anyway.

Thereafter the road led downward and the pace quickened. Two days later, the army camped by a shallow lake in the foothills of Lemodslope. The talk now was all of conquest and the joys of loot. The warriors assured one another that Lemodian girls were famous for their beauty.

Eventually the Sonalby troop received its turn to bathe in the now very muddy lake. The warriors stashed their arms, but did not bother to strip. They charged into the water with whoops and set about making it even muddier. Golbfish avoided the horseplay, but he enjoyed the soak and the chance to reduce his personal population of vermin. What small things could please him now!

He limped out to dry off in the sun. A gangly young man was sitting on the grass, leaning his head and arms on his bony knees, his bright blue eyes watching Golbfish with amusement. He must have been in the water also, for his hair and beard were wet.

"Congratulations, warrior!" he said. "You've done it, haven't you?"

"I think you deserve most of the credit, sir." One thing Golbfish had certainly learned, and that was humility. He knew he could not have managed without D'ward's help and inspiration.

"Nonsense! Sit down here and relax a minute. I said I could show you how, but you did it." D'ward chuckled, shaking his head at Golbfish's tattered appearance. "You just need to grow a new skin and you'll be done. How do you feel?"

Golbfish considered the question. It seemed like centuries since he had held a real conversation with anyone—meaning anyone with intelligence. "Surprised, mostly."

"But proud?"

"Yes," the new warrior confessed. "I wouldn't have believed that a fortnight ago—but, yes."

"You should be proud. Even the men are proud of you, you know! They were laying bets on how long you'd last. Nobody won—or rather you won! They admire courage. Anything you need?"

Golbfish smiled, and it was a long time since he'd done that, too. "Ymma or Uthin-ima or Osmialth."

The blue eyes blinked. "Who?"

"My concubines."

D'ward laughed. "You are better, aren't you! Sorry, I can't help there. Well, I just thought I'd congratulate you and tell you how much I admire what you've achieved. It would have broken most men. Well done!"

He moved as if about to rise.

"Sir?"

The hordeleader settled back with a wary look. "Yes?"

"May I ask . . . No. May I make an observation?"

"Observe away."

Golbfish turned his head to watch the splashing mob in the lake. "This is impertinent and rash of me, but I have overheard enough to know that you are not a native of Sonalby."

There was no reaction, just a terrible stillness that was more eloquent than a scream or a string of oaths.

"Sir! . . . I am sorry. . . ."

"I'm not originally from Sonalby, no," D'ward said, very quietly. "The Joalians don't know that, though. At least, I didn't tell them, and I don't think they know. Carry on."

"No. I should not have—"

"*Carry on!*"

"Sir!" Why had he been such a fool as to bring this up? "You arrived there in early summer. I suspect it was soon after the seven hundredth Festival of Tion, in Suss."

There was a long pause, and then the young man said, "Who says so?"

"Nobody. I worked it out. Very few of the lads can read. If they have ever heard of the *Filoby Testament,* they certainly know none of the details."

D'ward sighed. "But you do, of course. What details do you have in mind?"

"Oh . . . just that it implies the Liberator will be born then, but that isn't what it actually says. It actually says that he will come into the world naked and crying. Not quite the same thing!"

The piercing blue eyes raked the prince's face, then suddenly began to twinkle. "How else does one come into the world?" D'ward demanded with a grin that washed away the guilt and tension.

"Well . . ." Golbfish felt a twinge of nostalgia, remembering table talk in Joal, the long philosophical debates when every word must be combed for subtleties of meaning. He gazed for a moment at the peasants roistering in the water. "Those who enter convents or monasteries are said to leave the world. So I suppose a man who was, say, evicted from a monastery might be said to enter the world again?"

"You believe that is what is meant?"

"Perhaps. Or there may be an arcane meaning. Other references suggest that the Liberator is something other than a normal man."

"Are you trying to blackmail me?"

Golbfish looked around in horror, momentarily speechless. Even worse than the suggestion itself was the realization that a fortnight ago he probably would have been thinking that way. "*You?* When I owe you my life?"

His companion smiled again. "Sorry! I must have been consorting with that black-guard brother of yours too much. You don't really owe me anything, you know—but carry on."

"Nothing! I wish I hadn't mentioned it."

"Have you discussed this with anyone else?"

"No, sir! Sir . . . you can trust me!" Golbfish was suddenly seized with a need to weep. Why had he ever blabbed all this out?

"You are implying that I am something other than a mortal man?"

"I think you have powers that others do not."

D'ward said, "Damn!" and studied his toes.

"Are you a god?" Golbfish asked nervously.

"I'm definitely human. I am probably the man mentioned in the *Testament,* though.

Shrewd of you to work that out." He sighed. "I don't know if I shall ever be the Liberator. I have no ambitions to be any sort of liberator. I just want to go home! Will you keep this to yourself, please?"

"Of course. I swear it."

Obviously D'ward did not want to talk about the prophecies, which was a pity, because Golbfish did. The *Filoby Testament* never mentioned Nagland, so he had never paid much heed to it. It did mention a prince. About half the Vales were monarchies, so there must be many princes around, but he and Tarion were certainly the only princes available at the moment.

The blue eyes were smiling again, and D'ward unrolled, stretching his bony form out on the grass. "I trust you! So let me ask you something. The day I arrived in Sonalby, I saw a family murdered by a mob."

Golbfish shuddered. "Led by Karzon's priests? It happened all over the vale."

"Because they were heretics?"

"Yes. We didn't have very many in Nagland, but the Man decreed that they must be stamped out."

D'ward raised his head and frowned at the troops in the water. "I think we'll have company in a moment. The Church of the Undivided? Tell me about that."

"It's a new faith," Golbfish said hastily, racking his brains for the little he knew about it. "Where it started, or when, I don't know. It's fairly widespread in Randorland. It may be cropping up in other vales too—I have no idea. It preaches a new god, a single god. That sounds like Visek, but it isn't. All gods are the Five and the Five are the Parent, you know? But this god is none of them. His followers claim that he is the only true god, and all the others are . . ."

"Yes?"

"Demons," Golbfish said reluctantly. It was a heresy almost too foul to repeat. Why in the world was D'ward interested in that obscure sect of deluded fanatics?

"Has he a name, do you know, this new god?"

"Apparently not." Vague memories of drunken dinner conversation stirred. "If he has, it is too holy to be spoken. And his followers do not pray to him directly."

D'ward grunted. "This is very interesting! What are his teachings, his commands to the faithful?"

"I really don't know, sir! I wish I could be of more help! They wear a gold earring in the left ear."

D'ward turned his head and stared. "Even the men? And only one ear?"

"Apparently."

"Peculiar! That must make them very conspicuous. It will be dangerous, if they are being persecuted. Or is that the whole idea?" he added thoughtfully.

"Perhaps not all of them do," Golbfish suggested. He had always taken the gods for granted. Philosophy was interesting, but religion he had left to the priests.

"Perhaps not," D'ward agreed. He sat up as a mob of wet warriors emerged from the lake, eager to greet their former friend, now elevated to giddily high rank. "One last question. Quickly! If I wanted to find this church, where should I look?"

"Randorvale, I suppose," Golbfish said. "But we're going the wrong way."

# 23

"White tablecloths!" Edward said in a tone of wonder. "Silver cutlery! Civilization!"

Outside the dining car window, the Thames valley rushed by in a blur of hedgerows and hamlets, evening sun on woodlands and church spires. Even in the mere ten years of Alice's experience, rural England had changed, although much less than the cities, where the inrush of motor vehicles and power lines was more visible. Out here the plodding horses still hauled mountainous hay wagons, but lorries and omnibuses were proliferating on the country lanes. Tradition was a personal thing, she supposed. The landscapes Constable had painted had long since been blighted by railway lines and then telegraph wires.

The carriage swayed in hurried rhythm. *Clickety-click,* said the wheels, *clickety-click, clickety-click . . .*

"I think I'll try the Scotch broth," she said. "How long since you saw tablecloths?"

"Ages. We had them at Olympus, but I didn't stay there very long."

He had been attempting to turn the conversation away from his adventures, inquiring about her life in wartime London. She kept steering him back to Nextdoor. Even then, he would obviously rather talk about Olympus than relate his experiences as a warlord. She was curious to know why. Either he had something to be very proud of and was being typically modest about it, or he had done something shameful. Which?

Was he concerned that she would think he had gone native? Julian and Ginger had both been shocked by the little they had heard, although neither had said so. In their view, the code of the English sahib did not include self-mutilation and spear-throwing. Having spent much of her childhood playing in the dust of an Embu compound, Alice had few such prejudices. As far as she could see, Edward had had no choice. Marooned on another world, he could hardly have appealed to the British Consul.

"The lamb may be safest," she said. "Railway food is not what it was before the war. Tarion sounds like an interesting character."

Edward snorted. "He has charm, when he bothers to use it. He's a superb athlete and tough as an anvil. That about sums up his good points, I'd say."

"How about his bad points?"

"Please! That would take all night. I swear the man has not one trace of morals or ethics or scruples. Nothing is beneath him, absolutely nothing!"

"He tried to bribe you, I suppose?"

Edward looked up from the menu again and rolled his eyes. "Dozens of times. You can't imagine some of the offers he made me!"

Alice thought she could, but she knew he would not mention them in the presence of a lady.

She wondered just what it would take to bribe her idealistic cousin into doing something he felt was wrong. The Imperial Crown Jewels, perhaps, as a start? Edward had no family responsibilities; he was young enough to have few needs beyond his daily bread. He had been taught to believe that honesty and willingness to work would suffice to carry him through life. Vast estates would just seem a burden to him, and his education had armored him against depravity. He probably still took a cold bath every morning. He would be true to King and Country, decency and fair play—and seek nothing else. His education had been designed to turn out incorruptible administrators, the men who ran the Empire. Even Edward Exeter might slip in a year or two, when idealism faded in the light of experience, but at the moment he was as close to incorruptible as any mortal could be. The Tarion man must have been very puzzled by the response to his offers.

Where Tarion had failed, how could Alice Prescott succeed?

Whatever had happened to her patriotism all of a sudden? She recalled the recruiting posters of the early months of the war, before conscription: THE WOMEN OF BRITAIN SAY "GO!" She had been horrified when D'Arcy enlisted, and yet proud of him. Like everyone else, she knew the war must be fought and must be won—she just did not think that it was Edward's war. He had been called to other duties. The very laws of nature seemed to bend around him. But if she could not justify this feeling even to herself, how could she ever convince him? What would it take to change his mind?

"You declined, of course?"

"Alice, darling! What do you think I—Don't answer that! Of course I did. Even if he'd come up with anything really tempting, Tarion's promises are mere wind and always will be."

"Did you tell him so?"

"Of course. He would just laugh and agree. In a day or two he would try me again."

Edward smirked. He knew what she was thinking. He knew he was good. Well, she could deflate him. She could still make him blush.

"You're young and winsome," she mused. "I assume he also made indecent advances?"

He blushed an unbelievable scarlet. "How did you guess?"

"From things you didn't say. Golbfish was no pillar of virtue either, I gather."

"Not by our standards," Edward said primly. "But he was merely debauched, whereas Tarion was depraved. There was a real man inside Golbfish's blubber. He'd just never had reason to call that man out before."

*"Not for the sake of a ribboned coat,*
*Or the selfish hope of a season's fame,*
*But his Captain's hand on his shoulder—"*

"Oh, cut it out!" Edward said testily.

"So you turned a frog into a prince? And then—"

The waiter appeared beside them as if condensing out of the air. They ordered dinner. Up ahead, the engine came into view, snaking around a curve, smoke pouring from its funnel. Some poor devil of a fireman was shoveling his heart out there. The dining car rocked unevenly as it reached the bend.

They sat for a while in silence, Alice reviewing a mental list of things she should be asking. Talking was difficult in the crowded train; when they arrived at Greyfriars they would have Julian for company again, possibly Ginger, and also the formidable Mrs. Bodgley. Mrs. Bodgley would probably demand Edward's story from the beginning. She would certainly want an account of what had happened to her son. Alice must put this brief dining-car privacy to good use.

The waiter slid soup plates in front of them and departed.

"This is not bad at all!" Edward announced.

"But look at this awful wartime bread!"

Everything went black.

"Don't eat it!" he said over the racket. "It makes you go blind." The acrid reek of coal began to foul the air. Then the train burst out of the tunnel, gradually shedding its cocoon of smoke.

"You are still the idiot I used to know," Alice said affectionately. "Tell me. You want to get in touch with the Service? You said you had three ways in mind."

Edward nodded glumly. "They're all very flimsy leads, though. One of them is that letter I asked Ginger to post for me. Do you remember Mr. Oldcastle?"

"I remember you talking about him."

"He wrote to me just after—after the news." His bony face seemed to grow even thinner for a moment, remembering the bad times, when Cameron and Rona Exeter had died in the Nyagatha massacre. "Claimed to be with the Colonial Office. He wasn't, of course. He was with Head Office."

Alice had known only that Oldcastle had been an absentee father to Edward. In retrospect, he had been too good to be true. His Majesty's Government would never take so much interest in the orphaned son of a very minor official.

"When you disappeared, I wrote to Mr. Oldcastle."

Edward grinned, popping a crust in his mouth. "What address?"

"I tried Whitehall, and I tried the one Ginger had, at the school."

"Whitehall had never heard of him and the GPO had never heard of Druids Close?"

"Right on."

"There is no Druids Close. There was no Mr. Oldcastle. He was a committee, or so Creighton told me, although he always wrote back in the same hand. Head Office were keeping an eye on me, you see, as a favor for the Service. The Blighters were after me then, too."

*Clickety-click, clickety-click, clickety-click . . .*

"So if Oldcastle doesn't exist, how do you get in touch with him now?"

"I do what I always did—I write him a letter! I already have, and Ginger will have posted it by now."

"I thought Julian had already tried this for you?"

Obviously she had been expected to ask that.

"Ah! But this one has my handwriting on the envelope, which may be important, and it's going in the right box." Edward smirked like a schoolboy demonstrating his first card trick. "I know a little more about magic now, you see. It would take a great deal of mana to bewitch the entire postal service, but not much to do one pillar-box."

"That is certainly logical."

"And as soon as I worked that out, I remembered several times when Mr. Oldcastle warned me that he would be away—at about the same times I was going to be away from Fallow! So any postcards or letters I sent him, from anywhere else, might reasonably not get answered! Simple, isn't it?"

"And you think the magic is still on that box?"

"Well . . ." He frowned. "I have no idea. It may not be. I warned you all these ideas were dishwaterish."

"Let's hear the next one."

"The next one is even dicier. The, er, man who rescued me from the hospital was a numen. He used to go by the name of Robin Goodfellow, a fairish time ago."

Blue eyes studied Alice solemnly, waiting for her disbelief. The waiter removed the soup plates and served the roast lamb.

"*Puck?*"

"The same. One of them. A local representative of the old firm, was how Creighton put it. Forgotten now, and ignored, but still residing on his node, amid the bracken and brambles and the standing stones—husbanding scraps of the mana he received back in Saxon times or the Middle Ages, when people still believed in the People of the Hills."

Gods on a storybook world were one thing. In modern England they took more believing. "What was he like?"

"Nice enough old boy. At least, he was nice to me. Mad as a rabid bat, really, I think. He can't have had anyone to speak to in centuries."

"He's with this Head Office bunch?"

"He's a neutral, but he must know how to find them."

"And where do you find him?"

Edward shrugged, struggling to cut an extra tough slab of mutton. "Not sure exactly. I was half out of my skull with pain that morning, but not far from Greyfriars, on a little hill. I'll know it when I see it."

This sounded even weaker than the first idea. It would take time and transportation to inspect all the hilltops around Greyfriars. The police must be after Edward Exeter now. The ominous Blighters might be. Looking at him, it was hard to believe that he was twenty-one and a man of two worlds. She felt a motherly obligation to dispatch her hopelessly idealistic young cousin off to Nextdoor as fast as possible, whether he wanted to go or not. Details to be arranged.

"Will Puck help you again?"

"I can only ask. He's a stranger here, of course. Originally from Nextdoor. From Ruatvil, in Sussland. I could sacrifice a bullock, perhaps."

He was being remarkably generous with her money.

"A bullock? You'll get thrown in jail if you waste food like that, these days. There's a war on, my lad!"

"Oh. Well, I shall think of something."

"Tell me the third lead." Alice forked up some well-named string beans.

"I think I still remember the key I used with Creighton, the ritual. Anyone who goes to the same portal and does that dance will arrive at the Sacrarium—that's the ruined temple in Sussvale." He gave up on the mutton and poked angrily at a soggy potato. "But that's a fair way from Olympus, and who could I ask to risk it? Arriving naked, not knowing the language?"

"You'd have to go yourself!" Now they were making progress!

He must have sensed her approval, because he scowled. "No. It would take too long, and I'd have to find my way back here all over again."

"It would only be a flying visit, surely? There and back." Another three years and the war would be long over.

"I don't trust the Service! They wouldn't let me come Home before, and they might try to hold me again. You think Smedley really wants to cross over?" he added hopefully.

"I don't know. I don't know if he knows. He's pretty badly shaken, Edward. Don't think any the worse of him for that! He's got enough medals to start a pawn shop and lots of fellows have been—"

"Shell-shocked. Yes, I know. I saw some of them, remember." Again he hacked angrily at the meat. "Smedley's a brick, I don't doubt it. But I can't send him over alone, not knowing the language. I damned nearly died myself, and I would have if I hadn't had Eleal to help me."

"Suppose none of these plans work?"

"Then I can't warn the Service about the traitor, that's all."

"So you just stay here and enlist?"

"Enlist or hang. Or both."

"Where is this portal you mentioned?"

"Stonehenge." Edward peered out the window. "What town is this we're coming to? Swindon already?"

Alice laid down her knife and fork. "Edward, Stonehenge is on Salisbury Plain."

"Of course I know. . . . Why? Why does that matter?"

"The Army has taken over all of Salisbury Plain now. There's an aerodrome at Stonehenge itself. There's even talk of knocking down the stones because they're a danger to planes landing and taking off, it's so close."

He stared at her in frank dismay.

*Clickety-click, clickety-click, clickety-click . . .*

"You were counting on that one, weren't you?" she said. "Stonehenge was your trump card?"

"Final stand, more like."

"You won't get near it," she said.

"After the war?"

"Perhaps after the war, whenever that is."

He pushed the remains of the meal to one side of his plate and laid down his knife and fork. "Damn!"

*Damn indeed!*

Then he grinned. "So I can't go back! Clear conscience. Good!"

"Do you wish to try the sweet, madam?" the waiter inquired. "Dundee pudding and custard?"

"Cheese and biscuits, please," Alice said, suppressing a shudder, "and coffee."

"The same for me," Edward said, not even looking up.

Waiter and plates disappeared.

Edward poked at some crumbs. "Let's just hope the letter works."

"Yes."

"And let's hope that the Blighters don't get it instead."

"What! Is that possible?"

He smiled bleakly. "Definitely possible. Head Office suffered a major defeat. I don't know what their English equivalent of Olympus is, but it may have fallen to the enemy since I was a kid. If that's the case, then I just wrote to the enemy, saying where I am."

"Oh."

"I should have warned you."

Disbelief swirled around her like a sudden squall. Two days ago Ginger Jones had walked into her life and now she was a character in a John Buchan thriller. *The Black Stone is after you! Flee, for all is lost. . . .*

"In fact," Edward said sternly, "I should never have let you come. You had better catch the first train back to town."

"Not Pygmalion likely!" Alice said. "Tell me more about your experiences as Chief of the Headhunters."

He frowned.

"Sorry," she said. "That was a cheap shot. So what happened when the old queen died? Who got the crown? The reformed Golbfish or the unrepentant Tarion?"

Edward sighed and turned to look out the window.

"The news arrived early one morning, just after we reached Lemodvale, before we got trapped. Old Kammaeman called me in to ask my opinion—which brother should he send back? I couldn't help feeling flattered, although I knew it was nothing to do with me personally, just my charisma at work. I told him any man who trusted Tarion ought to be chained in a padded cell."

She could guess what was coming from his disgusted expression.

"But by then it was too late?"

Edward looked up with rueful surprise, spoon poised. "Right on! Tarion had taken his Nagian cavalry and gone. Deserted in the middle of a war!"

She sipped coffee. "You expected better of him?"

He tried to laugh and swallow at the same time, and shook his head. "No! It was perfectly in character. He got the news even before Kammaeman did, so he must have bribed somebody somewhere. Personally, I was glad to see the back of him, but it left us seriously short of cavalry. Moas are one-man beasts. They fix on one owner when they're only chicks—calves I mean, I suppose. They're closer to mammals than birds. English doesn't have the right words. Anyway, it takes fortn—months, that is, to imprint one to a new rider. The Joalians hadn't been able to bring very many over Thordpass— it's too high—so they'd been depending on Tarion's troop. He upped and left, and that put us in the soup."

# 24

"Wake up, beautiful," said a whisper.

Dosh jumped, feeling a hand over his mouth. "Mmmph?" The hand was removed. He could see nothing except a faint hint of moonlight under the flap of the tent. He was lying on his sleeping rug, and the ground below it was hard and stony. He heard the voice again, very close to his ear.

"Awake?"

"Yes, master."

"Good. Keep your voice down. It is time to play a little game."

"Again?" The man was insatiable! "How long have we slept?"

"I have not slept at all, and this is another sort of game. We begin by tying you up."

Dosh's heart made a mighty leap and began racing all around his chest, looking for a way out. "No, master! Please! I have had some very unpleasant experiences with those sort of—"

Tarion's strong hand pushed a cloth into his mouth, and Dosh's protests subsided into whimpers. It was the rag he used for cleaning the master's saddle. He did not resist as rope was wrapped around his ankles, harsh fibers biting into his skin. Tarion had never bound him before and had never really hurt him—not too much—but he was capable of anything. There were bloodcurdling tales of orgies at Bondvaan Ambassador's house. . . .

"Roll over!"

Dosh rolled over on his belly and put his wrists together. As the rope tightened about them and then was pulled tighter and even tighter, he said, *"Mmmph!"* urgently through the gag. It did no good. Then his elbows were lashed together also, and finally his knees. *Holy Tion, preserve me!*

For a moment nothing more happened. He lay in the dark and sweated, while his imagination rioted with macabre thoughts of what Tarion might be going to do to him. If it took very long his hands would fall off.

It started—Tarion flipped him over, so he lay awkwardly on his bound arms. There was a sharp rock under his shoulders. To make matters worse, the prince lay down also and leaned one arm heavily on Dosh's chest. Something cold caressed his neck.

"That is my dagger you can feel, lover," Tarion said softly, a few inches above Dosh's nose. "I'll take the gag out, but if you make any noise, I shall cut your throat while the second word is still in it. Understand?"

The cloth was removed. Dosh gulped and tried to work the taste away. "Yes, master," he whispered.

"Good. Now listen carefully. I must leave. My dear mother has been called to take her place in the heavens, among the shining blessed."

"I am sorry, master."

"You needn't be—I'm not. It is Thighday already and she died on Ankleday, so our beloved battlemaster should receive the news before nightfall. I prefer to depart before he does, just in case he makes the wrong decision."

"But how—"

Dosh felt Tarion's chuckle more than he heard it.

"Just say I have a premonition. I am quite confident that she died on Ankleday. A monarchy should not be left without a monarch any longer than absolutely necessary. And I cannot take you with me, dear boy, much as I long to, because you have no moa and we shall be going very fast. So what am I to do with you, *mm?*"

Dosh managed a small moan, but his throat seemed to have closed up completely.

A wet tongue touched his nose. "I love you so much," said the dread, mocking whisper close above him, "that I can hardly bear the thought of leaving you to another master. But we have had such good times together that it does seem unkind to put you to sleep. Do you wish to express an opinion on the matter?"

Dosh believed. He knew the prince was quite capable of killing him here, now, on the tent floor, in cold blood, with a single slash of his dagger. "I love you!" His voice quavered.

"And I love you, too, darling. I considered just cutting your beautiful throat while you were asleep, but there is something I am curious to learn, most curious to learn. Men always tell the truth on their deathbeds, did you know that? And wise men tell the truth to avoid deathbeds. So you tell me now, lover: Who are you spying for?"

"I've told you before! Anyone who pays me."

"My, you are sweating, aren't you? I have known you sweat often enough, dear one, but never quite like this. So you do understand that I am going to kill you if you continue lying to me? Last chance, Dosh Houseboy. Who are you spying for?"

Dosh tried to speak and discovered he was weeping. Sobbing was not easy with so much of Tarion's weight resting on his chest. "Nobody."

"Oh, now that is absurd! Really silly. Everybody spies for somebody. The day I hired you, you hid two stars and some small change under the Niolian vase in my bedroom. You now have five stars in the bottom of my brush case. Three stars in seven fortnights?

That isn't nearly enough for a clever sneak like you to earn by tattling. You probably made that much selling your pretty body around the palace guard, but you'd have gained far more if you were peddling information about me to anyone local. So you're spying for some outsider. Who?"

"I love you," Dosh whimpered. "I don't tell anyone anything!"

A sudden searing pain at his throat and he thought he had died. . . .

"That's just a flesh wound," Tarion said. "At least, I think it is. It's hard to tell in the dark. I may overdo it next time. You still alive?"

"Yes."

"Good. This is taking too long. Somebody sent you to Nag to worm your way into my service and spy on me. You were not exactly subtle in your approach, I'm afraid. You claimed to be a Narshian, but you're not. Now I shall put the gag back and rip your guts open and you will die very nastily—unless you tell me who it was that sent you."

Trouble was, Dosh knew he could not answer that question. He was not spying on Tarion at all, only on the Liberator, but he could not explain that either.

He was dragged out of the tent in the bitter light of dawn. He should have been ashamed of his nudity, his tears, the dried blood on him, but the pain in his limbs drowned out everything else. His legs would not support him, and when he was brought before Kammaeman Battlemaster, he collapsed in a sniveling heap.

"Oh, sewage!" said the general. "That will be all, Captain. You may go."

The tent flap closed. There were two other men there, and they stayed. Through the blur of his tears, Dosh recognized Kolgan Coadjutant by his great height. The other was wearing face paint and a loincloth and was almost certainly the Liberator.

"All right, scum," Kammaeman said. "Talk! When did he leave?"

Dosh's mouth was a foul desert, still tasting of the oily rag that had spent so many hours in it, but he managed to croak, "Middle of the night, sir. I don't know the hour."

"Who brought him the news?"

Normally Dosh would lie in response to such a question or demand money for an answer—or both, but he was too weak to maintain a good fiction, and his hatred of Tarion maddened him.

"I don't think anyone did. He said the queen died on Ankleday, as if it had been arranged."

The Joalian grunted. "That's entirely possible, I suppose. Coadjutant?"

"I agree."

"Hordeleader?"

"I'd believe anything of that one, sir."

Yes, it was the Liberator. Not that anyone but Dosh knew that D'ward was the prophesied Liberator, of course.

Kammaeman growled angrily. "If we believe this wretch, then they've got too good a start for us ever to catch them. Hordeleader, send for the other one."

The tent flap lifted, and the Liberator said something to someone outside. Then he returned. He came over to Dosh and offered him a water bottle. Seeing that Dosh's hands were not functioning yet, he went down on one knee and held it to his lips so he could drink. Water went everywhere, but some found its way down into the desert. Bliss!

"I'm not sorry to be rid of the royal bastard," Kolgan muttered, "but we can ill afford to lose the mounts. It leaves us too damnably short."

Kammaeman grunted agreement. "But it'll be much worse if I detach a troop to follow him." The Joalians moved away, to sit on the stools at the other end of the tent.

The Liberator was peering at Dosh's face. "Why did he cut you up like that?"

"Just his idea of fun, sir," Dosh mumbled, hoping nobody put a mirror near him. He did not want to know how bad it was. The slashes on his throat wouldn't matter, but Tarion had done things to his cheeks and forehead, and close to his eyes.

"Mm?" the Liberator said quietly. His paint wrinkled. "Did you tell him what he wanted to know?"

Startled, Dosh shook his head. He had tried to! He had tried desperately, but his real master had made that impossible. His real master could not be named. It was hard for Dosh even to think his name.

Of course the Liberator did not know that, and he misunderstood. "Good for you!" he murmured. "Amazing he didn't just kill you, then."

That was certainly true! Dosh shuddered at the memory and could not speak.

"There's a surgeon's apprentice in the Rareby troop. He could stitch those slashes so they don't scar so badly."

Astonished, Dosh said, "I'd be very grateful, sir."

The Liberator chuckled drily. "After all, your looks are your stock in trade, aren't they?" He stood up and walked over to the others.

Who was he to sneer? A warrior sold his body too, and in worse ways. Beauty was a talent like strength or courage. If the gods blessed a man with those, he was expected to use them to benefit himself and other people, was he not? Then why not the same with beauty?

What chance had Dosh ever had, an abandoned Tinkerfolk brat? His own people had thrown him out. His body was all he'd ever had to offer. It had needed to be fed, just like any other. He had served women just as willingly as men—more so, actually, because they were less dangerous—but he had never found a woman with the money and the freedom to offer him long-term employment.

For a few minutes the soldiers talked tactics and battle plans, while Dosh brooded, wondering what was going to happen to him now. He had been wondering that for hours, ever since Tarion had given up and left him. When he had decided that he was not going to bleed to death, he had concluded that he would probably be lucky if the Joalians just ran him out of camp at spearpoint. Then the Lemodians would kill him. He hardly cared anymore. He was desolated by the thought that he had failed his master, his real master. The pain in his hands was a sickening throb. He stayed where he was, keeping very still, hoping to hear something of importance.

Then the other prince was ushered in, gasping and coughing from running. His face paint was patchy, as if he had been interrupted during his morning touch-up. Nevertheless, even Tarion had conceded that the fat man was far more convincing as a warrior now than he had been in Nag. He was still just as fat, though.

Kammaeman informed him that the queen was dead. Golbfish expressed suitable regrets, but he was probably even less upset than his half brother had been. No one had ever described old Emchainne as likable, and she had conspired to have this son murdered in front of her eyes.

"So either you or Tarion must be recognized as her successor," Kammaeman announced, belaboring the obvious. "As he has betrayed our trust, you are our choice. Even if he hadn't, of course! I mean, we had already decided that. Long live the king!"

"Thank you, Battlemaster," the blubber-man said. "Joalia will find that her trust in me is not misplaced."

Kolgan chuckled in the background. "There may be some delay in arranging your coronation, though."

"Yes," Kammaeman said. "First we shall have to hang your brother. However, you have my word. As soon as we return to Nag, he is a dead man, and you shall have the throne."

"I am very grateful, sir."

"I suppose we had better have him proclaimed in the camp?" Kolgan said.

"I suppose so." Kammaeman sounded displeased.

There was a pause, then Golbfish said, "That will present difficulties. I shall automatically become hordeleader." He even sounded like a prince now. How extraordinary!

"You are welcome to it," the Liberator said.

"But I swore before the goddess that I would fight in the ranks."

Dosh looked up in amazement, and saw that the two Joalians were equally at a loss. As for the Liberator . . . Face paint tended to mask expressions, but his jaw was hanging down.

Then everyone spoke at once: "That is not necessary!". . . "Do I understand that you wish to remain a simple warrior?". . . "It does you great honor!"

Golbfish shrugged. "If you will permit it, Battlemaster, that is what I request. I wish to fulfill my oath. When we return to Nagland, then I shall be free to assume my new duties."

"By the five gods!" Kammaeman exploded. "I confess I did not expect this of you . . . Your Majesty."

"It is gravely out of character, I agree," the fat man said, and chuckled. For a brief instant that chuckle made him their equal, or even their superior, and they responded with smiles and laughter. Then he sank back into his humble warrior role. "But my people will approve. Lately I have been studying leadership, under a remarkable teacher. Do I have your permission to withdraw?"

He must have been given a nod of consent, for he went strutting out, stalking past Dosh without even a glance of distaste.

"Miracle!" the battlemaster said. "May the gods be praised! D'ward, what have you done to him?"

"Me? Nothing! Nothing at all!"

"Somebody made a man of him!"

"Well it certainly wasn't me!" Kolgan said, laughing.

They all stood up. Then, of course, they remembered Dosh.

"Yuuch!" Kammaeman said. "What do we do with this dreg? Either of you gentleman need a catamite?"

"Throw him out and let the Lemodians have him," Kolgan suggested, looking down from his enormous height. His red beard twisted in an expression of extreme contempt. "He can only tend to corrupt the camp if he is allowed to stay. I despise such degenerates."

That was hardly honest, Dosh thought, considering that Kolgan had borrowed Tarion's houseboy twice since leaving Nag, for massage and other purposes. He was a stingy tipper, too.

The Liberator sighed. "Can you run, lad?"

"Run, sir?"

"I could use a messenger." He looked to Kammaeman. "If I send warriors, they spend half the day chattering when they get there."

The battlemaster chuckled. "I believe you! Take him by all means. If he causes trouble, though, he'll have to go."

"I think he'll behave, sir. Will you, Dosh?"

Dosh stood up shakily, hardly able to believe his ears. "Oh, yes, sir. Thank you, sir!" Personal messenger for the Liberator? Wonderful! How pleased his real master would be with him!

"Come on, then. Here, you carry my shield until we can get some clothes for you."

They all went outside, blinking at the sunlight. As he set off through the camp with the Liberator, Dosh tried to hold his head up and ignore the laughter and jeering his appearance provoked. It wasn't easy, though. There was a lot of it.

"Clothes first," D'ward said. "Then we'd best get those stitches done as soon as possible." He grinned down at Dosh. He was tall. "Perhaps you'd better try some face paint!"

Dosh laughed as a good servant should when his master makes a joke. He discovered that laughter hurt his face.

"Then food," the Liberator went on. "I wonder if we can find you some decent boots? Hatchet, knife? . . . I assume you're going to make a break for it?"

"No, sir. I want to stay with you, sir. I'm terribly grateful for—"

"Stuff that! I don't need your flattery. Why didn't he kill you at the end, when you wouldn't tell him what he wanted to know?"

"I think he was fond of me in his way."

"Curious fondness. All right, stay. I do need a messenger. But you will not sleep anywhere near me, understand?"

"Yes, sir."

"He offered you to me several times, did you know that?"

"He offered me to many people, sir. Many accepted."

The Liberator pulled a face under his paint and looked away.

Then Dosh felt a sudden blaze of inspiration and joy. He had completed his mission! He had solved the riddle in the prophecy: *Eleal shall be the first temptation and the prince shall be the second.* Prince Tarion had tempted the Liberator by offering him Dosh. That was all there was to it! The prophecy had already been fulfilled, so now he could report back to his master, his real master, his *divine* master.

# V

## *Pawn Takes Castle*

# 25

A schoolboy of about thirteen came out into the corridor and offered Alice his seat in the compartment.

She smiled winningly at him. "That's very kind of you, but I'm all right here. Thank you, though."

Blushing, he went back inside and slid the door shut.

Since Swindon, the train was far less crowded. It was possible to talk in the corridor.

"Tell me what happened after you arrived in Lemodvale and Tarion departed."

Stooping to peer out the window, Edward scowled. "I'd just as soon not talk about it, actually. Have you noticed how much luggage everyone seems to have? I think they're running away from the air raids in London."

"Possibly. And you're running away from my question."

He sighed. "I'm not proud of what happened! It was a mess. Kammaeman may have been a crafty politician, but he was no general. He hadn't done his homework."

He drew cucumber shapes on the greasy window and explained the geography. "Thargia had taken Narshvale, which had been Joalian. The Thargians are the bullyboys of the Vales, like the Prussians in Europe or the Spartans in Greece. Nobody calls out the Thargians!

"But Joalia needed to save face to keep its other colonies loyal. The original plan was to cross over Lemodvale and attack Thargvale itself, while it was still digesting Narshvale. It was to be a punishment raid—loot, rape, burn, and scram. Of course, the Thargians would have retaliated, probably the next year. I expect Joalia was counting on Nagvale taking the heat. That's what junior allies are for, isn't it? It was all business as usual, and nasty.

"But Tarion took almost all of our cavalry, so the plan collapsed. Even hitting and running wasn't in the cards without cavalry. Kammaeman had to do something with the forces he had, or face impeachment when he went home. He decided to conquer Lemodvale instead. He probably thought he could trade it back to Tharg in return for Narshvale." Edward smiled quizzically. "Does that sound logical?"

"But not practical? Like offering to give Southwest Africa back to the Boche in return for Belgium?"

He grinned. "Something along those lines. Cavalry would be useless in Lemodvale, anyway, which probably convinced him, but Joalia had never conquered Lemodvale before, and that should have warned him. All the vales are different, and Lemod is more different than most. First of all, it's hilly. There's no—I suppose *Lemodflat* would be the English equivalent."

He paused to think. Alice watched the telegraph wires dip, rise, dip, rise . . . *Clickety-click, clickety-click . . .*

"Valian languages use prefixes where we have suffixes," he said vaguely. "Roughly—very roughly—it would go like this. Say Nagvale is the general term, the whole basin. The mountains all around it would be Nagwall, the foothills Nagslope. Roughly. The arable part would be Nagflat, and in most vales it truly is flat. In Nagland itself it's a plain, almost a desert. Everything that's habitable is called Nagland and everything that's not has another name—Nagwaste? The capital would be Nagtown, or just Nag. The political entity would be Nagia, I suppose. They have other terms. You could say that Nagslope is the usable foothills, and the higher bits are Nagmoor or something like that. It's not a bad system. English doesn't make so many distinctions."

"I imagine words like *ebb tide* would confuse the Nagians just as much as you are confusing me. What has all this to do with the war?"

"Just that Lemodflat isn't. Flat, I mean. It's all cut up by streams. There wouldn't be enough level ground in the whole country for a good nine-hole golf course. And the Lemodians don't have farms, they have trees. They're strange looking trees, but all their crops come from trees. Something rather like a breadfruit gives them their basic starch, but they have others that provide stuff like flax—also cotton and fruits and nuts and wine berries and things just like potatoes . . . everything. The whole country is one enormous orchard."

"Which isn't too good to fight in?"

"It's great to fight in," Edward said bitterly, "if you happen to be a guerrilla."

He sighed and turned around to lean on the brass rail across the window. He folded his arms. "I should have seen what was going to happen. I should have guessed. But, damn it all, Alice, I was only eighteen! I was a stranger in their world. I thought they knew what they were doing in their shiny armor and fancy helmets."

She had never known him to make excuses before. "You couldn't have done anything, surely?"

"Surely I could have! I still had the mana I'd collected in Olfaan's temple. It wasn't much by the gods' standards, of course. I knew it wouldn't build any magic castles, but I thought I might manage a faith healing or something, so I was hoarding it. But even with just my stranger's charisma I could have talked some sense into Kammaeman if I had seen the problem." He pulled a face. "The only man with any brains was Tarion, who got out while the going was good."

He turned back to the glass and added to his map. "Lemodvale's shaped like a snake, very long and thin. We came in here, at the eastern end. That's where the main passes are. Lemod, the capital, is up here, at the western end. Nobody thought to ask what sort of openings there were thereabouts. It was autumn." He frowned at the map he had drawn or perhaps at the scenery sliding by outside. The train was slowing for a station, but she thought he wasn't really looking, just reluctant to tell her more.

"You'd think Kammaeman would have studied the geography, wouldn't you?" he growled. "Or at least the history. He wasn't the first Joalian general to die in Lemodvale."

Houses flowed past the window, slower and slower.

"He wasn't the first Joalian general to be murdered by his deputy, either. And when the Chamber learned I was with the army, then we were fighting gods."

# *26*

Four days after the army reached Lemodflat, Golbfish had his first experience of battle. The battle itself was not nearly so bad as the getting ready for it.

He hated Lemodvale. All the Nagians hated Lemodvale. Their own land was flat, dry, and treeless, with rarely a day when a man could not see all the way to Nagwall in every direction. At night the stars and the moons roamed overhead like fireflies in infinite space.

Lemodvale was different. Sky and mountains vanished; the world became nothing but trees, with rarely enough space to pitch a tent and no level ground anyway. Lemodflat wasn't even a decent jungle, because the trees were planted in rows, curving around the slopes. Usually there was no undergrowth, but the lowest branches sprouted at shoulder height and men became hunchbacked from creeping under them all the time. There were no open fields and few trails wide enough to let the sun through. Day after day a man saw no farther than twenty yards, and then only in one direction. He could walk for hours and the view never changed. It was like being shut up indoors, in a maze of pillars, with the roof leaking all the time. Some of the Nagians were almost out of their minds.

Rain fell every day, sometimes only a brief shower, often a dawn-to-dusk downpour. Face paint washed off and stained beards like rainbows.

Droppings showed that wildlife or packbeasts grazed the orchards, but they were never seen. The Lemodians themselves had vanished also. When cottages were located, they were always deserted, often burned. The army advanced unopposed—except by cold and constant wet and the ravages of unfamiliar food.

The scouts had finally located a village, name unknown. At last there could be a fight.

Kammaeman Battlemaster had decided to attack at dawn. He had given the Nagians the honor of leading the assault because he thought they could approach more quietly than the armored Joalians, or so he had said. The rain had stopped. Trumb was almost full, his eerie green light filtering dimly through the foliage. It was just possible for a man to see the man in front of him, as long as he stayed close. It was not possible to move without walking into tree trunks and branches. By day the warriors held their shields up until their left arms were ready to fall off, but shields would make too much noise now. So they wore their shields on their backs and felt their way forward with their hands. Golbfish followed Pomuin, and Dogthark followed Golbfish, each trying to keep the other in sight and not ram him with his spear. It was easy to lose track of where those sharp blades were in the dark.

Feet squelched on dead leaves, but otherwise there was no sound. For all Golbfish knew, they might have walked in a circle and returned to camp. His back and neck ached from stooping.

He was shivering, telling himself that the clammy morning air was at fault and knowing it was not. His feet were icy. He did not think he was afraid of dying so much as of exposing himself as a coward in front of these young peasants. What would they think of their future king if he fainted, froze, or just soiled himself with terror when the fighting started? He was probably the oldest Nagian in the army, because only single men had been conscripted and villagers married young.

They were ignorant, uneducated. They took life as it came, not questioning its meaning or the gods' purposes, or asking about ethics.

Courage was easier for the young. Life felt permanent to them. Probably every one of those rustic warriors was a virgin. Back at the camp, they had been cracking cheerful jokes, speculating about the Lemodian women they would capture and the sport that would follow. Golbfish was no warrior. He was no virgin either. He knew that the transient pleasure was not worth the risk of being maimed or killed.

Pomuin stopped and turned. Golbfish moved closer, watching where he put his spearpoint, then swung around to find out where Dogthark was putting his. They stood side by side, then, listening to the footsteps dying away behind them. A faint rustle of sound came along the line as the men sat down in obedience to some whispered command at the front. The move was not easy in the dark with trees all around and a ten-foot pole spear attached to one's wrist by a leather thong. But Pomuin sat, Golbfish sat, Dogthark sat, the activity moving away into the distance.

They were under strict orders not to talk. Golbfish did not think he had enough saliva to move his tongue anyway. Fear was an awful tightness in his chest, a terrifying insecurity in his bowels. What if he shamed himself right here, with men on either side of him who could not fail to notice? Even in darkness they would hear him and certainly smell him. And could he ever bring himself to thrust this spear into a living man? He had no quarrel with the Lemodians. The Thargians had taken over Narshvale, so the Joalians attacked Lemodvale. Why should a Nagian care, any Nagian? He kept imagining his spear impaling some young peasant, blood and guts spilling out, the victim's scream of agony, the accusing look on his face as he felt himself dying . . . rank, uncouth barbarism!

He thought of his friends in Joal, poets and artists and musicians.

Or the peasant might impale him. Somehow that did not seem so terrible, or at least not so shameful. Then it would be over and there would be no memories.

He sniffed. Smoke? The landscape was waterlogged, so smoke meant hearths. The village must be very close. Downhill, Prat'han Troopleader had said. When the signal came, they were to move downhill, and they would come to the village by the ford. Kill all the men, even if they try to surrender. Don't touch the women until the officers give permission, and then wait your turn. Go easy on the children lest you anger the gods.

Golbfish could hear quiet whisperings to left and right. He thought he could hear something from downhill, but the trees muffled sound so much that he could not be sure. Running water, probably.

What would Ymma say if she could see him now, sitting on wet leaves in a dark forest, damned nearly naked, waiting to kill or die? She would roll around on the bed screaming in hysterics, with her big breasts flopping from side to side. . . .

He jumped as an icy hand took hold of his. He looked around, into Dogthark's eyes, glistening bright in the green moonlight.

Dogthark's hand was shaking. He squeezed Golbfish's fingers.

Golbfish squeezed back. "What's wrong?" he whispered.

"I'm thkared!"

Dogthark was one of the youngest, but big. He had lost all his front teeth, which gave him an idiot look and slurred his speech. He was a troublemaker, a bruiser. Golbfish was afraid of him and avoided him normally, not wanting to get involved in a pointless brawl he would certainly lose. Dogthark was just the sort of moronic kid who might find it amusing to beat up his future king. He was exactly the sort of dolt Golbfish had been envying for his unthinking courage.

"We're all scared!" he said.

"Not you, thir!"

"Yes I am."

"But everyone elth was making thilly jokes and you were jutht quiet, all confidence, quiet courage!"

How wrong could one be?

"I am scared shitless," Golbfish said. "Like you. Worse. I've never been in a battle either. Keep thinking about the girls down there. How many girls can you rape in one morning?"

Dogthark made a strange panting sound that was probably a laugh. "Three?"

"Oh, come on! Husky young fellow like you ought to manage four or five."

"You really think tho? I've never had a girl before, thir."

Golbfish sniffed again. Smoke! How long until dawn? "They're nice. Lot of hard work after the first couple, though. It'll really make you sweat."

"I think you're marvellouth, thir! A king fighting in the rankth! We're all tho proud of you!"

"I feel like a bloody fool," Golbfish confessed. "I . . ."

Only his own stupidity had brought him to this. Why had he refused royal rank and insisted on remaining a warrior? What did he really owe to D'ward that he so much wished to be worthy of that youngster's approval? He was certainly acting out of character these days.

Sounds. Men rising, unslinging shields. Leaves crackling underfoot. It was not dawn yet, but the attack had begun.

"Come on!" he said, clenching every sphincter. "Save a few girls for me."

A hundred yards downhill and they saw the flames.

There were no women. There was no battle. Half the cottages had collapsed into embers already. Howling and yelling in disgust, the Nagian warriors milled around in the single street that had once been a village.

"There'th no girlth!" Dogthark wailed. "No wariorth! They all ran away! Cowardth!"

Golbfish felt drunk with relief. No battle! No need to impale men, no men to impale him! He wanted to dance and sing with joy.

"Tie a knot in it until the next time, son!" he said. "Next time you can try for a dozen!" He laughed aloud. The warmth from the fires was a caress on his permanently damp hide. But, oh, all that warm, dry bedding going up in . . .

Dogthark said, "Huh?" He looked down in surprise at the arrow protruding from his chest. Then he dropped.

Golbfish realized that he was well illuminated. Pomuin toppled forward on his shield with a shaft sticking out of his back. Arrows were everywhere and men were falling.

That was how it began.

Sometime in the next couple of fortnights, Golbfish decided it was all just a matter of numbers. Nagland sent out its unmarried adult males to make war. The Joalians allowed any man to volunteer, but in practice few but young bachelors chose to do so. Those were barely a twentieth of the population. When a Lemodian village was threatened, everybody fought, even the children. Their bows were crude, homemade affairs and their arrows merely fire-sharpened stakes. That did not matter, because the range was rarely more than a few yards and often only feet. The guerrillas hid in the branches or behind the trunks and waited until a warrior came within reach. If the victim's companions gave chase, then as often as not there would be an ambush waiting.

Progress slowed to a crawl. Every morning the army marched; by noon it had to stop and begin chopping trees. It spent far more time building stockades and huddling inside them than it did waging war. It killed a million trees and hardly a single Lemodian.

With every precaution the officers could think of, sentries died at their posts, sleeping men had their throats cut, fire arrows came over the palisade. Moas and packbeasts were slaughtered in the night or driven off. Day after day the wastage continued, while the army blundered its way through the unbounded woods of Lemodflat.

Lemod itself was the answer, Kammaeman insisted. Lemod was a fair city. When the capital fell the country would fall. Lemod was the prize and the sanctuary. The army marched on Lemod.

But there was no road to march on. The trails and lanes wandered all around the countryside, and every mile brought another ambush. On rainy days—and most days were rainy that fall—even the leaders lost their sense of direction. Streams and rivers wound and twisted like tangled wool. In some lands rivers were highways; in Lemodland they flowed in gullies or gorges and were barriers.

Officially the sick and wounded who could not keep up were left to die, but in practice their friends made sure the enemy did not take them alive. Knowing how they themselves interrogated prisoners, Joalians considered such murders a kindness.

"There's a new plan," D'ward Hordeleader said.

He had called the troop in around him to hear the new plan. It was midday break, and raining. The closer ones sat down on the soggy ground, wet and dispirited. The rest just stood or leaned against trees to listen. The supply of face paint had run out, and now they had nothing to hide their despondency. They were cold and deeply frightened, naked before their unseen foe and the anger of the gods.

Golbfish sat in the front row. The closer he could get to the Liberator, the better he felt afterward.

Even D'ward did not look happy. His eyes were raw, as if he did not sleep much; he was leaner than ever. He came around at least once every day, and his daily pep talk always raised the men's spirits. It was the only thing that ever did. He visited every Nagian troop every day.

But today even he did not look happy.

"Casualties, Troopleader?" he asked.

Prat'han had been elected to lead the Sonalby contingent when D'ward had been promoted. He was a good kid, but he was not the Liberator.

"Just one today, sir. Pogwil Tanner. Booby trap."

D'ward bared his teeth in anger. "Just one is too many! Well, there is a change of tactics. We're going to make a forced march. We're going to outrun the monkeys."

He glanced around and won some smiles.

Golbfish did not smile. He sensed desperation. Regular forces could not outrun guerrillas. These peasants would not know that. They would find out soon enough.

"No more wasting half the day building forts!" D'ward said. "We're going to push on now until dark, at the double. Then we'll bivouac. Same thing tomorrow. We'll set triple watches all night. Grab any chance for sleep you can get! Some of you have complained about getting blisters on your hands. From now on you're going to get them on your feet—and you certainly won't get any on your backsides!"

More smiles.

"A few days and we'll be in Lemod itself. I told Kammaeman Battlemaster that we Nagians could run rings around his metal-plated Joalians. Was I wrong?"

Loud jeers . . . Golbfish wondered what the Joalian leaders would think if they heard this pep talk. Every one of them would just snap out the new orders to his troop and leave it at that. None would ever bother explaining an order—but D'ward always did.

"By the time the monkeys realize where we are," he was saying now, "we'll be miles away!"

What difference would that make? The whole of Lemodvale was full of people. The enemy was everywhere, endless as the trees.

D'ward began talking details—foraging must be done on the way, no squad ever to be less than six . . . He was proposing a rout and making it sound like storm tactics. Soon he had the men twitching with eagerness to try this new plan.

Eventually he even had them laughing. He did not speak very long after that. He rarely said even as much as he had today. It was the way he said it that left everyone smiling and chuckling.

At the end he caught Golbfish's eye and jerked his head in a beckoning. Then he left, and Prat'han ordered the troop to its feet.

The Liberator was waiting a few trees away, leaning on his spear. His sky-blue smile jerked Golbfish's backbone a few notches straighter and dispelled the cold. He wanted to ask if Kammaeman had gone completely insane, but he knew he wouldn't. D'ward would not criticize the battlemaster, even to a prince.

"How are you surviving, Your Majesty?"

"Better than I would have expected, sir. Er, may I ask that you not call me that?"

D'ward held the smile for a few seconds in silence. Then he said, "Warrior, then. It is a more honorable title, because it is one you have earned for yourself. Do you think this experience will make you a better king?"

"It will make me or break me, I suppose. Yes, of course."

"If it were going to break you, you'd have broken long ago. You even look like a warrior now, you know. You stand like one, walk like one. I suspect Joal may eventually find you a tougher nut than Tarion. If all kings were trained this way, there would be fewer wars. . . . But that wasn't what I wanted to talk about. How well do you know the *Filoby Testament*?"

Golbfish sighed. "Not at all well! I tried to read it once, but it's such a muddle I lost interest." He wished he could be of more help to this youngster who had helped him so much. "I've heard bits of it quoted, of course."

"Does it say anything about Nagvale?"

Golbfish shook his head. "Not a word. That I do know."

D'ward frowned thoughtfully. "How about Lemodvale?"

"I don't recall anything about Lemodvale. That doesn't mean it isn't— You mean you—"

The blue eyes twinkled. "No, I've never read it. None of it. I'm not sure I could, since it's written in Sussian."

"Oh, that's not so far from Joalian. But—" Golbfish choked off the question. Why would the Liberator not have read the prophecies about himself?

"I just wondered if there was anything that might be relevant." D'ward sighed and straightened up. He hitched his shield to a more comfortable position. He hesitated. "You haven't any idea how far it is to Lemod, have you?"

"None at all."

"Mm. Pity. Well, keep up the good work. You're a great inspiration to your countrymen, you know."

With an encouraging smile, the Liberator strode away.

Golbfish wondered afterward if he should have mentioned the *Filoby Testament*'s prophecy about a prince.

# 27

Less than three quarters of the original army arrived at Lemod. There it was thoroughly balked. Lemodwater, the main drainage of the vale, writhed like a mad snake in a deeply incised canyon. The city stood on a $\Omega$-shaped salient, practically an island, its fifty-foot walls poised on the brink of sheer cliffs, a hundred feet above the torrent. The only approach was along a narrow neck of land from the north, which dipped almost to river level, so that attackers must charge uphill to reach the gates. Needless to say, those gates were closed. Lemod had been starved into submission a time or two, but even the Thargians had never taken it by storm.

Lemod was a very easy city to invest, for the white-water river was neither fordable nor navigable. The Joalians settled in. Relieved to be out of the pestilential trees at last, they cleared a campsite and a safety zone around it. They set up barricades against any attempts at sorties; they laid out sanitary trenches and generally established a proper military camp. Then they sat back and waited—to sicken, starve, and rot.

At first it was not too bad. The orchards provided food, but five thousand men ate many tons of fruit a day. As days stretched into fortnights, the foragers must go ever farther in search of fresh trees to strip. The greater the radius, the greater the guerrillas' opportunity for ambush.

Attempts to storm the gates failed before a blizzard of arrows and missiles from the defenders. Casualties were heavy. The attackers began digging trenches, building breast-works and siege engines, and generally going through all the proper motions of invest-ment that Lemod had seen a dozen times before. Periodically the defenders would sally out to burn or smash what had been achieved. The earthworks crept steadily up the hill, but progress was desperately slow.

Disease spread through the camp. The temperature fell steadily, and the snow line slunk downward on the peaks of Lemodwall. Soon it became obvious that the city could endure the siege far longer than the besiegers could.

The mutiny took Edward by surprise. He had little to do with the Joalian officers and too much to do keeping the Nagians in line. He worked day and night at keeping up their morale. Without his steadying hand they would have broken long ago. They would have fled in a mob for home and been cut down in the trees. Old Krobidirkin had foreseen that.

Besides, Edward was not familiar with Joalian customs, and Kolgan Coadjutant had the law on his side. When he convened a meeting of the officer cadre, he invited the Nagian commander along to witness Joalian democracy in action.

The rain had stopped at last, but a bitter wind blew. Ropes creaked and canvas thumped. The meeting was held in the general's own tent. It did not take long. Kolgan denounced Kammaeman as incompetent. Kammaeman blustered. The troopleaders voted. Kammaeman was taken out and beheaded.

Kolgan assumed command.

"Thank you, citizens," said Kolgan Battlemaster. "I shall endeavor to be worthy of your trust. Pray inform the army of your verdict. Tomorrow I shall issue new orders."

The officers saluted and trooped out into the thin sunshine.

Edward wandered over to a stool and sat down.

The tall man scowled at him and then pulled another stool up close, very close. He sat down and said, "Well, Hordeleader? You wish to see me?" Their knees were almost touching.

"Very democratic!" Edward said. "How long do you have before someone pulls that trick on you?"

Kolgan glared. Facing challenge, he went on the offensive. "As it happens, I wish to speak with you. I hear reports that you have been releasing prisoners."

Who had been blabbing? "One prisoner."

The admission made the Joalian pause. "Any lesser man guilty of that offense would be executed on the spot. You had better explain, Hordeleader."

"I was out on patrol," Edward said, knowing that Kolgan would not have raised the matter if he were not aware of the details. "A couple of the fellows captured a girl. She was no more than fourteen, I should say. Not a warrior."

"She might have provided valuable information."

"Under torture?" Edward let his disgust show. "The only thing she could provide was sport. They told me I had the right to go first, as I was senior. I said that the gods damned men who made war on children and that a rapist was about the next lowest slime I could imagine. Then I asked who wanted to take my place. When no one offered, I told the child to make herself scarce and she did. What did I do wrong?"

Kolgan stared at him blankly. Finally he said, "Don't you have any balls at all?"

"The same number you have, I'm sure. But I don't let them rule me."

The big man curled his mustache up in contempt. "You prefer Dosh Houseboy?"

"I don't spin in that direction, Battlemaster."

"Ha! That reminds me—all this damp is making my back ache. I am told he is an accomplished masseur. May I borrow his services this evening?"

"No," Edward said. "You may not. That would be rape too."

The tall man flushed almost as red as his beard. For a moment the confrontation teetered on the brink of open quarrel. Then Edward turned on a grin, consciously using his charisma. "I am sorry about old Kammaeman," he said, "but not terribly sorry."

After a brief hesitation, the tall man grinned back. He was in armor but without a helmet. There was gray in his hair, and that was new. He was deeply worried, trying to hide the fact.

"Just an old Joalian custom, Hordeleader!"

There was another old Joalian custom that Edward did know of—betrayal of allies. He had even less confidence in Kolgan than he had lately had in Kammaeman. Too lately. Obviously this expedition was a disaster. His own loyalty was to his Nagians, and they were going to be slaughtered unless he could pull off something dramatic. He should have been smarter sooner; he felt responsible.

"So now it is your turn, sir. How long do you have to find a solution?"

"A fortnight at most, if I stay here." The new commander glanced around the unfamiliar command tent. His angular features were somehow reminiscent of a pointer sniffing the air. "The old fart used to keep some damnably good Niolian brandy hidden away somewhere."

"Not for me. What do you plan to do?"

Kolgan's gray eyes narrowed within their wrinkles. "What plan do you propose, Hordeleader?" He would put no stock in Edward's judgment. Charismatic or not, D'ward was merely another peasant.

"You summarized the situation clearly, sir. Winter is almost here. Food is almost out of reach. We take the city soon or we die."

Coppery eyebrows rose ironically. "I did not put the question quite like that. Have you a solution?"

"I am only a village laborer. Instruct me."

If the Joalian was needled by this sudden assertiveness from his colonial subordinate—his *juvenile* colonial subordinate—he was still sufficiently under the spell of the stranger's charisma to reply civilly.

"I must rescue the army. If I can lead it safely back to Nagland, or get even a substantial fraction of it back safely, then I shall be in the clear, and possibly a hero."

So his motives were purely personal, which Edward should have expected. "And how can you rescue the army?"

Kolgan scratched at his beard for a long moment, as if weighing his words carefully. "The prisoners tell us there is a rarely used pass to the north. Tomorrow we strike camp and head for it. The season is late."

"Your men are far better dressed than mine, Battlemaster. Can you supply us with warm clothing? Is this road passable for men going barefoot?"

"No, to both questions."

Without warning, fury was a tight hand around Edward's throat, making normal speech almost impossible. His voice came out so harsh he did not recognize it. "Are you certain this is not a trap? Can armored men carry enough food to cross the ranges? Do you expect the Lemodians to let you leave unopposed? What happens if a storm strikes while you are in the high country? Can you carry the sick and the wounded? What of *my* men? You just abandon your allies?"

Kolgan had paled until the rough weathering on his face seemed lit from within. He raised a clenched fist like a mace. "Have you a better plan, Nagian? If we stay we starve.

If we try to fight our way back the way we came, we shall be butchered in the woods. The Thargians will hold Siopass in force by now. Do you propose to parley? Kammaeman tried it and was refused. The Lemodians think they have us by the testicles."

And so they did, Edward thought, except for one factor. They could not know that the besieging army included a stranger with a store of mana. He did not want to use it for so fell a purpose, but he had been left no choice.

He sprang to his feet, rage pulsing in his ears and a sour taste in his mouth. "I need to borrow a bugle!"

Kolgan rose also, half a head taller. "What for?"

"Trumb will eclipse tonight?"

"I believe so. Why?"

"Tonight we Nagians will force the gates for you. When you hear the bugle, advance and take the city!"

Edward turned around and stormed out of the tent.

Cursing his folly, he stalked off through the camp, heading downhill. He could feel his store of mana like a pocketful of gold, but how much would it buy? Major gods like Tion or Zath would have power to blast a hole through a city wall as easily as Apollo leading the Trojans through the Achaeans' stockade. Or levitate the invaders to the battlements. Or just convince the Lemodian guards that they should throw open their gates, which would be the simplest solution. Edward did not think he could even do that much. If he tried and failed then he would have spent his mana to no purpose.

Nevertheless, he had taken up the ball and he would have only one shot at the wicket, so he had better think of something before dark.

The wind was icy on his bare hide. Fallow had encouraged toughness, but running around naked in winter was a little more stringent than cold baths. Lemodwall shone with fresh snow. The peaks to the north looked higher than any he had yet seen on Nextdoor. Those to the south were lower, but behind them lay Thargvale.

Kolgan's rumored pass to Nagvale might not exist; it might be already blocked; it certainly could not be attempted without warm clothes and stout boots. The Nagians were doomed unless their madcap leader could deliver on his boast. Probably the Joalians were too.

As he neared the edge of the camp, he sensed that he was being followed. It was Dosh Houseboy, of course, now formally Dosh Envoy, although no one but Edward ever used that name. Edward waved for him to come closer, and then walked on. In a moment the youth was pacing at his side, decently dressed in a blue Joalian tunic, yellow breeches, and a stout pair of boots. Where or how he had acquired those was a mystery. He might have stolen them. If he had bought them, Edward preferred not to know what price he had paid.

Except when running errands, Dosh clung to Edward like a shadow. None of the warriors would have anything to do with him, lest their friends suspect them of unmanly desires. He could not even find a meal or a place at a fire unless he was with the hordeleader. The Nagians left him alone because D'ward had commanded them to, but he had been punched up by Joalian troublemakers at least twice. Perhaps Dosh's life had never been easy. At the moment it was certainly not, but he never complained.

He might be years older than he looked. He refused to give his age, or say much about himself at all. He was short and slight, had fairish curls, and his face had been childishly pretty until Tarion took a knife to it. Now it was scrolled with crosshatched red lines that bore a bizarre resemblance to railway tracks on Ordnance Survey maps, although only one man in this army would ever notice the resemblance. He had let his downy beard grow in since his promotion to messenger, but it was invisible at a distance. At close quarters it made him seem like a boy playing at dressing up. He could be mawkish or servile or acidly witty as circumstances required. And underneath the professional softness, he was as hard and bitter as a harlot—at least, Edward assumed a harlot would be like that, having never met one. He felt sure that sweet little Dosh was as tough as any bruiser in the army and much less trustworthy than the average tarantula.

"How long would you need to round up all the troopleaders for a council?" Edward asked.

"An hour. Half that if you'll let me delegate some to fetch others."

"Have the forager leaders returned?"

"No. You want substitutes?"

"Yes. Stay with me awhile, though. I have a problem."

They came to the lowest point of the neck, flanked by the river on either hand and barely above its level. Beyond them the land rose steeply to the gates. Joalian soldiers were working on breastworks and siege engines just out of bowshot of the defenders. Edward stopped and stared at the activity without going any closer.

If he were defending the city, he would be about ready to make another sortie and burn those scaffolds. He wondered if they were dry enough for the attempt to come tonight. Probably not. It would take many fortnights for the earthworks to reach the gate. Winter was at hand. Tomorrow Kolgan was pulling out.

He turned his attention to the city itself, the high wall and the tall buildings within. The toothed battlements went all the way around, which seemed unnecessary—why build walls on the edge of vertical cliffs? Was there some reason to expect attack from the flanks, or was that merely an artistic conceit?

The cliffs were not perfectly sheer, and the plateau was irregular. In places the ground projected out beyond the walls, although those salients had mostly been beveled away to steep slopes. Between them, where the ground dipped, the walls were necessarily higher. An army could not march around the city, but possibly an active man could work his way along there, if he had time and was sufficiently suicidal. A squad of sappers might find a place to undermine the foundations, but how could they possibly do so undetected? The defenders would drop rocks on them. Still, there were spots where a man might stand back a short distance from the wall, so that he would not be looking straight up at it. Or shooting straight up it? Or? . . .

He felt that there was an idea there somewhere, but he could not find an end to tug on. Many generals much wiser than he must have considered all these possibilities in the past. Lemod had never been taken by storm.

"It should be possible to walk right around the base of the walls," he said, shivering.

"If they didn't see you. A couple of the Rareby kids claim to have done it."

Edward glanced down at the guileless blue eyes in their long golden lashes. "How do you know that?"

"Eavesdropping."

Obviously. Nobody spoke to Dosh unless it was absolutely necessary.

"Bring them to the meeting too."

"Want me to ask if any others have done it?"

"No." Edward chuckled. "Did you speak to Tarion this way?"

"What way?"

"All terse and efficient and military."

"No."

"How did you speak to him?"

Dosh looked away for a moment, then turned back to Edward with tears glistening. "I love you," he said with a break in his voice. "I will do anything for you, anything to make you happy." He seemed completely sincere. "I love you for your smile, for the touch of your—"

"That's enough, thank you! I get the gist."

"You asked."

"And I should not have. I didn't mean to humiliate you."

"How could you humiliate me? You don't know what humiliation is."

"No, I suppose I don't. I am truly sorry."

"Don't be," Dosh said. "*Sorry is a waste of time.* The Green Scriptures, Canto 474."

"Really?"

"Who knows? Who ever reads that junk?" He smiled ruefully at Edward's laughter. "What's your problem?"

"Can I trust you?"

"If you mean will I tell anyone in the camp what you say to me, the answer is no. Who would listen?"

"Can you talk to anyone outside the camp?"

Dosh flinched. "Of course not!" he snapped.

Which confirmed what Edward had suspected for some time. The wind was gnawing through to his bones now and he was probably turning bright blue, but this was important.

"You were spying on Tarion, weren't you? Who for?"

"I won't answer that."

"You *can't* answer that! And you couldn't tell him, either! That's why he cut up your face!"

"You calling me a hero?"

"No, I'm not. You're not spying for a mortal, are you?"

A spasm that might have been pain twisted the red scars beside Dosh's eyes. "Can't answer that," he mumbled.

"Then you needn't try. If I name a name, can you—"

"Don't, sir! Please?"

"All right," Edward said, still uncertain how much of this performance was real. "If you get the chance, will you stick a knife in my back?"

Dosh curled his cherubic lip in contempt. "You would be well rotted by now."

"Yes. I see. Thank you." Not Zath, then. "Did you ever wear a gold rose in your hair?"

Dosh stared at him, then nodded. A boyish blush spread around his scars. What did it take to make a harlot blush?

But the answer to the real question was obviously *Tion.* "Just snooping?"

"Just snooping. Now, what's the problem?"

He was a born spy, curious as a cat about everything. Even little Eleal had been no nosier than Dosh. Edward did not like to think about Eleal.

He hugged himself, hunching against the wind. "I told the new battlemaster that I would take the city for him tonight, and I don't know how. Haven't the foggiest."

"Oh, you'll find a way."

"You display a gratifying confidence in . . ." Edward stared at that cryptic, mutilated face. "What do you mean by that?"

Dosh smiled slyly, twisting the crimson railway lines around his eyes. "Nothing, Hordeleader."

"Out with it!"

"The prophecy?" Dosh said reluctantly.

"What prophecy?"

Surprise . . . disbelief . . . "The long one? The one about the city? The *Filoby Testament*, about verse five hundred, or four-fifty?"

"Tell me!"

"You don't know? Truly?"

"No, I don't know."

For a moment Dosh seemed to think Edward must be joking. He shook his head in astonishment, thought for a moment, then declaimed: *"The first sign unto you shall be when the gods are gathered. For then the Liberator shall come forth in ire and be in sorrow revealed. He shall throw down the gates that the city may fall. Blood in the river shall speak to distant lands, saying; Lo—the city has fallen in slaughter. He shall bring death and exultation in great measure. Joy and lamentation shall be his endowment."*

# 28

Too much happened that night. In retrospect, Dosh was not to recall ever panicking or disgracing himself. He was never to doubt that he had remained clearheaded during the events themselves. He did what was needed, with far greater courage than he had ever known he possessed.

It was his memory that betrayed him. Terror piled on terror and horror upon horror until his mind could not retain them all. Reality faded like a nightmare, so that afterward he recalled only glimpses, the highlights mostly, but also a few unimportant incidents like incongruous flickers of dream. It was as if the turning point of his life had been written in a precious book and then he had lost all but a fraction of the pages before he could even look at them. Long stretches were evermore blank.

It was a night of quadruple conjunction, a wonder that few mortals ever see, coming only once in generations. Even then, most people will not be alerted in time; it never lasts long. Neither Niol nor Tharg would admit afterward that the great event ever happened. The Niolians insisted that Ysh passed close by Trumb that night, but not actually behind, while the Thargians claimed it was Kirb'l who narrowly failed to cross over Trumb. In Joal the weather was bad and no one noticed anything at all.

Dosh knew better. He witnessed the gathering of the gods that had been prophesied, and his world was changed forever.

As for all the rest . . . just pictures on a wall.

The first picture: faces around a campfire at sunset. . . . He huddles silent on the outskirts, ignored. A dozen or more near-naked Nagians shiver in the dusk, their unpainted faces listening in awe as the Liberator promises a miracle.

He does not mention the word. He does not tell them he is the Liberator; he seems not to believe that himself. In his own mind he has no great faith that he can deliver a miracle—Dosh knows this from what he heard earlier—but certainly no one else around this fire will guess as much from D'ward's manner. He gives orders calmly, with perfect poise. He needs a miracle, so he will attempt one. To profit from it he must have his troops standing by, so he is promising them that he will open the city. If he fails he will have destroyed himself, but he is the Liberator and they believe him. It shows in their wild, childlike eyes. They would follow him into a furnace, these crude peasants. They are all muscle and faith and no brains.

They will be the Warband, the first of all his followers.

*Does Dosh sense that, even then?*

\*   \*   \*

What says the Liberator in this image by the campfire? Alas, most of that precious speech is written on pages lost. Dosh will recall no words, except a few, right at the end, when the Liberator turns and points at him and all the warriors scream in fury.

Their hordeleader has told them he will take only one man with him to help carry the ropes. A dozen strong voices have cried out, demanding the honor. No, none of them, D'ward has said. Not the troopleaders, for they must lead their men. Nor the prince, nor even Talba and Gospin, although they know the way. No, he will take Dosh Envoy and no one else. Only he ever calls Dosh by name. Everyone else has other terms for the despicable catamite.

This is the second picture—a dozen furious warriors howling in outrage and the Liberator shouting them down. To Dosh his words are to be the beginning of the other miracle, his personal miracle, but he does not know that yet.

"Because you ask," D'ward is saying in that second picture, "and only because you ask, I will tell you why. I need a man whose courage I cannot doubt. Be *silent!* Look at those marks on his face! They were made in the dark, while he was bound and gagged. See how close they come to his eyes? See how his throat was slashed? That man endured vile torture, yet did not tell his tormenter what he wanted to know. Will any of you now claim to be this man's better in courage? Will any of you exchange your merit marks for his? I will have Dosh Envoy at my side tonight, for I trust him beyond all others."

Another glimpse: Dosh weeping, as the warriors come, each in turn, to embrace him and beg his forgiveness for past slights. . . . Some also whisper in his ear that he will die most terribly if he fails D'ward this night, but he ignores that. He is finding the experience very strange, for many reasons. The body contact arouses him, and he knows that will disgust them if they sense it. Their admiration distresses him—why should he care what these bullocks think?

Not the least strangeness is that he knows the Liberator is lying. The Liberator is fully aware that Dosh could not have given Tarion the information he wanted. Dosh does not understand why the Liberator should tell such a falsehood now, nor why he apparently believes his own lie enough to trust Dosh, or why Dosh himself in his present terror is not refusing the suicidal honor. He has not been asked, and he does not refuse.

Do the wonders begin here?

The waiting in the trenches as the sky darkens . . . gut-wrenching anxiety. Dosh and D'ward crouch amid timbers and stonework while the weary soldiers trek back to camp for the night. Below an empty sky, the temperature drops by the minute. Trumb's green disk peers between the eastern peaks, huge and ominously perfect. Nights are bright when Trumb is full.

Has the Man already eclipsed? Will he wait for true darkness? The Liberator is counting on those few precious moments of distraction to let him approach the city unobserved. An eclipse of Trumb is a time of dread, when reapers claim souls for Zath.

The guards will be watching the sky and praying. It is a time of ill omen, the last time anyone should choose to launch a mission such as this.

Trumb did eclipse, of course. Trumb must have eclipsed. At D'ward's side, Dosh must have sprinted through the darkness under the stars, stumbling up the slope under his burden, forcing legs and straining lungs to greater effort before the brief blessing was withdrawn. He must have reached the base of the walls before the light returned and hence escaped the notice of the watchers above. If he hadn't, he would have died. He must have done.

He just lost the memory somewhere.

Terror.

Fingers scrabbling in dirt for purchase, feet fumbling and slipping, the coiled rope a crushing weight on his back threatening to pull him out into the abyss, a hundred feet of nothing above the rumble of the torrent. His face pressing into the rimy grass.

Why did he not remember sooner how much he hates heights?

His nose against the gritty surface of the masonry as he edges his way along, spread-eagled against the wall . . . Nothing below him at all, just a hundred feet of vertical rock in the ghastly green moonlight, and below it the raging cataracts of Lemodwater. How many seconds would a man have to scream as he fell? How often would he bounce on the ledges?

Wind.

Cold. Icy, biting cold, and he is swaddled in a double layer. He has wool underwear that nobody knows about, except the three Joalians who sold it to him all through one very hard night. D'ward must be frozen to the marrow of his bones.

Slippery wet grass and steep slopes. Not a bush, not a root.

Greasy rock with nothing to grasp hold of.

Always the smooth face of the wall above, merciless and uncaring.

Always the thought that someone up there may chance to look down and see the two intruders. They will be amusing target practice. Even in moonlight, fifty feet straight down is not a difficult shot.

Dosh will remember quite a lot of that journey. Too much.

The *dike* . . . that is the Liberator's name for it, not a word Dosh has ever heard. It is only a narrow buttress jutting out from the cliff face a few feet below the brink, a crumbly black rock about ten feet across. Here D'ward can stand a small way back from the wall to work his miracle. Of course they are much more visible here than they were earlier, directly underneath. Watchers on the battlements will see them easily if they look down.

That is what watchers on battlements are supposed to do, isn't it?

The wind tugs and pushes viciously, striving to throw them both from their perch. D'ward curses under his breath as he fights with the thin line and the wind tries to carry it all away or tie it in tangles. His teeth chatter. In the lurid green light he looks like a walking corpse.

Picture: Dosh unbuttoning his tunic and pulling it off—he offers it to his near-naked companion and it streams out sideways like a flag.

D'ward's angry snarl: "Stop that! Are you *trying* to get us killed?"

"You need it."

"No. The others do not have it. Put it on again." He goes back to tying knots with numb fingers.

The others are not crouched on this accursed ledge a hundred feet above the rapids.

The throw . . . the beginning of the miracle.

In the wind and the dark at that impossible angle, the Liberator succeeds at his first attempt. It is beautiful: the log rising into the night, trailing the string behind it, the wind arcing it away.

D'ward teetering on one leg, flailing his arms, and somehow recovering his balance. For a moment Dosh is sure he is about to fall. That image will remain always, one of the clearest—the Liberator poised over the abyss, with one leg and both arms outstretched, face rigid with terror, and Dosh leaping forward to catch him just in time. . . .

If the log makes a noise as it falls on the parapet far above, then the wind steals it away.

There must have been a hasty scramble then, back up to the base of the wall, into relative cover. Dosh does not recall it. That is a moment of terrible danger, for if anyone has heard or seen that log arriving then he must inevitably peer down to see where it came from.

The waiting.

How long it lasts, he will never know. The two of them huddling up against the cruel masonry, waiting, waiting . . . D'ward looking as if he will freeze to death. Again—perhaps several times—he has refused to accept a share of Dosh's garments. In the end Dosh wraps him in his arms, and the Liberator does not resist the embrace.

It is hardly romantic, anyway, like hugging a glacier.

The fading of hope. The despair . . .

The moons. Trumb's glare drowns out the stars, but Ysh had risen soon after him, and then Eltiana. Three moons shine together, close together: a huge green disk, a tiny blue disk, and a red star. In the required order. Not quite a straight line, but close enough, yes? Please! Imperceptibly but inevitably, the red and the blue catch up with the green.

The prophecy is being fulfilled. Three of the gods gather, as they do every few years. It is awesome and auspicious, but it is only three. Three are rare; four are epochal.

Where is Kirb'l, the Joker?

The Maiden and the Lady edge closer to the Man. Where is the Youth?

No one can predict Kirb'l. He moves in strange patterns, straying far to north and south. He appears and he disappears at will. Sometimes, at his brightest, he travels from west to east.

Dosh praying.

The Joker!

Dosh will never forget that dramatic entrance. It will be the sharpest of all his rec-ollections of that night—the tiny, brilliant, golden moon flashing into view ahead of Trumb, so that all four gods blaze together in the velvet silver of the sky. Kirb'l, visibly moving, moving *east!* Four lights. Four shadows.

Eltiana and Ysh on one side, Kirb'l on the other, almost in a line, in perfect order and relentlessly closing on the great disk of Trumb.

Quadruple conjunction, a gathering of the gods!

Wait for it . . .

The Liberator's sudden hiss, and the brightness in his eyes . . .

"What?"

"Someone's coming!"

Dosh peers all around, and of course there is no one on this accursed windswept cliff top. Someone up on the battlements, then? How can D'ward possibly know?

(Perhaps that was the beginning of belief.)

"He's found it!" D'ward pushing free, sitting up, tense in the moonlight.

"Here it comes!"

The *miracle!*

Some weary sentry, cold and bored, walking his beat on the parapet, has found a chunk of firewood. His superiors will not approve of litter where a fighting man may trip over it.

Perfectly natural for such a man to pick up the log and heave it over the side and then resume his march. He will be watching the skies tonight, like any other man.

Not natural for a sentry to overlook the twine attached to the log . . . that is the real miracle. Not entirely luck, either, that he does not throw it out the same crenel it came in by. But he does *not* notice the twine he is thus looping around a merlon, and he does *not* notice that twine running out as the log slides down the wall, snagged on a stone tooth.

He plays his part in history and walks away to die, and at the base of the wall the Liberator relaxes with a sob, a gasp of breath held far too long.

Miracle.

There are more pages missing here.

One of the two invaders unfastened the twine and attached it to the heavier rope. One of them hauled on the twine, muttering prayers that the string would not wear through on the crenelation or just break under the strain. One of them then grabbed the rope when it came and tied a noose in it and hauled it tight.

It may have been Dosh. It may have been D'ward. It must have been one of them.

*     *     *

The four moons closing.

Faint sounds of chanting coming down on the wind. The priests of the city are rousing the people to come and praise the miracle in the heavens.

They do not notice the miracle on the walls. So small a thing, to bear such fruit— a length of twine looped around the battlements, and then a rope.

The Nagians will be on their way now.

The quadruple conjunction.

Side by side, sapphire Ysh and ruby Eltiana vanish behind Trumb. A moment later Kirb'l slides in front, and the gold speck is lost in the green glare. Only Trumb remains.

A gathering of the gods, omen of great destiny.

No one ever forgets seeing that.

D'ward has gone, gone up the rope. His corpse has not come back on its way to the river; there has been no sound of challenge. He must still be alive up there. Dosh waits to show the way.

He is to remember that waiting as being worst of all, because D'ward is up there alone.

Then the cream of the Sonalby troop emerges out of the darkness in single file, bringing more ropes. Bringing no spears or shields, only their clubs, clambering along that same perilous road.

Dosh insists that he be allowed to go next, first after D'ward. . . . They argue and Prat'han concedes, letting him go.

Stripping off his clothes so that he will not be mistaken for a defender.

Climbing near-naked and unarmed up a vertical wall in the dark.

That image will remain, always.

And after that . . . a great blank.

The Sonalby troop followed the Liberator into the city. They overpowered the watch. They opened the gates for the rest of the Nagians, the spearsmen who had crept forward while the defenders watched the conjunction.

Someone sounded the bugle to summon the Joalians.

The Joalians arrived as the defenders rallied and began to slaughter the club-wielding, unarmored Nagians.

Dosh was to remember none of that. None.

The memories that came after drove them away, perhaps—bitter memories, better for-gotten: glimpses of battle in near darkness, blood splattering on walls, bodies in the streets, much screaming, panicking mobs. Dead babies.

A man run through dies cleanly, showing only surprise. Men dispatched with clubs have their heads beaten into shapelessness like broken jam pots.

Women cower in corners or lament over the bodies.

Children, tiny children, running, screaming. With blood on them. Clinging to their fathers' corpses.

Great fires stream up into the night as the failing defenders try to deny their city to the victors.

The chapel of Yaela Tion, the goddess of singing—an avatar of the Youth . . . Dosh has found it somehow, he cannot remember how.

The main temple is full of hysterical refugees, but this little crypt is deserted, dark and silent, lit by one flickering candle before the diminutive image of the goddess. He will not remember entering, kneeling, or performing the secret ritual given him for this purpose.

He remembers the coming of the god, the blaze of his beauty and glory . . . although that particular recollection may have blurred and merged with those of other, similar, occasions when the god has come in response to his call. He never can remember afterward just exactly what he has seen—only the impact and the beautiful voice of the god. Sobbing with happiness, barely able to speak because of the love that fills his throat to choke him, he whispers his report to the stones of the floor.

And is praised!

"You have done well so far, Beloved," says the god. "Quite well. The prophecy of the city is fulfilled, yes. I feel the prophecy of the prince is not. Tarion offered you to the Liberator, certainly. I expect he offered you to just about everyone, but you were no temptation to D'ward. There is more to come, and it would seem that Golbfish is the prince to watch now. Carry on."

Despair! Sorrow! "Take me, master! Take me with you!"

"No, dear boy! Not yet. You must stay and watch, for my sake. And report of course. When the prophecy is played out to the end, when you have completed this task I gave you, then I promise you will be reunited with me and my love. Stop slobbering . . ."

This above all will remain with him: the drab emptiness when the god has gone, the unbearable pain of knowing that his mission is not complete.

Later came an unfamiliar gnawing doubt, a reluctant, treasonous, blasphemous sensation that obedience to his real master, which formerly filled him with unalloyed joy and pride, now bore an odious aftertaste, the certainty that he is betraying the Liberator.

# *29*

Ysian Applepicker did not know the city well. She had arrived there only a couple of fortnights before the war came. She should have gone home again while there was time— her parents had written, urging her to do so—but the marriage had already been arranged and to leave would have seemed like terrible cowardice. Everyone had insisted that Lemod was impregnable. Soon all the rope bridges over Lemodwater had been cut down to prevent the invaders crossing, and then it had been too late. So she had remained at her uncle's house, patiently waiting until the siege was lifted and a day could be set for her wedding.

She had been all ready for bed when Aunt Ogfooth had come flustering into her room in great excitement to announce that there was going to be a holy event, a quadruple conjunction, and Ysian must come and watch. Such a once-in-a-lifetime opportunity was not to be missed; she had dressed in her warmest furs and gone out into the night with her uncle and aunt and with Cousin Drabmere, who wore his sword.

The best view would be from the battlements, Uncle Timbiz had explained, but the wall was off-limits in this time of siege. They had gone instead to the great square, which wasn't truly great, even to the eyes of a rustic orchard girl, but was the largest open space in the city. The palace fronted it, and the temple too. The entire population seemed to have had the same idea, so the crush was enormous.

To be perfectly honest—although Ysian already knew that honesty was one virtue that should be exercised with discretion—the quadruple conjunction was not especially impressive. She could recall a couple of triple conjunctions, and this was not all that much more. The excitement she felt came from the crowd itself, like an infection. People wept and sang hymns and called out praises to the gods who were thus promising to protect their loyal and faithful worshippers in Lemod. Ysian wondered if the besiegers viewed the sign that way or if their interpretation might be very different. Time would doubtless tell who was right.

The singing faded, the conjunction ended as Kirb'l parted from Trumb. Ysh reappeared shortly thereafter.

Ysian looked around and realized that she had become separated from her companions. Well, her highly respectable aunt and uncle could always be relied upon to do the right thing, and in this case the right thing was obviously to attend the inevitable service of thanksgiving in the temple. At least half the crowd had come to the same decision, so the squash inside was frightening, the air chokingly stuffy. The high priestess made the service brief, almost indecently brief, shorter than the conjunction itself had been. Soon, but not too soon, Ysian found herself back outside in the welcome cool of the night.

She could still see no signs of her family. Being all alone did not bother her unduly. Indeed it was an adventure. An unmarried maiden should not wander the streets alone, even by day, although that was more a matter of propriety than safety, for Lemod was very law-abiding. She hung around the square as the crowd dispersed, looking for her relations until she was forced to conclude that they must have gone home. Quite likely they had all been separated and each would assume she was safe with one of the others.

She set off to make her own way home. Lemod's streets were narrow and winding, all very dark, and she had no lantern. Anytime she had been out of doors in the past, she had been accompanied by her aunt or Cousin Drabmere or by *someone,* and everything seemed different by night, anyway. Propriety made her reluctant to ask strangers for directions. She wandered around for a while, and all the time the city was growing quieter and quieter around her, the roads emptier and emptier, as the citizens repaired to bed. Very soon her sense of adventure became a feeling of misadventure, of being incredibly stupid. Somehow or other, she had managed to get lost.

Then the shouting began. Alarms rang. People started running. She guessed what was happening, but soon she was caught up in the panic. There were still no lights, only the eerie colored glow of the moons. Even the few lighted windows winked out into darkness. She ran away from the clamor, but invariably it circled around in front of her again. Shouting became screaming, and the clash of steel. She could not tell if the screams came from men or women. Once she almost tripped over a body.

But then—Oh, praise the gods!—she recognized an elaborate marble horse trough. A few gasping minutes later, she stumbled against the great double doors of her uncle's workshop. To her intense astonishment, the little postern door was not merely unlocked, but ajar. She could clearly remember Cousin Drabmere locking it behind him when they left. She hesitated, wondering if this might possibly be some sort of danger signal. Common sense told her that the invaders were charging around the streets killing people, not lurking in dark interiors, but still she hesitated. Then a howling, battling mob surged around a corner into the street. Ysian jumped through the door and shut it behind her.

The big shed was as black as a cellar, but she knew her way, roughly. At the cost of a dozen or so bruises on her shins, she reached the stairs. She crept up them, making no more noise than a growing mushroom, stepping very close to the wall, so that the stair treads would not creak. The house itself was dark and silent. Only the big clock in the living room made any sound at all.

She crept into the kitchen and armed herself with the biggest, sharpest knife she could find. Then she explored every room, all the way to the attics. She found no one, not even the servants, which explained the unlocked door.

She worried about that door. Common sense . . . Her parents had been great believers in common sense and had made an appreciation of its importance a central element of her education—common sense told her to keep it locked. But suppose her aunt or some of the others in the family came home seeking refuge as she had done? That thought brought immediate nightmares of them being cut down on their own threshold. Furthermore, if the Joalians succeeded in seizing the city, they would mount a house-by-house search for defenders, while the Lemodians, if they won, would go around rooting out any stray invaders. The door could certainly be forced easily enough, which would mean damage to her uncle's property. To leave it open might divert suspicion. In the end she went back downstairs and opened it again, leaving it ajar as she had found it. Then she hurried back upstairs to find a hiding place.

The big closet in her aunt and uncle's bedroom seemed a likely choice, but when she went to look at it, she decided that it was all too obvious. She sat down on the edge of the bed in the dark to think. Faint but horrible noises kept drifting in through the open window, sounds of death and violence. As always, the big room was scented with her aunt's favorite perfume. It was warm, this room, never chilly. A soft, friendly room.

She wondered why she did not feel more frightened, even terrified. She decided that there was a blanket of unreality over the events of the night. Quadruple conjunction, big disappointment . . . on her own for the first time since leaving Great-uncle Gooba's orchard . . . unvanquished Lemod about to fall . . . at least it sounded as if it was falling. She really could not believe any of this! Some prayers to the gods would likely be a sensible precaution, especially to Eth'l, patron goddess of Lemodvale. . . . Eltiana had been eclipsed by Trumb tonight. . . . Ysian decided that praying could wait until after she thought of a good hiding place. She would likely have more than enough time for praying then.

A house was burning a few streets away, ruling out any temptation to consider the attics. The workshop downstairs? The big laundry copper where the clothes were boiled?

Cousin Drabmere was probably caught up in the fighting, although he had been an inoffensive, bookish man until the war came. If her aunt and uncle were not already dead, then they had probably fled. Common sense—Ysian could not help wondering now if common sense might be a poor guide to wisdom in such an *uncommon* event as a sack—common sense suggested that she ought to go out and discover who was winning. If the Joalians were, then she should flee also. Trouble was, she knew she could not find her way to the gate. Other refugees would guide her, but she would be just as likely to blunder into a gang of murderous Joalians or Nagian savages, who would be worse. She would be killed or raped or both.

Well, if she was going to be raped, she would rather it happened in a private bedroom than out in a cold public street. She might well be carried off into slavery. A virgin of sixteen was probably very valuable slave material, although she would not count on remaining a virgin much longer. She clutched the big knife tightly to her chest. The first man who tried was going to regret it!

The second one would probably succeed, though.

Probably her marriage had been postponed indefinitely. She might never even know the name of the man she had been about to marry! Aunt Ogfooth had revealed only that he was a widower, wealthy, and a prominent citizen. And a man of mature years . . . The one member of his family Ysian had yet met had been a nasty old harridan with a million wrinkles and few teeth, and even her name had not been disclosed. That was the custom in Lemodia. Ysian had assumed at the time that this antiquated crone was negotiating on behalf of a son or more likely grandson, but then Aunt Ogfooth had let slip the word *brother.* . . .

Why did Ysian not feel dismay at the thought of losing the advantageous marriage she had been promised? It was for that purpose she had been sent to the city. Her parents had very little money. A well-married daughter was their only hope of comfort in their old age. She should be heartbroken at the collapse of all her prospects, so what wickedness was this sense of relief she felt? Had she no shame?

It was at that point in her meditations that she heard men's voices downstairs.

# 30

" 'The city was sacked,' " Edward said bitterly. "You read about it in history books, but that doesn't prepare you for the real thing. Drogheda, Cawnpore, Boadicea in London, or the Goths in Rome . . . the Saxons, the Vikings. Just words."

The train had slowed to a crawl, waiting for a clear signal to pull into Greyfriars station. Only the grassy sides of a cutting crept by the windows, with a single church spire bright against the evening sky.

"It can't possibly compare with what's been happening in Europe lately," Alice said. She had been wrong to make him speak of it.

"In some ways it's worse, because it's more personal. You pull the trigger on a machine gun and you don't see the blood spurting, I suppose. But battering a man to death with a club—that's real."

"Well, don't talk about it anymore."

"Why not? If I'm ashamed to talk about it . . . I mean, I did it. I opened the city. I knew there would be killing, didn't I? I must have done, mustn't I? It was them or us. The old, old excuse. If I wasn't ashamed to do it then, why should I be ashamed to talk about it now?"

He was ashamed, she knew, deeply ashamed. This was part of the change she had sensed in him. He had brought about the death of thousands.

"Fire and slaughter?"

A clamor of couplings ran down the line and the carriage lurched. Picking up speed, the train began chuffing toward the station.

"There was some fire, yes, but the defenders did that. Men were slaughtered. Children and the old were mostly driven out. The thing had not been properly planned, of course . . . too many deaths. The Lemodians out in the woods reacted very quickly. They broke into the camp and killed all our sick and wounded. In the end it was a reversal of positions—us inside, them outside. But we had the supplies and could wait out the winter. That was what mattered."

People were emerging from the compartments, bringing their bags.

"And rape, I suppose?" she said. "You haven't mentioned the rape."

He shrugged. "That really wasn't so bad. Gosh, I know that sounds awful, but being gutted with a spear is frightfully permanent. There was no violence, no public violence at least. The women knew the rules. When the killing was over and the Joalians held the city, then every man just picked out a woman and said, 'I'm so-and-so. You're mine now.' They submitted and made the best of it."

"Edward! How can you be so . . . callous?"

He looked at her oddly. "That's how it's always been—in their world or in ours. That's more or less how the women were married in the first place. No one ever asked their opinions. Like in Africa, women are property; you know that. This isn't Kensington we're talking about. Even in Kensington it happens. Ask some of the debutantes! Valians live closer to the ground than we do."

She shook her head in disbelief. Was he serious?

"And the men were *dead*!" he added bitterly. "They had it worse, wouldn't you say?"

The station slid into view, and a sign saying GREYFRIARS. Some of the people standing on the platform were waiting to board, standing patiently until the train came to a stop. Others were there to meet friends, and were waving and running. Porters scanned the windows, hunting for hire.

"There was no numen in Lemod," Edward said, peering out the window. "That was probably lucky from my point of view. Most cities in the Vales are sited on nodes, and I think that's true here, too. Lemod had been chosen for its defensible location. It had just a trace of virtuality near the north wall, and there were shrines there and a small temple to Eltiana. But no numen."

Clattering and huffing, the train came to a stop. He slid down the window and reached out to the door handle. He went first with the suitcase and handed Alice down to the platform.

"So there we were, locked up snug in Lemod for the winter, knowing that the Thargians would arrive in the spring. I had fulfilled the prophecy and given the first sign, so I had advertised where I was to Zath. Apart from that— By Jove, there's Mrs. Bodgley!"

# *31*

Julian Smedley had had a bad day. The crowds niggled at his nerves; the close-packed mob in the train suffocated him. He felt as if everyone were watching him, especially men in uniform. He developed an absurd tendency to sweat whenever he saw a policeman. He was frightened he would suddenly start weeping in public.

Women bothered him, especially young women. He found himself staring at them, even while terrified that they would notice his attention. At his age he ought to have learned something about affairs of the heart, but the war had stolen those years out of his life. He was still the innocent virgin he had been when he left Fallow. How could he ever catch up now? No girl would be interested in a cripple—a cripple with no profession, a part man who burst into tears without warning.

His invisible right hand was tightly clenched, aching and cramped. He could feel the nails digging into his palm. Even if he pushed the end of his stump against something to make it hurt, he could not convince himself that those fingers had rotted away in the Flanders mud.

He exchanged little talk with Ginger, except when they changed trains at Chippenham. There they paced the platform together, but they seemed to have nothing left to say to each other. In the cold light of day, the previous night had taken on a tinge of nightmare. They did not mention Exeter at all. His story now seemed like the wildest sort of jiggery-pokery, a tale of the horse marines. Perhaps both he and Ginger were ashamed to admit having believed it.

Even now the cops might be informing the guv'nor that his lunatic son was not just a physical and emotional cripple but also a criminal.

The local train was as crowded as the express, puffing along from station to station, full of farmers and West Country burr. Jones disembarked at Wassal, hoping his bike was still where he had left it, chained to the railings. Smedley carried on alone to Greyfriars.

And there he was met by Mrs. Bodgley. Surprisingly, she was just as large and loud as he remembered her, a weathered dreadnought armored in Harris tweed. Her hair was streaked with silver now; there were lines like trenches radiating from her eyes. She beamed at him and boomed at him, saying nothing that might surprise anyone overhearing. Luggage? No luggage? Well, that made things simpler. The cart was this way, for of course motorcars were out of the question these days. He braced himself for questions about medals and the war, for mention of his mother's death or her husband's or Timothy's murder—and none came. He realized as they strode up the station stairs together that Ginger would have warned her about his nerves.

The dogcart might have belonged to Queen Anne, and the shaggy pony between the shafts was almost as ancient. Before Smedley could protest, Mrs. Bodgley scrambled up nimbly on the near side. There she sat, calmly adjusting her skirt, apparently engrossed in watching a gaggle of children playing hopscotch. For a moment he dithered. Of course, when a couple rode together the gentleman must drive, but . . . but she knew about his hand. With a rush of both gratitude and embarrassment, he heaved himself awkwardly into the driver's place. He almost tied himself in a knot reaching the brake. He jiggled the reins. The pony did not know he could not use the whip. It wandered off homeward, dragging the dogcart behind it.

Timothy Bodgley, poor old Bagpipe, had been Exeter's friend, not especially Smedley's. Smedley had never visited the Grange. He whistled under his breath when he saw it in the distance, a crenelated backdrop to a hundred acres of stately park. There were *sheep* grazing in that park! Nothing he had seen that day had so clearly shown him the changes that war had brought.

Now the Army occupied the Grange, and his destination was the Dower House—a gloomy, ugly box buried in monstrous yew trees, ancestral storage for unwanted mothers-in-law. As he drove into the yard, three enormous dogs came roaring to greet him.

"Down, Brutus!" Mrs. Bodgley bellowed. "Be *quiet,* Jenghis! Oh, do stop that, Cuddles! There was a most beautiful house here, you know, designed by Adam. There's an etching of it in the Grange library. But Gilbert's grandmother had it torn down and put up this *dreadful* Victorian barn. I shouldn't complain. I can't imagine what I should have done if the Army hadn't taken over the big house. Oh, these dreadful pigeons! They turned it into a hospital, you know. Can't get servants for love nor money these days, and with just myself, it would be far too . . . Heaven knows what I'll do with it after the war is over. Let me do that. And I'll give Elspeth her rubdown. Please don't argue. She's used to me. Just go on inside, dear boy. Captain, I mean. Make yourself at home. If you want to put the kettle on we can have a cup of tea. Jones said the others would be arriving on the four fifteen, so we've lots of time. . . ."

The Dower House was dark and smelled of damp. Its furniture was old and lumpish, its plaster stained. There was no electricity, not even gas. Smedley filled the black iron kettle from the pump and carried it indoors. He poked up a flame in the range, which would have roasted oxen in herds. Just a little place, this—only seven bedrooms. It was a mausoleum, but at least his nerves would not be troubled by crowds. The kitchen was the size of a ballroom, a vast expanse of shadow and stone. It echoed, full of emptiness. He thought of prisons. He sat on one of the hard wooden chairs and wondered what life should have been.

"There you are!" Mrs. Bodgley boomed, bustling in with the dogs all around her. "I can show you to your room if you like. No, don't thank me. It is I who should be grateful. I have so little company these days. Stop that, Brutus! One tries to keep busy, you know, and do one's bit. Knitting for the troops and war bond committees and visiting our poor dear boys up at the Grange, but I do confess that sometimes the evenings drag, so I was only too happy when Mr. Jones called, and I do so want to hear Exeter's story from his own lips because I never for one moment believed he had anything to do with what happened to Timothy. And where he went to! I have some Madeira cake around somewhere. That inspector man was utterly incompetent, and Gilbert himself was quite distrait at the time. Where did he disappear to so dramatically, do you know?"

Exeter, not the general. "He went to another world, Mrs. Bodgley."

Mrs. Bodgley had been rummaging in a drawer for spoons. She straightened to her full height and transfixed Smedley with a stiletto eye.

"Did you say, 'Another world'?"

"Yes, I did."

"Oh." Mrs. Bodgley pursed her lips and thought for a moment. "How very curious!" she murmured, and returned her attention to the cutlery.

He had never felt so helpless in his life. He was appalled to discover that his hostess had no resident servants, only "old Tattler's daughter who comes in twice a week to do the rough cleaning." Moreover, Mrs. Bodgley did not seem to find that situation remarkable. He had not realized how much the war had changed things.

She began peeling spuds. He could not help with that. He might possibly make beds, but she assured him the beds were already made up. There was no shortage of linen. She had *trunks* and *trunks* of stuff she had brought from the big house, she said. Perhaps he could just look through *that* one and find some more plates?

He had run out of fags. He could not even walk into town to buy some—partly because he was a hunted fugitive, mostly because he had no money. Oh hell! How had he ever blundered into this bog?

Rumbling nonstop as she prepared dinner, Mrs. Bodgley spouted news of his old chums, and he felt the chill of the war's grim shadow. Wounded, wounded, dead, dead, dead . . . She talked of the difficulties the school was having now, for although she was no longer wife of the chairman and hence Honorary Godmother, she had maintained her interest.

She asked what his plans were now. He had to confess that he had none. He had always assumed that he would return to India, where he had been born, following in the guv'nor's footsteps. The Government of India would probably prefer men with two hands, but he had some gongs and he was Sir Thomas's son . . . but the police were after him now. Whatever happened in the next week or two, that blot would never fade from his record. Scratch India.

He kept thinking of Exeter's Olympus—dressing for dinner in the jungle, house servants galore . . . but that mythical world was wilting under the clammy breath of reality. Magical powers and miracle cures, prophecy and vindictive gods . . . how could anyone believe such ravings?

Oh, for a cigarette!

The time came to harness up the pony again. Mrs. Bodgley set off for Greyfriars and the station. Smedley wandered out into the garden. The vegetables were well tended, the flowers needed work. He removed his jacket and tie. Clippers or lawn mower were beyond him, but he found a hand fork in the shed and set to work on the weeds. When that palled, he established that he could use a hoe, after a fashion, and even rake leaves.

The scent of fresh earth reminded him of the trenches. But this was an autumn afternoon in England. He was Home. Thick hedges and ivy-furred walls enclosed him like a womb. There were leaves overhead and white clouds. He could hear a chaffinch and the pigeons. He had done his bit, his war was over. Home! Blighty! A fierce contentment seized him.

After a while he realized that his invisible hand had gone, and he had not wept all day.

The trap came jingling back, with Exeter driving. Smedley went to open the yard gate for them, but of course Alice was there. Alice was a *girl*. Confused by the strange shyness that suddenly possessed him, he hastened back to his gardening. There, at least, he would not have to listen while Exeter discussed old Bagpipe's murder with his mother, if they had not already gone over that.

An hour or so must have drifted by before he heard a mechanical rattling. Exeter came around the corner, grinning cheerfully and pushing a lawn mower. "Escaped!" he said. "Tired of talking! You've got a good show going here."

He hung his jacket and tie on a branch. After a few passes across the straggly lawn, he stopped and glanced at the hedges. The lane outside was a cul de sac, with no traffic. He took off his shirt, to work in his undervest. The ladies were busy in the kitchen, he said. They wouldn't notice. It wasn't quite gentlemanly, but it did make sense. Smedley removed his shirt also, and went back to killing weeds.

His mood of lonely content had faded. Every time he caught sight of Exeter's bronzed shoulders he thought of those ritual scars the man must still have on his ribs. How could he have gone native like that? What little he had said about the Service had made it seem like a very worthy cause. Olympus had sounded like a true outpost of civilization. But spears and mutilation and painted faces . . . those were not pukka!

Dinner was a strange meal. Even with all the windows open, the sepulchral dining room was dim and breathless. Its monumental mahogany furniture would have seated twenty without trouble, so the four of them clustered at one end of the table, Smedley paired with—and tongue-tied by—Alice Prescott. If either of the ladies had ever studied the culinary arts, the food did not bear witness. They both wore dresses, but not evening dresses, and of course the men had nothing except the clothes that Ginger had acquired for them from the mythical barrow. The total absence of servants screamed wrongness.

As compensation, the wines were superb. Everyone became a little louder than usual.

Exeter hardly had a chance to eat. Whenever he paused, either Alice or Mrs. Bodgley would fire more questions at him. He repeated much that Smedley had heard before. He added a lot more. Mrs. Bodgley raised her eyebrows a time or two, but never expressed a doubt as the unlikely tale unfolded.

If Exeter was making it up, or had imagined it all, it was astonishingly detailed and consistent. Reluctantly, Smedley began to sense belief creeping back again, and odd stirrings of something that felt strangely like relief. He was too close to being tipsy to work that out.

After the cheese, the men declined port, and all four moved out to the little crazy-paving terrace to sit on a pair of extremely uncomfortable wrought-iron benches and watch the sky darken and the stars awaken. Alice brought coffee. Mrs. Bodgley disappeared and returned with cobwebs in her hair and a very dusty bottle in hand.

"This is older even than I am," she said. "It's part of a stock of wines and spirits that Gilbert laid down for Timothy when he was born. It seems only fitting that his friends should enjoy them. Edward, will you do the honors, please?"

It was an angel of a brandy.

There was only one thing wrong with the day now.

"Captain?" Mrs. Bodgley boomed. "Mr. Exeter? What am I thinking of? I do believe there are still some of Gilbert's cigars in the humidor. Would either of you care . . ."

It was a goddess of a cigar. Corona Corona, finest Cuban.

"Listen!" Alice said. "That can't be a nightingale? This late in the year?"

\*      \*      \*

"Well?" Mrs. Bodgley demanded, shattering a reflective silence. "What are your plans now, Mr. Exeter?"

Smedley jerked out of a reverie. Good question!

"I do wish you would go back to calling me Edward, Mrs. Bodgley."

He had asked that several times. Smedley was amused to see the redoubtable Mrs. Bodgley not in perfect control of her tongue, but he knew that this evening must be a devilish strain on her. She must feel haunted by ghosts of past, present, and future—son, husband, and better days. She deserved a medal for even trying.

"Tch!" she said. "I keep forgetting. What are your plans now, Edward?"

"I want to enlist, of course; do my bit."

"Naturally. I would not expect anything different of a Fallow boy."

Alice shifted on the bench at Smedley's side. He thought she was about to speak, but she did not.

"Preferably not in the Foreign Legion," Exeter added.

Mrs. Bodgley thundered a brief laugh like a signal cannon. "Indeed not! But from what you say . . ." She was talkative but her wits were not befuddled. "Oh, some of Gilbert's friends will help. I'll think of someone in the morning."

"That would be wonderful! Thank you." Exeter's gaze flickered toward Smedley's empty cuff—and then away again, quickly. "But I also must get word back to the Service, on Nextdoor. About the traitor. That is urgent."

Even the deepening twilight could not conceal the shrewdness in the old lady's stare. "But you say that only people can cross over? You cannot just drop a note?"

Again Exeter glanced briefly at Smedley.

"That is correct. All messages are verbal. Someone will have to make the trip there and back. One possibility would be Stonehenge, the portal I used before, but Alice says the Army has it shut off."

"I am sure that is correct."

Smedley waited for her to invoke some more of her late husband's friends, but she just sipped her brandy in silence.

Exeter scratched his chin. He had cut it while shaving for dinner, and now he was making it bleed again. "Another approach would be to get in touch with the, ah, the numen who cured my leg. The one I called Mr. Goodfellow."

"And where is he?"

"Not far from here, but I'm not sure where. Do you have any local Ordnance Survey maps around?"

"Gilbert had reams of them, but they're packed away in boxes somewhere. And I don't think you can buy any just now—in case of spies, you know. Why do you need them?"

"To find a hill with standing stones on it."

"Nathaniel Glossop."

"Beg pardon?"

"Nathaniel Glossop," Mrs. Bodgley repeated infallibly. "A neighbor. He knows all the local archaeology. I shall call on him in the morning."

"Oh, jolly good!" Exeter said. "Spiffing! That would be very good of you."

"No trouble, Edward. But tell me something. Why did it take you three years to return?"

His hesitation was interesting.

"Well, the Service weren't frightfully helpful, I admit."

"You were a prisoner?"

"Er, hardly! But they'd suspended all Home leave during hostilities, and the Committee didn't want to make a special case for me. They kept saying that the war would be over before I could do any good. Olympus doesn't keep up to date very well, you see. The *Times* doesn't circulate there. We knew the war was still going on, but months would go by without news, and the war always seemed to be on the point of ending. And . . . they had this conviction that I have a destiny to play out as the Liberator."

Mrs. Bodgley made clucking noises of disapproval. The moon was rising, silver behind the sable yews.

"Well, naturally they're more concerned about what's happening on Nextdoor than here," Exeter said defensively. "They're very dedicated to their own cause. And it did take me almost two years to arrive at Olympus in the first place."

"Why?"

He peered at his fingers and found the blood on them. Muttering angrily, he fumbled for a handkerchief. "What? Oh, the Vales are primitive compared to Europe. The distances are not great, but it's like wandering around Afghanistan or ancient Greece. Strangers attract suspicion. Unattached young men are apt to be taken for spies. Remember how Elizabethans felt about paupers—Poor Law, and all that—send them back to their home parish? There's slavery in some places. Thargvale, in particular."

"How barbaric!"

"Believe me, it is! And if not slavery, then military service. For the first year or so, I was caught up in a war."

Pause. "A war?" Mrs. Bodgley repeated the word with disapproval. The brandy was making her louder and more matriarchal than ever. Smedley wondered what Alice was making of her. Alice had not spoken in a long time. She was too close for him to see her expression. She was too close.

"'Fraid so," Exeter agreed.

"Like Afghanistan, you said? Bows and arrows? Some squalid tribal squabble?"

"Very much squalid."

"Edward, I'm afraid I feel a little disappointed in you! Could you not have left the natives to fight their own battles? I really can't see why it need have been any of your business. Your duty lay back here, surely?"

Smedley wondered what the good lady was going to say when she heard about the scars and the face paint. Perhaps Exeter could guess, because he did not mention them.

"I felt that way too, Mrs. Bodgley. But it wasn't so easy. First, no army tolerates deserters. Secondly, I—" Exeter shot another brief, cryptic glance at Smedley, as if checking his reactions. "Well, I had responsibilities there, too. I had made friends, you see, who had given me hospitality, so I could hardly just run away and leave them, could I?"

"You weren't fighting in the ranks, though, were you?" Alice said.

Exeter pulled a face. "Not in the end," he admitted.

"They elected you leader?"

He nodded unwillingly.

"Leader?" Mrs. Bodgley paused, as if rolling the idea around in her mind. "Leader of what?"

"The combined Joalian and Nagian armies. In our terms not much more than a brigade, five or six thousand."

"Indeed? Well, that does make a difference, I admit."

It certainly did, Smedley thought. Brigadier Exeter? Field-Marshal Exeter! Bloody good show!

"Of course, it would be just like a Fallow boy to take command," Mrs. Bodgley mused approvingly. "Leadership! Initiative! The traditions of the Old School. The school magazine will— No, I suppose not."

"Oh, it was nothing to do with me," Exeter protested. "It was just my stranger's charisma."

"You are modest, Edward. It is starting to get chilly, isn't it? But let's stay out here a little longer. I hate the smell of those paraffin lamps. Do tell us about this war of yours."

Exeter laughed unconvincingly. "It wasn't very noble. I worked my way up from the ranks. By the time they elected me supremo, we were locked up in a besieged city with the finest army in the Vales certain to come after us as soon as spring opened the passes. The seasons are running about three months behind ours just now, so that would have been roughly a year after I crossed over."

"Your cause was just, I trust?"

"My cause was just to save our necks. There was no hope of winning anything, nothing at all. All we wanted to do was get home safely."

"Xenophon and the Ten Thousand!"

"On a very, very small scale."

Better still! Smedley had always approved of wily old Xenophon, and he was intrigued by this charisma business—could use bags more of it on the Western Front! "How did you get them to elect you leader?" he asked.

Exeter shrugged. "I didn't. It just sort of happened. Joalians are great believers in *pour encourager les autres*. They'd already beheaded one general. They were ready to shorten his successor and put me up instead. I said I would help, but only if they'd just demote Kolgan back to being my deputy. . . . I told you, strangers have charisma."

"But you'd got them safely into the city in the first place," Alice remarked quietly.

"True. But that was a magic trick."

"So how did you get them out?"

Exeter scratched his chin. "By reading, mostly," he said vaguely. "We had a whole winter to kill, and there were books in Lemod—that was the city, Lemod. I did a lot of reading. And I had Ysian to help."

"Who's Ysian?" Alice asked.

"Er . . . a friend, ah, native, I mean. A Lemodian. Helpful."

"Describe this friend!"

Even in moonlight, his hesitation was obvious. "A girl. I—I found her under a bed, actually."

# VI

# *Pawn Promoted*

# 32

The west end of Lemodvale was very high and the climate was harsher there, but spring had come at last. Snow still lay on the hills, but in the last few days the temperature had risen dramatically, and now a drizzly rain had begun to fall. The world was about to turn green again.

Lungs strained and boots splashed in the slush as Dosh Envoy sprinted up the street. He could hear the heavy tread and labored breathing of Prat'han Troopleader at his heels. Prat'han was a bigger man by far, but he was weighted down by shield and club. Besides, while acting as D'ward's runner, Dosh had developed the best pair of legs in the army. Knowing that he could win and that winning would matter much more to the troopleader, he eased back slightly. Prat'han drew level. His face was bright red with effort and soaked with sweat. The idiot was wearing a fur suit he had looted somewhere and still persisted in wearing.

Their destination was in sight, and the two guards on the door were watching the race with interest. Prat'han put on a spurt; Dosh let him edge out in front. He was visibly in the lead as they stumbled up to the door and stopped, gasping. They leaned against the wall to catch their breaths. The guards cheered and clapped the winner on the back, but they had grins for Dosh also.

He was one of the boys, now. They spoke to him, joked with him, accepted him. If they were ever in doubt about what D'ward wanted, they would ask Dosh's opinion. He found the situation novel, amusing, and infuriatingly pleasant. He had never sought their approval—why should he enjoy it?

His sins had been forgiven the night he had helped the Liberator break into the city, almost half a year ago. They had been forgotten as soon as Anguan's pregnancy had become noticeable. Oh, once in a while one of the men would snidely inquire who had helped him with that, but the fact that it was cause for ribaldry showed that the former outcast was now accepted as a real man. Dosh's standard response was to explain that he was very versatile. That was absolutely true and always discomfited the inquirer.

"All here now?" Dosh asked as soon as he could speak. The guards nodded. "Come!" he told Prat'han, and led the way in. He was exceedingly curious to know what the Liberator was going to announce at this gathering. He hoped he had not missed anything important already.

The sign over the door said this was the house of Timbiz Wagonmaker, but now it was D'ward's. When Lemod had fallen, every man in the army had picked out a home and a woman to look after it—and him. The rest of the population had been slain or driven out, to conserve food. All the Joalian officers had moved into the palace, but the Liberator had chosen to reside with his troops. Although he had selected a home larger than most, he used it to hold meetings, and no one grudged him that symbol of rank. He was the hero who had taken the city.

He was the Liberator! Everyone knew it now, although he refused to accept the title.

The ground floor was one big workshop. There was no wagon under construction, but there was plenty of loose timber stacked around the walls. With the big double doors open the place was dim, and Dosh's eyes needed a moment to adjust. He realized how hard it had become to distinguish Nagians from Joalians. They had all survived the winter by dressing like Lemodians. In the last couple of days, some of the Nagians had begun to go around bare-chested. Not many, though. Dosh suspected that even full summer plumage would still leave the two armies looking much more alike than they had in the fall.

Everyone he had been told to summon had arrived—twenty-seven troopleaders, Kolgan, Golbfish. The new battlemaster preferred the Nagians' custom of informality, or else he refused to impose Joalian discipline on them. Everyone was sitting. Most of the Joalians were silent and ramrod stiff, while all the Nagians were chattering, and a few were lying stretched out on back or belly. Kolgan Coadjutant and Golbfish Hordeleader were seated on either side of a pile of planks, while D'ward himself sat cross-legged between them. He shot the newcomers a smile of welcome.

Dosh found himself a dark corner where he could watch the faces. He had not been specifically told to attend the meeting himself and could only hope he would be allowed to remain. He had nothing useful to contribute. Anyone he might conceivably be sent to summon was already present.

D'ward looked like a long-legged boy between the gangling, red-haired Joalian and the bulky prince. They were obviously in serious disagreement about something. His eyes went from one side to the other and back again as his deputies contended in angry whispers across him. He was saying nothing, and nothing in his expression revealed which side he favored, if either.

To see the flaccid, wide-hipped Golbfish resisting Kolgan was a phenomenon of note. Tarion would not recognize his half brother now; and when D'ward had been promoted to battlemaster, the Nagians had elected their prince hordeleader unanimously. If Golbfish ever returned to Nagland, Nag was going to be very surprised indeed.

D'ward threw up his hands to end the argument. Then he spoke to the assembly. His blue eyes twinkled. "To business! We have a slight disagreement here about the tactical situation. Let's have it out in public. Kolgan Coadjutant?"

The tall Joalian lumbered to his feet. He was scowling, but that was his customary expression. He wore armor over at least one layer of Lemodian woolens.

Dosh would love to know how Kolgan felt about the Liberator now—a juvenile savage from a minor colony running the Joalian army? The Clique would have his head when they heard of it. But Kolgan would have lost his head a fortnight ago if D'ward had not insisted that it remain attached.

"Honored Battlemaster," said the big redhead, "Hordeleader, and Troopleaders. The

Thargians may be in Lemodvale already. If they are not, then they will come over Saltorpass the minute it's open. They will secure Siopass to close off our retreat, and they will march west to Lemod." He glared over D'ward's head as if daring Golbfish to disagree.

The room was humming with tension. Everyone was aware of the peril. This was why Kolgan had been deposed.

"There are lesser passes closer to us," D'ward remarked, "closer to Lemod."

Kolgan sighed patiently. "But the lesser passes open later. And even if the Thargians do manage to come that way, they cannot cut off our retreat, because they would be on the south side of the river—the wrong side."

"They could cross the river."

"No, they couldn't! The only place Lemodwater can be crossed is at Tholford."

Kolgan sounded very sure of that. Dosh grinned to himself. One of the first things the Liberator had done when Lemod was taken was to set Dosh to work scouring the city for books on the history and geography of Lemodvale.

"And our best strategy?"

"Our *only* strategy is to wait until Joal sends a relief force. Probably it will come over one of the lesser passes from Nagvale, but those will not open for several fortnights yet—that side of Lemodwall is higher, as you may know. Or they may come over Siopass, as we did, and then follow our route here. In either case, we must wait for relief. Lemod can resist a siege indefinitely."

"Thank you. Hordeleader?"

Kolgan sat down. Golbfish stood up, swathed in Lemodian woolens of ill-matched colors. He looked very bulky in them, but his bulk was still visibly pear-shaped.

"I agree with Kolgan Coadjutant on what the Thargians are likely to do. I disagree with him about staying shut up in Lemod. We do not know if Joal will ever send reinforcements. If it does, they will have to fight their way to us, every step. Lemod has never been taken by storm in the past, but the Thargians can starve us out. I say we march out to meet them in battle! If we are going to die, then let us die bravely in the open, not trapped like rats, eating our boots! We fought our way in here, we can fight our way out again."

His Nagians cheered him, of course, but without conspicuous enthusiasm. He sat down. Half a year ago, who would ever have expected to hear such defiance from the fat man?

D'ward glanced around the big chamber, as if inspecting reaction among the on-lookers. Then he scrambled to his feet and stepped up onto the pile of planks. "My information is that the Thargian army is already in Lemodvale, and will be on our doorstep very shortly. Has anyone else heard similar rumors?"

There was a pause, a long pause. A few Nagian hands rose reluctantly. A moment later, some Joalian hands joined them. Angry whispers buzzed through the shop.

"Rumors!" Kolgan barked. "The city is sealed! Who can know?"

D'ward smiled down at the tall man's angry glare. "When we were the besiegers, the people inside the walls signaled back and forth to the Lemodians in the woods with flags. Did you not see them at the windows? And there are still many thousands of Lemodians here in Lemod. Those outside have been sending them messages. The rumors are well-founded."

Kolgan opened and closed his mouth a few times.

And so did Dosh.

The women!

The Joalian had worked it out also. "Can you trust a word they tell you?" he demanded angrily.

"Yes," D'ward said sadly. "Some of them. And I am not the only one who has been told, obviously. This is a problem, gentlemen. Some of you have won the love of your companions, and I am sure that hundreds of others have done so also. But most of those women are now with child. I am afraid that we must leave them all behind when we depart, and that—"

"Depart?" Kolgan shouted. "Go where? How?"

"Well, home, of course! You don't *want* to stay here do you?"

Even the Joalians guffawed at that, even Kolgan himself, but it was laughter with a brittle ring.

The Liberator folded his arms and looked around the room again. "A fortnight ago," he said loudly, "you honored me by electing me battlemaster. I asked you then to wait, and to trust me. You did both and I thank you for your faith. Now the time has come. This morning it started to rain."

He smiled faintly at the puzzled reaction.

"I am told, and I believe, that the Thargians outnumber us by three to one. The Lemodians must be even more numerous. While I respect Golbfish Hordeleader's courage, I refuse to send warriors against impossible odds. On the other hand, I also refuse to end my life as a slave in the Thargian silver mines."

The assembly growled agreement like a nest of fourfangs.

D'ward raised his voice. "When you have eliminated the unacceptable, you are left with the merely impossible."

He grinned and paused, as if waiting for suggestions. None came.

"No one's mentioned the rope bridges they maintain in peacetime. I looked into the possibility of building one, but it isn't practical. It would take days, and we'd need half the army on the other bank anyway, to defend the construction. If we could move half over, we might as well move all of it."

He waited a moment. Dosh wondered how many of the listeners had even known about the rope bridges. He had heard of them from Anguan and come to the same conclusion—they were not a practical solution.

Receiving no argument, D'ward continued. "It's true that the only permanent, all-weather ford on Lemodwater is Tholford. But at low water, there are other sites where active men can force a crossing. You may think that low water comes in late summer, as it does on most rivers. But Lemodwater is fed by glaciers. Its low point is right now! In a few days the rain and melting snow will start it rising again. Have none of you noticed?"

Dosh heard the mutter of surprise. Certainly he had not spared the river a glance lately, but he never stood guard on the walls. No one spoke up.

D'ward shrugged. "Well, you will see shortly. An army can go where traders and normal civilian traffic cannot. My information is that about three days ago, the Thargians arrived in Lemodvale over Moggpass, which is about twenty miles due south of us. That must have been quite a feat, but Thargians are a determined bunch when roused, so I'm told. They headed west, to Thimb'lford. Men can cross there at low water. They should be making their crossing today. Expect them at the gates by tomorrow night or the day after."

Dosh shivered.

D'ward waited until his audience fell silent. "Now do you see? They're going to be on our side of the river, the north side. So tonight we shall cross over to the south side! It must be tonight—the rain has begun. We jump the river, and then we make a forced march to Moggpass, which the Thargians have so kindly opened for us. Our only way out is to invade Thargvale itself."

The room exploded in tumult.

D'ward yelled, "Quiet!"—and won silence. "I am your battlemaster! You will take my orders now, or you will depose me and cut off my head! Which is it to be?"

He was younger than anyone present, an untrained youth garbed in a motley collection of cast-off clothes, and yet he seemed to blaze. Deadly blue eyes raked the room. Not a whisper . . .

"Very well. Why does the wall go all around the city? I wondered about that when I first saw it. The only possible reason is that sometimes the river can be crossed! And right now the water is as low as it ever gets."

Men stirred in excitement. Dosh thought of the cliffs and that roaring white torrent. He shuddered. There would be Lemodians over there, and probably Thargians. Not very many, perhaps, but some.

"We need planks," D'ward said, "and all the rope we can find. We can bridge some of the gaps with pontoons. It won't be easy in the dark, but tonight we cross Lemodwater. If we can get one man over, we can get all of us over. Tomorrow we march on Thargvale. The Thargian army will be on the wrong bank—and the river is rising!"

Escape! He was offering them hope—a slim hope, but a chink of light in a sealed tomb. So what was a thousand feet of roaring foam, sharp rocks, ice floes, and Lemodian arrows? Nothing, compared to the Thargian host. The troopleaders sprang to their feet and cheered.

D'ward waved impatiently for silence. "This is what we shall do. Secrecy is essential! Some of the women here now support us, but many are still loyal Lemodians, understandably. They will try to signal. When darkness falls, they may set the place alight. We must round up every woman in the city, so there are no signals passed. Every man will need warm clothes, good boots, four days' rations. . . ."

The implications struck home to Dosh like a kick in the belly. He was going to be parted from Anguan! He would miss that wiry little Lemodian wildcat. He would never see that child she carried. He had always known that this must come to pass, of course, but the actuality was an unexpected blow. Why? Affection? Gratitude for some wonderful copulation? It was no more than affection, surely?

Perhaps he was more like other men than he had realized.

He wrenched his mind back to the Liberator, who was spouting a fountain of orders
and directives. Obviously he had worked out all the details in advance. As soon as
darkness fell, Golbfish and Kolgan were to lead separate columns across the river. Before
then, they must obtain ropes and prepare floats, pontoons, and gangplanks. There were
tree trunks and ice floes caught amid the rocks. Of course it would be dangerous. They
could expect to lose men, drowned or frozen. The enemy on both banks would attack
when they learned what was happening.

If a contested crossing of Lemodwater had been achieved in the past, the Liberator
must have learned of it in his reading. He was not mentioning that, so it had never
been done.

The withdrawal of the forces on the gates . . .

Oh!

D'ward asked for volunteers for that contingent and got them—but who could doubt
that the rear guard was going to die?

Logic said it was impossible. The Liberator said it could be done, and his words
carried conviction. It was madness, and it was going to happen. It was going to happen
tonight. The troopleaders listened in stunned amazement. By morning they and their
army would be on the far bank, or they would all be dead. A lot of them were going
to be dead anyway.

Questions?

Most of the questions were about the women. The women were certainly a problem.
The women had been taken as slaves and booty, but copulation was not called "making
love" without reason. Many of the men were reluctant to leave their concubines now.
D'ward was adamant: The women must stay behind. Never see Anguan again . . .

The council took a long time, but the basic plan had been accepted. Only the details
needed to be hammered out, and D'ward had answers for every objection. Dosh sat
back in his shadowed corner and marveled at this spectacular display of leadership. He
could not recall any hint of it in the *Filoby Testament*. Success or disaster, the coming
night had escaped the seeress's foresight.

Eventually the Liberator had the troopleaders convinced—he had them roused to
quivering excitement. When he dismissed them, they stampeded to the door to begin
their preparations. Evening was coming fast.

"Dosh Envoy!" he called, and then he sat down on the pile of planks.

Dosh stalked forward expectantly. Only Kolgan and Golbfish remained.

"Battlemaster?"

The Liberator was hunched over and silent. He raised his head with what seemed a
great effort, and Dosh was shocked to see the change in him. The vibrant war leader of
a moment ago had disappeared. D'ward was only a haggard, exhausted boy, as if he had
been drained of strength.

Kolgan frowned, seeming as puzzled as Dosh was. "Something wrong, sir?"

"Just tired."

Was rhetoric such an effort? True, he had roused almost thirty men to wild enthusiasm, every one of them older than he. Some of them had been twice his age and far more experienced in warfare. He had inspired them to rush out and attempt the impossible, knowing that many of them were going to their deaths. It had been an amazing performance, but why had it left him looking like a corpse?

He smiled weakly at Kolgan, and then at Golbfish. "Thank you for keeping silent there. You have questions too, I know."

Kolgan laughed harshly. "I do. No women, no cavalry, no pack animals? Just a bunch of men on the run? What happens in Thargvale, if we ever get that far?"

A spark of blue fire returned to D'ward's eyes. "I don't know. Do you want to come with us to see, or would you rather stay behind?"

The big man recoiled. "I beg your pardon, sir. It is a bold inspiration! Of course I support you."

D'ward grunted. "Hordeleader?"

Golbfish said, "Did your reading tell you that the river can be forded here at Lemodvale?"

"No. It sort of implied that no one had ever been crazy enough to try it."

The prince's big, suety face split in a grin. "Then by the five gods, I should love to see those Thargian faces when they discover we've gone!"

D'ward chuckled. He rubbed his eyes with thumb and forefinger. "You two go and reconnoiter the best routes. I'll meet you on the battlements by the clock tower steps in an hour."

The two deputies saluted.

"Wait!" D'ward licked his lips. "One last thing before you leave. There's some rope over there." He pointed at Dosh. "Tie this man up."

# 33

Kolgan Coadjutant and Golbfish Hordeleader hurried over to the door and departed. Dosh sat in dread stillness, his wrists and ankles bound to a chair. Fear churned in his belly, making him nauseous.

D'ward was hunched over again, head in hands. After a long moment he looked up and forced a smile.

"Relax!" he whispered. "I'm not Tarion."

Of course he was not Tarion, but the memories were terrifying. "What are you going to do with me?" Dosh was ashamed to hear the quaver in his voice. "You won't leave me for the Thargians?"

"No! No, of course not!" The Liberator straightened up wearily. "I just don't want you rushing off to the shrine to report to Tion. That's what you would have done, isn't it?"

Dosh fumbled for words that would not come. "But . . . but, Battlemaster! Surely you don't think you can keep a *god* from knowing what's happening?"

"Yes, I do. Yes, I can, for a while anyway." He smiled thinly. "I know more about gods than you do, my lad! Why does Tion need you to report to him if the gods already know everything, *mm*? I don't think he would tip off the enemy, but one never knows. You won't be hurt if you behave."

He heaved himself to his feet and walked over to the stairs. He disappeared up them, moving like an old man.

Dosh strained at his bonds, with no success. He could probably trust D'ward's promise not to leave him behind, but he was still determined to escape. His master's orders gnawed at him, compelling him to rush to the shrine and report this new development. And just being tied up was a torment in itself.

He glanced around the shop. There must be something. . . . Yes, there had been a pile of scrap iron lying in the corner where he had sat during the meeting. If he pushed with his feet, he could tip the chair over backward. Then he would break his arms or wrists. Try something else.

If he could somehow tip himself forward to put his weight on his feet, then he might manage to shuffle across the room like a snail carrying its shell. He had been left some movement in his shoulders, so if he tipped the chair back a little with his toes, then threw his weight forward, he might manage to rock it enough to—

A voice said, "Stop that."

He stopped.

A girl was standing over him with a balk of timber in her hands.

"Hit him on the head hard enough to dent a cooking pot—that's what D'ward told me to do."

"Would you?" he asked.

"Yes."

"Then I'd better behave myself, I suppose." He had not met Ysian more than two or three times, had not exchanged a dozen words with her. Anguan alone took a lot of satisfying and for variety there had been other playmates around much safer than Ysian Applepicker—D'ward's mistress had been off-limits.

There was something different about her . . . her hair. She had gorgeous dark auburn hair, which she had worn in a thick pile on top of her head. He had often wondered how she would look with it hanging loose and no clothes on, and how it would feel to play with. Now she had cut it short. Criminal! It made her look even younger. It made her look boyish, for she was short and thin. Her nose was small and peppered with freckles. She wore a long dress of some dark material, a shadow in the fading light of evening. He could make out a tightness to her jaw, and he decided she was capable of carrying out her threat. The glint in her eye suggested that she might even enjoy doing so. Definitely boyish.

"Pull up a chair," he said. "I won't run away."

Ysian thought for a moment solemnly, then sat down on the pile of planks D'ward had used, watching Dosh fixedly and still holding the club.

"We may be here some time," he said.

"I expect so."

"Tell me about yourself."

She kept her eyes on him like an agate idol. "What is there to say? This was my home. When D'ward took it over, I came with it."

"What happened to your family?"

For a long moment she did not answer, but when she spoke her voice was unchanged. "My aunt and uncle are out there in the woods somewhere. My cousin died in the battle."

D'ward had been right, as usual. The guerrillas had been keeping the women in town informed; the women who had fallen in love with their masters had passed them the news. It was inevitable that Ysian would be one of those traitors. The Liberator's charm could melt warriors twice his age. A juvenile mistress would not have a chance.

"I am sorry," Dosh said. "Truly, I am! I did not start this war. I am not even a warrior."

"I know. You were the other prince's plaything."

He withheld the obvious retort that she was D'ward's. "You are well-informed."

"We women gossip."

That might be humor or cynicism, he could not tell. How much of his life story had he told to Anguan, and how much had she babbled to the women of Lemod? Ysian's features had not changed expression since she arrived. She was only a kid, but he sensed he was matching wits with a very shrewd woman.

"What else do you know about me?"

"That you are a liar."

"All men are liars!"

She did not reply. Admittedly his position put him at a considerable disadvantage, but he was annoyed that she was besting him in the conversation.

"I have never lied to D'ward."

"Yes, you have!" She glared. "He asked you to find him a copy of the *Filoby Testament*, and you told him there were none in the town. I know there were. You threw them in the river."

"That is not true!"

"I saw you. I followed you."

He gritted his teeth. "Does he believe that?"

"I told him about the books, but it was too late. You had found them all. He said he was not surprised. He said you had been sent to spy on him and that was why you had taken service with the prince, back last summer. He said there is a prophecy about him and a prince and you never mentioned it to him, so he knows you are not to be trusted. He thinks you are one of those people who cannot help lying all the time."

That was probably true. Telling the truth always seemed sort of risky. Still, lying was probably just a habit. He was as loyal to D'ward as his other loyalty permitted—but he could not explain that.

"You told D'ward about Moggpass."

She did not deny it, just sat and watched him as if he were a cake on a griddle.

"If he cannot trust me, how can he ever trust you? You betrayed your people to the leader of the army that killed your cousin. Why? What sort of woman does that?"

"He knows he can trust me."

Dosh snorted. "But you cannot trust him!"

"I trust him absolutely." Her confidence was stupidly childlike and infuriatingly unshakable. He felt a sudden urge to crack it, to hurt.

"He took the city! He slew your family! And you think you can trust him? What madness is that? He is going to leave you tonight! What will your own people do to those who have aided the enemy?"

"I am coming with you tonight. I shall be your guide."

"He told the troopleaders that none of the women would come."

"Except me."

"He will not take his own woman and make his men leave theirs. He is not that sort of leader!" Why else had she cut her hair off, though?

Ysian shrugged—the first gesture he had seen from her. "I was raised on the south bank. I know Moggpass. I can help."

"He is lying to you, you know."

*"No!"*

Aha! Now the tinder was starting to smoke.

He sighed with great sadness. "Women in love are rarely reliable judges of character, Ysian Applepicker."

She bared her teeth at him. He chuckled, imagining her as wrestling partner. Usually he preferred boys tough and girls tender, but he would relish a sharp tussle with this firecub.

"What makes you think I am in love, Dosh Envoy?" she demanded.

"Ha! He is the Liberator. No one can refuse that man! I just watched him twist thirty warriors to the shape he wanted, all at the same time. Even I really do try to please him, as much as I can. No woman could resist him for a moment!"

Ysian tossed her head, perhaps forgetting that she had cut her hair. "You are jealous of me, Houseboy! Jealous because I live with D'ward!"

He flinched at the use of his former name, then sudden inspiration. . . .

"Why are you laughing?" she shouted.

"I don't need to be jealous of you, girl! Do I? Nothing to be jealous of!"

She blushed furiously, confirming his guess. She really did look ready to club him, and for some reason that made him laugh even harder.

"We have more in common than I thought!" he taunted. "There's another way to win a woman's loyalty, isn't there?"

Only D'ward would have thought of that, or been capable of it.

# 34

Golbfish stood at Kolgan's side on the battlements, staring down at the river. He felt ashamed of himself. The flow was half what it had been when he first came to Lemod, and he had never noticed the change. Beaches of shingle fringed both banks; ledges and boulders dispersed the channel; tree trunks and ice flows bridged some of the narrower gaps. An agile man could certainly work his way to the middle. Beyond that, the widest, fastest stretch . . . well, that was what friends were for.

The sides of the gorge were vertical in places, and not much less than vertical everywhere else. He wondered who stood in the woods on the far side, watching the city.

He spoke for the first time since leaving Wagonmaker's. "By the five gods, he's right again! It is a way out, and the only way! He saw it and we did not."

Kolgan growled. "I wish I knew how he does that."

Golbfish had asked the Liberator that question once, but the answer had been something about a temple of learning somewhere, and he had not understood. "Where will you try?"

"Down there looks good," the Joalian said, "but how could we get to it?"

They paced the parapet for an hour, until each had chosen a point of attack. The Nagians would try downstream, the Joalians upstream. The leaders would have to guide their men across by memory.

"Think we can do it?" Golbfish asked glumly.

"Cross? Some of us, yes." The tall man glared across at the far cliffs and tugged at his red beard. "But to invade Thargvale with no cavalry, with very little surprise, with a larger army already in the field and able to cut our line of retreat . . . You know this is madness?"

The alternative was worse.

"Have you ever been to Thargland?"

Kolgan shrugged. "Once. As a youth, I accompanied an uncle of mine on an embassy to Tharg. I was not impressed."

"You are a Joalian. You would not be impressed by a Thargian shitting gold bars."

"I would certainly have them appraised by a competent minter."

Golbfish chuckled, but it was a social chuckle, and false. "Tonight the river. To-morrow the guerrillas, the forest, and the pass. We must take life one day at a time now and be grateful for it."

"Aye!" Kolgan said sourly. "And even if we fight our way home, Your Majesty, our troubles will not be over. Your brother will be well established on your throne now, with an army of his own, and my foes in the Clique will have drawn up detailed plans for my funeral."

This would not do. Leaders must maintain their own morale if they were to maintain their troops'. Golbfish squared his shoulders—as much as his shoulders would ever square.

"Look on the bright side. However it began, this is no longer a squalid territorial squabble. We are caught up in the affairs of gods. Many things are prophesied of the Liberator, some clear and some obscure. Many things are likewise prophesied for a man named D'ward, and now we know that D'ward and the Liberator are the same. The most famous of the prophesies is that the Liberator will bring death to Death. If you wanted to find Death, Kolgan Coadjutant, where would you go looking?"

Kolgan raised his eyes to the southern peaks, his red brows bunched in a fearsome scowl. "Are you suggesting he is going to lead us to the city itself?"

"What use is a prophecy that is never fulfilled? Tharg would not take us very far out of our road, as I recall."

"It would be a shorter road, because we should never return."

True! Golbfish admitted to himself that he held no great hopes now of ever seeing Nag again. "When you were in Tharg, did you visit the double temple?"

"I saw it, although it was not then complete. Not all the pillars were erected, K'simbr Sculptor was still working on the image of the Man as Creator. But I have looked upon the face of Death." He spat contemptuously. "No one but the Thargians would raise such an abomination!"

After a moment he added, "And their cooking takes the skin off your tongue."

Before Golbfish could comment, D'ward came stalking along the parapet. He seemed to have recovered his strength, although his face was still drawn.

"Possible?" he demanded.

"We'll take casualties," Kolgan growled. "But it won't be a massacre."

The Liberator nodded and leaned on the battlements. "Get as many men working on supplies as you can. Ropes, planks . . . food for the march, of course. Wineskins and barrels for floats. Have to lower the barrels down the cliffs in nets, but keep all prepa-rations out of sight until dark, of course. A swimmer won't last two minutes in that cold. Oh . . . I didn't say so, but Ysian comes with us. She knows the terrain."

Golbfish caught Kolgan's eye. When the Lemodians returned, they would be hard on traitors.

Kolgan was disapproving. "Sir, this will not be an easy march, even for battle-hardened warriors. For a girl . . ." He let the suggestion die aborning.

D'ward was staring down at the river. "Do you know the narrowest escape I have had in this campaign so far, Coadjutant?"

"Your entry into the city, I assume, sir."

"No." He looked up with a grin. "The next morning, when I first met Ysian. She came at me like a whirlwind. She very nearly skewered me with a butcher knife."

The men laughed as men do when their leader makes a joke. "You tamed her, sir!"

"Or she tamed me. Now, anything else?"

"What of Dosh Envoy?" asked Golbfish. "I thought you trusted him?"

D'ward smiled thinly. "In some things. He has a higher loyalty that you'd be happier not knowing about. He'll come. Don't worry about him once we're across."

He looked up at the drizzling clouds. "Pray for rain," he said. "Pray for lots and lots of rain."

Just before the light failed completely, Golbfish buckled on a sword. He sent a squad down the cliff face to rope out a path and string ladders. He followed with the next contingent, descending into black madness. Men kept coming steadily after that, with ropes, with timber, with anything that might float.

An hour or so later, bruised, battered, and freezing, he stood on the south shore.

He had been one of the lucky ones. Everyone went roped, with two companions feeding out the line behind him, but anyone who slipped landed in ice-cold water and was usually smashed into the rocks before he could be hauled back. Planks worked loose from their moorings, barrels sank, ropes failed, ice floes rushed out of the night like monsters. Men vanished in mid-sentence and were gone forever. Darkness and the roar of the river made communication almost impossible. The current brought down Joalian bodies.

As soon as he had a score or so of men with him, Golbfish secured ropes to guide the rest. Then he told a squad to follow him and set off up the cliff. When the Lemodians learned what was happening, they would start rolling boulders down on the invaders.

The slope was steep—rock and mud, dribbling water. He knew he was at the top when he banged his head on a tree root. He hauled himself over the lip and rose shakily to his feet. The darkness was absolute, but *something* alerted him. He ducked. A blade whistled overhead. He dragged out his sword and slashed at the night. He felt a sickening, squishy impact, heard a cry, and knew that he had just drawn his first blood. He moved quickly to the other side of the tree and peered around helplessly, listening. His victim was sobbing and muttering prayers, somewhere on the ground.

Again an unnamed sense warned Golbfish of movement, and he flailed his sword at the empty air. He was a warrior now, a killer. Behind and below him, he could hear his own men coming.

"Watch out!" he shouted, parrying blindly. His blade struck another with a loud clang. He dropped to a crouch and swung again, knee high. A man screamed and fell into crackling undergrowth.

The only way to tell friend from foe was by speech—challenge, and if he did not reply in the right accent, try to kill him. If he just tried to kill you, don't wait for the reply. But the resistance was surprisingly light and soon faded away completely.

Having secured a beachhead in the woods, Golbfish detailed a squad to accompany him and set off to establish contact with Kolgan.

The Joalians were having a worse time of it. There was another blind skirmish in the undergrowth, and again the defenders withdrew. Soon Nagians were hauling Joalians over the cliff edge and securing ropes for those coming after. There was no sign of Kolgan himself.

Golbfish returned to his own column and was dismayed to discover less than a hundred men in position. He waited for a while to see if the Lemodians would launch a counterattack. Nothing happened; the woods were silent. He scrambled back down to the river. The army was crossing, but at this rate it seemed likely to take days. He fought his way back across the river—an even more hair-raising procedure than the first trip, for he frequently had to work his way around other men clinging to the same rope or boulder.

He harangued the crowd milling on the beach. He assured them that their comrades were crossing safely and had not just gone to a watery grave. He ordered more lines set up, more avenues mapped through the maze.

He climbed back up the north cliff in a shower of gravel, mud, and descending warriors, and somehow even forced his way up one of the rope ladders dangling on the walls. More haste! he commanded. Faster!

He reeled off in search of D'ward and found him overseeing the defense at the gates, for the Lemodians had guessed what was happening. Even there, though, the assault was strangely halfhearted.

Golbfish reported. D'ward listened, thanked him, and ordered him back to the south bank. He set off to cross the river a third time. He saw with relief that the exodus was gathering speed.

There were no moons. By midnight the rain had become a downpour, making the darkness absolute. Undoubtedly many men died at the hands of their friends as gang-plank or rope failed and too many struggled to occupy the same perch. Hundreds drowned or froze or were smashed on the rocks.

At dawn Golbfish found himself in command of the army in the orchards of the south bank. Kolgan had fallen while climbing the cliff, breaking his shoulder. He was huddled in a daze of agony and shock on the shingle. The river was littered with bodies and the shore with wounded.

Rain still fell in torrents. The river was visibly rising. Lemod was back in the hands of its rightful owners, blazing in several places from fires set to slow down their return. There was no sign of pursuit. Praise the gods!

Dosh Envoy appeared in the first gray light, accompanied by a boy whom a second glance showed to be Ysian in male clothing. The sight of her blue lips persuaded Golbfish to let fires to be lit. The two camps had been amalgamated and he had posted a cordon around the perimeter, almost a solid fence of men. The Lemodians were still not at-tacking, not even reverting to their old guerrilla tactics. Why not?

Everyone was coated in mud. Half the survivors seemed to be limping or staggering blindly in deep shock. One skinny youngster arrived hobbling, with his arms around two friends. He pulled loose from them and steadied himself on one leg, hanging on to a branch.

"How many?" he barked, and Golbfish realized that the kid's eyes were blue.

"Casualties? Four or five hundred, I think."

The muddy scarecrow winced. "No opposition?"

"Very little. How many did you leave behind?"

"Damned few," D'ward said. "How many can't walk?"

Golbfish shrugged. "There are at least fifty still down on the beach. Up here . . . I don't know. Another fifty?"

The Liberator groaned and wiped an arm across his face. It remained just as filthy as before. "You all right?"

"A trifle fatigued, perhaps. You, sir?"

Chuckle. Another groan. "Twisted an ankle, that's all." The Liberator laid his injured foot on the ground and showed his teeth in a grimace. "My first battle," he muttered.

Golbfish saw how his eyes were glistening, and felt a curious twinge of sympathy. Like him, D'ward was not a genuine soldier, was not hardened to being responsible for the lives of followers. Most leaders would have been cheering madly at this point, exulting in a brilliantly executed withdrawal. Twice now, D'ward had pulled off stunning reversals; twice he had made brilliant generalship look like child's play, and all he was concerned with was the cost.

"The river has taken its toll, but it was not the massacre the Thargians would have inflicted."

"We must see they don't get their chance yet." D'ward eased himself to the ground. "Summon the troopleaders." Ysian came and knelt beside him. She tried to wipe his face with a rag, and he waved her away irritably.

Soon the troopleaders gathered around, a bedraggled, shaken retinue, barely half the number who should have been there. D'ward appointed temporary substitutes and sent for them—there was no time for proper elections, he said. He seemed to know the names and abilities of every man, Joalians as well as Nagians.

Still sitting in the mud, leaning against a tree, he outlined what everyone already knew and did not want to think of. They had escaped from one trap, but only into a greater. The Thargians might recross the river and try to intercept their quarry before it could reach Moggpass. If not, they would head east to Tholford and block the road back to Nagvale. There would undoubtedly be many more armed men in Thargland itself. The reckoning had only been postponed.

"Now we must march," he said. "Anyone who can't must stay. Form up."

The men were exhausted, but the alternative was death or slavery. The troopleaders exchanged glances, but no one objected.

D'ward hauled himself to his feet. Half a dozen men rushed forward to help, but he refused them. In obvious pain, he began to hobble forward. In a moment someone offered him a staff, freshly cut, and he accepted that. He was setting an example, but that was all he was capable of.

Kolgan had arrived, but he was still too shocked by pain and exposure to be any use at all. Marveling at the strange fate the fickle gods had thrust upon him—and cynically amused by it also—Golbfish took effective command and issued the necessary orders.

One woman and less than five thousand men set off on a journey of conquest and deliverance. The steady, chilling rain was both a physical torment and a promise of hope.

Behind them, the abandoned wounded screamed and pleaded until their voices faded into the distance.

# 35

"Thargvale is beautiful," Exeter said. "Naturally. It's very fertile, the climate is moderate, and it's ruled by an aristocracy."

"What has aristocracy got to do with beauty?" Smedley asked drowsily.

Mrs. Bodgley had shepherded her guests indoors to the drawing room and settled them in chairs. A single oil lamp cast a soft light on the four faces, while two moths held races around the glass chimney. Fortunately the chairs were excessively uncomfortable, or Smedley would not have been able to stay awake at all. Alice had reluctantly consented to play, insisting she was hopelessly out of practice. She had then executed a couple of Chopin études from memory. Very well, too, so far as he could tell. And now they were back on Nextdoor again.

"Oh, *really*, Captain!" His hostess's tone suggested that he was showing himself to be excessively ill informed. "It's a matter of tender loving care! The only people who can look after land properly are those who plan to hand it on to their children and grandchildren. Gilbert's father planted an avenue of oak trees, knowing he could never live to see their majesty. That was fifty years ago, and they need another hundred at least. Gilbert himself absolutely refused to countenance mining operations on our place in the Midlands. That sort of thing. Men who think only of their own lifetimes *exploit* land. Those who think of their families *nurture* it. Do help yourself to another cigar if you wish," she added, as though regretting her scolding.

Smedley thanked her and heaved himself out of the lumpy chair even more gratefully. He went to the humidor. No Bodgleys would admire the oak trees in their prime. The Bodgley line had died out when Timothy was murdered. There was no one left to smoke the cigars, even.

Alice's eyes were twinkling in the lamp's gentle glow. "You can carry it too far, of course, like anything else. William the Conqueror depopulated whole counties to make royal deer forests. People have rights, too."

Mrs. Bodgley considered the point and seemed to decide that it was a dangerous heresy. "Not necessarily. People come and go, but land is forever."

Exeter flickered a wink at Smedley as he returned to his chair. "Do you suppose that aristocrats' tendencies to make war all the time is a form of population control, weeding out the peasants?"

The lady saw the hook at once and bit it off. "Probably! Lancing a few of the men would be kinder than letting women and babies starve, wouldn't it?"

"Depends which end of the lance you're on, I expect. But land and war do seem to go together. The Thargian military caste is just as bad as Prussian Junkers."

Dogs of war howled in the night of the mind. "Dueling scars?" Smedley demanded.

"No, I don't think they go that far."

"Thargvale is like England?" asked Alice.

"It has the same organized, cared-for look. The vegetation is very different. Thargian trees are colorful. We have copper beeches and then dull old green. They have blue and gold and magenta and various other shades as well. But the great estates are beautiful. The farmland is one big garden. The wild parts are beautiful too—and yes, some of those are deer parks. There are no picturesque little villages, though, or not many. The slave barns are kept out of sight."

"Sparta?" Mrs. Bodgley murmured.

"Similar," Exeter agreed. "I didn't see much of it at first. Partly because it was raining cats and dogs, partly because I twisted an ankle leaving Lemod and it took everything I had just to keep walking. The river crossing was a tricky business all round. Old Golbfish was the hero of the hour, organized the whole thing and rallied the troops. We were lucky with the weather. The river began to rise, so the Thargian army daren't come after us. The Lemodian guerrillas left us alone. By the second day we were into Moggpass. The Thargians had opened a trail—bridging streams, cutting through the avalanches, and so on, and that helped a lot. By the fourth day or thereabouts we came panting down into Thargvale and could start the looting and pillaging. We were half a year late, but that's what the original intention had been. Everyone had a great time."

"Except you?" Alice asked.

"I healed up quite quickly, actually. The troops were feeding me mana, although they didn't know it. Not that I deserved it, but that made no difference."

Smedley fought down a yawn. The carriage clock on the mantel estimated the time at around eleven. As soon as he finished the cigar he would excuse himself and head off to bed. Exeter's little war was interesting, but he had no need to hear any more about war for the next hundred years.

Alice was wearing a dangerously sweet smile. "So Pocahontas led you to the pass, did she? Then she went back to her own people?"

In a very flat voice, Exeter said, "Yes, she led us to the pass. She couldn't go back to her family, although we went very near her home. They would have treated her as a traitor, even though she was only a child."

"I see. Sorry. I was being bitchy."

Mrs. Bodgley gulped audibly. "Er, what did these Thargian Junkers of yours have to say about the looting and pillaging?"

Looting and pillaging were not part of the Fallow curriculum.

"Almost nothing! That was very strange indeed! They shadowed us with cavalry, lancers on moas. We could see them in the distance, but they never closed. They picked off stragglers and patrols, but only Joalians. Nagian blood was never shed."

"Odd?"

"Very! Favoritism! It began to cause dissension, as you may imagine. Golbfish insisted that the enemy was trying to pry the allies apart, split the Nagians away from the Joalians, and he managed to keep the peace more or less—he was a wonder, that man! After a couple of days, when the pattern became obvious, he suggested that Nagians and Joalians exchange equipment, helmet for shield, spear for sword. We tried that, and even the army itself could hardly tell which was which. The Thargians stopped attacking at all.

"We kept up the pace. Forced marches, thirty miles a day. It was a race. Moggpass had held us up a little. After that we had a clear run across Thargvale to get to Saltorpass and home. Thargian roads are excellent, as you might guess. In order to cut us off, their main army had to run the gauntlet of Lemodflat, and I told you what that's like."

"Obviously you won the race, or you wouldn't be here."

Exeter rubbed his eyes. "No. We lost. Well, not exactly. The Great Game came into play again. I say, it feels deucedly late! We didn't get much sleep last night. . . . Do you think we could continue this breathtaking saga in the morning?"

"Well, of course!" Mrs. Bodgley said. "But you can't leave us hanging like that! Give us a clue. What do you mean by the Great Game?"

"The Pentatheon, the Five. I told you how Krobidirkin got me involved in the Joalian campaign, and possibly Tion was in on that also. I still don't know all the details. The Game is so complicated that even the players can't keep track of the rules, and everyone has his own way of scoring. But when Zath learned that the gates of Lemod had been opened under a quadruple conjunction, he knew exactly where the Liberator was. So he leaned on Karzon, who is the Man, who is also patron god of Thargland. That was why the Thargians weren't killing us—the priests in Tharg had received a revelation from Karzon."

"I'm lost," Alice said.

"Zath wanted me taken alive."

"Alive?"

"So he could make absolutely certain I died, of course. This time he was going to do it himself and see it was done right."

# 36

Noontime sun beat down on the dusty road. There were no mountains in sight to the south at all—a situation that seemed wrong to Dosh, as if a necessary part of the world were missing. Thargvale was very big, the army very small. With the scouts and foragers and skirmishers spread out amid copses, hollows, and hedges, five thousand men could vanish into the landscape. Trudging up the road with Ysian at his side, he could easily disbelieve in those five thousand men.

That was a delusion, a fancy. In fact Talba's squad was just ahead, out of sight over the rise. Beyond the hedgerows, patrols flanked the army's progress on either hand. Gos'lva and his cavalry troop were close behind—unfortunately.

Since Lemod the cavalry traveled on foot, like everyone else. They were close enough to call out ribald remarks, usually about the incongruity of the pervert squiring the battlemaster's concubine. Away from the city, out in the field again, Dosh was no longer one of the boys. Jittery men needed a butt for nervy humor, and he was an obvious target.

"Hey, Pogink Lancer?" bellowed a voice.

"Yes, Koldfad Lancer?" roared another.

"Tell me, Pogink Lancer, why Dosh hath no spear?"

"I don't know, Koldfad Lancer. Why hath Dosh no spear?"

The punch line was predictably obscene. The cavalry's humor had never been of the best; descent to ground level and the status of mere mortals had not improved it. Their current blisters, fatigue, hunger, danger, and other tribulations must be very good for their souls but were obviously failing to keep their primitive minds from carnal fantasies.

Dosh bore no weapons because D'ward still used him as a runner. He probably traveled twice as far as the rest of the Army did in a day. He didn't usually let the abuse worry him, and didn't know why he was feeling the bite now.

"Hey, Koldfad Lancer?"

"Yes, Pogink Lancer?"

"What do you think of the way those hips move?"

"Which hips are you admiring, Pogink Lancer?"

"You don't have to stay here and listen to them," Ysian said quietly.

Dosh glanced down and saw a puzzled look in her big, clear eyes—the eyes of a child. She had been limping along at his side in silence for some time, apparently paying as little attention to the humorists as he did . . . paying, it must be admitted, very little attention to him either. The pack she bore was as big as any man's, her boyish form bent almost double under it. Every man in the army was half again as big as she was, but she kept up. She never complained, so far as Dosh knew. He sought her out and escorted her when he wasn't running errands, but the two of them rarely spoke much. The only thing they had in common was that they were both misfits.

A runner could not carry a pack, either. Ysian had shared her rations with him.

"They're just getting randy," he muttered, and then wondered if she would even understand what he meant.

Apparently she did. "This rape and pillage expedition hasn't produced much of either so far, has it? And they are not as perceptive as you are."

"Don't let them vex you. D'ward had his own reasons for bringing you. It's none of their business. Want me to carry that pack for a while?"

Ysian shook her head, hefted the pack higher on her shoulders, and continued to limp along.

D'ward was bringing up the rear, as he usually did. He had given himself the task of inspiring the stragglers, the wounded and the weakest, although every day men would drop in their tracks and perforce be abandoned to the doubtful mercy of the Thargians. Golbfish was in the van, leading the rout.

The land was deserted. The Thargians had burned the houses and driven off all the livestock. There were no women to rape and precious few goods to pillage—which mattered little, as the invaders had no pack beasts to carry booty. Whenever the weary foot-sloggers did manage to catch a stray zebu or auroch, it went straight in the pot. The rations brought from Lemod were exhausted; the spring fields were bare. A few more days of this, and hunger would bring the army to its knees.

Thargwall to the north was a glittering parade of ice and fresh spring snow. Somewhere behind it the Thargians must be marching too. Mountains loomed to the east also, closer every day. Within those crags lay Saltorpass, the road home, but could the weary, starving invaders ever hope to force it, and then Siopass after? This campaign seemed destined for fame as one of the greatest military blunders in Valian history. Joalia had sacked Lemod, thanks to D'ward, but otherwise all it had achieved was to force the Thargians into wasting a strip of their own homeland. Dosh found that a very small consolation indeed.

Like the peaks of Thargwall, massacre and surrender loomed ahead, ever closer, and the survivors would go to the silver mines. The two misfits could hope for nothing better. Dosh was serving his chosen god, and to die for Tion would guarantee him an eternal place with the blessed among the constellations, but the girl had no reason to be there. She had been useful as a guide in Lemodvale—why had D'ward not left her there? Had he no gratitude at all? Dosh would have expected better of the Liberator, somehow. The *Filoby Testament* never mentioned any Ysian, as far as he could remember. That meant nothing; the prophecies were very patchy.

He was on top of the rise now, with Talba and his men in clear view ahead. He stared around at the countryside—half expecting, as always, to see a second Thargian army advancing in wrath. Specks in the far distance were some of their scouts, lancers on moas. They rode circles around the invaders, watching like buzzards, pestering like mosquitoes, and yet now they had stopped attacking at all.

A temple!

A cluster of trees and ancient stone buildings standing all alone, halfway up a hillside in the middle of a pasture, where there was no visible reason for any sort of settlement at all—that could only be a sanctuary of some sort. The trees' spring foliage was beaten gold, but so was the glint of the central dome, and gold said *Tion*. Dosh could not resist that call. He did want to; he was eager to serve his master.

"Better see if D'ward needs me," he muttered, and stepped to the verge.

Gos'vla and his men marched by; he gave them the finger and they shouted obscenities at him. As soon as they had gone past, he dived through the hedge. He sat down in the weeds and waited for the rear guard to pass. The last troop went by him singing lustily, which was reasonable evidence that D'ward was with them, encouraging and inspiring as only he could.

Dosh stayed where he was a little longer. Then he scrambled to his feet and began to run across the fields.

# 37

Smears of dust in the distance told Dosh that the Thargians were still skulking. They might very well intercept him before he could ever catch up with his companions again. He was neither Nagian or Joalian, so he could not guess how they would treat him. It was better not to speculate. No matter, he had news he must pass to his master.

Half a fortnight ago D'ward had asked an unsettling question: Why should a god need spies to tell him things? Dosh had puzzled over that a lot until he worked out the answer. A god did not *need* anything. Gods were omniscient. It was the act of service that was important, and it was important only to Dosh himself. As a huntercat was trained to fetch prey, so he was being trained to serve, so that his soul might be worthy of a place in the heavens. Sacrifice was of value to the worshipper, not the god. The more it hurt the better it was, whether the sacrifice was a scrawny chicken or an act of service. Tion did not need Dosh, but Dosh desperately needed Tion.

The settlement was an abbey, he decided as he drew close. A nunnery was possible but a monastery more likely for an avatar of Tion.

Gasping for breath, he trotted through the gateway, slowing to a respectful walk within the sacred precincts. The buildings were very old, thickly coated with moss—five of them crouching among the trees and one larger edifice standing off by itself in the open. From the size of its windows, that one was probably a scriptorium. The order could not be very large, a dozen monks at most, and he wondered what they did with themselves, all alone out here in the hills. He caught a glimpse of a gowned figure bent over, weeding a herb garden, but saw no one else around. Prosaic washing waved on a line.

The minster was recognizable by its dome and central location. His wet shirt flapped against his skin as he strode up the steps. One side of the double door stood ajar, and he stepped through into clammy dimness.

The little chapel was entirely barren of furniture, not even an altar. It held only the image of the god, lit by beams shafting down from high slits in the dome. It certainly represented some aspect of the Youth, but a chunky, unappealing carving in veined marble, with his customary nudity partly concealed by a scroll he held vertically in both hands.

Dosh had been given a personal ritual to summon his master. Gods always designed such ceremonial so that they would not be duplicated by any trivial accidental gesture, and in his case he had to begin by taking off his clothes. That required privacy. He stood on one leg to remove a boot and almost fell over as a tall figure floated forward out of the shadows. Where had he . . . Oh, there was a door in the corner.

The monk was elderly, but his back was straight and his shaven face and head made his age hard to estimate. The bones were well shaped under the parchment skin; in his youth he would probably have been worthy to serve the lord of beauty. His yellow robe shone in the gloom; his sandals made a faint shuffling noise on the stone floor. A glittering necklace dangling to his waist suggested that he was the abbot himself. He was frowning.

"You come to pay reverence to Holy Prylis, my son?"

Fortunately, long winter nights of pillow talk with Anguan had given Dosh a grasp of Lemodian, and Lemodian was not unlike that dreadful Thargian croak. He understood, if only just. Prylis was god of learning—hence the scroll.

Clearly the holy father did not approve of sweat-soaked worshippers arriving out of breath, shirt unfastened, muddy boots. He probably expected Dosh to kneel and kiss that chain now, and then he would order the peasant off to some freezing pond to bathe before commencing his worship.

Dosh made the gesture of Tion, but he used his left hand and simultaneously extended two fingers of his right. It was probably a recognition signal of one of the Tion cults, although Dosh had never been sworn to a mystery. Just where he had learned that sign, he could not recall. Perhaps the god himself had instructed him. It always worked.

It did now. The old priest bowed low. He did not even raise his head fully, did not look directly at his visitor again. Murmuring, "I shall see that you are not disturbed, my son," he departed, sandals whispering hurriedly on the flags. The outer door closed behind him with a thump, making the chamber even darker. Much better.

Dosh stripped, shivery in the dank cold. The series of postures he was required to assume would normally be regarded as utter blasphemy in a temple, but one of the

Youth's attributes was Kirb'l, the Joker. Dosh bowed to the idol, turned his back, bent over. . . .

*"What in the world are you doing?"*

He shrieked and jumped and twisted around. There was no one there. Furious enough to forget his nudity, he strode over to the little door in the corner and threw it open. Beyond it lay a small chamber containing a table heaped with books. There was no other furniture, no other door. The voice had not come from there.

Trembling now, he hurried back to the idol and abased himself on the cold stone floor.

*"Well?"* asked that same sepulchral voice. *"You have not answered my question."*

"Lord, I was merely performing the ritual that you taught me."

*"Oh!"* There was no doubt now that the voice was coming from the statue. *"Tion did, you mean?"*

Dosh gibbered for a minute. "But are you not Holy Tion also, Lord?"

The god uttered a peculiar *tee-hee* noise, almost a snigger. *"Well, not always. Not at the moment. What is he up to now? What in the world are those scars on your face? Start at the beginning and tell me the whole story."*

"But . . ." Dosh had performed his ritual several times, in shrines or temples, and always it had brought the Lord of Beauty himself. But of course this time he had not completed the ritual, had hardly begun it. Were not all Tion's avatars Tion? That was what the priests said. Why, then, did this one refer to the Lord of Beauty as "he"?

It was not his place to question. "Lord, I have been following the Liberator, as you . . ."

*"Yes?"*

"As you . . . I think you told me to. I don't remember!" He began to panic. "I have to report to you what the Liberator does, don't I? That's right, isn't it? You must have . . ."

*"When did it begin?"* asked the voice. It had lost some of its spooky, echoing quality. It sounded almost gentle. *"Did you by chance win the gold rose in the—our, I mean— festival?"*

"Yes! Yes!"

*"What year?"*

"Six hundred, ninety-seventh festival, Lord."

*"And then what happened?"*

"I . . ." Dosh moaned. He trembled. He felt faint. "I don't remember! I stood on the dais with the rose in my hair, giving out the prizes in the festival. Then . . . I don't remember!" The next day he had gone to the palace in Lemod and asked Prince Tarion for work and been hired on the spot. That was almost a year ago now. . . . But that did not add up! "Four years? That festival was four years ago, wasn't it?"

*"Yes, it was. Put your clothes on, lad."* The god's voice had lost its divine menace altogether and become almost chatty. *"I can see you're freezing. Don't worry about the missing years. You're much happier not remembering, I'm sure. Keep talking. You mean that the Liberator is actually here, in Thargvale?"*

Dosh confirmed that as he shivered into his wet garments. Three years! Three years stolen out of his life!

*"That's very serious! Dangerous! Did the Service send him here, so soon?"*

"The who, Lord?"

*"The Service! The Church of the Undivided, if you prefer. Hmph! Obviously you don't know about them. My mast—my senior aspect has not been totally frank with you. Well, this is all very interesting, yes? Tee-hee! I must meet the Liberator. Go and fetch him."*

Dosh gulped in dismay. D'ward and the army would be miles away by now. How could he, Dosh, ever persuade the Liberator to turn it around and come back? Even less likely was the possibility of his coming alone, with the Thargian cavalry prowling over the countryside.

But to disobey a direct order from the god was unthinkable. It might condemn him to more years of . . . of what?

*Hatred!* Three years of his life had been stolen!

Anger and sorrow burned up in his throat. He turned and stared hard at the inanimate image. This was another god altogether. He must not let his sudden fury at Tion spill over onto Prylis. He must not antagonize the god of learning, who had granted him this wisdom.

And the Liberator—D'ward had done far more for him than Tion ever had. Must he now lead D'ward to his death?

"Lord, how can I ever persuade the Liberator to come? There is danger!"

*"Mmph! See what you mean. Well, your new insight will be a sign to him, and . . . yes . . . we shall find you some assistance. Go outside."*

More bewildered than ever, Dosh genuflected to the god, then stumbled over to the door. He stepped out into blinding sunlight. A hand grabbed his hair and hurled him forward. He pitched down the steps and sprawled on the gravel. Through sudden tears of pain he saw shiny boots all around him.

". . . is no Nagian!" said a harsh voice.

"Not with hair that color," another agreed. "We can kill this one."

"Feed him to the worms."

"Sacrilege!" someone bleated. "You violate the holy sanctuary!"

"Take him outside the gate, then," said the first.

Dosh heard a strange moaning noise and realized it came from himself. Rough hands grabbed his arms and hauled him to his feet. He was surrounded by eight or nine Thargian lancers—hard, wiry men, in green and black leather riding gear, in bronze helmets, all clean shaven in Thargian fashion. He tried to speak and merely gibbered.

The abbot was flustering around in the background, wringing his hands and still protesting the sacrileges: violence on the steps of the minster, moas desecrating the gardens, general lack of respect. Followers of Karzon could not be expected to pay much heed to a priest of Prylis, and these troopers were not about to create precedents like that.

"Move, scum!" said the leader.

As Dosh was jerked forward, the minster doors behind him flew open with a boom.

*"Stop!"* roared a voice of thunder.

The hands released him. He staggered and almost fell.

*"Come in here, all of you!"* No mortal could be that loud.

The image still seemed to be marble, and yet it was also flesh. The scroll was almost vellum, and Prylis still held it before him. His eyes were more visibly alive than the rest of him, shining as blue as D'ward's. His hair had taken on a golden hue.

The abbot and the Thargians groveled before him. Behind them, Dosh knelt respectfully, then stared disbelievingly at the idol. That pose with the vertical scroll—it was deliberately obscene! Why had he not noticed sooner? *New insight* the god had said. . . . The Joker mocked his worshippers!

A voice of thunder rolled around the chapel: *"Barbarians! Say why we should not smite you for your sacrilege?"*

The lancers moaned and gabbled.

"Lord!" their leader croaked. "We followed orders. We were told that Holy Karzon—"

*"This place does not belong to Karzon! You, Ksargirk Captain, are sworn to his vile cult of the Blood and Hammer, we see. You also, Tsuggig Lancer, and Twairkirg Lancer . . . and Progyurg Lancer, too. Savages! Renounce your oaths!"*

The soldiers howled.

*"Abjure or die and be forever damned!"* the god screamed, louder than ever.

In quavering mumbles, the four men renounced their oaths to whatever the Blood and Hammer was—some warriors' cult of Karzon, presumably, probably nasty. Dosh decided he was enjoying this unexpected change of fortune. Prompted by the divine bellow, the bullyboys denounced the Man and swore never to seek his patronage again. They were practically wetting their breeches with terror now.

It was nice to have friends in positions of authority.

*"Now swear eternal obedience to us! All of you! Swear that forever more you will worship the Youth above all gods."*

Could it be that the god was enjoying this also? There was an odd timbre to his thunder, which in a mortal might have hinted of bluster. How often would an obscure, unassuming deity like Prylis indulge in such assertive behavior?

The troopers swore allegiance to Tion with great reluctance, some of them almost weeping. Dosh suspected that the apostates would arrive in the heavens most speedily if Karzon ever heard of this breach of faith—or if any of their friends as much as suspected, either.

*"Now,"* the god said in a slightly less deafening roar, *"there is a great evil abroad in the world, and you are called to strive against it."*

"Tell us its name, Lord," said the captain, sounding encouraged.

*"Its name is Zath!"*

The troopers exchanged horrified glances.

*"You are charged to give all help to our trusted servant Dosh Envoy, whom you sought*

*to slay. You will obey his orders without question or hesitation and if necessary to the death, until such time as he releases you. Rise, Dosh Envoy."*

Dosh stood up. One by one the Thargian lancers knelt to him and swore unlimited obedience. Yes, he was definitely enjoying this! He was going to continue enjoying it, too. That young one . . . Progyurg? Yes, Progyurg Lancer was a really cute-looking kid. . . . Obey without question or hesitation, *mm?*

For some reason, Dosh suddenly thought of D'ward. Tarion certainly saw nothing wrong in using the authority of rank to satisfy personal whims. Progyurg himself would certainly not argue, because Thargians put obedience to superior officers before anything else in the world, but D'ward would disapprove. Dosh felt sure of that, although he did not know why or how he knew. Well, he would think over the morals of the situation before he detailed Progyurg for special duties.

*"Holy Father Abbot?"* boomed the god.

The old man was still groveling. "Lord?"

*"Dosh Envoy may need your assistance also. Aid him. Um. That seems to be all, doesn't it? Tee-hee! Well, I suppose you are all our servants now and we give you our blessing."*

The image was marble again.

Poor Progyurg Lancer toppled to the floor in a dead faint.

# 38

The army had camped amid the ruins of a great manor. The big house was a smoking, stinking ruin, but some of the many outbuildings had survived. Together with stone walls around yards and paddocks, these gave shelter from the cool wind that had sprung up at dusk, and they concealed the little campfires. Eltiana's red eye stared down from the darkening sky; the stars were gathering.

The Sonalby troop was crammed into a tiny courtyard. Ysian spotted Prat'han right away, and began jostling her way quickly toward him, stumbling over legs. Nagians accepted her much more readily than the Joalians did. She was D'ward's woman, and if D'ward had chosen to bring his concubine along while forbidding anyone else to do so, that was his leader's privilege as far as they were concerned. They would be shocked speechless if they knew that D'ward had never as much as kissed her. Dosh Envoy had guessed, but Dosh was a creepily perceptive person.

The Sonalby troop especially regarded the Liberator as one of themselves; they seemed to approve of his choice of woman, and now they greeted Ysian with whoops and crude jokes in the gabbling Nagian accents. They were *definitely* not thinking of her as a baby sister, which was a nice change. When she said she was looking for D'ward, of course, the humorists shouted that she mustn't tire the poor man, should at least wait until bedtime, and so on. The others laughed and agreed. She was used to that now. In half a fortnight with the army, she had learned a great deal about men that she had never known before, and one of the things she had learned was they rarely thought of anything other than sex. Their single-mindedness was quite astonishing.

Big, gangling Prat'han was squatting by one of the fires, roasting something on a stick. He yelled at the jokers to be quiet. Then he shone big teeth at her. "The battle-master has gone scouting with the Thoid'lbians, lady. They wanted to see if they can climb that ruined tower. Should be back soon. Stay and keep us company, for we are all lonely for the sound of a woman's voice." The audience shouted agreement.

Ysian was very conscious of so many men close around her, a very odd feeling, and not unpleasant. Their attention was flattering. But she had come to see if Prat'han would help her rescue Dosh, and now she realized she could not ask him in public like this. Relations between Nagians and Joalians were bad. She knew D'ward was worried; she must not do anything to make matters worse. Prat'han must know that too, so he might refuse to get involved. Or too many of the troop might get too much involved, and she would have started a riot. Bother!

"I really can't stay just now, Troopleader. I'd like to. Maybe later."

Prat'han said that was a pity. The men needed the company of beautiful women to keep their morale up. Then he held out his stick to her. Sonalby, he explained, had met with good fortune that afternoon—a marshy pond, full of fat lizards. The tails were a great delicacy, and she must eat this one while it was hot. He smiled proudly.

She took the stick and tried not to look at the smoking lump on the end of it. She would not eat lizard if she were dying of starvation, but it might be just the excuse she needed to intrude on the terrible things she had seen happening.

"This is very kind of you," she said. "It smells delicious! You won't mind if I take it with me, will you?"

"Alas! We are heartbroken. Where must you rush off to so urgently?"

"Oh . . ." Ysian was already edging away over the tangle of legs. "A friend needs me. Something I must do before D'ward gets back."

Of course they chose to misinterpret her words, but nothing she could have said would have been proof against their coarse humor. With the raucous suggestions scorching her ears, she hurried off into the shadows. Her father had never talked like that. D'ward never talked like that. D'ward was different. She rather wished he were not quite so different. She thought he would approve of what she was doing now, because she knew he disliked deliberate cruelty as much as she did. She was so mad she did not care overmuch whether he would approve or not.

She detoured around the charred and stinking remains of a stable to avoid a camp of Joalians. She reached the shed she wanted. The door was ajar, casting a thin wedge of lamplight over the cobbled yard outside. The horrible noises had stopped. Ignoring sudden quiverings in her insides, she kicked the door open and marched right in. The hut was larger than she had realized, bare except for a workbench along one wall; from the smell, it was probably where wool was baled at shearing time.

Two of the Joalians were sitting on the bench, feet dangling. Two more were leaning against their shadows on the wall. Dosh lay curled up in the middle of the floor, his arms bound behind him and more rope around his ankles. The old scars on his face were hidden by blood and fresh welts, his legs were bruised and scratched. Rips in his shirt showed more bruises on his ribs, repulsively bright on his fair skin.

"Well!" One of the Joalians on the bench paused in licking his knuckles. "Brought us some supper, did you?"

"Not for you!" Ysian did not look at him. She knelt down beside Dosh and pulled out her knife. D'ward had given it to her when they left Lemod, telling her to keep it handy always.

"Hey!" the Joalian shouted. "What do you think you're doing?"

"He can't eat with his hands tied, Troopleader." She sawed at the rope around the prisoner's wrists. It had bitten into the flesh, and his hands were hideously red.

He peered at her out of the corner of his eye, looking very astonished. He gasped as the rope parted.

The Joalian leader pushed himself off the bench, his boots thudding on the flagstones. He was big and swarthy and hook nosed. His shadow leaped up behind him, huge and menacing. "Who said you could do that? And why should a traitor eat before honest men?"

However disgusting the grisly lump on the stick seemed to her, all four guards were eying it hungrily.

"He's not a traitor until the battlemaster says so! Here!" She thrust her revolting offering at Dosh, who was struggling to sit up.

"Need a minute," he muttered, chaffing his hands.

"You give that to me!" The Joalian bent to grab it from her.

Ysian whipped it around behind her back. "Go and get your own food! This is for Dosh Envoy." She tried to glare up at him, but kneeling was not a good position for glaring.

"Dosh Traitor you mean! Just because you're the battlemaster's harlot doesn't give you the right to order me around, missy!" He tried again to take the stick from her. "You don't have his authority to do that!"

"Yes, she does," D'ward said, marching in. Golbfish Hordeleader's cumbersome bulk filled the doorway behind him.

Ysian relaxed with a rush of relief. She had been starting to think that things might shortly begin to get somewhat out of hand. Dosh grinned at her, showing blood on his teeth. She handed him the stick. He took it in his swollen fingers but did not try to eat.

The Joalians had come to attention. Tall and fearsomely blue-eyed, D'ward glanced them over, then spared a longer, harder look for Dosh. He was making no effort to hide his anger, and it filled the shed like a winter frost. He spoke first to Ysian.

"What are you doing here, *Viks'n*?"

"I brought Dosh Envoy some supper."

"Why?"

"I thought they might stop torturing him if I was here."

D'ward sighed and gave her his exasperated look, which always annoyed her tremendously. "Well, cut his feet loose too. Now, Dibber Troopleader, I want an explanation. Report!"

"Sir! Saw this man consorting with the enemy, sir!" The Joalian waited, as if nothing more need be said. When nothing more was said, he spoke again, but with much less confidence. "This afternoon you passed the word for him, sir. He wasn't found, sir, was he? About sunset, sir, we saw him in the distance with a band of Thargians. We watched him try to sneak into camp unobserved . . . arrested him . . . sir. . . ."

D'ward's eyes shone like blue steel. "You did not report to Kolgan Coadjutant or Golbfish Hordeleader?"

"Er . . . waiting for you, sir . . ."

"So you questioned him yourself?"

"Er, yes, sir." The troopleader's face glistened wetly under the lantern—he was scared and serve him right!

"Did he tell you anything?"

"Some lies about acting on your orders, sir."

"And you know he wasn't, do you?"

An insect thudded into the lamp and bounced off. In the awful silence, it sounded like a drumbeat. When D'ward spoke, his voice was even softer but full of menace.

"Dosh Envoy, did any of them try to stop what was happening?"

"Not that I heard." Amazingly, Dosh was now nibbling at the lizard tail. He seemed remarkably cheerful, considering the beating he had suffered.

D'ward pronounced judgment. "Dibber, you exceeded your authority. Go back to your troop. Inform them that you have been demoted and they are to elect a successor. He is to report to Golbfish Hordeleader immediately with recommendations for your further punishment. That means all of you. Go!"

The prince moved his mass aside, and the four men stampeded out into the darkness. Golbfish pulled the door closed, with himself on the inside of it. He was smiling, yet somehow he did not look pleased. Ysian stood up, planning to leave the three men to their deliberations. She had done what she came for. She thought she deserved a little more appreciation for it, too.

"You'd better stay, *Viks'n*." D'ward heaved himself up on the bench, feet dangling. He stared down at Dosh with disgust. "Oh, you! What sort of mess are you in this time?"

"Got a message for you," Dosh said, still chewing. Apparently he was actually enjoying the revolting meal. He could not have been eating well lately.

Puzzled that she was wanted, but quite pleased, Ysian moved back against the wall. She caught the prince's eye. He nodded and smiled at her, and she did not understand that, either. She liked the big hordeleader. He always spoke to her as if she were a lady.

"From?" D'ward said.

Dosh glanced warily at Ysian and Golbfish. "A friend of a friend. A servant of a former master of mine. The one you guessed."

"Aha! You can talk about him now?"

Dosh nodded. "The servant removed the master's . . . directive." He choked. "That bastard! That mudpig! He stole three years of my life!"

He tried to rise. Golbfish went to help him, and he staggered to his feet. "This aspect's all right—I think. He wants to meet you."

D'ward raised his eyebrows.

Golbfish made a rumbling sound. "Now wait a minute! Let's hear where you went— and how you came back. And what about the Thargians?"

Dosh leaned both arms on the bench. He must be in a lot of pain, though he was trying not to show it. "Liberator—"

"Don't call me that! You'd better speak openly. I trust these two, and they deserve to know what secret they're keeping. Out with it!"

"Sure?" Dosh said impudently. He was never as respectful to the Liberator as everyone else was. "Well, I went to a temple, to report to Tion. I met his avatar Prylis—god of learning. I gave him my report, but . . . Well, he isn't Tion!"

"Of course he isn't. None of them are. What else?"

"He wants you to go to him. Very important, he said. Some Thargians had followed me. Prylis bound them to my service. They have to obey me!" Dosh tried to laugh, winced, and rubbed his ribs regretfully.

Ysian caught Golbfish's eye again. He was frowning, but he did not look as surprised as she would have expected. Perhaps D'ward had told him some of the strange things he had told her—things that would have shocked her parents to the core, things she would have believed to be dreadful heresies had she heard them from anyone but D'ward.

"I saw that temple," Golbfish said. "If you went there, then how did you catch up with us?"

Dosh twisted his bruised lips into a parody of a smile. "I rode a moa."

"That's impossible!"

"That's what I thought, but it isn't. Not if you ride double. The brute didn't like it, but it brought me."

After a moment, D'ward said, "I'll have to trust you. What does this Prylis person want with me?"

"Dunno. Don't question gods."

"Maybe you should." D'ward stared down at his knees for a while, swinging his feet. "How far away is this temple?"

Dosh shrugged, wiping his mouth. "Ten miles, maybe. My lancers will take us. You can be back before morning."

"Battlemaster!" Golbfish exclaimed. "You cannot seriously . . ."

But obviously D'ward was planning to go. How could he trust his life to Dosh Envoy? Ysian did not *like* Dosh. D'ward had told her why the other men disliked him, but that should not matter to her. There was just something *wrong* about him—not wrong enough to justify what had been done to him tonight, though.

"I have to risk it, Highness," D'ward said. "It could be very important. If I'm not back by dawn, lead the army into the pass—and keep going, understand! On no account wait for me or look for me!"

"Battlemaster—"

"Can't pass up a chance to have a god as an ally, can I? Consult Kolgan, but you make the decisions, apart from the orders I just gave you. I'll tell him." He turned to Dosh, who was trying not to show his pleasure at the Liberator's faith in him. "You coming too? Can you make it in your condition?"

"I'm the toughest bastard in the whole army."

"I know you are. Very well, I'll make my rounds now, and you get yourself cleaned up. Nobody else must know I've gone, or half the Nagians will come after me, no matter what I say! As soon as—"

"Me too!" Ysian said. She was *not* going to be left behind like a child!

The three men all turned to stare at her; she racked her brains for some convincing reason why she should not be left behind like a child.

"Now, ma'am!" Golbfish said. "This is no expedition for a—"

"Me too! D'ward, you told me where the safest place was!"

The safest place was next to him, he had said, because the *Filoby Testament* predicted many things he would do before he died. Besides, even if the army escaped back to Nagvale and Joalvale, what would become of her, a Lemodian traitor? Even if she could ever return to Lemod, no decent man would marry her now. Next to D'ward was the only place she wanted to be, ever. She could never tell him that, but if he ever asked . . .

He was grinning. "Quite sure, *Viks'n*? It'll mean a couple of hard rides and no sleep all night."

"Quite sure!"

"Thargian patrols may catch us and kill us."

"You don't believe that or you wouldn't be going!"

He chuckled and gave her one of his rare, wonderful smiles that always lit up the world. "Come, then." He gestured at Dosh. "Help this traveling disaster clean up, will you, *Viks'n*?" He jumped off the bench and disappeared out the door, leaving the two men staring after him in disbelief.

"What's this *Viks'n* he calls you?" Dosh demanded.

"Just a pet name."

Golbfish shrugged. "In classical Joalian, '*viksen*' means 'courage.'"

Dosh said, "Oh."

Ysian had not known that and felt pleased. D'ward had told her it was the name of a small animal with red hair, and her hair was *not* red. It was dark auburn.

# 39

As they crept out of the camp, D'ward took Ysian's hand. She thought *progress!* Then she decided he was just being protective again, babying her. The only time he had ever touched her was when they had been crossing Lemodwater, escaping from the city. His strength on that occasion had impressed her a lot, but she would not agree that he was necessarily more surefooted in darkness and rough terrain just because he was a man. Not without a demonstration, anyway.

And this could never be a truly romantic stroll, since Trumb had risen, three-quarters full above the branches. His eerie green light made people look like corpses, definitely not romantic. Eltiana's rosy glow was the moonlight for lovers. Besides, Dosh was there too, leading the way. He was moving like a corpse, or at least a half-dead person, and ought to be in bed. So not romantic. More like goose-pimply and exciting. Nevertheless, she let D'ward continue to hold her hand, squeezing his fingers discriminatingly from time to time.

They avoided the sentries' notice—which annoyed D'ward a lot. Then Dosh said he had better go ahead in case of accidents, and in a minute she had D'ward to herself.

"Are you being romantic or just baby-sistering me again?"

He released her hand. "Sorry."

"Sorry for what? You really are the most maddening man!"

His eyes and teeth showed bright in the moonlight. "Now what have I done?"

"It's what you don't do that bothers me! It is very insulting for a woman to find herself ignored like this when she has made her inclinations perfectly clear!"

"With the knife, you mean? Oh, I certainly understood the message. I have never been so scared in my life!"

"That was before I got to know you. Why don't you even kiss me?"

He sighed. "I've told you, Ysian. I am promised to another. You're a sweet kid and—"

"I am not a kid!"

"And rarely sweet?"

"Exceedingly sweet. Try me."

"I ought to put you over my knee and spank you."

"Promise to take my pants off first?"

"Ysian! You should be ashamed of yourself."

"I am ashamed of myself. I've tried everything I know—" At that point she tripped and almost fell. D'ward did not even try to catch her.

It was humiliating.

After twenty minutes or so, they came to a bridge over a stream. A voice from the shadows up ahead demanded, "Password?"

"Flower of shame," Dosh replied. "Captain Ksargirk?"

"Yes, sir."

"There are three of us. You take this man. And the, er, boy can go behind Tsuggig. I'll ride with Progyurg."

"His mount is only a five-year-old, sir. Better to—"

"That's an order!"

"Whatever you say, sir."

Ysian grinned to herself, wondering if D'ward noticed how much Dosh enjoyed flaunting his authority; the Thargian certainly had.

A chance to ride a moa had seemed like a big adventure. Moas were big—she had never realized just how big. More Thargians led the steeds in from the darkness. The long necks seemed to stretch halfway up to Trumb, and the saddles were higher than the men's heads, even D'ward's! How was she ever going to get up there? More important, when and how would she come down?

The lancers began hauling on reins, some of them lifting themselves right off the ground and hanging there. The moas snickered complaint, then one by one reluctantly folded their huge legs and sat.

"Ready, boy?" the Captain asked Ysian. "Hold on for your life, now!"

"Er, me? Ready for what?"

The nearest lancer vaulted into his saddle and at the same moment Ksargirk Captain and another man lifted Ysian bodily and more or less *threw* her at his back. She flung her arms around him and the moa went mad. It leaped straight up into the sky, while the other men cleared rapidly out of the way. It came down and went up again. It shrilled and brayed, kicked and cavorted. She clung grimly to the rider, her face pressed hard against his tunic. She clung so hard she wondered he could breathe, and yet she was bounced madly for what felt like several hours. Sometimes she came down on the moa's hairy rump, sometimes on the edge of the saddle, which hurt. Her legs flapped up and down like wings. Tsuggig cursed a stream of guttural Thargian that she could not understand and the moa ignored. She heard a few cries of pain from Dosh—he really ought not to be doing this in his condition! D'ward made no noise, but soon the whole night seemed to be full of bucking, rampaging moas. Oh, poor Dosh!

All nine moas made a fuss at being mounted, but the three with passengers were by far the worst. The other six calmed down after a few token leaps. Her lancer was the last to bring his mount under control, perhaps because it was the biggest, perhaps because both Dosh and D'ward weighed so much more than she did. When it began to behave itself, tired by its antics, he was given his lance, which one of the other men had been holding for him. Then Ksargirk Captain shouted an order, and the troop set off along the road. *Streaked* off along the road! Never had Ysian traveled so fast in her life. The moa seemed to cover eight or ten feet in a stride, but its gait was amazingly smooth. Hedges and trees went hurtling past, a blur in the night. The wind blew cold on her face, and although the saddle was too small for two, she soon decided that she was enjoying herself after all.

Clouds had covered most of the green moon when the weary moas strode into the grounds of the monastery. Two elderly monks were waiting with lanterns at the door of the temple, and one of them wore a golden chain, so he must be the abbot. Ksargirk Captain reined in at the steps, and then sprang nimbly from his moa's back. He made a very graceful landing, and saluted the abbot. A lancer dismounted the same way and took the captain's reins. Ysian looked down at the ground thoughtfully.

Tsuggig Lancer twisted around to peer at her. He was older than she had realized, clean shaven in Thargian fashion, but not really ugly. "You're no boy!" He had not spoken a word to her until then.

"I wasn't the last time I looked."

He made a growly sound, and then chuckled. "If you were when you got on, then you might not be now. But you did good. My pleasure. Can you get down without help?"

"Of course." Ysian pushed herself off and slid spryly down . . . down . . .

Her legs buckled under her and she fell flat on her back, banging her head on the gravel. Bother! The moa shrilled mockingly and shifted its hooves as if readying a kick. She scrambled up and moved to a safe distance to dust herself off, feeling oddly shaky. The ground seemed too close, as though her legs had shrunk, and much of the rest of her felt as if she had been flogged by the public executioner. D'ward had already dismounted and gone to help Dosh. She took a hard look at the forbidding figure of the old abbot and decided he might not approve of women in his monastery. She had better remain a boy.

Four of them went into the temple, for Dosh was barely capable of standing on his own, let alone going anywhere. He gave the abbot some very snappy orders to look after "his" men, then called on Progyurg Lancer to dismount and help him walk. He hobbled inside with one arm draped over the Thargian's shoulders and the other on D'ward's. Ysian followed.

No one had said she shouldn't.

Her experience with temples was limited. This one was small and dark, no more than a barren stone box, chilly and dusty smelling. It was not nearly as impressive as the temple of Eth'l in Lemod. As the lancer brought the lantern closer, the image of the god emerged from the gloom. Being an aspect of the Youth, Prylis was depicted in the nude, but he held a scroll of learning in a strategic position. Progyurg and D'ward lowered Dosh to his knees.

"Good lad," Dosh whispered. "Leave the light here."

"Sir!" The lancer departed. He was a nice-looking boy, not much older than Ysian herself, she thought. Not as handsome as D'ward, of course. The door thumped closed behind him.

She knelt and was surprised to see D'ward still standing. He had his arms folded and seemed to be shivering. The temple was cool but not as cold as that.

"Holy Prylis!" Dosh proclaimed. "I have done as you commanded."

Silence.

The flame in the lantern danced. Highlights squirmed on the shiny surface of the statue, but nothing else happened.

"I am the Liberator," D'ward said. "You summoned me."

More silence.

"Perhaps he's asleep," D'ward said.

"Gods don't sleep!" Ysian protested.

"I'll bet they do!"

"This is annoying!" D'ward added, but she could tell that he was more angry than that. "I have an army to look after and a war to fight. We must get back before dawn. How do you waken a god, Dosh?"

"Nibble his ear?"

"I'd break my teeth. No better ideas? What's behind that door?"

"A little room with a table. Nothing else. It doesn't go anywhere."

"Prylis!" D'ward shouted. "We've come!"

Even more silence.

"What if you try your ritual? No, I suppose not."

"Definitely not!" Dosh groaned and eased himself down into a sitting position. "Looks like we'll have to wait for morning."

"Damned if I will . . . Ah!" D'ward walked over to the door in the corner. He opened it, went in, closed it behind him . . . and again there was silence.

After a minute or so, Dosh said, "Go and look for him, *Viks'n.*"

"That's not my name! Only D'ward calls me that!"

"Then, my lady Ysian, will you go and look for him—please?"

She clambered to her feet and walked over to the mysterious door in the corner. Behind it there was only darkness. She went back to Dosh and fetched the lantern. Shadows leaped around the edges of her vision as she carried it. As Dosh had said, there was a little room there, with a table piled high with books. Apart from that, there was nothing at all—no other door, no window, and no D'ward.

Ysian and Dosh waited. After half an hour or so, she realized that she could hardly keep her eyes open and he was unconscious, or at least he could only groan when she tried to rouse him. So she went out and asked the abbot to send some monks in to get Dosh—he should be put to bed and cared for, she explained. She told Ksargirk Captain that he and his men could stand down; she asked the abbot, very politely, if she might have something to eat and a place to sleep. She thought nothing more was going to happen before morning.

# VII

## *Revealed Check*

# 40

Smedley came down very late for breakfast. He had a sour, sandy feeling behind his eyes, and he had cut himself twice while shaving. Worst of all, the underwear he had rinsed out before going to sleep had not dried completely in the night. He would not be able to hire a valet until the war was over. Of more immediate importance were adequate clothing and some fags.

The great Victorian dining table would have seated at least a dozen. Exeter sat alone at it, poring over a thick book propped amid a field of dirty dishes. He looked up wryly.

"Morning," Smedley grunted.

"Good morning! *Beautiful* morning! Lovelier now for your presence, of course."

"Put it where the monkey put the nuts. Any tea in the pot?"

Smirking, Exeter removed the cozy and swished the teapot. He removed the lid and peered inside. He pulled a face. "Lots, but I think someone's been washing boots in it."

"Just what I need!" Smedley sat down.

Exeter poured. "The ladies have gone off to shop and call on the erudite Nathaniel Glossop. There's a couple of congealed eggs there and some petrified bacon. I'll warm it up for you—seems there's laws about not wasting food. . . ."

"Just the tea will do, thank you."

Mercifully Exeter said nothing more for a while. He closed his book and carried it out of the room. When he returned without it, though, he was still infernally cheerful. "Looking up Prylis. Not the one I met."

Smedley ended his contemplation of the heap of soggy toast. "Prylis?"

"Chappie who invented the wooden horse. Didn't take out a patent, though, and Odysseus swiped the idea. Probably spoke much better Greek than the one I met. Sure you don't want eggs and bacon?"

"Quite sure."

"We both need our shirts ironed. I'd try it, except I don't know how."

"Me neither," Smedley lied. To avert further small talk, he said, "Tell me about Olympus."

Exeter crossed his legs and hugged one knee with both hands. He stared for a moment at Smedley with his impossibly blue eyes.

"Told you, old man. It's very much like a station in the colonies somewhere, an outpost of civilization in the bush. The *tyikank* and *entyikank* live in nice houses, the natives are the servants. Like Kenya, India, or all those other places. Main difference is the natives are as white as we are. Redheads, most of them. The *tyikank* are a mixed bunch, but a lot of them are English originally. Recruited here. Some aren't. A couple are from other worlds altogether. Some of them have been on Nextdoor a deuce of a long time, but the Service itself isn't all that old. The guv'nor was one of the founders."

"But what do they do?"

"Argue. Plan. Squabble. Go out on missionary work." Exeter continued to study Smedley as if watching his brain cells twitch. His own face was illegible as the Sphinx. "One committee's still working on the True Gospel. Another runs an intelligence branch, tracking what's going on—politically and theosophically both. Anything that may help overthrow the Pentatheon."

That steady gaze was starting to get under Smedley's skin. "You make it sound as if you don't approve."

"Oh, it's a wonderful idea. A worthy cause. The strangers are definitely parasites. Some of them do a little bit of good in passing, like Tion and his festivals. A lot of them are . . . well, horrors."

Smedley poured another cup of tanning fluid. "I suppose if you're going to live forever you don't rush at the hedges?" He looked up, and the blue eyes were still boring into him. "If it's such a wonderful idea, why are you being so shifty about it?"

Exeter sighed, put his foot back on the floor, and turned to stare out the window. "It's just not that simple, old man. It's not like Dr. Livingstone and the witch doctors. It's not Saint Eggbeater burning down the druids' grove. These Johnnies have *power!* Real power. Start blaspheming in their temples and you're liable to drop dead. Nothing like a public thunderbolt to impress the masses—and then the mana just pours in to replace what's been spent."

"So start a new religion, a good one! You mentioned a Church of the Undivided. The Service is behind it?"

"It *is* the Service. The trouble is that the old gods have cornered the market. Say you find yourself a node—there's still good ones around—and you set up a new god, then you get asked what is he the god *of*? Anything worthwhile will have its own divinity already, and he or she will be an avatar of one of the Five. The Pentatheon have all bets covered. Even the Undivided tends to get identified with Visek, the Parent, so the mana benefits them . . . him? Her? Visek's sort of androgynous. . . . Visek hasn't taken sides yet. I think the Service does him more good than harm. More good than they want to, certainly."

It was definitely not the right time of day for riddles, but Smedley had started this. And he did want to know more about Olympus and the Service. If he didn't find out from Exeter now, he would probably never have another chance. Who could resist the chance to learn about an alternative world?

Or was he just looking for a cause?

"You said some of the gods—strangers—some of them are all-right types?"

"A few." Exeter began fiddling with a spoon, drawing lines on the tablecloth. "A few are secretly Service supporters. Lukewarm, mostly. Fence-sitters. One or two have converted, but not many have got away with it."

"Converted?"

"Mm. Like the Irish goddess Bríg, who became Saint Bridget. Or Cybele becoming the Black Madonna—back in the Dark Ages, scores of pagan deities became Christian saints. But in the Vales they're all vassals of the Five. If Tion, say, catches one of his minions consorting with the enemy, then he is seriously peeved."

"If Christianity did it in Europe, then why not try Christianity on Nextdoor?"

Exeter looked up with a smile. "And where exactly is Jerusalem? Who did you say these Romans were? Egypt? The Red Sea? I've been on the other side of this conversation a few times. What I got told then was that one big advantage Christianity had over the pagan gods was that it had a real historical basis, instead of just myth. But that's in this world. On Nextdoor it isn't."

"So what is the Church of the Undivided?"

"A hodgepodge. A Unitarian concoction of ethics and morals: Christian, Socratic, Buddhist, et cetera—the Golden Rule plus a universal god too holy to be named. That's an attempt to shut out Visek. As I said, that doesn't seem to work awfully well. It's a frightfully antiseptic sort of religion. No passion, you know?"

Smedley reached for toast and butter. "You're saying there's really nothing you can do, then?"

Exeter sighed. "There's nothing *I* can do, no. I'm branded as the Liberator and anything I tried to do would be warped by the prophecy and lead to killing Zath. That brings on catastrophe."

"Why?"

Exeter looked irritated. "You'll see if you just think about how it would have to be done. It would need an enormous amount of mana. How do I get that? What would I have to become?"

Yes, Julian should have seen that. If Exeter had invented all of this, he must have spent a lot of time working out the details. It was as logical as whist. "You'd have to start playing by their rules, you mean?"

"Playing their game. That's why I shan't ever go back there. As to whether there's anything *you* can do, old man . . . you want to try?"

Smedley was not ready to face that question yet, but his pulse rate had jumped a fraction. "I'm asking what the Service can do."

"Keep trying and hoping." Exeter's eyes were gleaming. Was he poking fun at the Service? Or at Smedley, for believing this fantasy? Or was he a supporter, coolly understating his enthusiasm? No way to tell, with him.

"But not praying? How do the faithful pray to a nameless god?"

"The whole point is that they don't. They pray to the apostles to intercede for them, because only the apostles can speak to the god. The apostles are not gods themselves, because he's Undivided; they're just the Chosen. Strangers from Olympus, of course." Exeter smiled wryly. "The Service doesn't have the manpower to put a missionary in every pot, but they do try to have someone drop by every couple of fortnights. You understand why they have to do it that way?"

"So everybody shares in the mana? Does that work?"

"It works after a fashion. A chicken sacrificed to the Undivided in Joal, say, will not provide the Service with anything like the mana it would give Astina if it died to her glory in her temple there. Mana will flow between nodes, but there's a lot of steam leaks out. No other reason?"

Then he raised a quizzical eyebrow and waited.

Smedley began to feel nettled. "You're three years ahead of me and it's too early in the morning."

Exeter laughed, taking pity on him. "Right-oh! The real problem, my boy, it that we're all human. The reason the apostles are set up as a sort of nameless divine committee is that power corrupts, as Alice said the other night. The Service has had agents go over to the other side. They discover what they can do with mana and they like it. Set a chap up in his own chapel and pretty soon he begins to feel like it's *his* chapel, and these are *his* people. Sooner or later one of the Five will send a henchman around. Some of our chaps sell out. There was an Italian named Giovani who became Jovanee Karzon, god of wagons. All the best attributes have been taken, but there's always room for more. Did you know the Romans had a patron goddess of the-light-in-rooms-where-women-are-giving-birth?"

"No," Smedley said grumpily, thinking that he did not want to. Having buttered the toast, he supposed he had better eat the horrid stuff. "You're saying it's hopeless?"

"No. Here's what I think, on the level: It may work! They may overthrow the Pentatheon. They're not fools, they're dedicated and well-meaning, all of them. But it's going to be a long, long struggle. Two or three hundred years at the least. Christianity took longer. Islam was faster, but more brutal. If you think of mana as being like money, then the Five are stinking rich and getting richer. The Undivided is scratching for crumbs. . . ."

The doorbell rang.

The two exchanged glances. Then Exeter pushed back his chair and stood up tall. He adjusted his tie and straightened his jacket. "That may just be the Women's Institute soliciting contributions for the church fete. Or it may not be." He strode out, closing the door.

Smedley continued to masticate long-dead toast. Why was he so fascinated by the idea of Olympus? Was he just trying to flee from reality—the war, his mutilation, lost friends, the changed face of England? If he nurtured secret fancies of magic giving him his hand back, then he was seriously bonkers. Cold logic said he should not make any decisions yet, not for a long time. On the other hand, his nerves were improving. He had not wept since leaving Staffles. Dreaming of Olympus and Exeter's fantasy world was probably a lot healthier for him at the moment than brooding over his own reality. He had always been too prone to introspection.

He heard voices as the door began to open.

"I'll put the kettle on, then. You go in."

In came portly Ginger Jones, attempting to polish his pince-nez with a silk handkerchief and keep hold of a pair of bicycle clips at the same time. He looked hot. "Morning, Captain!"

"Morning, sir. Any news?"

Ginger put his specs on his nose, his handkerchief in one pocket, and his bicycle clips in another. "No. Oh . . . thought you might need these." From yet another pocket, he produced two packets of Player's.

Smedley's heart melted. "May you be blessed with many sons and your herds prosper!" He fumbled for matches.

"Lord, how would I explain that to the Head?" Ginger sat down chuckling. "Thought I'd drop over and hear some more of the Exeter-Through-the-Looking-Glass saga." He glanced up as the man in question returned. "I posted your letter. Caught the evening collection, too."

"So it should arrive today," Smedley said, "if it is going to arrive?"

Exeter sat down. "If it's going to arrive, then it has already arrived. It wouldn't even hit the bottom of the pillar-box. It would go straight to somebody's desk."

The others each waited for the other to comment. Eventually Ginger said, "Explain that, would you?"

"I can't. The magic may have been removed, since it does no good now, or it may be still there. But when I was a kid at Fallow and Head Office were keeping an eye on me, then the letters I put in that box went straight to them. I hope there was a spell invoked by that address written in my handwriting. I may be wrong—there may have been a guardian living in the neighborhood, in which case he or she will likely have gone now. I think Creighton would have told me if there had been, but I don't know. Told you it was a long shot." He shrugged.

"Indeed!" Ginger muttered. "I'm trying to remember if I heard the letter drop."

Smedley did want to believe. "It's rather like the portal idea, two worlds touching at a point."

"Mana can certainly be used to warp space," Exeter said, "especially on nodes. The inside of Krobidirkin's tent was bigger than the outside."

"Wonderful idea for luggage."

"Or blocks of flats." He grinned. "Imagine the rent you'd collect! You remember that business with the long strip of paper you give a twist to and then paste . . . ?"

"Möbius strip?"

"Probably. Sounds right. Old Flora-Dora spent half a term trying to get the idea into my skull. All I remember now is that you start at a point and go all the way round, and when you come back you're on the wrong side. It gave me nightmares. Now the chappie Prylis I mentioned last night had a library, a corridor lined with books. At the end you turned right, and there was another corridor lined with books. At the end of that you turned right again. You went around and around in a square—round and round and round, and you never came back to where you started. All the windows had a north view. This was all behind the church, and yet there was nothing there."

"I hadn't thought of the Fallow postbox in quite that way," Ginger said. "No use taking it apart to look?"

"None. The question is," Exeter added, "if it works as I hope it does, then whose desk does it lead to? Head Office or the Blighters? I warn you—this may turn out to be a jolly interesting day."

# 41

Golbfish moved the army out at dawn. He did not like doing so, but the Liberator's orders had been explicit. No one demanded to know why he and not D'ward was setting up the order of march; among five thousand men, the commander's absence would not be noticed for a while yet.

Golbfish himself stayed near the front with Kolgan at his side. The big man's sword arm was in a sling, his face haggard with pain. When the inevitable battle came, he would not be able to fight. If the gods were merciful and the army miraculously won its way home to Joal, he would certainly be put on trial before the People's Assembly. The verdict and sentence could never be in doubt. His beard showed more white than red now.

Food supply was becoming critical. Armies usually went marauding in the autumn, when harvests still filled the barns; no sane infantry ever went anywhere without cavalry to support it. Even Golbfish knew that. Plumes of dust in the distance showed where the Thargian scouts were tracking the invaders and watching their progress. The enemy had mobility—if the Joalians turned aside to pillage, the livestock was removed and the stores destroyed long before men on foot could reach them.

"Why don't they attack?" Kolgan demanded more than once. It was all he ever spoke of. "Why don't they harass us? Why not molest our patrols? Why are they letting us go?"

To that paradox there was no answer. At first the enemy had picked off Joalians whenever they could and left Nagians alone. Now they ignored Joalians also, not meddling even with small bands. All they did was ravage their own land, then stand aside to let the invaders pass. No people should behave like that, least of all the proud and warlike Thargians.

Around mid-morning, the road crested a height of land. Golbfish paused a moment or two to look back at the weary multitude trailing behind him. "It shows already," he muttered.

"What does?" growled Kolgan.

"Yesterday they sang as they marched. Today they're not singing. They're slouching and straggling more than marching."

"They're hungry." Kolgan turned away. Golbfish stayed to watch a little longer, but then he too resumed the journey. Yes, lack of food was a major problem, but lack of D'ward was a greater one. The army might not be aware yet that he was absent, but it was missing him.

The road curved down into a wide valley, but instead of crossing the river, it turned to the north and headed straight toward Thargwall. Consulting his maps as he marched, Golbfish concluded that the river must be Saltorwater; a conspicuous notch in the peaks probably marked Saltorpass itself. If the army could cross over that and reenter Lemodvale, then there was some hope of Joalian reinforcements coming to the rescue. Unless his slimy half brother had changed sides already, Joalia must still hold Nagvale and probably Siopass.

But Saltorpass was the first problem and a perfect site for an ambush. Thargia was in a much better position to bring up reinforcements than Joalia was. If Golbfish were running the Thargian campaign, he would let the invaders into the pass and then bottle them up from both ends. A few days' starvation would force complete surrender, which would yield the maximum harvest of slaves. Golbfish was certainly not running the Thargian campaign, and the men who were might prefer a more violent ending, with Saltorwater running red. That would be more Thargian, more traditional.

The valley was wide and relatively treeless, the fields divided by unmortared stone walls. Here and there, ruined farms still smoked, but the people and their livestock had gone. The only consolation Golbfish could find in the situation was that his right flank was now protected by a raging milky torrent. He withdrew the patrols from that side and spread others farther to the left, but he sensed the jaws of a trap closing around him. He was hungrier than he had ever been in his life.

Wherever D'ward was, he would not be able to rejoin the army until darkness shrouded this barren landscape. He had said he would return, and he had meant what he said, but Golbfish could not help but wonder if the Liberator had gone to meet his ordained destiny elsewhere.

About noon, patrols signaled enemy activity to the north. Shortly after that, forces could be seen gathering on the height of land to the west. There was a lot of dust to the south, too.

The herald came in the middle of the afternoon, and he came from the south. By then every man in the army knew it was surrounded. He was a welcome sight, so he was allowed to pass unmolested. Talking would at least put off the battle for a while. Riding a white moa and bearing a flag of truce, he raced along the columns, being waved forward with no worse abuse than jeering and insults. Undoubtedly he was counting and assessing as he came. He would not be much impressed by that footsore, bedraggled array. Joalians had lost their shiny smartness; Nagians were no longer painted savages. They had merged into a hungry, hopeless rabble.

Advised of the herald's coming, Golbfish hurriedly summoned a few of the closer troopleaders to form a retinue. The Liberator's absence was obvious now. They growled mutinously when he refused to explain. He had no time to explain and no explanation that he was willing to give them anyway. Kolgan sneered in the background, saying nothing to help. D'ward had left Golbfish in charge and Kolgan knew that, but Joalians found loyalty an elusive concept. The Thargians would insist on dealing with a Joalian, so Kolgan was going to be battlemaster again by the end of the negotiations.

What was there to negotiate, though?

Shogby?

Centuries ago—according to a legend that the Thargians insisted was vile slander—they had surrounded a Randorian army at Shogby and had offered mercy. If one quarter of the invaders would surrender and go voluntarily as slaves to the silver mines, they had said, the remainder would be allowed to depart unharmed. After long debate, the Randorians had accepted, drawing lots among themselves to select the sacrificial victims. The next day the Thargians had surrounded the departing three quarters and offered the same terms again.

The first ice of winter and the word of a Thargian, said the proverb.

The herald reined in before the leaders. His ceremonial whites were drab with dust, his mount was labored and steaming, but he stared down from its back with predictable arrogance and the traditional sneer of his craft.

"I come in the name of Holy D'ward!"

Not the Liberator—D'ward Tion, god of heralds. His ritual was brief and to the point. He leaned down, holding out a leather bag. Golbfish dropped a silver coin in it. The herald shook it to demonstrate that there were now two coins in there and that he was therefore bound equally to both sides. He straightened up and came right to business.

"I bring terms from the ephors to your commander."

Golbfish held a spear and shield, wore a loincloth. At his side, Kolgan was clad in Joalian armor and helmet. Around them stood the motley retinue of both peoples, most wearing a random assortment of garb and weapons so that their individual races were not immediately evident—but the herald's gaze was fixed on Golbfish alone.

That was odd. No, that was bad. It probably meant that the Liberator had been captured and interrogated. But apparently the envoy wanted to deal with Golbfish, and D'ward had left him in charge. His childhood ambition, he recalled, had been to write great poetry. "I am leader. Speak and be brief."

The herald's grim smile implied that there was very little to argue about. "The noble Ephors Grarknog and Psaamb send these words: They have twice your number at your rear. Your flank is held by an army little smaller. The noble Ephor Gizmok blocks the pass ahead with a force greater than any I have yet named. The ephors would—"

"That's good!" Golbfish barked. "Glad to hear it. We have been getting very bored lately." His companions laughed on cue. The sound was brittle.

"The ephors would meet with you at sunset. In—"

"The usual Shogby terms, I presume?"

The herald scowled. "Will you hear my message or not?"

"If you will stop insulting my intelligence I will give you a few more minutes." Being deliberately rude was a new experience and quite enjoyable.

"Then hear. In token of their good faith, the noble ephors have refrained from attacking your men these past several days, as you must know. Moreover, they have now halted all movement of their forces and will not advance farther until after the parley. They point out that you are totally at their mercy. Nevertheless they wish to offer you terms."

"Women chatter, men act. Tell them to write their terms on their swords and deliver them in person." Golbfish gestured dismissal and started to turn away.

"They will offer safe passage for all your men, back to Joaldom!"

Golbfish returned to his previous orientation. He was ignorant of military matters, but he did know history and he did know politics. He also knew how the haughty Thargians must feel about the presence of invaders within their home vale. Nothing in the world would persuade the ephors to let them escape scot-free.

"Oh, begone!" he shouted. "You foul the air with your lies and posturings."

"You will not even agree to a parley?"

"I have better things to do with my time than talk about Shogby!" Golbfish was amused how airily he threw that mortal insult at a Thargian warrior. Even a lifelong coward could be assertive when he had an army at his back. "Go tell the Milogians of mercy!"

That was worse. The herald's pallor showed even under the road dust. "You may yet suffer the fate of the Milogians!" His voice croaked with fury.

Golbfish had run out of insults. "Begone!" Again he started to turn away.

"Hear me out!" the herald yelled. "The ephors will come in person to your camp. They will bring with them the Most Holy K'tain Highpriest, primate of all Thargia." He swallowed as if the next part was going to taste ever worse. "In support of the terms they will offer, the ephors will furnish whatever hostages you demand, including their own sons if necessary."

Golbfish realized his mouth was hanging open and closed it quickly. He glanced at his companions and wondered inanely why he had not heard the clatter of jaws dropping all around him. "Ah . . . That's all?"

The herald shuddered. "Could there be more? In all our great history, no such offer has ever been made to an enemy of Thargia. I agreed to deliver it only on condition that my tongue will be cut out when I have returned with your answer. This has been promised me."

Golbfish looked at Kolgan, but the Joalian seemed to be too shocked to speak. He felt little better himself. Even if this was all a trick, merely to make such an offer should be suicidal humiliation for the ephors.

"Why?" he demanded of the herald. "Your words are beyond belief. You claim to have us at your mercy and then throw yourselves at our feet? You will have to explain, or I must assume that Thargians have merely discovered humor."

The man wiped his forehead, where sweat had turned the dust to mud. "I have exceeded my mandate. Pray ignore what I said about tongues. Grant me your answer."

"At sunset . . . within our camp . . . How many?"

"I am to ask for twelve, but accept fewer if necessary."

Either the herald was insane, or Golbfish himself was. He made the stiffest demand he could imagine. "You will deliver fifty fat bullocks to our lines within the hour. Your forces will hold their present positions. At sunset you may send just five suppliants—two ephors with one son apiece, plus the priest. Unarmed, on foot, in civilian clothes."

An army crushed by defeat would have howled at such humiliation, but the herald barely hesitated. "You are leader of the Nagians and you grant them safe conduct upon your personal honor?"

Odder yet! Why had the man been told to make that strange stipulation? Why *Nagians,* when the Joalians were the real enemy?

Then Golbfish realized what was different this time, what was warping warfare, history, religion, and politics into this nightmare tangle. He licked his lips to hide a sudden smile. "I am leader of the Nagians and the Joalians both, and I grant safe conduct upon my honor."

"Then it is agreed! The curse of Holy D'ward to Eternity upon him who says otherwise."

The herald wheeled his moa and flashed away like a leaf in a whirlwind. He was only a speck on the horizon by the time Golbfish emerged from a screaming, cheering riot of Joalians and Nagians. They were clapping him on the back and pumping his hand; they were hugging him and kissing him.

Nobody, they exulted, had ever humbled a Thargian emissary like that. Never. Fat bullocks within the hour? Ephors unarmed and on foot! Ephors surrendering their sons? In the end he was hoisted shoulder-high and paraded through the army as his feat was shouted from troop to troop. They seemed to believe that he had suddenly become a military genius. He found it amusing. He knew D'ward would, if he were there.

He did not try to explain to them. The herald had spoken with the leader of the Nagians. *The Thargians thought they were dealing with the Liberator.* What was going to happen when they discovered their error?

# 42

"That's it!" Edward said. "Harrow Hill! What else?" He jabbed a finger at the map and looked up, beaming triumphantly.

Alice doubted things could be so easy. "They show standing stones there," she agreed, peering. "Why Harrow?"

"Anglo-Saxon. *Hearh* meant a hilltop sanctuary."

"Is there any language you can't speak?" Julian demanded.

"Chinese. And I'm not much good in Thargian. You need a sandpaper throat to pronounce it. But this looks right, and here's the village where we met the Gypsies—Vicarsdown. See the meadow by the river? It all fits."

The five of them were gathered around Mrs. Bodgley's dining room table, examining the maps Mr. Glossop had provided. He had also sent a list of half a dozen megalithic sites around Greyfriars, but obviously Edward was already convinced he had found the one he wanted.

Alice distrusted enthusiasm. "Second choice, just in case?" she asked. Harrow Hill was only nine or ten miles from the Dower House, so she could guess what was going to happen this afternoon.

She had had a busy morning, visiting old Glossop with Mrs. Bodgley and then shopping in Greyfriars. The town itself had not changed in three years, but the effects of the war had been depressingly obvious. That a wealthy lady would have to fetch her own groceries instead of having them delivered—that had been one big difference. The eerie scarcity of young men had been another. Not that their absence had been all bad. Buying men's underwear in Wickenden Bros. Gentlemen's Outfitters might have been a lot more embarrassing had the clerk not been a woman.

Edward completed his survey of the list and shook his head. "Looks like Harrow Hill or nothing. We can run over there after lunch. It's a lovely day."

"Is old Elspeth up to another outing?" Smedley asked.

Mrs. Bodgley shook her head. "Better not. Her wind isn't what it used to be. Mr. Glossop allowed us to borrow his bicycle, though. It's a lady's model of unimpeachable antiquity, but if you don't mind being seen on it, Edward, it should take you there and back."

"I don't mind being *seen*. Being *noticed* might be sticky. Running into old Inspector Leatherdale, for example."

"Why don't you take my bike?" Ginger suggested. "Miss Prescott will doubtless be pleased to accompany you." His expression was unreadable, light reflecting off his pince-nez.

About to suggest that Julian go in her place, Alice caught herself in the nick of time. She had not brought any clothes suitable for cycling, but Edward was beaming at the prospect. "I'd love to," she agreed. "Very kind of you."

"Then that's settled!" Mrs. Bodgley said heartily.

"Ripping!" Then Edward frowned. "One thing, though . . . we shall have to take an offering."

The lady blinked. "What sort of offering? Kill a white lamb, you mean? Or a five-bob note?"

"Something significant." He looked apologetically at Alice. He was flat broke, of course.

"I think I may have something." Mrs. Bodgley swept from the room.

An awkward silence remained. This was the twentieth century. Pagan gods were a permissible subject for conversation, but actually making sacrifice to one would be behavior beyond the bizarre.

"Blood, of course," Edward muttered, "but it would be more fitting to have brought something tangible in this case, I think. . . ."

Alice decided that blood sacrifice was out of the question. She could not possibly summon up enough faith . . . which was the whole point, presumably. Half a crown in the plate was as far as she would go for a pre-Christian woodland numen.

Mrs. Bodgley sailed back in majestically. "I presume you can deliver an offering from me, on your behalf?" She might have been referring to the church jumble sale.

"Certainly."

"Then take this to your, ah, associate." She handed Edward a small silver tankard. "Timothy's christening mug. As a token of my gratitude for his helping my son's friend. And this . . . I gave you this once, so it is yours, but it still has Timothy's name on the flyleaf and Inspector Leatherdale returned it to me. It has no real value, yet I expect it could be termed significant under the circumstances."

Edward took the book and glanced at the title. Then he blinked several times and swallowed, at a loss for words. Eventually he mumbled, "Thank you very much. It's a wonderful choice."

Alice looked away. Probably they all did, for nobody said any more. The English were never very good at dealing with emotion.

It was indeed a lovely day. Mr. Glossop's bicycle was Jacobean, or even Elizabethan, with a pedal brake and a flint saddle; but it worked. Despite a niggling worry that her skirts would catch in the chain, Alice realized that she was going to enjoy this outing. Three days ago she had believed her cousin dead, and here she was cycling along a country lane with him, under beeches and elms just starting to blush with autumn. Wild roses and chestnut trees were laden with fruit.

In the Grange park, the sheep had been herded aside, and the convalescents were indulging in a strange sort of cricket match. With half the players in bandages or even casts, the rules must have been specially devised. She turned her mind from them; she wanted to forget the war today.

"England!" Edward sighed.

"Are the Vales comparable?"

He pulled a face, as if that was the problem he wanted to forget, but he answered. "Not many. Thargland comes close. The colors! I suppose a blue and purple forest sounds grotesque, but it has its own beauty."

A hill intervened then, and they concentrated on pedaling. As they started downhill, Alice put her doubts into words.

"Edward? This is fun. I am enjoying it, but are you seriously promising to introduce me to a genuine woodland spirit? Human originally but from another world and endowed with magical powers? Centuries old? I must admit—"

"No. Probably not. If we went at night, perhaps, but he's very shy. I don't think he'll appear in daylight."

That was a relief. "So what are you hoping to achieve? What will you do, actually?"

"Pray," he said solemnly. "Thank him again for what he did for me three years ago. Leave the offerings, explain that I need to send a message to Head Office. Tell him the message, probably, and just ask him to pass it on. That's all."

Even that sounded weird. With almost anyone else, she would have wondered about sanity; she would have suspected obsessions or just tomfoolery, but Edward had never been a leg-puller. Even as a boy, he had been trustworthy.

"So how will you know if you've been heard?"

"I think I'll know."

And then he would set off to wangle his way into the Army! She did not want to think about that. Why fight for a homeland that wanted to hang you? A hay wagon loomed in the road ahead, rumbling along behind a solitary horse. They pulled out to pass it and started up another slope. On either hand the fields were golden.

"You can't predict strangers," Edward said. "They don't face early death as we do. Their viewpoint is so different. . . ."

"How many have you met?" she asked. "Just Puck in this world, but how many on Nextdoor?"

"Four or five. That's if you don't count the Service people, of course. Most of them haven't been strangers long enough to lose their humanity. They're communal, too. That helps. The god types are solitary."

"Skulking on their nodes like spiders in a web?"

"Exactly! Well put. Mad as March hares, a lot of 'em. But charming! They all have charisma, you see, so you can't ever dislike them."

He frowned at some memory or other and fell silent.

She prompted. "Tion and the herder one?"

"Tion and Krobidirkin. Then Prylis—delightful, entertaining, and a thoroughgoing rotter!"

Intrigued, Alice said, "In what way?"

Edward pedaled in sulky silence for a while. "I suppose I shouldn't judge him," he said—but so reluctantly that he obviously did. "He was just playing the Great Game as he thought it should be played, and he did save my life because of it. A real Zath hater."

More silence.

"Tell me about him."

"Prylis? He's one of Tion's minions, god of learning. Originally he was from somewhere in Macedonia, I think. Don't know exactly when. His ideas of history and geography never seemed to match mine. He was delighted to have a visitor from his old world, more or less. The last one had brought him up to date with current affairs at the time of Charlemagne. We talked in a wild mixture of Greek and Thargian and Joalian, but his Joalian was centuries old, and whenever he got excited his Macedonian and Thargian accents combined to make him completely incomprehensible. He had more books than the British Museum."

It was not like Edward to hold a grudge, and he was not explaining this one.

"He sounds no worse than eccentric."

"Oh, he was personable enough—and knowledgeable, as you'd expect in a god of learning. He showed me maps of the Vales, he talked of the lands outside—deserts to the southeast and Fashranpil, the Great Ice, to the north. There are jungles west and south, with travelers bringing back tantalizing hints of salt water beyond, but even Prylis can't tell if it's an ocean or a closed sea. There's a trickle of trade goods coming across the desert: sapphires and spices, carved onyx and amber, but nobody knows who or where they come from.

"He spilled out centuries of history for me, biographies of gods, legends and beliefs, great poets and great art, politics and customs. I learned more about the Vales in those two days than I had in the previous year. Just about anything I wanted to know he could tell me . . . except where Olympus was, oddly enough. The Service wasn't in his books and didn't interest him. Reforms had been tried before, he said, and he quoted some examples, but whenever they became a serious nuisance the Five just took them over or stamped them out. But the quirks of the Vales and the vagaries of its peoples . . . anything I wanted to ask he would answer. Thargvale wasn't such a crazy place to put a temple of learning as it seemed. Thargians are Philistines who care about little except war, but they're usually strong enough to keep the war in other people's vales. Prylis had been left undisturbed for centuries. By arriving with an army, I'd earned a spot in the history books already, just out of ignorance. Lovers of learning shouldn't mind the pilgrimage to his digs anyway, he said, which was true enough. He did have humor! We sat up all the first night, talked all day, two days. He charmed me, beguiled me."

Edward scowled darkly. "He kept me from my duty."

Ah! That was the crime he could not forgive.

# 43

Being tough had its limits and Dosh had reached them. He had reached them once or twice before in his life, but never so convincingly. Dibber Troopleader and his sadists had enjoyed themselves very expertly under the guise of questioning him, and then the ride on the moa had completed the job. He remembered bringing D'ward to the temple, but that fulfillment had released the compulsion the god had put on him. After that, not much registered for a while.

He could recall being carried somewhere and laid on a bed. A wizened old man who must have been the house leech had tended him, strapping up his broken ribs, poulticing his well-kicked knees, salving his abrasions, dosing him with sour-tasting potions to ease the agony in his belly. Mercifully, he had slept after that.

He had awakened in confusion and a great deal of pain. Sunlight trickling through a high grating had revealed rough stone walls, bare floor, and a few dry sticks of furniture. For a long time Dosh had just lain on the boardlike bed, not daring to move a single tortured muscle and unable to hazard a guess as to where he was. Then the old man had come back and insisted on fussing with bandages; but after that he had spooned warm broth into the patient, which had been welcome. The man's yellow robe had reminded Dosh of where he was, but he had asked no questions. He was too weak to do anything about the answers.

He had slept again, wakened in darkness, slept more.

The next time he was conscious, a boy was standing over him, frowning. Good-looking lad, er, lass. It was Ysian in a skimpy tunic, standard male attire in Thargland. Women wore long skirts, which in Ysian's case would be a shame.

"Good morning," he muttered. His lips hurt. Everything hurt. He was afraid if he moved a finger he would start having cramps, and that would be disaster.

"It's afternoon."

"How long have we been here?"

"All yesterday."

"What's Ksargirk Captain doing?" A good commander always thinks of his men, especially Progyurg Lancer.

"They've all gone. The abbot sent them away."

"What right does he have?"

"He said the god told him to."

"Oh. Where's D'ward?"

"I don't know! He went through that door and disappeared. The abbot says he is with the god and not to worry."

Obviously she was worrying, though. The army would be a long way off by now, and the moas gone. Didn't matter about the army, Dosh thought. Much safer away from the army. His job was to keep watch on the Liberator, not the army.

In a startling flash, he remembered that his job was over. He was no longer bound to report to Tion, that unspeakable . . . Words failed him, thoughts failed him, hatred choked him when he tried to think of Tion. Prylis had removed Tion's binding. So Dosh was a free man again, for as long as he could stay out of the god's clutches. He had never been a free man before. Was he free now, for the first time in his life? The Liberator . . .

"What's wrong?" Ysian demanded.

"Not much, except I'm one big bruise. I have to get up. Don't be alarmed if I scream."

"I'll help you."

"I'd rather do it at my own speed." He flexed an arm. Ouch! "So are you having fun?"

"What does that mean?" she snapped.

"You're the only woman in the place, aren't you?"

"Sh! I told them my name was Tysian. They think I'm a boy."

He tried the other arm. Worse. "Do they? Do they really?" Could even monks be in doubt about those legs?

"Well, I think one or two suspect, but they're very kind."

"Mm? Found any good-looking young novices?"

Ysian said, "Oh, you're horrible! Don't you ever think of anything else?"

"Not unless I have to. Have you even looked?"

Without a word, she spun around and left. She slammed the door behind her.

Pity. He had been going to ask her to send them his way.

Ironically, the young novice who came to feed the invalid shortly thereafter was a very good-looking youth indeed, which was not unexpected in a devotee of Tion's. He showed no personal interest in Dosh, and while teasing Ysian was possible, Dosh in his present condition dared not venture advances that might be taken seriously. He felt quite disappointed in himself. He dozed off the moment he finished the meal.

The ensuing night was long, broken by sleepy thinking-times into several nights, end to end. He thought a lot about this strange notion of freedom and what it might be good for. He had had many masters before Tion—mortals all, but masters—plus a very few mistresses. He must have been about ten or so when his father sold him to Kramthin Clockmaker. He could still recall his joy when he learned that he would be able to stay in Kramthin's warm, comfortable house, eating fine food, never being hungry. What Kramthin had required of him in return had been much less unpleasant than his father's drunken beatings. Kramthin had been the first. Dosh had been traded a few times and then decided to handle his own affairs thereafter. Whenever he had tired of one master, he had just run away and found another. They had not owned him in law, for only Thargia of all the lands in the Vales permitted slavery, and he had stayed away from Thargland until now. They had not bound him as Tion had. He had bound himself to them voluntarily, for food and shelter and affection.

The last of his masters, Prithose Connoisseur, had gone visiting Suss to enjoy the artistic offerings at Tion's Festival. He had entered Dosh in the contest for the gold rose, much as a breeder might enter livestock in a show. Dosh had been seventeen. He had won the prize easily and apparently that prize had made him Tion's own prize. Three years missing . . . What had he been during those three years? Servant? Plaything? Wallpaper?

Prylis had broken Tion's spell. Would he impose one of his own, and turn Dosh into a monk, copying manuscripts to the end of his days? Would he return him to Tion? Or was Dosh now a free man for the first time in his life? Could he survive without a master?

At some later point in the night, his mind returned to the problem. All men but kings served other men, for that was the way of the world. The talent that had supported him until had become a doubtful commodity when Tarion ripped up his face. Copy manuscripts? Dig and reap?

Chastity or monogamy? Fun though lechery undoubtedly was, it had brought him more than his share of grief. D'ward seemed to get by without it at all. That was going too far in the opposite direction, much too far, but perhaps Dosh ought to introduce a little moderation into his life.

Who—him? Honest labor? Nothing like a few aches to bring on repentance, he decided. In a day or two he would be his old self. He went back to sleep.

# 44

The next time he awoke there was light behind the grating and birds were creating a damnable racket outside. Dawn. What morning? It had been Heelday when he first came to the monastery. Had it been Ankleday when Ysian came? This must be Shinday at the least. The army was either well out of Thargland by now or all dead. If the gods dispensed justice, though, ex-troopleader Dibber and his bullyboys were just settling in to a long, hard lifetime in the silver mines.

Dosh stretched. He sat up with a jerk. He fingered his ribs and detected only a trace of soreness under the bandages. He pulled down the blanket and looked at his knees. Not a mark. Not one bruise on him. His fingertips went to his face. It was smooth.

He leaned his chin on his arms and pondered. In among the litter of forgotten dreams, he found vague memories of voices in the night. Two men? He was able to raise no details, but he knew who one of them must have been, and could guess at the other. Well! So what about breakfast?

He swung his feet to the floor and saw that someone had been leaving him presents: on the solitary chair lay a brown Thargian tunic, a sword, sandals, a belt pouch with an intriguing jingle. The sword annoyed him, but he knew that Thargian law required freemen to go armed. He had no skill or experience with a sword. His weapon of choice was the concealed knife. He was quite good with that.

He had just finished counting the money—sixteen silver marks—when the door creaked open and a Thargian stalked in. No, it was D'ward, with his face clean shaven and his hair cut short, wearing a tunic and a sword. He even had the mean Thargian scowl—or at least an icy glitter in his eyes. When he saw that Dosh was awake, it thawed a little.

"Sleep well? Feeling better?"

"Did you come calling in the night?"

"Yes."

"With a friend?"

The angry glint returned. "*You* could call him that. I . . . He paid you for services rendered."

"I'd better go and thank him, I suppose."

"I suppose so too, but don't make an epic of it. Some merchant's just donated a very rare book to the temple, so the god is undoubtedly too engrossed to hear you. We're not wanted in the refectory for the same reason—the abbot's entertaining the wealthy gent, trying to squeeze an endowment out of him to enlarge the scriptorium. There's grub in the kitchens, cold water in the washhouse. You'd better shave off your beard if you want to pass as a local. Prylis removed your scars. I expect you'll want to thank him for that, too." He turned to the door.

Too much too soon! "Wait a minute!" Dosh caught his breath. It sounded as if D'ward was extremely knowledgeable about the workings of the monastery and the habits of the resident deity. What had been happening? "Where are we going?"

D'ward drummed fingers on the door before he looked around. "I know where I'm going. You can please your own sweet self, as far as I care. Pick a direction and start walking. If you want to come with me, we can chat on the way, but I won't loiter. I plan to eat on the hoof."

Dosh bit back a snappy retort and asked, "Any news of the army?"

"Yes."

"Well?" What was gnawing at the Liberator? Dosh had never known him to be crabby before.

"They're safe."

"*Safe!?*"

"I'll tell you later. Jump to it!" D'ward pulled the door open.

"Wait!"

He looked back with a glare. "Now what?"

Dosh smiled cherubically. "Has anyone ever told you that you have beautiful legs?"

D'ward could slam a door even louder than Ysian.

Chewing on hard bread and hunks of cheese, three wayfarers strode along the track in the dewy dawn. D'ward was in the middle, setting a murderous pace with his (beautiful) long legs. Despite his considerable handicap in height, Dosh was prepared to take him on at distance sprinting any day, but Ysian was struggling to keep up. To look at, they were a trio of young men, with no packs, one long dagger, two swords, three money pouches. Dosh still had his favorite knife, which didn't show. All in all, Holy Prylis had done them proud.

Apparently the war was over, at least so far as they were concerned. The future shone much brighter without a massacre in it. There seemed no obvious explanation for D'ward's vile mood, unless he was concerned about getting safely out of Thargvale, which certainly might pose problems. By law, strangers were spies unless they could prove otherwise.

"Where are we going?"

"Down to the river," D'ward said. "Thargwater. There I'm going to catch a boat. It's downhill all the way—I should be in Tharg in a couple of hours."

Tharg itself? "And what are we going to do in that city of celebrated boredom and illustrious ugliness?"

D'ward wrinkled his nose. "You please yourself. Ysian and I are going to the Convent of Ursula."

"*We are going where?*" Ysian screeched.

"Goddess of justice. I have been assured that her convent is a worthy sanctuary, and the sisters will take you in and care for you. I have a letter from the abbot."

Dosh strode along in silence as the ensuing altercation waxed loud and long.

Seemingly D'ward regarded Ysian as a child and felt responsible for her. Some child!—Dosh had known women who had borne two children by her age, but apparently the Liberator had other standards. He had sacked Lemod. One result of that act had been to brand all women remaining within the walls as ruined, harlots beyond all hope of marriage. For that reason, he had allowed Ysian to accompany the flight and guide the fugitives to Moggpass. He had then accepted her word that her family would put her to death for treason if she went home. Dosh suspected that she had been exaggerating there. But D'ward felt responsible, and now he had decided to hand his burden over to the stern nuns of Ursula. In a few years she would be old enough to make up her own mind what to do with her life, he said.

Ysian's rebuttal began quietly, but his stubborn responses soon had her yelling, interrupting the last of the birds' dawn chorus in the branches overhead and scaring the leafeater lizards in the ditches. She was a mature woman, she screamed. She would make her own decisions right now. He would have died in Lemod without her help. He was utterly heartless and she hated him. She loved him more than life itself. The nuns of Ursula were notorious sadists. She would follow him to the corners of the world. She would sleep on his doorsteps forever, anywhere he went, and haunt him for the rest of his life, and she was going to kill herself before nightfall and him soon after.

There was more, but suddenly both she and D'ward collapsed in helpless, hysterical mirth. Dosh was shocked to realize that she had been putting on an act and it had fooled him completely. Admittedly she was on the far side of D'ward, so he had not been watching her, nor listening very closely either. Yet he felt peeved at being fooled. He felt like an outsider in the presence of lovers—which was exactly what he must be. *Jealous, my lad?* He had never really seen these two together except in very public settings. Observing them now—leaning on each other for support, gasping for breath, tears of laughter streaming over their cheeks—no one could ever doubt that they were hopelessly in love. Ysian knew. D'ward was apparently not ready to admit the obvious.

The nervous release did not last long. Soon he returned to his angry urgency, and the three of them resumed their progress. Abandoning the argument, D'ward turned to Dosh. "Where are you headed?"

"I want to stay with you."

"Why?"

Interesting question! Dosh debated several answers, and then decided to tell the truth, just for once. What was the truth, though? The silence dragged out for half a mile before he found it.

"I want to learn from you. You're different."

D'ward said, "Hmm?" The river was in sight in the distance, a line of trees twisting along the valley floor. "How does it feel?"

"How does what feel?"

"Telling the truth."

"Dangerous. Like being naked in a crowd."

Ysian laughed.

"Have you a trade you can take up?" D'ward said. "Or a skill of some kind?"

"I'm good at massage."

He winced, misunderstanding. "Where are you from? Where was your home?"

Dosh decided to push the experiment in veracity a little farther. "Never had one. My people were Tinkerfolk."

"What are Tinkerfolk?" Apparently the query was serious and he really did not know.

"They're nomads. Wanderers. They mostly live in tents or wagons, although every city has a tinkers' hole somewhere. They do odd jobs, poach, steal. Most people think they're all liars, whores, thieves, and spies."

"What are they really?"

"Spies, thieves, whores, and liars."

The others both laughed at that, which felt good. The road led to a hamlet with a jetty. There were boats there, waiting for hire.

"Listen," the Liberator said, serious again. "You can't come where I'm going. You've got the same problem Ysian has. I'm sorry, but I can't help either of you. I have a potent sort of charm that I can't control and I really can't explain to you, either. You saw how it worked on the army—I began with a spear and ended up as battlemaster. I had five thousand men all wanting me to scratch them behind the ears. Ysian thinks she's in love with me, and so do you. I like both of you, but I can't return the sort of love you want and I am promised to another woman, so I can't help her, either. I'm truly sorry, but that's the way things are. *Viks'n*, you're better at this local snarl than we are. See if you can hire a boat to take us to Tharg."

"How many?"

"Two."

"Three," said Dosh.

Marg'rk Ferryman was not much more than a boy, built of sticks and string as if he had not eaten in several fortnights. His skiff was a smelly, leaky little hulk, and its sail bore innumerable patches. He toadied and groveled for passengers rich enough to pay him a whole silver mark for a half-day's work. He addressed each of them as "Warrior," which was the correct honorific for Thargian freemen. Had he known Ysian was a woman, he would properly have called her "Mother." That said a lot about Thargian values.

Propelled much more by the current than the forlorn breeze, his boat drifted out into Thargwater and headed southward. Marg'rk clutched the tiller with a bony hand, smiling obsequiously whenever anyone looked in his direction. Wide, swift, and smooth, the river oiled through a rich countryside. The banks were ornamented with fish traps and jetties, water mills and multicolored trees. High-horned kudus plodded along tow-paths, hauling barges. Cargo boats crawled upstream under the muscle power of slaves. The hills beyond were figured with vineyards and orchards, or fields being plowed and sown. Here and there, grand aristocratic mansions graced the landscape.

Ysian sat amidships, being unusually quiet. Even cropped short so barbarically, her hair shone with red-gold highlights. She was brooding ominously. Dosh suspected the convent would have to survive without a new postulant, whatever D'ward might think.

The Liberator sat beside her, the mast between them, crouching to see under the edge of the sail. He scowled, fidgeted, and squirmed. He had not yet explained why he so urgently wanted to reach Tharg. Impatience was out of character for him.

Dosh sprawled in the bow with his feet in a stinking litter of nets and baskets, pots and bilge. After a while he removed his tunic and leaned back in his breechclout to soak up some spring sunshine. His two companions carefully avoided looking at him. Prudes! He had all the essentials covered. They wouldn't care about anyone else; they just knew he would accept any reasonable offer and were frightened to look in case they were caught window-shopping.

"Warrior D'ward?"

"Yes, Warrior Dosh?" D'ward had developed an intense interest in the reflections of windmills.

Dosh peered past Ysian at the boatman, who leered back nervously and mawkishly. That lout would not understand Joalian. "Are you going to Tharg to bring death to Death, as has been prophesied? And when you have that one stuffed and mounted, will you do Tion too, as a favor for me?"

"That's not why I'm going to Tharg." D'ward straightened his long back, and the sail hid his face.

"You told me our former comrades-in-arms are now safe. You promised to say how."

D'ward sank back into a slouch, and his scowl became visible again. Why was he so edgy? "Prylis told me. The Thargians gave them safe conduct back to Nagvale."

"More miracles? The *Thargians* did? You're serious?"

"They sent emissaries, a couple of the ephors in person. That alone is unprecedented. Golbfish did the negotiating. He demanded the whole world and they gave it to him: food, hostages, formal oaths sealed with sacrifice. The Thargians will hold back the Lemodians to let the Nagians go by. They groveled, they implored. Anything he wanted."

That ought to be unbelievable or else hilariously funny, and yet D'ward was disconsolate. Obvious question: "Why?"

"Plague," D'ward said, staring blankly at the left bank. "People are dying by the hundreds all over Thargland. They take ill in the night, and they rot for three days and then die. Funeral pyres bejewel the night and sully the sun by day—Prylis's words, not mine."

"Padlopan's the god of sickness, but—"

"This is Zath. The people think it's an epidemic, but Prylis says Zath's called in his reapers from all over the Vales, brought them here into Thargvale, and he's taught them a new form of sacrifice. A reaper death used to be quick. Now it's slow and even more horrible. And they're working overtime."

Zath was an aspect of Karzon, the patron deity. Why would a god destroy his own people? Dosh caught Ysian's eye; she looked away quickly. She was frightened about something.

"Human sacrifice?" he said with disgust. "You're saying that what reapers do is human sacrifice?"

"What else would you call it?"

"I don't know. I just never thought of it that way. Human sacrifice is something done by the savages in the southern jungles or read about in old, old history. Uncivilized. We don't do that anymore!"

"Reapers do," D'ward said grimly. "Zath does."

"I suppose you're right. What has this plague of reapers got to do with—Oh, my god!"

"Not your god, I hope. But you've got the idea. Karzon—or Zath—the distinction seems to be getting blurry . . . One of them has sent a revelation, telling the priests how to turn aside the divine wrath and end the epidemic."

"Deliver the Liberator's head?" Dosh said.

Ysian's face was sickly pale.

D'ward's mouth twisted in a mirthless grin. "That's not what he said. Gods have pride. Everyone knows what the *Filoby Testament* prophesies about the Liberator and Death, although most people believe that the Liberator is still a year-old baby somewhere in Sussland. For Zath to name the Liberator would be a confession of weakness. He might have named D'ward, but even that would draw attention to the prophecies. He didn't have to name names. He knew I was responsible for the fall of Lemod. He knew I would be acclaimed leader—that was inevitable, although you won't understand why. So the revelation just demanded the leader of the Nagians, no name mentioned."

"That's why the Thargians stopped killing us?"

"That's why. They didn't want to kill me by mistake. The leader of the Nagians must be brought to the temple and sacrificed there. Death in battle will not suffice. The ephors were willing to let the whole Joalian army go—willing to feed them and escort them home, do anything they asked. They demanded only one thing in return."

Dosh rubbed his oddly smooth cheek—no stubble, no scars. "So Golbfish gave himself up?"

D'ward nodded miserably. "He's on his way to Tharg right now. We should arrive about the same time he does."

"He's going to die by mistake?"

"No. Well, a Thargian mistake, but the prince is quite smart enough to have worked this out for himself by now. He must know that he's the wrong man, but his captors don't. He was in command and he has Nagian merit scars on his ribs—that would be enough for them. Zath may guess when he gets a look at him, but a god can hardly back down at that stage. So Golbfish will die, and the plague will end, and meanwhile his men are on their way home already, escorting enough hostages to make sure they get there."

D'ward licked his lips. "It's a good deal from Golbfish's point of view. He dies, but he would likely have died anyway. This way his entire force gets home safely. No honorable leader would refuse such an offer. I'm sure he didn't even argue."

"You don't seem very satisfied by the arrangement."

"Prylis pulled me out of the trap and put in Golbfish instead." D'ward bared his teeth.

"You enjoy being bait?"

D'ward did not deign to answer. For a while nobody spoke. Dosh registered vaguely that the boat was tacking and the river had turned to the west already. The city might be coming into view. He did not look around—he was too busy trying to work out why D'ward should be so upset.

Baffled, he finally asked.

The Liberator looked at him oddly. "What don't you understand?"

"He's going to the temple," Ysian said bitterly, "to give himself up, tell them they got the wrong man!"

"But that would be utterly insane! D'ward . . . ? Really?"

"Aren't you?" she demanded.

"I must, *Viks'n*." He was looking at Dosh, not at her, and there was a curious appeal in his cerulean eyes, as if he wanted approval or reassurance. "A man's got to have honor. Right, Warrior?"

"No!" Dosh said. "No! No! Not right! What you're planning won't work, and even if it would, I'd still think you're bloody crazy."

# 45

"I think you're crazy!" Alice said angrily. "It won't just be Boche bullets you'll have to avoid. All those hundreds of boys who knew you at Fallow are all out there now, subalterns, mostly. It will only take one: 'By Jove! That fellow looks just like that cricketer chappie, Exeter. I say! Wasn't he the one who murdered old Bagpipe Bodgley?' And then, my lad, you'll be in the—"

"You're nagging," Edward said.

They were in Ye Olde English Tea Shoppe in Vicarsdown. The village was bigger than he remembered, he said, and she had retorted that it would still fit inside Piccadilly Circus, which was not true. But the tea shoppe was an authentic Elizabethan building and delightful, although it must have had some other purpose originally, because authentic Elizabethans had drunk ale, not tea. It was tiny, cramped, and rather dark—pleasantly cool. They were drinking tea. They were eating homemade scones spread with strawberry jam and cream thick as butter. It was too precious a moment to waste quarreling.

Edward's eyes were cold as a winter sea. "Furthermore, those hundreds of boys are not all out there now. Half of them are dead. And you persist in treating me as your baby brother, which I'm not, anymore."

She lifted her cup. "Yes, you are. You always were my baby brother to me, and you always will be. When we're both a hundred years old, with long white beards, you will still be my baby brother." She took a sip of tea, watching to see if he would accept the olive branch.

"I don't think I'll like you in a long white beard," he said reflectively. "Promise me you'll dye it?"

She laid down the cup and reached across for his hand. "I promise I shall stop thinking of you as a baby brother if you'll tell me about Ysian."

"What about her? I didn't take advantage of her. I hope that doesn't surprise you."

"Not in the slightest." She knew it would surprise most people, though. "Did you love her?"

He pulled his hand away and began heaping cream on a scone like a navvy loading a wheelbarrow. "I've told you everything. She's a very determined young woman—I have rather a weakness for those, you know. She was sixteen and I was a stranger. She fell for me like a ton of bricks, naturally. It wasn't me, just the charisma."

"You haven't answered the question."

"No, I didn't love her."

"What happened to her? When did you last see her?"

"About a year ago. Mrs. Murgatroyd took her on as cook, at Olympus. She's a good cook, although of course she knew only Lemodian recipes."

Romance cracked and shattered into fragments. "But not educated? Just a native wench? Not good enough?"

He stared at her in disbelief, face flaming cruelly red. His knife clattered down on the china plate.

"Oh, Edward, I'm sorry!" she said quickly. "That was abominable of me! I'm sure you behaved like a perfect gentleman. Oh, I mean—"

"I was a stranger," he said in a very quiet, tight voice. "Strangers never die, except from boredom or violence. I know I don't look any older than I did when I left here. Ysian is eighteen or nineteen now, I suppose. Ten years from now she will be twenty-nine, and ten years after that, thirty-nine. Had I stayed on Nextdoor, I would still be much the same as I am now. Why do you think the Service sends people Home on leave—especially bachelors? One reason is that they have to marry other strangers! Love between stranger and native is unthinkable. It leads to unbearable heartache. It leads to . . . to abominations. The Chamber— Never mind."

"I hadn't thought of that. I'm sorry. You didn't let yourself fall in love with her, you mean?"

He went back to destroying scones. "I did not tell her I loved her. I never gave her any encouragement whatsoever. I used you as an excuse, actually. Hope you don't mind.

Had I been free to react to Ysian like a normal man, I'd have thrown my heart at her feet and rent my garments and piled ashes on my head and writhed in the dirt until she promised to marry me. That wasn't possible, so nothing was possible. Just friends."

How wonderful the world would be if emotion could be dosed with logic so easily! *I am sorry, Sir D'Arcy, but your married status inevitably precludes any further communication between us. . . .*

"Look!" Edward pointed out at the sunlit village beyond the little diamond-pained windows. A Gypsy wagon was being hauled along the street by an ancient nag. Dogs barked, small boys ran after it.

He watched as it disappeared around the corner. "Last time I was here, a Gypsy told my fortune. That's a different wagon, though."

"You believe in that stuff?"

He twisted his face. "I didn't used to, but that one hit the mark pretty well. She said I'd have to choose between honor and friendship. Sure enough, I was forced to abandon Eleal when I might have been able to help her."

"Come off it, Edward! That might just as well have applied to Ysian."

His eyes glinted like razors. "I don't rat on my friends very often. Abandoning Ysian, if that's what I did, was the honorable thing to do. You might like to know the rest of the prophecy, though—Mrs. Boswell the Gypsy also said I'd have to choose between honor and duty, that I could only find honor through dishonor. Explain that one, because I can't!"

Was there a chink here to work on? "Well, if your duty is to enlist, but the honorable thing is to avenge your parents' murder—"

"Never give up, do you?" Even Edward could lose his temper. If that happened she would have lost any hope of making him see reason.

"You haven't seen Ysian in a year?" The girl was the only bait she had to coax him back to Nextdoor and away from the Western Front.

He flashed a look of exasperation at her. "Told you," he mumbled. "She's at Olympus, working for Polly Murgatroyd. She's very nice—Polly, I mean. I wrote to her before I crossed over—to Ysian, I mean. . . ." He frowned, dabbing at his mouth with the napkin. "As the man who promised to deliver the note then tried to kill me, she probably never got it."

"You weren't at Olympus?"

He shook his head, chewing. "I took two years to get there and when I did, I didn't stay long. The Committee decided it was too dangerous, both for me and for everybody else—didn't want Zath sacking the place in the hope of catching me. I was packed off to Thovale, which is very small and rural, but not too far away. I helped set up some chapels there. I became a missionary!" He laughed gleefully. "Holy Roly must have turned in his grave! But we all do . . . they all do it."

"You'd make a good preacher." She could just imagine him running his parish like a school dormitory.

"I didn't! I can't ever believe that I know better than everyone else. I don't like telling people what they must think. It's immoral!"

"Doesn't a stranger make a good preacher?"

"Yes," he admitted glumly. "I could pack in the crowds. I converted heathens to the Church's new and improved heathenism. My heart wasn't in it, though. Jumbo Watson can convert a whole village with a single sermon. I've seen him do it."

Alice abandoned the Ysian campaign. If he could stay away from the girl for a whole year to do something he did not believe in, then thoughts of Ysian were not going to discourage him from enlisting.

"The Liberator?" she said. "It's a noble title—calls up memories of Bolívar, William Tell, Robert the Bruce. Doesn't it tempt you at all?"

He rolled his eyes in exasperation at her persistence. "Not too terribly frightfully, no. There were a couple of times—and the *Filoby Testament* predicted them both. I almost gave in to Tion, because he said he would cure Eleal's limp. That was a very close-run thing! And then in Tharg, the prince—" He popped a jammy, creamy morsel in his mouth and chewed blissfully.

"What about the prince?"

"That didn't work either, but it came close, too. That particular prophecy ends, *but the dead shall rouse him.* That's me, rouse me. And that part did work, Alice, because I saw the dead—in Flanders. How many lives has this war cost?"

"No way of knowing. What you read in the papers is all censored."

"Well, the dead speak. They say it's my turn. I have to do my bit, and that's that." He glanced at his wrist and then at the grandfather clock in the corner.

She sighed. Two more miles to Harrow. Her legs ached already. "Time to go, isn't it?"

Edward nodded. "Wish I hadn't eaten so much." He surreptitiously slid the last scone into his pocket. He grinned sheepishly when he saw that she had noticed. "Another offering."

Alice shook her head in disbelief. It was Friday afternoon in England and they were on their way to meet a god.

# 46

*Shame! Shame! To the Man goeth D'ward, saying, Slay me! The hammer falls and blood profanes the holy altar. Warriors, where is thine honor? Perceive thy shame.*—Verse 266.

The divinely inspired gibberish echoed and reechoed in Dosh's head as he was swept along a milling street in Tharg. Insects droned, people shoved and jostled; heat and noise and stink. That passage made no sense at all at this point in history. How could the prophecy of D'ward's death be fulfilled before all the others about him? The trouble with the *Filoby Testament* was that too much of it made sense only after it had happened.

What about Verse 1098, then? That was the one that intrigued Tion so much. Something about the Liberator being slow to anger, and then, *Eleal shall be the first temptation and the prince shall be the second, but the dead shall rouse him.* It certainly referred to the Liberator. It might well apply to this very afternoon. Something was about to happen, something so momentous that it had caught the eye of the seeress all those many years ago.

Tharg was the largest city Dosh had ever seen, bigger even than Joal. It well deserved its reputation as the ugliest. The buildings were of somber stone, with high plain walls and tiny windows, every house a fortress. There was no color, no decoration, not a carving in sight. The men wore tunics of drab brown or khaki, boys yellow or beige, although all had a touch of the sacred colors at the neck. Women were not in evidence. Doors and shutters were tarred, not painted. The streets were narrow trenches, hot and airless, straight as spears.

They were also thronged with huge crowds of impatient, hustling, urgent freemen, all hurrying in the same direction he was heading, and most of them much taller than he. He was having trouble keeping D'ward in sight. Fortunately the Liberator was taller than most, his distinctive black hair bobbing above the tide like a cork. He was gaining. He seemed not to care that every man in the crowd bore a sword and aggressive jostling might be fatal. Very likely he was deliberately trying to lose his unwanted follower.

*Gods did not make mistakes.* That thought, too, Dosh kept repeating like a mantra. Prylis had extracted the Liberator from the army so that the ephors would abduct the wrong leader. When Prylis had released him this morning, had he not known what D'ward would try to do? Because he had let him go, then he must have been certain that it was now too late—mustn't he? Golbfish must be dead already, mustn't he? *Could gods make mistakes?*

Maybe a minor god like Prylis could. Everyone was heading for the temple, because there was to be an announcement—Dosh had gathered that much from remarks overheard. He dared not ask questions, lest he be denounced as a foreigner. Thargians were never nice to foreigners, especially Thargians in mobs, and the air stank of dangerous passions already. Angry, armed male mob . . . no women, no slaves? The women would all be at home in those narrow-windowed prisons of houses, being mothers.

Now where was D'ward?

Dosh rose on tiptoe as he walked, peering through the jungle of heads. Gone! No! There he was.

He had stepped into an arched doorway, and Dosh was almost past him. He pushed his way across the stream of the crowd, bumping and apologizing, being shoved and cursed and threatened. Thargians never apologized. He reached the wall and was flattened against it by the crush, then began edging his way back to the arch.

A flash of color above it caught his eye, a festoon of faded blue ropes. Blue was the color of the Maiden, and a net was the symbol of justice. He had always thought that was inappropriate. In his experience, the little ones got caught and the big ones got away. That wasn't what it meant, of course.

D'ward was speaking through a grille in the door. Ysian stood at his side, her face pale and rigid. She looked up at Dosh and bared her teeth. D'ward passed the abbot's letter through the grating. Dosh eased nearer in the hope of hearing what was being said. As he squeezed by Ysian, a sharp pain stopped him. He glanced down and confirmed his gut feeling that the problem was her dagger.

"Go!" she whispered.

He stammered and then decided that he had seen that expression in her eyes once before, when she had threatened to club him senseless. D'ward was still talking, pleading for haste. The pain came again. She could puncture Dosh's bowels with one swift jab. He stepped back. She followed, urging him on at knifepoint.

"Go!" she insisted. "Move!"

He turned into the crowd and was swept away. He felt her hand grab hold of his belt, but at least the dagger was making no more holes in his hide. In moments they were being rushed along the street by the sweaty tide.

"What do you think you are doing?" he demanded, twisting around to see her.

She was smirking triumphantly. "I am not entering any flea-infested convent! D'ward will go on to the temple. We are going to catch him before he gets there and stop him making a fool of himself!"

It wasn't a fool he was going to make of himself, it was a corpse. "By the five gods, girl, how do you ever expect—"

"Don't you call me a girl!"

"I call you an idiot! We'll never find him in this—"

The crowd had slowed to a crawl. Dosh stumbled into the man in front of him, and a vicious elbow rammed into his solar plexus, knocking all the breath out of him. He staggered.

"Watch where you're going," Ysian said, pushing him forward again.

In all cities, the holy places tended to huddle together. Temple Square was just around the corner from the convent. It was now full. Refusing to be balked, the mob in the street continued to press onward.

It occurred to Dosh that women might well be prohibited by law from entering the Man's holy place. If Ysian's deception was discovered, then he would be held responsible. On the other hand, he was more likely to die in the crush. It was already hard to breathe, and the crowd continued to squeeze tighter and tighter. It oozed ahead like a human glacier, a paste of compressed bodies. He wished he were taller.

"This will kill us!" he groaned, feeling the start of panic. Two hands gripped his arms and pulled them behind him. "What in eternity are you doing?"

"Cup your hands!"

"What?"

Ysian pushed his hands together. Somehow she squirmed and struggled and got one foot in them. Then she wriggled up his back and seated herself on his shoulders, her fingers locked in his hair and her weight threatening to buckle his knees.

"There!" she said. "Now I can see. Keep moving!"

The ancient temple of Karzon in Tharg, dating from the days of the kings, had been built of wood. During the Fifth Joalian War, it had been struck by lightning and burned to the ground. This evil omen had caused great despair among the Man's Men on the eve of the final campaign, but the famous Goztikon, thirteen times ephor, had declared the sign to be one of hope. He had publicly pledged his life and the lives of his seven sons that the god was promising renewal for Thargia; the Man's Men would prevail, he swore, and would return to build a new and mightier temple to the glory of their god.

So it had transpired. The armies of the Joalian Coalition had been crushed in the bloody battle of Suddopass. The survivors had worked out their lives in the quarries to further the building of the temple. Artisans and craftsmen from all over the Vales had spent twenty years on it. The indemnities levied on Joalia by the peace treaty had included the greatest artist of the age, K'simbr Sculptor, who had been specifically requisitioned so he might raise fitting images of the god.

Gods. Whereas the Man in his primary aspect had always been god of both creation and destruction, he had hitherto been represented by a single likeness. In the new great temple, he was shown twice. One giant image was plated with copper, which would weather to the green of his color. The other was of silver, to turn black. Officially both were Karzon, but the ignorant multitude soon spoke of the second image as being that of Zath, his aspect of Death. The avatar had been promoted to equality.

Eased forward irresistibly by the bodies pressed in all around him, Dosh shuffled into the southwest corner of the square. Over the shifting oceans of heads he saw the temple towering into the sky, two walls of stupendous pillars running off to east and north. They were so thick and the gaps between them so narrow that from his angle they completely blocked the interior from view. They were oppressive, domineering, overwhelming. The temple of Karzon was a giant gray granite cage, the ugliest structure he had ever set eyes on.

The crowd pushed relentlessly at his back, urging him closer.

"Not yet!" Ysian proclaimed, having to shout over the din. She twisted Dosh's head around. "Wait over there!"

"I can't get out."

She took hold of his ears and pulled. He yelled, causing his nearest neighbors to look at him in surprise. He blinked away tears.

"I shall pull them off!" Ysian said, kicking him with her heels.

She probably meant it. He began to fight his way out of the crowd.

He broke free of the main current after a considerable struggle and reached the shallows at the edge of the square. There were many people there too, but they were mostly not moving, just staring at the temple, fearing to risk their lives in the compacted mob. He leaned back against the wall, gasping and sweating. His shoulders were breaking.

"Get down!" he groaned. "You're crushing me."

"Stop whining! You said you were the toughest man in the army, didn't you?"

"I'm not a fornicating moa!"

Other children in yellow tunics floated above the crowd, riding their fathers' shoulders. None was anywhere near Ysian's size. He would wager that none was a girl, either. Many older youths had clambered upon the plinths of the columns, and some had scrambled even higher, apparently finding toe- and fingerholds within the carvings, clinging there like human lichen. Every few minutes one would lose his grip and fall, dragging others with him, down into the melee. Whatever screams or oaths resulted were lost in the steady, torrential roar.

Dosh was farther from the corner now. He could see through the closest pair of pillars, and what he saw was the back of the statue of Zath. Silvery black, it stood ten times the height of a man, muffled in a reaper's cloak and ominously stooped, as if to study the multitude huddled around its feet. He was happy not to be there, looking up at the face of Death. Beyond it he could see an edge of the statue of Karzon, mostly just the great hammer he held, his symbol.

Ysian kicked her heels into Dosh's ribs. "Here he comes!"

If he had room to move, he could grab her arms and flip her off him, but in this mob she would fall on top of at least one man, probably two, and then there would be reprisals. As it was, his arms were so tightly crushed against his sides that he could not raise them even to defend himself from her attacks.

"D'ward's coming!" she insisted. "Move. This way." She took him by the ears again and twisted his head to the left.

He yielded to the inevitable, starting to shoulder himself forward. He would probably have made no progress at all had Ysian not begun using her feet with deliberate savagery on the innocent bystanders. The inevitable retaliation was all directed at him, of course—he was jostled, jabbed, punched, cursed at. Any minute someone would manage to draw a sword and gut him.

"Faster!" she demanded. "We'll lose him."

Of course they would. There was no chance of catching him. D'ward was bigger and taller, and he was the Liberator. He had admitted that he had a special sort of charm. He would charm his way through the crowd. He was not carrying Ysian.

Yet Ysian did add some weight to Dosh's efforts. He discovered he could lean on the men in front of him and they would pull away to avoid being pushed over and trampled. If he lost his footing, that would happen to him.

Ysian yanked at his left ear. "That man in green coming! Catch him!"

In a moment, Dosh saw the man she meant. His green tunic marked him in the drab brown crowd and probably meant that he was some sort of temple flunky—priest or guard. He was very large, very beefy, and obviously very determined to move closer to the temple. That meant closer to D'ward.

Somehow Dosh managed to slip in at his back, and after that they made better progress. The big fellow did not seem to register that he had acquired two hangers-on as he wrestled his way toward the pillars. Dosh leaned on him, urging him forward.

The noise was fading, and now there was another sound, a steady drumbeat. Dosh had no idea what was happening inside the temple, but the ominous *boom-boom-boom* made his scalp prickle. Was Golbfish being brought in now? Human sacrifice? No god of the Vales had demanded human sacrifice in thousands of years. What would they do to him? Cut off his head? Tear out his heart? Burn him alive?

Poor old Golbfish! He had turned himself from an effete slob into a warrior and a leader. He had made himself worthy to rule the kingdom that was his by right, and now he was dying to save his men. What must he be thinking?

"Almost there!" Ysian bounced a few times with excitement. Dosh shrieked at her. He thought she meant the great pillars now looming over them, but then he saw the familiar black hair just ahead. Perhaps this madness was going to pay off after all. Then what? D'ward had refused to listen to reason on the boat; he was not likely to be amenable to logic now.

But Dosh had not been joking when he told D'ward he knew massage. He also knew a few sneaky tricks of self-defense that had come in handy more than once when the romping had become too rough. *If* he could actually get within reach of D'ward and *if* he could then work his arms free and *if* he could put his hands around D'ward's neck—then he could put D'ward to sleep very easily.

Then . . . then D'ward would slump to the ground and be trampled to paste? That part of the plan needed more work. The drums were beating faster. All that was needed was to delay D'ward a few more minutes and it would be too late for him to stop the sacrifice. Now the man in green had caught up with D'ward and was right behind him. He had become a barrier instead of a trailblazer, for Dosh could not get by him.

They were within a few feet of the pillars when the man in green abruptly caught hold of D'ward's arm and jerked him around. He himself twisted to the right. Dosh stumbled to catch his balance, recovering to the left. The crowd surged back in tightly around them again, packing all three men in together, face-to-face, with Ysian's legs between them.

The whole congregation had fallen silent under the surging *boom-boom-boom* of the drumbeat.

"What?" D'ward demanded angrily, struggling to break free of the grip. He had not even glanced at Dosh or Ysian. "Oh—it's you!"

"Who did you expect?" the man in green demanded, in a voice as thunderous as the drums. "What in creation do you think you're doing here, you young idiot?" He was the taller by two or three inches and considerably huskier. He had a dense black beard and a jutting hooked nose. He seemed young, yet he was the sort of man one instinctively addressed as "sir" . . . or "master," in Dosh's case.

Ysian's fingers were knotting painfully in Dosh's hair. He could hardly breathe in the crush, glancing from the Liberator to the other man and back again. Their faces were directly above his, yet neither of them seemed to know he was there. He did not want to guess who this other man might be.

D'ward smiled, but the effect was grotesque—all eyes and teeth, as if the skin of his face had shrunk. "You've got the wrong man in there!" His voice was hoarse.

"I know that, fool! And tomorrow he dies. You think that's an accident? Have you any idea of the trouble that cost us? What do you think you can achieve, coming here?"

"I can take his place. My place!"

"You won't save his life if you do! Even if Zath chose to spare him, which he wouldn't, the ephors could not forgive the humiliation. He's dead now, dead as surely as he will be when they dash out his brains tomorrow."

D'ward grimaced. "I won't let them!"

"And how are you going to stop them now?"

The drumming was a continuous menacing roll, rising louder, echoing among the pillars.

"I can go there and say who I am! I can tell them they have the wrong man. If I say I'm the Liberator—"

"You would drop dead."

D'ward's face was white with misery or terror or fury—Dosh could not tell which, and perhaps it was all of them. "Then if you helped me, stood beside me—"

"Fool!" The big man roared the word, yet none of the surrounding crowd paid him any heed at all. How could anyone resist his authority? "Zath has more power than all the Five together. *You can do nothing here except die as well!*"

"There must be something I can do!"

"No, there isn't! Maybe one day, but not today, nor tomorrow." The massive fingers squeezed harder into D'ward's arm. The man seemed ready to bite him. "Now—will you live or die? Must I force you?"

D'ward's eyes glinted feverishly. "Use mana here and you'll attract his notice, won't you? We're on the node."

"Why are you so anxious to die?" They were bellowing at each other now, yet the mob packed around them seemed oblivious.

"Why should it matter to you if I die?"

"Because we want you to fulfill the prophecy! Your time is not yet, that's all."

D'ward closed his eyes and shuddered. He slumped in despair, as if only the press of the crowd held him upright. "All right! If that's your price, I'll do it. I'll be the bloody Liberator, I'll take your orders, I'll do whatever you want, but you've got to pull the prince out of there. I *won't* let another man die in my place."

"Sorry. I can't do that."

*"Then damn you!"* D'ward screamed. "Let me go!"

Before the man in green could answer, the drum roll stopped. A brief silence . . . a faint voice making an announcement . . . the crowd within the temple screaming in joyful unison . . . the crowd outside howling for the news . . .

The man in green heaved his great shoulders back to free his other arm and cracked his fist upward against the point of D'ward's jaw. D'ward's head jerked back. He went limp, held upright only by the man's hold on his arm and the squash of bodies.

Nobody could move, or the crowd would have been dancing. As it was, they all kept bellowing their lungs out. The news spread: The sacrifice would be made. The plague would end.

The man's eyes came down to Dosh with no surprise or sudden recognition. It was as if he had known all along who Dosh was and that he was right there.

"Bring her and follow me," he growled.

Then he hoisted D'ward effortlessly onto his shoulder and plowed off through the crowd, parting it like tall grass.

Still unconscious, D'ward dangled head down in a sandwich between the man in green and Dosh, who clung tightly to the man's heavy leather sword belt and let himself be dragged. He was barely supporting himself, sagging under Ysian's weight. As the crush began to slacken, he crumpled to his knees. Ysian broke free and tumbled. The big man turned and hoisted each of them in turn upright. His strength was . . . superhuman?

Who was he? Better not to wonder . . . but he probably was . . . Who else could he be? Why?

"Hang on!" the man commanded, leading the way again.

Dosh was certainly not about to disobey, lest hard experience prove his suspicions correct, and of course Ysian would not let D'ward out of her sight. The crowd was dispersing in jubilation, flowing out along the streets from the temple, cheering and singing. Dosh clung to the man's belt, towing Ysian by the hand. Gradually the mob thinned. South, east, two more blocks south . . . the man (the Man?) knew exactly where he was heading.

He turned into a dark opening. "Stairs!" he growled, and headed down them into blackness. Dosh and Ysian descended warily, fumbling at the rough stone wall for guidance. They descended three sides of a square well, into a littered and putrid-smelling hall. A door creaked open, and they followed their guide into a dim crypt, full of people.

The air was heavy with a multitude of scents: the dank rot of the chamber itself and its sweating walls overlain by odors of candles; bodies and unwashed bedding, herbs, and strongly spiced cooking—especially cooking. They brought back a rush of memories that stunned Dosh. He recoiled, cannoning into Ysian.

Men were scrambling to their feet, women hastily covering their heads, small children scampering to the comfort of mothers. There were easily thirty people in that dingy cellar, barely visible in the faint light of a few high ventilation slits. The men crowded forward—stocky men wearing tatters that seemed ready to fall apart, men with golden hair and beards. Their eyes were pale in the gloom, shining like their knives.

As soon as they had formed a cordon between their families and the visitors, they halted, deferring to an elderly man in the background. He stood amid a litter of bedding, bundles, and broken furniture. He was spare, silver haired, and dignified. He alone wore a rich robe, amid this ragged rabble. He bowed stiffly.

"You do us honor, noble Warrior."

It was a tongue Dosh had not heard in a score of years. The lump in his throat was already agony, and it seemed to swell at the sound of those words.

"Call off your panthers, Birfair Spokesman!" the man in green answered in the same speech.

The old man barked a single word. The other men reluctantly sheathed their knives.

Their pale eyes moved to inspect Dosh. He knew he was in grave, grave danger now. He edged closer to the big man. The Tinkerfolk were granting him respect, although they obviously did not think he was who Dosh thought he was, or they would all be flat on their faces.

Whoever he was, he slid D'ward loosely to the floor. "This is the one I told you of. He is resting. I suggest the women bleach his hair before he awakens. It will save argument."

The old man smiled and bowed again.

"The others—" The big man gestured to indicate Dosh and Ysian. "That one is a woman. The other is one of your own. Take them also, if you will."

Birfair rubbed his hands. "At the same price, noble Warrior?"

A snort. "Very well. For the woman." The big man tossed a pouch to him. It struck the floor with a loud clank. "See she is not molested—she may be important. The man can pay his own way."

"Certainly, if he is one of ours, as you said." The old man's poxy, palsied face was more apparent now, as Dosh's eyes adjusted to the dark. "He is a diseased whelp of a degenerate sow, spawned in a cesspool."

"I shall rip out your stinking guts and thrust them down your throat with your feet," Dosh retorted. It was only a language test. His accent was rusty.

Karzon shrugged. "How touching to restore a lost son to the loving bosom of his people! I want all three of them out of the city as fast as possible. I don't care how you arrange it. After that, your brother can work for his gruel. He may have some skills you can use, if you're not too fussy. The other two will need your charity."

"The noble warrior has already provided most generously."

"And I expect value! When my muddle-headed young friend awakens, explain to him that he must stay away from Lympus."

"Lympus," the old man repeated.

"Yes. A place. It is being watched and will not be safe for him to approach for a long time."

"We shall obey."

"You'd better!" The man in green turned to the door.

It closed in Dosh's face as Dosh dived after him. Mysteriously, the door was now locked. It had probably been locked earlier, which would explain why the Tinkerfolk had been taken by surprise.

He spun around to get his back against it, knife in hand. Three young men were moving in on him already, coming cautiously but steadily, eyes and teeth shining. Birfair had made no promises about him. He had gold, a tunic of fine cut, and a valuable sword he did not know how to use. He also had his life. Whether he would be allowed to keep that would depend on how much he charged for the others.

# VIII

## *Endgame*

# 47

Lunch had been bad enough, because everyone had wanted to talk about the war news—rumors were floating around Greyfriars that Passchendaele had fallen—but whenever anyone had mentioned it, someone else had changed the subject. *Mustn't upset our hero in case he starts weeping!*

That had been bad enough, but after Alice and Exeter departed on the bikes, Smedley found himself alone with Ginger Jones and Mrs. Bodgley, the three of them fighting their way through conversational swamps—nothing safe to take a stand on, nothing safe to talk about.

He went outside to try gardening, not that he could do much good. Black Dog really hounded him then. His hand hurt. His leg throbbed. He thought of challenging Ginger to a game of one-handed croquet, and that brought on visions of one-handed golf, one-handed grouse shooting, one-handed cricket, and one-handed loving . . . as if he would ever find a gal interested in a cripple. One-handed car driving?

He went for a walk, but it did no good.

He came back to the Dower House, flopped down on one of the garden benches, and wondered why he had ever been crazy enough to let himself become involved in Exeter's affairs and how he was going to extricate himself. There was no decent alternative in sight, either, just the family mausoleum in Chichester. The last meeting with the guv'nor had ended in both of them yelling and Julian sobbing at the same time. Thousands of aunts. Sunday was his birthday. . . .

"Cut it out!" said a voice.

He whipped his head around and saw that Ginger Jones was sitting in a deck chair under a tree. He had a newspaper spread over his chest, as if he had been napping under it and just pulled it down.

"Beg pardon?"

The old man's glasses flashed in the sun. "You were never a moper, Julian Smedley. Don't be one now!"

"I'm not moping." Smedley turned away.

"It's just another stage," Ginger said. "I've seen dozens like you these last couple of years." There was a rustle of paper and a grunt as he heaved himself out of the deck chair. "At first you're so relieved to be out of it that you don't care what it cost." His voice came closer. "Then you begin to realize that you have the rest of your life to live and you are not as other men. You think it isn't fair. Of course it isn't fair." He was right behind Smedley now.

"I'll try to do better next term, sir."

He might as well have saved his breath.

"I've seen dozens, I say! Lots of them would be delighted to give you a hand in exchange for what they've lost. Lungs, eyes, both legs . . . There's one chap who was a fairly close chum of yours—I won't tell you his name—and he looks absolutely splendid. It's just that he isn't a real man anymore, at least not as he sees it. Care to swop with him?"

"Why don't you go and help Mrs. Bodgley knit some warm woolly undies for Our Brave Fighting Men?"

"Because I'd rather stay here and carp at you. I'm telling you that you were never a whiner and you won't be in future. It's just a stage. It will pass. Soon the real Julian Smedley will surface again."

"I really can't tell you how much I look forward to that."

"And then you will start to do what we all have to do, which is play the cards we are dealt. I should have had Exeter give you this lecture. He's better at it than I am. He says he will get you to Nextdoor if you want to go."

"What!?"

Ginger shuffled to the other bench and sat down, moving as if his back hurt. "I asked him before lunch. He'll do anything for you, Captain, because of what you did at Staffles. If Nextdoor's what you want, he says, then he'll help. He thinks you would do well there. The Service will take you at his word, he thinks. But is that really what you want?"

Smedley was, for a moment, speechless. Then, "Do you believe him?"

"Yes, I do. Don't you?"

"I don't know. It all fits . . . but it's fantasy, Ginger! Ravings! Opium dreams."

"I believe him."

"You're not just saying that to cheer me up?"

Jones shook his head. "You knew him when he was a caterpillar. You were chrysalises together and now you're both butterflies. You know him as well as anyone will ever know him. You shared adolescence. You will never know any man better than you know him. Is there anyone, anyone at all, whose word you would take over the word of Edward Exeter?"

Smedley considered the question seriously. He had to. After a while he said, "Probably not."

"Me too. Now come indoors with me, because I want to take a look at that leg of yours. Have you changed the bandages today?"

The gashes were swollen and inflamed. Ginger wanted to phone for a doctor and only agreed not to when Smedley promised to do so the next day if things got any worse.

Then they went downstairs for tea.

It was cooler in the sitting room than in the garden, Mrs. Bodgley said, because it faced east. Smedley thought it gloomy, unlived-in, lonesome. The crumpets were from Thorndyke's, Mrs. Bodgley said, and Wilfred was an even better baker than his grandfather had been, although of course nobody would ever tell the old man so. The jam, Mrs. Bodgley said, had come from the county craft fair and she thought it must be Mrs. Haddock's recipe. The gentlemen agreed it was excellent jam.

Mrs. Bodgley then narrated several tales of events that had happened when she was in India. The viceroy's court in New Delhi, some jolly times up in the hills in Simla. Something about her visit to Borneo . . . the Raffles Hotel in Singapore . . .

The Empire on which the sun never sets.

Smedley laughed at the jokes, taking his cue from Ginger.

But his mind was on Nextdoor, a whole new world. Civilizing the natives, a worthy cause. His missing hand wouldn't matter there, because he would be *Tyika* Smedley and have house servants. The war would never be mentioned. He would dress for dinner and the *entyikank* would wear long gowns. He would do good for the people. He would live forever. He would gain mana and get his hand back.

Dream.

Gravel scrunched.

A car?

Mrs. Bodgley frowned. "That sounds like a car."

Inexplicably, the muscles in Smedley's abdomen all tightened up like wire cables. He remembered the bombardment at Verdun.

The doorbell jangled.

Mrs. Bodgley rose. "I am not expecting visitors. Do you wish me to introduce you by an assumed name, Captain Smedley?"

"No," he said. "If that is necessary, then it will do no good."

Which made no sense, but his hostess nodded her chins and sailed from the room. He glanced at Ginger, who was scratching his beard, light reflecting inscrutably on his pince-nez. Neither of them spoke.

Voices in the hall . . .

". . . the year Gilbert was elected chairman," Mrs. Bodgley was booming. "I was probably more nervous than you were!"

They both rose to their feet as she cruised in again, followed by a man. A man with fishy, protuberant eyes—eyes with a jubilant gleam in them.

"Of course the captain and I have met." He extended his left hand. "And Mr. Jones! Or may I call you Ginger now, as we always did before, behind your back?"

"If I may call you Short Stringer, as *we* always did behind *your* back. Oh, blast!" Ginger's pince-nez fell to the floor.

Stringer reached it before he did, wiped it on his sleeve, and returned it. "Yes, thank you, tea would be wonderful. Driving is dusty work."

Smedley felt ill.

Ginger had lost the ruddy glow that the sunny afternoon had given him. He pawed at his beard.

Mrs. Bodgley seemed quite unconcerned, happy to welcome an old acquaintance, one of her uncountable honorary godchildren. Perhaps she really was unconcerned—

had anyone ever given her the Staffles part of the story? Did she realize how impossible this situation was, how deadly? She went to the china cabinet with a hesitant glance at the open door. "Do be seated, please, all of you. Your friend . . . ?"

"I'm sure she will find us," Stringer said blandly, selecting a chair. The gleam was back in his eyes again. His flannels and blazer were immaculate, but he seemed weary— as he should if he had driven across the width of England.

"Just freshening up," Mrs. Bodgley murmured quietly. "One lump or two, Mr. Stringer? Or would you rather I also called you Short?"

"Not unless you wish to be challenged to pistols at dawn. My friends all call me Nat. Only a few old Fallovians call me Shorty. Captain Smedley, I fancy, calls me an impossible coincidence."

"I might call you other things were Mrs. Bodgley not present," Smedley said, crossing his legs. His fist was clenched. Both fists were clenched. He consciously relaxed the visible one. The other he could do nothing about.

A teacup rattled on its saucer. He had shocked Mrs. Bodgley. Alerted to the conflict, she glanced from face to face in bewilderment.

"Nothing to what we were calling you two nights ago," Stringer said with asperity. "That was hardly pukka, what you did, Captain Smedley."

"You were long past due for a fire drill. Your presence here demonstrates that my suspicions were well-founded." Julian toyed with the idea of blacking one of those piscine eyes, and it tasted good. He was shaking, but that was only anger and all right.

"Well-founded but misdirected. Ah!"

A woman marched into the room and stopped, raking it with a glower like a burst of fire from a Hun machine-gun nest. She was tall, angular, unattractive. She wore a cheap-looking brown dress and carried a cumbersome handbag. Her hair was bound high in a bun. Smedley had last seen her behind a desk outside Stringer's office at Staffles.

The men started to rise again. Mrs. Bodgley said, "Ah, there you are. May I intro—"

"Where is she?" Miss Pimm demanded harshly. "Where is Alice Prescott? Is she with him?" She glared at Smedley.

He had nodded before he realized.

"Who?" Ginger said loudly.

She did not look at him, as if his effort to deceive was beneath contempt. "The Opposition has a mark on Alice Prescott, has had for the last three years. She went to Harrow Hill with him?"

Mrs. Bodgley made a choking noise and sank back in her chair.

"Where?" Ginger said.

"Oh, don't be childish!" Miss Pimm snapped. "I can tell that Exeter is a few miles southwest of us. *We* have a mark on *him*! I assume he went to Harrow Hill to consult the presence again. If his cousin is with him, then he is in deadly danger."

"How do we know," Smedley's voice said from where he was sitting, "that you are not the Opposition?"

"You don't. But it makes no difference. You will cooperate anyway."

"Mana!" Ginger said, and sat down hurriedly. "You have this mana he talks about!"

She looked at him seriously for the first time. She was the only one standing; the others sat and stared like children in a classroom.

"Yes, I am with Head Office, although you will have to take my word for that."

"I don't think I understand," Mrs. Bodgley muttered faintly. Had her self-possession ever failed her before? "Will you sit down and have a cup of tea, Miss Pimm?"

"No. There is no time. Mr. Stringer, we must hurry."

The famous surgeon sighed and drained his cup. He muttered, "You're sacked!" half under his breath.

Smedley and Ginger exchanged glances of panic.

"Perhaps you could explain?" Mrs. Bodgley said with an effort.

Miss Pimm slung the strap of her bag her shoulder. "I repeat, there is no time. Nine years ago, I promised Cameron Exeter that I would guard his son. I almost failed. The boy is back again, and I still have some residual obligations to fulfil. I don't believe the rest of you are in any danger now. I shall intercept Exeter before he returns here. Even if the agent the Opposition has sent is a vindictive type, he will have no reason to vent his spite on you. Come, Stringer!"

"Wait!" Smedley barked. "What exactly are you planning to do?"

She stopped in the doorway and turned as if to give battle. "I am going to do what I was planning to do at Staffles before you stuck your oar in and disrupted everything, Captain Smedley. It was your blundering intervention that alerted the Opposition."

"The Blighters, you mean?"

"We sometimes call them that. Stringer?"

"Exeter says he will never go back!" Smedley shouted.

"I fail to see that it is any business of yours."

"I do. I want to go."

He had said it. He was shocked to hear it.

But he had said it, so he must mean it.

With the reluctance of a frozen pond melting, the formidable Miss Pimm's pale lips thinned into a faint hint of a smile. "After all the trouble you have caused me, you demand favors? Talk about brass! I know you are a man of initiative and fast decisions, Captain Smedley, but do you know what is involved? Do you understand that it means considerable danger and to all intents and purposes is irrevocable? It means loss of family and home and friends. It is a leap beyond the bounds of imagination."

He nodded. His heart was beating a mad tattoo. Damn Chichester and the old man! Damn the aunts! Sunday was his birthday—twenty-one, key of the door. He smiled, to see if he still could. "Just show me."

"You are ready to come now? Immediately?"

"Yes."

"Then you impress. Very well. Come along and we'll see if it is possible. I make no promises." Miss Pimm summoned Stringer with a flick of her head and stalked from the room.

Everyone stood up again.

*"La Belle Dame Sans Merci!"* the surgeon growled, following her. "Thanks awfully for the tea, dear lady. I have so much enjoyed our long chat this afternoon. Don't bother to see us out. We really must do this more often. Get the lead out, Captain! She won't wait for you." He disappeared into the hallway.

Smedley was shivering like a dog in the starting gate. He looked to the others. "Anyone else feeling suicidal this afternoon?"

Neither had any close family. They were both aging. Ginger at least believed the tales of Elfenland—Smedley wasn't sure if Mrs. Bodgley did. Get away from the war! Live forever! Be restored to youth and health! How could anyone refuse the chance, no matter how long the odds?

Ginger removed his pince-nez and rubbed it vigorously on his sleeve. Then he replaced it and sighed. "No. I think not. Not me."

Outside, the car engine rumbled into life.

"Mrs. Bodgley?"

The lady was pale. She bit her lip. Her hesitation was longer, but then she shook her head. "No. At my age . . . no. My memories are here."

"Then I must run. Thank you, Mrs. B. Thank you both for . . . everything." Oh, God! His eyes were flooding. He grabbed her and kissed her cheek. He clutched Ginger's outstretched hand awkwardly and pumped it, thumping the man's shoulder with his stump.

"Bye!" he shouted, and ran out of the room. He blundered into the umbrella stand, ricocheted off it, raced along the hall and out the front door. The great silver Rolls was just starting to move along the driveway. He sprinted after it, and a door swung open for him.

# 48

The road was narrow between tall hedges. It was canopied by branches of great trees and full of fragrant green coolness. But it was steep. Alice gasped a final, "Whoof!" and gave up. She put her foot down and wiped her forehead.

"From here I walk!" she said. "How much farther?"

Edward halted at her side. "Just around this corner, I think."

She dismounted, pulled her skirts clear, and began to push the bike.

He took it from her, pushing both. "Look on the bright side. We can freewheel on the way back!" He was grinning, quite unwinded. He was in much better shape than she was.

"Mmph! Well, you can do the talking on the way up. You have never told me how you found Olympus."

"There isn't much to tell. You've heard all the exciting bits. How far had I got? Karzon? Well, he dumped us on a band of Tinkerfolk—"

"Why? I mean, I thought he was the Man, and Zath was one of his."

"Ah! Zath's supposed to be, but he hasn't been for quite a while. There had never been an actual god of death before him. Who would want to be? There are several fictitious deities like that, just a temple or shrine with no stranger behind them. People worship there just the same. In every case, a member of the Pentatheon will claim suzerainty, so not all the mana is lost. I think Death was merely an abstract notion until some minion of Karzon's asked for the title and Karzon let him take it. What his real name was, I don't know and it doesn't matter.

"Anyway, Karzon had made a bad mistake. Zath founded his own cult, bestowed the Black Scriptures on it, sent out the reapers. Human sacrifice is an enormously potent source of mana. Even though the murders were not committed on his node, he gained power from every death. By the time the Pentatheon realized what he was up to—and that probably took half a century or so—none of them dared challenge him."

"They couldn't combine against him?"

Edward guffawed. "Combine? After thousands of years of playing the Great Game? No, they can't think like that. They let Zath continue on his jolly way, all trying to get on his team. About fifty years ago, he arranged for a new temple in Tharg, with himself as co-deity. The Five, in effect, have become six."

"I think I get the gist. So Karzon supports the Liberator and the *Filoby Testament*!"

"Enthusiastically! He daren't let Zath know that, of course. He was hoping that little old me would achieve what all the gods of the world were scared to try. Well, I won't!"

Alice groaned. They had rounded the corner. The road ahead was straight—and straight up.

"Oh, I remember this bit," Edward said. "The gate's at the top."

"I hope my heart will stand it. Do you think we ought to be roped?"

They began to climb. Edward continued to push both bikes, yet he still had enough wind to talk.

"Karzon shipped us out of the city, disguised as Tinkerfolk. They're very much like our Gypsies, only more primitive, because the whole culture is more primitive. They wander all over the Vales, trading, stealing, spying. They're all blond as Scandinavians. It's said they abandon any baby who isn't, in the belief that it must be a half-breed. I wouldn't put it past them. Dosh was borderline, only just blond enough. He probably had a rough childhood because of that.

"By the time I woke up, he'd already been in a fight. He'd killed one, wounded three others, and was just about a goner from lack of blood himself. I still had some of the mana the army had given me, and I used it to revive him instead of curing my own headache, which at the time felt very altruistic, believe me! They were a rough-and-ready bunch of scoundrels."

Obviously! Alice had no breath to comment.

Edward chuckled. "But I had an interesting summer, that year! We crossed a pass into Sitalvale, then another into Thovale, and eventually wandered over into Randorvale. I passed very close to Olympus, although of course I didn't know that, and in any case Karzon's warning to stay away from it made good sense. Dosh disappeared in Thovale. By killing a man of the tribe, he'd acquired a wife, and she was a genuine, steam-powered firecat. Or perhaps it was just the primitive living conditions he didn't like. I don't know where he went, but I'm sure Dosh will survive. He's incredible."

"How?" She panted. Running with Gypsies! She wondered what Julian Smedley would think of this confession if he knew. Or the masters at Fallow.

"Just tough! All the Tinkerfolk are, but he could out-tough most of them any day. As for morals . . ." Edward fell silent for a dozen paces, and apparently decided not to discuss morals. "At first they treated me as a baby, but they had accepted gold and sworn oaths to cherish me, and they kept their word. They didn't know the man who had hired them was Karzon, but they knew he was somebody to fear. I wanted to earn my keep, so I became an expert in livestock trading. Every vale seems to have a different collection of herdbeasts, none of which look anything like our horses and cattle, but they're all traded in much the same way. Charisma came in very useful there, and I cheated outrageously—a stranger can be so plausible! I could extract more money for a worn-out useless runt than even old Birfair himself could, or buy a champion for less. Eventually they came to accept me as useful, a real man."

Alice decided that her cousin had depths she had not suspected and would prefer not to know about. Julian's hair would turn white if he heard this, an English gentleman going to the dogs, becoming a vagrant huckster.

"By autumn, though, I'd had enough of rags and dirt and hunger. Ysian was pining. We were in Lappinvale by then, which at the moment is a Thargian colony. And one day I saw a man I knew."

Alice stopped to catch her breath. He looked at her with concern.

"I'm all right," she said. "What man?"

"You can wait here while I go and see Mr. Goodfellow."

She shook her head. She wouldn't mind being winded were Edward not so confoundedly cool looking and relaxed. He turned to stare up at the hill ahead, and then peered around at the distance they had come, but his mind was away on another world. He smiled in secret amusement.

"I had never met him, but I had been told of him. In the higher, cooler vales, they have a riding beast they call . . . Well, there are a lot of different names for it. It's the Rolls-Royce of Nextdoor. It's enormous, big as a rhino. It's pretty much a mammal, but it looks like a cross between a stegosaurus—that's one of the dinosaurs in *The Lost World* with a row of bony plates down the middle of its back. . . . It's a bit like that and also like a Chinese dragon. It has scales, yet it's warm-blooded. It eats grass, and it's a wonderful steed—gentle, intelligent, willing, the only thing better than a terrestrial horse. I thought of them as dragons, so that name will do.

"One day I saw a herd of them just outside a village we had been cadging off. There were tents there, and I guessed soon enough that this was the encampment of a man who traded in them. I sauntered over to take a closer look.

"I got shouted at, of course. I was a tinker. I had bleached hair and blue eyes and my clothes were mostly holes held together by hope. I would have made a scarecrow look like a lord. The wranglers tried to chase me away, because I must be a thief and a ne'er-do-well. Most of them had a little gold circle in their left earlobe, and they all wore black turbans. That told me this was the outfit Eleal had described. Ready?"

"Think so." She began plodding again. He sauntered along at her side, still pushing a bike with each hand.

"So I withdrew to a safe distance and squatted down by some bushes and waited. After an hour or two, the man I wanted came marching back from the village. He was very big, and he had an enormous copper-colored beard. You know the legend of the sailor who has a girl in every port? Well, this fellow has one in every village. . . . I assume that's where he'd been, but perhaps I'm doing him an injustice. He may have been there on business. I doubt it. Anyway, I cut him off before he reached his tents.

"He barked an obscenity and tried to go round me.

"I said, 'T'lin Dragontrader? We almost met, once.' That stopped him!

"He scowled at me and said something I won't repeat.

"I said, 'How are things with the Service these days?'

"He went back two steps with his eyes almost popping out of his head. I knew that he was an agent of the Service, you see, because Eleal had told me. He's a native, not a stranger, and he spies for the political branch. He threw some sort of password at me then—'The grass grows softer when the rain is cool,' or some such gibberish.

"I said, 'Frightfully sorry, but I don't know the answer.' I gave him another code that I'd been told once. He recognized it, although he didn't know the answer, because it was for the religious branch and he's political. In the end I just said, 'I am D'ward Liberator.'

"I thought he was going to faint. We sat down beside the bushes, and we had a long chat. He admitted that the Service was hunting for me—they'd heard of the fall of Lemod, too, of course, and realized I was still alive. He knew they were not the only ones after me. I asked him to pass the word. Then I remembered Ysian and decided that being a dragon trader would be nicer than being a tinker. So I informed T'lin that he had just acquired two more hands.

"He didn't argue, actually. He's a very loyal follower of the Undivided—a likable rogue, very shrewd. I went and got Ysian. Old Birfair and the gang were genuinely sorry to lose us, and I had to write a note to Karzon, testifying that they had fulfilled their side of the bargain. I doubt if any of them could read, but they were grateful for the insurance. Then we went to T'lin's camp and put on some respectable clothes and became dragon traders. Look out."

They moved to the side of the road as a car came growling up the hill to pass them. It was a bright red roadster, puffing stinking clouds of exhaust. The driver wore goggles and a sporty cap.

"May his radiator boil and his tires all burst!" Edward said cheerfully as he strode out again. "Only a real bounder would drive a motor that color. We wandered around the Vales a bit, and settled down in little Mapvale for the winter. By then I'd been almost two years on Nextdoor and was getting pretty desperate, but we got no word back from Olympus before the passes closed. I loved the dragons, though."

They walked for a while in silence. They were past the worst. The gate must be just around the corner, set back in the hedge, probably.

"Did you meet Eleal again?"

"No, never. T'lin had changed his schedule, and he had not run into the troupe since the reaper almost got him in Sussvale. He thought they were still in business."

"And Olympus?"

"Ah! One morning, early in the spring, I was exercising a couple of bulls—boars—stallions? What the deuce do you call a male dragon in English? Anyway, I ran into a chappie riding a beautiful young female, of the color they call Osby slate. Of course we stopped to admire each other's stock, and of course I asked him if he would like to sell or trade.

"He was a lanky, rangy youngster with sandy hair and a notably big nose. Well fitted out. He admitted he would consider an offer. . . ."

Something funny was coming, judging by the grin.

"We must have stood there and haggled for two solid hours. I tried every trick I knew. I really wanted that filly! I blew my charisma to white heat. I argued and wheedled. I kept going up and up, and he wouldn't come down one copper mark. I was completely flummoxed. And finally he held out a hand and drawled in perfect English, 'I don't believe I want to part with her after all, old man. I'm Jumbo Watson. I was a chum of your father's.' "

Alice chuckled at Edward's infectious glee. "Nicely done?"

"Oh, beautifully! I wanted to melt and soak into the sand." He laughed aloud. "You should hear Jumbo tell the story! He puts on this incredible Tinkerfolk accent, although we'd been speaking Joalian. I have died a thousand deaths at dinner tables over that episode. But that's Jumbo."

"What's wrong?"

"Nothing. I took to him right away. We got along like a house on fire. We rode dragons over the ranges to Olympus, which was a corker of a trip at that time of year, and he was absolutely solid. He was gracious to Ysian, which is more than can be said of some. . . . He has the most marvelous dry humor, a regular brick.

"There you are—that's how I got to Olympus. It's a charming spot, very scenic, a little glen tucked away between Thovale, Narshvale, and Randorvale. Didn't dare stay more than four or five fort . . . about a couple of months." He fell silent for a moment, and then seemed to discard what he had been about to say. His smile had gone.

"I'd been two years on Nextdoor, and that was the first time I'd had any news of Home. I was horrified to hear that the war was still on and at the same time glad that I hadn't missed it all and would still be able to do my bit. I sat around for a few days, bringing them up to date on what I'd been doing and learning about the Service and so on. Then I politely asked for the first boat Home. That's when the wicket got sticky.

"The Service is badly split over the Liberator prophecies, you see, and always has been. The guv'nor had never gone for them. Once I got to Olympus and learned all the ins and outs of the business, then I was thoroughly against it, too. Break the chain and be done with it! Jumbo was pretty much leader of the anti faction, and I agreed with him wholeheartedly. Killing Zath would only lead to worse trouble. I wanted to come Home and enlist.

"Creighton, incidentally, had been one of the pro-Liberator group. In spite of what he told me, he came Home in 1914 specifically to make sure I crossed over on schedule. Much good it did him personally! But the pro-Liberator forces were in a majority, and they kept me dangling, on one pretext after another."

They were almost at the summit, and Alice decided she could cycle again. Before she could say so, she saw that Edward's mind was very far off.

"And what happened?"

"Mm? Oh, well, I did come back, didn't I? Eventually. And here I am. It's a beautiful day and I'm Home and I want to enjoy every minute of it."

She sensed evasion there and went after it—instinct, she thought, like a dog chasing anything that runs. "How, Edward? How did you come back?"

Long pause . . . Then he shrugged. "That was Jumbo's doing, too. One day he turned up at the chapel where I was massaging the heathens' souls for the Undivided and more or less said, 'If you wait for a flag from those blokes on the Committee, you'll wait a thousand years. I can fix it up for you.' He took me to another node and taught me a key to get me Home, and he swore that there would be people waiting at this end to help."

"What! You mean he deliberately dropped you on that battlefield in Flanders? He's the traitor you've been talking about! *Jumbo* tried to kill you?"

Edward nodded. He stared at the road ahead with eyes as hard and cold as sapphires. With a shock, she remembered that her young cousin could be dangerous. He was a sacker of cities.

"You see why I need to send word back?" he said. "And it may be worse than that, even. Five years ago, when the coming of the Liberator was almost due, the Service sent a couple of men Home to talk to the guv'nor, to see if he still felt the same way about matters. They wanted to meet me, too. I was sixteen by then, and they thought they should be allowed to inspect me. The guv'nor forbade that, although the only one who ever learned his reaction was Soapy Maclean. Jumbo came straight to England. Soapy went to Africa."

She took her bike from him. "And died at Nyagatha!"

Again Edward nodded. "The Blighters roused the Meru outlaws. But who tipped off the Blighters? Who told them where Cameron Exeter was? I think that must have been Jumbo, too. I think he was working for the Chamber even then. He killed our—"

She looked where he was looking. They had come to the gate. It was no farmer's gate. It was a steel gate, with a padlock. It bore a sign that said, WAR DEPARTMENT and POSITIVELY NO ADMITTANCE EXCEPT ON HIS MAJESTY'S SERVICE and other stern things. Beyond it, a freshly paved road climbed across the field to the crest of the hill—once, she assumed, crowned with a copse of oaks and a few immemorially ancient standing stones. Now it was surrounded by yet another fence and a gate with a sentry box. The woods had gone. In their place was an antiaircraft battery, a twentieth-century obscenity of iron sheds and repulsive ordnance.

"Puck!" Edward said with cold fury. "They've despoiled his grove! It's all gone. They drove him away."

First Stonehenge, now this. Another of the roads back to Nextdoor had just closed. But obviously that was not what was distressing him. He had just stumbled on a friend's grave.

Alice fumbled for words of comfort. "He had lived beyond his time, Edward. All things pass."

"But he was such a likable old ruin! Harmless! He helped me—a kid who meant nothing to him at all but was in serious trouble. He wouldn't have hurt a fly!"

"On the contrary, Mr. Exeter," said a voice from the other side of the road, "he was a meddler, and for that he had to pay."

# 49

It was the motorist whom Edward had called a bounder. He was short and thick, standing in the weedy grass of the verge, half hidden in the hedge. He wore his floppy cap at a cocky angle above a haircut short enough to be called a shave; his brown tweed suit looked absurdly hot for the weather. He had removed his goggles. Despite his breadth, his features were not flabby. They were hard, and his eyes were a peculiar shade of violet.

He was smiling and he had his hands in his pockets, yet Alice had an inexplicable feeling that he was pointing a gun at her.

"Should I know you?" Edward drawled.

"If you believe in knowing your enemy. I have been waiting for this meeting for a long time, Exeter. The prophecy has run out of mana at last."

Fighting to quench panic, Alice wondered why she did not turn around to face this threat. She had not moved her feet, and neither had Edward. They were both standing in an awkward, twisted position, holding their bikes; they had not moved their feet.

"You needn't worry about the prophecy," Edward said calmly. "I will never go back. I will never become the Liberator. You have my word on it."

"Ah! The word of an English gentleman!" The bounder sighed dramatically. He ought to be an artesian well of perspiration in those tweeds on a day like this, but his face was pale and dry. "So you say now. Forgive my doubts. I had rather make sure." She could not place his accent.

"Then let Miss Prescott leave. She is not involved in this."

"I think it will be neater to include both of you. Turn your bicycles around, please, and prepare to mount."

Alice did as she was bid, and so did Edward. Why had she not refused? Why did she not simply climb on the saddle and pedal away? Why didn't Edward? Of course the nasty red roadster was parked just over there, so the bounder could run them down, but why should they not at least try to make a break for it?

Rabbits hypnotized by snakes?

Oh, that was absurd!

Then why not just go? Why not just scarper?

"What are you going to do?" she demanded, and was disgusted by the shrillness in her voice.

"Very little." The bounder shrugged his broad shoulders. "I've already done it, actually. I just have to say the word. An Army lorry is starting up the hill. You and Mr. Exeter are going to pedal down. You will pedal as hard as you can, both of you. When you reach that bend down there, you will cut the corner, over to the wrong side of the road."

"Humor him, darling," Edward said. "He's funnier as Lady Hamilton, but that's on Tuesdays. His keeper gets Fridays off."

"Ah, the impeccably stiff upper lip!" the man agreed in the same dry tone. *"Toujours le sang-froid!* I estimate you will be doing between forty-four and forty-seven miles an hour when you stop. That is quite adequate to remove most of the rigidity from your ossiferous framework, if you will pardon the euphemism."

"Never," Edward said. "I had better warn you, I suppose. You have overlooked something. The *Testament* is a self-fulfilling prophecy. Every time someone tries to break the chain, he just strengthens it!"

"A few more minutes," the bounder said casually.

"You don't believe me? Then consider: If Zath had simply ignored the whole damned rigmarole, then nothing would have happened. But he tried to kill my father to prevent my being born. The attempt failed, and it alerted the guv'nor to the prophecy. The guv'nor left Nextdoor in case Zath tried again, but that meant he met the mater in New Zealand and got married and I transpired. If he'd stayed on Nextdoor, then any son he might have had would be a native, and harmless. Don't you see?"

"Ingenious. But not convincing."

*Leave!* Alice thought. Just perch on the saddle and pedal away. Freewheel sedately down the hill, staying safely on the left side of the road, and this whole insane conversation will fade away like moonbeams. Why did she not do that?

"It goes on and on." Edward was still speaking quietly, but faster. "The massacre at Nyagatha was supposed to kill me, but it killed my parents instead. If my father had lived he would have told me the whole story and I would never have crossed over! I would have taken his advice. I worshipped him and would never have gone against his wishes. So you outsmarted yourselves again. Then you tried to kill me in Greyfriars, and the result of that was that I did cross over and the prophecy was fulfilled. If you'd left me alone, I'd have enlisted and probably died last year on the Somme!"

The bounder had barely moved since Alice first set eyes on him, but now he raised a hand to smother a yawn. "Sorry to drag it out like this. Another minute or so and you can be on your way."

"I'm warning you!" Edward said, louder. "The same thing happened in Thargvale. Zath tried so hard to snare me that he let the whole army escape, and me too. By trying to break the chain, you will only strengthen it. Don't, please! I'm on your side! I want out. I want my own life. I don't want this damned prophecy coiling around me like a serpent all the time. Just ignore it and it will go away. It will wither. I want to stay here on Earth and serve my King. *I do not want to be the Liberator!*"

"You won't. We are about to make quite sure of that."

"Then leave Miss Prescott out of it!"

The bounder chuckled, but his ugly purple eyes did not smile. "If you believed your theories, you would not ask that."

"Bystanders get hurt! That's why you should listen to me. You may get caught in the backlash yourself. Dozens died at Nyagatha, thousands at Lemod. I sail through unscathed, and the innocents get mowed down!"

"You won't sail through this time," said the bounder. "Pedal as hard as you can and cut the corner at the bottom. No braking! It won't hurt."

"Let Alice go!" Edward shouted.

"You both go. Ready? Now!"

Alice swung up on the saddle and began to pedal as if her life depended on it. She was just trying to deceive the man. She would stop pedaling in a couple of minutes, as soon as she was safely away. They could freewheel almost all the way to Vicarsdown from here, and perhaps even have another cup of tea in the Tea Shoppe.

Edward went by her, head down, legs going like aeroplane propeller blades.

How dare he! Show-off brat! She forced her legs to move even faster. The wind was whistling by her. Never had she known such a sensation of speed. The hill unrolled below her like a death warrant. The hedges on either hand streaked past in green blurs. Wind caught her hat and snatched it away. Faster, faster! Harder, harder! Steeper, steeper! Edward was still gaining, his long legs giving him an unfair advantage, his jacket flailing behind him like Dracula's cloak.

She could no longer move her feet fast enough to do any good. Her hair was unravelling. Her eyes were full of icy tears, and she could hardly see. The bike hammered so hard she could barely hang on to the handlebars. The corner was rushing up at her.

Edward was there already. He leaned into the curve, cutting across to the inside— and vanished behind the hedge. She struggled to stay on her own side of the road, but at that speed she dare not. Despite all her efforts, she was turning to follow exactly where he had gone. The lorry leaped into view, growling up the hill, dead in her path, filling the road. Alongside it, cutting out to overtake it blind, came a huge silver-gray Rolls-Royce. There was no sign of Edward at all and she closed her eyes.

# 50

In one corner of the back seat, Miss Pimm snapped commands: "Faster! Cut this corner! Go faster!" Her voice was soft and yet it carried the authority of a sergeant major's. In the driver's seat, Stringer was howling in terror, but apparently doing exactly what she wanted, like a puppet on strings. The big car swung around the bends, trees and hedgerows streaming past in an impossible blur. Thank the gods there was no other traffic . . . so far.

In the other corner of the back seat, Smedley had clenched his real fist until the nails dug into his palm, and he could not feel his imaginary one at all, just when he needed it. This was downright maniacal! A country lane like this was only safe at about twenty miles an hour, and they must be doing seventy at least. And uphill at that! The engine would boil. Even a Rolls made a din at this speed.

"Prepare to overtake!" Miss Pimm said. She seemed quite relaxed, holding her over-sized handbag on her lap. "There is a lorry ahead."

God in heaven! What had got into the crazy old bat? She had been perfectly sane until about fifteen minutes ago. And then . . . well, they had gone through Vicarsdown like a Sopwith Camel. A miracle they hadn't killed someone. When he had expostulated, she had told him to stuff a sock in it.

"Pull over—*now!*"

The Rolls seemed to tilt almost onto two wheels as it hurtled around the corner on the outside. The back of an Army lorry swelled instantly from nowhere to fill the gap from hedge to hedge. Stringer shrieked and somehow shot the Rolls into the slit on the right. Branches snapped and whipped along the coachwork.

"Stay on this side!"

*Straight ahead!* A cyclist! Smedley yelled, "Look out!" Stringer screamed at the top of his lungs. There was a momentary image of an impending disaster, a loud impact of metal against metal, and Edward Exeter was sitting alongside Mr. Stringer in the front. *Then another!* More noise . . . something like a wheel whistled past the window . . . and Alice Prescott was on the back seat between Smedley and Miss Pimm. "Stay on this side!" Miss Pimm repeated. A bright red roadster rushed straight at the windscreen, veered at the last second, missed the lorry by inches, and plunged headlong into the woods with a noise like an artillery barrage at close range. Smedley caught a glimpse of its wheels and chassis as it reared vertically, plastering itself against a tree. Then the Rolls was around the bend and humming up a long, straight hill on a peaceful, sunny afternoon.

"I think that went well, don't you?" Miss Pimm said, in the tones of one who had just pulled off a daring finesse in a game of auction bridge. "You may pull over to the left now, Mr. Stringer, and reduce speed."

Alice opened her eyes. Exeter said something in a harsh foreign tongue and twisted around to look at her. They were both brightly flushed and apparently out of breath. He studied Alice, then Smedley, and finally Miss Pimm.

"Is it legal to enter a car at that speed?" Smedley inquired weakly. His heart was doing a thousand revs. If he had been skeptical of magic before, he must certainly believe now. Those two had been *outside,* on *bicycles,* and boring straight into the lorry like *howitzers* and here they were quietly sitting . . .

"Mr. Stringer, why are you stopping?" Miss Pimm demanded sharply.

"I'm a doctor! There has been an accident. And, by heaven, the police are going to ask some—"

"Drive on! We need not worry about the law. Unfortunately, nobody was injured. The soldiers will discover that the other car had no driver, whatever they may have thought they saw before the crash. They will not be able to explain the bicycle debris either, but that is not our concern. Pray continue." The class will now hand in its dictation.

"I'm alive?" Alice whispered.

"Only just!" Miss Pimm said. "I apologize for my tardy arrival and the unruly procedure."

Exeter squirmed around to kneel on the seat, leaning over the back. "I saw you at Staffles!"

"Being a guardian dragon? And now I am the *deus ex machina.*"

His eyes gleamed with delight. "*Dea,* surely? And *in machina,* not *ex?*"

How could he possibly be capable of making jokes already? Alice was still paralyzed. Smedley had just discovered that he had bitten his tongue.

Miss Pimm smiled her barely visible, thin-lipped smile in appreciation. "At the moment I am going by the name of Miss Pimm."

"But when I was at Fallow, I used to address you as Jonathan Oldcastle, Esq?"

"You did indeed! Well done." *Move to the top of the class.* "I don't suppose your handwriting has improved at all, has it?"

Exeter was grinning as if all this insanity were just enormous fun. "Unlikely. Colonel Creighton said you were a committee."

A faint spasm of annoyance crossed her face. "I was chairwoman."

"Was it the pillar-box? You had a spell on it?"

"No, Edward. It was your fountain pen. Turn left at the intersection, Mr. Stringer."

*"You read my diary?"*

"No. It was excessively uninteresting."

Exeter scowled and looked at Alice. "You all right?" He reached out a hand, but the car was too big for him to reach her.

She let out a long sigh. "Yes, I think so. I need an explanation!"

"We have time for that!" Miss Pimm adjusted her handbag on her lap. "The real credit goes to Mr. Stringer's brother, the brigadier. He recognized Edward. He guessed that whatever had happened was beyond the scope of normal military procedures and very gallantly took the risk of shipping him home, notifying—"

"Dumping the whole mess on me!" Stringer snarled, turning left at the intersection. "I will kill him! Where are we going?"

*Nextdoor!* Smedley thought. *Olympus!*

"Straight on until I say otherwise. I became aware of your cousin's return when he reached England, Miss Prescott. I placed a mark on him many years ago. It is not operative outside this world, and even here its range is limited. I investigated. I decided he was in no immediate danger. It took me a few days to make arrangements—"

"My secretary eloped with a sailor!" Stringer growled.

"Quite so. Love at first sight. The very morning I took up my new duties—"

"Excuse the interruption," Exeter said softly. "But what do you do when you are not being my nursemaid?"

"Many things. I am with the organization you refer to as Head Office, of course. My portfolio is the British Imperial Government, excluding the Government of India. Mostly I burrow around Whitehall like an invisible mole, arranging this and that. For example, it was I who was responsible for your father being appointed D.O. at Nyagatha. That was an interesting challenge, as he was twenty-five years old, with thirty years' experience."

She smiled her schoolmistress smile again—Smedley wondered what age she was. He realized that he could not tell. At times she seemed quite young, and at other times quite old. Dowdy and unattractive, she was yet lording it over all of them. Charismatic?

"We wanted to see if we could demonstrate the advantages of nondisruptive techniques in elevating the social systems of subject races. But I digress. As I said, that very first morning Captain Smedley came blundering in."

Exeter looked at Smedley and smiled fondly. "Bless him!"

"He turned out to be a confounded nuisance," Miss Pimm said sharply. "But he has named his reward, and we shall see what he does with it."

Exeter's smile widened. "What did he do wrong?"

"He involved Miss Prescott. The Blighters have a mark on her. When she suddenly left London on a weekday, they were alerted. The rest, I think, you can work out. Right at the junction, Mr. Stringer."

The surgeon snorted. "You haven't asked me what reward I want!"

"I catch images of myself being burned at the stake," Miss Pimm retorted, "so I shall not inquire about the details. Try to concentrate on the interesting weekend you are having."

"We must need petrol."

"No, we don't. We have a fair distance to go, and the Opposition will be after us. Did you get a good look at their agent?"

Exeter scowled. "If you mean that joker driving the fire engine, then I think so, yes. He had mauve eyes."

"Ah! Then it was Schneider himself. I thought as much."

"He's dead now?"

"Not at all. And as soon as a suitable vehicle comes within his reach, he will be on our heels. He has probably summoned reinforcements. You have bruised his vanity too often, Edward."

"I did warn him!" Exeter glanced at Alice. "And that is not all I should like to bruise."

"But you are a native here, so you have no chance whatsoever of doing so. You must leave him to us. Now I have to teach you all the key to the portal—"

"Not so fast! You want to cross over, Smedley?"

"All three of you will cross over!" Miss Pimm said sharply. "It is the only way to put you out of the Blighters' reach. I have better things to do than guard you twenty-four hours a day, Edward."

"Not me! My duty is to enlist. I will not return to Nextdoor."

Miss Pimm's eyes narrowed dangerously, as if she considered ordering him to wash out his mouth with soap. "Then why did you go to Harrow Hill?"

Exeter was looking dangerous himself, or at least implacably stubborn. "I have a message to send, that is all. There is a traitor in Olympus, but if Julian is going, then he can tell them for me."

"Who?" she demanded.

"Jumbo Watson!"

"Absolute rubbish! I have known Mr. Watson for—for more years than you would believe."

Exeter sighed and shook his head. "I would very much like to agree with you, ma'am. I like Jumbo personally, like him a lot. But remember he was Home in 1912? Somebody tipped off the Blighters where the guv'nor was hiding."

"No, they didn't. Soapy Maclean came over by way of the Valley of the Kings. That portal had been compromised. We did not confirm that until much later. The only person to use it since was Colonel Creighton, in 1914, and there was so much confusion that summer that he managed to shake off the followers he had acquired."

"Really?" There was an oddly pleading expression on Exeter's face.

"Certainly. Jumbo was confident that your father would still oppose the Liberator prophecies and would try to prevent your fulfilling them—he had no motive to kill Cameron and Rona Exeter. Furthermore, the Blighters obviously believed that they had caught you in the massacre. They ignored you for two years after that. Jumbo knew you were at school in England, although I would not tell him where. You cannot blame Nyagatha on Jumbo, Edward."

Exeter sighed. "I'm glad! But he was the one who dumped me on the battlefield. It was a deliberate attempt to kill me, and it was certainly Jumbo who did that. Even if he wasn't the rat at Nyagatha, he's a rat now."

Miss Pimm frowned and bit her lip. After a moment she said, "I cannot recall anyone from Nextdoor ever crossing over by way of Belgium. That is not a portal known to the Service. So who told Jumbo about it?"

"Zath, I expect. The Chamber."

"Of course. Cannot we go a little faster, Mr. Stringer? We have a long way to go."

"I am a nervous wreck!"

"You will be a physical one also, if you try to resist me now."

Exeter caught Smedley's eye and grinned. Miss Pimm was a most formidable lady.

"Faster!" she said. "Undoubtedly the Chamber informed Jumbo, Edward. But how? They must have an agent within the Service, but who? If Jumbo were here, we could ask him who told him about that portal. We could ask him who taught him the key, and who assured him that there was a tended node at this end—which I assume he told you was the case? You were deceived by someone you trusted, but perhaps that person had been deceived also?"

Exeter was nodding.

"You are making charges of the most serious nature," she continued. "Undoubtedly, the Service will bring whoever is responsible to trial and impose the death penalty if he is convicted."

"I will drink to that."

"But is Jumbo the culprit, or was he duped? Captain Smedley is an unknown on Nextdoor. He is also—forgive me, Captain—a man who has recently undergone a grave ordeal. If he turns up unannounced in Olympus mouthing accusations of treason against one of the Service's oldest and most senior officers, then he is not likely to receive a serious hearing. At the very least, the individual responsible will have enough warning to make his escape. If you want revenge, Edward, if you want justice, then you must deliver the message yourself. An accused person has the right to face his accusers."

Now that was telling him, Smedley decided joyfully. Exeter obviously agreed, for his frown was thunderous.

Alice was smiling. She was pretty when she smiled, not at all horsey.

Exeter said quietly. "My duty is to enlist."

A shadow of exasperation passed over Miss Pimm's crabby face. "Spoken like a true Englishman," she said cryptically. "But to do so here would be rank stupidity. I cannot guarantee that I shall always be available to pull you out of the wreckage. I will make you a much better proposition. Do you know the sacred grove of Olipain?"

"In Randorvale? I know where it is."

"And you can get there from Olympus?"

"It's not far. Three or four days' walk."

"Very well. I shall teach you the key to it. It leads to a tended portal in New Zealand. In fact, that was how your father came Home in ninety. Your mother was born not far from there."

She paused, but Exeter just waited for her to finish, eyes steady and unreadable.

"You will return to Olympus this evening, taking Miss Prescott and Captain Smedley. When you have laid your charges and given your evidence—when honor is satisfied, and I know I can trust your judgment on that—then you can make your own way to the grove of Olipain. You will not need to ask the Committee's permission, fair enough? That key requires no additional drummer. You will enlist in New Zealand. The Dominion forces are playing a noble part in this war. The chances of your ever being recognized in their theaters of operation are remote. That is a reasonable compromise, is it not?"

"I have no intention," Exeter said icily, "of sitting out this war guarding some bloody sheep farm on the wrong side of the—"

Smedley exploded. After he had outlined the Gallipoli Campaign and the reputation Anzac forces had earned on the Western Front, he subsided as suddenly as he began. He apologized to the ladies for his language. He had rather surprised himself, and he had certainly astonished Exeter.

"I didn't know!" He swallowed. "I'll have to swot up on all this! But I apologize. I accept your generous offer, ma'am."

"That is settled then!"

"Not me!" Alice roused herself for the first time, sitting up straight and seeming to pull herself together. "I stay here."

"Alice!" Exeter said.

Smedley wanted to tell him that he was being a fool. She kept a man's dressing gown in her flat. A woman had greater loyalties than cousins. For a moment nobody spoke.

At last Alice said, "No, Edward. I warned you. I have my reasons, Miss Pimm."

Miss Pimm nodded.

Exeter moaned. "Alice? Please? The Blighters may come after you!"

"No, Edward. If they are using me as a Judas goat, then I think I will be more valuable to them alive than dead. Correct, Miss Pimm?"

"I hope so. One cannot tell, but it may be so. You must go faster, Mr. Stringer. I shall warn you if there is any traffic coming."

"There is a car behind us. It has been there for some time, a Bentley, I think. Is it a threat?"

She closed her eyes for a moment. "Nobody I recognize. I shall watch them, though. Carry on. Now, do not be tiresome, Edward. Your cousin is quite old enough to make her own decisions."

"But—"

"No buts. Attend carefully, please, Captain Smedley. All portal keys are very ancient and very complicated. They involve rhythm, words, and a dance pattern. They arouse primitive emotions to attune the mind to the virtuality. Think of that as sanctity."

"Exeter described them." Smedley had begun to feel excited again. "He mentioned beating drums, though, and I'm short a few fingers now."

"I don't think that will matter, as long as someone is drumming for you. Have you ever felt a sense of *uplift* in church, when the anthem soars?"

"Um. Yes, I suppose so."

"You are not tone-deaf, I hope? You can dance?"

"No and yes, respectively." His leg was throbbing like the dickens, but he could move it.

"Then I foresee no difficulty. Your wrist has healed sufficiently that it will not open if the sutures are lost. We shall begin with the words."

# 51

*O mbay fala, inkuthin,*
*Indu maka, sasa du.*
*Aiba aiba nopa du,*
*Aiba reeba mona kin.*
*Hosagil!*

The gibberish ran round and round in Smedley's head. Fortunately there were only three verses to that key, each ending in the same shout of *Hosagil!* He thought he had the words, but the beat was nastily complex and contrapuntal, and of course the steps and gestures would have to wait until they arrived at St. Gall's. Even a Rolls was not spacious enough for dancing.

*Ombay fala* . . . Screw *Hosagil,* whoever he was.

Exeter ought to be in worse shape, because he was having to memorize two keys. Smedley could not imagine how he would manage that without mixing them up, but he had not changed a bit from their schooldays—cool, calm, and accomplished. He caught on to the rhythms right away, claiming a knack acquired during his Africa childhood, and he had always been a whiz at languages, which must help with the words. He would probably come first in the exam. Just like old times! In fact, Edward Exeter would be a downright pill if he wasn't always so straight and square, such a brick. No one could ever dislike him.

The sky was trying on pastel colors as evening approached. Stringer clung grimly to the wheel, rarely speaking. If Miss Pimm was not supporting her driver with spikes of magic, he must be well beyond the end of his tether. There had been no break for tea.

Now Exeter was prying information out of her, a process much like opening oysters with bare hands.

"And what is St. Gall's?"

"A church."

"Very old, of course?"

"Of course. There are," she continued in an obvious diversion, "two standing stones remaining in the churchyard. It may well be that some of the keys we know date from megalithic—"

"Do you use this portal often?"

"Quite often," she admitted with the reluctance of a biology mistress being asked to explain the function of reproductive organs.

"It leads directly to Olympus?"

"Yes."

"And back?"

She sighed. "Yes. We know keys for translation in both directions. That is rare."

"Then why are the Blighters not aware of it?"

"They are."

"They have sentries?"

"No resident stranger, no. No traps I cannot handle. Normally they don't care a fig about Nextdoor, remember! It was only the Chamber's appeal for help in destroying you that roused the Blighters' interest. They care more who comes in than who goes out, in any case. Anyone departing who has not entered will be marked in some fashion."

"Will that Schneider man have guessed it is where we are going?"

"Oh, yes. He may have alerted others to intercept us there."

Cheerful thought!

The car wound down a steep hill. Now Stringer was being allowed to proceed at his own pace, for there were cyclists, horse traffic, and a few cars. With all the *Ombay fala* guff, Smedley had lost track of what county he was in, but the building stone was the right buff color for the Cotswolds, and the landscape was picturesque enough. A large plate of hash and a tankard of bitter would go down very well about now. Would there be such a thing as beer on Nextdoor?

Waves of unreality . . .

At times he believed. Then it felt like the night before a big push, with the barrage to begin before dawn. Then a man looked at his watch every half minute and wondered if he'd ever see another sunset. Not quite that bad, but his gut was tight and his palm damp. *Aiba aiba nopa du* . . . Tonight he might meet the suspect Jumbo Watson face-to-face. Tomorrow go for a nice ride around on a dragon.

Other times he just couldn't. Then it all felt like an enormous leg-pull. *Aiba, aiba,* up your nose. Shamans and fakirs. Witch doctor dances moving people to other dimensions? What utter gullage that was! If such things were possible, then hundreds of people would have disappeared over the centuries.

But if they had, what evidence could there be? You couldn't prove it wasn't true!

Not in that direction, whispered his doubts, but when was the last time you read about a naked, shocked, bewildered foreigner stumbling out of the woods somewhere, unable to speak a word of the language? That ought to be easier to disprove, because at least you could demand to have a body produced. *Habeas* the bloody *corpus*!

"Sharp left at the end of this wall, Mr. Stringer," Miss Pimm said. "There is room to park."

Smedley snapped out of his reverie, realizing that the spire he had seen over the trees a moment ago must be St. Gall's.

"The vicar is expecting us." She did not deign to relate how she knew that. "But I ask both of you to be discreet in what you say to him. 'Them as asks no questions isn't told no lies,' or, 'No names, no pack drill,' as Captain Smedley is fond of remarking.

This is a small parish, not well endowed. The Service supports his church with generous donations. He knows we use the building for unorthodox purposes, but it is easier for him if he can pretend to turn a blind eye. The current bishop is notoriously conservative in his views."

Exeter had twisted around to stare at her again. "You mean we are actually going to go through with this inside the church itself? Dancing around with no clothes on?"

Miss Pimm sniffed. "Would you prefer an audience? On a fine evening like this, the grounds are a favored locale for courting couples."

"Too many bodies in the graveyard," Stringer remarked loudly. It was comforting to know that he was still conscious.

She ignored the comment completely. "The node overlaps the building itself, especially to the east, so we could perform our ceremonies outside. However the center of the virtuality is just in front of the altar. That is where in-comers materialize, and you will translate more easily from there."

There was a stunned pause, and it was Alice who sniggered first. "Do they ever drop in on Sunday mornings?"

The old bag did not crack even a hint of a smile. "Olympus keeps careful track of the clock, naturally, and times its deliveries for the small hours of the morning. The vicar is accustomed to receiving unexpected visitors."

Stringer was braking. Smedley caught a brief glimpse of some houses about a half mile away, then the car turned into a narrow lane, lurching to a stop beside an iron gate set in a high stone wall. With a long sigh like a deflating tire, Stringer sprawled limply over the steering wheel. Miss Pimm uttered a snort of disbelief. About to say something cheerful to Exeter, Smedley took a second look at his expression, then at Alice's, and didn't. Instead he opened the door and clambered down. There would have to be an awkward farewell here. He had no taste for public sentiment. . . . She kept a man's dressing gown in her flat, dammit! He hurried around to open the door for Miss Pimm.

Someone had beaten him to it. As that someone was wearing a cassock, it would not be unreasonable to assume he was the vicar. He was short and plump, elderly and fatherly, white-haired and rubicund, obviously not a stranger but a *native*. Smedley's heart did a little jump at that thought. It meant that he really did believe.

*Ombay fala, inkuthin . . .*

He fumbled shakily for cigarettes and matches.

All five of the occupants had emerged from the car. Edward hovered very close to Alice, Stringer was stretching and rubbing his eyes. Miss Pimm and the vicar had obviously met before. They exchanged congratulations on the weather. She did not introduce her companions and he ignored them—extremely odd behavior for a cleric—then they all converged on the gate, with Miss Pimm and the vicar in the lead. Smedley found himself being squired by the surgeon, crunching along a gravel path. He could not hear Alice and Exeter following.

The churchyard was dark and rather spooky, overhung with gigantic yews and studded with headstones, half of them weathered to shapeless boulders. Rhododendrons had taken over much of it, while the straggly grass in the remainder badly needed cutting. Someone had made a start on that, and then abandoned the lawn mower in its tracks. There seemed to be no lovers dallying amid the shrubbery or skulking in the shadows, but the vicar's sudden conversion to gardening would have blighted the romantic atmosphere of the evening.

The church itself was small and extremely old, or at least the west front was, because the door was set in a rounded arch. "Norman, I see!" That was about the limit of Smedley's architectural expertise.

But not Stringer's. "More likely Saxon. That transept is younger, Early Gothic. Middle thirteenth century, probably. The spire can't be older than fourteenth."

"And the railway station beyond the far wall? Late Victorian?"

"That's probably the vicarage."

*Garn!* "Or the county jail."

"Ah, yes. By the way, Captain, I congratulate you on the way you spirited your friend out of Staffles. Adroitly done!" The surgeon's hearty tone was belied by his fishy eyes, which were friendly as barracudas'. "You did not limp on Wednesday."

"I scratched my leg going over the wall."

"We wondered which of you that was. Have you had it seen to?"

"I plan to have it cured by magic in another world."

Stringer snorted. He walked on in silence for a long minute, then sighed. "I think I need a holiday."

Yes, the war was tough, wasn't it?

Four of them had reached the steps. Alice and Exeter still loitered by the gate, staring into each other's eyes and whispering earnestly. He must still be trying to talk her into coming. Why could he not understand that the lady hankered after what came wrapped in that dressing gown?

"Hurry, please!" Miss Pimm called. "Reverend, we have had no chance for a meal and some of us have a long drive ahead of us yet. Would there be any shops still open in the village to buy something we could eat on the road?"

The little man looked alarmed at being required to make such a decision. "Not shops. I have some ham . . . or you could inquire at the Bull. Mrs. Daventry might run up some sandwiches for you."

Smedley suppressed images of a buxom lady climbing a mountain of sandwiches. He must be windier than he had realized. He took a long draw on his fag.

"You could pick me up back here in half an hour or so," Miss Pimm informed Stringer with a meaningful look.

He frowned at this cavalier dismissal, but obviously he had learned not to argue with his new secretary. He offered his left hand to Smedley. "Thank you for a most interesting few days, Captain. Do drop in if you're ever in my neighborhood, won't you?"

"And you likewise," Smedley said.

Alice and Edward arrived hand in hand, very tense about the eyes.

"I will send you a postcard as soon as I, ah, return," he told her.

"No, you won't!" Miss Pimm snapped. "That would be insanely unwise. I shall see she is informed of your whereabouts. For goodness sake, kiss her and go inside! Thank you for your help, Reverend."

"Oh, very welcome, I'm sure, Mrs.—er . . . If you need me, I shall be cutting the grass out here."

Better than trying to cut the grass in there, Smedley thought. Lord, he was getting hysterical! He pecked a kiss on Alice's cheek, nodded politely at the vicar, who jumped and returned a nervous smile.

He stamped out his cigarette. Then he followed Miss Pimm up the steps and into the cold gloom of the church. Edward came trotting after them and closed the heavy door with a slam. It echoed like a knell of doom.

# 52

Smedley tossed his shirt into the chest. There was a strange assortment of clothes in there already, male and female both, plus a couple of small drums. He sat on a chair to remove his shoes and socks. The floor was icy.

Damn it all! No matter what she had said, he would not remove his pants! Not yet.

He limped out into the nave. He could hear the rattle of the vicar's lawn mower outside, very faint and distant. With a drum slung around her neck, Miss Pimm was poised on one foot, left arm raised and head thrown back. "Ogtha!" she proclaimed, and brought her hand down to the drum, and raising the other. "Ispal!" She was teaching Exeter the gestures for the key that would take him to New Zealand. He was watching intently, showing no sign of discomfort at being stark naked.

Writhing with embarrassment, Smedley slipped by them. He wandered along the aisle, studying the pictures in the stained glass windows and the nosegays of color they shed. The arches at the east end were rounded, then they became pointed, Gothic. Either the original church had been extended, or a new generation of builders had taken over at that point. The oaken pews displayed prayer books and hymnals, laid out at even spacing, ready for the next day's service. The pulpit was modern and grandiose, perhaps a result of the Service's generous contributions, and too big for the church.

This was a very little church.

But it was a church, a recognizable C. of E. place of worship, and its like could be found all over the world. The sun never set on the Anglican Communion. It was all the things he had been brought up to revere, had taken for granted and respected all his life. His family went to church every Sunday. They almost never discussed religion. It was just there, part of a man, like breathing. Dancing around in the nude was not in the cards. It was uncivilized. Gentlemen did not do such things anywhere, least of all in a church.

*"Umbathon!"* said Miss Pimm in the background.

This was not going to work. This was a gigantic confidence trick. This was insanity. *Ombay fala, inkuthin . . .*

He had not wept in days. Was he past that, now? Had he sunk to a whole new level of madness, with delusions of flying to other worlds and people leaping from bicycles into cars without actually moving through space? Was he, despite all the evidence of his senses, bound up in a straitjacket inside some padded cell?

He could feel his right hand again. It didn't exactly hurt, but he could feel it. He looked down at the bandage disbelievingly and tried to flex invisible fingers. He was in front of the altar rail already. This was the center of virtuality, she had said. Bunkum!

He shivered.

He turned away from the altar. Fresh yellow roses and chrysanthemums in brass vases. A fellow should not go mucking around in a church in a state of undress. Not proper! What in heaven would the guv'nor say? Or the mater, if she were alive—she would be truly shocked. Or the aunts, the monstrous regiment of aunts?

The other two were coming up the aisle. "Captain Smedley!" Miss Pimm's harsh voice took on a notable resonance in this old stone cave. "I asked you to remove your clothes."

"After the dress rehearsal."

"No, Captain—now! You will not achieve the correct state of mind if you are distracted by trivia. It will take you time to adjust. Off with them!"

He glared at her, then turned his back on her, pulling off his braces. But when he had everything off, he did not know what to do next. He could hardly leave bags and underwear for the congregation to find in the morning. He glanced over his shoulder. Miss Pimm was watching him with her arms folded. He could imagine her toe tapping.

"Give them to me," she said impatiently. "I'll put them in the chest as I leave. Oh, Captain! I saw my first naked man several hundred years ago, and none of the equipment has changed since then."

He gave her the bundle.

"Thank you. And your bandages. Then we can begin."

The governess instructed her pupils in the proper ritual movements for *Ombay fala.* They took it in slow motion, gesture by gesture, and Smedley felt worse and worse as the farce progressed. His nerves were not going to take much more of this. Exeter, he was glad to notice, was starting to shiver. At least when they began to dance in earnest, they both should feel warmer. He was shivering too, and he did not think that temperature had very much to do with it in his case. It was funk.

Oddly, Miss Pimm seemed colder than either of them, and she was fully dressed. She was snappier than a vixen in heat, shouting at them when they got it wrong. She kept glancing at her watch.

For once, Smedley realized, he was picking up something faster than Edward Exeter.

Exeter was distracted, thoroughly miserable. Pining for Cousin Alice? Had he just realized that he could never see her again? He could not even send her a postcard. The
Blighters would never stop hunting him until he fulfilled the prophecy or died. Or was
he just unwilling to cross over?

Miss Pimm made herself comfortable in the front pew and adjusted the drum on
her lap.

"Now we'll try it with music. First verse. Ready? One, two—"

"*Ombay fala*," Smedley chanted, lifting his left foot and raising his stump overhead,
"*inkuthin.*" Exeter followed him around the circle. Surprisingly, they went right through
the first verse without an error—at least it felt as if they got it right, and Sergeant Major
Pimm did not interrupt.

"Not bad!" she admitted as they bellowed out the closing, *Hosagil!* "Edward, you
forgot the words a time or two, didn't you? Captain, your timing is erratic. Is that leg
going to be a problem?"

The scar on his wrist was blood red, but a neat piece of sewing. The trivial scratches
on his leg looked much worse, ugly and swollen. He compared his two arms, wondering
if the right one was already wasting away.

"Let's try again." Miss Pimm stole another glance at her watch. "Smartly! I certainly
don't want to have to fight my way out of here. Take it right through, now. Keep on
going until something happens. Ready? Oh, I almost forgot . . . *bon voyage!*"

It was the first real smile Smedley had seen on her face. It made her seem almost
pretty, in a way he would never have guessed, but he was not in a mood to return
smiles. He was expecting her to break into howls of laughter any minute, and start
shouting *April fool!* "Thank you in anticipation," he said coldly.

Exeter said, "Thank you for everything." But he did not smile either, and Miss Pimm
responded with a rolling tattoo of fingers on the drum.

Smedley shivered and waited for the rhythm to begin. This was all wrong! He had
taken religion seriously as a child, because his parents had. Here it came. . . . *Dum-de
dum-de dum-dum-dum* . . . At Fallow he had done what all the others had done. "*Ombay
fala, inkuthin,*" he chanted. In the senior forms he had joined the conventional rebellion
into Buddhism, atheism, agnosticism, Unitarianism, or any esoteric -ism that had turned
up. *Right leg, left arm.* Smedley himself had never been quite sure which of the -isms
he favored. When he enlisted he had given his religion as C. of E. without thinking
about it. "*Indu maka, sasa du.*" He had attended church parade on Sundays. In Flanders
he had prayed his heart out a few times, screaming and sobbing to a merciful god, any
god, any god at all. No atheists in foxholes . . . *Hop, bow, hop, bow.* When the danger
had passed, he had always felt ashamed of his cowardice, and less of a believer in
consequence. What sort of merciful god would have allowed the war to start in the first
place—and why? Just so some terrified sods would repent of their sins? "*Aiba aiba nopa
du.*" What sins had he ever had a chance to commit?

But even so, a chap ought not to profane a holy place. Even a heathen temple deserved
respect. Even if it was a mud hut, even if only one single curly-haired darkie thought
it was sacred, then a fellow ought to have the grace not to mock it. *Head back, elbows*

*out.* St. Gall's was a Christian church, the sort of place his ancestors had worshipped in for hundreds of years. It deserved better than this obscene posturing, these primitive antics. *Echoes rolling back from the ancient stones.* It was holy. He could almost smell the sanctity. Normans had worshipped here, maybe Angles and Saxons. "*Aiba reeba mona kin.*" That meant *nine centuries* of humble people bowing down and glorifying their God. Their worship alone made it sacred. The thought was suddenly terrifying. Light blazed. He screamed and stumbled and fell facedown in the grass. *Hosagil!*

Bewildered, not understanding, he raised his head and blinked at the painful brightness. He lay in the exact center of a circular lawn, about the size of his parents' dining room, and the surrounding hedge was the color of a blue spruce, with the sheen of holly. He heard sounds of chirping, whistling, and hooting. He blinked harder to clear away tears. Beyond the hedge soared the most incredible snow-capped peak he had ever seen, blushing orange against a pale blue-gold sky. The air was tangy with a scent of wood smoke. It was evening or early morning.

He had done it! He had done it! He had done it! Yes! It was true. He had crossed over to another world. Grass. Odd, mint-scented grass. Daylight. The war, England, the guv'nor, the aunts, medals, the dead, the maimed—all gone. He had really done it. He wouldn't have to go to the Palace for his bloody gong after all. He had done it, really done it.

He laid his face on the back of his hand and started to sob.

# 53

I t was the cold that stopped him, the unpleasantness of lying on dewy grass at dawn. He sat up and rubbed his eyes with the back of his hand and almost laughed. He hadn't had a weep like that since Wednesday's lunch in the Black Dragon. Done him a world of good, it had! *Two* worlds of good. Now he needed to find some clothes before he caught pneumonia.

He had done it. He had done it.

Behind him stood a small kiosk of unpainted wood, like a summerhouse. Alongside it was the only break in the hedge, through which he could see only a gravel path and more hedge on the far side of that. Assuming this place was not somebody's idea of a joke, it must be a secluded, private aerodrome for travelers arriving in a state of undress—which was a reminder that Exeter would be dropping in any minute, and the exact center of the circle might become crowded.

Miss Pimm had issued somber warnings of the aftereffects of passing over, and especially a first trip. Cramps and nausea and despair, she had said, and Exeter had nodded grimly. Usually it would last only a few minutes, but it was as unpredictable as seasickness. Smedley felt none of those, unless his weeping fit qualified. He felt fine.

So he scrambled up and limped over to the gazebo. The orange fire had already faded from the mountain and the sky was brightening. There were several other peaks to admire as well, painted in blinding white and ice blue. The hedge was high enough to hide everything closer, except a trailing, lazy cloud of white smoke, which accounted for the tangy smell in the air. Someone was having a bonfire.

What could be keeping Exeter? It was jolly good to have pipped him like this, and him on his third trip, too.

The gazebo contained a comfortable chair with a book lying on it, and a wooden chest. Like the one in the vestry of St. Gall's, that chest probably held all sorts of Apparel Suitable for the Discerning Traveler. The book was heavy, leather-bound, and apparently written in Greek, but yet no Greek Smedley had ever seen. Odd! When he looked inside the chest, he found one shoe and three socks. He took two socks and put them on, but that hardly seemed adequate wear, no matter how temperate the climate.

Undoubtedly the little kiosk was a sentry box. Someone was supposed to be sitting here, reading that book, keeping watch in case visitors dropped in. The rotter had deserted his post. Having breakfast, likely.

What on Earth, real Earth, could be delaying Exeter? Had the effort of learning two keys at the same time confused him, mixing them up in his mind? Or was he so reluctant to leave Alice and return to Nextdoor that he could not summon up the correct mental attitude? Bother the man!

So what did Julian Smedley do now, poor thing?

He went to the gap in the hedge and—being extremely cautious not to expose too much of himself—peered around the edge. He looked straight into the face of a young man doing the same thing from the other side.

The other man yelled. They both jumped back in alarm.

Smedley broke into roars of laughter.

Slowly the newcomer edged into view around the hedge, one big, wide, green eye at a time. He was barefoot, wearing only a loincloth. His beard was close-cropped, while his hair hung down his back like a woman's. Both were a startling shade of copper, and his very fair skin's efforts to tan had coated him in several million freckles. He was one all-over freckle. He was also jumpy as a field full of grasshoppers, ready to flee at the slightest provocation.

He said something, but the only word Smedley caught was *tyika?*

"Sorry, old man! Don't speak the lingo. Got any English?"

The man nodded vigorously, still jittery, but apparently reassured. "I am speak English well, *tyika!*" He had a singsong accent. "My name is Dommi Basketmaker, but once Dommi Houseboy, and having hopes again to be so." He was no older than Smedley himself, short and broad shouldered.

"I'm Captain Smedley. Dommi, you said? Weren't you bearer for, er, *Tyika* Exeter?"

A huge grin split Dommi's face into unequal halves, revealing a set of perfect white teeth. "Indeed I had that highly pleasurable honor a year ago, for a transitory time only.

*Tyika* Kisster a most felicitous *tyika* to serve, a very benignly inclined *tyika!* I had been informed that his honor will be returning shortly and have had apprehension of perhaps being permitted again to serve him, which I would be most earnestly appreciative." His joy wavered into sudden despondency. "But, alas—"

"Well, he's due any moment now." Smedley wondered how that information could have reached Olympus ahead of him, though. "And he will be arriving in the same state of undress I am. And I am deucedly cold, to boot. Why don't you run off and dig up a couple of sets of clothes for us, soonest?"

"But . . ." Dommi's gaze wandered over Smedley, noting the missing hand and the gashes on his calf. "Of course, *Tyika Kaptaan!* At once, most imminent!" He spun around and vanished. Sounds of feet running on gravel faded into the distance. *Bare* feet? Ouch!

Well, that took care of clothes.

Exeter was taking a damnably long time! He had two translations to his credit already, so he ought to be able to manage another, surely. Had he changed his mind? Having seen Smedley cross first, was he going to rely on him to unmask the traitor, whether Jumbo or another? No, he would not go back on his word to Miss Pimm. Or had Schneider arrived at St. Gall's and queered the show? She had said: *I don't want to have to fight my way out of here.*

Smedley decided that there was nothing he could do about that. He had no idea of the return key, and he could have contributed nothing to the fight, if fight there was. He might never know what had happened after he left.

He might have to introduce himself to the Service, instead of being recommended by Edward Exeter, Liberator. Should have brought his *curriculum vita.* Damn! That could be unpleasant. He'd have to talk about the war. Well, one day at a time . . .

He should have asked Dommi to bring some breakfast. His mouth was watering. He sniffed. Mm. Yes, there were definite hints of meat in the all-pervading smoke. Perhaps someone was roasting an ox on that bonfire? Or frying bacon.

Curiosity took him back to the gap in the hedge. He peered again, and this time there was no other face advancing to meet his. As he had suspected, the other hedge was just a screen across the entrance, providing privacy. The gravel path curved out of sight and his view was blocked by shrubbery and tall trees. They were not English trees, but a tree was a tree anywhere. Some of the colors were a bit off.

He looked the other way.

A body sprawled on the path about twenty feet away, but there was no doubt that it was dead. It had been hacked to pieces. Hair and clothes were unrecognizable, black with dried blood, and he could not tell whether it had been a man or a woman. He could hear insectile buzzings even at that distance. A couple of things like feathered squirrels were chewing at it.

He looked beyond. Smoke drifted up from the remains of a house, a black field of ruin. He retched at the memory of the odors that had made his mouth water. In the background, amid the trees, other houses smoked, many other houses, all razed. Black specks on the ground might well be other bodies. Olympus had been sacked.

A few men were moving around, and although they were far off, he could see that they were not dressed like Englishmen. They were dressed like Dommi, meaning virtually undressed. The natives had risen against the *tyikank*. It was Nyagatha all over again.

Now one of the savages had learned that there was a *tyika* who had been missed. Dommi had not gone to fetch clothes, he had gone to fetch his friends, with assegais or machetes or whatever they used to kill white men . . . *tyikank* . . . Dommi was as white as Smedley, but he was a native, and there could be no doubt what had happened here yesterday, or perhaps the day before.

Smedley was alone, naked, penniless, and friendless on a strange world where he could not speak the language and the native population was out to kill him.

He really ought to have settled for Chichester.

He ought to disappear into the woods as fast as he could move.

But what if Exeter arrived as soon as he left?

How long until Dommi and his pals arrived?

Somebody screamed, but Smedley did not think it was him.

# 54

Edward Exeter was thrashing like a landed fish in the middle of the grassy enclosure. He kept on screaming.

Smedley ran over to him and knelt down, having to ward off flailing arms and legs. He shouted a few times, but it did no good. In a few moments, though, the paroxysms grew quieter. Exeter subsided into a twitching heap. His muscles kept knotting and unknotting horribly, and he cried out every time.

"Exeter? It's me, Smedley. Anything I can do to help?"

*Anything I can do to shut you up?*

Exeter's eyes were closed. He was obviously trying not to move. "Julian?" he whispered. "Hold me."

Hold him? He was a *man*, dammit! And neither of them had any clothes on. With distaste, Smedley lay down behind him and tried to put an arm around him. All he did was set off another riot of cramps and spasms, and more shrieks of pain.

"Keep it down!" he hissed. "They'll hear you!"

"Hold me, damn you!"

Right. Smedley rose to his knees, took hold of Exeter's hair, and hauled him up into a sitting position. Exeter screamed. Smedley wrapped both arms around him and hung on as tightly as he could.

The fit passed. Exeter gasped and leaned his head back on Smedley's shoulder. After a moment he whispered, "Thanks! Just keep holding me."

That was all very well, but there was a band of headhunters on the way. This did not seem like the moment to explain that, though.

"What delayed you?"

"Dunno," Exeter whispered. His eyes were closed, and he was barely breathing. "Just couldn't get it to work."

"I thought the Blighters had got you."

Exeter shook his head, and that small movement set him off again, thrashing and moaning. Damn! but he was loud. He was going to be sore for days after these cramps. He was knotted like a fishnet.

"I do believe we have run into a spot of trouble here," Smedley said.

Footsteps on gravel! He looked around in alarm, bracing himself to face a murdering mob, but it was only Dommi, alone. He came hobbling in, clutching a bundle. He was covered with soot, streaked pink with sweat, and he had developed a severe limp.

"*Tyika* Kaptaan!" he cried. "I was as quickly as I could. And *Tyika* Kisster! It is most fortuitous to set eyes on your honor again, but at such a sad timing. I have brought the clothes, *tyika*, but I fear they are only the best I could find in the house of *Tyika* Dunlop, and many of them have singe marks upon them, and are soiled. It was the only house I was able to make entrance to."

Exeter's eyes opened wide.

"That's great, Dommi!" Smedley said hoarsely. "Could you hold *Tyika* Exeter for a moment for me?"

Muttering solicitously, Dommi knelt down and relieved Smedley of his burden. The exchange set off another round of cramps in Exeter, but he bit back his screams. Grateful, Smedley crawled away and rummaged through the bundle the bearer had dropped. He found typical tropical kit: shorts and shirts and sandals and long white socks. No underwear. As Dommi had said, the white cloth was scorched and soot stained. He began to dress.

Dommi was spilling out the horrible story between sobs. "It was a great madness, *tyika!* On Necknight, a great madness came upon us in the village. We gathered torches and all weapons which were at hand for us, and we marched in whole company upon the compound of the *tyikank*, singing hymns in the praise of Holy Karzon, whom our ancestors were ignorant to worship, but we know well to be the Demon Karzon and yet did not hail as such that night." He was weeping like a fire hose. "There was terrible slaughter, *tyika*, and raping of the *entyikank*, and, oh, awful things were done. The houses were all been burned. I cannot explain this madness, *tyika!* There were others there, not belonging to us, not Carrots like us but strangers. They wore black, *tyika*, all black! I fear they were the dread reapers of whom our mother would frighten us when children we only were. It is most likely that they were the cause of our madness, *Tyika* Kisster, is it not? All of us Carrots are most humbly disposed toward the great *tyikank* who have done so much to educate us and civilize us, and we are very truly grateful for what you have done for us. It must have been the robed ones who provoked us."

The reason he had been limping was that he had a bloody great burn on his foot. He must have gone into one of those smoldering ruins to find the togs.

"There's a body just outside," Smedley said. "The houses have been burned."

Exeter licked his lips. "Zath again," he whispered. "It's all over now?"

"Indeed yes, *tyika!* We Carrots are remorseful in the most extreme about what we have done, but we could not help ourselves. I myself was one of them who did these terrible things. Now we are chagrined most deeply and wish to make amends. It is to be hoped that many of the *tyikank* and *entyikank* and domestic Carrots managed to escape out into the woods, *tyika*. We have been trying to count the bodies, but we also slew all the Carrots we found wearing the noble liveries you *tyikank* had so generously provided for us, and it is hard to tell who is among the dead and who is not there. Many escaped, I am hopeful . . ."

He choked down more sobs. "We even burned the library, *tyika!*"

Very gingerly, Exeter eased himself into a sitting position. Blood dribbled from his mouth, shockingly red against his pallor. "I am sure it was the reapers who were to blame."

"It had been reported that you would have imminent return." Dommi whimpered. "I am most glad that your honor did not return sooner and so share in this unfortunate killing."

Exeter hugged his knees, staring blindly across at the hedge, not moving. "The house of the *Tyika* Murgatroyd? Was this attacked?"

"Indeed yes, *tyika*. No house escaped."

"The servants of *Entyika* Murgatroyd? Ysian, the cook?"

Dommi covered his face with his hands.

"Well?" Exeter demanded, not looking at him.

Ysian? Wasn't that the name of the girl Exeter had found hiding under a bed somewhere? How had she ever got to Olympus?

"No, *tyika*. She did not escape. I saw."

"How did she die?"

"Not to ask, *tyika!*"

Exeter's eyes were burning cold, but he was still gazing at the hedge, or through it. "Tell me, Dommi. Please tell me. I know it wasn't your fault."

"*Tyika*—there were awful things done. Please not to say them."

Exeter mumbled something that made no sense, but sounded vaguely like, "Oh, Vixen!"

"What? Smedley demanded.

"Nothing. Pass me those bags, will you, old chap?" Moving very deliberately, he began to dress. "Dommi, go and collect the Carrots."

The valley was narrow, less than a mile wide. From a flat floor, the sides rose precipitously, soaring almost unbroken to the incredible peaks all around. It held a river, open meadows, and many-colored woods. It would have been spectacularly beautiful two days ago.

They walked past burned ruins and trampled flower gardens, many strewn with dismembered bodies. By the time they emerged from the trees, Exeter was able to walk on his own, just steadying himself with a hand on Smedley's shoulder. They had come to tennis courts, where a band of terrified natives awaited their arrival, two score or more. Men, women, and youngsters, they all had red hair. Many carried shovels, but seemed unsure what to do with them or where to begin. They all looked ill with guilt and horror. Even Smedley, hardened campaigner from the Western Front, was utterly nauseated by what he had already seen, and that was only a small part of Olympus. Plumes of smoke were still fouling the valley.

Exeter was greeted with apprehension and relieved murmurs of, "*Tyika* Kisster!" Others were running in through the trees. He waited as the crowd grew, leaning on Smedley. He was still trembling and very weak. It had been a bad crossing.

"Self-fulfilling!" he murmured.

"What?"

"The *Filoby Testament*. It seems to be self-fulfilling. Dommi said he was expecting me back from Thovale, so the Committee must have summoned me—but I'd gone to Flanders! If Zath hadn't sent me there, I would have arrived here in time to die, you see. And if he hadn't done this, I would still be going on to New Zealand."

Smedley looked at him in surprise. "Now you won't?"

"If Zath can't break the chain, then how can I?" Exeter released his grip on Julian's shoulder and straightened up to address the nervous mob of Carrots.

"It was not your fault!" he shouted. "It was Demon Karzon who drove you to this, Demon Zath. The saints will not abandon you, for it was not your fault. The Undivided knows the truth and where the guilt lies."

They reacted with screams of joy, like children.

"But you must demonstrate your grief. You must bury the dead with honor. Women go and start digging graves in the cricket ground, big graves. Men collect the bodies. We shall bury each household together, *tyikank* and servants together. The saints and the Carrots who lived together shall lie together. It must be done by sundown!"

It was done by sundown, when the snowy peaks of Kilimanjaro and Nanga Parbat turned to blood. The dead could not be numbered, for many bodies had been piled in the burning houses and others had been butchered into anonymous lumps of meat. Nevertheless, it was clear that many more Carrots than *tyikank* had died—most of the strangers would have been able to use their mana to escape, Exeter said. The remains were tipped into pits and covered over. Olympus was a ghost settlement.

Almost out on his feet with exhaustion, Smedley watched and marveled as Edward Exeter conducted a funeral service over the mass burial. He faced a congregation of several hundreds, probably the entire population of the native village, and he spoke in the local tongue, so that Smedley did not understand any of it, only the tears of the assembled Carrots. Whatever Exeter said, he began softly and ended with great vehemence, and his audience was impressed. When he had done, they cheered wildly, which seemed like a very peculiar closing for a funeral.

*     *     *

The next day some of the surviving *tyikank* came creeping out of the forest, hungry, frightened, and exhausted. Missionaries began returning from duty in the field. They were all surprised to find work gangs already clearing away the ruins, cleaning up, erecting temporary dwellings. They were even more surprised that the leadership was being provided by a young man none of them had ever met, an officer in the Royal Artillery, known to the Carrots as *Tyika* Kaptaan. The lad was doing a fine job, too.

Exeter had gone. He had departed in the night, alone, and nobody knew where. According to reliable Carrots, he had revealed to them in the eulogy he had delivered over the graves that he was the prophesied Liberator. They were not supposed to know that, of course, but it had always been impossible to keep the English-speaking domestic Carrots from eavesdropping and passing rumors, so many of them had already known. Now, apparently, Exeter had sworn that he was destined to bring death to Death, and thus fulfil the prophecies.

It was, he had said, an affair of honor.

He had not said where he was going.

As the fortnights passed with no news of him, a consensus arose that either Zath's watchers had caught the fellow on his way out, or else he had just gone native again. He could safely be forgotten.

Some of the pessimists would not believe that, especially Jumbo Watson. He predicted that Olympus had not seen the last of Edward Exeter. He pointed to the *Filoby Testament* and in particular to the cryptic Verse 1098:

*Terrible is the justice of the Liberator; his might lays low the unworthy. He is gentle and hard to anger. Gifts he sets aside and honor he spurns. Eleal shall be the first temptation and the prince shall be the second, but the dead shall rouse him.*

# 55

*47 Bamlett Road,*
*London, W1*
*16th September, 1917*

*Dear Miss Prescott,*

*With very deep regret, I must inform you that word has been received that my brother, D'Arcy, has made the Supreme Sacrifice. A telegram from the War Office reported today that he has been killed in action. We have no further details at this time.*

*I was at the house when the telegram arrived. My sister-in-law was, as you will understand, quite distraught, as were we all. I have only just got home, and have written to you as soon as I could. You may have seen the news in the evening papers already.*

*A memorial service will be arranged and announced in the usual way.*

*I am sure that you share our grief, even if you will not be able to acknowledge it in public.*

*I am,*
*Yours sincerely,*
*Anabel Finchley (Mrs.)*

# *Appendix:*

# *The Moons*

Nextdoor is a probability variant of Earth. The stars visible from its surface are the same as those visible from Earth; the sun is apparently the same.

However, Nextdoor has four moons. Prof Rawlinson's theory that they might have been gouged out by the impact of one or more meteors is not without merit. The Pacific was commonly believed in his day to be the scar left when the Moon was torn from the Earth. Modern theory supports an impact origin for the Moon, although the Pacific is now known to be billions of years younger. The impacting body would have had to be the size of a small planet, considerably more than a meteor, but in some respects Rawlinson was ahead of his time. He was particularly perceptive in anticipating recent insight on chaotic systems; even a minute difference in the size, velocity, or angle of such an impact could generate enormous variations in the final results. This would account for not only the varying number of satellites but also the slight discrepancies in the length of the day and year on Earth and Nextdoor.

Only Trumb displays a sufficiently large disk to hide the sun and create a solar eclipse. This occurs on every orbit, but is visible only in the daylight hemisphere. The following refers mainly to eclipses of the respective moons by the shadow of the planet, lunar eclipses as we know them.

The outermost moon, Eltiana, has a period of twenty-eight days, very similar to Earth's Moon, but it is much less conspicuous, little more than a bright red star. Its equatorial orbit causes it to be eclipsed every month, although on average only each alternate eclipse will be visible from a given location.

Ysh displays a small blue disk. It has a useful and dependable period of almost exactly fourteen days, the origin of the fortnight used as a basic division of time. Like Earth's Moon, Ysh has an inclined orbit and therefore is likely to be involved in eclipses only two or three times a year. Many eclipses will be obscured by weather or their occurrence during daylight hours. An observed eclipse of Ysh is a rare and ill-omened occurrence.

Trumb, the green moon, displays a large disk. Its synodic period is 4.44 days and its orbital inclination too slight to matter. It is eclipsed on every orbit, although half the eclipses occur below the horizon.

The tiny yellow moon, Kirb'l, may be a captured asteroid. Its orbit is elliptical and inclined at 15°, which is close to the latitude of the Vales. To complicate matters, its orbit precesses rapidly under the influence of the other moons, and the body itself is asymmetric, rotating every two hours with marked changes in albedo. It has a synodic period of 1.5 days.

At perigee, it appears to move from west to east. This may occur almost overhead, at times of minimum declination, or may be invisible below the horizon. Eclipse is very common at perigee, but Kirb'l is never eclipsed at apogee. At intermediate positions it moves north or south and may or may not be eclipsed.

The astronomer priests of the Vales find Kirb'l completely unpredictable.

# *FUTURE INDEFINITE*

*In dedicating books I have too long overlooked someone who deserves a dedication more than almost anyone—my agent, Richard Curtis. He not only makes my job more profitable, he also makes it much more fun.*
*One day his Collected Correspondence will be the humorous bestseller of the twenty-first century. So, thanks, Richard! This one is for you.*
*(Have you sold the Swahili rights yet?)*

Men say I am a saint losing himself in politics. The fact is that I am a politician trying my hardest to become a saint.

MAHATMA GANDHI

Saints should always be judged guilty until they are proved innocent.

GEORGE ORWELL

In wrath the Liberator shall descend into Thargland. The gods shall flee before him; they shall bow their heads before him, they will spread their hands before his feet.

FILOBY TESTAMENT, 1001

# Contents

IX. We can see why throughout nature the same general end is gained by an almost infinite diversity of means, for every peculiarity when once acquired is long inherited, and structures already modified in many different ways have to be adapted for the same general purposes.

939

# I

Behold! Exalted, I have come. I have escaped from the nether world. The roads of the earth and of the sky are open before me.

THE BOOK OF THE DEAD, 78

# 1

Prat'han Potter was growing tired of waiting to die. He had been standing in chains in the courtroom since dawn, and pretending to be brave for so long had turned out to be much more wearing than he had expected. Seventeen of his age brothers had already been tried, convicted, and taken out to be whipped. But he had been the ring-leader and this was his third offense, so he had been assured he would be found guilty and put to death. He was starting to think it would be a welcome release, the sooner the better, and if the Joalian crotchworms had not gagged him, he would be telling them to get on with it. He hoped his martyrdom would be the spark to light the revolution that Nagvale so badly needed.

"Granted that death is the only possible sentence in this case," the advocate for the defense said in a bored voice, "impalement is an exceptionally painful, lingering form of execution, and I would ask the court to stipulate more merciful means for this defendant, if My Lord Judges will permit me a brief word on the subject."

"Briefly, then," the president conceded with poor grace. All three judges were Joal-ians, as were all the other court officials. Most of them were sweltering in formal robes and floppy hats, for the courtroom was as hot as a kiln. Indeed, Prat'han's only con-solation was that he was clad in nothing but his usual leather apron. And chains, of course, lots of chains.

The courthouse was the largest and most splendid building in Sonalby, recently erected by the Joalian overlords as a symbol of the enlightenment they brought to their colonies. It contained at least four rooms, all with shiny plank walls and windows of stained glass. This room was the largest, but even with only one defendant remaining, it still contained far too many people for its size—the judges up on their bench, two advocates, four clerks, half a dozen sword-bearing guards. Although the door in the tiny area railed off as a public gallery stood open in a vain attempt to let in some air, it admitted nothing but a view of the village huts of wattle and thatch. The street was deserted. There was not even a mongrel cur left in Sonalby today to hear the victims howl at the whipping post or watch Prat'han die. The inhabitants had vanished before dawn, to show what they thought of Joalian justice. It was not much of a rebellion, but it was the best the poor sheep could manage.

"My Lords are gracious," said the advocate. He had not spoken ten words to his supposed client, and all they had in common was that they were both bored. "First, I respectfully point out that the only crime the defendant committed was to paint his face. My Lords will forgive me if I concede that I might be tempted to do the same if I had such a face."

The judges smiled thinly. There was absolutely nothing wrong with Prat'han's face except that he was not allowed to paint it the way his forefathers had done for a thousand years. Women told him he was handsome even when his face paint had been smudged to a blur. He tried again to lick the roof of his mouth and was again balked by the foul-tasting wooden bit. His jaw ached from being held open so long.

"Objection!" said the prosecutor, half rising from his seat. "The paint is itself not the issue. The issue is that the governor has prohibited a specified list of barbaric tribal customs such as ritual self-mutilation. Face painting is one of the forbidden procedures."

The left-hand judge smothered a yawn. "And the law specifies impalement. Have you anything else to say?"

"Yes, My Lords," the advocate for the defense said hastily. "Briefly, the accused, Prat'han Potter, had a distinguished military career in the recent war against Thargia. He was troopleader for Sonalby during the campaign in Lemodvale and the subsequent glorious and historic invasion of Thargvale, fighting alongside our noble Joalian warriors. When the victorious joint army returned to Nagland three years ago and was forced to suppress the usurper Tarion, the accused strangled the usurper with his own hands during the assault on the palace. He acquitted himself throughout with great distinction, receiving a commendation for personal bravery from our own noble Kalmak Chairman."

The judges exchanged annoyed glances. They were all political appointees, and Kalmak was currently top dog in the Clique and hence effective ruler of both Joalia itself and its colonies.

Prat'han made loud protesting noises around his gag and rattled his chains. If the court decided to refer the appeal for mercy all the way to Joal, then he might have to wait two or three fortnights for an answer, and he could not see that strangulation would be enough of an improvement to justify the delay.

"Silence that man!" said the left-hand judge.

A guard punched Prat'han in the kidneys. Taken by surprise, he screamed and fell to his knees in a rattle of chains, choking for breath, fighting nausea. The courtroom floor swam before his eyes. Long before he was ready to be brave again, he was hauled to his feet to hear the sentence. He could barely straighten up properly or control his breathing.

". . . previous convictions," the judge president droned, "have used up any goodwill earned in the war. You have been found guilty of treason against the Nagian People's Democratic Republic. The sentence of the court is—"

"Wait a moment!" said a new voice.

It was not a loud voice, but all heads turned. The speaker was a tall youth standing in the hitherto deserted public enclosure. Lean as sinew, tanned to walnut, black haired, empty-handed, naked except for sandals and a leather loincloth—just a typical Nagian peasant in from minding the herds? But Prat'han recognized him instantly and forgot the sickening throb of pain.

"You have a very short memory, T'logan," said the newcomer. "So have you, Dogurk. I remember when you were T'logan Scribe and Dogurk Scholar. Have you forgotten so soon, My Lord Justices?"

He swung a long leg over the railing, revealing a glimpse of very pale thigh under the leather. As he brought the other leg over, one of the guards lurched forward, drawing his sword. D'ward just looked at him, and he stopped as if he had hit a wall.

D'ward resumed his approach to the bench. Two of the judges had lost color, even in that steaming sweat house. Where had he come from? All this time and never a word—yet he walks in at this very instant . . .

"Three years ago, My Lords, you were under my command, remember? Not quite four years ago, you were about to die outside Lemod, trapped by a guerrilla army and the onset of winter. The only thing that saved you—and all the rest of your great Joalian army—was that the Nagians took the city in the nick of time and found you safe haven. That is correct, isn't it?"

He was in the center of the courtroom now. He folded his arms and scowled up at the bench. Judges T'logan and Dogurk nodded in horrified silence.

D'ward, D'ward! Where had he come from? He had vanished in Thargvale three years ago, and no one had heard anything of him since. He had not changed at all. Prat'han knew how his own once-taut belly had begun to thicken and how the hair had crept back from his temples, but D'ward was still that same wiry youth he had been then—a boy with a black-stubble beard.

The third judge began, "What is the meaning of this—"

"Shut up!" said D'ward. "I *respectfully* remind the court that Prat'han Potter was the third man up the rope in that assault. He saved your lives, you miserable slugs! And you, T'logan—I remember him jumping into the freezing torrent and lifting you out bodily when we were making our escape from Lemod in the spring. I saw it with my own eyes! He saved you again."

The judge president made incoherent choking noises.

"And now?" D'ward added enough scorn to turn the oven into an icehouse. "And now Joal has enslaved the entire population of Nagvale. Oh, I know! I know you think you're raising them from barbarism to civilization, but they don't see it that way, and the complete suppression of a culture seems like enslavement to me. Civilization, you call it? Because Prat'han Potter is a proud man as well as a brave one and chooses to decorate his face with what he regards as sacred symbols of his manhood, you plan to put him to death in the foulest way you can think of?"

An agony of silence filled the courtroom.

Then Judge T'logan spoke the forbidden name: "The Liberator! What are you doing here?" He glanced uneasily around the courtroom, as if expecting to see reapers assembling.

D'ward Roofer, D'ward Troopleader, D'ward Hordeleader, D'ward Battlemaster . . . D'ward *Liberator!* He had never accepted that title before, but this time he did not refuse it.

"Just passing through. But if you harm my age brother Prat'han, then I may decide to stay here and organize the Nagian Freedom Fighters. And if I do choose that option, My Lord Justices, I will throw every last Joalian out of the vale inside two fortnights. I will trample you as I humbled the might of Thargia. *I am the Liberator foretold!* Do you doubt my word?"

The three judges shook their heads in unison, although they probably did not know they were doing so.

"So, My Lords, you will now issue the prisoner a severe reprimand and release him."

Judge T'logan spluttered and drew himself up. "That is not—"

*"Now!"*

The judge subsided again. He glanced at his associates. Dogurk nodded. Trillib nodded, more reluctantly.

"Release the prisoner!"

Two minutes later, Prat'han staggered out into the blinding sunlight, leaning on the Liberator's shoulder.

Five minutes later, the two of them arrived at his shop and he could drink his fill of tepid water, cleanse his mouth, slump onto his work stool and gape at D'ward. The stabbing pain in his back had faded to a dull ache.

No one had seen them, of course. No one had screamed out D'ward's name, or even Prat'han's own, for he would be something of a hero himself now, being so unexpectedly alive. The people would not return until after dark, and the rest of the senior warriors must be off tending one another's stripes.

Under its thick reed-thatched roof, the shed was cooler than the sun-drenched street outside, but not by much. The heavy smell of clay that always hung in the air had faded in the last fortnight, while the potter languished in the village jail. Sunlight blazed in through the open door, glowing on the warm pinks of the wares that cluttered the floor—dozens of jars, bowls, jugs, plates, all waiting for buyers. Flies droned around or walked on the wicker walls. Prat'han was both surprised and delighted to see his spear and shield still leaning against the wall. He would feel castrated without those old friends, although it was illegal to take them outdoors now, and rumors persisted that the Joalians would soon confiscate every weapon in the vale.

D'ward inverted a ewer and sat on it. He sighed deeply and wiped his forehead, then grinned at Prat'han as calmly as if he were one of the regulars who dropped in to chat every day. There was no need to ask how he had worked that miracle in the courtroom. He was D'ward Liberator. The shockingly blue eyes and unforgettable white-toothed smile could spur a man to do anything.

"The years have been good to you, old friend?"

"You . . . you haven't changed!"

D'ward's smile narrowed a little, but it was still a smile. "Not on the outside, I suppose. You're not much different yourself, you big rascal! Married now?"

Prat'han nodded, while his gaze wandered over D'ward. His beard was trimmed close in Joalian style. His ribs . . .

D'ward looked down where he was looking. "Oh. I seem to have lost my merit marks, don't I? Well, you know they were there once. I can't help it if I'm good at healing, can I?"

The potter pulled himself together. "I owe you my life again, Liberator, and . . . Oh! I must not call you that, must I?"

"Yes, you can!" Blue eyes twinkled. "My time has come! As of today, you may call me the Liberator. From now on, I bear the title proudly and will teach the world to respect it. I am happy to start by liberating you. It was pure chance; I came by four days ago and heard what was bubbling."

He stared thoughtfully at Prat'han, who felt a thrill twist his gut. Why had the Liberator come? Was there blood on the wind again? He said, "You have been away too long! We are your family."

"Always! But I have many sad things to do in the world. I came to see my old comrades in arms and discovered that most of them were in jail. I had hoped that the old Sonalby Warband might be willing to help me in a dangerous venture, but . . ."

There *was* blood on the wind! Prat'han crossed the shack in three long strides to snatch up his shield and spear. "Lead, Liberator! I will follow."

D'ward rotated on the ewer to face him. "I'm afraid not. Not you. And none of the others either. You see, brother, now I march against the gods themselves. I can't lead followers who sport the symbols of the Five—green hammer, blue stars, the skull of—"

"Faugh! Face marks do not matter. If you want me like this, then you get me like this."

"Oh?" D'ward seemed to be having trouble keeping his lips in line. "But do I want a helper so fickle? Ten minutes ago you were prepared to die horribly for the right to paint your face. Now it doesn't matter?"

Of course it didn't! But Prat'han was not accustomed to thinking *why*, and he had to rummage frantically in unfrequented corners of his mind before he could say, "You offer me a choice. Joalians tell me. Quite different."

D'ward laughed. "I see! But the next problem is that you and the brothers seem to have a revolution of your own under way. What I'm planning has nothing whatsoever to do with throwing the Joalians out of Nagvale."

Prat'han shrugged to hide his chagrin. "I only fight Joalians from boredom. Whatever your cause, I will support it. Your gods are mine."

"It will involve long travel and grave danger."

"Good!"

"But you said you were married. As I recall, married warriors are reserved for defense."

Why had Prat'han been such a fool as to admit to Uuluu? "I am only very slightly married—a matter of a couple of fortnights." Or thereabouts. "No children! My wife can go back to her father unchanged."

D'ward raised his eyebrows in disbelief. "That she may go back I will believe, but unchanged? This I doubt, you big male animal, you!"

"Not much changed." Feeling as if he had been counting every hour in three long years for this moment, Prat'han fell to his knees. "Liberator, I would kneel to no other man. I would not plead with any other, either, but I swear that if you leave me behind, then I shall die of shame and despair. Take me, Liberator! I am yours to command, as I always was. I will follow you wherever you lead."

"Don't you even want to know what I'm planning?"

"You are going to bring death to Death, as is foretold in the *Filoby Testament?*"

"Well, yes. If I can."

"I wish to help. And all the others will, too! Gopaenum Butcher, Tielan Trader, Doggan . . ."

D'ward grimaced. "I let them all get flogged today. I dared not intercede for them, Prat'han, because I wasn't sure I had enough . . . had enough power to rescue you. It was a damned close thing, there, you know! A couple of times I really thought you and I would be gracing adjoining fence posts. How long until they'll be well enough to travel?"

"They are well now! I've had those beatings. Nagians shrug them off. We have thick skins."

"You have thick heads, certainly." D'ward ran his fingers through his hair—curly, bushy, shiny black. He pulled a face. "What is your wife going to say? I warn you, this will be bloody. Many who go with me will not return. Perhaps none of us will."

Prat'han rose. He put his heels together and laid his spear against his shoulder, as D'ward himself had taught him, long ago. Staring fixedly at the far wall, he said, "Lead and I follow."

D'ward rose also. They were of a height, the two of them, both tall men, although Prat'han was thicker.

"I can't dissuade you, can I? Never thought I would, actually." He took Prat'han's shoulder in the grip that brother gave to brother in the group. "You have been a shaper of clay, Prat'han Potter. Follow me, and I will make you a shaper of men."

# II

And he is the guardian of the world, he is the king of the world, he is lord of the universe— and he is myself, thus let it be known, yea, thus let it be known!

KAUSHITAKI-UPANISHAD, III ADHYAVA, 8

# 2

Ripples raised by that encounter in Sonalby were to spread throughout the Vales in the fortnights that followed and give rise to major waves. Before the green moon had eclipsed twice, they disturbed the normal calm of a certain small side valley between Narshvale, Randorvale, and Thovale, whose only claim to distinction was that the little settlement near its north end was home to the largest assembly of strangers on Nextdoor. They called it Olympus.

The Pinkney Residence was not as grand as the palaces of the monarchs or high priests of the vales, but it was spacious and luxurious by local standards, having recently been rebuilt from the ground up. In design it more closely resembled the sort of bungalow favored by white men in certain tropical regions of Earth than anything a native of the Vales would have conceived. Within the oversized and overfurnished drawing room, lit by a multitude of candles in silver candlesticks, a man with a fair baritone voice was singing "Jerusalem" accompanied by a lady playing a harp, because the Service's efforts to instruct their local craftsmen in the construction of a grand piano had so far failed to meet with success. The audience consisted of eight ladies in evening gowns and six gentlemen in white tie and tails.

" 'I shall not 'cease,' " the singer asserted, " 'from mental fight, Nor shall my sword sleep in my hand. . . .' "

Two more men had slipped out to the veranda to smoke cigars and contemplate the peace of the evening. The warmth of the day lingered amid scents of late-season flowers and lush shrubbery, although the sky was long dark. Amid an escort of stars, red Eltiana and blue Astina peered over jagged peaks already dusted with the first snows of fall.

"It is a rum do." The taller man was spare, distinguished by an unusually long nose. He had grace and confidence and—on appropriate occasions—a wry, deprecating grin. Like most strangers, he did not discuss his age or past. Although he appeared to be in his middle twenties, he was rumored to have participated in a cavalry charge at the battle of Waterloo, more than a hundred years ago. "Never expected him to start that way."

"Never expected him to start at all," his companion complained. "Thought we'd heard the last of him. Thought Zath had got him, or he'd gone native."

"Oh, no. I always expected Mr. Exeter to surface again. I just didn't expect him to cock a snoot at the Chamber quite so blatantly or quite so soon." The taller man drew on the cigar so it glowed red in the gloom. Then he murmured, "Very rum! I wonder how he went about it."

"I wonder how he's managing to stay alive at all." The other man was shorter and plump, although he appeared to be no older. He parted his hair in the middle and tended to close his eyes when he smiled.

"That's what I meant. Zath should have bowled him out in the first over. Think we ought to stop him, do you?"

"Stop who?" demanded another voice. "What are you two plotting out here? Arranging a little something behind the Committee's backs?" Ursula Newton came striding out and peered suspiciously at the two men, one after the other. She was below average height, but her evening gown revealed very muscular arms and unusually broad shoulders for a woman. She was loud and had never been compared to shrinking violets.

"Certainly not!" said the shorter man.

"Jumbo?"

"Of course we were," said the man with the long nose, unabashed. "Pinky was just about to ask me to name the most efficient assassin on our staff at the moment, weren't you, Pinky?"

His companion muttered, "I say!" disapprovingly. "Nothing like that."

"The fact is," Jumbo explained, "that young Edward Exeter has surfaced up in Joalvale, preaching to the unwashed, openly proclaiming himself to be the Liberator foretold."

"Great Scot!" Ursula frowned. "You're sure?"

"Quite sure," Pinky said fussily. "Agent Seventy-seven. He's a very sound chap, knows Exeter quite well. Very well, actually."

"And how long has this been going on?"

"He'd been at it about three days when Seventy-seven saw him. Seventy-seven scampered back here right away to let us know. Very sound thinking. I commended him on his initiative. It did take him four days to get here, though, so the situation may have undergone modification."

"Exeter may be dead, you mean. But if we've heard, then the Chamber's heard, sure as little apples."

"Oh, quite, quite."

The patter of applause having died away, the baritone had unleashed his next song.

> " 'And this is the law I will maintain,
> Until my dying day, sir. . . .' "

The men smoked in silence, and Ursula leaned on the rail between them, scowling at the night.

"Could be serious," she said.

> " 'That whatsoever king shall reign . . .' "

"Absolutely," Pinky agreed.

*" 'I will be the vicar of Bray, sir. . . .' "*

"You're going to send someone to bring him in?"

"That was what we were debating when you arrived," Jumbo remarked, sounding amused.

"It's a matter for the Committee," Ursula said, "but of course you haven't told Foghorn yet, have you? Want to get it all settled beforehand, don't you? You two and your cronies."

"Not settled," Pinky protested. "Dear me, no. Not settled. Didn't want to spoil a delightful evening by bringing up business. But I knew Jumbo would be interested. Thought he might have a few ideas. And you, too, my dear. You agree we ought to send someone to have a word with Exeter?"

"Just to have a word with him?"

"The emissary's terms of reference would have to be very carefully drawn," Pinky said cautiously. "A certain amount of discretion might be permitted."

Jumbo coughed as if he had swallowed more smoke than he intended. "Spoken like a true gentleman—Cesare Borgia, say, or Machiavelli. Well, he certainly won't let me near him. Not after what happened the last time."

"If he has any brains at all," Ursula said, "he won't let any of us near him. Except Smedley, perhaps. Old school chum? Yes, he'd listen to Julian."

Pinky closed his eyes and smiled beneficently. "Captain Smedley is an excellent young man. But he is rather new here. Do you think he could comprehend all the ramifications of the situation? I am sure he would deliver a message, but would he plead our case with conviction?" He peered at her inquiringly.

"He certainly won't do the dirty work you've got in mind. But remember he has no mana. I think you need to send two emissaries to Exeter—his friend Smedley and someone else, someone who can help the captain out if there is need for a little muscle."

"Ah! Brilliant! I expect we should have seen that solution in time, Jumbo, what? Two emissaries, of course! And who should the other one be? What do you think?"

Jumbo sighed. "I don't like this. Not one bit. Rosencrantz and Guildenstern. We need someone with damned good judgment."

"And very few scruples?" Ursula inquired scathingly.

"Now, now," Pinky said soothingly. "Don't go jumping to conclusions. I am quite hopeful that Mr. Exeter will see reason."

"It's a matter for the Committee. Let them decide. Now come on back inside, both of you, and stop this inner-circle intriguing." She spun on her heel and strode off into the drawing room, a surprisingly abrupt departure.

Two cigar ends glowed simultaneously. Two smoke clouds wafted into the night air.

"Obvious!" said Pinky. "We'd have thought of her on our own, wouldn't we? Eventually?"

Jumbo sighed again. "Truly it is written that the female of the species is more deadly than the male."

"Oh, quite," said Pinky, smiling with his eyes closed. "Quite."

# 3

Seven Stones in Randorvale had only four stones—one vertical, two leaning, and one fallen. The missing three were either buried in undergrowth or had been carted away in past ages. The remaining four were set in a grassy glade walled around by enormous trees like terrestrial cedars that crowned the level summit of the knoll. It was a spooky place, dim and pungent with leafy odors, stuffy as a Turkish bath on this breathless autumn afternoon. Staying well back from the crowd, hidden behind shrubbery, Julian Smedley could feel his skin tingling from the virtuality.

Using the fallen stone as a pulpit, Kinulusim Spicemerchant was thundering the gospel of the Undivided at a flock of forty or so people sitting cross-legged on the grass. Men and women, even some children, they were a fair sampling of the local peasantry from Losby and other nearby hamlets. Forty was a good turnout at Seven Stones. Julian had already identified a few familiar faces, the faithful. Others were here for the first time, investigating this strange new religion their friends now professed. Soon it would be his turn to try to convert them.

Meanwhile he was changing into his work clothes. Standard Randorian dress was a single voluminous swath of flimsy cotton, apparently designed to keep off insects, as Randorvale was well supplied with bugs, but its main attraction for Julian was that it had no tricky buttons or hooks. Feeling like a human Christmas present, he unwrapped yards and yards of gauze, enough bunting to decorate a battleship. When the silkworm finally emerged from its cocoon, Purlopat'r solemnly held up his priest's robe for him to step into—hood, long sleeves, girdle. He thought of it as his Friar Tuck costume. It was a drab gray, because the Pentatheon had already appropriated all the better colors.

Purlopat'r Woodcutter was a nephew of the spice merchant, somewhat more than life-size. He had the face of a boy of twelve, but from the neck down he was about seven feet of solid muscle, which gave him a certain air of authority, and he wore a gold circle in the lobe of his left ear, the sign of a convert to the Church of the Undivided, so Kinulusim must regard him as an adult. Purlopat'r was serving no real purpose at Julian's side. He had probably volunteered to wait on the saintly guest so that he need not suffer through another of his uncle's interminable sermons.

Kinulusim was a convincing lay preacher, one of the best the church had. His faith was strong; he proclaimed it in rolling, sonorous torrents of words, waving his fists in the air as he denounced the evil demons of the established sects of the Vales. If he became any more heated, his beard would burst into flames. The old boy was always a tough act to follow. Julian was neither a natural orator nor truly proficient in the

Randorian dialect, and he lacked Kinulusim's faith. He also considered the Church of the Undivided to be a load of guff.

"Holiness?" Purlopat'r spoke in a high-pitched whisper unsuited to his size. He was one of those people who can rarely remain silent for two breaths at a time. "Did my uncle tell you about the troopers he saw?"

"Yes, brother." Julian smiled up at the worried young face. He wanted to run over his sermon notes again, but apostles were expected to demonstrate both patience and faith. Troopers were worrisome news.

"Do you suppose King Gudjapate has been misled by the demon Eltiana?"

"Undoubtedly. The demons will mislead anyone who listens to them."

Purlopat'r nodded, rolling his eyes. "If the troopers come against us here today, the Undivided will defend us, Holiness?"

Julian sighed and adjusted the tie on his gown, mostly to give himself time to think. The young woodcutter had just thrown him the worst paradox in monotheism: Why does an all-powerful god tolerate evil in the world? That was not something to be answered off the cuff, even if Julian had had a cuff handy.

"I do not know the answer to that, brother. We must do our duty and have faith that the One will prevail in the end, even if sometimes our limited vision does not reveal all the details to us."

"Oh, yes, Your Holiness. Amen!"

Julian thumped the kid's shoulder, curious to know if it was as solid as it looked. It was. "We are both humble servants of the Undivided, brother. We are in this together."

*And in this case, laddie, you can be confident that your apostle will not vanish in a flash of magic and leave you in the lurch, as slimy Pedro Garcia did down in Thovale. This apostle hasn't got any mana.*

He took a quick look through the greenery to see how Kinulusim was doing. The audience seemed suitably impressed.

Julian liked Randorians, who were mostly simple peasants, working the land in the ways of their ancestors. Their dialect was more tuneful than those of vales closer to Tharg, whose harsh, guttural tongue seemed to have infected all their neighbors. They were taller than most Valians and laughed a lot when they were not engaged in solemn activities like worship, and they had wonderful folk music.

Having been allowed to choose between Randorvale, Thovale, Narshvale, and Lappinvale for his missionary work, Julian had selected Randorvale and proceeded to specialize in its dialect. He was happy with his choice, perhaps because most of the natives had faces a tone darker than his. Preaching to them, he could almost convince himself that he was back Home, in some remote colony of the Empire, enlightening the heathen, bearing the White Man's Burden. With people the same pale pink he was, he would lose that illusion. Then he might wonder about historical accidents, the possibility that some flip of a divine coin might have gone otherwise and resulted in Narshians and Randorians saving souls in England—a discomfiting thought.

Like most of the Service, he had little faith in souls anyway. He did not promote the Church of the Undivided for theological reasons, but because it was the only possible way to undermine the tyranny of the Pentatheon. Only when the Five had been over-thrown would the Vales ever progress to true civilization. It was the worldly lot of the natives he sought to promote, just as the European powers bettered the economies of their colonies. Here in Randorvale, Julian Smedley would preach with a clear conscience, doing what he did for the good of the natives, the *lesser breeds without the law.*

Already he could feel mana flowing. As the spice merchant worked up to his thun-derous peroration, his listeners' veneration for the Undivided god was becoming infec-tious, magnified by the virtuality of the node like organ music reverberating in a church.

Purlopat'r had been silent for thirty or forty seconds. The strain must have become unbearable, for again his whisper came from somewhere above Julian's head. "Was it not most wonderful what miracle the most holy Saint Djumbo performed in Flaxby two fortnights ago?"

Julian craned his neck. "I don't think I heard about that. Flaxby, in Lappinvale? What happened?"

The boy's eyes widened. "It was a mighty miracle, Holiness! The laws in Lappinland now proclaim that all the faithful are to be rounded up and punished most barbarously."

"Yes, I know. That, too, is the work of the demons. But what about Saint Djumbo?"

"A magistrate sought to arrest him, Holiness! He had two soldiers with him, and he accosted the holy apostle as he was leaving a prayer meeting like this one. But Saint Djumbo called upon him to repent and instructed him, and lo! the magistrate and his companions fell upon their knees and heard the word of the True Gospel. Then all present departed in peace, singing the praises of the Undivided!"

The devil they did! "Saint Djumbo has true modesty, brother. He has never reported this to us, and I thank you for bringing it to my attention."

Purlopat'r beamed. He was no more pleased than Julian was, although Julian inter-preted the story differently. Obviously Jumbo had used his stranger's charisma—and perhaps a shot of mana as well, because even for Jumbo, those three together would have been a tough egg to crack. He had not abandoned his flock, a bloody sight better performance than Pedro's craven desertion! But to hear of persecution in Lappinland was bad news. The Pentatheon's pogrom against the Undivided heresy had begun in Thargland half a year ago, then spread to Tholand and Narshland. Today Kinulusim had reported troopers in the vicinity. Had the poison now reached Randorvale, too?

Ah, the old windbag had run out of steam at last. He wiped his hairy face with a corner of his wrappings and drew breath.

"We are most blessed today, brothers and sisters! Come among us to honor us is one who can speak to you with true authority. I am but a humble merchant, no better than any of you, perhaps worse than some. Most of you have known me all your lives. How can this man have wisdom of holy things? you ask, and you are right to ask. But now I give you one of the blessed apostles themselves, one chosen by him whose name may never be uttered, chosen to lead the rest of us into righteousness and save us from damnation. He is already one of the saved. He can speak to you with authority. He can teach you holy matters with the voice of perfect truth. Brothers and sisters, hearken unto the words of the most holy Saint Kaptaan." He raised his hands overhead to form the circle. Then he stepped down from the pulpit rock.

Julian straightened his shoulders, confirmed that his long sleeves hung straight, and walked out from behind his tree. As he came into the worshippers' view, he felt the rush of mana like a tingle of electricity, a surge of exaltation. He sprang up on the stone and smiled benevolently at all the earnest faces.

This was always the moment when he wondered what his father would say if he could see him now—bearded, dolled up in a long robe like an illustration from a children's Bible, a Moses from Hyde Park Corner. Actually, he had a fair idea what his father would say. Sergeant-Major Gillespie of His Majesty's Royal Artillery would be even more explicit. What of himself? What did he say? Did he really want to spend the next few centuries like a horoscope huckster, touting nostrums and panaceas like a monkey up a stick?

No time for doubts; he was here to do good. He raised his arms briefly to make the circle. The congregation bowed their heads for that blessing, so the chances of his maimed hand being noticed were slight. He had already settled on sermon six, but before he got into that, he would have to correct Kinulusim's minor theological error.

Standard opening first: "Brothers and sisters in the true faith! To be here with you all today gives me wondrous pleasure and a great sense of humility. The first time I visited Seven Stones, there were only three of you. . . ." He droned his way through that, and yet his stump was already aching by the time he had done.

Then to Kinulusim's slip. He slowed down, wrestling his thoughts into singsong Randorian. "Our virtuous brother Kinulusim spoke well, revealing many great truths to you. Carry them with you in your hearts when you leave this place. He is a worthy servant of the Undivided. In his humility, he may have given you the impression that I am in some way more worthy than he is. Do not let his modesty deceive you into believing so. I am one of the apostles, yes, but this does not make me any better than Kinulusim—or any of you—in the eyes of God. The Undivided chose me to bear his word to the world, but not because of any great virtue of mine. I am a sinner, too. I am only a man as Kinulusim is." And so on.

Having spread that little fiction, he began the sermon. He had rehearsed it many times and the dialect came readily. Number six was his favorite, straight plagiarism of the Sermon on the Mount. The Service's synthetic theology always made him feel hypocritical, but the ethics were fine. He had believed in these ethics all his life.

Blessed are the poor. . . . Blessed are the meek. . . . It worked. Of course it worked! Fascinated bright eyes stared at him out of brown faces.

Soon the mana was pouring in. His stump burned as if it were dangling in molten lead. He could feel the fingers of his right hand, which had rotted away in the Belgian mud, back in 1917. At least the pain reminded him to keep his arms at his sides. He need not draw his audience's attention to the fact that he wore gloves, and hopefully few of them would notice or guess why. There was nothing in doctrine to say that apostles must be perfect human specimens, although in practice their steady diet of mana kept them ageless and healthy. He would not create theological paradoxes if he displayed his mutilation. He would if he cured it.

Many of these worshippers had seen him before, and he hoped most of them would see him again in future. A visible miracle of regeneration would not fit the Service's definition of sainthood. If such a miracle became known, Julian Smedley would be promoted in the eyes of the people into a supersaint or even acquire godhood, and the Service was very much on guard against that. It had lost too many missionaries to the opposition already, most recently the mealy-mouthed Doris Fletcher, who was now the divine Oris, avatar of Eltiana and patron goddess of the newfangled art of printing.

He was hitting his stride. "Murdering chickens in a temple will not save you from the wrath of the Undivided, brothers and sisters! He does not judge you by what you sacrifice to the demons but rather by every moment of your daily lives. Virtue and kindness are the offerings he demands of you. . . ."

It was hackneyed stuff to a man raised as a Christian, but to many of his listeners it must be startlingly new and unexpected. They had been brought up to respect the rich and powerful, not to pity them. The Pentatheon did not teach compassion or humility. The Five demanded only obedience, for that brought them mana.

"Not great temples!" Julian thundered. He liked this bit. "Pouring your alms into stones and gilt does not honor the Undivided! Rather use that money to feed a starving child or ease the lot of a cripple. This is the road you must take to find your place among the stars. . . ."

That was pure bunkum, but for centuries the Pentatheon had bribed their victims with a promise that the obedient would dwell evermore amid the constellations. To remain competitive, the One True God must offer nothing less, and it had seemed safer to adopt the local faith than invent a new afterlife. Potential converts might hesitate to accept an unfamiliar heaven.

The words drifted away through the steamy glade; sweat streamed down Julian's face. Then a flicker of movement caught his eye. And another. In the patchy shade at the outskirts of the wood, sunlight glinted on metal. All around the grove, soldiers were moving in, pushing their way through the shrubbery. They held naked swords in their hands.

Oh damnation!

His audience was waiting, puzzled by his sudden silence. He had lost his place. Where in Hades had he got to? He smiled comfortingly at his frightened flock and jumped a few mental pages to be certain he did not repeat himself. Meanwhile his mind was racing.

So was his pulse. He had not felt terror like this since the day a Boche shell had buried him alive.

He was not Jumbo Watson, who could preach a magistrate and two soldiers to their knees, and there must be thirty armed men out there, maybe more. He was not Pedro Garcia, who had magicked himself out of danger in similar circumstances. Julian Smedley could not save himself with mana, even if he wanted to. Every scrap of mana that came his way went into healing his hand—that was not a conscious decision, it just happened. When he had come to Nextdoor a year and a half ago, his arm had ended at the wrist. Now he had a palm. On his last circuit, it had begun to sprout five stubs. He assumed that one more tour would give him recognizable beginnings of fingers and thumb.

Wrong! This tour was going to kill him. He was likely to die on the wrong end of a bloody sword unless he could do something dramatic.

Right. The first thing was to keep control of the meeting. So far the congregation had been too intent on his words to notice the intruders. If they leaped up in panic and tried to flee, they would undoubtedly be hacked down in a bloodbath.

He stopped preaching. He raised his arms in the sign of the circle.

"Brothers! Sisters! We are greatly honored. We have visitors. See the noble company of His Majesty's brave soldiers come to join our worship. Nay!" he shouted over the sudden screams. "Do not be afraid!"

In one simultaneous surge, the worshippers were on their feet. Damn!

*"Stay where you are!* Welcome these worthy men; admit them to our fellowship in the name of the True God! Enter, friends!"

The captain, distinguished by a scarlet plume on his helmet, was emerging from the undergrowth almost at Julian's side. A grizzled boar of a man, in leather and steel, he was showing his teeth in a gloat of triumph at having cornered his prey so easily. "Desist in the king's name!" he bellowed, raising his sword.

Julian bellowed right back at him. "God save the king!" He turned to his cowering, paralyzed flock again. "God save the king!" he repeated.

Wily old Kinulusim echoed him at once: "God save the king!"

"Long live His Majesty!"

This time the response was stronger. "Long live His Majesty!" The congregation had huddled in around Purlopat'r and his uncle, with the young giant towering head and shoulders over everyone else. All those frightened eyes stared at Julian in mute appeal.

"Let us pray, brothers and sisters. Let us pray that good King Gudjapate be granted long life and wisdom to reign over his people. Let us pray that he be granted health and prosperity and true counsel, that his beloved queen . . . that the noble young prince . . ." And so on and so on.

The captain was nonplussed, unwilling to interrupt these patriotic sentiments. His band had come to a halt, all in full view now, a ring of dangerous young men waiting for the word to begin the roughhousing.

Julian roared on. He prayed that the king might continue to be a beloved father to Randorland. He prayed that the king be saved from the wickedness of evil demons. The faithful would know that he referred to Eltiana, the Lady, patron goddess of the vale, but he was careful not to mention her by name nor any of the other local deities either, not even the Undivided. He gave the captain no excuse to interrupt. Gathering words from the wind, he gradually edged his prayer into a sermon again, and this time he used number three.

Julian disliked sermon three more than any other of the current year's issue. He had spent little time studying it, because he had not truly believed that he would ever use it. Just to read the words made him feel more than usually hypocritical, although he had known that three would be a good crowd rouser, pure hellfire: The Five promise you an afterlife of bliss among the stars—they lie! The Pentatheon and all their avatars are not gods at all, they are foul demons, who will be destroyed by the One True God at the Day of Judgment, and all who worship them and serve them here will be similarly wiped out. Solid stuff. Solid balderdash! Who could know what happened after death? Certainly not Prof Rawlinson or the other scribblers of the Service who had written the True Gospel. At least they had not designed a god so malicious that he would torment sinners forever. An eternity of black and solitary boredom was the Valian concept of hell, and the Service had been content to stay with that.

Julian tossed in a little brimstone for good measure.

What he could not remember, he improvised, ranting and roaring. With one small, unoccupied corner of his mind, he registered that it was working. He was holding his own. Sheep and wolves alike, his listeners were rooted to the spot, intent on the torrent of words. Three cheers for charisma!

But it was not enough. He could not go on forever. As soon as he stopped, the captain and his men would snap out of their trance and remember their duty.

He was starting to repeat himself.

His stump had stopped hurting. He was soaked in nervous sweat, but he was also soaked in mana, loads of it—this was a node, after all, and a powerful one. He could feel mana like crackling static in the air, and he must be spewing it right back at the worshippers so fast that his mutilation had no chance to steal it on the way.

There was the answer! For the first time since he crossed over to Nextdoor, he was capable of working a little magic. If he were Pedro Garcia he might use the trapdoor, but he was a true-blue Englishman, who would never desert the ship.

"You ask for proof?" he demanded, although no one had spoken a word. "You want evidence of the powers of the Undivided? Then behold and I shall show you." He thrust out his arm. "You—Purlopat'r Woodcutter! You have known me for a year now, have you not?"

The big youth nodded, eyes wide as soup bowls.

"Then tell your brothers and sisters why I wear a glove!"

"You have only one hand, Holy One," Purlopat'r cried out squeakily.

"Wrong! I did have one hand. My right one was cut off at the wrist, wasn't it? See now what is there!" He ripped off the glove. "My hand is restored to me. My fingers are coming back. Next time I visit you, brothers and sisters, I shall have a hand here as good as the other. This is how the One Who Cannot Be Named rewards those who serve him."

The Service would disapprove thoroughly. The Service would accuse Julian Smedley of promoting superstition, raising false hopes, seeking self-aggrandizement. Under the circumstances, he could not care less what the Service might think. He just wanted to keep on breathing.

"A holy miracle!" yelled old Kinulusim, falling to his knees.

"A miracle!" chorused the faithful, copying him. Young Purlopat'r actually prostrated himself full-length, like a falling cedar. Only the soldiers remained standing.

The captain stood openmouthed and irresolute. Julian swung around to flaunt his maimed—his partially unmaimed—hand at him. He gathered up all that crackling sense of mana and mentally hurled it at the man in desperation. *Kneel, damn you! Kneel!* It was doubtless a very tiny ray of mana by the standards of the Five or their avatars, but it was enough to overpower one crusty, intractable old veteran. *Repent! Repent!*

Slowly, reluctantly, the captain sank down on his knees, and all around the glade, his followers followed his example.

*Jesus!*

"Let us pray!" Julian barked. "Let us give thanks for the evidence of mercy and goodness—"

He gasped as flames of agony enveloped his hand. Then he caught his breath and plunged ahead. The mana was boiling in now, not just from the already overawed believers, but from another thirty converts also. He had worked a miracle. He was a holy man. The captain was weeping and half his men had thrown away their swords.

# 4

Amorgush had gone to sleep on Dosh Coachman's arm, but he managed to slide it free without waking her. She rolled over on her side, breathing loudly. He slid out of the bed and wriggled his toes in the thick rug.

Sunlight streamed in through the windows, gleaming on silk sheets, marble walls, and furniture polished to a glassy luster. Just one of those gold-framed paintings would keep him in luxury for the rest of his days, or possibly get him hanged. Outside, acres of manicured garden swept down to the shores of Joalwater. A small fortune in jewelry lay scattered on the dressing table, making his fingers itch.

He must resist the temptation if he wanted to continue living on old Amorgush. He stooped for the clothes he had dropped on the floor an hour ago. They were fine clothes. Give the old bag her due—she was generous. That was about the only good thing to be said of Amorgush, though. She claimed to be forty, and the gods should strike her dead for perjury. She was reputed to be the richest woman in Joalvale. She was certainly one of the stupidest, although not quite stupid enough to believe the words of adoration he whispered to her every day about this time. She knew he was only a hired man.

He slipped into his pink linen breeches and kid shoes, fastened his wide leather belt lovingly. That did not come from Amorgush. It was probably of Randorian make, although he had stolen it in Mapvale a couple of years ago. A twist would bring the ornate buckle free, bearing a thin strip of steel, flexible yet razor sharp on both edges, a beautiful thing. He loved it. Poor little Dosh always felt naked without at least one weapon concealed somewhere on his person.

He donned his silk tunic—a delicate lilac shade, exquisitely embroidered with many-colored wildflowers—and admired himself in the mirror for a moment, then looked more carefully, checking for love bites. He found none. What he did notice, with annoyance, was the gleam of scalp through his curls. Blond men always went bald young, and he was no longer as youthful as he liked to think he was. There were faint lines starting on his forehead. He turned away angrily from his reflection.

The old hag was still asleep, snoring now. That relieved him of the obligation of a sticky, hypocritical farewell embrace. Amorgush was a good living, but he felt he earned every crust of it, and he headed for the door with the conviction that he had just done a noble day's work. After such a session, his nominal duties in the stable always seemed positively recreational.

The corridor was deserted. He strode along it, admiring the pillared grandeur, intent on a quick bath to get the stench of her perfume off him. All things considered, though, his position in the Bandrops household was the most enjoyable sinecure he had found in his highly varied career. For one thing, Joal was the finest city in the Vales, with every facility a man could dream of. He was paid enough to indulge his versatile taste in vices. Best of all, he need not fear the wrath of a jealous husband, because Bandrops knew exactly what his coachman did during siesta hour.

It had been Bandrops who had first brought Dosh into the house. Bandrops Advocate was an up-and-coming politician—which in Joal meant a man with the instincts of a killer spider—who was widely expected to bribe his way into the Clique when the next vacancy occurred. He had married Amorgush for her money, as his personal tastes ran more to the likes of Dosh than to matrimony. For a while poor Dosh had been required to satisfy both of them regularly, which had been hard work, but now the master had found himself a tender juvenile page, and his calls upon his coachman's evenings were much rarer.

As Dosh reached the head of the staircase, who should be trotting up it but that very same Pin't Pageboy, looking hot and flushed and positively adorable. He stopped, and the two of them appraised each other warily. Dosh had a faint worry that Pin't was after his job with the mistress. Pin't was distrustful of Dosh's own advances, although he had so far managed to resist them admirably.

"Feeling the heat?" Dosh inquired. "It's a remarkably warm fall."

"You don't look very cool yourself," the brat retorted. He had a dark curl trailed artfully over his forehead—Dosh wished he knew how the kid organized that so consistently. "I was looking for you."

"Wonderful! I'm just heading for the bathhouse. Come along."

Pin't curled a lip in refusal. "The master wants you."

Dosh regretfully dismissed the thought of cool water. At this time of day, Bandrops would be wanting a coachman, not a catamite—probably. He shrugged. "Then I'd better go to him. But keep my offer in mind."

"I can't think why I should."

Dosh trotted down. "Experience, my boy!" He reached out in passing, aiming an affectionate pat, which Pin't foresaw and dodged. "I could teach you some very useful tricks."

"I doubt it," Pin't retorted.

He was certainly wrong.

Dosh knocked and was bade enter. The master's office was a sumptuous, sun-bright room overlooking a manicured garden. The rugs alone represented more wealth than most men earned in their lifetimes. Amorgush left all the financial decisions to her clever husband.

Bandrops's perpetual stoop seemed only to emphasize his bulk. He sported the thickest, blackest eyebrows Dosh had ever seen, under a shiny bald pate, although every other part of him sprouted dense black hair. He had a mellifluous, orator's voice, a raging ambition, and sadistic tastes in recreation. He was wearing a loose silk tunic of sky blue and leaning his fists on his ornate desk.

He greeted his coachman with a disagreeable scowl. "I am sorry to drag you from your work."

"I am entirely at your command, sir, of course," Dosh remarked airily as he crossed the sumptuously colored Narshian rug. He was much more interested in the other man standing near the window.

The other man was younger, leaner, even harder, with a cold intensity in his face to warn the discerning observer of potential trouble. He, too, wore the standard Joalian tunic and breeches. In contrast to Bandrops's, his forearms were almost hairless, well muscled, and also much paler than his hands. As were his shins. His cheeks above his close-trimmed beard were darker than his ears and forehead.

"This is the boy, Kraanard," Bandrops declaimed. "Dosh, this is Kraanard Jurist. He has need of your services."

"As my master bids me, sir." Dosh bowed to the stranger, wondering what sort of services were implied. He wondered, too, why an obvious soldier, a man who normally wore greaves, vambraces, and helmet, would be masquerading as a jurist.

Kraanard regarded him with unconcealed contempt. "Have you a moa, boy?"

If Dosh wished to be impertinent, he could now ask where a lackey like him could ever acquire the wealth to own a moa, but that was not what was meant. Moas resisted new riders with murderous zeal; it took months to attune a moa to a man. Dosh was skilled at many things other than seduction. He could harness the household stock to the master's coach and drive it. Officially, that was all that was expected of him.

When Bandrops had hired him, though, he had set out to imprint one of the household moas—mostly because he thought the brute would make suitable severance pay if he had to leave without notice. Bandrops knew he had been trying, because he had commented on the numerous bruises and tooth marks poor Dosh had acquired in the process. What he did not know, apparently, was that Dosh had persevered. There seemed no reason not to tell the truth in this instance, for the other servants knew.

"There is one I can usually manage, sir."

The other men exchanged pleased glances.

"You will come with me," Kraanard announced. "We shall be gone only a few days."

Dosh had survived so long in his perilous career only because he possessed an acute sense of danger. Now tocsins clamored in his mind. There was something extremely fishy here. He contrived an expression of youthful anxiety, which had always been one of his most effective.

"I doubt I can handle Swift for that long, sir. I am only an amateur on a moa."

Bandrops reddened, but it was the soldier who answered.

"The matter is extremely important. Even if you suffer some scrapes, you will be well rewarded."

"I am sure to be thrown a few times, sir. Then Swift will escape."

Kraanard's eyes narrowed. "We shall have others with us. We shall round it up for you. They never go far."

Now the details were starting to take shape—a troop of lancers!

"If you need a moa rider, sir, surely there must be hundreds of native-born young Joalians far more expert than I am."

Again the two men exchanged glances. Then Kraanard strode across until he was right in front of Dosh and could stare down at him with cold gray eyes and unmistakable menace. He was considerably taller.

"But I understand that you are familiar with a man named D'ward."

If he wanted to shock, he succeeded. Dosh felt as if he had been dropped into ice water and for once his self-control failed him. *The Liberator?*

Kraanard was pleased by the reaction. "Some call him that. He is here in Joalvale, somewhere over by Jilvenby."

D'ward! It had been more than three years. They had been traveling with a band of Tinkerfolk, Dosh's own people. Dosh had tired of the grinding poverty and run out on them. But before that . . .

"No!"

A dangerous silence . . . Kraanard said, "What does that mean?"

Dosh himself did not know what that meant. He did not know what he was thinking. D'ward!

"It means he wants money," Bandrops growled in the background. "He's a greedy, grasping scoundrel with the heart of a whore, but he'd sell his own mother for a few silver stars."

Mother certainly, but not D'ward!

Why not D'ward? Dosh did not know. He needed time to think.

Kraanard smiled. He closed a fist in Dosh's hair and bent his head back. "How does thirty stars sound, boy? All you have to do is identify him for us. We'll handle the rough stuff. You won't be hurt."

Dosh uttered the plaintive cry he used to indicate pain or fear, but at the moment he was feeling neither. He was filled with an inexplicable fury. Thirty stars? That was too much. What sort of gullible fool did they think he was? Far too much! Thirty stars was more money than he'd ever owned in his life.

"What's the Liberator to you, boy?" Kraanard demanded. His breath stank of fish.

Good question! "Sir, you're hurting me!" Dosh wailed, but his mind was churning. What, indeed, was the Liberator to him? Betraying friends had always been one of his specialties, so why should he feel so different about D'ward? Was it because D'ward, although he had known exactly what Dosh was, had always treated him as an equal, another human being? He was almost the only person who ever had. Dosh slid the knife out from his belt.

The trooper did not notice the movement. Snarling, he twisted Dosh's hair harder. "Answer me!"

Dosh gave him his answer. Flexible blades were tricky for stabbing, but he drove it expertly between Kraanard's ribs. He had a very intimate knowledge of anatomy—he knew the way to a man's heart. The knife came free easily as the body dropped. Bandrops gaped, then dived around the desk, heading for the door and opening his mouth to shout, but he should have done the shouting first. Dosh leaped, took him from behind, and cut his throat.

He had wiped the blade clean on Bandrops's tunic before the blood stopped pumping out of its owner. Meanwhile, he was thinking hard. Killing had never bothered him— nor excited him either. His heart was beating quite normally—but he had certainly behaved in a very uncharacteristic fashion. Why refuse an offer of thirty stars, however remote the chances of collecting?

More to the point at the moment, how had the authorities known that Bandrops Advocate's coachman could identify the Liberator? He could think of no reasonable explanation in mortal terms, which meant the gods must be meddling again. Dosh revered no god. He despised most of them—especially Tion, the Youth.

Which god was mixed up in this? Many men and women affected special loyalty to a specific god, swearing allegiance to a mystery. Tion had the Tion Fellowship and probably several other cults also; Thargian warriors would belong to the Blood and Hammer, loyal to Karzon. Dosh knelt beside Kraanard and peered carefully under the neck of his tunic, looking for a chain. Not finding one, he undid the laces, but then he was forced to conclude that the late, unlamented Kraanard had not been wearing an amulet. He stripped the tunic off the corpse and began to inspect it—a nice, well-muscled body. He noted with approval how tiny the wound was and how little it had bled, like a deadly snakebite, he thought proudly.

He did not find what he was looking for until he removed Kraanard's breeches. High on the inside of the man's right thigh he discovered a small red birthmark in the shape of an Ø. Dosh would bet his ears that the man had not been born with that birthmark.

Well! He had expected a five-pointed star, symbol of the Maiden. Astina was presiding deity of Joalia, her resplendent temple standing not a mile away. In her avatar of Olfaan, she was patron goddess of soldiers. If a Joalian trooper was sworn to any deity, it should be Astina, but Ø was the symbol of Eltiana, the Lady. The label was so inconspicuous that the cult must be a very secret one. The Lady was goddess of such things as passion, motherhood, and agriculture. None of her aspects was especially threatening, so far as he could recall; a few of them demanded ritual prostitution from their worshippers, but Dosh had no quarrel with that.

He patted the dead man's cheek. "You rascal! You're a spy—or even an assassin, perhaps? I misjudged you!" But the evidence was clear—the Lady was after D'ward and could be assumed not to have his best interests at heart.

He rose and surveyed the carnage. Moments ago those two had been rich and powerful, and he a lowly flunky. Now they were dead while he was still alive. Such is life. Situations change, though—having slain a prominent citizen and a soldier, poor Dosh would soon be as dead as they were if he lingered long in Joalvale. All he would have left to look forward to would be a prolonged and very public death.

Besides, whatever D'ward was doing in Joalvale, the lunatic ought to be warned of Eltiana's concern. It would be an hour or two before anyone thought to interrupt the master at his business. That was long enough for him to get well out of town. Amused by a sudden inspiration, he took the time to undress Bandrops's corpse also—that should confuse the issue a little.

Investigating the secret compartment in the desk, Dosh found a bulky purse he estimated must hold fifty or sixty stars. Unfortunately the jewelry he had seen there on earlier inspections was absent. He considered the possibility of running back upstairs to collect Amorgush's, but concluded reluctantly that the old cow might be awake by now. Hanging the bag on his belt, he headed for the door. Jilvenby lay to the northeast, near Joalwall. A fast moa ought to make that in a day, and despite his earlier disclaimers, he was now extremely skilled at handling Swift.

He was skilled at many things.

# 5

The sun hung low over the snowy peaks of Randorwall as Julian Smedley headed back to Losby through a green jigsaw of paddy fields and orchards, divided by winding hedges of bloodfruit bushes. Here and there between the trees, he could see small groups of the faithful making their way homeward. Randorvale was very lush, vaguely reminiscent of the south of France if one did not look too closely at the vegetation or question what mountains those were.

His stump ached fiercely—the finger stubs were already visibly longer than they had been this morning—but all in all he felt as if his feet were barely touching the ground. His dander was still up, a fizz of mana. The old spice merchant trudged along at his right in triumphant silence, while on his left, young Purlopat'r ambled with gigantic strides that would not have shamed a moa, prattling shrilly about the glorious miracle the One had vouchsafed his believers.

It had been quite a good show, actually. Before setting out from Olympus three days ago, Julian had equipped himself with two dozen gold earrings for converts he might bring into the fold during his two-fortnight circuit. He had thought he was being grossly optimistic, but he had used up eighteen of them already. Eighteen in one day was certainly a Service record—he had heard of Pinky Pinkney managing twelve. Seventeen of the troopers, including Captain Groud'rart himself, had also clamored to join the church on the spot, but the rules required them to take a course of instruction first. Some of them would change their minds, of course, but some would not. To have believers within the royal army could be a tremendous advantage for the Undivided, perhaps leading to infiltration of the Randorian government itself. When Julian Smedley returned to Olympus and submitted the usual report, it was going to be a very unusual report. The new boy had scored a stunning success. It was too bad that he had done so by flaunting his personal miracle cure, and there would be whispers about that. Shag 'em! The alternative had been martyrdom, and the Service did not demand that of its agents. He had not used the trapdoor like Pedro Garcia. He had turned certain disaster to pure triumph. He had even outscored Jumbo Watson.

There was Kinulusim's cottage now, on the outskirts of Losby, flanked by his storage shed and the paddock. There were two rabbits in the paddock.

"Someone has come," Purlopat'r squeaked.

The someone would be from Olympus, almost certainly, and Julian's first thought was that now he had an audience to brag to. His second was that of course a fellow didn't brag, and his third was perverse annoyance that whoever it was would get the story in spades from Purlopat'r and Kinulusim. Dammit! He wanted to slip his miracle into his written report without comment, not make a great shemozzle out of it.

Their approach had been observed. The man heading out to meet them was short and stocky, wearing brown breeches and tunic—Joalian garments that were well suited to riding but which at once made Julian acutely conscious of his own absurd Randorian draperies. In a moment he identified the newcomer and his mana fizz flared close to anger.

Alistair Mainwaring was a plumpish, brown-haired man of indeterminate age. His English bore a faint Highland brogue that showed up even when he spoke Joalian and quite strongly in Randorian. He was one of the most effective missionaries the Service possessed, known around Olympus as Doc and to the natives as Saint Doc, although his degree was in anthropology, not medicine. He was also head of the Randorian section, thus Julian's boss, and a sanctimonious twit. Had he come all this way just to check on his most-junior assistant's progress?

They met, and Julian raised his gloves overhead to make the circle—thereby demonstrating that he had no fears of unfriendly onlookers and had the district under control. The other three copied him instantly. Kinulusim and Purlopat'r would be much impressed to have two holy apostles honoring Losby at the same time. The old spice merchant would also be frantic with curiosity to know why.

Disturbingly, Doc looked about fifty. Strangers' apparent ages were defined by their current mood, and the fatigue of the journey alone should not be so evident. He was also grimy and windswept, so he must have just arrived. He spoke curtly. "Blessings upon you, brothers, and greetings, Saint Kaptaan."

"Your Holiness is most welcome at my humble abode." Kinulusim rubbed his hands eagerly. "May we hope to be honored with your company for an extended period?" He would expect to prolong the greetings with flowery phrases for at least ten minutes, but Doc was clearly in no mood to soft-soap the natives.

"Possibly—that will indeed be a pleasure—but it is likely that Saint Kaptaan will have to leave very soon. I need a quick word with him."

Failing to hide his affront at this summary dismissal, Kinulusim assured the honored apostle that of course he understood and would at once see about preparations for refreshments, and so on. He stumped angrily off along the road, accompanied by the titanic woodcutter, who peered back in juvenile curiosity at the guests.

Alistair sank down on the grass with a weary sigh. "How did it go, old man?" He looked as if he expected a string of excuses.

Still tipsy on mana, Julian felt absolutely no need to sit and was quite certain he had nothing to excuse. "Not bad."

"I hear there have been peelers seen in the area—no trouble, I hope?"

"Nothing we couldn't handle."

Doc dismissed the matter with a shrug. "I've got some queer news. Your chum Exeter is reported to be on the loose up in Joalvale, marching up and down telling everyone he's the Liberator of the *Filoby Testament*."

Julian was too astonished to say anything but, "I beg your pardon?" Exeter? Come out of hiding? Parading around in public? Godfathers! He was going to be frightfully dead frightfully quickly if Zath heard of it. Somebody would have to do something. Oh, it couldn't be! He interrupted Doc's explanations. "There's been a mistake! That would be suicide! I mean, he would never—"

"Sorry, old son. No bally doubt about it."

"It can't be!"

"It is. Seventy-seven says so, and he knows him as well as any. It's definitely Exeter and he's definitely calling himself the Liberator, quite openly."

Julian felt sick. "Zath will fry him."

"The tough one, old chum, is why Zath hasn't fried him already."

"What does that mean?"

Alistair raised a sardonic eyebrow. "Our information is that Exeter started a week ago or longer. It's old news, of course, but if he's still alive, then he must have made himself reaper-proof, mustn't he?"

"I fail to follow you." Julian would gain nothing by losing his temper. Nor could he defend Exeter's behavior when he did not even know what it was.

"You've been here long enough to know the rules. If Exeter can protect himself against Zath's killers, then he must have picked up some jolly powerful mana. I mean, little things like the trapdoor are fine if native bullyboys come after you, but you'd need a sight more heft to take on Zath. How can he have done that?" Doc's upper lip was very close to a sneer.

Julian caught his temper just before it escaped. So that was what was in the wind, was it? The Service had never done a damned thing for Edward Exeter, although his father had been one of the founders. It had kidnapped him, ignored him, hindered him, and tried to kill him. Now, apparently, he was going to be maligned as a turncoat. That would be a good excuse to give him even less help in future.

"Mana? Human sacrifice or ritual prostitution. Like the Chamber does. He took the medal in sixth form for human sacrifice."

A long ride on a rabbit was not the best sauce for humor, and Doc's eyes glinted angrily.

Julian pressed on. "I haven't heard a word from him, if that's what you're wondering. I don't know what he's up to any more than you do." Almost two years ago, right after the massacre at Olympus, Exeter had walked out of the station and disappeared. Perhaps he had gone insane. That felt like a very disloyal thought. "So why come to me?" Was he going to be tarred with the traitor brush, too?

Doc shrugged. "Committee wants you back at Olympus. For consultation. I'll take over your tour here." He did not add that he would do a much better job of it, but his manner certainly implied that.

Dammit! The Committee was probably chasing its tail, trying to decide what to do. Because Julian had been at school with Exeter they would assume that he knew him better than anyone else did, but that had been a long time ago. Rivers of blood had flowed since those days. Still, orders were orders, and he couldn't deny any call that involved Exeter, however unlikely the story sounded at the moment.

"Then I'd better scoot."

Doc blinked. "Tonight, you mean?"

"It's a fine night. Should be lots of moonlight. Why not?"

"It's your arse." Doc hauled himself painfully to his feet. "I'm going to stagger down to the village bathhouse and thaw mine out."

"Then I'll see you when the nabobs have done with me," Julian said cheerfully. With luck he could disappear over the horizon before anyone told Alistair about the eighteen converts. That was a pleasing thought.

# 6

It was close to midnight, and Cherry Blossom House was having a poor night. Half the tables were empty, the roar of conversation was so muted that Potstit Lutist's playing was audible at the far end of the big dark room.

The true artist, so Grandfather Trong had always said, regarded a poor audience as a challenge to excel. Thus Eleal Singer was working the crowd, making her way from group to group, smiling, laughing, chatting up the clientele. The paying customers were all men, of course, a galaxy of hairy, flushed faces under the hanging lamps—young men, old men, just men. The women beside them or draped over them were staff. The air stank of cheap wine and stale cooking, lamp smoke and unwashed bodies.

The tables were very close together, by design, but that let her lean on chair backs or men's shoulders as she moved, concealing her limp. She wore a black leather bra and a short leather skirt, both studded with brass. It was not the sort of outfit a normal girl would wear outside a nightmare, but an actor dressed as the part demanded, and this was the only costume that could justify the heavy boots she needed. Her hair hung lush and raven dark around her shoulders. Apart from her short leg, her body was the best in the house, which explained the deadly stares from the harlots at the tables. And they couldn't sing.

Eleal could. She was going to sing in a few minutes.

She knew most of the regulars by sight, but they were not what she was looking for. She flirted and taunted them a little, relishing the wistful lechery in their eyes, but she was not for them. They knew she was not one of the whores. Suddenly she had a chance to prove it. A calloused hand slid up her thigh. She swung around on her good leg and struck as hard as she could. Fingers almost fell off his chair, and the slap was clearly audible over Potstit's lute playing. So was her roar, professionally projected to reach the farthest reaches of Cherry Blossom House.

"If that's what you want, there are those here who sell it. I do not!"

Fingers's companions yelled with laughter and pulled him down on his chair as he tried to rise. If he got out of hand, Tigurb'l Tavernkeeper would send in his notorious bouncers.

Under the cluster of lamps hanging over the little stage, Potstit ended his solo and reached for the bottle beside his stool. There was no applause. Tigurb'l appeared beside him—a gray, lizardy man like something dreamed up after drinking too much perfumed wine. He rubbed his long thin hands together and flicked a pale tongue over his lips.

"My lords!"

His customary salutation was met with the usual hoots of derision. He proceeded to give a long buildup, introducing Yelsiol Dancer—the *great,* the *sensuous,* the *seductive* Yelsiol Dancer, and the audience responded with drunken whoops. Yelsiol was a great, sensuous, seductive barrel of grease with the wits of a cockroach. Her legs looked fat as full-grown hogs, but they must be solid muscle to stand the pace. Tonight was a real stinker if Yelsiol had to come out again so soon.

Potstit struck a chord and began the beat. Eleal Singer started heading for the front. She was on next, and she still had not found one single friend. Most nights there would be half a dozen of her admirers scattered through the audience, those who came here especially and only because of Eleal Singer, and on a good night . . . Wrong! There was one, sitting alone at a table next to the wall. She changed direction. What *was* his name again? It was only four or five nights since he had been here. A perfect memory is the absolute first requirement of an artist, Trong had always said, but she couldn't remember.

*"Darling!"* She slid gracefully onto the next chair and pecked his cheek. "Darling, how *wonderful* to see you again!"

He was fiftyish, flabby, and vaguely frail, as if his health was poor. His mustache was silvered and his face lined, but he would have stood out in Cherry Blossom House just from the quality of his attire. He was obviously a very successful businessman, which explained how he could afford to patronize the arts so expansively.

He smiled and squeezed her hand and they exchanged pleasantries. In the background, Yelsiol dropped a veil and the audience cheered and yelled for her to get on with it. Fat rolled and pulsed.

Potstit flubbed a few notes and recovered. Potstit had played at court when he was younger, long before Eleal was born. When on form, he was still good, but he was rarely on form. His pay and the rare tips he received, he converted at once to wine. His fingering was very shaky early in the evening, became reliable or even inspired around midnight, and went into eclipse before dawn. Tonight the tempos seemed to be deteriorating faster than usual. Time to go.

Ah! She had it—Gulminian Clothier.

*"Darling* Gulminian, I really *must* rush! I'm on next. But *it's* been *ages!* Don't you *dare* run off without a word. *Do* come and see me *right* after my number, won't you? I shall be *heartbroken* if you don't."

Gulminian promised. Greatly relieved, Eleal heaved herself up with a friendly hand on his shoulder and resumed her journey toward the front. She would be so humiliated if not a single admirer came to congratulate her after she sang! It had never happened yet. It would certainly give Tigurb'l Tavernkeeper ideas if it did.

She reached for another chair back and lurched to the next table, turning on her smile. Again, only one man . . .

"Eleal?"

Oh, by all the gods! For a moment she turned away, as if to flee. Then she forced herself to meet his eyes, while her innards curled up in knots.

It was Piol Poet. How he had aged! A thousand years old—tiny and shriveled. His face was as white as his hair and as thin. He hunched over a beaker clasped in both spidery hands, with no bottle in sight. Normally he would not rent his chair for long at that price, but the house was so poor tonight that he was welcome decoration. He stared up at her with a strange appeal.

She forced the smile again. "Piol!" She squeezed down on a seat beside him, too shaky to stand. "It's been a long time! How are you?"

"I'm well." He wheezed. He did not sound well. He did not look well. "And you?"
"Oh—I'm very well!"

The audience screamed enthusiasm and hammered on the tables as more of Yelsiol came into view. Potstit lost the beat and then found it again.

"What are you doing these days?" Eleal said hurriedly. "Who's performing your plays now?" She wondered if he was eating regularly.

He blinked a few times. "No one at the moment. I have several being considered. I hope to hear shortly on two or three of them. You may be confident that my name will appear at the Tion Festival again next year."

"That's wonderful!" Wonderful hogwash. Piol's plays needed Trong to direct them, and Trong was no more.

The old man fumbled inside his robe. "And I had a book published. Here—I brought you a copy."

She took it, thanking him, congratulating him, remembering how Piol had always despised printed books. Like its author, this one was notably thin. "I shall enjoy this. Will any of them make songs?"

"Possibly. Feel free to use any of them that take your fancy." His wizened lips smiled uncertainly. "And you?"

"Oh . . . It takes forever to get one's name known. But I have had quite a few auditions in the last fortnight." More hog, more wash. She dismissed Cherry Blossom House with an airy wave. "This is just to keep my hand in, you understand. I get so bored otherwise." Unless old Piol had lost every last wit in his head, he knew that the only money in music was in dramatic roles and a crippled singer had no real future.

"I remember you singing in the king's house," he quavered.

"But only as a member of the troupe. I plan to win my way back there on my own merits." That would certainly be the day water ran uphill. "Er . . . Have you heard any news of the others recently?"

He sighed and shook his head, a skull balanced on crumpled parchment. "You know that Golfren went back to farming? Sharecropping, of course. And Uthiam gave him a son at last? Klip joined the Lappinian army."

None of that was new. To think of Uthiam, that beautiful, wonderful actor, working in fields, probably as fat as Yelsiol now, nursing babies! Gartol had died. Eleal had even heard a rumor that young Klip had been killed in a minor mutiny, but she would not pass on such tidings. She wondered how much bad news Piol was keeping from her.

"Those were the good old days!" she said brightly.

It had been the Trong Troupe, but it had not been her grandfather who held it together. None of them had really appreciated that fact until Ambria had been carried off by a sudden fever and the troupe collapsed like a puffball. Trong had died of a broken heart. The troupe had been Eleal's family, the only life she knew. They had never had money, even in the good times, but they had had fellowship and good cheer.

"At your age, the good days are still to come, dear Eleal."

She laughed. "I certainly hope so." It wasn't the good days, it was the bad nights. . . .

Yelsiol was working up to a frenzy now, thumping around the stage, raising clouds of dust and yells of encouragement. Only two wisps to go. Eleal must get up there and wow the fans. No time for finesse.

"Are you eating regularly? Where do you live now? You need money, Piol?"

He shook his head violently, pulling back his lips in a grimace. "No, no! I'm very comfortable."

"Look, this isn't much of a scene, but it pays well. Are you sure—"

He continued to shake his head, pointing at the chapbook she held. "I have a room above the print shop . . . help set type, proofread sometimes."

A deafening howl . . . Yelsiol was down to the last wisp. Eleal pushed back her chair.

"That's my cue, old timer! It's wonderful to see you again, Piol." It was, too, however unwilling she was to be seen in a place like the Cherry Blossom House. She wondered how Piol had found her, and how many of the other survivors of the troupe knew. "I want to have a long talk with you, I really do."

He smiled eagerly. "I look forward to hearing you sing again, Eleal. Come back here after you're done?" For a man who had been a literary genius in his day, Piol had always been blessed with an astonishing streak of naiveté.

"Er, not tonight, I'm afraid. I—I promised my boyfriend. Sorry. One afternoon, maybe?"

Whatever he tried to say was lost in the roar as all of Yelsiol came into view. A couple of her admirers rose and hurried forward through the storm of applause—hoping to visit the star's dressing room and congratulate her, of course, as admirers did. As Gulminian Clothier and hopefully some others would come to visit Eleal. Tigurb'l Tavernkeeper's terms would be reasonable tonight.

Eleal patted Piol's bony, blotched hand and stood up. "Come back one afternoon!" she shouted. She began to hobble away, heading for the stage.

He twisted and reached out to her. "Eleal!"

She looked around. She should be up there by now.

"Eleal," Piol quavered. "I forgot to tell you. Have you heard the news about the Liberator?"

She staggered as if he had struck her with a rail. *"Who?"*

Piol blinked rapidly and beamed. "There's rumors in town that the Liberator's appeared in Joalvale. I wondered if you'd heard."

*"D'ward?"*

"I assume it must be D'ward."

She stood frozen, barely aware that Tigurb'l was already onstage, introducing her. D'ward! After all these years! The floor rocked under her boots. D'ward! That *slime?*

Piol had not noticed her reaction. "It's very strange! I can't imagine how he would dare to flaunt that name when he knows about the *Filoby Testament.* I mean, Zath is certain to hear. So maybe it isn't D'ward at all, just an imposter, although even an imposter would be very stupid to call himself the Liberator. But just in case it really is D'ward, I thought you might like to know, because I remember how fond you were of—"

*"Fond!* Fond of D'ward you mean, you old fool?"

Piol's face fell. "What's wrong? I thought you'd like . . . What's wrong?"

He was so stupid that she wanted to grab his stringy neck and shake him. She tried to scream and her throat produced only a whisper. "Nothing's wrong, Piol. Nothing's wrong at all! I'd love to meet D'ward again!"

*And I will tear his lungs out and make him eat them and then there will be even less wrong than there is now. It's all his fault that I work here as a harlot in a brothel.*

# III

Rise up and get ye forth from among my people.

THE PENTATEUCH: EXODUS XII 31

# 7

All morning, Dosh Coachman had been enjoying a leisurely ride across Joalvale. He arrived at Jilvenby around noon. The moa could have made the journey faster, but he had not pushed her, for he was not worried about pursuit. Yesterday's little episode would not have been discovered for hours, and who then could have known that the murderer had headed east? Kraanard had been a soldier, certainly, but even if he had been acting in an official capacity, his superiors would need time to organize a pursuit. His brethren in the Eltiana cult would be equally eager to peg out the culprit's hide, but they might not hear the news for days, so Dosh had every reason to believe he was free and clear. His life to date had been a hard one. He deserved some good fortune, and now he had earned it with quick wits and the foresight to imprint a moa.

Jilvenby was an unprepossessing hamlet, much what he had expected—a cluster of adobe hovels and waving palm trees set in the middle of farmland. Its inhabitants could be assumed to be honest, hardworking, impoverished, and dull as mud. The only good thing that might be said about the place was that it had a spectacular backdrop of jagged mountains already topped with the first snows of winter, but the same could be said of almost anywhere in the Vales.

The problem would be to locate D'ward. That would not be difficult in a place so small, except that he must be living under a false name—obviously that was why Kraanard had needed a witness to identify him. A man who had the god of death as his sworn foe could not survive for long otherwise. He might have been hiding out in this pigpen for years, earning his bread with honest sweat—horrible thought! Rural yokels did not take kindly to strangers, but that difficulty cut both ways. If D'ward had won some sort of acceptance from the locals, they would be even more suspicious of another foreigner asking questions about him. Silver would usually loosen tongues.

The village stood on the far side of a small river. As Swift waded across the ford, Dosh noted a peasant eating his lunch in the shade of some parasol trees. The evidence lying around this stalwart yeoman indicated he had been repairing a rail fence. Common prudence suggested that Dosh interrogate him before venturing into Jilvenby itself.

He rode over and bade Swift crouch. He slid gratefully from the saddle and hobbled her by tying the reins around one of her hocks. Taking his lunch from the saddlebag, he strolled over to the native, affecting the aloof bearing of a man rich enough to own a moa.

"Care for some company this fine day, my good man?"

The good man in question was a grizzled, overweight specimen wearing a loincloth and a surly expression. He was hairy and none too clean. Taking another bite from a hunk of bread, he continued to chew in relative silence.

Prepared to be patient with the bumpkin, Dosh chose a patch of shady moss on his upwind side and settled down with relief. A moa was a comfortable ride, but he was not accustomed to long journeys and had sprouted blisters. He unwrapped his bundle, selected a slice of sausage, and began to eat, admiring the fall sunshine much more now that he was not exposed to it. This part of Joalwall looked higher than he had expected, leaping from the narrow green foothills in shards of dark rock and sparkling snow. The frondy trees swayed in lazy dance. Swift hobbled around, crunching grass in its big teeth.

"You're too late," the yokel announced. "He's gone."

Now it was Dosh's turn to ruminate. "Who's gone?" he asked eventually.

"The Liberator."

*Well!* More chewing. "Who's he?"

"The one prophesied. Been here three, four days. Him an' his rabble. Locusts!" The workman spat.

This information would require more digesting than the sausage. Dosh rejected his previous theories on D'ward's activities. He discovered he had nothing to replace them.

"Never heard of him. What rabble? What're they up to?"

"They're up to trampling my field to mush, knocking down my fences, camping, littering, singing hymns half the night, preaching a lot of heresy." The peasant was becoming disturbed, working himself up to righteous wrath. "Must've been a hundred of them by the end, more trooping in every day." He skewered Dosh with an accusing glare.

"Not me! I never heard of any Liberator. Where'd they go to, so's I can avoid them?"

"Said they were heading over Ragpass."

"To Nosokvale? Oh, that's all right then. I couldn't take my moa over Ragpass, anyway, could I?"

"Why not?"

"Thought it was too high for them."

"No." The inspection continued. "Where're you heading, then?"

That was a valid question that must not be given a valid answer.

If D'ward had publicly declared himself the Liberator and was leading some sort of religious uprising, then all of Dosh's previous assumptions were trash. The Joalian government would move far more swiftly and drastically to crush a potential rebellion than it would to flush out a solitary fugitive in hiding. If the late trooper Kraanard had been acting officially in a case of suspected insurrection, then his death might be taken as evidence that the conspiracy had reached into the capital already. The authorities would view the affair much more seriously than Dosh had expected.

In other words, pursuit might be a lot closer than he had been counting on. He had better start laying a false trail.

"Me? I'm heading down Sussvale way."

"Can't take your moa over Monpass," the oaf said triumphantly. "Nor over Shampass neither!"

"I have a friend near there, who'll look after her for me while I'm gone."

The yokel scratched himself busily, not commenting, more obviously suspicious than before.

If D'ward was not in hiding and already had a hundred followers, then he was in much less need of Dosh's information about the Eltiana cultist, and the emblem on Kraanard's leg might be totally irrelevant anyway, because his military superiors were far more likely to be worried about an uprising than the Lady would be. But now poor Dosh was trapped in eastern Joalvale, with only one pass out that he could take with his moa. It seemed he was going to follow the Liberator to Nosokvale whether he wanted to or not.

He began to eat more quickly. "And what exactly are these crackpots preaching?"

"I don't know," retorted the peasant. "And I don't shitty care. The Maiden's good enough for me, praise her name."

"Amen!" Dosh said piously. He wondered how far it was to Ragpass and how much start D'ward had. He wasn't about to ask anyone in Jilvenby.

# 8

In Joalian, the principal dialect of the Vales, the animal that members of the Service termed a "rabbit" was a *rabith*. English dictionaries traced "rabbit" back to old Flemish and dismissed earlier etymology as unknown, but undoubtedly the word came from some native of Nextdoor who had crossed over to Earth centuries ago and applied the Joalian name to the comparable animals he found there. Nextdorian rabbits were considerably larger, of course.

They also had tusks. From tusks to bunny tail they were longer than horses, but only about half the height, so that their riders must sit with feet raised in a posture that became very uncomfortable after a few hours. Although they had amazing endurance and an incredible turn of speed, they could not maintain a steady pace. They would flash over the ground for fifteen or twenty minutes, then slow down until another sharp kick sent them off again at their original breathtaking rush. Every hour or so, they needed a break to eat. They were steered—and only constant attention would keep them on a straight course—by gentle tugs on their long ears. Julian thought of them as hay-powered motorcycles. They were certainly no smarter.

For a man with only one hand, a rabbit was a much harder ride than a horse would have been. Braking required tugs on both ears simultaneously, so the only way Julian could stop was to steer straight at a high wall. Even then, Bounder would sometimes try to jump the obstacle, with unpredictable results. A rabbit must be tethered before its rider dismounted or it would run away, and Julian had difficulty doing that. Experience had taught him that it was easier to keep on going until he arrived at his destination, and thus he was very glad to arrive back at Olympus at dusk, after almost twenty-four hours on the road.

He was always happy to return to the station, though. The air alone was worth the price, as Jumbo said. Cosy and wooded, the little glen nestled between the peaks the Service called Mount Cook, Nanga Parbat, the Matterhorn, and Kilimanjaro—native Valians rarely gave names to mountains; there were just too many of them to bother with. Julian's pleasure now was marred only by the knowledge that the person he most wanted to see would not be here, because she had set out the day before he had, on a mission to the Lemodians.

He had given much thought to the Exeter problem and had concluded that the man up in Joalvale must be an imposter. Zath would probably welcome a few fake Liberators showing up to discredit the legend; he might well have set up this false Liberator himself, as some sort of trap for the Service or for Exeter.

The one time Julian had heard Exeter discuss the prophecy, he had been adamant that he would never try to fulfill it. He could not bring death to Death, he had said, because the only way to do so would be to become a more powerful pseudogod himself, and the only way to acquire such mana would be to stoop to the rotten tactics the Chamber used. Out of the question, Q.E.D.

But of course, if this reported Liberator was the real McCoy, then Exeter must have found another answer, and in that case Julian had a worthy friend engaged in a worthy cause. He would have to go and help, whether the Service was willing to support him or not.

Or had the man just snapped under the strain? For almost five years Exeter had known that the Chamber was after his blood; he had been harried from world to world and watched his friends die in his stead. Julian Smedley had seen enough of the effects of war to know that even a regular brick like Edward Exeter must have a breaking point. He had seen it happen to dozens of men almost as good.

Same answer—rally round and help!

Bounder loped wearily along the banks of the Cam, past the Carrots' village. Copper-haired children gawked at the *tyika*. A few adults bowed or made the circle sign. Soon after that, Julian came in sight of the station itself, a cluster of villas grouped around the node. The first time he had seen it, a year and a half ago, it had just been sacked by Zath's henchmen, but it was all rebuilt now. There was even a new cricket pitch, and a few chaps were still out there, practicing in the fading light. The latest addition was a polo field. The first thing he would do when he'd finished growing his hand back was take up rabbit polo.

He rode straight to the paddocks, where he steered Bounder into a corner and then turned him over to the Carrot grooms. He set off on foot for his own bungalow, staggering with fatigue but knowing he could not have come so far so fast on a horse, or even a relay of horses. He had a recurring dream where he somehow took a rabbit

Home and rode it in the Derby, leaving the rest of the field at the post. Alas, the dream must remain a dream, for only people could cross between worlds.

He had not even reached the gate when he saw a man he knew in the next paddock, leaning on a fence and chatting with a couple of stable hands.

Julian bellowed, "Dragontrader!"

T'lin looked up, said a word to his companions, and clambered over the gate. He came trotting in Julian's direction, not moving quite as fast as Julian would have liked.

Political Branch's Agent Seventy-seven was a huge man with a monstrous ginger beard. His origins were obscure, although his habit of wearing a turban suggested that he hailed from Niolland or one of its neighboring vales. His fur jerkin had once been dyed blue, his voluminous bags were a faded green, his boots had started out as scarlet, and he would have some yellow and white about him somewhere. Those were the sacred colors of the Pentatheon, but the tiny gold circle of the Undivided glinted in his left earlobe.

He arrived, stopped, and made the sign of the circle. Julian ignored it, for the Service did not bother with religious mumbo jumbo within Olympus.

"I understand you met *Tyika* Kisster in Joalvale?"

T'lin stood well over six feet tall and could look down on Julian easily, even at his present respectful distance. His expression gave away nothing. "That is correct, Saint Kaptaan."

"Did you speak with him?"

"I did, Your Holiness."

"Just call me '*tyika*' here, Seventy-seven, if you please. Did he say what he was doing?"

T'lin's emerald eyes regarded him coolly under hedges of russet eyebrows. "I asked him. He just said, 'Preaching,' Holiness. I already knew that, because I had watched him. I heard little of what he was preaching, although I believe it was the True Gospel."

"Did he say anything else?"

The green eyes twinkled. "He asked how you fared, Holiness, and if your hand had healed."

Damn! Julian was momentarily thrown off balance. His hand slid behind his back without any orders from him. "You have no doubt that it was the real *Tyika* Kisster?"

"None, Your Holiness. He reminisced extensively about the days when he traveled with me, pretending to be one of my men. No one else could have known the stories."

Damn again! And damn Exeter for foreseeing this very conversation! "Thank you. That will be all."

"Holiness." T'lin hinted at a bow and stalked away. *Tyika*, of course, meant "master." Red beard or not, Dragontrader was not a Carrot.

Julian resumed his walk home.

As he trudged up the bungalow steps, Dommi Houseboy appeared on the veranda to greet him, bowing respectfully. The groom handed him Julian's bag and hurried off. Like almost all the natives of the valley, Dommi had flaming copper hair, although as a domestic he was required to keep it cut short. He was losing the all-over freckles of youth, but he was just as eager to please as he had been when Julian first hired him. As always, his white livery was faultless.

"Evening, Dommi. How's Ayetha?"

"Oh, she is indeed most well, *tyika*, thank you. And you are very welcome back."

"And glad to be so," Julian admitted, heading straight for the bathroom. "I need to shed about twenty pounds of dust."

"I have a warm tub waiting, *tyika*."

He did. The big copper basin was steaming. How on Nextdoor had he ever managed that? He could have had only a rough idea of when Julian would turn up and likely was not supposed to know even that much. He must have arranged for someone in the village to signal to him somehow. Couldn't keep secrets in Olympus—damn Carrots knew everything.

Accepting help to undress, three hands being faster than one, Julian caught a glimpse of his bristly beard in the mirror. Shave? Usually when he came home to Olympus, a smooth chin stood right at the top of the order of battle. Doc had taken over his tour . . . but there was still the Exeter problem. Think about it. He sank blissfully into the water. Dommi bustled around, laying out clothes and towels.

Now for the news, which Dommi must be eagerly waiting to impart.

"The Peppers back yet?"

"No, indeed, *tyika*. They are now four days overdue."

That was odd. Normally members of the Service went Home on leave every couple of years, but the Great War had interfered. Now that it was over, everyone was very eager to catch up. The Peppers had won first slot and were making themselves extremely unpopular by being late returning. It would be at least eighteen months before Julian's number came up.

"There is many excitements around, *tyika*. You are not the only *tyika* to be summoned back. *Tyika* Corey, and *Tyika* Rollinson, and *Entyika* Newton, and *Votyikank* Garcia, and *Entyikank* Olafson and McKay." Dommi's head disappeared into the linen cupboard for a moment. "But *Entyikank* Corey and Rutherford have not been summoned for, nor *Tyikank* Newton and McKay."

It sounded like the Committee was in one of its paper-throwing frenzies, but it would not be good form to say so to Dommi.

Julian rolled an eye to inspect the garments awaiting him. "Dinner?"

"You are invited to *Votyikank* Pinkney, *tyika*."

Julian groaned. He needed sleep! "What time is it?"

"It is approaching six. I checked our clock with the sundial this morning, *tyika*." Olympian clocks were individualists and rarely agreed with one another about anything.

"Then I will have a nap and arrive late." Reaching wearily for the soap, Julian recalled his adventure of the previous day. "Blast!" The Randorian intervention would have to be reported. Political Branch would be interested, and the other missionaries must be warned. "Take down a letter for me, will you?"

Dommi beamed. "Of course, *tyika!*" He loved to demonstrate his literacy, although his spelling was legendary. In seconds he was sitting cross-legged beside the tub, with pen, paper, and ink.

"To *Tyika* Miller. Dear Dusty. Some Randorian soldiers intruded on the meeting at Seven Stones yesterday. Fortunately they proved amenable to reason and did no harm. Doc knows, of course, but we must expect trouble in future. Yours."

Dommi carefully blew on the paper to dry the ink, then held it up for Julian's inspection. Had he really said "enterooded"? or "iminiable to reesson"? or "I have the oner to be uor most humbille and ubidiant sirv'ntt"?

"That's fine. Thanks. Remind me to sign it." He realized that Dommi had not produced the razor. "How about a shave now?"

"If the *tyika* feels it is advisory."

Julian contemplated that remark sleepily. "Or perhaps I'd better keep the beard."

"It might be for the best, *tyika.*"

So Julian was not going to be staying long in Olympus and the Carrots knew it. They had ears like hawks!

"I'll need a snack before I turn in. I'm famished."

"At once, *tyika*. Would tea and bubbler sandwiches be sufficiencies?"

"You know I love bubbler sandwiches." Julian roused himself to attend to his ablutions.

Dommi headed for the door, then paused. *"Tyika ?* If it is not too much presumptuousness . . ."

"What say?"

"When you go to meet the *Tyika* Exeter . . . may I come also?"

Julian was so startled he rubbed soap in his eyes and swore. The Liberator problem was none of Dommi's business! He could not recall Dommi ever leaving the valley before, and Ayetha was close to term. But he had been Exeter's houseboy once, and Exeter had always had a gift for inspiring loyalty—when he had been house prefect at Fallow, the juniors had worshipped him. If the *Filoby Testament* had not kept him out of the war, he would have made a great officer. None of which concerned Dommi.

"I haven't been told I am going anywhere to meet anyone."

Dommi murmured, "Of course, *tyika !* I beg the *tyika*'s pardon," and padded away.

Julian began contemplating a long evening. The dinner at the Pinkneys' might be more important than any formal Committee session, for the real decisions would be made there, over port and cigars. And of course Dommi had been careful to tell him that his mistress was back, but her husband was not.

# 9

A cruel wind wailed along the street, inciting dead leaves to run races, whipping up the rank smell of horses from the stones. It tugged at Eleal's cloak and tried to snatch her precious load from her arms. It threw dust in her eyes. In this corner of the town the evening's activities would not normally begin for hours yet, but twilight was coming early under the storm clouds and she must complete her business and be well away before it did. Bending into the gale, she trudged with her uneven gait—*clip-clop, clip-clop-clip*. The wind repeatedly tried to push her off balance or rip the cloth wrapping from the burden she carried.

Jurg was a fine town, her favorite town in all the Vales, but all towns had seamy corners and River Street was seamier than the backside of a patchwork quilt, a fetid alley that made the area near Cherry Blossom House seem dull as a virgin's diary. She had only ever ventured here before once, and then in broad daylight. The Cherry Blossom whores came regularly, but always around noon, and even then Tigurb'l Tavernkeeper sent bouncers along to protect them. Eleal could have asked a couple of those thicks to escort her this evening, but they would have been more dangerous than the ill-reputed denizens of River Street. They would have demanded to know what she carried wrapped in that rag and then promptly relieved her of it. The brighter ones would also have cut her throat so she couldn't tattle back to Tigurb'l.

It had cost more than five Joalian stars. If she let it slip, it wouldn't be worth a copper pig. If she fell and went down on top of it, she might not be, either. The sucker was as tall as a two-year-old child—and *heavy*. The push of the wind was uneven. The cobbles were uneven. Her legs were uneven. *Clip-clop . . . clip-clop . . . clip . . .*

There were few other people around. The town mice had fled the coming dark and the cats had not yet emerged. The one or two men who came hurrying past all looked at her as if they could not believe their eyes—this was no place for a woman alone. She should have borrowed some less pretentious garments, too. Her cloak alone had cost almost half a star, burgundy-colored Narshian llama wool with white goose-fur trim.

But here was her destination. Amid all the shabby tenements, run-down stores, and mysterious anonymous doorways stood a grand pillared entrance, far older than all of them. The original proprietor was still in business, for the portico bore a massive metal hammer, the symbol of Karzon. Usually the holy buildings in a city were clustered close together. Isolated temples like this one were so rare that Eleal knew of no others—it was as if the god who lived here had been spurned by the other gods of the city, as if they would not associate with him. This was the home of Ken'th, avatar of the Man in Jurg.

She dared not pause to catch her breath, although her heart was racing like a cheetah. One more effort to think this project through and her courage would fade like mist. Blinking the wind tears from her eyes, she hurried up the steps, clutching her precious bundle. *Clip-clop, clip-clop . . .* The old tiled steps showed signs of wear. That amused her, because no one ever admitted to worshipping at the temple of Ken'th. Mother Ylla, that horrible hag, had told her once that only boys and old men did—she had overlooked harlots.

The door stood open. It was a small door for so large a portico, and the interior beyond seemed dark. Again, Eleal felt her nerve waver. Her insides had tied themselves into hard knots; her arms shook so violently that she feared she was about to drop the figurine. That would ruin all her plans! But gods should be approached with humility and reverence, not this burning anger, this vitriolic craving to *get even.* Who ever brought a plea for justice to the Man? Justice was the prerogative of the Maiden, especially her aspect of Irepit, who had once sent one of her nuns to save Eleal from a reaper and must therefore be well disposed toward her. Unfortunately, Astina's aspect in Jurg was Agroal, goddess of virginity, not at all the right goddess to handle a problem like this— nor one that Eleal Singer would dare to petition, whereas she had a special call on Ken'th. *Get even!* I will be revenged on D'ward! She clenched her teeth and lurched forward into the temple. *Clip! Clop! Clip!*

The circular chamber was small for the home of an important god, but that was because Ken'th attracted solitary worshippers, not great congregations. To her intense relief, it was presently inhabited only by a restless wind, which rustled leaves it had brought in as offerings and stirred the draperies covering the walls. High, narrow windows above them shed little light on the gloomy hall. In the center, two oil lamps burned on the low dais, their flames jumping nervously—they could not be half as nervous as she was! Above them stood the figure of the god.

Unlike the Youth, the Man was normally portrayed clothed, but of course this was Ken'th. Lit mainly from below by the lamps, the carving was impossibly priapic. She had been only a child on her previous visit, yet even then she had been confident that the anatomical details were based on wishful thinking. Now she knew that from experience, but she could also tell that the sculptor had been much more skilled than whoever had painted the pornographic murals in the upper rooms of Cherry Blossom House. The musculature was superb. The set of Ken'th's hands on his hips and the tip of his head demonstrated male arrogance beautifully—man the irresistible. The face bore an expression at once sensuous, demanding, and callous. She thought of her mother, wondering if she had come here of her own free will, or if the god had sought her out somewhere else.

Eleal limped closer. She should kneel, she supposed, and yet she felt strangely reluctant to do so. Her heart was fighting to escape, a terrified bird in a bony cage.

A curtain swished open, revealing a dark little room behind. She jumped, almost dropping the figurine. A man strode out silently on bare feet—a priest, of course, although he did not look like a priest. Male servants of other deities wore long robes, and most shaved their scalps and faces. Being Ken'th's and on duty, this one had only a green wrap tied around his loins. His hair hung to his shoulders, his beard merged with the fur mat on his chest. He was tall and well-built, an exemplar of young manhood, but the temple of virility would have many more applicants to choose from than most did.

He came around the plinth and stopped near one of the lamps, regarding her with approval. "You are welcome to this holy place, beloved."

Eleal clutched the figurine tighter—much tighter and she would break it. "Thank you, father," she said, and was annoyed to hear the quaver in her voice.

He nodded slightly, eying her burden curiously. "I see you bring a substantial offering. How may I aid you? What mercy do you seek from mighty Ken'th?"

"I wish to speak with the god himself."

"An elderly husband, perhaps? An embarrassing delay in conceiving?" He would be willing to remedy the matter, with the god's help and a suitable fee. He might even waive the fee in her case.

"No, father."

He smiled, unable to conceal his eagerness. "Then too much success in conceiving? You wish the god to withdraw his blessing? This, too, may be arranged, beloved."

That was why the harlots came. It would be all much the same to him, for although that ritual included some complicated preliminaries to appease the god and ensure the required result, all Ken'th's rituals included coitus. All that involved women, anyway. What happened with the boys and old men, she did not know and did not want to.

"Not that, either. I wish to speak with the god."

A flicker of impatience. "Present your offering, make your prayers, and then I shall aid you in the rites."

"No. I—I wish to meet him in person."

The man blinked. Then he grinned broadly. "You are ambitious, daughter! Whatever your need, I am authorized to represent the god in the performance of his sacrament."

Eleal had never met a man who did not think that of himself, and she could recognize the too-familiar eagerness in the priest's manner. He advanced a step. She backed away. He noticed her limp and frowned.

Unable to think of anything more to say, Eleal pulled the cover from the figurine, a female dancer poised on one toe, about to take flight from its plinth, carved Niolian crystal flashing in the lamplight. Its beauty was heart-stopping. She had spent all afternoon haggling with the dealer, and even then he had emptied her purse to her last twelfthpiece. Surely such an offering would earn the god's attention?

The priest sucked in his breath. "You bring a rich gift, lady!" he admitted. "It is fitting." He tore his eyes away from the carving to study her again, noting the quality of her robe. She could almost hear him concluding that a woman who wore such a garment to visit River Street must be out of her mind.

He reached out. "Let me take it for you."

"No!" She moved it away.

"Then lay it on the dais, carefully."

"No! I wish to give it to the god in person. *I want Ken'th in the flesh!*"

"You are verging close to blasphemy, daughter!"

His tone annoyed her. He was little older than she was.

"Tell the god that—"

"Give me that carving before you drop it." He reached out again.

Again she lurched back. Seeing she could not evade him any longer, she turned and hurled the figurine at the feet of the idol. The crash echoed from the stone walls; a hail of diamonds danced across the floor. The priest cried out in horror.

"There!" Eleal shouted. "I have given my offering to the god! Now let him hear my prayer!"

The priest backed away, watching carefully where he put his feet. "You are crazy, woman!" His voice was unsteady. "You commit sacrilege and blasphemy! Begone, lest Holy Ken'th smite you in his wrath!"

"I want Ken'th!" she yelled. "I have words for his ears alone!"

"Go! You are out of your wits, I say. Beware that he does not curse you, so that no man will ever consummate his holy sacrament with you."

"He is my father!"

The young priest curled his lip in disgust. "One of those, are you? Be thankful to mighty Ken'th for giving you life and do not trouble him further." Coming around, staying clear of the shining fragments, he grabbed her arm so hard that she cried out.

"I have a special service to offer him!"

"Begone, madwoman!" He began pulling her to the door.

She struggled and clawed at him. He took hold of her other wrist and manhandled her easily, practically carrying her.

It was not working out as she had planned. She had thrown away everything she had ever earned and would have nothing to show for it. She was going to be balked of her revenge. "I want to tell him of the Liberator!"

"I am sure you do. And you doubtless have a few prophecies he should hear also. Pray to him in the privacy of your bedroom, and he will hear." They had reached the door. "Out with you!—and do not linger in these streets, for the god's presence here makes men bold. It is no place for a woman alone."

With that cold warning, the priest threw her out. The door slammed behind her as she sprawled down on the rug.

# 10

*Rug?* Not a woven rug but a thick alpaca fleece. She raised her head to look into a cheerful log fire, crackling and sputtering in a stone fireplace. She could have sworn that the priest had thrown her outside on the steps. His words had said so. To her left, a leather couch . . . another couch on her right. She was indoors in a large and comfortable chamber.

She moaned in fear and pushed herself up on her arms. She had sung in the king's house when she was a child and she gave private recitals now, so she knew how the rich lived. She had seen nothing to better this: floors of polished wood overlain with soft fleeces, walls bearing shelves of books, racks of bows and spears, mounted trophy heads. The furniture was solid, upholstered in browns and russets, subdued and harmonious. Scents of beeswax, leather, and wood smoke hung in the air. Bewildered, she rose to her knees. This was very much a man's room, a rich man's den, cozy and friendly and appealing.

She peered around for a door but saw only full-length drapes of umber velvet, which might equally well conceal windows. None was close enough to explain how she came to be where she was. This was certainly not that fusty little cubicle she had glimpsed in the chapel. On the shelf above the fireplace stood two gold candlesticks, a golden vase of autumn flowers—and a carved crystal figurine of a dancer poised to fly. She scrambled to her feet to stare at it. It stood a little higher than eye level, and with candlelight dancing over the shiny facets, she could easily imagine that it was already flying. There could never be two identical and yet she had smashed . . .

"Thank you. It's very beautiful." The voice came from somewhere behind her.

There had been no one there a moment ago. She knew who must have spoken, who must have re-created the dancer. Her prayer had been granted. She spun around and simultaneously sank to her knees, touching her face to the rug, not daring to look upon the god without permission. Her heart thundered in her throat.

The Man was an ambiguous deity. Creator and destroyer, he must be both feared and adored. As D'mit'ri he was the builder of cities; as Krak'th he shook them down. As Padlopan he was sickness; as Garward, Strength. He was husbandry and battle. As Zath he was Death, as Ken'th he quickened the womb to bear new life. As Karzon he was all of them.

Piol Poet had written the Man into his plays many times, but never as Ken'th, although there were many fine legends of the Lover. Most were variations of the tragic tale of Ismathon, the mortal who pined away and eventually slew herself rather than live without his love. The Trong Troupe would never have performed any play with Ken'th in it.

"It is an exceptionally fine piece," the god said, his voice coming closer. "It cost you dearly, so whatever it is that troubles you must be a serious matter." Then he chuckled. "Are you comfortable down there?"

She had not expected a god to *chuckle*. "Er . . . yes, Lord." She raised her head a fraction and saw two bare feet. A strong hand reached down and raised her. She kept her face lowered until a finger lifted her chin and she met his smile.

Back in her theater days, she had seen Karzon in his various aspects depicted by many actors—Dolm, Trong himself, Golfren, men with other troupes. He was always portrayed with a beard, often in armor, and whenever possible by a large man. Ken'th did not look as she expected at all. He was younger, for one thing, and not especially big, although his arms and shoulders were solid enough. He had curly hair and a Niolian-style mustache. He wore a sleeveless shirt and knee-length breeches—in green, of course. At least the color was right. But there was no sense of divine majesty about him. Nor did she sense any stunning, overwhelming sexuality. He was just a chunky, cheerful young man, handsome in a rugged sort of way, faintly scented with musk and lavender. He was smiling reassuringly. His eyes . . . perhaps the eyes . . .

"Why not begin by telling me your name?"

She struggled to find her wits. "Eleal Singer, Lord."

"Welcome to my house." He unfastened her cloak, glanced at it approvingly, and tossed it over a couch. He took a step back to look her over. "Mm! You are not only a startlingly beautiful woman, Eleal Singer, but you have exquisite taste in clothes!"

She gasped out her thanks. She had money to indulge her whims now, and this gown was her newest and best, just bought for winter. She had not worn it before—fine white wool, decorated only with big rhinestone buttons down the front and brocade on the collar. She always chose clothes with long skirts to hide her boot; she suspected that the long sleeves and high collar were a reaction to the skimpy things she wore to perform. It was snug around the bodice, though, with a high, tight waist supporting her breasts, and from there it fell full and loose. To have her clothes praised by a god was a heady sensation. She avoided his eye, feeling herself blush.

He led her to a russet leather couch, seating her next to the fire and settling down beside her. She clasped her hands on her knees and stared at them as if she were a fourteen-year-old with her first man.

"And you claim to be my daughter? Who was your mother?"

"Itheria Impresario." When there was no reaction, she continued. "She disappeared for a fortnight, here in Jurg. I know very little about her. She bore me and then she just died, and I was reared by my grandfather, Trong Impresario, and his wife—his second wife, Ambria. She said my mother hadn't been a bad woman, she had . . ." Been seduced by the god, but she couldn't say that. "Pined away for love?"

Ken'th sighed faintly. "That does happen, I'm afraid. I don't recall the name. It could have been me. I'm not usually quite that fickle—only a fortnight? But it is possible, I suppose." He slid an arm around her, making her heart flip. "You are certainly beautiful enough to be the child of a god. You sing for a living?"

"Yes, Lord."

"Where?"

"Oh, all over the place. I have performed in many of the Vales and at many places here in Jurg." That was all true. The Trong Troupe had traveled. Tigurb'l often arranged for her to perform in private houses.

"Fascinating!" the god said softly. "And you mentioned the Liberator! Are you the Eleal named in the *Filoby Testament?*"

"Yes, Lord."

"Father?"

"Yes . . . Father." She glanced sideways.

He raised dark eyebrows and waited. He was smiling, but his amusement held none of the mockery the priest's had. He was taking her concern seriously.

Talk . . . "I did what was prophesied. When the Liberator came, I tended him, washed him. He fell very sick, and I nursed him. I did everything I was supposed to, Father!"

Ken'th frowned. "You know, I find I dislike that title? I have no experience at being a father, Eleal. That's not my job. For that you need Visek."

"Of course, Lord!"

"I am god of virility," he said apologetically. "I do have duties. If I tried to keep track of all the bastards I have fathered in the last few hundred years, I would have no time for anything else. You do understand?"

"Yes, of course, Lord!"

"Call me Ken'th."

She hesitated, appalled.

"Go on!" he said, teasing. "You wanted me in the flesh. You have me in the flesh, so call me Ken'th!"

"Yes, Ken'th."

"That's better."

For a moment he just smiled at her. She smiled back with mounting confidence. He was handsome, now she saw him close—handsome and attractive. His face did not at all resemble the face on the statue. Not arrogant, not callous, but kind and trustworthy and sympathetic.

"How old are you?"

"Seventeen . . . Ken'th."

"So when the Liberator came you were only a child. He was not a baby, of course, although the text implied he would be. How old was he?"

"Eighteen, he told me."

"Lovers?"

"Oh *no!* Of course not!"

The god's arm tightened around her. "And what did you want to tell me about him?"

This was where matters might become just a trifle delicate. Her heart began to speed up again. "He's reported to be up in Joalvale."

"That's the story that's going around, yes."

She drew a few long breaths, as she did just before starting to sing an especially difficult song. "I thought . . . perhaps . . . I wondered if you might want to get in touch with him. If you do, I could identify him for you . . . if you wish. . . ." Of course it was Zath who would be interested in catching the Liberator, but Zath was Karzon and Karzon was Ken'th, although she couldn't in any way relate this chunky, likable young man to the dread god of death.

"An interesting offer!" the god said thoughtfully. "What is wrong with your leg?"

Normally she was furious if anyone mentioned her impairment, but this was her father, so his interest was excusable. "One's shorter than the other." She raised her leg so he could see the thick sole on her boot. "I fell out a window when I was a baby."

"It does not hinder your ability to perform?"

"Not— Well, yes, of course it does! My ambition has always been to be an actor, but I can't clump around a stage like this! I would not be allowed to enter the Tion Festival!" There, she had told him!

And Ken'th murmured sympathetically. He understood! "Let's hear you sing. Sing for me—nothing elaborate, something simple. Something unusual." He took his arm away and reached over the back of the couch to produce a lute. He strummed expertly; it was in perfect tune. "What'll it be?"

She had not expected this! To sing for a *god!* She racked her brains. " 'Woeful Maiden'?"

He smiled and played a verse, although it was an obscure song, one that not many people would know. He was much better than Potstit had ever been. "Higher? Lower?"

"No, no, that's just right!" Daringly, she added, "You play divinely!"

He laughed. "Well, of course!" He began the introduction.

She sang the first verse, but then he stopped and put the lute away.

"Just what I expected. Your voice is reedy, your timing eccentric. You put terrific feeling into the words and get by on drama, but you wouldn't be admitted to the Tion Festival in a thousand years."

"Lord! I mean Father . . ."

He swept her into his arms and squeezed her tightly. He kissed the tip of her nose playfully. "You must be very hot in that dress?"

"I'm your daughter!"

His eyes gleamed in a look she knew well. "And I'm a god! Gods do not have to obey petty little rules!"

Then he kissed her lips.

It was not an especially long kiss. It did not have to be. When he had done she leaned back and gaped at him. She was limp. No man had ever kissed her like that.

He chuckled with satisfaction. "Now, Eleal Singer, let's have the truth. Not just what you want to believe is the truth, but the real truth. Where do you sing?"

She clenched her teeth. And her fists. But the god was waiting, regarding her with big brown eyes. "Well, several places. I mean . . . sometimes . . . well, Cherry Blossom House."

"So you are a whore!"

"Certainly not!"

He raised his eyebrows. "My, you are a determined little prickleback, aren't you? We'll try some more, then."

He was firm; he did not hurt her, but her struggles were useless against his strength. His lips pressed on hers, his hand stroked her breast—the dress was down around her waist, although she did not know how that had happened. Tingles rippled through her, from her scalp to her toes. She was melting and struck by lightning, both at the same time. Excitement surged through her in fiery waves. No man had ever taken over her body like this, nothing like this had ever happened to her before, she was floating away in clouds of pink fog—but then he stopped.

"Oh, Ken'th, Ken'th . . . Darling . . ." She reached down to remove the dress completely.

He took her hands between his and clasped them. "The real truth now!"

She heard her own voice from far away. "Yes, darling. Yes, I'm a whore. After I sing, Tigurb'l sends men back to my dressing room. I bring in three times what anyone else does, he says. Sometimes he sends me to perform in private houses . . . just for men, of course. I don't want to do these things, but there's no other work for a crippled singer. I was so hungry! Kiss me again, please."

He uttered that surprising chuckle again. "You don't shock me, Eleal. Did you think I would disapprove? You are doing what women should do—aiding men in the performance of my sacrament. And the Liberator?"

One of her hands broke free and began to unbutton his shirt. "I don't care much about him," her voice said. "He was supposed to go to Tion's temple. This was in Sussvale, where the Youth is patron. The priests commanded that D'ward—that's the Liberator's name, D'ward—that D'ward come to the temple, and Kirthien Archpriest said I had done well and Holy Tion would heal my leg, but the Liberator just ran away. He disappeared! So my leg didn't get cured . . ." The memory of that awful injustice flickered faintly through the pink fog. *Coward! Ingrate!* "He ran away! He betrayed me. I want. . . . You're my father. When I learned that, when we came back to Jurg, I came and prayed to you, here in the temple. Until a priest found me and said I was a dirty little girl and threw me out!"

"I didn't hear you," Ken'th said grumpily. "I may have been away. Or busy."

"Well, this morning I decided you might hear me if I mentioned the Liberator. And if I brought a big offering." She hoped she could stop talking now and he would kiss her again. She had his shirt open and could run her fingers through the manly thatch on his chest.

"You want revenge on the Liberator. . . . No, mostly you hope to bribe me to heal your leg."

"No, no, no! I just want to help you, because you're my— I want to help you!" She tugged one-handed at the big gold buckle of his belt.

Ken'th was frowning, though. "I could cure you, of course, but I'm god of lust, not god of healing. That's one of Tion's attributes. I suppose I could claim that repairing a harlot was within my field, because he certainly plays around in my garden when he's in the mood. Damn you, you little shrew-cat, you've put me in a confounded mess!"

Eleal choked. "M-mess?"

"Mess. If Zath ever finds out I had a lead like you and didn't follow it up . . . Never mind. You can't understand."

Why did he speak of Zath as if he were someone completely different, not just another aspect? She had thrown away her savings, angered a god, probably angered Tigurb'l Tavernkeeper, too, because she was going to be late—and she still had to get out of River Street without being raped. But at the moment none of those things mattered. "Kiss me again. Please!"

"No. I need you with some wits about you. Here's what you're going to do, Eleal Singer. You're going to go and find this D'ward Liberator, you hear? You're to go up to him and put a hand—"

Black panic cut through the pink fog like a sword blade.

*"No, no!"* She writhed and struggled. "You're not to turn me into a reaper!" A reaper like Dolm Actor, with all those horrible rituals he had known—to slay people with a touch, to walk through locked doors, even to summon Zath himself . . .

"By the Five, you do have resistance, don't you? Tough as marble!"

"Not a reaper! I won't, I won't!"

"I couldn't make you a reaper. That's Zath's speciality. But I have a trick or two of my own. Don't I?" Ken'th smiled and removed her hand from his belt. He spread her arms wide and leaned on her, bringing his lips to hers again.

The world danced for her. She soared into heavens of delight. She melted. But it was all too short, only seconds. When he pulled back from her, she could see his big brown eyes appraising her calmly. She was gasping for breath, soaked all over, quivering violently. More, more!

"Now, Eleal Singer. I shall give you money and have the priests escort you safely back to the whorehouse. Tomorrow you will go and find the Liberator. Get very close to him, touching him. In his bed would be best, but a hand on his arm will do. Then you will sing that song you sang for me. You must never sing it again until you are touching D'ward, you understand? And when you come back, I shall heal your leg for you. I'll find you a nice rich husband—rich, anyway, the two together are rare."

He released her hands, which immediately reached for her bundled dress, to push it off her completely.

He chuckled. "No! Put it on again. Do as I say, and I'll give you what you want when you come back. Truly, I look forward to it! But now you will leave here at once and you will not remember this conversation. When the priests deliver you to your door, you will forget ever coming here. But tomorrow you will do as I have told you."

# 11

Dosh knew most of the official passes in the Vales and a few unofficial ones also—the secret "back doors" patronized by smugglers and Tinkerfolk, who were frequently the same people. Although he had not crossed Ragpass in years and had only vague memories of it, he remembered it as soon as he saw it. The Nosokvale end, he now recalled, was quite gentle, but the Joalvale side angled up a sheer cliff. In many places the trail had been notched into the buff-colored rock like a half tunnel, and those artificial parts were too narrow to let two men pass. The natural ledges were mostly wider but often canted unpleasantly toward the scenery. The only good thing to be said about the ascent was that it zigged and zagged so much that anyone who blew off could have some hope of flattening a fellow traveler or two as he bounced his way down.

Convinced now that his continued survival depended on leaving Joalvale with haste and as few witnesses as possible, Dosh had not paused to talk with any more natives. His Tinkerfolk childhood had given him skill in tracking, but any fool could have read the footprints in the dust, and they would have been erased by the wind if the Liberator and his gang were more than a few hours ahead of him. When he drew near the base of the cliff, he could see small groups of people like mites, trailing upward, far above him. In the warm glow of a setting sun, he proceeded to ride his moa up the nightmare.

The first third or so went comparatively easily. All he need do was urge his mount on and resist a temptation to close his eyes. Being suspended seven feet above the path was much worse than having one's own feet on it, and he had to curl into a knot at the overhangs, but at least he need not exert himself. Joalflat began to expand below him like a painting. He caught up with some of the stragglers and passed them. They were mostly old folk or families with children—not the normal run of travelers at all—so he assumed that they were the tag end of D'ward's army. He did not stop to speak with them, merely shouting at them to stand aside and let him pass.

The moa repeatedly battered his knees and ankles against the rock. As he drew higher, the wind flapped at his clothes and ruffled his curls.

The rule of thumb in moary was that moas would go no higher than the tree line. Swift must have read the rule book, because she suddenly concluded that the total absence of trees hereabout meant that she was excused from further effort. She stopped dead and tried to bite him.

Dosh kicked hard, winning another few minutes' progress. Then Swift stopped again. Wishing he had thought to wear spurs, he pulled out his dagger and gave the brute a jab in the shoulder. The result was a hair-raising tantrum of leaping and bucking, followed by a serious effort to run back down to Joalvale. Pebbles flew over the edge and rattled away into space. Dosh wrestled the beast around and jabbed again. Swift took off like a Nagian warrior's spear. Warned by his yells, other travelers cleared the way, and he went by them in a blur.

It could not last, of course. Eventually they reached an impasse. Swift absolutely refused to budge any farther. Concluding that more jabbing would merely exacerbate her already vicious temper, Dosh dismounted.

Moas could be led, in which case they tended to bite. Their teeth were blunt and rarely drew blood but could certainly hurt. Moas might also be driven, in which case they would kick with their sharp hooves. Dosh elected to drive, untying the reins and using the thong as a tether. As he had hoped, Swift was too winded and too unsure of the footing to do much serious kicking. They proceeded up the hill at a reasonable pace.

The sun was drawing unpleasantly close to the horizon. Joalflat stretched out to infinity, vanishing into haze to the west. Moa or not, Dosh was determined to reach the top of this accursed ascent before dark.

He passed a few more of the Liberator's rabble, which was a fair description of them. A majority seemed to be women, and none of them looked prosperous. Obviously no one with a good living would throw it up to follow the Liberator, although why anyone at all should want to follow the Liberator just because he was the Liberator escaped Dosh completely. D'ward had been a superlative leader when he was battlemaster of the combined Joalian and Nagian armies, but these derelicts were no army. And who was the enemy? *Zath?* That seemed like a war to avoid at all costs. Dosh wished wholeheartedly that he had washed his hands of the Liberator and headed west to Fithvale.

As the sun swelled to a scarlet cushion on the skyline, he reached the top of the ascent. Suddenly there was no more cliff above him, only trees and two great peaks flanking the pass. A gale was howling through the gap. As far as he could recall, though, from here the road wound gently downward all the way to Nosokflat.

"There, you brute!" he told the moa. "Trees! You're back on duty."

She kicked at him and he dodged.

He paused to catch his breath and look back, letting his sweat cool. Half of Joalvale was visible, its shadowed landscape a tapestry of green and gold fields, woodlands, blue waters. The rivers were silver ribbons, the roads red threads. If the light were better, he would probably see Joal itself.

He saw dust. Something was raising a smudge of dust on the road he had come. It might just be a caravan of wagons, but his instinct for self-preservation told him not to bet on that. Far more likely it was a troop of Joalian cavalry. They probably would not attempt the ascent in the dark—he hoped. They might not be after him or the Liberator.

Pig puke! His lifelong motto had always been to assume the worst, and it had never failed him yet. He should have heeded it sooner.

The sky was cloudless. Trumb had risen, almost full, and could be counted on to bathe the world in bright green light until dawn. Dosh turned to give battle with the moa. "You," he said grimly, "are going to run as you have never run before."

Swift expertly kicked him on the shin, hurling him to the dirt, and then landed another kick on his ribs as he rolled away. Fortunately it broke no bones and he did not let go of the tether.

Who owned a pass was a question that had started many a war, but the ultimate answer depended on the relative strengths of the parties involved. When the neighboring states were Joalia and Nosokia, there was no argument. The Nosokian rulers were Joalian puppets and would not talk crossly to Joalian troopers if they pursued a fugitive into Nosok itself and hacked him to bits on the main street. When the fugitive spoke no Nosokian and knew of no back doors out of Nosokvale, his only option was to head east as fast as possible. If he could reach Rinoovale, he would be into Niolia's sphere of interest, safely out of Joaldom.

All four moons graced the night. Although Kirb'l, Ysh, and Eltiana combined could not match the green glare of Trumb, they did help lighten the shadows, and Dosh rode swiftly along the valley. Mainly the track clung to the banks of a chattery stream, avoiding the head-smashing branches of the forest. He passed more of the Liberator's followers. If the Jilvenby peasant's numbers had been anywhere near correct, there could not be many more of them ahead.

After a mile or two, Dosh rounded a bend into a section of the valley that was more open. Its walls rose steeply from a flat floor, carpeted by shrubs but few trees. He saw the flicker of fires ahead, a cluster of fallen stars among the bushes. There were many more of them than he would have expected.

There was nothing to stop him riding right on by. He could be in Nosokland by morning, whether or not it killed his moa. That was what he should do. On the other hand, he must have at least an hour's start on the Joalians, even if they risked the ascent in moonlight. He had come this way to warn D'ward, so he might as well do so.

His sentimentality would be the death of him.

He even decided as he turned Swift off the trail that, if he were to be completely honest—not something he encouraged in himself—he would admit that he would dearly love to spend a friendly evening with D'ward beside a campfire, chatting of old times and finding out just what all this Liberator racket was about.

He headed for the fires and the sound of crying babies. He noted people moving around in the shrubbery and guessed that they were gathering berries. How many berries would it take to fill a hundred empty stomachs?

A man appeared as if from nowhere, right in his path. He wore only a leather kilt—chilly covering in the mountains at night—and he carried a spear and a round shield. He said, "Halt!"

Dosh halted. The spear was a serious matter.

"State your business!" The sentry had a familiar accent, and suddenly his face was familiar also.

"Doggan! Doggan Herder! It's me—Dosh!"

"Five gods! I mean, *Bless me!* It's the faggot himself! What you doing here, slime?"

"I could ask the same of you." Dosh considered dismounting, but he was more worried now by Swift's teeth than Doggan's spear. He wondered how many more of D'ward's old Warband might be around and concluded that there would probably be quite a few of them. Nagian age groups were fanatically loyal and did everything in bunches. "Where's your face paint, warrior?"

"Face paint is out!" Doggan said firmly. He was a short, broad man, more notable for muscle than brains. He seemed unaware that what he had just said was rank heresy to a Nagian. "I asked you what you wanted."

"I came to see D'ward."

Doggan thought about it. Then he gestured with the spear. "Follow me. And if you let that brute bite me, then it's cutlets."

"Lead on." Dosh began rethinking strategy. A troop of Nagian warriors would be a fair match for the Joalians. If D'ward was willing to protect him, he might be out of danger.

A few minutes brought them to a campfire. Having hobbled Swift, he limped wearily forward into the light, his leg throbbing like hammers where the moa had kicked it. Half a dozen shivery-looking Nagians squatted around the flames, apparently listening intently to D'ward, who was sitting on a rock, expounding. He broke off what he was saying, his teeth flashing in a smile.

"Well, see who's here! Our old messenger! Welcome, Dosh!" He was dressed in a dark, long-sleeved priest's gown. He wore a close-cropped beard and hints of black curls showed under his cowl, but he would look more like a priest if he shaved both his face and his head. That would be a pity.

"Thanks." Dosh moved closer to the fire and the others quickly made room for him, lots of room, as if he carried some contagious disease. He crouched down to warm himself, registering that these men were all from the old Sonalby troop—Prat'han Potter, Burthash Wheelwright, Gopaenum Butcher, and the rest. Every one of them would cut himself into small cubes if D'ward asked.

Silence alerted him; he looked up and saw that D'ward was waiting for him to speak.

"I heard you were at Jilvenby. A trooper in Joal told me. Thought I'd come and warn you."

Even in the flickering firelight, D'ward's eyes showed blue, twinkling with amusement. "That was very friendly of you, Dosh. The Joalians were no threat to me—but it was a kind thought."

He had not changed at all. If he wanted people to think of him as a leader, he ought to let his beard grow longer. No, that might be true of other men, but it wasn't true of him. He seemed too young, yet he was completely calm, absolute master of the group and of himself. Dosh felt the old magic at work again. This was a man who commanded respect and loyalty without ever asking for it. He talked with gods. He was foretold by prophecy. He elicited trust—and also confidences.

"He wasn't quite what he seemed," Dosh said. "He bore the mark of the Lady."

Big Prat'han grunted, but what he meant remained unclear.

D'ward pursed his lips. "The only male Eltiana cult I know of is the Guardians of the Mother. They're said to wear her symbol in a very intimate place."

"That's it."

The smile faded. The stare seemed to sharpen. "And how did you discover that, Dosh?"

A couple of the men muttered inaudibly.

"No," D'ward said. "If he was sworn to Eltiana, then he wouldn't be doing that. Well?"

"I killed him."

D'ward sighed. "Why?"

"He wanted me to betray you." Dosh looked around the group hopefully. If he expected approval, then he was disappointed. These lunks had never approved of him. They had let him continue breathing only because D'ward had told them to. He cared nothing for their opinions, but he would like to think D'ward appreciated what he had done. He had felt that way about very few men in his life . . . no others at all that he could think of just at the moment.

D'ward said, "I suppose it explains why you ride by night. How did you ever get a moa?"

"Stole her, of course."

"You haven't changed a bit, have you?"

"No, I just got better at it."

D'ward scratched at his beard, seeming more exasperated than anything else. "I appreciate the news about Eltiana. The Guardians are her doers of dirty work—not as bad as reapers, but they can be dangerous. I just wish you hadn't gained the information the way you did. Will you spend the night with us or are you in a hurry to admire new scenery? 'Fraid we can't offer much in the way of hospitality."

All the eyes turned toward the intruder, waiting for his reply. The Nagians were hoping he would leave very soon and thus clean up the neighborhood. He could not tell what D'ward wanted.

Wearily, he held out his hands to the fire again. The air was cooling off, leaving the night cold and dark. And lonely. "There's a troop of Joalian cavalry—" His tongue was not usually so eager to run away with him, and he reined it in.

Gopaenum threw more brush on the fire. Smoke and sparks billowed up to the stars.

"Not after us," D'ward said. "I doubt they're even coming to make sure we've left, because our safe-conduct runs for three more days yet. Are they on their way up the pass now or waiting for daylight?"

"Don't know." Dosh rose stiffly, wincing at the pain in his leg. "Well, I've told you my news. I'd best be going." He thought of the long, lonely ride to Nosokvale.

"We welcome recruits," D'ward said quietly. "You're welcome to join us."

Prat'han growled.

D'ward said, "Hush!" and Prat'han flinched as if he'd been slashed with a whip.

Dosh went down on one knee by the fire as a sort of compromise between going and staying. "Join what? What are you up to?"

"Tell him, big brother."

The muscular potter scowled at Dosh. "The Liberator is fulfilling the prophecies.

We are the Free, and we are on our way to Thargvale, where he will bring death to Death, as is foretold."

That was utter insanity, but Dosh knew better than to argue with Prat'han. His head was as empty as his pots.

"What conditions?"

"Ah!" D'ward thought for a moment. "You're a murderer, a thief, a liar, a sexual pervert of every description, and a traitor. Does that about sum you up?"

Burthash guffawed. D'ward looked at him sharply.

He shriveled guiltily, muttering, "Sorry, Liberator."

"I think you've covered all my good points," Dosh said. "I also drink to excess and smoke poppy when I can afford it."

"We can't accept a man who does any of those things."

"Then why are you wasting my time?" Dosh began to rise.

"Because you could promise to stop doing them."

Dosh wondered if he'd heard correctly, and the others looked equally bewildered. With anyone but the Liberator, he would have assumed that he was being mocked, but D'ward's eyes held no ridicule, only challenge.

"I don't care what a man was, Dosh, only what he is now."

"You mean you'd take my word for it? Mine? You think I could possibly keep such a promise, even if I wanted to?"

"Yes I do. You once told me you were the toughest bastard in the army, and I said I believed you. I'd believe you now. If you'll tell me now that you'll give up all those vices, then you'll keep your word."

The fire began to crackle more loudly, its smoke drifting away in the wind. Out in the dark valley were low voices, children, and someone singing what sounded like a hymn. Who were the Free? Just the Sonalby troop or all that ragtag collection of humanity? Join them? Him?

"Gods!" This was the greatest insanity yet.

"Only one god here. Your decision." Suddenly D'ward laughed. "I've never seen you look scared before, Dosh!"

He *was* scared. His hands were shaking. "I couldn't!"

"I think you could."

That was what he'd wanted D'ward to say, but he still didn't believe it.

The Liberator was watching him very closely. "We knew you as Dosh Envoy. If the troopers ask for you by whatever name you're using now we can say we don't know you." He grinned faintly. "Besides, you'll be a new man altogether, won't you?"

New man? This was the sort of decision that needed a lot of thinking over. Dosh wouldn't be a loner anymore. He would be one of this harebrained Liberator cult, heading for certain death in Thargvale or sooner. He had been one of the gang, once. Briefly.

"Why haven't the reapers caught you already?"

D'ward shrugged.

"Reapers?" Gopaenum laughed raucously. "You want to meet some reapers? We've got a dozen or so around somewhere. Soon as they get near the Liberator, they aren't reapers anymore."

"Huh?"

"Never mind that," D'ward said. "You're avoiding the issue."

Dosh looked uncertainly around the firelit faces. He couldn't actually *see* the scorn and contempt, but he knew it was there. They were hiding it out of respect for D'ward, that was all. He heaved himself to his feet, feeling as if he weighed more than all of them put together.

"I wish you luck. You're all crazy. Go and bring death to Death if you can. Me, I want to keep life in the living."

He turned away. He had taken only a couple of steps when he heard D'ward call out, "See you in Nosokland."

He walked on, paying no heed.

# *12*

The first *tyika* houses at Olympus had been laid out on the perimeter of the node. When that loop was full, an outer circle had followed, forming the other side of a street, and after the Chamber had sacked the station, it had all been rebuilt to the same plan. Being "Boots," the junior officer in the regiment, Julian lived even farther out, in a new suburb just beginning. A man's residence defined his status very clearly, but it wasn't all swank, for the innermost locations provided a distinct occult advantage. When followers of the Undivided anywhere in the Vales prayed to the apostles, a little mana would flow to those located on a node. It would not compare to the power the gods received from the worshippers in their temples but, year in and year out, it must mount up.

As the sky flamed blood red behind the peaks, he headed inward, feeling the first tingling of virtuality as he paced up the Pinkneys' garden path to their front door. Through the open windows, he heard the polite laughter of the *tyikank* enjoying themselves. Three minutes later, he was clutching a glass of the sickly fluid that passed for sherry in Olympus and pretending breathless interest as his hostess described the new rock garden her Carrots were building for her.

Escaping from Hannah Pinkney's horticultural saga as soon as he decently could, he began to circulate from group to group. He was required to discuss polo and cricket— the Carrots had taken it up and were becoming too bally good at it, old man—and of course the weather. Not a word was said about the Liberator.

"Fascinating news from Fithvale," Prof Rawlinson declaimed. "Seems that Imphast has ordered her clergy out of red and into blue!"

Delores Garcia said, "Really!" Then she added vaguely, "Who's Imphast?"

"Goddess of, um, female puberty. Obviously she's changed allegiance from Eltiana to Astina! A major move in the Great Game!"

"Gracious!"

Prof began to explain, at great length. Julian knew nothing of Imphast and cared less. He moved on, analyzing who was there and who was not. Some people were only window dressing, not relevant to the Exeter problem—people like Hannah, for instance. Ineffectual people, gossipy, garrulous people. Some undoubtedly were relevant: Prof Rawlinson, Jumbo Watson, and a couple of the others Dommi had mentioned as having been recalled. In the background he could hear Foghorn Rutherford, this year's chairman.

About three of the women might be significant: Delores, who had a body to drive men out of their wits and was reputed to be the only faithful wife in Olympus; Ursula Newton, with the shoulders of a wrestler and the unerring competence of a sergeant-major; Olga Olafson, who was unmarried, voluptuous, and a nymphomaniac. Scandal whispered that she even pursued Carrots.

He detoured away from Foghorn, who was leering at Cathy Chase, who in turn was portraying bored indifference, although they were current lovers. Extramarital affairs were the main source of entertainment in Olympus, but it was understood that they must be kept strictly confidential in case the Carrots gossiped. That deception was the second most popular game. Admittedly, there were few other games to play in a land so backward, but Julian considered it absurd early-Victorian hypocrisy. Of course, many of these people *were* early Victorian. In practice, everyone knew exactly who was sleeping with whom. If they didn't, they could always ask their Carrots.

The Service were a very rum lot, and somehow that was even more obvious than usual tonight, but it took him a while to work out what was different. There was nothing conspicuously wrong with the dinner party—a dozen men, a dozen women, two Carrots serving drinks and probably twenty or more laboring away behind the scenes. Conversation swung from triviality to banality and back again.

Under the glitter of the chandeliers, the men wore tails, the ladies long gowns. This sort of dinner party happened almost every night of the year, for there was no restricted social season in Olympus. No one would ever mistake it for a formal dinner in Town. The discerning London hostess would look askance at the outdated fashions. She would eye the furniture with curiosity and inquire politely where in the Colonies this or that had come from, although she might well praise the Narshian rugs or the Niolian brasses, which were as good as anything from Benares.

On the other hand, the gathering was a reasonable facsimile of a social occasion in an outpost of Empire almost anywhere on Earth—dinner with His Majesty's district commissioner. The Service did not serve the Empire on Which the Sun Never Sets, but it had the same altruistic motives as those who did. Like them, Olympians were dedicated to uplifting the benighted savage. They were just exiled a little farther away, that was all, or no distance at all, if one preferred that view of the paradox. The node here was a portal. Walk out on the grass, perform the key ritual, and you could be Home instantly. Unless you had made arrangements to be met by Head Office, you would be naked and penniless, of course, and you would certainly be mortal again. No fear! It was a lot better to better the lot of the natives here in the Vales.

Then he realized what was wrong: A party that should be as lively as gaudy at Oxford was as flat as a geriatric Mafeking reunion. Strangers never revealed their age, and to discuss it was strictly off-limits, always, but he was the baby of the group. None of the rest of them would ever see twenty-two again. Olga had probably weathered several centuries. Jumbo and Pinky and Ursula Newton had been co-founders of the Service, along with Cameron Exeter and Monica Rogers, fifty years ago. Nonetheless, at a do like this strangers ought to be sparkling like a gang of adolescents. Tonight they seemed middle-aged. They displayed no wrinkles or silver hair, and their bodies were still trim, but their mood gave them away.

Joalvale was not the problem. The Church of the Undivided had no significant presence there and nothing to lose if Exeter provoked the civil authorities into repression—in fact a few martydoms were good for business, although it would be poor form to say so. No, the Chamber was the danger, and always had been. The Service feared the prophecies of the *Filoby Testament* almost as much as Zath himself did, for any attempt to fulfill them must provoke an all-out war that Olympus could not hope to win. Then the men and women of the Service would be faced with a choice between death and flight back to Earth and mortality. Their cosy fiefdom here would be wiped out.

They had the wind up!

He discovered Marcel Piran and Euphemia McKay in a secluded nook behind some potted shrubbery and invited himself into the conversation. Euphemia was a right-down stunner with green eyes and hair so authentically Irish red that it made the Carrots' seem drab by comparison. Culture and intellect were not her strong points, but she had a devilish wit and a keen sense of mimicry—she was, in fact, a bundle of fun. Unfortunately she also had the worst clothes sense in two worlds. Tonight she was squeezed into a satiny gown of royal blue, which should have flattered her coloring and figure but made her seem frumpy and hippy. She looked much better without any clothes on at all.

In a few moments, Marcel tactfully eased away to speak to Hannah.

"And how is my delicious Wendy?" Julian assumed a lecherous growl, while pretending to study the shrubbery.

Euphemia peered around the room indifferently. "Randy as an alley cat. How about my Captain Hook? Ready for boarding? Got your cutlass well sharpened?"

"Primed, loaded, and cocked. Why don't we nip behind the sofa and have a quick one?"

"I'd rather wait for a slow one later."

"Just one? It's not like you to settle for just one, Wendy."

"Well, think what you tempt me with! How's a girl expected to refuse that?"

This verbal foreplay was interrupted by the arrival of Olga and the evening's host, Pinky Pinkney. Conversation veered to a discussion of the latest news from Home, which was over a fortnight old.

"It is most unfair of the Peppers to keep the Goldsmiths waiting like this!" Pinky proclaimed. "Deborah is desperate to see London again."

"You haven't heard what's delayed them?" Euphemia asked.

"Of course not. The Montgomerys are due back in a couple of days—perhaps they'll know what's keeping them."

"No word from Head Office?"

"I'm afraid Head Office has been badly disorganized by the war. They're not what they used to be."

She sighed, and her dress struggled to contain the movement. "William and me aren't due to go for years!"

Pinky made sympathetic noises. He was as slick as an oiled eel and parted his hair in the middle. "Are you quite sure of that, my dear? I think there were some changes made to the schedule while you were gone."

"Really?" Euphemia asked with surprising interest.

"Dolores will know. Let's go and ask her, shall we?"

Without a word of apology, the bounder led her off across the room. Julian sipped some of the nasty sherry.

"Don't glare, darling," said a throaty murmur. "People will think you're jealous."

He jumped. Olga was a heart-stopping Nordic blonde, a female Viking—something Wagner might have invented if he had dared. Tonight she wore a scarlet gown in a way that implied one deep breath would cause it to explode.

"Jealous? Of Pinky and Euphemia? There's nothing between them."

Olga fluttered golden lashes. "The way Pinky was looking at her, darling, there won't be anything at all between them in a few hours."

Julian drained his glass in one great Philistine gulp. Olga unnerved him on several levels. First, he had no idea whatsoever of her background—her English was too perfect to be her genuine mother tongue; she might not even be from Earth at all. Second, she was probably the oldest person in the Service, because she was a convert. Before changing sides, she had been a minor goddess, an avatar of Eltiana.

And third, she was blatantly promiscuous. No other woman on the station would dare to look at a man the way she was looking at him right now. She was probably not serious, because she had hung Julian's scalp on her belt years ago, a few days after he arrived. He hoped she wasn't serious, but at least a fellow need not watch one's tongue with Olga. She was unshockable and never took offense. And at the moment she was trying to put the boot in.

"I think you are attributing unseemly motives to a perfectly innocent conversation. Mrs. McKay and Mr. Pinkney are—"

"Are rutting, dear. He is, anyway. He's as loud as a wapiti."

"What the deuce is a wapiti? And even if he is, why should Euphemia—"

Olga rolled her sea-blue eyes dramatically. "Julian, darling, I thought I cured your innocence years ago. Don't tell me all my work was wasted! Weren't you born in India? You should know that imperial exiles are the same everywhere."

"Nextdoor is hardly a blooming colony," he protested. "The Empire doesn't reach quite this far—not yet, anyway."

She smiled sardonically. "They like to pretend it's a colony, though. Olympus is deliberately modeled on a British government station somewhere in the bush, isn't it? Don't deny it; you know it's true. Lording over the natives, dressing for dinner . . . I remember Foghorn trying to get us to put up a flagpole so we could fly the Union Jack. Cameron threatened to strangle him with it if he tried."

Julian blinked. He had not known that Olga had been around Olympus so long, for Cameron Exeter had gone Home thirty years ago. "What has that to do—"

"You're not worried, darling?" she purred.

"Not about Pinky," he said staunchly, fairly sure he was not even blushing, which was a jolly sight different from how he would have reacted to Olga's claws two years ago. Pinky would get nowhere tonight—or any other night either—because Euphemia considered him a bore and a toad in the grass. It would not be Pinky skin to skin with Euphemia tonight, it would be Captain Smedley (Royal Artillery, ret.), and the sooner the better.

He made his escape from Olga as soon as he could without seeming to be running away. No one had mentioned the reason for his recall yet or told him whether he was scheduled to appear before the Committee itself. If he were, it would be an irrelevant formality, because decisions in Olympus were made by the inner circle, Pinky and his cronies. That was another characteristic of the Service—nobody trusted anybody; too many had gone over to the opposition. There had been traitors, one of whom had very nearly scuppered Edward Exeter by sending him Home into the middle of a battle in Flanders. Mana was addictive, and the Pentatheon could offer better sources of mana. Even a very minor god with his own temple collected far more of it than a preacher holding secret prayer meetings in the bush.

Euphemia and Pinky reappeared, but Julian's efforts to resume his wooing were persistently defeated by Pinky, who clung to her like a treacle shampoo until his wife announced that it was time to go in to dinner.

Julian was alarmed to discover that he was paired with Olga, who proceeded to flirt shamelessly with him. Fortunately they were seated across from Jumbo and Iris, who were good company. Euphemia, he was annoyed to notice, had been placed next to Pinky.

Dinner went off as usual, with inconsequential small talk. It was all frightfully civilized—damask tablecloth, silver plate, hovering servants—and a welcome relief from the peasant hospitality he should have been enduring in Randorvale right now. The only time anything approaching business was discussed was when someone brought up the story of Jumbo's miracle at Flaxby, deflecting a magistrate and two soldiers. Julian had learned of it from Purlopat'r, but apparently the news had leaked out just after he left.

It was impossible to dislike Jumbo. He was tall and lean and had gained his nickname from the length of his nose. He had a notably wry sense of humor and a becoming modesty.

"It was nothing much," he protested. "I didn't set out to work any miracles. I was so scared at the sight of those jolly swords that I started babbling my head off. Before I knew it, the chaps were on their knees, begging for mercy—wanting me to shut up, I expect. If I did spend some mana, then I got a whole lot more back in return. Jolly fun, actually. You should have seen the magistrate's face. . . ." He made a good story out of it, everyone laughed.

Julian did not mention his adventure in Randorvale. The conversation veered to the unusually warm weather.

If it was impossible to dislike Jumbo, it was still possible to distrust him. He had been the one who sent Exeter to what should have been certain death in the battle of Third Ypres. He claimed that he had been deceived by Jean St. John, but Jean had either died or done a bunk when Zath's reapers caused the sack of Olympus, so there was no way to confirm the tale. Jumbo had been friends with both Exeters, father and son, during their respective times in Olympus. He was an adamant opponent of the Liberator prophecy.

Julian struggled not to yawn as he kept up his end of the conversation. The people around the table were all worried; they were all scared. It showed.

The meal was over, decanters waited on the sideboard. The hostess glanced around the table to make sure everyone had finished. Hannah Pinkney was a lightweight, far more interested in her proposed rock garden than in the Service's mission to save the heathens or her husband's slimy advances to Euphemia. Tonight she was dressed in lace and chiffon, all pink and fluffy, well suited to her personality.

"Well!" she said brightly. "Shall we leave the men to their cigars, ladies?"

The expected shuffle of movement as men rose to lift back their companions' chairs . . . Olga removed her hand from Julian's thigh.

"I should like a cigar tonight," said a loud voice.

Hannah tracked it down to Ursula Newton and stared at her in consternation. Julian struggled against an urge to burst out laughing.

Ursula had not been drinking unduly. She was merely irate and consequently dangerous. Although not unattractive, she was too broad for her height, built like a Victorian mahogany dresser—muscle, not fat—lacking feminine grace. But she could preach damnation with the best of them or raise hell with a tennis racket, being aggressively good at anything she cared to try and inclined to bark at those who were not. Tonight she wore a lilac gown that displayed her powerful arms and shoulders and clashed with her dark coloring. Where Euphemia lacked taste, Ursula didn't give a damn.

"You're not serious, are you, dear?" Hannah bleated. "I mean, I'm sure we can find a cigar for you if—"

Ursula ignored her, scowling at Pinky. "No, I'm not serious about the cigar. I am serious about the Committee. I am very tired of discovering that every matter brought before it has already been settled. You men are planning to cross-examine Captain Smedley tonight and tomorrow you will tell the rest of us what to rubber-stamp."

Pinky smiled graciously, but when Pinky smiled nothing showed of his eyes, only their heavy lids. "Aren't you being a little unfair, my dear? You must agree that we men are free to discuss whatever we wish, as are you ladies. Surely you are not suggesting we should banish Captain Smedley from the table, mm? Wouldn't that be unkind? Of course it would. If you have complaints about the way the Committee is being run, then you should address them to the chairman. Formally, I mean. In writing."

Foghorn Rutherford was this year's chairman. That did not matter. Despite the Service's professed determination to remain a democratic association of equals, Pinky Pinkney was the one who pulled the strings, this year and every year.

Foghorn was loud, large, windy, and uncouth, a rubicund human bagpipe, likable in an uncomplicated sort of way, typecast from birth to be captain of a county rugby club. Now he harrumphed a steam-hooter noise. "I assure you that the Committee will have ample opportunity—"

"I don't believe you!" Ursula snapped. "You are going to deal with Captain Smedley exactly the way you did with the man who brought in the news."

Rutherford guffawed like a mule. "Ursula, old girl, if you imply that Pinky invited that rascally dragon trader to dinner, then he will demand pistols at dawn on the croquet lawn."

Hannah tried to start a laugh, but no one picked it up.

Ursula returned her fearsome glare to Pinky. "If you will give me your word that no one here will as much as mention Edward Exeter for the rest of the night, then I shall happily withdraw. If not, I stay. So does Olga."

Like the rest of the men, Julian had resumed his seat. Olga had resumed her fondling. Olga would certainly be involved in the ad hoc group dealing with the Liberator crisis— he should have realized that. She would have been coopted at once, for she knew better than any how the Pentatheon thought.

Pinky surrendered, smiling sleepily. "Stay by all means. Yes, I expect we shall talk shop. Why not, mm? Don't we always? Any of you who want to stay, may stay. If shoptalk bores you, you may depart in peace and migrate to the drawing room. Is that fair enough? Very fair, I'd say." He nodded to the waiting Carrots to bring out the port.

Everyone elected to stay, of course, and the men all refused cigars, which annoyed Julian, who needed a smoke. Nextdoor's equivalent of tobacco tasted like burning pine needles, but it did pack a wallop of nicotine. The port came around, Ursula pouring herself a glass and passing it on with the correct hand; most of the women just passing it. Small talk fluttered like awkward moths until the Carrots had departed. Then Pinky nodded to Foghorn who boomed obediently, "I expect Doc told you, Captain? Edward Exeter is on the loose up in Joalland, proclaiming himself the prophesied Liberator chappie."

With T'lin Dragontrader so sure of himself, there was no use trying to cast doubt on the identity of the culprit. "Yes, sir."

"What's he up to, hm?"

"I have no idea. I haven't heard from him since he left here." Julian could feel that statement being weighed all around the table. They didn't trust him, which was fair enough, because he did not trust them.

"You know him better than any of us, Captain." The speaker was Pedro Garcia, who had done a bunk in Thovale and left his flock to pay the piper.

"We were school chums, yes, but I've hardly seen him since—once, very briefly, two years ago. You lot know him better than I do, actually."

Guff! Exeter in 1917 had been exactly the same person as the house prefect who had left Fallow in 1914. He was one of those people who never change. He had been as self-reliant at eighteen as he would be at eighty—or eight hundred, if he stayed on Nextdoor that long. He would sail his own course, guided by his own sense of what was honorable, letting nothing sway him. He had been upright, unassuming, admirable—all those proper things—and thoroughly square on top of it. He would be till the day he died.

Garcia shrugged, greasy as a Dago fish fryer. "He went native."

Julian's fist clenched. "Did he? I thought he went off back Home, to enlist and do his bit in the war. That was the plan." Olga squeezed his thigh, but whether that was intended as a warning or encouragement, he did not know. Or care.

"Indeed, Captain? In his farewell address he told the Carrots he was going off to fulfill the prophecy."

"What if he did? That prophecy has blighted his whole life. It killed his parents. It branded him a murderer in England. It kept him from enlisting. It cut down his friends like corn." It had even killed the girl he loved, although Ysian had been a native and to mention her would do no good. "He walked out of Olympus to save the rest of us. If he'd stayed here, Zath would have struck at the Service again."

Directly across the table from Julian, Jumbo said, "Hear, hear! You're not being fair, Pedro old man. Exeter survived his first two years on Nextdoor without any help from us. It's hardly cricket to call that 'going native'! I'd call it 'surviving under adverse conditions.' Adopting local color, if you prefer. When he finally did get here to Olympus, he was a perfectly civilized young gentleman again."

Julian smiled gratefully at him and reached for his port. He hoped the discussion was now over and he could trot off to bed. Euphemia's bed.

Rutherford broke the awkward pause with a throat-clearing like a carillon of church bells. "We were wondering, Captain . . . Do you know a young lady named Alice?"

Julian took a sip of port. They were ganging up on him. "Sounds like a limerick. Did she live in a palace?"

"We can all think of a good rhyme for the last line," Jumbo said, "but I don't think that was what the chairman was getting at."

"Alice Prescott, Exeter's cousin? Yes, sir, I've met her. Why?"

"Just wondering!" Foghorn boomed. The port was turning his red face redder. "If we asked for her help to make Exeter see reason, do you suppose she would cooperate, what?"

Not in a thousand years. Alice had far more respect for her cousin than that. At least, Julian thought she probably had. Alice was on another world anyway.

"I really could not say, sir." That sounded uncooperative. "I only met her once or twice."

"We just wondered. Well, that ought to conclude the shoptalk, so—"

"No." Apparently Jumbo had other ideas. Jumbo was quick; he had a sight more gray matter than Foghorn, perhaps even more than Pinky. "Let's review the problem. I have never made a secret of my dislike for the prophecy. Exeter's father agreed with me all the way."

Heads nodded, but the eyes were on Julian. He said nothing, waited for the haymaker.

"First," Jumbo said, "it's crazy to take on Zath. He's not officially one of the Pentatheon, but he's undoubtedly stronger than any of them. The Five are scared stiff of him."

"Human sacrifice!" Olga said. Her hand was exploring busily. She must have decided that Julian's scalp had grown back in again. "None of the others stoop to that."

Jumbo nodded. "And it won't only be Zath. The Pentatheon may not like Zath, but they won't approve of an upstart stranger preaching reform, so Exeter can't hope for much help from the Five. Second, the civil authorities will not take kindly to hundreds of people galloping off after a new prophet. We're already meeting resistance, and we're nowhere near to being the sort of threat that the Liberator would be."

"Powers that be always want to go on being powers, you know," Pinky remarked sagely.

Pinky himself was a prize example, so Julian couldn't argue with that. They were picking on him because he had been Exeter's friend. A chap must stand by his friends. "Civil authorities can be diverted, sir. You proved that yourself in Loxby."

"Not if the Pentatheon throws its weight behind them!" Jumbo shook his head wearily, looking twenty years older than usual. "The next stage is likely to be plague and thunderbolts, you know. We don't have anything like enough mana to protect the church against direct assaults."

"The argument cuts both ways. Exeter as Liberator may draw the Chamber off. They won't worry about us while he's on the rampage."

Jumbo was unconvinced. "They're more likely to lump both heresies together and declare a general pogrom. Exeter's a threat to all of us and everything we're trying to do. We're still terribly vulnerable. A hundred years from now, things may be different."

Heads nodded solemnly all around the table. Bloody bunch of chickens!

Olga spoke up demurely. "Historically, if any one of the Five began to grow too powerful, the other four have always combined against him or her. They didn't spot what Zath was up to until it was too late."

She unfastened a button in Julian's fly. He removed her hand and refastened it. She'd had her chance at what was in there two years ago.

Farther along the table, Prof Rawlinson took up the argument. "There is another point. Didn't T'lin Dragontrader say that Exeter is preaching the Undivided?" Rawlinson was colorless, owlish, and clever in an impractical sort of way. He had the pedantic manner of a divinity student, but in the past he had been one of the pro-Liberator group. The Service had always been divided over the Liberator; now it seemed to be united. No one was on Exeter's side except Julian Smedley.

"He could hardly do otherwise, I fancy," said Pinky smoothly. "He did do some missionary work for us, remember? Mostly in Thovale, was it not? Yes, mostly Thovale. He will need a gospel to preach. The *Testament* by itself would not be enough. Couldn't work just from that. He'd need something more, mm? So it's quite natural that he would adopt our theology. Ready-made for his purpose, I'd say."

"You mean he is stealing our church?" Hannah cried. She subsided into blushing silence under her husband's frown.

"So if Exeter tries and fails," Jumbo said, watching Julian, "he may bring us down with him."

"Worse!" Prof chirruped. "Suppose, against all odds, he succeeds? If he does fulfill the prophecy, then he'll be stronger than Zath. What will he become? What could he do with such power?"

No one seemed very worried about that improbable hypothesis, but Jumbo said, "That's what bothered his father. Cameron didn't want his son to become another pseudogod."

Obviously everyone was against Exeter, whether he won or lost: Zath, the Pentatheon and their lesser gods, the various rulers of the Vales, the Service—they were all opposed.

Julian decided it must be his turn.

"You are asking my opinion?"

"Go ahead," said Pinky. "You have the floor. The port is with you, Duffy."

"I don't believe it. I know Edward Exeter, and he was as much against the prophecy as anyone. There's been some mistake."

"Seventy-seven's a sound chap."

"But a native, sir. Would you expect Exeter to confide all his plans to T'lin Dragontrader?"

"That's an interesting point, Captain. Very interesting." Pinky filled his glass. "But the fact remains that Exeter is calling himself the Liberator. In public. Do we have a consensus that he should be stopped? Is that the sense of the meeting?" He glanced around with a smile, his eyes seeming to be shut. "Unless anyone has changed his mind, of course?"

What did *stopped* mean? Julian risked another glass of port as the decanter went by him. "Sir, Zath has been trying to break the chain of prophecy for thirty years. It's too late to work on any of the other stuff in the *Testament*. The only way to stop it now would be to kill Exeter himself."

Hannah and a couple of the other women gasped.

Foghorn boomed out, "Balderdash!" without meeting Julian's eye.

Only Jumbo was looking at Julian, staring challengingly across the table at him. "Perhaps Exeter himself is trying to break it by committing suicide."

"Not the Edward Exeter I knew."

"That's how it looks," Foghorn said firmly. "Damned fool stunt! We owe it to him for his own sake to bring him to his senses."

Here it came. It was Jumbo who put the question. "Are you with us on that, Captain?"

Julian held up a hand, the one without fingers. He sensed the surge of anger and embarrassment. "I agree with everything you've said about the dangers of the prophecy, yes. I support what the Service stands for absolutely—and so does Edward Exeter, as far as I know. I also feel that Zath is the embodiment of all that's evil in the Pentatheon and we have a duty to overthrow him as soon as possible. I hope *you* are all with *me* on that! It would be the greatest service we could perform for the people of the Vales." Was the Service really interested in the natives' welfare or only in its own survival? "He's not unlike the Kaiser, really. We've been fighting a hellish war to stop him, back in Europe. Victory did not come cheap."

He glanced around the table. He wasn't increasing his popularity terrifically. "The war cost millions of lives, but it was worth it. Destroying Zath may be worth some sacrifice too, so I cannot dismiss whatever Exeter is doing without knowing more about his thinking. He may have seen something that the rest of us have missed. I think you owe him a hearing before you condemn him out of hand."

Pinky drooped his eyelids again. "Quite right. Very sound. We ought to find out how the land lies. Would you be willing to go and talk to him, Captain, mm? Drop in on him, feel him out?"

"I'd be glad to. Always wanted to see Joalvale. I'll leave first thing in the morning."

Pinky nodded graciously. "Very obliging of you, Captain. It would put our minds at rest. But that's quite a long jaunt. You will pardon my mentioning this, but you don't have the experience some of the rest of us have. Two heads are always better than one, what? Not that we don't trust you, of course."

They trusted Julian as far as they could throw Kilimanjaro. He decided to make it easy for them. "I'd be very happy to have company, sir. You all know I can't use mana. It won't stick to me—or it sticks too well, rather."

His preferred companion would be Euphemia, of course, and everyone could guess that, but he must not say so. The watchdog they chose would be Jumbo. He had been Exeter's closest friend, his father's friend, and a founder of the Service; he was adamantly opposed to the prophecy. He was a jolly dog, though, and a journey with him would be fun.

Foghorn Rutherford recalled that he was chairman of the Committee and fired a broadside of decibels. "That's damned white of you, Captain! The sooner you can go and talk some sense into our young friend the better. We may send someone Home to seek out Miss Prescott and enlist her help, too, but that will take time."

That was pure bosh, designed to lower Julian's guard. The Service had already condemned Exeter. How far were they prepared to go to stop him? Jumbo was looking a bit shifty—were they setting Julian up as a Judas goat? Dammit, a chap ought not to go calling on a chum with an assassin in tow.

But obviously the business of the evening had been concluded. Tomorrow Julian Smedley would head north to find Exeter. The only remaining problem was to escape from Olga and find his way to Euphemia's bedroom to do his lover's duty.

# *13*

"I shall be leaving in the morning," Julian said, pulling on his pajama jacket. "Pack a bag for me, will you?"

Dommi closed the wardrobe door and turned with a smile. "It is already taken care of, *tyika*. I have laid out winter garments in tribute to the advanced season and in presumption that you will be dragon traveling and may therefore cut short across country."

"Good show. Um, Dommi . . ." It had occurred to Julian on his way home that, whatever dark deeds Jumbo Watson might have in mind, there was one person in Olympus who could be trusted to support Edward Exeter through Hull, Hell, and Halifax. Not that a native could do much in practice against a stranger, but a friendly face was worth a third arm on a black day. "I'll be heading up north, going to find *Tyika* Exeter. I'm not sure there'll be a spare dragon, but if there is, then you're welcome to come. If you still want to, that is."

Dommi beamed. "I shall be most and assuredly honored, *tyika*."

Why would the man leave his wife at such a time? Carrots were not expected to have such unexpected foibles, but it would not be right to ask. "I'm sure you'll be a great help. I think that's all, thank you. Night, Dommi."

"Good night, *tyika*. Do you wish me to open the window wider?"

"Yes. It's a little stuffy in here."

Dommi pulled the sash up another foot and departed, closing the door in silence.

Julian snatched up his dressing gown and headed for the window.

It was a black dressing gown.

Love was a rum business, and even rummier in Olympus than anywhere else. "Till death do us part" became meaningless frippery when life expectancy stretched out to three or four digits. All evening he and his sweetheart had smiled politely across the room at each other, exchanged meaningless small talk, behaved just like all the other guests. Thus was the game played, and everyone played it. But every dressing gown on the station was black.

He clambered over the sill. There was no reason why he should not just walk out his own front door, except that certain things should be done in traditional ways.

The night was a symphony, cool without being chilly, lit by the red and blue moons and a million stars and scented with the innumerable night-flowering blossoms of the Vales. The mountains looked as if they had been arranged by an expert stage designer, and the squirrel-like nightingales caroling in the bottle-gourd trees were almost as tuneful as the birds of the same name back Home. He hurried along the road, keeping to shadows as much as he could, seeing no one. It was embarrassing to meet a friend on such occasions, although by convention neither party would take notice of the other. The total absence of lights in the station did not mean that all the inhabitants were sleeping the sleep of the innocent.

His quest led him inward again, and soon the ancient thrill of lover hurrying to meet beloved was augmented by the familiar skin-tingling awareness of virtuality. As he passed Olga's house, a bat-owl soared overhead, circled a few times to decide if he was prey, then decided he wasn't and floated away behind the trees. Reaching the McKay residence, he picked his way around the side path until he came to a garden bench, which just happened to be under a window.

Which just happened to be closed.

Well, bother the woman! What was she thinking of? She knew he was coming. They'd been doing the drink-to-thee-only routine all evening, making sheep's eyes and sending just-wait signals. William was still away exhorting the unbelievers—not that William cared two hoots who tumbled his wife. He slept with Iris Barnes these days . . . these nights.

Julian stepped up on the bench and rapped fingernails on the glass. He waited. Nightingales serenaded. He was tingly and twitchy already.

He knocked harder, with knuckles.

Light flared as the heavy drapes were moved, then vanished again. Now a pale figure knelt on the other side of the pane. It lifted the sash about an inch.

"Go away," it whispered through the gap.

"No. What's the matter?"

"Nothin'. Everythin'. Please! Not tonight." The lilting Irish voice thrilled him as always. He had told her it was the sound of rain on peat, although then he'd had to explain that he'd meant it as a compliment.

She was crying!

"Darling Euphemia, tell me what's wrong. No, let me in first."

"Just go . . . please!"

"I will not go." A nightmarish vision of Pinky in pink pajamas . . . "Not unless you have another man in there."

"No! But please, Julian? Not tonight. We can talk when you come back from Joal-vale."

"Why? No! There's something wrong? Look, if you don't let me in here, I'll go 'round and beat on the front door until I waken every Carrot in the house." That ought to do it, for every woman in Olympus lived in dread of what the Carrots might be saying about her, even though she knew that every other woman was doing exactly the same thing and the Carrots really did not care anyway. The only thing that was *not* done was doing it with Carrots. "You're upset. I want to help. I love you, darling!"

Euphemia made unromantic sniffing noises.

"I'm not going to rape you!" Julian protested, mentally reserving seduction as a definite option. "We can just talk, if that's all you want." If that was all he could achieve. She'd never been unwilling before, not once that he could recall. She would enthusiastically try anything he suggested, which had been almost anything he'd ever heard of or could imagine. . . .

She rose and the light flared again as she departed, but she had left the window open. He slid a hand and a half under the sash and lifted. A moment later he pushed through the drapes and blinked in the glow of the candles on the dresser. She was standing in the middle of the room with her back to him, wearing a diaphanous pink nightgown, half transparent and completely the wrong color for her, but her gorgeous hair hung almost to her waist, a Titian waterfall that excited him as much as the glimmer of milky skin through filmy fabric.

He put a hand on one shoulder and a stump on the other and tried to turn her. She resisted and moved away. He restrained himself.

"What have I done?" Had any man since Adam not asked that question at some time in his life?

"Nothing, nothing at all. Just not tonight, darlin'. When you come back from Joalvale."

"Right-oh!" he said thickly, although everything was obviously wrong-oh. "You sit there, and I'll sit over here, and you tell me what's the matter." He went over to the chair. He wished he knew more about women.

She sank down on the edge of the bed, hunching herself small, arms tight around her breasts and face down. Candlelight on that hair was enough to detonate him all by itself, but there was also the deep cleavage, the bulge of nipples like pale strawberries, the russet shadow at her groin. His heart was running the Grand National, jumps and all. He adjusted his dressing gown to hide the incriminating bulge.

"Now Wendy can tell Captain Hook what's wrong."

For a long time she just sat there, heaving with dry sobs, not speaking. He had very little experience with women. Olga had bedded him a few days after he had arrived in Olympus—just once. That once had satisfied Olga's curiosity. It had been a devastating experience for a crippled, shell-shocked, war-damaged virgin of twenty-one. He had not begun responding to the hints again for several months, and even then he had not dared risk a commitment until that magical day when he had gone for a walk up the hill and had run into Euphemia purely by chance. One thing had led very quickly to the next thing, and they had ended up lying in some badly crushed wildflowers clad only in a healthy perspiration. Since then there had been no one else. She was everything he had ever hoped a woman would be.

She was not, by any stretch of the imagination, a lady. Her father had sold fish in Donegal. The other women tended to snub her. Bill McKay had gone Home on leave and returned with this common, working-class slip of a girl and . . . Lord knew how long ago that had been. One did not ask. Back Home, Julian would not even have considered her. His monstrous regiment of aunts in Cheltenham would succumb to mass hysteria if he ever brought home a woman like Euphemia McKay. The thought of her at the opera or even helping out the ladies at the church garden fête just did not pass muster. But this was Olympus, not Cheltenham, and she was his mistress. His, not Pinky's!

"I've been greedy," she whispered.

"What say?"

"I've been greedy." She glanced up briefly, eyes red-rimmed, then dropped her gaze to the floor again. "I shouldn't be keeping you all to myself like this." *Sniff, sniff!*

"You are not communicating, darling."

"Why don't you understand? I've had my turn. They all want you! You're young, really young, not just stranger-young. You're handsome and a wonderful person and really no older than you look and so innocent, and Olga's told them all about—about what a man you are, and you're a hero, a real hero! So you ought to share yourself around and—"

Julian spoke a word he had not used since he left the Western Front. Then he stood up and began to pace back and forth across the room. He wanted to sit down beside her, but if he ever got his hands—hand—on her in his present mood, he wasn't sure what might happen. Well, he knew what might happen, but not how.

"This is absolute——" He used another expression ladies were not supposed to know, although Euphemia would. "Am I a bloody stud horse? They think they can pass me around like a good book? Don't I have any say in who I sleep with? Whom, I mean. Hell's bells, woman, I want you, not anyone else. And screw Olga and all the rest of—" He choked and then laughed nervously. "I mean, no, I won't. Screw them, that is." Let them suffer. Flattering to think they might be thinking that way, even if he didn't believe it. Did they really? Strewth!

No answer except more snuffling.

"What's Pinky been telling you?"

She made a sound that was half sob and half gasp, but she did not look up.

"Well?"

"You're going off to Joalland tomorrow."

"So? I'll be back. I'll take you with me gladly if you'll come." It would cause a scandal, but he wouldn't care if she didn't.

"With Ursula Newton."

Julian stopped pacing. "I thought I was going with Jumbo." But no one had said so. He'd just assumed.

Euphemia shook her head, making the curtain of hair sway. He could not see her face at all. "Ursula."

"Darling, that was not my choice! And if you think there's anything between me—" He shuddered, and there was no faking required. Never Ursula! That female blacksmith?

She hit a tennis ball harder than any man on the station. Mannish women repelled him. "I'd sooner crawl into bed with Foghorn."

"You think it'll matter what you are thinking?" she demanded, suddenly loud. "She's been around longer than any of us!"

"Yes, but . . . What do you mean?"

"I mean no one's ever known Ursula to work any miracles, have they now?" Euphemia's brogue grew thicker when she was excited, and she was excited now, even if she was still wringing her hands and talking to the Narshian rugs. "She must have more mana saved up than any livin' soul on the station, and if she wants you—and she does, I know it—then she'll have you and you won't have any say in the matter."

Godfathers! That would be rape.

There were even nastier implications. "Why are they sending Ursula?"

After a moment, Euphemia whispered, "To stop Mr. Exeter."

Julian shuddered again, even harder. He was being sent along to get Ursula Newton in under Exeter's guard so that she could nobble him with mana? Judas goat! He sat down on the bed beside Euphemia and put an arm around her to comfort her. He really wanted her to hold him and comfort him, but she squirmed away, not understanding.

There was a very nasty taste in his mouth. He had to solve the Euphemia problem before he could even think about the Exeter problem. He cleared his throat harshly. "What else did Pinky say to you tonight?"

Silence.

"What did you say to Pinky, then?"

Another silence, then she said softly, "Go away, love. Stop asking questions. I don't want to be hurting you."

"You can't hurt me more than you're hurting me now."

She sniffed and wiped her eyes with the back of her hand. "Yes I can."

"Try. I want the truth, Euphemia, the whole truth."

*Sniff!* She rubbed her nose. "They're going to send someone Home to see Alice Prescott, ask her help. Just a very quick trip, there and back."

He waited, not understanding. Again he tried to put an arm around her, but she pushed it away. He noticed that his dressing gown no longer bulged.

"William and me won't be going for months yet. There's someone I . . . someone I haven't heard from since the Great War started. Not a word. I asked the Peppers, but they may not remember . . . and they had so many requests. I only need a few minutes on the phone, just one call. . . ."

"That filthy devil is blackmailing you? I'll rip out—"

"No, no!" She squirmed around and clapped a hand over his mouth. "All he said was that they were going to choose someone to make a quick trip Home. Then he said he always sleeps with his window open. That was all."

That was enough. Julian could hear Pinky saying it, in his sly way.

"That sleazy, slithering bugger! I'll—"

"No! You mustn't, or he won't let me go! There's lots of people want the chance, but he said he thought he could arrange it—"

He pulled her hand away. "Jolly right he can! He can arrange anything for a price, can't he?"

"Oh, it isn't the end of the world, Julian. I've done it before."

"What? With Pinky? No!"

"Yes!" she shouted.

"You said you never cared for him."

Her laugh was bitter as lemons. "Oh, you young idiot! I've cared for almost all of them at one time or another. Haven't you guessed that yet? You think you got me as a virgin?"

One never asked. "It doesn't matter." It did, though. He wished she hadn't said it. How many? Who? They all did it, all the time. He was the baby. "Who is it that you're so thumping keen to get news about?"

"A—a relative."

"What relative?" He jerked on her wrist. *"Answer me!"*

"All right with you, then!" she shouted. "I'll tell you and you'll wish you'd never asked. It's Tim—Timothy Wood, my son!"

"Son?"

He always thought of her as being younger than himself. His rational mind knew that was nonsense; but his emotions went by appearance and behavior. She had never seemed any more than eighteen to him, and often less, but staring at him now, green eyes awash with tears, inflamed with weeping, red blotches of anger burning on her cheekbones, she was much more than eighteen, much much more.

"He's older than you, Julian Smedley."

"Your son is? Not William's son?"

She shook her head, eyes searching his face. "Big, strapping broth of a lad, he is. Has red hair. Like his mother."

He guessed from her eyes. *Don't say it!* he thought, *please don't say it.*

But she did. "And like his father."

She did it with Carrots.

Julian's world collapsed.

It wasn't just that Carrots were natives. At least they were white. They were rustics, primitives, uneducated. . . . But Mrs. McKay was working class herself, wasn't she? No, the snake in the grass was that Carrots were mortal, and romance between mortal and immortal was simply not on. Inexcusable. Exeter had discovered that.

"You see why you should go now, Julian? You go and have a brave holiday in Joalvale with dear Ursula, and I'll go and be nice to darling Pinky."

Still he hesitated. She pushed him roughly. "Be gone with you. I tried to save you, and you so innocent, but now you know I was breeding Carrot bastards before you were even born, my lad. So be off with you."

He stared. How old was she? How many dozens or hundreds of men had gone where he had gone? Some trick of the candlelight made her a nightmare hag.

"If that's what you really want." A gentleman could hardly stay around a lady's bedroom when he wasn't welcome. He stalked over to the window, climbed out, and went home, feeling about a thousand years old himself.

# 14

The fair city of Jurg was just awakening for business as Eleal Singer came limping along Market Street, weaving between the carts, being jostled by fresh-scrubbed apprentices hurrying to their labors and maidservants out buying fresh bread for their masters' tables. A few late-rising roosters still crowed in the yards and alleys.

She labored under the weight of a pack that held all her worldly goods: spare clothes, three books, two spare pairs of boots, and a few keepsakes. She was also suffering from some very painful bruises, although her face was unmarked, fortunately. To compensate, she was buoyed up by a strange exhilaration, a sense of destiny, a conviction that her life was about to turn an important corner. The sunlight seemed strangely bright, the day itself sweetly scented. Cynical inner voices told her that she was merely suffering from lack of sleep, for dawn more usually marked the end of her working day than her time for rising. That was all behind her now, though. She was a new woman.

A new life beckoned. She had resigned, retired, absconded. Last night she had gone for a stroll and returned late for her gig, something she had never done before. Tigurb'l Tavernkeeper had been unreasonably annoyed. He had not struck her himself, but he had an infinite number of ways to punish, and he had chosen to send some very nasty customers to her dressing room. After the second one, she had packed up her valuables and departed by way of the window.

Here was the place she sought. A garishly painted sign in the shape of a book hung from a bracket above the leaded windows: BALVON PRINTER, MAKER OF EDIFYING TOMES, TEXTS, & TRACTS. The wide door stood open, so she marched right in.

She had never been in a print shop before. It was surprisingly large, with seven or eight people already hard at work. The heavy brass contraption in the center must be the press itself. The air bore an aromatic tang of mingled dust and ink. She glanced around, trying to figure out what everyone was doing so busily at tables and benches around the walls. Two men seemed to be setting type, fishing letters out of rows of boxes. One boy was spreading ink, another carrying away freshly done sheets to dry, another cutting the dried sheets into pages. An old man was pushing a broom around. Three men seemed to be sewing, and one with a mallet was pounding leather on a bench. Fascinating! All this fuss to produce silly little books?

A heavyset man swept forward to greet her. His arrogant demeanor and domineering eyebrows suggested that he might be Balvon Printer himself. She braced herself to meet his inspection. She had shed all her paint and perfume. She was a respectable woman again and need not let this artisan bully her. What if she did carry her own luggage?

Her cloak was a great deal grander than his ink-stained apron, even if he did have a jewel in his turban.

His bow was peremptory, but it was a bow. "How may we be of service to my lady?"

Not bad! She savored the respect. Then she wondered if that was suspicion glinting in his eyes—or recognition, perhaps? Could he be a patron of Cherry Blossom House? Might he have recognized her? Might he even have been one of her admirers? She could not recall his face.

She would not consider such a possibility. She must be the daughter of a wealthy landowner, a patron of the arts. She assumed a suitably ladylike manner. "Good morning, my man. I am sorry to disturb you at your labors. I merely wished to speak for a moment with . . ."

The old man holding the broom was staring at her in rank dismay.

Before she could prevent it, a very unladylike blast of laughter erupted from the patron of the arts. "Piol!" She composed herself. "I wish to have a quick word with an old friend." Seeing a glower of disapproval compressing fat old Balvon's heavy features, she raised her chin again and hid her amusement.

"I shall not keep him long from his duties, master. Surely your janitor's time is not so valuable that I need buy a library to earn the privilege of a moment with him?" That seemed like a good exit line, so she turned and swept out into the street.

Piol followed her out, trailing his broom, and blinked at her ruefully in the sunshine.

"Good morning, Piol!" She could not keep her mirth from her voice.

He looked even frailer in daylight than he had under the lamps two nights ago. His straggly white hair was awry, his skin yellow as old parchment, his wrinkles were deeper than Susswater Canyon. His robe was a shabby, dusty thing, and he was barefoot.

"Good morning, Eleal."

"Now we share each other's dreadmost secret, don't we?"

He nodded, smiling without much conviction. "I'm afraid we do." He made a few desultory strokes with his broom, as if he had come to clean the doorstep.

"Oh, Piol!" Where had that terrible lump in her throat come from?

He glanced around, perhaps afraid his employer might be standing at his back, glaring at him. "What is it, Eleal? Be quick, please."

For a moment she could hardly remember what it was she wanted. Piol Poet, who had won the playwright's rose at the Tion Festival an unprecedented twelve times! Piol Poet sweeping floors!

"I want you to come with me."

"What? Where? It is not much of a job, Eleal, but even old men must eat. I don't need much, but I do need a dry, warm place to sleep."

"You shall have it!" she said hurriedly. "Piol, I have decided to go for the big time! Joal beckons! I shall seek to further my art in the artistic capital of the Vales!"

He smiled uncertainly. "Well . . . well, that is wonderful news, my dear! I am sure you will prosper there. Joalians appreciate talent."

"But I need company on my journey. You!"

His toothless jaw dropped, and he stared at her as if he had taken leave of his wits or thought she had lost hers.

"I am on my way to Joalvale, Piol. It was your mention of the Liberator that gave me the idea. It will be fun to see D'ward again, so we shall contrive to meet him there. But I need a companion, and you are the only one I can trust. Besides, I feel my career requires a manager. Come with me!"

"The Liberator?" He shook his head in disbelief, then made an effort to straighten his bent shoulders. "But that isn't necessary! The Liberator is coming here. All you need do is wait in Jurgvale. He will come. No need to go to Joalvale. In fact, he probably isn't even there anymore."

She felt an inexplicable stab of dismay. "Not there? But you said he was in Joalvale!"

"He was. He will certainly have moved on by now. And what use can I be? I am old. I am not very well, Eleal. . . ."

"Nothing a good meal or two won't fix! If D'ward isn't in Joalvale, then where is he? And how do you know?"

"From the prophecies, of course. He is on his way here, I am sure of it."

That would not do at all! "Then we shall go and meet him in Fionvale."

Piol's eyes narrowed. "I doubt he will be coming that way. He will be coming around by Niolvale, I'm sure. Are you especially eager to leave Jurg, Eleal?"

She laughed and glanced around nervously. The bouncers were not usually operational so early in the day, but Tigurb'l must be very, very mad. She had no time to waste. "You're still as sharp as ever, you old rascal! Yes, I do believe a change of scenery would be beneficial and absence thereof detrimental. Let us head for Niolvale, then. There will be opportunities for an artist there, too. I shall require a good manager—I see now that that was where I made my mistake. How do you know D'ward will come that way?"

Piol blinked his rheumy eyes. "Verse six sixty-three: 'In Niol's shadow, by the silver waters, multitudes shall flock to hear him, and the sharp swords shall drink, spilling blood into the sands. Young men leave their bones where the Liberator has passed.'"

Oh! "Well, we're neither of us young men, are we? Please, Piol! I am carrying quite a lot of money. I do need someone with me, and who else can I trust?"

"Not me! Eleal, what are you planning? Who has put you up to this?"

She had expected him to leap at her offer, but he seemed ready to flee back into his cage.

"No one except you! I'll explain all that when we're on the road." Some of it, anyway. "I need you, Piol. Surely you'd rather come adventuring with me than stay here sweeping dirt? It'll be like old times, Piol! A little like old times, at least. The trader caravans leaving at noon from . . ."

Piol was shaking his head. "I can't leave, Eleal," he whispered.

"Can't? Why not?"

He glanced behind him again, having to turn his whole body in the manner of the aged. Then he looked back to her, his face crumpled with shame. "It costs money to print a book. I still owe rather a lot of it, I'm afraid."

She reached for the money bag under her cloak. "How much?"

"I can't take your gold!" He recoiled from her.

"Piol! Whatever do you mean? Are you implying there is something shameful about my money? I earned this with my singing."

Still he hesitated, shaking his bony head.

"How much do you need? I have lots of money! On a long journey I need a man to accompany me. Go back in there and shove that broom down old Balvon's throat, then gather up your things and come with me! Meet me over there in that bread shop. We'll have some fresh hot rolls and plan our journey. Please, Piol?"

The bakery was hot and rather dark. It was thronged with servants and housewives impatient to acquire their daily bread, but it did have a few rickety tables and chairs. Eleal sat in a corner and fidgeted. She ordered rolls and some of the weak, sweet beer that Jurgians drank in the morning, although she was neither hungry nor thirsty. She had spent the night at a very fine inn, a hostel patronized by gentry, and had eaten well this morning.

Tigurb'l did not own her, but he behaved as if he did. Furthermore, in a few frantic minutes just before leaving her dressing room, she had achieved a remarkable amount of destruction—it was quite amazing what could be achieved in complete silence with a sharp knife. The thugs would be trying to find her to take her back. Definitely a change of scenery was called for.

And it would be fun to see D'ward again. Perhaps he had a very good explanation for running out on her in Suss. She should not judge until she had heard his excuses.

She stifled yawns. What little sleep she had achieved had been broken by strange dreams of an admirer she could not place, a chunky, ruggedly handsome young man with a mustache. It was odd that she could not remember his name or anything more about him except his face and his very hairy chest.

Piol appeared at last, staggering under the weight of a bulky bag. His robe was a threadbare rag, well patched and faded until its original color could not be guessed at. He had wrapped up his head in a whitish turban, which was a Niolian custom, but not uncommon in Jurgland. He tucked in to the buttery rolls with his scanty teeth and ample enthusiasm as if he had not eaten for two fortnights.

He showed much less enthusiasm for her project. "By all means try your luck in Joal, my dear. I shall be happy to help in any way I can. I probably still have friends in the artistic community there, and as you say, it is the greatest of them all. But D'ward . . . I was wrong to mention him to you. Now I think you should avoid opening old wounds."

Whatever could be worrying the old coot?

"Oh, bygones are bygones. It will be fun to see him again."

"You didn't seem to think so when I told you about him."

"Nonsense! I was merely surprised. Tell me why you think he is coming here."

"He must," he mumbled with his mouth full, "go to Thargland, right? That's what the *Testament* says. You can work it all out from the places named."

"Tell me."

He glanced down at his bag. "I have a copy . . . but I think I can remember. You have to fit them together in the right order. . . . Verse one thousand and one: 'In wrath the Liberator shall descend into Thargland. The gods shall flee before him; they shall bow their heads before him, they will spread their hands before his feet.' Tharg is where Zath has his temple, the temple of Karzon, so that's where D'ward must seek him out."

"But if he's in Joalvale, then the quickest way for him to go is through Nagvale and Lemodvale."

"He isn't going the quickest way!" Obviously Piol had been giving much thought to the prophecies. However old and sick he might be, his brain was still working. "Verse two twenty: 'In Nosokslope they shall come to D'ward in their hundreds, even the Betrayer.' "

She forced herself to meet his stare. "Who's the Betrayer?"

"I don't know." He was wondering about it, though.

She shrugged uneasily. "Then let's not go to Nosokvale. What's next?"

"Then the one about Niol—the sharp swords and the young men leaving their bones."

She did not think that could apply to her. She certainly had no sharp swords to hand. "Niol won't get him any closer to Thargland."

"Then Verse fifty-six: 'The Liberator shall hail the Free in Jurgland.' There's a lot more about him promising to bring death to Death and being acclaimed by the multitude. But that one must come next. There's a verse about the king of Randoria and one about hunger in Thovale."

Eleal took a large bite of bread and chewed busily to keep her face occupied. "Prophecies aren't inevitable, though, are they?"

Piol sighed and took a gulp of his beer. "No. If you can break one link in the chain, all the rest must fail. If I were Karzon, I would be trying to kill D'ward before he killed me." He watched carefully for her reaction.

She laughed gaily. "You don't look much like a god to me!"

"You know what gods look like, Eleal?"

"Well of course—I mean, no. Only in general. Why mention Karzon? It doesn't say D'ward will kill Karzon! Only Death, and Zath is just one of the Man's aspects. Of course I don't know what gods look like, except on stage."

"Where did you get so much money, Eleal?"

"I earned it, of course." At least, she thought she had. In her hasty flight, she had emptied all the little caches where she kept her savings hidden. When she went to count it this morning, she had discovered that her money belt contained about four times as much as she expected. It was odd but certainly nothing to complain about. She could live for a year on it.

"So if you're right, then I don't need to go all the way to Joalvale. We can just go over Lospass to Niolvale. If he isn't there yet, then we'll go on to Rinoovale."

"I thought you were going to Joalvale and the Liberator was incidental?"

"Well . . . It would be nice to see him again."

The old man nodded in resignation, making the flaps of his neck wave like flags. "If you insist. Have you enough money to buy a sloth and cart?"

"What do I need a cart for? Or a sloth?"

He smiled for the first time since he had arrived. "If you have money, Eleal, then you always have trouble. If you can't find a better defender than me, then you have serious trouble! You need to discourage the young and greedy. Let's buy a sloth and cart and load it up with sewerberries."

"Yuck!"

This time he actually chuckled, just like his old self. "Exactly! Nobody's going to dig through a load of sewerberries looking for gold. Nobody will come within yards of us! It's a profitable cargo, too—we may make money, which is better than paying for a ride in a caravan and for guards whom we couldn't trust anyway."

Suddenly she felt much better. She leaned over and squeezed his hand. "Brilliant! That's the Piol I used to know! You write the play and we'll star in it together. Two tragic figures? You shall be the noble old campaigner, called forth once more to bear arms in a worthy cause! And I shall be your granddaughter, perhaps? A forsaken maiden going in search of the man who betrayed her but whom deep in her heart she still . . ."

Then fell one of those deathly silences, as if someone had forgotten his lines. A shadow had settled on Piol Poet's face.

"I will write that role gladly, Eleal, if you will play it."

# 15

Overhead the sky shone pure Wedgewood blue, although the sun had not yet cleared the peaks. Morning was a symphony of pearly light and cold as a bugger. Rimy grass crunched underfoot as Julian trudged along, shivering inside his furs and fleece-lined boots. He was in no mood or state for an argument, but he could see one coming whether he wanted it or not.

His eyes were gritty. He had slept very little, tossing the night away thinking about Euphemia prostituting herself to bloody Pinkney just for a chance to make one phone call. It made him feel so bloody inadequate, a man who couldn't defend his woman! It wasn't the ritual that was the problem—she must know at least one of the keys as well as bloody Pinky did—it was the timing. The Olympus portal connected to St. Galls in Wiltshire and a cemetery in Edinburgh and other places as well. You had to know what hour of day or night it was at Home now and when Head Office would have helpers standing by, or you could find yourself in very hot water indeed. The Committee kept all that information under its hat.

Well, it was over. Pinky had had his fun by now. And here came more trouble. Dommi was at his heels, bent almost double under a bag as big as himself. Pind'l and Ostian, Dommi's juvenile assistants, brought up the rear with the rest of the baggage. The air was sharp as swords, and yet they wore only flimsy cotton livery. Dommi was bareheaded, although the rest of him was swathed in a ragtag assembly of moth-eaten furs.

The dragon paddock lay upstream from the station, far enough off to muffle the brutes' incessant burpings. Four dragons were being loaded by a group that included two men in black turbans—simple arithmetic foretold trouble. Turbans came from Nioldom, black was the color of Zath, to be displayed with caution. The only men who ever wore black turbans were T'lin Dragontrader and his hands; it was a sort of uniform with them, dating back before T'lin's conversion to the Undivided.

Julian was in the soup because Dommi expected *Tyika* Kaptaan to keep his promise. A man's word was his bond, and all that. Dommi's furs must have come from the Carrot village, so the whole valley would know that he was bound for Joalvale with *Tyika* Kaptaan. He had roused Julian before first light, having already laid out the *tyika*'s warmest garments, heated a tubful of water, packed the bags, summoned bearers, and prepared a hot breakfast. But two and two made four, on any world, and there were only four dragons in the pen. Olympus owned three of its own, but it was not unusual for all of them to be absent from the valley, as now. Most of those half-clad redheads bustling around would be grooms or polishers or whatever the correct name was for men who shoveled dragon shite, but the dragons themselves all belonged to Agent Seventy-seven, alias T'lin Dragontrader. And both the black-turbaned men were armed, dammit! Julian hadn't even thought of that problem.

Dragontrader himself he could override; Ursula was another matter alto-blooming-gether, especially at this time of day, after two nights without sleep. Blast Edward Exeter and his blasted prophecies! Still, a man's word was his bloody bond.

"Dommi?" he croaked.

Dommi took two fast steps to draw alongside, craning his neck to peer up at him from under the pack. *"Tyika?"*

"You know how to handle a sword."

A worried frown disturbed Dommi's honest freckles. "Is regretful, *tyika*, that I have never had experience with weapons, excepting the short bow for bird-hunting and—"

"Don't argue. You know how to handle a sword."

"As the *tyika* wishes."

Dragons were hay-eating nightmares, a cross between a rhinoceros and the Loch Ness monster, but gentle, helpful creatures in spite of it, the only species capable of crossing from vale to vale without using the standard passes. Exeter had once referred to the dragon as the Rolls-Royce of Nextdoor, and Julian was looking forward to his first real chance to ride one. With his entourage at his heels, he strode into the center of group. Amid a crowd of freckled, lightly clad Carrots, Ursula was well bundled up in white fur with only her face visible. She looked as friendly as a rabid bulldog, and T'lin's expression was equally hostile. They disapproved of Dommi's costume.

"Morning all!" Julian chirruped. He jumped as the two youngsters' packs hit the ground beside him, shaking the valley. Dommi lowered his more circumspectly. "You're looking very charming this morning, Mrs. Newton, an Eskimo's dream. Everything all ready to go there, Dragontrader?"

T'lin raised his massive arms to make the sign of the Undivided. "We are honored to serve, Holiness."

"Rather! Well, sharp's the word! Let's get this stuff loaded, shall we? Then we can be on our way, what?"

"Captain," Ursula growled, "what does this mean?" She spoke in English, aiming a loaded finger at Dommi.

"What? Dommi, you mean? Oh, need a valet. Can't handle buttons and all that, you know." Julian waved his right hand, making the fingers of his glove flap.

Her glower darkened perceptibly. "I am sure Dragontrader won't mind helping you dress, Captain." Was she implying that she would help him *un*dress? *From ghoulies and ghosties and long-leggèd beasties . . .*

"Humbug! Dommi's an excellent cook, and I'm sure he can help out with the livestock too. Can't you, Dommi?"

With great eagerness, Dommi said, "Indeed, *tyika,* I had experience many years as a stripling here in the paddock, helping tending with the dragons."

"There! That's settled." Julian turned away.

"No!" Ursula barked. "This is not a Sunday school picnic, Captain Smedley. We have only four mounts. Goober Dragonherder is a skilled swordsman. So is Seventy-seven, of course, but an additional guard will be invaluable. We won't take any houseboys."

The surrounding Carrots raised their pink eyebrows at her tone, although few of them would understand the words.

"Dommi can handle a sword. Can't you, Dommi?"

Dommi favored Ursula with a gaze of earnest innocence. "Most assuredly, *Entyika* Newton, I was juvenile fencing champion of the village running three years in my youth, and my father sent me out to Randorvale to study with the noted blade-master—"

She uttered a snort that startled even the dragons. "Tell it to the marines, boy! We're going to Joalvale. You're going back to the kitchen. Now, Dragontr—"

"Joalvale, *entyika?*" Dommi exclaimed. "But *Tyika* Kaptaan told me that Niolland would be your most primordial destination, because of the notorious prophecies."

*Tyika* Kaptaan had said no such thing and wondered if he looked as surprised as Ursula did. Dommi glanced from one to the other, apparently worried that he might have revealed a confidence.

"Prophecies?" she demanded. "What prophecies?"

Totally at sea, Julian sighed. "Oh, go ahead, Dommi. You tell her."

Dommi beamed with innocent youthful pleasure at this honor and began to gabble. "*Tyika* Kaptaan explained to me, *entyika,* how the words of the *Filoby Testament* can be construed to elucidate the route that Liberator must follow to reach his intended dread purpose in Thargvale, *entyika,* which is where he must be going if the slaying of

Zath is his object, which we are all knowing it is, yes? Likewise, *Tyika* Kaptaan was instructing me how there are eight references only to the Liberator and twelve to D'ward, whom we know to be the same with *Tyika* Kisster and also himself the Liberator, overlooking a few ambiguous abstrusenesses that may also refer but not specify by name, yes? And of the twenty, fifteen either specify a place or imply one, *Tyika* Kaptaan says."

Julian wondered if perhaps he had not awakened at all and was dreaming this. In that case, why was Ursula gaping like a dead fish?

"Incontrovertible it is," Dommi continued, flushed with excitement until his freckles hardly showed, "that numerous of these place-naming verses may be ordered so as to predict *Tyika* Kisster's chosen path, and while it is not certain that he has already left Joalland, where he was observed in motion a half fortnight ago, *Tyika* Kaptaan pointed out that his chances of interception to the Liberator would be magnified by regressing this indicated itinerary backward, and consequently it will be advantageous to make progression directly to Niolvale—or perhaps Jurgvale, even—and retracing his tracks before he makes them."

Ursula looked aghast at Julian. "Damn my eyes! You mean he isn't just *letting* the prophecies happen, he's going to fulfill them *deliberately* to prove he's the bloody Liberator?"

"Well, surely that's obvious, old girl?" It was obvious to Julian now that his bottle washer had pointed it out. Resourceful chap, Dommi, the perfect gentleman's gentleman. Of course Exeter would make it his business to fulfill all the prophecies—half a Liberator would be no bally good to anyone. And of course he would have to do it in some sort of geographical order, and why the blazes had the Carrots worked that out before the *votyikank* did?

Ursula's eyes burned dark with suspicion. "Why didn't you mention this last night?"

Julian shrugged. "I assumed you could all see it as well as I could, old girl." Nothing untrue there.

"Niolvale or Joalvale, wherever we're going, we still only have four dragons."

Not trusting his Joalian, Julian switched to Randorian, which he knew T'lin understood, and flourished his crispest military tone. "We'll head for Niolland. Dommi, get our kit loaded." Immediately a wave of gleeful Carrots swept through, bearing away all Julian's baggage—and Dommi's also, of course—to pack it in the dragons' panniers. "I'm sure someone will turn up with another mount in a day or two, Dragontrader, and your man can follow us then." Before anyone could argue further, he added, "Oh, and do get him to lend Dommi his sword, will you? No use taking along a first-class fencer without arming him."

# 16

It was not Dosh's fault—he could have gone on for hours and almost certainly escaped from Nosokvale, free and clear. The festering moa failed him in the night. Just where Ragpass widened out and merged with the foothills of Nosokslope, the brute began staggering, stumbling, and falling over things. Reluctantly, he rode off the trail and took refuge in a wood. There he unsaddled and hobbled her, then stretched out under a bush and slept.

By the time he awoke, it was well into morning. He ate his last scraps of food before doing battle with Swift, who was still lame and did not want to go adventuring again. When he returned to the trail, he saw at a glance that a company of moas had passed recently. If they weren't the Joalian troopers, he was a virgin. He considered turning back and decided against it. He had no supplies, he was hungry, and he felt strongly disinclined to run into D'ward and his ragtag rabble again. More to the point, if the cavalry leader knew his business, he would have foreseen the possibility of the fugitive doubling back and left a squad behind to guard the pass.

So Dosh went on, riding down to Ragby, which was a sorry little excuse for a village. Nosokvale was a shoddy land altogether. It must have been fertile and prosperous once, for there were more ruins around than houses, but it was too close to Joalvale for its own health. The Clique and their friends had exploited it, evicting the inhabitants and setting up huge ranching estates. Amorgush owned great tracts of land in Nosokvale.

Knowing no back doors out, poor Dosh had no option but to head east to Lampass with all the speed he could force out of Swift, who no longer deserved her name. He was not so stupid as actually to go into Ragby itself, for the troopers would certainly have mentioned blood money in the village, but the nagging hunger in his belly forced him to stop at an isolated hovel and buy a meal. Either the old couple there betrayed him or he was just observed on the trail; Nosokflat was a tablecloth of grass with very little cover, and by noon Dosh knew he was being watched. He saw isolated riders tracking him in the distance—herders, probably, servants of the absentee landlords. No one was closing in on him, but he must assume that they had sent word ahead to the Joalians. He wondered if there was more than mortal justice hunting him now, if Kraanard's murder had brought the wrath of the Lady upon him.

When pursuit became chase, he would have no chance at all. Most of the troopers' moas must be as exhausted as his, but some of them would still be in working order. Reluctantly, he turned around and headed back. In an ironic echo of the previous day and at about the same time in the evening, he entered Ragpass from the opposite end, confident that he must have the same hunters on his trail again by now.

As the track wound up through the Nosokslope foothills, he began to see people, scores of people in small groups, all heading in the same direction he was. They could not be planning to cross Ragpass tonight, for already the grasping shadows of Nosokwall were reaching out over the landscape. Most were clearly local peasantry, the same sort of rabble that had been following D'ward from Joalland—looking even more impoverished and downtrodden. Others were astride llamas or rabbits or rode in carriages. Apparently, word of the Liberator's arrival had preceded him, and the gentry were also assembling to view the wonder.

Regrettably, he saw not one solitary moa to make his own less conspicuous. He went with the crowd, which merged with the tail end of the self-proclaimed Free coming down from Joalvale and then flowed off into a side canyon. There, obviously, D'ward had set up camp again, and so had his followers. Fires twinkled in the dusk. Dosh met tantalizing odors of cooking, noting that they were mostly associated with parked wagons or coaches and hobbled animals. Those must belong to Nosokians who had brought provisions, although some enterprising groups were selling meals from carts. What were those without money eating? Probably nothing. There were no berry bushes here—precious little of anything except grass and a few emaciated trees. He could hear children crying, but when did children not? Soon he drew near a steep hillside closing off the little valley. From the ruined walls of some ancient building at its base came the sound of many people singing. If they were singing for their supper, they would have to sing much louder than that.

His situation had improved very little. True, there must be three or four hundred pilgrims here to hide among. He could buy himself a meal from one of those entrepreneurs and pick out some respectable citizens to blandish with his polished charm. If that would not uncover a few temporary brothers or cousins to vouch for him, then his money should, provided the price on his head was not too high. The main thing would be avoid the notice of the Liberator and his—

"Dosh!"

Too late. The three men running toward him bore spears and circular Nagian shields. The big one in front was easily recognizable as Prat'han Potter, and behind him came Gopaenum Butcher and Tielan Trader—all from Sonalby, all veterans of the Thargian campaign.

Dosh barked at Swift to crouch, and she seemed to collapse under him. He slid down from the saddle, not worrying about hobbling or tethering, for the brute was too spent even to try to bite him. Feeling just as weary himself, he leaned against her flank and waited for the warriors, wearing an unfamiliar sense of failure like a shroud. He had been in tight corners often enough in his life, but rarely had he lacked confidence in his ability to wriggle out again. Now he was too tired to run and could not hope to hide. These men had always despised him; now they could turn him in as soon as the troopers appeared. Here he was, with more money than he'd ever had in his life, trapped by idiots too stupid to be bribed.

Prat'han arrived first, with the other two close on his heels. They grounded their spears.

"Greetings!" the big man said.

Dosh looked for the mockery he expected. Surprisingly, he did not find it. "Greetings to you," he responded warily.

Tielan chuckled. "The Liberator said you would turn up! Been a long time, Dosh!" The trader was a small, wiry man. He had always had a flippant, juvenile air about him and he had not lost it. Yet even he did not seem to be gloating. He stepped forward and grasped Dosh's shoulder in the Nagian greeting. Prat'han and Gopaenum quickly did the same, as if caught out in a breach of manners. Dosh responded doubtfully.

Well, well! All old friends together now?

"You look as if you've had a hard day." Prat'han peered at the moa and frowned. "You've ridden that poor brute into the ground!"

"It was it or me."

"The troopers came by not long after you left us last night," Gopaenum said. "I'm surprised they missed you. And pleased too, of course!" he added without much conviction. In the last few years he had gained weight and moved most of his hair from his scalp to his chest.

"You told them where I'd gone, though?"

The three exchanged glances.

Prat'han shrugged. "You'd refused the Liberator's offer."

Dosh waited for more, but they waited too.

"And what happens when they turn up tonight? Will you tell them I'm here?"

Gopaenum and Tielan looked expectantly at Prat'han. The big man was their leader, after D'ward. He sidestepped the question.

"We were hoping you'd changed your mind, Dosh."

"You're lying. D'ward may be hoping that, but you aren't, none of you. Join you? Why should I trust you?"

"Because we're prepared to trust you, of course."

"You are or D'ward is?"

Prat'han put his weight on his spear as if he expected to be there for a while. "Whatever D'ward wants is enough for us. He said we were to look out for you and make you welcome if you want to join the Free."

Dosh snorted in disbelief. "I just have to promise to be a good boy in future and you'll accept me as your long-lost brother? You?"

The big man bared his teeth. "I'll try. I really will try. You were our friend once."

His memory was very selective. Friend? Never. After the sack of Lemod, they'd stopped spitting at Dosh Catamite but that was about all.

"You mean you'd defend me from the troopers? You'd lie to them? You'd *fight* for me?" Dosh laughed.

The other two scowled at him. At least Prat'han was trying, although the effort was making his forehead shiny. "We'd do that for a friend, of course—for a brother, I mean. D'ward says you weren't a Thargian spy at—"

"Ha! But I was a spy. Did he mention that?"

"Yes. But he told us to remember how you proved yourself at Lemod, how you went out with him that night, how you went over the wall right after him. He said if you do want to join the Free, you'll prove it."

Startled and then suspicious, Dosh said, "Prove it how?"

"He didn't tell us that."

Tielan said, "He said it's up to Prat'han. You gotta convince Big Pots here. Go ahead and convince. I'm sure it will be an interesting performance."

Gopaenum chuckled. "I'm looking forward to it, too. Actions speak louder than words, the Liberator says."

The bastards were really enjoying this. Dosh peered around, hoping to see some alternative. He didn't. The valley was almost dark now, so that the scattered fires shone brighter. The singing had stopped. The crowd at the ruins had fallen silent, listening to someone speaking—D'ward, probably, but the snatches the wind brought were too faint to make out. The only other sounds were thuddings of axes as the last trees turned into firewood. The moa was useless; if he took off on his own feet, he'd be run down easily. The Nagians knew he was here and would tell the troopers. It was join them or die. He was shaking now from cold and exhaustion, but these boneheads would think it was from fear. Maybe they were right. He'd have to join the Free, at least until morning.

Join them how?

"You're going to bring death to Death?"

"To try," Prat'han said. "We're not fools, Dosh. We know this is dangerous. Some of us may die. All of us may die. We think it's worth the risk, that's all—no more reapers."

"If it scares you, you don't have to, of course," Tielan added.

There was one thing he could do, but his whole self shied away from the prospect like a fiery death. "Suppose I agree now and change my mind tomorrow?"

Prat'han chewed his lip unhappily for a moment. He was having to *think*, and he usually managed not to get involved with that. "Suppose you'll be free to go. Anyone's free to go. One or two of us turned back; missed their wives, they said."

Gopaenum shivered noisily. "You going to stand there all night? Come on—convince!"

Dosh thought it over again and reluctantly came to the same conclusion as before. He sighed. "You still a butcher?"

"I was until a coupl'a fortnights ago. Why?"

"Lot of hungry people out there tonight. I don't need this moa if I'm going to join you, do I? Take it, kill it, share it out. The saddle can go to make shoes for some of the kids."

Gopaenum and Tielan looked inquiringly at Prat'han.

"Doesn't prove much, Dosh. It makes you conspicuous and it's half dead already."

"I haven't finished!" Dosh snapped, although he'd had hopes. "And it's still worth a hundred stars! Here, I've got some cash, too." He pulled out his money bag, wishing he'd had the foresight to divide his riches between two bags.

Tielan snarled, "We don't want your filthy gold!"

And him a trader!

"Not for you, shitface. For those hungry people. Come and watch."

Hardly able to believe he was letting himself be suckered like this, he stumbled off into the gloom, heading for the nearest campfire, Prat'han and Tielan stalking along at his heels. Gopaenum stayed with the moa, and it cried out briefly in the background as Dosh handed the first coin to an astonished child. More children flocked around; he gave them silver. He strode over to the next fire and the next, choosing those that were not cooking food. He dropped coins to mothers with babies, laid others beside sleeping children. He found himself laughing rather shrilly at the expressions on the adults' faces. Then the bag was empty. He turned to the two Nagians.

"Well? Have I convinced you now?"

Tielan beamed and opened his mouth.

"Why stop now?" Prat'han demanded, frowning. "That's a pricey-looking outfit. What's in the pockets?"

"Nothing, you stupid ox!"

"Well, you can't cross a river halfway, D'ward says. Finish the job, Dosh. Do it all."

Cursing under his breath, Dosh stripped. He gave away his tunic, his boots, his precious knife belt. He exchanged his fine linen breeches for a grubby loincloth off an astonished beggar. Then, penniless and barefoot, he turned on Prat'han. "Well? You want my skin, too? Because that's all I've got left. You want to pull out my toenails, you, you . . ." He wanted to scream.

With a bellow of joy, Prat'han enveloped him in a bear hug so tight his ribs creaked. "Well done, Dosh! Well, well done! D'ward said you'd prove yourself and none of us believed him!"

Then it was Tielan's turn. He not only hugged Dosh, he kissed his cheek. "Welcome, brother! Come and meet the others, Brother Dosh."

They led him back to where Gopaenum was passing out hunks of still-warm meat to an excited throng. More of the Warband emerged from the darkness. Told what he had done, they embraced him and bade him welcome to the Free. They all smiled as if they meant it, although he couldn't see their faces clearly. It was easy enough for them. They hadn't had to throw away a fornicating fortune to join a madhouse.

# IV

Now this, O monks, is the noble truth of the cessation of pain: the cessation, without a reminder, of that craving; abandonment, forsaking, release, non-attachment.

BUDDHA

# 17

It was February. It was almost dark. It was raining. To say rain was falling would be inaccurate—it moved in gray sheets parallel to the ground, sweeping horizontally across the sodden flatland of Norfolk so that it could needle into Alice's face, insinuate its cold presence under the edges of her sou'wester to soak her hair, creep down the tops of her Wellingtons, trickle icily into the neck and sleeves of her raincoat. The wind tugged and wrestled at the coat, which was much too large for her and probably Tudor, or at least Georgian. She had found it hanging on a nail in the cottage, overlooked or unwanted by those who had taken all the other contents. No wonder the English had conquered half the world—a race toughened by such weather could overcome anything.

Her hands and face ached with the cold. She had been a fool to come out for a walk and an even bigger fool to head downwind. Now she had the gale in her face all the way back and the going was much harder. She had wanted some fresh air, but not quite this much, thank you. She was still so weak that it had blown her over twice already, sliding her feet from under her in the mire, so she was almost as muddy as the track itself. She would have no one to blame but herself if she caught a chill; the doctor had warned her not to get overtired, but he had not thought of hypothermia. Wistful dreams of hot, steaming tea in large quantities drove her onward.

But not far now. She turned into the little driveway to her door. The hugely overgrown hedges on either side gave her shelter from the wind.

She ought to fill up the coal scuttle before she went in, while she had her coat on. Had she ever truly appreciated the gas fire in her flat in London, or the roof there that did not leak? Even the screaming boredom of the office had taken on a certain nostalgic glow now. Frailty, thy name is Alice! She had made her decision and would live with it. Tonight she would finish painting the ceiling if it killed her. She had started four days ago and she could still see more mildew than paint.

As she left the shelter of the hedges, the wind grabbed at her, flapping her coat, making her stagger. She almost walked into the car before she saw it. She stopped in astonishment, wiping rain from her eyes.

It was a very large motorcar, parked right at her door. Large and black. Just for a moment, it reminded her of D'Arcy's old Vauxhall. A wild, crazy fantasy . . . *It was all a horrible mistake, darling. I've been in a German prison camp. . . .*

No, that was madness. Even if it were true, she had seen the Vauxhall wrecked by bombs in Greenwich eighteen months ago during those few chaotic days when Edward had returned from fairyland. And the other, corresponding, daydream, of Terry turning up saying, *No, love, I wasn't drowned* . . . that was even more impossible. If Terry were to come back from the dead, he would not do so in a car.

But who did she know who had an automobile and access to petrol? No one. The war had not been over long enough for such luxuries to have reappeared. And almost nobody would have known where to find her anyway. She had not yet written all the letters she meant to write, ought to write, must get around to writing.

A neighbor coming to call? Leaving cards? She would not expect the locals to drop around and leave cards—that seemed a ludicrous idea in a rural wilderness like this. She had been expecting someone to drop in before now, just to check out the newcomer. She had not been expecting a car to come by itself, and this one was certainly unoccupied.

She fingered the big key in her pocket. She was quite certain she had locked the door, although that would probably seem an unfriendly act to the locals. There were no other houses within a mile of her and she had no telephone. Until now, that situation had not bothered her. She really should not let it trouble her now. . . .

But where was the driver? In the outhouse? In the shed at the back? It made no sense to take shelter in either of those, for the car itself would be more comfortable. If her visitor had evil intentions, it made even less sense to lie in wait for her somewhere with the car standing in full view. She moved slowly to the door. The cottage's two tiny, secretive windows both faced the front, and few people would be able to clamber in through them anyway. Neither was broken or showed conspicuous signs of tampering. The long grass under them had not been trampled.

Very gently she depressed the latch; the door was still locked. More relieved than she cared to admit, she twisted the key in the keyhole and heard the antique lock clatter. The wind hurled her into the cottage in a cloud of rain. She heaved the door back and slammed it. She shot the bolt.

Panting and shivering, she stood for a moment, hearing the patter of mud and water on the newspapers covering the floor at her feet, grateful to be in out of the storm, unable to see anything except the twinkle of firelight. Bring in more coal? Coal could wait. If her unknown visitor had merely gone to visit the privy, she would hear him return to the car.

She hauled off her hat. The reek of turpentine in the room was sickening. Gradually her eyes adjusted to the light and she saw the sink and counter in the corner, the stepladder, the tins of paint, the paraffin lamp, the sofa and chair draped in dust covers as if veiled for a funeral. All the rest of the furniture had been crammed away into the bedroom. The woman on the sofa was drinking tea.

Yelping with shock, Alice jumped back and cannoned into the door.

The visitor frowned and lowered her cup into the saucer she held in her other hand. "Good afternoon, Miss Prescott. I'm sorry if I startled you." She sat tall and erect in a sensible brown tweed coat with a fur collar. A cumbersome handbag lay beside her on the sofa. Her bright-glinting eyes and angular features were oddly birdlike.

For a moment Alice had no breath to speak but every muscle in her body tried to move independently in all directions. Then she croaked, "You're younger!"

The visitor raised carefully penciled eyebrows to suggest that the remark was in questionable taste. "Younger than what? Magna Carta?"

"Than when I last met you, of course. Are you still Miss Pimm?"

She was completely dry, from her neat hat to her practical, square-toed shoes, although the path outside was awash in mud. There was no sign of moisture on her fur collar.

"That name will do, I suppose, Miss Prescott."

Suddenly shock gave way to anger. "And mine is Pearson." Alice struggled with the buttons on her coat.

The witch glanced briefly at the ringless fingers and considered that information for a moment. "You are living alone, though, Mrs. Pearson. I take it that condolences are in order?"

An explanation would be much more in order. Not the locked door. That was easy enough to understand, for Miss Pimm had once removed Alice herself from a bicycle and placed her in the backseat of an automobile while the two vehicles were approaching each other at a hundred miles an hour. Why, though, had she invaded Alice's hard-won solitude in the depths of darkest Norfolk? Could she not recognize a hermitage when she saw one?

Then understanding and excitement: "Edward? You have news of Edward?"

"He is alive and well, as of a couple of weeks ago. And he is the reason for my intrusion, of course. He always is, isn't he?" Miss Pimm shook her head in mild exasperation. "I must have an impacted mother instinct where that boy is concerned."

"He has returned?"

"No. He is still on Nextdoor. He never came Home, as he promised. I should have informed you promptly if I had had word of him. This is the first definite news I have heard."

And the first Alice had heard of either of them in years. She hung her hat and muddy coat on the nail by the door. "You had had *in*definite news?"

"I received a report that he had announced his intention of fulfilling the prophecy and had then left Olympus. The details were so vague and so unlikely that I chose not to trouble you with them."

Alice chafed her cold and aching hands, then pulled her feet out of the Wellingtons. "And what is more definite this time?"

"I shall get to that in due course. I made some tea." Obviously. And the teapot in its cozy was perched on the ladder, one step up from the milk jug, the sugar bowl, and a second cup and saucer. All those things had come out of the jumble in the bedroom. Miss Pimm was a very efficient busybody, for Alice had not been gone more than twenty minutes.

"It was very kind of you to come so far to let me know," she said sweetly, heading for the tea. She had no need to ask how the old hussy had tracked her down.

"You have been ill."

"Is it so obvious?"

"Not to most people, no."

"I had a touch of the Spanish flu."

"You were in good company. You must find this place very lonely after London?"

"By choice." Anger made her hands shake as she poured the tea. In the month she had been here, no one had come to call except tradesmen: milkman, butcher, grocer, and the postman twice. Not a single neighbor. She had wanted solitude and found a ton of it. Until now. Now her privacy had been raped. She sat down on the lumpy, shrouded chair and sipped at the tea while trying to face down Miss Pimm's penetrating scrutiny. "How is Head Office?"

Miss Pimm pouted. "Licking our wounds."

"But you won, didn't you?"

"The result might best be described as a draw. We won in the West. We definitely lost Russia and we are seriously concerned about the Peace Conference. The struggle against evil continues; the Blighters have regrouped. They outwitted us with the Spanish flu."

"*That* was their doing too?"

"Indeed it was—influenza is not normally so deadly. It was an attempt to keep the Americans out of the war. It began in America, you know, and turned up in all forty-eight states within a week. It has already killed more people than the war did. It may not be over yet. Does that sound like ordinary flu to you?"

A tale so outrageous ought to defy belief but did not when spoken by Miss Pimm. "Pestilence! The fourth horseman?"

"Quite. In the end, it backfired. It was the flu that crippled the German Army and ended the war." A thin, gloating smile came and went quickly.

"That is not true!"

"That is what General Ludendorff says." Miss Pimm dismissed the German High Command with a shrug. "But we did come out better in the war than we initially feared, yes."

The light from the window was failing. The fire threw the visitor's shadow on the wall, larger than life and ominously like the shape of a bird of prey. "Why Norfolk?" she demanded.

"I inherited this place. It has been in the Pearson family for generations." Irrelevant! Alice took another sip of tea, feeling its warmth running hot down inside her.

Miss Pimm eyed the ceiling acerbically. "Obviously none of them believed in paint. So why did you throw up your London job and bury yourself here in the swamps?"

That was absolutely none of her business, but one did not say such things to Miss Pimm.

"I'm not sure. The war was over. I needed a new start? Turn a new leaf? Or just postflu depression. Now, what news of Edward?"

Miss Pimm nodded briskly, as if agreeing that the time for small talk was now over and the meeting could get down to business. "He has apparently decided that he is Jesus Christ."

"I consider that remark to be in poor taste."

"Moses, then. Or Peter the Hermit. He is trying to fulfil the *Filoby* prophecy." Miss Pimm might have shed thirty years, but she had not shed her stranger's authority.

"He swore he never would."

"Apparently he has changed his mind."

"His privilege," Alice said carefully.

"Not if his whim endangers others, it isn't. We have a visitor from the Service, a Mrs. Euphemia McKay. She says that your cousin is now openly proclaiming himself the Liberator of the prophecy. He is going up and down the landscape preaching a religious revolution."

"*Edward* is?"

"Apparently."

"Well, I expect he has his reasons." Alice's memories of her cousin and foster brother were mostly memories of a boy, but she had seen a very strong-willed young man in 1917. He would not do anything lightly.

Miss Pimm sighed. "I am sure he does have reasons, and I must confess that my presence here today is largely prompted by sheer curiosity. I should love to hear what those reasons are. His father was most adamant that the Liberator gambit would be a grievous error, and from what I know of the matter, I tend to agree. That is irrelevant. Mrs. McKay was sent over because the Service are seriously worried. What Edward is doing could have catastrophic consequences for them."

"In what way?" Alice asked. And why should that concern her? Why, even, should it concern Edward? The Service had done nothing for him except shanghai him to Nextdoor and then frustrate his efforts to return Home. It had also tried to kill him—or one of its members had. She could not see that he had any obligations to the Service. She certainly did not.

"I believe they are mainly concerned that he will fail," Miss Pimm said thoughtfully, "and that their work to date will thereby be discredited. That is a charitable view. I could present less favorable hypotheses."

Alice decided not to pursue that train of thought. She did not like the direction this conversation was taking. "I am glad to hear that he is alive. It was kind of you to bring the news in person. Thank you." *Good-bye.*

Again, Miss Pimm's smile was fleeting but sinister. "Mrs. McKay crossed over to this world specifically to appeal to you for help."

"Me? How? Write a letter . . . No, that's not possible, is it? My help to aid Edward or try and stop him?"

"The latter."

"Why should I? I fail to see that whatever he is up to is any concern of mine."

"Or of mine. I am becoming a trifle peeved that the Service keeps appealing to us for help. We did not seek to involve them in our struggles with the Blighters."

That remark seemed irrelevant, so Alice ignored it. "He is of age. I have every confidence in his judgment."

"So do I. That is why I am curious." The admission was appealing, suddenly making Miss Pimm seem almost human . . . normal.

For a moment, neither spoke. It was Alice who looked away first, of course. She discovered that her cup was empty, but the effort of going for another was beyond her.

"The suggestion is absurd. For me to intrude on him, to presume to advise him, when he knows the situation—indeed the whole world—so much better than I do . . . it would be an intolerable presumption. I refuse. Please indicate to Mrs. McKay . . . Where is this Mrs. McKay?" Alice glanced uneasily at the door to her bedroom.

"I left her prostrate on a bed in the Bull in Norwich. She is suffering from lack of sleep, because Valian days do not coincide with ours at the moment. She also wanted to make a telephone call. You wish me to convey your regrets to the Service, then?"

Alice wondered if it was possible to shock this formidable lady. "You may tell them to go and get stuffed."

The basilisk expression did not change. "The sentiments, if not the precise phraseology, are exactly what I predicted."

Again, a silence, and this time longer. Miss Pimm appeared to be waiting for something, but Alice could not imagine what. She was certainly not going to go and wag her finger at Edward on behalf of strangers. Even if she knew all the facts, which she certainly did not, and even if she thoroughly disapproved of his actions, which she might, she would not presume to meddle. So what was there left to discuss?

"Have you anything planned for this evening?" Miss Pimm inquired softly.

Try to finish painting the ceiling and the cupboards, by the light of the paraffin lamp. Then open a tin of sardines or something for supper. Whatever it was, it would taste of turpentine. And then go to bed with a candle and *Wuthering Heights.* She could not even play the gramophone, because it was packed in under the bed behind her books and pictures and general paraphernalia. Come to think of it, the kitchen table and the rug were on top of the bed.

"Not much," Alice admitted.

"Then you shall come and have dinner with us at the Bull. I can bring you back afterward, if you wish."

Why should she not wish?

"The last time we met, you didn't drive."

"'Didn't' and 'couldn't' are not the same," Miss Pimm said firmly. She rose and headed for the teapot. "Go and change."

Alice opened her mouth and then closed it, knowing that arguing with a *stranger* was not likely to be productive. Besides, the thought of a decent meal in civilized surroundings had a definite appeal. She hauled herself out of the chair and walked across to put her cup and saucer in the sink.

"Don't," Miss Pimm added, "put on anything you would mind losing. Just in case you change your mind."

Alice swung around, fright and anger boiling up together. "Are you planning to abduct me? Is that what you're hinting? Because—"

"Of course not. If I planned a kidnapping, Mrs. Pearson, I should not have wasted all this time in conversation."

# 18

"Mrs. McKay, Mrs. Pearson," Miss Pimm said.

Alice was cautious at first, unsure of the correct protocol. "I trust you had a comfortable journey?" seemed a peculiarly banal question to pose to a traveler from another world—but the mysterious Euphemia turned out to be extraordinarily ordinary, almost disappointing. Her dress was dowdy, her accent working-class Irish, and her manner decidedly unladylike. If she had been smitten by fatigue earlier, she had now recovered, for she sparkled with prankish humor, openly teasing Miss Pimm and making racy little remarks about the handsome soldiers she had seen hanging around the Bull. At a guess, she was in her very early twenties, but she had the confidence of a much older woman.

"The news was good?" Miss Pimm inquired archly.

"Oh, it was grand!" Mrs. McKay said. "They say he's doing just splendid. Telephones are marvelous, aren't they?"

The three ladies proceeded to the dining room. It was gloomy and low ceilinged, but it was warm and did not reek of turpentine. At this early hour they had the place to themselves and were granted a table next to the fire and tended by an antiquated and very deaf waiter. As soon as they sat down, Miss Pimm withdrew from the conversation, behaving as if she had cast an invisibility spell on herself. Mrs. McKay, in contrast, began chattering breezily about the rigors of occult travel, how wonderful it was to be Home in England, even if only for a brief stay, the disgraceful weather, the changes she had seen already, and the misfortunes of a couple named Pepper, who had won the lottery for the first postwar leave and had both been stricken with flu a few days after they arrived.

Olympus would not have sent an unprepossessing ambassador, and Alice soon realized that her first impressions had not done Euphemia justice. She was personable and witty in a sharp, juvenile way. If she would just get a fashionable haircut, if she weren't wearing too much powder, an ill-fitting dress of dowdy brown, and a rouge that clashed horribly with her coloring, then she would be quite a beauty. Men would probably regard her as a stunner already, for her hair was a cascade of fiery auburn and she had an impressive figure. To be fair, her makeup and clothing must be other peoples' castoffs, for she could have brought nothing with her from Nextdoor. Who was Alice to criticize when her own hair was full of paint?

The food was vastly better than wartime London had offered, although the only vegetables available in February were turnips and soggy potatoes. Alice gorged herself on roast pork, washing it down with an excellent white wine. Her indulgence in the wine might possibly be an aftereffect of Miss Pimm's driving—just because the old witch could see around corners did not mean that she had to keep proving the point— but by the time Alice realized that alcohol might be unwise under the circumstances, it was too late to care. Much to her surprise, she discovered she was enjoying herself more than she had in months.

Eventually, of course, Mrs. McKay got down to business. She confirmed what Miss Pimm had said about Edward—he had returned to Nextdoor in 1917, then walked out of the station and disappeared. Since then there had been no word of him at all. Now, according to reliable reports, he was openly preaching to the natives in some place called Joalvale, professing to be the foretold Liberator.

"He is taking a terrible risk," she proclaimed earnestly, although it sounded more like *turrible roosk.* "I just don't know why Zath and his gang did not kill him imme-diately. It may very well be too late already."

Too late to do what?

The green eyes widened—she really ought to try mascara on those sandy lashes. "You do know of the prophecies, Mrs. Pearson?"

"Roughly. Please call me Alice."

"And you must call me Euphemia!" Euphemia took a sip of wine, then leaned forward with a conspiratorially intent expression. Here came the grifter's patter. "You understand that what he's doing could have serious repercussions on the poor natives?"

Whose vocabulary was that? Not hers.

Alice said, "I know that Edward insisted he would not do what you say he is now doing. If he has changed his mind, then he must have good reasons for doing so. Did he take anyone with him when he left Olympus?" He had spoken of a girl Ysian, who had become somebody's cook. . . .

"Oh, no. Well, at least I don't think so." Either Mrs. McKay had never considered that possibility or she had not been briefed on it. "There was a lot of muddle just then, of course. . . ."

The query had thrown her off balance and Alice followed up her advantage. "Muddle? What can muddle a coven of sorcerers?"

"A what?" Looking startled, Euphemia took another drink of wine, then began to speak in her normal manner again, as if abandoning a prepared script. "We're not that! The Chamber attacked Olympus while Edward was away, and he was the first one back after it happened. Just terrible! The houses were all burned. We've only just got the place shipshape and Bristol fashion again. And there were deaths! Not all of us managed to escape in time. Several people were never accounted for. We think one of them was a spy who ran away with the killers, but I suppose it's possible that one of the others went off with Edward. . . . Why are you asking?"

Alice chewed for a moment while she tried to think of a tactful way of inquiring about Edward's possible romance. She couldn't find one. "It must have been quite a shock for him to cross over and find himself in that. And a worse shock for Captain Smedley." She had forgotten to ask for news of Julian.

"Oh, yes! They organized the Carrots to bury all the dead."

"*All* the dead? It was that bad?"

"Dozens! Only four of them were strangers, though."

"And natives don't count, of course?"

"They count with me!"

Oh lordy! "I beg your pardon. That was unforgivable. They would count with me, too, and I know they would with Edward. We were both raised in Africa, you know. . . ." As Alice struggled to extricate herself from her embarrassment, she noted that Mrs. McKay was blushing bright enough to make the rouge on her cheeks seem pale, but she was sure that she must be as pink herself. How could she have said such an appalling thing? *Alice, you have been drinking too much!*

Mercifully, the waiter arrived then and interrupted the conversation. When he hobbled away, leaving offerings of trifle, generously laced with sherry, Alice tried a fresh start.

"Doesn't one of the prophecies say that the dead will rouse him? The Liberator, I mean. Two years ago, I thought that referred to the dead he saw in Flanders, but perhaps the seeress meant the dead in Olympus?"

Mrs. McKay shrugged vaguely. "Oh, I don't pretend to be understanding the prophecies."

*Dead* plural, the massacred Carrots? Or *dead* singular, the girl Ysian? To ask that of this twittery woman would be a waste of time, but obviously something had roused Edward.

Two other parties entered the dining room and were seated. Euphemia seemed to have forgotten or postponed her mission, which Alice had begun to suspect mattered much less to her than the unexplained good news she had received earlier. She was tossing down wine wholesale, as if celebrating something more than a flying visit to England—not that Alice herself was far behind. Drinking had been frowned on during the war, but now it was all right again.

"It is wonderful to be Home again, even if it's so brief-like. The war must have been terrible?"

Yes, Alice found herself agreeing, it had been very bad. Millions had died. At the end, the flu had come and killed millions more. Even here in England, it had been bad—food shortages, bombs, the daily casualty lists, women working in factories, social upheaval.

"But it is getting better?" Euphemia demanded. "The men are coming back? Things are getting back to normal?"

"Things will never get back to normal, if you mean what was normal before the war." Somehow—was it the wine talking or reaction to the loneliness of the cottage?— Alice found herself describing the past bombings, the continuing shortages, and now the strikes, the frustrations, the eternal squabbling that filled the newspapers with gloom and made one wonder what good four years of slaughter and sacrifice had accomplished.

Euphemia made sympathetic noises, her green eyes wide. "And the war touched you personally?"

"Too personally."

"I was told to find a Miss Prescott. Of course, if you would rather not talk about it . . ."

"There is hardly anything to talk about," Alice said bitterly. "I was married for less than a week. I had lost a very dear friend in Flanders. He was killed in action the very day that Edward returned to Nextdoor. I married Terry on the rebound, one of those crazy wartime affairs. You probably won't understand. He was young and brave and terrified. They had this awful urgency, you see, this sense that every day might be their last. They were all so tough and so frightfully fragile at the same time." The wine drove her onward. "It sounds terrible to say, but it may have been for the— I don't mean that. It was tragic and I mourn him, of course. What I mean is just I can see now that our marriage was foolish, one of those impetuous wartime romances that might have turned out to be a mistake—"

She clenched her teeth as one might rein in a runaway horse. She had been starved for company so long that her mouth was going to make an ass of her if she gave it half a chance. So much had happened since that bewildering day when Miss Pimm had saved her life and Edward's with a display of magic. First D'Arcy, then Terry . . . It was D'Arcy she thought of most, still. Terry had been a transitory madness. The only thing they had had in common was a complete lack of family. A smile, an aura of vulnerability, a lightning romance, a wedding, five frenzied nights of love, a frantic farewell, a telegram . . . and a cottage.

"I inherited the cottage. It was all he had to leave, his grandfather's home. His ship went down six days after our wedding. A U-boat. I get a small pension. . . ." She felt guilty every time she spent a penny of it.

She stared down at her empty plate and bit her lip until the pain brought tears to her eyes. Then she took another drink. Her plate was removed. Cheese and biscuits and coffee arrived. The dining room buzzed with conversation, an unfamiliar sound.

After the silence, Euphemia said, "I am terribly, terribly sorry. Our troubles must all seem very trivial to you."

"No. Not at all. Tell me about Olympus itself. Edward was confoundedly vague about it, and he had so many other things to tell us."

"Olympus? It's a monkey house!"

Bewildered, Alice said, "In what way?"

Euphemia seemed to have second thoughts. "Oh, you know—outpost-of-Empire stuff. Exiles in the bush going wild-crazy from boredom. There's no other stations to visit, no big, fancy Port Said or Singapore within reach. The climate's so darlin' that we don't need to rush off to the hills in the hot season. The men can't go big-game hunting, because the only weapons around are bows and arrows. There are no letters from Home."

"And the *Times* is never delivered?"

"Never. Olympus is worse than a lighthouse. We inmates may not admit it, but at times we all became bored to madness. That's why the Service allows women to be missionaries, dear. Try leaving the little women at home all the time, and they get the crackers. We're bored, we gossip, we squabble. We—" Euphemia hesitated, then said bitterly, "Monkeys in a monkey house." She drained her wineglass.

"Oh!"

"The rules don't apply there, you see. We don't grow old. The fires don't cool. We don't settle into comfortable, down-at-heels middle age."

Alice was annoyed to discover that this frankness discomfited her. She liked to think of herself as modern. "Edward definitely did not mention that."

"Ha! No, he was different. Of course he wasn't there very long, but he was definitely the only man who ever refused Olga Olafson."

Nettled, Alice said, "I'm not surprised. His morals were always the most rigid thing about him."

Euphemia found that remark hilarious, and Alice laughed with her.

"To chastity!" Euphemia said, raising her glass, which had mysteriously refilled itself.

Alice clinked it with her own. "In moderation!" They drank. "And how has Captain Smedley fared in Olympus?"

"Oh! Um. Jolly well. Just went off to see if he could help Mr. Exeter. Very popular . . ." Euphemia's already flushed complexion became noticeably pinker. "His hand is growing back, you know."

"No! Really?" Magic in a vague, general sense was hard enough to swallow, although Alice had seen enough of it now to believe in it. To associate a miracle with someone as ordinary and practical as Julian Smedley was somehow more difficult.

"Of course," Miss Pimm said quietly. The other women both jumped, as if they had forgotten she was there. "Did you ever doubt that it would, Mrs. Pearson?"

"Yes."

"You should have more faith! A stranger can always heal himself—or herself." She skewered Alice with an extremely disconcerting stare. Had she grown taller since the evening began or was that just an illusion?

"What—what do you mean?"

"I mean that what you need is a nice tropical vacation."

"Me?"

"You. Soldiers are not the only people who suffer from battle fatigue. The whole world is suffering from battle fatigue. You have experienced two bereavements in eighteen months. You lost your uncle not long before that, and you thought your cousin also. I suspect your encounter with the Spanish flu was more serious than you admit. Your decision to seclude yourself here in Norfolk was probably very sound, but the vacation I have suggested would be a better alternative."

*Battle fatigue? Shell shock?* Alice had never thought of applying those sinister terms to herself. They seemed like a very glib excuse. What she had experienced was nothing to compare with the hell the men in the trenches had endured. " 'Nervous breakdown,' we used to call it."

"The name does not matter," Miss Pimm said firmly. " 'Emotional exhaustion,' would suffice, and you are probably badly run-down physically, also. So why not a holiday—all expenses paid? A few weeks in exotic surroundings? Perhaps not quite as relaxing as a Mediterranean cruise, but probably more enjoyable at this time of year. It is late autumn in the Vales, but the weather will be clement."

"Much better than this," Euphemia agreed hopefully.

Alice struggled to adjust to the concept of holidaying on another world. Her mind slithered helplessly, like a puppy on an icy pond.

"Very beneficial for the convalescent," Miss Pimm remarked. "Of course, if you do decide to go on and see Edward, the journey may be strenuous. The Vales are a more primitive land than England, so it would be foolish to deny that there may be risks, but no more than you would incur on a safari in Kenya or yachting on the Broads, for that matter. At this time of year you would have to travel on dragonback. A chance to meet your only living relative?"

"But I refuse to—"

"I do not believe the Service's invitation has any strings attached to it. You can make it quite clear that you do not commit yourself to supporting any particular viewpoint in the dispute. Is that not correct, Mrs. Mackay?"

Euphemia started to shake her head and then nodded uncertainly.

"Jolly good!" Miss Pimm said as if the matter was settled. "And if you do agree to go and see your cousin, you can explain your motives to him. I am sure he will accept them and be very glad to see you again."

The dining room rocked in waves of unreality and disbelief. To hear Edward talk of crossing over to other worlds had been bad enough. For Alice to consider actually doing so herself was a unicorn of another color.

She glanced suspiciously at Euphemia, who seemed to be having trouble keeping up with the conversation. "What guarantee do I have that I shall be allowed to return?"

Miss Pimm pursed her lips. "I can give you mine. The Service personnel are all eager for Home leave, now that the war is over. For that they require our cooperation. If you do not return in a month or so—or whatever time you stipulate beforehand—then I can arrange for serious consequences. Take hostages, in effect. We can set up a code message for you to send me if you wish to remain longer."

Gibber! Alice thought of the cottage: dark, damp, dingy, and drear. No one would care whether she finished the painting now or months from now—or never. No job. No friends who would notice her absence unless it was prolonged. Why could she not jump at this incredible offer?

Miss Pimm frowned. "I honestly do not believe that the Service will make trouble for you. They are basically decent people, perhaps a little out of their depth at the moment."

Euphemia said, "Ha!" and emptied her wineglass.

Alice drained her coffee cup. Outside was rain, loneliness, mud, and skeletal, leafless trees. To see a warm, tropical land again! How long since she had enjoyed a real holiday? She could not recall one, not ever. A week now and again visiting great-aunts at Bournemouth. Stolen weekends with D'Arcy before the war. The fire hissed and smoked.

"The milkman," she muttered. "The butcher . . ."

"Your bills are all paid up? We can go past the cottage on our way. You will leave a note on the door, requesting no deliveries until further notice."

"An invitation to burglars?"

"I can make the cottage secure against intruders. Now, is it settled?"

Alice looked doubtfully at Euphemia. "As long as I am not committing myself. I trust Edward. I won't betray him."

# 19

*Ombay fala, inkuthin . . .*

They had not long left the cottage for the second time, passing through Norwich again and heading southwest toward Cambridge, when Alice's sense of collapsing reality made her wonder if her mind had come unhinged completely. Or was the wine wearing off? She huddled in the back of the car with Euphemia McKay, while Miss Pimm drove like a maniac through the night. Rain streamed on the windscreen, mocking the wipers' efforts to clear it; the fancy electric headlights showed nothing ahead but silvery torrents.

*Indu maka, sasa du.*

Teeth chattering, slapping her hands on her knees to beat time, Euphemia was attempting to teach Alice the words of the key, the age-old chant that would open the portal at St. Gall's and lead them through to another world. Alice could recall a similar drive, a year and a half ago, when it had been Miss Pimm instructing Edward and Julian in the same gibberish. Words from before the dawn of history, a complex, troubling rhythm. But that had been a sun-baked summer afternoon and the driver had been the solid, sane Mr. Stringer. He did not overtake on blind hills in pitch darkness or cut corners on the wrong side of the road.

*"Hosagil!"* Euphemia cried triumphantly. "That's the first verse. You want to try it now?"

No, Alice did not want to try it. Alice wanted to go home to her lonely hermitage and jump into bed and pull the blankets over her head. She wanted this insanity to stop. Now! Instantly. The wine had scrambled her brains or she would never have agreed to this madness. Vacation on another world? They had no luggage, either of them. They weren't going anywhere. They couldn't be. It was all just a gigantic hoax; it must be. Now the wine was wearing off, she could see that.

"Let me try it one line at a time first, please."

"Right-oh!" Euphemia chirped. *"Ombay fala, inkuthin."*

*"Ombay fala, inkuthin."*

In Cambridge they were going to pick up Bill and Betsy Pepper, the couple who had come Home from Nextdoor on leave and then succumbed to the flu that still lurked around England. Euphemia had explained at great length how the poor Peppers' failure to return on time had made them very unpopular back at Olympus.

Bugger the poor Peppers! Why, oh why, had Alice ever consented to this?

> *"Aiba aiba nopa du, Aiba reeba mona kin.*
> *Hosagil!"*

"Now the second verse—"

"Just a minute. Shouldn't I learn this beat you're doing, too?"

"Oh, you'll pick that up. Miss Pimm will drum for us. Won't you, Miss Pimm?"

The car tilted into a corner and slewed sideways before accelerating again into the rushing, silver-streaked darkness. Alice's half-formed scream failed as she realized she was still alive.

"Do you *have* to go so fast?"

"Yes, I do!" Miss Pimm said loudly. "We have a long way to go. We must complete our mission, and I must be gone, before the locals wake up and notice odd things going on."

*Odd* things? Neolithic shamanism in this day and age? In a *church?*

"The vicar will be celebrating matins," Miss Pimm added, as if that excused everything.

"St. Gall's is still in use," Euphemia said cheerfully. "The center of the node is right in front of the altar, but there are some standing stones in the churchyard. It's been a holy place for thousands of—"

"I know. I've been there."

"Oh, yes. You said."

Alice had witnessed Edward and Julian go into that church. To the best of her knowledge, they had never come out. It was in the Cotswolds, somewhere. That was right across England: Cambridge, then probably through Northampton, and Oxford. Wiltshire? It was going to take hours.

"Let me get this straight. We dance and chant, and then the magic comes and we find ourselves on Nextdoor? Just like that?"

"Just like that. One second you're in St. Gall's, and the next you're on the node at Olympus. On a lawn with a hedge round it."

In Colney Hatch with a straitjacket on, more likely.

"There will be four of us," Euphemia continued blithely. "It's much easier with a group. Coming over I was all alone and it was frightfully hard. It took me at least twenty minutes before I could catch the mood. I was absolutely fagged out, all that dancing. . . . Now the second verse—"

"Just a minute! If Miss Pimm's doing the drumming, what's to stop her passing over with the rest of us?"

"It's happened," Miss Pimm bellowed from the front. "The wrong person going through, I mean." She swerved to avoid a suicidal lone cyclist fighting his way against the wind and rain with no light on his bicycle. "But I shall stay well back from the center of the node, and I shan't be singing or dancing."

Pagan orgies in a respectable rural Anglican church?

"Besides," Euphemia added, and the tremor of amusement in her voice should have been a warning of what was coming, "Miss Pimm will have her clothes on."

"What? You mean we have to . . . in this weather?"

"Oh, yes. So let's learn our chant, shall we, so that everything goes off smoothly and quickly and we don't have to hang around too long."

"No clothes at all?"

"Not a stitch. But it will be almost dark. Don't worry about Bill. He's done this lots of times and seen everything there is to see. First verse again. . . ."

# 20

The night went on forever, to the limits of unreality and fatigue and then beyond, into total madness. As morning neared, Alice found herself cavorting around with three other lunatics before the altar of a respectable little country church, an ancient, down-at-the-heels conventional place of worship like a thousand others scattered over the face of England. The first rays of dawn showed the tints of stained glass in the eastern windows, the glimmer of a sputtering acetylene lantern cast wild shadows over oak and flagstone and memorial tablets.

And this was only the dress rehearsal! She mumbled the gibberish as well as she could, she copied the others' movements as the four of them leaped and gestured and gyrated, dancing around in a circle between the pulpit and the front row of pews. Miss Pimm sat farther back, thumping intricate rhythms on a drum. No one else seemed to recognize the insanity of what they were doing. None of them even seemed to see that it was rank sacrilege.

Alice never thought of herself as religious. What her true parents had believed, she could not remember. Uncle Cam and Aunt Rona had been upright, moral people, but not members of any formal sect. They had taught her that deeds mattered more than words, that love and duty counted more than ritual or any specific creed. Like Edward, she had been repelled by the overt fire-and-brimstone dogmas preached at them by their Uncle Roland. She had entered a church only once in many years, and that had been only because Terry had wanted a Christian marriage. She had mourned him without clerical assistance.

Nevertheless, St. Gall's was a church, a place of worship sanctified by the devotions of humble, honest people over many centuries. To profane it with this mumbo jumbo was not merely disrespectful, it was horribly wrong. The sense of wrongness grew steadily stronger until she felt she could endure it no more. She was just about to stop dancing and say so, when Miss Pimm ended her tattoo.

"That will do. We'll try it now."

Alice said, "But . . ." and then her courage failed her. She stifled her protest and followed the others back to the vestry, picking her way along the dark nave by the light of the lamp Euphemia was carrying. She waited at the door with the other women while Bill Pepper went inside. She averted her eyes when he emerged without his clothes. She kept telling herself that she had had enough, that she was not going to play this stupid game any longer, and yet she entered with Euphemia and Betsy—who still had a racking cough and certainly ought not to be exposing herself to the icy cold in this unheated church on a rainy February night. Cursing herself for a dupe, a gullible maniac, Alice undressed with them and hurried back to the altar when they did, shivering at the touch of dank air on her skin and the cold stones underfoot. If it had been wrong before, how much worse it must be now!

"Ready?" Miss Pimm boomed, and began the beat without waiting for a reply.

"*Ombay fala, inkuthin . . .*"

Jump, twist, wave arms.

"*Indu maka, sasa du . . .*"

Mr. Pepper was a tall, hollow-chested man, but he had an astonishingly loud bass voice. Supposing some early riser happened to be passing the church and saw the light of the lantern flickering through the stained-glass windows or heard the drumming and all this gibberish? Next thing anyone knew, the police would be at the door. The gutter press would shriek about satanic orgies. Bare limbs and torsos writhed like pale ghosts in the darkness. It was wrong! It was sacrilege. It was obscene.

With no warning, the gloom split, as if the fabric of reality had ripped. A brilliant jagged rent opened overhead, too bright to look upon. It spread instantly, down beside the pulpit, across the floor, dividing the world in two halves. The ground vanished below Alice's feet and she fell through into hot daylight, rolled on grass. A wrench of anguish twisted through her. She screamed and heard others screaming also. Brightness blinded her. Pain, despair . . . Then someone enveloped her in a blanket and hugged her tight, lying beside her, clasping her.

"It will be all right, *entyika,*" said a gruff female voice in her ear. "I will hold you and it will pass in a minute."

# V

Where are the fiends? Where are the worshippers of the fiends? Where is the place
whereon the fiends rush together? What is the
place whereon the troops of the fiends come
rushing along?

THE ZEND-AVESTA: VENDÎDÂD, FARGARD VII, 8

# *21*

Dosh had not visited Rinoovale since his childhood. Braced against the wind on a vantage where Lampass road emerged in Rinooslope, he stared down at the flats with disgust, seeing it as even bleaker than he remembered—a small, drab basin wedged in the teeth of gigantic peaks. Cowering under those terrible white fangs, the land was more gray than green, smallholdings and pastures struggling to survive between the mounds of slag that would eventually engulf them all, tiny isolated hovels spread like pepper grains, plumes of dust drifting from the active mines. He thought he could recall trees, but there were no trees now. The only touches of color were specks of lurid reds or purples on the slimy, poisonous ponds in abandoned workings. At the hazy limit of vision, he thought he could make out a village. That must be the only real settlement in the vale, the self-proclaimed city of Rinoo, where the Niolian military governor ruled.

Of more immediate interest, sunlight was flashing off a troop of bronze-mailed soldiers about half a mile ahead at the base of the long descent. They were lined up across the trail, so the Liberator's entrance was going to be disputed. This would be interesting. Would D'ward loose the Warband on them or talk his way through or turn back? Having no weapons other than his fingernails, Dosh did not intend to get involved, but it would be interesting to watch.

He turned away, blinking back tears and wishing he had more clothes than one threadbare rag. Twice in his life he had gone adventuring with D'ward Liberator, and twice he had ended up poor as beggars' lice. Some people never learn.

To his left, the Warband had come to a halt on the top of a little knoll and formed up around the leader. That seemed to be the warriors' main task—to keep the crowds away from D'ward when he wanted some peace. The rest of the time, he was buried in eager pilgrims, mobbed by them. Dosh had not spoken with him since he had joined the Free. He had just hung back and watched, trying to understand this madness. He sat on the edge of the crowd when D'ward preached, which he did two or three times a day. He was a wonderful speaker, of course. In the old days, Dosh had watched him inspire an army often enough, and he was even better now.

He spoke Joalian like a native, but if anyone addressed a question to him in Niolian, he would reply in that tongue. He was very slick at answering trick questions. He told stories. He uttered homilies, enjoining faith, humility, honesty, chastity, and other absurdities. He disapproved of fun things like lechery, avarice, and gluttony. He quoted the *Filoby* prophesies that he would bring death to Zath, so that there would be no more reapers collecting souls by night. Much of what he said was pure blasphemy, denying the gods, the Pentatheon and all their lesser avatars. He insisted that they were merely mortals with magical powers, sorcerers. That should have provoked his listeners to riot and stone him to death, but so far they hadn't. A surprising number of them seemed to believe him and believe in him.

Dosh couldn't. He knew something of the gods; he did not like all of them and he hated the Youth especially, but he knew enough to fear them. He would love to believe D'ward's claptrap heresy, but he could not. It would be even more wonderful to be able to swallow the Liberator's idealistic moral drivel, but he knew too much of the world, and it just wasn't like that. The world was made up of wolves and sheep, and wolves could not eat grass, no matter who preached to them. He wasn't about to tell D'ward that, though.

And he certainly would not say so to Prat'han or the other henchmen. Dosh's only contact with the Sonalby Warband had been when he dropped in at their campfires to eat. They fed him willingly, kidded him a little, and in general were friendly enough. They had concealed him from the troopers. They even seemed prepared to trust him, but he was not at all sure he trusted them. Their fanatical faith in the Liberator proved that they were all crazy, and a prudent man did not consort with armed lunatics.

From habit, Dosh had kept himself to himself. He had been a loner all his life, a man of unnumbered lovers and no friends. Now Prat'han Potter was heading his way, striding purposefully over the grass, tall and dangerous with his spear and shield. Evidently he had been sent to summon Dosh. Dosh waited for trouble to arrive in its own good time.

Behind them, the ass end of the procession was still trickling down the trail from the pass—the runts, the women with babies, the old men on canes, the cripples and invalids. The Free had increased in Nosokvale; there must be half a thousand people following the Liberator now. Most of them had no food and no money. Many of them were wearing no more than Dosh was. They were going to pour into barren little Rinoovale like a plague of locusts if the soldiers let them. If the soldiers turned them back, they would starve or freeze in the hills. Winter was coming.

"Greetings, Brother Dosh!" Prat'han boomed. It was still surprising to see a Nagian warrior without face paint.

"Greetings to you, Troopleader."

"I am no troopleader. The Liberator is our leader. I am but one of the Free, like you." The big man grounded his shield and surveyed the vale. "You been here before?"

"Long ago."

"What place is that?" The spear pointed.

"Rinoo."

"That's the city?" Prat'han snorted. "That? Who owns the temple there?"

"There isn't one that I know of. Just a few shrines. There's a temple a few miles east of Rinoo, though, to Gunuu. He's god of courage, an avatar of the Youth."

"No gods!" Prat'han snapped menacingly. "Enchanters. Imposters, all of them!"

"If you say so."

"D'ward says so! That's good enough for me, and for you now."

One of Dosh's personal rules was not to argue with armed young men more than three feet tall, and Prat'han was twice that. "Sure. The main, er, enchanter's foundation in Rinoovale is the convent of Irepit."

Prat'han sneered. "And what does she claim to be?"

"Goddess of repentance. You've heard of the Daughters of Irepit?"

"No. And I do not wish to. The Liberator wants you."

Obviously Dosh had no choice. They began to walk back up the knoll.

"What's the matter with this land?" his companion demanded. "It looks like a well-used feedlot."

"It is overblessed with mineral wealth. Dig anywhere and you turn up nuggets of gold and other metals, even jewels."

"A waste of good grazing."

"Niolians don't think so. They strip it down to the water table, so nothing ever grows again. Why don't you ask D'ward these questions? He's been here more recently than I have."

The warrior glanced down at Dosh suspiciously. "How do you know?"

"Well, I assume he has."

Prat'han thought about that and frowned. "Don't *assume* about the Liberator." End of conversation.

To anyone with less muscle and more brain than an ox, it was obvious that D'ward knew exactly where he was going, in precise detail. He chose the damnedest places to make camp, but he set off every morning straight to the next. Some days he would walk his ragged congregation to exhaustion and others he would hardly go any distance at all. If Dosh were a gambling man—and he must assume that now he wasn't, at least not at the moment—he would bet everything he owned—which was currently nothing, of course—that D'ward had walked out his entire route from Joalvale to Tharg in advance, using the *Filoby Testament* as a guidebook.

When Dosh had first met him, he had known almost none of the prophecies. He must know them all by now. He must know the one that said, *In Nosokslope they shall come to D'ward in their hundreds, even the Betrayer.* Dosh himself had joined the Free in Nosokslope.

He reached the outskirts of the crowd behind Prat'han and began to pick his way through. Whenever D'ward stopped moving, a halo of followers would gather on the grass around him, sitting patiently, their numbers steadily growing as the stragglers arrived and settled at the edges. The Warband stood guard in the center, clustered around D'ward, who was sitting on a rock, talking as always. His gray robe flapped and billowed in the wind, he had his cowl up, and yet he seemed oddly hunched, as if he felt the chill more than the men around him, who were all nearly naked.

Seeing Dosh slipping in between the shields, he jumped up with a smile. He grabbed Dosh's shoulder in a Nagian greeting.

"Welcome! How are you feeling?"

"Cold and hungry and poor."

D'ward grinned, as if truly pleased to see him. "But not hunted? You've been lying low! But we're not in Joaldom anymore. If you want to slide over the horizon, now's your chance."

Dosh glanced at the frowning faces of the Warband all around him. Even the smallest of them was at least a hand taller than he was. "With no clothes and no money? You think I'm crazy?"

"I think you're just fine. Tielan? Give him the bag."

As if he had been expecting the order, Tielan Trader stepped forward, pulling a strap over his head. He handed Dosh a leather satchel—small, well worn, and so unexpectedly heavy that Dosh almost dropped it. He looked up at the Liberator in bewilderment.

"From now on," D'ward said, "you hold our purse."

"What do you mean? This is money?"

D'ward nodded, seeming amused. "That's the war chest of the Free. It's everything we've got. You can look after it for us."

"How do you know I won't vanish with it?"

"I don't, but I'm willing to gamble." His blue eyes sparkled brighter than the sky. "Most of it was yours originally, you know. We pass the hat after the sermons, and just about every coin you gave away came back eventually."

Why did he have to say so? Oh, temptation!

"And what do I do with it?" The warrior animals were scowling at him because he was talking back to their precious Liberator.

D'ward shrugged. "Keep it safe."

"Set a thief to catch a thief?"

"Of course. Everyone has his own talents, Dosh. You can count, which some people can't. You still got those great legs you had once?"

Dosh had done no real running since those far-off days when he had been D'ward's messenger; his feet were soft and already blistered, but he wasn't going to say so in front of the louts. "Sure."

D'ward smiled as if he saw through that lie. "Then when we get down to Rinooflat, I want you to run on ahead to Rinoo. Tonight we'll camp at the burial ground at Thothby—"

"Burial ground? Why camp in a burial ground?"

The answer was a flicker of authority from those sky-blue eyes. Dosh's spine chilled all the way down. "Sorry," he muttered.

"All right." The Liberator scanned the vagabond army sitting patiently around the knoll. "How many are there now, do you suppose?"

"Five or six hundred. At least."

"Well, it's your job to feed them tonight. Buy livestock, buy grain, buy firewood— arrange for it all to be delivered to Thothby. There's no village left, but they'll know where it was. All right?"

Dosh nodded. He could run to Rinoo, certainly. Then perhaps just keep on running? He would decide when he got there. "You still have to get us down to Rinooflat safely."

"Ah!" D'ward said, and pushed back his cowl so he could scratch his head. "I was just explaining when you got here. There isn't going to be any trouble. I had a safe-

conduct for Joalvale and Nosokvale. I've got another for Rinoovale. Once we get to
Niolvale, things may get sticky." He glanced around at the listening warriors. "That's
when you sharpen your spears."

" 'bout time!" said Gopaenum and the others laughed nervily. Did they know verse
663, the one about young men's bones?

"Safe-conduct from whom?" Dosh demanded.

D'ward hesitated and then replied to the group, not just to Dosh. "The authorities.
Not all the enchanters are totally bad. Remember that always—nobody is totally bad!
Nobody is totally good, either, of course. Some of the enchanters are on our side. A
few of them are helping us." He looked around the Warband to locate Prat'han, who
was the senior, even if he would not admit it. "Remember, no bloodshed!" His eyes
glinted mischievously. "But perhaps we can start to stir up a little trouble now."

Prat'han chuckled throatily. "What sort of trouble, Liberator?"

D'ward scratched his bushy black locks again. "Only the Thargians keep slaves, right?
Do any of you know who those miners are down there?"

Silence. These Sonalby rustics knew of nothing outside Nagvale.

"Convicts," Dosh said.

D'ward turned a sky-blue smile on him. "And what does it take to become a convict
in Niolland?"

"Forgetting to bow when the queen's name is mentioned? Life sentence in the mines!
Having a pretty wife that some official fancies? Ten years for that, I expect."

"Probably. With time off for good behavior on her part? Understand, lads? Rinooland
is nothing but a Niolian penal colony. Now, if a multitude of pilgrims like this just
happened to swarm right through one or two of those pits on their way by, then I don't
think the jailers would be able to do very much about it, do you? And there might not
be any miners left when we'd gone by, right?"

The oafs all guffawed and thumped their spears against their shields.

D'ward grinned at them. "But, please, no bloodshed! Stun them if you must. No
more than that. Recruit them if you can. They'll be in deep trouble with their superiors
after we've gone, so they may be open to reason. . . . I think we've had a long enough
break. Let's move on. I'd better stay in front this time."

At that he strode forward and the Warband opened to let him through. The massed
pilgrims began scrambling to their feet, some of them running forward to accost the
Liberator and ask him questions. D'ward waved them away, the warriors blocked them,
and soon most of them had been left behind. Very conscious of the weight of the money
bag on his shoulder, Dosh found himself hurrying along at D'ward's side, while the
armed band escorted them both. That might not be a good place to be when they
reached the checkpoint at the bottom of the hill, but it would do for now.

He asked the question. "What do you really want of me?"

The Liberator looked down at him for a moment in silence, his stare strangely
frightening.

"Bagman?" Dosh demanded. "Runner, like before? I'm not a kid any longer,
D'ward."

"More than those, Dosh. I think you have a really important part to play in this." Suddenly D'ward smiled, and it was as if the heavens had opened. "Just be a friend, if you want. You're under no compulsion to stay, but I do hope you will."

Dosh looked away to break the spell. Time had not blunted his feelings toward the Liberator. D'ward could still melt the flesh off his bones with that smile. *Idiot! He didn't want you even before you started going bald.*

"What happens when you get to Niolvale itself?" Dosh was surprised to realize how little he doubted that the Free *would* get to Niolvale, despite that army ahead blocking their path.

For a moment D'ward stalked on down the track, staring straight ahead and not replying. His bony features seemed oddly shadowed. He still had his cowl back, and the sun glinted on his black hair like starlight. "That's when we start playing the Great Game with real money."

"Verse six sixty-three says that in Niolvale the bones of young—"

"I know that, Dosh. I just hope it won't be too many young men. The trouble will start in Niolvale, though. There must be visitors on their way to see me by now. The kings and politicians are starting to take notice. More than all that, Niolland is Visek's turf. Visek can nip me in the bud if he wants."

Visek the Parent, Father and Mother of Gods, greatest in the Pentatheon, patron deity of Niolvale, god of destiny, god of prophecy . . . The Liberator was not going to bring death to Death if Holy Visek did not want him to.

"So you'll go and pray to Visek?"

"I may go and have a chat with Visek. Not quite the same."

"But you do cooperate with the gods when you want to?"

"They're not gods, Dosh. Just enchanters, sorcerers, magicians."

"Tion? Or Prylis? He cured my scars!"

"That doesn't make him a god. He's at least a thousand years old, I agree, but he's human. They all are. They can die, as Zath will die when I kill him. They will all die one day. They were born of woman, every one of them—wet and bloody and screaming, just like us. One day they will die, whimpering and frightened, just like us."

"They are gods!"

D'ward shook his head sadly. "No, they're not. They want you to think they're gods, because that gives them power. When you believe they are gods, you expect them to judge you. Accept that they're mortals and you can judge them. Some things they say are true always. Some aren't true, ever. And some were true once and now aren't true anymore. Watch out for those. Those are the tricky ones."

It took Dosh some time to think through the words and discover that they didn't mean anything much. "Forget Visek. What about Elvanife?"

"Who? Oh, the queen?"

"Yes, the queen of Niolia! She's just a kid. Too young, and female."

D'ward shot a puzzled glance down at him. "Why does that matter, Dosh?" Sometimes he seemed incredibly naive.

"It matters because she's not safe on her throne! The nobles are conspiring against her. Haven't you heard? She's been throwing her weight around, showing how tough she is, stamping out dissent. You're going to present her with a peasant revolt! She'll have no choice but to jump on you."

D'ward shrugged. "She'll do what the priests tell her, I hope, and the priests will tell her what Visek tells them to tell her."

Maybe, but then Dosh realized that they were almost at the base of the hill and there was someone else stalking along on D'ward's other side. He hadn't seen where she had come from. She was tall, shrouded in a long blue nun's habit, her face concealed by a voluminous blue hat whose flaps tied under her chin. At her side dangled a long, shiny naked sword, so she must be a nun from the convent he had mentioned to Prat'han, one of the Daughters of Irepit. They had a very sinister reputation. D'ward must know she was there, yet he was ignoring her.

They had almost reached the roadblock. Dosh tried to ease back, only to discover there were spears and shields close behind him. He was trapped out in front, where he had vowed not to be at this point. The Warband was at his heels, but there were only twenty of them, whereas the force facing him was at least a hundred shiny bastards, all glittering with bronze, their shields blocking the way like a wall. Each man was set with one foot forward, javelin poised to throw. Their leader waited a couple of paces in front of them, sword drawn.

Niolia was not engaged in any war at the moment, so far as Dosh had heard, and only when engaged in active hostilities would a ruler muster the peasants. This must be a sizable portion of Elvanife's permanent army, the Royal Niolian Guard.

"Halt in the name of the queen!"

D'ward halted. Everyone halted. Dosh pressed his knees together to steady them and glanced around to plan his escape. There was no cover anywhere. Good legs or not, if he took off over that stony plain, he was going to have an ash shaft sticking out of his back in seconds. The pilgrims, he noted, were well behind the Warband now, waiting to see what would happen. If it came to bloodshed, they weren't going to throw any stones to help their precious prophet.

D'ward drew a deep breath and then out-bellowed the captain. "Stand aside! I am the Liberator."

"Turn around and liberate elsewhere! You and your followers are forbidden entry to Nioldom, on pain of death."

"It is prophesied that I shall go to Tharg and bring death to Death."

"Go another way, then. I shall count to three. *One!*"

In the terrible silence, Dosh could feel the sweat running down his ribs. D'ward seemed to have run out of bright ideas. The way the wind played with his curls was very appealing, but it wasn't going to be enough to get him past the Niolian military.

"*Two!*"

Dosh prepared to throw himself flat.

The nun laughed. "Well? Do you want my help after all?"

D'ward sighed. "Yes please, ma'am."

She took a step forward. She had her sword in her hand and she raised it, pointing it straight at the captain. Dosh didn't think he could have held such a weight steady, but the point was not wavering. In a voice as strong as the men's she cried, "Repent!"

It was if the soldier had not noticed her until then. He started violently and dropped his sword. It fell on the stones with a clang. His lips moved, but no sound emerged. Behind him, the bristling ranks of javelins wavered, their blades glittering like shards of ice in the sunlight.

"Repent!" she cried again. "You dare oppose the Liberator who is prophesied? Rather you should join his ranks and march in his service. Repent, I say! Throw down your arms or die on them. Stand aside!"

The captain spun around and screamed orders. The Royal Niolian Guard dissolved in panic. In seconds the road was clear, while on either hand men were tearing off their armor and hurling it down on the weapons that now littered the ground.

"Thank you, ma'am," D'ward said quietly.

She glanced at him. Dosh had a brief view of a face both surprisingly youthful and yet ageless, beautiful but stern—sad, lovely, unforgettable. "I keep my word. Go with my blessing, Liberator."

He nodded, then raised his arms in benediction, hiding the nun from Dosh's view. He called out to the soldiers over the clatter of metal and the moans of fear.

"Brothers! We are the Free, for we go to bring death to Death. Your repentance has been accepted; you are forgiven. Those who wish to join our pilgrimage are welcome. Leave your weapons, arise, and follow me."

He began to move and at once pebbles rattled under the Warband's horny feet behind him. Dosh was butted forward by a shield, so that he had no choice but to follow. Smiling, D'ward marched along the road, his arms outstretched to the Niolian military that knelt on both verges. A few were still armored, many had stripped almost naked, almost all of them were sobbing with terror, hands reaching out to the Liberator and beseeching his blessing. The blue nun was nowhere to be seen. A horde of excited pilgrims came yelling and jabbering along behind.

Thus did the Liberator enter into Rinoovale and Nioldom.

# 22

Lospass, between Jurgvale and Niolvale, was neither very steep nor very high, one of the easiest passes in the Vales. Sloths, on the other hand, were well named. If they moved faster than mushrooms, it was not by much. Eleal Singer and Piol Poet had been on their journey for several days, and only now were they truly into Niolvale. The air was muggy, scented with a vegetable odor that seemed alien to her. In her childhood, the troupe had rarely visited Niolland. Most years they had returned home to Jurgvale from Jiolvale by way of Fionvale.

Piol had been clever to suggest the sloth and cart. As they rattled out through the city gate of Jurg, Eleal had seen a couple of the Cherry Blossom House bouncers inspecting passersby, but they had not looked twice at her or her malodorous conveyance. She was used to the stench of the sewerberries now, although they had nauseated her for the first couple of days. They certainly deterred everyone else. Other people went by the wagon like birds in flight, no brigand had accosted them to poke through their cargo in search of gold. Niolians used sewerberries to make the patina on their famous black bronzes, Piol said, and only Jurgvale could grow them. No matter. No matter, either, that the travelers were both so saturated with the foul stench that no inn would admit them. They had been blessed with fair weather; they had slept under the stars or under the cart, and they had eaten as well as could be expected when Eleal herself was doing the cooking.

Now they were in Niolland, the sun shone, the road stretched out level before them, winding between little lakes, fording streams. Niolvale had more water than any other vale, Piol said. Men wearing only turbans were harvesting rice from paddy fields. The villages were blobs of white walls and red tiled roofs against the green and silver landscape. It was very idyllic.

But not too helpful.

Eleal awoke from a wonderful daydream of . . . of what? She wasn't sure. Her nights were full of dreams of D'ward, but a strangely changed D'ward—thick and chunky, instead of tall and lean, and wearing a floppy mustache. Lack of sleep seemed to be catching up with her, for the curiously wrong image had started haunting her days too.

A fragment of melody surfaced and then submerged again. . . . The name escaped her.

"Piol?"

"Mm?"

"Do you know a play called *The Poisoned Kiss*?"

The old man blinked at her. "No. Who wrote it?"

"I have no idea. Perhaps there isn't one. I just thought it sounded like a good title. Um . . . Where does one start looking for a Liberator?"

"Don't know. There is only one road, so we may as well stay on it until it forks. Then we ask someone, I suppose."

"Who will let you near them?"

He chuckled toothlessly. "I can stand downwind."

True. She looked around. Niolwall was retreating behind them. To the east it disappeared completely and the bottom of the sky was flat. Niolvale was the largest of all the Vales, rich and prosperous—as was only to be expected of a vale whose patron god was the Parent. There was a village ahead, with a high-spired temple. It must be Joobiskby, and the road would certainly divide there.

After a few minutes, Piol began to cackle softly to himself. She demanded to know what was so funny.

"Remember the time we were playing *The Fall of the House of Kra* in Noshinby? Trong was playing Rathmuurd and he went to draw his sword—"

"No!" Eleal said firmly. "I do not remember that and I certainly do not know who had put the molasses in his scabbard. She must have been a real little horror, though!"

They laughed together. They had been doing this for days—reminiscing about the old times, the good times, the plays, the actors, the places, the crowds, the triumphs, the catastrophes.

After a moment, she said, "Do you remember Uthiam doing *Ironfaib's Polemic*? She won a rose. . . . That was the year I missed the festival, but I shall never forget her in rehearsal. Oh, she was marvelous!"

"That she was," Piol agreed sadly. "Do you know it?"

"Most of it, I expect." Every word!

"Let me hear it."

"Oh, you don't need to suffer through that," Eleal said hastily. She had just remembered that the reason she had missed seeing Uthiam perform at that festival was because she had been away tending D'ward, which was probably why the lines had come to her mind.

"Look!" she said. Two ancient, harmless-seeming peasants were tottering along the road ahead of them, moving even more slowly than the sloth. "Why don't you go and ask them if they've heard any news of the Liberator?" When she thought Piol might argue, she added, "You can easily catch up with the cart again if you run hard."

This was taking too long! She felt an itchy-scratchy urgency to meet D'ward again.

# 23

" ' A jug of wine beneath the bough,' " Julian intoned. " 'A loaf of bread and thou/ Beside me singing in the Wilderness/Oh, Wilderness were paradise enough!' That last rhyme needs *work!* I mean, it *looks* all right—"

Ursula peered across the table skeptically. "You left out the book of verse."

"Would depend what's it's printed on. Might make good bumf."

She laughed. Ursula's laughter had all the innocent gaiety of a child's, quite out of keeping with her normally gruff manner. "You're impossible!"

"I'm extremely easy, as you well know!" He raised his glass and she clinked hers against it. They sipped in mirror image, smiling the contented smiles of lovers.

The sun had set; the red moon, Eltiana, hung amid the wakening stars. Location? The side of a small, unnamed, and apparently uninhabited valley somewhere south of Niolvale. The air was cooling rapidly, but the campsite lay well below the snow line, and the weather had cooperated splendidly. For several days—Julian was deliberately not keeping count—they had ridden their dragons over glaciers, icefields, ridges, plateaux. They had gone up and down vertical cliffs. It had all been thumping good fun. The days had been thumping good fun, and the nights even more so. Spiffing!

This was how to rough it. This was how fieldwork should always be. Just the two of them, face-to-face across the little table, sitting on their folding chairs, eating off china with tableware that was a very good imitation of sterling silver. The wine was chilled. The turkey-shaped thing that T'lin had run down had been expertly fricasseed by the indomitable Dommi. The campfire crackled and blazed cheerfully nearby, its smoke drifting upward in a breeze so gentle that the flames above the candlesticks hardly wavered. Doubtless there would be cheese and coffee in a few minutes, as soon as Dommi finished erecting the tent. T'lin was a few hundred yards off, still polishing his precious dragons.

Meanwhile, a man and the woman he loved, the stars, the jagged peaks, the trees . . . Odd sort of trees, not quite conifers. They looked pinelike at a distance, but their needles were tiny stars and the fragrance they put out smelled more like incense than pine. No matter, they would do.

Wary of tearing their frills, dragons shunned forest, but T'lin had found a convenient avalanche path down from the icy highlands to a meadow beside the little river. Ursula had fretted that the woods might be inhabited by the nasty cat things called jugulars. Julian refused to worry about them, on the grounds that if you had to worry about a jugular, it was already too late.

She looked up and caught him studying her. Her chin was too square to be classically feminine, yet it suited her. She wore her hair shorter than he usually liked to see, but that, too, suited her, and it shone like jewels in the firelight. Her eyes were very large and all womanly mystery. She was more Venus de Milo than Mona Lisa, but beautiful in a way all her own. And she was a herd of tigers at lovemaking. Tigresses?

He thought of Euphemia and wondered for the thousandth time what he'd ever seen in the slut. It wasn't just that she fulked with Carrots—she just wasn't good for anything else. His Omar Khayyam joke would have floated clear over her pretty head, whereas Ursula knew a hawk from a handsaw and probably what act and scene they came from. She understood that John of Gaunt wasn't necessarily very thin. . . .

"Happy?"

He jumped and glanced around. "Ecstatically. Night is my favorite time of day. I'm ready for my coffee now, though."

Dommi was still tightening the tent ropes. He wouldn't be long.

"Perhaps we should have coffee in the lounge?"

Julian frowned at the dark mass of the trees around them. "I think we forgot to pack the lounge. How about the palm court? Or the croquet lawn? I'm sure Dommi brought the hoops and mallets."

"It's the Service makes it possible, love," Ursula said softly.

"Makes what possible?"

"All this. Dragon rides and servants. A touch of civilization in the bush—lady and gentleman on safari. Without the Service and its mana, you and I would be hacking our way through jungle and eating roots and sleeping under bushes."

Wanting to talk business, were we?

"If it wasn't for the Service," he countered, "we wouldn't be here at all, my little turtledove. Would we?"

"But we mustn't let Edward Exeter mess it all up, must we?"

He sighed. The moment was too precious to spoil with reality. He did not want any pikes in his millpond tonight.

"Is that the nub? 'I say, old man, you've got to put a sock in this Liberator prank, you're queering our pitch with the natives!' Is that what we tell him?"

Ursula placed her glass down carefully on the spotless white tablecloth. "Yes, that is part of it for me. We live well, I admit. But we work hard for it. You know how bloody rough the missionary cycle can be at times—rough and dangerous, too. You know how boring it can be, studying the language, learning all those sermons, spouting them. You know what homesickness is. We do good, dammit! We don't get paid in pound notes, but we are entitled to compensation, and I don't feel one damned bit guilty about it. So, yes, that's a consideration for me. Isn't it for you?"

Julian shrugged and evaded the question with a mental image of a toreador and his cape. "I don't think that argument will impress Exeter."

"Which one will?"

"Dunno. I'll decide when we've talked with him and I know how his wheels are turning. Do we have to discuss it now, when I'm halfway through composing a sonnet to your eyelashes?"

"We'll be in Niolvale tomorrow."

"And he may still be in Joalland. Or he may be bloody dead already."

She nodded. Dommi materialized in the firelight like a ghost. At some point during his preparation of dinner, he had contrived to change into his white livery. He removed the plates.

"That was delicious," Ursula murmured, although she kept her eyes on Julian.

"Thank you, *entyika!*"

"Listen," Julian said. "Let's not argue. Let's not even talk about it until we find out more facts. When we've heard Exeter's reasons, then we can see whether or not we agree with them. If we don't, then I'll try to talk him out of the whole business, I promise you." Offhand, he could think of no one less likely to be talked out of anything once he had made up his mind than Edward Exeter, Esquire.

"And if you don't succeed?"

"You're jumping to hypothetical conclusions."

"Answer me." Her voice was soft, but there was a lot of power behind it. All sorts of power.

"Then what I think won't matter, will it?"

"No, it won't."

And what Exeter thought wouldn't matter either. That was a skin-crawly idea—using mana to change a man's mind. Nasty. Not nice. It was more or less what he himself had done to the troopers at Seven Stones, of course, but that had been self-defense. He didn't like to think of Ursula doing it to Edward . . . or to any man, of course. He wondered what it would feel like, and whether the victim would even know it had happened.

Dommi laid out cheese and biscuits and butter, poured coffee. When he left, the silence seemed to remain, hanging over the table like a mist. The night was cooling rapidly.

Julian said, "Darling? What exactly happens in a battle of mana?" He saw her mouth tighten and went on quickly, "I mean, if Exeter does go up against Zath, one-on-one—"

"Then he dies! Zath's been at the business for years. Whatever scheme Exeter may have concocted to gather mana, he can't possibly match what Zath has collected from those thousands of human sacrifices. It would be like you taking on the German army single-handed, armed with a penknife."

"I realize that," Julian said, knowing that Exeter must think otherwise, "but in the general case? Forget Zath. If two strangers have a magical donnybrook, what actually *happens?*"

Ursula drank coffee. Eventually she said, "They almost never do, because it would be a leap in the dark. You can't tell the flyweights from the heavyweights in that league without actually throwing a punch and seeing what comes back. That's why the Five play the Great Game with human chessmen. They never go for one another."

Julian hacked savagely at a piece of cheese. She was being evasive. The Service must know the answer. Prof Rawlinson would have investigated, even if no one else had. The library had been burned when Zath's thugs sacked Olympus, of course; that was frequently offered as an excuse when the new boy asked too many questions.

The stars were coming out in thousands now, but the romantic aura had faded. "So you don't know?"

"No."

"I bet Exeter does."

"What?" Ursula looked startled, surprisingly so.

"He's very chummy with Prylis, the so-called god of knowledge. Didn't you know that?"

She stared hard at Julian while she dabbed invisible crumbs from her lips. "No, I didn't." She was narked at being caught offside.

He felt oddly smug and annoyed with himself because of it. "Read his report on his first two years here—oh, I suppose that got burned? Pity. He told me about it before we came over. He spent two or three days with Prylis. He may very well have gone back there when he left Olympus. I'm sure Exeter knows what a mana battle would be like."

Ursula had her demon-tennis-player look on. "I think I can handle Edward Exeter, no matter what he's been up to these last two years."

"You can certainly handle me all you want," he said happily. "You ready to start now? We ought to let Dommi get on with the dishes."

"You never stop, do you?"

"You want me to?"

She laughed. "No. It's what I like about you."

He jumped up and went around the table to her. "Then let's go, lover!"

# 24

"They are no gods, they are imposters! All that lets them act like gods is that fools worship them. I tell you that they are mere enchanters, fakes, evil people masquerading in the guise of gods . . ."

D'ward was nearing the end of his evening sermon, building to the usual climax where he would promise to bring death to Death and invite his listeners to join the Free and follow him.

Dosh had heard it all before. "Time to take up your stations, sisters and brothers!" His helpers looked around in surprise, some of them seeming to start out of a trance. Then they scrambled to their feet and moved off in pairs.

The Free had come to Niolvale. The sun was setting behind the ragged summits of Niolwall, painting the sky in lurid reds and orange, turning the leafless trees into arabesques of shadow and silhouetting the tall figure of the Liberator. He stood on one dominant rock with a thousand people huddled together on the grass below him, all spellbound. As he so often did, he had chosen a curious place to camp, a boulder-strewn slope. There was a much better site half a mile away, a level meadow alongside a river. Perhaps he had thought the noise of the water would drown out his preaching or that he would be less visible there.

As soon as he finished, Dosh's helpers would start moving through the throng, taking up the collection. Dosh had selected them all with care and always sent them out in pairs to keep watch on each other. He believed that nine tenths of the money the pilgrims contributed was being turned in as it should be. *Set a thief to catch a thief!* Tonight's take should be better than usual, for a large part of the congregation were newcomers, Niolians who had heard of this latter-day legend and wanted to see him with their own eyes.

Yes, the crowd had grown during the day. Just from where he stood, Dosh could tell that it was also becoming more varied. The ragtag poor were still there in droves— the old, the crippled, the penniless, women with too many babies, convicts snatched from the Rinoovale mines—but he could see sturdy, healthy farmers. He could see artisans and merchants from the city, escorting plump, well-dressed wives. Some had come by carriage or on rabbits. Mingled among them, of course, were the weird. Always the weird: the lost, the dreamers, the lonely, the failures, unworldly intellectuals, fanatics. Especially fanatics. At least ten members of the Free claimed to be reformed reapers who had been sent to collect the Liberator's soul for Zath but had changed their minds when they came into his presence. In Dosh's view those were the weirdest of the lot.

Or perhaps the Niolian soldiers were. Of the troop that had so dramatically failed to stop the Free entering Rinoovale, almost half had then enlisted in it themselves. Most of them were more fanatic than anyone, even the Warband. At least the Warband mostly demonstrated its loyalty with actions, not floods of words, while the Niolian deserters went around all day babbling their wonderful new vision of life and the universe to anyone who would listen. They seemed to have a need to justify their change of allegiance to every mortal in the Vales. Or were they just trying to convince themselves?

Most interesting at the moment was a nearby dozen or so men and women wearing the gold earring of the Church of the Undivided. They were taking a risk in flaunting their allegiance here in Niolland, but perhaps they felt safe within this multitude of heretics. Huddled in a circle on the grass, they were arguing in fierce whispers, and Dosh could guess why—the Liberator had his own brand of heresy. His theology was not Undivided orthodoxy. It was still all heresy to Dosh, though. He was D'ward's friend and a senior helper, but he was not a believer, and if D'ward chose to change his dodge and start touting Gramma Oriilee's homemade herbal impotence potion, that would be all the same to Dosh.

"Now you have heard!" the Liberator proclaimed. "You have heard the truth, you have heard the call. Now is the moment when you must decide . . ."

This was the finale. Many of the listeners would hurry home now, but some would adhere. More followers would need more to eat, and that also was Dosh's responsibility. It was a sign of the Liberator's continuing success that Dosh now needed assistants, and the Warband was run off its feet trying to keep so large a throng organized. Prat'han had begun enlisting locals to help with the crowd control. Niolvale was large and heavily populated; the numbers could only continue to grow in the next few days.

Unless the queen intervened. Monarchs did not approve of mass gatherings raised by anyone but themselves. The court in Niol must be hearing tales of invasion and uprising, which it could never tolerate, and D'ward had not only spurned Elvanife's warrant, he had subverted half her army. No official welcoming party had graced the mouth of Thadrilpass this morning as the Liberator led his band into Niolvale. There had been no phalanx of warriors, either. Possibly the military had learned its lesson, but more likely it just needed time to muster larger forces.

*The sharp swords shall drink, spilling blood into the sands. Young men leave their bones where the Liberator has passed.*

Who needed the dread forecasts of the *Filoby Testament* to know that trouble must be brewing? Think of the gods and the priesthood! So far they had ignored this rampant heresy, but he was preaching rank blasphemy not a dozen miles from the temple of Visek, greatest deity of all the Vales.

The sermon ended as the Liberator touched his hands together overhead in the benediction of the Undivided. The crowd sighed like the sound of wind in a distant forest.

Dosh's bagmen moved in. He watched to make sure that they were following the drill D'ward had stipulated—no entreaties, no harassment. Just hold out the bags and keep smiling. If asked, explain that the money goes only to feed the pilgrims. Above all, give thanks for every coin, no matter how small. If offered only rags or scraps of food, accept them as gratefully. Strange man, D'ward!

The Liberator departed, heading for his tent within a group of the Warband. The congregation was rising to its feet, stretching, muttering incredulously at what it had heard. Dosh was about to scramble up on a rock to gain a better view of his collectors, when he saw Prat'han approaching, towering over heads.

He waited.

"What're you grinning at?" he demanded.

"You. You're smiling."

Dosh was disconcerted. "What's unusual about that?"

"Lots. You never used to."

"Well, I'm planning to run off with the loot tonight." He felt himself grin as widely as the big lout. "You think I'm lying?"

"Not seriously." The big man leaned on his shield and glanced around. He lowered his voice. "The Liberator wants you to meet him at the pulpit rock when Trumb rises."

*An odd thrill of surprise.* "Why?"

"He didn't say. Just you, so far as I know. Said to leave the purse with one of us." Prat'han glanced down narrowly at Dosh; his mouth twisted. "I wouldn't get my hopes up too high if I were you."

Dosh pulled back an angry retort as he noted the twinkle in Prat'han's eye and recognized that the mockery held no real intent to hurt. Even stranger, his own face returned the grin. "A man can dream, can't he?"

Prat'han laughed and jabbed a friendly punch at his shoulder, then turned and stalked away. Fornicating porcupines! Where had that big ox learned sympathy for others' problems? Or had Prat'han developed a sense of humor? The Liberator had certainly taught him a thing or two.

And Dosh also, perhaps. What did he want with him tonight?

# 25

"Nobody knows what's happened to the Czar and his family," Alice said. "The Bolsheviks have been running a reign of terror since the attempt on Lenin's life last year, so they may well be dead. Britain and France have troops in the north and some in the south too. We're very much afraid that we shall be drawn into the civil war in earnest."

Mr. Rutherford said, "Good God!" loudly. He was usually loud, a heavyset young man with the bemused air of a bull that genuinely liked china and wasn't sure what he was doing wrong.

All around the table, faces frowned at the terrible tidings from Home. Alice felt as if she had not stopped talking for three days. The newly returned Peppers were probably being subjected to the same intense interrogation, but their knowledge would be scanty compared to hers. The Olympians had an insatiable appetite for news of Home and accounts of the war. Their incredulous reaction to her stories made her appreciate how much the England and Europe they knew had changed.

Realizing that everyone else had finished the soup course, she set to work on hers hurriedly. Yet another dinner party! The faces and the houses varied, but she seemed to repeat the same words every night and all day too, on an endless circuit of dinners and tea parties. When she wasn't being wined, dined, or pickled with what passed for tea here, she was being escorted around the station on sight-seeing strolls, answering interminable questions. A thousand times she had cursed Julian Smedley, who should have brought the Olympians up to date on events prior to his arrival in 1917; but Julian had been unable to talk about the war. He was over his battle fatigue now, she gathered, but every audience wanted her to start at the beginning, 1914, and deliver an intensive history lesson on the worst four years the world had ever known.

She laid down her spoon. Footmen paced forward to remove soup bowls and serve the fish. Euphemia had described Olympus as an imitation outpost of Empire—Alice had not seen Euphemia since the day they arrived—and, yes, Olympus did bear a slight resemblance to Nyagatha, where she had spent most of her childhood, and even more to some of the neighboring stations that she had visited a few times. There were overtones of British India, which she could vaguely remember. The formal evening wear and the innumerable liveried servants were familiar, although the natives were as white as the sahibs.

But there were differences also, not all of which she could quite identify. One was certainly the era. The residents seemed oddly old-fashioned, Edwardian or even Victorian. The women's gowns were historical, the manners stilted. The wealth was over-done, too. Even in India, few Imperial Government officials would live as well as these people did, every one of them. They all seemed about the same age. Scanning the Chases' dining room—"banquet hall" might be a better description—she could see no one she would classify as junior recruits and no middle-aged seniors either. It reminded her of a rugby club dinner that she had been taken to once, before the war.

"Do tell us about these tank things!" demanded Prof Rawlinson from the far end of the table.

Obediently, Alice began to talk about tanks and aeroplanes and poison gas. They were an unsuitable topic for polite dinner conversation, but she had been seated between Foghorn Rutherford and Pinky Pinkney, with Jumbo Watson opposite her. She was beginning to learn who turned knobs and pulled levers in Olympus, and she suspected those three intended to bring up the purpose of her being here: Edward. She did not want to talk about Edward.

If this was a relaxing vacation, it had not achieved its purpose yet. She had been billeted on Iris Barnes, whose husband was off on the missionary circuit somewhere, enlightening the heathens. Iris was pleasant enough, in a prudish sort of way. Her house was extremely comfortable, although the walls were not totally soundproof and the lady entertained gentleman visitors at unconventional hours. No matter—the hospitality could not be faulted, and it was certainly pleasant to have an army of servants eagerly satisfying one's slightest whim. But relax? No, not yet. The crossing had been a gruesome experience of massive disorientation, followed by nausea and muscle cramps. For the first couple of days Alice had hardly been able to stay awake, only to discover that she could not sleep at night. The chronic exhaustion that had burdened her since her bout of flu still oppressed her.

The fish was delicious, a sort of trout. She was queried about food rationing in Britain. Red meat and red wine appeared. The wine had never known Bordeaux, but she had met worse. She was asked about the war in Palestine and the charismatic Colonel Lawrence. Then came the sweet, a berry tart with cream—she certainly should be able to recover the weight she had lost. It must be about time for the U-boats.

No, not U-boats. Even before the footmen stepped back from the table, Mr. Pinkney said, "By the way, Mrs. Pearson, were you informed of the latest news about your cousin?"

"No."

The room fell very still.

"One of our agents arrived tonight. Just before dark. Exeter has left Joalvale by way of Ragpass. That is the story. He is in Nosokvale." Pinky Pinkney was a quiet-spoken, rubbery man, whom Alice had already identified as one of the powers in Olympus. What his title was she did not know, but everyone else seemed to defer to him, even the resonant Foghorn Rutherford, who was official chairman of the committee that ran the Service—and whose tight-lipped expression hinted that this news was news to him too.

She could feel all eyes upon her. "He is in good health?"

"Oh, yes. Apparently. The news is a week or so old, of course. He is collecting quite a following."

Alice decided she did not like Mr. Pinkney, his silky, self-satisfied manner, or his center parting. She did not like his habit of smiling with his eyes closed, nor his bombshell public proclamations. To have passed on news of a missing relative in private would have been better form. If she did not like him, she need not pander to his feelings.

"I never doubted he would."

Pinkney's smile was as polished as the silverware. "Oh?"

"Edward has always chosen his goals carefully and always achieved them."

"But what exactly is his goal this time, mm? This is what we should all like to know. You understand?"

She shrugged. "I know no more than any of you, probably a lot less." She caught her hostess's eye. "This tart is delicious! What sort of fruit is it?"

Mrs. Chase said, "Lobsterberry," in very flat tones and without a smile.

"It tastes much better than it sounds, then!" About to take another mouthful, Alice realized that everyone else was just watching. Pinky had the floor, and they were all waiting for him. He was apparently waiting for her. She put the fragment of pastry in her mouth anyway.

"What we do not understand, Mrs. Pearson," Pinky said, "and what we hope you may be able to explain to us, is why your cousin has declared war upon Zath. The so-called god of death. The self-proclaimed god of death, mm? He would have more luck trying to knock down the Tower of London with a crowbar. What he is attempting is certain suicide."

Appropriately, a small pink butterfly swooped a few times around the nearest candlestick and then plunged into the flame, vanishing in a brief flash. The dinner guests remained silent. They were all very solicitous about Edward's well-being, all of a sudden.

Alice swallowed her mouthful. "As I understand the matter, it was Zath who declared war on him, before he was even born. I don't believe Edward would ever be suicidal, under any circumstances. He might undertake something extremely hazardous if he thought the stakes justified it." She went on the offensive. "Explain to me how this mana affair works. I know that he can collect it from his followers and in large amounts it can act like magic. I know that Zath is supposed to have more of it than anyone else. Suppose Edward does challenge him to a duel? What happens? Do they toss thunderbolts at each other?"

Pinkney frowned, drumming fingertips on the tablecloth. "Perhaps, if he ever got that far. Strangers have certainly slain natives that way. It is, however, extremely rare for one stranger to assault another directly. A duel, as you put it. I'm not sure I can truly answer your question." He hesitated, then turned his head to peer along the table. "Prof? You're our expert in such matters."

The one they called Prof was slender and sandy haired, with a pedantic, donnish manner. Alice had already decided he was no leader, for men would trust his memory and intellect but not his judgment. He gave the impression that he should be peering at the world through very thick glasses, yet none of the Olympians wore glasses. Now he brightened at this invitation to pontificate.

"There isn't much known, just hearsay. I doubt thunderbolts, because it would take as much power to throw one as it would to block one. Both sides would lose mana. . . . I'm assuming that the contestants are rather evenly matched, of course, which would not be the case here. I think it would be more like arm wrestling—they both push until one goes down. Then the loser is at the winner's mercy."

Pinkney aimed an oily, I-told-you-so look at Alice. "One thing Zath does not have is mercy."

No one was eating, all waiting for her reply. They wanted her to say something like, "Oh dear, then I had better go and find Edward and tell him to stop it at once."

She was damned if she would. Whatever he was up to, he would have calculated the odds, weighed the ethics, and made his decision in ice-cold blood. It was none of her business and she would not interfere.

She spoke along the table to Prof Rawlinson. "How fascinating! Then where does the mana go? If I have—Say I have five pounds of mana, and you have seven, and I challenge you to a duel. Then you win, so I have none left and you have two? Pounds of mana, that is."

Prof blinked a few times. "No, I don't think so. I think you have none and I have twelve."

That remark elicited a few surprised glances.

The foghorn boomed out again. "Really? You sure of that, old man?"

"Fairly sure."

"Dammit! So Exeter is not just likely to die, he's liable to make Zath stronger than ever?"

Pinkney also seemed to doubt. "How can you know that?"

Prof shrugged. "I told you it was hearsay. Don't think of it as arm wrestling, then. Think of a tug-of-war. Winner gets the whole rope. It's the Great Game!" he protested, apparently feeling his word was being doubted.

Alice detected an open goal and kicked. "Well, you admit you are not sure. Perhaps Edward knows something you don't?"

That remark provoked an ovation of sniffs and stuffy looks. The diners turned their attention to the lobsterberry tart.

"I think Prof is correct!" The voice came from a striking blond woman sitting across from him. Alice searched for the name. . . . Olga somebody. "Years ago one of Tion's flunkies changed sides, and Tion turned on him. He bragged to me afterward that he had *sucked the bastard dry.*"

This time the disapproval was even more general. Alice wondered why, and tried another broadside. "Tion's the one they call the Youth? I didn't realize that you were on social terms with the opposition."

"Talking of news," Jumbo Watson said loudly, "I suppose you've all heard about poor Doc? He's been arrested, you know. Blighters down in Randorvale raided a meeting at—"

A strange tremor seemed to strike the company. Every head turned to stare at the same corner of the room, like two rows of weathercocks in a sudden gust. Alice shivered as if cold fingers had touched her skin. Then everyone relaxed again in a buzz of comment, no longer at all interested in the Randorvale problem.

"What?" she said, annoyed at being the only one not in on the secret.

Across from her, Jumbo laughed. "Did you feel that, Mrs. Pearson? We are just inside the edge of the node, here. Someone just arrived."

"Arrived? From Home, you mean?"

"Where else? The node is a portal, of course. When people come through, it sort of shimmers. You felt it?"

"The Montgomerys!" Foghorn proclaimed loudly. "They're due back. Who's next on the roster?"

The Olympians were all on tenterhooks over the prospect of leave, like kids waiting their turns for a ride on a pony. Excited conversation had erupted all along the table. The unfortunate business in Randorvale was conveniently forgotten; even Edward was forgotten. Alice was happy to be offstage at last, but she was peeved at Mr. Jumbo Watson for so clumsily cutting off her question to Olga whats-her-name.

Furthermore, she thought the Randorvale incident deserved more serious consideration. She had heard the news the previous day, and no doubt everyone else had, too. One of their own, a Dr. Mainwaring, had been thrown in jail and at least a dozen native converts had been killed or injured. If she were a member of the Service, she would be demanding to know What Steps Were Being Taken. She had, in fact, asked that question several times, without receiving an answer. It was none of her business if she were merely a guest on holiday, but if they were going to drag her willy-nilly into their dealings with Edward, then she had a right to know just what sort of organization the Service was and what sort of protection it could provide for its own people.

In her books, "people" included natives.

She finished her sweet, dabbed her lips with a napkin, and waited until she could catch Jumbo's eye.

Edward had mentioned Jumbo Watson more than once. Charming, he had said, good company, a friend of Uncle Cam's many years ago, but possibly a traitor. Yes, he was charming. He was the only person Alice had yet met in Olympus who fitted that description. She enjoyed his humor. She could imagine being friends with Jumbo Watson, were she quite certain that he had cleared himself of the taint of treason, and she would trust nobody's word on that but Edward's.

He finished what he was saying to Hannah Pinkney and saw Alice looking at him.

"Tell me about Randorvale," she said. "What are you going to do about Dr. Mainwaring?"

Jumbo's long face seemed to lengthen even more. "Frankly, Mrs. Pearson, we don't know what we can do. We're not His Majesty's agents here, you know. We have no legal authority whatsoever. Quite the reverse, indeed. As far as the law is concerned, we're heretics, and that means we're criminals. We have no legal recourse, and illegal methods do not look promising. Our best bet may be to try to bribe the guards to let Alistair escape. We're going to try that first."

"Soon, I hope?" As soon as she spoke, she realized she was being presumptuous, but Jumbo just smiled.

"We have people on their way there already."

"And what about the natives who were—"

A thunderous crash from the direction of the kitchen sounded like a tray of dishes falling. Several voices screamed. Doors slammed. All heads in the room turned in unison once more.

In through the serving door strode a tall figure, swathed in black, too tall to be a woman. The hem of his robe swept the ground and long sleeves concealed his hands. He stopped and folded his arms. Although he held his head erect, his face was a mere blur within his hood. Yet he seemed to rake the company with invisible eyes.

After a first frozen second, pandemonium broke out. The red-haired servants shrieked and fled. One dived straight through a window, in a shattering smash of glass. Chairs toppled as diners leaped to their feet. Two or three men and at least half the women winked out of existence altogether. Crystal, china, and silverware clattered and danced on the parquet floor. Footsteps and screaming died away in the distance, leaving silence.

Alice stayed where she was, too astonished to move, the only person still seated.

"Leader?" demanded the newcomer. "Which one of you is leader?"

Foghorn was on the far side of the table, next to Alice. His burly face was ashen, but he lifted a fallen candlestick and set it on its base before it could start a fire.

"I am the current chairman, sir. Rutherford, Bernard Rutherford, at your service. I don't believe we have been introduced?"

"I am Zath," said the intruder harshly.

Hannah Pinkney slumped in a faint. Jumbo caught her with a remarkable display of reflexes and strength; he lowered her into a chair as if she weighed no more than a blanket.

"Good evening, Your Excellency," Foghorn said in unusually quiet tones for him. "Since you are here, will you take a glass of wine?"

"No."

Rutherford resumed his seat, and at once the others copied him, finding chairs still upright if they had knocked over their own. He leaned back and studied the dread figure. "Then pray state your business."

Still the face showed as only a pale smudge, the eyes as darker patches, and yet the creature radiated contempt. "I came to tell you to call off your dog or pay the penalty. I hold Olympus ransom for his behavior, and every soul in it."

"My dog? Would I be correct in assuming that you refer to Mr. Edward Exeter, commonly known as the Liberator?"

Beautiful! Loud and even obnoxious Rutherford might be in normal times, but he was hitting straight sixes now. Alice felt an insane desire to clap.

"Yes, you would!" Zath snarled. "Stop him any way you like, but stop him, or I shall blast this valley to embers."

Foghorn smothered a yawn. "I am frightfully afraid you have been misinformed, Excellency. Edward Exeter is none of ours. Not one of us has seen him in years, as I am sure your spies have reported. He is a free agent. Pray address your complaints to him in person."

"Then I may as well slay the lot of you now?"

Foghorn shrugged. His color was returning. "I am sure you can—but be warned that this is a node, sir, and every one of us will die believing we do so for Edward Exeter's cause. You wish to make us martyrs?"

Silence—as if that irrelevancy had somehow been a threat.

The god of death growled deep in his throat. "You have been warned. Heed my words!"

He wavered like a pillar of black smoke and wasn't there anymore. Alice felt the icy touch of the portal on her skin. For a moment the tension held as minds adjusted to this miraculous release, then everyone seemed to breathe at the same moment.

"Very nicely done, old man," Jumbo said.

"Bloody good show!" Pinkney agreed. He rose and hurried around to his wife, although some of the ladies had already reached her. "You wouldn't have a drop of brandy handy, would you, Larry?"

Their host opened his mouth and bellowed, "Tramline!"

Alice wondered why she had not felt more frightened. She could not recall being frightened, although she was a little shaky now. Had the whole charade seemed too unreal, or had she just gone into shock?

"Unmitigated bounder!" Foghorn said. His face was bright red now. "What do you make of that, Prof? Prof?"

Rawlinson was no longer present.

The butler swept in, his features as white as his starched shirt front, and his coppery hair askew. He bore a silver tray with a decanter and a dozen glasses, which rattled as he set it down.

"Good man, Tramline!" Chase said heartily. "We could all do with a snifter, I think. Anyone hurt backstage?"

"A few cuts, *tyika*. Nothing serious."

"Issue a noggin to all hands, then. Splice the main brace, what? I'll talk to you about a bonus for the staff in the morning."

Amid the general hubbub that now ensued, Alice registered Jumbo gazing quizzically at her. His eyes twinkled.

"Apart from that, Mrs. Pearson, how are you enjoying your holiday?"

She had been through the Great War; she would not let these bush babies outdo her in upper-lip stiffness. "It's interesting, Mr. Watson."

"Isn't it, though?" He reached over to the tray where Tramline was pouring brandy and passed Alice a glass with conspiratorial glee.

Alice laid it down carefully, hoping her hands were not jiggling too noticeably. She waited until Jumbo had obtained one for himself and then offered hers to clink. They smiled and sipped in unison.

Other people were chattering loudly, inspecting damage, picking up debris, gulping brandy. She and Jumbo sat opposite each other, ignoring it all.

"You probably didn't register it," he said, "but that little episode just vindicated Prof Rawlinson beautifully."

"Explain."

He smiled wryly. "When that blighter charged in here, we all thought it was a reaper. Most of us have managed to collect a little mana, as I expect you know. Half of us used the trapdoor—teleporting out, which is not too difficult when you're on a node, like this. The rest of us tried to clobber the bugger, if you'll pardon my Thargian."

She took another drink of brandy, feeling its warmth tingling in her mouth and down her throat. "And?"

He glanced around. "Don't know about the others, but mine just vanished. My power, I mean—it disappeared. That's when I knew we had more than a reaper to deal with. It felt as if Zath swallowed it, just as Prof said would happen. Interesting!"

"I hadn't realized that Zath was a fellow countryman. I find that rather disappointing."

"Why do you think that?" Jumbo drained his glass and somehow contrived to shake his head at the same time. "Oh, the language? Don't think he's one of us. Certainly hope not! He wasn't speaking English. He was speaking in tongues, glossolalia. It's quite a minor use of mana, making everyone think he's hearing his own language. Acts, Chapter 2, if I remember correctly. I've done it myself once or twice. But what are we to make of this curious event, Mrs. Pearson?" He quirked an eyebrow.

"I can't believe the Service will capitulate before the crude threats of an obvious bully."

"Not by a long chalk! Zath just made enemies out of allies, had he only known. More than that, Mrs. Pearson, wouldn't you say our deathly friend has got the wind up?" He narrowed his eyes in a smile that hinted at real excitement bubbling underneath.

"I received the distinct impression," Alice said solemnly, "that Edward scares the shite out of him—if you'll pardon my Joalian."

The rest of the room was still ignoring them. Foghorn was in full spate, drowning out two other men and the Olga woman in a ferocious argument. The Pinkneys had gone home, others had left in search of missing partners. Newcomers were pouring in, men in tails, men in dressing gowns, some carrying swords, all demanding to know what was going on, by Jove or by George. The servants had almost restored order, except for the litter on the table between Alice and Jumbo, which they had refrained from touching yet.

"What do you make of it, Mr. Watson?"

"I want to know what Exeter is up to that could so alarm his opponent. Obviously you were right. Zath doesn't see him as the pushover we all did." Jumbo fell silent, unconsciously rubbing his prominent nose. Was he wondering if he had been wrong all along about the *Filoby Testament*? What did it take to change a man's mind after thirty years? "Captain Smedley thought Exeter might have a trick or two up his sleeve," he muttered, more to himself than to her.

"So you're going to go and visit Edward."

He looked up with a gleam of challenge in his eye. "He should be informed of what happened here tonight. There are two dragons in the compound and the moon is bright."

"Only two?"

Jumbo pushed himself to his feet. "Only two. I'm going to change, pack a bag, and leave. No signed orders, no arguments, no good-byes."

No conditions, no questions, only challenge. She should have expected this from Jumbo. If he was a traitor . . . if Edward believed that Jumbo was a traitor, then he would not believe the message he brought. If he was not a traitor, then there was no danger. To her astonishment—perhaps it was the brandy—Alice stood up also. "Sounds like an excellent plan. Lead on, my dear Watson."

# 26

For some time, Dosh had been leaning against the boulder, watching great Trumb rise over the watery lands of Niolflat and wondering if he would eclipse before dawn. He had been studying the stellar twinkle of the pilgrims' fires in the meadow and wondering how many nubile maidens and lithe youths there were down there and how much longer he could maintain this unfamiliar chastity he had undertaken. He had been wondering why he did not have the sense to vamoose clean out of this peripatetic prayer meeting before it hatched into full-scale bloodbath and disaster.

"Dosh?" said a whisper, and he jumped like a cricket.

He had not heard anyone approaching. It was D'ward, of course, but he had discarded his priestly robe and wore nothing but a loincloth. His limbs and chest gleamed very pale in the lurid green light. D'ward in disguise must mean serious trouble. Had he decided to vamoose also, while the going was good?

"D'wa—Liberator?"

"How're your legs tonight?"

"Beautiful as ever."

A chuckle. "That was not what I meant, you scoundrel. Can you run as far as Niol and back before dawn?"

*Once I could have done.* "I can try."

"Then let's go!" D'ward turned and began loping down the hill.

That was tricky, stony going, but when they found the trail Dosh was able to move to D'ward's side. He was setting a mean pace, if he truly planned to keep it up all night.

"I didn't know you were a runner too."

"I may have to cheat a bit."

What did that mean? Dosh added another question to his already large collection, but before he could ask any of them, D'ward said, "This may be dangerous."

"I sort of thought it might be. Who're we going to call on?"

"Visek."

"Great gods!"

"No, they're not."

They jogged on for a mile or so while Dosh rolled this astonishing development around in his mind and wondered why he had not already turned on his heel and taken off in the opposite direction. Now he knew why the Liberator had not brought his bodyguards—the Warband could do nothing against the Parent. But dangerous? That was an understatement of enormous proportions. "Suicidal" would be more apt. The least the Liberator could hope for was to have his tongue cut out for blasphemy; his accomplice would be lucky to get off with a life sentence in the mines.

"This may be a turning point," D'ward said.

"Or an ending point!"

"Certainly. But it should be interesting. I thought you'd be interested. I'd appreciate your company, but turn back if you want to."

They kept on running. The farms they passed were dark. There was no one else on the road. Trumb lit the world with unworldly light and flashed off ponds, canals, and ditches, while the red moon was just setting at their backs. Niolvale nights had a heavy scent of damp vegetation that was all their own, very distinctive.

Dosh found his second wind. For once he had D'ward to himself and might get some answers. "According to the *Testament,* the Liberator was to arrive in this world five years ago and be tended by someone called Eleal—aided by a Daughter of Irepit."

"It happened."

"So you knew there was one god—enchanter—who was on your side?"

D'ward chuckled. "Go to the top of the class. No, you've always been top of that class. You're right. When I decided to stop fighting the prophecies and become the Liberator, I first went back to Thargvale, to call on our old friend Prylis again. He helped me shape my plans. Then I came north to Rinoovale and Irepit. She gave me her support. She sent me to Joal, to see her boss."

"You mean the Maiden?"

"Of course. Astina was not quite as supportive—she's the weakest of the Five at the moment, and nervous. But she did promise to deal with any reapers Zath might throw at me in Joalvale."

That explained a lot. Dosh jogged on, hearing only their breathing, the slap of their feet on the dirt, and distant nightingales. There were no clouds, and few stars could compete with Trumb when he was near the full.

"So those churn-brains who claim to be former reapers—"

"Don't mock them! Pity them. Astina de-spelled them—they're genuine. They have terrible, terrible memories to live with."

Their problem, Dosh thought, not his. "That was Joalvale. How about Nosokvale?"

"There too. Astina promised to keep me breathing in all Joaldom. Irepit did the same in Rinoovale. They gave me time to get the boat launched."

"And here in Niolvale?"

"Here I'm on my own. Remember I warned you we'd be playing with real money here? If you see any black shadows moving, speak up promptly."

Dosh felt the sweat freeze on his skin. He almost did turn back then.

"Can probably handle one"—D'ward panted—"or even two."

"No one can stop a reaper!"

"Not true. Killed one once . . . with a rock."

Impossible! but after that, D'ward saved his breath for running and would answer no more questions.

The greatest temple in the Vales stood a short way north of Niol, which was one of the three great cities. The runners approached from the southwest, slowing to a walk when they reached the holy grounds. They had not met a soul the whole way. The night was very still—ominously still, in Dosh's opinion. Trumb's great disk soared almost full through the sky and he would certainly eclipse before the sun rose. An eclipse of the green moon was a sure portent of reapers.

"You've been here?" D'ward was limping, panting, with sweat shining on his skin like silver, but Dosh was in no better shape.

"Course."

"Describe it."

Between puffs, Dosh tried to do justice to the temple of Visek. The innumerable minor buildings—shrines, barracks, libraries, colleges, refectories, dormitories, observatories—sprawled over many acres of tended parkland, interspersed with lakes and pools. There must be three or four thousand priests, priestesses, monks, nuns, and associated characters in residence.

"The main sanctuary is over there?" D'ward pointed a long arm.

"Probably. Yes, I think so. How'd you know that?"

"I can sense the holiness. What's it look like?"

"Columns. A rectangle of them supporting a lintel, but no roof. It's not like that hideous thing of Karzon's in Tharg, though! Visek's is bigger, white marble, breathtaking. One of the wonders of the world."

They trod along a wide avenue flanked by night-scenting shrubbery and tall statuary. To Dosh's nervous gaze, some of those mysterious figures tended to look very much like waiting reapers, although he was trying to assure himself that Zath would not dare seek out sacrifices in this place.

"How about an altar?" D'ward asked. "A holy of holies?"

"Don't know."

"Where's the god, then?"

"They're in the middle."

After a moment, D'ward chuckled. "The Parent—the Father *and* the Mother? You know, Joalian's a very handy sort of language! 'Visek' is abstract, so applied to a person it can mean masculine or feminine, singular or plural."

"That's true in all languages: Sussian, Randorian, Nagian, Thargian. . . ."

"I know some that won't work that way, but carry on. Where are they?"

"In the middle. On the throne at the top of the steps. Back to back. If you come in from this end, you're facing the Father. From the other end, you see the Mother." Dosh pointed. They had come around a curve, bringing the main temple into view, glimmering faintly in the moonlight. Even at this distance, its size was obvious, larger even than he remembered. It made the trees seem tiny.

D'ward muttered, "Mmph!" admiringly. "We'll deal with the Father, then. Or would you rather wait outside?"

Oh, no! Dosh was too conscious of the lurking shadows in the gardens. His skin crawled and he wanted to stay close to the Liberator. He just kept on walking, trying to match his companion's greedy strides.

As they neared the pillars, he made out a twinkle of lamps and vague shapes of people moving around just inside. There would be priests in attendance, even at this time of night, and they would certainly have some means of summoning guards. If they knew that the Vales' most prominent heretic was within the sacred precincts, they would take him faster than a fish snapped gnats. D'ward must know what he was doing, mustn't he? He must have plans or knowledge that he hadn't bothered to pass on, mustn't he?

Dosh worked a painfully dry mouth. "Does he know you're coming?"

"He claims to be the All-Knowing, so I didn't bother to write. We have no choice but to walk in the front door? We can't sneak in through the side pillars?"

"Not unless you're totally crazy. Nothing attracts attention like furtive."

"I'll trust your judgment and experience on that, Brother Dosh."

"And we'll have to make an offering, you know! Why didn't you warn me to bring some money?"

"Because that money was not given for that purpose."

Crazy! "They'll still demand an offering," Dosh muttered. His feet were sore and his legs ached.

Somewhere far off, someone was singing. There was no accompaniment, just a single voice in the night, soaring high in a lonely, wistful anthem, a woman or a boy caroling praise to the greatest of the gods. Or the greatest of the evil enchanters, if you believed D'ward. Dosh didn't—not here, where the sanctity was as palpable as rock. Even the air felt old and holy.

Side by side, the newcomers mounted the steps—long, shallow steps that did not fit a man's stride, with uneven risers so he had to watch where his feet were going and could not move with grace or ease. The marble was cold on bare feet, the night air even colder on bare skin and sweat-soaked hair. They reached the bases of the great pillars and entered a black puddle of shadow cast by Trumb. The lamps were obvious now, revealing turbaned, white-robed figures waiting within the entrance. The visitors would be questioned or at least asked to define their business.

Suppose the priests became suspicious? Suppose they began serious interrogation or called in the guards? D'ward would certainly give a false name, so what if poor Dosh were asked to confirm it? Then he would have to decide where his loyalty was and which side he believed in. *In Nosokslope they shall come to D'ward in their hundreds, even the Betrayer.* This might be where he discovered if he had ranked a mention in the *Filoby Testament.*

They passed between two marble piers, each larger than a house and taller than a tree. A white-ghost priest took a step toward them, touching his forehead. Dosh automatically responded with the same gesture. He did not quite see what D'ward did, but he thought the movement was not exactly orthodox—more like rubbing an eyebrow. The elderly priest could not have noticed the difference, for he held out his leather bag expectantly and his expression was benevolent . . . so far.

"Your troubles must be great, my sons, if you seek solace at this hour."

"Our labors by day make us keep strange hours, Father." D'ward spoke in Niolian, just as he had in his evening sermon. He never slowed his pace, striding past the priest and onward into the sanctuary.

Dosh sweated along at his side, resisting the temptation to look back. He could not believe it had been that easy!

"I just rang the doorbell," D'ward murmured in Nagian, which was his preferred dialect.

"What do you mean?"

"Visek probably heard me get by that old fellow. . . . Never mind. I'm just whistling in the dark."

He was not whistling and it was not dark! It was not bright either, of course, but Trumb was flooding the great space with light, and large candles burned around the holy figure ahead. They did not look large at this distance, but they must be. The great rectangle of white pillars and polished floor contained nothing except the plinth in the center, a truncated pyramid about half the width of the enclosure and not much over head height. On the top sat Father Visek, a marble god on a marble throne. Dosh had seen other gods much larger—the grotesque colossi of Karzon and Zath in the temple of the Man in Tharg, for example. Visek, he knew from memories of past visits, was scarcely more than life-size, or at least did not seem so from ground level.

The singing came from a boy at a corner of the pyramid, kneeling on the lowermost step. Then another boy walked out of the shadows to kneel at another corner. The first rose, touched his forehead in obeisance, walked away, and the second began to sing. Kids that age ought to have been in bed hours ago. There was no sign of anyone else nearby, but there must be at least a choirmaster skulking in the shadows and doubtless more singers awaiting their cue. The second singer was not as tuneful as the first, unsure of his key.

D'ward continued to stride forward. Dosh shuffled along at his side, wishing he had even an inkling of what was going to happen. He knew the Liberator provoked strange reactions from gods. With his own eyes, Dosh had seen Irepit appear to lend him a hand in Nosokvale only days ago. In a past that now seemed almost historical, Prylis had hailed D'ward like a long-lost friend. Karzon, the Man himself, had punched him on the jaw. That did not mean the Parent would not smite him with lightning or burn out his tongue and cut off his hands, which was the standard penalty for blasphemy.

The Father loomed above them, a majestic seated figure, hands on knees, flowing beard. If the marble had ever been colored, the tints had long since weathered away, but the features were still discernible, stern but loving in the warm glow from the tall gold candlesticks. Reaching the base of the steps, Dosh prepared to kneel—and D'ward kept moving. Dosh grabbed him and hauled him back. "You can't go up there!" he whispered. "Only the high priest—"

"Come along!"

D'ward seized Dosh's arm in a painfully powerful grip and urged him up the stairway. The singer missed a note and then continued. Oh, gods! This was forbidden. The priests must be able to see. They would call in the guards. Dosh tried to look around and stumbled when the next step wasn't where he expected. . . .

Moon and candles had disappeared. He was in a tunnel. No, not a tunnel, for there was carpet under his feet. Somewhere indoors, though, being hurried along a level floor. Where had the god gone? The throne? The temple?

"Where are we?" he squeaked.

"Damned if I know," D'ward said cheerily. "Watch out!"

Dosh sensed a very large place, a hall. The only light was a faint glow from up ahead, and D'ward released his grip to lead the way along the narrow path, twisting through a maze, a forest of miscellaneous objects, curved or angular, some very large, others small and heaped on top of one another—statues, tables, huge jars, candelabra, chairs, cauldrons, musical instruments, rolls of fabric, piles of what might be clothes, suits of armor, and thousands of other things, all pushed in together in no sort of order and in many places stacked higher than head height. The air was dry and musty. It was a gigantic storeroom, a junk merchant's cellar run riot.

"What is this?"

"Damned if I know that, either. A museum? A kleptomaniac's hoard? Offerings, I suppose. People keep bringing things, one must collect a lot of stuff over the centuries."

Trying not to whimper, poor Dosh followed his guide. Why had he ever let himself get involved in whatever this was he was involved in? He needed to pee.

The light came from a wide doorway. D'ward walked through it. Dosh crept in behind him, trying to be inconspicuous. D'ward stopped.

Dosh peeked over his shoulder. The light would be too dim to read by. It cast no shadows and he could not see its source. The room was large, as big as Bandrops Advocate's study, and just as cluttered and heaped as the antechamber. The only clear space was roughly triangular, its corners being D'ward himself and two huge chairs, angled toward each other. Everywhere else was packed with the same mindless jumble as the antechamber: furniture, figurines, boxes, pottery, birdcages, crystal, scrolls, weapons, and just about anything else a man could think of or ever want. Gold and gems glittered dimly under layers of dust. The air was stuffy, with the stale, acrid smell of a tomb.

The chairs were occupied. One held a man, the other a woman, both lying back motionless, with their hands folded in their laps. Their hair fell in frozen white waves to lap on their shoulders, their skin was as smooth as vellum, and their robes had long since faded to an indeterminate gray. The man's beard reached to his waist. He rested his chin on his chest, seeming to stare at the woman's feet, while she had her head back, gazing fixedly into space above him. Neither was heeding the visitors at all.

Silence. Dosh shivered violently. These could not be real people, of course, merely more images of the Father and the Mother, representations of the same dual god. They must have lain there for years, gathering dust, although they seemed to have escaped the film of cobweb that coated all the hodgepodge and bric-a-brac. Yet what sculptor could shape so convincingly and in what medium? Hair rose on the nape of his neck.

"Who is it?" muttered the man, not looking up, moving nothing but his mustache. His voice creaked, as if it had dried up from disuse.

After a long moment, the woman muttered, "A stranger. Come looking for a job, I expect." She continued to stare blankly at nothing.

Pause. "Have we any vacant aspects now?"

Longer pause. "Don't remember." Very slowly she turned her head to stare at D'ward. Her face was unwrinkled, yet it conveyed a sense of age beyond imagining. Her eyes were dull—not filmed with cataracts, as old people's often were, just lifeless glass. "Go away. . . . We are busy. . . . Come back in a hundred years."

"I am D'ward Liberator, the one foretold in the *Filoby Testament.*"

The woman's head drifted back to its original position.

Even D'ward seemed nonplussed. When nothing more was said, he bristled, putting his fists on his hips. "I am the Liberator! It is prophesied that I shall bring death to Death."

"A reformer," the woman muttered.

"Another? It never works. Send him away."

Dosh's teeth were trying to chatter. He took hold of his jaw with both hands and held his mouth open. His bladder felt as if was about to burst from sheer terror.

"I am D'ward Liberator. You two are Visek? How long have you been sitting there?"

"Go away," the woman murmured.

"You are dying of boredom! I offer you a little excitement for a change, something new. I am going to slay Zath."

The man sighed, stirring the silver hairs of his mustache again. "Who?"

"Zath!" D'ward was not even trying to hide his exasperation. "The one who calls himself the god of death. He sucks mana from human sacrifices. He is evil, a blot upon the Vales and your religion."

Long pause. With glacial slowness the man looked up, his eyes showing the same dead indifference as the woman's. "Then go and do it and stop bothering us."

"I do not yet have the power. I need more mana. I go from node to node, recruiting followers, preaching my purpose, but I need help. Will you aid me? Will you lend me mana?"

Another sigh. "No."

"Will you at least grant me protection while I am here in Niolvale, so that Zath's minions cannot—"

"No. You are intruding. Play the Game like the others or pay the penalty. Begone." The man closed his eyes and lowered his chin again.

"*Strewth!*" D'ward said angrily. "Play the Game? Zath has more mana than you do! He has more power, probably, than the whole Pentatheon together! What if he decides he would like to be Visek? He'll kill you and take your place! What do you think of that move? Or don't you care anymore?"

The awful, stuffy room swayed around Dosh. His blood hammered in his ears. These talking mummies could never be divine, so D'ward had been right all along, and the gods were merely human enchanters who had stretched out their lives for untold centuries. Spiders caught in their own web, dying of boredom! Everything he had ever believed was totally false, criminal rubbish. His stomach heaved.

It was the woman who reacted first to D'ward's taunts, although reluctantly and with irritation. She peered at him. "You blaspheme against Visek."

"It is the truth! Talk to Karzon or Eltiana or Astina! Damn, talk to crazy Tion if you trust him! Every night more people die so that Zath can suck mana from their deaths. Prylis told me that it was Visek, three thousand years ago, who banned human sacrifice in all the Vales—was that you or one of your predecessors?"

"It was us, I think," the man mumbled, with the first hint of interest that he had shown. "Wasn't it, dear?"

D'ward snorted. "Then Zath defies your edict! He is evil and deadly and dangerous to you. The prophecy—"

"We are god of prophecy. Among other things."

"Others also prophesy. The prophecy says that I will bring death to Death. If the one who calls himself Zath were to become Visek, then he wouldn't be Death anymore and he would be safe, wouldn't he?"

"Blasphemy!" the woman quavered. Both of them were looking at D'ward now. Both were showing signs of anger, or at least disapproval.

"Astina will confirm what I say."

"We must talk with the Maiden one day, dear," the man mumbled.

"Yes, darling, we must."

*They would never get around to it. . . .*

D'ward thumped his fists against his hipbones. "I ask from you only what Astina granted me: first, that she would defend me from his reapers within her domain, second, that she would issue a revelation to her priests to hold back the civil—"

"No," said the man, closing his eyes again.

The woman uttered a creaky chuckle. "If you can't defend yourself from those, how can you hope to handle a god?"

"But it will waste mana! You know that the more I have, the faster I will be able to garner more. I need help to build my—"

"Revolution?" The man yawned. "It doesn't work. We built too well."

D'ward swore under his breath, words Dosh did not know. "No one has ever managed to preach rebellion in more than two vales, so Prylis says."

The woman moved her lips for a moment. "True."

"I am in my fourth! I have lasted almost two fortnights already. I am something new, do you hear? Something you have never seen before! I am foretold by a chain of prophecy Zath has not broken in thirty years of trying. If you won't guard me in Niolvale, will you at least watch my efforts? Will you watch to see how far I get, when and how I die?"

With glacial slowness, the man raised a hand and scratched at his beard with nails like small horn daggers. "That might be amusing," he conceded.

"Haven't seen anything new in a thousand years," the woman muttered.

D'ward released a deep breath, as if he had won a victory. "Astina promised me one more thing. If I do survive to confront Zath on his node, then she will lend me some mana for the final—"

"Oh, no!" snapped the woman, and this time she actually stirred in her chair. "How could we ever trust you to pay it back? You say that Zath is a threat to us, but if you won, you would be stronger than he."

"I gave my solemn word that—"

"Dragonshit." Her pebbly eyes shifted to stare at Dosh, peering around the Liberator, and they seemed to come to life. "Who's he?" Her voice rose to a screech: "You brought a *native* into our sanctum?"

The man heaved himself erect in his chair to glare at Dosh, and his robe crumbled away to dust.

Without turning, D'ward whispered, "Go!"

Dosh spun around and shot out of the chamber.

# 27

In panic, he fought his way through darkness, finding the tunnel by ricocheting off furniture, bouncing against tall urns, stumbling over chests, tripping on goblets and vases, knocking down giant candelabras and suits of armor. Debris cascaded to the floor behind him, and his flight must have sounded like an earthquake. He had no idea what sort of a door he would find, or if he would be able to open it. In the end there was no door—he flailed out into moonlight and rolled head over heels down the steps.

That was not the last of his troubles. Evidently the trespassers' violation of the sanctuary had been observed and all the available clergy had assembled to beseech Visek's forgiveness. At least forty white-robed priests and priestesses were on their knees there, chanting a lament. Dosh plowed into them like a runaway snowball, bowling over seven or eight before he came to a stop.

The green moon whirled in the sky above him, accompanied by flashes of flame and more stars than he had ever seen before. Three or four men threw themselves on top of him to restrain him, although he would not have been capable of even sitting up, let alone making a run for it.

The singing ended. People shouted. Order of a sort was restored.

Dosh found himself lying on the floor, with his arms and legs pinned. A burning agony in his nose was spraying blood. He peered up groggily at a ring of irate faces. Several tried to speak at once before one elderly man established his seniority.

"Where is your accomplice?" he screeched. He was standing between Dosh's widespread legs and looked dangerously liable to start kicking if he did not receive a satisfactory answer.

Dosh licked his lips, choking on blood from his nose. His left ankle throbbed. "With Holy Visek, of course."

The old man hesitated, considering the implications.

Poor Dosh had been in tight spots before, although probably none tighter than this. He groped for self-confidence, which was not readily accessible in his present condition. "He will be along shortly. Is this how you normally treat the Great One's guests?"

Amazingly, it worked—or at least the old man did not lash out with his feet, which was the most immediate danger. He scowled uncertainly and then stepped back. "Get him up!"

The hands holding Dosh's legs were removed. Those on his arms heaved him erect. The whole temple swayed vertiginously and a spasm of agony shot through his ankle. He stumbled and was held upright, balancing on one foot, nauseated by the battering and the blood he had swallowed.

"Who are you?"

That was a very good question, but it did not seem to have a suitable reply. "Tion," came to mind. No one would question a god's right to come calling on another, but a god would not fall down a flight of steps; a god would not arrive cut, bruised, and unable to put any weight on his left foot.

"A friend of the Liberator's," was another possibility. It had the advantage of being the truth, but it would lead to extremely unpleasant consequences.

"I am not at liberty to answer that," Dosh said.

Someone struck him and the temple rocked again. This time he did throw up, which at least made the senior priest back away and held off further questioning for a moment.

But not for long.

"Guards!" squealed the old man, almost gibbering in his fury.

The cordon of priests and priestesses parted to admit a squad of armed men, moonlight glittering on blades and armor and reptilian eyes.

"Interrogate this criminal!" the high priest quavered. "Find out who he is and what he is doing. Get the truth out of him."

The shiniest guard looked around uneasily. "Here, Venerable One?"

"Yes, here! Now! Immediately!"

As soldiers replaced the priests holding his arms, Dosh braced himself for unpleasant experiences. Oh, poor, poor Dosh!

"What are you doing?" demanded a voice from the throne. D'ward came striding down the steps. "Release that man!"

He wore nothing but a peasant's loincloth, but his voice rang with the brazen prestige of bugles. The crowd opened, men and women and even soldiers backing away. Dosh swayed and steadied, teetering on one leg.

Blue eyes seared the onlookers. "Stand back!" They all retreated one more step. "Farther!" The clearing widened. Then D'ward turned to Dosh and pulled a face at what he saw. He reached out and touched his throbbing, burning nose. The pain stopped instantly. Dosh wiped off the blood with his arm.

"And what's wrong with your foot?"

Dosh felt better already. This breather might not last, but every minute he was not being questioned by those thugs was an improvement. "I broke my ankle." He thought it was only sprained, but that was a mere quibble.

"Who are you?" The high priest had lost much of his screech.

D'ward turned and studied him for a moment. "Who do you say is the god of prophecy?"

The old man twitched in indignation. "Holy Visek in their avatar of Waatuun."

"And I am D'ward Liberator, the one foretold."

Screech became scream. *The heretic?*

Without deigning to answer, D'ward dropped to one knee and took Dosh's ankle in his hands. His fingers felt ice cold on the hot swelling. He pulled the foot down to the floor.

"Try that."

Dosh put his weight on it and nothing nasty happened. "That's fine now," he said calmly. "Thank you." He must have banged his head harder than he realized, for obviously this could not be happening. On the other hand, there was not a closed mouth in the audience.

D'ward rose and regarded the onlookers as a proud housewife might inspect cockroaches in her larder. He was taller than almost all of them, which helped. "I am the Liberator. I had business with Visek. Is that any concern of yours? It is prophesied that I shall bring death to Death. And it is written, 'Hurt and sickness, yea death itself, shall he take from us. Oh rejoice!' "

The high priest's knees began to buckle, but a younger, larger man beside him caught him by the elbow and held him upright. "The Liberator preaches foulest heresy against the Holy Gods!"

D'ward's eyes spat contempt at him. "How often have you heard the Liberator preach?"

"I would not let his lies foul my ears!"

"Then let his deeds open your eyes! 'Rejoice!' the prophecy says. You have just seen a wonder. What does it take to save you from your ignorance and error? I tell you to rejoice!"

The man looked at Dosh's nose, down at his ankle. Then he sank to his knees. The high priest followed more circumspectly, and all the rest also. Bronze helmets and white turbans dipped to the floor. Oh, that was much better!

"Rejoice!" D'ward snapped. "Rejoice until the sun rises to warm your cold and unbelieving hearts." He nudged Dosh and strode away.

Amazingly, no one tried to stop them. Soldiers and clergy cowered on their faces and the most notorious heretic in the Vales walked away unchallenged, his companion at his side. As they trotted out between the pillars and down the steps, he remarked casually, "You know, that was a lot closer than it looked."

But the priests were not the only ones troubled by ignorance and error. Dosh's eyes also had just been opened. "I have been a fool!" he wailed. "Lord, forgive—"

"Never mind that now! Can you run? Because I haven't got anything left! We'll have to manage on honest sweat and muscle. Can you run?"

"Yes, master."

"Good man. Then let's get out of here before they change their minds."

They ran. The way back was a thousand times longer than the way there had been. Trumb dipped to the west and duly eclipsed, becoming a black moon against a glory of stars, and only the cold blue glow of Ysh lit the road. Dosh should have worried about reapers then, but he was beyond such trivia. As the eclipse ended, clouds moved in; rain began to fall, slowing the pace even more.

He was tortured by both remorse and fury at his own blindness. He had known D'ward for years and identified him as the Liberator earlier than anyone else. He had seen him perform miracles before—they had all been unobtrusive, deniable miracles, but they should have been enough. Lack of morals never bothered him, but he hated to think of himself as lacking brains. In the last half fortnight he had heard D'ward preach about a dozen times, and yet he had let the words roll off his mind like water off a candle. Now he tried to recall all those words, to understand just how much he had missed.

What was D'ward, then? Was he a man sent by the gods, or was he a god himself? Surely only a god could have healed that ankle? Yet D'ward denied the gods. There was only one god, he said, a god Undivided, indivisible. The puzzle was too great to solve on a cold, wet night, jogging along in the mud. Fatigue blurred his mind until he could not think, could only slog along, following the pale glimmer of D'ward's back in the darkness.

The first time they stopped at a stream to drink, even before he had washed off the dried blood, he tried to ask for guidance and forgiveness.

"Don't worry about all that now," D'ward said. "There is time yet to straighten it all out. How are your bruises?"

As the hours passed, Dosh began to stumble more and more often. D'ward would hear his steps falter and come back and help him up, plastered with mud, and get him moving again. And then even D'ward seemed to run out of strength—although his strength was much more strength of will than of body, for he too was reeling on his feet. And the rain was becoming a downpour.

They took shelter under a bridge at a place where the road ran straight, a low causeway crossing marsh and lakes. At intervals it rose on timber bridges to let the wandering streams drain through, but at this time of year the water was low, exposing sand. The two of them crawled underneath and stretched out between the weed-furred piles with groans of contentment. Rain drummed on the planks only inches above them, but they were out of it.

Almost out of it—Dosh eased away from a dribble.

"Sleep awhile," D'ward mumbled.

"One fortnight or two?"

"Just one. When Prat'han wakes up and finds I'm not there, he's going to murder me."

After a bemused moment, Dosh worked out why that sounded funny, and surprised himself with a chuckle.

"Mm?" D'ward said. "Oh, well, when I get back he will. He'll have to manage somehow, won't he? Trouble is, we have a long trek to do today."

"Skip it," Dosh murmured. The Liberator had told Visek that he went from node to node. He wondered what a node was. "Rest today, go tomorrow."

D'ward began muttering about winter being due and the problem of finding enough food if the Free stayed in one place, but his voice came from a long way away. . . .

"Watch it!" A warning hand caught Dosh's head just before he jerked it up and cracked it against a beam.

He blinked in alarm, wondering where he was, why he was so confoundedly cold, wet, and sore, and who the bastard was who was sprinkling water on him. Then he heard the noise, and registered the vibration in the timbers above him that was shaking off the moisture. Green moonlight shone on the stream beyond the bridge, so they had not slept very long. An hour, perhaps, not as much as two. The rain had stopped.

"What . . . ?"

"Soldiers!"

Many hooves tramping across the bridge.

Dosh heaved himself up on an elbow to peer over his companion and study the shadows on the water. He saw shapes of lancers on moas, heading west. He looked at D'ward, two eyes shining in the darkness, and asked, "They're after us?"

"Not us two, I think. The Free. We'll have to wait until they're gone, and then go back and try to cut around the lakes."

"No!" Dosh said. "Once they're off the bridge, they'll speed up again. We'll never get there before them, no matter what way we go."

D'ward groaned. "Suppose you're right."

The rear guard passed and the noise faded into the distance.

Why go on? If the Niolian cavalry was moving against the Free, then the Liberator would return to find his followers massacred, arrested, or scattered. But of course D'ward would go back. There would be no talking him into deserting. And if he were there, then he might work another miracle, even without the help of Irepit. He was the Liberator.

Dosh thought back to his servitude with Tarion, the Nagian cavalryleader. "It may be possible. They'll bivouac before dawn to rest their mounts. We may get in front of them then."

It sounded impossible. It was impossible, for two exhausted men on battered, bleeding feet. But they did it.

As dawn was painting rosy tints on Niolwall ahead of them, they trotted past a field where moas were grazing on stubble and men huddled around campfires. Those proud lancers showed no interest in two peasants going by on foot and did not challenge. As soon as they were out of sight, D'ward quickened the pace. Somehow Dosh kept up with him on his shorter legs.

The campsite of the Free was much less organized and covered a far greater area. The pilgrims were awake, most grouped along the riverbank, washing, rolling up bedding if they had any, singing hymns, or eating whatever scraps they had saved from the evening meal. Few of them noticed the two bedraggled, mud-splattered young men walking along the road, and probably none recognized their leader without his priestly gown.

On the other side of the trail, on the boulder-strewn slope with the Liberator's tent near the pulpit rock, the Warband with shields and spears was moving over the ground like foraging ants, as if searching for bodies. Prat'han was the first to recognize the newcomers. The big man shouted and came leaping down the hill to greet them, looking ready to weep with relief—and also about ready to run his spear through Dosh for having abducted the Liberator. The rest of the warriors came running in to cluster around. Dosh flopped down on the grass.

D'ward remained standing, drooping with fatigue. "Water, please, food if there is any. I've got to clean up and dress. Pass the word that I will not preach this morning and get them moving. We're going to have trouble."

Teeth shone. "We can sharpen our spears now?" Gopaenum demanded.

"Yes. Yes, you can sharpen your spears. And I fear you may blunt them, too, before the day is out. A troop of lancers'll be here very shortly." D'ward rubbed his eyes wearily. "We mustn't lie around here like fish on a slab. Get everyone moving." He pointed.

The trail ahead crossed the river at a ford and then wound off through a watery morass of lake and sedge.

"Can't ride moas through that!" Part'han said, sounding disappointed.

"Can't follow us more than two or maybe three abreast, either!" crowed little Tielan Trader, who had more brains than was thought seemly back in Nagvale. "You want us to hold the bastards off, Liberator? Hold the road?"

"No. I'd rather we got ahead of the crowd. Or as much of it as we can." D'ward limped off toward the tent. Prat'han snapped orders and then followed him.

Suddenly alone, Dosh lay back on the grass. In the last horrible hour he had been unable to think at all. He had almost forgotten the lancers. Now he had arrived, the Liberator had arrived, and the Niolian cavalry would doubtless arrive very soon.

He ought to go back down to the river and clean up, but he did not think he could move another step. He could just curl up where he was and hope the lancers did not notice him or care about one heretic—or would at least not wake him before they skewered him. A loud jingling . . . He forced his eyelids open. Prat'han Potter was squatting beside him like a small mountain, shaking the money bag and grinning like a rock eater.

"Don't you want this back?"

Dosh's mouth felt full of sand. "Not especially. You hang on to it. I'm in no fit state to guard it."

The big man chuckled and produced a hunk of bread as big as two fists. "How about this then?"

Instantly Dosh was aware of a monstrous hunger raging inside him. He heaved himself up on an elbow. "Now that does look interesting!"

"Cheese? Pickles? Smoked fish?"

Afraid he might drown in his own saliva, Dosh sat up. "Brother Prat'han, you have just earned a place among the stars of heaven." He bit greedily. "I mean, you will be united forever with the True God," he corrected.

His companion grinned approvingly at this declaration of Liberator creed.

Already D'ward was striding down the hill to the river, conspicuous in his hooded gray robe, surrounded by the Warband. Perhaps a hundred of the Free had already crossed the ford and were moving off along the road into the marshes. All the rest would follow the Liberator and the lancers would come and that plan seemed totally wrong. Dosh thumped his sleepy brain; he had just worked out the answer when Prat'han put the question, frowning.

"What happens when the troopers get here?"

What he meant was, "D'ward doesn't usually hide behind his friends."

"They'll use a lot of military jargon," Dosh said, munching. "Technical terms for *feces* and *impregnation* and *unnatural sex* that god-fearing people like you don't know. They won't fancy charging two or three abreast along miles of track with swamp on both sides and lots of cover for archers or spearsmen, not to mention a thousand pilgrims getting in the way. If they do try it, the pilgrims can jump into the water and escape."

Prat'han grinned, a mouthful of ivory. "So they'll have to go the long way round and catch us at the other end? Wherever that is?"

"Probably." Dosh groaned and began to rise.

Prat'han offered a hand and hauled him upright. He handed over his spear. "Take this. Your feet look like raw meat. We get down to the river, I'll clean them up for you. Wrap them, too."

Dosh mumbled thanks, eating with one hand and leaning on the spear with the other. He hobbled down the slope, feeling every muscle, every joint. And a long way to go today, D'ward had said.

"Food? Can you organize the food? Someone'll have to get out ahead and buy— How much money is there?" Shamedly, he said, "I'm all in, brother! I need help." He mustn't let D'ward down, but asking for help was not something he was good at.

"Course. Soon's I've seen to those feet."

Giving thanks wasn't something Dosh was good at, either. He tried.

As they neared the trail, "While we're at the river, Brother Prat'han, would you do me that water thing you do with converts?" He received a thump on the back hard enough to knock his knees together.

The big man laughed delightedly. "I think D'ward would like to baptize you into the Church himself, Dosh."

"He won't mind, and I'd sort of like it from you, I think."

"I'd be honored to! Can—can you tell me even a little?"

Little what? Then Dosh saw the torture of curiosity in the Nagian's dark eyes. Oh, that!

"We went to Niol, to the temple. He announced who he was, but they didn't even try to arrest him. They didn't *dare!* Wonderful things . . ." Where could he even start? "I *saw Visek!* Not a god, just two old mummies. Oh, Prat'han, he's right! Everything he says is true! I was so wrong and all of you weren't. You believed and I didn't. I do now. I've been a fool, a terrible fool!"

The potter laughed and squeezed his shoulder. "I asked D'ward about that a couple of days ago. He said bigger brains need more evidence and I ought to mind my own business."

"Bigger *fools* need more evidence, you mean."

"True. But that's not what D'ward said."

They looked at each other and grinned. And then they laughed.

# 28

Julian and Ursula had arrived in Nosokvale the previous evening, only to learn that the Liberator had already passed through. They had followed his trail over Thadrilpass, and now they were descending into Niolvale.

An hour or so ago, Julian had been greatly impressed by his first glimpse of it. For one thing, it was much larger than any Nextdoorian basin he had seen so far, its encircling walls dwindling away to vanish over a flat horizon. For another, it was superbly fertile. The bare, dry foothills of Niolslope plunged abruptly into a flatland symphony of green and silver. To the north many little white villages shone like pearls in the morning sun, and from higher up he had seen a city that T'lin said was Niol itself. Southward lay lakes, swamps, and rivers, with only scattered islands cultivated.

Now he was less concerned with geography than demographics. Just how many people were in that crowd down there? It wasn't a full battalion, he decided—closer to three companies, say seven or eight hundred. The vanguard was almost out of sight already, advancing into the marshlands along a narrow, winding track.

Dragons disliked traveling in close order, so conversation was rarely possible except at halts. While still a thousand feet or so above the road, T'lin Dragontrader shouted, *"Zappan!"* Starlight stopped obediently. The other dragons closed in around him, puffing and belching, peering at one another and their riders with their intelligent, jewel-bright eyes.

"Dragons do not like water," T'lin said, scratching at his coppery beard and scowling.

Why should that be a problem? "I don't suppose there's any doubt that's *Tyika* Kisster's band, is there?"

"No, Saint Kaptaan. I have never seen a gathering like it before. It must be."

"But larger than it was in Joalvale?"

"Oh, many times, Holiness."

"Where are they going?" Ursula sounded grim and looked grimmer.

"The Thadrilpass road divides here, Holiness. That way leads to Niol. I think the other must go to Shuujooby. That would be the shortest road to Lospass and Jurgvale. . . . I am not sure. I have been to Shuujooby, but not by this way. Dragons do not like water."

"Probably stiff with mosquitoes," Julian suggested cheerfully. He did not see why Ursula should be in such a sour mood all of a sudden. She had been enthusiastically playful in the tent before they emerged for breakfast, which might be one reason he was feeling so jovial himself. Was she piqued that Edward had collected so many followers so quickly? That seemed rather petty of her. Bloody good show and more power to him!

"Exeter will be out in front," she said crossly.

"Can't imagine a prophet not leading the chosen people in person, certainly not Edward. Let's amble on down and find out."

T'lin rolled his eyes, clawed at his beard with both hands, and growled, "Dragons do not like water!"

Oh. Now Julian had caught up with the parade. "You mean we should have arrived a little earlier and cut him off?"

Ursula shot him an exasperated look. "A brilliant observation." She turned to survey the ridges of Niolslope behind them and then addressed T'lin again. "What is there at that Shuujooby place?"

"Just a village, Holiness." T'lin thought for a moment. "There is a ruined temple, half buried in sand."

Ursula nodded to herself. Julian could guess that she was thinking *node!* If Exeter was gathering mana and followers by preaching, then he would certainly do so on nodes whenever possible.

"But we can cut back through the hills and get in front of him?"

"Certainly, Holiness."

It was a reasonable suggestion, for dragons were the ultimate in cross-country transportation and the barren hills ideal terrain for them, but Julian was damned tired of sitting on a Brobdingnagian lizard all day, strapped in place like luggage with nothing to do except shout the occasional *"Zaib!"* or *"Varch!"* or "View halloo!" "Let's send T'lin and the mounts around that way. I wouldn't mind a chance to ride shanks' pony for a change."

"Walk?" She snorted. "In the middle of that rabble? You'll get your wallet lifted and fleas in return."

Julian refused to be nettled. "I haven't got a wallet. We came to find out what Exeter's up to, remember? Be a jolly good idea to hear what his crusaders think of him first."

She pouted, apparently unable to refute his arguments. The more Julian considered what he had just suggested, the wiser it seemed, but obviously Ursula would not back down and agree with him. She just did not want to walk and he did, and he could profitably investigate what Exeter was up to. Language might be a problem. His Joalian was still sketchy and there would be no Randorian-speakers this far from Randorvale. He knew someone who could get by in Joalian, though.

Dommi was sitting impassively on Bluegem's back, waiting for the *votyikank* to issue orders. His copper hair shone in the morning sunlight because he had removed his hat, but his face glowed almost as redly, because he had refrained from removing anything else. Which reminded Julian that he too was clad in mountain furs and liable to melt at any moment. He unbuckled his saddle belt and called over to his valet.

"The blue Joalian breeches, if you please, Dommi. And the orange smock. Or do you think something more conservative for a religious convocation? Possibly the forest green?"

Dommi was already standing by his stirrup to help him dismount. "The orange might be an overly brightness, *tyika*, if you wish to remain inconspicuous. And may I suggest the bubblerskin half boots? If I might have a moment, I could give them another coat of wasp oil, although I believe they are watertightest already."

"Oh, I'm sure they are. And I trust you to tie me a hanky-spanky turban."

As his batman headed for Bluegem's panniers, Julian began loosing a few buttons and eying the nearby boulders to decide which one was the gentlemen's changing room. "A snack for me to take with me, too, Dommi? And one for yourself if you want to come along."

Dommi looked around, beaming. "I shall be most honored to accompany you, *tyika*."

Ursula was still mounted, still scowling, staring down at the disappearing multitude. If Exeter had been drawing mana from so many for the last few weeks and not spending any of it on miracles, then he might not be the pushover she had anticipated. Then there would have to be honest negotiation, not any Svengali-type mesmerism.

"Look, old girl," Julian said, "I'm not trying to queer your pitch. I swear I won't even mention you, all right? No hints, warnings . . . I just want to sound him out.

Dommi and I will walk. We'll meet you at Exeter's headquarters this evening. At Shuujooby or wherever."

She surrendered with a shrug, as if it didn't matter what he did. "Don't bring the
fleas with you."

Dommi had produced the required clothes, all seeming new-washed and freshly
pressed. Time to change.

"You could ride as far as the river, Holiness," T'lin suggested, looking worried at
this sudden change of plan.

That was only half a mile or so, and by the time Julian got there the stragglers would
still be crossing. "No, I'd attract too much attention. You'll take good care of Saint
Ursula, won't you? What's that striped thing? Not my turban? For crying out loud,
Dommi, you don't expect a gentleman to appear in public in that, do you?"

An hour or so later, Julian began to wonder if his decision to walk had been unwise.
Two hours later, he was sure of it. The steamy air reeked of wet vegetation and was
every bit as well supplied with mosquitoes as he had predicted. Reflecting off the water,
sunlight came at him from both above and below. His sweat-soaked smock and breeches
clung to him like leeches. So did the leeches. The track was narrow, muddy, winding,
and crowded; he could make little progress in his efforts to work his way to the head
of the line and steal a private word with Exeter. Here and there the trail would cross
an island, and then he could speed around the other travelers, except when the adjacent
land was planted in crops. The inhabitants had emerged from their bushy little shacks
to stare at this mysterious migration passing through their lonely little world. It must
seem like a strange dream to them.

Still, he was moving faster than any, so he would catch up with the leaders sooner
or later. The only people who passed him were two men running, both carrying spears
and shields. They shouted to clear the way and trotted through, dribbling sweat in the
sticky heat but soon vanishing beyond the crowds ahead. No one else seemed to be
armed, and yet no one had reacted to them with surprise or alarm.

"Interesting!" Julian said. "Wonder who those jokers are?"

"I saw them when we started, *tyika,* up a tree. I am believing that they may be
Nagians, *tyika.*" Dommi's face bore no expression at all, only freckles. He must know
as well as Julian did that Exeter had spent his first year on Nextdoor in the Nagian
army.

Scouts, perhaps? Left behind to watch where the dragons went?

By and large, the pilgrims were not nearly as helpful as Julian had hoped. Their
Joalian was more idiomatic and very much faster than the Joalian he had studied at
Olympus—even Dommi often failed to understand their accents. When he could, the
halting translation made the conversation stilted and awkward. Most of the crowd
seemed to have very little idea why they should be part of this strange expedition, except
that Holy D'ward was the prophesied Liberator, he would bring death to Death, he
had called on them to join the Free and follow him. It was a perfect example of charisma
at work. They were following Exeter because he was a leader, which Julian had known

already. Most of the strangers in Olympus could have achieved the same effect as easily, had they ever had cause to risk the wrath of the Pentatheon and the civil rulers of the Vales.

The congregation was a curious cross section of Valian society. Some were in rags, others plump and prosperous. Julian saw ancients staggering along on canes and the arms of younger folk, sturdy young adults with children, babes at their mothers' breasts. He began to have misgivings that had not occurred to him before. Did Exeter have any ideas of how drastically he was disrupting the lives of all these hundreds of people? Where was he leading them and what was going to happen to them? Whether he won or lost his insane gamble, he was creating social chaos. However one regarded the justice of his cause, he was being blasted unfair to the participants. Damn it, they were more victims than participants! Julian could not recall anyone at Olympus offering that argument.

Around the middle of the day, many of the pilgrims settled themselves in the shade of trees or bushes to rest. That thinned out the crowd on the road considerably. Musing that mad dogs and Englishmen could take the same attitude to the noonday sun on this world as well as any other, Julian increased his speed. Dommi produced lunch from his pack, and the two of them ate as they went.

Then Dommi suddenly whispered, *"Tyika?"* and stopped. Here the road ran over a low, rocky island, too small to cultivate. It was graced with some willowlike trees, though, and a group of ten or twelve pilgrims had halted there to rest. There was an argument in progress. Julian could not follow the jabber, but apparently Dommi was picking up at least some of it. He was frowning.

The center of the squabble was a short, blond youngster perched on a boulder. He had no turban; indeed, he wore only a loincloth and sandals, and his feet were bandaged in bloody rags. The others were clustered on the ground around him, like pupils around a teacher. The class was definitely unruly, though, shouting objections. Then Julian saw what Dommi had perhaps noticed right away—most of the audience wore the gold earring of the Undivided. They did not like what they were hearing.

Obviously the kid waving his hands and bellowing was a native; if he had the charisma of a stranger, his message would not be meeting such resistance. Equally obviously, he was sincere in whatever he was saying, growing louder and more flushed by the minute with the righteous anger of a fanatic. He was not really a kid, although his small size and fair coloring made him seem boyish, a slightly balding cherub. A very angry cherub! He might be a Pentatheon believer denouncing the Service's imported theology or perhaps a Liberator disciple. The hitherto simple theology of the Vales was starting to become complicated.

After a few minutes Dommi jerked his pack higher on his shoulders and shot Julian an apologetic glance to indicate that he was ready to move on.

"Stay longer if you want."

"I have heard it all, I think, *tyika*. They are repeating themselves."

"Right-oh!" As they resumed their march, Julian waited for enlightenment. Dommi remained silent.

"What was the argument all about?"

"I think it was theology, *tyika*."

"You astonish me. Actually, you don't surprise me at all. Who was arguing what?"

"I only caught a few words, *tyika*."

"Let's have those, then."

Dommi became surprisingly reticent, his English even more convoluted than usual. Eventually he admitted that the little preacher had claimed to be a close follower of the Liberator and the bone of their contention had been the nature of the afterlife. Until now the Church of the Undivided had followed the Pentatheon's example in promising that the faithful would find eternal bliss among the stars of heaven, while the evil would linger alone forever in darkness. The Liberator apparently had other notions of what the Undivided intended, although Dommi seemed genuinely uncertain what those were.

That explained his troubled frown. The *tyikank* were now disunited, so his loyalties to the Service and to Exeter, his former master, were being put in conflict. Certainly Olympus would not be happy to hear that the Liberator was splitting its Reformation into rival sects. The Pentatheon might be very pleased.

"It's probably just a misunderstanding," Julian said airily. After trudging along for a while, hearing nothing but footsteps squelching in the mud, he decided that the contention he had witnessed required a bigger bone. And obviously Dommi still had misgivings.

"There was more to it than that, though, wasn't there?"

More hard work on Dommi eventually extracted an admission that the afterlife had been a side issue. The main debate had concerned the nature of the traditional Valian gods. According to the Church of the Undivided, Visek and Co. were demons. The Liberator was teaching that they were human enchanters.

That was the truth, of course. It was also a major difference in doctrine.

Julian said, "Damn!" This was much more serious. Prof Rawlinson and the others who had written the True Gospel had thought hard and long before introducing a deliberate falsehood, but they had eventually concluded that it would be simpler and safer to invoke demons than try to explain charismatic strangers, because demons were evil by definition. That was the official explanation. Julian was quite certain that their real reason had been that the apostles themselves were charismatic strangers. To equate the leaders of one side with the leaders of the other would provoke questions about the difference between them. Better to brand the opposition as demons than to argue that they are the baddies and we are the goodies. The obvious answer to that was: "Sez who?"

"Damn!" he repeated. "What the blazes does Exeter think he's up to?" He did not realize that he had spoken aloud until Dommi gave him an answer.

"He is taking help from them, *tyika!*"

"He's *what?*"

Dommi nodded miserably, his face so wobegone that it seemed surprising all his freckles did not jump off and run for cover. "The man on the rock said that the Demon Irepit appeared in Rinoovale at the side of the Liberator. She dispersed a troop of the queen's soldiers for him. And he said that he himself went with the Liberator last night to Niol and saw the Demon Visek in the temple with his own eyes, *tyika!*"

Julian used some words he had not uttered since the Battle of the Somme. Had Exeter sold out to Zath's opponents in the Pentatheon? Foghorn and the others had been absolutely right. The Liberator was going to bring the Church of the Undivided crashing down like Samson's temple.

Ursula would have forty purple fits.

# *29*

The trail rose over an island, which bore a small farm at one end, the rest being upholstered in shoulder-high bushes. Five men with spears and big round shields stood guard along the west side of the trail. No napoleonic genius was needed to surmise that Edward Exeter might be taking a siesta in the shade somewhere at their backs.

Julian arrived in the company of Dommi, Garhug'n Papermaker, Garhug'n's wife, and their three children, the youngest being around four. Garhug'n spoke a Joalian that Julian found intelligible—most of the time. He had recounted at length how they had been returning home to Niol from visiting his elderly mother, how they had seen the unexpected assembly at the mouth of Thadrilpass the previous evening, how they had stopped to listen to the Liberator's sermon, how their eyes had been miraculously opened to the truth. Garhug'n had at once decided to follow the Liberator, bringing his family with him. He was floating on a cloud of religious ecstasy. His mousy, unassertive wife looked worried out of her mind. The children were muddy, hungry, tired, and bewildered.

The first guard was a stocky young man with dark hair and beard. His skin had been burned to walnut by the sun, about the color a Spaniard or a high-caste Hindu might be, had either ever condescended to live outdoors in a leather loincloth. His spear was a wrist-thick pole about six feet long, topped with a shiny metal blade that looked both sharp and deadly. He bared an excellent set of snow-white teeth in a cheerful smile and recited a formula greeting in the pidgin Joalian that served as lingua franca of the Vales.

"The Liberator will preach tonight at Shuujooby. Food will be available. Please move on and let him rest. The blessings of the Undivided be with you."

Garhug'n complied immediately, chiding his youngest to stop that wailing, urging the rest of his family along.

Julian returned the smile. "He will wish to see me. We are old friends. If he is asleep, of course—"

The smile shrank. "Move along please, brother."

"I assure you that I have known the Liberator since boyhood and he will be very pleased to see me." Julian took a step forward and found his way blocked by a large bullhide shield.

The teeth above it were no longer smiling. "Move along, I said."

Julian was momentarily shocked speechless. Even at Home, a former army officer could expect to bluff his way past a naked savage without raising more than an eyebrow. On Nextdoor his charisma ordinarily gave him the persuasive power of a charging tank.

"Now look here, my good man—"

The guard twirled his spear around in his fingers as if it were a twig and rammed the metal blade into the ground at Julian's toes. He jumped back instinctively, bumping into Dommi.

"Tonight, in the ruined temple at Shuujooby." The guard pulled his spear free and aimed the point at Julian's belt. His teeth smiled again. His eyes did not.

Another Nagian, if that was what they were, strolled over to reinforce him. He was considerably larger. Saint Kaptaan's charisma was not going to work here. These warriors had been exposed too long to Exeter's, and he had left orders.

Dommi cupped his hands to his mouth and bellowed, in English: "*Tyika* Kisster! It is me, Dommi Houseboy, from Olympus!"

The warriors frowned at each other, momentarily nonplussed. The first raised his spear as if he were about to use it as a club; the second snapped a word and stopped him.

Julian drew himself up, although he could not meet the taller one eye to eye. "Go and inform the Liberator that Kaptaan Smedley and—"

A voice called out from the bushes, not fifty feet away. It began, "Dommi?" and then became unintelligible. Whatever the language, the guards reacted and Dommi seemed to understand. With an enormous grin, he hitched his pack higher on his back and plunged into the undergrowth. The guards made no move to stop him.

Julian took half a step and was again blocked by a shield of wood and bullhide.

"You were not summoned."

Ridiculous! Absurd! That had been Exeter himself calling. So now Julian was going to have to yell out his name also, hawking like a bloody peddler selling fish? He would be damned first. The alternative was obviously just to cool his heels here on the road, and that was almost as bad. He felt his temper rising. He wished he had a store of mana, as Ursula and the others did. It would not take much to jerk these flunkies' chains, but his magical resources were precisely zero. Dommi would presumably inform Exeter that he was here right away.

Or very soon.

The warriors were starting to grin.

"Move along, please," said the taller in the exact tone used by London bobbies.

An instant before Julian began bursting blood vessels, Exeter's voice called out again. The guards stepped aside at once.

"The Liberator summons you!" snapped the big one. "Move!"

For a moment Julian was tempted to tell them that Edward Bloody Exeter could come and deliver the invitation in person, but then common sense prevailed. He stalked into the bushes with as much dignity as he could muster, going where Dommi had gone.

The ground dipped abruptly to a small pond. Shrubs overhanging a low wall of rock threw narrow shade on a sandy beach, where a dozen or so of the Nagians were relaxing, some sitting up, alert, others lying down and apparently snoozing, although they all had their spears within reach. In the middle of the group, Dommi was on his knees with his pack beside him, chattering excitedly to Edward Exeter. Julian scrambled down the little slope and picked his way over outstretched brown legs. He sensed a faint tremor of virtuality. This snug retreat was a very minor node.

The Liberator wore a gray robe, which might be uncomfortably warm in the sticky heat but would at least keep the sun off. He had the cowl back, revealing a shock of wavy black hair in desperate need of a barber. He was jabbering at Dommi, the two of them grinning and talking all over each other like bosom friends, but speaking Randorian so fast that Julian could make out little except proper names. Seemingly Exeter was being brought up to date on events in Olympus since he had left. Almost all the names being bandied to and fro were names of Carrots, not strangers.

For a moment neither paid any heed at all to Julian standing over them. Then Exeter looked up. His brilliant blue eyes studied the newcomer warily before his mouth quirked in a smile.

"Dr. Livingstone, I presume? Or is that your line?"

Feeling oddly at a loss, Julian said, "Cheers!"

"Good to see you, old man." Exeter reached up a hand to shake. " 'Scuse me if I don't leap up, won't you?"

His eyes were bloodshot and sunken. His beard was better trimmed than his hair, but the cheeks above it seemed pale below their tan. His feet were bandaged—just like those of the blond man they had seen earlier who had claimed to have visited Niol last night. . . .

Julian sank down on one knee and accepted the shake with his right hand. Exeter had momentarily forgotten, obviously. He reacted with shock. Then he kept hold of Julian's flipper while he inspected it.

As he let go, he smiled approvingly. "Bloody good show! Nextdoor agrees with you, I'd say."

"It's an improvement." Julian sat down, crossing his legs and pushing Dommi's pack out of the way. "What the blazes is the matter with you, though?"

Exeter shrugged. "Too many late nights." He yawned, and then yawned again, even longer.

Assume a man walked all day, day in, day out. Assume he left his followers one evening and went on foot to Niol and back. . . . Any man might justifiably look all-in after thirty hours on the road. But Exeter was not any man. He was the Liberator.

He was also memories—school days at Fallow in the golden glow of youth, the too-brief trip to Paris that the War had cut short, the frantic few days in 1917 when Julian Smedley had rescued him from a mental ward and he had opened the door to another world for Julian Smedley and thereby saved his sanity. Was that still less than two years ago?

Julian pulled himself together. "No mana?"

"Not just at the moment. So it was you they sent. I rather expected Jumbo or Pinky." There were questions hidden in that remark, questions about loyalty and old friendship.

Why had Julian ever promised not to mention Ursula?

"They asked me to come and find out what you're up to."

"And *Entyika* Newton also," Dommi said quietly.

Whoops!

Exeter compressed his lips so that they vanished briefly between beard and mustache. He said, "A formidable lady, Mrs. Newton, as I recall." Again there were hidden queries in that steady stare.

Relieved that the cat was out of the bag—although he would not use those exact words to Ursula—Julian said, "Ursula will be waiting for you—us—at Shuujooby."

The reply was another cavernous yawn, which effectively masked any reaction the information might have produced.

Damnation! Exeter *must* have been collecting mana these last few weeks. He should be able to banish his fatigue and heal the blisters with a snap of his fingers. Surely he could not have been crazy enough to squander it all on fancy miracles to impress the peasants? Or had he spent it fighting reapers?

Ursula would see right away that he was vulnerable. She would eat him alive. The toughs with their spears and shields would be no defense against her, for Exeter would order them all to go home, dismiss his crusade, and follow her back to Olympus like a pet dog. Hell!

No mana at all? Had it been stolen from him?

"I understand you dropped in on friend Visek last night."

"Oh, blast!" He rubbed his eyes wearily. "How did you hear about that?"

Touched a nerve, have we? "A little bird told me."

The warriors sprawled nearby were frowning at their inability to understand the conversation, but Dommi knew English. He was gazing at Exeter with idiotic adoration. "We overheard a fair-haired man narrating this incident, *tyika*. He had sore feet likewise."

Exeter said, "Thanks!" without taking his eyes off Julian, and smothered another yawn. "Remind me to invent taxicabs sometime. Yes, it's true. His name's Dosh Envoy. I should have told him to keep his mouth shut. He usually makes oysters sound like starlings."

"He was babbling brookily this morning. So is Visek male or female?" Julian could win a sizable bet or two in Olympus with that information. Even Olga claimed not to know for certain.

"They're both—Jack and Jill. So where's Mrs. Newton?"

Julian's gaze wandered to the brown-leathery hills, which must be five miles away now, or more. From this distance, bluish ice-clad crags showed above them. "Riding around."

"Who else is with her?"

"Just T'lin Dragontrader. We came to—"

"That's all right then. Good."

"What do you mean, 'good'?"

A gleam showed in the tired cornflower-blue eyes. "I mean T'lin's dragons can probably outrun Queen Elvanife's moas, as long as he doesn't wander too far into the plains."

It was Julian's turn to jump. This was the meanest game of verbal tennis he'd played in years. "That's why you left two of your Trojans up a tree? You blocked the road with disciples and forced them to go around another way?"

"I detect the mind of a professional strategist."

Which was no answer. Julian shrugged. "There's a nasty prophecy about young men's bones in Niolland."

Exeter nodded, stretched his arms, yawned some more. He glanced briefly at his entourage, smiled at Dommi, turned his calculating gaze on Julian again. "Time to hit the road. It would be gentlemanly to be there to greet Mrs. Newton when she arrives, wouldn't it?"

Julian rolled a few curses around in his head. He had promised not to issue any warnings. . . . If only Exeter didn't look so damned played out . . . Hell! He could drop a hint. "Why don't you take a break, old man, and go on tomorrow, when you're fresher?"

Exeter seemed to understand, because his smile depicted gratitude like an illuminated vellum scroll. Then he shook his head. "I'd best be on my way. I'm expecting a squad of Niolland's finest, and it wouldn't be fair to let them run into Ursula without warning them, would it? Tell me, is it only Mrs. Newton I have to fear, or have the others loaded her up with their mana, too?"

Julian gaped. "Is that possible? You can *give* mana to someone?"

"Yes, it's possible. That's how the little gods pay their dues to the Five." He reached stiffly for his sandals, and his bodyguards scrambled to their feet, even the ones that had seemed to be asleep. "There's a whopper of a node at Shuujooby. I want to get there before the troopers do."

A node would be a fortress for him, but only if he had a store of mana to exploit it. Julian had no mana either, so he couldn't help, whatever happened.

# 30

Exeter limped back to the road, obviously finding walking an ordeal. His praetorians fussed around him like mother hens, but he ignored them, pulling up his cowl to hide his face. They would gladly have carried him shoulder-high, of course, but what sort of prophet would he seem then? Soon he called Dommi to his side. The road was narrow and crowded again, now that the sun was past its height, so Julian found himself excluded, walking behind his own houseboy and hemmed in by the armed escort like a felon being led to the gallows.

He tried to make conversation with the spear carriers on either side of him, but he could understand little of their heavily accented Joalian. They were loathe to speak with him anyway, being uncertain just who he was or how their leader regarded him. The red-haired one was obviously the boss's favorite.

Julian had made no progress with Exeter so far. He still had no idea why the man had changed his mind about the *Filoby Testament,* nor did he know what could be done about Ursula. He had been expecting to find the Liberator all charged up with mana, capable of at least putting up a fight. Watching the gray-robed figure striding along in front of him, though, he could see charisma at work. Even though they were not on a node, Exeter was bearing himself straighter already, drawing strength from the devotion of his bodyguard and the adoring pilgrims he passed. That would doubtless carry him as far as Shuujooby. It wouldn't help much with Ursula, or Queen Elvanife's lancers either.

For a sweaty, mosquito-laden hour, they trudged through the swamp, looping around toward the rocky gullies of Niolslope again. Finally Exeter remembered his manners. Leaving Dommi to walk alone, he dropped back to partner Julian.

"Dommi tells me the war is over." He looked fitter than before, his blue eyes twinkling again. Perhaps he felt better able to battle wits.

"Apparently. The Huns lost. We haven't heard much detail yet." Julian told what he knew, marveling how little it touched him now. He rarely even dreamed of the hell he had known in Flanders anymore. "And you've started another," he concluded. "Another war, I mean."

"Dear me! The Service is upset?"

"Very. When they hear how you're changing their doctrine, they'll all spit fire and brimstone."

"Their own fault for inventing the demons. What sort of religion is based on lies and slander?"

"Try telling that to Ursula."

Exeter did not answer. His cowl concealed his face. He had been a devilish-good bowler back at Fallow, never much of a batsman. When he was on bat, he had consistently stonewalled. He had not lost that ability, for he now proceeded to stonewall every question Julian threw at him.

"You don't hand out gold earrings to your converts?"

"Ain't got no gold."

"But you've imported baptism!"

"Water's cheap."

"I suppose every cult needs some sort of initiation," Julian mused. "And circumcision would be messy?"

Exeter shuddered. "Please!"

"So you went into partnership with the Pentatheon?"

"They're not all monsters."

"And they deal with any reapers Zath sends after you?"

"They have so far."

If the Five were frightened of upstart Zath, they might accept the Liberator as an ally or use him as a stalking horse, although only a congenital idiot would ever trust any of them. What promises had Exeter made to win that cooperation? How long a spoon was he using? How far had he bent his principles? To ask those questions would be to end the conversation and trample the fragile reawakening of friendship.

"I thought Zath was stronger than any of them, perhaps even stronger than the whole caboodle?"

Exeter shrugged. "Who knows? Who can possibly know, without trying? No one plays the Great Game with his cards showing."

Julian persisted. "So why doesn't he come and get you, now that he's aware where you are?"

"You're the military man. You send out skirmishers and they fail to return. Do you march your whole army after them?"

"No. I send a stronger force to reconnoiter."

"I expect he'll get around to that."

Reapers were only natives, enslaved by mana. They were armed with rituals that could direct the power of their god, but all their strength came from Zath himself.

"If he sends that stronger force, will you be able to detect them? Will the spells show?"

Exeter took a while to reply. Julian could not tell whether he was thinking over the question or just delaying.

"If I have mana of my own, I may be able to detect them."

"Why don't you have any mana now?"

"Used it up."

"Doing what? Turning rods into serpents?" He knew he was prying dangerously, but he got a civil enough answer.

"Running. I did heal an injured ankle, but it was on Visek's node."

"Why did that matter?"

"All the witnesses were Visek's clergy. They gave all the credit to Visek."

"You'll gain some back tonight, when you preach at Shuujooby?"

"Hope so."

Ursula might get to him before he even opened his mouth, unless Julian himself could distract her somehow. To a large extent, mana was its own fertilizer, like money— the more one had, the easier it was to gain more. Physical exhaustion was not the best state in which to preach a religious revolution. Bloody idiot!

Julian realized he was starting to lose his temper, which was the worst way to deal with stonewalling. "You're heading for Tharg? You're going to knock the chip off Zath's shoulder, aren't you? Where the hell are you going to get the mana from?"

Exeter hit that one for six. He turned his head and flashed a smile at his tormentor. "From the *Filoby Testament,* of course."

Julian said, "What?"

"The prophecy itself has mana, old man. Haven't you realized that yet? It takes a ton of mana to prophesy—so where does it *go*?"

"Haven't the foggiest."

"Into the words! Every time the prophecy is vindicated by events, it collects more mana from all the people who know about it. Zath's been trying since before we were born to break the chain. He fails every time, and every time the prophecy grows stronger."

Julian stepped in a pothole and stumbled into a leather shield, which helpfully thumped him back to the vertical again.

"That's bizarre! I never heard that theory before. Who told you that?"

"Thought it up by myself," Exeter said with a shrug.

"I don't believe it!"

"I'm not sure I do, actually. But perhaps Zath does? I thought there was at least a fifty-fifty chance he'd come after me right at the start—nip me in the bud in Joalvale with *donner und blitzen* and fiery whips. He didn't. So perhaps he's learned his lesson."

"He'll just let all those things happen, you mean? Let the play be acted out? Hell's bells, man, the finale is his own death!"

Exeter chuckled. "Which means that he won't have dared do a foreseeing of his own. Did you know that, old man? Foreseeing your own death is fatal. He may have had someone else do it for him, of course. No, I'm sure he'll fight at the end. Now he knows I'm coming for him. He knows I have allies, but he doesn't know how many or who, and he'll want to know that for settling scores later if he wins. He may try another jab or two, but I do believe he'll save his strength for the final innings."

The idea of the *Filoby Testament* as a sort of active participant did make a wildly improbable sort of sense. Julian himself had postulated that Exeter might have seen something nobody else had. Was this it? More important, would it deter Ursula from meddling?

"That valley?" Exeter was pointing a long, gray-sleeved arm at the hills that now loomed over them, surprisingly close again. "Shuujooby's at the mouth of that."

"You've reconnoitered the whole route, haven't you? That's what you've been doing these last two years?"

Exeter just smiled.

# 31

Where the river emptied out of the hills to feed the lakes and marshland, its course was almost a mile wide. At that time of year it was all sand, brilliant white quartz, with only a few silver pools and shallow braids holding water, and nothing flowing except an invisible, tangible torrent of air, the breath of the mountains pouring out of the gorge to blow grit in men's eyes. The only relief from the glaring whiteness was a speckle of shadow under isolated dead trees, stark bleached skeletons.

The trail ended on the northern bank at a rickety jetty and a couple of stranded ferryboats. The celebrated metropolis of Shuujooby was a cluster of driftwood hovels cowering low in the long, rank grass, each hoarding a snowy drift of sand on its leeward side. About a score of ragged villagers stood gaping at the Liberator's crusade going by. They must have been puzzled by the pilgrims who had already passed and dwindled to specks in the distance, trooping over the shining white desert to reach the designated stopping place. The Warband with their spears and shields were an even greater wonder, and there were hundreds of followers to come yet.

The far bank was a faint green line of brush and woodland, before which stood the remains of the temple, half buried in the sands of the floodplain. Even at that distance, Julian could see that it had been picked clean, as if by giant vultures. Every stone must be burnished smooth, and few seemed to be standing in their original positions. It would have been built on a node, though, and the virtuality would remain. A whopper of a node, Exeter had called it.

He had gone forward to rejoin Dommi, so Julian was alone again. He did not mind, for he had much to think about. Ursula would certainly try to block Exeter's revolution. Julian found that he was hunting for arguments to stop her, so he must want it to continue. Why? Could he really believe that it had any chance of success? It seemed horribly like a children's crusade, a massacre of innocents. Whatever damage it was going to do to the Church of the Undivided was probably inevitable now. Whether the heretic sect was smitten by Zath in Thargvale or just discredited and dispersed when Ursula betwitched its leader, the Pentatheon and their traditional religion would be seen to have triumphed.

That was a very cynical attitude! At the rate Exeter was going, he would have gathered a huge following by the time he reached Thargvale. Better, surely, to abandon a few hundred people here than let thousands be slain there? Unless Julian could convince himself that the circus held some reasonable chance of success, he would never convince Ursula—and should not even try.

Ignoring Shuujooby and the watching Shuujoobyites, the Warband arrived at the riverbank and the jetty. The lead warriors jumped down from the spiny grass to the white plain. Exeter and Dommi followed, then Julian himself slithered after them in a shower of hot sand. As he recovered his balance, he saw Ursula a hundred yards or so off to his right, beyond the hamlet. For a moment he felt a strange reluctance to speak with her. He had sworn not to warn Exeter and then broken his word.

She saw him and waved. She ran down the bank, wheeling her arms for balance, and then stood waiting. He slipped neatly between two of the Nagians and started to run. If anyone tried to follow and was called back by Exeter, the wind stole away the words. He staggered and stumbled in the soft sand, his aching feet reminding him how far he had walked that day.

As he drew close, he saw that she was barefoot, clutching her shoes in one hand; the other held her wide-brimmed hat in place against the mischief of the wind. She was wearing a white dress of the flimsy Nextdoorian fabric the Service called cotton, although its fibers came from a tuber. Her arms were bare and the billowing of the material revealed her ankles and half her shins. It also displayed the curves of her hips and thighs and breasts, the unusual width of her shoulders. He had never heard of such a garment in the Vales, but he would not complain about it. She looked for all the world like a girl playing on a beach at Blackpool or Frinton, and must feel like that, also, for she was laughing as she watched his labored approach, her face flushed by the wind.

Instinctively he reached up to remove his hat and remembered that it was a turban. Good Lord! Kiss a woman with his hat on?

He did. She folded into his embrace and returned the kiss willingly, thumping her shoes against his flank in a one-armed hug. Then she applied her other arm as well, and in seconds the wind stole her hat. She swore. He broke loose and ran to catch it, noting that the Warband was tramping along in the same order as before, heading for the distant ruins. Had Exeter observed the meeting and drawn the appropriate conclusions? No matter—Dommi would certainly have told him how the land lay.

Julian brought back the hat and kissed her again.

"Mm! Walking must agree with you," she said breathlessly.

"Actually, I was dead on my feet until I saw you." And now he wasn't. Ursula Newton intoxicated him.

He exchanged the hat for her shoes, which he held in the crook of his right arm. Hand in hand, they plodded over the riverbed, heading for the ruins. He could think of no reasonable excuse not to.

"Those Zulus are Nagians, I suppose?" she said.

"Right on. His old comrades from the Lemond campaign."

"And how is General Exeter?"

"As well as can be expected." He was lying already.

Ursula glanced up at him quizzically. Her eyes were hazel with tiny golden flecks in them. "Did you discover the argument that will convince him to stop this madness?"

He hoped he had found an argument to stop *her*. "Not really. I—We really had no chance for thorough discussion."

She made no comment. The brim of her hat concealed her expression.

"Remember that night at the Pinkneys'?" he said. "I suggested that Exeter might have seen something the rest of us had missed?"

"Do tell." She sounded skeptical already.

"Well, he's got an interesting theory that the *Filoby Testament* itself may be a reservoir of mana. We know it was an accident; we know it drained Garward so he almost died of it. Mana certainly went into its making. Exeter thinks that every time it's been proved right, it's grown stronger."

"You believe this?"

"I don't know. I think we ought to get back to Prof Rawlinson on the subject before we take any action." Hearing no wild cheers of agreement, Julian pressed on. "I was sent out to reconnoiter, remember. We're scouts, not an assault party."

He was a scout. Ursula might think of herself otherwise.

"Fiddlesticks! It's enough to send Prof into delirium. You honestly think that a prophecy can somehow take on a life of its own and then gather strength from its own success? You're anthropomorphizing an idea!"

"I'm not the first to do that, old girl. A faith is an idea, and lots of faiths have been anthro-whatever-you-said. Religions and nation-states are ideas." Then Julian thought of something else. If he wasn't convincing Ursula, he was at least beginning to convince himself. "Look at it this way—if Zath had never tried to invalidate the *Filoby Testament,* then a lot of things wouldn't have happened. D'you see? Such as Exeter's return Home. That wouldn't *dis*prove anything, because the prophecy gives no dates or order. As far as the world's concerned, those things just wouldn't have happened *yet,* see? But Zath meddled and they did happen, and everyone says, 'Oo! There goes the *Filoby* thing again, ain't it wonderful?' People talk. Its reputation gets boosted. Fame is a source of mana—you've got to admit that."

"Pull the other one! Trafalgar Square's famous. You think it's got mana?"

"It may," Julian protested. "It makes me feel pretty proud to see old Horatio up there on his bally chimney. It's at least got virtuality." Was virtuality in places the same as mana in people? Did a place gain virtuality from worship as people gained mana? That was an intriguing idea, by George! When he got home to Olympus, he wouldn't just ask Prof about it; he'd work it all out in a paper and present it for discussion. But the problem at the moment was Ursula. "Besides, mana doesn't obey the laws of logic. Nor does charisma. Or nodes or portals."

"Or Captain Smedley."

They were halfway across already. The Warband had almost reached the temple, trailing a snake of pilgrims in its wake. The broken walls and stark, tilted columns were a pale yellow stain on the whiteness of the sand. Julian thought of streaky yolk in a fried egg and realized that he was hungry.

The Nagians might keep visitors away from the Liberator until he had delivered his promised sermon. He doubted they could stop Ursula from gate-crashing if she wanted to.

"What else did you learn?" she asked, not looking up.

"Not much. Well . . . he has allies. Astina and Irepit have been helping him. Apparently he had an audience with Visek."

Now she tilted her head and her eyes glinted angrily. "Is this common knowledge?" She had seen the asp in the basket already.

"Some of it," he admitted.

"And how does he rationalize consorting with demons?"

"Um, you'll have to ask him. Look, darling, just promise me that you won't do anything hasty, because—"

"I won't promise a blasted thing!"

"Dammit, Ursula, it's dangerous!"

"What is?"

"Tampering with the prophecy! Zath's been trying for years. All he ever managed to do was kill a lot of innocent bystanders—Exeter's parents, Julius Creighton, poor old Bagpipe. . . . You're likely to get your own fingers burned if you start meddling. All I'm asking is that you—*Oh, Hell!*"

Never mind Ursula. A column of lancers on moas was pouring down the far bank and across the sand, heading for the Liberator and his Warband. There were at least a hundred of them.

# 32

Back in 1916, on leave in London, Julian had visited a moving-pictures theater. This was just like that. There the screen had been canvas, here it was a glare of sunlit sand, but he saw the same black-and-white images—jerky, silent, and hard to make out, varnished in the same unreality. Only the thundering pipe organ was missing.

Moas stood ten or twelve feet high. They were bigger than ostriches and even faster, which meant they made a terrestrial horse seem like an arthritic Shetland pony. A man on a moa's back was out of reach of a foot soldier and his fifteen-foot lance was tipped with a triangular blade of razor-sharp steel. In full charge, he moved at around fifty miles an hour, a bloody near impossible target for bow or javelin.

This was a charge. Riding three abreast with pennants waving, the column swept across the riverbed like an express train, undulating over the low dunes and ridges. A cloud of dust from the hooves floated away in the wind, adding to the train illusion. The three files began to spread out, opening like talons, bearing death to all in their path.

Julian stood rooted. The Warband was sprinting to the temple—a man with solid rock at his back would be a harder target, although he would have little room to handle his own weapon. Within the ruins, the lancers would lose their advantage of speed, but not that of height, and moas were as nimble as men at dodging and cornering. The odds were five or six to one anyway. Two files were moving to encircle the temple. The third was heading for the long rope of pilgrims, which began to disintegrate as the prudent took to their heels, fleeing back toward Shuujooby. The procession became a rout.

"This should be an interesting test of Mr. Exeter's abilities," Ursula remarked acidly.

That broke the spell. Julian almost screamed as he realized their peril. He and Ursula were just standing there, two isolated onlookers in the middle of the empty field of sand. They could never be mistaken for ragged Shuujoobian peasants, so they would be assumed to be Liberator supporters. They were sitting ducks. He dropped Ursula's shoes, grabbed her wrist, and began to run. She must have come to the same conclusion at the same instant, for she did not resist.

Running in the hot, soft sand was pure nightmare. The hamlet seemed a million miles away, and it would provide no real cover anyway. The moas would move on the grass as easily as on the riverbed. Julian could not recall how far beyond Shuujooby the edge of the swamp was—he just knew that it was too far, so running was useless. No matter, they had no alternative. The shell burst of pilgrims was throwing fragments in their direction, a few agile youngsters overtaking them. So now they were within the fleeing mob itself, part of a designated target.

Out of the corner of his eye he saw a long shadow hurtle over the sand. He turned his head in time to see a boy die—a lad of about fourteen, a brown, skinny adolescent flailing his long legs, floundering as fast as he could through the powdery sand. The moa flashed in from behind him and past him and was gone before his corpse even hit the ground, hosing a crimson jet. The lance blade had severed the kid's neck. One of the flashing hoofs struck the falling head and hurled it in a long arc like a soccer ball. There was no sound at all.

The moa spun around ninety degrees and accelerated straight for Julian and Ursula without missing a stride. Mount and rider seemed to explode out of the distance, from small to huge in an instant, filling the sky. Julian pushed Ursula behind him. He caught a brief glimpse of the trooper crouched alongside his mount's long neck: bronze helmet, leather tunic, shiny boots in stirrups. He saw the moa's yellow eyes and teeth and the froth around its bit, saw human eyes slitted and teeth bared as their owner aimed his bloodstained lance straight at Julian's chest.

Shells and bombs he had survived, bullets and poison gas, and he was going to be stuck like a pig by this medieval nightmare, this anachronistic cowboy. He closed his eyes.

He felt the wind of the beast's passing; he caught a whiff of its animal scent. Hot sand sprayed against his shins.

He opened his eyes and looked around. The lancer had just caught an elderly, silver-haired woman. His blade took her in the back, lifting her bodily off the ground like a rag, then cutting loose through meat and bone. The body dropped free and the rider changed direction slightly, aiming at another target.

Julian peered at Ursula's chalky face. His mouth felt drier than the sand. "You did that?" he croaked.

She nodded.

"Thanks!" He wrapped a shaky arm around her shoulders, and she huddled in tight against him. Most of the fleeing peasants had been run down now. The last few were being skewered as they tried to scramble up the sandy bank. Some had taken refuge under the jetty, but the troopers had seen them.

There was still activity at the temple. There the butchery had not been so easy. Several dead moas lay in clear view and more wheeled around riderless. That would be the Nagians' work, of course, but spears were shorter than lances; they would have had to throw their spears. Even if you were good enough to hit such a target, what could you do for an encore?

The numbers had been impossible from the start. Even if every Nagian managed to kill one lancer, he would then be left with no weapon except a knife, facing three or four more. How many civilian pilgrims had gone to the temple ahead of them? A hundred? Two? Julian could see people scrambling up the walls in search of shelter, swarming ants. He supposed that the troopers would now draw their swords and go after them on foot. Exeter would certainly be dead, of course—prime target. Dommi was in there somewhere, poor sod.

He stood with Ursula on a white desert blotched with corpses. He supposed they should be moving, but shock had addled his wits. He couldn't decide what to do, which way to go.

"How long can you hold that invisibility trick?"

She shivered against him. "We're not invisible. I just distracted that one. It won't work if there's more than one or two of them. Besides, there aren't any more decoys to use."

"You mean you—" Don't ask! The old woman would have died anyway. "Then we ought to . . ." He looked around again to make sure no murdering Lancelot was heading their way. He could hear faint screams from the jetty. Some of the troopers had dismounted and gone in after the refugees. He looked away.

He blinked. He looked again and blinked again. It was real. "By Jove, I do believe that's our bus coming!"

Four dragons running over the sand, coming from the gorge mouth. T'lin's black turban and copper beard on the lead dragon. Julian waved and T'lin waved back, so he had seen them. How long had Ursula known? Never mind. Saved!

Well, perhaps saved. In a race on this terrain, the smart money would back the moas. Fortunately, dragons were hellishly expensive. No trooper was going to mistake a gentleman on a dragon for a penniless vagrant pilgrim. It would be like driving up to the scene of the crime in a Rolls—the bobbies would salute you and call you sir.

He saw the woman's body, and the boy's head lying in a puddle of water, a long way from the corpse. Murdering swine! Yes, artillery killed people too, but that had been on a battlefield, those had been soldiers. This was deliberate slaughter of unarmed women and children. *Damn Edward Exeter and his bloody peasants' revolt!*

Their butchery at the jetty complete, the Shuujooby troopers had formed up and were coming across the plain at a slow lope. They would certainly pick off the two they had missed on the first pass.

T'lin and Starlight came racing over the sand, with Bluegem, Blizzard, and Mistrunner spread out behind. Julian bellowed a wordless welcome as the dragontrader went by, barking commands that hardly seemed needed. Dragons often showed surprising intelligence, and Mistrunner was already heading for Ursula. Blizzard came straight to Julian and skidded to a halt on his belly, ready to be mounted. He was obviously suffering from the heat, puffing hoarsely, his long neck frills flapping like wings.

Julian threw himself across the saddle and scrabbled wildly until he could grip the pommel plate with his good hand and swing his leg over. *"Wondo!"* But Blizzard was already heaving himself to his feet. Now where? Stand and face down the troopers or make a run for the hills? While Julian was still trying to make up his mind and find his left stirrup, he heard Ursula's voice raised in command and a cry of protest from T'lin, "Dragons cannot *zomph* in this heat!"

But Mistrunner shot off in a shower of sand—heading for the temple.

"Dommi!" Julian shouted in sudden understanding. "Dommi's in there. *Zomph!*" Good for Ursula!

Blizzard's game leap forward hurled him back against the baggage plate. To make a run for it would likely have brought on pursuit anyway, and Dommi certainly deserved rescue if he were still alive. Edward Bloody Exeter did not! His crazy messiah delusions had provoked this bloodbath. Jumbo and the other antis had been right all along.

Ursula and Mistrunner were drawing out ahead. Poor Blizzard was managing no more than a *varch* and probably could not keep even that up much longer; he was blowing out more steam than the Flying Scotsman. T'lin drew up close on Starlight, the unladen Bluegem following.

"This will kill them!" the Dragontrader howled.

"It may kill us too," Julian said cheerfully. Though he still had no weapon, there was something about being mounted that stiffened a chap's spirit. Being the man on the ground when the cavalry charged was a ruddy poor show. That was what the Middle Ages had been all about, of course.

He passed the first dead moa, its rider sprawled nearby with his throat cut. The footprints showed where the Nagian victor had departed, taking his spear with him and apparently the trooper's lance also, for it was missing, but one down did not change the odds very much.

He went by more bodies: men, women, even small children, many of them horribly ripped by the force of the lances; blood-soaked sand. The fighting was still going on—he could hear shouts and screams from the ruins and he wanted to scream. There was nothing he could do to help. Now, if only Nextdoorian dragons were real fire-breathing monsters instead of hay-eating softies . . .

A whopper of a node, Exeter had said, and already Julian could feel his skin prickle at the awesome touch of virtuality. A great holy place, an ancient sanctuary . . . The temple remains were bigger than he had realized, so scattered and shattered that he could form no clear image of its plan. In places the original carvings still showed; in others the stones had been fretted into grotesque shapes; yet others had been polished smooth. Centuries of wind had pushed the sand into waves, leaving columns and walls sticking up at random from the dunes, many of them now bearing bizarre headdresses of refugees. There were people perched on every high surface. He saw one canted column with two women and a man on the top of it. How had they climbed up there? They looked as if one sneeze would hurl them all off. He sought vainly for a sign of Dommi's red hair.

T'lin had disappeared. Blizzard was following Mistrunner through the labyrinth—around a corner, then another, over a dune, and almost into a squirming, bleating herd of moas, which had been packed into a dead-end corridor and were being kept there by two mounted lancers. Their job had probably been hard enough even before the dragons appeared, but then the moas began to panic. The soldiers reacted with roars of anger. Ursula turned Mistrunner and put her straight at a wall. Blizzard followed without waiting to be told. Julian's hill straps dangled unfastened and useless behind him—he grabbed at the pommel plate with his good hand just as he was tilted onto his back and almost tipped off.

No human could have climbed that stonework and even the dragons took it slowly, their long claws scraping and scrabbling for purchase. He twisted his head around to see if he was about to be skewered, but the troopers had their hands full with the moas.

Then Blizzard reached the top of the wall, balancing precariously on the stony ridge at Mistrunner's side and belching clouds of steam. Ursula did not even look around. She was watching the drama in what must originally have been a great hall and was now a shadowed courtyard. The sandy floor sloped down to a slimy green pool at the far end, making a sort of amphitheater, and above the pool rose a high wall, bearing a few stumps and buttresses that had once supported a ribbed roof. The rest of the walls were a jagged sawtooth, all the higher points loaded with Exeter's pilgrims, feet dangling. More were perched on any ledge or sill that had a chance of being out of reach of lances.

The entrance was an archway blocked with drifted sand almost to its keystone. No moa could pass through that. Even men on foot would have to crouch to enter, so there the Nagian spearmen had been able to hold off the Joalians' greater numbers. At least three had died doing so, yet all their lives had bought was a little time for their friends, for now they had been outflanked. Now the troopers were swarming in through window apertures and breeches in the walls. The Nagians had shields, but their spears were much shorter than the lances. They were hopelessly outnumbered. Brave defiance became instant rout. Soldiers yelled; onlookers howled; dying men screamed. It could not compare with the Western Front for sheer horror, but it was still bloody murder.

And there was idiot Exeter in his monk's robe, floundering and splashing through the water of the pond, accompanied by two of his henchmen. The others were trying to cover his retreat and being cut down. Running away? Being unharmed, Exeter had little choice but to run away; even so, it was not what Julian would have expected of him. He watched in grim despair as the trio reached the wall, assuming they would now turn at bay. Instead, the larger, brawnier Nagian dropped to hands and knees in the water, the other jumped up to his back and pulled his leader up after him. He cupped hands; Exeter scrambled to the man's shoulders and reached for a ledge overhead. There was a window opening higher up. He might even reach that, but did he really think he would be allowed to escape so easily?

The top half of his human ladder jumped down, the other man stood up. They had just time to grab up their spears again before the last surviving half dozen of their companions fell back and joined them in the water. Then the Joalian pack was upon them. The troopers came in a bristle of blades, offering no quarter. The pond became a bloody froth as the victims fell, most of them stabbed by four or five lances simultaneously.

Julian shuddered and looked away. Ursula's face was haggard, her lips drawn back in a grimace. He glanced quickly around the watchers on their perches, hoping for a glimpse of Dommi's red hair, but could not see it. He looked down at the cavorting, cheering victors and felt the cold familiar breath of mortality on the back of his neck. The civilians would be next, for the carnage at the jetty showed that someone had ordered a massacre.

"Think we'd better get the devil out of here. The show's over for the Liberator now."

"Wait!" she said.

Exeter had reached his objective, a circular opening about fifteen feet above the pool. It must once have been a great window. He stood within it, outlined against sunlight, balancing himself with outstretched arms and feet. He had his cowl back. The wind was billowing and tugging his gray robe, as if trying to dislodge him. He was a perfect target, an X in a circle. The Joalians had seen him.

An officer began shouting orders, calling upon his men to clear a space and give him a fair shot. It would not be a difficult one, for although a lance was too heavy to be thrown far, in this case it need go only a few feet. He hefted the pole and prepared to run.

"Stop!" Exeter roared. "Don't you realize what you have done, you fools?"

The scene shifted and shimmered as if a stone had fallen into a reflecting pool. Suddenly he was not a target anymore.

"Even Karzon forbids the slaughter of penitents and pilgrims! Have none of you read scripture? Have you forgotten your oaths?" His words echoed and reverberated, magnified into a knell of doom by strange acoustics and the intense virtuality. He loomed over the assembly like an avenging angel. The captain dropped his lance in dismay, staring up openmouthed at his accuser.

"Repent, repent!" Even Julian, perched on a puffing gargoyle atop the far wall, could feel his scalp prickle at the power of the call—and he was only a bystander. Exeter lambasted the lancers, berating them for the massacre. He quoted their own Valian gospels at them: the Green Scripture, the sacred words of Karzon, god of war; the Blue Scriptures of Astina, goddess of warriors. He reeled off passage after passage to show the sinners how they had sinned, the laws they had broken. He even quoted the secret oaths of the soldiers' Karzon cult, the Blood and Hammer. How did he know all that?

Julian glanced again at Ursula, but she was intent, as mesmerized as any. He ought to be making his escape or searching for Dommi among the living and dead, yet he could not move. The waves of charisma and authority streaming from Exeter were mind-numbing.

"So if those misguided teachings denounce your conduct, what then must the One True God think of you? The Undivided, the one who must not be named? Open your ears to the truth and tremble! Hear his commands. . . ."

Why was the idiot speaking English to Niolians?

No, he wasn't. It was Joalian. No, Randorian . . . Whatever it was, the audience understood. Julian watched the soldiers cringe lower; he heard them sob. He felt his own eyes prickle with tears, and still Exeter lashed the guilty. The rest of the troopers, the contingent from Shuujooby, came filing in through the arch, falling to their knees as they, too, heard this awful judgment. At last the anathema ended.

"Yes, there is forgiveness! Yes, you still have hope! If you truly repent, the Undivided may yet turn aside his wrath. . . ."

This was the most incredible display of mana Julian had ever heard of. An hour ago—nay, much less than that—Exeter had been exhausted, able to walk only because he could draw strength from his devoted supporters. Now he blazed within that window like the sun at noon. He thundered with the authority of God.

"Will you accept my judgment?"

"Yes! Yes! Tell us!" The troopers howled agreement, reaching up their hands in supplication.

"Are there any among you who did not shed blood today?"

Six or seven men timidly raised their arms. The rest subsided.

"Then this be your penance. Go now. Find your mounts and ride with all haste to Niol. Take word to Queen Elvanife herself. Tell her to her face how she has offended against the people who were her children. Tell her that she must come here at once to weep on their graves—walking, barefoot, with her hair unbound. Tell her that only thus may she have hope for her soul. Go!"

The half dozen men reeled to their feet and fled from the courtyard, stumbling over the sand. The rest remained, waiting to hear their fate.

The Liberator had cowed a victorious army into a pack of sniveling penitents.

"And when you have gathered them up and prepared the graves . . ."

He was ordering the rest of the troopers to bury the dead.

But the greatest concentration of corpses was directly below him. There, in that scummy puddle of water, the last of his Warband had made their stand, defending their leader. There the Nagians had bled to death or drowned, and now only a few shields and lifeless limbs protruded from the bloody surface.

The bubble burst. Julian clapped his hands over his ears. His throat knotted in waves of nausea. Monster! Contemptible murderer! Hypocrite! The prophecy had warned Exeter that there would be killing in Niolvale. He had foreseen the carnage, and he had used it for his own ends. He had sacrificed his followers, the peasants—men, women and children—and especially his old comrades from Nagvale.

There was the source of his new mana.

The Liberator was no better than Zath.

No, he was worse. When Zath wanted human sacrifice, at least he did not slaughter his friends.

# 33

The wind dropped soon after sunset, letting the muggy air of the swamps drift in with its bugs and pungent leafy scents. Julian had wandered off alone, away from the ominous virtuality of the node. Having found a trunk of driftwood on which to sit, he watched unseeing as the sky turned bloody above Niolwall and then dimmed to black, and stars came out like a million shiny tears. The green moon would not rise for hours yet, but Ysh, Kirb'l, and Eltiana shed enough light to reveal the activity on that plain like a stark etching, ebony on silver. The troopers labored to gather the bodies and dig graves. They toiled in silence, dark gnomes in a milk-opal world, anxious to work the bloodstains off their souls.

T'lin and the dragons had been sent off to high ground, where the poor brutes could rest and graze, and would return in the morning. Ursula was still somewhere around the temple. Dommi was alive and well.

Exeter must have dispatched messengers to tell the rest of his followers that it was now safe to continue the pilgrimage. Probably some had chosen to flee back through the marshlands, but an amazing number had trusted his word, and they came trudging in over the riverbed—hundreds of them, hour after hour.

At dusk, two Nagians had appeared with their spears and shields, driving a small herd of sheeplike animals. Julian had wondered how those two lone survivors must feel, then realized that he knew exactly how they felt, because he had felt the same way on the Western Front every day for two years. They would be feeling enormously relieved to be alive when their chums were all dead, and guilty as hell because of it.

How did Julian Smedley feel? He could not put words to his disgust, his sense of betrayal, his shock, anger. . . . Power could corrupt, but the greed for power corrupted more. He would not have believed that any Old Fallovian could have sunk so low to gain it, let alone Edward Exeter. He wished he had left his former friend in the psycho ward at Staffles, back in 1917. A cell in Broadmoor would be even better, beside the rest of the criminally insane.

His reverie was broken by singing. The funeral service was under way. Irony! The last time he had seen Exeter before today, he had been conducting a funeral for some of Zath's victims. Now he was burying his own.

This time Julian Smedley would not attend.

\*     \*     \*

The service was brief. As soon as it ended, campfires flickered into life all around the ruins so the sheeplike things could furnish the funeral feast. Reluctantly admitting to himself that he was giddy from lack of food, Julian hauled his weary bones upright and set off in search of charity, but the scent of charred meat at the nearest campfire turned his stomach and he went on without stopping. Shunning the crowd, he wandered into the temple. He found the big courtyard, deserted now. The bodies had gone from the pool and only stars filled the empty window where Exeter had stood. The stonework was still warm, the air cool. Somehow the virtuality seemed even greater by moonlight, stark walls against the sky, black velvet shadows on the sand. It made his flesh crawl. Even the natives had sensed it and stayed away.

Except one. Tracking a flicker of light, he discovered a smaller courtyard and a man alone, lying prone before a small fire. He was obviously alive and conscious, because one of his feet scuffled busily in the sand, but his head and shoulders were hidden by a boulder. Curious, Julian walked over to him, silent on the ever-present sand. He recognized that what he had thought was a boulder was Dommi's pack at the same instant as the copper glint of Dommi's hair came into view. He was writing busily, his paper and writing board so close to the fire that they might become part of it at any minute.

"Hello."

His houseboy let out a gasp of surprise. Then he recognized Julian and showed all his teeth in a beam of welcome. "*Tyika* Kaptaan!" He squirmed around and sat up cross-legged, clutching his writing board to his chest. "I am most joyful that you and *Entyika* Newton escaped the villainous event."

"And I'm very glad that you did." Julian wanted to know what was so important that it had to be written by firelight and could not wait until daylight. "I expect we'll be returning to Olympus in the morning."

Dommi's face did not react and that very blankness was a reaction.

"We've done what we came to do," Julian added.

"Yes, *tyika.*"

Oh, blast! "You want to stay, I suppose?"

Dommi nodded and bit his lip.

Julian stepped closer and sat down. He leaned his arms on his knees. "Tell me. You can't expect *Tyika* Exeter to need a valet when he owns nothing but a gown. Your wife is very near her term. Tell me why you want to stay."

"It is most difficult to describe in words, *tyika.*"

There, for a moment, the conversation rested. As a stranger himself, Julian was almost immune to Exeter's charisma—he could feel it, but he understood it and could resist it in ways that a native could not. To explain the mechanics of charisma or mana and what had happened in the temple that day would not cure Dommi of his enchantment, any more than a child could believe that the rabbit had come out of the conjuror's sleeve. Did Julian feel like this just because he didn't want to lose a damned good houseboy? No, he was honestly concerned for Dommi himself, and Ayetha. The Liberator's cause had always been doomed to failure, and now its black heart was cursed by a terrible crime.

"You realize that there may be more danger, don't you?"

Dommi smiled. "Not from soldiers, *tyika!* Twice Queen Elvanife has sent her warriors against him, and twice they have failed her. What army will challenge the Liberator now?"

"I suppose you do have a point there." The tales of haughty cavalry officers weeping in contrition and digging graves for their victims would sweep through the Vales. The kings and magistrates might still try assassins, but they could send no more armies against Exeter's crusade. "Writing to Ayetha, are you?"

Dommi clutched the papers closer. "I am making some notes, *tyika.*"

"Sorry. None of my business. I'll leave you to your task, then. We can talk in the morning, when *Entyika* Newton and I have decided what we're going to do." Julian began to rise.

Dommi looked up. "I am recording the words of the Liberator, *tyika.* While they are remaining green in memory."

Julian subsided again. The Gospel according to Saint Dommi? With his appalling spelling? But Julian had seen enough of the paper to know that Dommi was not writing English. He was using the Greeklike alphabet of the Vales.

"In what language?"

The question produced surprise. "In Randorian, *tyika,* of course. As he spoke. He numerously revealed things about the Undivided that are not told in the True Gospel."

Of course! Exeter had been making it all up as he went along, and he had been speaking in tongues, not Randorian. Among other things, he had completely scuppered the Service's teaching on the subject of the afterlife and the nature of the Pentatheon. The Undivided Reformation was now split into two opposing sects.

There was one question that Olympians never put to Carrots. Prophets had no honor in their own country and no man was a hero to his valet—except perhaps Edward Exeter. The Carrots knew that the apostles were only human and did not practice their public religion in the privacy of Olympus. Now, on impulse, Julian asked the forbidden question. "Dommi, what do you believe in? What god or gods do you follow?"

The freckled face glowed in the firelight. "I am believing in the Undivided, *Tyika* Kaptaan, although it is admissible that my faith was a most frail wisp until this afternoon when the Liberator spoke to my heart."

Which was to be expected. Exeter had a hell of a lot to answer for!

"Good," Julian said, and this time he did stand up. "I understand, and if you wish to remain with him for the time being, then I don't mind. You have been an exemplary houseboy, Dommi. I could never hope for better service. I shall miss all that you do for me at home very greatly, but I shall keep your position open. It will be yours again any time you wish to return. And if you do want to write a letter to Ayetha, give it to me and I will see she gets it."

"That is most kindly of you, *tyika!*" Shyly, Dommi released his writing board so that he could raise his arms and touch his hands together in the sign of the Undivided.

Julian nodded and turned away.

"*Tyika?*"

"What?"

"What god do you follow?"

The question left Julian at a loss. Certainly not Edward Exeter! "I'm not sure, Dommi. I'm still thinking." He beat a fast retreat.

He began wandering between the campfires, looking for Ursula, but it was she who found him. Shimmering like a white ghost in the darkness, she caught him by the arm and pulled him close.

"There you are! Have you eaten?"

"Not hungry."

She leaned back to study his face and said, "Mm!" thoughtfully.

"You can't stop him now, can you?" he snarled. "If we'd arrived here a day sooner . . . but not now?"

"No, not now. Come along, he wants to see you."

"I want nothing to do with him!"

"Now, now!" She sounded like a nanny. "Every man is entitled to face his accusers. Come and tell him what you disapprove of." She was urging him forward, over the sand.

"Disapprove of? Ursula, don't tell me you're on his side now?"

She squeezed his arm. "Not on his side, exactly, but now I don't think we can stop him. Zath probably can . . . but I'm not even quite certain of that anymore. I want to learn more of what he's up to. I underestimated him."

"I overestimated him. Christ, did I overestimate him!"

She pinched him. "Stop that!" They were heading back to the temple, back into the virtuality. His scalp prickled and sweat trickled down his ribs.

"What do you mean you underestimated him?"

She took a moment to answer. "He's done some things I never thought were possible."

"Such as slaughtering his friends? God! Don't you feel that's letting the side down a bit?"

"I wasn't thinking of that. He's won the support of the Pentatheon, or some of them, or at least he's won their neutrality. That's clever, darling! He must have impressed them. We know they're frightened of Zath, and Exeter's managed to capitalize on that."

"The devil you know is better than the devil you don't. The Pentatheon may decide Zath's a better bet when they hear how the Liberator treated his own supporters today."

*Horrors!* Obviously Ursula had switched sides—did that mean Exeter had bewitched her as she had planned to bewitch him? Would he now twist Julian's mind in the same way? For a moment, Julian considered doing a bunk, and then pride stiffened his spine. If he had not run from the Boche guns, he would not run from this.

They walked around a tent and there was the messiah, safely hidden from prying eyes in a private little sanctum. The tent and a fallen pillar and two ruined walls formed its sides; a fire of driftwood crackled and sparked on the sand in the center. The Liberator sat well back, in the corner of the two walls, his head bare and yet tightly hunched in his robe as if he were cold. Julian had seen that look on strangers before and knew it came from too much exposure to virtuality.

About a dozen Nagian shields had been laid out around the fire like hour markers on a giant clock face, with a disciple sitting by each—a new Round Table to replace the slain Warband. The two surviving Nagians were there, with their spears beside them. Another was the blond boy with the bandaged feet, Dosh Somebody, who looked as if he had been weeping. The rest seemed to be equally divided between men and women. They had been listening to their peerless leader talk, but he broke off when he saw the newcomers, and all eyes turned to study them.

There was a gap opposite Exeter, and Ursula's hat lay there—but no shield, Julian was relieved to see. The women on either side moved to make the space wider. Ursula sat down, adjusting her white dress, leaving room for him, but he remained on his feet and folded his arms, scowling over the campfire at the man he had hitherto called friend.

Exeter did not even appear weary. The exhaustion he had displayed so many hours ago had been washed away by his gluttonous feast of mana. Charisma and authority had replaced it.

For a long moment the two stared at each other. It was Julian who looked away first, of course.

"Tell me what troubles you," Exeter said, in English.

"Murder. Betrayal."

"Be more specific."

Julian glared at him. "You knew from the *Filoby Testament* that there would be bloodshed in Niolvale. You deliberately let it happen—hell, you invited it! You offered up your own team as human sacrifice, you sucked mana from the deaths of women and children and innocent men. You are no better than Zath himself!"

Exeter pulled a face, as if he felt the acid burn. "I knew there would be bloodshed, yes. 'Young men's bones,' was what the prophecy said. I told them that back in Sonalby. Some of them must die, I said. They knew."

Julian shuddered and swallowed against a surge of nausea. "A few days after you went away, Prof Rawlinson gave me the standard welcome-aboard pep talk in Olympus. I'm sure you had it, too, once. The source of mana is obedience, he said—the greater the pain, the greater the sacrifice, the greater the mana. And I said, 'And human sacrifice is the greatest of all?' He told me there was one much greater."

The blue eyes were steady and unreadable. "Martyrdom."

"Yes, martyrdom! The greatest source of all. 'Greater love hath no man.' . . . You let them die for you, so you could have their mana!"

The onlookers were frowning at this unfamiliar tongue and at the heretic who used so disrespectful a tone to their leader. Ursula was studying the fire. Standing over her, Julian could not see her face.

Exeter sighed. "I knew some of the Warband must die. I honestly did not expect so many. I honestly did not expect the others—the prophecy did not mention them.

But"—he spoke quickly, before Julian could interrupt—"but I have been hearing tales recently of the Church of the Undivided coming under attack. Will you swear to me that the Service makes no use of martyrs?"

Unfair! "We try to defend our own. I never took mana from a killing. I never—"

"No." Exeter smiled grimly. "You aren't one of the inner circle, are you? But you aren't guiltless. You live your parasitic life in Olympus on the fruits the others gather. You eat with your silver spoons in your fine houses, tended by your servants. Very fine houses! What exactly has the Service achieved in fifty years, apart from that cushy little settlement at Olympus? I'd ask you to explain to me just how the strangers of the Service differ from the strangers of the Chamber, but I know the answer already. It's a matter of degree—that's all, isn't it? None of you are virgins, some are just more pregnant than others. And the martyrs are all on your side, aren't they? The Pentatheon doesn't dabble in that. Never mind. Swear something else to me, Captain Smedley. Swear that your guns in Flanders never killed a civilian."

A jolt of fury made Julian break out in cold sweat. "If they did, I never benefitted from the death!" he yelled. "I took no blood money!"

"You took your pay! You took your medals. Your side benefitted, your team—your cause, dammit!"

Julian opened his mouth and was shouted down. The blue eyes blazed brighter than the fire.

"I know you weren't in the trenches with the infantry. You never ordered the lads to go over the top, did you, but—"

"British officers don't order their men to *go* over the top, you bastard! They *lead* them over the top!"

"Like Field Marshall Haig, I suppose? Like Asquith or Lloyd George?" Either mana or the walls behind him made Exeter's voice thunder. Even the fire seemed to bend away from the blast. The disciples gaped, aghast at this quarrel. "The real leaders stand well back and *order*, Captain."

"If you're content to be compared with them, then may you rot in hell with them! I'll ask some questions now! I saw you in that circular window. I know a symbol when I see one. . . . Chose that in advance, didn't you? Scouted out this node and decided this was a good place to hold your bloodbath, didn't you?"

Exeter's lips vanished into his beard. He nodded to concede the point. Bastard!

"And your god is undivided?" Julian roared. "But you're not claiming to be a saint, Mr. Exeter. You're not quoting ancient prophets. You're issuing wisdom on your own authority! 'Verily I say unto you,' and all that. Where does your authority come from? If you're not a saint and your god is undivided, then what does that make you—*Christ?*"

"I am the Liberator."

"But are you human or divine? Are you god or prophet? Buddha or Mohammed or Jesus or Zarathustra or Moses?"

He had scored again. Exeter said, "I am human, Julian, you know that." But he had hesitated.

"Have you told them that? Go ahead and tell them now. I want to hear it. Speak nice and slow, in Joalian."

Exeter stared at him for a moment and then said, "No."

"Ha! Then I rest my case." Suddenly all Julian's anger drained away in a rush, leaving bone-aching weariness and a sick regret like the pain of bereavement. That it had come to this! "Remember that morning at the Dower House at Greyfriars? Two years ago. At breakfast. You explained all this to me. You swore you'd never become the Liberator. You asked what it would do to you. 'What would I have to become?' you said. Well, you did it and it happened, damn you!"

The onlookers could not be following the words, but they must be reading the tones and the expressions. They all turned to hear what their tin-pot deity would say next. He spoke very quietly, as if his anger, also, had turned to sorrow.

"The game isn't over yet, Julian. It's hardly begun. All I've done so far is jostle the board."

"And Zath will burn you in the end."

Exeter shrugged. "I have to trust the *Testament*. Remember it said that the dead would rouse me?"

"Ysian?" Julian laughed his scorn. He wanted to hurt, to wound. "Have you avenged her yet?"

"No, not Ysian. Not even the Carrots you helped me bury. Well, maybe a little. But mostly it was Flanders, that hell at Ypres. I saw a few hours of it. I saw fields turned to mud by human gore. I saw boys blown to bits or blinded by gas or driven insane by terror. I passed out cold from the shock of it. You must have seen a million times more than I did. You were there for two years. What can excuse that, Captain Smedley?"

"Nothing! Absolutely nothing!"

Softly, gently, Exeter drove in the dagger. "So the war was wrong?"

"You bugger! Wrong for the side that started it, yes. Not wrong for those who resisted the evil!"

"Then I, too, rest my case."

Julian turned and walked off into the night.

Ursula did not come after him.

# VI

And he goeth up into a mountain, and calleth unto him whom he would: and they came unto him.

THE NEW TESTAMENT: MARK, 3:13

# 34

Eleal awoke with a start. For a moment she just lay and stared at the roof overhead, heart pounding, soaked with perspiration. She had been dreaming about D'ward again. Rather, she had been dreaming about that mouthwateringly romantic admirer whom she knew to be D'ward although he did not look in the slightest bit like him. He might have grown broader in the last five years, might have grown a mustache and hairs on his chest, but he could hardly have grown shorter. Nor could he have changed the color of his eyes. And why, when they were locked in a passionate embrace, had she been *singing?* Oh, dreams were stupid!

It was very nice to wake up in a bed again, and even nicer to know that the stench of sewerberries had gone . . . almost gone. Never mind. She was awake now. Close above her hung a gable ceiling, with sunbeams angling through the dirty little skylight. From the street below came a faint racket of voices, wheels, and hooves as the world roused itself for business. This was not a luxurious inn, but it was not a slum, either. And she was in Niol! Today she would be able to explore a city as big and grand as Joal, one she had never visited before. She raised her head to peer over the edge of the blanket and make sure Piol Poet was still asleep, so that it would be safe for her to get up and dress.

Piol's bed was empty. That was exceedingly annoying. He must have risen and departed without waking her, and who knows what he might have learned by now? She threw off the blanket and sat up. Why, he might even have solved the Liberator puzzle already! She reached for her dress.

There had been no shortage of news of the Liberator in Niol last night. The rumors were thicker than flies in a butcher's, but no two of the stories agreed. She had dragged herself off to bed without reaching any conclusion.

With the inevitability of a glacier going downhill, the sloth's snail-slow progress had brought them to Niol itself, the only place in the world where sewerberries were used or bought, so that a cartful of them going in any other direction would have provoked questions. Here, they had sold the stinking mess, cart and sloth and all, making quite a good profit. They had spent about a third of it replacing their ruined clothes and getting cleaned up, as no bathhouse had wanted to admit them, and the rest she had shared with Piol, since it had been all his idea.

*Clip! Clop!* She lurched down the steep little staircase to the barroom, which was gloomy and deserted. It stank strongly of wine, with lesser odors of urine and vomit. Deciding that she was not quite ready for breakfast yet, she clumped over to the big door and heaved it open, blinking as the sunlight caught her in the face. Niol was famous for the width of its streets. Porters trudged past in twos and threes, carrying bales on their heads and moaning away in their lazy Niolian singsong. A few smelly, humpy bullocks crawled by, hauling wagons. She could hear peddlers hawking their wares in the distance, and the shutters were coming off the little shops opposite. Half a dozen juvenile beggars flocked around her at once, shouting for alms. She cursed at them and slapped them away before their prying little fingers could discover her money belt.

"The gods be with you, my lady," said a Joalian voice.

She spun around. Piol Poet sat on a bench outside the inn door, legs outstretched, back against the wall. He was munching on a roll.

"And with you, my lord." She smiled at him and joined him. The journey had done wonders for Piol, but whether it was rest, food, or just a sense of purpose that deserved the credit, she did not know. His eyes were brighter, his skin less jaundiced. A clean new robe certainly helped, and his turban was neatly bound.

He tore the doughy bread in two and gave her half. "Lots more where this came from. Be off with you!" he snapped at the beggars.

She bit, eying him thoughtfully. "You've got news."

He pouted. "Am I so horribly transparent?"

"No, I am excessively perceptive. Tell me."

He finished a mouthful with the patience of the toothless. "I have ascertained that the Tion Champions are in town, and there is to be a festival next fortnight in commemoration of—"

"Never mind all that! What have you learned about the Liberator?"

He raised a silvery eyebrow. "I thought you wanted me to be your manager in the furtherance of your artistic career?"

"Later. First, what news of D'ward?"

He sighed. "Eleal, *why* are you so concerned about him?"

"He's an old friend! I mean, those days in Suss were the most exciting time of my life. There's nothing wrong in wanting to meet up with an old friend, is there? Now, what's the news?"

He frowned at her doubtfully. "It makes sense now. The winds of truth have winnowed the chaff of rumor."

"Spare me the poetry." She caught his hand as he moved to take another bite. "Talk first."

He chuckled at her impatience. "He's been here, in Niol! He was seen in the temple. He's also been reported in the queen's palace, but that story seems altogether too farfetched. It does sound as if he came into the city three nights ago, went to the temple, and pulled the priests' noses. Then he ran away before they could catch him. The next night he was at Shuujooby."

"Doing what?"

"Preaching heresy."

"Oh!"

Piol shook his head sadly. "Can't say I'm surprised, not really. He was never a strong supporter of the gods, you know. Remember, he wouldn't go to the temple with you when you went to give thanks to Tion for your safe deliverance?"

That's right, she thought, he didn't. And when the high priest summoned him to the temple, he ran away altogether, so her leg didn't get cured. But to support those awful heretics! T'lin Dragontrader had joined them, too, she remembered. The last time she had met him, they had quarreled over that.

"Well, I certainly will have nothing to do with heresy!" she said firmly. "I believe in the gods!" After all, her father was one.

"So we can forget about D'ward?" Piol beamed with relief.

"No!" Again she waylaid the bread on its way to the old pest's mouth. "If he's a heretic, why isn't he being thrown in jail?"

"Well, that is an interesting question! The queen sent her household cavalry to arrest him at Shuujooby. Apparently there was some fighting, just as the *Testament* predicts, but the accounts vary from hangnail to hangman, as they say here. In the end the guard failed to obey orders and most of them threw in their lot with the man they were supposed to apprehend."

"That doesn't sound likely."

Piol shrugged his thin shoulders. "It sounds like a miracle. There are rumors of other miracles, too." He hesitated, then added softly, "They say he is healing sick people, Eleal—and cripples."

With professional skill, she suppressed an impending shiver and laughed scornfully. "But you don't believe such tales, do you?"

"I don't know." Piol frowned and bit on his roll. Mouth full, he mumbled, "We have seen miracles of healing in Tion's temple. . . . All these stories are incredible, yet they seem to hang together too well to be completely wrong."

She nibbled at her own hunk of bread. "So where is he now?"

"Yesterday he left Shuujooby on the road to Mamaby. . . . If he keeps up his progress, then today he'll be going on to Joobiskby, and tomorrow he'll head over Lospass to Jurgvale."

If Piol Poet wasn't adding that he'd advised her just to wait in Jurgvale until the Liberator arrived, that didn't mean he wasn't thinking it. Bother! It had taken them *days* to come from Joobiskby. If D'ward ever got ahead of her, she would have to chase after him, and he was obviously covering the ground much faster than a sloth did. Almost anything would, of course, and she did not own a sloth anymore anyway.

Eleal sighed. "Speak up, old man. You're my strategist. Advise me."

Piol chewed for a long time. She curbed her impatience until he was ready.

"My advice to you, Eleal Singer, would be to go on to Joal, as you said you would, or else let me arrange some auditions here. In some of the temples, perhaps. Niol also has many fine pleasure gardens where an artist may earn a good living with her art, not with—"

"Forget that. How do I catch the Liberator now?"

He sighed deeply. "You always were a wayward child, you know. Follow the crowds, I suppose. And they are heading for Lospass."

"Crowds?"

"Hundreds of people are going to hear the Liberator. They're leaving their jobs, their friends, their families. . . ."

"You have been busy, old man! How long have you been up and about? Never mind that. We can't go on foot, either of us. How?"

With his mouth full, Piol mumbled, "There are people organizing wagon trains. One silver star there. Two for a return ticket."

"That's daylight robbery!"

He chuckled wheezily. "I'd pay the two, I think. The return price may be a lot more when they've got you there."

"We'll pay for one-way trips," Eleal said firmly, "and worry about the future when it comes."

# 35

A tusk ox walked faster than a sloth, but not as fast as a man. All day Eleal watched in frustration as people on foot caught up with the wagon, passed it, and eventually disappeared into the distance ahead. Were it not for her deformed leg, she would be out there too, striding along with the best of them. It was all D'ward's fault.

Piol had been well-informed when he reported that hundreds were going to see the Liberator, for the southbound traffic was much greater than the northbound—and not merely foot traffic, either. The wealthy swept by on moas or rabbits or in coaches pulled by them, spraying dust or mud. For the first time Eleal wondered if this legendary crowd-drawer might not be the same boy she had known. D'ward had always tried to avoid attention, not attract it. He had been retiring, almost shy—although a wonderful actor, of course. Among all these people, how was she ever going to get close to him for a private little chat about old times?

Having been queried to death by the mob ahead, the meager wayfarers heading back toward the city were mostly uninformative, responding to shouted questions with oaths or angry silence. A few reported that the Liberator had reached Mamaby yesterday and might either be still there or have gone on to Joobiskby and Lospass. One or two spoke briefly of miracles, but none claimed to have actually witnessed one.

The ox's name was Tawny. Its owner, shuffling along at its ear, was a grubby, some-what battered-looking man named Podoorstak Carter. Eleal had seen his like around the Cherry Blossom House often enough to be very glad she had not prepaid her return journey. The lumbering, bone-rattling wagon had been smelly even when it set out. After a day of baking sunshine, packed to suffocation with fourteen people, it reeked. Its cargo included two elderly nuns, who spoke only to each other in whispers. A very loud matronly lady, whose son had been slain by a reaper, wanted to give the Liberator her blessings and wise counsel on his campaign to slay Death. An addlepated, hunch-backed young man babbled nonsense about prophecies, rolling his eyes and slobbering. A girl of thirteen who had seen a vision she must describe to the Liberator was accom-panied by her proud mother. There was a very sick baby, clutched by an underfed, worried-to-death woman who hoped that the Liberator might bring death to Death before her child died. The baby coughed a lot and threw up everything the woman fed it. There were two overweight, green-robed priests of Padlopan, the Niolian aspect of Karzon, who indicated grimly that they were going to beat the heretical manure out of the Liberator as soon as they got their hands on him. Unfortunately, their neighbors were an elderly couple wearing the gold ear circle of the Undivided. Their conversation with the priests was strained.

Healthy, wholesome people had gone on foot or stayed home.

The priests and the nuns, of course, were intent on stamping out heresy, and therefore traveling on the gods' business. They regarded their companions as wastrels, sensation seekers, and potential heretics. When Eleal explained that she hoped to use her former friendship with the Liberator to recall him to the true faith, their manners improved a little. But not much. She did not mention that she was the Eleal of the *Filoby Testament*.

Lubberly lot though they all were, they were a potential audience, and no true artist could resist an audience. So Eleal sang for them from time to time. They all seemed to enjoy that, excepting the baby and the straitlaced nuns. Later, she and Piol performed brief excerpts from some of his plays, and everyone enjoyed those except the priests, the baby, and the girl with the vision, who had an epileptic seizure halfway through *Hollaga's Farewell.*

The wagon rolled ever more slowly as the tusk ox tired, but evening came at last, bringing them to Joobiskby. It had been a sleepy, peaceful little place when Eleal and Piol had slothed their way through it a few days ago, but now the only thing she could recognize was the spire of the temple. The inhabitants, male and female both, had built a barricade across the road and manned it, brandishing forks and mattocks to repel the intruders. It was fortunate that the harvest had been gathered in and the paddies, which in spring and summer had been thigh-deep in water, had dried to mere mud at this time of year, for the horde of visitors had trampled over everything, knocking down hedges and dykes, leaving a wasteland.

Podoorstak halted the wagon a cautious quarter mile or so away from the ramparts, at the end of a long line of parked carts and coaches. The bored drivers and servants left to guard them ignored these latest arrivals.

"Ain't going no nearer," Podoorstak announced. "We'll leave from here at dawn, them as wants to come. Fend for yourselves till then."

His passengers burst into complaint, but to no avail. Obviously the village was sealed and his ox could not drag the wagon through the soupy morass that surrounded it. Sighing, Eleal scrambled down and offered a hand to Piol. It was good to be out of the wagon at last, but she was not looking forward to the last stage of the journey. Her ultimate destination was obviously a small hillock to the north, for there the crowds had gathered. That must be where the Liberator was.

Piol wanted to carry their little pack; she insisted on taking it. Side by side, they clambered over the remains of a ditch and set off across the fields. They moved more slowly than most, faster than some, and still pilgrims were arriving behind them. The going was hard—red mud sucking at her boots with every step.

An old refrain was going around and around in her head: *Woeful maiden, handsome lad. . . .* She had not heard that song in years.

"How many?" She puffed.

"Thousands! Can't see them all from here." Piol chuckled wheezily. "Trong never drew a house like this one. We should have kept D'ward in the troupe!"

His good humor shamed her. "But are these people the audience or the extras, old man? Even Trong couldn't have directed so many."

The situation seemed more and more hopeless the closer she came to the hillock. There was a building on the crest of it, perhaps an old shrine. The flanks supported a few scattered trees, but whatever else they might have borne—grass or fences or berry bushes—had vanished under the human tide.

"This is madness! What do they all want? Just to see him or touch him?"

"The madness of multitudes," Piol murmured. His eyes were bright with a faraway look she could recall from her childhood, a sign of inspiration at work. "It will pass. Nectar-ants swarm so in spring. The Liberator is their queen and they must be as near him as they can."

"If he speaks, most of them won't even be able to hear."

"But he is something new in their lives. They will go home and tell all their friends. And when the world doesn't turn upside down in a fortnight, they will forget him. It will pass."

As they reached the trampled lower slopes of the knoll, and then the edge of the horde, Piol took hold of Eleal's hand. There they stopped, seeing that any attempt to push into the throng would be not only fruitless but dangerous. She could hear a menacing rumble mixed in with the normal crowd buzz as those higher on the hillock resisted efforts to displace them or pack them tighter. Already more people were jostling in at her back. She exchanged rueful glances with the old man—neither of them was exactly tall. They would not even see the Liberator, let alone hear him. She assumed that he would speak. He would have to do something or the crowd would riot.

"Sh!" said a few hundred voices all around her. Someone was making an announcement. She could not make out the words, but she sensed that the crowd was breaking up, somewhere off to the right.

A moment later, she heard the speaker again, and this time he was closer.

"There is food available around the other side. The Liberator will speak now, and later he will speak again for those of you who did not hear. Go and eat now, and come back."

Eleal and Piol exchanged questioning glances. They had thought to bring food, so they were not hungry. How many would be tempted away?

Then the speaker came in sight, walking around the outside of the gathering. He was a short, fair-haired youth, wearing only a loincloth, burdened with a leather satchel and a large round shield slung on his back. Slight though he was, he projected well. He made his proclamation yet again.

The crowd began to roil, some fighting their way out to go in search of the promised meal, others pushing in to take their places higher on the hillock. Dragging Piol behind her, Eleal lurched over to the herald. She banged a hand on his shield just before he disappeared.

"You!"

He turned around and regarded her with soft blue eyes. His face was drawn with fatigue and reddened by the day's sun; he was spattered with mud. She expected annoyance, but he spoke with surprising patience. "Sister? How may I help?"

"I need to speak with the Liberator."

He even managed a smile, although her request was obviously insane, and raked fingers through curls that might be pure gold on a better day. "We all do. I have been trying to get a word with him myself for three days. I wish I could be more helpful."

Eleal was impressed. He was really very cute. He would make an excellent Tion in the right sort of play.

"I am Eleal."

A guarded expression fell over his face like a visor. "Sister, I am very honored—"

"Really I am. The Eleal of the *Filoby Testament*. I cared for him and washed him . . . almost five years ago. I want to see him again."

A faint smile of doubt. "Do you know his name? Can you describe him?"

"His name is D'ward. He is tall. He has black hair, quite wavy, and the bluest eyes I have ever seen. When I knew him, he was very—lean, I suppose is the nice way of describing it. I expect he will have put on weight since then."

The boy clicked his teeth shut. "No, he hasn't. You are Eleal!" He fell on his knees in the mud.

"Er . . ." Eleal looked to Piol for guidance. He seemed equally astounded. The milling bystanders had noticed, and a ring of the curious was solidifying around them.

"Don't kneel to me!" she said firmly. She found that strangely disturbing. "Get up, please! But I would like to see my old friend."

The boy stood up, having trouble managing the big shield. He glanced around at the audience. "A moment!" He made his proclamation again, and again the people within earshot began stirring like vegetables in a boiling stew pot.

He turned back to Eleal, biting his lip. "I cannot get you to him now. After he has spoken the second time, he will bid the crowd disperse or sleep. Then we have a—" He smiled a rueful smile. "Well, usually we have a meeting. The numbers are becoming so great that I can't even count on that today. But look for me, or for people carrying shields like this. Tell any of them what you have told me, or tell them I said so. My name is Dosh Envoy. I am sure that they will get you to the Liberator then."

It was as much as she could have hoped for. "I thank you, Dosh Envoy."

He nodded. "The blessings of the Undivided upon you, sister." Then he eased his way off through the crowd.

She would have to be content with that, and she supposed she would not die of impatience. Her craving to meet D'ward again seemed to be growing stronger all the time. The closer she came to him, the more eager she felt.

# 36

Some of the places D'ward chose to pitch camp were bizarre, but Dosh could not have faulted the knoll at Joobiskby. It was a natural theater, for the little ruin at the top made an excellent stage and the slopes could have held even more thousands than had turned up. The problem was not the campsite but the wind and the size of the multitude. Loud as D'ward could be, he could not make his voice carry upwind. Those who had heard the first sermon—a necessarily brief one—were reluctant to move away and make room for others who had not. The lower slopes were muddier than the top, an unsavory place to sleep.

Patience. Understanding. Tact. Above all, patience.

Even with a manageable crowd, the shield-bearers would have had trouble, for they were all new at the job, other than Dosh himself and the two surviving Nagians. D'ward had appointed the shield-bearers the previous evening to replace the Warband, naming four women and six men, promising to add more soon. He had chosen well, Dosh believed, but dedication was no substitute for experience. Even Prat'han and his brothers would have been out of their depth shepherding this multitude. In retrospect, the band that had followed the Liberator through Nosokvale and Rinoovale seemed like a family on an outing—already those were the good old days, fond memories shining through golden haze. Now the greater burden had fallen on shoulders unprepared to take it. Dosh had not been off his feet since dawn; Tielan Trader and Doggan Herder were doing their best, but they were still numb with grief and shame at being alive.

Dosh had shame to bear also, for he had not believed in the Liberator until their audience with Visek, so he had never had a chance to tell most of the Warband that they had been right all along and he had been wrong. He had not appreciated their courage and loyalty. Now, for the first time in his life, he knew what guilt was.

Patience: "I know you are tired, brothers and sisters. There are many down there who have come just as far as you and have not yet had a chance to hear the Liberator.

It would be a demonstration of the understanding he described if you were to give them a chance. . . ." And so on and so on.

As he repeated the same carefully phrased and reasoned request for the thousandth time, Dosh wondered where he had learned patience. Not just patience, either. If the Dosh who had left Joal a fortnight ago were to meet himself now, they wouldn't know each other. They wouldn't like each other much, either. Fortunately, he was too accursedly busy to wonder whether he enjoyed being this sort of person. He supposed he would eventually weaken and revert to lechery. Meanwhile, he must keep on being a good boy, because there were whiffs of riot in the night air. He had broken up three fights already.

The sun had set. There was not a single moon in sight, and D'ward had just begun his second speech. The wind was still rising, snatching his words away. The clouds that had been gathering at sunset over Niolwall portended the start of the winter rains—that would thin out the crowd in a hurry.

Dosh began to work his way up the knoll. He had done all he could down here. He moved quietly and with exceeding care, literally stepping between people's legs, being careful not to bang any heads with his shield. A shield was a great honor, but a demoniacally heavy and awkward honor. In his case the honor was especially great, because he had been granted Prat'han's. The hole in it marked the blow that had felled the big man and the stains were his life's blood. To carry such a relic was honor and privilege.

Dosh wondered if Queen Elvanife had obeyed the Liberator's edict and gone to Shuujooby to do penance. He wondered if D'ward would move on again tomorrow, as he usually did. He wondered how many of this horde would choose to join the Free and march with the Liberator. They would have to be fed, but his satchel was quite empty, although the collectors would soon have money for him. He wondered when he would get a chance to sit down.

He reached the crumbled walls of the old shrine just as Kirb'l flashed into view in the east, shedding a welcome yellow light on the hundreds of upturned faces paving the sides of the knoll. D'ward stood on the highest corner, lit from below by a bonfire, casting his message to the night air.

Amazingly, Kilpian and the others had managed to keep the crowds out of the shrine itself. Most of the walls had long since collapsed into heaps of stones, but even those were a barrier and gave a sense of privacy. Dosh climbed over a low spot and slithered down inside, spilling onto the grass. He detached himself from his shield and relaxed with a long sigh of wearied contentment.

A portly, gray-haired woman came to him, offering a gourd of water. He accepted gratefully, trying to remember her name. She was a friend. D'ward had appointed shield-bearers and friends. The friends were supporters not yet quite ready to profess their faith or to assume authority, he had said, but they were to be admitted to the evening meetings.

Dosh drained the gourd and muttered thanks. The Liberator's voice rang out over-head.

"Food?" she asked, smiling at his woebegone manner. Hasfral, that was her name, Hasfral Midwife.

"Food? What's that? Has D'ward eaten yet?"

"No."

"Then I'll wait till he does."

She shook her head as if puzzled. "That's what you all say."

"Because we know there wasn't enough for everyone out there today."

"Lots of them brought their own."

"But some will go hungry, and D'ward won't want to eat if he knows that. The only thing that will make him eat then is if the rest of us haven't eaten either and he knows we'll do whatever he does."

"Will you? Will you go without if he does?"

Dosh sighed. "Let's hope we don't have to find out."

He glanced around the little group. Quite a few missing still. Doggan Herder was brooding in a corner by himself. No sign of Tielan Trader. Kilpian Drover and Kondior Thatcher and Bid'lip . . . Bid'lip Soldier had been one of the troopers who had defected in Nosokvale. He was a bear of a man, with the thickest eyebrows Dosh had seen since Bandrops Advocate's. He wasn't Prat'han, but he would be a strong arm for the Liberator. Half a dozen others . . . A red-haired youngster sitting close by the fire was writing so busily that he must be trying to take down the Liberator's words verbatim.

"Who's he?" Dosh whispered, pointing at the scribe.

"Dommi Houseboy. A friend."

It was becoming hard to keep track of everyone.

And there was Ursula Teacher. Dosh disliked her without quite knowing why. Perhaps it was a relic of his old days of lechery, when he had preferred women pliant and muscles on men. Her jaw was too square, her hair too short, her manner too domineering, but none of that should matter to him now. Or perhaps he just wasn't sure what to make of her—she spoke with the Liberator in a language unlike any he had ever heard. At least her insolent male friend had departed, heading out at dawn yesterday on a dragon; good riddance, whoever he was.

The sight of Ursula suddenly reminded Dosh of Eleal Singer. Bother! Well, it would be useless to go and look for her in that mob out there. If she really was the fabled savior mentioned by the *Testament*, then she would find her way here somehow. Must remember to tell D'ward about her . . . Screw it, but he was tired . . . !

The sky was clouding over. No matter—no deluge would keep Dosh from sleeping tonight. He eyed the baggage heaped in one corner. With a groan, he sat up and prepared to rise.

"Bid'lip? Give me a hand putting up the tent."

The soldier shook his head. "D'ward said to leave it. Said we can all use it as a cover when the rain starts."

Dosh sank back to where he had been before. He suspected that the Liberator rarely slept in the tent and it was only a decoy to deceive the reapers. There had been no reapers for several nights. What was the enemy up to now? While worrying about that, he almost dozed off. A jingling sound roused him when Kondior Thatcher dropped a cloth poke at his feet. The Liberator had just finished his speech and was clambering down from his vantage point, being steadied by Kilpian Drover. More shield-bearers and friends had arrived. The crowd on the slopes of the knoll rumbled like a great beast as it tried to make itself comfortable for the night.

Hasfral Midwife and Imminol Herbalist were handing out the evening meal: beans and tubers and some pieces of fruit. D'ward accepted his gourd, looking around his followers, studying each in turn. When everyone had been served and no one had begun to eat, he smiled as if he knew what they were thinking.

"Praise the food the Lord sends; may it give us strength to serve Him."

A chorus of amens became a fanfare of crunching.

D'ward made himself comfortable and nibbled on a pepperroot. "Well done, all of you! You've had a brutal day, and I appreciate how hard you've all worked. I think it will get easier now. Not many of those city folk will follow us over Lospass. Who has anything to report?"

Dosh remembered Eleal, but others spoke up first, complaining about problems sharing out food equitably, assigning toilet areas, dealing with troublesome delegations of priests.

Nothing to be done about any of those now, D'ward said cheerfully. Let tomorrow look after its own afflictions. Had everyone met Dommi Houseboy, a new friend? The youngster blushed in the firelight and beamed toothily.

More shield-bearers and friends came scrambling in over the walls. D'ward made more introductions, announced a couple of promotions. People brought money to Dosh and he began dumping it into his satchel. Even so, there would not be enough to feed everyone tomorrow unless the crowds thinned out considerably.

Then a loud, clear female voice cut through the mutter of conversation like lightning through a cloud: "D'ward?"

The Liberator looked up. He started violently, dropping his gourd.

Tielan Trader had arrived at last. He had brought the girl who claimed to be Eleal and the little old man who had been with her, who now carried her pack.

"D'ward? Slights live long in memory, but debts die young?"

"Eleal!" D'ward scrambled to his feet. "Eleal Singer! And Piol!"

She lurched forward a few steps to meet him. Kondior Drover moved to block her and she stopped.

Dosh had expected the stunned expressions on the rest of the faces, but why did the Liberator look so strange? There was something odd here. What did it take to bring such a pallor to D'ward? Everyone knew the prophecy about Eleal and the coming of the Liberator, but the *Testament* did not mention anyone called Piol. Was the old man the problem?

Eleal was a pretty enough young piece, certainly. Had he still been that sort of man, Dosh could have gone for that sort of woman. In fact . . . It takes one to know one. . . . Just what grade of woman was she? Studying her in the uncertain flicker of the firelight, he decided that if he had still been that sort of boy, he would have been prepared to gamble that she was that sort of girl. No blushing virgin, certainly. Younger than he would have expected, for "Eleal shall be the first temptation." . . . It was almost five years since the seven hundredth festival, when the Liberator had come into the world. She would have been only a child then.

"Eleal!" D'ward repeated. He shook his head as if breaking a trance. "I forgot how long it's been. The years have blessed you greatly."

"They haven't changed you." She smiled and held out her hands in greeting. "Aren't we still friends?"

D'ward did not order Kondior to move out of the way. "You are very welcome. Sisters, brothers, this is Eleal Singer, the Eleal named in the *Filoby Testament*. Piol, it is good to see you also. What news of the others?"

"Time enough for prattle and idle gossip later," Eleal said with a toss of her head. Her eyes were flitting around, appraising the group. "I doubt that your entourage would be interested in our bygones. Are you going to offer us hospitality or not?"

D'ward laughed. "You are still Eleal! And I am a boor. Come and join our feast by all means, both of you. Make room there for Eleal Singer and Piol Poet. Welcome to the Free." His laughter had not rung true, though. Dosh was very intrigued. He had studied the Liberator long enough to sense a mystery here.

Then the girl walked to the place cleared for her and her lurching gait drew all eyes down to her feet. The sole of her right boot was built up. Hasfral and Imminol moved apart to make a place by the fire. Eleal sat and the old man eased himself down beside her, wriggling out of his pack straps.

D'ward picked up his gourd and held it out to Bid'lip Soldier, his neighbor. "Pass that to our guests. We live simply, Eleal, as you see."

Bid'lip tipped in what was left of his own meal and passed the gourd.

The sharp-eyed Eleal had noticed. So had the old man, and he began fussing with the tie on the pack.

"Pray do not let us deprive you," she said haughtily. "As it happens, we have some provisions of our own remaining."

D'ward sat down without a word, and perhaps only Dosh noted his smile, for it was a brief and private smile. When his gourd returned, he shared out its contents with Bid'lip and began to eat again, without taking his eyes off Eleal.

"Excuse us if we talk business at mealtimes. Has anyone else anything to bring up?"

Bid'lip said, "I heard a rumor tonight, Liberator. I was told that Queen Elvanife remains in her palace."

"I'm not surprised." Still D'ward studied the girl, as if every mouthful she took was a revelation. "She is not our concern. The One God will deal with her—probably through her courtiers, would be my guess."

"Tomorrow, master?" asked someone else.

"Tomorrow we keep going. We can't inflict this torture on Joobiskby any longer. I hope the weather holds for the pass."

*Fornicating scorpions!* Where was Dosh going to find provisions for several thousand people marching over Lospass? It was at least a two-day trek to Jurgvale, so he could not run ahead and buy there. He would have to accost the Joobiskbians on their barricades. They might demand totally unreasonable prices to compensate for the damage the crowds had done, but he could argue that the alternative was to have the Free stay where they were, starving. That ought to convince them. . . . The Liberator had spoken his name.

Without taking his eyes off Eleal, D'ward said, "I need you around. I want you to keep the purse, but we'll let someone else take over the commissariat. Any suggestions?"

Dosh tried not to show the warm rush those words had given him. To be needed, trusted, asked . . . "Doggan knows livestock—"

"No. I need him around too."

"Hasfral, then?"

"Will you take on the provisioning, Hasfral?" D'ward asked, still staring at Eleal.

"I'll be glad to, master," Hasfral said.

"Then I'll promote you to shield-bearer, if you won't mind carrying one."

"Anything to keep her from doing the cooking," said Imminol. Those two were old friends, so it was all right to laugh.

A drop of rain struck Dosh's leg.

D'ward must have felt one too, for he glanced up at the sky, frowning. "Tomorrow we'll camp at Roaring Cave. At least we'll be dry there. It's a short trek. You can pass the word in the morning. Bid'lip, when we get near the tree line, see if you can get every able-bodied pilgrim to pick up a branch and take it along for firewood. Anything else?"

"Yes, Liberator," said a Nagian voice. Doggan Herder hauled himself to his feet like an old man, yet once he was upright he stood straight enough, holding his spear and shield in proper warrior style. "I wish to go home."

So it had come at last. Dosh had been expecting it for two days, and D'ward showed no surprise. He glanced at Tielan, and the trader's face was a blank slate. Assume that Tielan had known and D'ward had expected. . . .

"Go then, but nevermore count yourself my friend or brother."

Doggan had not expected *that.*

"I know what you're thinking," the Liberator said quietly. "They were my brethren too, remember. I threw my first spear at Gopaenum, then watched Gopaenum throw it back at me. Had I known then how much beef the butcher packed in that arm of his, I'd have turned and run straight up Nagwall. Burthash and Prat'han drew the lines on my ribs for me to cut when I earned my first merit marks. We were all brothers together. Side by side we marched and fought. When I came asking aid a couple of fortnights ago, they threw down whatever they were doing and came without question, as you and Tielan did, as brother should for brother. I told them there was danger and they scoffed. At Shuujooby they died, all of them except you two, but that was God's election, no shame on your heads. I underestimated the evil, so if anyone is to blame . . . No, hear me out. History will not judge me blameless. And now you feel it is your duty to bear the tidings back to Sonalby so the rest of our brothers can take up arms to spill the guilt blood. Against whom will you lead them, Brother Doggan? The lancers who did the slaying? But most of those men are out there now, shamed and penitent and doing whatever they can to aid our cause. Against Queen Elvanife, who gave the orders? I doubt very much that she will still sit her throne by the time you fetch the brothers to Niolvale. Against Zath, whose evil moved the queen? He is the true source of darkness, but what hope will you have against him? I have promised you that he will die when we come to Tharg. I need your help on the way, but if you will not trust my word—if you think that Sonalby has not suffered enough—then go. But do not expect my blessing."

Doggan stood in silence. His mental processes had never been speedy.

"He is right," Tielan said. "I told you. Sit down."

Doggan sat down. He laid his spear and shield on the ground. Then he doubled over, weeping onto his knees. Tielan put an arm around him.

No one spoke for a while. Embarrassed and mourning, they finished eating. For dessert, Dosh decided, he would really appreciate a thick, juicy steak. He had not overlooked the rolls and meat that Eleal and her elderly friend had been devouring, and he wondered what else might remain in their pack. He was not the only one watching the two of them with hungry thoughts.

Eleal gulped down her last few bites and licked her fingers. "Well, D'ward?" She smiled nervously. "Can we retire somewhere more private and reminisce about the old days? I can enlighten you about the fates that have befallen so many we held dear."

"No!" D'ward said sharply. Then he gabbled something in that strange other language.

The mysterious Ursula Teacher had been watching and listening in silence. She, too, had kept her attention on Eleal Singer. Now she nodded and replied briefly in the same tongue. Whatever the words, her frown made them a warning.

D'ward rose and walked over to the girl. He stood between her and the fire. Eleal looked up at him warily, then began to rise.

"Sit down!"

Surprised, she sank back.

"Take off your boots," he said.

"What? I certainly will not do any such—"

*"Take off your boots!"*

The order cracked like a cane on a tabletop. No one could resist an order from the Liberator when he used that tone. She paled and obeyed, and then looked up at him again with fury and defiance and shame.

It was cruel. Everyone could see the comparison—the deformed leg, horribly shorter than its companion.

D'ward glanced at Imminol and the old man on either side of her. "Hold her hands."

Eleal began to protest, but the others seized her hands. "D'ward! What are you—"

The Liberator raised his eyes as if studying the sky. He lifted his arms overhead in the circle. A flash of revelation told Dosh what was going to happen an instant before the girl cried out. She struggled against her captors.

D'ward lowered his hands. "Give thanks to the True God."

He turned and walked back to his former place, his robe swirling in the rising wind. Raindrops hissed in the fire. Imminol and Piol released their hold on Eleal. She had turned ashen pale, staring down at her feet.

"A blessed miracle!" Ursula said in accented Joalian. "Praise to the Undivided for this sign to us."

One or two voices muttered, "Amen!" Everyone else was too stunned to speak. The girl's legs were now the same length.

"It is written," Ursula continued. " 'Hurt and sickness, yea death itself, shall he take from us. Oh rejoice!' "

Then Eleal reacted. She screamed, "D'ward!" and scrambled to her feet. She started to move toward him and lurched, almost overbalancing.

"No!" D'ward snapped. "Come no closer!"

"But—You cured—" She looked down at her feet, as if unable to believe her senses.

It would feel very strange, Dosh thought. Even having a sprained ankle cured had felt strange, and she must have lived with her deformity all her life. It felt bizarre even to witness such a miracle. His scalp prickled, although he had seen the Liberator use his powers before. The effect on the others would be even stronger.

Ursula laughed, and the sound was as shocking as it would be in a temple. "That was foolish of you, Kisster. You should have done that where the world could see."

D'ward scowled at her. "I did not do it for that. It was recompense for an old offense. Tielan, can you take that extra sole off her boot? Eleal, I have repaid some of my debt to you. Go now."

Eleal's face glistened wet in the firelight, and that was not all rain on her cheeks. She trembled visibly. "D'ward, D'ward!" She took a tentative step.

"No closer! I am happy to see you again, and even happier that I could do what I just did, but you are not welcome here tonight. You must find a place outside. Piol . . . What do you think, Piol? Am I being foolish?"

The old man was pale also. He shook his head.

D'ward pulled a face, as if that confirmation of whatever troubled him was highly distasteful. "Bid'lip, Doggan . . . will you see that Eleal Singer and Piol Poet find a place to lie tonight?" He did not add, "Far away from me," but the implication was obvious.

Tielan had pried the lift off Eleal's boot with the blade of his spear. He handed the boot to her in silence. The rain was starting to sting on Dosh's shoulders.

"The rest of us," D'ward said, "will use the tent cloth as a blanket. It won't be very comfortable, but it will cover more of us that way, and we shall be a lot better off than most of the people out there. If you see any small children, invite them in. Farewell, Eleal and Piol. I wish you safe journey home."

# 37

Showers came ever more frequently as the night passed, growing heavier, colder, and more persistent. The fires went out early, starved for lack of fuel or just drowned by the rain. Strangers huddled together, grumbling and muttering, sharing their misery. Few slept much.

Eleal slept hardly at all. She would no sooner start to nod than something would disturb her—if not a dream then rain on her face, a child wailing, or someone moving beside her—and instantly she was wide awake, thinking *my leg is cured!* She was no longer a cripple, a freak, a monster. Now she could plan a career as a singer or actor. She could dream of entering the Tion Festival. She could make plans for husband, family, children. She could imagine herself as beautiful, attractive to men, a complete person.

And it had been D'ward who had done this. Not Tion or any of the other gods. D'ward, who preached heresy. How could she reconcile this miracle with the terrible things he said? How could she tell evil from good anymore? Five years ago D'ward had betrayed her trust. Now he had granted her dearest wish without a word from her, asking no favor or service or pledge, repaying in one stroke everything she had ever done for him.

How? Who was D'ward? She had been thinking of him as man born of woman, and yet she had seen him come into the world, materializing out of empty air. If he was not mortal, then he must be divine or demon, and why should a demon grant such a blessing?

As the first faint hint of day began to seep through the sodden clouds, the multitude on the knoll stirred and crumbled. People rose shivering to their feet and headed for the road, jostling and disturbing any who remained asleep. From the angry mutters she had overheard around her in the night, Eleal knew that most would be heading straight back home to Niol. D'ward had dismissed her, refused to meet with her alone. She had saved his life once and yet he did not trust her! He had bade her leave.

Piol came awake with a paroxysm of wheezing and coughing. How could so few teeth chatter so loudly?

"You all right?" she asked.

"Apart from rheumatics and frostbite and double pneumonia, yes. How about you?"

"Mental confusion and moral uncertainty, mostly."

He turned to peer at her in the gloom and then chuckled. His bony hand found hers and squeezed. "A new life opens its doors?"

She hugged him. He was a bundle of faggots and cold as a fish. "I don't know, Piol, I don't know! Explain it to me."

He hacked again. "Wish I could. Where are we going now?"

After a long moment, Eleal whispered, "I want to follow the Liberator."

"I was afraid of that. Why, Eleal? What is driving you? You told me you wanted to go to Joal, but all you really seem to want—"

"D'ward cured my leg."

"That's no reason. Even before—"

"Yes, it is!" But was it? Her dream had changed. In the night it had really been D'ward in her arms, not that unknown admirer with the mustache—D'ward as he was now, with his trim beard. *Woeful maiden, handsome lad . . .*

Piol was waiting for more. What could she tell him? It was ridiculous to think of revenge now. However D'ward had harmed her in the past, he had made redress. But how could she ever be friends with a man who uttered such frightful blasphemies? Furthermore, he was leading his army to Jurgvale, and in Jurgvale was Tigurb'l Tavernkeeper. She had not told Piol about him, but he had guessed enough. There was absolutely no reason for her to join this crazy heretical pilgrimage.

There was no way she could not. "I never thanked D'ward properly."

"Yes, you did."

"Well, I'd like to talk with him. Talk about old times. He's an old friend, isn't he? I like him. He's nice. Let's eat something." She reached for the pack they had been using as a pillow, and he caught her wrist.

"Not yet. Too many eyes and mouths here. Let's start walking. It'll warm us."

The crowd was already flowing down from the hillock, dividing into two streams. The larger by far was the stream heading for the Niol road, but a surprising number were making for Lospass. Eleal and Piol moved more slowly than most—he because he was old, she because she had to learn how to walk all over again. As soon as her mind wandered, she tripped or staggered as if she were drunk. It was funny, really, and once or twice she laughed aloud.

Daylight came grudgingly, a drippy, gray morning. It must be Twenty-second Fortnight already, so bad weather was hardly surprising, even in Niol. Narshvale would be thigh-deep in snow by now. So might Lospass. She was not dressed for winter and neither was Piol.

The road wound across the flats. Rain clouds drifted overhead, trailing gray tendrils. Niolwall and most of Niolslope were hidden. Just as the marshy paddies began to give way to gently rolling pastures, she noticed that the Liberator and his bodyguard were coming up behind, and drawing closer. They moved in spurts. It seemed as if D'ward was hailing almost everyone he passed by name, sometimes striding on by, other times slowing for a few minutes' chat upon the way. Then he would lengthen his stride again and so would the shield-bearers, and he would move on to the next group.

Perhaps he would be in a better mood today—a hug and a kiss for old times' sake. . . .

Piol was managing well. He was slow but sure, he said; he could keep this pace up all day, just as long as nobody rushed him. They ate the last of their rations without stopping.

D'ward's party caught up with them before Eleal expected. The first she knew was a voice at their heels:

"Piol Poet?"

Piol was too unsteady to look around while walking. He stopped and turned to peer at the speaker inquiringly.

"I am Dosh Envoy. The Liberator asks a word with you."

Piol said, "Oh?" and "Oh!" and "Of course!"

"And I will keep you company, Eleal Singer." The little blond man smiled pleasantly enough, but he nudged her forward.

"Why Piol? Why doesn't he want to speak with me?" She allowed herself to be conducted along the road while Piol fell back to be immersed in the bodyguard.

"I don't know, lady. I would love to know that. He granted you a miracle and then threw you out. I was sort of hoping you would tell me why. Are you a reaper?"

"A *what?* Of *course* not!"

Dosh was not the stripling she had thought. Seen by daylight, he was undoubtedly older than she was, and while that might be innocence steadying the gaze of his baby-blue eyes, it was creepily like the cynical contempt she had seen so often in Tigurb'l Tavernkeeper's.

"I'm the Eleal of the prophecies. That's why I got the miracle."

"And I'm nosey. That's why I'm asking. Would you tell me what happened at the seven-hundredth festival, when the Liberator came into the world?"

"That's a very good smile—most winsome. Have you acted professionally?"

He laughed, not at all abashed, pushing wet hair out of his eyes. "Lady, I have done things professionally that would shock you to the core." His teeth gleamed. "Or would they?"

"I ought to slap your face for that."

"Go ahead. I deserve it. D'ward has shown me the light; I'm trying to reform and it's harder than I expected. I am sorry if I offended."

"Did he tell you to cross-examine me?"

Dosh nodded cheerfully, hitching his shield higher on his back. "He said I would find your story interesting, if you would tell it. I met him not long after you did, a few fortnights later, in Nagvale."

"Oh, that was where he ran to, was it?"

"Wouldn't you run if Zath were after you?"

Eleal walked at least a hundred steps on her new leg before she could answer that question. It opened doors she had never thought of. She had always thought of the Lord of Art as a defender, but he might not defend heretics. "Would Tion have betrayed him to Zath?"

"Very likely. I would trust almost any of them before Tion."

She shuddered at the blasphemy. "You are personally acquainted with gods, are you?"

"I thought they were gods, too," Dosh said calmly, "until a few days ago. I've met at least four, probably five, because I think I was Tion's pathic for a few years. There's a chunk of my memory missing. I'll tell you about them if you'll tell me how D'ward came into the world."

"You first."

"No, you first."

The trail rose gradually into the hills. Forest closed in. The rain became colder.

Dosh was granted a very brief account of the Liberator's arrival in Sussvale. Eleal was a shrewd little minx, and he had to hammer her with questions to obtain a reasonably full account of what had happened. She was astute and willful and pretty, he decided, but not as worldly wise or ravishing as she thought she was. He found himself almost regretting his present state of grace, for there could be no doubt who would have been ravished had she met the old Dosh in a mood for girl.

He eventually decided that she genuinely did not know how D'ward had managed to escape from Sussland. That was a nagging mystery, because the Youth must have known the Liberator was prowling on his turf. It was very much out of character for Tion to ignore a handsome young innocent, which was what D'ward had been in those days, and to let the Liberator leave in peace would have been rank defiance of Zath. Eleal had no inkling of Pentatheon politics, though.

When he was satisfied that he had learned as much as he was going to, Dosh picked up the story. He was just describing the army's escape from Lemodvale when a group of shield-bearers moved past them to take up station ahead. D'ward himself arrived, walking at Dosh's other side, using him as a barrier between himself and the girl.

She said, "D'ward!" Her smile was quite convincing. It didn't quite convince Dosh, though.

"Stay there, please," the Liberator told her. He had his hood back, and his black hair was sparkly with rain. "Why didn't you go back to Niol?"

"Aren't you pleased to see me again?"

"You I am delighted to see, and Piol too. What I don't welcome is your curse."

"Curse?" If that reaction was faked, then she was first-class.

"There's a spell on you, Eleal. I'm not quite sure how I know that, but I do, and my friend Ursula agrees. She is wise in such matters."

"I don't know what you mean! That's a ridiculous, horrible idea."

D'ward sighed. "Who did it, Eleal? Which of your supposed gods?"

She grew shrill. "You're talking nonsense! Curse indeed!"

"Piol says you were living in Jurg, so the most likely culprit is Ken'th, who happens to be your father, as I recall. Why did you throw up your job and come looking for me? Come on, Eleal, we're talking murder here. . . . Do you really want to kill me?"

"Of course not!"

"Would you let me kiss you?"

"Of course . . . I mean perhaps." Now she was certainly hiding something.

D'ward sighed. "We'll be in Jurgvale tomorrow. You can go home and resume your career."

"I can *start* a career, you mean! Didn't Piol tell you? I sang in a brothel. I was a whore, D'ward! That's what cripples do to eat."

There were other ways to earn a living, Dosh thought, although he had heard that they paid poorly. She was limping again, but he could not decide whether that was from habit or because her muscles were unaccustomed to an even gait. Or it could be just a ploy to win sympathy.

"No troupe would hire me. I was starving in the gutter, D'ward! But now that's all behind me, thanks to you, and you think I want to kill you?"

The Liberator had turned his face away and pulled up his hood against the rain. "I see why you would have wanted to."

"But I didn't understand!" she proclaimed. "I admit I felt hurt when you ran out on me, D'ward, but I was only a child. Now I am a mature woman and can see things more clearly. I didn't know Tion would have turned you over to Zath."

"Well, I thought he might. What do you think, Brother Dosh?"

"About what, master?"

"Can I trust her?"

"I'm sure you're going to. I wouldn't, of course. How does one recognize a curse on someone?"

The Liberator shrugged. "It isn't something you could ever learn to do. I couldn't have seen this one if it had been done properly—which is another reason to think that Ken'th is the culprit. He's quite a minor sorcerer." He nodded to the girl. "You can come as far as Jurg with us, Eleal Singer, and welcome." He strode forward very quickly, and the shield-bearers followed.

"Which brothel?" Dosh asked.

"Mind your own business!" Eleal spun around and limped back down the road to where the old man was following.

It wouldn't be the one Dosh had worked in.

Different clientele.

# 38

Alice came awake suddenly, in the shocked where-am-I? awareness of a strange bed. The room was almost dark, with just a hint of light around the shutter, and the rattling of that shutter had wakened her. The weather had broken; she sensed a strong wind gusting outside and the dampness of rain. Unfamiliar scents of spice or potpourri added to the strangeness, and someone very close to her ear was breathing in a measured half-snoring rhythm. There was a man in her bed.

Then her memory awoke also and began supplying answers. She was in Boydlar Rancher's house in Jurgslope, the foothills of Jurgwall, and the man on the other side of the bolster was Jumbo Watson. Valian peasantry were always willing to offer hospitality to wayfarers, and Jumbo was not above using his charisma to obtain the best. The best in this case was Boydlar's own feather bed, for although Boydlar had a large rambling house, he had an even larger rambling family to fill it. Jumbo, always the gentleman, had announced that he would roll up in a blanket on the floor. Alice had told him to put the blanket between them, and she would trust him to behave himself. So here she was, bundling with a man she had met only a week ago.

Her affair with Terry had gone even faster, but that had been a wartime emergency. Jumbo Watson was not a terrified, doomed boy. Gentleman or not, he had taken more than his share of the covers. She pulled gently. He snorted, but in a moment he was snuffling regularly again.

Boards creaked overhead. Something mooed or lowed in the distance. The Boydlar family would be astir at dawn, she supposed, but there was no reason why she should not go back to sleep for an hour or so.

A week ago she had been hiding in her hermitage in the flats of Norfolk. Now she was roaming the ranges of another world on the back of a dragon. And loving it! Miss Pimm had been absolutely right. This impossible adventure had jolted Alice Pearson right of her depression. If that rain she could smell was going to hang around— from the look of the clouds at sunset, Jumbo had predicted that it would—then future days might not be quite so much fun as the last few. But a little damp wouldn't kill her, whereas Norfolk might well have driven her loopy.

Jumbo rolled over. She could not have found a better guide or traveling companion than Jumbo. She wished she knew how old he was. He seemed about twenty-five and yet he told tales of Uncle Cam, who would be almost eighty if he were still alive. She wondered if Edward looked his age now. Trying to imagine the expression on his face when she turned up to meet him, Alice went back to sleep.

Breakfast was served in a huge, stone-flagged kitchen that could have belonged to any prosperous rural family in Europe. Kettles simmered on the great hob, metal pans hung gleaming on the walls, and the Rancher family swarmed in and out: husky workers, frail old crones, wet-mouthed toddlers. Things that looked like cats snuffled under the table like dogs. Boydlar's wife—named Ospita or Uspitha or thereabouts—was a red-faced, cloud-shaped woman, who seemed to be everywhere at once, tending children, dropping loaded platters on the table, pushing reluctant adolescents out the door to attend to chores, and talking all the time very loudly, mostly to Jumbo.

Alice understood less than nothing of what was said. On the first night of their journey, Jumbo had tried to pass her off as his sister from Fithvale, which was a long way away. That ploy had not worked very well, because everyone in the Vales spoke at least a few words of Joalian. Since then she had been his sister who had been deprived of speech by a sickness, and whom he was taking to the temple of Padlopan in Niol to be healed. So Alice communicated in gestures and everyone was duly sympathetic.

Three children were chased out. Two more appeared, followed by Boydlar himself, all wet and pink from the weather, with his scanty hair hanging in streaks. Ospita made a comment; he laughed and riposted, setting his listeners laughing louder. It was an idyllic scene of rural domesticity. Whatever the evils of the Pentatheon, this section of the Valian peasantry seemed happy and prosperous, and a great deal healthier than any working-class family back in England's city slums. No world wars troubled them, no clamoring traffic or industrial strikes. If she had to spend the rest of her days in rural solitude, she would prefer the Vales to Norfolk.

The food she had been given was delicious, even if it did seem to be the illegitimate offspring of an omelette and a meat pie. It was also four times as much as she could eat. While she was forcing down a few last mouthfuls in an effort not to insult her hostess too much, there came a stamping of boots outside. The door flew open to admit a swirl of wind and rain, plus a tallish young man in a leather cloak and hat. The usual jovial greetings flowed to and fro. Then he removed his hat, shaking the rain from it.

Alice realized she was staring and looked down at her food hastily, only to discover that her appetite had gone completely. The unintelligible conversation eddied around her without pause, so her rudeness had either not been noticed or was being ignored. The newcomer seemed to be conveying some news to Jumbo, speaking in a slurred gabble. Her eyes kept stealing furtive glances. She should have known that every Eden had its serpents—the young man was missing half his face, his left arm, and most of his shoulder too. In a nightmare leer, his mouth reached back to where his ear should have been, showing teeth and parts of his skull. The injury was not recent, but it was very horrible. Not high explosives, not machinery . . . The only explanation she could imagine was some sort of wild beast, some monster like the bears and wolves that Europe had killed off centuries ago.

What you gain on the swings, you lose on the roundabouts.

Clouds had settled in around the Boydlar house, reducing the ranch buildings to faint ghosts and the scenery to nothing at all. The rain was a steady fine drizzle but not as cold as it looked. Migraine and Apocalypse, who preferred their water solid, were belching and burping in disgust. They set off at a moderate run, but a mile or so along the trail, as soon as they were safely out of sight of their former hosts, Jumbo called a halt for talk.

"You going to be warm enough?"

"I shall be both warm and dry," Alice assured him from within her voluminous furs. "I cannot guarantee that I shall not smell abominably, though."

He laughed. "A hazard of the road, my lady! That one-armed chappie was Ospita's nephew, and he brought news. Your cousin was in Niolvale two days ago, with a large following. Thought to be heading for Lospass."

Alice released a long breath. She was surprised how welcome that news was, how much she had secretly dreaded news of another kind. "Then we should meet up with him tomorrow?"

"We should meet up with him this afternoon, I'd say. Jurgvale's quite narrow. Yes, easily."

"Good!" Nevertheless, Alice wondered how Edward was going to react. She would have to explain right away that she had not come to meddle.

Jumbo was eying her quizzically. He must guess what she was thinking. "Right oh? Ready to *zomph?*"

"Yes . . . no. One thing. What happened to that poor boy?"

"Which—Oh, Korilar? From the look of him, I'd say he'd had a very narrow escape from a *mithiar.*"

"What's a *mithiar?*"

"Well, that's the Joalian name. Don't know the local term." Jumbo pulled a face. "If you can imagine a ten-stone tarantula, or a black panther with saber teeth and six legs, you'll be getting close. We call them jugulars. They attack on sight—grab you with their claws and tear you to bits."

Alice glanced around at the fog. "You never mentioned those before, Mr. Watson."

"They're not very common," he said solemnly. "I've never spoken with a man who's met one, except possibly Korilar just now."

She distrusted the twinkle in his eye. "I can guess why not. Have you spoken with people who met one later?" She realized she was inviting him to display his humor. Jumbo had a very good sense of humor and knew it. The fastest way to a man's heart was always through his vanity, but why was she playing up to him like this? She had caught herself at it several times yesterday.

"Of course. Seriously, you don't see jugulars very often—and never for long."

"Only when they spring at you?"

"No, only when they spring at other people!" Jumbo laughed and shouted to the dragons to *zomph.*

# *39*

When Julian Smedley told T'lin Dragontrader that he wanted to go home as fast as possible, the big man took him more literally than he intended. T'lin made a beeline for Olympus with very few stops, and four dragons could transport two riders much faster than four. Julian discovered that he was expected to eat and sleep in the saddle, but pride would not let him countermand his own orders, so he ate and slept in the saddle. The fine weather had broken at last, and the dragons raced joyfully through driving snow, over crag and crevasse. How they managed to stay in contact, Julian had no idea. Most of the time he seemed to journey entirely alone through a blinding white fog, but T'lin and the spare mounts always reappeared eventually.

He had leisure to brood on Edward Exeter's megalomania—the disease was obvious enough, the cure was not. *You call him crazy because he used to be your friend. You would label anyone else as straight evil and not beat about the bush.* Crazy or evil, he was a mass murderer and must be stopped before he did more damage. How, though? With all the mana he had sucked up by martyring his friends, it would take the entire Service to have any hope of overpowering and defanging him, but the Service had already tried and failed. There was no way to tell whether he had recruited Ursula to his team honestly or by using mana on her, and it did not matter. Obviously his Olympian opponents would not have sent her against the Liberator without giving her all the mana they had been able to supply. The Service had shot its bolt. Only Zath could stop the Liberator now.

Julian had never thought he might find himself cheering for Zath, but if there had to be one supreme homicidal maniac slaughtering innocents all over the Vales, he would rather it not be a former friend of his.

He also had time to meditate on his own folly. He had behaved like the crassest of boors to Euphemia, walking out on her in her distress, and then he had compounded his sins by bedding Ursula—whom he had never cared for, never lusted after, and now detested. Oh, what a muggins he had been! One little waft of mana and he had run to her side like a lapdog. She had used him all the way to Niolvale. He could not have resisted the mana, but he ought to have guessed what she was doing to him. He would never be able to hold up his head again. Euphemia had warned him, and he had forgotten her warning. He could certainly never look Euphemia in the eye after this.

It felt like a broken heart, but it was probably only wounded pride.

Groggy with fatigue, he did not realize that his journey was over until Blizzard, scrambling down a sheer cliff, emerged from the clouds directly above the paddock at Olympus—about a thousand feet above. Julian closed his eyes and kept them shut until he was safely delivered to the grassy valley bottom. Belching triumph, Blizzard raced to the gate, where Mistrunner and Bluegem were already gorging on hay and T'lin was stripping off Starlight's tack.

Julian tried to dismount with grace and dignity, but his legs failed him and he sat down abruptly in the mud. Green eyes glinting amusement, T'lin took hold of his arm and heaved him to his feet.

"Thank you, Seventy-seven," Julian said staunchly. "You made excellent time. Good show."

A broad grin of satisfaction split T'lin's ginger beard. "The dragons enjoyed it. A record, I believe, Saint Kaptaan."

"I really do not doubt that. I'll have someone collect my kit, if you'll just leave it here."

T'lin promised to have it delivered. Julian thanked him again and trudged off, already sweltering in his furs as the packed snow fell off them in handfuls. One of the joys of

Olympus was the mildness of its climate, even in winter. While storms raged on the peaks all around, here only a faint drizzle was falling, but the sky was overcast and darkness not far off.

He reached his house by blind reckoning and had stumbled up the steps to the veranda before he remembered that Dommi would not be there to care for him. Still, young Pind'l and Ostian ought to be able to manage for a week or two, until Dommi came to his senses and returned. Throwing open the door, Julian bellowed, "Carrot!"

He marched through to his bedroom, fumbling one-handed with his buttons. Receiving no response, he bellowed again.

Still nothing.

That was definitely odd! Where were those two? Then he recalled that there had been no one but T'lin at the paddock, and he had met no one on the road, either, neither Carrot nor *tyika*. Up welled sinister memories of his first, disastrous arrival at Olympus, with Exeter. Oh, ridiculous! On that occasion the whole station had been burned to the ground. But still . . . He went over to the window and peered out. No lights showed in any house he could see. Well, it wasn't really dark yet. But still . . .

Hauling off his coat, he went through to the kitchens. Everything was tidy and spotless as if no one lived here, and the grate was cold. No hot water, not a crust in the larder. Feeling more and more uneasy, he returned to his bedroom and dressed in fresh clothes. Taking an umbrella from the stand by the front door, he tramped out into the dusk.

He had trudged halfway around the node before he saw any lights in windows, and still he had not met a soul—definitely odd! The first inhabited house was Rawlinson's, so he went up to the door and rang the bell. He heard it jangle in the distance.

After a minute or so, he pulled again.

At last bolts and chain clattered and the door opened. Prof himself peered out, wrapped in a black dressing gown. He held an oil lamp in his hand and had an open book pinned between his ribs and his elbow.

"God bless my soul! Captain Smedley?"

"Who else? What the deuce is going on, Prof? Since when have you locked your door? Where is everybody?"

"Oh, you don't know, of course, do you?"

Julian almost exploded. The maniac Seventy-seven had brought him all the way from Niolvale in three days. He was beat and in no mood for any of Prof's confounded puzzles. But all he said was, "I have news of Exeter and his crazy Liberator crusade."

Rawlinson coughed wheezily. "Excuse me. I've got the flu, though I think I'm over the worst of it. Wouldn't you rather try one of the others? The McKays, or—"

Julian pushed the door. "I must talk with you about Exeter. And I need a drink."

Prof retreated in disorder. "Well, if you insist . . ."

"I do insist," Julian said.

Five minutes later, he was stretched out in a leather armchair with a glass of spirits in his hand, staring in stark disbelief at his host. *Götterdämmerung?*

Prof's wife had died in Zath's assault on the station and he had not remarried. According to the Carrots, he was regularly consoled by the tender embraces of Marian Miller. His living room was a bleak, empty-looking place, because he had rebuilt it with an immortal's lifetime supply of bookshelves but had not yet had time to acquire books to fill them. His taste in furniture ran to London club style, heavy and dark. The single oil lamp within this barn cast an apologetic glow on a scattering of discarded clothes, books, dirty dishes. The fireplace held only ashes, although the winter air was dank. Prof, in other words, appeared to be just as bereft of domestic servants as Julian.

More surprising even than that was his fevered look and racking cough. Under his robe showed mauve pajama legs and green bedroom slippers. He had put a bookmark in his book and poured his guest a drink without taking one for himself. Now he was huddled in a corner of the sofa, looking wan and ill in the lurid light. The big house echoed with lonely emptiness.

"You're not well!" Julian said.

Prof scowled at him balefully. "I did mention flu, did I not? Does the simple term 'flu' not find suitable referents within your English vocabulary?"

"Well, then, cure it! Dammit all, man, you're a stranger. You're not even supposed to catch head colds." Julian looked down at his crippled hand. "I thought healing just happened."

"Not always." Prof coughed painfully. "Sometimes it requires conscious application of power. I think your suggestion is an excellent one. I do believe I might have thought of it myself, given sufficient time. The only trouble is that I have no mana at present."

"Then ask someone else. . . ." Julian realized that he was being excessively stupid and Prof's sarcasm was not unwarranted. He took a long draft, feeling the brew burn all the way down inside him. " 'Scuse me, I'm all in. What's going on?"

"There is something of a mana famine in Olympus just now."

"You gave it all to Ursula to use on Exeter, you mean?"

"Er . . . That is part of the trouble, yes. But then Zath came to call."

"*Zath* did?"

Prof greeted his astonishment with a gleam of satisfaction. "Indeed. You have missed eventful times, Captain. Zath transported in by the node one evening and gate-crashed a dinner party at the Chases'. He demanded that the Service restrain the Liberator, otherwise he, Zath, would take it out on our hides. Burn us to the ground. Then he transported out again." Prof pouted balefully. "I see from your bemused expression that I shall have to be more specific. I personally did not hear the intruder's words. I confess that when he appeared, what I should like to refer to as a reflex for self-preservation came into play. I hit the ground almost at the dragon paddock. It took me fifteen minutes to walk back. I am not proud of that, but I was certainly not alone in using the trapdoor. About half of those present did the same. The rest reacted by trying to subdue what they assumed was only a reaper—vainly, of course, because he wasn't. The long and short of it was that everyone who was present at that dinner party was totally stripped of mana."

Julian stared at his host. He certainly did look ill, but could he be delirious? Was any of this nonsense true? "But—but that can't have been everyone!" The Chases' dining room was not big enough to have held the whole of the Service.

"No. But we are extremely short-staffed now. That is another development you missed. A great many people were suddenly overcome by a fervent calling to minister to the benighted heathen. They did a bunk—vamoosed, scarpered."

"You mean they let Zath scare them away?"

Prof scowled. "No. They let the flu scare them away. This is no ordinary flu. Back Home they call it the Spanish flu. It's killed more millions than the war, and it especially strikes down young adults. It's incredibly infectious—it circled the Earth in five months, Betsy says."

"I thought only people could cross over! You're saying that germs can?"

"If by germs you mean bacteria, then influenza is not caused by a bacterium."

"What is it caused by?"

"A *filterable virus,*" Prof said smugly.

"What's that?"

"No one knows. It can't be seen in a microscope but is infectious. And obviously it can cross over between worlds. The Peppers caught it, but they had recovered before they came back." His voice was becoming hoarser and weaker. "That's why they were late. It must have been Euphemia. She went Home for just a few hours, to fetch Exeter's cousin. She noticed nothing herself, but her Carrots all came down with it, and it spread through the valley like a flash of lightning. Those who still had mana tried healing. They could not keep up with it." He coughed several times painfully. "I don't know how many Carrots have died, but a lot, certainly. And some of us, too: Foghorn, Olga, Vera, Garcia. Very suddenly, all of them."

"Good God!" Julian took a long drink. *Strangers* dying? Of *flu?*

Prof seemed to find his astonishment amusing, for he bared his teeth in an ironic smile. "Götterdämmerung, Captain? The Carrots are naturally somewhat disillusioned. Their idols have feet of clay. The immortals are mortal after all. They have withdrawn their services. Personally, I am surprised that they have not driven us out of the valley, lock, stock, and barrel. They may do so yet."

Julian drained his glass to help him digest this incredible news. Prof blinked blearily at his guest. Then he hauled himself off the sofa and shuffled over to the sideboard. He poured himself a drink and brought back the decanter, depositing it alongside Julian. He returned to his seat and was convulsed by a severe spasm of coughing.

"Alice is here?" Julian asked.

"She is on Nextdoor, yes. She's gone off to see Exeter. What news of the Liberator, then?"

"His belfry is jam-packed full of bats. It's every bit as bad as Jumbo and the others predicted. He thinks he's the messiah. He's marching on Tharg, dragging a ragtag rabble of peasants behind him. I was hoping . . ." But any lingering hopes of the Service being able to stop Exeter were now dead. "He's ripping up all your work on the True Gospel. He calls the Pentatheon and the others enchanters, instead of demons, and you know where that leads. He's in cahoots with some of them, so God knows what sort of bargains he's been making. He's invented some kind of reincarnation claptrap to replace the afterlife among the stars. He's issuing divine doctrine on his own authority. He's mad as a whirling dervish." Julian refilled his glass.

Prof rubbed his chest as if it hurt. "I shouldn't worry about him too much. I think Zath has his number." He smirked, which meant he thought he was being especially perceptive.

Fatigue and liquor were making Julian's head spin. "Let me get this straight. First of all, what the hell was Zath up to, coming here? That kind of threat is just the thing to get all our backs up and turn us into Exeter supporters!"

"Well, of course. You're quite right there. Bluster will work on natives, but Zath can't know much about the English. Even Pinky was sounding pro-Liberator next day."

"And second . . . why would he? Why try to stop the Liberator by threatening us? That's even rummer! It almost sounds as if Zath has the wind up!"

Prof nodded and leaned back, closing his eyes. "Of course. That's what we all thought. I'm afraid it was what we were supposed to think." Ill as he was, he was not beyond playing stupid games.

"What's missing?" Julian barked. "What haven't you told me?"

"Jumbo. Jumbo and Alice Pearson—Exeter's cousin—that's her name now, Pearson. She's a widow. They were present, of course. Later that night the two of them swiped a couple of dragons and took off."

The implications took a moment to register. Then Julian said, "Oh my God!" and drained his glass. *Alice, what have we done to you?* "This was not planned?"

"Not at all. Zath asked who was in charge and spoke only to him. He wasn't in the room more than a minute or two, I'm told. But Jumbo was there, and Mrs. Pearson was there."

"You think Jumbo's . . ." How could a man put it into words? "You think he's a traitor? You think Exeter was right all along?"

Prof rubbed his eyes without opening them. "I know he was. The Jean St. John story was a blind. It was Jumbo who tried to queer Exeter by dropping him in Belgium—he admits it. The point is that Jumbo couldn't help himself. He's been around a long time, so he's well known to the opposition. Zath trapped him, installed a compulsion, and sent him off to be Judas."

Julian shuddered. Much as Exeter ought to be stopped, there was something peculiarly repellent about a trusted friend turning Brutus, even if that friend was not responsible for his own intentions. Mana had not seemed like an utter evil when he had used it to convert the troopers at Seven Stones, but Ursula had turned him into a gigolo with it, Exeter had slaughtered his friends to obtain it, then used it to unman the Niolian cavalry—and now this tale of Jumbo being bent, at least once and probably twice. No one was safe when there was mana around.

"You think Zath chose Jumbo again? Seems odd. Exeter will be suspicious this time, won't he?" Then he shuddered a second time, feeling his skin crawl as if he had just fallen into an especially foul pit. "You don't mean Alice?"

"I don't know." Prof peered blearily at him. "Jumbo's more likely, because Zath would know he was a senior member of the Service. He shouldn't have known who Mrs. Pearson was—but I fear it is a great mistake to underestimate him. Hell, Captain, maybe he did come just to make threats."

"But you don't think so. You think he came to hex Jumbo again."

Rawlinson struggled with a cough and took a drink. "I think one of them's a poisoned pawn, probably Jumbo. He may not even know it himself, but I think he's a loaded gun, and when he meets the Liberator, he'll fire."

"And he took Alice along to allay suspicion? As a decoy?" Just as Ursula had taken Julian himself. "Exeter'll be so surprised to see her that he won't pay much attention to Jumbo."

"That would be Jumbo's thinking," Prof agreed in a whisper, "although not willing thinking, if you follow me. But it could have been Alice who talked Jumbo into taking her."

Julian cringed. "Exeter has buckets of mana of his own. Whichever one of them is the hemlock, he'll detect the hex . . . won't he?"

Prof heaved himself upright with a groan. "If you'll excuse me, old man, I'm going back to bed." He was swaying on his feet. "Stay and finish the bottle if you want. There's more in that cupboard. No, I don't think Exeter will detect the trap. With the kind of power Zath has at his disposal, he won't have left any fingerprints."

# 40

Julian spent the night on Prof Rawlinson's sofa and went home through a drizzly dawn to clean up as best he could. Even the water supply had failed, though. Exploring his own house in a way he never had before, he discovered that the taps were supplied from a tank in the attic, which was charged by hand-pumping from an underground cistern— how it arrived there was not clear, but he managed to fill a bucket from it without falling in. There was no firewood cut, and he could not handle an ax.

Clean but shivering, he had just conquered the last shirt button when he heard the doorbell jangle. On the veranda stood William McKay, unshaven and rumpled as a wet cat, beaming in his usual witless fashion and holding out a covered basket.

"Heard you were home, old man. Brought you some brekker."

Julian was nonplussed. "That's extremely kind of you."

"Oh, don't thank me, old son. Thank the Reformed Methodist Ladies' Good Deed and Morris Dancing Society, Olympus Branch. They distribute gin to the needy. I'm just the messenger boy. You can tip me a tanner if you're feeling generous. Need the basket back."

"Come in a moment."

McKay stepped over the threshhold and stopped. He was a tall, vapid man and the best linguist in the station, able to speak at least twelve of the Valian dialects without saying anything of substance in any of them. His only interest was fishing and he was of interest to Julian only because he was Euphemia's husband. She swore they had not shared a bed in years, but how did one cross-examine a man about his own wife?

Lifting a corner of the cover, Julian found fruit, bread that smelled newly baked, and a stoppered bottle hot enough to contain tea. His mouth began watering enthusiastically. He thought of Prof. "You do this gin-distributing to all us worthy poor?"

"Well, it makes sense to have a central mess. Got to ration the supplies, what? All hang together. Polly organized it." McKay's gaze wandered past Julian and back again. "You—you're alone?"

"Yes. Come and sit a moment. I need to talk to you."

"Oh. Should be getting back. Just wondered if you had news of Euphemia. We're a bit concerned, you know."

"What? Why? Come in here," Julian said firmly. Taking the basket, he led the way into his drawing room. It was small and rather sparse, for he had no skill at homemaking and rarely entertained, but he noted that it was at least tidy. He waved his guest to a chair and took one himself. He began emptying the basket. "Tell me."

McKay folded himself down into the chair and stared at the floor uncomfortably. "Well, she went back Home briefly to fetch Exeter's cousin. . . ."

"And brought the Spanish flu back. Yes, I heard. Where is she now?"

"Don't know. Just got back from Thovale myself yesterday. Haven't caught it yet, but I expect I will. She'd gone already. Thought you . . . Well, you know. Thought you might know."

Julian gripped the bottle between his knees and pulled out the stopper. An intriguing wisp of steam emerged. "No." He took a swig of tea and burned his throat satisfactorily.

"Ah. Seems she managed to sweet-talk the Carrots into supplying us with some grub a couple of days ago, when we ran out. Then she did a bunk. Didn't tell anyone where she was going. Left no note." McKay was looking everywhere except at Julian. "Unless you . . . ?"

"None here, I'm afraid. Look, McKay. . . . You know we're lovers."

The tall man shrugged at the fireplace. "No moss. We've gone our own ways a long time. You made her very happy, old man. More than—er, well, you know."

More than half the other men in the station in their respective times? How *old* was she? Pride would never let him ask.

"We had words. I'm deucedly sorry and I want to make up. You have no idea where she's gone?"

"Not a bally notion. She works Lemodvale, you know. She'll have contacts there. Or—" He bit his lip. "The Carrots may know, I suppose. She gets on better with them than most of us do."

"She told me about Timothy."

Suddenly it was eye-contact time, man to man stuff, stiff upper lips. McKay colored, then clasped his hands together so tightly that the knuckles showed white. "Long time ago. Look, I should be getting back. . . ."

"It makes no difference to me, what she did. Like to hear your side of it, though."

"Dang it all, old man . . . !"

"Please?" Julian said, feeling his own face burning but utterly determined to see this through. "For her sake? I love her, but I hurt her feelings without meaning to. Want to make up. I want to understand her."

"Don't we all! Men can't understand women, laddie. Women are a mystery in all worlds. Can't live with 'em, can't live without 'em." McKay stared at the empty fireplace, chewing his lip. "It may not have been entirely all her fault, actually. I suppose. One of those things . . . She didn't fit in, really. The women were pretty bad to her."

Idiot! What had he expected? How long ago? Twenty years? Fifty? Even now it was easy to imagine the ladies of Olympus snubbing the fishmonger's daughter from rural Ireland, a pride of cats sharing a mouse. It was also easy to see that such stupid class prejudice should mean a lot less to Julian Smedley, who had been through the Great War, than it did to all those Victorian fossils. If the war had decided anything, it had brought England together. Things would be different from now on. But even if Euphemia might still be a misfit back in Cheltenham, here on Nextdoor she was his woman and that was all that mattered.

"I may not have been as much help as I should have been," McKay said gruffly. "She went native. Moved in with a Carrot woodcutter."

Where else could she have gone? "She—they—they had just the one child?"

"Well, yes. Then her big buck Carrot got eaten by a jugular. A year or two later she came back to me, brat and all." He shrugged. "Took her in. Separate rooms, you know? We got along better like that. And Tim. Jolly good kid, actually. Brought him up as a gentleman. Taught him fishing. He went off Home a few years ago. Last we heard he was with Head Office. He's a stranger over there, of course. Well, mustn't point fingers, old man! I'm pretty sure I've fathered a few by-blows around the Station myself." McKay lumbered to his feet.

Obviously it still rankled that his wife had gone native, left him for a Carrot. He probably didn't even appreciate the courage it must have taken for her to come back to him and his precious friends. Well, what she had done or not done did not matter now to Julian. He'd rather think of the young Euphemia having a love affair with a young Carrot than of her being blackmailed into bed by slimy Pinky Pinkney. Nothing wrong with Carrots except that they were mortal. Dommi, for one, was a hell of a lot better man than Pinkney or even this bat-brained William McKay.

"What news of Exeter?" McKay asked, shambling toward the door.

"All bad." Julian told him the tale. "It's Alice Prescott I'm worried about. Pearson, I mean."

McKay nodded vaguely. "What are you going to do?"

Julian took a moment to digest what he had learned. If Euphemia was not in Olympus, then there was no reason for him to stay. With only one hand, he was limited even in the help he could give to the sick. "I think I'm going to head back to Exeter's crusade again. Alice is an old friend, and Exeter may be dead. I sort of feel responsible for her. If Zath bewitched her, then she may be dead, too, or crazy by now. Or Jumbo is, if he was the poisoned pill. The flu must be all over the Vales already. She doesn't know the language, she has no money." That bitch Ursula might not help her.

"Better you than me, old man. I must get back to Kingdom Hall. Good luck." McKay held out a limp hand. "Don't count on finding much here when you come back, what?"

"No. I won't."

Götterdämmerung!

# *41*

A quick reconnaissance of the Station confirmed McKay's report. Polly Murgatroyd had organized meals and care for the sick, but the Carrots controlled the food supply and might cut it off at any time. There was nothing Julian could do to make things any better. He discovered that three quarters of the strangers had fled and not one of the remainder was able or willing to accompany Captain Smedley on a hundred-mile walk. All the rabbits had gone from the paddocks and when he continued on up the valley to the dragon compound, he found that deserted also. Seventy-seven must have discovered the situation and chosen the logical course of action.

He gathered a blanket, spare clothes, and some money, and walked out his front door with a pack on his back and an umbrella in his good hand. He could reach Randorvale before dark. He might be carrying the infection with him, but so many of the Service had preceded him that he was not going to make matters any worse. From Randorvale he would go by Lappinvale, Mapvale, and Jurgvale—none of those passes was beyond a man on foot. If necessary, he could carry on to Niolvale, but before then he ought to have news of the Liberator. He should also have learned just how badly the Spanish flu had struck Nextdoor. An epidemic that could circle the Earth in five months would have spread across the Vales in days.

Fifteen minutes brought him to the Carrots' village. His approach was noticed, and a delegation of three elderly men came out to meet him on the road. Two he could not recall ever seeing before, but the third had been the Pinkneys' butler, although Julian could not recall the man's name. When he was still about twenty or thirty feet away, that one shouted, "Stop!"

Julian stopped and stood there in the mud, facing rebellion while rain pattered on his umbrella. "How many of you have been stricken? How many have died?"

"Too many! Let the *tyikank* attend to their own sick and leave the Carrots alone. You are not welcome." Their green eyes were uniformly hostile.

"I do not understand. We have brought much prosperity to this valley, and done much good for your people. Just because a sickness comes, you suddenly turn on—"

"Go away, Kaptaan!" said another. "You have brought the wrath of the gods upon us. Many of us think we should burn your big houses and drive you out. Do not tempt our young men to rashness. Go!"

"I am trying to."

"Go by the river trail, then," said the former butler.

That was a sizable detour, but evidently charisma was not going to work.

"Is *Entyika* McKay with you?"

"No."

"I have two letters here—one for her, if she comes back, and one from Dommi for Ayetha."

"Leave them on that stump and begone."

Julian did so and trudged back to the turnoff. The Carrots' attitude was infuriating but understandable. It was only natural for them to attribute the pestilence to Zath and the anger of the Pentatheon. Perhaps the storm could have been weathered if the *tyikank* had stood their ground and not been so craven. As it was, the Service was wounded mortally. It could not blame Exeter or the Pentatheon, for it had brought götterdämmerung upon itself.

# 42

No one knew how Roaring Cave had earned so inappropriate a name, for nowhere contained more silence. It was a huge cavern in a hillside overlooking Lospass, much used by travelers. Eleal had overnighted in it and explored it a few days ago on her way to Niolvale. She was greatly relieved to see it again, for her muscles were not accustomed to her new leg; they throbbed as if tortured with red-hot pincers. Old Piol seemed to be in no worse shape than she was, but they were both chilled to icicles by the rain. They scrambled up the slope to the cave mouth in the company of a dozen or so other pilgrims, being met there by one of the Liberator's shield-bearing deputies. He wore a shabby, incongruous military tunic.

"We have just lit a new fire," he announced pompously. "Follow me and I will lead you to it. Try not to make unnecessary noise."

The floor was generally level, but littered with boulders of all sizes, which must have fallen in past ages from the soaring roof. The uneven path was tricky going in the gloom.

At first Eleal could see nothing except Piol's back directly ahead of her, but gradually her eyes grew accustomed to the dim light of many fires, each one surrounded by several dozen people. The warning against noise had been given because everyone was trying to listen to D'ward himself. He was sitting with one group but speaking loudly, apparently not preaching as much as answering questions.

Led to a smoky, crackling heap—more fuel than flame as yet—Eleal huddled in as close as she could and shivered strenuously. Between the snapping of the twigs and the chattering of teeth all around her, she could not make out what was being said at all. The air smelled very strongly of wet people, but she was glad of the company. As the flames leaped higher and the heat penetrated, her bones began to thaw. It was then she realized that one of the men pressed against her was Dosh. His eyes shone in the firelight as he saw that she had noticed him.

"Are you keeping watch on me?" she whispered angrily.

He nodded and held a finger to his lips.

She looked around. More and more people were trickling into the cave. Another fire had been lit nearby, and newcomers were led to that one now. The overall silence of such a crowd was quite eerie.

D'ward had risen and was moving to another group. They cleared a boulder for him to sit on. Now he was closer, and she could hear better.

"Well?" he said cheerfully. "No questions?"

"I have a question, heretic!" The harsh voice came from a large man in a dark robe. Eleal would not have been sure of its color had she not recognized its wearer as one of the priests of Padlopan who had shared the wagon with her yesterday.

D'ward's voice was no softer. "You waste your life worshipping a false god of sickness! I doubt that mere words can penetrate so many years of wrongful thinking, but ask."

The priest rose to his feet, a massive dark shape against the dancing firelight. "You say you go to slay Death. Then tell us what happens after, when Death is dead! Shall we all live forever?"

The Liberator sighed. "Whatever I answer, you will not believe. Come with us and see for yourself what happens. Who else has a question?"

"I have not done," the priest bellowed. "Nay, I have many other queries!" The reaction was a roar of fury from the audience. The priest was clearly shocked but undeterred; then D'ward said something sharply to him and he sank down out of sight.

Eleal discovered she was on the verge of sniggering. She caught Dosh's eye and saw he was grinning as if he had heard such exchanges before.

The next query was inaudible.

"Ah!" D'ward said. "Not everyone heard that. You, priest, have an excessively brazen voice. Repeat for these good people what the lady asked."

The priest did not rise, but he made himself heard. "Gladly, I will, gladly! The woman said her babe is dying and can the Liberator slay death in time to save it? Yes, answer that, Liberator!"

D'ward did not reply for a long moment, and Roaring Cave was very silent. Only faint crackling from the fires disturbed the hush. Then he said, "Pass me this child."

Eleal rose up on her knees, hoping to see more, but there were too many bodies and boulders in the way and people behind her began hissing angrily until she sat down again. All she could make out was D'ward's familiar face, framed in a narrow gap, lit from below against darkness. He looked up from whatever he had been doing.

"There!" he said. "I think that will answer your question, mother, and answer yours, too, priest. The poor mite is hungry. Has anyone a scrap of food for a hungry child? Thank you, brother—a blessing upon you. And back to your mother with you, kitten."

Roaring Cave did not exactly roar, but a whirlwind of whispers seemed to sweep through it, and then some voices cried out, "A miracle!"

Eleal looked around, and Dosh's expression was as mocking as she had expected. "Like me?" she said. "He cures others? He does this all the time?"

Dosh nodded. She cowered down low, thinking furiously.

D'ward waited until the reaction died away. "It was a blessing from the Undivided upon our quest. Who else has a question?"

He kept it up for more than an hour, moving around from fire to fire. In that time he apparently cured a woman's paralyzed arm and another fevered child and gave a blind man back his sight. Sometimes he would laugh and joke, sometimes be solemn. Often his replies took the form of little stories that made a point but left no handhold for the priests wanting to contest it. He was unfailingly gracious to everyone except clerics, and to them he was scathingly rude. That was understandable, as they kept trying to trap him. None of them ever seemed to catch him out, although some of his answers were evasive, like the one he had given the priest of Padlopan.

His mastery was amazing. Eleal had seen audiences held spellbound before, but never for so long and never by an extemporaneous performance, for obviously D'ward was following no script. His progress would eventually bring him to her fire, and she waited with trembling anxiety lest he break off and go elsewhere.

By the time he arrived, dusk was falling beyond the great arch of the entrance—and not just dusk, for the rain had turned to snow. People squirmed out of the way to make a place for him. Instead of sitting, he remained standing, his arms folded. She remembered the time he had played Gunuu in *The Tragedy of Trastos*. Then he had not worn a robe, only a loincloth, and the magic of firelight had made him shine like the god he portrayed. Oh, what a triumph that had been! A lump arose in her throat, and she trembled with a fierce longing to jump up and throw her arms around him.

He glanced at her without expression, then looked around the group. "Who asks here?"

An old man beside him cried out in the loud, flat tones of the deaf. "There is a storm coming! My bones know it! My bones always tell me when there's bad weather coming. Will you lead us onward again tomorrow, young man, or stay here and wait it out, mm?" It was a good question. He looked even older than Piol, and he was wearing no more than the legal minimum. At a guess he was just a beggar who had joined the Free for the food.

D'ward shrugged. "We're warm here now, there's fuel in the woods, water in the stream, meat walking in our direction—why run to meet tomorrow's troubles?"

"Because I don't have many tomorrows left, young man! That's why!"

D'ward laughed gleefully and reached over to clap the man's bony shoulder. "You have all eternity to look forward to, grandfather! But if your bones are telling us the truth, then I think we'll have to wait out the storm. You're not the only one without proper clothing. I don't want to see anyone freeze. Now, if we have any rich people here who would like to contribute money or spare clothes to the Free, that would be a very meritorious deed in the eyes of the Undivided."

He glanced over the group as if looking for another question, but it seemed to Eleal that his eyes momentarily flashed sapphire at her. Could he know about her money belt? She must have more wealth to hand than anyone else in the cave. She would not let D'ward have that money to foster his blasphemies!

But if she did, would he forget his unfair suspicions? Would he accept that she only wanted to be his friend now?

Would he even give her a hug, just one brief hug, to say that he knew he could trust her?

"May I ask?" The voice was that of Piol Poet, who had somehow become separated from her and was now on the far side of the fire. "I fear it may be an impertinent question, master."

D'ward chuckled. "But coming from you it will be an astute one, old friend. Ask."

"You teach things that are not written in any scripture. By whose authority do you speak?"

The Liberator's dark eyebrows rose very high. He lifted his head to address his answer to the whole cave. "Piol Poet asks by what authority I speak. Oh, Piol, Piol, do you really put so much trust in books? You know how often a scribe will make mistakes when copying a text. You know that even the original was written by mortal hand, for gods do not stoop to writing their own scriptures. Is it not better to hear the words of the teacher at firsthand than at innumerable repeats? My authority comes from the One True God, who sent me."

Several voices began to speak at once. D'ward nodded at the loudest, a burly, sullen-looking man who had been sitting with his arm around a girl no older than Eleal. Perhaps she was the only reason he was here, for his manner did not seem at all respectful.

"You claim to be the Liberator foretold in the *Filoby Testament.* But according to the *Testament,* the Liberator was born less than five years ago. How then can you be the Liberator?"

D'ward did not take offense, although several of the listeners growled angrily. "That is not what the *Testament* said about me, and I can call a witness to what did happen. Eleal Singer is here, the Eleal prophesied, the Eleal who fulfilled that prophecy. Rise, Eleal, and tell the people what you saw."

Eleal had almost forgotten what stage fright felt like, for she had not experienced it since she was a child. Now she cringed away in shock, staring aghast at D'ward's twinkling blue eyes. She could not follow an act like that!

Dosh pinched her. "Up with you! Give them the performance of your life, Singer. But keep your clothes on."

She slapped him away angrily.

Then D'ward smiled at her. She had forgotten his smiles. The beard hadn't changed their impact. She rose unwillingly to her feet.

"Come and bear witness," he said. "Up here! Excuse us, grandfather."

He meant her to stand on the flat rock the old man was now vacating. She held out a hand so he could help her up, but he ignored it. Then Dosh gripped her waist and lifted her onto the makeshift podium. A great cavern, full of twinkling fires, bright now against the evening . . . innumerable intent faces. She had never performed before an audience this size before, and she did not have her lines memorized. Piol had not even written her part yet. The pounding of her heart seemed to fill the cave; something was building a nest in her stomach.

"Begin at the beginning," D'ward said below her. "Like you told Dosh." He smiled again.

She turned to the audience and drew a deep breath. "My name is Eleal Singer." She heard her voice echo back satisfactorily from the rocks. "Five years ago, I came to Narshvale with a troupe of strolling players. Innocent child that I was, I never dreamed that evil forces conspired to slay me, nor that I was destined to play a starring role on the stage of history. . . ."

After that it was easy. She told everything, or almost everything. She did not describe D'ward's hasty departure from Suss, but she included the first miracle, when he had cured Dolm Actor of his curse, and the miracle yesterday that had cured her leg. By the time she had finished, the sky outside was black. She expected an ovation, for she was sure that it had been the finest performance of her life. She was greeted by a numbing silence. Well, no matter! People did not applaud in a temple, and today this cave was a temple. Silence itself was appreciation; the cave was very still. Not a cough. She had preached for the heretic. She had no regrets—although she wondered what her father thought of her now.

She spun around on her podium, planning to jump down into D'ward's arms for a little hug and a whispered congratulation, perhaps even a quick kiss.

But D'ward had gone.

# 43

As Eleal Singer began working up a serious sweat in her highly dramatized version of *The Coming of the Liberator*, D'ward nodded to Dosh to follow him and slipped away from the little group around the fire. Unnoticed by the intently listening pilgrims, he moved off into the dark. Doing the same was not quite so easy for a man loaded like a turtle with Prat'han's great shield, but Dosh accepted the challenge.

He reached the toe of the rockfall first. D'ward arrived, then turned around to look for his missing follower. Like an unusually silent shadow, Dosh stepped in close behind him and whispered, "Master?"

D'ward jumped rewardingly and then laughed. "You trying to frighten me to death?" In the faint glimmer from the many fires, his face was hardly more than a blur, but he was smiling, and if anyone's smile could glow in the dark, it would be his. "You know this cave?"

"Best lodgings in the Vales, for the price."

"True. So you know the little hollow back there?"

Dosh nodded. "It's called the Fleapit."

"Probably well deserved. I asked Kilpian to get a fire going. Try and keep everyone except friends and shield-bearers away, will you?"

Oh, blazes! The cave was fifty strides wide, and although the main path over the rockfall was well defined, there were other low spots. Dosh had spent days exploring Roaring Cave in his youth, for it was a favorite Tinkerfolk campsite. He knew six or seven passable routes to the Fleapit. Dusk was falling, but with so many fires burning, the cavern would not be truly dark. Intruders could manage the barrier without a torch if they took it slowly.

He sighed. "You always give me the tough ones!"

"I do," D'ward said solemnly. "That's partly because I can rely on you to tackle them better than anyone else. It's also because I know you like getting the tough ones." He grinned again. "Don't you?"

"No!" But then Dosh realized that he did enjoy the unfamiliar sensation of being trusted, which was probably the same thing. "Well, maybe. I suppose I do." He hadn't really known that, but it was true. Not for the first time, he wondered if the Liberator knew him better than he knew himself. "I'll see you're not disturbed, master."

D'ward squeezed his shoulder. "Good man. You never let me down, Dosh." He faded away into the gloom.

Dosh stood for a moment, savoring those final words. *Never let him down!* How good that felt! And how strange that he should think so—he, Dosh Envoy, who had never before cared for anything except carnal pleasure, the kinkier the better. Some miracles were less obvious than others. . . . Then he heaved Prat'han's shield straight on his shoulders, adjusted the (horribly light) money bag on his belt, and set off to locate some helpers.

He enlisted shield-bearers Tielan and Gastik, two friends, and also three Niolian youngsters he'd picked out earlier as promising recruits. Then he found Tittrag Mason, a new shield-bearer who was big enough to move the whole rockfall single-handed.

He posted them in pairs to cover the most likely paths over the pile. None of them was very happy at the prospect, thinking of reapers.

"Don't worry about them," he said. "A reaper can go by without being seen if he wants to, and in this case he won't want to leave bodies around to raise the alarm, right? The same thing's true of Eltiana cultists or Blood-and-Hammer thugs, or any other assassins the evil sorcerers may send against D'ward. Don't worry about them, because they won't worry about you, and you can't do anything about them anyway. If they do turn up, D'ward will deal with them. Your job is strictly pest control. Be polite and understanding, but firm. If you have any trouble, shout for me. I'll be going up and down the line."

Pest control. Some people just *had* to speak to the Liberator personally, to explain their problems, the gods' truth, or his mistakes. D'ward dealt with most of those during the day, but that sort could never understand that he might have more important business to attend to, such as sleeping. The worst pests by far were the priests. There were dozens of priests around now, every one of them determined to stamp out his heresy.

Dosh began patrolling back and forth across the toe of the rockfall, keeping both eyes wide open, watching anyone who headed deeper into the cave and also watching his helpers. He was annoyed to discover how easily he could work his way past them without their seeing him. He was a very good sneak, of course, after a lifetime's practice, but others might be just as good.

There was too much cover, too many people in the cave, too little light. Even if he had the fuel to build a chain of fires from one wall to the other, there would still be too many shadows. The job D'ward had given him this time wasn't just tough, it was an eyelash short of impossible.

# 44

"Crikey!" Jumbo said. "For a native, she's quite a performer!" He was sitting near a smoky little fire at the far side of Roaring Cave, leaning his arms on his knees and looking as totally relaxed as if he were watching a cricket match on a village green.

Alice refrained from comment. He was referring to the famous Miss Eleal, who had certainly grown up from the child Edward had described in 1917. She had grown *out,* too, in conspicuous places.

Riding a dragon had been a very strange experience, but this cave was stranger yet. Never would Alice have believed that her next meeting with her cousin would take place in such grotesque surroundings. When she came in, she had known his voice at once, even reverberating in that huge, echoing space, even speaking whatever dialect that was. He had not been speaking in tongues, as Zath had, yet she had often been able to catch the gist of his words. Later she had seen him in the distance. He had not changed a bit, except that now he had a beard. It did not suit him, but it might be required wear for the unlikely career he had chosen. He was obviously doing very well in it. Hundreds of people were grouped around dozens of twinkling fires under a blue haze of wood smoke.

It all looked rather like one of Uncle Roly's more lurid descriptions of Hell, except that no one was screaming or suffering. Quite the reverse—this cavern was a node, and the virtuality added an unnerving aura of holiness to the proceedings. She had been tempted to stand up and shout, "He's only Edward! I knew him when he picked his nose and woke up crying from nightmares."

She hadn't, of course. Nobody would have understood her anyway. But it was definitely an odd feeling to have a holy man in the family.

A woman with a shield on her back was shouting over the rising buzz of conversation.

"Now what's going on?" Alice demanded.

"She says," Jumbo drawled, "that the train on platform four is the express to Pontefract and Llandudno."

"I shall ask my cousin to turn you into a pillar of salt."

"Actually she said that there's food coming, that the ladies' room is over that way and the gentlemen's that way, and could she have some volunteers to fetch firewood?"

"Go ahead and volunteer," Alice said. "Shouldn't we be checking on the dragons, anyway? Suppose somebody steals them?"

"Then we walk home. They'll be all right. I think it's time to go and have a word with our esteemed Liberator." Jumbo sprang nimbly to his feet and held out a hand to aid her. All over the cave, people were rising to stretch their legs. The darkness seemed to move in as bodies blocked the firelight.

"I don't see him now," she said.

"I know where he went. Come on. If we get separated, I'll meet you underneath that molar, all righty?" Gesturing at a prominent stalactite, Jumbo took her hand and set off confidently across the cavern floor. His strong left arm cleared a way through the milling throng while he growled peremptory apologies. It seemed odd that he should be so little concerned for the safety of the livestock he had left to graze unattended outside the cave. Until this evening he had fussed over them as if they were prize racehorses. Still, he must know what he was doing. All the way from Olympus, he had been a competent guide and an enjoyable companion.

She was about to meet Edward. That was why she had come. Would he feel she was meddling? That had been a danger all along. Now there was something new. Now she had seen a blind man given back his sight and a feverish, whimpering baby come suddenly to life and start laughing. Faith healing might explain the man, but not the baby, and she wasn't sure how far she believed in faith healing anyway. Had anyone else staged those miracles, she would have been sure that they had been faked, the "invalids" being accomplices planted ahead of time in the audience.

Edward wouldn't do that. If he had worked miracles, then they had been genuine miracles. Magic, of course—Miss Pimm could use magic and the rules of the parallel worlds would give Edward on Nextdoor the powers Miss Pimm had on Earth. All the same, it was disturbing to see the cousin she had known all her life, her foster brother, deliberately playing Jesus. There could be no doubt that that was what he was doing. Although she thought of herself as a Christian, she liked to believe she was tolerant and broad-minded. His performance made her uneasy, but it could hardly be blasphemous in a world where Christianity did not exist—or could it? She must not jump to conclusions. Doubtless he would explain his reasons to her. Even if he wouldn't, she would trust him and not ask.

She felt a vicarious pride at the numbers he had collected. My cousin the messiah . . .

She followed Jumbo through the crowd, weaving between clusters of people, heading for the depths of the cave. Soon their way was blocked by a wall of rubble and megalithic blocks and frozen rivers of stalagmites. The ominous irregularities overhead showed where masses of stone had fallen off and crashed to the ground. This cave was old. The odds of another fall happening just as she was passing underneath were remote—remote but still hard to ignore. There was almost no light here, far from the arch and the fires. She had never suffered from claustrophobia before, so why start now? It was only virtuality making her skin crawl, wasn't it?

As she neared the foot of the rockfall, she heard voices raised in argument. Suddenly Jumbo halted, listening. In front of a wall of cyclopean boulders, three figures in gowns were confronting two men, one of whom bore a round shield and a dangerous-looking spear. Even without understanding the words, it was obvious to Alice that the three were demanding and the two were refusing. The subject of their disputation seemed to be access to an ominous dark notch.

"What's going on?" she whispered.

Jumbo said, "Sh!" In a moment, though, the three turned away and headed back to the main gathering, muttering angrily. The two stayed where they were.

"It appears," Jumbo said quietly, "that our reverend friend does not wish to be disturbed. Those monk-chappies were priests—Tion's I think. Let's see if we can do any better."

He led her forward again, passing the three grumbling clerics, heading for the two gatekeepers.

"They don't look much like a welcoming committee," she murmured.

"Just keeping the riffraff out. I'm sure they'll recognize a lady when they see one."

Alice did not feel much like a lady. The last few days had done nothing for her coiffeur or complexion; she was still bundled in heavy, waterlogged furs, smelling strongly of wet sheep. The guards did not spring smartly to attention at the sight of her.

Jumbo drawled an explanation as he went by—tried to go by. He stopped at the sharp end of the spear. His tone changed, but still displayed the blithe arrogance of strangerhood.

The spear did not waver. The other guard growled a response.

Jumbo tried again, in yet another voice. That one worked no better. He was obviously taken aback by this failure of charisma.

"You're not wearing the old school tie," Alice suggested and gave her knuckles a mental rap for tactlessness.

Jumbo shot her an acid glance. "I'm tempted to turn them both into pumpkins."

"An intemperate response . . . Can you?"

"Not until midnight." He launched into a longer, quieter speech. That one at least produced a civil reply. It even had hints of regret in it, but it was still clearly a refusal.

Then a third man drifted in out of the darkness. He was short and very blond, and at first glance Alice thought he was just a boy. Then she noted that he, too, bore a shield on his back. He had no spear, but he was obviously in charge.

Jumbo began again, and this time Alice heard her own name and others: "Ursula," "Captain," and "Jumbo." He was having to beg, and he would not like that. Something he said impressed the blond boy, who snapped out an order, and the guard who did not have a shield turned and disappeared into the opening between the two great rocks.

That was progress. It left four people standing in near darkness: two very vigilant and suspicious guards, one toe-tapping, heel-cooling, icily furious Jumbo, and one Alice trying not to let her amusement show.

"Where are we trying to get to, anyway?" she asked.

"*Hrnnph!* There's an inner cave here behind this rockfall. I've slept there many times. Travelers prefer it, because it's cosy. Tends to be warm in winter and cool in summer. Obviously that's where Exeter's hiding out."

Jumbo fell silent again. Minutes dragged by. In the outer cave, the pilgrims had begun singing. The tonality was strange, but the beat was rousing enough—possibly the Valian equivalent of "Onward, Christian Soldiers." Had Edward taught them the Fallow school song yet?

"There are other ways over this junk heap," Jumbo growled.

"Patience!" she said soothingly. "He's a celebrity, remember. He can't let himself be pestered all the time."

Light flickered. Out of the canyon emerged a flaming torch carried by a woman. She came to a halt and raised it to inspect the supplicants.

"Evening, Jumbo. And good evening to you, Miss Prescott. I'm Ursula Newton."

"Charmed," Alice replied, blinking against the light. "Actually, I'm Mrs. Pearson now." Why the devil should that matter here? "But still Edward's cousin, of course."

At that point, Jumbo should have spoken, or Mrs. Newton should have offered to lead the visitors to the holy of holies. Instead, she just stood and looked hard at each of them in turn. Alice felt twinges of apprehension. She had come so far. What could be wrong now?

"Is Captain Smedley with you?" she asked.

"No, he's on his way back to Olympus." Ursula Newton was a solid, powerful-looking woman, wearing a thick woolen robe of Valian cut. Her hair was unusually short and her manner definitely suspicious. "Forgive me if I ask you a couple of questions?"

"Dammit all, Ursula!" Jumbo said. "What's got into you?"

"Prudence." She turned her watchful gaze on Alice. "Who was Bujja, Mrs. Pearson?"

"Who?" Merciful heavens! "Edward's nursemaid at Nyagatha."

"And Spots?"

"That was a leopard cub we tried to domesticate once, without much—"

"Wrong answer!"

For a moment Alice just stared at the woman, quite unable to believe this was happening. Then she said, "Oh! It was also Julian Smedley, when he was national acne champion."

Ursula relaxed visibly. Her smile was not exactly winsome, though. "Thank you. The Liberator has to be extremely careful, you see, and news of your arrival here was a surprise."

Jumbo laughed. "Oh, he's 'the Liberator' now, is he? Have you changed sides, Ursula, darling?"

Her eyes narrowed. "Not really. I still think he made a serious mistake in launching this crusade. Now he's done so, I believe it must be carried forward as well as possible. And you?"

"Much the same. We didn't come to try and talk him out of it, whatever you may have told Exeter. We have some interesting news for him."

"Then Mrs. Pearson can pass it on. He prefers not to meet with you, Jumbo."

"I quite understand." Spoken like a gentleman, but even in the flickering light of the torch, Jumbo's flush showed. "Give him my regards, won't you?" He turned and stalked away before Alice could think of anything to say. How awful!

Ursula gestured for Alice to follow. Holding the torch overhead, she led the way up a steep, narrow trench. The rocks pressed closer, looming, threatening. Alice could feel them all around her and overhanging, grinning at her—claustrophobic! The floor was steep and uneven.

"I apologize for that inquisition," Ursula said over her shoulder. "The Chamber has been sending human time bombs after him. Your presence here was so unexpected that I insisted he take some precautions."

And Jumbo's presence was definitely unwelcome. Alice would have to have a word with Edward about that, and build some bridges. "Quite all right. Understandable. What exactly are human time bombs? I presume they don't have fuses dangling from their ears?"

"Not so easy, I'm afraid. They're people enslaved by mana to kill the Liberator. If it's any comfort to you, I can't detect any sorcery on you—nor on Jumbo, for that matter—but that doesn't mean much. Only a very clumsy curse would be detectable."

"Well, I assure you that I truly am his cousin. Fresh from England. I'm here on holiday, surprising as that may seem."

Mrs. Newton uttered a loud snort of laughter. "You have strange tastes in vacation spots! We have to squeeze through here. Watch your footing." She held the torch higher to illuminate the gap. Then the path led steeply downward, and Alice had to hold back to avoid the heat of the flames ahead of her.

Her guide stopped and turned around. "Almost there," she said quietly. "One final request, Mrs. Pearson—please do not go close to your cousin. His bodyguards have been warned to block anyone who tries to touch him. They might not be overly gentle."

Alice was becoming very tired of this nonsense. "Is it necessary for a human time bomb to touch him to kill him?"

"Probably not, but that would be by far the easiest way to set up the sorcery. It is how Zath always primes his reapers. You might not even be aware that such a curse had been laid on you." Ursula Newton was obviously quite serious, despite the unbelievable words she was speaking. "You would be given an irresistible compulsion to touch him and then complete some deadly ritual, although whatever it was might seem quite harmless to you."

"I shall be extremely careful to keep my hands to myself, then."

"That would be advisable. Follow me, please."

As Jumbo had promised, the air was appreciably warmer here. Summer lingered on, deep in the bowels of the hill, and yet the virtuality seemed even stronger. Then a faint glimmer of light showed ahead, and Alice found herself stepping down into a hollow that could almost count as a separate cave. Obviously it was a well-frequented campsite, its floor littered with old chips of wood and bark. In the center was a fireplace of blackened stones, surrounded by a circle of low rocks for sitting. Beyond that, in turn, lay heaps of frondy leaves for bedding and a miscellaneous clutter of gourds and logs.

Half a dozen people were grouped around the twinkling fire, their faces dancing in and out of the dark like ghosts. Edward was on the far side, speaking softly while the others listened—the king and his court. He looked weary but not as weary as might have been expected for an actor resting after such a performance.

Her arrival made them all scramble to their feet, but she had eyes only for the tall man in the prophet's robe. Yes, she wanted to run to him and hug him, but she did not think there was anything sinister in that urge, just normal affection for her only living relative after a long separation. She sensed the others' hair-trigger vigilance, watching to see if she would try it.

"Alice!"

"Edward! It's wonderful to see you!"

"And you. Er . . . won't you sit down?"

She moved to the closest seat, a flat rock upholstered with a scrap of fur. After a moment, everyone else sat down also, all except Ursula Newton.

Nobody spoke. Edward was just staring at Alice as if she were a ghost, the Holy Grail, or King George himself, and she was similarly tongue-tied. There were so many things to say that they could not even begin. She sensed an invisible wall of distrust between them.

Norfolk seemed very far away now.

She found her voice first. "I'm not here on business, Edward. Just on holiday. I'm not carrying any banners. Funny—you haven't changed a bit!" The beard was not all that bad at close quarters, hardly more than a heavy stubble. With a patriarchal bush like Tennyson's, he would look like a character in a school nativity play.

Behind her, Ursula coughed harshly. "Well, I'll leave you to have a private chat, shall I?" The guards, three men and one woman, would not understand English. She must have left, then, but Alice did not turn to see.

"Sorry about the cloak and dagger," Edward said. "Ursula . . ."

"It's a good idea. I don't mind."

"You're thinner. Keeping well?"

"Splendid, thank you." Under the circumstances, this was an absurdly banal conversation. It was wonderful to see him again. There was an extraordinary pain in her throat. "And you?"

He smiled wistfully across the fire at her. "I'm ever so homesick! Tell me about England."

# 45

The Free had begun yet another hymn. Eleal did not know the lyrics to this one either, and she was not in a mood to sing the praises of the Undivided anyway. She was still struggling to accept the idea that the gods she had always believed in might be imposters. The fire was burning low, but she was not cold now. She was hungry, and the supplies in her pack had run out. A shield-bearer had come around promising that the food would appear shortly, so meanwhile she must just huddle in miserable solitude amid a crowd of tunelessly chanting believers, wrestling with her faith and her conscience.

Old Piol squeezed himself onto the rock beside her. She glanced sideways at him, unsure whether she wanted his company.

He smiled—not the smile of the naive dreamer Piol Poet but that of the other Piol Poet, the genius who knew the human heart and could lay it bare in a carillon of silver words. "Talk it out," he said. "The first thing to do with problems is to list them in order of worrisomeness."

"They're all worrisome." And some she couldn't tell even to Piol. "Who is D'ward? What is he—human or god?"

"You told the crowd that he almost died once. If you believe that, then you must believe that he's human."

"Well, he was human then," she admitted. "But in those days he didn't go around performing miracles . . . at least, not like he's doing now."

Piol nodded, cannily waiting for her next problem.

She said, "I can't believe both him and the Pentatheon, can I?"

"Not both, no."

"But Tion heals cripples too!"

"D'ward calls that sorcery."

"And Tion would call what he does sorcery. Their words cancel out."

Piol rubbed an eyebrow. "Then look for other evidence."

That was obvious, but she had not thought of it quite that way. What was he hinting at? "Which of them do you believe?"

Piol was not to be trapped. He grinned, gap-toothed. "Tell you later. I won't make up your mind for you."

She pulled a face at him. "Their words cancel out and their miracles cancel out. What else is there to consider? Well? What other evidence is there?"

He probably wouldn't have given her a straight answer, and he was saved from having to reply at all, because a shield-bearer came by the fire with a bag, soliciting money. He didn't speak, because most people were singing. A few found coins for him, most just shook their heads sadly to show they had nothing to offer. Eleal declined too. She carried a fortune around her waist, but she was not about to expose it to so many curious eyes in this cave. The shield-bearer flashed her a smile and went on by.

He had reminded her of another problem: D'ward was worried by the weather. He needed money to clothe and feed his followers. She had money. Could she force herself to give away so much, even to D'ward?

Piol was waiting. "What will you do tomorrow, Eleal? You can be an actor now, a great actor. Frankly, you always had more talent for acting than for singing. Will you stay with the Liberator or set off to seek your fortune?"

"That's the whole problem, you silly old goose! What I believe doesn't really matter— I can take years to decide that. What I need to know is what to *do!*"

"Good! You're getting closer."

She debated wringing his scrawny old neck—affectionately, of course. "You? What will you do?"

"Me? Oh, I shall join the Free. Whether I believe D'ward or not, what he's doing is the most exciting thing I've ever seen in my life. I shall follow him to Tharg and witness the fulfilment or failure of the prophecy." Piol sighed and clasped her hand in his cold fingers. "But I am an old man, with few years left to me. In your place I might not make that choice, because it may be very dangerous. If I am spared, I shall try to write an account of it all." After a moment, he chuckled. "Maybe when I have done that, I shall know what I really believe, mm?"

He already knew, of course. He just wasn't saying.

Tharg would supply the answer, but Eleal could not wait for that. She could not live with this awful predicament. She had to make her decision sooner. Now! To follow D'ward or go her own way? D'ward had told her to leave. He had definitely not made her welcome. That was one point. She dare not return to Jurg itself, and the clutches of Tigurb'l Pimp. That was another. D'ward seemed to avoid cities, so he would probably just cut across Jurgvale and carry on to Mapvale. She could risk that. Or she could go back to Niol and try for auditions there, as Piol had suggested several times.

"I can't decide!" she moaned. "*What* other evidence is there?"

"Actions, of course. Judge people by what they do, not what they say."

"Miracles? Sorcery?"

"What else do they do, apart from miracles?"

Eleal shivered. "Zath, you mean? Reapers?" She could never imagine D'ward sending out reapers to kill people. "Give me a clue, Piol!"

He sighed. "Girls with problems should ask their mothers. I'm afraid yours would not be much help to you, even if she still lived."

Eleal gulped. "You knew her? I thought that was before you joined the troupe."

"No. Just after. For a whole fortnight we searched Jurg for her, all of us and all our friends. She was nowhere to be found. Nowhere! Suddenly, out of the blue, she just wandered up to the door of the house where we were staying."

"Mad! Mad for love of the god?"

"Mad for someone. All she would ever say was, 'He kissed me!' "

"He did a lot more than that!"

"Perhaps he did, but the first kiss was what she remembered. From then until the day you were born, those were the only words she ever spoke. No matter what we asked her, or how your grandfather raged, all she would say was, 'He kissed me!' Dreamily. She wasn't really unhappy. She tended to wander away and hang around his temple, and of course we had to try to stop her doing that or fetch her back right away if she had eluded us. After you were born, she said nothing at all. It was not a hard birth, but it killed her. No, it *released* her. She had just been waiting for you to arrive, and after that she faded away, her job done."

"Ken'th!"

"Well, she never said so, and Trong would never admit that a god would do such a thing."

Eleal squeezed her eyes tight shut in case they started leaking. "D'ward would never—" Her voice broke.

D'ward would never do that sort of miracle, or that sort of sorcery. A shiver of revulsion racked her. Her mother: a woman starved for the love of a god or a woman enslaved by a poisoned kiss?

Lecherous Ken'th. Murderous Zath. Depraved Ois, with her holy whorehouse. Or Gim Sculptor, whose beauty had won him the right to represent the Youth at the prize giving in Tion's temple? Two years later, his parents had still been hunting for him.

"Trust their actions, not their words!" Piol said firmly.

"Gods who kill people, gods who hurt people—those are not good gods." She gripped his hand in gratitude. "I choose D'ward. I believe him, not them!"

"I do too."

Eleal straightened up. Good! Then her choice was easy. She must go and find D'ward and tell him that she believed in him and his Undivided god. She would give him her money, every copper of it. Then, surely, he would let her stay and be one of the Free. A shield-bearer, even? She could help him, too! She could repeat her witness of his coming, as she had done today, to help convince others. She could imagine his astonished thanks, his hug of thanks . . . a quick kiss. . . .

She mumbled some words of thanks to Piol without thought. She rose and walked away, heading for the inner cave, for she had explored this place on her way to Niolvale and could guess where the Liberator would rest after his marvelous performance. The greenroom, she thought with a smile.

The fire had almost gone out, so her eyes were well adjusted to the dimness. As she reached the rock pile that divided the cavern, she saw the guards before they saw her. She stopped, unwilling to face an argument or make long explanations to underlings.

Well, there must be other ways around. She turned off to the left, moving with care, for the going soon became very tricky. She scrabbled up between the boulders, frequently bumping her right foot, for it was farther away from her now than it used to be. That did not matter, though. All that mattered was that she would be able to renew her friendship with D'ward. How could she have ever doubted him?

She need not dream of making love to him, though. Dosh had told her how the Joalian-Nagian army had sacked Lemod, and how every man had taken a Lemodian girl to be his concubine, all except D'ward. D'ward had taken a girl and never laid a finger on her, even when she begged him to, Dosh said, although Dosh had probably been guessing there, for how could he have known? Still, he was undoubtedly right when he said that D'ward was a very holy man, with strict standards.

So they would not be lovers, only friends.

No passion. Just a quick hug? And a little kiss, to let bygones be bygones?

She clambered over a smooth, rounded boulder and peered down at the drop. It looked about five feet, but she could not see the ground clearly enough to risk a jump, even with two legs of the same length. This little canyon led directly down to the inner cave, with its ancient ashes and its circle of rocks to sit on.

A pebble clattered. Someone was coming.

She hunkered down on the rock, willing herself to be invisible. And then, in the frail glow of reflected firelight, she saw him, working his way cautiously along the path below her. He wore a long robe with a hood. A gray robe! It was D'ward himself, all alone for once. The urge to leap down and surprise him was absolutely irresistible.

# 46

One of the shield-bearers tossed a log on the fire, sending sparks swarming up into the dark. Alice felt as if she had been talking for hours. Any time she hesitated, Edward demanded more. She had described the horrors of war, the unexpected horrors of peace, the new war in Russia, the terrible flu epidemic, the changes that had come and would probably never go. . . . She had talked of the few acquaintances they had in common, like Mrs. Bodgley and Ginger Jones, and even, reluctantly, told him about D'Arcy and then Terry. He had responded with concern and no maudlin formulas.

There were a million things she wanted to ask him, but his need was greater. He had been trapped on a faraway world for five years now, with one brief break. He was starved for information. She could see that being a prophet must be a desperately lonely business, with a thousand followers and not a single friend. She forgot her doubts and was glad she had come, for she was uniquely able to be the confidante he needed. He hung upon her words, staring at her as if she were a dream who might vanish if he even blinked, but his face said everything needful.

Then the log went into the fire.

"I'm hoarse!" she said. "You talk now."

He glanced around at the four disciples, who had lost some of their coiled-spring alertness, doubtless bored to distraction by the newcomer's incomprehensible jabber. He turned a look of wide-eyed innocence on Alice. "What do you want to know, child? What wisdom would you seek from the master? How it feels to out-hypocrite Holy Roly himself, for instance?"

"Uncle Roly wasn't a hypocrite, he was a fanatic. You're not."

He pulled a face. "Don't talk to me about fanatics! I'm creating fanatics, Alice! My helpers—disciples, I suppose. They believe every word I say, and I see it happening to them, day by day. They're becoming fanatics, all of them, and I feel like a terrible hypocrite."

Surely My Cousin the Messiah was not suffering doubts? Was he asking for Alice's approval? That did not sound like Edward.

"What do you teach them? The Service's universal Unitarianism?"

He shrugged as if the question was irrelevant or the answer obvious. "Pretty much. Ethically it's the Golden Rule, the stuff that's common to all religions—concern for the sick, alms to the poor, smite not thy neighbor with thine ax. . . . It's Christianity mostly, because that's my background, but I think any Moslem, Buddhist, or Sikh would recognize it."

"And theologically?"

"Monotheism." He paused for a moment, frowning . . . looking for all the world as though he had never really thought about it before. "And reincarnation."

"Why that?"

"Not sure . . ." He ran a hand through his hair and grinned. "Because Uncle Roly gave me a fixed picture of heaven as an endless ghastly Sunday morning of psalm singing. Because reincarnation seems a happier creed than hellfire. Why should God insist we get it right the first time?"

"And if we have only one chance to get it right, that gives the priests much greater power over us, doesn't it?"

"By Jove! You know, I hadn't thought of that. Jolly good! I like it. Besides, you can't prove I'm wrong, can you?"

"No. So why are you worried if you create a few fanatics? You don't encourage violence or persecution, do you? You don't tell outright lies."

His mood turned glum again. "Yes, I do. I use the magic they give me to heal babies and then tell them that this is a miracle sent by a god I don't believe in myself."

"What would happen if you told them the truth?"

"What is truth? That all my power comes from their belief? They wouldn't believe me. Even charisma has its limits."

No faith, no mana. No mana, no crusade.

"Are you quite sure God *didn't* send you?"

"Alice! *Please!* If I start thinking like that I'll turn into a total theomaniac."

"You're not the type. I'd say you're a pragmatist. You're doing the best you can in the circumstances. The object of the Game is to kill Zath, isn't it? And thereby rid the world of a monster?"

Again he ran a hand through his curls. He needed a haircut. "So the ends justify the means?"

Memories, memories! "You're playing devil's advocate, my lad. You always did that." She saw his shy grin flicker and that, too, was heart-stoppingly familiar from years gone by. "And you've had a lot more time to think up the answers than I have. You tell me."

He stared sadly into the fire for a moment. "I think that sometimes life forces us to choose the path of least evil. How's that for rationalization?"

"It sounds sound to me," she said loyally.

"It didn't convince friend Smedley the other day. It's not the way a saint thinks. A saint won't bend his principles no matter what the cost—to himself or anyone else. I'm just a political revolutionary masquerading as a prophet."

"You're more saintly than most. You've always had strict principles."

"So did Holy Roly. You know, I used to think the old bat enjoyed heaping brimstone on his wayward nephew's head? Now I'm not so sure."

"Good heavens! You really have been gathering insights, haven't you?"

He laughed, probably not noticing the surprised smiles of his guards. "Wonderful to see you here!" Abruptly he turned serious again. "Dear Alice, I don't doubt that you are the true, dear Alice. I don't doubt your motives in the slightest, and yet your arrival here leaves me a teeny-weeny bit suspicious still. Are you quite certain that the Miss Pimm you met was the genuine Miss Pimm?"

Alice opened and closed her mouth a couple of times. "Well, I suppose the answer to that is No! I mean, how could I ever be *certain*? She did seem younger than she was two years ago. I assumed that was because she'd been playing a role then, and wasn't now—or at least not the same role." She realized that she had not told him about Zath's appearance at Olympus, which was the reason for her coming here at all.

Edward bit his lip. "Doesn't really mean anything," he muttered. "So you went to Olympus. Whose idea was it for you and Jumbo—"

He was interrupted by shouts and a clatter of boots. His bodyguards sprang to their feet. The little blond disciple she had seen earlier came running into the hollow, waving a flaming torch. Right on his heels came Ursula Newton. Much singsong jabber was exchanged. Edward rose and began to move toward the exit. At once two of the guards set themselves between him and Alice. She stayed put on her nice, comfortable rock.

The torchbearer ran out again, probably taking word that the Liberator was coming.

"You'll have to excuse me a moment," Edward said. "There's a young girl out there having some sort of seizure, and everyone thinks she's about to die." He grinned ruefully as he passed her. "A god's work is never done."

"As I recall," she countered, "under similar circumstances, Jesus did not need to go to the centurion's house."

Edward's smile vanished. "But that was Jesus. This is only me." He disappeared, too, into the passageway. Well, at least he wasn't a total theomaniac yet.

The sound of singing was still drifting in over the barrier. Most of the Free must be quite unaware of the current medical emergency. The bodyguards all sat down, not following the Liberator. Did that mean they were now jailers? Ursula Newton had stayed behind also. She made herself comfortable on the next rock with a sigh of wearied satisfaction, like a schoolmistress after the final bell of the day, and fixed Alice with a gaze as steady as a recruiting poster's.

"I assume you're now certified as the genuine article, so may I start all over? I'm Ursula Newton, and I'm very happy to meet you." She leaned over to offer a hand. Her smile was more hearty than winsome, but that was because her face would never manage winsome. The smile itself seemed genuine enough. She had a grip like a blacksmith.

"No offense," Alice said. "You're quite right to take precautions. He's a pretty important man, now." The significance of her own words seemed to ricochet back at her from the megalithic walls. Important? Edward was working his way into the history books of a world. "I mean he will be if he succeeds, like Moses."

"He'll be Jan Hus if he fails."

Alice shuddered. "Meaning?"

"Martyrdom, murder, massacre, and mayhem. He knew the risks when he burned his first bridge. He had no choice, you know."

"Edward or Jan Hus?"

"Your cousin, of course!" Mrs. Newton glowered belligerently. "Julian has told me what happened back Home, how the Blighters almost caught him—and you too. Obviously Zath will never stop trying to kill him. He was forced to defend himself, and this was the only way open to him."

Alice was taken aback. She could not recall saying anything critical of Edward's crusade and did not see why Mrs. Newton need defend it to her so aggressively. Besides, she found the proposed defense repellent.

"I can't believe Edward would have involved so many innocent people just to save his own skin. I am sure he seeks some greater good than just his personal survival."

Her companion conceded the point with a faint pout. "He chose a more daring path than I anticipated. I expected him to begin by freeing the slaves in the Thargian mines."

"Being Moses?"

"Exactly. 'The Liberator,' you see?"

"But you don't have a Red Sea handy. I suppose the pursuing Thargians could have been buried in a landslide instead."

Mrs. Newton was not amused. "He elected instead to be Christ, which is a bolder concept altogether."

It certainly did not lack ambition, but putting it in words raised worrisome questions that Jumbo had not been able to answer. "What will happen when he reaches Tharg itself? I understand crucifixion is not a Valian custom."

Ursula grimaced. "They've never heard of it. Thargians execute criminals by dashing their brains out on an anvil. They'll have to catch him first, won't they? I don't believe your cousin has anything so barbaric in mind for Zath or so suicidal for himself, Mrs. Pearson. I do wish the cooks would hurry up. I'm hungry."

The guards had begun whispering, perhaps discussing the strangely ill-tongued intruder.

"But he may fail?" Alice said. "How do you rate his chances?"

"Impossible to say."

"You must have a better idea than I do, for I have no way of judging at all. If you thought he had no chance you wouldn't be here, would you?"

"On the face of it he doesn't, frankly." Ursula folded her arms and thought for a moment, scowling at the fire. "There are three unknowns. The biggest is the Pentatheon. If enough of them rally to Exeter's side in the final scrum, then they may tip the scales. They're scared of Zath, but they have no real reason to set up your cousin in his place, which is basically what they'd be trying to do if they intervened."

"I suppose they're fence-sitting at the moment?"

"Absolutely. Don't expect a peep out of any of them until the last possible minute. I expect every one of them has a spy or two within the Free, though. They're watching. And there's no way to know how they're judging Edward's performance, which is what this parade is." She seemed to be warming to her lecture. "The second factor is the *Filoby Testament* itself. It hasn't hit a wrong note in eighty-five years. That's impressive! Prof Rawlinson estimates that three quarters of the prophecies have already been fulfilled."

"But there can always be a first time failure?"

"Oh, crikey, yes! And I'm a little bit suspicious of the way verse three eighty-six is worded. It doesn't say that the Liberator will slay Zath, or that he will win a fight. It just says he will bring death to Death. I only hope that isn't to be interpreted in some sort of mystical way. Nevertheless, I'd much rather have the *Filoby Testament* working for me than against me."

"It saved my life once," Alice said. "Or, rather, it saved Edward's and I was with him. The third factor must be his own mana?"

"Right. No way to measure that, either, of course. Can't stick a thermometer in a man and test his mana level. Drat them, I wish they'd bring the tuck basket around!" With a sudden show of irritation, Ursula grabbed up a log and hurled it on the fire. She was concealing something, or trying to detour the conversation away from something.

Alice prompted. "Edward's obviously collected great power if he can give a blind man back his sight."

"True."

"And the miracles inspire the crowd to provide more mana? He gets it back?"

Ursula nodded, beating her hands on her knees and staring angrily at the rocks as if trying to glare through them. "All that singing going on out there doesn't sound like anyone's doing much eating yet."

"What's wrong? Why don't you want to talk about it?"

"I never . . ." The doughty Mrs. Newton scowled at this frontal attack. She glanced at the wall around them as if looking for listeners. "You really want my opinion, no matter what?"

"Please."

"Well, I suppose you are his next of kin. I wouldn't say this to anyone else. You won't repeat my words to Jumbo or your cousin?"

"Certainly not."

"Rain, Mrs. Pearson! The rain's bad news. He's lost a lot of people since yesterday. If the weather continues bad, he's going to come a cropper. He can't travel as fast in the rain, he can't attract enough people. So he won't collect enough mana—or even enough money. If he can't feed his flock, it'll wander away. He's certainly not strong enough yet to do loaves-and-fishes miracles, not on that scale."

Ursula scowled at the fire for a moment. "And that's not all. I keep telling him he's not ruthless enough. As you said, when he uses mana to perform miracles, the resulting adoration should give him back more than he spent. That's the way it should work. But he's too softhearted. It begins that way, but it's astonishingly easy for people to become . . . um, saturated. Blasé. The first couple of miracles today, I could feel the whole node tremble with the surge of mana. Did you notice?"

"I felt something."

"That was just a whiff of spray we were getting—the waves were hitting the Liberator and they must have rocked him to his toenails. Did you notice how much less the response was the fourth time?"

"He overdoes it, you mean?"

"Absolutely. The Pentatheon's god of healing is Paa, one of Tion's. We estimate he grants about one real healing miracle a year, plus a few minor, show-offy things: squints or harelips or measles. Those keep the crowds coming. Tion himself does one miracle cure every year at his festival. By definition, miracles need to be rarities."

"I suppose Edward can't refuse suffering babies."

"He could tell them to wait until tomorrow," Ursula growled. "Listen!" She waved a hand at the dark. "They're still singing! He went out there to perform a miracle. He can cure an attack of epilepsy with a snap of his fingers, if that's all it is. But why do it that way? Why hasn't he ordered the singing stopped and made everybody gather round to watch? He's not enough of a showman! Oh, he does quite well, but he could do a lot better."

Showing off would go against everything he had ever been taught. "So you think he isn't gathering mana fast enough?" But if there was no way to measure mana . . .

"I'm very much afraid he's *losing* it. I don't think he has as much now as he did—"

She was interrupted by a scream. It began, very briefly, as a yell of outrage or anger. It immediately shot up to the unmistakable shrill note of mortal terror, four and a third octaves above middle C, the universal alarm cry of the human species. It came from somewhere very close, amid the encircling maze of rocks and stalagmites. It reverberated through the cavern, doubled and redoubled by its own echoes. It froze the blood. Alice and Ursula and the four bodyguards leaped to their feet, peering around, trying to locate the source.

Then the human scream was joined by a sound much greater, an earsplitting animal roar. The two swelled in chorus, alternating, combining, mingling with mighty cracks and thumps.

Alice clapped her hands over her ears. "What in the world is that?" she howled.

Ursula yelled back through the din. "A *mithiar!* What they call a jugular. It's killing someone."

Judging by the noise, it was tearing someone apart.

As suddenly as they'd begun, the sounds stopped. They were replaced by the blurred roar of a multitude of terrified people on the far side of the rockfall. Their screams, too, echoed everywhere, but at least they were not as close. Roaring Cave suddenly justified its name.

Alice uncovered her ears. Ursula was ashen. She could not possibly be more shaken than Alice, though, and the men looked no better, apparently torn between a desire to flee and a need to stay close to the light. One of them had hauled a burning branch from the fire, but he wasn't going anywhere with it.

Ursula snatched it from him and headed toward the source of the trouble. The men all yelled and tried to stop her. Shouting and shaking her head, she cleared them out of the way with her flaming brand and kept on going. Shamed, perhaps, they followed. Alice did too, determined not to be left alone in this nightmare.

They did not have very far to go, and then they all stopped dead, blocking the way and also Alice's view of what they had found. She scrambled up on a table-high ledge and peered over their heads. Steep walls rose to shoulder height on one side and even higher on the other, forming a narrow canyon that continued on, twisting out of sight. The rocks were pale gray, mottled and cemented together with oozings of white stalagmite like melted candle wax, but now all splattered with sheets of shocking red as if a whole barrel of blood had exploded. In places streaks of blood and blobs of flesh had splashed ten or twelve feet up, glittering wetly in the light of Ursula's torch. Surely it would have taken a dozen victims to produce so much blood?

The shouting in the main cave had almost stopped, probably because most of the Free were outside in the rain by now. Flickers of light reflecting from the roof showed that more people were coming to investigate.

A woman's body lay facedown in the center of the shambles. It was naked and smeared with gore, but it bore no obvious wounds. How was that possible? Ursula and the men were all talking at once, not a word intelligible to Alice. Some of those lumps were not rock. A leg. An arm. A couple of the men cried out at the same moment, pointing at a small boulder, coated with blood. Its eyes were open.

Revulsion! Nausea! Suddenly every shadow held a monster, every rock was a tooth. Alice half fell, half jumped from her perch and went stumbling back to the fire, moving as fast as she dared and banging her shins and elbows in the process. She threw a heap of sticks on the blaze to try and make it brighter, then hunkered down beside it, shivering. Two victims, one torn to pieces, one not visibly harmed. That made no sense at all! The sort of claws Jumbo had described could never rip a woman's clothes off without tearing her skin to ribbons as well. Where had the jugular gone?

Where had it come from?

The crowd in the main cave was silent now or else had fled out into the night. She heard voices nearby, and recognized Edward's, issuing commands. She was shaking from shock and nausea. Even the smoke from the fire seemed tainted with the reek of blood. She could make no sense of the talk, and no one was going to be speaking English for a while. She considered going in search of Jumbo, but she could not be sure he was still in the cave. With Edward's snub still rankling, he might have taken the dragons and ridden off in a huff. No, Jumbo was too much a gentleman to do that, but she had better wait here until Edward had straightened out the emergency. Her vacation was turning out to be more stressful than she had expected.

A moment later, light advanced out of the passageway. Ursula appeared with her torch, followed by Edward himself carrying the woman's body in his arms. Other men came after. As he lowered his burden to one of the heaps of bedding, Alice snatched up a blanket and went to cover her. She was only a girl.

Edward straightened, wiping bloody hands on his robe, which was already well smeared. "Thanks."

"She's alive?" Of course. He would not have brought a corpse.

"Eleal Singer. She was starting to come around. I've put her to sleep. See if you can clean her up, will you?" He turned to his followers and began giving more orders. He was paler than before, but calm, completely in command. Though they were all older men, they did not argue or hesitate. Most went out by the way Alice had entered, others returned to the scene of the accident—of the *murder?*

Ursula came to help, dragging a water skin. Alice chose a tattered cloth that might be somebody's bedding and ripped a strip from it. Together they began washing away the bloodstains. Eleal muttered and stirred as they wiped her face but did not awaken. There was little they could do about her long hair, which was caked and matted. Her skin bore only a few scrapes from contact with the rock, and there was a reddening welt around her waist that Alice could not explain. When Ursula started work on Eleal's hands, she moaned and tried to pull them loose. The tips of her fingers were swollen, some of the nails broken. Her toes were the same. Alice exchanged shocked glances with Ursula and thrust away the impossible suspicions that kept boiling up in her mind.

"How are you doing?" Edward asked.

He was standing with his back to the proceedings. This absurd display of modesty almost provoked Alice to sniggers, but she fought against them. That way lay full-blown hysterics.

Ursula pulled the blanket over the patient again. "You can look. She has serious bruising around her middle. There's something wrong with her fingers and toes."

Edward knelt down and considered Eleal's draped form. "A couple of broken ribs, too." He touched the blanket over her waist for a moment. Then he lifted one of her hands and gritted his teeth. "Swine!" He covered the girl's hand with both of his and healed the finger wounds, even the broken nails. He moved on to do the other hand, both feet.

Ursula was watching intently, but she looked more angry than impressed.

"What happened?" Alice demanded. "Can either of you explain? Does this sort of thing go on all the time?"

Ursula shook her head. "It was aimed at him, definitely. Ken'th?"

"Probably," Edward said. "Stand back and I'll—"

Pebbles rattled. The young fair-haired disciple came hurrying in. His face had a sickly pallor and there was blood on his knees and hands. He held a long strip of blood-soaked leather. From the way he offered it to Edward, it was heavy.

The two spoke for a moment. The disciple pulled a face, but nodded. He dropped his burden—it fell with a metallic clunk—and headed back out the way he had come. Someone was going to have to organize a burial for that other victim, and probably he had just been given the horrible job.

A rising murmur of voices indicated that the disciples were coaxing the crowds into the cave again.

Edward turned back to Eleal. Ursula caught Alice's arm and led her out of the way, over to the fire. Her fury was obvious now. She nudged the mysterious parcel with her foot.

"That's what did the bruising. A money belt."

Alice's brain resisted the implications. "How? And how can you know that?"

"The buckle's ripped right through the leather."

"Yes, but—" *No, don't think about it.* "Where did the jugular come from? Where did it—"

"It's sorcery," Ursula growled, "very horrible sorcery. You think I'd have gone after a real jugular with nothing but a burning stick? If there had been a jugular in the cave, it would have attacked somebody hours ago."

"But where did it go?"

The answer to that was a disbelieving glare. "Dosh has found another body, a priest. Someone bashed him on the head with a rock and took his gown."

"I don't understand!"

"Oh, work it out, girl!" Ursula shouted. "All cats are gray in the dark. All robes, too. If you wanted to get by the guards . . . We knew Eleal Singer had some sort of spell on her. We knew it made her come looking for the Liberator. We knew there was a compulsion, we just didn't know what else it did. Even I could see traces of it on her. I couldn't see one on you or Jumbo, but that didn't—"

"Jumbo! Shouldn't one of us go and find Jumbo and—"

Ursula threw up her hands and turned away. "Oh, go right ahead! Go and find him. I can suggest a good place to look. Are you completely stupid? Must I carve words in stone for you? Go to Jumbo by all means. He was a good friend of mine, Mrs. Pearson. A good friend for almost a hundred years. He deserved better than that horrible, *shameful* death. It's one more reason to settle accounts with Zath. Go to Jumbo. Tell him we're sorry. Tell him he's forgiven. There's no hurry. He isn't going anywhere now."

# 47

Eleal floated back up to consciousness, aware first of a revolting taste in her mouth. She tried to spit out whatever it was. A strong arm reached under her shoulders and raised her; someone held a gourd of water to her lips. Water dribbled down her neck, between her breasts. Coldness, darkness, and her eyelids seemed to be crusted with mud. She forced them open, shivered convulsively. Faint light, coldness again, and awareness that she wasn't wearing anything. She was on a very lumpy, prickly bed . . . someone holding her upright.

"Relax, relax!" said a voice. A man's voice.

She clutched at the blanket and pulled it up to cover her nudity. She turned her head and found herself looking into a concerned pair of very blue eyes.

"You're all right," D'ward said. "You're not hurt. You'll be quite well in a moment. We're trying to help you. Wash your mouth out again."

She discovered more aches and scrapes. Her elbows and ankles, especially. Her teeth felt as if someone had worked them over with a mallet.

D'ward holding her up. Her head against his bony shoulder. D'ward wiping her face with a wet, pink cloth. Had she been injured, somehow?

"What?" she said, and her tongue felt wrong in her mouth. "What happened?" She tried to focus, but his face was too close, a blur.

"You had a brush with very nasty sorcery, but you're all right now."

He lowered her. She still held the blanket under her chin. He was kneeling beside her.

"Relax! You're still not thinking straight. Take a little longer."

Why did her teeth hurt so? Vague, confused pictures whirled in her mind: D'ward in his priest's gown with the hood over his head, walking along a passage below her . . . a man with a mustache . . . take money to D'ward . . . *Woeful maiden, handsome lad, Met on lonely way* . . .

She peered up at him. He smiled at her, and she could make out the smile. How had she come to be lying in bed with no clothes on and D'ward beside her? She smiled back. If that was about to happen, then she would as soon it was D'ward as any. . . . What was wrong with her teeth?

"Starting to feel better?"

"Yes. What—what happened?"

"You saw a man in a robe and thought it was me."

She closed her eyes. That did sound right, but where? And what had she been doing? She opened her eyes again and tried to nod.

D'ward blinked at her a few times. "You're all right, Eleal. It's all gone now. The curse is gone."

Then the missing pieces dropped into place. She stiffened in horror. "D'ward! I came to find you! I jumped—"

"Never mind. It's over."

"Just going to surprise you . . . *I started to sing*—"

He seized her shoulders and squeezed them hard. "It's all right, I say. It wasn't me! It's all right."

"I didn't *want* to sing . . . didn't *mean* to sing—" Her voice was shrill. She felt tears, panic, and terror. Her limbs thrashed and trembled.

He steadied her, strong hands on her shoulders. "It is all *right*, Eleal! It's all over!" He made soothing noises, whispering. She calmed abruptly. The whirling terrors settled like leaves after a gust of wind has passed.

He said, "Oh, Eleal, Eleal, darling! You saved my life and—"

"What?"

"Yes! There was another curse, see? A man after me. So you saved my life again, and this time it was my turn to wash and nurse you. . . . Well, it was my helpers—not me. I mean, I didn't even peek . . ."

That struck her as funny. She laughed. "You think I would mind if you peeked?"

"Perhaps not as much as some," he agreed awkwardly.

"You think I didn't peek at you when I had the chance?"

"Er . . . That was a long time ago. The main thing is that the curse is gone."

She closed her eyes and saw the man with the mustache.

"He kissed me!"

"I expect that's his preferred technique."

"He sent me to find you, kill you?"

"Don't worry about it."

She shivered and lay still, thinking hard. "I was coming to tell you that I believe in you, not in the imposters."

"Good. Truly that makes me very happy."

"I came to give you my money."

"You don't have to."

"Some of it was his. He gave me money!" Memories were coming back. The room, the crystal figurine.

"I'll certainly take his money, if you like. And put it to a good use."

"And let me stay with you? Keep me safe, in case he tries to—punish me for failing?" She opened her eyes and watched to see what he would say.

He looked worried. "You don't have to stay, Eleal. You have two good legs now. You can go and chase that acting career you wanted."

She wanted to stay. Very much she wanted to stay, and things that worked on most men would not work on D'ward. Not quickly, anyway.

"But most of those plays—they're lies! They're about the evil sorcerers who pretend to be gods. Those plays are bad, D'ward, aren't they?"

He rubbed a wrist across his brow and looked even more worried. "If you take them seriously they are."

"Then what's to become of me!" A sob escaped her.

"Join us if you want. Glad to have you. I need someone to help with the preaching."

"Preaching? Me? You don't have to mock me." She writhed under the blanket.

"I'm not mocking you at all. You heard me last night at Joobiskby—I'll bet you could repeat almost everything I said and bring the house down with it."

She had been doing better with her eyes closed, so she closed them again. "He kissed me! I still feel his mustache on my lips. I dream of him. I'll never forget how he kissed me." She squeezed out a tear.

D'ward chuckled, very close to her ear. "You haven't changed a bit, you minx!" he whispered. "You've just learned a few more tricks. I'll see if someone can find some clothes for you."

His lips touched hers for a moment. She grabbed with both arms but he was gone already.

# VII

And now we have sent down unto thee evident signs, and none will disbelieve them but the evildoers.

THE KORAN, II:99

# 48

On the third day of his quest, with rain still sheeting down as hard as ever, Julian Smedley trudged into Losby. He found the church there in disarray—which was hardly surprising, for all Randorvale was in disarray. A third of the hamlet was stricken; a dozen people had died already. Old Kinulusim Spicemerchant wheezed and sweated on his sickbed. His equally aged wife was up and about already, but still weaker than wartime beer, while young Purlopat'r Woodcutter, the baby-faced giant, had fled to the hills with his wife and children. Julian summoned a few of the faithful to Seven Stones and held a brief service to cheer them up. Then he went on his way. Having no mana, he could do no healings.

He had gathered more discouraging news: Rumors were flying that this inexplicable pestilence was the work of the Church of the Undivided. He was not too surprised. People always found scapegoats for disasters—Christians burning Nero's Rome, Jews causing the Black Death by poisoning wells. Whether or not the orthodox clergy had originated the slander, the Pentatheon would certainly use it to good effect; the Service's efforts to humanize the religion of the Vales were utterly doomed now. They might have survived the Liberator himself, but in trying to stop him, the Service had brought in the Spanish flu and was going to die of it.

On the fourth day, Julian came to Thurgeothby, a homely little ranching village at the mouth of Soutpass. The rain had ended, leaving behind a bone-chilling wind. Randorwall towered above him in the crisp sunshine, white and almost painfully beautiful against a pale winter sky. He was not looking forward to the long climb and even less to the vale beyond it, for Lappinland was not a happy place. Beyond Lappinvale lay Mapvale, and then he would be into country new to him.

In Thurgeothby he could have dropped in on the local preacher and would certainly have done so had he wanted lodgings for the night, but the day was young yet. Instead, he went to see Urbiloa Baker, who was agent Twenty-nine in the political arm of the Service and should be able to advise him on current affairs in Lappinland. She was a tall, angular widow of middle years, white haired and customarily well dusted with flour. Both residents and transients frequented her shop, and she had a gift for extracting significant information from idle chatter. She greeted him blankly, as if she had never set eyes on him before, so they went through the cloak-and-dagger rigmarole of exchanging passwords. Then she took him through to her kitchen, hot and smelling deliciously of baking bread, sitting him at a table with some hot, soft rolls and a pitcher of buttermilk.

The news she broke to him while he ate was general knowledge that he could have gained from almost anyone in Thurgeothby. The flu was raging there as it was everywhere in Randorvale, with the deaths, as usual, especially high among young adults, the mainstay of the population. The pestilence was at least as lethal here as it had been back Home: healthy one day, bedridden the next, often dead in three. Children and old folk were mostly recovering, although slowly. The Church of the Undivided was being blamed—nonsensically, for its members succumbed like everyone else. Many had fled, some been driven out. Houses had been burned.

As if that were not bad enough, Soutpass was closed. Lappinvale was a Thargian colony, ruled by an iron-fisted military governor, and he had sealed off the pass to keep out the infection. Travelers from the south were being turned back. That was typical Thargian despotism and it wouldn't work—information traveled the Vales only by word of mouth, so the flu would arrive at the same time as the news. In retaliation, the Randorian government had forbidden entry to anyone coming the other way, but the king had not sent enough soldiers to enforce his decree and the permanent garrison was too incapacitated by flu to do anything. So a few traders were still trickling into Randorvale.

Julian leaned his elbows on the dough-stained table and gazed bitterly at the twinkling grate under the oven while he pondered his alternatives. There did not seem to be any. He knew of no other pass to Lappinvale; if there was one, the Thargians would certainly have blocked it. He could backtrack almost all the way to Olympus and then try the Narshvale road, but there he would be into the highest ranges of the Vales. Even if he could get through to Narshvale in this weather, there were no roads at all from Narshvale to Lappinvale or even Mapvale. Only dragons could cross that country. To reach Jurgvale, he would have to go round by Sussvale and Fionvale, which would take far too long and was probably impossible at this time of year anyway. He was apparently doomed to wait here in Thurgeothby until the Thargian garrison lifted its useless quarantine.

Of course the Liberator's crusade might eventually come to him, but if Exeter did make it this far, it would mean he had survived Zath's efforts to murder him. Then Alice would need no rescuing by Julian Smedley. His situation tasted nastily like failure.

He sighed and accepted it. Only fools struggled against the inevitable. Within the next couple of days, the Thargians would certainly learn that the pestilence had outflanked their swords.

He looked up at Urbiloa, meaning to ask her if he might lodge with her until then. The calculated suspicion in her shrewd eyes stopped the words in his throat. Urbiloa wore no earring. Political ran its own stable of agents, separate from the church. They all had their own agendas, their own motives for spying, although most were rewarded with gold as well, so they could be blackmailed if necessary. Some of them were not even aware that the Service and the church were related. For all Julian knew, the Thurgeothby baker was a devoted follower of Eltiana, mother goddess of Randorvale.

He reached for his purse. "Well done, Twenty-nine. Good report. I must be on my way."

She did not try to stop him leaving. She sent no pursuit after him.

He headed east, along the mountain front, and found shelter at the lonely home of Tidapo Rancher. Tidapo was a hearty, brawny man, full of joviality and self-reliance, always glad to offer hospitality to a visiting apostle. His wife was the Undivided supporter, but he tolerated her whims, probably from a total lack of interest in anything as impractical as theology. He greeted Saint Kaptaan cheerfully and made him welcome. At dinner he apologized for the way the children were coughing, but no one in the household seemed to have heard of the plague sweeping the vale, or at least no one took it seriously.

Two mornings later, Julian had had his fill of both the rancher's trivial chatter about livestock and his wife's religious fervor. The children and the hired men were all abed with flu by then. The sun was still shining and it was time to try the pass again. Julian thanked his hosts, blessed their house, and retraced his steps to Thurgeothby.

As he had hoped, southbound travelers reported that the blockade had been lifted. They said that half of Lappinvale was down with the sickness already, which was certainly an exaggeration but bad news anyway. The Liberator had left Niolvale, last reported at Roaring Cave, on Lospass, several days ago.

That night Julian camped with a band of traders, who charged him extortionately for the privilege of bedding down at their fire. They were very worried by the damage that the sickness would do to business. Like him, they were bound for Jurgvale, so their knowledge of the Liberator came only from hearsay. They did not think he would do business any good, either.

Julian descended into Lappinvale the next day. There he began to have trouble with the language and was repeatedly forced to exercise his limping Joalian. Even that was of less use than he had hoped, because the Thargian overlords discouraged its use— Thargian itself being a throat-burning screech that he could not even attempt. He found the natives sullen but with good reason, for Thargians were hard taskmasters, and they had ruled the land for more than a century.

Two more hard, cold days brought him to Mapvale. Smallest of all the vales, it was famous only for its blossoms, which were not in evidence at the start of winter. Historically, Mapland had always been too trivial to interest the great powers, so it had rarely endured conquest—invading armies just walked across it and up the other side. Of course, on the way through they conscripted boys as soldiers and girls as harlots, but everyone expected that. Those were predictable perils in a primitive land.

The natives wrung a subsistence economy from the export of fruits and nuts. Although very poor, they seemed happier than the Lappinians—smiling, chanting greetings in an incomprehensible dialect that must be close to Niolian, for it had a singsong lilt to it. They struggled to understand his Joalian and to reply in kind. He did not think this friendly reception was all due to his stranger's charisma; they were a genuinely friendly people. He asked what they knew about the Liberator but could not follow their answers. Much pointing to the north and sign-talk of walking suggested that Exeter's crusade was still in progress.

Julian supposed that was good news.

Hamlets were few. There were no decent roads at all. He spent the day trudging along lanes that wound like snakes through trees and across fields of leafless shrubs. The ruts were frozen hard under his feet, so that he was in constant danger of twisting an ankle. Hour by hour the snowy ranges marched with him on either hand. When he met anyone or saw a man at work—usually gathering firewood—he would ask for Thamberpass and always the finger pointed east. Onward he would go again. The air smelled of snow. The weather was turning colder.

His mood was turning blacker. Regardless of what the Mapians were trying to tell him, if Exeter was still alive and his crusade still proceeding, Julian should have run into it by now, for he was much closer to Shuujooby than he was to Olympus. Admittedly, the Liberator's pace would be dictated by the slowest of his followers, but Julian had lost two days to the Thargians' quarantine. The absence of any indication that the prophet was approaching was a very bad sign. It strongly implied that he had died at the hand of either Jumbo or Alice, whichever was the poisoned pawn.

Julian supposed that was bad news.

The familiar tremor of virtuality awoke him from his gloomy reverie. He stopped and peered around at the darkening trees, trunks and branches iron black in twilight. He realized that his legs and feet ached and his belly was growling. It was past time to find shelter.

A node might contain a temple or monastery, either of which would likely offer some minimal hospitality to wayfarers. If the price was an obeisance to some idol or other, he would not be unwilling to pay it at a pinch. A resident numen, if any, would probably detect Julian as a stranger, but then Julian might do quite well out of the encounter. Being a god was a lonely business, all visitors welcome. While natives were fair game for anything, strangers were protected by the club rules.

He could not be certain which way the center of the node lay, but a faint scent of wood smoke hung in the air. Turning to windward, he set off through the trees, ducking under branches, pushing aside twigs. The virtuality grew stronger. A few minutes later he emerged in a wide clearing and abandoned hopes of a temple. There was nothing there but a desolate patch of moorland in the winter dusk: a few acres of withered weeds and an ice-bound pond. Then he noted animal dung and a tiny hovel at the forest's edge, which must be the source of the smoke. He headed straight for it, confident that his charisma would be irresistible on a node.

His approach was challenged by a flock of white, shrieking things. They looked and sounded much like geese, although they had teeth and fur. He shooed them away with his umbrella.

By then a woman stood in the door of the hut, watching him. She was small and stooped, dressed in rags. Her sparse white hair hung limp and her eyes did not meet his. Old, certainly harmless . . . and yet she made him think of the nursery tales of his youth: Hansel and Gretel, the gingerbread house. The sinister implications were not reduced by the acrid clouds pouring out around her, for this witch's cottage had no chimney, only a smoke hole.

He tried his Joalian. "Greetings. I am Julian Teacher. I seek shelter. I will gladly pay."

She stepped aside. He took one last deep breath of fresh air and stooped through into the shed.

She shared the one-room hovel with a boy and her livestock—the goose things and a rack-boned ungulate. The floor was filth. A fireplace of stones, a shelf with a few bundles of edibles, a heap of twigs for fuel, a water skin and a couple of gourds, bedding made of two piles of frondy leaves plus scraps of uncured hide . . . nothing more.

The billowing smoke stung Julian's throat and eyes, although the tiny fire barely gave light, let alone heat. Nonetheless, he sank gratefully to the ground, leaned back against his bedroll, and crossed his aching legs. Soon he was coughing his lungs out, but he was off his feet and that was all that mattered.

The woman tipped water into a small gourd and handed it to him; he drank it, assuming it was a symbol of hospitality. It tasted bad but went down well, soothing his throat. Her hands were gnarled. Indeed, her whole body was twisted. He wondered if she was eighty, as she looked, or just a badly used forty.

She knew no Joalian and he no Mapian. He established by signs that her name was something like Onkenvier *Orliel,* although he had no idea what an *orliel* did. When he pointed inquiringly at the boy, she said, "Thok," and thereafter no one spoke at all. The boy's age was a mystery too. He would have matched an English twelve-year-old in size, but if that was fuzz and not dirt on his lip, he was both older and seriously malnourished. He did not speak. Perhaps he could not. What sort of a name was Thok anyway? A nickname? It was neuter. In Joalian, a *thaki* was a cub.

The silence dragged on, broken only by stray crackles from the fire. The woman sat and stared at it with rheumy eyes. Thok sat and stared at nothing. Julian sat and shivered. He considered unrolling his blanket and wrapping up in it, but the effort seemed too enormous to attempt. The smoke had already given him a headache. Was there a husband somewhere or more children? No, because there were only two beds. How could such a life even be worth living? Earth had poverty to match this, he supposed, but he had never met it. Exeter might have done so, in his African days. The Liberator could do nothing about the plight of these people. They could have no interest in religious reformation. One of Zath's reapers might seem like a welcome release to them.

Onkenvier produced a knife made from a piece of a rib and stabbed at something in the fire. She pulled out a charred tuber, which she proceeded to hack into three pieces. Then she skewered the largest fragment, blew on it to cool it, and offered it to Julian. His stomach heaved. He shook his head, pointed to the water and made a sign for drinking. Onkenvier said something to Thok; Thok poured another drink for the visitor.

He started to cough and almost choked on it, spilling water into his beard. Again he refused the tuber. He could not imagine eating anything, the way he felt. He had walked too far, obviously. It was not only his legs and feet that ached. Everything ached. He ached all over.

Thok and Onkenvier began chewing on the smaller fragments of the tuber, eating even the charred crust. Julian wished he could call over a waiter and order a couple of steaks for them—although meat would probably make them as ill as the sight of their normal diet was making him feel. Still, he was immensely grateful just to be here. He fumbled in his purse and found a coin. He held it out to the woman.

She stared at it as if she did not know what money was, then turned a puzzled gaze on him, meeting his eyes for the first time.

"For you," he said. "Take it."

She did, peering at it wonderingly.

Thok was looking at Julian. His face bore no expression at all, so it was impossible to judge what thoughts were writhing inside that undernourished mind, but Julian realized he had made a serious error. Sleeping men had no charisma. He might wake up with a bone knife through his heart.

The prospect was strangely unworrying. He made a huge effort and rolled his bundle away, so he could lie down and lay his head on it. He did not need it as a cover, certainly. Despite his shivering, he was pouring sweat as if he were in a Turkish bath.

# 49

By next morning, he was almost too weak to stand. He had to lean on Thok's shoulder when he went out to the pit, and thereafter he just lay on the smelly heap of bedding and waited to die.

Onkenvier would not let him die. She stripped off his clothes, wrapped him in his blanket, piled ancient furs over him to keep him warm. From time to time she bathed his face and rubbed foul-smelling grease on his chest. She forced him to sip a thin soup while Thok held his head up. When he needed to relieve himself, Thok held a gourd for him.

He slid into delirium. "Fools!" he told them. "You are fools. Let him die and you can bury him and keep all the money. It isn't much to him, but it's more than you have ever seen in your lives." They did not understand, so they continued to nurse him.

In his lucid moments he wept at his incredible weakness. He could hardly find the strength to cough, although the pain in his chest was unbearable and every breath rattled like a cart on cobbles. He did not want to die lost among strangers in a strange world. He would never tell Euphemia how sorry he was. She would never know what had happened to him; he would never know what had happened to her. To have lived through the Great War, to have adventured to another planet, then to die like a rat in a sewer . . . it wasn't right. It wasn't fair.

Night came again. He faded in and out of consciousness, but always when he stirred,

Onkenvier was there. Did she never sleep? Breathing was an impossible effort. He was drowning in mucus. Eventually she seemed to realize that, for she roused the boy so that together they could pull Julian up to a sitting position. They propped him there somehow, and then he could breathe. Just. He wandered away into delirium that was worse than the pain. He was a kipper in a smokehouse, being eaten alive by earwigs.

Morning at last . . . He was aware of sunlight streaming in at him when the door opened, which it did a few times. Onkenvier was still fussing around him with her broth, but he was too weak to swallow it. He was dying—dying nastily, messily, irrelevantly, as everything must die. King or worm, it always came to this. He had been granted more time than those poor sods at Ypres or the Somme. A lot of them had died more disgustingly even than this, but at least they'd had the consolation that they were dying for King and Country. The universe would roll on without Julian Smedley and never notice the loss. He would leave no fame, no children, no great works. Laugh all you want at this fevered, suffering relic, but your turn will come. . . .

"*Tyika* Kaptaan!"

Julian prized his sticky eyelids open. There was nothing there but a blur. How stupid of Dommi to wander into such a nightmare! How stupid of himself not to hallucinate someone more interesting.

"*Tyika!*" Someone was shouting. Someone was trying to rub the skin off his hand. "Hold on, *tyika!* He is coming, *tyika!* The Liberator is coming. We have sent word for him to hurry."

Julian tried to explain that it was too late, but he couldn't make the words. It didn't matter. He didn't care. He wanted it to end. Come to think of it, a chap couldn't possibly accept a favor from a man he'd accused to his face of being a murderer, so it was just as well that prophet chappie wasn't there, couldn't help, wouldn't arrive in time. . . . He had probably died already anyway. See you when I get there, old man.

When the release finally came, it was almost sexual in its intensity. The end of all the harsh, labored breathing, the pain and striving, the pounding fever, the desperate effort—the sudden peace, the wonderful, wonderful peace . . . the unbearable joy.

There was a cool hand on his forehead. There were a devil of a lot of people making a damnable lot of noise outside somewhere, and the door was open again, although the sun wasn't shining on his face anymore. He opened his eyes.

He licked his lips. He swallowed. He forced himself to meet that familiar smile. "Thank you."

The blue eyes sparkled strangely. "My pleasure entirely," Exeter said. "You are a thousand times welcome."

# 50

"It was most fortuitously, was it not," said Dommi, "that I was given assignment on the advance team to this campsite and were thus identifying you?" He was methodically going through Julian's bundle, squatting on his heels to keep his fastidious self from coming in contact with that floor.

Julian pulled his blanket tighter around him, shivering now not because he had a fever, but because he did not have one to keep him warm. He was still adjusting to the idea of being alive. He was also trying to reconcile that miracle with the deaths he had witnessed at Shuujooby, for if Captain Julian Smedley (retd.) was now living on the avails of martyrdom, then he was as guilty as Exeter and a hypocrite as well. He wasn't going to tell Dommi all that, though.

"I trust that *Tyika* Kisster would have come to the aid of any invalid, not just a personal friend?"

"Oh yes, *tyika!* Many hundreds every day are succored in this wise. But I have never seen the Liberator ride any rabbit quite so hard." He laughed. "These appear to be the best of a sad assembly, *tyika.*" He held up a smock and breeches.

When had anyone ever heard Dommi laugh before? His flaming hair had grown perceptibly longer since leaving Olympus, and he had sprouted an impressive layer of copper beard. Now he proceeded to hand the disparaged garments to his former employer and head for the door.

"You didn't mention where the hot tub is."

Dommi paused in the doorway and then laughed again, a fraction too late to be convincing. "Hot tub? I barely have recollection of what this is."

Mm? Times they were a-changing! "Then before you go, tell me of *Entyika* Alis and *Tyika* Djumbo."

"The *entyika* is well and keeps very busy with meritorious service. I regret to be informant that the unfortunate Djumbo has departed his recentest incarnation."

"He's dead?"

"Indeed so." Dommi's face had twisted itself into an expression of such heartrending solemnity that it looked ready to shed a few freckles for the departed. "His soul has moved to the next rung of the ladder, as the Liberator has instructed us, and because the madness into which he had fallen was a repercussion of invidious sorcery, no blame must be attached to his memory and we may be confident that his progress upward will continue. Now, if you will excuse, I have many important duties, Kaptaan."

The doorway was then empty.

Musing upon Dommi's strange transformation, Julian reached for the water skin. There was no sign of either Thok or Onkenvier, and the door had mysteriously been ripped from its worn old leather hinges. He was unbearably sticky and scratchy, so he proceeded to clean up as well as he could, although the clearing was now crowded with people. No one came to applaud his striptease. Everyone must be fully occupied. He could hear mallets thudding on tent pegs, axes cracking on trees, carts rumbling, and people singing hymns.

He dressed, combed his hair and beard, and stepped out into the brightness of a winter afternoon. The extent of the activity astonished him. He could see lines of tents, with more going up, makeshift paddocks holding at least a dozen rabbits and a few moas, five or six parked wagons, and the beginning of a camp kitchen—fires and spits and tables. His stomach growled wistfully. Hundreds of people were bustling around, all seemingly performing duties with eagerness and good cheer, even if they were doing nothing more than singing hymns. This was the county fair or the circus come to town, and the British Army could have organized matters no better. Exeter's crusade was prospering, far removed now from the turmoil of Shuujooby.

Details could wait. Julian's first duty was to find Onkenvier and give her money, all the money he had. He peered around carefully, but he could not see her. Perhaps she and Thok had fled into the forest when this unexpected invasion overthrew their world. The crisp winter air, which two days ago had been crystalline and silent, now rang with hundreds of voices. The carpet of low weeds and shrubs had been trampled flat and patterned with innumerable long shadows by the waning sun. If not terrified, she would be at least bewildered.

Another wagon rolled into camp, drawn by two rabbits. People ran to help the occupants disembark, lifting some of them out on litters, then carrying or escorting them over to the hymn singers by the pond, where Exeter in his gray robe stood ready for them. In moments the healing began, with shouts of jubilation and surges of mana that made the node tremble. The Spanish flu had met its match.

The largest group appeared to be made up of initiates; they were being harangued by an adolescent girl. On the far side of the pond, converts were being baptized. Unless Julian's eyes deceived him, one of the officials in charge was Dommi Houseboy with a shield on his back. Well, well, well! Piccadilly Circus.

The Onkenvier business would have to wait. If she failed to appear before the Free departed, Julian would just leave his purse in her cottage. Meanwhile, he was painfully aware that he was not as fit as a Stradivarius and had not eaten in at least two days. He headed for the commissary, where people were already lining up to be fed.

He had to stop for a long line of newcomers, bent under their bundles, being led by a shield-bearer to a campsite. Then he narrowly escaped being run down by a gang towing newly felled tree trunks in from the woods. He detoured around a construction site where young men were exuberantly wielding picks, hammers, and shovels, slamming posts into the ground like nails, hurling dirt with the enthusiasm of dogs going after rabbits. Their excessive energy was clearly inspired by the presence of young women, who were officially weaving withes into makeshift screens, but also commenting back and forth about muscles and stamina and related matters. It seemed like a jolly way to build latrines.

Within fifty yards he saw a dozen styles of clothing and overheard a whole Babel of dialects. The nasal Randorian accents he could identify exactly, but the others displayed varying tones of Niolian singsong, Thargian growl, or the terse staccato of Joal, as if every one of the twenty-seven Vales was represented here already.

"Captain?" caroled a voice. "Oh, Captain Sm*ed*ley! I say! Hell*o-o-o!*" The hand waving the lacy handkerchief belonged to Hannah Pinkney. She stopped waving it and metronomed her sunshade instead, until she saw that Julian had changed direction.

Hannah Pinkney! Muddled, twittery Hannah Pinkney? How the devil had she found her way to this battleground? There was no mistaking her, though, swathed in a spectacular robe, an Eiffel Tower–shaped sweep of white fur, plus a straw hat with pink bows. The effect was neither Valian nor European, but something disconcertingly in between—Ascot Week in Thargia or the Randorian Embassy at St. Moritz.

Then Julian thought, *Oh my ears and whiskers!* because the man at her side was Pinky himself—Pinky the gray eminence, the manipulator, sly Pinky, smooth Pinky, Pinky as greasy as a ha'pennyworth of cold chips, Pinky all dapper in a fur-trimmed leather greatcoat, unbuttoned to display the leather jerkin and heavy wool knickerbockers beneath, the knee-high boots, Pinky clutching an official-looking notebook, Pinky smiling a greeting without showing more than his eyelids.

"Captain Smedley! My word! Good to see you, Captain."

Julian shook Hannah's hand while he discarded all the nasty remarks lining up in his gullet: *Not good to see you!* or *By Jove, I never knew a man switch sides faster!* or even *How long do you think you can hide here before Exeter finds you?*

He said, "Pinky, old son! What brings you here?" Possible answers would be: *Pure funk!* or *Crass opportunism, old man!* or *If you can't beat 'em, join 'em.* Yet who was he to accuse Pinky of changing sides? He'd switched sides himself, and now apparently he'd switched back again, because he'd accepted a miracle cure from First Murderer himself. He was as guilty as anyone.

Pinky said, "Logistics, actually." He waved the notebook as if he were bidding on a picture at Christie's.

Julian said, "Oh my word! What sort of logistics?"

"Mm, the usual stuff. You know, Captain. You'd probably have set it up better than I did, you with your military experience. We can't afford to have the Liberator wasting time shuffling around on the roads any more, can we? Can't afford to have him waste mana doing cures in jolly ditches, either." Pinky sighed to indicate the labor involved. "We move him from one node to the next as fast as possible. That means rabbits, sometimes relays of rabbits. It means having one camp set up before we tear the last one down, and then moving it ahead to be set up for next day. It means getting all the sick to the right place at the right time. It means transportation for the halt and the lame, so they don't slow us down too much. It keeps us busy." Pinky beamed modestly, displaying his eyelids again.

Pinky, in short, was all ready to take over the Free and run them as he had run

Olympus. The Pinkneys of this world—or any other world, for that matter—gravitated naturally to the bridge. Did Exeter have any say in this? Did he even know who was doing what in his name anymore, or was he so intoxicated on mana that he had lost touch with his own revolution?

Why should the prospect worry Julian Smedley? He had wanted to nip the entire Liberator fandangle in the bud, but his narrow escape from death had changed his spots. Now he wasn't sure what he wanted, except that he felt an unreasoned resentment at the thought of slippery Pinky Pinkney taking over the whole shebang.

"Us? Who's us?"

"There are quite a few of us helping out," Pinky agreed. "The Chases are here and the Coreys."

Goodness! That sounded like a lot of wedded bliss all of a sudden. "Have you seen any sign of Mrs. McKay?"

"She was at Olympus when we left."

"Don't forget the Newtons, darling," Hannah said without a blush.

*Damn!* The last person Julian wanted to meet now was Ursula.

"Ah, the Newtons!" Pinky said blandly. He opened his book and found a page. "Yes, the Newtons are currently with advance party two. They ought to be in Lappinvale by now, getting everything shipshape for tomorrow. Dawn departure: We shall move the Liberator over the pass in one day. That is the plan. Have to wait a couple of days for the supporting cast to catch up, of course. He will have plenty to keep him occupied in Lappinvale."

It was a good job Julian's stomach was already empty. "I take it you now support Exeter as the Liberator?"

"Oh, he's doing splendidly, splendidly! The mana's just pouring in. The flu was a godsend, of course."

"Now, now, darling!" Hannah murmured. "You know the Liberator doesn't like you saying that."

Pinky chuckled. "Well, it's an ill wind that blows nobody good, what?"

Some winds were iller than others. "Well, it's such fun to see you," Julian said. "But I mustn't keep you from your important duties. If you need a fourth for bridge anytime, just shout. Cheerio!"

He stalked off in search of food.

Hypocrite! He had been projecting his own sense of guilt onto Pinky. Healing influenza was a morally acceptable source of mana, but Exeter had begun by martyring his own bodyguard, and that was definitely not on. The martyrdom mana had been diluted by the influx of influenza mana. So what? Julian Smedley had accepted his life back, knowing where the miracle had come from. Actually, he'd had no choice at the time, but he wasn't planning to cut his throat now, so he was just as guilty as if he had agreed in advance. When the root is evil, the plant is evil. Wear gloves, Lady Macbeth, and no one will notice the bloodstains.

He went by a makeshift log table where three husky butchers were hacking a carcase into pieces. Small wonder the Liberator's cause was popular if he was giving *meat* to all who asked for it! At the next, two men and two women were chopping vegetables. One of the women was vaguely familiar—quite good-looking in a horsey sort of way. . . . As if his stare had alerted her, she looked up and their eyes met. It was Alice Prescott.

They met halfway and embraced like long-lost lovers. A trio of passing youths whooped in approval.

Then they stood back to inspect each other, holding hands, both a little breathless and flushed and abashed at having made such an un-English scene in public. She was weather-beaten and faintly bedraggled, indistinguishable from any young woman of the Vales. At school, Julian had been rather awed by Exeter's cousin—older, mature, worldly. Two years ago, he had kissed her, but only once and then only to distract her attention from something else. Perhaps he should consider making a habit of it.

She laughed. "I like your beard better than Edward's, I think. And your hand? It's growing back! That's wonderful!"

"You haven't changed a bit!"

"Crikey, it's only been two years! How are you?"

"I'm splendid, thanks to Edward. And you?" He looked down at the work-ravaged fingers he was holding. "Scullery maid? Is that the best job he can find for you?"

She cocked her head and looked at him inquiringly. "It's not unworthy! I can't speak the language, so my qualifications are limited. I look after babies sometimes, help load and unload the wagons. Don't worry about me, Julian! I'm having the time of my life."

Was she? Her eyes were steady; he couldn't tell if she was lying.

"That's good. But I'm starving!"

"So am I! Let's eat and talk." She urged him in the direction of the queue. Side by side, they walked over the frosty scrub. "You went back to Olympus?"

"It's in pretty bad disarray, I'm afraid."

"Pinky told us," Alice said offhandedly.

"Pinky! How does your cousin feel about that lot being here?"

Again she gave him an appraising look. "He welcomes anyone. Why shouldn't he?"

"Because Pinky will try to take over the whole show, if I know Pinky."

Alice looked away. "I don't think anyone is going to take anything away from Edward now, Julian."

"Good. How is he?"

They joined the end of the line, edged forward as it moved. They were speaking English, so no one could eavesdrop, yet she took a moment to answer, and then she spoke softly.

"Changed, even since I came. At times he's just Edward, but not often. I'm sure he sleeps no more than two hours a night. Most of the time he's the Liberator, whatever that is. I don't mean he's acting a part. He *is* the part."

"Too much mana?"

"Overdose? What are the symptoms?"

"I have no idea. I didn't get a decent look at him." Julian's stomach rumbled loudly, having sighted the food.

Alice said, "He is different. You'll see. And of course he's collecting lots of mana from all this healing. Funny, at first it didn't work too well. He spent more than he earned, was how Ursula put it. Now . . . It doesn't take much mana to heal influenza, apparently. A lot less than blindness, say. And the audience . . . is different, somehow."

"More supportive?" Julian looked over the clearing and the crowds. "I can believe that. Watching a blind man being given his sight is impressive, true, but most of us aren't blind and never expect to be so. Pestilence is different; it can strike down anyone." He suppressed a shiver. "They're scared, all of them!"

"I expect that's it."

"The Pentatheon can cure flu too."

"They can," she agreed. "But Zath can't! You don't go to Zath for a healing. And what temple can hold a crowd like this?"

Yes, the flu had been a godsend, but Alice was not going to admit it. And it must have brought money as well as mana. There was more to this assembly than just good organization: tents, transportation, abundant food, the equipment to process it. Most of the Free were much better dressed than the rabble Julian had seen in Niolvale.

"He's certainly doing very well. The boodle must be rolling in too."

"Oh, yes!" Alice would rather discuss money than mana. "It began with a windfall from Eleal Singer, of all people. But now the rich are flocking to him. The flu brought them as nothing else could have done. Mana and money and followers."

Julian asked the question that had been hovering unsaid between them. "You think he's going to make it?"

Her face was unreadable. "He certainly has a better chance now than he did a couple of—a fortnight ago. Ursula says it's still impossible, though. Zath's been at the game too long. Edward still can't hope to win without help from the Five, she says."

And what would the price of that help be? They had reached the front of the line and were about to be served. Julian was saved from having to comment on that.

The food helped, but after he had eaten, he realized how weak his brief illness had left him. Tomorrow he would have to start walking again, for he had no doubts that he wanted to stay with the Free now, if only to watch what happened as this juggernaut rolled onward through the Vales. He did not think he would be granted a mount or a place in a wagon—not with Pinky organizing matters.

The numbers were staggering. People continued to limp in long after the sun had set, although he could not tell whether they were newcomers or stragglers from the day's march. Nothing like this crusade had ever been recorded in Valian history before, and he wondered what the Pentatheon was making of it. Trying to put himself in Zath's position, he could think of no way in which the blighter could fight this mass assault except by throwing the full Thargian army against it when it arrived on his doorstep. He was certainly powerful enough to control the weather to some extent, but the cost in mana would be frightful. If he sent reapers to nip at the edges of the crowd, he would merely create more martyrs for the Liberator, who would be so much closer to the sacrifices that he would glean more benefit from them. Exeter had found an unbeatable strategy. The big question now was how long he could hold his army together—the influenza epidemic would not last forever, and winter was coming. Like a plague of locusts, this horde must keep moving or starve. If he miscalculated, he would create a famine.

After a long search, Julian found Onkenvier, huddled down in a vast crowd of singers. She was chanting along with them, although he did not think she was making words. She looked at him blankly, not seeming to know who he was, and she stared uncomprehendingly at the purse he thrust upon her. He left it with her, sure that somebody would relieve her of it fairly soon. She remained as he had found her, in a mindless, chanting trance.

He went off to speak with Exeter. He must give proper thanks; he must try and apologize for the angry words he had said, for now he shared in the blood guilt. But getting close to the Liberator was far from easy. Even when the camp was settling down for the night under the frosty stars, he did not stop working. He preached, he answered questions, and he healed the wagonloads of sick that were still arriving.

Julian cut no corners; he joined the throng and sat with many others, all wrapped up in blankets, all spellbound, listening to a sermon. It was an astonishing performance. The words were simple, the ideas simplistic, and yet the authority in them was utterly compelling. Even a stranger could barely resist the charisma now.

"There is only one god. God is Undivided. Yet there is a spark of godliness in all of us. Have you not seen it in others? Have you not felt it in yourselves—sometimes? Not often. It rarely shows, but it is there. We strive and sometimes we succeed. We are all evil at times; none of us is evil always. And when we die, as we all must die, do you think that spark of godliness is lost? Of course not! Our bodies die, but the god-stuff in us does not die.

"So where does it go, that spark? The sorcerers promise you a place up there in the heavens, twinkling away every night. Did you ever think to ask: *Doing what?* Just watching the world snoozing far below you? Have you never wondered if perhaps you might eventually get *bored?* Doing nothing, just watching? The first week it would be nice, yes. To be free of the fear of death, to be free of pain and sickness and suffering— wonderful! But for how long could you be satisfied with that? A month? A year? A century? A thousand years? A million? I tell you that what the evildoers offer you is illusion. I tell you that their paradise of unchanging perfection would soon become a hell, and their eternity would be a torment of boredom! Fortunately the truth is otherwise."

He began to outline his doctrine of successive rebirths, and Julian found himself intrigued, despite his utter disbelief. Exeter's idea of reincarnation was not the bound-to-the-wheel sort of reincarnation from which the only escape was to a nihilist Nirvana. It was a cheerful, progressive, ladder-to-God reincarnation, a collect-your-Boy-Scout-badges-and-get-promoted reincarnation. It did not deny the world, for the world was where the medals were won. It promised that all souls could merge with the godhead in the fullness of time—apotheosis, not annihilation—and it came from no earthly creed that Julian knew. He wondered where Exeter had found it.

Who knows? said the sceptic in him, it may be right. Who ever comes back to report?

It was as appealing a blueprint as any, and that would be exactly why his old friend had chosen it as the keystone of the new faith. To overcome Zath he needed followers, to gain followers he needed a faith, and all faiths needed to explain about the party after the game.

It would be wonderful to believe stuff like that, said the cynical Julian—believe wholeheartedly and permanently. In Flanders he had seen sheer terror create some steadfast, if temporary, believers, even himself. Unfortunately, God had not designed the world quite so neatly as people like Edward Exeter thought He should. At that point Julian was shocked to realize that he was now crediting Exeter with believing what he was preaching.

When the sermon was over, the disciples organized a reception line for those who felt they had a special need to meet the Liberator. He spoke a few words to each—quietly, confidentially . . . soothing, blessing, comforting, encouraging. Then the supplicant moved on, walking a little taller, and Exeter spoke to the next.

While waiting his turn, Julian studied that tall, gaunt figure in the leaping glow of the fires. From many yards back he thought he could see a difference, as Alice had said. Exeter had changed, even in a brief two weeks. Confidence, yes. Authority, without question. Certainty, certainly. But there was more, somehow, and Julian could not put a finger on what it was.

Too much mana? Was Exeter becoming a god, or at least thinking of himself as a god, just as the others did? Could occult power corrupt as inevitably as temporal power did? So soon?

Whatever had happened, this was not the Exeter he had expected to meet, and as his turn came nearer, his determination wavered. He began to feel more and more as he had in Buckingham Palace, waiting for King George to pin a medal on him. There was no need to give thanks to this person. His thanks were so insignificant that to mention them would be to waste the Liberator's time. The bitter accusations of a fortnight ago now seemed not merely irreverent but totally irrelevant, just as Pinky's petty manipulations were irrelevant. Exeter did not need anyone's apologies. Exeter had been right all along, and the sacrifice his followers had made had been as justified as the similar sacrifices so many had made on the Western Front. He had seen through the smoke to the flame, which Julian had not. Desperate evils may require desperate remedies.

Almost, he turned and fled. But in the end he stayed, and a last step put him in front of the Liberator. Tongue-tied and dismayed, he stared into those piercing sapphire eyes—and was unable to remember even why he had come.

The spell snapped like an icicle. It was only the old familiar Edward Exeter who laughed and took his hand. "Now you're a thousand and one times welcome, old man! Come. Let's talk." He gestured to the closest fire.

"But . . ." There were hundreds still waiting to meet him.

"They won't disappear. Time for a tea break."

Thus Julian found himself sitting at a fire with the Liberator, served a hot, spicy beverage by worshipful disciples, while a few hundred envious worshippers watched like tigers peering through bars.

"I never doubted you would return."

"Actually I came to check up on Alice. Since I'm here, I'd like to stay and do my bit."

Smile. "Very glad to have you."

"Look, old man, I'm frightfully sorry about—"

"Stow it!" Exeter said sharply. Then he grinned sheepishly. "If I can't let bygones be bygones, then I'm in the wrong trade."

"You're doing very well in it."

"Got a few lucky breaks. How bad are things in Olympus?" He seemed totally relaxed, fresh, ready to cruise along all night.

His humor was a twinkling armor, deflecting all effort to pry. Only once did Julian manage to nudge the conversation close to Exeter himself.

"Your blueprint for the afterlife intrigues me. It isn't any form of Buddhism I've met. Is it Hindu? Where'd you find it?"

Just for a moment, Exeter seemed startled. "Find it? I don't really know. It just sort of came to me one day when I was preaching. Felt like something they'd like to know . . ." Then his eyes focused on Julian again and suddenly flickered amusement, as if he had a very shrewd idea of what his old chum was thinking. "It's all this mana, you know. I take dictation directly from God now."

He didn't *seem* to be serious.

When the brief audience was over, the prophet returned to the reception line to greet the next devotee. Julian walked away into the darkness, humming cheerfully. He paused once to look back at a scene made bleary by wood smoke—the Liberator foretold, receiving the adulation of his admirers by night. There were a dozen people grouped in the warm gold glow of the fires against the dark. It could have been a picture from an illustrated Bible, or even a study in chiaroscuro by some would-be Caravaggio, but the light did not shine any more brightly on Exeter than on the rest. Despite Alice's misgivings, he had not really changed. Exeter was playing a role and playing it magnificently, but he was still the same old Exeter underneath.

A little later, when he had found a cramped corner of a crowded tent in which to curl up, Julian Smedley discovered that he now had two normal hands.

# VIII

He leaves his own country and goes to
    another,
But he brings the five evils with him.

ADI GRANTH: PRABHĀTĪ M.V.

# 51

Give Pinky his due—if it was his due—the organization was impressive. Pilgrims were already starting to move out when Julian awakened at first light. He had promised to wait for Alice, and by the time she and the other commissariat staff had struck camp and loaded up their wagons, Onkenvier's clearing was almost deserted again, a wasteland of gray mud dotted with smoking ash piles and abandoned latrine fences. Snow was falling gently but with persistence, as if determined to hide the mess the Free had left behind them. The Liberator himself was still there, healing some last patients straggling in, while a fleet of moa taxi chariots was being assembled to carry him and his handlers to the first staging point.

Alice explained that she normally walked with the pilgrims, helping the old or the very young, but that morning she was scheduled to ride with other kitchen workers in a rabbit cart, and she insisted on Julian's joining her. He suspected that she was not being completely truthful, but accepted gratefully, feeling very much a scrimshander because there were thousands of other people who had been just as sick as he. He promised himself that he would pull his weight tomorrow.

The express could not travel very fast through the multitude packing the Fainpass trail, but it did arrive at the next campsite soon after the vanguard. When Captain Smedley offered to assist, he was armed with a knife and aimed at a mountain of several tons of a tuber much like a potato. It was one of the most joyful moments of his life: He had been assigned a job that needed two hands and he could do it.

The node Exeter had specified was marked by a single standing stone in the center of bleak winter pasture a couple of miles from a small village. Soon the Free were settling on it like flies on a cow pat. There was no snow in Lappinvale; the sun shone at times. Seated on an upturned bucket with his back to the wind, Julian peeled spuds into another bucket to his heart's content. He had companions—two women jabbering away in Lappinian, a very deaf old man, and three disgruntled girls who thought they deserved much better. He was quite happy to ignore them and just peel spuds.

Then a shadow fell across his bucket and a voice spoke his name. He looked up in fury. She was swaddled in moth-eaten furs like a shapeless teddy bear, her hair blowing untidily across her face. She wouldn't care how she looked, though; she never had. And she was actually smiling at him as if he should be pleased to see her!

Never in his life before had he wanted to hit a woman, but he did now—very much. "Go away!" he shouted. "Get out of my sight!"

She backed a step. "What's wrong?"

He rose to his feet, trembling with fury. "The word is rape, Mrs. Newton. You raped me!" None of the onlookers would understand English, but he would not have cared if they did.

"Oh, that."

"Yes, that!"

She looked at him uncertainly. "That's a rather extreme way of describing what happened. I suppose I used mana on you. I didn't mean to, Julian."

"Didn't *mean* to?" He took a step forward, and she retreated again. He was glad to see that she was starting to look alarmed. His anger had surprised her.

"No," she said. "You know how . . . Perhaps you don't. You never had much mana, did you? When you have mana and you want something, it's very difficult not to cause it to happen. The power leaks out. You couldn't stop your hand healing, could you? I wanted you to come to my tent. You did. I wanted you to—"

"I did not want you!"

She frowned as if he had said something a gentleman should not. "I suppose I should have been more careful. I'm sorry, Captain Smedley, truly I am."

But she didn't care. She would have been much more sorry if she had knocked over his teacup. Now he was waving his knife at her, and the onlookers were becoming alarmed. The deaf old codger had struggled to his feet. Julian was so furious he could not find words.

"When I saw what was happening," she said patiently, "I should have stopped, I suppose. Or asked you, perhaps. I didn't think you'd mind. Men usually don't." She smiled knowingly.

"You make a habit of it? Is that the only way you can get a man?"

"Oh, your hand!" Ursula cried, changing the subject. "It's better!"

Julian threw down the knife and made a fist. "A present from an old friend. I should hate to put it to work by knocking your teeth down your throat, Mrs. Newton, but if you don't get away from me now and stay away from me in future, then the Liberator is going to have more healing to do. Now go to hell and stay there!" He was bluffing, of course. She could bring him weeping to his knees with a whiff of mana.

She didn't, but she obviously thought he was making an awful fuss. "I am sorry, truly I am. I just didn't think you'd mind." With a shrug, she turned and walked away.

Shivering with frustrated rage, Julian resumed his seat and began hacking madly at the tubers.

# 52

Light snow was falling as the Free crossed Fainpass, but the weather was fine in Lappinvale. Alice had heard predictions that the Thargians there were sure to cause trouble. They would try to block a mass invasion heading for their homeland, and they certainly did not want their Lappinian serfs taking the opportunity to escape over the border.

The doubters had forgotten that the pandemic still raged in Lappinland. Governor Kratch himself brought his wife and children to be healed by the Liberator. Gratitude was not a prized virtue among Thargians, but they always put expediency ahead of principle, and their garrison was outnumbered a hundred to one. The Free marched on unopposed, gathering recruits as they went. These refugees were free to desert as soon as they reached Randorvale, of course, but surprisingly few of them did.

Alice was enjoying herself enormously. London seemed far away now, but she had never truly been a Londoner. Tents she associated with childhood safaris, Uncle Cam and Aunt Rona in Kenya. The climate and the scenery were different, but roughing it did not bother her. Her Norfolk depression forgotten, she helped with the cooking, tended babies, cared for the sick waiting for Edward to arrive, and generally did work that felt more useful than any she had done before in her life. Now that she knew how much fun crusades were, she could understand why the Middle Ages had put on so many of them.

Even so, having Julian Smedley around was an improvement. She needed an interpreter to help her learn some basic Joalian. During her first few days with the Free, she had been forced to rely on Ursula, Dommi, and Edward himself, and they were all too busy with other duties to spend much time with her. Various Olympians began turning up and enlisting after that, but they were quickly put to work as well. Julian was not fluent in Joalian and usually enlisted a native as tutor, translating back and forth and learning along with her. It ate up the hours on the daylong treks and the sometimes monotonous toil, for he pitched in with the lowly work of the commissariat, leaving religious affairs to others.

Captain Smedley qualified as an old friend. Alice had more in common with him than anyone else in this world except Edward, and she rarely saw Edward. Julian had flicked in and out of her life for years, her cousin's closest chum, a different person every time she met him: bean sprout boy, then spotty, unsure adolescent, debonair youth, shell-shocked hero. And now? Now a lean, competent young man, not quite handsome but certainly attractive, old beyond his years. If he still had daylight nightmares, he hid them behind a cheery façade. He never discussed his own affairs, but he was too personable not to have at least one sweetheart somewhere. Recalling the bed-room roulette that Mrs. McKay had described that long-ago evening in the dining room of the Bull, Alice concluded that Julian Smedley would be regarded as a prime target but might not be ruthless enough to play such games well.

From Lappinvale by Soutpass into Randorvale—and still the sun shone. Randorland might be tricky, Julian warned, because it was home ground for the Lady, the Church was being persecuted there, and Doc Mainwaring still lay in jail. But the prophecy was encouraging, verse 318: "From Randor the mighty shall seek out the Liberator, sleeping in the woods and ditches, crying: aid us, have mercy upon us, and they will shower gold upon him."

The first thing that happened in Randorvale, though, was that Ursula and Dommi disappeared.

"They'll be back," Edward promised. "Dommi's appointed himself apostle to the Carrots. Ursula's going to report to whatever's left of the Service."

The following morning, King Gudjapate summoned the Liberator to an audience and the Liberator declined the invitation.

Two days later, the king tried again, delivering an emaciated but otherwise unharmed Doc Mainwaring as a peace offering. Edward still refused, although he kept Doc.

On the Free's fourth night in the vale, when they were camping close to the western end and thus not very far from Olympus, several hundred copper-haired Olympians poured into camp and greeted the Liberator with hysterical adulation. With them came Ursula and some familiar faces: Betsy and Bill Pepper, Iris Barnes, Prof Rawlinson, and others.

Julian learned of the evangelists' return as he was wrapping himself up in a fur robe beside a campfire. There were still not enough tents, and he could not see why a seasoned campaigner like himself should be given preference. He was quite healthy now, just a little weak, and Flanders had been much worse than this. A man knelt down at his side and grinned at him like a starving crocodile. He sat up quickly.

"Dommi! You're back? How's Ayetha?"

"Indeed she is most excellently in good health, Brother Kaptaan. And I am very proudest father of very loud son."

Julian, formerly *Tyika* Kaptaan, thumped him on the back and shook his hand. "Congratulations, Brother Dommi! And what is his name?" He could guess the answer. The Vales were going to be swarming with D'wards from now on.

"By gracious permission he is named after our esteemed Liberator."

"And was *Entyika*— Was she there?"

Dommi grinned even wider and nodded. "I have brought missive for you."

Julian snatched it from his hand and ripped it open. He forgot to say thank you, and he did not see Dommi depart.

*my dearest darling captain hook,*
*it was very clever of you to guess were i had gone. i am staying hear with one of tims ants not a man. i would have staid in olimpus if i new you were coming back so soon.*

*and i am sorry to miss you. i miss you very much. i am sorry we quareled but all lovers*
*quarel sometimes. all your promises made me cry and i wont hold you to them because*
*i think you will repent at leshur but if you do realy mean them then i am yours always*
*on any world. body and soul and espeshly body.*

*your ever loving*
*wendy*

That letter very nearly cost the Free one of their number, but in the end he decided to stay aboard. The crusade would not last very much longer, whereas his future with Euphemia could be stretched out for centuries. A few days more would be very little by comparison, however long they might seem.

The following morning, the royal family and most of the court drove into the camp in a caravan of fine carriages. Edward greeted them politely, cured every last runny nose, and did not insist that they sleep in ditches. He accepted their gold and gave it to Dosh to buy more food and more pack beasts.

Prophecy was a two-edged weapon, and next stop was Thovale. By now everyone knew that verse 404 of the *Testament* held some ominous words about D'ward and hunger in Thovale. The encounter was unavoidable—a man of destiny could not pick and choose.

"Should make an early start in the morning," Julian said. "Beat the rush."

Alice could see only a sheer wall of mountain, fit to challenge a fly. "Certainly. How is the pass rated?" She knew now that Joalian had a dozen words that might be applied to a mountain pass, depending on its difficulty. Difficulty was a matter of judgment, though. If it couldn't stop a mountain goat, then it ranked as easy.

"Figpass is a *jaltheraan.*"

"I'm not familiar with that one. What does it mean?"

"Bloody-awful-even-in-summer."

"Will an hour before dawn be early enough?"

The Figpass trail began rising at once, climbing steeply through scrubby trees, and it soon opened out to reveal vast hills of an impossibly green green under a pure white sky. The Free were a gray rope dropped by a giant, scrolled over the mountain face and ultimately vanishing into clouds thousands of feet above. And that was only the vanguard. There were many, many more behind.

Alice leaned into the slope, trying to keep up a steady plod. In an hour or two she would stand up there and look down to see the masses following. "It seems so unreal! I keep trying to think of earthly equivalents and I can't find a single one. Visigoths . . . the Children of Israel . . . Xerxes crossing the Hellespont—none of them quite fits."

Julian puffed, his breath already white in the cold. "Peter the Hermit?"

"Don't even think that!"

"Right-oh, I won't. It is real. It is also very transient. All of us will remember these days for the rest of our lives. A century from now one or two of those children may still be alive, bragging that they marched with D'ward, following the Liberator into Thargvale."

These days were also the most important of Alice Pearson's life. If she lived to be a hundred, like those hypothetical children, everything else would be anticlimax. The Vales were only a small part of the world, and only a tiny fraction of their population was actually involved, but surely this was a moment in history. Who would refuse a grandstand seat at the Hegira, the parting of the Red Sea, or Caesar crossing the Rubicon? She tried not to include the People's Crusade or the Crucifixion in that list. Whatever was going to happen at Tharg, she would never again see anything to match this. She assumed she would eventually go Home. She had already overstayed the four-week limit she had set with Miss Pimm, but it was certainly not time to leave yet.

No one, even Edward, knew how many followers he had now. The organization alone was a miracle, growing of itself to keep pace with the mushrooming numbers. Having learned over the past five years how incompetent armies were, Alice would not have believed that a large group of people could cooperate so well. The credit was all Edward's, for he had chosen a superlative team of disciples and inspired them with fanatical loyalty. There were no personal feuds or squabbles over precedence among the shield-bearers.

Their strength as a team sprang from their differences. No one understood human weaknesses better than Dosh, the reformed criminal and libertine. Dommi had scaled up his experience at running households to run the commissariat. Ursula Newton was an irresistible force, a human tidal wave to overcome all resistance, while Eleal's preaching could wring tears from a field of rocks. Of Edward's two age-group brothers from the old Nagian days, Tielan was a shrewd trader and Doggan was dogged and untiring in humdrum tasks that drove others crazy. Piol Poet was official archivist, keeping Eleal's sermons theologically orthodox. Pinky Pinkney moved people as the wind moves snowflakes, usually without their knowing it. Bid'lip had been a soldier, Kilpian a drover, Hasfral a midwife, Gastik a farmer, Imminol a herbalist, and Tittrag a mason.

The Liberator himself could outperform any one of them at anything, but he could not be in a dozen places at once. Whatever he needed done, he had a disciple to do. There were twenty shield-bearers in all, and Edward remarked to Alice in one of his wry asides that he could not imagine how Jesus ever got by with only twelve.

In the last two weeks, she had seen very little of Edward. When he offered apologies, she refused them. "You are working; I am on vacation. I can't speak the language, so I can't help much. If you want to talk, then send for me and I'll come gladly. Otherwise, do what you must do and don't give me a thought. One thing I am not is bored."

He did send for her a few times, always late in the day, when others were ready to relax. He seemed to need no rest, but his helpers did, or perhaps he chose the hour merely from habit. She was amused to notice that the two of them were never completely alone, so no tongues would wag, and yet she doubted that the danger of scandal had consciously occurred to him. His instincts were perfect.

At those sessions he would always inquire if she was happy, and she would always assure him that she was. She let him lead the conversation, and thus they talked of England, of the war, of poetry, of their childhoods. Only once did he mention what might happen when the Free arrived in Tharg, and then almost offhandedly.

"They can only be a cheering section," he said, "but of course it is their cheers that make it possible. There is just one event on the bill—the heavyweight championship of the Vales, between the reigning champion, Zath *(boo! hiss!)* in the black corner and the Liberator *(hip! hip!)* in the gray. We've all read the result in the *Testament*, so it should be a very dull. . . . What's wrong?"

"Nothing. I just tend to forget that Zath is a real person, not just an allegory."

"Oh, he's real all right." Edward's eyes narrowed, and for a moment he stared out bleakly at the night. "But what I'm planning is not murder, it's execution. You know which victims' names head the indictment."

Then he shrugged and changed the subject. If he had any doubts about the outcome, he could hide them even from her. But he must know that the battle was not always to the righteous and that most popular uprisings ended in disaster: Wat Tyler, Jan Hus, Peter the Hermit. The People's Crusade had taken thirty thousand people to slavery or slaughter.

Sometimes he was the Edward she had known. He had shown this same courage and quiet determination when the Blighters were trying to kill him. Sometimes she sensed more, a fearsome coiled power waiting to be unleashed, a calculated hatred for an evil foe—unless that was only her imagination seeing what it wanted to see. Yet, sitting demurely across the fire from him, she would watch the play of light on the angular planes of his face and wonder what her cousin had become.

Once, and only once, he let his inner feelings show. He fell silent for a while, staring at her. She waited, pretending to watch the flames, and finally he said wistfully, "Dear Alice! What would have happened if the war hadn't come? Happened to us? If there had been no *Filoby Testament*? Do you ever wonder?"

"I can't imagine." She studied the pictures in the embers, which was just as practical an occupation as indulging in useless might-have-beens.

Softly, he said, "I was very much in love with you, you know. I still am, but now . . . well, things are different now. Let's not complicate matters by talking about that. Would you ever have taken me seriously?"

"I always took you seriously, Edward, dear. Very seriously. I was very frightened of hurting you. I was sure you would find another girl soon enough, probably lots of girls. I was the only one you'd ever known."

"One's enough. I don't think I'd have found another. I don't think I'd have given up—not even when I learned about D'Arcy."

She met his eyes then, and the question in them. "I was in love, too. Crazily in love."

"And if the war hadn't come?"

"I would have continued to be a fool, I suppose. His wife's still alive."

"Were you really a fool? Do you think that now?"

"Yes." She felt disloyal to the memory of a man who had given her so much happiness, but she owed loyalty to Edward also. "He wouldn't risk losing his career and her money."

"Jolly watery sort of love!"

"Yes. I suppose I'd have come to my senses eventually. Why I didn't become pregnant, I can't imagine—that would have done it! Too late, of course. I should be grateful that the war did come."

He pouted. "Don't think that! And Terry?"

"Rebound, only rebound." Terry had been even younger than Edward, with the same black hair and blue eyes—an odd coincidence. "A wonderful man, and yet in the end that would have been worse. We were madly in love, both of us, but we'd nothing else in common. It wouldn't have lasted. We'd have lived unhappily ever after."

After a moment, he said, "Thank you."

For what? Sauce for the gander? "What about Ysian? Didn't you love her?"

He shook his head in sad amusement, as if unable to credit her disbelief. "No. I told you. Love between native and stranger is unthinkable. It doesn't matter which world you choose, one must age while the other doesn't. I could have loved her. I didn't *let* myself fall in love with Ysian."

"Then what of Miss Eleal, who follows you around all day with those big, big mooncalf eyes?"

His eyebrows arched. A corner of his mouth quirked. "Alice, darling, you're not, um, just a little bit—"

"Me? Of course not. As far as I'm concerned, she's perfectly welcome to her classic profile and her overabundant mammary tissue and her life as one vast dramatized tragic *tableau vivant.* I just wish she'd keep it a little farther away from me, that's all."

"Her own father bewitched her," Edward said. "Can you imagine that—his own daughter? I took the spell off."

"With another kiss?"

He laughed aloud. "Don't blow steam at me, Mrs. Pearson! Yes, if you must know. I didn't enthrall her, though."

"She managed that all by herself?"

"Yes, she did! She was hurt and vulnerable; she picked the first man she could find to fill that terrible gulf in her soul. And the answer is still the same—love between stranger and native is unthinkable."

Alice was still winding herself up to apologize when he shrugged and said, "I just hope she's strong enough not to turn suicidal when—when she discovers I can't respond."

"Or when—what?"

"Let's talk of happier things," he said. "Do you remember . . ."

How many men could resist a piece like Eleal? Life would be much simpler if more of them were like Edward.

Figpass was bad going up and worse coming down. Alice stopped in the shelter of a rock to take a break, while wet-flannel mist drifted by and the column of Free trudged past without a break. Julian was looking very weary, but his sense of humor was still operational.

"Thovale?" he said. "It's very small and very strategic, because it connects to several other vales. The Thargians have always known the gods meant it to belong to them; they have never quite convinced the Thovians of that self-evident truth. Thovians are wild hill men. They make the Scots or the Afghans look like bunny rabbits.

"Thargia has tried to annex the vale several times. The clansmen came down from the hills by night and cut throats. The Thargians couldn't do much to retaliate, because they prefer to fight in straight lines and the terrain here won't allow that. Their armies had to cut their way through every time, both going and coming, which cramped their foreign policy *vis-à-vis* everyone else. So they came to a gentlemen's agreement. Thovale is officially independent, but it won't hinder Thargia marching through and won't support its enemies. Now the Thargians are free to bully everyone except the Thovians and the Thovians can carry on feuding among themselves. Everybody's happy, doing what they enjoy most."

She laughed. "You are a cynic!"

"I learned that on Earth," he said grimly.

Even as the Free poured down into Thovale in their thousands, a sudden blizzard closed the pass. Snow fell in shiploads, day after day after day, trapping the pilgrims within their camp.

Very few of the wagons had arrived in time. Fuel ran out first, but that hardly mattered. People had crammed into every available tent and the tents were buried in snow, so although their interiors were dark, damp, and stank horribly, they were not really cold. Walkways between them became trenches through the drifts. The food ran low. Rations were cut and finally stopped altogether, with the last reserves being issued only to children and nursing mothers—for there were even nursing mothers on this crusade.

Edward came around regularly, visiting every tent at least once a day. Shield-bearers came more frequently, especially those who were good preachers: Eleal, Pinky, Dommi. Influenza came, and was dispatched by the Liberator. Boredom came also. Hymn singing palled. Doctrinal arguments palled. Alice was very glad she did not understand enough of the language to have to listen to all that. Tempers grew shorter as the hunger bit harder.

Gradually fear began to seep into the Free. The *Filoby Testament* said that the Liberator would take death to Death, but it did not mention his followers. Perhaps they would all die first? Alice worried about that, having heard of the fruits of martyrdom from Julian, and she was certainly not alone. A word from Edward or even a shield-bearer cheered everyone up again, but the doubts returned.

It was night on the second day without food. Tempers were brittle. Somewhere in the pitch-black tent, two men were arguing, ignoring the rising grumbles of their neighbors. Alice was cramped from sitting with her knees up, but it was not her turn to stretch out yet. The shapeless furry lump she was leaning against was Julian, leaning against her. She was fairly certain that there was no one else in the tent who understood English.

"Julian?"

"Mm?"

"He's been imitating Jesus."

"Mm." Meaning, *yes.*

"How far do you suppose he's willing to go?"

"Driving out the money changers? Last Supper?"

"You know what I mean. Being crucified."

He sighed. "I wouldn't put it past him if he thought that was what was needed. Fortunately, I don't think it's relevant. I asked Prof and he agrees. There's no way that the Liberator's death would in itself destroy Zath. Edward's in terrible danger, of course. The odds are still long against him, so he may well die. If he does, I'm sure it won't be by his own wish."

The argument in the corner sounded as if it was about to come to blows. The protesters were growing louder too.

"He might pull down the temple, like Samson?" Alice asked.

"No, that won't work. It's got to be a straight, heads-down contest of mana. The stronger wins, the weaker loses. If Edward isn't powerful enough to win that, then he would gain nothing by pulling down the temple. Zath would just trap-door himself out of there. Edward would have used up far more mana than he would."

She thought of the other two men she had lost in her life and wondered if she was about to lose a third. Not a lover like them, of course, but a very dear foster brother. Just that. It was enough. Of course, if Edward survived his ordeal and then renewed his suit . . . She shied away from such thoughts.

"You still believe he needs help from the Pentatheon?"

"Zath has been collecting mana for a hundred years or so."

"But Edward has done far, far better than anyone expected, hasn't he?"

"Thanks to the Spanish flu, he has. I know we mustn't say that, but it's true." Julian chuckled, and Alice felt it through her backbone. "Fallow always claimed it taught us leadership, but no old Fallovian has ever led anything on this scale before. He's done far, far better than the Service ever dreamed possible. I think the only one who foresaw this was Zath himself. I hope the bastard's been worrying about this for thirty years."

"How do you think the Pentatheon feels?"

"Pretty bucked, if we're right in thinking they don't like Zath."

"But the more powerful Edward is, the greater the risk they take if they help him, surely? They'll just create another Zath to threaten them, and they must know Edward doesn't approve of them either." His own success might doom him.

"I don't know." Julian squirmed into a new position. "Nobody knows. It's a waste of time theorizing." He wasn't contradicting her. He couldn't, because he had said much the same things himself in the past. "I will say this: Prof and I went over the *Testament,* and this is almost the end. This is verse four-oh-four, hunger in Thovale. There's only one prophecy left. Edward's fulfilled all the rest—all those that mention the Liberator, all those that mention D'ward, all those that seem to be relevant but don't name him at all. The only one left to go is verse one thousand one: 'In wrath the Liberator shall descend into Thargland. The gods shall flee before him; they shall bow their heads before him, they will spread their hands before his feet.' "

"That's certainly encouraging, but you're forgetting three eighty-six. It's not finished yet."

"Well, of course."

Everyone knew verse 386:

*Hear all peoples, and rejoice all lands, for the slayer of Death comes, the Liberator, the son of Kameron Kisster. In the seven hundredth Festival, he shall come forth in the land of Suss. Naked and crying he shall come into the world and Eleal shall wash him. She shall clothe him and nurse him and comfort him. Be merry and give thanks; welcome this mercy and proclaim thine deliverance, for he will bring death to Death.*

The arguing men had been forced into silence by their neighbors. People were whispering and coughing, and a child wailed in another tent somewhere. Snow smothered all other sounds.

Thinking over what Julian had said, Alice realized that there was another verse in the *Testament* that had not been completed yet, one that mentioned someone called the Betrayer. Who was he?

# 53

Dosh had set off over Figpass with fifteen helpers and ten wagons. Five men and six tusk oxen froze to death on the way, but four days later he led the survivors into Thovale, arriving two hours after dawn, just as a warm wind mockingly turned the snow to rain. A crowd of men and women ran out to meet the train, shrieking and cheering, slithering and stumbling through drifts already shrinking. The famine was over.

Dosh was dead on his feet, soaked and frozen and exhausted, aching in every bone. If he were in a fit state to find anything amusing, he would be finding that welcome amusing, for the rescuers were being greeted like the long-lost son in that parable D'ward told. Tielan and Doggan were the first to locate Dosh himself amid the bedraggled band of rescuers. They embraced him as if they were planning to rape him. Doggan kissed him. Tielan screamed that he loved him. Oh, how times changed! The last time the three of them had been in Thargdom together, those two would not have been seen within arm's length of Dosh Houseboy. That was what the Liberator had wrought.

That was what virtue was all about, and it felt good. He could not deny that it felt good.

More people flocked around him to pummel, hug, and congratulate. He was too weary. He shook them off, turned away . . . and came face-to-face with the one man he really wanted to see.

"Well done!" D'ward said harshly. "You delivered the goods again. You saved the day!" He clasped Dosh's shoulder briefly, a squeeze hardly detectable through its covering of wet fur.

Dosh stared up at him in dismay. "Master? What's wrong? What have I done?"

"Nothing! I mean everything. We've got a famine on our hands, and you've saved us. You're the best, Dosh! I can always count on you."

The Liberator bared his teeth in a death's-head grin, thumped Dosh's shoulder again, and trudged away to greet the others. His eyes had not said what his voice had. Something was wrong.

Dosh found a tent and fell into the bottomless sleep of total exhaustion. By the time he awoke, it was the following morning and the Free were already on the move, under a roof of cloud that seemed to rest on the treetops. A steady drizzle still fell; slush had become a soup of mud, black and pungent and knee-deep. Most of the tents had been struck; all the livestock had gone. The remaining wagons were being hauled away by teams of men.

Stiff as an oak rafter, he limped off in search of food and news. The rumors were thicker on the ground than the mud. The Thargian army was holding Mestpass. The Thargian army had been devastated by the sickness. No, it had been devastated a fortnight ago but was now recovered. The ephors had sent word that the Free were welcome to enter Thargia, or must not enter Thargia. The ephors had demanded D'ward be handed over to them. D'ward had demanded Zath. The ephors were dead and Tharg was burning. All guesswork, obviously.

The poles were genuine, though. Men had been tearing down a forest, cutting poles. D'ward had decreed that every able-bodied pilgrim should henceforth bear a pole topped with the circle of the Undivided. He had demonstrated by cutting a sapling, trimming off all the branches except one at the top, curling that one around, and tying it with a length of creeper. The camp was full of them. They were being issued to everyone departing.

"What the blazes are those for?" Dosh demanded of the Fionian woman who heaped his platter with boiled vegetables. The meat he had brought had not stayed around long enough for him to share.

"Symbols of the One, dear." Fionians called everybody "dear."

Dosh considered the matter as he headed off to find a seat. The Free had never needed such emblems before; D'ward spurned even the earrings that the old Church of the Undivided had issued to its followers. So what was he really thinking?

Thargia maintained the only real standing army in the Vales, commonly estimated at no less than ten thousand men. That number might be doubled or tripled in an emergency, but what had the pestilence done to Thargland's fighting strength? Moas would not accept substitute riders, so the cavalry had certainly been weakened. It was not impossible that the Free would outnumber whatever forces the ephors sent against them, although numbers alone were misleading. A trained Thargian soldier could eliminate half a dozen peasants without spitting on his hands. When every peasant bore a quarterstaff, the odds were a little better. Moas had very fragile legs.

So D'ward was anticipating trouble. What of morale? Would even Thargians fight for the hated god of death? Furthermore, the Liberator had gone from strength to strength for the last three fortnights, from nothing to leader of a mighty host. This was the hand of the One, of course. Even the pagans must be wondering which side their phony gods supported.

If he were one of the ephors, Dosh concluded, he would let Zath and the Liberator settle their own quarrel first. Then he would decide whether to let the Free go or round them up and send them to the mines.

He was still very shaky, but his duty lay with D'ward and Dosh did not want to be left out of the excitement. Having checked on the condition of his helpers—because that was what D'ward would have done—he acquired one of the circle poles and set off in pursuit.

Mestpass was classed as easy, but no pass was truly easy in winter. Much of the trail ran through a broad, flat valley, made difficult now only by mud, but in some places it narrowed to a canyon. Normally placid Mestwater had become a boiling torrent, glutted with melted snow. Half the bridges had gone and must be replaced before the Free could cross. Consequently, they had not progressed very far, and Dosh caught up with the main body before midnight. The next morning he was ready to resume his duties.

By midday, he was walking over the green hills of Thargslope. Snowy peaks dwindled away to west and south, for Thargvale was so wide that its far side was hidden beyond the horizon. The sun shone in a sapphire-pale sky as if spring would jump out of the ground at any moment. Yet this was midwinter! Thargvale was blessed with a much finer climate than its inhabitants deserved.

"The old place hasn't changed much, has it?" D'ward said cheerfully.

"No, master." Dosh eyed the Liberator's smile and decided that there was nothing wrong with it. He must have been imagining that odd greeting two days ago. He had been very tired, after all. "I don't suppose the people have changed much either."

"Well, you never know. It does look as if they're up to their old tricks, though, hiding the silverware."

"Master?"

"No welcoming committee, no livestock in sight. You think perhaps they don't trust us?"

"We're being watched," growled Bid'lip Soldier from D'ward's other side. "I'd swear I saw something on that hill a moment ago. And the back of my neck's itching."

"Fleas," D'ward said. "Fleas in bronze armor. You can see the sun flashing off them every few minutes. Watch over there."

Four years ago, Dosh had traveled across Thargvale with D'ward—and with Tielan, Doggan, Prat'han, and all the others. Then it had been springtime, with the trees shining in a million shades of green and gold and purple and blue. Then he had been young and crazy. Now most of the woods were bare, although here and there he could see patches of evergreens—also everblues and everpinks, for all Thargian vegetation was colorful. A few patches of snow still lingered in the hollows. Mestwater swirled along the valley floor, deep and dark, spread beyond its banks. It was burdened with floating logs that had been cut in the summer and were now on their way to market.

By marching into Thargvale, the Free were blatantly provoking a fanatically xenophobic warrior state. This was the second time in four years that D'ward Liberator had led such an invasion. The air seemed to crackle with danger.

The countryside was much as Dosh remembered it: prosperous, well-tended farms in the lowlands, stone walls trailing like pencil lines over the fertile, rolling hills. The big houses of the nobles were more noticeable with the trees bare. Silos, haystacks, windmills. As D'ward said, no visible people or animals. Since Jurgvale, his progress had been marked by groups of the sick and their attendants, waiting for healing: people on foot or in wagons or even in tents, camped out until he should arrive. Here, there was no one. Had the pestilence avoided Thargvale, or were the people forbidden to seek the aid of the heretic?

No one in sight except the Free themselves, a wide column that stretched back out of sight, many thousands, carrying thousands of circles . . . or quarterstaffs, if that was what they were. With them came their wagons and pack beasts, oxen and llamas, and even a few moas and rabbits that had appeared after the snow melted. It must be the greatest movement of people in the history of the Vales.

Where was D'ward taking them? That morning he had placed himself at the front and given orders that the inevitable stragglers be herded up as much as possible. He was setting a very gentle pace. He had detailed no advance party and had refused Bid'lip's request to send out scouts. Obviously he anticipated trouble, but he would have to be insane not to anticipate trouble in Thargvale. A little while ago, he had passed the word for Dosh and Bid'lip, but so far he had said nothing of substance.

Then he did. "How's the money?"

"All gone, master."

He nodded. "Thought it would be. Well, Bid'lip? You're our expert on strategy. How does our situation look?"

The big Niolian scrunched up his luxuriant black eyebrows. He had been known to remark that he had the sort of face that looked best when he put his helmet on backward, but he was not in a joking mood today. "Shaky." He pointed to the river. "Mestwater's in spate. Somewhere up ahead it must join Thargwater. There'll be other tributaries, I expect, and likely all of them in flood too. The Thargians can cut down the bridges, if the rivers haven't done it for them. Is Tharg on the south bank or the north?"

"North. But you're right about the tributaries."

When D'ward said no more, Dosh spelled out his own worries.

"No supplicants, no fresh recruits, so no source of funds. Buying food in Thargland won't be as easy as it's been in other vales. There's no villages here, only those big estates. They trade with one another or send their produce directly to the city. Dommi's moaning about supplies, master."

Still the Liberator continued to stroll along in silence, wielding his pole like a staff. His face was giving nothing away. He seemed to be enjoying the walk and the sunshine.

"But we have the One True God to rely on?" Dosh snapped.

His impudence earned him a reproving frown. "He doesn't expect to do all the work, Brother Dosh. Good intentions are not enough by themselves." Then D'ward smiled to take the bite out of his words. "Yes, I know it looks bad. I'm not unaware of that. Here's what I want you to do. See that little hill? The one with the trees and the house on top? We're going to camp there. Bid'lip, I want you to post guards around the house to keep people out. I'm going to use that as my headquarters. I think it'll be empty. It was half a ruin when I last saw it. Don't let anyone except shield-bearers in . . . and anyone else I send for, of course."

The soldier nodded. "Yes, sir."

"And post guards around the perimeter. I don't expect an attack, but they may try a feint or two, just to see what our reaction is."

"And what is it?"

"We can defend ourselves, if we must. Try to avoid violence."

The big man rolled his eyes as if to imply that he would not attack Thargia with a force comprised of civilians and two armed Nagians.

"I'll want you at the house," D'ward continued, "so appoint deputies. Tell them to let any sick people into camp, of course, as usual—any genuine supplicants. They're to escort those to me in the usual way. But if messengers come or emissaries, they're to make them wait and send to the house for Dosh. All right?"

"Yes, sir."

"Good. Then go and get started."

D'ward sent him on his way with a smile. Dosh waited for his orders. And waited. The Liberator continued to walk in silence. He was frowning now, though.

Eventually Dosh couldn't stand it any longer. "How many days from here to Tharg?"

"I don't know. Four, maybe?"

Dosh almost gasped aloud. That was a shock! Until now, the Liberator had always known exactly where he was going. Sometimes the weather or the crowds had delayed him unexpectedly, but always he had known the route he was going to follow. He had scouted it out in advance. Now he did not know.

D'ward glanced behind him, as if making sure that there was no one close enough to overhear. "Dosh?"

"Master?"

"We've been friends a long time."

"The only real friend I've ever had."

D'ward winced. "Surely not?"

"It's true."

"I wish it wasn't."

"Well it is! Everyone I've ever been close to just wanted carnal pleasure of me, one way or another. You're the only person I ever knew who liked me as a person. I have friends among the Free, now, of course. But they wouldn't be my friends if I wasn't the new man you made me."

D'ward's face twisted as if he was in pain. "Well, you've certainly been a good friend to me, these last few fortnights. I don't think I'd have managed what I have without your help. I want you to know that, Dosh. I wasn't nearly as sure as I pretended I was that you'd manage to reform. You've succeeded beyond anything I ever dreamed of. You've been wonderful."

"It was you, master. D'ward, I mean. Or it was God. You brought me to God, and every night I thank God for sending me to you."

D'ward groaned. "Well, I need your help again. I need you to do something for me."

"Anything. Anything at all."

"Oh, Dosh, Dosh! It isn't going to be that easy. It may cost you your life, or worse."

How could he doubt? "Just tell me, master! I swear I will do it, exactly as you tell me. I know I failed you in Roaring Cave, letting those intruders—"

"You did *not* fail me! Those two both had magic to help them. Don't blame yourself for that. But I said then that I gave you all the tough ones. There isn't another soul in all the Free that I could trust to do this."

Dosh laughed aloud. He felt almost as excited as he'd ever felt in all his years of perversion and debauchery. "Tell me! Tell me!"

D'ward put an arm around his shoulders. "I'm not clear on the details yet. But if I give you an order tonight or perhaps tomorrow . . . We'll need a signal. Suggest one."

" 'Good old days'?"

The Liberator's brief smile acknowledged the humor. "Yes, that'll do. So if I mention the good old days, that means I want you to do whatever I ask then, however wrong or crazy it may sound. Or it may seem absolutely trivial, but it will be deathly important. Whatever it is, will you do it with no argument?"

"Yes, master. Of course."

"Thank you. That's all I can tell you now."

"I promise."

The Liberator gave Dosh's shoulder another squeeze and then took his arm away. He had left a burden there, though. What orders could possibly be so terrible that Dosh would be tempted to refuse them?

# 54

"I know you are hungry!" Eleal cried. "So am I. So, I am sure, is the Liberator, for he will not eat when you cannot. Remember how he spoke to us in Thovale, saying that those who hunger and thirst after righteousness shall be filled?"

She must hurry up and finish now, for it was almost dark and she was supposed to be up at the house. Pity! Her speech was going very well. She was enjoying it, and she thought her listeners were enjoying it too. They were certainly attentive. The little clearing was so packed with people that she could barely see the campfire. The woods all around were packed also, and yet when she paused for breath the night was still. Barely a cough, only the ticktock of woodcutters in the distance. Earlier she had caught snatches of other shield-bearers preaching elsewhere on the hill, but not anymore. Hurry.

"But he has also warned us that mortification of the flesh can be carried too far. And so that message I gave you, that you will feast tonight!" She paused while a sigh of wonder swept the wood like a breath of wind. Did they think the Liberator might have changed his mind since she began her talk? "Be patient, therefore, brothers and sisters! It will be a sign unto you! Tonight Trumb will eclipse."

They all knew that. The great moon hung over the jagged teeth of Thargwall like a green plate, glistening in the winter night. Before dawn it would certainly fill out to a circle and then fade to black.

"No matter the misguided pagans worship that disk as one of their false gods, for the Liberator has taught us that it is only a blessing from the One, to brighten darkness. Is not the circle His symbol? It is a sign of God, not of the so-called Man. You know how the pagans tremble when that light is eclipsed, believing that Zath will send reapers to steal away souls. Well, Zath's days are numbered. It is written that the Liberator will slay him, and he has come to Thargvale to do that."

Another sibilant murmur.

"We are greatly blessed to have traveled with him, all of us. Friends and family behind at home will revere us all our days because we are here and they are not. Harken to what the Liberator said to us at sunset! He said that before Trumb eclipses again, *Zath will be dead and there will be no more reapers!*"

Louder, longer, came the reaction. Naturally—the shield-bearers themselves had cheered when they heard that news. Trumb's eclipses often came nine days apart, sometimes only four, rarely more than a fortnight. She raised her voice over the rumble.

"And therefore tonight, when the green moon darkens, we feast! We are the Free, and we shall celebrate tonight the certain death of Zath! So promises the Liberator, in the name of the One True God. He bids us remember this night all our days and all our years, so that evermore, when midwinter comes and the sun turns, we shall feast and make merry in remembrance and thanksgiving. This be his command to us. Let us pray."

She kept the prayer brief, made the circle sign, and stepped down from the stump. Her head was pounding with reaction as if she had just come offstage after playing some great role. Which was apt, she supposed. What greater part could there ever be than this? Voices were rising excitedly all around. She looked for her shield before remembering that it was still slung on her back. Willing hands passed her staff and her pack. The crowd parted to let her through. She saw eyes glinting with tears in the moonlight, she felt hands reach out to touch her gently as she passed. She did not enjoy that for it reminded her of how men had fondled her flesh in the Cherry Blossom House. Here they were doing it for other reasons, of course, but she still did not like it. She was only D'ward's mouthpiece, unworthy of such adulation. She hurried off, up the hill.

Since she had joined the Free, she had never known D'ward take over a building. It was yet another sign that things were changing. The absence of any new recruits today, the fact that they were now in Thargvale, which had always been their objective, D'ward's unique promise of a feast . . . events were hastening toward their climax, and one tiny part of it was Eleal Singer.

Singer? She did not sing now, except when everyone else did. She really ought to change her name. Eleal Preacher? She considered asking Piol's advice and chuckled as she imagined his reaction, telling her not to get swelled-headed. Eleal Actor? She performed before great audiences now, greater than any Grandfather Trong had ever imagined, but she wasn't really acting. Plays were fiction, mostly sinful nonsense about evil people who claimed to be gods, but every word she spoke now was true. She only repeated what she had heard D'ward say, or what Piol and Dommi had written, which again was only what D'ward had said in public or in private instruction.

Puffing and leaning on her staff, she emerged from the wood at the entrance to the house. It was a spooky place, two storeys high, long abandoned. The windows were empty eyes, the door a vacant mouth. Once there had been gardens around it, but they had run to weeds, dead winter straw crackling under her feet. Stark, unsightly trees raised branches against the sky in frozen agony.

Two young men sat on the steps, chatting. They jumped up when they saw a shield-bearer and made the circle. She, having both hands full, raised her staff in salute instead. She paused to catch her breath. "Blessings of the Undivided! Am I the last?"

They exchanged worried glances. One said, "Don't know, Mother. There's another door."

*Mother?* Now that was amusing! She was younger than they were. Mother Eleal? Eleal Mother? "Well, D'ward says that the last shall be first." Making a mental note to ask him or Piol what that meant, she went on up the steps.

She found the others gathered in a large, high-ceilinged room. A fire crackled cheerfully in a fireplace at one end, but most of the light came from Trumb's great disk, blazing in through three huge windows. Cobwebs festooned the gaps between jagged edges of glass, and the mullions cast hard shadows on the floor. The floor, she noted, had probably been a fine expanse of mosaic at one time, but it was so littered with a mulch of dead leaves that little of it was visible. Someone had thought to sweep a clear space in front of the hearth, or the first spark would have sent the whole place up. The air was musty and earth scented.

She made a hasty count and decided she was not the last. In the absence of furniture, the shield-bearers were sitting in twos and threes on their own bedrolls, not clustered at the fire but grouped around the walls. Seeing Piol's shiny scalp alongside Hasfral Midwife's silver mop, she went to join them, dropping her pack and sitting on it before she dealt with shield and pole. She released a sigh of content.

"I heard you speak," Hasfral said, leaning around Piol. "Some of it. You were marvelous! I do enjoy your sermons!" She patted Eleal's knee and smiled her motherly smile.

Eleal mumbled thanks. She would have been ecstatic to receive such praise had she been *acting*. For preaching, it seemed inappropriate. All she did was quote the Liberator. With a little practice, anyone could do the same. Besides, talent was a gift from God, D'ward said, more an obligation than anything to get swelled-headed about.

"Where's D'ward?"

"Out there," said Piol, "with Kilpian and Dommi. And don't ask us what they're doing, because we don't know."

"Not so," Hasfral corrected. "We know what they're doing. We just can't decide why."

The windows looked out on a courtyard enclosed by two wings of the house and a high wall. Like the gardens outside, it had degenerated to a wilderness of trees and shrubs run riot. In summer it would be a dense jungle of greenery. In winter it was a brown tangle of death and decay. What might have been a lawn had become a small hayfield. Three men were moving around there—dragging away thornbushes and brushwood, apparently.

"They can't be planning a bonfire. It'd burn the house down."

"They're clearing a space," Hasfral said. "I think we're going to have a ball. May I have the first dance, Piol?"

He coughed his dry little laugh. "If you promise not to tramp on my bunions. Personally, I hope we have the feast first."

"Has D'ward ever promised a feast before?" Eleal asked. She could eat a mammoth, medium rare with lashings of mapleberry sauce.

The others said, "No," in unison.

"Must have been a lovely garden once," Hasfral said wistfully. "That's a lantern tree and a giant spindle nut. Those small ones are sesames; beautiful in spring, they are."

Footsteps scrunched outside. A small man marched in, his blond halo identifying him instantly as Dosh Envoy.

"Twenty!" said Tielan, from somewhere near the fire. "Now we can start."

"Twenty-three," Dosh retorted. Two others followed him in. "Alis and Kaptaan, and you mustn't forget D'ward himself."

While Tielan protested that he hadn't, the newcomers found places. The men outside must have concluded their work, for they were approaching.

Eleal had almost never seen all the shield-bearers gathered together like this, with nobody else. Well, almost nobody else. Alis and Kaptaan didn't count—they were special. They were not shield-bearers or friends. They did not preach or undertake specific responsibilities. They just were. The Liberator knew what he was doing. Laws were for evildoers, he said. The righteous were guided by principles.

Kilpian and Dommi stepped over the low sills and stamped across the room to their bundles. D'ward followed, looked around, counting. He remained standing.

"Blessings!" he said. "Are you hungry?"

"Yes!" said almost everyone.

He sighed. "So am I! We'll have to wait awhile yet, I'm afraid." He strolled over to the fireplace and turned his back on it. "A few of you may be worrying that I'm about to produce a sacramental supper. I'm not. That is not what we're here for. We have no bread and no wine, anyway."

He began to move again, sauntering along the big room. "You wonder what's going to happen. The One will provide. Bid'lip? Any signs of trouble?"

The soldier's deep growl came from the darkest corner. "No, sir. But they're out there. Lots of 'em. You can smell moa on the wind."

"I'd rather smell a moa than its rider! Colleagues . . ." D'ward turned and started wandering back, peering at faces. "Yes, I am proud to call you colleagues. You have all realized, I'm sure, that we have arrived at an ending. I marvel that the Thargians let us come even this far. I will not tempt them further, for there are thousands of people out there who would make good mine workers."

He continued to wander, speaking now to one group, now to another, but audible to all. "Yes, this is an ending. All those good folk we brought with us have played their part. Like wedding guests who lead the bride and groom to the chamber, they must now depart in peace, their portion done."

And would the Liberator also depart? Vanish in a blink as he had come into the world, the Free dispersed, scattered, perhaps persecuted. What then of Eleal Singer? She could not go back to the Cherry Blossom House. There was little call for a preacher of heresy. Although her leg no longer barred her from the stage, her eyes had been opened and she knew how evil most of the plays were, filthy pagan legends; she would certainly never dream of entering Tion's Festival. As for marriage, a woman's normal lot . . . no matter what husband she found, she would compare him with D'ward every time she looked at him. She must pray, and the One would provide.

Even if He didn't, D'ward would never forsake her.

He was still talking. "An ending but also a beginning. I was told of this house by a friend who lives not far off. He said that its owner and his sons were taken by reapers, many years ago, and the old place had remained deserted ever since, as no one knew who owned it. It was a noble place once and it will be noble—Aha!"

Footsteps crunched on dry leaves outside the door and then halted. Eleal could not see who was there, but D'ward could, and he smiled a welcome. "Kuchumber Boatman, isn't it? You came for Dosh, I assume."

Dosh was already on his feet, heading for the exit. D'ward watched them go until there was no more sound, and then began to pace again.

"That means we have visitors, so the house must wait till later. Let us plan the feast. How much food is left?"

Dommi said, "None, master!" and a few others muttered agreement.

"None at all?" D'ward stopped in the center of the room. "No food! There is no food, but the Liberator promised us a feast, so now he will call on the One, who will shower miracle wheat from the heavens like hail?" His voice was soft and bantering, yet it had a razor edge. "Oh, my friends, have I not told you that you were given brains to think for yourselves? You would die of thirst underwater. The Lord has already provided what you need, if you will but look. Did I not just tell you that we have reached an ending? Dommi, how many wagons would be needed just to haul the infirm and small children?"

"Four, perhaps five—"

"So save five oxen and— Ah, now you see?" The Liberator smiled as the old house rang with laughter.

# 55

Julian whispered a quick explanation to Alice. She chuckled. The shield-bearers began planning the feast, joking about the best ways to cook llamas, rabbits, and tusk oxen. They would be edible but tough as rope, likely. D'ward listened with tolerant amusement.

What a performance! Could have used more like him in the trenches to buck up the lads and lead them into battle with their heads high. But this wasn't really funny, dammit! The Liberator must meet Zath alone, man to man—that was the sword above the throne. That had always been the plan, David and Goliath. Exeter had specifically not staged a travesty of the Last Supper, but he was sending the Free home, and he'd dropped bags of hints that he was pulling out.

Alice tapped Julian's shoulder. "He said *all* the rabbits?"

"Yes. Why? What's wrong?"

She frowned. "Nothing."

Yes there was. What?

A quick look the other way showed that Pinky was wearing his sleepy-eyed thoughtful look as he watched the byplay. He, too, had noticed something awry.

"Tell me," Julian whispered.

Alice shrugged. "If they slaughter the excess oxen and *all* the rabbits, then how is he going to Tharg?"

"Good question." Julian mentally kicked himself for not seeing that. It would take days on foot, and Thargians did not tolerate strangers wandering around their vale. They would especially resent the man who had laid a historic humiliation on them only four years ago. Zath would lay his own traps. Of course Exeter had enough mana now to defend himself from mundane attack—or even teleport himself across country from node to node if he chose—but either would be a foolish waste of power. He might have hidden one rabbit away somewhere for his own use.

Alice had been expecting to go to Tharg with him.

And so had Julian Smedley. Damn! He didn't want to be sent home with the children. Exeter knew what he was doing, certainly—clearing ground in the courtyard, sending Dosh off on a secret errand. How and where did he expect to meet Zath? Was he even going to Tharg at all?

Now he was raising a hand for silence. Ye gods, but he was a cool one! Only his tendency to pace around showed the strain he must be feeling, and that might be due to the virtuality of this node. It was localized, but very intense.

"We are about to have visitors." Exeter walked over to the central window and sat on the sill, so that the light was behind him, leaning against a mullion and stretching out his legs, cool as the proverbial cucumber. The great room fell silent. A bat-owl warbled its ghostly call out in the trees. Farther off, some of the Free had begun a singsong. Footsteps approaching. . .

Dosh entered first and stepped aside. Three men followed, coming to a halt just inside the doorway, looking around for the leader.

None of the three was dressed for riding moas. The chappie in the center was a massive figure in full armor, boots and crested helmet making him tower over the others. His clean-shaven chin showed he was a Thargian, had there been any doubt. His scabbard hung conspicuously empty at his side. Wee Dosh had done extremely well to persuade him to disarm. From a Thargian point of view that would be a very poor start to negotiations. The other two wore civilian garb: fur hats, long fur robes. The one on the right sported a trim, gray-streaked beard, the one on the left a heavy black mustache. Now there was a surprise! Julian glanced at Alice, but she was still studying the visitors and probably did not know the significance of that facial hair.

If they were waiting for introductions or words of welcome, they were evidently going to be disappointed. No one spoke a word. Then the soldier picked out the man in the window as the likely head boy and marched forward, his heavy boots scuffing up dust clouds from the litter of humus. When he was in the center of the room and just into the moonlight, he stamped to a halt. His greaves flashed streaks of Trumb's green fire.

"I am Kwargurk Battlemaster, ephor of Thargia." His accent was as thick as road tar, but— Good Lord! An ephor *in person?* And speaking Joalian, too!

"I am the Liberator." Exeter showed no awareness that he was being granted an unprecedented honor.

Kwargurk grunted contemptuously. He waved a hand to indicate his companions. "Petaldian Ambassador from Joalia and Tanuel Ambassador from Niolia." Neither moved.

"I am the Liberator," Exeter repeated. He crossed his legs. He was in the presence of one third of the Thargian government and representatives of the other two great powers. Julian suppressed a strong desire to whistle a cheery tune.

The ephor growled deep in his throat. "Let us speak in private."

"No. These are my friends. I hide nothing from them."

"Friends? How many cohorts can you field?"

"None. I am armed with the word of the One True God."

The ephor glanced around the desolate, unfurnished chamber and then down at the young man lolling on the windowsill. His voice was a sneer. "He does not pay you well."

Exeter's voice was higher pitched and quieter, but it was steady and plainly audible. "He pays better than you can imagine, Ephor Kwargurk, but you did not come here to trade insults. State your business."

"You and your rabble have violated our borders. Your persons are forfeit. The penalty is death or slavery."

"I know that."

"Why? What is the reason behind this insanity?"

"Our business is God's business. It does not concern you, Ephor. You came to offer terms. State them."

"Not offer, heretic—dictate! Hear, then. You who call yourself the Liberator will proceed to Tharg with all deliberate haste, taking no more than ten companions, and will present yourself there to the authorities, who upon examination may decide to put you on trial. The rest of your followers have two days in which to leave Thargvale or endure the consequences."

Julian heard Pinky utter a faint hiss of surprise or relief. Make that both. By letting the Free leave unscathed, the irascible Thargians were breaking all their own rules. If Exeter had not been tipped off in advance, he was a fantastic guesser. Obviously this was how he planned to journey to his rendezvous with Death—as a guest of the Thargians. Would he accept the offer of ten companions or insist on going alone?

Julian whispered a hasty explanation to Alice: "He's done it! He can go on to Tharg and everyone else is free to depart!" He squeezed her hand and she returned his grin. Triumph!

Exeter uncrossed his legs and rested his forearms on his knees. "What are Joalia and Niolia doing in this?"

The ambassadors exchanged glances. Tanuel cleared his throat loudly, or perhaps he was just blowing his mustache out of the way. "You have deluded many citizens of Nioldom and even some of Niolia itself into following your mirage. I made representations on their behalf to the noble ephors and their excellencies agreed to treat the matter with the outstanding leniency that Ephor Kwargurk has just described. You have many persons from Joalia here also. Honorable Petaldian Ambassador will confirm, if you wish, that his government's views are concurrent with mine. We have assembled a stock of foodstuffs to provision the refugees' return journey—at no small cost, I may add. You should know that the Thargian government's concessions are historically—"

"I think we understand. Thargia would love to load up its slave pens, but it doesn't want to antagonize all the Vales at the same time. The chance to take so many hostages must be mouthwateringly tempting, though. A more weighty consideration would be that the omens and auguries are especially ambiguous just now?" Edward stood up, revealing that he was as tall as the ephor. His next words cracked out like pistol shots. *"Your terms are rejected. Leave this camp."*

Alice understood the tone, and her nails stabbed hard into Julian's hand. Pinky gasped. Others among the shield-bearers were reacting similarly. Petaldian Ambassador uttered undiplomatic obscenities. A six-foot pillar of bronze viewed from the side in partial moonlight should not be able to express astonishment without speaking, but somehow Ephor Kwargurk managed it.

Tanuel Ambassador hurried forward, his voice emerging as a trembling bleat. "Young man, you will have the blood of innocent thousands upon your head! Ever since your destination became obvious, I have worked night and day to persuade the Thargian—"

"Your motives are honorable. The One will not be unmindful of them, nor of Petaldian Ambassador's. But we will be guided by our God and heed not the butchers who reign in Tharg, worshipping evil. The blessings of the Undivided go with you all."

"You really are insane," Kwargurk growled. "My colleagues and I did not believe that so many would follow a maniac." Turning slowly, he surveyed the hall. "Will none of you break free from the madman and seek to avert bloody catastrophe?"

No one spoke. Not that Julian was not tempted . . .

"Truly," Exeter remarked, "this concern for the welfare of others is a welcome innovation among Thargians. There is hope for you yet, when I have ripped out the foulness that contaminates your city. Go, ephor. Go back to Tharg and tell your murdering Zath that his hour has come."

For a moment the giant seemed to balance on his toes, poised to seize the insolent preacher and snap his neck. Possibly he tried to, although no tremor of mana disturbed the virtuality of the node. Then all three envoys turned and stalked away. The two diplomats were doubtless downcast at their failure. It was hard to believe that the Thargian was feeling anything short of homicidal mania. All three vanished out the door, crackling dead leaves into the distance.

As Dosh was about to follow and see them off, Exeter called him over. For a moment the two conferred, then Dosh departed also.

Julian was returning Alice's wide-eyed stare. "He had it all! They gave him everything he could have asked for, and he turned it down flat. This is insane! He's bloody bonkers."

"It's a rum go," Pinky muttered.

"Never thought I'd agree with a Thargian. He *is* crazy, as the man said. He must be."

Alice chewed her lip. "He knows what he's doing, I'm sure."

"I'm not," Julian growled. He turned to regard Pinky. If anyone had a mind devious enough to understand this, then he did. "You make head or tail of it?"

Pinky lowered his eyelids dreamily. "Indeed we must suppose a complex gambit, mustn't we, mm? A ploy being made on several levels, I suspect. Wouldn't you agree with that? Different message being passed to different listeners, as it were . . ."

Alice said, "Sh!"

Exeter had moved to the center of the hall. He had just declared war on Nextdoor's equivalent of the Prussian Empire and now he was talking of trivialities as if nothing at all had happened.

". . . was telling you of this fine house, fallen on hard times. We must now consecrate it to greater service than it knew before. Let us make this building the first temple of the Undivided, to give witness to the Truth, to minister to the suffering and unfortunate. A temple must have a high priest or priestess, some holy person well fitted. Who among you is most worthy?"

He stopped and looked around. No one spoke. Julian wanted to scream, Who cared about a bloody temple? He glared at Pinky, but Pinky was frowning at this latest Liberator outrage. The Church of the Undivided had staunchly refused to establish permanent chapels in the belief that they would attract persecution like wasps to a picnic.

Exeter sighed. "No nominations from the floor? Oh, my friends, do you not see yet? Is it not obvious? Only two of us here are mentioned in the *Filoby Testament*. She knows what it is to be penniless and wretched. She knows what it is to be crippled. I have even heard tell of those who mutter that she should not hold up her head among *honorable* people. Shame, shame! It is those proud popinjays who should hang their heads in her presence. Eleal Highpriestess, come forward."

At the far end of the hall, Eleal clambered to her feet, apparently being pushed by her companions. She walked forward slowly, shoulders hunched, her arms tight around her breasts. Superb actress that she was, she could not possibly be faking that shock and reluctance. Exeter embraced her.

"Now, priestess," he said, releasing her, "we need a Circle. There is a nail in the wall above the fireplace, and you have a shield that would sanctify this hall without any further words from us. May it ever remind us of the Warband who fell so bravely as the first martyrs of our church. . . . They will not be the last. I shall consecrate it and this temple in the name of the Undivided and all of you shall watch and listen and remember, for soon you will carry the word to all the Vales and to lands beyond."

Horsefeathers! Either the blighter had come completely unhinged or he was killing time until something happened or . . . or . . . or Julian Smedley was a monkey's uncle. *Why had Exeter spurned the ephor's offer of safe conduct for the Free?* Pinky knew, or suspected, if he could ever be persuaded to get to the point.

But Pinky was glaring at the ceremony now being organized before the fireplace. Again Exeter was going his own way with his own schismatic sect—the Church of the

Liberator, probably. . . . And Eleal as high priestess! Not a stranger, even. A girl in her teens, a native, and an actress! A former harlot! No wonder Pinky was seething. It was surprising the man hadn't turned in his shield already. Of course, he must assume that he would be able to overrule a mere—

No! If Exeter cut loose and left the Church of the Liberator to fend for itself, then certainly Pinky would expect to run it as he had run the Service, the rat behind the wainscot. But that program depended on the believers surviving tomorrow's apocalypse. The Thargians would come at dawn in fire and slaughter. The old, the infirm, the children, would be put to the sword and the able-bodied marched off to the mines in their thousands.

The awful truth reared up like a monster in a nightmare: Exeter had brought all those innocents here to die for him, just as the Warband had died. That was why he had refused the Thargian terms. More martyrdom, more human sacrifice! Wholesale massacre—wholesale mana! He was going to try and beat Zath at his own game.

# 56

Dosh trotted down the steps and set off after the Thargians, crunching leaves under his boots. The night was calm but turning cold, and Trumb's disk was almost a perfect circle, so the eclipse would start soon. He could find his way along the path by moonlight. If it had gone by the time he returned, the fires twinkling among the trees would guide him. Snatches of hymns mingled with popular folk songs told how the Free were celebrating the Liberator's triumphant promises. They were showing their faith.

Shamefully, Dosh's faith had not been as strong as it should be. He knew Thargians and how jealously they guarded their borders. He had been very relieved when he heard them promise to let the Free depart unmolested but also very astonished, which he should not have been. He should have trusted more in D'ward and the power of the Undivided.

Catching a glimpse of the envoys in front of him, he slowed down. D'ward had told him to speak to them when they had left the woods and not before. He could hear the mutter of their conversation, the clink of the ephor's armor.

When D'ward rejected their terms, Dosh had been as surprised as everyone else. He should have had more faith. Just why the Liberator had chosen to proceed in the way he had was still a mystery, but he always knew what he was doing. Trust in the One! It would be the Thargians who would be surprised when they heard the message Dosh brought. They would curse, undoubtedly, but they would certainly accept, and it would be fun seeing their faces.

The real mystery was why D'ward had made so much of this mission. He had used the code words that meant Dosh was to obey without question, but it had not been necessary. Dosh would have been overjoyed to undertake this task without that. He could not imagine what problem D'ward had foreseen. Perhaps he had expected something else to happen, or had been considering several plans, and the worst had not happened. Why, then, had he used the code words "Good old days"?

"Dosh, darling?" A figure stepped out of the trees before him, from deep shadow to bright moonlight.

He yelped in horror and reeled back. His heel caught against a root and he fell, landing on his seat with an impact that knocked all the breath out of him. He gaped up at the apparition.

She was stark naked. She was hardly more than a child. She was also very pregnant, her breasts and belly distended. Her golden ringlets hung below her shoulders.

He turned his head away and closed his eyes. "Sister! You must not display yourself like that! It is unseemly. It is contrary to decency."

In midwinter, too! She must be having some sort of brainstorm. He'd heard that imminent motherhood could have strange effects on women. He was not sure if this sort of madness was commonly one of them, but madness was the only possible explanation. She was in need of help. He scrambled to his feet.

She laughed, a laugh like a tinkle of silver. "You always liked me like this before, lover."

Dosh reached out and clutched a tree for support. The roughness of its bark under his hand reassured him that he was awake and not dreaming. The voices of the Thargian embassy had faded into the distance. He stole a quick glance out of the corner of his eye and she was still there. In fact she was closer.

"Go away! Go back to your husband at once!"

"Husband?" She laughed again, nearer than ever. "Don't you remember me, Dosh? After all the happy times we had together?"

He stole another glance—at her face, only her face. It was a very lovely face, soft and fair and smooth. She was much too close. He looked away.

"I have never seen you before in my life!" he squealed.

"Well not like this," she admitted. "This is last year's model. Lovely, isn't she? Or she was. One of the guardsmen did the damage, I think."

Dosh's knees trembled with the shudder of terror and horror that ran through him. Oh, God preserve me!

She laughed again, and somewhere in the deep crypts of his mind, down in the foulness where the nightmares lurk, there was something unbearably familiar about that laugh. "Memories starting to come back, are they?" she teased. "It's easier to wipe them clean than bring them back, but we'll see what we can do. Aren't you going to kiss me?"

Nausea burned in his throat and cramped his gut. He pressed his face against the prickly tree bark. "Go away! In the name of the One True God, I bid you begone!"

He began to pray, but silently, so she would not hear how frightened he was. God would hear. God would help him.

After a moment, she said sweetly, "I'm still here, Dosh. Are you sure you don't want to kiss me?"

Never! Never, never again! That sort of sin was all behind him now. He had a job to do, a very important job. D'ward was depending on him. He spun around the tree, bypassing the girl, and sprinted away along the path, stumbling and staggering, trying to fend off the trailing branches but missing some of them, which stung him across the face.

"Goodness, what a hurry!" she trilled, right at his back. "It isn't very good for this body to run like this, Dosh. Suppose it drops its brat right on the path here? And you won't get away from me like this, you know. What a surprise the ephor will have when we turn up together! Will he take your message as seriously as he should, do you suppose?"

Dosh stopped dead. The girl cannoned right into him and wrapped her arms around him, laughing gleefully. He struggled to free himself, and of course she was far stronger than she looked. She weighed as much as he did, and her mountainous belly seemed to get in his way more than in hers. The two of them staggered to and fro, banging into branches and saplings. He cursed between clenched teeth, he tramped on her bare toes, and she just trilled her ghastly mocking laugh. At last he managed to free an arm. He punched her in the face as hard as he could, hurting his knuckles.

She released him and fell back a step. Again she was in full moonlight.

"Darling, does this mean you don't love me any more?" Her smile displayed a missing tooth and blood coursing down her chin from a gashed lip. Her swollen bosom heaved as she panted. "Or are you just remembering how I enjoy rough play? Hit me again. Kick me!"

He was trembling so hard now that he could barely speak. "You are not a god! You are a foul, evil sorcerer—like that pair of mummies that call themselves Visek!"

"This is true," she said, looking down at the dark stream flowing over her breast and splashing onto her protruding belly. "It was naughty of D'ward to tell you, but it is true. That needn't come between us, lover. We can still do all the things we used to do."

"You bewitched me!" His voice broke. Tears of frustration blurred his sight. Memories were starting to writhe in his mind like worms in rotten meat. Naked girls, naked boys . . . Worse, the faces were starting to come back, and the sounds of laughter and screaming and gasping and pleading. "You cast spells upon me. . . ."

She stepped forward. He retreated until he ran into a tree and could go no farther. She was so close that her nipples touched his coat and he could smell her sweat.

"Sometimes I did," she said huskily. "But you didn't really need them. You were the most inventive playmate I have ever had, Dosh. So tough, so versatile, so resilient. You're too old to be Tion now, of course, but we could still have fun together. Even if all we do is just watch the others—"

"Go away!" He closed his eyes. His fists hurt, he was clenching them so hard. "I will have nothing more to do with you ever again!"

"You will if I want you to!" she said sharply. "I can take you away from here before D'ward knows a thing about it. Well, if last year's model doesn't interest you, how about this year's?" A man's voice added, "These ones wear better."

The change of pitch warned Dosh what had happened. Reluctantly he looked. Now Tion was a boy—slim, narrow shouldered, dark haired, and startlingly handsome. Naked, of course. He pursed his lips invitingly.

"Go away!" Dosh screamed. He was powerless against such sorcery, and yet D'ward was relying on him. If he failed to deliver the message, thousands would die and all the Liberator's plans be ruined.

The incarnation shook his head pityingly. "You are being terribly foolish, Dosh. You want to go and tell the ephor that the Liberator was only pretending and really does accept his terms. But you haven't seen what that message is going to do to *you*, Dosh. D'ward is being very nasty and unfair to poor Dosh. Can't you work it out?"

"What if he is? I don't care! I'd do anything for him because he is my friend, a true friend, not a blood-sucking lecherous monster like you, Tion Sorcerer!"

The boy pouted. "I never treated you any worse than D'ward is treating you now. For your sake, you really shouldn't deliver that message, love."

Dosh clung to the thought that Tion the Youth was evil incarnate. Whatever he wanted was wrong, wrong! To escape by force was impossible, so deception was the only alternative.

"What message should I deliver then?"

"Let's see. You could tell them that D'ward says Thargians are cowards. You could tell them he's calling Ephor Kwargurk a turd in a tin tankard." The boy chuckled and then his eyes narrowed. "Don't try to fool me, love. You never could before, and you're terribly confused at the moment. D'ward is just another sorcerer, like me. That invisible god he's invented doesn't exist. D'ward doesn't even believe in him himself."

"That's not true! You're lying. You're on Zath's side! You want D'ward to die!"

The kid sighed, fluttering his long lashes. "No, love, no! You're wrong again. I am on D'ward's side, believe me! I always was. I had him in my power years ago and I let him go. Didn't you know that? I set you to spy on him, but just out of curiosity. I never tried to stop him, did I?"

Dosh moaned, unable to speak. His mind was whirling like a moth as it tried to find some way out of this. His efforts to pray were being choked off by all those ghastly memories bubbling up in his mind. D'ward had told him many times that the Youth was crazy. He'd said so to Visek, and they hadn't denied it.

"So you see," Tion said, "I really do want to see that horrible Zath dead, and this is the only way to do it. D'ward himself still isn't strong enough. He has to do one of two things. Either he lets the Thargians kill the Free, or he gets help from me and the others—all of us, the Five he has been slandering so nastily. I'd gladly help him, truly I would, but I won't dare to, because I know that the others won't. It would take all of us, all Five together and all our flunkies as well. And that won't ever happen, because none of us trusts the others enough. Somebody would be sure to break faith and help Zath, and then Zath will win."

He reached up a hand to stroke Dosh's cheek. Dosh jerked his head away and banged it on a branch hard enough to make stars fly in front of his eyes.

The boy tweaked Dosh's beard playfully. "You can guess what Zath will do then! It's called the Great Game, lover. The secret is to always choose the winning side, and D'ward isn't the winning side."

"You're lying!"

"No, Dosh, dear, I'm not. So I'm not going to let you deliver that message. We're going to let the Thargians think he meant what he said the first time. The silly boy changed his mind, but they're not going to hear that. You won't understand, but this way D'ward may just have a chance without our help. Zath will outsmart himself, and that will be a very elegant solution."

Dosh tried to lunge past. The kid caught him with one hand and held him like a steel bracket, so his feet shot out from under him and he thought his arm had been jerked from its socket. Tion supported the weight without even tensing his slender muscles. Dosh regained his footing and swung a punch at the beautiful face. He howled as his fist cracked into something as hard as a stone wall. Tion apparently felt nothing at all.

"Oh you do want to play rough games?" He glanced up at the sky and frowned. The light was fading fast as a stain of black spread over Trumb's great disk. Stars were returning.

"Well!" the sorcerer muttered. "Now that's interesting!"

Dosh squirmed, trying to pry the slender fingers loose and failing utterly. Tion ignored him, apparently staring at the eclipse.

"Very interesting! That changes things." The sorcerer chuckled. "All right, Dosh. You go and deliver your message. Stop the massacre if you can."

With that he vanished, fading away even faster than the green moon.

# *57*

The ceremony was over. Alice had understood not a word of it, but the actions had been plain enough. Eleal, that silver-tongued ingenue, had now been installed as bishop of Thargvale or perhaps archbishop of the Vales. She had recovered from her shock and was already warming to her new role, accepting congratulations from the shield-bearers with matronly grace. Edward had certainly made some very odd decisions tonight. Pinky's face was a picture. Ursula's would rank as a whole art gallery. Even Julian had gone into a black sulk about something. With the fire shrunk to a few red embers, some subtle difference in the overgrown garden beyond the windows hinted that the eclipse had begun.

Edward must have given orders to start the feast, because people were leaving. He was standing by the door, speaking to each shield-bearer in turn, but his tone sounded cheerful enough, more like personal instructions than final farewells. He would not dispose of Cousin Alice quite so easily. She wanted to know what he was planning to do next, and she was not leaving until she found out, so there! She stood up and eased her stiffened limbs.

She peered up crossly at Julian's scowl. "What's the matter? Don't you think Eleal will make a good pope?"

He shrugged, not caring about that. "I wish I knew why he rejected the Thargian offer. And the way he did it! Dammit, Alice, an ephor is like a king or a president, one third of an absolute tyrant."

"I think I know why. I'll tell you if you promise not to repeat it."

Julian said, "Right-oh!" too quickly. He obviously thought he did know the answer and she didn't.

She looked around. Edward wouldn't hear her. He was saying good-bye to Eleal at the door, but she was the last.

"It's the old problem of church and state. . . . This isn't easy to put into words. I'm not sure Edward could, even. I think he was acting on instinct—"

"Instinct! *Instinct?* He's likely to get us all killed or enslaved with his bloody instinct."

"In a sense that almost doesn't matter." She wondered if she could ever explain to a man who couldn't see it already. Julian was a downright, earthy Anglo-Saxon. Edward was a realist too, but he also had a Celtic streak in him, an artistic undercurrent that defied logic. "The point is that this is the climax of everything he's worked for, yes? So even details are very important. What we saw tonight may become legend for thousands or millions of people. This was his night, his apotheosis almost, and he would not be seen currying favor from the Thargians."

"If you think that, then you're as mad as he is! This is Thargia, woman!"

It must be her turn to shrug, so she did. "I just don't think Edward saw that man as Ephor Kwargurk. I think he saw Pontius Pilate."

Julian's mouth opened. Then closed.

"He was irrelevant," she explained, "like Pilate. Sometimes military force just doesn't matter. Generals and armies are forced to dance to other tunes and serve purposes they cannot comprehend."

Julian was a former soldier. "That is the most ridiculous—" His eyes shifted to look over her shoulder.

She turned. Edward was approaching, but he wasn't looking at them, he was staring out the windows. He spoke as if one of them had said something.

"It's too late to ask questions."

Julian said, "But—"

"No. There's only faith left now." Edward glanced briefly at him and held out a hand, but his attention went back to the garden.

Julian ignored the hand. "Just tell me why—"

"No. Good-bye, Julian. Thank you." Edward put his arm around Alice as if to lead her away.

"Thank me for what? I haven't done a thing, and—"

"You will." Edward steered Alice over to the wall. "If you stand back here in the shadows you should be safe. Don't draw attention to yourself."

She put her hand over his. It was icy. His face was rigid.

"Edward! What's . . ." She grabbed his shoulders as he tried to leave. "What are you going to do now? Tell me!"

"You must have faith, too." He flashed her a grotesque smile and left her there, heading for the windows. His sort might die of fright, but it would be on its feet, doing its duty.

The ghastly green moonlight was fading fast. She folded her arms tightly around her and watched as he stepped over the sill. He strode through the weeds and brambles, hastening to the patch he had cleared earlier.

She had thought Julian was leaving, but he changed his mind and came and stood beside her. Neither spoke, but her hand found his to hold. She was grateful for the company.

Dimmer and dimmer grew the light. The night seemed to close in, growing colder as well as darker. Edward was standing with his arms folded, waiting, barely visible through the branches. Waiting for what? Clocks in the Vales were primitive contraptions. With no uniformly accepted standard time, how did one set up an appointment? *Meet me when Trumb eclipses* would do very well. Waiting for whom?

It could not be Zath. He would not have let her stay if he expected Zath. He did anticipate trouble or danger. No one had ever said that his campaign would be anything other than dangerous, but she had been thinking that the threat was still a few days off. The sudden urgency had caught her unaware. It could not possibly be Zath, the main event. It must be vital, or Edward would not have been so tense. She said a small prayer. *Lord, two men I loved have been taken from me. Be with him and keep him safe.*

Another man stood in the clearing, facing Edward and about ten feet from him. He was slim, dark haired. . . . He had no clothes on.

Julian sucked in air through his teeth. "Tion! It must be!"

Alice edged closer to his side. Cold and tension were making her shiver. That boy out there would freeze to death unless he was using mana to keep himself warm, or unless he wasn't really there at all, just some sort of moving picture.

The Liberator and the Youth might be exchanging words, but if so they were too soft to hear. Then another figure . . . This man was larger, husky even, decently clothed and black bearded. That must be Karzon, the Man. Two more people appeared almost simultaneously. They were only vague shapes, but they could have been a girl in a blue robe and a mature woman in a red. That was what the mythology of the Vales would dictate.

"It won't work!" Julian whispered.

"Sh!"

"No Visek, see! The Five can never all cooperate . . . been squabbling for centuries . . . won't trust each other, let alone a . . ." His voice trailed away.

What was being said out there in that unworldly meeting? Alice would give her front teeth to be allowed to eavesdrop. And where was the fifth, Visek? The Free had a legend that the Liberator had met with the Parent in Niol. As far as Alice knew, Edward himself had never described such a meeting. The story was attributed to Dosh—the gospel according to St. Dosh.

The light had almost gone when the node shimmered again and the gap in the circle was closed by two more figures. Their arrival showed only because they were wearing white or something close to it. Starlight glimmered on silver hair. Seven people—the Liberator and the Pentatheon.

"There!" she whispered. "He's got all of them!"

Julian snorted. "He'd be crazy to trust them. And why in hell should they trust him?"

"You think he's asking for their help? He wants to borrow their mana?"

"What else? But all he has to offer them in exchange is Zath removal, and they have to gamble that he'll pay them back afterward. They'll stick with the devil they know."

Alice did not reply. She had no idea, really, but she was confident that Edward had worked it out a long time ago, before he even started his crusade. He had gambled his life to arrive at this one point, so he would not let the Pentatheon cheat him out of everything he had won. Yet they must know he had his back against the wall. Events were rushing to a climax and if he needed their help, he needed it now or never. That was not a good bargaining position.

Have faith!

The darkness was total. This, above all, was the time when the reapers pursued their grisly work, when Zath might be distracted by the inflowing surges of mana. Was that another reason to choose the eclipse as the time of meeting? Starlight showed only as a gleam on rimy branches and on the walls around the courtyard. Whatever was happening, whatever was being negotiated, the scene was invisible and inaudible. She wanted to run out there and shout, "You can trust him!"

For Edward *was* trustworthy. An Englishman's word was his bond. That creed had been drummed into him all his life, and no one believed it more strongly than he did. If he borrowed mana on a promise of returning it later, then he would do exactly that, even if it killed him. He would repay every penny of it. Yet how could those age-old pseudogods ever believe that? He had set out to prove himself to them, but why should they believe? Far more likely, they would judge him to be what they were themselves— sly, devious players of the Great Game. The whole point of that game was to lie and cheat. It would be no fun at all if a promise could not be broken at will.

"This is crazy!" Julian muttered at her side. "They'll cross their hearts, but when the chips are down, they'll pull the plug on him and leave him holding the bag." Metaphors were never his strong suit.

"Wait!" she said.

They had no choice but to wait. Even the fire had disappeared. They stood in darkness, broken only by faint outlines of windows. She could not have found the door had she wanted to. Oh, what a wonderland this Alice had found! She did not belong here in the dark and cold, on another world, meddling in tumultuous events; she never had. She should return to her own place soon, as soon as possible, if indeed it was still possible at all, for the Service had collapsed. The old Church of the Undivided had been overthrown and Edward obviously intended his new church, whatever it would be called, to be a populist movement with little place for world-jumping elitist strangers. Go Home. She tried to frame a prayer in her mind, for the act of putting her fears and wants into words often clarified her thinking. First, let the good triumph here on Nextdoor. Let Edward survive, his purpose achieved. Go Home, yes—she did not belong here. Go Home with Edward . . . yes again, wonderful! If he still wanted her. His name was still on a murder warrant, but the trail was cold, and perhaps Miss Pimm could solve the matter anyway. Norfolk? The cottage? It would be spring there now. London was gorgeous in spring, and this first spring after the war it should blossom beyond imagining. But neither prospect thrilled her. Africa did; return to Nyagatha. The war was over; it should be possible. No warrant would find them there. Heat and starkly brilliant sunshine and the scenes of their childhood. That was really Home. *Thy will be done, but if I had my dibs, Lord, it would be that.*

The light had begun to return. The trees came first, then the roofs and the general shape of the courtyard. Soon she made out the ghostly glimmer of Visek's robes, the pallor of Tion's bare flesh. The circle was still there, still presumably negotiating—the Liberator and the six who made up the Five.

Tion sank gracefully to his knees. Mana rippled. Then more. Julian gasped. The node writhed with surges of power, wilder and wilder until reality itself seemed to twist and the house undulated. Karzon went down, then the Maiden, the Lady . . . and finally, slowly, the two who were together Visek. A silent thunderstorm of mana rolled through the courtyard, dim flickers of sepulchral color playing over the kneeling Pentatheon and the one triumphant figure looming over them.

"My god!"

Edward Exeter stood in the clearing and the paramount sorcerers of the Vales knelt before him, fulfilling the prophecy: *They shall bow their heads before him, they will spread their hands before his feet.* Then, suddenly, everything vanished again into darkness, blacker even than before.

Alice and Julian had their arms around each other, although she could not recall who had started it. "He's done it! They have agreed to help!"

"Shush! And don't be so bloody sure! I wouldn't trust any one of that lot as far as I could throw a battleship."

The scene changed almost too fast to register, the Five gone and Edward trudging back to the windows. Alice ran forward to meet him as he stepped over the sill. She hugged him. He drooped in her arms like a man exhausted. There was no doubt now—he was shaking. Relief, of course!

"You did it!"

He sighed, leaning his head on her shoulder. "Think so," he mumbled.

"Oh, Edward!" There was nothing else to say. Just hug him, hold him.

He endured her embrace without returning it. She discovered she wanted to tell him to get a good night's sleep, so he wasn't the only one suffering from reaction. She had not realized how taut her nerves were. She clung as he made a halfhearted effort to break away.

"Things to do, Alice."

"But the worst is over, isn't it?"

He made a sound that was half a laugh and half a sob. "The worst hasn't even started."

She looked at him in alarm and did not like what she saw. His forehead was beaded with sweat like dew.

"What more? What happens now?" she demanded.

He shook his head. "Have faith, remember?" Then he did laugh, a bitter, hollow laugh. "What does it matter? Even if Zath wins, he can't stop what I've started. The Five can't. They've pushed their own theology so long that they have no idea how flexible faith can be. Even if I die tomorrow, some people will go on believing I brought death to Death in some mystical way. *I am the resurrection,* or something. They'll find a faith to fit."

"Stop that! You're going to fight and win."

He pulled free and straightened up to his full six feet. "Even if I do, what do you suppose they'll make of it all? What will the Church of the Liberator be like a hundred years from now? Religions don't spring up fully armed. They sprout, they grow, they change. They split off heretical sects and persecute them until the best creed wins." His voice was dangerously shrill. "As soon as the Caesars stopped torturing Christians, Christians tortured Christians. What would Jesus of Nazareth have thought of the Inquisition? What would Saint Paul have said to a Borgia Pope? Will the Free do that now? Or have I convinced them enough? Do they believe my lies about the Undivided? Have I convinced anyone? Who really believes in that hodgepodge god of mine?"

"I do."

"No, you don't!"

"Yes, I do! Details don't matter. The principle does. I believe a god sent you to them."

He studied her for a moment, as if trying to decide how serious she was. Then he forced a smile. "Wish I did, but thanks anyway." He kissed her.

Well! If that was the best kiss he could manage at his age, she ought to be ashamed of herself. She pulled him back to her and showed him what a real kiss was. Eventually he put his arms around her and cooperated clumsily.

Afterward he just said, "Oh!" For a monosyllable it seemed to convey an awful lot of meaning.

"You need lessons." She was breathless herself.

"Would you give me lessons?"

"Gladly, oh gladly!"

He glanced around the big, empty room. Julian had gone. Another man stood in the doorway, leaning limply against the jamb as if he had just run over Figpass. It was only Dosh, with his blond hair awry and some lurid welts across his face—how long had he been there? Why did little Dosh look so sinister, so ominous, waiting there?

Edward shuddered and broke free from her embrace. "Too late. Time to go."

"Not just yet!"

He took a step or two and stopped. He looked back unwillingly and bared his teeth in a snarl. "I have to go, Alice. Got a job to do. I promised. God knows I don't want it but I asked for it and I can't evade it now."

"What job? Promised what? Promised whom?"

"Pray for me," he whispered.

Then he turned and hurried over to join Dosh. The two of them went out together.

# 58

There was prickly grass in his face, an earthy smell in his nostrils. The back of his head thumped a sickening beat, keeping time with his heart. He was cold.

"I don't think you should lie there like that, love," said a man's voice. "It isn't good for you, and it's likely to get a great deal worse very shortly."

Dosh groaned. If he spoke he would throw up, or die. Dying would be better. He opened his eyes a crack and made out a bare knee close by. He closed them and tried not to groan again.

"I suppose I can waste a little more mana on you, just for old times' sake," Tion said. "There, how's that?"

Cool fingers touched his scalp. The pain and nausea disappeared. Dosh felt infinite relief and then shame at having accepted a favor from the sorcerer. "Go away."

"Oh, I shall! But I do think you ought to make yourself scarce, too, lover. They're going to tear you into small pieces if they catch you."

Dosh raised his head. He could hear a strange, low roaring noise in the distance. Like a waterfall. He did not know what it was. Come to think of it, he didn't know what he was doing here or how he had come here or even where here was.

Keeping his face averted from the sorcerer, he scrambled to his feet. Trumb blazed green in the sky again, drowning out the stars, shedding its unholy light on the peaks of . . . er, Thargwall. Yes, this was Thargvale. He was in a meadow, just below the wood where the Free were camping. He turned around to look for the two lonely bristlenut trees, and they were right beside him. This was the rendezvous he'd set up with . . .

He spun around. "D'ward? Where's D'ward?"

Tion was on his feet also, wearing the same appearance as before, the dark-haired boy of ethereal beauty. He shrugged. "Almost at the river. But I think you ought to worry more about those irate peasants, lover."

Reluctantly, suspecting a trap, Dosh glanced again toward the woods. It was shedding a tide of stars, a dark flood full of twinkling lights, flowing down the hill. The roar was growing louder. The dark mass was . . . people with torches.

"The Thargians! They took D'ward?"

"Well, of course. They cracked you on the head. You're of no value to them. You are to me, of course, lover, but not to them. They broke your skull with a sword hilt. Didn't want to get the blade dirty."

"But it was a parlay!" He had delivered the Liberator's message. He had promised that the Liberator would come in person to confirm the agreement, as D'ward had told him to. They had agreed on these two trees as a landmark. . . .

"Dosh, Dosh! You know Thargians!"

"They took him! They're taking him to Tharg?"

Tion rolled his eyes. "I can't heal stupidity, lover."

"They can't kidnap the Liberator! He'll perform a miracle. He'll escape!"

"No he won't. He promised not to."

"Promised who?"

"Me—and my associates."

Filthy lies! Who would ever believe Tion?

"The river?" Dosh looked at Mestwater, a brilliant silver highway looping through the valley. It was in flood, deadly—but it would lead to Thargwater and then the city. "They've got boats?"

"Even ephors can't walk on water, Dosh, dear."

Treachery! If the Thargians had boats ready, then the perfidy had not been a sudden impulse. The swine had planned it. Rescue? Rescue! There might be time for the Free to overtake them before they reached the water with D'ward and were swept away to safety.

He had taken two steps when Tion's hand closed on his shoulder and effortlessly stopped him in his tracks. "Think, Dosh, think! Somebody saw you. They're coming already. But I really don't think they want your help now, darling."

"But—"

"Think! You haven't forgotten verse two twenty, have you? 'In Nosokslope they shall come to D'ward in their hundreds, even the Betrayer'? Where did you enlist, Dosh?"

Dosh screamed. "I was only doing what D'ward told me to!"

"But they don't know that, do they, dearest?" Tion chuckled. "You were seen leading D'ward out of the camp. Now the Thargians have got him. What would you think? If you want to die horribly, then I suggest you stand pat, and your wish will be granted very soon. If you want to live, then your best course is to get down to the river before the last boat leaves and before D'ward's friends can catch you."

The lights were much closer. The roar was louder, and distinguishable now as the sound of mob fury. Being a loner, Dosh had always hated mobs. Panic! He turned and sprinted downhill, running as hard as he had ever run in his life, leaping and stumbling over the rough pasture. When he came to a stone wall, he hurdled it recklessly and kept on going. His shadow raced ahead of him. The river was a hatefully long way away.

Tion loped along easily at his side. "I did warn you that you shouldn't deliver the message, didn't I, dear? I told you it wouldn't do you any good."

Dosh tripped, regained his balance, and went on. He thought he could feel a stitch starting in his side. He had no breath to argue with the evildoer.

"I did tell you D'ward was being nasty to you, didn't I?"

And so had D'ward. D'ward had warned Dosh that the mission might kill him. He had known.

Dosh ran. He had always hated mobs. They would never give him a chance to explain. He thought of Tielan and Doggan, of Bid'lip. . . . They wouldn't stop to listen to reason or explanations. It wasn't fair. But he'd always done best when he expected the worst. D'ward knew the truth. If he could get to D'ward, he would be all right.

It wasn't D'ward's fault, it was Tion's. If Tion had left him lying unconscious in the field, then the Free would have found him like that and known he hadn't helped the Thargians. He would have been a *betrayed,* not the *Betrayer.* He ran. D'ward had known the physical danger. He had foreseen the probability of Thargian violence. He couldn't have expected Tion's meddling.

The river was closer. Dosh looked around, and the pursuit was closer also. There were hundreds of them, spread out now. Some of them would be younger and faster than he. The leaders carried no torches, and they were gaining on him rapidly. It would only take one stripling to bring him down and let the others catch up.

"A little more to the left," Tion said quietly, "over by those sheds." That was the last Dosh heard of him. At some moment after that, the sorcerer disappeared. Soon, though, Dosh made out the Thargians, two or three score of them, dragging boats across the grass to the river. The boats had been beached for the winter, pulled up high, away from floods. As he ran, he watched one after another being launched and swept away in the swirling torrent. He could not see D'ward, but he would have been loaded into the first. Tree trunks and ice floes and ice-cold water: Without a boat, the river was death.

Reeling and gasping, he arrived at the bank just as the last boat was loading. The men were armored and armed. A couple of them drew their swords. Somewhere he found breath enough to scream, "They'll kill me!" in Lemodian, which was close to Thargian. Men laughed, but someone shouted an order. The soldiers sheathed their blades and vaulted over the side as the dory began to move. Dosh splashed through water so cold that it burned his legs. He grabbed hold of the gunwale and tumbled over it headfirst.

Howls of fury and frustration from the shore faded swiftly into the distance as the little craft was seized by the current and swept away on its long trek to Tharg.

# 59

Whatever Edward was doing, Alice knew she could be no help, only hindrance, but she wished she knew what it was, where he was. She strongly suspected he had set off for Tharg already, with only Dosh to keep him company. That would explain Dosh's mysterious errands—filching a couple of rabbits and concealing them somewhere.

Lugging her bedroll along on her shoulder, she went in search of the feast. She investigated two or three campfires, hoping to find Julian, Ursula, or anyone she knew who could speak English. In a community of thousands, that was not very easy. Eventually her hunger drove her to join a group of—she thought—Lappinians. They jabbered at her cheerfully, laughed at her halting efforts to reply in Joalian, and presented her with a slab of roasted meat on a scrap of bloody hide as a plate.

It was disgusting and absolutely delicious. She ate all the meat, handed the skin on for someone else to use, and licked her fingers. A woman offered her a rib to chew on, but she declined with thanks. She had a strong desire just to lay out her blanket and go to sleep. Her eyelids weighed tons.

On the other hand, her nerves were still jangled and jumpy. She heaved her bundle up on her shoulder again and renewed her search. She had not reached the next campsite when the shouting began. It spread like ripples on a pond. Soon the whole camp was in an uproar, people racing around howling and waving torches that threatened to set the entire hill on fire. Unable to understand a word of what was going on, she just stood her ground, a rock in a whirlpool, and watched the faces streaming by. Were the Thargians attacking already? Should she flee with the mob or go to the house for a last stand?

Then a woman with carroty red hair going past in a shrieking crowd . . . Alice grabbed her arm.

"You speak English?"

The woman glared at her, then at her vanishing companions.

"Yes, *entyika*. I must go."

"Just tell me what's happening!"

She did, then she ran.

In some sort of herd reflex, Alice found herself racing down the hill with thousands of others. The night was a madhouse. People were falling and being trampled, screaming, yelling. Others were pushed by the mob into the freezing river. A few crazier souls went as far as the Thargian army camp, four miles away, and were repulsed with heavy casualties. It was useless, of course. The mob rampaged along the flooded meadowland for hours, but their Liberator had long gone.

As the sky began to brighten toward a chilly dawn, Alice trudged wearily back into the grove. The fires had gone out, the landscape looked as if a plague of Brobdingnagian locusts had slept in it. Not many people had. Now they were returning, as she was, broken and bewildered. Exhausted children clung to their parents and wept. Lost children howled in terror for theirs. Adults prowled the ruins in search of scraps left over from the feast.

Someone was trying to restore order, though. Tracking down the shouts, she found a shield-bearer, but it was Kilpian Drover, who knew no English. She could just make out enough of his words to understand that he was trying to collect all the Niolians.

Farther up the hill, Ursula Newton was bellowing for Joalians, Lemodians, and Nagians. There was nothing wrong with her voice, but her eyes were red-rimmed pits, her hair a briar patch, and she obviously had not slept. She paused, leaning on her pole and staring blearily at Alice.

"You heard what happened?"

"I heard. Can any boat survive in that torrent?" That was the first danger—that the fates had made a mockery of human ambitions once again and the Liberator was floating facedown in some weedy backwater, his mission forever incomplete. (But mana should have taken care of that danger, shouldn't it?)

Ursula pulled a face that declined comment. Then she seemed to change her mind. "It's possible. That river's flowing forty miles an hour or I'm a Dutchman. He could have reached Tharg hours ago."

"So what are you doing?"

Another pout. "I'm carrying out the last orders he gave me. I'm to lead the exodus to Joalia. Can't leave the kiddies here for the Thargians."

Alice looked over the group Ursula had collected so far and concluded that she might be several hundred short, although who knew how many Joalians had come to join the crusade? "Will they let you go?"

"Can't know till we try. Excuse me." She started shouting at a group of men, gesturing vigorously with her pole. They nodded reluctantly and moved off, separating and starting to shout in their turn. "Bid'lip and Gastik are taking the Niolians. Don't know who else is doing what the hell else." She thumped the end of her pole at a helpless rock a few times. "Shite, what a mess! I hope those ambassadors come through with the rations they promised."

"And that the Thargians cooperate too. Who's staying here?"

"Don't know. I imagine Eleal Highpriestess will be wanting to put her temple in order. Don't know if the Thargians will allow that either, of course."

Alice rubbed her eyes and thought about it. "That will probably depend on what happens when Edward gets to Tharg, won't it? Once he's killed Zath, he won't have to tolerate backtalk from the ephors."

Ursula responded with long bellows of, "Joalians! Here, Joalians!" like a bull elk summoning his harem. She resumed the conversation in her normal voice, eying Alice pensively. "You really think he's still alive?"

"I'll believe it until I know he's dead."

Mrs. Newton pursed her lips skeptically. She was a hardheaded, practical woman, not given to wishful thinking. Julian detested her for some reason he would not discuss, but she would do as good a job as anyone could in shepherding a few thousand pilgrims back to their homes.

She said scornfully, "With the mana he had, the Thargians should never have been able to ambush him, you know. And certainly not overpower him. Doesn't that suggest that it was Zath's doing?"

"Why abduct him? Why not just kill him and leave his body for the Free to find?"

"I don't know." Ursula sighed. "Because Zath wants a public execution in Tharg, perhaps. It'll take a few days for them to get back with the news."

Ah! "Someone did go?"

She nodded absently. "I heard Doggan, Tielan, and Julian. Possibly Dommi. They may have had a few others with them, I don't know. They found a boat farther upstream. Shouted to someone as they went by."

Alice's knees trembled with weariness. If she didn't sit down soon she would fall down. She compromised by leaning against a tree.

"That doesn't sound like enough people to stage a rescue, and I don't imagine Edward needs rescuing anyway. I mean, if he overcomes Zath and gets all his mana—that is what's going to happen, isn't it?"

Ursula was peering around as if to spy out ill-intentioned Joalians hiding in the bushes. "I don't think rescue was uppermost in their minds. They wanted to catch that scummy, yellow-haired Tinkerfolk pervert and knot his guts round his throat."

"What? You mean Dosh?"

"Dosh! Dosh the Betrayer! He turned Exeter over to the Thargians—didn't you know that? Well he did! And if I ever get my hands on him, he'll rue the day he was born, I'll tell you. Where are you going? You want to go Home? There's a portal over in Thovale we know the key for."

Alice shook her head. "Not until I find out what happened. Are you quite sure Dosh . . ." The look in Ursula's eye was answer enough. But it still seemed incredible. "Edward valued Dosh very highly. He put him in charge of the money, remember."

"Christ trusted his to Judas!"

"Hell! So he did." Alice felt very, very weary. "Think I'll go up to the temple and help the bishop with the housework. If I don't ever see you again . . ."

They made a subdued farewell. Leaving Ursula Newton to her bull moose impressions, Alice dragged herself up the hill on aching feet.

# 60

The soldiers had apparently been launching the boat stern first, because Dosh found himself in a pointed end, which he assumed was the bow. He huddled down on the thwart and hoped to be forgotten and overlooked—not an unreasonable ambition, for the helmsman would be fully occupied in trying to steer by moonlight and the four oarsmen must face the rear. His first thought was to pull off his wet boots and massage some life back into his toes, but he discovered he needed both hands just to hold on. Even then, the boat rocked and pitched so violently that he was hard put to stay on his seat. Besides, there was bilge slopping around already, so he might as well keep his boots on. Then something hit the side with a shuddering crash and the sergeant screeched something in Thargian.

Dosh realized it was intended for him. He also realized that the other four were not rowing, they were frantically fending off logs, ice, and other debris, using the oars as poles. Both ends of the boat were pointed; he was at the stern. A shower of spray half blinded him. The thwart tried to buck him overboard.

"Speak slowly!" he said and repeated it in Lemodian, which he had learned in bed from Anguan, four years ago.

One of the sweating troopers knew enough Lemodian to swear in it vividly. He concluded his invective with, "You want us to sink?"

Dosh turned his attention to the river. It was a ghastly heaving soup pot of black water, surging in glistening waves, frothing and juggling tree trunks, many of which were bigger than the boat, some still furnished with branches and roots. Uphill one minute, downhill the next. They wanted a lookout? No. When a trooper kicked a wooden bucket at him, he realized they wanted him to bail. He should have known not to expect charity from Thargians.

He reached for the bucket and promptly tipped headlong into the bilge and a melee of struggling men. Spluttering and cursing he sat up, edged back out of the crew's way, and began to bail.

He bailed until his arms were ready to fall out of their sockets, until the night became a nightmare of bailing. The ancient cockleshell sprang more leaks with every impact. Bilge surged back and forth, drenching him. One moment he was half afloat, the next he thudded down on the boards again, and then another wave would throw him over backward against the thwart.

Mestwater flowed into Saltorwater which flowed into Mid'lwater which flowed into Thargwater, spreading out to a great width, drowning fields and forests. The current seemed just as fast, if a little smoother. Collisions became less frequent—fortunately so, because the little craft was steadily settling lower in the water. The troopers began using their oars more for rowing and less for fending, struggling to keep the waterlogged boat in the main channel, away from the half-submerged trees and fences that marked its normal banks.

Dosh's cramped muscles moved more and more slowly. The bilge grew deeper, tipping the boat as it surged. Eventually one of the Thargians snatched the bucket away from him and started throwing water overboard at three times the rate Dosh had been managing. He hauled himself up on the thwart out of the way and curled into a knot to try and get warm.

The first light of morning was brightening the sky now, but a mist was rising from the river. A bridge came hurtling out of the fog. The sergeant screamed orders. Oars creaked in the oarlocks. The boat wallowed sideways, straightened, and hurtled between two piers on a long spout of water. The underside of the bridge shot over their heads with inches to spare, and they plunged down into foam. For minutes it seemed they must founder. Dosh clung to the gunwale to avoid being washed overboard. Then the man with the bucket gained on the flood and the boat was still floating. Another man took over the bailing.

Soaked and shivering, Dosh peered out at the ghostly fog and wondered about escape. The troopers were shouting and pointing, identifying landmarks. Obviously they were very close to Tharg itself now, but they were also very close to sinking. If they decided to lighten the boat, Dosh knew what they would throw overboard first. The water was running very close to the top of a levee, well above the countryside beyond. Vague shapes of trees and buildings loomed out of the murk and then vanished again.

The troopers were as exhausted as he was. The sergeant's yells grew louder and more urgent. The two men still rowing strained to obey and the helmsman leaned on a third oar, but their efforts had no effect. The irresistible river swept them straight for a levee— steep, muddy, and partially undercut, so that great trees had canted outward and overhung the water or floated in it like booms, still anchored by a few roots. The boat struck just upstream, stabbing into the mud, tipping perilously. The current spun the stern around into a tangle of branches and twigs, slapping and cracking over them. The Thargians threw themselves flat. As the boat began to pick up speed again, Dosh saw a thick trunk across his path and stood up.

The impact winded him, doubling him over. He scrabbled with frozen fingers as someone's head knocked his feet from under him. Then he was sprawled over the log and the boat had gone. His perch trembled ominously; black water raced past underneath him. He managed to get a leg up and lay there, nauseated and shivering, but safe from the Thargians.

The tree creaked and shuddered as more roots pulled free. He worked his way in along the trunk to the bank and clambered up to a footpath. The river raced by below him, and all the rest of the world was washed away to shadows by white mist. Deathly cold had seeped into his bones and his whole body was shaking. He must keep moving or freeze. He removed his boots to get the water out of them, then found his fingers were too stiff to retie the laces properly. Letting the boots flap, he began to jog. By the time he realized that he was heading toward Tharg, he had gone too far to think of turning back.

Besides, he probably had more chance of finding some food and shelter in the city than in the country. And there was D'ward. Unless his boat had sunk, he was probably in Tharg now, perhaps already confronting Zath. When the prophecy was fulfilled, he might have a moment for Dosh.

D'ward was his only hope. The Free assumed he had betrayed the Liberator. Why in the world would he ever do such a thing—for money? That was infinitely unfair, because it had been a Joalian's offer of thirty silver stars to betray the Liberator that had led Dosh to him in the first place. He hadn't taken that money, so why would he have changed his mind after all that D'ward had done for him? He must find D'ward to clear his name.

Tired, cold, starving, he staggered on as well as he could, muttering prayers through chattering teeth. As the day brightened, the fog grew thicker not thinner. Nothing was clear or solid anymore. His repentance had brought him no better luck than his former sins.

He met no one on the path; he seemed to inhabit a ghost world all his own. All the friends he had cherished would be against him now; he was a traitor to the Free and a heretic to the Thargians. The track became a road, then a street. His story was repeating itself. Four years ago he had come to Tharg with the Liberator. Then the ephors had been planning to execute poor old Golbfish, thinking he was the Liberator, and D'ward had wanted to take his place on the anvil. The Man himself had stepped in to stop him throwing his life away. Golbfish had died anyway, fulfilling the prophecy: *Shame! Shame! To the Man goeth D'ward, saying, Slay me! The hammer falls and blood profanes the holy altar. Warriors, where is thine honor? Perceive thy shame.*

Now D'ward was again coming to Tharg. . . . Had he planned this? He might have done. He had warned Dosh of the dangers of those orders, so he must have had an idea of what was going to happen. Would Karzon interfere again? But D'ward wasn't asking to be slain this time, was he? Or was he?

*Which visit had been prophesied?*

Ugly, ugly city! Narrow streets, houses like fortresses with barred windows and armored doors. The fog didn't really help, it just laid a wet dreariness over everything. Cheerless, gloomy place! Very few women to be seen, just smooth-faced, grim-faced Thargian men. Every one of them bore a sword, for only slaves went unarmed. They all wore the same brief tunics they wore in summer, scorning to cover their legs. Drab, brown colors. Drab, brown city. Fog.

Where to go? Dosh slunk from doorway to doorway, careful not to antagonize those strutting warriors, not even by meeting their eyes. He knew no one in Tharg. He did know where the Tinkerfolks' hole was, but anyone there would likely be some of old Birfair's band, and they would cut out poor Dosh's liver before he could speak a word.

He doubted he could make it that far in any case. If he did not eat soon, he would faint. If he fainted, he would be thrown in the river or slapped into a chain gang.

"I see you made it." Tion was dressed like a Thargian youth, but only just, because his buttercup tunic was indecently skimpy and practically unlaced, while his soft leather half boots barely covered his ankles. The rapier at his belt, in contrast, reached almost to the cobbles. The too-beautiful face wore an authentic-seeming Thargian sneer.

Dosh leaned against a doorpost and shivered. The street rocked, wet clothing clung lankly to his skin. "Where is D'ward?"

"He's presently standing trial for blasphemy against the beloved gods."

"And what's going to happen next?"

"Well, he's not being very cooperative. I'll bet he'll be acquitted if you'll give me ten million to one." Tion simpered.

"And then?"

Mist swirled along the alley. The Youth moved closer, but grew no more solid. He draped an elbow against the wall and smiled down at Dosh. "You know the Thargians. A court can impose capital punishment for public farting if it wants to. They'll smash his brains out in the temple, right in front of Zath's statue."

"You, boy!" A burly Thargian had stopped in front of Tion.

Tion raised his classic eyebrows. "Warrior? How may I serve you?" He did not move from his languid posture against the wall.

"Fasten that tunic! It's indecent to expose yourself like that!"

"Oh, dear!" Tion sighed. "That is the whole idea. Do go home and disembowel yourself, Warrior."

The Thargian saluted smartly. "At once, Warrior!" He turned and hurried back the way he had come.

Tion shrugged. "Now, Dosh, darling, where were we?"

"D'ward came here to kill Zath!"

"So he did. And Zath is definitely going to die. He doesn't know it yet, but he is. Probably. He has become a serious nuisance. The problem is that D'ward is going to die too."

"No!"

"I'm afraid so, Dosh. It's a shame, don't you think? He's such a *nice* boy! But he's much too dangerous for the Pentatheon to let him live. He's too good at the Game! Why, in only four fortnights, he's managed to outmaneuver Zath himself, the greatest player of us all. Who knows what he might try next? D'ward must die, dearest!"

"No!"

The sorcerer displayed a hint of interest. "No? I promised ever so faithfully that I would not try to rescue him. I should hate to break my word on that, Dosh!"

Dosh shuddered. To trust Tion was insanity. He was total evil. He did not know what truth or fair-dealing were. "Can you rescue him?"

"Probably not. It would be very tricky. But if I were to try . . . What would it be worth to you, Dosh dear?"

"Anything! What do you want—my soul? My body?"

"Probably both," Tion admitted. "And your life too?"

"Yes!"

"My goodness! Love is a beautiful thing." The sorcerer held out a slender hand.

Dosh took it in his own, which Tion raised to his lips.

"Well, we'll see what we can do. It certainly won't be easy. I only say I'll try, not that it'll work. Now why don't you run on up to the temple and find a good spot to watch the proceedings? Close to the altar at Zath's end would be best. Very close. The crowds are starting to move already, so you'll have to hurry."

"You're coming?" Dosh demanded suspiciously.

"Not just yet. It would not be wise for me to come too close yet. But I do hope to see you there, love." A pained expression . . . "Trust me, Dosh! I haven't told you a lie yet. Not recently, anyway. Off with you now!"

History repeating . . . Isn't this the same trench of a street he came along four years ago? Then, too, he was following D'ward. The crowds were thicker then, but there are crowds now—a crackle of excitement in the air, people heading for the temple . . . Do they know of the Liberator, or does any public execution bring out the vultures? There is the Convent of Ursula, with the festoon of blue net over the door, unchanged. So much else has changed in four years. Here D'ward had brought Ysian. *Oh, Ysian, little firecat, it was your death that roused him!*

*Crowd's growing thicker, almost no women. Yes, jostle me, see if I care.* Draw your swords, it hardly matters now. All this swirling fog, is it real or is poor Dosh faint? People recoiling off him in disgust because his clothes are wet. The great square, with men hurrying across it like scurrying bugs. The huge pillars of the temple, tops almost hidden in the fog, giant granite cage, ugliest building in the world.

Cold, oh so cold. Poor Dosh. Is there any warmth left in the world? Has there ever been warmth since he left Amorgush's bed? Climbing the steps. Passing between two great plinths. The temple floor packed already, a-buzz with whispers . . . Karzon . . .

Zath . . .

The Man, taller than a tree, green-stained copper. The mighty bearded face with its hooked nose—a fair likeness—the hammer clutched against the brawny chest in two hands, the draperies of his wrap exquisitely rendered by the great K'simbr Sculptor, trailing from the belt to the ground to support the weight, one foot forward, one shin bare. A noble work.

Turn, damn it, turn! Look at the other end of the great rectangle. The matching colossus in blackened silver, swathed in a cowled robe, one hand holding a marble skull . . . stooped, head bent, looking down on the altar. Splendid evil.

Shivering, teeth chattering, must go to that end, must meet Tion. Drums starting, crowd reacting, announcement coming. People don't like wet bodies against them, edge aside, let me through, not enough room to draw swords, ignore the looks, the oaths, the jabbing elbows. Getting closer.

The altar is an anvil, set on the plinth, a black altar, or is it all old blood? Coming to the edge of the steps, crowd jam-packed, unwilling to be pressed up onto the steps, closer to that awesome, dread god. Go on, look! Look up at the face of Death.

*No, no!*

Don't look again. Men coming out, priests coming out, coming around the base of the silver statue, soldiers. D'ward, bound, limp, bloody. What have they done to him? Roll of drums. Silence, hushed, pregnant. White fog, black fog. Is it only the crowd swaying or the temple? Proclamation.

"In the name of the ephors and people of Thargland, in the name of the Man, the heretic D'ward convicted of blasphemy and condemned to die on the anvil. To the glory of Zath, the Last Victor, so be it."

Rumble. Whispers. *Where is Tion? Can't see Tion. They have D'ward on the anvil.* The masked executioner with the hammer. Coming forward. *Where is Tion?! He tricked me.* D'ward prone on the great anvil. *Is he even conscious? They've beaten him. Can't fight Zath if he isn't conscious. So tiny below that titan. Evil, evil.* Black fog swirls. White fog swirls. Executioner coming forward. *Up, D'ward! Arise. Rise up like a giant, a giant of fog. Grapple with him. Choke him.* White fog, black fog. *Don't lie there waiting for the hammer! Rise as the Liberator, great as the One God. Tower over the temple, D'ward. Awe the crowds, D'ward. Seize the monster Zath. Crush him. Strangle him.* Feel the ground sway. Hear the people cry. *Help him, God. You are mightier, greater. Stand tall, D'ward. Fulfill the prophecy. Reveal the Liberator. Come, brothers, save him from the anvil. Leave him not there as the hammer falls. Cry out. Cry out. Let Karzon come striding over the multitude. Let Visek appear white as fog bright as sun through cloud. . . . They come. They come. See Eltiana red as blood, see blue Astina and her sword of justice. Shake the pillars. Heed the cries of the people, God. Zath trembles. He's failing. It's not enough. . . . Where is Tion? Where is the Youth? He needs you, Tion. Come now, Tion. Save him, Tion. Don't let him die, Tion. If you want me I am yours, Tion. Anything anything . . . Help him, Tion! Save him. . . .*

# IX

We can see why throughout nature the same general end is gained by an almost infinite diversity of means, for every peculiarity when once acquired is long inherited, and structures already modified in many different ways have to be adapted for the same general purposes.

CHARLES DARWIN, THE ORIGIN OF SPECIES

# 61

Tiny flames flickered in the dry grass, stroked the shreds of bark, grew taller and braver, and reached up for the twigs. Alice blew. The bark began to burn hotter, brighter. She laid a thicker twig across the logs, then another. The fire uttered a crackle like a baby's first cry, and she sat back on her heels to admire her handiwork. There was something very satisfying in building a fire this way, much more satisfying than putting a sixpence in a gas meter. It came with the world. She began building a castle of thin branches. That should keep it going until she returned. Beyond the high and narrow windows, clouds blushed red in a winter sunset.

She stood up to survey her day's work. This chamber was now the refectory, by decree of Eleal Highpriestess, and for the time being would also serve as chapter house. It was a mess, but this morning it had been a disaster. The floor lacked so many of its tiles that not all Alice's hours of sweeping and scrubbing had made it look clean. Half the plaster had fallen off the rough stone walls; what was left resembled mange. The men had brought in four benches and a couple of tables they had found upstairs, badly worm eaten but apparently safe enough to use. Well, it wasn't the Savoy, but it beat camping in the woods. She hoped the chimney was not plugged with birds' nests.

Now for the little ritual she had promised herself. She walked out the door and along the corridor. Here the filth had been swept to the sides, leaving a narrow path in the center, but tomorrow or the next day it would be cleaned out properly. She passed the chapel, hearing a murmur of voices from Eleal and a translator as Br'krirg and some of his people received instruction. Someone—almost certainly Tittrag Mason—was chopping wood in the courtyard beyond, clearing out the firetrap. If the monotonous thumping did not bother Eleal, then it should not bother Alice. She peered morosely at the blisters on her palms. They were taking a long time to turn into calluses.

Arriving at the main door, which was only an archway with nothing to open or close, she was met by the cool evening breeze. The red-tinged clouds to the west were a sailor's warning if she had ever seen one, not that Nextdoor had any sailors to speak of. She did what she had come to do—walked out and stared down the long, overgrown driveway. It was deserted, as she had expected.

"You too?" Pinky Pinkney stood on the steps, resting one foot on a bulky roped bundle of sticks, calmly smoking a cigar. Where the blazes had he acquired that? Trust Pinky! There was an ax at his feet, though, and she could not deny that he had been pulling his weight these last few days, working as hard as any native.

He smiled smugly and blew a stream of smoke. "Watched roads never, um, get traveled. That isn't a very melodious proverb, is it? I really cannot imagine a road ever *boiling,* though, can you? Not that one, at any rate."

"This is the first time I've dared look. Three days at the very least, we were told, so I swore I would not start looking until the end of the third day." Alice felt unreasonably irritated at having been caught doing so, and even more annoyed at herself for making excuses.

"But four was described as much more likely, was it not? And six or seven quite possible. Considering the floods. And even that assumes that they did not stay more than an hour or two in Tharg. But where are my manners?" He took his boot off the bundle. "Do sit down, my dear Mrs. Pearson!"

She declined, being quite certain that the sticks would be an intolerably uncomfortable seat. Pinky replaced his foot on it and leaned an elbow on his knee to help support the cigar.

"I am reasonably confident that they will have decided to remain in Tharg. For a day or two. I should allow no less than two. So we may anticipate hearing the news, whatever it may be, from our local friends. Br'krirg has promised to inform us right away if he hears anything. Anything at all. Right away."

"I shan't mind, so long as they don't remain in Tharg permanently, six feet under."

He drew smoke, closing his eyes in rapture. "This is a concern, of course. A real concern. The hazards of the river journey disturb me more than the civil authorities do. Much more. But the other is a factor, definitely. Not under, by the way. Thargians cremate their dead. Almost all vales do."

That information was hardly comforting. "I must get back to work. I was lighting a fire."

He chuckled. "May I offer you some firewood, then? Very reasonable! My rates are competitive."

"I shall have to requisition funds from the temple bursar. Do we have one?"

"I am prepared to serve, if asked. When we have some funds. Ahem! I understand that you plan to return Home, Mrs. Pearson? Ultimately."

She felt her defenses rise like a drawbridge. "Well, that depends on what the news is when it comes." If Edward was now safe from Zath's murderous attentions and if he chose to settle down on Nextdoor and if that kiss had meant anything more than a farewell . . . "Possibly."

"Of course," Pinky said blandly, as if he were not capable of interpreting implications, which he certainly was. "That is understood. There is a portal in Thovale, only a day or so from here, which connects to a provisioned portal in the New Forest. The Goldsmiths were planning to use it. When they went Home on leave, you understand. The Peppers inspected it and confirmed that it is still in operational condition."

"What exactly is a provisioned portal?"

"One not actively tended by Head Office but with clothes and money to hand. Not one where you will drop in unexpectedly on a funeral. Or Divine Service, what? General consternation. Let us give thanks for this sign unto us! You are expected to restore whatever you take, mm? At your convenience. I should be happy to instruct you in the key. And guide you there of course."

"That is most kind of you, Mr. Pinkney." She would not have expected it of Pinky, somehow. She had underestimated him. Or overestimated him, if his interest was in watching her dance around in the nude. "My fire will be pining for attention, so I— *Someone's coming!*"

A rider had just turned the corner at the far end of the driveway. A rabbit, not a moa, so not military. Only one, but a rabbit was not a herd animal and chose its own pace. There might be others following.

"Bless my soul!" Pinky stood up straight. "Not one of ours, surely? Where could they have acquired a rabbit? They had no money. Cannot be one of ours."

The rabbit was halfway to the temple now, and a second had come into view behind it.

"Red hair!" Alice shouted. "It's Dommi!" She leaped down the steps and raced to meet him.

# 62

Halfway up the drive, Julian's rabbit saw the people ahead and tried to bolt off the road. Julian reined it in and just sat there, not sure if he was too weary to fight with the stupid beast any longer or too cowardly to help Dommi break the news. Soon a boy he did not recognize came trotting down the road, gangly and bare legged. He said something in Thargian, smiling and obviously offering to take charge of the rabbit. Utterly disinclined to argue, Julian exchanged places with him, and the boy rode the brute off to be confined somewhere. That chore complete, Julian had no choice but to totter up the driveway and join the wake. Lordy, but he was stiff! Also filthy, hungry, exhausted, and in dire need of a pint of bitter.

Alice was coming to meet him.

He saw that she knew.

When they met he hugged her. She accepted the hug, ear to ear.

"He did what he set out to do." He was surprised at the harshness of his own voice. "I don't think he would have . . . I mean, even if he had known what the result would be, he would have accepted . . . He would not have done things differently."

"He did know." She pulled back and looked at him. Only her pallor and a sparkle in her eyes betrayed her. "I'm sure he did. There is no doubt about Zath?"

"Well, there was no corpse. Not in public, anyhow. But the statue fell. I mean, that's pretty definitive, isn't it? There were many reports of former reapers confessing. I believe it, Alice: Edward killed him somehow. I'm convinced."

She was pale as a corpse herself, but her chin was steady. "And no doubt about Edward?"

He shook his head. "None at all."

She nodded and took his hand. "You must be all in! Come on up to the temple and we'll find you something to eat."

They began to walk. Her fingers were icy. He knew that she had not had much luck with men lately: her secret lover, her husband, even her former guardian the Reverend Roland—and now her cousin . . . foster brother. She must be used to bereavement, and she was certainly bearing up admirably. Wonderful pluck! Why wasn't she asking questions? Dommi could not have told her everything in those few minutes.

He found the silence unbearable. "Who are all those people?"

She smiled witlessly at a passing tree. "Believers! When the Free left, the army followed. As soon as they had gone, the locals began coming to investigate. The white-haired one's Br'krirg Something, a big landowner. He's been wonderful—sending men over to help with the clearing, providing food and tools and things. And Eleal's been giving him lessons in the new faith. We're short of Thargian speakers, but she can pretty much make herself understood, and he found some people who understood Joalian. They translate, sentence by sentence."

The Thargians would be the men with bare legs and the two women with shawls over their heads. That left Dommi and four of the Free, distinguishable even at that distance by clothing that was an obvious rag bag of castoffs. The group divided, the Thargians taking their leave with much bowing and curtseying, disappearing around a corner of the house. The others headed for the doorway.

Alice continued to chatter. "We've been terribly busy ever since you left! The place is almost habitable now apart from the beetles and I had no idea that Nextdoorian beetles had eight legs. The Thargian army did let the Free go and the ambassadors did come across with the food they promised, or at least they were doing so the first day. We haven't heard since, but we assume they're all safely on their way home now. And the few of us left here have been working our fingers to the bone getting the place Bristol fashion and Eleal makes a slamming good highpriestess. Even Pinky addresses her as 'Your Holiness'! Dommi says you cremated him?"

"That's the law there. I don't think he would have minded, do you? We arrived just after it happened. There was a frightful shemozzle, people fleeing in thousands, so it took us a while to fight our way through to the temple. . . . You want to hear all this?"

"Tell me everything."

They began to climb the steps. The others had disappeared inside.

"It was rather like a very local earthquake. Zath's statue collapsed, Karzon's turned on its plinth, some of the pillars shifted. The Convent of Ursula next door sustained some damage, and a couple of the minor shrines were badly hit. The rest of the city was not affected at all. In other words, it was pretty much confined to the node. Edward was right in front of the idol."

"In front of Zath?"

"In front of Zath. That's where they do all their executions. That idol was sixty feet high, Alice! The inside of it was masonry, covered with silver plating, and it collapsed like a heap of rubbish. Why there weren't a lot more deaths, I can't imagine. Apparently it rocked a few times, and the priests and people had enough time to run."

Her grip tightened on his hand. "And why couldn't Edward run?"

"He'd been laid out on the altar—"

"Bound?"

This was the part that did not bear thinking about, Exeter just lying there while it happened. "When we found him, his hands were tied, but his legs weren't. The witnesses agree he was conscious—although the buggers had roughed him up a fair bit, I'm afraid. So why didn't he run? Or at least roll off the anvil? I don't know. I can only assume he was too busy dealing with Zath somehow."

"Go on!" she said dully.

"Well. You know how they do it. The executioner uses the hammer of Karzon to crack the victim's skull. But he didn't hit Edward! When he raised his hammer, the temple began to shake. Zath's idol collapsed in a storm of dust and rubble. No one else was hit. Everyone else fled in terror, of course. Even more amazing, nobody was trampled in the panic. There were a few injuries, I heard, but no deaths."

"You found him?"

"We found him quite easily, lying beside the remains of the altar. He looked very peaceful." Julian concentrated on memories of the face, suppressing thoughts of the rest. "He couldn't have felt a thing. A big block crushed him; he must have died instantly." A marble skull the size of a potting shed—no wonder the damned statue had been unstable. "We just took him. The priests were too dazed to object. . . . I think everyone who was near the altar got blasted by mana—they were gibbering and babbling, not making much sense."

He paused to peer into the big chamber he remembered. It was swept and clean, furnished with some plank benches. The shield above the fireplace was the only decoration. The courtyard outside had been stripped of much of its jungle and now two rabbits were grazing on the rest. "By Jove, you've been busy here!"

"It was Pinky and Tittrag's doing. We call this the chapel. Eleal has designs for stained glass in the windows. It'll look very . . . Well, come along. The chapter house is this way."

A bloodcurdling scream echoed through the empty house.

Julian's nerves were at breaking point. He jumped. "What in hell was that?"

"I think," Alice said drily, "that Eleal Highpriestess has just been told."

An hour or so later . . .

Fire crackled irascibly in the fireplace, two candles twinkled on one of the tables, but most of the light still came from the windows. There were half a dozen or so people standing inside the doorway, all talking at once in a jabber of Joalian, Randorian, and English. Julian did not want to attend this inquest. He wanted to go away and lie down—sleep, yes, but mostly just stare at the ceiling for a fortnight and let his jangled thoughts settle. Alice seemed to want him, so he must stay.

"You are a most welcome sight, Brother Kaptaan."

He turned and looked blankly at the girl who had spoken. Recognition came as a sudden shock: a taller, older Eleal Singer. She had lowered her voice to a contralto and tied up her hair in a bun on top of her head. It suited her; she had pretty ears. Her robe was faded, patched, and threadbare as if discarded by some convent after generations of use, the staff she wielded like a jeweled crozier was only a pole and a loop of twig, and yet she portrayed real dignity. Her eyes were rimmed with scarlet, but she was in control of herself. Embarrassed by his failure to identify her at once, Julian bowed low.

"Thank you, Your Holiness."

She nodded graciously. "We seem to be assembled. Let us begin." She walked to the head of one of the tables—where the only chair in the room happened to be located— and thumped her staff on the floor for silence.

Dommi was recounting the boat ride in staccato Joalian. Alice said, "Where did you get the rabbits?" just as Prof Rawlinson exclaimed, "Captain Smedley!"

"Almighty God!"

Everyone jumped, turned, fell silent, bowed heads.

"We give thanks for the safe return of these, our brothers Dommi and Kaptaan and for the glorious news they bring us. Let us see Your purpose through our grief and may our joy at the destruction of the evil Zath be tempered by recognition of Your hand in all things. Guide our debate, we pray You, and lead us in the path of Your truth and justice. Amen."

"Amen," chorused the congregation. They shuffled to the benches along the sides of the table. Julian caught Alice's eye, and for a moment a twinkle of laughter shone amid the grief. This stripling bishop knew what she wanted! Eleal took the chair and called the meeting to order.

So it had come to this. Only nine of them left, out of thousands! Julian was seated between Alice and the intimidating bulk of Tittrag Mason, who completely hid Prof Rawlinson at the end. Opposite sat the saturnine Kilpian Drover, Pinky Pinkney, Piol Poet, and Dommi—whose freckles were barely visible through his windburn. The church itself was down to six, since Prof, Alice, and Julian himself were not officially disciples, not shield-bearers. Yet there were both natives and strangers gathered here, sitting as equals—that was one of Exeter's legacies. How long would it last? How long before Pinky had the Church of the Liberator knocked into shape? Charisma would soon bring back his bearers and silverware and freshly ironed sheets.

At the moment, the Church of the Liberator did not have two coppers to rub together. All religions began in poverty.

"We wish to hear the whole story," Eleal proclaimed. "But first, tell us of Brothers Tielan and Doggan who went with you?"

Julian did not want to talk at all, not to anyone, not for a long time, so he silently tossed the query to Dommi, who might even enjoy being raconteur.

"They stayed behind, Your Holiness, hoping to find the trail of the accursed Dosh Betrayer. They promise to return very shortly, having both received directives from the Liberator—as I did myself, and must attend to."

"We are glad to hear that they did not come to grief. Would you begin at the beginning now, please, Brother?"

Dommi spoke Joalian, with an occasional repeat in Randorian. When he wasn't strangling English, he was notably articulate, was Dommi. At his side, old Piol Poet scribbled frantically on scraps of paper, his nose almost on the table and his wispy hair in danger of catching fire from the candles. Pinky had his eyes closed; Kilpian Drover wore his usual morose expression, which didn't mean anything. Eleal was engrossed, but remembering to keep her chin up. Whatever Prof Rawlinson was doing was concealed by Tittrag's Himalayan mass. Alice . . .

Julian stole a few sideways glances at Alice. She was chewing her lower lip as she struggled to follow the story. He suspected she would decide to go Home now, for götterdämmerung had taken all the fun out of Olympus. In fact he would not be surprised if the station was abandoned completely. He really ought to take her off somewhere and tell her the whole story in English. He was just too tired. He was oppressed by guilt and sorrow. Why, why, why had he not guessed sooner what Exeter was up to? It was obvious now, but if no one else could work it out, then he wasn't going to tell them, not even her.

Dommi had run into trouble, hemming and hawing.

Julian stirred himself with a mental pitchfork. "I'll tell this bit. We loaded the Liberator's body onto a sheet of silver plate from the Zathian junk heap and carried him out of the temple. We stopped to rest outside, at the edge of the big square. A crowd gathered, and Dommi began preaching to them. He was absolutely wonderful! He told them of the death of Zath and the prophecy fulfilled and how the Liberator had laid down his life for it. He had them all weeping. He had me weeping, dammit! And I think he stumbled onto . . . No, I think he was inspired! He said, 'D'ward Liberator sacrificed his life to show us the way to the One True God, for now he assuredly has reached the top of the ladder and is united with the Undivided. By following his teachings we shall also climb until we are united with Him. He brought death to Death— not in the sense that our bodies shall not die but in the sense that death is no longer to be feared. We, too, shall become the Liberator. We, too, shall become God.' I think that should be the creed of our Church, Your Holiness."

Who had ever guessed that Dommi was so fluent in Thargian, or that he could be so convincing? Dommi was a miracle, and Exeter had seen that years ago. Julian had not. Eleal was another, of course. She was still inexperienced and impetuous, but she would soon grow out of that. Pinky would take her in hand.

Piol was busily writing down the new official creed, aided by Dommi and Eleal. Exeter would probably have hated it. He had never claimed to be Buddha or Jesus, but all sects must attribute perfection to their founders. Even Mohammed, although he had remained human, was a unique human.

Hesitantly, Dommi took up the story again, telling how the crowd had built a funeral pyre right there in the plaza. His voice broke and the room fell silent. The candles burned brighter in the deepening darkness.

Prof Rawlinson was eternally impervious to atmosphere. "And where did you find the rabbits?"

"Some of our new Thargian supporters provided them," Julian said. "They showered us with hospitality. Doggan and Tielan are still with them. You may expect a flood of pilgrims to arrive within days, Holiness."

Eleal nodded. Her eyes were brimming, but she recalled herself to her role. "We give thanks for this wonderful story."

Prof cleared his throat. "Three days ago?" he muttered in English. "It should be about time, shouldn't it?"

Alice gasped and looked at Julian.

He peered around Tittrag. "Time for what?" he snapped. "What are you implying?"

Rawlinson pursed his lips and blinked as if he had mislaid a pair of very powerful spectacles. "Come, come, Captain! We all know the model on whom Exeter based his actions. The saga is not yet complete."

Julian ought to be angry, but he was too numb to feel anything more than disgust. "If you're expecting a resurrection, Rawlinson, then you will be disappointed. Exeter isn't going to appear as Christ appeared to the Apostles, showing his stigmata. Exeter was smashed to pulp. We watched his body burn away to ashes. Don't be obscene." He leaned his head on his hands.

"You are overlooking the logic of the confrontation, Captain." Prof had assumed his lecturing mode. "Zath is dead, we agree. So Exeter killed him. So Exeter was the survivor and acquired all the mana. With that kind of power, it would be fairly simple to fake one's death, I am sure."

The Valians were looking puzzled, all except Dommi, who understood English. "I am assuring you, Brother Prof, that the person we found was most assuredly the *tyika*, and he was most assuredly dead. His face was not damaged. He had a birthmark on his leg, often which I have been observing when he was bathing."

"I remember it from school days," Julian said. "And I noticed it too."

The infuriating drawl would not be hushed. "Mana could simulate that. It would be easy enough to alter the appearance of some other corpse—"

"There were no other bodies."

Prof laughed. "Precisely! A most fortunate miracle? Or does it sound like the hand of our friend, taking charge of events when he had overcome the opposition and was free to exercise his powers as he wished?"

Sudden fury blazed up in Julian. He slammed a fist down on the table with a crack that made everyone jump—his right fist, which the Liberator had given him. "No!" he roared. "It sounds like plain, damned, good luck! I tell you that Edward Exeter was not a shyster! He would never stoop to that sort of deception. However powerful he became, he would not have been immortal, so to stage a resurrection would have been the cheapest sort of trickery. *He would not have done that!* Don't you see? Don't any of you see? He knew he was leading his Warband to their deaths in Niolvale, and he did so *because even then he knew that he would have to die himself!*"

Alice whispered, "Oh, no!"

"Oh, yes! Those were the only terms on which he would ever have sacrificed his friends. He wouldn't just send them over the top without him. He avenged his parents and all Zath's other victims, but he knew the necessary price and paid it. Zath died and so did he!"

Prof was shaken but not convinced. "Simultaneously? How is that possible? Where did the mana go?"

Julian wanted to scream.

"For heaven's sake, man—*Exeter didn't have any mana!* Haven't you worked it out yet? We all wondered how he could ever convince the Pentatheon to support him, to give him enough mana to win the battle. We all knew that the stronger he became, the less likely that they would ever trust him."

Pinky's eyes were open wide, for once. "And how did he persuade them to trust him?"

"He didn't!" Julian shouted, leaping up. He was horribly afraid he was about to start weeping as he had wept in Tharg, as he had wept when he was shell-shocked. Shell shock felt just like this. He yelled louder. "He summoned the Five here, to that court-yard. Alice and I saw them, right out there. But he didn't ask for their help. He didn't ask them to trust him. *He* trusted *them!* He didn't beg mana from them. *He gave them his!* All of it. That was why the Thargians were able to arrest him and drag him off to a fake trial and beat him and take him to be executed. He had no mana left! Zath had never thought of that gambit. Nobody had. But Edward planned it right from the beginning, as the only solution to the problem. Remember the prophecy that the dead would rouse him? He saw the war in Flanders. If millions of ordinary men could lay down their lives to defeat an evil cause, then he would do no less, and he could avenge his parents and the friends who had died. . . ."

He took a deep breath and forced himself down on the bench again, shivering like the guv'nor when his malaria took him. "Zath must have been horribly puzzled when his mortal foe was delivered to him bound and helpless. He must have suspected a trap. And while he was engrossed in watching Exeter die, the Five took the chance that Exeter had given them, and the extra mana he had given them, and *they* killed Zath!"

He stopped, choking. Alice put a hand on his arm.

"You imply that they cooperated?" Pinky asked dubiously. "The Five?"

"They had to! Edward had left them no choice, because the winners would share out Zath's mana, so none of them could afford to be left out. They took the only opportunity they would ever get to deal with Zath. The opportunity Exeter gave them as a gift, no strings attached."

After a moment, Prof said doubtfully, "I suppose that is possible. But . . . You'd have thought one of them would have had the common decency to save the Liberator's life."

"That bunch? Oh, no! They don't know what gratitude is. And they certainly did not want Exeter running loose again. He could play their game better than any of them.

He would have gathered more mana next year and then pulled them all into line, at the very least. They got rid of the two men they feared at one stroke. I bet they're all celebrating like a bunch of drunken sailors."

But they would never again make the mistake of permitting human sacrifice. That was one good thing.

"Julian is correct," Alice whispered. "There was another prophecy, you see. A gypsy told him he must choose three times: honor or friendship, honor or duty, and finally honor or his life. He chose honor every time. He knew he must die."

This time the silence was longer. At last Pinky said, "I do believe we should speak in Joalian. Holiness, brothers, we were just discussing the evil sorcerers, and how much they may have come to the Liberator's assistance. We conclude that they did not, of course."

"They are doubtless rejoicing in their wickedness," Eleal agreed majestically. "But the good shall triumph, as the One wills."

"Yes, it will," Julian said hoarsely. Tears ran cold on his cheeks; he felt nauseated, ashamed of his outburst, ashamed that he could not conceal his grief as the others could. "And they don't know the power of an idea. What D'ward has left us is a church built on a true historical event, whereas the pagans' beliefs are merely legend and deceit. We must build in his memory." There would be persecutions and martyrdoms, and the church would feed and grow on them. . . .

"I believe—" Piol Poet said. From somewhere he produced a wad of papers and began to thumb through them. "I believe I have some . . . Ah! Yes, these were words the Master spoke regarding a church." Holding a sheet dangerously close to the candle and his nose even closer, he read, "In Jurgvale on Thighday, the Master said:

" 'Is not a church a living thing? It is conceived in union, when a father drops a seed in a ready womb. It comes forth in pain and blood, and they smile who hear its first cries. Is not a church like a child, for it grows and changes and makes errors and learns? Is not a church like a young person, zealous and vigorous to improve the world, but apt to blunder into violence? Is not a church like a mother, who should love her children but not smother them? Is not a church like a father who should defend and discipline his family without hurt to them or others? Is not a church like anyone of us, who may grow in wisdom and compassion or sink into lazy and meaningless old age? Wherefore judge faiths as you judge persons. If they are greedy for gold, spurn them. If they lie, deny them. If they threaten, defy them. If they slay or harm or persecute, seek other counsel, for a false guide is worse than ignorance. And if they repent, forgive them.' "

Julian could recognize Exeter's sentiments, but the actual words were Piol Poet's. The evangelists were ornamenting already.

Eleal was beaming at the old man. "Assuredly, that was his hope. He entrusted me to guide his followers here in Thargvale, and he instructed Ursula Teacher to found a temple in Joalvale."

"And he directed me to do so in Niolvale," Dommi said quietly. "I have been remiss, but I shall leave at dawn."

"And you, Kaptaan?" the high priestess inquired.

Julian shook his head. How shameful his repeated lack of faith seemed now! He had never truly trusted Exeter—he who had known him since boyhood. Oh, how he wished now that he could call back those angry words he had spoken after the death of the Warband at Shuujooby! "I am no shield-bearer, Holiness. In fact, I have never even been formally baptized into the Church. I ask now for that honor, although I do not feel worthy of it."

She gave him her best reverend-mother smile. "Indeed your request will be granted! Is there one among us you would especially ask to perform this sacrament?"

Julian looked hopefully at Dommi.

Dommi beamed wider than ever. "I shall be most honored, Brother Kaptaan!"

Eleal nodded approvingly. "In his last words to me, the Master said that he hoped you would go into Randorvale and found a church, Kaptaan, because he thought you would be a very great apostle. We have one shield with no bearer. He said that if the previous bearer did not return to claim it, then it was to be yours. It is the most cherished shield of all, for it belonged to the holy Prat'han, first among the Warband."

For a moment Julian just stared at her. Then he babbled, "I should like nothing better than to take the Church of the Liberator into Randorvale. I shall be honored." Yes, he would take on Eltiana and her gang and stuff Edward Exeter down their throats. And one day he would burn her filthy brothel temple and dance on the ashes. If it took him a thousand years.

"Previous bearer?" growled Pinky. "You mean Dosh Betrayer, of course? Was that his shield? I just hope he had the grace to hang himself, like the original Judas."

Unfair! It was possible, of course, that Dosh had taken silver from the Thargians to betray Exeter, but Julian was fairly certain that he had only been following orders. In order to deceive Zath, Exeter had been forced to deceive everyone else as well. It would be better not to say anything to damage the burgeoning legend. The calumny would not matter unless Dosh himself showed up, and he must know that he would be torn to pieces if he did. Better to have poor Dosh remembered as a traitor than to admit that the Liberator had set up his own martyrdom. Julian decided he must tell no one about that, not even Alice.

Nor even Euphemia. But on his way to Randorvale, he would stop in at Olympus and assure her that he had meant all the promises he had made in his letter. And he would hold her to hers. No one had suggested that the Liberator's clergy were required to be celibate.

# 63

When the usual waves of nausea and despair had faded and her muscles stopped trying to knot her up like a string bag, Alice gingerly raised her head to survey the clearing. It was very small, tightly encircled by dense trees and shrubbery. There was blue sky above her and dew below. The fresh air on her skin was a little too fresh for comfort, but this was an April morning in England. She could probably have guessed that from the smells alone. By the time she had struggled to her knees, she had spied violets, primroses, and cowslips. The branches were dipped in the first green fuzz of spring, and a cuckoo hooted its demented refrain not far off.

Muttering, "Too true!" she staggered to her feet.

The hut was so small and overgrown that she might have overlooked it had she not been told of its existence. The key, they had said, was in the squirrel hole in the third tree to the left. The Service had never outgrown a juvenile obsession with cloaks and daggers.

Half an hour later, she was trudging north in clothes that were at least a generation out of date, but the buttoned boots fitted tolerably well and she had several gold sovereigns in the pocket of her coat. A lorry driver gave her a lift into Southampton and was much too polite to inquire why a lady should be tramping the New Forest dressed for a masquerade ball. Such things had never happened before the war.

She took the train to Waterloo and crossed London by bus, breaking her journey to visit Thomas Cook and Son and inquire about passage to East Africa. At Liverpool Street, she caught the 4:15 for Norwich with seconds to spare. The travel information would wait; she divided her time between a selection of newspapers and just staring out the window. England had not changed in two months, not as much as she had. Spanish flu was raging again, although in a less deadly form. It had almost killed the American president.

On another world, it had killed Zath.

By evening, she was sitting in a rattling, wheezing taxicab, bound for her cottage. The driver himself belonged in a museum. He looked too old to know much about trains, let alone motorcars, and when he tried to make conversation, his lack of teeth combined with his scrambled Norfolk accent to defeat her completely. Worse than Thargian. She gathered only that this was the first sunshine in weeks, and it had been the worst April since Noah.

The shops were all shut, but she could eat sardines tonight and face the real world tomorrow. London had seemed even more of a madhouse than she remembered it. Not

London. And not Norfolk. If she shut herself up in her hermitage with her memories, she would be talking to the gulls inside a week. No, it must be Africa. What she would do there she could not imagine, but she'd find something. She would look when she arrived.

One thing she would not look for was romance. Three men in less than three years! She was Lucretia Borgia. She was Typhoid Mary. One heart can only break so often before it forgets how to heal. She would let no more men enter her life, not ever again.

Methuselah stopped at the end of her muddy little drive, perhaps not trusting his chariot to extricate itself if he went in. She overtipped him, and he sprayed her as he gushed his thanks, touching his cap. His rattletrap ground its gears and roared away, one wheel wobbling precariously.

She trudged up the driveway, unburdened by luggage but still feeling the aftereffects of her cramps. Miss Pimm had promised no intruders—and there were the tire marks from Miss Pimm's motorcar, still showing in the mud outside the door. The garden . . . oh, dear, the garden! Tomorrow the garden. Home was where your heart was? Not in her case, because she had left her heart in Thargvale. But the little place was a welcome sight. After all those weeks of sleeping in tents, it would feel like the Ritz. It did seem quite homely, with the smoke drifting from the chimney. . . .

A broken heart could still leap into its owner's throat. Alice did not need to be an Embu or Meru tracker to know that those tread marks were recent, or that an untended fire did not burn for two months.

Three empty paint tins lay by the doorstep. There was a muddy footprint on the step itself. *Panic!* No, steady . . . Think this out. . . . There's nowhere to run to anyway. Concentrate! Miss Pimm herself? Getting it ready for its owner's return? Nobody except Miss Pimm knew of this place, but even Miss Pimm could not have known she was coming, not today, not to have a fire ready. It was a man's footprint.

Faint strains of music . . . That was why he hadn't heard the taxi. He was playing one of her records, Galli-Curci singing "Un bel di vedremo." Even as she listened, the soprano dwindled to a mournful baritone and then soared triumphantly again as he wound up the gramophone.

Paralyzed, Alice could only stare at the door. D'Arcy, the horrible mistake and the prison camp fantasy? Or Terry? But Terry's ship had gone down in the Channel, not off some desert island. Edward? Julian and Dommi had vouched for the body and watched it burn. . . .

Magic? Mana? He had given all his mana away to the Five. Prof Rawlinson had said: *It should be easy enough to alter the appearance of some other corpse. . . .*

He had said: *You'd have thought that one of them would have had the common decency . . .*

Alice threw open the door.